Flowers on the Mersey

JUNE FRANCIS

Allison & Busby Limited
13 Charlotte Mews
London, W1T 4EJ
www.allisonandbusby.com

First published in Great Britain in 1991.
This edition first published by Allison and Busby in 2011.

A CIP catalogue record for this book is available from
the British Library.

10 9 8 7 6 5 4 3 2 1

ISBN 978-0-7490-0859-8

Typeset in 10/14.2 pt Sabon by
Allison & Busby Ltd.

The paper used for this Allison & Busby publication
has been produced from trees that have been legally sourced
from well-managed and credibly certified forests.

Printed and bound in the UK by
CPI Bookmarque, Croydon, CR0 4TD

In acknowledgement of the special ties that exist between Liverpool, America, and that island across the Irish Sea.

If they had been thinking of that land
from which they had gone out,
they would have had the opportunity to return.
But as it is, they desire a better country,
that is, a heavenly one.

Hebrews 11: 15-16

PROLOGUE

Esther Clark placed the letter from Ireland on the green chenille tablecloth and rested her chin on her hand. What to do? There must be something. She sat there for several minutes before rising to her feet, unable to stay still any longer, and went to the sitting-room door. 'Hannah!' She had to call several times.

'What is it thou wants?' The maid's voice was disgruntled as she came into the sitting room. She swiped at a fly with her duster and smiled with satisfaction as it zigzagged like a drunken man on to the floor. She picked it up and deposited it on the coal fire before looking at her mistress. 'If it's the shopping thou's after, then thee'll just have to wait. I haven't finished upstairs.'

'I'll do the shopping.'

'You! Thee, I mean.' Hannah looked startled. 'Are

yer going on thy own then for a change? Thee hasn't dun that for a while.'

'Yes. I'm going on my own,' said Esther, despite being all of a dither but determined that Hannah would not have the upper hand for once. The maid had entered her life one stormy night when she had come into the Quaker-run St Anne's Citizen's Institute, situated in one of the worst slum areas in Liverpool. Esther had been a voluntary helper and had fed the hungry young woman. Now, fifteen years on, Hannah was supposedly one of the Quaker faithful.

'Thou's up to summit.' The maid scowled and folded her skinny arms across her chest. 'What is it?'

Esther drew a deep breath. 'I'm going to St Anne Street, and I want to go alone.'

'Whatever for?' Hannah's tone was curious. 'If thee'll just hold thee horses, 'I'll cum with thee. Don't want thee having one of thy queer dos.'

I'll be all right,' insisted Esther, reaching for the letter on the table. 'I can always go to the Centre if I'm not. Tina will give me a cup of tea.'

'Hmmph!' Hannah's sharp eyes glanced down at the letter and her thoughts shifted. 'It says Dublin. Is it from that sister thee were speaking about?'

'Yes. Sarah hasn't been at all well.' Esther picked up the letter and placed it in her pocket.

'Not surprising,' sniffed Hannah. 'They should shoot the lot of them rebels. The way they snipe at

8

our soldiers . . . hanging's too good for them.'

'Just thou finish upstairs and don't thee be concerning thyself with such things,' ordered Esther, her plump cheeks turning pink as she hurried out of the room. There were times when the struggle to impart pacifist beliefs into Hannah proved too much, but having said that, the maid's words had given her something to think about.

Esther put on her coat, found her handbag, took a couple of Dr Cassell tablets to calm her nerves and stood quietly for a few moments in the lobby, aware of Hannah's overwhelmingly silent presence behind her. Then she opened the front door and went out.

Esther sat on the tram, her gloved hand nervously twisting the ticket between her fingers. It was twenty years since she had last seen her sister and in all that time her father had only mentioned Sarah's name once. Esther had watched him withdraw into himself, shutting even her out. It made it all the more difficult to understand why he had kept the letters her sister had sent and which Esther had not known existed. Yet she could only be glad that he had not got rid of them. Otherwise she would never have been able to trace Sarah after he had died. As it was her letter had needed to be forwarded because her sister had moved with her husband and daughter to a different address in Dublin. Esther now had a nineteen-year-old niece, a member of this wild post-war generation. A young mind whom she might be able to influence as she had once tried to influence Sarah, ten years her younger. She looked out of the window, remembering.

Her stop loomed up and Esther got off the tram and walked quickly in the direction of St Anne Street, which not only housed the Institute where she had met Hannah, but also the wholesale and general merchant store which her father had once owned. It was here that Sarah had met the handsome young Irishman, who had swept her off her feet.

How contented Esther's life had been before he had come on the scene. Mama's passing had been a blow, of course, as had the deaths of the three tiny boys, at each of whose births Papa had dared to hope that here was a future heir to his tiny kingdom. He had borne each terrible death stoically and resigned himself to the care of his older daughter. As for Esther, she had known it was her duty to tend her father and small sister.

They had lived in rooms over the shop, sharing them with the stock that Papa imported on ships from every corner of the British Empire. Brought on horsedrawn carts from the Liverpool docks, the boxes, tins, bottles and casks had always provided an exciting diversion from her bookkeeping. Life had been busy and fulfilling, so that sometimes there had been no time to give Sarah the discipline she needed. Her sister had got away with much that their mother would never have allowed. Esther's only excuse was that Sarah was always so cheerful and bright about the place that she and Papa found it difficult to scold her when she did do wrong. (There had been the episode with a bicycle and a boy.) She had been forgiven much, but not falling in love with Adam Rhoades, a member of the Church of Ireland. He had refused to accept the tenets of the Quaker faith and Sarah had been lost to them. Esther's fingers crumpled the ticket. Adam had caused a lot of pain and she still had not forgiven him.

She reached the shop to notice that the partially black-painted windows still bore in gold lettering her father's name and the year in which he had established his business – 1870, the year of her birth. Despite Hannah's company in the house she had felt very alone since her father had died in the flu epidemic which had swept Europe last year, killing more people than the Great War had soldiers. It made it seem all the more terrible that across the Irish Sea the rebels and the Black and Tans were playing all kinds of dirty tricks on each other.

Esther thought of her sister's letter and the unexpected tone of it. There was no note of brightness in it at all. It was obvious that her sister needed looking after but it was no good going herself. Her nerves would never stand the terrible sniping and explosions. She pursed her lips. There was only one person who was fit to go and that was Hannah, who claimed to be scared of nothing and who had nursed her mistress through flu. Hannah who could wear you down once she was determined about something. It was very tiring, but it was that trait that had made her a survivor and so suitable for the task Esther had in mind. Hannah was the second eldest of six children, whose mother had taken to the bottle after her husband left. Hannah had reared the younger ones in a filthy court in the vicinity of Gerard Street. Those houses were one room above another with an earth closet beneath the bedroom window shared between several families. For coping with such horrors, Esther could not fail to admire her maid, despite the underlying aggression in her manner. Hannah waged war on dirt, strong drink and men. Esther did not doubt that her nerves would stand up to bullets and bombs. There would have to be some extra money in her wages, of course. She was as sharp as a knife where money was concerned because she was saving for her old age.

But Hannah was not the only one growing old. Esther would be fifty in August and wanted her family near her. She would send a note with Hannah suggesting that as soon as her sister was fit to travel, she and her daughter Rebekah should come to Liverpool on a visit. Surely Adam would see no wrong in that? He would want his wife and daughter in a place safe from violence – and hopefully it would be the first step in persuading them to stay in Liverpool for good.

PART ONE

CHAPTER ONE

Rebekah Rhoades walked soft-footedly along the lobby and opened the front door as Hannah came out of the dining room.

'It's fellas, isn't it?' demanded the maid, bustling towards her. 'That's what's taking thee out?'

'I've told you where I'm going.' Rebekah's voice was controlled, not revealing the annoyance she felt. 'Not that it's any of your business, Hannah.'

She closed the front door and hurried down the street, her russet and black skirts flapping against her calves. How dare Aunt Esther in Liverpool send that self righteous, prying old . . . old harpy? As if Rebekah had not been able to cope since her mother took ill with her nerves. It was boring being stuck in the house at times, but she had given up a job working in her father's government office to do the housework and look after Mother. Now Hannah had taken over and she was fed up with it. She glanced behind her, not putting it past the maid to follow her, but there was no sign of Hannah's bony figure.

Rebekah relaxed slightly, enjoying the sun shining through the autumn-tinted leaves in St Stephen's Green. She had arranged to meet Willie, one of the lads from the street, by Nelson's monument in O'Connell Street, but first she had to pay a visit to an old lady, who was her excuse for escaping the house. Since Hannah had caught her passing the time of day with a boy by their front doorstep, she had watched her like a hawk. It maddened Rebekah, and it was that more than anything that had caused her to take up with Willie. It was nothing serious but she needed some young company. The worry over her mother and the fighting had got her down. Like most people in Dublin her nerves were stretched to the limit. She was convinced that those in authority had lost control of the lower ranks on both sides and anarchy had taken over.

She felt a familiar sense of apprehension as she went along the High Street, and tried to concentrate on thoughts of Willie. He was fair and good-looking; a would-be poet who considered himself another Yeats. He had a swaggering manner which sometimes amused, sometimes irritated, but she would not have to put up with it much longer. Besides, not every girl had verse written in praise of her eyelashes!

Going down towards the Liffy she passed a couple

of Black and Tan auxiliaries, so named because of the combination of khaki uniform with police cap and belt. A number of them were ex-soldiers from the Great War. They looked at her and she stared through them, determined not to show nervousness or irritation at their scrutiny. She was doing her good deed for the day by visiting the elderly grandmother of a young Irish soldier killed on the Somme.

Aware that they had stopped a little further up the street while one of them lit a cigarette, Rebekah hesitated in front of Old Mary's door, which opened directly on to the pavement. The wide brim of her black hat with its rust ribbon blocked her vision slightly and with one hand she eased it back as she knocked.

The door opened quicker than was normal, but before she could take in that it was not Old Mary standing in the doorway, she received a push that felled her to the ground. Two shots rang out and she lifted her head in time to see one of the auxiliaries crumple in a heap while another pulled out his revolver and pressed himself against a house wall.

Scared to death, Rebekah buried her head in her arms as several more shots rang out. An angry voice hissed, 'You bloody fool, Shaun. You'll have a whole heap of them down on our heads now!'

'Not if I stop the other one getting away!'

Rebekah forced herself to look up as the gun fired again, and she saw the Black and Tan fall. She wished she hadn't looked. A hand took her arm, lifting her to her feet and the hat was removed from her head. She stared into the face of a dark curly-haired man, who returned her scrutiny with a mixture of annoyance and concern. 'Are you all right?'

She bit her lower lip. 'My knees hurt! And I think I've laddered my stockings,' she stammered.

'I'm sorry about that.' His gaze took her in slowly. 'You were coming to visit I take it?'

'Y-yes!' She smoothed back her hair nervously. 'I'll come back another time – when Old Mary's alone!'

'I'm sure she'd like that.' He handed back her hat and smiled.

'Danny, what the hell—!' The voice was angry.

Rebekah jumped and her gaze darted to the other, younger, face. It was spotty and there was a trickle of blood at the temple.

'Who are you? Speak fast and say the right words, or I'll blow you to pieces,' said its owner.

'Shut up, Shaun!' ordered Daniel in a weary voice. 'Can't you see that she's terrified out of her wits.' He turned to Rebekah. 'You've got nothing to be frightened of. We won't hurt you.'

'You mightn't!' Her voice shook despite all her efforts to control it. 'But he'd kill me if he had half the chance. And I know why! But I only came to say goodbye to Old Mary. I'll be leaving Dublin in a day or two.'

'You're leaving?'

'Yes!' She did her best to infuse assurance in her voice. 'So you see, I won't be around to tell anyone.'

'She's only saying that,' interrupted Shaun, scowling. 'Listen to the way she speaks. She's one of them.'

'I'm half Irish,' said Rebekah desperately. 'My father's family have lived here for hundreds of years. We're for Home Rule! And Mama is too. Although she's from Liverpool and was a Quaker, so she hates the fighting.'

'A Quaker! Maybe you're one of Cromwell's soldiers' descendants?' Shaun spat on the ground at her feet and his eyes darkened. 'We haven't forgotten what he and his troops did to our ancestors, have we now, Danny?'

'You're not listening, Shaun,' said Daniel, frowning. 'Her mother's a Quaker and she's from Liverpool. Cromwell's men were mainly Puritans. There's a difference. She's not involved in our fight.'

'She's still a witness.' The other's expression was stormy. 'And how do we know she's telling the truth about her father? He doesn't sound like one of us.'

'She's not going to say anything.' Daniel's eyes met Rebekah's again. 'Are you?' he said softly.

'I'm leaving, aren't I?' she retorted swiftly, but determined to say what she thought. 'I will say, though, that I just can't understand why he had to fire on them first when there wasn't a fight. It'll cause reprisals, and you must know how savage and bloody they can be.'

Daniel's expression tightened. 'We've lost two brothers in an ambush. You'll have to forgive Shaun his desire for revenge.'

'It's not for me to forgive,' she said, flushing. 'But what about those two mothers in England who've now lost their sons? It's just so pointless.'

Daniel shook his head slowly. 'If you're a Quaker then you can't begin to understand what drives a man in such a situation. You'd best get going.' He turned away, but Shaun made an exasperated noise.

'Are you bloody crazy, Danny? You can't take her word that she'll keep quiet. Let's at least tie her up until we get away. If she'd been one of our women caught by the Black and Tans, they'd treat her different. See the flesh on her!' His hand moved unexpectedly to squeeze her breast.

Rebekah gasped and instinct brought up her hand but she gained control of herself before the blow could land. Even so Shaun raised his gun, and she felt sure he would have hit her if Daniel had not turned and gripped the back of his collar, dragging him backwards. 'Go, girl!' he said, spinning his brother round and forcing him into the house.

She stared at him a moment longer, then went off in the direction of the river. When she reached the quayside her knees gave way unexpectedly and she sank on to the ground. She felt sick, thinking of how close the bullets had been and of the two men's blood on the ground. Then she heard running feet and turned and saw Daniel.

'I just wanted to check you were all right,' he said.

'Of course I am!' There was a touch of anger in her voice as she began to struggle to her feet. He took hold of her shoulder and helped her up.

'Leave me alone.' She was near to tears as she pulled herself free. 'Why bother with me? You must see dead men all the time. What's one stupid girl, sickened by the sight of blood?'

'I didn't fire the gun,' he said in a low intense voice. 'And I don't see death as often as you seem to think. I've said I'm sorry. I can't do anything else, except perhaps see you home?'

'I don't want you to.' She turned her back on him and looked over the river. 'Just go away.'

There was a silence but she knew he was still standing there behind her. She was filled with a strong feeling of apprehension. He was not going to go away. Why? And why be scared? She only had to scream and someone would come to her help. 'Please go,' she whispered unevenly.

'I'll see you home,' he insisted. 'Could you wait here for five minutes?'

'No.'

'Why not?'

'That's a daft thing to say.' Her tone was incredulous.

'I suppose so. You could still wait. Or is it that you're going for the soldiers?'

'It's what my father would have me do.' She paused, thinking of the brutality of some of the Black and Tans. 'But I don't like what the soldiers do either.'

'Good.' There was relief in his voice. 'My brother's a hot head and he shouldn't have done what he did, but I'm glad you're not a girl who'd go screeching to the military.'

At that she turned and looked at him. 'Maybe I should have screeched when you brother first fired. Sniping at people is despicable! Or perhaps, when he touched me, I should really have yelled. He should not have hurt me – where he—' Her voice tailed off and a line of colour ran up under her skin.

'No, he should not have,' said Daniel, shoving a hand into a jacket pocket. 'And I know it should be Shaun saying sorry, but I couldn't get him to do that. Surely you'll accept my apology?'

'I don't know why you think I should,' she said coolly. 'But it does say in the Bible that we should forgive our enemies, so I suppose I've got to accept your apology.'

A smile lightened his expression. 'I'm no enemy of yours. And I'm thinking that some girls would have made a worse shananakins of it all, but you're a rare one with a head on your shoulders.'

She frowned at him. 'If I had screeched like a

banshee then I don't doubt your brother would have shot me.'

'Perhaps. He's more nervous than he appears, you understand.' His voice was serious.

She raised her eyebrows. 'He surely has cause to be if he goes shooting off guns! Someone else might have seen him.'

'They'll keep their mouths shut,' he said with a certainty that she understood.

They fell silent and she looked away, flustered by his stare. 'Your brother said that Old Mary was your aunt.' Her tone was stilted. 'She never mentioned having family alive.'

'She isn't a real aunt. Was it her soul you were after?'

Rebekah felt like laughing hysterically. 'That's the kind of thing you Catholics said to my great-grandmama who came over from Lancashire during the Great Hunger to help feed the starving! Your faith is priest-ridden so I know when I'd be wasting my time.'

He grinned. 'What's your name?'

She hesitated before saying clearly, 'Rebekah.' There was a hint of hauteur in the look she gave him. 'And yours, I remember, is Daniel – a good Bible name.'

'Aye. He had to go into the lions' den.' His smile faded. 'I've got to get my brother away, but I'd still like to see you home.'

Her eyes narrowed thoughtfully. 'You don't trust

me, that's what it is. You want to make sure that . . .'

'No!' he interrupted. 'That's not my reason. Think, girl. There was no need for me to follow you here. I could have just run.' He added in a softer voice. 'Wait for me here by the river. Give me a quarter of an hour.'

She laughed sharply. 'You said five minutes, five minutes ago! There's no cause for me to wait. I can't wait! I'm meeting—'

But he was already running up the street. 'Wait!' he called.

For several minutes Rebekah stood looking after him. He was crazy to think she would hang about for him. Her father would be furious if he knew that she had said as much as a good morning to a rebel. He had been paranoid for months, fearing a shot in the back because he worked for a British civil administration in utter chaos due to Sinn Fein's refusal to accept the ruling of British law courts and the collection of taxes. Besides, Willie would be waiting for her. It would be sensible to go right now. She chewed a strand of her hair. He had probably only told her to wait to give him and his brother time to get away. She should have marched straight to the barracks and told the soldiers what had happened, never mind standing and listening to his excuses. He didn't fire the gun . . . So? He had still been there, and his brother had. Why had she stayed listening to him? He was not even what you would call devastatingly handsome or even very tall. The dark part she would grant him, and he had brown eyes that had a way of looking at her that made her – No, she would not think of how he made her feel. He was not worth wasting her thoughts on. She shifted her feet restlessly. He had a button missing from the top of his shirt and wore no collar. Wasn't there a woman in his life to sew a button on?

A tap on her shoulder caused her to whirl round. 'I'm glad you waited,' said Daniel. He had been less than ten minutes.

She tilted her chin. 'Who said I was waiting for you?' She turned and began to walk away.

He fell into step beside her. 'If you were waiting for someone else, he obviously hasn't turned up.'

'I wasn't meeting him here.' She did not wait for him to ask where but said stiffly. 'Is Old Mary all right? The Black and Tans will search the street and ask questions.'

'I doubt she'll tell them anything.'

'Probably not.' Rebekah pushed back a strand of blonde-streaked brown hair from her eyes and sought safety in thinking of the old woman. 'Her memory's queer. She can talk about the old days like they were yesterday, but yesterday might never have happened.'

He nodded. 'You must have a lot of patience. I found it hard going because she kept thinking I was a lad after I told her who I was.'

'I listen more than talk.' She glanced at him and

then away. He looked like he needed feeding up.

'Why do you visit her?' His voice was curious. 'How did you get to know her? It couldn't have been through the priest if you're a Quaker.'

'Her grandson's name was on the list of those killed fighting for the British in the war,' she said in her quick, light manner of speaking. 'Mama and I started visiting. It was our bit for the war effort. We'd heard that the Friends – Quakers to you – were visiting families in Liverpool, you see.'

'I see.' He made no further comment as they came to O'Connell's Bridge with its customary collection of beggars, some with missing limbs. One was selling shoelaces. Rebekah paused and bought some and Daniel followed suit, murmuring, 'Bloody war. Why did they go and volunteer?'

She remained silent, although she could have said there had been plenty in Ireland glad to take the King's shilling during the Great War because they were unemployed and their families hungry. It made her angry that those in Ireland killing each other could not use their energies to join forces and fight those kinds of evils in both countries.

Daniel said, 'Do we cross for where you live?'

'No,' she said shortly.

'Then are you really wanting to go straight home?' He smiled and she thought it was enough to charm crows from the trees and was suddenly wary.

'Why do you ask?'

'It's a fine day and I'm free for a few hours.'

People's suffering was still on her mind. 'Free from what – ambushing people?'

He frowned. 'Why go on about it? I didn't ambush anybody, as you know. If you feel that bad about me, why did you wait?'

'I don't know why I waited,' she said honestly.

His frown vanished. 'Don't you?' He seized her hand and pulled her on to the bridge. She had to run to keep up with him and was confused as to why she bothered. She was definitely annoyed at his presumption in taking her hand; it simmered just below the surface, but mingling with it was an unfamiliar excitement because what was happening was so out of the ordinary and he was so different from the boys she knew.

She sought for something to say to stop her mind dwelling on the effect he had on her. 'Do you know Dublin?' She asked that because he did not have the Dubliner's way of speaking.

'Sure. I used to come more often when Mam was alive.' He slowed down and matched his easy gait to her hurrying steps, guiding her round a mess on the ground. 'Would you like to go a different way than this?'

'No.' She glanced over her shoulder. 'Hannah just might come looking for me.' She did not like mentioning Willie now.

'Who's Hannah? Your sister?'

'I have no sister.' A grim little smile played round Rebekah's mouth. 'Hannah's a real live gorgon who'd turn you to stone as soon as look at you. She's from Liverpool and all she does is go on about the place. My Aunt Esther, whom I've never met, sent her because Mama isn't well. I think it's all a trick. For weeks she's worked on Mama until all she does now is talk about when she lived in Liverpool. You'd think the place was the promised land to hear her. And then doesn't Hannah suddenly start on Papa, but it's a different story with him! It's America, and the ships that sail from Liverpool to New York taking emigrants. You'd think she'd been there from her talk of what a great country it is. I've never known my parents to disagree but now, although they don't exactly argue, you can tell that one wants to settle in Liverpool and the other in America.'

'Who do you think will win?' He sounded amused.

Rebekah flashed him an embarrassed look and tried for a light note. 'Papa, of course. Doesn't the man always get his way? I take Mama's side, and maybe that's why Hannah doesn't like me. When she first came she was all smiles – but that was when she thought we were only going over to Liverpool for a visit. When it became a possibility that we might live there for good, she changed. For some reason she doesn't want us settling in Liverpool.'

'What reason can she have for not wanting you living there?'

She shrugged.

'Perhaps she's jealous of you?' he suggested with a smile. 'You're young.'

'Why should she begrudge me that?' Rebekah's eyes sparkled. 'No, it's because I don't behave as she thinks a good little Quaker girl should. In her opinion, I talk too much, I fidget, I've taken up my hems – that's the last word in flightiness according to her! I said I'd like to go dancing so she says it's because I want to flirt! She spies on me when I talk to the young men in the street.' She stopped abruptly and looked away over the glistening peaty waters of the river. She was talking too much. What would he think of her?

'Go on.' He was looking at her again with that expression in his eyes that made her feel – she wasn't sure exactly how she felt. It was odd.

'It's not important,' she murmured.

'What *is* important?'

'Mama getting better.'

'What's wrong with her?'

'The fighting's made her ill. She jumps if I drop a fork.'

'That's really why you're leaving Dublin?'

'Yes. Aunt Esther made us realise that there's no need for us to stay.'

There was silence and she was very aware of his eyes on her. 'I suppose you were against Pearse and the Easter Rising four years ago?'

29

She looked at him, puzzled by the question. 'Not really. I thought it wrong that the British executed him and the other leaders. It turned them into martyrs, and people felt sorry for them then and angry with the British Government. I wish Pearse and the others had been patient and then Ireland wouldn't be getting torn apart.'

His eyes narrowed thoughtfully and he kicked a pebble. 'Frustration. What do you do when you feel like you'll never get what you want? People lose patience.'

'They act stupidly instead, like your brother,' she said without thinking.

'We've lost two brothers,' repeated Daniel, his tone rebuking her. 'I'm sorry he frightened you.' His hand brushed hers and she drew back.

'Let's not talk about it.'

He nodded. 'Let's carry on talking about you. These lads – are you walking out with one of them?'

'Oh no!' she said quickly. Their eyes met and there was a churning feeling in her stomach. 'Have you a wife?' she blurted out.

He raised his eyebrows and his fingers caught her fingertips. 'I was thinking about marrying once but she married someone else. I'm glad now that I didn't.'

'Why? Has she changed? Is she not so pretty? Has she put weight on?' Rebekah freed her hand, but she was glad that he was not married.

'It had nothing to do with looks. But wouldn't

you stop right now walking with me if I had a wife? That's why I'm glad.' He caressed her cheek with the back of his hand, causing her to jump. 'Your skin's so smooth and you're the pretty one.'

She blushed. 'You shouldn't say that. I don't need flattery.'

He looked disbelieving. 'Don't you like nice things being said to you? One of those boys must have said something?'

Rebekah thought of Willie and his poetry about the length of her eyelashes. 'They tease. One tried to kiss me but I didn't want him to.'

'Why?' His shoulder touched her upper arm and she looked away. 'Because I'm waiting for Mr Right to come along.' Her voice was deliberately firm. 'And Hannah was watching through the curtains, and she'd tell Papa.'

'Has Papa someone in mind for you then?'

'Not that I know of. He's just old-fashioned! You wouldn't think that him and Mama ran away. She says that he was very handsome when he was young, and although she was brought up to believe that it's more important to see the beauty of the soul shining through a person's eyes than for them to be good looking, she couldn't resist him.'

'Fancy that!' His face drew close to hers, almost touching it. 'I can see the soul in your eyes.'

Her heart suddenly felt as if it was beating on the outside of her body and she murmured, 'Hannah

says that if a man kisses you, he can give you a baby.'
She did not know why she said it.

'It takes more than a kiss to make a baby.' His voice was expressionless.

Colour flooded her cheeks again. 'I'm not stupid! Why are we talking like this?' She stopped abruptly, knowing that she should never have come with him.

'Perhaps because kissing is on your mind?'

She gave him a look. 'Only because we're talking about it.'

'Only talking.' His eyes gleamed. 'There's no danger in that, is there?'

Rebekah thought it wiser to remain silent and considered turning back, but he made no more comments guaranteed to make her blush, and soon the sweep of Dublin Bay was before them.

Ships were at anchor and a lone yacht flew before the stiff breeze that whipped colour into Rebekah's cheeks and set her skirt flapping against her lisle-clad legs. She glanced at Daniel and was surprised by a grim expression on his face as he looked not at the sea but to the hills. 'What's wrong?' she demanded impulsively.

'I'm thinking of the blood that's stained those hills. And how it must tear at a man's heart to leave Ireland for good.'

She caught on to his last words. 'Are you leaving Ireland too?'

He did not answer but said instead, 'You said you were leaving. When?'

'The day after tomorrow. We'll be taking the steamer to Liverpool and staying with my aunt. Perhaps we'll go to America from there – who knows?' She shrugged.

'There's plenty of opportunities for a man to put the past behind him in America,' he murmured. 'Did you know that the old Celts believed that the Land of the Ever Young existed westwards across the Atlantic? There's a story about Oisín, a knight of the Fianna, who went there and lived with the beautiful princess of Tír na nÓg, never growing old.'

She smiled. 'Everlasting life. It's what a lot of people are looking for.'

He dug his hands deep into his pockets. 'In this story it didn't do them any good. Their love couldn't be consummated because she was immortal, and he a man. If he left her world then he would die, while she carried on living forever without him.'

'What happened to them?'

He stared at her. 'It's a romance. Oisín was heartsick for Ireland. So he left her and they never saw each other again.'

'How sad for the princess,' she said quietly.

'It was sad for both of them.' He surprised her by taking her hand. 'I wish you weren't leaving so soon.'

She did not know what to say to that or whether to snatch her hand back. His skin was warm and rough, his grip firm. 'I have to go,' she said at last.

'It doesn't give us much time to get to know each other better.'

'There's no point in doing that, anyway,' she said.

'You don't think so?'

'No.' Her tone was positive. 'I can't stay long. There's a hundred and one things to do before we leave.'

'And I suppose your papa wouldn't like you being here with me?'

'Yes.'

He toyed with her fingers. 'You won't want me to be seeing you home then?'

'I didn't say that. But maybe it's not sensible. If my father—'

He interrupted her. 'Then perhaps we'd better say goodbye here.' He leant towards her and kissed her briefly. She stared at him. Part of her had been waiting for it to happen. Hannah would say that she'd been asking for it. Glancing about them she saw that there were only seabirds gliding overhead to take notice of them, so that when he drew her closer she made little resistance. She wanted him to kiss her again and for longer this time. It was foolish but that was how she felt. The next kiss proved more than nice and she responded, but not for long. She placed her hands against his chest and he lifted his head and looked at her. She found herself with nothing to say and he kissed her again. She was almost breathless by the time that kiss came to an end, and decided that it better stop now.

'It's time I was going home.'

He hugged her close. 'You don't want to go home?'

'No. But I'd better.' Her tone was grave.

A slight smile lit his face and he let go of her and sat on the grass. 'You liked it though.'

'Yes. But I wasn't brought up to think about my own enjoyment.' She knelt on the grass. 'It's different for girls.'

'Of course it is.' He stretched out. 'And as well as that, I'm Catholic and a rebel.'

'Yes.'

'You think they're insurmountable objects to our getting to know each other?'

'What do you think?'

He leant on his elbow and his expression was thoughtful. 'They probably are.'

She frowned. 'Yes. Although you act like they're not there. It's the same with the shooting earlier. You seem to be able to brush it aside. I saw it and it's the kind of thing that makes me glad to be leaving.'

'You've made your point.' He looked over the sea, his expression sombre.

Rebekah's eyes followed his and she considered it wise to change the subject. 'Papa says that America has breathtaking scenery.'

It was a couple of minutes before he responded and then it seemed it was with a struggle. 'Would you mind going to America?'

'I haven't thought about it much.' She twisted her hat between her hands. 'Liverpool – Ireland –

America,' she murmured. 'They have strong links. Mama was telling me about her side of the family. My grandfather had some kind of wholesale shop. He came down from Bolton in Lancashire during the American Civil War because thousands were out of work. The ships blockaded the Southern ports in America, which meant there was no cotton for the mills. They were hard times. So he went to Liverpool looking for work.'

'How did he make the money to buy the shop?' Daniel broke off a blade of grass and chewed on it.

She leant towards him, her expression lively. 'He went to the Meeting House on first-day – that's Sunday to you – and the owner took him on. He worked hard. When the boss died he married his daughter. Papa wasn't so lucky. He'd hitched a ride on one of the wagons up from the docks to my grandfather's shop. He'd just got off the boat from Ireland after a quarrel with his brother. Till then he lived on the family farm. He came in looking for a job and met Mama. They married against my grandfather's wishes. Because he was Quaker, she was treated like she didn't exist by him and the Friends.'

'What made your father come back to Ireland?'

She smiled. 'Mama says it was to put the sea between them and her father. But his mother had written to him. He had two brothers and one had sickened and died. What about your family?'

He threw the grass down. 'There's only Shaun

and me now, although we have relatives in Liverpool. My mam's sister's family.' He stared down at his hands. 'There was money once. My great-grandfather had land. Out of his own pocket he drained a marsh to grow more crops. The only trouble was that the landlord owned the land. During the potato famine he took it back.' His expression darkened. 'D'you know what it does to a man to lose his roots? The land which his family has farmed for generations?'

'It happens in Ireland.' Her tone was philosophical. 'Papa's family farm has gone now. I'm sorry that you lost your land.'

Daniel's eyes softened. He took her hand and kissed it. She ran her fingers over his mouth. The next moment he pulled her down and she sprawled on top of him. He kissed her forcefully and she responded with a slowly growing passion. His hands roamed her back, coming to rest on her covered bottom. Instantly she was alerted and attempted to push them away, aware of a hardness beneath her. She felt the sigh run through him and then he pushed her off.

'We'd best get back.' He stood up, holding out a hand to her.

She took it. 'I've been thinking that for the last half hour,' she murmured.

'I know.' He grimaced. 'Where do you live?'

She hesitated, considering how her father had

always stressed not giving their name and address to strangers.

'You don't trust me, do you?' His dark brows drew together.

'My father – he's getting almost as nervous as Mama,' she excused. 'But if you still want to, you can walk with me as far as Trinity College.'

He nodded but his expression was angry. 'When I was a lad and we had nothing, I wished I could have killed that landlord who took our land. But now I'm just wishing that you could believe in what I believe. Understand why we have to fight against British Imperialism.'

'Vengeance is mine saith the Lord,' she murmured.

Daniel's laugh had a bitter sound to it. 'But who's to do His dirty work?'

Rebekah shook her head, feeling unexpectedly depressed. 'I only know that killing creates suffering and it is destroying Ireland. Will that do for an answer?' She turned and walked away.

Daniel caught up with her. 'I hate violence as much as you do. It's just that there's no other way.'

'Don't lets talk about it any more. There's no point.'

'I suppose not if you're leaving. I'll walk with you as far as Trinity.'

She nodded and silently they began the walk back, side by side.

CHAPTER TWO

Rebekah was out of breath with rushing by the time she reached the red-brick Georgian terraced house where she lived. Pausing on the step, she pressed the palms of her hands to her hot cheeks in an attempt to cool them as she tried to empty her mind of Daniel and everything that had happened since she left the house, but he was still in her thoughts when the front door with its shiny brass knocker was pulled open.

In the doorway stood the tall, soberly clad figure of Hannah. Her coal black eyes bored into Rebekah's. 'So thee's come back after all. I bet yers been with a fella!' she declared triumphantly in her mixture of old-fashioned Quaker speech and Liverpudlian. 'It's written all over thee so don't be denying it! It's one of those lads from up the street, isn't it? One of those clothes horses! One of those strutting peacocks!

39

Well, yer father's been home, and in a right mood he was – even before I told him that thou hast been missing all afternoon and still not home! He's gone to look for thee.'

'What did you tell him?' demanded Rebekah, pushing past the maid. 'Where's Mama? You didn't say anything to either of them about fellas? Because it's all lies.'

'Of course I did to yer father.' Hannah hurried in after her and would have closed the door, but suddenly it was taken out of her hand and slammed.

Rebekah turned swiftly, her heart sinking at the grim expression on her father's still handsome features. 'Go and tell my wife that her daughter's home, Hannah, and then go to the kitchen.'

'Yes, Mr Rhoades.' Hannah shot a triumphant glance at Rebekah before disappearing into the dining room.

Her father's hand fastened on Rebekah's arm, causing her to wince. 'Up the stairs, miss. I don't want your mother hearing what I have to say. She's been worried about you.'

'But I told Hannah I was going to see Old Mary earlier on,' she said, almost tripping over her feet as he hurried her along the lobby past the solemnly ticking grandfather clock. 'Honestly, Papa, I did go there.'

'Old Mary didn't remember you being there – but then that's not surprising according to your mother,

40

and considering the soldiers were searching the houses,' he muttered, dragging her up the stairs. He was breathing heavily and paused for breath on the landing, leaning against the brown-painted wall next to an oil painting of Kingstown harbour.

The painting instantly reminded Rebekah of Daniel kissing her and her cheeks warmed. She was aware of her father's regard. Had someone seen her with Daniel? 'Papa, I dawdled home,' she said hastily. 'It's been a lovely day.'

He straightened and his expression was thunderous. 'You weren't dawdling alone, though, miss, were you?' He pushed her with some force along the landing. 'I saw you as you came past Trinity College, his hand on your arm and you looking up at him.' His bedroom door yielded beneath his touch and sunlight touched them as it filtered through the lace curtains and heavy dusty velvet drapes that adorned the multiple paned windows that reached almost ceiling to floor.

Rebekah closed her eyes against the sun's brightness and sought for words. 'I can explain!'

'I'd be interested to hear a reasonable explanation for you being in Daniel O'Neill's company,' he said through his teeth, the palm of his hand in the small of her back sending her flying across the room onto the patchwork quilt of the old mahogany bed.

She gasped with shock, pushing herself up, and turned her head just in time to see her father take a switch from the wardrobe. Both belonged to the owner of the house and the switch had never been used on her, although her father had told her how he had been beaten as a boy. Her eyes dilated with apprehension. 'What are you doing?'

'Down, miss. This is going to hurt me more than you.' He swiped the air with the switch, making a whooshing noise, and took a deep breath. 'I should never have listened to your mother when she said that we shouldn't heed the scriptures where they say spare the rod and spoil the child, but I did because you were a girl.' He advanced towards the bed. 'But I never thought a daughter of mine would be cavorting with the likes of Daniel O'Neill! Didn't you think of the danger you could be putting us all in?' he shouted.

'He only walked with me to Trinity!' She struggled as he forced her face down on the bed and flung her skirts up. The first stinging blows landed on her cami-knicker clad bottom and she yelped. Never before had he raised a hand in violence against her.

'You should not be walking with him at all!' he cried. 'There's a price on his head, and if you had been seen by either side you could be dead! We could all be dead!'

The blows, and the words, sent shock waves through her. 'How do you know he's got a price on his head?' she gasped, trying to free her head from the folds of her skirts.

'How do I know? Because I've seen the poster. His brothers had prices on their heads. The whole family's rotten. His two older brothers are dead, but he and his younger brother are wanted. One of the soldiers said the one you were with is like the bloody Scarlet Pimpernel because he keeps disappearing.' His swearing shocked her as much as being beaten. 'Have you been meeting him regularly? What have you been saying to him?' he panted. 'Is it you that has been providing the Sinn Feiners with information?'

'What information? I don't know what you mean,' she croaked, catching her breath as another blow landed.

Adam Rhoades leant against the foot of the bed, the switch dangling from his hand, and said harshly, 'Did you know that another army barracks has been attacked and several men killed? Also a goods train has been derailed. Becky, Shaun O'Neill is implicated, and if he's involved then it must go without saying that his brother is as well.'

Rebekah was filled with dismay. 'I don't know anything about that! I only met him today outside Old Mary's. She's an old neighbour of his mother's.'

There was a silence and she felt the bed give as her father sat on it. 'You're telling me the truth about only meeting him today?' His voice was a little more controlled.

'Yes!' She struggled again to free her head. How

dare he degrade her in such a way at her age? She would never forgive him! Never!

'Perhaps it was him the soldiers were looking for?' he muttered angrily. She remained silent and when she did not answer the switch came down again but there was less strength in the blow. 'Don't you know better than to get involved with a man like that?' His voice trembled. 'Why was it you took so long to reach Trinity? Did you flirt with him?'

'No!' She stopped struggling and lay still.

'I can't emphasise too much, Becky, the danger you could have been in. We've had friends disappear. He could have known who you were and tried to get to me through you.'

'Papa, he didn't know who I was!' she cried, her fingers clenching on the bedspread as she searched for the right words to channel his thoughts into a different direction. 'It wasn't like you say at all. We walked as far as the bay because it was such a nice day, and he told me a story about the Land of the Ever Young.'

'What?' He sounded disbelieving.

'It's the truth.' She crossed her fingers.

Her father made a disgusted noise. 'Faery tales! The man's a dreamer and a fool. That's the trouble with some of these rebels. They lack a sense of reality.'

'Yes, Papa.' She was suddenly thinking that Daniel had seemed the most real person she had ever met.

There was a silence and she felt her father pull down her skirts. Relief made her body sag. Then he demanded, 'But why did you go with him in the first place?'

Rebekah tensed again but thought quickly. 'He wanted to know how Old Mary had been. He hadn't seen her for a while.'

The room was silent again but for the sound of his heavy breathing. 'I hope that's the truth, Becky. I've never known you to lie to me before, but—'

'It is the truth,' she said in a low voice. 'And don't be thinking, Papa, that he'll try and see me again because I told him that we were leaving Ireland.'

'Good!' He sighed. 'Thank God we're going at last. Your poor mother worrying about everything and everybody. The never knowing who might be next.' He wiped a hand over his sweaty face. 'We should have gone years ago.'

'But we're going now,' she said. 'Mama will get better.'

'Yes. But there's nothing definite settled. There'll be uncertainties still, but I've been thrifty so that's in our favour.' He stared at the switch in his hand and violently threw it across the room. 'I shouldn't have hit you so hard,' he said jerkily. 'I'll send Hannah up and she can wash and anoint the weals.'

'No!'

He stood up, frowning, 'I don't want to be upsetting your mother. There's been enough of that lately due to that aunt of yours – so no mention of this, and I'll expect you down to dinner.' He held out a hand. 'I'll see you to your room.'

She ignored his hand, shrinking from physical contact with him, and got herself up.

He left Rebekah outside her room and within moments she was lying on her stomach on the bed, easing off her T-strap shoes. She was in pain, and her emotions were a tangle of hurt, anger, guilt and resentment. She could understand her father's fears but was still shocked by his violent reaction to having seen her in Daniel's company. He had never been an over-indulgent father but he had been approachable, if on the whole leaving most of the decisions concerning her upbringing to her mother. Only in the matter of religion had he insisted that she attend his church, although he had never quarrelled with her mother's insistence that teaching her something about Quaker beliefs would not harm her. Only in the last two years had father and daughter rubbed each other up the wrong way. He had found her a job in the tax department where he had a position of authority. (The previous man had left because of the tenuous hold the British government had in Ireland.) Making friends had not been easy and young men had been wary about approaching her. In a way life had become simpler when her mother had collapsed while shopping and she had to give up her job.

As Becky remembered the tedium of those earlier

months of her mother's illness, she compared her life then with what had happened today. Her mother had been frightened to be in the house alone, and scared of going outdoors. Becky had been almost completely tied to her. She remembered how relieved she had been when Hannah first arrived, until she had got to know her better. As an example of a Quaker and Liverpudlian, Becky could have been put off both if it had not been for her mother. Being cast out of the Liverpudlian meeting house had not embittered her. She had a genuine love for her home town, a belief in the brotherhood of all men and women, and abhorred violence. If Becky had not met Daniel she would have had little to regret in leaving Dublin. It was no longer the safe place of her childhood.

Were her father's suspicions about Daniel true? She did not want to believe that he was a killer. The word sent a shiver through her, conjuring up images. Then she remembered his words and the feel of his arms and decided that it was a good job that they were going because she would have found it difficult to turn him down if he had asked her out again. She forced herself on to her knees. It would have been much more sensible if she had not waited for him and gone to meet Willie, who, because he was unexciting, caused little disturbance to her emotions.

As Rebekah began to undress, Daniel's words about the softness of her skin came to mind. She imagined his mouth on her naked flesh and grew hot and damp and tingly. She gave up undressing to reach for her brassbound leather Bible on the old-fashioned bedside cabinet. Her sleeve caught the angel holding a candle and she dropped the Bible quickly to save the candleholder from breaking. It belonged to the owner of the house as did most of the furnishing in the place. He had left for England when the troubles started and as they had been living in a small damp house, her mother had coaxed her father into renting this one, even though it was too large for them, the furniture old-fashioned, and only downstairs lit by gas.

Replacing the angel, she picked up her Bible again. She should be asking God's forgiveness for lying, seeking perfection instead of thinking thoughts which she felt sure her parents wouldn't approve of. She remembered the girls who had come to the house during the war to fetch their younger brothers and sisters whom her mother had taken in, fed with soup and bread, and attempted to teach them their letters. The girls had talked about boys and men, love, and how babies were made.

A door downstairs opened and Becky heard Hannah's sharp tones mingling with her father's deeper ones. Quickly the Bible was placed haphazardly on the bedside cabinet and she rushed over to the half-empty wardrobe and brought out a primrose-coloured georgette dinner frock, the only such garment she had. From the dressing table she took some cotton knickers and a scarf. For a moment she stood naked, twisting to see and gingerly feeling the weals across her lower back and buttocks. Then she dragged on a white cotton robe and went over to the mahogany and marble washstand.

By the time Hannah knocked on the door, Rebekah was washed and dressed, with the scarf providing a little extra padding beneath her knickers. 'Come in!' she rose from her seated position in front of the oval mirror on the dressing table. 'What is it, Hannah?' she asked cheerfully.

The maid's face fell. 'I thought I heard—'

'Heard what, Hannah? The noise I made earlier because there was a spider in the room?'

'A spider?'

'Yes. I can't abide the creatures. All those legs!' She shivered.

Hannah sniffed and her dark eyes were disappointed. 'It's downright foolish to be scared of an insect. Just put yer foot on them and squash 'em – that's what I do.'

'You're so much braver than me.' Rebekah smiled sweetly, wondering how the Quaker maid taught to abhor violence could find pleasure in the idea of her suffering and the death of a spider.

The maid did not smile back. 'Yer father said that thee wanted me.'

'It's all right now, I managed without your help, but if you could take my dirty clothes, please?'

Hannah sniffed and did not move. Instead she

folded her arms across her non-existent bosom. 'Talked thy way out of trouble after all, did thee?'

Rebekah raised her eyebrows. 'What trouble, Hannah? I told the truth – that I went to see Old Mary and walked for a while in the fresh air. That was something you could have told Mama and Papa about earlier,' she rebuked gently. 'Now – my dirty clothes.' Adding, just to make the maid squirm a little, 'Watch out for lice. Old Mary isn't fussy when it comes to washing.'

The maid hesitated, then moved to pick up the untidy sprawl of clothing on the floor. 'Yer father's still annoyed about something,' she muttered, straightening. 'Came in earlier with his face all twisted and slammed his paper down on the hall table – nearly knocked off the lamp that I'd trimmed and filled this morning – but he keeps hold of a piece of paper and he was looking at that very letter when I left him just now. I wonder what's in it?'

'If it's something bad, I'll soon find out,' murmured Rebekah.

'I suppose so,' grunted Hannah, moving towards the door. Rebekah returned to twisting her heavy tawny hair in a coil at the nape of her neck. For a moment her fingers itched for the scissors before common sense asserted itself. Papa would only see cutting her hair as an act of defiance and the thought that he might again respond violently was enough for her to put the notion aside.

He was standing on the landing when she came out of her bedroom. He had changed into grey flannel trousers and a clean shirt and collar. His dark hair was parted neatly on one side and he had shaved. For a moment she wondered if he was going to bring up the subject of Daniel again and tensed, but he said nothing, only flicking the embroidery round the neck of her frock before proceeding downstairs.

They entered the dining room, to find her mother fiddling with an arrangement of scarlet and lemon dahlias. The gaslight glowed on cutlery and glass and turned Rebekah's mother's complexion the colour of parchment. She wore an Edwardian dark green frock with a high neck, and a heavily fringed crochet shawl was draped about her shoulders. Her slender hand was cool where it touched Rebekah's. 'Such a worry you've had me in, Becky, but your father's explained that you were with Old Mary so let's eat. I suppose you're hungry as usual.'

Rebekah avoided looking at her father, trying to control the anger that rose inside her, and schooled her features as she seated herself on a balloon-backed chair.

Hannah bustled in carrying a tureen. 'Here's some pea soup for yer and I don't want it getting cold,' she grunted. 'It's full of the juices from the beef that I boiled yesterday.'

It smelt delicious and there was silence as Rebekah's father said grace. There was no conversation while they ate their meal. After the soup came cold beef, potatoes and mashed turnip. For pudding there was stewed plums and baked custard. It was not until tea was poured that her father spoke. 'I've had an answer from the agent, Sally.'

His wife looked across at him hastily. 'What agent?'

'The shipping agent.' His tone was irritable.

'Why should you write to a shipping agent?' Her voice trembled.

'For berths to America, of course,' he said in a tightly controlled voice, stirring his tea jerkily so that it spilt in the saucer. 'I wrote to Cunard's in Liverpool, thinking that way I could get preference and the most comfortable passage for you. No expense was to be spared. I even gave them a draft on my bank. Now they write and tell me that all berths on their ships were taken up weeks ago. That I should have booked a passage earlier.'

Rebekah exchanged glances with her mother, who was obviously trying hard to conceal her relief. 'Does that mean we won't be going to America then?'

'Of course it doesn't!' Her husband slammed the table. 'How many times do I have to tell you, Sal, it'll be a better life for us there. The Ireland we know is finished. And England's going to find it difficult financially. The war cost them! America's the place.'

'But if there's no berths,' murmured his wife, pleating a fold of the tablecloth. 'What can we do?'

'There's other shipping lines,' he said firmly. 'They probably won't be as comfortable but we'll have to put up with that.'

'Adam, if you're doing this for me,' she said hesitantly, 'as I've said before, there's no need. A new life in a new land is for those just beginning. I feel too old to start up again. Liverpool would suit—'

'No!' His mouth thinned and he scrunched the letter in his hand, 'I don't feel too old, and you only feel like that because of what it's been like here for the last couple of years. You'll soon perk up once we're away from the fighting. There's lots of folk emigrating who are as old as us, and travelling further. Since the War they want to leave Europe. It's that sister of yours who wants you to stay in Liverpool. And why should we, Sal? For years, nothing! We were treated like lepers. Not a penny farthing did your father ever give you. We had to struggle when he could have made it a bit easier for you.'

'I know, I know!' She put a hand to her mouth and her throat moved jerkily. When she spoke again, her voice shook. 'Don't let's go over all that again, please. Will you still allow me some time with Esther? She was like a mother to me, if you remember?'

'Bossy enough!' he interposed.

'She couldn't help that.' A shadow crossed his wife's face. 'You had your mother to old age. Can we still stay with Esther? Once we leave for America, you know that it's unlikely I'll ever see her again.'

He nodded slowly. 'I won't deny you some time with your sister. But if she upsets you by playing her tricks, like she did when she tried to separate us when first we met, then we'll find lodgings elsewhere.' He patted her hand before taking up his teacup. 'It might be best for me to see if we can leave tomorrow.'

'But I haven't finished packing,' said Rebekah in a startled voice, her thoughts moving swiftly into the present instead of dwelling on her parents' past.

Her father's eyebrows came together. 'Then you shouldn't have wasted time visiting that old woman and going for walks,' he said fiercely. 'Get a move on, miss, because what doesn't get packed will be left behind.'

Rebekah decided it would be wisest to show willing and rose with stiff awkward movements, hoping that her mother would not see anything amiss. She was in pain and did not want to go to America. It would be even stranger than Liverpool and so far away from home. As for Daniel, there would be no chance of ever seeing him again. Her resentment against her father hardened as she went as quickly as she could out of the dining room, barely able to take in that such great changes in her life were happening. Soon they would leave Ireland for ever.

CHAPTER THREE

The Irish ferry boat steamed up the Mersey, having safely manoeuvred the sandbanks in the estuary and avoided the numerous craft in the river. Rebekah had never seen so many ships and growing excitement now replaced the regret she had felt when she had seen Ireland becoming a tiny smudge on the horizon. They had not departed as early as her father had wished because there had been too much to do.

Yesterday, tempers had been fraught and only Hannah had gone about her tasks with a smile on her face that had maddened Rebekah. She had handed back her discarded clothing, saying that there was no way that she could get them dry if she washed them. So Rebekah's dirty clothes had been stuffed in a cloth bag with her nightdress, tortoise and ivory dressing table set, her Bible, and an old doll given her by her dead paternal grandmother which she could not bring herself to part with.

Now her father's hand descended heavily on her shoulder and she tensed. 'You must stay close to Hannah. If you get separated in the crush, wait outside the Riverside Station and we'll find you there.'

'Don't thee be worrying, Mr Rhoades,' said Hannah with a satisfied smile. 'I'll watch her like a hawk.'

Rebekah contained her impatience. 'Papa, I do have a tongue in my head. I'm not a child.'

'It might be better if you were,' Adam said shortly, and before Rebekah could say another word he was gone.

She frowned, guessing that he was making an oblique reference to the episode with Daniel O'Neill. She had not been able to get him out of her mind, but now she gave her attention to Liverpool. Along the seafront sprawled its famous docks and its bustling landing stage. It seemed enormous after Dublin.

'Soon be getting off now, and thou wilt be needing all thy wits about thee then,' said Hannah, picking up her bag. 'Babylon it is all around dockland. There's pickpockets and lads wanting to carry thy bag who'd have the last farthing off a one-legged beggar. Stick close to me as thy father said, and hold on to everything.'

Rebekah noted the change in the sound of the ship's engines and watched the sudden surge of foaming water about the hull. Now they were only yards from land, and ropes thicker than a man's arm were being thrown from ship to the landing stage. On shore, a little way back, she could see a roof with the words RIVERSIDE STATION painted on it.

Hannah seized her wrist. Irritated, Rebekah pulled herself free, not seeing any reason to hurry as she gazed on the people that crowded the deck. She spotted her mother, a little more colour in her cheeks than normal, who gave her a faint smile. 'Stay close to Hannah,' she called, before suddenly disappearing from Rebekah's sight as people surged towards the gangway.

No sooner did Rebekah and Hannah set foot on land than they were besieged by several youths. A huge burly lad, with a thatch of red hair, freckles, and an ingratiating smile which revealed several gaps where teeth were missing, shouldered his rivals out of the way and laid a hand on Rebekah's luggage. 'Carry yer bag, miss?'

'Thou wilt not,' Hannah intervened sharply, poking her elbow into his upper arm.

He barely spared her a glance, but thrust a widespread hand on her face and pushed hard. She went toppling backwards. 'If yer in need of lodgings I can show yer a decent place,' he said, as if Hannah's interruption had not taken place.

Rebekah had no time to enjoy the spectacle of Hannah sprawling but had to tug hard on her bag. 'Will you let go? I can carry my own bag – and I don't need lodgings because I'm staying with my aunt.'

His smile slipped. 'That's alright, luv. I'll still get yer a cab.' And he gave a heave that took the bag clean out of her grasp.

'Hey, give me it back!' she cried indignantly.

He did not even spare Rebekah a backward glance but was away. Her temper rose and she gave chase. It was not easy keeping her quarry in view. The Prince's landing stage was a busy place at most times and it was worse today because several large ships had docked. Still she managed to weave her way through the crowd to catch up with him and seize hold of her bag. 'Got you.'

Several heads swivelled in their direction as he turned with an ugly expression on his face and surprised her by sneering. 'Hey now, what's this, little thief! Have yer seen this one, folks?' he yelled, looking about him. 'Real barefaced she is.'

'It's you that's the thief,' she panted, enraged, swinging her free hand and punching him on the nose.

Tears started in his eyes and an ex-serviceman, selling matches, chortled, 'Serves yer right, Joe.'

'Yer little cow,' he said in a muffled voice, covering his nose a moment before bringing down his fist. The blow would have stunned Rebekah if she had not swerved while tugging at her bag. The clasp gave and out tumbled a flesh-coloured lawn nightgown.

She snatched it up from the damp, dirty ground. 'Whose bag is it?' she cried triumphantly. 'Do you wear skirts?' Several people laughed.

'It's me mam's,' he snapped, obviously determined not to be bested as he struggled with her.

'Yer haven't a mam,' called a voice. 'Give the girl her stuff back.'

'That's right,' said Rebekah. 'Give me it back.'

Joe's eyes narrowed and he pulled so hard on the bag that she was catapulted against him. 'I take orders from no one. Yer've got a bloody nerve, girl,' he hissed in her face. 'I could squash yer as soon as look at yer. Yer don't think any of this lot'll help yer.'

'Get your hands off me.' She was proud that her voice did not betray her.

He stared at her, almost eyeball to eyeball, and laughed. 'Yer gonna make me?'

Before she could speak, a voice said, 'She mightn't be able to but I can.' The words uttered in the familiar Irish brogue took both of them by surprise and Rebekah twisted in Joe's grasp.

Daniel did not pause in his advance on them. 'It's a fine mess your father's making of looking after you.'

Rebekah felt a lifting of her spirits. 'He's with Mama. I was with Hannah but this – this person pushed her in the face.'

'Hardly friendly.' He clenched a fist. 'If he doesn't take his filthy hands off you, I'll knock his block off.'

'I wouldn't try it, Paddy.' Joe eyed Daniel up and down uneasily. 'You might be taller than me but I've got the weight, see – as well as a pile of mates I can call on.'

Daniel shrugged, 'I don't like fighting a lad of your age but if you're so keen, boyo, I've got a few friends I could whistle up. So let her go.'

Joe reached for his belt but before he could pull out the knife that was there, Daniel made his move. Rebekah was forcibly swung out of the way and his fist made contact with Joe's jaw. He crumpled slowly to the ground.

'Let's get out of here,' said Daniel, seizing her wrist and getting them lost in the crowd in seconds.

'Where are we going?' Her grip tightened on her bag as she almost fell over her feet in her attempt to keep up, cram her nightdress back in her bag, and look at him at the same time.

'Out of sight, out of reach. Joe's a regular here. He's bound to have mates somewhere.'

'I shouldn't have got you involved in a fight,' she said, her breathing flurried.

He smiled. 'That was a good punch on the nose you gave him.'

'You saw it?' she gasped. 'Perhaps if I hadn't hit him, he mightn't have got tough with me. I lost my temper.'

'You've got to stand up to some people.'

She shook her head. 'I should have turned the other cheek.'

He ignored that remark and said, 'Where are your mama and papa?'

'Seeing to the luggage, I suppose. I'm to meet them

at the Riverside Station if I get lost.' She looked about her. 'I *am* lost.'

'We're only going to the end of the landing stage.'

'You've been here before?'

'I told you, I've got relatives in Liverpool.'

There was a pause before she said, 'Why didn't you tell me you were coming?'

'I wasn't sure if it was the right thing to do.' He glanced at her. 'Mam always said, "When in doubt, say nowt." Besides, I had our Shaun to get out of trouble.'

'He's here?' Involuntarily she glanced about them.

He grimaced. 'Not right here and now. We came yesterday.'

She stopped abruptly. 'Then there is a price on your heads?'

He halted. 'Now who's told you that?'

'My father.' Her voice was low. 'I hoped it wasn't true. But it is, isn't it?'

Daniel was silent for several minutes, then he said vehemently, 'I'm no killer! My brothers gave the family a bad name. What made your father mention it? Did you tell him about us?'

'No!' She frowned. 'He saw us together. I got a hiding just for being in your company.'

'I'm sorry.' He squeezed her fingers.

'It's not your fault. He thought I'd been passing you information for IRB activities. He's been overwrought lately. I told you that the other day.'

'I'm still sorry he hit you. What did you tell him

61

about us?' They had halted almost at the far end of the landing stage and her gaze took in the khaki-coloured waters and beyond them Birkenhead and its new shipyards. 'I told him I'd met you at Old Mary's – that I'd walked with you because you wanted to know how she was.'

'He believed you?' His gaze followed hers across the water.

'I don't make a habit of lying. For the first time in my life he hit me – then asked questions.'

He held her hand tightly. 'I'm sorry again.'

'I know. You don't have to keep saying it. Will you be staying in Liverpool?'

'I'm not sure what I'm doing. You?'

'Father's determined that we're going to America.' She told him what had passed at the dinner table.

'He'll get berths,' said Daniel positively. 'There's other shipping lines.'

'I don't know how quickly, though. It could take time.' She glanced at him and he shook his head.

'You mustn't be thinking what you're thinking.' He released her hand. 'We both agreed that it's pointless us getting to know each other.'

She tossed her plait back over her shoulder, surprised at his perception. 'I know. And it would be difficult meeting.'

'It could be dangerous too.'

'Even here?' she whispered.

He added hastily, 'If your father saw us together

again, it wouldn't be much fun for either of us.'

'Could he have you arrested?' She moved away from him and he followed.

'Probably.'

They were both silent, and she felt if he did not speak and say something positive then she would burst. He did not and she rushed into saying, 'Where are you going now?'

'To my aunt's. I only came to see if—' He stopped and stared over the river.

'To see what?'

'The ships.' He glanced at her. 'What are you doing tomorrow?'

'I don't know,' she said quickly. 'If you wanted to—'

'Aye! I'm prepared to take a chance.'

'Where do we meet?'

'You don't know anywhere.' He smiled.

'Here?' Her eyes were bright.

He nodded. 'One o'clock?'

'Fine.'

He leant towards her and their lips met briefly. 'Till tomorrow then,' he said, and vanished into the crowd.

Rebekah wondered if she was quite mad, but she was smiling as she turned and ran towards the customs shed. She went through and headed for the railway station. As she neared it she saw her mother and Hannah waiting. 'Where have you been? We've been worrying, thinking you might have been carried off and shipped to China!' Her mother's voice was lively.

'China?'

'Tea clippers used to race there and back in the old days.' Her mother put a hand through her arm. 'Oh, it's so good to be home! Do you know, Becky, the Liver building wasn't built when I was last here. Isn't it grand? And the docks – they seemed to have spread out.'

Hannah interrupted her with a sniff. 'I was robbed lying on the ground. Sum things don't change.'

'Poor Hannah!' Rebekah could spare her a smile. She was thinking no further than tomorrow and nothing could cast a cloud on her spirits. 'Did you have much stolen? I got my bag back.'

The maid sniffed again. 'Me purse. Yer father and mother came before I could suffer any more insults from those black-hearted scoundrels. Not fit for mackerel bait, they ain't.'

'Where is Papa?' asked Rebekah, quickly changing the subject.

'Arranging transport for the bulk of our baggage,' replied her mother. 'He said that we were not to wait but to get a taxi to your aunt's. But I was just thinking, love, if your legs are like mine then a walk will do them good. Hannah can get the tram if she wants.'

'I will,' said the maid, and accepted her fare and left them.

Rebekah thought about warning her mother

against walking too far, she had been resting a lot since her illness. But then Rebekah considered how useful walking about the town might be in getting to know her way about.

They went under the overhead railway and passed the sailor's church. Her mother told her that just over a hundred years ago there had been a terrible accident during Sunday service when part of the steeple had collapsed, killing more than twenty people. Further on she pointed out the town hall. 'When my father tried to stop me going out with your papa, he told me how there'd been a Fenian plot to blow up the town hall in 1881. You know that the Fenians were sort of forerunners of the Irish Republican Brotherhood?' Rebekah nodded. 'They caught the men, and thank God the town hall is still here. But Father thought the telling might prevent me wanting to marry your papa. He had a habit of tarring all the Irish with the same brush.'

Rebekah said nothing, but she was thinking of what her father had said about Daniel. By the time they came in sight of the Graeco-Roman style St George's Hall, built during Victoria's reign, her mother was tiring so they caught a tram in Lime Street. Rebekah asked about places and roads, some of which her mother did not know, although she pointed out the Royal Hippodrome in West Derby Road. 'When I was about twelve, my father's sister came down from Bolton. She took me to a variety show. It was a revelation. I enjoyed the acts and went again with a friend when I was older, but I never told Papa or Esther. Aunt Maggie wasn't a bit like other Quakers I knew. She had a yen for the stage, and soon after left the Society of Friends and went to London. The only time Papa mentioned her again was years later when he said I was as flighty as her. I remember I replied that I looked upon that as a compliment. That she was the best in the family.' Her eyes gleamed. 'He nearly hit me. Sad. I would have liked to have seen her again.'

Rebekah smiled. Liverpool seemed to be bringing out a different side to her mother and she was glad to see it.

They descended from the tram a couple of stops later and walked up a road of red-brick houses with long front gardens. Rebekah had visualised something grander because her father had told her that Aunt Esther had come into the family fortune and it had been quite substantial. They stopped at a house with a green front door with a black wrought iron knocker on it.

Footsteps hurried in response to their knock and the door opened to reveal Aunt Esther. She was small and round, with fluffy yellow-white hair. The three of them stared at each other then the two sisters flung their arms around each other.

'Oh, Sarah,' cried Esther, tears in her eyes as she crushed her against her black serge bosom. 'It's so good to see thee. If I'd know that thou were definitely arriving today, I would have come to meet thee.'

'It doesn't matter. We're here now.' Sarah's voice was unsteady as she disentangled herself from her sister's arms and seized Rebekah's hand. 'This is Becky. I think she's got a look of our side of the family, don't you?'

'Oh, yes! She's got Mother's eyes. Thou art very welcome, Rebekah.'

'Thank you.' She suffered her aunt's embrace, then was pulled inside the house.

'It's been so long, Sarah,' said her aunt. 'I hope thee can stay for weeks and weeks. Hannah was saying something about America?'

'Yes,' Sarah sighed.

Rebekah squeezed her hand. 'It's Papa's idea, Aunt Esther.'

Her mother nodded. 'We've tried our best to dissuade him, but there's no moving him. He's adamant.'

'Adam always was,' said Esther, her lips compressing in an uncompromising line. 'Hannah said that he left thee to fend for thyselves at the Pierhead. No doubt it's his selfishness as well as the fighting that's worn thy nerves down. Did Hannah give thee the Dr Cassell's tablets I sent? I know plenty of people who swear by them, and I've taken them myself since Papa died.'

Sarah said warmly, 'I've taken the tablets, and I

believe they have done me some good. It was kind of you – and to send Hannah too. She's such a good worker. But please don't speak of Adam in such a way.'

'Thou still won't have a word said against him,' said Esther in resigned tones. 'Such loyalty does thee credit, sister.'

'A wife has to stand alongside her husband.' Sarah smiled. 'Try and get on with him, Esther. I know the pair of you could never see eye to eye in the past, but do try now. Papa tried to browbeat Adam into doing what he wanted and it was the biggest mistake he ever made.' She paused long enough for her sister to nod, then added, 'Now how about a cup of tea? I'm parched.'

'Hannah will make us a cup,' said Esther, leading the way. 'It was quite a sacrifice sending her to thee. The girl I've had to put up with in her place doesn't do half the work, and walked out this morning just because I rightfully complained about the way she hung the clean curtains – she said she'd be happier working at that new Woolworths! Young girls these days! It's the war and this suffragette movement. It's unsettled them.'

'The movement was going in our day,' murmured Sarah, entering a back room and looking about her, before sinking into an armchair.

'Yes, but we didn't get involved. There was too much work to do.'

'That's true. But it's no different for women today.

They still work hard.' She smiled at her daughter. 'Some have to work harder.'

'But there's many who are just out for a good time,' protested Esther.

'It's the war,' said Rebekah, who had knelt on a tiger rug at her mother's feet.

Her mother nodded. 'Thousands of women have lost the chance of marriage, and there's thousands more who have to be father and mother to their children. Even if more women get the vote, there's no easy cure for what ails most girls today.'

'Let's not talk about it,' said Esther, sitting in the other armchair. 'Instead tell me what hast thou been doing all those years in Ireland, and why that husband of thine wants to go to America.'

Sarah shook her head, 'I'm not ready to talk about Ireland. You've no idea how the fighting—' Her voice trailed off.

'Thou should never have left Liverpool.' Esther's voice held a fierce note. 'Adam could have accepted our ways.'

'Don't let's go over that again.' Sarah's face stiffened. 'Why not tell me who bought the shop? And what happened to . . .'

Rebekah leant back against the leg of her mother's chair and listened to the two sisters talk. They gossiped about old times and old acquaintances, and not for the first time she wished that she had a sister to confide in. To talk to about Daniel. She let her mind drift, wondering how she could escape tomorrow.

Hannah brought tea and toasted buns. The door knocker sounded and it was Esther who went to answer it because the maid was occupied. Rebekah and her mother exchanged glances and her mother put a finger to her lips.

Rebekah could hardly prevent a smile when she heard her aunt's disgruntled tones, 'It's thee! I suppose thou had best come in.'

'You always did have a warm welcome for me, Esther,' said Adam in a surprisingly pleasant voice. 'You'll be pleased to know that I won't be staying above a day or two.'

'Why is that?' Esther's dismay was obvious, 'I haven't said anything so terrible yet.'

'No, but you will,' he said grimly. 'I've booked berths for us on a ship going to America.'

'Not already,' cried Esther. 'Thou could have given Sarah and me some time. We've hardly had chance to—'

'There's been plenty of chances for you during the last twenty years,' he rasped.

'No, there wasn't. Thou never did try to understand our way. And now—'

Rebekah got to her feet at the same time as her mother, who called, 'Will you two please stop! My nerves can't stand it!'

Her father came into the sitting room. There was a sullen expression on his face.

Rebekah said quickly, 'When are we going, Papa?'

His expression lightened, 'I can see you're as impatient as I am to be on our way, Becky. I'm glad you're coming round to my way of thinking.'

'I didn't say that, Papa,' she murmured, 'I only asked when we were leaving Liverpool. And how did you manage to arrange it so quickly?'

He looked towards her mother, 'I put it down to the hand of God myself,' he said with heavy humour. 'No doubt, Sal, you and Esther will disagree.'

'Maybe,' said her mother, unsmiling. 'Just answer Becky's questions.'

Slowly he took his pipe from a pocket and placed it between his teeth. 'When I was seeing to our luggage I literally bumped into the son of the man who bought our old farm.' He paused to search for matches. 'The father's dead and the brother who inherited was killed in the war. The second son now owns the father's shipping line as well as the estate in Ireland. Joshua remembered me.' He lit up. The three women waited in silence for him to continue, and once he had his pipe going to his satisfaction he did so. 'We now have a cabin to ourselves on one of his ships. With a bit of luck we'll be leaving on Monday.' There was the slightest hint of defiance in his tones. 'The ship is still short of crew but they should be signed on over the weekend.'

Rebekah glanced at her mother and on seeing her expression, anger bubbled up inside her. 'Couldn't you have allowed Mama a few more days?' she hissed. 'Why the rush to get to America?'

Her father turned on her. 'You wouldn't understand! It was bad enough when we left for Ireland twenty years ago. Your mother was homesick for ages. It's better my way, you'll see. Now how about a cup of tea?' His gaze passed over the three of them just as Hannah came into the room.

'Tea! I know what I'd like to do with you and a cup of tea,' said Sarah in a seething voice. 'How could you arrange everything without consulting me? You could have given me more time.' She swept out of the room. Esther glared at Adam and followed her sister.

There was a silence. 'Well,' he snapped, 'are you going to walk out too, miss, or are you going to show me some respect and gratitude by pouring me a cup of tea?'

Before Rebekah could say or do anything, Hannah chipped in 'I'll do thee a cup of tea, sir.' She picked up a fine bone china cup decorated with red-purple roses and filled it to the brim. There was a wide smile on her bony face. 'I'm sure thee's right and are only doing what yer think best for thy family. As yer know, two of me brothers are in America. It's a fine place. They never want to come home.'

'Who'd want to come home to you?' Rebekah could not resist saying, and walked out of the room. Her aunt's voice could be heard from the direction of the parlour, and although the door was shut

Rebekah could clearly hear what was being said.

'There's no reason why thou hast to go to America, Sarah. I've got enough money to keep the three of us.'

'You're suggesting I leave Adam!' Her mother gave a sharp laugh. 'It's easy to see that you've never married, Esther.'

'I looked after Papa and that was no piece of cake,' retorted her aunt, 'I know what men are like. They like their own way. Only thinking of themselves. Papa treated me like a skivvy, and from the look of thee Adam hasn't behaved any better in that Godforsaken country.'

'You know nothing about my life there, only what I've told you of in the last year and that's not Adam's fault! You don't know him.' Her mother's voice had altered, and sounded weary.

'A handsome face and a beguiling way with him.' Her aunt sniffed.

'There's more to Adam than that but you never wanted to see it.'

'I'd brought thee up. I didn't want to lose thee.'

'I can understand that.' There was a pause. 'Don't let's quarrel. We have to make the most of the time we have.'

'Then thou art going to America?' The words were uttered in a disgruntled voice.

'I can't leave my husband just because you want me to stay here!' There was silence and her aunt murmured something Rebekah could not catch. Then her mother said, 'I'll try and make him change his mind but I think it'll be a waste of time.'

There was movement towards the door and Rebekah backed away and sat on the stairs as the two women came out. 'Hannah's making up to Papa,' she murmured.

Esther stared at her. 'Hannah! Not her! She doesn't like men.'

'I thought that myself but perhaps it's Papa's handsome face,' she said lightly.

Her aunt's mouth tightened. 'Handsome is as handsome does. He won't get much change out of Hannah, whatever he says and does. I'm not going back in there right now. If thou likes I could show thee thy rooms?'

'I think we could all do with time to calm down,' said Rebekah's mother. 'Come on, Becky. Grab your case.'

She nodded, considering it wiser to do as suggested, and followed the two sisters upstairs.

As Rebekah unpacked her nightdress, toothbrush and toothpowder, her aunt came back into the room. She sat on the bed, her expression determined. 'Thou doesn't want to go to America, does thee, Rebekah?'

'It doesn't matter what I want,' she said honestly.

Esther nodded and sighed. 'It's always been that way. Girls have to do what they're told. Duty – it's a burden. But thou cares what thy mother wants? Thou wants her to be happy?'

'She wouldn't be happy without Papa,' said Rebekah positively. She glanced at her aunt. 'I heard you and Mama talking. It's no use, Aunt Esther. If Papa has made up his mind, I don't think he's going to change it. Especially when he's already got the tickets.'

Esther played with the bobbles round the shade of the bedside lamp. 'Thou doesn't think thee can change his mind?'

'Me?' Rebekah was startled. 'I doubt it.'

'Some fathers and daughters are very close.' A frown creased her plump face and she added with apparent difficulty, 'Papa was very fond of thy mother. As I was. The light went out of our lives when she left. If thou could persuade—'

Rebekah shook her head. 'I'm sorry, Aunt Esther, but Mama's your best bet. Papa and I aren't the best of friends at the moment. Now, is there any chance of my having a bath?'

Her aunt nodded and with a gloomy expression took her outside, indicating the bathroom before going downstairs.

Rebekah lay in bed, listening. Eavesdropping had always been the only way she could obtain the information that her parents thought they should keep from her. Even here in her aunt's house it did not seem to have occurred to them that they could be overhead. Her bedroom window was slightly ajar and theirs next door must also be open. Her father was speaking, stressing each word. 'Why did we leave Dublin, Sal? To get away from the fighting, that's why. And Liverpool isn't far enough away for me. Joshua Green told me that there's cells of the IRA over here, causing as much trouble as they can by arson and cutting telegraph wires. You know the way they work to create chaos.'

'Esther hasn't mentioned anything about that,' responded her mother in that controlled way of speaking she had when her nerves were fraught and she was on the brink of tears.

'She wouldn't, would she?' he insisted. 'It's in her interests to keep quiet.'

'She wouldn't think of that!' Her mother's voice trembled. 'Esther might have her faults but she wouldn't deliberately keep something like that to herself.'

'Perhaps not,' he said mildly, before adding, 'What I'd like to know is, if she cared so much about you, why haven't we heard from her in all these years?'

'You know why! Father didn't tell her about my letters.'

'So she says. More likely she wanted to keep all his money for herself.'

'You can think what you like. I don't believe that.'

'You wouldn't.' His voice had softened. 'You like to think the best of everybody. Believe me, Sal, it's our future I'm thinking about in going to America.'

'I don't doubt that.' She sighed. 'But what if Esther takes ill? She has no one close.'

'She has Hannah. She'll be all right.'

There was a short silence and her mother said something Rebekah did not catch because she was distracted by her own thoughts about Hannah. When her father spoke again, his manner had changed altogether. He sounded excited. 'There's a good chance of my already having a position to go to in America, Sal! I'll be seeing Joshua Green tomorrow about it. You said that you wanted to do some shopping. Well, that fits in fine with my plans. I'll give you some extra money and you can go into town with Esther and Becky and buy some new clothes.'

'Becky does need some new things,' said her mother thoughtfully. 'She's had little chance in the last few years of going on a shopping spree.'

'Aye, well, there's been little chance for any of us to go on shopping sprees and have a good time. It'll be different in America, you wait and see.' The voices grew faint and Rebekah presumed they had moved away from the window. Everything else was inaudible.

She lay staring out the window at the night sky, thinking that it was a real shame they were not staying in Liverpool. Still, at least they were going shopping in town tomorrow. Surely there would be an opportunity for her to get away and meet Daniel? All she had to do was to watch out for it.

CHAPTER FOUR

'I'm sure Papa would be against you having your hair
cut.' Rebekah's mother looked at her anxiously as
they stood in front of Hill's Hairdressers in Ranelagh
Street not far from Lewis's great store where Sarah
had just purchased a pair of black glacé kid shoes
with patent leather toecaps for her daughter.

'But everyone's cutting their hair now,' insisted
Rebekah.

'You've got such lovely hair,' protested her
mother. 'Your father wouldn't like it cut. Besides it
would be such a shame to—'

'Please, Mama,' she said coaxingly. 'It's always
braided and generally hidden under a hat so nobody
sees it.'

'The girl has a point,' interrupted her aunt. They
both stared at her. 'Why shouldn't she have her
hair bobbed?' She bristled. 'If it's good enough for

78

the upper classes, then who's thy husband to speak against it?'

'The upper classes!' snorted Sarah. 'That argument won't wash with Adam. You're a snob, Esther.'

'No, I'm not,' said she. 'The trouble is, Sarah, thou hast been in the backwoods in Ireland. If thou wants to find a husband for the girl, she has to make the best of herself.'

Her mother gazed at Rebekah and said softly. 'Of course I want a husband for her, but I don't think Adam wants her to marry just anybody.'

Her aunt sniffed. 'He's just the kind of father who doesn't want to see himself replaced in his daughter's affections!' Her gloved fingers twisted her handbag chain so that it dug into her hand. 'Let the girl get her hair cut if she can make an appointment today. If she can't – well, then, her hair will have to stay the way it is.'

Sarah's uncertain gaze went from her sister to Rebekah.

She smiled at her mother. 'You can tell him that I went missing and did it without your knowing.'

'I'll do nothing of the sort,' said Sarah with an outward show of calm. 'We'll go and have another look in Lewis's windows while you find out if you can get it cut.'

'Thanks, Mama!' Rebekah hugged her and stared once more at the picture of a fashionable young woman with a cap of deeply waving dark hair before entering the hairdressing salon. If she was lucky then she would tell her mother and her aunt not to wait, that she would find her own way home.

An hour and a half later, Rebekah came out of the shop, carrying her hat. Her head felt so light that it might not have been there. She had been told that if Madam was prepared to wait, then they would fit her in. Well, Madam had waited and they had done her a treat. And, she told herself with fingers crossed, she did not care if Papa hit the roof because she was certain that Aunt Esther would take her side.

Setting out for the Pierhead, and knowing that there was plenty of time, Rebekah enjoyed looking in the shops, not only at her new reflection but at the clothes and fancy goods. Her gaze was riveted by a French voile hand-embroidered blouse in George Henry Lee's window but she knew the chances of her buying it were remote. She turned away only to collide with two men deep in conversation. All her brave resolutions vanished and her heart sank as she recognised her father. She averted her face and mumbled an apology, and would have passed unrecognised if his companion had not seized her arm and enquired if she was all right.

Reluctantly she glanced up to see a man, probably of about thirty, pleasant-looking, fair-haired and moustached, with pale blue eyes. At the same instant she heard her father's quick intake of breath and knew him to have identified her.

'Rebekah!' His mouth pursed in the way that she had become familiar with during the last months.

'Yes, Papa?' She forced a smile and pulled her arm out of the man's hold. 'I'm in a hurry – to meet – Mama and Aunt Esther in Kardomah's cafe.'

'Never mind that!' Her father's voice cut through her explanation. 'You've had your hair cut! Does your mother know about this, or have you—'

'I think it looks charming,' interrupted his companion, smiling. 'You never told me your daughter was so pretty, Adam. Introduce us.'

Grudgingly her father said, 'Rebekah, this is Joshua Green, the owner of the shipping line we're sailing with. Say your how do you do's.'

Knowing that her father could hardly upbraid her in his presence, Rebekah held out her hand and said warmly, 'How do you do, Mr Green? I'm happy to meet you.'

He raised his hat and the blue eyes took on a look of startling awareness as his fingers fastened about hers. 'It's a pleasure to meet you, Miss Rhoades.' His voice was deep. 'It's a pity you're to be in Liverpool such a short time because I would have asked your father's permission to show you the sights.'

'That's kind of you,' she said, surprised.

'I would have enjoyed it.' He smiled and pressed her fingers.

'It's nice of you to say so, but I must go. Thank

you.' She withdrew her hand and before her father could say anything else she hurried away, resisting a backward glance to see if they were watching her.

The exchange had wasted time and then she had to stop and ask someone if she was going the right way for the Pierhead. They said she could not miss it if she kept walking straight ahead and down towards the river.

Rebekah did just that but was getting anxious as she neared the Mersey. She glanced up at the Liver clock. It was five past one and immediately she made haste, running up the covered passenger way that led to the landing stage. She need not have worried. Daniel was waiting.

'I thought you mightn't have been able to get away.' His eyes searched her face and she knew it had been right to come.

'I almost didn't get here.' Rebekah took off her hat and shook her head.

'You've had your hair cut!'

'Don't you like it?' Her voice was anxious. 'It was my excuse for getting rid of my mother and aunt. And, besides, I've wanted to get it cut for ages. Long hair is a nuisance.'

'I thought you were perfect as you were. But, yes, I like it.' He smiled as she blushed.

'Papa almost didn't recognise me. I bumped into him in Church Street. Now I'm in trouble! If he had known I was coming to meet you, he'd have gone up in smoke!'

'Then we'd best avoid Church Street if we don't want to see a fire-breathing papa,' he said, offering her his arm. 'Where would you like to go?'

'I'm still only a little the wiser about places,' she murmured, taking his arm. 'All my family seem to be in town so window shopping is out.'

'Best get out of Liverpool then,' said Daniel. 'I'll take you on the Overhead Railway to Seaforth Sands. It's the fastest electric train in England, and the first. We'll be there in no time and you get a great view of the docks and the river.'

'That sounds fine. I've never heard of Seaforth.' She was very aware of the muscular arm beneath her fingers and the smell of his shaving soap. He was all spruced up – clean collar, blue tie, well-brushed dark jacket and grey flannels. She was glad that she had on her best yellow organdie frock and her only pair of silk stockings. They made a fine couple, she thought, feeling warm inside.

'It's a good place for an outing,' he said. 'The tide's out so we'll be able to stroll on the sands.'

'You know it well?'

'Well enough. I've been coming on and off since I was thirteen. Liverpool has some nightmarish spots but I like the place. There's always something going on. But I was telling you about Seaforth – Prime Minister Gladstone lived there for a while, you can see his family house, and a ship called the *Dicky Sam* went aground on the sands during Victorian times. Straight from Virginia it was, and full of tobacco.'

'Was anybody drowned?'

'I don't know about that. Only that the villagers stripped the ship of its tobacco.'

'They stole it?'

'What the tide washes up and leaves—' He smiled.

'It's still stealing,' she said slowly. 'The shipowners and the merchants would lose money.'

'They can afford it.' He glanced at her. 'Sweated labour, Becky, that's how they use the poor. A working man isn't paid what his labour is worth.'

'I know that. Are you a union man?' She hoped he would tell her more about himself.

'To be sure I am when I get the time. You're not against the unions?'

'I know hardly anything about them. What union?'

'I'm a seaman,' he said. 'What other job would keep bringing me back and forth to Liverpool and Ireland?' He took her hand and led her up the steps to the station as she digested the unexpected information, considering how it put a different light on things.

'I suppose your being a sailor is what makes the soldiers think you're like the Scarlet Pimpernel,' murmured Rebekah, as they settled themselves in a second class carriage.

He stilled. 'What makes you say that?'

'My father said it.' She cleared her throat. 'He also said that the IRA have cells in Liverpool. I wasn't sure if he was saying it just to make Mama not want to stay here. Do you know—?'

A frown creased his forehead. 'Look out of the window, Becky. You'll be getting a good view of the river and the ships. As well as that, there's the warehouses for storing the cargoes to see. They're enormous, aren't they? They hide some terrible housing. As bad as any you'd see in Dublin.'

'You don't want to talk about the IRA?' she said quietly.

'No.' He looked out of the window. 'Did you know now that Liverpool has the biggest tobacco warehouse there is?'

She recognised his determination not to talk about the troubles, but his involvement was there between them even though they were away from Ireland and it bothered her, really bothered her. 'I thought cotton was the biggest commodity Liverpool handled?'

'Sure it's huge.' He glanced at her and the frown was still there. 'But there's more than that to the Port. You have your rubber – your timber from Canada – vegetable oils for soap. And there's granaries for the cereals from Canada and America.'

She looked down at her hands. 'I have to know, Daniel. Have you come to Liverpool because of the IRA?'

A muscle tightened in his cheek. 'And there's the emigration trade. It's bigger than cotton now.'

'I suppose you think it's none of my business,' she said.

'I wouldn't say that exactly. But can't you allow me to forget that side of my life? I thought meeting you was the best thing that ever happened to me. That's why I wanted to see you again. Now—' He shrugged. 'I didn't know you wanted to pump information out of me.'

Rebekah felt awful. 'I'm not trying to get information,' she murmured. 'I came because I wanted to be with you. Do you think I'd have bothered otherwise?'

His face softened. 'Then why go on about the—' he hesitated '—the organisation.'

'That's what you call it?'

'It's safer.'

She raised her eyebrows. 'And you ask me why I go on about them! I don't want you hurt.'

He smiled. 'I'm not going to get hurt. If I tell you that I'm not as involved as Shaun – that I've never killed a man in ambush – will you believe me and drop the whole thing?'

'I'll try.'

'Good girl. Now tell me what your father's doing about going to America?'

'He's got tickets on a ship.' She pulled a face. 'It's probably sailing the day after tomorrow. Aunt

Esther was livid, and I wasn't too pleased as you can imagine.'

'Damn!' he exclaimed in a low voice. 'It doesn't give us much time.'

She shook her head. 'And I daren't be away too long. I'm a coward, you see. I can't imagine how Papa could get to know I'm with you but it worries me in case he does.'

Daniel's hand tightened about her fingers. 'He won't get to know. Stop worrying.'

She smiled and gave his hand a squeeze in response. For several minutes they did not speak and she was content just to be in his company. Then he began to talk about Seaforth again.

'The Marconi Wireless Company was stationed there, you know. It was there that the captain of the *Montrose* radioed the information about the murderer Crippen being aboard his ship. Unless you've been aboard ship and in trouble, you can't imagine the difference radio makes to being at sea.'

Rebekah was interested. 'I heard someone once say that it was love that got Crippen hanged.'

'They must have thought what they had was worth murdering for.'

'Love does strange things to people.'

'Sure does.' He smiled and she smiled back. She felt happy just looking at him and listening to his talk about Seaforth and his relations in Liverpool.

They clattered down the steps from the station

and immediately felt the breeze from the river blowing sand into their faces. The sun had come out from behind white clouds and there were lots of blue patches. It was turning out to be a lovely day and Rebekah tried not to think that it could be the only one they had.

Daniel ran her down to the beach and she laughed for the sheer pleasure of being in his company, out in the fresh air with no fear of snipers or bombs going off.

He brought her to a swinging stop when they reached the shore, pointing out the high tide mark at the foot of the cobbles. 'The tide comes sweeping in fast all along the coast for quite a way. There's sandbanks so you have to be careful.'

They strolled along the deserted beach. The tide was way out and sky and sand seemed to stretch for miles. Her nerves were soothed. Across the water she could see the low green Wirral coastline and the hills of Wales. It was different to Ireland and yet in a way similar. There was a joy inside her that she had never experienced before and every time she looked at Daniel, her heart seemed to swell.

The sun grew warmer and they took off their shoes and stockings and paddled in water in a shallow gully left behind by the tide. They did not talk about anything serious, only of shells, crabs, fishing and swimming. He told her tales that made her laugh. Uncomplicated laughter, but at the back of her mind all the time was the knowledge that there was little time for his tales and the simpler things that couples did together. Probably they would never do this again and she could not bear the thought.

They walked on, barefooted, and when Daniel's arm slid about Rebekah's waist, she leant against him. 'There's sinking sand somewhere,' he murmured. 'My cousins used to warn me about it. They told me that a donkey was swallowed whole into a pit of black mud.'

She shivered. 'If you were wanting to bring me down to earth then you've done it, Daniel O'Neill. Imagine losing someone you love in such a way!'

'Do you love anybody that much, you couldn't bear to lose them?' He turned her towards him and his expression was intense as his eyes scanned her face.

'Do you?' she whispered.

'I'm starting to think I might.' He stroked back her hair.

'Me as well. But what can we do?'

'I don't know. But don't you be worrying about what I said about the mud. It's probably not true. My cousins are terrible exaggerators. If they caught a tiddler it would end up a whale.'

She smiled as he had intended and he kissed her open mouth, long and deep. They both dropped the shoes they carried and their arms went round each other. She rubbed her cheek against his and kissed it, tasting the salt on his skin. Then she pressed her mouth against his and he pulled her against him with insistent hands, and kissed her back. His passion dissolved any sensible thoughts she might have had and she responded with hungry enthusiasm. For what seemed ages they only kissed. Then, 'You're lovely,' he said, 'I want to make love to you.'

He pulled her down onto the sand and her heart pounded. Their hands explored, undoing buttons. He had hair on his chest and his skin was cool with the wind from the sea. He touched her breast and a few moments later there did not seem anything terribly wrong about him rubbing his chest against her breasts. It was at least five minutes before he stroked her skirts up above her thighs. For a moment she did think that really she should say something to stop him but there was such desire inside her that although she protested and he hesitated, removing his hand, it was not long before he was back again and caressing between her legs. She was surprised at how pleasant it was and how weak her resistance. She did not want him to stop. Her pleasure was growing, overwhelming her, until she had no control over the movements of her body. When he stopped she wanted him back and said so. 'If you're sure,' he murmured, and took off his pants. She stared up at him from dazed eyes, not so certain when she saw him naked. She liked the look of the strength of him, but before her mind could touch on the consequences of what might happen next, he was beside her again. His fingers touched her and she quivered with anticipation, closing her eyes and her mind as he straddled and slowly penetrated her. It barely hurt, and as he moved, the pain mixed with the pleasure that still lingered, and her desire for more caused her body to match his movements. Her arms went round him but he removed them one at a time and withdrew quickly. She reached up for him and his mouth touched hers briefly.

Luxuriating in a sense of relaxation that she had never felt before, it was several minutes before she opened her eyes and saw for the first time what had entered her. It didn't look as big as it had felt inside her and now her mind took over. 'Will I have a baby?' Her voice was low and slightly apprehensive.

He shook his head. 'I made sure I wouldn't do that to you.'

'How?' She sat up.

'Just take my word for it.' He pulled on his trousers, then passed shoes and stockings to her.

She stared at him. 'We can't just say goodbye,' she insisted.

He wiped sand off his foot with his sock, not looking at her. 'I've nothing to offer you, Becky.' His voice was taut. 'I'm a man with a price on my head.'

For a moment she could think of nothing to say. All the pleasure had dissolved and all she could feel was a great big lump in her throat. 'I don't know what to say,' she gasped. 'After what we've just done, how can you just leave me?'

'What else can I do?' He glanced at her, frowning. 'I'm sorry.'

'Sorry?' She put a hand to her mouth and closed her eyes, forcing back tears.

'Becky! Becky, don't cry.' He dropped his sock and put his arms round her. 'This ship you're going to America on—'

She rubbed her eyes against his bare chest. 'I don't know the name of it.'

'God, you must!' he said urgently. 'Think!'

'It's no use my thinking,' she cried, pushing herself away from him. 'We were all so annoyed with Papa that we never asked!'

'The line – what's its name?'

'I don't know that either!' She hunched her legs, aware of her nakedness, and dropped her chin on her knees.

'Don't you know anything about it at all?'

'Only the name of the owner.' She lifted her eyes and looked at him.

'Well?' he said, smiling.

'Joshua Green.'

'Hell!' His smile faded, and reaching out for her clothes he threw them at her. 'It just would have to be Green's, wouldn't it! He sank back on to the sand, a moody expression on his face.

'What is it?'

'It's him, that's all.' He looked up at her. 'He has land in Ireland, you know.'

'I know. Apparently he owns the farm that was once my grandma's. I don't know the hows and whys. It was years ago, when I was a child.' She bit her lip, clutching her clothes to her breast. 'Does it matter to us?'

'It matters to me.' He picked up his sock again. 'Can you find out the name of the ship and meet me at the Pierhead about two o'clock tomorrow.'

'I'll try.' She began to dress 'It won't be easy getting away.'

'If you can't make it, you can't,' he said grimly.

'But that would mean we wouldn't see each other again,' she stammered.

'You really do want to see me again?'

At a look from her a slow smile lit his face. 'Trust me, Becky. I'll think of something. Now hurry up! There's a man with a dog coming along the beach.'

She hurried.

Rebekah walked swiftly up the road in the direction of her aunt's house, hoping her father had not arrived home yet.

Hannah opened the door and sniffed. 'Thee's here at last, are thee? Yer hair's a mess.'

'It's because of the wind.' Rebekah flashed a honeyed smile and pushing past her went on into the house.

Her mother and aunt were having tea. 'Sorry I'm

late,' she said breezily, pulling off her gloves, hoping that they couldn't tell anything from her face, 'I'm completely windblown because I've been down by the river watching the ships. Is Papa in?'

'Not yet.' Her mother stared at her, fidgetting with the neck of her dress. 'I hope he's in a good mood.'

'I saw him in town. He was with that shipowner he mentioned – Joshua Green.'

'Green's?' Her aunt shook her head and picked up her knitting. 'Such a small company. I hope his ships are up to scratch.'

'Oh, do stop going on, Esther!' Sarah's attention was still for her daughter. 'What did he have to say about your hair?'

'What you'd expect.' Rebekah took a scone from a plate. 'Mr Green said he liked it.'

'I doubt that would weigh with your father.' Her mother bit her lip.

Rebekah shrugged, and tilted her chin. Being with Daniel had put strength in her somehow. She was ready to confront her father, and anyway doubted he would hit her while staying in her aunt's house. Anyway, she intended to be nice to him because she needed the name of the ship and a chance to get away tomorrow.

It was not long before he came in. 'Well, miss, I can't say that I liked it at first sight,' he muttered, accepting a cup of tea from Hannah and standing in front of the fireplace.

'I consider she looks extremely neat,' put in Esther, her blue eyes determined.

'It's tidy, Adam,' said his wife quickly, 'and will be easier for Becky to take care of on the voyage.'

His gaze fell on his wife. 'No doubt she did it without your approval?'

'Yes!' said Rebekah swiftly.

Her mother shook her greying head. 'No, Adam.'

'I persuaded her to let the girl get it done,' put in Esther. 'Lots of women are having a bob these days. I've been thinking of it myself.'

His mouth thinned. 'They say there's no fool like an old fool, but for pretty young things I suppose it's acceptable.' He looked in Rebekah's direction. 'Joshua Green's sister has had hers done recently. She's not very well apparently since her husband was killed in the war, and lives quietly. For some reason Joshua believes that a visit from you would cheer her up. As I've some business to discuss with him, he suggests that we spend the afternoon at his house and have tea with him tomorrow.'

'Surely if you've business to discuss you'd be better going alone,' said Rebekah swiftly, her heart sinking. 'There's things I'd much rather be doing than visiting strangers.'

Her father's mouth pulled down at the corners. 'I said Mr Green's sister is ill,' he said emphatically. 'Surely if you had time in Dublin to visit that old woman, Mary, you can spare time to relieve the monotony of the day for a sick young woman? I insist on your coming with me.'

'Mama, couldn't you?' Rebekah sent her mother a look of entreaty.

Sarah shook her head. 'Your aunt and I are visiting an old friend. I would gladly take your place otherwise.'

'That's settled it then,' said her father, his eyes steely. 'You come with me, Rebekah, and I want no arguments or trying to get out of it. I'll be keeping my eye on you.'

'What time is this visit?' Her hand curled tightly in her lap.

'After lunch.'

Rebekah could have screamed. She was already missing Daniel. 'Where do they live?'

'Not far. The other side of Newsham Park. Joshua's brother made the move out of the town centre for his sister's health a couple of years back.'

She tried one last time. 'If she's been married, Papa, then she must be a few years older than me? She might not want my company.'

'She's twenty-two.' He gulped his tea and reached for a scone. 'Young to have suffered so much. But perhaps Joshua's right and you can cheer her up. Whatever you do, don't be talking about the fighting at home. It could upset her.'

'Perhaps you'd like to tell me what I can talk to her about?' Rebekah said acidly, 'I doubt we'll have much in common.'

His mouth tightened. 'I'm sure you'll find something. Now let's drop the subject. Tell me, Sarah, did you get all that you went for in town?'

Rebekah went out of the room and up to her bedroom. What was the point of asking her father the name of the ship now? Was it worth her trying to get out of the house earlier in the day? She thought of his expression and voice when he said, 'I'll be watching you.' He would too. She sank onto the bed. She could only put her trust in Daniel as he had said she should.

Joshua Green's house fronted an expanse of green parkland. A gravelled path flanked by rhododendrons wound round the side of a large red-brick porch, and there were several steps up to the entrance. A ship's bell swung from a wrought iron hook.

Rebekah watched, one white-gloved hand clasped about the Barker & Dobson chocolates that her mother had insisted she took for Joshua Green's sister. This was more the kind of house that she had thought Aunt Esther would have. Her father pulled the short rope that set the bell clanging. Nothing happened. She felt fidgety and checked that the yellow ribbon threaded through her short hair was lying flat and fastened the top button of the brown jacket over her primrose-coloured frock. Adam rang the bell again and for good measure banged the knocker. Moments later the door was opened by an elderly maid.

The hall seemed dark after the brightness of the sun and their feet made a ringing noise on the tiled floor as they followed the maid to a back room where she announced them. A yawning voice bid them: 'Come in.'

Warmth hit them and Rebekah's eyes went involuntarily to the fireplace where one of the latest gas fires burnt. Then her gaze moved quickly to the woman lying on the sofa with her mousy head nestling against several cretonne cushions. On the plaid rug that covered her legs lay the magazine *Vogue,* a blue-black Persian cat and a half-empty bowl of grapes.

'Josh shouldn't be long because he's been gone ages,' she murmured, staring at them. 'The vicar rang up, wanting something or other, and he said it would be easier if he went round to sort it out.' She sat up and Rebekah was able to gain a better view of the pale face and nondescript features of their hostess. 'You don't mind waiting for tea? If you're hungry, help yourself to a grape.' Limpid grey eyes seemed to gaze past them as with a slender hand, adorned only by a wedding and an engagement ring of rubies and pearls, she offered them the bowl of black grapes, still with the bloom on them.

Her father declined politely and nudged Rebekah's arm. She hesitated before refusing. The girl shrugged. 'We grow them ourselves – or at least Fred the gardener does.' She gathered the bowl to her beige jersey-clad bosom and lowering her head took a grape from the bowl with her teeth.

Involuntarily, Rebekah glanced at her father, who nudged her again. 'Give her the chocolates,' he muttered beneath his breath.

'Chocolates?' Their hostess stared vaguely at them. 'For me? What sort are they?'

Rebekah handed them to her and she smiled, gazing down at the box. 'How kind! I'll eat them now.' She dropped the bowl of grapes on the Indian carpet, then opened the box of chocolates. She bit into one before looking up abruptly and saying, 'I've forgotten to ask you to sit down, haven't I? Do sit and have a chocolate.'

Adam refused but this time Rebekah did not. She was hungry. Her father sat ramrod straight in an armchair, his expression unusually blank. Rebekah, who was finding their hostess more interesting than she had expected, relaxed in a leather-upholstered chair, and waited for her father to speak first.

There was a silence while Mrs Richards ate the chocolates, flicking over the pages of the magazine, giving them only a perfunctory glance. Rebekah decided to break the silence and sought for something safe. 'Does your cat have a name?'

Joshua's sister looked up at her from beneath pale lashes. 'Bloody foreign moggy,' she said, seeming to relish the words. 'That's what Fred calls him when he mucks up the garden. My name's Emma. Dicky calls me little Emma. His proper name is Richard Richards. Silly, isn't it? He'll be coming home soon now the war's been declared officially over.'

'The war finished ages ago,' said Rebekah, startled. 'In 1918.'

'No!' said Emma softly, her hands moving restlessly. 'Not properly it hadn't, and Dicky signed up for the duration. The other day I read in the paper that officially it's over. You'll see – he'll be back soon.'

Rebekah glanced at her father and saw that his colour was high. He looked away and stared out of the window. Oh Lord, she thought, what do I say next? 'Your hair's nice. I had mine cut at Hill's yesterday. Where did you get yours done?'

Emma did not answer right away but ate another chocolate before saying, 'Upstairs in my bedroom. A man came. He had dark shiny hair and talked and talked until my head started aching so much, I threw the hairbrush at him.'

Rebekah was startled into asking, 'Did you hit him?'

'Yes.' A mischievous expression suddenly lit Emma's face. 'He said that he wouldn't come again and I said good. That I would let my hair grow and grow until it reached my bottom.' Her mouth trembled and an apprehensive expression replaced the mischief in her eyes. 'Josh was annoyed and lost his temper. He said that it's all gone on too long – that I've got to pull myself together or else. "Or else what?" I asked, and he said that I'd soon see.'

'He probably didn't mean anything by it,' said Rebekah, suddenly feeling out of her depth and wishing that Joshua Green would come back.

There was a silence which seemed to stretch and stretch. Her mind drifted to thoughts of Daniel, hoping that he had been disappointed when she had not turned up and that he would think of something so that they could be together again.

Suddenly there was a sound of the front door opening and the murmur of voices in the hall. There came hurried footsteps and several seconds later Joshua entered the sitting room. He was dressed in grey flannels and a navy blue blazer with silver buttons. His pleasant face clouded as his eyes flickered over his sister's prone figure. 'Still resting, Em?' he said lightly.

She murmured indistinctly, but his attention had already passed to the others. 'I hope you haven't been waiting long?' He bowed slightly in Rebekah's direction, and smiled. 'I was unavoidably detained. After persuading me to let him have one of my boats for a day's cruising on the Mersey next year for some of the orphans, the Reverend droned on and on. He's a real windbag, but not a bad chap as clerics go.' He waved a hand in the direction of the window. 'Let's go outside. Because it's such a fine day I've told Janet to serve tea outside.' Moving swiftly, he crossed the room. As he passed his sister he murmured, 'I presume you are joining us, Em?' He switched off the gas fire before going towards the french windows, opening them and beckoning the others out into a large walled garden.

Rebekah was glad to be outdoors. The room had been stifling hot. She paused on a paved area where a white table and four chairs stood close to the wooden figurehead of a mermaid from which the paint was peeling.

'Once she graced the first sailing ship that my grandfather commissioned,' said Joshua, coming to stand at her shoulder. 'Andromeda, my brother called her.'

She looked up at him. 'I doubt if Perseus will be coming to her rescue.'

He nodded seriously. 'Too late for the old girl. I suppose I should really get rid of her but father was a bit superstitious where Andromeda was concerned. He reckoned that she brought the family luck.'

Rebekah placed her hand on the mermaid's dirty yellow hair. 'You should give her a new coat of paint. I'm sure she'd enjoy that.'

He smiled. 'You think so?'

'If I was her I would.' She ran a finger over the beautifully carved tresses and facial features. 'I'd want golden hair, bright blue eyes, red lips – and a sea green tail.'

'What nonsense you talk,' said her father, coming

up to them. 'Take no notice of her, Joshua.'

The light died in Rebekah's eyes. 'It was only a bit of fun,' she murmured, turning away from the two men and walking over to where Emma stood with the cat bundled in her arms. The fragrance from some late-flowering roses filled the air.

'They smell nice, don't they?' said Emma, her expression sombre. 'I had some in my bouquet when I married Dicky before he went to France.'

Rebekah could think of nothing to say but felt deeply sorry for her. To lose someone you love, so young – no wonder she'd gone funny. Daniel came to mind and she stood close to Emma, absently stroking the cat up the wrong way until Joshua called them to come to tea.

Emma ate little which was not surprising, thought Rebekah. Conversation between her father and Joshua seemed to be about politics and shipping. Afterwards they disappeared inside the house and Emma unexpectedly gripped her hand tightly and stared at her with dilated dark blue eyes. 'It'll be our fifth wedding anniversary next week. Perhaps Dickie will be home for it,' she whispered. 'Will you remember me when you're out in the middle of the Atlantic, and pray?'

Startled, Rebekah replied, 'If you want me to.'

'Thanks.' She wandered back into the house.

Rebekah followed. Not long after that her father called that it was time to go. She walked down the front path to where he waited with Joshua, who held out his hand. 'The *Samson* will be sailing tomorrow. Until next we meet, Rebekah.'

'What?' she asked in a vague voice, thinking that it was too late to get the name of the ship to Daniel. She could only hope.

'Sometimes I come over to America on business,' he answered, squeezing her fingers.

'Oh, I see!' It seemed ages since she had actually thought of what it would be like in America. 'That will be nice,' she added politely, freeing her hand and moving to the other side of the gate.

He raised an arm in farewell and as they turned the corner into the main road, she was aware that he still stood at the gate, watching them.

CHAPTER FIVE

Daniel had not been on the landing stage and although Rebekah scoured the decks, staring at every sailor she encountered, she had not seen him anywhere on the ship. As she gazed at coasters and dredgers, ferry and cargo boats, tall liners and tiny river craft, her vision blurred. He must not have been able to find the right ship in time. Or else – terrible thought – he had not wanted to. She felt quite desperate, especially when she caught a glimpse of Seaforth. The tide was in and although she could not be sure of exactly where they had walked and made love, she had not forgotten what it felt like. She tried not to think of never seeing Daniel again but could not stop. She scrubbed at her eyes and was aware of her mother weeping by her side. She could no longer bear her own thoughts. 'Mama, shall we go to our cabin?'

'In a minute.' Her mother wiped her face with a handkerchief and then blew her nose. 'I'm sorry to be such a misery but it's just really hit me that I'll never see Liverpool again. When I went to live in Ireland, I always believed that one day I'd return.' The tears flowed again and the next words were muffled by her handkerchief. 'But America, Becky! We'll never come back from there!'

'We might,' said Rebekah in bracing tones, determinedly quashing her own misery and slipping a hand through her mother's arm. 'Never say never, Mama.'

Her mother sniffed and dabbed at her nose and eyes again. Rebekah thought of Daniel's words about leaving Ireland and wondered sadly if the Americas were full of emigrants still mourning the countries they had left behind.

They passed down a companionway and Rebekah barely noticed that her mother's colour was changing until she felt her pressing her arm and saw that her face looked clammy and pallid. They managed to reach the cabin before Sarah was sick in the basin. Rebekah helped her to undress and soon had her lying between the sheets in the bunk bed. She rang for the steward and cleaned out the basin before sponging her mother's face and hands. The steward came and soon her mother was comfortably settled with a couple of arrowroot biscuits and a cup of weak tea.

Her father arrived from seeing one of the officers.

'Not feeling so good, Sal?' He patted the hand lying on the cover. 'Don't think about it. Mind over matter and you'll soon feel well enough to see over the ship,' he said cheerfully.

'Not yet I won't,' muttered Sarah, giving him an exasperated look. 'You've never been seasick, you've no idea. Pass me my bag, Becky. There's a book I can read. And I need my glasses.'

Her husband frowned and sat sideways on the bunk. 'Joshua arranged with the captain for us to see over the ship. One of the perks of my new job, Sal. I'd like you to come.'

'Well, I'm not.'

'It's not until after dinner. You might feel better then.'

'I won't,' she said determinedly.

'You're not sulking, are you?'

She looked at him. 'What would be the use? Take Becky.'

'Me!' Rebekah had no desire to be in her father's company.

Her father glared at her. 'And why not, miss? If you think you're going to be let loose on this ship to flirt with all and sundry, then you've got another think coming! You'll come with me and like it.'

'I might come but I certainly won't like it!' retorted Rebekah, handing the book to her mother.

'Like it or lump it,' muttered her father, his eyes

narrowing. 'You are definitely coming. It could be useful to you in the future. Mr Green bought the ship from one of the big companies and changed her name. She was designed and built at Harland and Wolff's Belfast shipyard and used to carry first and second class passengers.' His voice had risen as if he was trying to impress the knowledge into her. 'He's had her converted to transport single class emigrants, knowing he couldn't compete for the upper-class tourist trade. He's just had oil-fired boilers installed. It's a good investment! Coal's a bulky, dirty fuel to load and carry. Try and remember all that, daughter! It might come up in conversation in shipping circles and you'd know what a man was talking about. A man likes a woman who can listen intelligently, instead of babbling on about mermaids wanting to be painted.'

'Mr Green knew it was a bit of fun,' she said hotly. 'He probably hears enough about boilers and engines in his office.'

Her father stared at her and there was that pinched look about his mouth again. 'This is one of the times when I wish you'd been a boy!'

'Being a girl was hardly my choice,' she said, tilting her chin. 'You can blame that on God.'

'That's enough, Becky,' murmured her mother, without lifting her head. 'Go with your father and give me a bit of peace.'

Rebekah wanted to say more but considered her

mother was upset enough at leaving Liverpool. She went with her father to dinner and ate the soup, roast lamb and tapioca pudding with a lack of her customary enthusiasm for food, taking little notice of the company at their table. Afterwards, her father steered her hurriedly to the bridge.

It soon became obvious to Rebekah that the officer, Mr Eaton, who was acting as guide on their tour of the ship, was out to please her father. He listened with flattering attention to all his questions and she wondered what the job was that her father had mentioned. The way Mr Eaton was behaving, her father could have been buying the ship!

They climbed down into the engine and boiler rooms. The pumps were slightly noisy and there was a strong smell of steam and oil. It was hot and Rebekah felt a bit sick as she politely tried to pay attention to the conversation between her father and the second engineer as they discussed valves, pistons, pressures and boilers. Depression clouded her spirits. As her eyes roamed the pipes which seemed to snake everywhere they fell on one of the overalled men. His eyes were fixed on her, the whites gleaming in a face that was shiny with sweat and smeared with grease. A smile drew oily lines in the grease and her misery evaporated. She could hardly believe it but she had found Daniel!

Rebekah glanced at her father and jumped when she realised he was watching her. Quickly she looked away and smiled at Mr Eaton, praying that she had not given the game away. She forced herself to look subdued and followed her father up the ladder out of the engine room. Even so, her mood was buoyant. Daniel had done it! He must really care! He had told her to trust him and backed his words up with action. Hallelujah!

As she stood in the tiny space that housed the ship's wireless, she wondered how he would be able to get in touch with her. It had to be soon! Mr Eaton, who it turned out was a cousin of Mr Green, was at her shoulder, telling her about the advantages that a smaller ship could have over the larger liners when it came to knots per hour. They could be in New York within the week. Rebekah had expected it to take much longer and the news gave a greater sense of urgency to thoughts of seeing Daniel.

When the tour came to an end her father gave Rebekah no chance to escape but took her upper arm in a grip so tight that she winced. 'I saw the way you were looking at Mr Eaton, my girl, and I'm telling you now that I have someone better in mind for you.' He gave her a shake. 'Just behave yourself! I haven't forgotten what happened in Dublin and I'll not be having you making a name for yourself among the crew!' He slackened his grip slightly. 'Now let's go and have our tea.'

She stared at him defiantly. 'I'm not hungry, Papa.'

'I've paid for this food so you'll eat it,' he said, his fingers tightening again on her arm. 'Now, move.'

She moved, realising that it was unlikely that Daniel would have left the engine room yet.

She was toying with a smoked herring, thinking of how she was to get away from her father, who was talking engines to the man opposite him, when a pleasant-looking girl with auburn hair twisted in a knot on the top of her head, grimaced and said, 'All this talk of engines is double dutch to me, even though me brother Pat's a deckhand on the *Gideon*. A sister, or brother, whatever you call it, to this ship. Yer'd sure and think I'd have picked up some know-how, wouldn't you?' she said in a Liverpool accent.

'I beg your pardon?' said Rebekah, gathering her wandering thoughts.

'My name's Brigid O'Shaughnessy.' The girl's eyes were warm. 'The trouble is I never listened to Pat when he chunnered on. All I need to know about a boat is that it'll get me to where I'm going. Not that I was in any rush to leave Liverpool, but as my Keith said, they promised him a land fit for heroes. And while round Mere Lane isn't too bad, it's hardly Paradise. Even so I kept telling him it was home, but he wanted a better future for our kids when we have 'em, so I had no choice but to pack me bags and come.' Tears welled in her eyes and her voice wobbled when she spoke again. 'He might be right, but I'm already missing Mam and me sisters.' She sniffed and wiped her eyes with the back of her hand. 'He'd like a bit of land to farm, and a cow. I'm not keen on cows. I've lived next door to the dairy all me life and the smell was something awful at times. They're dangerous as well.' She nodded sagely. 'One of the cowmen had his eye flicked out by a cow's tail. That wasn't much fun for him, I can tell you.'

Rebekah suppressed a giggle. 'Do you have to keep cows?'

Brigid raised her eyes ceilingward. 'It's what he wants! But I'll get to work on him. You can change a man if you go the right way about it, so Mam always said.'

Rebekah gave up all pretence of eating the smoked herring. 'Are there lots of things you want to change about him?'

'There's never been a perfect man.' A dimple appeared in Brigid's cheek. 'Are yer leaving someone behind?'

Rebekah glanced in her father's direction. 'There's someone. Papa doesn't approve.'

'Dads are like that.' Brigid's tongue darted out, licking the jam at the side of her mouth. 'I used to nip down the yard to the lav meself and sneak out the back way.'

'Not a bad idea.' Rebekah smiled and stood up, murmuring her excuses to her father. He nodded but told her that he'd expect to see her back in the cabin in ten minutes. She smiled a goodbye to Brigid and left.

Rebekah walked the promenade deck but saw no sign of Daniel. He was not in the general saloon either. She wondered whether the crew were allowed in such places. Continuing her hunt she gazed through the door of the smoking saloon and withdrew her head, coughing, after a hurried review of the few men's faces present. She was starting to believe she was wasting her time and that Daniel must still be down in the engine room when he came up a companionway, talking over his shoulder in an emphatic voice. He stopped in mid-sentence when he saw her and there was a brightness in his eyes.

She felt as if the whole of her body was smiling and without hesitation flung her arms around him. 'I'm so glad to see you!'

'Same here.' He hugged her.

'I was so worried Papa might have recognised you.'

'I'd heard he was coming so I had my disguise ready.'

She spoke against his shoulder. 'Your own mother would hardly have recognised you.'

'But you did.' He held her off from him and her smile deepened.

'You were staring at me.'

He grinned. 'You had the best legs in the engine room!'

'You shouldn't say things like that,' she said

demurely. 'You'll have me blushing. How did you find the ship?'

'I had a mate check the passenger list – then I signed on. Crazy though it might be.'

They continued to stare at each other, smiling until a voice said, 'Danny, isn't this the girl who was in Dublin? Did she tell her father about us and that's why you said—?' Rebekah jumped. It was Shaun.

Daniel frowned. 'No, she didn't. Her and me are none of your business. Go for a walk and I'll find you later.'

Shaun did not move. 'Mam would want me to be looking out for you, and I know for sure your taking up with a Quaker wouldn't be to her liking.'

Daniel's mouth tightened. 'Go away, Shaun.'

His brother jingled the change in his pocket. 'I knew she was trouble as soon as I saw her.'

'It's you that's trouble,' said Daniel grimly. 'Now, go.'

He scowled. 'What about our business? I hope she's not going—'

'She has nothing to do with our business,' said Daniel emphatically. 'And if anyone was going to get us into trouble, it would be you!'

Shaun's face reddened and he scuffed his feet before turning and walking away. He looked back several times with an angry expression.

Daniel pulled Rebekah down on to a bench. 'I'm sorry about that.'

'It's all right,' she said in a low voice. 'I understand why he doesn't want me around. But what's he doing here?'

'He's the only brother I've got left. I thought it less likely that he'd get into trouble if I brought him.'

'Papa might recognise him. You'd better warn him.'

He nodded, 'I never thought.'

'It doesn't matter,' she said softly, squeezing his hand.

'Let's forget them both. I'll enjoy seeing your pretty face after being down in that hellhole every day. But don't expect to see much of me. We work long hours.'

'I'm just glad you're here.'

'Me too.' He stared down at her and she wondered what he was thinking, just before he kissed her in a manner as starved as her own.

It was the sound of children's voices that caused them to draw apart. As soon as the girls and their mother had passed they turned to each other again, but the sight of a man coming up the companionway to stand at the rail, puffing his pipe, was enough to make Rebekah draw back. 'You'll have to go,' she whispered, 'it's my father.'

Daniel looked down at her. 'D'you think I'm the kind of man to run from your father?'

She lowered her gaze. 'Do it for me. If he discovers you're on this ship, there'll be terrible trouble. I know him, you don't.'

There was silence and her father turned his head and glanced idly about. She pressed herself against the back of the bench, hoping that Daniel's bulk would conceal her, and did not dare look in her father's direction again.

'I'll go,' murmured Daniel, 'I've a few hours before I've to be down in the engine room again. If you can make it, we can meet on the boat deck after supper.'

She nodded. 'I'll find a way.'

He turned up his jacket collar and went in the opposite direction from her father. She watched him go, thinking that some women were being emancipated but that didn't make most of them any freer than in Victorian times.

Her heart thumping, Rebekah rose to her feet and went over to her father, standing at the rail.

He turned and frowned at her. 'Your hair's a mess. What are you doing here? I thought you were going to see your mother.'

'I got lost.' Relief lightened her voice.

'After having a tour round the ship?' he said sarcastically. He prodded the hollow beneath her collar bone with the stem of his pipe. 'If I catch you flirting, you're in trouble.'

'You won't catch me, Papa,' she retorted.

'What's that supposed to mean? That you think you're too smart for me?' His eyes narrowed as he put his pipe back into his mouth and his teeth bit into the end.

'No, Papa. I mean that I have no intention of flirting with any man,' she said, adding with a self-assurance that she was far from feeling, 'You should trust me, Papa.'

'Hmmph!' he grunted. 'Let's go and see your mother.'

Sarah still showed a wan face. 'Was it a good tea?'

'Kippers, and bread and preserves. I didn't eat much.' Rebekah sat on her bunk and spoke about the people at their table, but it was not long before her mother's eyes closed and she dozed off. Rebekah sighed and hoped that she would be able to get away after supper.

At the dining table Rebekah got into conversation again with Brigid, who asked her, 'This fella you spoke about, will he be following you out?'

Rebekah whispered, 'I'm seeing him after supper. He's one of the engineers.'

Brigid's brows arched. 'Oh! So you haven't left him behind.' Her voice was low. 'Is he your first boyfriend?'

Rebekah's head lifted. 'My first real boyfriend.'

Brigid smiled. 'Well, yer probably in luv with luv, as me mam used to say. Enjoy it while it lasts, but be careful because yer know what they say about sailors.' At that point in the conversation her husband nudged her arm and she turned to him.

Rebekah noted that her father was talking to

someone else and swiftly left the dining room.

Up on the boat deck she looked about for Daniel.
The wind was cold and it was almost dark. She
shivered and huddled inside her coat. Suddenly a
hand seized hold of her shoulder and she was pulled
into the space between two lifeboats. She trembled
as she held up her face to Daniel's kiss. Was this being
in love with love? Would it pass as Brigid had warned
her? She did not want it to because it was wonderful.

His head lifted and he rubbed his cheek
languorously against hers. 'You had no trouble
getting away?'

'No. Although—'

'Good.' He undid a couple of buttons on her coat
and she remembered what Brigid had said about
sailors. He looked down at her, and there was the
slightest gleam in his eyes. 'You don't mind?'

'No,' she whispered. 'Although with Papa aboard,
I'm a bit nervous.'

'I don't plan on taking any risks with you.' His
arms slid about her waist beneath the coat. 'It's just
that it's warmer this way.'

It was, and she snuggled her head against his
shoulder, breathing in the mingled faint odours of
oil, soap and damp wool. 'When do you have to go
on duty?'

'An hour or so.'

'It's not long.'

'No.' His mouth moved over hers with a sensuality

that was enjoyable. As their kisses grew more torrid, she forgot everything but the physical sensations she was feeling. His hands shifted until they rested just beneath her breasts, which seemed to be swelling, and her breath caught in her throat as his fingers explored them. Then came the sound of footsteps, a man's cough, the smell of pipe smoke. She stiffened and Daniel's hand pressing against her breast seemed to be attempting to stifle the heavy beating of her heart. Neither of them moved or spoke until the footsteps retreated.

Daniel took her hand and began to walk with her. She was glad of the chance to let herself calm down. Her blood still seemed to be pounding in her head but as they slowly walked, the sea breeze cooled her hot cheeks and gradually she felt more in control. She sought for something to say that would take her mind off her father and what he might say when she got back to the cabin. 'What made you become an engineer?'

'It wasn't anything I planned.' He squeezed her fingers. 'Life was awful at home, despite Mam trying her best. My brothers were always fighting so I ran away to sea when I was thirteen. I wanted to see the world.'

'And have you?'

He smiled. 'You don't see much of it from an engine room. And one port's pretty much like another when a ship's only turning round.'

'You sound disillusioned.'

'It's not as bad as I make it sound,' he drawled. 'A ship's something special.'

'Do you have a woman in every port?' She had heard that about sailors.

'What a question!' He brushed her cheek with his fingers.

She caught his hand and suddenly remembered Shaun. 'Is it a taboo like the IRB? The business with your brother—'

His brows furrowed. 'Forget what Shaun said. Forget them. I never go to any of the meetings. It's Irish people having a complete say in their own country that's important to me.'

'Why don't you get out then?'

His mouth twisted. 'You've lived through the last few years in Dublin and you ask me that? When it's all over and Ireland's free, there won't be any need for killing or secrecy.' He hugged her to him. Talk of something else.'

'Tell me more about yourself. Did you go to school?'

Daniel stared past her at the sea. 'Sure. But my brothers were there before me and a priest decided he was going to beat the wickedness out of me before it got a firm hold.'

A shudder ran through her. 'Don't talk about it if you don't want to.'

He shrugged. 'The parents of another boy

complained. He was replaced. My mam, though, would never go against the priests, whatever us boys said.'

'It's a wonder you learnt anything,' she whispered.

Daniel smiled, 'I liked learning once I was allowed to do just that. The priest that replaced Brother Jerry was well-read and had been about the world a bit. Spent time in Africa and South America. He liked nothing better than to talk about travelling and ships. It sounded like a different world.'

'That's what made you run away to sea?'

He nodded, remembering the horrors of that first ocean voyage. The seasickness and the yearning for home. The hard work and the men who had wanted sex with him. At first that had terrified him more than any beating, but he soon learnt from a couple of seamen that he did not have to use his fists and feet. 'Sod off, mate, I'm not that way made,' caused them to back off.

Rebekah nudged his arm, sensing his withdrawal from her. 'Was it what you expected?'

'Is anything,' he said drily. 'And why are we wasting time talking about the past?'

'Because I want to know more about you, of course. Have you had many girlfriends?' she blurted out.

'I've had other things on my mind each time I've docked in Liverpool and New York, so there's no need for you to be jealous.' He sounded amused.

'I'm not jealous. It's . . . I don't like to think that I might just be one in a line. You could have had more than one in each port?' she said jocularly.

'I could have half a dozen, but I haven't!' He pulled her into his arms but she warded him off.

'What do you have on your mind?'

He sighed. 'I've never known anyone like you for asking questions – except perhaps our Shaun.'

She did not enjoy being linked with him, and thought of what her father had said. It made her uneasy, 'I'm not likely to tell anyone.'

'I'm not giving you the chance.' His face was set. 'I'll not be having you knowing anything about that side of my life. It's safer for you and safer for me, as I've told you before. Just take my word that I'm not involved in anything violent.'

'You said New York. Eamon de Valera, the President of Sinn Fein, is in America.'

He frowned. 'Don't pry, Becky.'

She was silent, but all the fear and anger of the last year or so bubbled up inside her. 'I don't know why, when he was legally elected, he couldn't have taken his seat in Westminster.'

His arms dropped. 'You must know!'

She shrugged. 'Because he wants an all Irish parliament – Dáil Éireann.'

'There you are then. Having Irish M.P.s in London hasn't done us much good, so we have to take the other way, however much I hate it.'

122

'But why be involved?' she said urgently. 'You don't have to be! There's no need for you to set foot in Ireland ever again. What's to take you back? You have no mother and your other brothers are dead.'

He stared at her. 'You know what takes me back. Have you no feeling for the place at all? I seem to remember your saying that you believed in a Free Ireland.'

'I do.'

'But you're not prepared to help bring it about.'

There was silence before she said, 'I pray. Isn't that what women have always done when men went off to war? Violence is what drove my parents out of Ireland, and I'm past caring if I ever see the place again.'

He looked as if she had smacked him in the face but she could not stop. 'It'll be a half empty country Dáil Éireann will be ruling over, the way things are going.'

'But you believe we'll win?' His voice was strained.

'I believe that the British will hand over some kind of self-government because they're fed up to the back teeth with the Irish problem. Shall we not talk about it any more?'

'That's all I ever asked,' he said intensely. 'Not to talk about it.' He stared at her a moment, and thrust his hands into his pockets. 'I'm going to have to go. Maybe I'll see you tomorrow.' And without touching her, he walked away.

Rebekah wanted to call him back but she had a feeling it would be of no use right now. A shiver went through her. If he was not careful he could end up getting himself killed.

As quietly as possible Rebekah entered the cabin. Her mother looked up from her knitting and her father from a sheaf of papers. 'Where've you been?' he demanded.

'Walking,' she said shortly.

'I didn't see you and I've been over most of the ship.'

'You can't cover the whole ship at one time.'

'Don't be impudent, Rebekah!' He flung the papers aside. 'I've warned you – if I catch you up to anything, you'll regret it. If this happens again you won't get off so lightly.'

'Don't you think you're over-reacting, Adam?' murmured her mother. 'It's Becky's first night at sea, and if I was her age I might find it exciting and not want to go to sleep yet.' She smiled at Rebekah over her glasses. 'But there are men about, love, and lots of them have probably been drinking. We worry about you. Now get into bed and think about what we've said.'

Rebekah nodded, and before her father could say any more she dived under the bedcovers to change. She wriggled into her cambric nightgown as the light went out. Years ago she had longed for a sister to talk to, and cuddle up with, when night terrors held her frozen between chilly linen sheets. She had made do with a dog when staying on her grandma's farm. She sometimes dreamt of the summers spent in Wicklow. That had been Ireland at its best. If only it could always be like that. But it was not, and Daniel's wanting to go back scared the life out of her.

'Now I'm feeling better, you can accompany me round the promenade deck,' said Rebekah's mother, tucking her hand into her arm. 'Your father's having a word with one of the officers but we must get exercise and fresh air while the weather's not too bad.'

'What's this job he mentioned?' Rebekah began to work out the odds of seeing Daniel on their tour of the decks, or the possibility of him attending the entertainment in the General Saloon that evening.

'Mr Green has asked him to replace the shipping agent, whom he considers too old for the job. It's quite an important position, with the emigration and tourist trade getting into its stride. It'll keep him very busy. What we're supposed to do while he's busy I've no idea!' There was an unaccustomed hint of sarcasm in her voice.

'You still don't want to go to America?'

Her mother shrugged. 'I know it's not my fault, but I feel mean leaving our Esther the way we did. She's not getting any younger.'

'Papa would say—'

'I know what your father would say. "She hasn't

bothered with us for years and she's got Hannah."
Hannah's a worker, all right, but she's not family.'

'I think she's after Aunt Esther's money,'
murmured Rebekah.

Her mother halted and stared at her. 'What
makes you say that?'

'She was glad to get rid of us and annoyed that
Aunt Esther bought us presents.'

'The presents were nice,' said her mother. 'You
must write to your aunt – keep in touch. We never
saw much money from your father's side of the
family so I'd like you to get some of your aunt's.
You have a right to it.'

'What happened that Papa never got any money?'

'His older brother drank and gambled all the
money away. That's how your father's Mr Green got
his hands on the farm. I've told him if we do ever
get rich and influential from this job he's got, I'd like
a ship named after me. In my younger days—' She
did not finish because a sudden gust of wind took
her old-fashioned, wide-brimmed hat from her head
and sent it careering along the deck, bringing the
conversation to an end.

It was evening and Rebekah had not seen Daniel all
day. She frowned as she fastened a white belt about
her hips and smoothed the tan dress of cotton and
silk down over her thighs. She was supposedly going
to the Entertainment. Her father had left her and

her mother, saying he was going to the smoking saloon to see a man from Manhattan. Presumably he believed her mother would not let her out of her sight, but Sarah had tired of her fidgetting and told her to go out but not be late.

Rebekah took a brown handbag by its chain and twisted it round her wrist. Her mother looked up from a book. 'I suppose I've got to accept that fashions change. When I was young—'

'When you were young – I know, Mama – your skirts were down to your ankles.' Her eyes softened, 'I won't be late.'

She looked in on the Entertainment – a girl singing, 'I'm forever blowing bubbles' – but there was no Daniel. She found him on the boat deck, leaning on the white-painted rail, gazing out over the dark sea. She took a deep breath to steady herself as he turned and looked at her. 'Daniel, I'm sorry about last night. What you do is your business.'

'Thanks.' He was still smarting from her words. 'Do you really mean that about not caring if you never saw Ireland again? Don't you have any feelings for your birthplace?'

'Of course I do. But my future's in America now.' She hesitated. 'Yours could be, too. I don't like thinking that you might be killed.'

He turned slowly. 'No one can be completely immune from suffering and death. It's all around us.'

'That's not quite the same.'

Daniel put his arm around her. 'Don't look so sad, Becky. Let's forget about Ireland and America and live life while we've got it.' He turned her towards him.

'That's easily said,' she murmured. 'But you want to live in Ireland. You're like that Oisín in the legend.'

'But you're no princess.' He kissed her neck. 'You're real, thank God.' They kissed once, twice, and before long were back to where they had been the evening before, except this time no footsteps disturbed them. In an atmosphere of dark skies and slapping waves their passion for each other seemed at one with the elements.

She gasped as his tongue ran over her nipples and her fingers laced through his curly hair and held his head against her breast. With her other hand she pulled out his shirt and stroked his bare back. She wanted to be part of him just as she had been on the beach, and pressed against him.

A soft sigh escaped him. 'Becky, love, do you know what you're doing to me?'

'Tell me,' she whispered. 'Tell me that you love me, that you want me.'

He lifted his head and gazed into her face. 'I love you, I want you.' His voice was husky. They kissed and she could feel the heavy thud of his heart against her bare breast as his hands took hold of hers and guided them to his trouser buttons. He nuzzled her neck and with an accelerated pulse and shaking fingers, she forced the first three buttons through holes, brushing the swelling beneath with the tips of her fingers several times. Abruptly he pressed her hand so that she could not move. 'Keep still. Let me calm down,' he said against her ear.

'What do you mean?'

A chuckle sounded in his throat. 'It's too nice.'

'What is?'

'What you're doing.' He took her hands away and held her at arm's length. 'I don't know what we're going to do. I want you, but we could end up in trouble.'

'Can't we get married?' She struggled to get close to him again but he continued to hold her off.

'It's not that easy and you know it,' he murmured. 'I'll have to do some thinking. It's getting late. I'll have to go.'

'Already?' She could not hide her disappointment.

He kissed her and she clung to him. He released her with obvious reluctance. 'It's time you were getting back or we'll have your father breathing brimstone and fire.'

'Shall I see you tomorrow?'

He nodded. 'I'm on in the early hours but I'll hope to see you here towards the end of the morning.'

They parted at the head of the companionway that led to her parents' cabin. Rebekah began to think up excuses.

She was not far from the cabin when she collided

with a staggering Shaun, who stared at her from bleary eyes. Thinking that in his drunken state he had not recognised her, she would have passed without speaking but he dragged on her arm and stuttered, 'Why don't you leave my brother alone?'

'I don't think it has anything to do with you.' Rebekah's voice was curt. She made to pull away but he stumbled into her and she fell against the wall. Suddenly his hands and mouth seemed to be everywhere and she was slapping at him. 'I'll scream,' she hissed, 'if you don't stop it!'

'And wake everybody?' he sneered, and rammed her against the wall.

She screamed.

A couple of doors opened and Shaun removed his hands as if she was a burning chestnut.

'Rebekah!' It was her father's voice.

She turned on Shaun quickly. 'Go! Or you'll get what for!'

Her father had seen them and was hurrying along the corridor.

'I'll bloody get you,' said Shaun, before making a stumbling retreat.

Her father would have pushed by her if Rebekah had not seized his arm. 'Papa! A complete stranger, and he wouldn't let me past.'

He wrenched his sleeve out of her grasp. 'A stranger?' he said sardonically. 'I thought I recognised him as one of those damned O'Neill boys.'

She felt a chill of apprehension, realising her mistake in screaming. 'How could it be?' she said, her voice quivering. 'You've got O'Neills on the brain, Papa!'

'Don't be impudent!' His eyebrows hooded suspicious eyes. 'I'll check the lists – and if it is him, I'll have something done. It's a good job it's not nine o'clock yet or you'd be in worse trouble. Now get into the cabin.' He gave her a push that sent her stumbling along the passageway.

That night she dreamt of Trim Castle in Ireland where her father had taken her as a girl. It was large and forbidding and frightening. She was looking through an opening at the sea far below, knowing that Daniel had gone somewhere far away while she was locked in a tower. It was all her father's fault and she had to get out before he came back. Suddenly the window wall vanished and she was airborne, flapping her arms as she sped over the sea, but there was someone behind her. That someone took on the shape of a banshee and her fear grew into an overwhelming panic. It would catch her and she would never see Daniel again!

CHAPTER SIX

Scared by her dream, Rebekah could hardly wait to meet Daniel the next day and she was halfway up the companionway to the boat deck far too early when she heard footsteps behind her.

Daniel took her hand. 'I nearly bumped into your father. He came into the smoking saloon so I made a quick exit.'

'Shaun wasn't there?' Her voice was strained.

'He told me what happened,' said Daniel, his expression suddenly vexed.

She felt certain his brother had not told him everything. 'This morning Papa's going to check the passenger list to see if you're both on it,' she said quietly.

'He'll find no trace of Shaun. I smuggled him aboard.'

'Papa's very determined.'

He nodded. 'He'll still have difficulty. I wish I'd left Shaun at home now. He's always been trouble. I spent more time getting him out of fixes than myself when we were kids.'

'I thought it was your older brothers who were the troublemakers?'

He grimaced. 'They were, but Mam always said it was Daddy's fault. When he got drunk he was like a mad hog. I remember kicking him back once when he hit me. I was about five, and he landed me such a clout that my ear swelled up and I couldn't hear properly for days. It got so bad in the end that I was glad when he became ill and died.'

She was horrified. 'Papa was never like that! It's just lately that—'

'He's frightened and worried,' interrupted Daniel in a positive voice. 'He's not young to be taking such a big step as emigrating.'

'He doesn't seem to be bothered about that,' murmured Rebekah.

'He wouldn't tell you.'

'No.' She was silenced for a moment, then she murmured, 'What will we do if he does find out you're on the ship?'

'He hasn't yet. Let's worry about it another day.' He pulled her towards him and for a while there was no more talk.

They resumed talking about her father when some

people came up on deck. 'If you weren't a Catholic and a rebel, he might accept you,' said Rebekah.

'But I am,' Daniel said emphatically.

She stared at him. 'People do get round the religious thing. My parents did.'

'Nobody's ever done it in our family.'

'There's always a first time.'

Daniel shook his head at her. 'Do you realise me mam would spin in her grave? She was always wanting me to settle down with a nice respectable Catholic girl, schooled by the nuns and as innocent as a newborn chick. In fact I know one in Liverpool. A friend of me cousin. She'd bear me numerous children, all to be raised as good, clean-living Catholics.'

Immediately Rebekah felt threatened. 'What's this girl's name?'

'Marie. She's got the softest brown hair and goes to mass every day.' His eyes twinkled. 'She knits me socks and prays that I'll be a reformed character. Me cousin Maureen told me that's so.'

'Her prayers don't seem to be working very well,' said Rebekah, raising her eyebrows. 'Have you kissed her?'

'Only the once.'

'Oh?'

'She didn't take to it like you. All screwed up for it she was. It was like kissing a prune. But I'm sure she'd make a faithful, dutiful wife.'

'She sounds too good to be true.'

'Sure, and she's an angel.'

Rebekah looked him squarely in the face. 'Then she should be in Heaven – with your mother, if she's the kind of girl she wants.'

He shook his head at her in mock reproof. 'If I had any sense and was a good, clean-living Catholic, she's the girl I should think of marrying. But when a man's in love it's not clean living he's thinking about. It's kissing and cuddling, and—' His look said the rest and she could only agree with him because inside she had that physical ache for him again. She tried not to think about the future but went into his arms.

It was on the way down the companionway that they met Rebekah's mother going up. She wished desperately that she could have escaped with the barest, 'Hello, Mama.' And she did press Daniel's arm, hoping he would take the hint and go ahead, but he did not.

'I've been wondering where you were,' said her mother, addressing Rebekah, but staring at Daniel.

'I'm hoping you won't mind my walking with your daughter?' he said, taking off his cap. 'It's nice and fresh on the boat deck. Unlike the engine room.' He held out a hand. 'I'm—'

'This is – Willie Smith, Mama,' interrupted Rebekah. 'I met him at the Entertainment. He asked me to walk round the deck with him.'

Her mother shook Daniel's hand. 'How do you do, Mr Smith?'

'Very well, thank you.' He avoided looking at Rebekah and she did not look at him as he exerted his charm. 'And yourself, Missus? Miss Rhoades was telling me that you haven't been well.'

'I'm much better, thank you.'

'I'm pleased to hear that. If you aren't minding, I'll be leaving Miss Rhoades with you as I'm on duty within the half hour. It's been nice meeting you.' He looked in Rebekah's direction. 'I enjoyed our walk.' She murmured polite agreement and did not watch him go.

'A nice-looking and polite young man, but not Mr Eaton,' said her mother calmly.

'I never said I'd been with Mr Eaton.' Rebekah fiddled with her glove, and looked down the steps.

'So you didn't. Shall we see if the air is still fresh on the boat deck?' Her mother ascended the stairs.

Rebekah followed her. 'Where's Papa?'

Her mother ignored her question. 'I presume that you were with Mr Smith last evening?'

Rebekah was about to tell a lie but changed her mind. What purpose would it serve. 'Yes, Mama.'

'Your father's worked up about some young man.'

'Mr Eaton?' Rebekah picked a piece of cotton from her sleeve.

Her mother looked at her severely. 'I was your

136

age once, Becky. I saw the way the pair of you didn't look at each other.'

Rebekah dropped the thread. 'Didn't look at each other?'

'Yes! It's in case you give anything away. If two people like each other, they can't easily hide it. They try. How your father and I tried to keep it from our Esther and my father!'

'Mama—' began Rebekah.

'I won't say don't see him,' interrupted her mother, clasping her hands. 'In fact, I won't even say bring him to meet your father.'

'I wouldn't,' said Rebekah quietly. 'We've made no arrangements. He has duties.'

'Duties.' Her mother smiled. 'Of course, he's a sailor. I used to adore sailors. We had plenty of them coming into our shop, trying to sell us things. The ones I met always had exciting tales to tell. The only trouble was that our Esther would always hover. But he seems a decent enough young man. Irish blood somewhere, I think.'

'He has family in Liverpool,' said Rebekah quickly.

'Don't half the Irish?' Sarah hesitated. 'Anyway, next time you see him, if it's evening have him escort you to our cabin. That way you'll be safe from drunkards. Now let's go and have some of that fresh air.'

She put her hand through Rebekah's arm and urged her out on deck, changing the subject to talk of apartments in New York. Rebekah let her talk flow over her, trying not to worry whether her mother would tell her father about the meeting with Daniel.

'Well, Becky, there aren't any O'Neills down on the passenger list,' said her father, at the lunch table. 'But don't be thinking I've given up. They could be using a different name. Or they could be crew working as deckhands.'

Trust her father to put them down as deckhands, thought Rebecca mutinously, aware of her mother's gaze.

'Who are these O'Neills, Adam?' asked Sarah.

'Bloody rebels.' he muttered, putting down his teacup.

'Language, Adam,' murmured Rebekah's mother. 'What would rebels be doing on a ship going to America?'

'Their president's in America. They could be taking messages.'

His wife's hand slackened on her fork. 'I don't think that's going to affect us, Adam. Shall we talk of something else.'

He changed the subject and Rebekah breathed easier. She caught Brigid's eye but the Liverpudlian remained silent and later followed her out of the dining room. 'I take it,' she said, 'that the fella you told me about, and one of the O'Neills yer dad mentioned, are one and the same person?'

Rebekah leant on the rail, and put her chin in her hand. 'How did you guess?'

'I know a Daniel O'Neill.' Brigid's elbow nudged hers. 'His auntie lives in our street.'

'That's a coincidence,' said Rebekah, not sure whether she was pleased or not that Brigid should know Daniel.

'They happen. He's a nice bloke. Friendly like. No sides.'

Rebekah sighed. 'We bumped into my mother and I wanted him to make a quick exit, but he didn't budge and had to go and be nice to her. I'm worried in case she tells Papa.'

'I presume he didn't use his own name.'

'I introduced him as Willie Smith.'

'Smith? Real original.'

Rebekah allowed herself a smile. 'It was the best I could do on the spur of the moment.'

'What are yer going to do? Yer dad seems pretty determined to find Danny.'

'I know.' Rebekah bit on a nail. 'I'll have to wait and see.'

'It might be best if you stopped seeing him.'

Rebekah's eyes clouded and she took her finger out of her mouth. 'I can't! I just can't! Even if Papa beat me—' The words were low and intense.

Brigid's expression was concerned. 'I'd think about it if I were you, luv.'

'I already have,' said Rebekah, and walked away

to make a fruitless search of the decks for Daniel.

Supper passed without incident and she decided after listening to Brigid's talk about the Entertainment and the dancing that followed, she might as well go along and see what went on. She changed into a new skirt and the eau-de-Nil crêpe-de-Chine blouse her aunt had bought her. On her way in she met Daniel, who immediately led her outside.

'Why did you have to interrupt me when I was talking to your mother?' he demanded.

'I thought—'

'I know what you thought.' He pulled her hand through his arm. 'If you'd waited for me to finish, Becky love, you'd have heard me tell your mother that my name was Peter Riley. You saying Smith complicates things. There isn't one on this ship.'

'I'm sorry. Papa said that you might be going under another name, and that you could be members of the crew! He's not going to give up, Daniel.'

'Well, he's not going to find an O'Neill amongst the crew.'

'If he gets at the truth—' Her expression clouded.

The corners of his mouth tightened. 'I don't want you getting hurt because of me.'

'He mightn't hit me,' she said with difficulty. 'He could just try and make sure that I don't see you again.'

He nodded. 'I'd prefer that.'

'You would?'

'There's always a way round things. Didn't I get on this ship?' He pulled her into the shadows and into his arms.

Rebekah held him tightly, still scared. 'It'll be New York soon and Papa'll make sure he keeps me away from you.'

'I'll think of something.'

She hoped he could but was still worried. She kissed him with a desperation she had never felt before.

Their kisses became more passionate, grew wilder, and his hands began to roam her body. He unbuttoned her blouse and eased the garment down to her waist, flicking off the straps of her underskirt. She looked into his face and it was soft with desire. She felt a quivering sensation in her stomach and a rush of anticipation. His mouth was on her neck, throat, breasts, covering her with little kisses, sending tremors through her. She felt like a volcano on the simmer and was aware that he was trembling with desire too.

Then unexpectedly he drew away and turned to the boat on their right. He climbed up and began to unfasten its covering, threw it back and pulled her up and inside the boat.

It was not the most comfortable place she had ever been in, but she rid herself of her clothes. Her breasts tingled as they brushed his bare chest and then his mouth was fastened on hers again and he began to explore and caress her all over as he had done once before. They moved together as if their bodies were moulded out of the same clay and she held on to him with all her strength. When she finally arched against him, he kissed her to drown the cry that rose in her throat and then withdrew quickly, moaning.

Afterwards they lay in each other's arms. 'We can't risk that again, Becky love,' murmured Daniel. 'It was a near thing. I wouldn't shame you.'

'It might mean that they would have to let us marry.'

A sharp laugh escaped him. 'He'd lock you away first. It's not going to be easy.'

'I know.'

'I have to go back to Ireland.'

'I'll go with you.' She hesitated. 'There or Liverpool.'

'You still don't want to go back to Ireland.' His voice suddenly sounded weary.

'I'll go wherever you want me to.'

He sighed and sat up. 'I should give you up.'

'But you won't?' There was a note of panic in her voice.

'Not if I can help it,' he said soothingly.

They kissed and got out of the boat. He fastened the cover back. His hand caressed the side of her face. 'I love you, Becky.' He kissed her again. 'I've got to go. I'm on duty soon. I'll see you early tomorrow evening. Perhaps we can go dancing? It would be more sensible.'

She nodded and they parted.

Rebekah had hoped that her father might still be in the smoking saloon when she returned to the cabin but he was lying on his bunk, fully dressed, filing his nails.

'Where were you, miss, when I looked in on the Entertainment?'

'What time was that?' She slipped off her jacket and placed it on the top spare bunk.

'It doesn't matter what time it was, you weren't there. With Mr Smith, were you, on the boat deck?'

She glanced quickly at her mother, who did not lift her eyes from her book, but Rebekah could tell from the stiff way she held her shoulders that she was no longer reading. She moistened her mouth. 'I was with Mr Smith. He's good company.'

'He isn't on any of the lists!' Her father flung the nail file on the bed and sat up. 'Perhaps it was Mr Jones? Maybe Mr Riley or Mr Merriman? Then again it might be none of them but Shaun O'Neill's brother!'

Rebekah cleared her throat. 'I thought you said there were no O'Neills on this ship?'

'That was before I saw one of them standing at the bar in the smoking saloon. He had gone before I could get to him but I'm sure it was the younger one.' He slid down from his bed. 'If I find the other one, I'll have them both clapped in irons.'

Rebekah moistened her lips. 'You're being

melodramatic, Papa. We're not in England now. You can't just arrest people!'

'I have influence on this ship,' he said in a manner that was very convincing.

She threw a look at her mother, who had put down her book and was twisting a long strand of her loosened hair in an agitated manner.

'Come here, miss.' Her father's words were quietly spoken.

To Rebekah they seemed all the more threatening than if he had shouted, and she stayed where she was.

'Don't provoke me, Becky,' he said. 'I only want to ask you a question and get an honest answer from you.'

'Adam, don't you think it's a bit late—' began his wife.

'Don't interfere,' muttered her husband, covering the couple of feet that divided him from his daughter. His expression darkened as he seized hold of her arm. He fingered her blouse, which was open at the neck, and pushed her head to one side. He prodded his thumb against her skin. 'What's this? And where did you get this thing you're wearing?'

'It's a blouse that Aunt Esther gave me, Papa!' She attempted to pull away.

'I know it's a blouse,' he whispered. 'D'you take me for a bloody fool. But what's the mark on your bloody neck? You look like you've been bloody bit.'

'It was an insect.' It was the first thing that came into her head.

'At sea? You wore the blouse for him, I suppose?' he said in a seething voice, and caught her a blow across the side of her head. 'Get it off and don't let me see you wearing it again. It's cheap and it's nasty and makes you look common.'

'It is not cheap,' said Rebekah, suddenly firing up. 'It cost Aunt Esther a lot of money!'

'Esther!' He seized on the word. 'It's her influence that's caused you to defy me. She's never liked me.'

'Can't this all wait till in the morning?' said his wife in a trembling voice. 'You'll be waking people.'

He stared at her and visibly controlled himself, releasing Rebekah's arm. 'You get ready for bed, Sally. She can go to bed too, but she can give me that blouse first. It's too provocative.'

Rebekah rubbed her arm. 'What are you going to do with it?'

'Just give it to me,' said her father.

She eased her throat. 'It's mine. Aunt Esther bought it for me. You've no right—'

Adam's face began to change colour. 'Don't tell me I have no rights! Women have got too much to say for themselves these days. Now give me that blouse,' he thundered.

The colour ebbed from Rebekah's face and she went behind the bunks and, turning her back on him, took off the blouse. With one hand she reached under her pillow for her nightdress. Expecting her father to do something at any moment she quickly exchanged one garment for the other before sitting on the pillow.

'Well, miss?' he said, ducking his head under the top bunk and thrusting his face close to hers. She drew back hurriedly and pulled her nightgown down over her underwear. He slapped her face. 'I said, where is it?'

She said nothing, waiting for the next blow. He thumped her on the upper arm, and she would have fallen off the bed if she had not clutched the post that held the bunks together. The patter of bare feet sounded on the floor.

'Adam, what d'you think you're doing?' His wife heaved on his arm. 'Can't we talk about this sensibly?'

'Let go, woman!' He tried to shrug her off but she hung on grimly and their struggles took them further from Rebekah's bed. She watched them until they broke apart and began to argue in fierce whispers. She could not make out what they were saying, but hated to see them arguing and slid beneath the bedcovers, pulling them over her head. Eventually, they both fell silent.

With a thumping heart, Rebekah waited for her father to make a move towards her. The bunks creaked. She held her breath for what seemed an age but he did not come. Slowly she relaxed and her fingers gingerly touched the sore part of her arm. It could have been worse. She supposed it had been stupid not to give him the blouse and she did not really know why she had been so stubborn about hanging on to it. He would not forgive her, nor would he forget that he had seen Shaun.

She fell asleep, only to dream about Trim Castle and escaping the banshee again. She woke with a headache and a nightmare feeling still in her limbs. She tried to rationalise the dream, remembering that outing to Trim Castle again. It was huge and grey, and her father had told her that during the Middle Ages the Anglo-Normans had kept hostages there.

And damsels in distress, she supposed, when knights were bold and their menfolk locked their women in chastity belts! Oh God, she was no longer a virgin! What would her father do to her and Daniel if he knew that? Irish rebels were sometimes hung for treason against the British Empire. In the grip of her dream, her fear of her father's power was beyond sensible thought or reason.

CHAPTER SEVEN

'Your father has Joshua Green in mind for you.'

Rebekah stared across the cabin at her mother. It was the next day.

'He wants you to be comfortable,' Sarah said earnestly.

'Joshua Green!' Rebekah laughed sharply and lifted her gaze from the magazine she was trying her best to read. 'So he's acting the Victorian papa! It's outdated, Mama. This is the twentieth century.'

A look of resignation crossed her mother's face. 'You might as well say it's what my father did, and perhaps if he hadn't behaved in such a way, we might not have run away the way we did. Believe me, I sometimes wonder whether it was worth it.'

For a moment Rebekah was dumbfounded. She had always believed that her mother thought the world well lost for love. 'You love Papa!'

'Love doesn't pay the rent.'

'Daniel's got a job,' said Rebekah.

Her mother raised her eyebrows. 'So you're admitting that the young man you introduced me to is the O'Neill rebel your father mentioned and not Willie Smith?'

Rebekah flushed. 'Yes!' she said defiantly.

Her mother groaned. 'He's a sailor and of a different faith. You do realise that would mean bringing up children on your own. Catholic children.'

'At the moment I don't care about any of that.'

Her mother's mouth firmed. 'Well, you should!' She got up from the bunk. 'Think! And do the sensible thing before your father does something we'll all regret.' She packed up her knitting and left her daughter alone.

Rebekah did not want to think, and hoping that maybe Daniel had got off duty earlier than he had said, she hurried up to the boat deck. She walked up and down, gazing at the single funnel which was almost midship. There was little wind and smoke hung in the sky, its acrid smell tainting the chill salty air. She counted the lifeboats. Daniel had told her that since the sinking of the *Titanic* the safety regulations had changed. Once it had been the ship's tonnage that decided the number of lifeboats, now it was how many passengers were aboard. She paced the deck several times, exchanging greetings with other people taking the air, but did not see Daniel. She did not go back to the cabin, though but walked around despite the cold.

It grew misty and she turned up the collar of her coat, hoping that Daniel would not be much longer. He wasn't.

Rebekah took his arm. 'Let's not go to the dance. I've got a feeling that Papa might turn up.'

He nodded. 'We don't want a confrontation on the dance floor.'

'Definitely not!' She shivered at the thought.

He glanced down at her. 'New York doesn't mean the end of everything for us. You might want to pretend to play it your father's way, for safety's sake. We could give things time. In a few months the fighting could have finished.'

She gripped his hand and said forlornly, 'I don't want to play it his way. Anything might happen. I'm prepared to turn round as soon as we get to New York and go back across the Atlantic. I can get a job. I have worked. I can type! We can save up.' A flush darkened her cheeks. 'When you dock, I'll make a home for you. I'm not asking you to marry me. There's the religious thing, and I'm not twenty-one.'

Daniel stared at her, a gleam in his eyes. 'Just like that, you'd live with me? I can just see me going to confession and saying, "Father, I have sinned by not only falling in love with a *Protestant* girl, but living with her as well." The priest would love that!'

She stared at him and smiled. 'Would you really say that to the priest? What would he say back?'

'Never mind. But we couldn't do it. It's a mortal sin and so is preventing babies.'

'But we did it and you said I'll be all right. We don't have to have babies until we get married. We could still do it lots of times.'

He grinned. 'You're a terrible girl, Becky. We'll have to wait and get married properly, but I don't know when.' He frowned. 'Your father's been asking questions in the crew's quarters.' He fell silent.

'And?'

'He's offering money for information about two Irish brothers. A couple of the lads know about Shaun. Any time now they're going to take the money.'

She was scared for him. 'What do you want to do? Papa's planning to take over Green's agency in New York so you'd know where to find me if—'

'That's why you had the guided tour?'

'Yes. Papa's going to be Joshua Green's agent. He took me to see his house in Liverpool.'

His eyes flickered over her face. 'A huge place, is it?'

'It's nowhere near a mansion. It's not as big as the houses in Merrion Square in Dublin. He has a sister living with him. Widowed. She's a bit – queer. I felt sorry for her.'

'Who wouldn't.'

'What do you mean?'

'It doesn't matter. Green and I were on the same ship once, that's all. It was torpedoed.'

'And?'

'It has nothing to do with now,' he said softly. 'Can you hear the music? Shall we dance here on deck?'

'I can't.'

'I'll teach you.'

She wanted to ask more about Joshua Green but was wise enough to know he did not want to talk. She wanted to go on about marrying but knew that would have to wait too. She gave herself up to the moment.

Despite the cold and the mist which had thickened she enjoyed learning to dance with him as teacher. Everything seemed unreal, including the mournful sound of a foghorn in the distance. They were so wrapped up in each other that at first the footsteps coming in their direction did not register. As they drew closer she opened her eyes and looked over Daniel's shoulder. Instantly she recognised the shadowy figure behind. 'It's Papa,' she said through lips that quivered.

Daniel looked down at her and for a moment his hands held her tightly. 'It's all right! Don't look so scared. It's happened now. There's nothing we can do.' He dropped his arms and they turned around.

For a moment nothing was said. Then her father addressed Rebekah. 'Your mother's in the cabin. You can go there.'

She shook her head. 'No. I want to hear what you say to Daniel.'

Her father's expression seemed to set like stone. 'You will do as you are told,' he said, stressing every word. 'I told you to have nothing to do with this man.'

'Papa, I'm nearly twenty. I'm not a child to be ordered around.' Her voice shook with sudden anger. 'The world has changed since the war. Women—'

'I don't want a lecture on emancipation.' A tic twitched his left eye and his fists clenched. 'This man's a traitor and a murderer, and you'll do as I tell you.'

'He is not a murderer!' she said hotly. 'Just because his brothers – You judge him without knowing him!'

'I don't have to know him!' Her father's voice rose. 'You're talking to a man who belongs to an organisation that wears a mask to cover up its activities! So get away from him and go to your mother!'

She tilted her chin. 'No.'

Daniel spoke. 'Becky, go.'

She looked at him but before she could speak or move, her father's hand shot out. The force of the blow knocked her head back against Daniel's shoulder. 'I will not have you speak to me like that!'

Her father's whole body seemed to loom larger with uncontrollable rage.

Daniel steadied her. 'Don't you ever hit her again!' His voice shook with fury.

'Don't you tell me what to do with my own daughter, you filthy rebel.' Her father's fists clenched.

'Papa, please!' Rebekah held a hand to her head in an attempt to stop it spinning. 'I'll stop seeing him. Just don't hurt him.'

'Hurt me!' cried Daniel, putting her on one side. 'It's me that'll bloody hurt him. Hitting you! He's a coward!'

'I'm no coward, you turf hopper!' Her father swung his arm.

Daniel easily parried the blow before lunging forward and catching him a punch on the chest. 'You're a bully. One of Green's yes men!'

Her father staggered slightly before making a recovery and coming forward with surprising speed. 'I'll have you know, boy, that I have shares in the company,' he panted. 'I'm one of the bosses. I'll have you fired! I'll see you never work again!'

Daniel was so surprised that he dropped his guard slightly and was caught a clout across the mouth. He began to bleed.

Now the two men grappled with each other, trying to throw each other off balance. Her father caught Daniel a vicious kick in the shins and he stumbled backwards. The blood from the blow on his lip was running down his chin. He prevented himself from falling and ran at the older man with his head down. Her father doubled over but soon straightened up to ram his fist at Daniel's mouth again. More blood!

Rebekah screamed. She had had enough. 'Stop it! Stop it!' She jumped on her father's back but he flung her off. Daniel's fist caught him on the jaw.

She drew back, her heart pounding. She would get Mama! She would stop Papa before either of them did each other a real injury.

She fled along the deck, only vaguely aware of a flurry of whistles blowing somewhere nearby. A foghorn sounded, then came what seemed to be an answering blast of sound. Her hands shook as she sought to open the cabin door but her fingers were shaking so much that it took her longer than usual.

At last it opened. 'Mama!' she cried. 'Come quickly!'

Her mother's pale face stared at her from the bunk. Rebekah took a few steps forward. 'Mama?' The eyes were red-ringed, as if she had been crying. Suddenly they widened as there was a noise like an explosion and then a dull, roaring sound. The whole ship seemed to shake. Next came a tearing and rending, a crunching and rippling noise. Rebekah wanted to call out but was abruptly flung to the floor. Her bunk crashed down on her. A dark object came through the side of the ship and crushed her parents' bunk beds against the wall.

CHAPTER EIGHT

Daniel became aware of the fog whistles at the same time as he noticed that Rebekah had gone. He swung her father round by the lapels of his coat and brought his fist back ready for the blow that he hoped would finish the fight. Then suddenly he saw, terrifyingly close, the prow of a ship looming up through the fog. 'Holy Jesus!' he whispered, crossing himself and taking a step back.

'Ha!' exclaimed Rebekah's father triumphantly through swollen lips, and punched him with the last of his strength.

Daniel staggered back as the ship hit, lost his footing and went head over heels backwards. Momentarily he rested on his haunches, trying to get his breath back. Then he sprang to his feet as the other ship crunched its way through steel and wood along the side of the *Samson* towards him. He turned and fled from its destructive path, down the nearest companionway. He had to find Rebekah! Thank the Holy Mother she had left! Her father . . . He didn't want to think of that. Where they had fought was just a tangled mess.

The lights had gone out and doors were opening. There were shouts. A woman screamed. People were running along corridors in panic, fighting to get past him as he searched and called, went up and down corridors, feeling his way. He realised that what he was doing was crazy. He presumed that Becky had gone back to her cabin but didn't know where that was exactly.

A light from a torch suddenly shone in his face, half blinding him. 'Is that you Riley?' The voice was incredulous.

'Yes!' He knocked down the torch with bloodied knuckles.

'You look a mess. Not that it matters. Come with me!'

'What?'

'Yer wanted, mate! In the engine room! It's flooding down there and there's a boiler making a funny noise. They need your expertise.'

'Hell!' Daniel groaned, and clutched his hair. 'I have to find someone.'

'You won't be finding anyone if you don't come. That boiler could blow.'

Daniel took a deep breath and told himself to calm

down. The odds were that Becky was all right. There were a heck of a lot of people running around.

'Well! Are you coming?' demanded the mate, shining the torch into his face again.

Daniel nodded and went with him.

For a long while Rebekah lay stunned, her thoughts incoherent. She was aware of a crushing weight on her right arm. Then there was a babble of voices outside along the passageway, hurrying footsteps and the sound of rushing water.

Fear was blighting her courage and it took several deep flurried breaths to calm her nerves and enable her to try and move her legs. At least they seem uninjured. She tried freeing her arm but the pain was excruciating and caused sickness and dizziness. Dear God, was she going to die? No, please! What had happened to Mama! She called to her mother but there was no answer.

Lifting her head she stared in the direction where she had last seen her mother and slowly, as her eyes became accustomed to the dark, could just make out the shambles that was her parents' bunk. She did not want to believe that her mother could not have survived. It was a nightmare. What about Daniel? What had happened? She must get out of here.

She screamed and carried on yelling for help until at last someone did come. The door was forced open and two men came in. One picked her out by torchlight and came over to her.

'You all right, luv?'

She laughed weakly. 'Oh, yes. I'm just lying here for the good of my health.'

'Glad you've still got your sense of humour.' He turned to his companion who had gone over to the other bunk and was trying to prise it away from the wall. 'Give us a hand here, vicar.'

The parson delayed several moments and could be heard praying. Then he came over, still in his pyjamas. Rebekah cleared her throat as the two men began to lift the weight from her. 'Mama's all right, isn't she?'

'Sorry, my dear.' The parson's hand was gentle on her cheek. 'It must have been almost instantaneous if that is of any comfort to you.'

She did not answer but a sob swelled her throat and tears blurred her vision. A few moments later she was free and one of the men was saying that her arm was broken. The parson was wrapping her in a blanket. The other man lifted her and she recognised him as their steward. 'I have a friend. He's an engineer. Da – no, Peter Riley,' she croaked. 'He's one of the engineers. He was with my father.'

'The engine rooms are flooding but they're getting it under control,' the steward answered. 'He should be all right. Ain't seen no sign of your father, though, miss. But that's not surprising, the panic everyone's in with the dark and all.'

She closed her eyes briefly, pressing down *her* panic, and said huskily as he helped her up, 'What happened?'

'This other ship came out of the fog and hit us. It's ripped this side open, but there's nothing for you to worry about. We're in no immediate danger.' His voice sought to soothe.

'No. I've got nothing to worry about.' she whispered before bursting into tears. He patted her shoulder and the parson told her that she would be all right. They would see that she was taken care of.

The passenger alleyways were still in darkness. 'Why aren't the lights on?' she stuttered.

'Water's short-circuited the dynamos,' said the steward cheerfully, flashing his torch. 'We'll take you on top. Don't worry.'

She wished he would stop telling her not to worry. What was happening to Daniel? Where was her father?

The decks were crowded with people in various states of dress. Some were crying. One man sat calmly playing solitaire, sitting on a lifebelt. An elderly woman was putting up her hair. It was still foggy and the ship's whistles played a mournful tune. The doctor came and put her arm in splints and a sling; gave her a couple of tablets. She asked him about the water coming into the engine rooms and he said he knew nothing about it. She looked round for a sign of someone she recognised and a few feet away saw a white-faced Brigid with a blood-stained bandage tied round her bright hair.

Rebekah struggled to her feet and stumbled light-headed over to her friend. She slumped down next to her and put her free hand through Brigid's. 'Mama's dead and Papa's missing.' She barely recognised her own voice. 'Are you badly hurt?' Brigid shook her head. 'Keith?' asked Rebekah. There was no answer but the Liverpudlian's eyes were filled with tears.

'Oh God,' whispered Rebekah, and gently drew Brigid's head down on to her shoulder.

She did not know how long they sat there while the deck started to empty. Mr Eaton came up to them. 'Miss Rhoades, will you and the other lady come with me, please? We want to get you off the ship.'

She stared up at him in a daze. 'Off the ship?'

'Yes. It's sinking. But you don't have to worry,' he said quickly. 'It'll take some time and the wireless operator's wired for help. There are several ships on the way. It shouldn't be long before you're picked up.'

Rebekah nodded and took a deep breath. 'Daniel O'Neill . . . no, Peter Riley! He's one of your engineers. Is he down in the engine room?'

His smile fixed, he said reassuringly, 'Yes, he is. It's a bit fraught down there with the pumps being worked overtime, but I don't think any of them are in danger. There was a bad moment I believe when the

161

boiler could have blown, but Riley managed to turn some valve or other and prevented it happening.' He hesitated. 'He said when I found you – that he's sorry, but your father didn't see the ship coming. I presume—'

'He knows I'm all right?' Rebekah whispered.

He moved his shoulders in a gesture that revealed his discomfort. 'Not yet.' He offered her his arm and she accepted it with gratitude.

'What happened to the other ship?' she stammered.

'What?' He seemed distracted but answered, 'She drifted off, but we've had a message from her. Her bow's badly damaged but she'll keep afloat.'

'Was there anybody hurt?'

'Several of the crew were killed.' He hesitated. 'I'm sorry about your parents.'

'Thank you,' she said woodenly. They both fell silent.

It was no simple task getting on her lifebelt. Neither was it easy or pleasant having to climb down the ladder into a small bobbing boat.

Rebekah and Brigid cuddled up to each other because it was freezing cold. The fog lifted a little, and although their boat had been rowed away from the *Samson* they could still see the great rip in her side. She was listing badly to port and Rebekah felt taut with apprehension. It began to rain.

People moaned and groaned, and Rebekah felt

she had never felt so miserable in the whole of her life. Time passed slowly and pictures from her childhood drifted through her mind. It occurred to her that now her father was dead, he could not stop her seeing Daniel. She tried to draw comfort from the thought even as she wept.

It grew lighter, and although there was no sign of the sun, several people said they felt better. After what seemed hours someone said the crew had begun to leave the ship. That it could not be long before the *Samson* went down. An exhausted and soaked Rebekah peered through the rain, trying to make out the faces of the figures climbing into the boats. Water was washing the ship's decks and some of the men jumped into the sea. A cheer went up suddenly, and the sound of the ship's whistle and siren were heard. Distracted, she turned and saw a steamer looming up through the downpour. When next she looked at the *Samson* there were only two figures clinging to her rigging. She presumed one of them was the captain. The next moment they were in the water – had gone under – came up. Under – up. They were swimming for the nearest lifeboat. There was a great cracking and a gurgling sound as the *Samson* sank, and for a while the sea was a great churning mass.

Brigid sobbed, clinging to Rebekah, who clung to her just as desperately. Had Daniel got off? How could she find out? Dear God, please let him be safe.

Within half an hour they were taken aboard the S.S. *Reliant* and wrapped in rough warm blankets. Rebekah's teeth chattered so much against the rim of the cup of hot sweet tea that she spilt it. Her head felt as if it was splitting and her throat felt raw. She fought to keep burning eyes open for sign of Daniel. Then she saw Shaun.

Three times she had to call his name before he showed any sign of hearing her. Then he sauntered over, cup in hand, blanket about his shoulders. Close up, she could see the strain in his face.

'Is Daniel all right?' she stammered.

He scowled. 'Didn't you see him in the water?'

'No.' She felt as if her heart was being squeezed and she feared his answer. 'He was rescued?'

There was a pause. 'If he was, I didn't see it,' said Shaun with a tight smile. 'He could be drowned. All I do know is that he's not on this ship.' Without another word he turned and walked away.

Rebekah stared after him. She felt as if *she* was drowning in a sea of misery, pain and discomfort. It couldn't be true! It just couldn't be true! He was meant for her. God couldn't take him away. That wasn't fair. She loved him, needed him, wanted him above anything else in the world. She would die without him.

'I don't know if I can bear it.' Brigid's voice was low. 'Keith, your parents, Daniel. I think I'll kill myself.'

'Don't say that!' Rebekah eased her throat and

attempted a smile. 'I think I'm going to die anyway.'

A corner of Brigid's mouth lifted wearily. 'I won't kill myself if you don't die on me.'

'Is that a promise?' A cough was tickling her throat.

'Cross my heart,' Brigid's voice wobbled.

'Right. That's it,' murmured Rebekah. 'We stay together.'

Brigid nodded and the pair of them sat on, sipping their tea with the tears dripping into the cooling liquid.

A doctor came and spoke kindly to them. He examined their injuries and told Rebekah to follow him. Brigid went with her.

Rebekah watched as he sprinkled plaster on strips of bandage then dipped them in water before wrapping it around her broken arm. She was a mass of aches and her throat and head felt worse. Her heart felt like a lump of stone. After the plaster set they were taken to a cabin and given warm clean nightwear, a hot milky drink and some tablets.

The last memory in Rebekah's mind before the tablets took effect was of Daniel saying, 'I love you, Becky.' Then it was overlaid by the grey rain-splattered scene of men struggling in the water while Shaun's words ran through her head.

Rebekah woke in a small room to a conversation going on in the distance. Her head turned on the smooth cool pillow and for the first time in what seemed forever there was no pain in her chest or her head. Where exactly was she? Who was talking? The memory of her arrival was hazy but she did remember that she had seen Brigid since coming here. Was that her she could hear talking? She tried to call her friend's name but her voice was only a whimper.

There was a glass of water on the cabinet by the bed but it was an enormous effort to hold it, and then another to lift it to her lips as she sagged across the bed, her broken arm held awkwardly against her chest. She sipped slowly. That was better. She cleared her throat. 'Brigid'. The voices stopped abruptly and there was the sound of heavy footsteps and lighter hurrying ones moving towards the door.

Rebekah squinted at the door, trying to recall who had brought her to this clean blue-painted room. One of the voices had said something about nearly dying. Were they talking about her? She had been having terrible dark dreams. Daniel and water . . . the ship . . . Mama and Papa! It was as if there was a blizzard in her head. A moan issued from her lips and her face turned into the pillow.

The door opened. Rebekah's wet cheek rubbed against the white cotton before she twisted to see who had entered.

'How are you, Miss Rhoades?'

She made no answer, staring at the man. He was familiar but she could not place him.

'Becky, Mr Green says he wants to take you back to England.'

'Who? What?' Rebekah's gazed shifted to Brigid's pale thin face.

Joshua, who was wearing a black suit, removed his hat before approaching the bed. 'Surely you haven't forgotten me? I've come to help you.'

There was a brief silence before she murmured. 'I haven't forgotten. You're the owner of the *Samson* . . . or you were.'

His expression was grave. 'It's a sorry business. A terrible thing to happen. I don't know what to say—'

'I don't think you can be blamed for the fog or for the other ship hitting us, Mr Green,' she said quietly, easing herself up against the pillows with difficulty. Brigid rushed forward to help her.

He looked relieved. 'I'm glad you can look at it like that, Miss Rhoades. We are, of course, taking legal action against the other ship. We want damages for the loss of the *Samson* and her cargo – as well as for the lives lost and passengers' belongings.'

She eased her throat. 'I would like to go to church.'

He nodded. 'We'll have a memorial service for them.' His voice was sombre. 'And for the others who died . . . as soon as you feel able to cope with it.'

Rebekah looked at Brigid. 'You do know that Mrs O'Shaugnessy's husband—'

'Yes. We've been talking.'

'About going back to England?' she asked.

'I didn't think you would wish to stay in New York.'

'No.' She stared down at the bedcover and her fingers plucked at the sheet. 'Mr Green, one of your engineers helped save a boiler from blowing. He was Irish and I knew him in Dublin.' Her pleading eyes were lifted to his. 'His name was Daniel O'Neill but he went by the name of Peter Riley. Last I heard, he was in the water. I don't know if he was rescued.'

For several moments Joshua did not speak. Then, 'I knew an O'Neill in the war, if it is him you're talking about. We were on the same ship for a while, I haven't had time to see if there's been any losses among the crew because I've only been in New York a few hours, but I'll certainly find out for you.'

She smiled faintly. 'Thank you.'

'It's the least I can do.' He returned her smile. 'I was told by the nurses not to stay long so I'll leave you now but I'll be back later.' He held out his hand. She took it, comforted by its strength and warmth.

The moment he left Brigid came and sat on the bed. 'Well that's that,' she said.

'What's what?' murmured Rebekah.

'Him! His lordship coming to see yer. Apparently it was on his orders that yer got moved from the hospital to this rest home. They only just about allowed me in.'

Tears filled Rebekah's eyes. 'I'm glad they did.' Her voice was unsteady as she squeezed Brigid's hand, noticing how bony it felt. The bandage on her head had gone but there was a yellow bruise and a healing cut on her forehead. She wore a black coat which hung on her. 'How are things? It's the first day I've felt myself enough to consider you.'

Brigid's eyes, with the dark pouches underneath, avoided hers. 'I'm surviving. But don't let's talk about it.' There was a pause while they sought strength from the other's presence. Then the Liverpudlian said in a bright voice, 'I haven't told yer but me brother came in on the same boat as his lordship.'

'Your Pat?'

'Yeah! We'll probably go back on the *Gideon*.' She hesitated. 'How d'yer feel about going on a ship?'

'I haven't thought about it.'

'I don't like it,' said Brigid bluntly. 'But if it's the only way to get back home, then I'll just have to put up with it.'

Rebekah rested her head against the pillows. 'At least you've got a home to go to . . . and your sisters and your mam.' It hurt when she thought of her own mother and she wanted to weep.

There was another pause. 'What about that posh aunt of yours?' asked Brigid.

'Aunt Esther?' She supposed that she had to

consider living with her aunt. 'She's family, of course.'

'Better than none.' Brigid hesitated. 'D'yer really believe that Daniel could be alive?'

'You think I'm clutching at straws?'

Brigid's answering silence was frustrating.

'His brother didn't see him drown,' said Rebekah, tilting her chin. 'He could be alive.' Her mind refused to accept that she would never see Daniel again.

'I'm not saying he couldn't be,' muttered Brigid as if the words were forced from her. 'But don't build up yer hopes.'

'Have you seen any sign of Shaun?'

Brigid shook her head and freed her hand. 'I think yer'd be better resting. Short visits – that's what I was told. Yer haven't been well and yer don't want to have a relapse.' She hugged Rebekah and went out.

For a long time Rebekah lay there, fighting back tears and a terrible sense of desolation. Then two nurses came in, one carried a basket of fruit which she said was from Mr Green. The other brought a bowl of broth. She had a nasal twang to her voice and spoke cheerfully about the visitors and how lucky Rebekah was to have an excuse to stay in her nice warm bed as it had begun to throw it down outside. Rebekah let the words flow over her as she drank several spoonfuls of broth voluntarily, and was coaxed into swallowing the remainder.

Afterwards, she was left alone, which was the last thing she wanted as thinking only served to depress her spirits further. What if Daniel was dead? How was she going to live without him?

The morning sun put a bit of heart into her and Rebekah felt less inclined to accept the worse. She managed some porridge, a cup of coffee, three grapes, and a trip to the lavatory on her own. Joshua came to visit, and because everything and everybody else was unfamiliar, he seemed to represent reality.

'Did you find out anything about Daniel?' she demanded as soon as the pleasantries were observed.

He paused in the act of sitting on the chair beside the bed and said in deep tones, 'No. I can't find anyone who has seen him since the *Samson* sank.'

'Oh!' She almost fell back into utter despondency, but not quite. 'Have you seen his brother?'

'Brother?' He seated himself, his expression severe. 'Should I have?'

His reaction gave Rebekah pause for deliberation and she lowered her gaze. 'I suppose not. Have you seen Brigid since yesterday? She won't have to pay to return to England, will she?' Her voice was concerned. 'They didn't have much money, and now she has nothing.'

'You're very friendly with this woman?' There was a note in his voice that caused her to slant him a challenging look.

'Mama and Papa didn't object to our friendship and I don't see why you should. Or that it has anything to do with you, Mr Green.'

There was a silence and she saw a brief flicker of annoyance in his face. 'Your father named me as your guardian.'

'You!' She was dismayed and the fingers of her left hand kneaded the sheet as she remembered what her mother had said about her father's plan for her. 'I thought my aunt—' She stopped abruptly. 'No! Of course not Aunt Esther.'

'I know it will come as a shock to you, but it seems there was no one else.' His expression was affable once more as he withdrew an envelope from his pocket. 'I went to see your aunt as soon as I had the news about the *Samson*. She was concerned for you and gave me this note. I was to tell you that her home is now your home, and I consider the way matters lie at the moment, that's not a bad idea.'

Rebekah took the letter and placed it on the bedside cabinet. 'When can I leave for Liverpool?'

He turned his hat between his hands. 'I've arranged the memorial service for the day after tomorrow. You'll need some clothes. I've asked for some to be brought in for your inspection – and some footwear as well. We'll be leaving the day after the memorial service.'

'Thank you. How long have I been here?'

'Two weeks.'

'Two weeks!' She was aghast. Surely if Daniel was alive she would have heard from him? The realisation sapped her newfound strength and she sank back against the pillows, closing her lids tightly on the tears of weakness.

Joshua leant forward and took her hand. 'There now, Rebekah. Don't be upsetting yourself. The service will be an ordeal, I know, but I'll be with you. Don't be worrying about anything.'

Her wet lashes lifted. 'I wish people would stop telling me not to worry,' she said through gritted teeth. 'I'm frightened, and terribly unhappy, and I don't know what I'm going to do with the rest of my life. I've got loads to worry about!'

'You're overwrought.' He patted her hand. 'You've suffered a great shock as well as your injuries. It's natural you'll feel this way. What you need is building up. I'm certain your aunt will see to that.'

'Aunt Esther?' Rebekah laughed slightly hysterically. 'She'll expect me to become a Quaker. And I'm not a good girl.'

'Shh! I'll get the nurse and she'll give you something to calm you down.' he said soothingly, dropping her hand and going out of the room.

Rebekah sobbed into her pillow. What was life going to be like with Joshua Green in charge of her affairs, and her having to live with Aunt Esther? She could not see it being exciting or fun. All her dreams had sunk beneath the stormy waters of the Atlantic. She wanted to die, die, die. She thumped the pillow and unexpectedly remembered that was what Brigid had said too.

By the time Joshua and the nurse entered the room Rebekah had gained some control over her emotions. Willingly she took the tablets that would give her brief respite from her misery. 'Good girl,' she heard Joshua say as her eyes closed, and then she drifted, was whizzing across what appeared to be a misty sea. For an instant she recaptured the dream in which she had escaped from the castle and her depression was if anything worse than it had been waking. Then unconsciousness claimed her.

CHAPTER NINE

Daniel was tired when he alighted from the train at Penn station in New York City, but a restless anxiety drove him on through the bustling sidewalks to the vicinity of West 19th Street. It was a fortnight since he had been plucked half-drowned and concussed from the sea to be laid in the bottom of a lifeboat by one of the passengers. He could remember little of what had happened after that but later was told in hospital that the wind had risen and they had lost an oar. The boat had drifted but eventually they were picked up by a liner heading for Philadelphia. The captain had refused to take them to New York, saying his first duty was to his own passengers. He would wire to Green's agency in New York that they were safe, and once they were fit for travel they could make their own way there.

Daniel reached the agency with its rather pretentious frontage and went in. A fiercesome-looking female stared at him over steel-rimmed spectacles and he wished he had taken time to freshen himself up. 'Can I help you?' she said frostily.

'I'm looking for a Miss Rebekah Rhoades and Mrs Rhoades. They were passengers on the *Samson*.'

Suddenly it appeared that she knew whom he was talking about because her expression thawed slightly. 'Are you a relative? Because if you are you've just missed the memorial service. It was this morning. Perhaps you'd like to talk to Mr Green?' She stood, and before he could answer, hurried through a doorway behind her.

Memorial service! Daniel sat on one of the chairs in the reception area and put his head in his hands. Dear God, he hoped that was just for Mr Rhoades. He had heard that several passengers had been killed but had hoped . . . could not believe that . . .

'Oh, it's you, O'Neill. Or is it Riley? What can I do for you?'

Daniel lifted his eyes and met Joshua's cool gaze. 'Miss Rebekah Rhoades?' He stood up.

Joshua feigned surprise. 'You knew her?'

'Yes. From Dublin.' He cleared his throat. 'That woman said something about a memorial service.'

'That's right. Friends of yours, were they, O'Neill?' There was the slightest hint of derision in his voice.

Daniel's back stiffened. 'I wouldn't be saying

that of Mr and Mrs Rhoades. But Rebekah—'

'The daughter? She's dead,' said Joshua, watching him intently. 'They're all dead. The cabin was smashed to bits. I'm sorry, O'Neill, if she was a friend of yours. Tragic. But there it is. I knew them myself, you know.'

For a moment Daniel just stood there, his face quivering, then he turned and made for the door. Joshua hurried after him and thrust an envelope in his hand. 'Here's your pay, O'Neill. I'm sorry I can't offer you another berth right now.'

Daniel thrust the envelope into his pocket without looking at it or Joshua, and walked out. He had not gone far before he heard the women from the agency calling after him. 'There was a message for you, Mr O'Neill. From a Shaun Riley. He said that if you turned up, to look for him at Kelly's place.'

Daniel gave no sign of hearing but carried on up the street. He could not get the image of Rebekah out of his mind. God, God, God! He wanted to smash something! Anything! Anyone! He wished now he had hit Green's smirking face. The coward didn't give a damn that he was suffering, and Daniel had known it. Aye, he'd known the pain he'd been inflicting, Daniel thought grimly. Becky! Oh Becky, love! That swine didn't care that you were dead!

A long time ago, he had liked Joshua. Funny, that. They had been on a ship leaving Pennsylvania then, carrying a cargo of horses, wheat and oil. It was

1916 and they had been intercepted south-east of Cape Race by a German submarine. They had taken to the lifeboats – or what was left of them. That was when Daniel had discovered a different facet to Mr Joshua Green. If he hadn't been so bloody-minded then, they wouldn't have lost so many men. It had all come back to Daniel when he had been struggling in the water.

Becky . . . Funny, lovely, warm, sexy Becky! He could hear her now saying that she loved him – offering to live in sin with him. He scrubbed away the tears with his coat collar. He would find his brother and get rotten drunk. His fingers searched for the hip flask in his pocket. He hoped that Shaun had not drunk any of the so-called whisky on offer at Kelly's. Some of it could blind a man. He had given his brother fair warning.

Daniel carried on through the wet streets, shivering with cold and shock, until he came to Kelly's. Inside there was a strong smell of sweat and wet wool but the room was warm, if smoky and crowded. Daniel's eyes scanned the room and saw his brother over in a corner with another man. He pushed his way between tables until he reached them. 'So you survived then,' said Daniel, in a voice slurred with grief and weariness, looming over his brother.

Shaun slowly got to his feet, his face alight with relief. 'I knew you weren't fish food! I just knew it!' Awkwardly the brothers hugged each other and then sat with knees touching in the confined space. Daniel exchanged greetings with the other man, whose name was Brendan O'Donovan.

He was a large man with a balding head and several chins. 'Tell us what happened to you, Danny boy.'

Daniel told his tale succinctly. 'Green told me that the Rhoades' cabin was really smashed up. That they were all dead. Did you see it, Shaun? Did you see any sign of Rebekah?' His voice shook. 'Did she suffer, would you say?'

Shaun's throat worked and he avoided his brother's eyes. 'Are you meaning that Quaker that you'd taken a fancy to?'

'Aye.' Daniel's mouth set in a hard line. 'You're knowing right enough who I'm talking about.'

Shaun swirled the beer in his glass. 'I'm knowing nothing about her. I was worrying myself enough about you without caring about her. If Green says she's dead then she must be. Will you have a drink?'

Slowly Daniel shook his head. 'And rot my guts? Get me a coffee.' He took some coins from his pocket. His brother sloped off. Daniel sat, staring at nothing in particular, his thoughts turned in on his own misery, until Brendan jogged his elbow.

'A beauty was she, Danny? English?'

'I'd rather not talk about her.' Daniel's eyes

focussed on the American. 'How are things with you? Did Shaun manage to save the goods?'

'He got them to me. Although how much longer De Valera will be exchanging Irish Republican Bonds for dollars, I don't know. Word's out that he's fallen out with the IRB and Devoy. And he didn't do well politically in Washington, as you know. He's not liked for whipping up enthusiasm for the interests of what many in the Senate see as a small, unimportant country on the other side of the ocean.'

'You think there might be a chance of him returning to Ireland?' Daniel frowned and gnawed at his inner lip. 'God knows, from what I've seen of the mess everything's in, they need him. It's anarchy there, and something's got to give. You can't govern a country by bullying methods and the law of the gun. In the end it's got to be done above board. I think it's time de Valera went home.' Daniel stopped abruptly as his brother placed his coffee in front of him. He took out his flask and poured Irish whiskey into the dark liquid. It felt good going down.

'What's this about going home?' asked Shaun eagerly, seating himself. 'I'm game if you are.'

Daniel exchanged glances with his brother and forced a smile. 'I'm all for going home. But I won't be trying for a berth with Green's again. I'll get us on another ship. I've friends.'

Brendan shook his head. 'Well, boys, don't go getting yourselves into trouble.'

Daniel laughed harshly. 'Perhaps this time I will.' He gulped at the hot drink and started to feel the sharp edges of his grief change shape. The room had begun to spin slightly already. He had not eaten all day, but it did not seem to matter. He was thinking that at least talking about Ireland, he had found some outlet for his anger and sorrow. Hadn't he spoken to Rebekah about Oisín and his love for his princess and country? Loss of love might break your heart but the land was always there. Rebekah had said it was sad for the princess but Oisín had gone back to Ireland – found faith, only to die.

Life was bloody unfair! Just when you started to believe there was a chance of something different – something sweet, something good – it all went bloody wrong. Rebekah was dead and nothing seemed to matter any more.

PART TWO

CHAPTER TEN

'I never thought I'd cry my eyes out at the sight of the Liver birds.' Brigid wiped her damp face with the back of her hand as she hung over the ship's rail.

Rebekah smiled faintly. 'What are they supposed to be?'

'Our Pat says they're cormorants. I wouldn't know. I always thought they were mythical.' Brigid switched her attention from the Liver building to the waiting crowd below, and suddenly her face brightened and she waved madly. 'Me mam's down there, and our Kath and her kids!' She put a hand over her mouth. 'Oh Mary, mother of God, they're all there! I think I'm going to howl again.'

'What's wrong with that?' Rebekah straightened her shoulders. 'Of course you're pleased to see them, and I hope they spoil you soft.' She moved away from the rail. 'We'd better say goodbye now.'

Brigid stared at her and said unsteadily, 'Yer'll be all right? You have me address?'

'Yes!' Rebekah hugged her awkwardly. 'Now go to your family.'

'They'll probably be fed up with me by Monday and Mam will be brushing me out of the house, saying that hard work's the cure for all ills . . . to go and get meself a job,' said Brigid in a muffled voice against her shoulder. 'What about that aunt of yours and his lordship?'

'What about them?'

Brigid held Rebekah off from her and said sternly, 'Yer not to let them boss yer about.'

'Fat chance,' said Rebekah.

'Hmm!' Brigid frowned. 'Yer not as tough as yer make out.'

'I'm tougher than you think.' She smiled. 'Now are you going or not?'

Brigid grinned. 'I suppose I'd better go and show me face.'

'And I'd better find his lordship.'

'He's got his eye on yer, so watch yerself.'

Rebekah grimaced, 'He's got no hope.'

'Good.' Brigid gave her one last hug. 'Keep yer chin up.'

'And you. Now go or you'll have me crying.'

'It'd do yer good to cry.'

'I've cried enough to fill an ocean. Go!'

Brigid went but kept looking back and waving

until out of sight. Rebekah knew that she was going to miss her terribly, but also that it was wrong to depend on her when she had her own family. She blinked back tears, tilted her chin and went in search of his lordship, Joshua Green, who was escorting her to her aunt's house.

'Thy father should have listened to me,' said her aunt, standing in the doorway looking like a plump blackbird in mourning clothes.

'So you said three times in your letter,' murmured Rebekah.

'It's because I felt it so deeply.' Her aunt dabbed at her eyes. 'My poor Sarah. Men! They think they know it all.'

'Some think they do,' agreed Rebekah, remembering how she had struggled against blaming her father for what had happened all the way back across the Atlantic and the Irish Sea. 'But Papa couldn't have foreseen the other ship ramming us,' she added. 'And anyway it's no use going on about it. Think about how now you've got to bear with me. I'm sure Hannah's told you just what you're letting yourself in for.'

'Fellas,' muttered Hannah, glaring at her.

'Hundreds of them,' said Rebekah drily, noting Joshua's look. 'I eat them for breakfast.'

'Now thou art just being plain silly.' Her aunt blushed.

Hannah grunted. 'Thee'll rue the day, Miss Esther. Trouble, that's what thee's taking in.'

'Mind your place!' intervened Joshua in a sharp voice. 'You have no right to speak like that about Miss Rhoades. She has been through a lot and needs sympathy and care.'

The maid sniffed and without another word went back indoors.

'I've had to speak to her severely myself the last week,' murmured Esther, looking at nobody in particular as she picked up Rebekah's bag. 'Perhaps thou would like to come in, Mr Green, for a cup of tea?'

'Some other time,' he said brusquely. 'Your niece is tired and I have to get home.'

The blush which had just begun to fade in Esther's cheeks surged up again. 'Suit thyself. Rebekah shall we go inside?'

Rebekah nodded but held out a hand to Joshua. 'Thank you for looking after me. Could you let me know when everything is sorted out?'

He inclined his fair head and from his pocket took several banknotes, pressing them into her palm and folding her fingers over them. He held her hand longer than was necessary. 'I'll be in touch.' His voice was warm.

'I'll look forward to it,' she said politely. He hesitated, then kissed her cool cheek before striding off in the direction of West Derby Road.

Rebekah quickly dismissed him from her thoughts, pocketed the money and followed her aunt up the dark lobby into the sitting room. Somehow she had to cope with the next few weeks. The minister who had taken the memorial service had told her to think no further than one day at a time. Good advice, when even the simplest tasks were made difficult due to her broken arm! She struggled to undo her coat and her aunt hurried to help her.

Hannah stood watching them. 'At least that broken arm will stop thy gallop.' Her small dark eyes were unsympathetic. 'That is, unless we're gong to be having Mr High and Mighty Green calling every hour God sends.'

'Hannah,' protested Esther. 'That's uncalled for.'

'Don't worry, Aunt, we understand each other.' Rebekah smiled at the maid. 'Your condolences are really appreciated, Hannah.'

'Hmmph!' The maid turned her back on them and began to make tea.

Esther stared at Rebekah and shook her head. 'I'm sorry, dear. But do sit down and tell me if we will be seeing much of Mr Green. He told me that he's thy guardian. Is it true?'

'It seems so.' Rebekah prepared herself for another attack on her father.

'It's all wrong,' cried her aunt, folding her arms across her bosom. 'I'm thy next of kin! If my dear Sarah had had any say in the matter—'

'If you go on about Papa again, I'll scream,' interrupted Rebekah in a firm voice. 'And I can really scream if I want to. Ask Hannah! If I see a spider, I scream. If a man attacks me, I scream. Moaning and groaning, nagging and lectures, make me scream and want to carry on screaming. What I need is to be looked after, as Mr Green said.' She sat in an armchair. 'Am I allowed any of that food? I'm hungry.'

Her aunt appeared dazed. 'Of course thou art, dear. Help thyself.'

'It's difficult with my broken arm,' she said softly.

'I'm sorry. I wasn't thinking.' Her aunt placed a couple of sandwiches, a slab of gingerbread and two scones on a plate, putting it on Rebekah's lap. 'What thou needs, my dear, is God in thy life. I remember going through a time when there was a big scream inside me.'

'What happened to it?' said Rebekah, forcing herself to eat a sandwich. Brigid had told her that she had to build herself up, although she had little appetite. 'Did you let it out or did you swallow it?'

'I am a Quaker,' Esther said proudly. 'Due to meditation and prayer, it went. We'll take thee to Hunter Street, Rebekah, and there thou wilt find consolation. Then perhaps thou might wish to help out at St Anne's Centre?'

'Hunter Street?' Rebekah's eyes lifted from contemplation of her plate. 'That's the Friends' Meeting House?'

Her aunt nodded, blue eyes fixed on her niece's face. 'Thy mam spoke of it?'

'Yes. I don't exist in their eyes, do I?' said Rebekah, biting into a scone. 'Mama went and did wrong, and was thrown out.'

'I wouldn't have put it quite like that,' said her aunt, going red again. 'Besides – that's in the past. Thou can start with a clean slate.'

'That's nice.' Rebekah's voice was emotionless.

Her aunt seemed disconcerted and there was silence while she ate a scone. She dabbed her mouth with a napkin. 'Perhaps thou would prefer going to the adult class in Breck Road?' she suggested. 'Thou could learn more about our ways there, and of the Bible.'

'I know my Bible, Aunt Esther. Mama and Papa read it to me when I was young, and I also went to church. What I need at the moment is a bit of peace.'

Her aunt took a quick sip of tea before saying, 'Peace! Thou should have been at the Peace Conference of all Friends in August. Rufus Jones gave the lecture. He compared the conscience to a lantern. Emotions upset our judgment – but we must see the light from God.'

'God gave us our emotions,' countered Rebekah.

Her aunt ignored her remark. 'Thou must meet Ellen Gibbs who's the same age as thee. She's very keen on fighting for peace. She and her mother attend my sewing circle on Monday afternoons. I take it thou can sew?'

'I don't think I'll be sewing on Monday.'

'We make garments for the poor but I presume from the only baggage thou hast, thou must be short of clothing. Perhaps thou can sew for thyself? I have some material. Thou wilt need some good combinations. It's almost November and we can't have fires in every room. Good thick wool will keep the draughts out and will see thee through more than one winter.'

'I've silk underwear,' murmured Rebekah, gazing down at her silk-stockinged legs and her small neat feet in the black crocodile skin boots with the tiny buttons up the side. 'Mr Green had some brought into the nursing home for me to choose from.'

'Silk! Mr Green!' Her aunt's brows shot up. 'Thou wilt catch thy death of cold!'

Hannah tutted. 'Disgusting! I told thee what she was like with fellas, Miss Esther.'

'My knickers were bought with my money,' said Rebekah, flashing them both challenging looks. 'Papa purchased shares in Mr Green's shipping line. They're worth something . . . and not everything was lost when the ship went down. There was time to recover some property from the ship's safe. Apparently Papa had been thrifty all his life.'

'He had?' Her aunt looked startled but her expression soon changed to one of satisfaction. 'That explains a lot!'

'What does it explain?'

'It's in Mr Green's interests to be nice to thee if he knows all this.'

'Of course it is,' said Rebekah, determined to behave as if she had already thought of that herself. 'And it's also in my interests to be nice to him if I want money to spend. Until I'm twenty-five he controls the purse strings – but he seems a reasonable man so far, and charitable. He was telling me about the Seamen's Orphanage that he takes an interest in.'

Her aunt seemed lost for words for a moment but not for long. 'He wants to appear in a good light to thee.'

Rebekah took a firm hold on her patience. 'He only told me about the orphanage because I asked about the collection box on the ship.'

Her aunt sighed. 'It wasn't right thy father leaving him – almost a stranger – in charge of thy affairs.'

'I suspect Papa had an ulterior motive.' Rebekah rose and went over to the window.

'He did it to annoy me,' said Esther.

'I don't think so,' murmured Rebekah, remembering a conversation with her father on the ship. 'There'll be insurance as well, Aunt Esther. I could be a rich woman one day, so I think Papa thought it best to have a man in charge of my affairs.'

'Fortune hunters!' exclaimed her aunt. 'And if they knew about my money—'

'I told thee, Miss Esther,' grunted Hannah, 'just like wasps round a jam pot the fellas will be. We'll have no peace.'

'There'll be no fellas – fellows, I mean – coming here,' said Esther. 'Does thou hear that, Rebekah?' Her expression was severe.

'I heard.'

Her aunt's face softened. 'My poor dear, thou can find satisfaction in other things. Perhaps it would help if thou involved thyself in the peace movement? I have a book written in the last century, called *Wanderings in War Time*. The author visited the Franco-Prussian battlefields. It'll make edifying reading for thee when thou goes to bed.' Rebekah murmured a thank you.

That night she found it difficult to sleep as she had on board ship. The mattress was as lumpy as ever, and the room was decorated with heavy floral wallpaper that looked as if it had been there since Queen Victoria's Jubilee. Her mother had said that the furniture had come from the rooms above the shop. She decided that as soon as possible she would buy a new bed.

Her gaze washed over the ceiling and she was wishing that time could be switched back . . . that she was with Daniel gazing over Dublin Bay. Had he thought of her or never seeing Ireland, when he had been swamped by the freezing waters of the Atlantic? Oh God! Her sorrow seldom ended in tears now. It was as if frost had blighted her capacity to cry. She picked up the edifying book on battlefields, began to read, was depressed even further, and threw it across the room.

Despite her aunt's coaxing words, Rebekah did not go to the meeting house the next day. She had no desire to be welcomed back into the fold of the Quakers in the manner of a prodigal daughter. She doubted her ability to cope with people's sympathy and well-meant suggestions. It was difficult enough dealing with her aunt's overwhelming desire to have her as one of them. Nor did she attend the sewing circle. Instead she went walking in the park.

Her aunt was annoyed with her. 'Ellen wanted to meet thee. She suggests that thou joins the Women's International League for Peace and Freedom.'

'Not now,' said Rebekah in a lifeless voice. 'I just want to be left alone. Can't you understand that, Aunt Esther?'

'No. I can't,' retorted her aunt, pursing her mouth. 'I would have thought it easier to forget in the company of others.'

'I don't want to forget,' said Rebekah, hugging her broken arm to her chest. 'However much it hurts, I want to go on remembering.' She walked out of the room, wishing she had Brigid to talk to, knowing that she would understand.

Yet over the next weeks Rebekah did not get

in touch with her friend, believing that she might not want her company now she was back with her family. The fact that Brigid did not write or visit only seemed to confirm that belief. Neither was there word from Joshua Green, which surprised her.

Rebekah's arm was freed from plaster and to her relief she was able to use it without much difficulty. She helped with the housework, which did not please Hannah.

'Always under me feet thee are,' muttered the maid, giving her a look that was positively poisonous. 'Why don't thee get yerself a proper job or go and see that man? No doubt he'd enjoy looking at thee legs. Short skirts! Sinful, I call them. But some girls would go to any lengths to get a man.'

'I don't want a man,' said Rebekah, outwardly calm as she polished the walnut sideboard.

Hannah's look was disbelieving and she sniffed in a way that expressed exactly what she was thinking.

Rebekah was determined not to let the maid drive her out of the house but even so she began to scan the columns of the local paper in search of a job.

'Housekeeper wanted.' Pity she couldn't send Hannah after that. 'Situations required by ex-officers and other ranks.' Poor soldiers! At least she was not desperate for work because she had a family dependent on her. She read on. Charlie Chaplin was getting divorced from Miss Mildred Harris, who was not to use his name in her profession. What happened to a marriage to make the scandal of divorce more preferable?

A couple more weeks passed and Rebekah continued to look in the *Echo*. Joiners throughout the country went on strike. The papers said that it was a bad look out for Christmas. She was terribly lonely and despaired of ever feeling normal or even mildly cheerful again. The days stretched ahead of her like a dark tunnel with only night at the end.

December came in and she read that there was talk of an Irish truce . . . that there could be peace. She considered how she and Daniel had spoken of such an event and could have wept. In the same paper there was an article about the funeral of a Sinn Fein victim. A young man had been shot dead in Liverpool when the Sinn Feiners had set fire to buildings. Hundreds had attended the requiem mass despite the gales that had swept Merseyside. Rebekah remembered the day in Dublin when Shaun had shot the Black and Tans and she experienced a heaviness that seemed to weigh her down. Even in Liverpool people were not completely safe. She was filled with a sense of restlessness and a need to talk about Daniel. Her aunt was no use. She would surely disapprove. Brigid! She had to talk to her. Before the doubts started crowding in again, she wrote to her.

Brigid replied by return of post. 'Of course I want to see you, you dafty! I thought you'd found some posh friends and didn't want me.' She gave arrangements for a meeting, and for the first time in a long time Rebekah looked forward to the days ahead.

At breakfast three days later, and two months to the day since the *Samson* had set off to America, Esther voiced her plans for the day. 'We'll go shopping, just for a few essentials. Then after a quiet time and dinner, we'll walk in the park. Exercise is essential for a healthy body.'

Rebekah had heard similar sentiments every day for the last few weeks. 'No thank you,' she murmured. 'I'm meeting a friend.'

'A friend?' Esther stared at her.

Hannah paused in doling out the porridge. 'It's a fella.'

'It's half a dozen,' said Rebekah mildly. 'We're going to dance ragtime in Woolworth's threepence and sixpence store.'

'I don't believe it,' said her aunt, obviously startled.

'I do,' said the maid in a satisfied voice, slamming a dollop of sticky porridge on to Rebekah's plate.

Rebekah's smile was genuine for the first time in weeks.

CHAPTER ELEVEN

'Where next?' Rebekah put her arm through Brigid's and smiled at her. They had done some of Brigid's Christmas shopping and then had coffee and cakes in Cooper's café before strolling round the Bon Marché where Rebekah had paid twenty-one shillings for a jade crêpe-de-Chine blouse – all due to Brigid's persuasive tongue, and the fact that she had spent little of the money Joshua Green had given to her. 'Yer looking real drab,' her friend had said, and Rebekah, who had stopped feeling drab from the moment her letter had arrived, agreed and bought the blouse. Now she was wondering why they had stopped in front of the flower girls outside Central Station.

'D'yer realise it's two months to the day since we sailed for America?' said Brigid.

'Yes.' The smile faded from Rebekah's face.

'I want to buy some flowers. I'm going to throw them on the Mersey.'

Rebekah stared at her. 'It's a lovely thought, but won't the tide wash them back?'

Brigid shrugged. 'I know it's daft but I want to do something.'

A sharp laugh escaped Rebekah. 'But I thought you'd lit candles in church and had masses said?'

'I have.' Brigid's voice was fierce. 'But it's not enough! I feel so frustrated, Becky. So angry with God.' She fumbled inside her handbag. 'He could have allowed me at least a grave to tend! But then, I suppose I'm no worse off than the thousands of women who lost their men in the Great War. Although they do have the new cenotaph.'

'We'll have a whole armful!' Rebekah found her own purse. 'I think lovely big yellow chrysanths are best.' She pointed out the flowers to the woman wrapped in a thick black knitted shawl. 'Yellow's for remembrance, you know, Brigid.' Her tongue was almost tripping her because she felt like crying. 'Not that I've forgotten Daniel or Mama or Papa – or your Keith.' She handed a pound note to the woman.

Brigid took some of the flowers and dropped a halfcrown in Rebekah's pocket. 'Yer don't have to pay my share.'

She shook her head but it was no use saying anything to Brigid. She was proud, and as she had a job as an all-purpose maid for a doctor with an invalid daughter, Rebekah presumed she must have some money.

They dodged a horse drawn wagon and a delivery bicycle as they crossed the road, laden down with parcels and flowers.

They walked in silence, deep in memories. 'I see in the paper the troubles in Ireland might be over,' said Brigid at last.

Rebekah nodded. 'I wonder if Shaun's back in Ireland or whether he stayed in America?'

'I haven't heard anything. D'you want me to find out?'

'No,' she said shortly. 'I never did care for him and I don't know why I'm bothering my head thinking about him now. Let's get a tram to the Pierhead. I don't know about you but my feet are killing me.'

As the Birkenhead ferry discharged people at the landing stage, throwing flowers into the Mersey did not seem such a good idea.

'People'll think we're mad, won't they?' said Brigid.

Rebekah looked at her, pinched with the cold, miserable of face, and was angry. 'Who cares?' She began to run and Brigid followed her.

Rebekah stopped on the spot where she had stood with Daniel a little longer than two months ago. Was it crazy to feel so lonely for someone she had known so briefly? She looked up at the sky, searching for she did not know what. God could not be pleased with her. She had broken his rules. He was supposed to be a forgiving God, but was she sorry for what she had done with Daniel? Did she have any regrets about defying her parents? She bit her trembling lips. She and Daniel had become part of each other and she could not be sorry about that, though she did regret hurting her parents. For a moment longer she searched the clouds, needing reassurance, but there was no sign from the heavens. Stupid of her. God's spirit was within you. It was an inner voice that she needed to listen to, but how did one know what were just one's own thoughts and which God's? She sighed, then put down her parcels and cast the chrysanthemums one by one on to the water.

It was the first of many outings with Brigid and when Rebekah mentioned that it was her birthday the week before Christmas, her friend said, as she paid twopence for *The Penny Magazine* in the newsagent's: 'You can't just let your birthday go by.'

'What's there to celebrate?'

'Yer aunt not doing anything special?'

'She hasn't mentioned it, but that could be because she's cross with me. She thinks I've got a fella.'

Brigid's eyebrows shot up. 'Why does she think that?'

'Because I pretend I have – just to get Hannah going.

She was actually croaking around the house yesterday. You couldn't call it singing. Besides, Quakers don't sing. Nothing would please her more than to see me married off – preferably to someone not of the Quaker persuasion. You're tall, dark and handsome, and after my fortune.'

Brigid grinned. 'Yer joking!'

'She believes it because she wants to, of course. Aunt Esther doesn't know what to believe. I've denied that you're a man but she's not sure because Hannah's gone on at her about my flirting with boys in Dublin. I'd ask you to visit, only she'd bombard you with questions. Wanting to know about your family and all that. Religion, you know.' She smiled. 'I think on my birthday I'll tell them that we're going to the theatre.'

'Are we dollying ourselves up?'

'Of course! We've got to put a good face on things.' Rebekah held her head on one side. 'Where shall we go?'

Brigid hesitated. 'If yer like – instead of doing that – yer could have a birthday tea in our house. Mam would like to meet yer and she'd be pleased to do it.'

Rebekah stared at her. 'What does she feel about my not being a Catholic?'

'As long as yer not Orange, that's all she cares. If yer were a fella, of course, it'd be different.'

'That's reassuring,' murmured Rebekah.

'Our Pat'll be home.'

'It'll be nice to see him again,' said Rebekah politely. She had little recollection of what Brigid's brother looked like, despite having met him aboard ship.

Brigid put her hand through her arm. 'He'll cheer us up. Even if he has yer crying at the same time. He left the money for our Kath's kids to go the grotto last time he was home so I'm taking them next week. Would yer like to come? I've got a half day off.'

'If I haven't found a job by then,' said Rebekah, not having much hope of doing so.

'Right! It'll soon be Christmas.' Brigid sounded cheerful but Rebekah knew exactly how she was feeling. She watched her open her magazine and start reading as she walked. 'What's so fascinating?'

'It's the new Ethel M. Dell romance.'

'Will there be any kissing?'

Brigid gave her a mock disapproving look. 'If you want lots of kissing you should read *The Sheik*. Although they do more than kissing in that! Mam sez it's immoral. She's read it because she sez it's her duty to know what kind of rubbish us girls read.'

Rebekah smiled. 'Ethel M. Dell's not immoral?'

Brigid returned her smile. 'They pray and struggle with their consciences. Yer should read Elin Glyn's *Three Weeks* if yer want immoral. Not that there's anything real descriptive. She's a princess and older. He's young and handsome. They're not married and they make love on a couch of roses. Have yer ever heard the like?'

Rebekah thought of a sandy beach and the hard wood of the lifeboat. 'It's not realistic'

Brigid's glance met Rebekah's and her voice quivered when she said, 'Who wants realism?'

Rebekah squeezed her arm and wondered if the pain would ever go.

The days passed less slowly. Rebekah went with Brigid and her niece and nephew to the grotto to see Father Christmas. Afterwards she took them to the cocoa house on the corner of the Haymarket and Manchester Street. They had hot drinks and Wet Nellies, a sort of stale bunloaf, which dripped treacle. In their company she momentarily forgot her grief. On the way home, Brigid told Rebekah that she had met Daniel's cousin and mentioned Shaun to them. 'They hadn't heard nothing from him! The news about Daniel came as a terrible shock!'

That night, Rebekah could not get to sleep at all and in frustration picked up Florence Barclay's *The Rosary* which Brigid had lent her. It was said to have been read and wept over by every housemaid in the British Isles. Even Hannah had read it and told Rebekah that it would do her soul good – which had not particularly recommended it to her. Rebekah wondered if there was something wrong with her because she was already bored with the lovers and their blindness to each other. When it came to the end, with the hero on his knees in front of the heroine, Becky wanted her to pull him up and have him demanding her all!

She put the book down, remembering the passion there had been between Daniel and herself. It seemed evil that it should have been suppressed so soon. Evil because that passion still existed. The yearning to give herself – to be taken. She turned off the gaslight and remembered that first meeting with Daniel. Had she fallen in love with him then? She recalled all their meetings. Her eyelids dropped and she dreamt that he was alive again, that they were making love on a bed of roses. Stupid! Roses had thorns. Even in dreams she could not escape reality. She woke up and wondered if the day would ever come when being alive did not hurt.

CHAPTER TWELVE

It was one of those glorious winter days, crisp but sunny, that catches at the throat, and is all the more welcome because one knows that the bad weather will soon be back. In a few days it would be Rebekah's birthday and she felt older than her twenty years. She almost wished herself as young as the girls, who could not be more than ten years old, importantly wheeling baby sisters or brothers in high prams. Several boys, on the way to the park not a couple of hundred yards away, kicked a ball up the middle of the road. A horse waited patiently between the shafts of a coal wagon as the coalman heaved a hundredweight sack of coal on his back and carried it up the long path to a house. Steps were being sandstoned and brass knockers polished as Rebekah walked past gardens where a few chrysanthemums still bloomed. A middle-aged man tying up flowers called, 'Good morning.' He had given her a friendly wave in the past but her aunt had always hurried her past.

Rebekah stopped. 'It's a nice day.'

He grinned. 'It is that. I'm Mr McIntyre. You're Irish? Never knew there were Quakers in Ireland until I heard about you.'

Rebekah returned his smile. 'There's a few but I'm not really one of them, although Mama used to be. It's nice to meet you, Mr McIntyre.' She held out her hand. 'I'm Rebekah Rhoades.'

He hesitated and wiped his own hand on well-worn grey flannel trousers before taking hers. 'It's terrible the things that have been going on over there, and it doesn't look like the peace talks are getting anywhere. They say that peace would be more likely if Lloyd George's didn't expect them to lay down their arms before handing only part of Ireland over to them!'

'Unconditional surrender,' said Rebekah. 'I can't see it coming off.'

He nodded and leant on the gate. 'I see they've got two sisters on conspiracy charges to do with that Catholic lad's murder in town. Apparently there was a framed Irish Republican Declaration in their house in Seaforth, as well as lists of arms and explosives. I ask you, women! I thought our Edwina was mad enough when she got herself involved with that suffragette movement before the war. You've never been involved in anything like that, Miss Rhoades?'

'No, but I admire her courage. I read some of my mother's leaflets about what was done to Emily Davison.'

He nodded, his expression grim. 'They force-fed my daughter once. That was enough for her. It was peaceful means after that.' He nodded vehemently. 'But I shouldn't be keeping you if you've the messages to get. You aunt'll be after me.'

He moved away and she carried on up the road, stricken with pain at the sudden memory of that afternoon with Daniel in Seaforth.

The smell of freshly baked bread did not rouse Rebekah from her thoughts, but as she entered the bakery she collided with a young woman in a brown tweed costume. Around her neck she wore a complete fox stole with glassy eyes that seemed to fix on Rebekah's face at the same time as the woman's. She looked to be in her late twenties. 'You're the Irish Quaker,' she said.

Rebekah grimaced. 'No, I'm not. My mother was, and so is my aunt. I'm not sure what I am.'

The woman raised thick eyebrows. 'My mistake. I'm Edwina McIntyre.' She possessed her father's strong bone structure and squarish face. 'Has your aunt been saying anything about me?'

'Nothing,' said Rebekah, taken aback. 'But your father's been telling me about your being a suffragette.'

Edwina's smile became fixed. 'Oh, that! Being

in prison isn't seen as so bad by your aunt because some of the Quaker men were jailed for being conscientious objectors during the war. It's my having had a baby and not being married that makes her look on me as a scarlet woman.' She paused. 'Am I shocking you?'

'Are you trying to because you don't like my aunt?'

Edwina laughed. 'How clever of you. She makes me squirm, the way she stares. You'd think I was the serpent in Eden.' She pressed Rebekah's arm. 'You must come and have a cup of tea with us one day. You can tell me all about yourself.' She waved a hand and strode off.

Rebekah stared after her. She could not see herself and Edwina having much in common, and the other woman had shocked her a little by her openness. Although who was she to judge? How would it have been if she had had Daniel's baby? How would her aunt have reacted? Perhaps she would have taken her in still, but a baby? And Joshua Green, what would he have said and done? She fancied a scandal would be the last thing he would wish for. Probably he would have sent her away to a quiet discreet Home and had the baby put up for adoption. Hers and Daniel's baby – how would she have felt about that?

It was strange, never having met Edwina before, that Rebekah should bump into her that evening when buying the *Liverpool Echo* from the newsvendor.

Edwina was reading the front page. She looked up. 'Oh, it's you again. I'm just reading about that poor woman they pulled out of the Mersey. I bet some man's behind it. They've named her as Emma Richards. Her brother's a shipowner and lives not far away. He goes to our church.'

'What!' Rebekah handed over the money for a newspaper and found the article. She began to read: 'According to her brother, Joshua Green, his sister had been staying with friends in Formby-by-the-Sea. She had been unwell for a while. They had not become worried immediately as she often wandered off on her own.'

'You look like you've seen a ghost,' said Edwina, staring at her.

'I've met her,' murmured Rebekah, folding the paper. 'Her brother's my guardian.'

'Her brother is – not your aunt?'

'My father and aunt never got on.'

Edwina nodded, but asked no questions as they began to walk. 'I see there's to be an inquest. Do you think it was suicide?'

'You mean, did she kill herself?' Rebekah's back stiffened.

'That's what suicide is,' said Edwina drily. 'And you can't exactly fall into the sea at Formby. Of course, she could have been trapped by the tide on a sandbank if she'd gone paddling – but the time of year's all wrong.'

Rebekah said woodenly. 'It's been a lovely day today.'

'Cold, though. It's been quite a year for the poor man.'

'You mean with one of his ships sinking, and now this?'

Edwina wrinkled her nose. 'I meant his being jilted at the altar last April. They make jokes about that sort of thing happening, but he was actually left waiting in the church. I mean, men can be swines – but to humiliate someone like that is all wrong.'

Rebekah nodded. 'I'll have to go and see him.'

'I don't envy you.' Edwina smiled. 'By the way, that invitation still stands. Just drop in when you feel like it.'

'Thanks.'

They parted at her aunt's front gate.

Rebekah told her about Emma. 'I'll have to go and see Mr Green.'

Esther looked up from her sewing. 'Not a nice thing to happen. Couldn't thou just send a letter and flowers.'

'There's to be an inquest, which means funeral arrangements won't have been made yet.'

Her aunt sighed. 'Well, if thou must, thou must. But don't linger.'

Rebekah said that she had no intention of doing so and went out of the room before her aunt could say more.

Rebekah stared at the ship's bell on the side of the red-brick porch, and then at the cat miaowing on the doorstep. She remembered how her father had tugged on the rope and set the bell clanging. She thought of Emma and her cat, and a heavy sigh escaped her. 'Bloody moggy', that's what Emma called it. So wrapped up in herself had she been during the last weeks, she had almost forgotten that Emma existed. She pulled on the rope and knocked on the door. Twice. Then she picked up the cat which was winding about her legs, and stroked it. Bloody Moggy began to purr.

Joshua opened the door. He looked angry and seemed about to say something but checked himself when he obviously recognised Rebekah's slight figure in the shadows. He said lamely, 'It's you, Rebekah. What are you doing with that cat?'

'I've just come to say how sorry I am. About your sister, I mean.'

'That's kind of you. I intended coming to see you this week. It's your birthday on Friday, isn't it? You'd best come in.'

'I expect you're busy,' she said, suddenly nervous.

'Don't be foolish.' He smiled and put his hands on her shoulders. 'I should have come to see you sooner but I've been busy organising new schedules and trying to buy another ship. I have the chance of purchasing an elderly lady with a good record and having her overhauled. Now the joiners have gone on strike and messed matters up. Put the cat down and let me take your coat.'

'I think he's missing Emma.' She released the cat which ran inside the house.

'I'm trying to keep him out!' Joshua made an exasperated sound which he turned into a laugh as he hung her coat on a stand. 'Sorry. It's not your fault. It's just that it miaows all round the house and drives me mad.' He led her into the front room where a fire burnt in the grate. He remained standing, resting an elbow on the mantelshelf.

'Poor cat!' Rebekah looked up at him from beneath her lashes and said impulsively, 'Can I have him if he's a nuisance?'

'He has a pedigree, you know.' He hesitated. 'But I'll be glad to get rid of the creature, if I'm honest.' He pressed an electric bell on the mantelshelf. 'We'll have a cup of tea and I'll take you home in the car afterwards.'

'Thanks.'

There was a discreet knock on the door and the maid entered. She glanced at Rebekah as Joshua asked her to bring tea. Rebekah remembered her from last time. Janet, that was her name.

After she left there was a short silence before Joshua said, 'I was going to suggest a visit to Crane Hall to see *The Gondoliers* on your birthday, but under the circumstances I suppose that's out of the question.'

She smiled. 'I would have had to refuse, anyway. I've been invited out.'

He lifted his head. 'Oh? By whom?'

'My friend Brigid. I'm having a birthday tea at her house.'

'You're still seeing her then?' He frowned into the fire. 'I would have thought—'

'What?' He did not answer and she added in a light voice, 'I like Brigid. She's gutsy and makes me laugh. I wondered if there was any news about the compensation?' She had not intended asking.

'These things take time.' His fingers toyed with a porcelain shepherdess on the mantelshelf. 'I will say, though, that it's unlikely there will be any.'

She stared at him, unable to conceal her disappointment.

'I'm sorry.' His expression was bland. 'I'm likely to receive the value of the *Samson* and its freight, but passengers will probably only receive the price of their fare.'

'But that's unfair!'

'It's a disgrace, but that's the way things are. We do urge people to get themselves insured.' He moved to stand in front of her and bent to peer into her downcast face. 'It's not my fault, Rebekah. If I could afford it, I'd pay the compensation myself. As it is, I need the money to buy a replacement for the *Samson*.'

'I understand that, but what about Brigid's

husband and the crew who were lost?' She lifted her head and caught his change of expression.

His eyes glinted, 'I presume we're talking about O'Neill?'

'Daniel,' she said firmly. 'He has a brother, Shaun.'

'He's the one you mentioned in New York?' He moved back to the fireplace. 'Haven't been able to trace him, I'm afraid.'

'He has relatives in Liverpool. They live in the same street as Brigid's family.'

'Do they now?' His hand stilled as it reached for the silver cigarette box on a small table. Then he took out a cheroot and lit it from the fire with a spill from a jar in the hearth. 'Have they heard from the brother?'

'No.' Rebekah sat on the sofa. 'Would it be worth telling them if they do hear anything, to get in touch with you?'

'Definitely,' he said without hesitation. 'Not that I can do much. Still—' He shrugged and there was a pause before he murmured, 'I suppose you learnt about Emma from the newspaper?'

'Yes. I wondered when the funeral would be, and where?'

'It depends on the findings of the inquest.' He sat down on the other end of the sofa. 'If you were thinking of attending, I don't consider it a good idea. You've been through enough.'

She swung one leg, gazing down at her foot,

finding it difficult to say what she wanted. 'I felt sorry for your sister. A woman I was talking to thought it unlikely that she could have drowned by accident.'

There was a pause as he inhaled deeply before letting the smoke drift slowly out through his nostrils. 'And what do you think?'

Rebekah moistened her lips. 'She was very confused.'

He gave a high laugh. 'She was crazy! Living in a different world to the rest of us most of the time. I find it quite believable that she could go walking on the sands and forget how swiftly the tide comes in.'

'But what about her friends?'

'Friends?' He looked startled.

'Didn't they warn her of the danger?' Rebekah was puzzled by his reaction.

He shrugged his shoulders. 'I should imagine so. But Emma could easily forget what she was told.'

'When you say it like that, it sounds the most likely explanation.'

'It's what I'll be saying at the inquest.' The creases about his pale blue eyes deepened. 'I want my sister buried in holy ground. No scandal.'

There was another discreet knock at the door and the next moment Janet entered with a tray. Rebekah did not press the subject further.

While they drank tea and nibbled chocolate biscuits, they discussed the weather and how she was settling in Liverpool. 'I've been looking for a job,' she murmured.

'What kind of job?' He leant towards her. 'Perhaps I can help you?'

'I was thinking of office work. I can type and know a little shorthand.'

'I'll ask around.'

She was surprised. 'You aren't against women working?'

He laughed shortly. 'What's the point of swimming against the tide? If my sister had found herself a job, then maybe she wouldn't have ended up the way she did. A child would have been best for her. Anyway, I'll see what I can do for you.' He put down his cup and stood up. 'I'll have to take you home now if you don't mind? I'm expecting callers.'

She got to her feet. 'The cat?'

'The cat.' He sounded amused and put an arm about her shoulders. 'I'll get Janet to find it while I bring the car round.' He kissed her forehead. 'Wait for me in the porch, and while I'm driving you home perhaps we can make some arrangements for having your birthday treat in the New Year.'

'That would be very kind,' she said in a polite voice before hurrying out of the room.

It was Rebekah's birthday and she was getting ready to go to Brigid's. She gazed at her reflection, remembering how thrilled she had been with her appearance after her hair was cut. Now it gave her no pleasure. The ends were straggly. She should have gone to the hairdresser's and had it trimmed. The jade green blouse made her skin look pale, almost translucent. She wondered about touching up her cheeks with rouge but decided to leave them alone. Standing, she smoothed the black serge skirt over her hips before picking up a black hat and cramming it on to her head. She pulled a face then smiled as Moggy bumped noses with his reflection in the dressing-table mirror and miaowed. She blew him a kiss. He had cheered up her life, despite Hannah's moans about: 'The lazy do nothing cat!' and 'Feeding it on best cod's head, are we now? I could make soup out of that!'

Rebekah put on a coat and kid gloves, and went downstairs.

'Dressed to kill,' sniffed Hannah.

'I suppose thou wilt be going out with him on Christmas Day?' muttered Esther, pleating a fold of her skirt.

'No.' She deliberately looked pensive. 'I said I'd be spending it with my rich aunt.'

Esther looked startled. 'Thou means that?'

'Of course. You're my only close kith and kin, barring Grandpapa's relatives up north – or so you keep telling me. Who else should I spend Christmas with?' She smiled and went out through the doorway.

Rebekah was not so cheerful as she walked the dark streets, passing children swinging on a rope tied to the bars of a lamp post on the corner of a street, and others chasing and hiding up entries and garden paths. Should she tell Brigid about the compensation or leave it until it was official?

She caught a tram and got off near the Mere Lane cinema. A week or so ago she and Brigid had seen *When Men Betray*. The poster had proclaimed it: 'A stirring drama of women's frailties!' The film had made a couple of girls behind them in the cinema say, 'It makes you wonder if yer should ever trust a man.' How trustworthy was Joshua Green? Her father must have trusted him, but Daniel had not liked him. She felt the familiar aching emptiness. Had that been only because Joshua owned property in Ireland? Or was there something else?

She peered at the numbers on the houses and began to count. Her nervousness grew at the thought of facing Brigid's family. What did they really feel about Brigid's friendship with her?

A cow's lowing startled her, as did a series of yells. She realised that she was passing the dairy. The next moment out of the darkness hurtled Brigid's niece and nephew, Jimmy and Veronica. The boy skidded to a halt inches from her but the girl flung her arms about Rebekah's skirts. 'We were told to watch out! Jimmy's shouted to them yer coming.' Rebekah swung her off her feet and round and round until they were both dizzy.

Jimmy seized her hand and pulled, causing her almost to fall over her feet in sudden haste. 'Happy birthday to you! Happy birthday to you!' he chanted. 'Me mam had the shop make yer a cake and Auntie Bridie paid for it! But there's only one pink candle on it. Me Uncle Pat said it's just as well because we didn't want to set fire to the house. That's a joke,' he said earnestly, his eyes shining in the lamplight. 'It's a joke because he said yer only a chicken yet. Scarcely out of the egg!'

Rebekah laughed because she was so relieved by the warmth of their welcome. The next moment Brigid was on the doorstep and pulling her inside the house. 'Yer found us! I was just saying to our Pat that yer might find it difficult in the dark. I never thought. I should have gone to meet yer.'

'I was all right. Jimmy's been telling me about the cake. You shouldn't have gone to all that trouble and expense, with it being Christmas soon and all.'

'Nothing's no trouble, girl.' A thin figure wrapped in a flowered pinafore came bustling across the kitchen floor. Her face still bore traces of the pretty girl she must have been. The tightly curled reddish hair showed few grey hairs.

'This is me mam,' said Brigid, the affection clear in her voice.

Rebekah was momentarily struck dumb, never having known Brigid's maiden name. Then she held out her hand. 'Hello, Brigid's mam. It's really kind of you.'

Her hand was taken and shaken vigorously, 'It's sad times we're living through, girl, and if we can't do a kind deed, then life's not worth living. Some people call me Ma Maisie, so you might as well. I feel like I know yer already through our Bridie.' She released Rebekah's hand but urged her over to the fire. 'The table's already set. I've done us something hot as it's a real cold night. Now get yerself warm. Our Pat's just making us a toddy. Yer'll take a drink with us?'

'Thank you.' Rebekah did not like saying that she had never touched alcohol before.

A man was standing on the rag rug before the glowing fire. He was good-looking with wide-set brown eyes and very white teeth. Rebekah remembered Brigid's brother Pat. 'It'll warm the cockles of yer heart,' he said. 'Bridie, have yer got the cups ready?'

'I got them ready, Uncle Pat.' Veronica came dancing into the kitchen from the scullery where she had vanished immediately on entering the house. She was followed by Kath, a ginger-haired woman, who nodded in Rebekah's direction and murmured what she took to be some kind of welcome. There was a subdued air about her. Brigid had said that her husband had died last year as a result of wounds inflicted during the war.

Pat poured the steaming liquid into the cups standing on the white tablecloth. 'Lots of water in that drop I've given the kids, Ma. A toast and then we'll sit down and eat. You've never lived, Miss Rhoades, till you've tasted Ma's spare ribs and cabbage.'

'Call me Becky,' she said, warming her hands on the cup.

'Becky it is then.' He chinked his cup with hers and smiled into her eyes. 'Drink up! I hope you'll be having lots more birthdays.' She drank up, determined to try and enjoy herself.

It was a birthday like no other that Rebekah had ever had. Nothing exciting but she felt part of a real family. Although, if she had known that she would have to join in taking a turn to entertain the rest of the gathering, she might have had second thoughts about accepting Brigid's invitation. But not knowing, and the drink, and the fact that Jimmy could do a fair imitation of Charlie Chaplin and Veronica recite a skipping song 'Eeper-Weeper Chimney Sweeper' about a man who shoved a wife up a chimney, made her feel that she had no choice but to sing a rather shaky 'Keep the Home Fires Burning' – the only song she could think of on the spur of the moment and one which Old Mary had once sung.

'Not bad,' said Pat, who played the piano.

Rebekah flushed. 'I'm not as good as Kath. She sings lovely.'

'Mam could have been on the stage,' stated Veronica proudly.

'No,' protested Kath. 'I only came second in a talent competition, and I couldn't have done that if it hadn't been for our Bridie, who pushed me into it.'

'Never mind that now,' said Pat, holding up the jug. 'Who's for another drink and a game of snap?'

Jimmy held out his cup but was refused. 'You've had enough me lad. Go and get the cards.'

The boy went and they settled round the table. It was soon obvious to Rebekah that the game was played so that the children could win. By the end of the evening her heart had warmed to the whole family and she was sorry when it was over.

She walked home arm in arm with Brigid on one side of her and Pat on the other. All the way he bellowed at the top of his voice, 'Swanee, how I love you! How I love you! My dear old Swanee!' It did not seem to matter that it was December and freezing cold. She suspected that they were all slightly drunk but did not care. It took the edge off her grief.

When they reached Aunt Esther's house she thought of asking them in but before she could voice the words, they both said they would have to be off home. 'See you New Year's Eve,' said Pat, tickling her under the chin. 'We'll have some fun then.'

'I'll see yer on Monday,' said Brigid, hugging her.

'I'm working all weekend. There's a dinner party on.'

They both waved and left her standing at the gate.

The week before Christmas passed swifter than Rebekah had hoped. There were sad moments. Shopping in town she was conscious of the constant trickle of people laying flowers in front of the new Cenotaph in Lime Street for their dead loved ones.

She bought *The Boy's Own* for Jimmy and a doll for Veronica. There was a tin of Mackintosh's toffee de luxe for Ma Maisie and perfume from Luce's perfumery in Ranelagh Street for Brigid. A scarf for Kath, cigarettes for Pat, and several sets of the best woollen combinations for Aunt Esther. She did not dare to forget Hannah and bought her one set of the thickest, itchiest unmentionables.

In the *Liverpool Echo* it was stated that a verdict of accidental death had been passed on Mrs Emma Richards. Rebekah was relieved. She ordered flowers to be sent and remembered to buy Joshua a present just in case he called. He came when she was out and left her a silk scarf.

Christmas was quiet and Rebekah was glad when it was over. Ireland's Yuletide had not been so peaceful. A constable in plain clothes had been set on outside the Gaiety Theatre in Dublin, and the Hibernian Bank at Drogheda had been robbed of thirty-six thousand pounds on Christmas Eve. Rebekah was glad that she was out of it all, and vowed to stop reading the newspaper, as well as deciding to look forward to the January sales. She would allow having money to go to her head.

New Year's Eve started quietly but her aunt was not pleased when at nine o'clock in the evening Rebekah started getting ready to go out with Brigid and her brother. 'If thou art not in by midnight, I'll lock thee out,' threatened Esther.

'But I'm twenty now – and midnight is when the fun starts,' insisted Rebekah, with her shoulder wedged against the front door as she pulled on her gloves. She was not really worried because she had had a copy of the front door key made. 'Don't be a spoilsport, Auntie,' she said in a coaxing voice. 'There's lots of Scots in Liverpool and first footing is popular, as you should know.' She straightened. 'You need all the good luck in this life that you can get.'

'Superstition!' said Esther, a worried frown puckering her plump face. 'Thy grandfather would turn over in his grave! What would thy mother think? Thou art supposed to be in mourning! That frock thou art wearing – it's green.'

'Green for grief, some people say, Auntie dear,' retorted Rebekah, her eyes shining with sudden tears.

'Oh, Rebekah!' exclaimed her aunt in a despairing voice. 'I hope thou doesn't come to grief.'

'I won't.' She suddenly felt sorry for her aunt and kissed her cheek before hurrying down the path.

Ma Maisie's kitchen and parlour were crowded and the party had spilt out into the street. People were dancing to the tinkling ragtime piano music of Scott Joplin. Rebekah had watched for a while but then Pat had partnered her. He was a showy dancer and because of that she had to concentrate on her own steps – steps taught her by Daniel. Then he handed her over to a shipmate at ten minutes to midnight, saying, 'I've got to first foot. I'm the only dark-haired one in the family.'

The blast of hooters and whistles from the ships on the river, and the clanging of church bells, heralded in the New Year. Pat reappeared, carrying a slice of bread, a piece of coal, a lump of salt and a shiny sixpence, which he handed to his mother standing just inside the front door. Then he kissed every woman and girl at the party, including Rebekah whose head felt airy despite the aching regret gripping her. Glasses and cups were filled again and toasts drunk.

'You're still looking bright-eyed,' said Brigid, yawning and coming to lean against the railings next to her. 'I thought you'd be ready for yer bed. It hasn't been too much for yer, then?'

Rebekah rested her head on her friend's shoulder. 'It's better than sitting at home, moping. But I suppose I'll have to make a move.'

'Stay here,' said Brigid. 'Doss down with Mam and me. It'll be a squash, but snug as a bug in a rug.'

Reluctantly Rebekah shook her head. 'Aunt Esther just might be waiting up.'

'I'll get our Pat.'

'No.' Rebekah seized her arm. 'He must be tired.'

'Aren't we all? I've work early this morning. Nineteen twenty-one! Another year to get through.' She squared her shoulders. 'Our Pat won't mind, and I wouldn't trust yer with anyone else. At least he's not lying down drunk.'

Rebekah resigned herself to being seen home by Pat, not so certain as Brigid that he could be trusted. She was proved right when he pulled her into a doorway halfway along Breck Road, holding her so that her arms were wedged against her sides and kissing her in a far from brotherly fashion. She stamped on his feet twice before he released her. They looked at one another. His teeth gleamed in the dark. 'So it's true yer still carrying a torch for Daniel O'Neill then?'

'Is that what Brigid told you?' she parried.

'Who else?' He shook his head sorrowfully. 'You women! Yer not like our Bridie now, and believing you're a one man woman?'

'I could be. Besides, it's only three months.'

He smiled. 'Early days. Yer'll get over him. In the meantime there's plenty of other pebbles on the beach I could pick, yer know.'

'Pick one up then!'

'I could do that.'

'You're handsome enough.'

He grinned. 'That's right enough. But if yer wanting the truth I'm not after getting meself shackled and there's too many girls since the war who are desperate – if yer peck them on the cheek they think it's a proposal of marriage. I've no mind to settle down just yet. And I'm not wanting the kind of girls who hang around Lime Street because yer never know what yer going to catch.'

Rebekah knew from Brigid about the women of the streets and did not know whether to be shocked because he had mentioned them. 'Should you be talking to me like this?'

'Why not?' He took her hand. 'Yer a woman of sense. I've heard yer talking. You've got a head on yer shoulders.'

'Is that supposed to be a compliment?' She was amused.

'You got it first time.' He squeezed her fingers. 'We could have a good time when I dock.'

'I'm not so sure,' she said, considering it might be worth experimenting to see if she could feel anything for another man. 'Besides, what about Brigid? I go out with her.'

'I've friends,' he said softly. 'Yer both need cheering up. Laugh all your troubles away, that's what I say.'

'Smile, though your heart is aching?'

'That's the ticket.' He pulled her hand through his crooked arm and she did not desist. They went on their way, with Pat insisting on arranging to meet when next he docked.

Although Brigid was dubious at first about the whole idea of going out with a shipmate of her brother's, her own philosophy was similar to his: Pack up your troubles and smile.

Rebekah's life took on a different colour. She was often out and her aunt moaned that she never saw her – said that she was becoming flighty. Joshua called, but Rebekah was not there to see him. Her aunt complained on his behalf even though she was still annoyed that he was Rebekah's guardian. She shrugged the complaints aside because, like keeping Pat at arm's length, it was good practice at hardening her heart against other people – that way you didn't get hurt so easily.

If sometimes she wanted to cry when waiting for Pat's ship, because this would have been the kind of life she would have had to get used to with Daniel, she never spoke of it to anyone. She was too busy pretending that she was coping with life.

CHAPTER THIRTEEN

'So I've caught you in at last,' said Joshua, one foot jamming the door open. 'About time too! It's been months!'

'Time does fly,' murmured Rebekah, opening the door wider. 'You never did take me out for my birthday.'

'No,' he said shortly. 'Your aunt was saying you've been burning the candle at both ends.'

'Aunt Esther would.' She deliberately put an amused note in her voice. 'Did you want me for anything in particular or just to tell me off?'

'Something in particular!' The lines about his mouth and nose deepened. 'Can I come in or are you going to keep me standing on the doorstep?'

'Come in by all means.' She led the way into the sitting room. 'Aunt Esther's at one of her meetings and Hannah's out, so you'll be able to scold me in peace.' She plumped up a cushion and removed the tin of Mansion polish and a duster from the arm of a chair, putting them on a shelf.

He took off his trilby. 'You're expecting me to scold you?'

'I knew you'd catch up with me sooner or later,' She waved him to a chair but remained standing herself. 'I suppose it's about money?'

Joshua's eyes narrowed. 'There's something different about you. You've changed.'

She shrugged peach cotton-clad shoulders. 'I've had to grow up quickly over the last few months. Come to terms with life.'

He nodded. 'That's a pretty frock you're wearing.'

Rebekah raised finely drawn eyebrows. 'It's going to be the soft soap first, is it? Thank you, kind sir.'

He smiled. 'You are pretty and I don't begrudge you buying new clothes. But little as I like to say this, Rebekah, you can't carry on the way you have been. The letter you sent me two days ago requesting an advance on your allowance I can't let you have it. What are you doing with your money?'

'I gave some away.'

'What?'

The corners of her mouth lifted. 'Don't look so shocked, Mr Green. I can give my own money away, can't I?'

He had been in the act of sitting down but straightened up again. 'No, you can't! I do have a say in the matter. Who did you give it to?'

She hesitated. 'A good cause.'

He stared at her and Moggy, brushing past the fire irons, made their clatter sound loud in the silence. 'What good cause?'

Rebekah sighed. 'Brigid's mother took ill unexpectedly and had to have an operation. If Brigid had had the compensation money, it would have paid for it. I thought it only fair that—'

He made an exasperated sound. 'She talked you into it, I suppose? Made you feel guilty!'

Rebekah fired up. 'No, she didn't! If she'd known it was my money she wouldn't have taken it. I told her that it was the compensation. The operation was serious and it's still dicey whether her mother will pull through.'

'Even so—'

'Even so nothing!' She slammed her hand down on the mantelshelf, her expression mutinous. 'What's the use of having money if you can't help your friends?'

'You won't have any money to help yourself if you don't stop spending it,' he said stiffly. 'It doesn't grow on trees, you know.'

She brushed his words aside. 'You care about those orphans of yours, don't you? Surely you understand—'

'Yes, yes,' he said impatiently, looking down at the carpet. His head lifted. 'But you're too soft-hearted, my dear. That's why your father made me your guardian. I'm going to have to be firm for your own sake. If you want any money you'll have to apply to me in person – no letters – and I'll want to know exactly what you're spending it on.'

'What?' She was filled with dismay. 'I'm not a child!'

'Don't I know it.' His glance flicked over her body.

She had seen that look often in Pat's eyes but so far had managed to keep him under control, his kisses doing little for her. 'Well then?' she murmured. 'Can't you trust me to act like an adult?'

'I'd like to,' he said softly. 'But you are still a comparative stranger to Liverpool, and if your aunt can't keep a proper watch on you, then I'll have to do so.'

'I've already decided that I'll spend less,' she insisted. 'I'm really quite sensible. You shouldn't take any notice of what Aunt Esther tells you.'

'I'd expect her to see things differently so I don't take everything she says to heart.' He took a cheroot case from his pocket. 'I presume that you haven't found a job yet?'

'No.' Rebekah was not going to admit that she had not bothered looking for a few weeks. Instead she had been spending a fair amount of time at Brigid's, looking after the children while their mother was at work.

'Perhaps I can help you with a job.' Joshua lit up. 'Sit down, Rebekah, and let's talk.'

She shook her head. 'I'm in need of a drink. Would you like one?'

'Thank you.'

Rebekah made a pot of tea and placed on a plate some jam tarts that she had baked. After she had poured the tea, she murmured, 'Now tell me about this job.'

He patted the arm of his chair. 'Come and sit here.'

'I'm quite comfortable here, thank you,' she said.

Joshua shrugged. 'It's a very worthwhile job but there's not much money in it.'

'Aunt Esther hardly takes a penny from me so the money isn't my main concern. Although—'

'If your aunt is supporting you, that's good.' He looked pleased.

Rebekah grimaced. 'Let me finish. She has threatened several times that if I don't pull my socks up—'

'I can't see her being other than pleased with you if you take on this job. It's to do with the Seamen's Orphanage.'

'That's in Orphan Drive on the other side of the park.' She leant forward eagerly. 'Not too far. Good.'

He held up a hand. 'Wait until I've finished. You wouldn't be working at the Orphanage. The job I'm talking about involves visiting the widows and children of men who lost their lives at sea. You can find out what financial help is needed so the children can remain at home.'

She nodded her head slowly. 'I'd like to help. As long as they don't look upon me as a snooper.'

'You're too young and pretty for anyone to see you in such a light.'

Rebekah avoided looking at him. It seemed Brigid, and her father, had been right and his lordship did fancy her, but she would not let that influence her decision. 'When do I start?'

'I'll have to find out.' He sipped his tea. 'Remember I was going to take you to see *The Gondoliers* at Crane Hall? Well, it's being performed once again. We could have supper afterwards if you'd like to come? I could let you know then.'

'All right.' She tried to sound enthusiastic. 'That would be lovely.'

Joshua arranged a time and soon afterwards left, saying he did not want to have to listen to a sermon from her aunt again on the folly of her father leaving a young girl in the charge of a bachelor.

After he had gone Rebekah stood with Moggy clutched tightly in her arms, staring into the fire, thinking about Daniel, Pat and Joshua, and how she would not mention the job to her aunt yet. Then resumed her polishing.

'I don't know why yer have to go out with his lordship,' said Brigid, frowning, as she and Rebekah left the Royal Infirmary in Pembroke Place.

'Money and a job.' Rebekah smiled. 'Honestly, Brigid, I'd sooner go out with the Emperor of

China! But Joshua holds the purse strings.'

'He's after yer. I've said it before and I'll say it again.'

'I hadn't seen him for months,' said Rebekah impatiently. 'Talk sense.'

'But that's not his fault.' Brigid tucked her hand in Rebekah's arm as they crossed the road. 'You've been gallivanting with our Pat. Does his lordship know about that?'

'Why should I tell him? Your Pat's intentions are perfectly dishonourable, as your Mam was relieved to hear tonight.'

Brigid grinned. 'If you'd said it like that she would have worried.'

'I guessed she was going spare every time Pat came home and we went out.'

'Well, she's not going to be worrying now,' said Brigid positively. 'I told her that there was no need . . . that you're still carrying a torch for Daniel.'

Rebekah sighed. 'If you know that, I don't see how you can go on about his lordship, although I think my father had him in mind for me to marry. I feel bad about my father now. I wish we hadn't been out of friends when he died.'

Brigid squeezed her arm and her voice was brisk when she spoke. 'There's nothing you can do about that now. So let's go for a walk in the park before it gets dark and forget our problems.' Rebekah agreed and they went on their way.

Despite what Rebekah had said to Brigid about the outing with Joshua, she began to look forward to it. She had never seen a Gilbert and Sullivan performance. Her aunt, though, was not pleased about her going.

'I don't know why thou hast to go out with the man.' Esther agitatedly plied her needle through the hem of a plain brown skirt.

'It's having her hair cut – it's given her brain fever,' interpolated Hannah. Rebekah and her aunt stared at her. 'Tis true,' added the maid, a gleam in her eye. 'Head feels cold, blood rushes to it to warm it.'

'That would mean a good half of the women in the British Isles have brain fever then,' said Rebekah, a smile in her voice.

Her aunt sighed. 'Let's not get silly, Becky dear. Do consider. Thou'd be more inclined to stick to the straight and narrow if thou came to the meeting house instead of just enjoying thyself gallivanting here and there.'

'I'll go tomorrow,' murmured Rebekah in an attempt to placate her, and swallowing her annoyance. First Brigid and now her aunt! Why couldn't people just let her make her own decisions?

Her aunt looked at her. 'Thou means it?'

She nodded. 'Cross my heart.'

Esther smiled but Hannah, who was clearing the table, grunted, 'I'll believe it when I sees it. All this dollying thyself up for a man. Thee'll cum to a bad end.'

'Didn't you ever dolly yourself up, Hannah?'

enquired Rebekah, experiencing another flash of annoyance. She was not dollying herself up for a man but for herself. She smoothed the boat-shaped neck of the mauve georgette dress, and glanced at Hannah who had not replied. 'Well? Didn't you ever walk out with a young man in your day?'

'I could have,' said Hannah gruffly, staring down at the white starched tablecloth and brushing crumbs off it on to a plate. She flung them on the fire, then looked at Rebekah, a hard glint in her eyes. 'But we's had no muny and I had thems that relied on me. Thou knows nuthing about such things, Miss Fancy Pants. Going here, going there. Thee thinks thee has suffered. Thee knows nuthing about real suffering and what it is to do without!'

'Hannah!' Esther's voice was sharp. 'That's enough! Miss Rebekah isn't to blame for thy misfortunes.'

'Aunt! It's all right!' Rebekah shrugged herself into her coat. 'I'm sorry, Hannah, I shouldn't have said what I did.'

'No, thee shouldn't.' Hannah glared at her and went out of the room as the knocker sounded.

'I really should get rid of her,' said Esther, shaking her head and wincing as she got up. She rubbed a knee.

'Don't do it because of me,' responded Rebekah swiftly, picking up her handbag and wondering where Hannah could go. 'Better for us to suffer her than to inflict her on someone else.' She kissed her aunt's cheek, who followed her slowly up the lobby, gave a barely civil greeting to Joshua, and stood watching her get into the car before she turned and went back into the house.

'Poor Aunt Esther,' murmured Rebekah as they drove off.

'Why do you call her poor?' asked Joshua sharply. 'She looked blue murder at me. I wonder if she realises I could take you away from her.'

Startled, Rebekah looked at his nice-looking, clean shaven profile. He was wearing a navy lounge suit and oozed masculine power, 'I don't think the thought's occurred to her.' She paused, wondering why he had said what he did, and added in light tones, 'When it does, she might just beg you to take me away. I'm not the easiest person to live with. At the moment she considers it her duty to care for me because I'm her only sister's daughter.'

'You want to keep reminding her of that,' said Joshua in a pleasant voice. 'She must have some money tucked away from when your grandfather died. You don't want that prune-faced maid getting it all.'

Rebekah's hands tightened on her handbag. 'Money's useful but it's not everything,' she murmured.

He glanced at her. 'That's a nice sentiment but it's not true. If you hadn't a penny you'd realise that there's nothing lovely about being broke. Be nice to your aunt.'

She looked out of the window, so that he would

not see her expression. 'I'm as nice as I can be. If I was any nicer she'd smell a rat.'

'Not her. She'd believe her influence was having a good effect on you.'

'You're probably right.' Her voice was non-committal and she changed the subject, asking where was Crane Hall.

'Near the Bold Street end of Church Street. If you know the Lyceum Newsroom, it's not far from there.' He added good-humouredly: 'I keep forgetting that you're a foreigner. Your accent's so faint.'

'I've been mistaken for English in Dublin.'

He flashed her a look. 'Do you miss Ireland?'

'Sometimes.'

'I have a place there.'

Rebekah swallowed an unexpected lump in her throat. 'Your father bought Grandmama's farm.'

'You know about that?' He sounded surprised.

She wondered why he should be and how he would respond if she told him about her conversation with Daniel concerning him, but thought it wiser to say, 'My father told me. I remember Grandmama always trying to build me up on buttermilk and porridge.'

He frowned. 'She was a fearsome woman. She made up for what your uncle lacked, so my brother said.'

'I was fond of her.'

'Why shouldn't you be? Family.'

She hesitated before saying, 'You must miss your family. Your sister, your brother—'

'Of course,' he said in a voice that did not encourage further questions.

They fell silent and did not speak again until they came to Crane Hall where Joshua tried to explain the plot of *The Gondoliers* as she attempted to read the programme. She was glad when the music began and she could give all her attention to the entanglements of the various lovers.

When they came out of the Hall she was humming beneath her breath 'Take a Pair of Sparkling Eyes'.

'You'll have some supper?' Joshua helped her into the car and she was conscious of the warmth of his fingers through the thin silk of her stockings when they brushed her leg as he moved her skirts out of the way of the door. She thought of Daniel and how the least touch of his hand could make her quiver.

'I'm not hungry.' She shrank back against the cool leather seat. 'And I'd better not be back late.'

The light from a street lamp reflected in his unusual pale blue eyes. 'You're not frightened of me, are you, Rebekah?' he surprised her by saying. 'I know I'm a few years older than you.'

'Frightened?' Was she? If she was it was only a fear of being pressurised into doing what he wanted just to keep on the right side of him. She closed her eyes. 'Why should I be? I'm just tired that's all. I'm not used to all this excitement.'

'I thought you had been having an exciting time lately.' He straightened. 'Your aunt said that you've been going out with some man for ages.'

She stilled, wondering if – as her guardian – he could stop her seeing Pat. 'It was a joke at first,' she murmured, 'Hannah has this thing about me and fellas so I pretended I was meeting someone.'

'Your aunt says that someone has been seeing you home,' he said emphatically.

'Does she?' She opened her eyes. 'He's Brigid's brother. His mother insists he sees me safely to the doorstep.'

'You don't find him exciting?'

She looked at him. 'Haven't I just explained?'

He stared at her and said abruptly, 'Did you find O'Neill exciting?'

'What?' Her heart gave a peculiar lurch.

'You heard me, Rebekah.' He vanished out of sight to crank the car, leaving her wondering why he had to mention Daniel right now. What was the point? He slid into the driving seat and drove away from the kerb. 'Well?' he murmured.

'Well what?' Her pulses were beating uncomfortably fast.

'O'Neill? You were very concerned about him in New York.'

'I don't want to talk about him.'

'Why? He didn't do anything to you, did he?'

Rebekah felt heat rising in her face. 'Why are you talking like this?' she whispered. 'He's dead.'

His gaze was on the busy street and she thought

that was why he did not answer immediately. 'I believe he had a way with women. Irish charm, I suppose. You'd appeal to him. Young! Innocent! You're lovely, you know. I bet he told you that.'

Suddenly she experienced a deeper darkness than she had suffered since first hearing that Daniel was dead. 'You're trying to turn me against him – why?' Even to her own ears she sounded bewildered.

'Because I don't want you wasting your thoughts on him,' he muttered, his neck reddening. 'I could tell you things—'

'No!' Her voice trembled. 'Please take me home.'

'I'm only thinking of you.' The tone of his voice had changed almost to a caress. 'If you can't accept the truth you won't get far in this life, my dear. You're so trusting.'

She stared at him and then away. 'I loved Daniel but he's dead. I accept that and don't need to know what you want to tell me. Can we talk about something else? What about the job you mentioned?'

For a moment she thought he was going to ignore her words then he shrugged. 'You can start on Tuesday, seeing as it's Whit this weekend.' He told her where and what time, and after that did not speak but drummed the fingers of one hand on the steering wheel. She sensed he was still annoyed because she refused to listen to what he wanted to say about Daniel but she was determined not to revert to their previous conversation or to begin a new one.

At last he broke the silence. 'Are you sure you wouldn't like some supper? I don't like eating alone and it hasn't been easy since Emma died.'

Rebekah was uncertain whether he was attempting to elicit sympathy but she was in no mood to feel sorry for him. 'I'm not hungry.'

He sighed heavily. 'What a pity. I was going to take you to the Oyster Rooms. You'd have liked oysters.'

'I hate the thought of eating them.'

'Do you hate me as well? Just because—'

'Don't say it,' she interrupted wearily. 'Talk about something else. Ships! Or what about Andromeda – your good luck charm? Is she still languishing in the garden?'

'I've had her repainted.' His expression brightened. 'That should please you.'

'It does.' She smiled. 'I hope she does bring you luck. I reckon you could do with some.'

'There's always an element of luck in life. Look at the *Samson*. A few minutes either way could have made a tremendous difference. You wouldn't be sitting next to me now.'

'No.' The word was muted.

There was a silence but she could imagine his thoughts. You could have been with O'Neill. Or could you?

He glanced at her. 'Sailors are notoriously superstitious. I know because I've lived among them. I'll take you to see Andromeda.'

'Not now,' she said, relieved that he had not mentioned Daniel but alarmed at the thought of going back to his house at this time of night.

He patted her hand where it rested in her lap. 'Forgive me, Rebekah, if I've upset you. It's just that I have your welfare at heart.'

'Apology accepted.' She removed his hand. 'But can I see Andromeda another day?'

'Tomorrow,' he said firmly. 'Why don't you come along to church? It's time you got yourself known and involved in the community. There's people worth your while getting to know. We could have dinner afterwards and—'

'I told my aunt I'd go with her to the meeting house in the morning.'

He scowled. 'I really do think you should do what I say.'

'I promised. Would you have me break a promise?'

'Of course not,' he said dourly. There was a short silence, 'I suppose we could go to church in the evening and have supper afterwards?'

She supposed that she should do something to please him and she was interested in seeing Andromeda. 'OK.'

'Good girl.' He drew up outside her aunt's house. 'I'll see you tomorrow then.' He leant towards her but she retreated.

'Tomorrow.' She gave him a sparkling smile from the other side of the gate and waved but did not stay to watch him drive away.

CHAPTER FOURTEEN

The church in Anfield was a beautiful building, but Rebekah was more conscious of its being High Anglican with its confession boxes, priest in fancy vestments, an incense-swinging choirboy and a highly decorated altar, than of its stonework. What would her parents have thought of it all? What would Aunt Esther think? The Quaker meeting house that they had attended was a plain brick building in a run-down part of the town off Byrom Street, not far from the notorious Scotland Road. There had been a scripture reading meeting half an hour before the meeting proper with no more than eighty people attending the main service, which concentrated on silent communion with God. Her aunt had told her that once numbers had run into the hundreds and the meeting house had been on the edge of town, but as Liverpool's prosperity had grown, so had the population risen. Housing had spread into the surrounding countryside enveloping the villages of Walton, Kirkdale and Bootle. Many of their members had moved out of the city centre, and once smart districts of Liverpool had turned into slums housing the poorest of the poor. She had pointed out to Rebekah the area where Hannah had once lived and for the second time that weekend she had experienced a flicker of sympathy for the maid.

Rebekah rose and went up the long aisle alone, Joshua having left her to her so-called prayers. At the door she exchanged a few words with the vicar and came out into a warm spring evening.

'God in Heaven, fancy meeting you here!'

Rebekah turned and was surprised to see Edwina McIntyre with her father.

'Hello,' she said, feeling instantly guilty. 'It's my first time. There was quite a crowd, wasn't there?'

'Too many to know everyone,' said Edwina briskly, clutching a large handbag. 'You never did have that cup of tea with us.'

'I'm sorry.' Her expression was contrite. 'I've been busy.'

'Come back now,' said Mr McIntyre eagerly, 'I want to know what you think about the meeting between Sir James Craig and Mr de Valera?'

She stared, barely able to believe what he was saying. Sir James Craig was Premier Elect of Ulster.

'Is Mr de Valera back from America then? I haven't been reading the papers.'

Mr McIntyre nodded with obvious satisfaction. 'Sir Edward Carson of the Ulster Unionist Party says that de Valera could do something to bring North and South together.'

Before she could respond Joshua came up to them. 'Rebekah, I was just coming to find you.'

She touched his arm. 'Joshua, this is Mr McIntyre and his daughter. They're neighbours. Mr McIntyre's just been telling me that President de Valera's met with Sir James Craig. Perhaps the fighting will stop at last?'

Joshua smiled but did not shake hands. 'It's nice to meet you. I'm sorry I've got to drag Rebekah away but there's someone I want her to meet.' Before another word could be spoken he hurried her away.

She turned on him. 'Didn't you hear what I said?'

'About Ireland? Of course. I hope there will be peace. Then I can sell my place over there.'

'Sell it?' Rebekah stopped abruptly. 'You mean – get rid of Grandmama's farm?'

'Not your grandma's, Rebekah. Mine,' he said with a smile. 'And what's the point of keeping hold of it now? Ireland will never be what it was in the days my father used to talk about. Now let's forget the place. Liverpool's your home.'

She could have said more and asked who was

this person she was supposed to be meeting, but he was talking about Andromeda as he led her across the road in the direction of the park, and she guessed that it had been a means to get her away from the McIntyres in a hurry.

'She's lovely,' said Rebekah, stroking the green tail of the mermaid figurehead.

'She looks a lot better than she did,' agreed Joshua, hovering behind Rebekah. 'Let's hope she works some magic. I could do with it.'

She glanced over her shoulder. 'Has something else gone wrong?'

'You may well ask,' he said, his mouth tightening. 'The ship repairers are on strike over wages and the Stewards' Union are threatening to come out over a pay cut.'

'Does that mean your ships won't be sailing?'

'It means that no liners will be sailing if the stewards refuse to sign on this week. Although, if they signed their articles on Friday they're bound to go. Unless the union can be persuaded there's no money available, we're in trouble.'

'It must be hard on the men having their wages cut.' She moved away from him and down the garden.

'Life's hard for all of us.'

'It's harder for some. We have it easy in comparison.' She stood on tiptoe to inhale lilac blossom.

He broke off some for her. 'My family worked for what I've got.'

'They had more luck than others, perhaps?' She eased the lilac stem through a button hole.

'It's not all luck,' he said shortly. 'And the men should be glad to have jobs when times are hard.'

Rebekah frowned, 'I'm sure they are glad. But after all, they are only asking for what's theirs. How much is this pay cut?'

'Something like eight shillings a week.'

'Eight shillings! That's a lot for a man with a family to feed!'

'It's happening all over the country.' He scowled. 'You don't have to glare at me like that, Rebekah! There's troublemakers stirring up the men and it's not only in shipping. It's the miners and the railwaymen. Nobody seems to be content with what they've got anymore.'

Times are changing in England just as they are in Ireland,' she retorted. 'The working classes no longer believe what the so-called upper classes tell them about their place in life. The war saw to that when it killed and maimed thousands of men! And for what?'

He seemed about to blurt something out but instead compressed his lips. After several seconds his expression relaxed and he placed his hands on her shoulders and shook her gently. 'You're a woman and can't begin to understand these matters.

251

But you're more of a fighting Irish colleen than I credited. It's a wonder you're not over there battling against the so-called president of the Dáil in Dublin. A schoolteacher for a President, I ask you! What can he know about governing a country?'

'He knows more about Ireland than Lloyd George,' murmured Rebekah, concealing her impatience. 'There's nothing wrong with its being a republic if that's what her people want.'

His smile faded and his eyes glittered. 'I suppose it was O'Neill who filled your head with such nonsense? Your father wouldn't have liked your supporting terrorists.'

She pulled away from him, her anger barely under control. 'Not all those who want an independent Ireland are terrorists! Lots of honest decent people want it too! And they want to keep the ties with Britain strong. When were you last in Ireland that you're such an authority on the subject?'

For a moment she thought he was going to strike her and drew back, watching him struggle with his emotions. At last he said in a tight voice, 'You're right, of course. I haven't been to Ireland for a long time. At most I've spent two years there and I did meet honest, decent people. Your grandmother was such a one.'

She recognised the olive branch. 'I wish I'd known her better.' She sighed. 'Just as I wish I'd known my mother's mother. I kept the doll Grandmama

Rhoades gave me for years – in memory of her – but it went down with the *Samson*.'

Joshua put his arm around her. 'We'll get you another.'

She forced herself not to stiffen and gave him a look. 'I'm too old for dolls. Besides, it wouldn't be the same.' She hesitated. 'There is something you can do for me, though.'

'Tell me.' He pressed his lips against her left eyebrow.

She wanted to move away but realised that would not improve her chances of getting what she wanted. 'The ship that's replacing the *Samson* – you'll change its name, won't you?' He nodded. 'Could you change it to the *Sarah Jane*? It was my mother's dream and I'd like to see it come true.'

'You don't know what you're asking,' he said bluntly. 'I'd be breaking with family tradition. All our ships are named for biblical heroes.'

'Sarah's biblical.' Determinedly, she put her hand through his arm and said in wheedling tones, 'Please, Joshua.'

He stared down at her. 'I'll have to think about it. How about coming out with me tomorrow? We could go for a spin in the country.'

'I can't. I'm meeting Brigid.'

'Don't go.' He squeezed her hand against his side. 'We could discuss your idea.'

'I can't let Brigid down.'

'Oh, come on, Rebekah!' he exclaimed impatiently. 'You're going to have to cut that connection sooner or later.'

'Am I?' Apprehension tightened her stomach muscles.

'Dammit, of course you are! And better sooner than later.'

'Better sooner than later, you say?' Her brow furrowed.

'Yes. You can't move in two different worlds,' he muttered, and kissed her with a passion that took her completely by surprise.

Early on Monday morning Rebekah gave a threepenny bit to one of the boys who played in the road, to take a note to Brigid. She leant on the gate in the sunshine, not wanting to go back inside the house to face her aunt's long face because she was going out with Joshua. As she waited for him to come, her feelings were mixed.

His desire to blacken Daniel in her eyes upset her, and yet she thought she understood it. After all, she had told him that she loved Daniel so that went some way to explaining it. Yet she felt there was something more. She frowned and shook her head and passed on to the next aspect of his character which she did not like: his attitude towards the men who worked on his ships. She had seen for herself how hard they worked, and surely so must he. He ought to realise they deserved what they earned. Neither did she like his insistence that she keep the right side of her aunt for mercenary reasons. Although she had no intention of allowing Hannah to get her hands on what she considered was rightly her own inheritance. But back to Joshua . . . She did not like his wanting her to cut her connections with Brigid. It was something she just could not do.

Yet he had his good points. There was his interest in the Seamen's Orphanage and the fact that he had given her the money she had asked for last week. He had found her a job and taken note of what she said about Andromeda. And he did have some kind of physical attraction for her, although she had resisted him when he had kissed her yesterday evening. He had apologised, saying that she had gone to his head. She pulled a face at the very idea.

There was the hooting of a horn and a motor car drew into the side of the road. Rebekah opened the gate, went over to the car and got in. She noted that Hannah was watching through the net curtains and waved to her. Her eyes gleamed as the maid's face quickly disappeared.

Some twenty minutes or so later they were rolling along the cobbled Walton Road with the hood of the Oxford Morris down. 'I thought I'd take you north of Liverpool,' said Joshua. 'It's nice countryside and coming this way I can show you where part of my family originally came from.' He waved a hand in an easterly direction. 'See that old mill? It's mentioned in a diary of my great-great-grandfather's. Springfield Mill, it was called. He passed it when he came to Liverpool seeking his fortune.'

Rebekah tightened the scarf to secure her new cream straw hat against the wind and gazed at the decapitated mill. In another age it would have been picturesque with its sails turning but with them missing it had a forlorn air about it. 'I take it he made his fortune?'

'He became a deckhand, but worked hard and was eventually the captain of a slave ship. He just about managed to make some money before slavery was abolished.'

'Did you know that the Quakers were involved in slavery at one time?' murmured Rebekah. 'I discovered that yesterday. And that they had dummy guns on some of their ships to trick privateers into believing that they were armed.'

'Never heard of that. But getting back to my family – even though slaving finished, there were still plenty of other cargoes to carry across the Atlantic. Earthenware, steel, glass, machinery, fish hooks, chemicals – you name it, we shipped it.'

Rebekah listened as he continued to talk about ships and cargoes, interspersing it with information about various landmarks. They passed a church. 'That's St Mary's. This is Walton-on-the-Hill where my great-great-grandfather came from. There's been a church here for over a thousand years. Well before Liverpool was more than a dot on the map. Now this place is a backwater, while Liverpool's thriving and a good place to live.' He smiled at her and drove on, humming.

He was full of smiles today, thought Rebekah, obviously enjoying driving and being away from his office. She had to admit to feeling some excitement herself, finding the speed of the car exhilarating. It was fun bowling along the road faster than anything else on it. She watched Joshua's hands as they moved from steering wheel to different levers and wished she could have a go.

Soon there was little else on the road. Housing became sparse and after Joshua pointed out Aintree Racecourse where the Grand National was run, it almost petered out altogether. As they travelled along country lanes where the hedgerows were white with hawthorn blossom and fields showed cowslips and daisies, he said, 'My grandmother on my father's side was Anglo-Irish, you know. Her family bred horses. That's how she and my grandfather met – at some horse race in Ireland.'

'You've never mentioned that before,' she said, surprise in her voice.

'Never saw the need.'

'But it explains why your father bought land in Ireland.'

'It would have been better if he'd ploughed the

money into the business,' he said in clipped tones. 'Are you hungry?'

'Yes.' She would have liked to have asked him more about his family but now received the impression that he did not want to talk about them.

'Janet made us up a picnic. I thought we'd have it on top of Clieves Hill. It's not a difficult walk and there's a good view.'

He brought the car to a halt and lifted the picnic basket from the back seat, telling her to get the rug. She did so and followed him up the hill. They could have been the only people in the world. She stared at the view. The flatlands of coastal Lancashire spread below them and the dark huddle that was Liverpool was visible far away, as were the Welsh Hills and the Irish Sea shimmering in the distance.

Suddenly Joshua's arms slipped about her waist from behind and she realised that subconsciously she had been waiting for it to happen. She attempted to release herself but he laced his fingers and she could not unlock them. He said against her ear, 'Isn't the view worth coming all this way for?'

'Yes. But can we look at it while we eat, please?'

'Give me a kiss first.'

'Mr Green, you're taking advantage of me,' she said indignantly, digging her fingers into the backs of his hand. 'Now let me go at once.'

'Don't do that.' His voice held a warning note.

'Just one kiss, Rebekah. It's not much of a reward for bringing you all the way out here.'

'I didn't know that I'd have to pay!' she said. 'I thought you brought me out of the kindness of your heart.' She twisted in his hold, trying to free herself, and ended up facing him.

He smiled. 'That's a good girl. I like you. That's why I brought you. Now be a sensible child and kiss me.'

She frowned but puckered her lips, thinking it quicker to get it over. She suspected he would spend time arguing with her rather than give in. He laughed, brought her close and almost ate her. Her mouth felt bruised and she was trembling when he released her.

He rubbed his hands together in a satisfied manner. 'Now food. Spread the rug, Rebekah.'

She did as she was told, watching him as he unpacked the picnic. There was tongue and beef sandwiches, homemade meat patties, fruit cake, scones, apples, and a bottle of white wine.

They did not speak while they ate. He filled two glasses with wine. It was sweet and she enjoyed it but refused a refill. 'Come on, Rebekah!' he said. 'It'll relax you.'

'I'm relaxed enough,' she murmured, determined that he was not going to get her drunk. Her gaze took in the view again and the car below them on the road. 'I enjoyed the drive. Do you often come out here?'

He shrugged and filled his own glass. 'I go to different places. I enjoy driving.'

'I wouldn't mind learning to drive.'

A little of his wine spilt as he turned and stared at her. 'But you're a woman.'

'So? I didn't imagine you'd have brought me out here if I wasn't. I imagine it's not that difficult. I'm sure I could get someone to teach me. In fact, I wouldn't mind having my own car.'

His expression grew wary. 'They're expensive. You can't afford—'

She knew that but was determined not to give up her idea. She wanted to drive. It would be exciting. 'I could ask Aunt Esther about buying one. I've noticed lately that her knee hurts her. Probably rheumatism. I could take her places.'

His mouth tightened. 'I don't know if it's a good idea, your having a car.'

'Why? Saying I'm a woman isn't a good reason. Women drove during the war, trams and all sorts of vehicles.'

'That was different,' he muttered. 'There weren't the men.'

She stared at him. 'That's no excuse. I'll ask Aunt Esther and I'm sure the dealer could arrange for me to have a few lessons.'

He stuck out his lower lip and it was several seconds before he said, 'I'll teach you.' He drained his glass.

'You?' She laughed. 'Wouldn't it go against the grain? You don't want to teach me.'

'Better I do than someone else.' He refilled his glass. 'Besides, your aunt mightn't buy you a car.'

That was true, she thought, but to go out with him again in his car was asking for trouble. He would probably believe that she did not mind his kissing her, and she did mind his presumption that he could kiss her when he felt like it. 'I'll think about it,' she said.

'You'll come.' His tone was positive. He flicked her cheek with his finger.

She rubbed her cheek but made no reply and began to collect the remains of the picnic together, aware that he watched her as he drank his wine. She was half expecting him to attempt to embrace her again but he did not. Soon afterwards he led the way down the hill and she followed, wondering whether he would suggest a lesson next weekend. She would have to make up her mind whether to go with him but before then she had her new job to think about, which started in the morning.

CHAPTER FIFTEEN

Rebekah hesitated at the foot of a flight of well-worn stone steps at the end of a row of dilapidated landing houses in Everton. She was aware of the curious stares of several small children sitting on the edge of the pavement. They had their bare feet in the gutter and were playing with stones. A couple of women who had paused in mid-gossip outside a front door set in the wall beneath the outside landing, watched her. She smiled but they looked through her and carried on with their conversation. She shrugged and looked up. Level with her head was a window with the curtains drawn. One of the panes of glass was missing and the space was blocked with a sheet of grubby cardboard. She glanced down at the paper in her hand and read the name and address again then began to climb the steps.

As she reached the landing a boy, whom she

estimated to be twelve years old, came out of the second house. He leant his back against the wrought iron railing opposite the front door, coughing and wheezing. He was pale and thin and wore grey trousers too short for him and a darned V-necked sleeveless pullover next to his skin. His eyes were unfriendly as they took in her appearance. She had dressed in her plainest and cheapest black frock but realised that here it would not be regarded as cheap. 'I'm looking for Mrs Rimmer,' she said, determinedly controlling her nerves:

'Ma's out.' He moved in one fluid movement back in front of the doorway from which he'd emerged. 'Yer'll have ta cum back tomorra.' His chest heaved.

'I can't,' said Rebekah, remembering how in Dublin there had been occasions when she and her mother had been informed that Mam was out while she had been in. 'If I can't see her today then I'll have to go to the next name on my list.'

'She's norrin, I tell yer! Why can't yer go away and leave us alone?' He coughed and twitched a shoulder in the direction of the floor inside the entrance. 'We've even had to sell the oilcloth,' he spluttered. 'There's nuffin else we got to pay yer.'

'Who said I want paying?' she said grimly. 'I've come to see your ma about giving her money.' She glanced down at the paper again although there was no need, she knew the words off by heart. 'Your father was drowned when an enormous wave swept over his ship, dismantling its steering apparatus and considerably damaging the deck,' she recited.

The boy nodded. 'The *Magnifique* the ship was called. Ma's inside with the baby. Me brothers and sisters are at school. Wait here.' He vanished inside the house to reappear a few minutes later, smiling. 'Ma said to cum in but don't go expectin' anythin' fancy.'

Rebekah went inside expecting nothing at all in the way of frills and she was not disappointed. The room she entered was furnished with one chair and a rickety card table. In a corner a couple of grey and black army blankets lay on the bare wooden floor. A woman in a grubby blue frock nursed a whimpering baby. She stood next to a grate in which the fire was dead. From the ashes it looked as if it had been made up mainly of cardboard, paper and wood.

'Billy sez yer from the Seamen's, miss,' said the woman eagerly. 'Will we get summit? Yer see, I need muny for medicine for Billy's chest. Bad it is still, but always wurst in winter. Goose grease me cousin gave me to rub on it after Christmas, and I'm sure it must have dun it sum good.' She paused for breath.

Rebekah nodded. 'I'm sure we can give you some money for medicine. I take it Billy hasn't seen a doctor?'

'Doctor!' A harsh laugh escaped her. 'Can't afford doctors. Daisy needs shoes and I owes the corner shop. Never clears that amount, but Mrs Murphy's got a good heart. As long as I pays summit she lets us buy on tick. If it wurn't for that swine of a man of mine, we'd never have got inta this state.'

'That's me dad,' said Billy, nodding. 'Always in the ale house. Never saw hardly any of his money, did we, Ma?'

'No, son.' She smiled at him and then at Rebekah as she continued to rock the baby which had fallen silent. 'He's a good lad. If his chest wasn't so bad he'd gerra job. Fourteen he is but nobody'll take him on. Andy cud have dun more for him but all he ever had on his mind was bed and booze. Eight kids I've got. Lost three.' Her expression turned ugly. 'Bed and booze. He was a bluddy animal.'

'No use my offering you condolences then,' said Rebekah as cheerfully as she could.

'What?' Mrs Rimmer stared at her. Then she began to laugh. 'Best bluddy thing that ever happened to me!'

Rebekah lay in the lukewarm bathwater, thinking of Mrs Rimmer and the lives different people lived. Her story was nothing new to Rebekah. Living in Dublin had accustomed her to inebriated men and worn down women, and she had seen more than a few drunken sailors since living in Liverpool where pubs were as plentiful as pigeons. She had slipped the woman a pound of her own money to tide her over until her application went through, and had gone on to the next family, glad of the street map book her aunt had given her, and thinking about what Daniel had told her of his own childhood. Poverty was a terrible thing. She had been a fool saying to Joshua that money was not important.

She pulled out the bath plug and with a towel wrapped about her went into her bedroom, thinking about her next port of call. She had felt sorry for Mrs Brown who ran a small shop wedged in a row of houses in Edge Hill. It was obvious that she missed her husband, that money was tight, but also that the family of four were managing. Mrs Brown worked long hours and the two boys, although only ten and twelve, helped with deliveries. The eldest girl of eight was already a good little housewife, according to her proud stepmother. Mrs Brown had married late in life, the widower of her best friend who had died in childbirth. Only the youngest child belonged to her but she saw it as her duty to do her best for all the children. They were not in dire straits so Rebekah could not recommend their receiving much financial help, but what she did so was put in for new boots for the boys. With that small offering their mother had seemed grateful. Tomorrow Rebekah would work in the office, writing up her reports.

She frowned at her reflection as she rubbed her wet hair, glad that it was short but knowing it needed trimming again. She smoothed merculised wax on to her face and tried not to dwell on thoughts of the place that the Rimmers lived in or on meeting Joshua next weekend. Liverpool, as Brigid had once said, was no Paradise. Its people were no angels, but Rebekah was starting to feel at home in it. She glanced at the clock and realised that she had better hurry or she would be late meeting her friend outside the Olympia.

Rebekah was surprised to see Pat and Joey when she reached the theatre on West Derby Road. 'What are you two doing here?'

'I thought you'd have heard from the bossman,' said Pat, the slightest sneer in his voice. 'The blinking stewards are on strike so we're not sailing.'

'I heard that the *Aquitania* had sailed,' said Rebekah, ignoring the tone of his voice. 'There were orphans on it who have been adopted by some rich Americans.'

'They were taking bets on the *Aquitania* going out, and the owners went and got a volunteer crew,' said Joey, Pat's mate, in a gloomy voice. 'Some of the stewards signed on at the lower rate of pay when Cunard's own clerks rushed to fill their places.

'You're going to be short of money.' said Brigid thoughtfully. 'We'll go Dutch if we go out again.'

Joe shook his head. 'I'm not having you paying for yourself. If I can't afford to take yer out, I won't go at all.'

'That's stupid!' said Brigid in a low voice. 'I'm earning so it makes sense I pay my way.'

'So I'm stupid,' said Joe, his thin face set stubbornly. 'That's the way I am and you won't be changing me.'

'Oh, Joe!' cried Brigid, giving him a gentle punch.

'Shut up, you two,' muttered Pat, taking some change from his pocket. 'Are we going in or not? The queue's moving, so make up your minds.'

'We're going in,' said Rebekah, putting her hand through his arm. 'I'm in need of a good laugh.' She knew better than to offer to pay for herself.

'You've been with his lordship today and all, have you?' said Pat, his mouth tightened.

'No, I haven't.' She squeezed his arm. 'I've been working.'

Brigid smiled. 'So yer got the job? Difficult day, was it?'

'Not really but it makes you glad of what you've got.'

Pat glanced at her and his face softened. 'What is it you're doing, luv?'

'I'm working on Outdoor Relief for the Seamen's Orphanage.'

'You're joking!'

'What's there to joke about?' Her look was puzzled.

'You're a blinking do-gooder!'

'You'd rather I was a do-badder?' She was irritated.

'You know what I mean,' he growled. 'You're

working for the bosses. They give to salve their consciences. Do you realise, Becky, if they paid the workers decent wages, there wouldn't be any need for charity. We could look after our own.'

'You might look after your own, Pat, but not all workers do,' she said indignantly. 'A family I visited today were that poor you would have wept for them. And most of their poverty was because the blinking husband drank his wages away and she had too many kids. Nearly every time he docked she was off again. What chance has she of coping without help? He wasn't looking after his own, only satisfying himself!'

He flushed. 'Hey, come on now, luv! That's life. Most women expect to have babies when they get married. You're sounding like—'

'Women don't went ten and twenty, though,' interrupted a female voice from behind. 'If you men had the babies it'd be different, I bet.'

Several people looked in their direction and Pat's face went redder. 'See what you've started,' he hissed.

'Me started!' Rebekah's eyes sparkled. 'It's you that thinks women should produce babies like a baker turns out loaves.'

'That's a good one,' approved the voice from behind. 'Even when love goes out of the window, sex never goes stale on men. Even if they're a hundred and two!' There were several titters from the queue.

'Mother of God!' said Pat through gritted teeth.

'Women! A man's better off without them. I'm going.'

His sister seized his arm. 'Now yer'll just stay here! You started this, our Pat, by calling Becky a do-gooder. What's wrong with helping people? Yer just downright jealous if the truth's known.'

'Jealous? Of Mr Bloody Green!' He gave a strangled laugh, dragged his arm out of his sister's hold and walked away.

Rebekah stared after him. 'What do I do, Brigid?'

'Go after him,' intervened Joe in an earnest voice. 'Prove to him that yer didn't mean any of it. Kiss and make up, luv.'

'But I did mean it,' said Rebekah, her expression fixed.

'Too right, yer did, love,' said the voice from behind.

'Oh shut up, yer old bag!' shouted the normally passive Joe, and seizing hold of Brigid's hand he marched her out of the queue. She turned and called, 'I'm sorry, Becky, but it looks like it's not on tonight. I'll see you on Thursday. Meet you outside Lyons in Church Street at seven o'clock.'

'Oh, all right!' Rebekah was annoyed with her friend. She moved out of the queue.

Her supporter, a plump woman with a feather in her hat, patted her arm as she took her place. 'He'll come back, luv. Jealous as hell. Not the easiest type to live with but I bet you know that.'

'I didn't but I'm learning,' murmured Rebekah,

and went in the direction of the park, deciding that she had better kill some time, otherwise Aunt Esther would be asking questions.

She walked to Newsham Park boating pond, and paused to watch boys send small yachts skimming across the water. At that moment she wished that she had never agreed to go out with Pat and felt like never bothering with him again. Maybe she would not have the choice. Did she care? She shrugged. Was he really jealous of Joshua Green? Damn! The two men were creating complications in her life that she would rather live without. If only Daniel . . . The ache which never completely left her made itself felt. Why had he had to die? Oh God! There was a lump in her throat and she wanted to hit something or throw things.

She went home and asked her aunt about buying a car.

'What for?' said Esther, stabbing herself with a needle.

'To ferry you around,' retorted Rebekah, leaning against the mantelshelf, her hands in her pockets.

'Chariots of the devil, that's what them motors are' said Hannah, her dark eyes darting dislike at Rebekah as she poured the tea and spilt it in the saucer.

'Rubbish!' Rebekah glared at her. 'You just don't like the thought of Aunt Esther spending money.'

'A motor car would cost a lot of money,' said her aunt, sucking her finger. 'And who'd drive it? I don't want to hire a man?'

'I can learn.' said Rebekah, her anger lifting. 'Would you buy one? I could take you shopping and for drives in the country. I've noticed your knee—'

Hannah interrupted her. 'A bit of rheumatism, that's all. She doesn't need mollycoddling. Needs to keep it moving or it'll seize up.'

'I'm not suggesting she glues herself to the car,' retorted Rebekah, glaring at Hannah again.

'I'll think about it,' said Esther hurriedly before Hannah could respond. She looked at her niece. 'It's not a decision to be made in a moment, dear. It would be nice to visit the country, but aren't cars dangerous?'

'It depends who drives them,' said Rebekah.

'Exactly,' muttered Hannah, thrusting a cup at her. 'And there's them that thinks they knows it all and knows nothing. When has thee ever driven a car, miss?'

'Starting from next week I'll be learning.' She smiled sweetly. 'So put that in your pipe and smoke it! Mr Green is going to teach me.'

'Perhaps thee'll crash it,' said Hannah, and walked out of the room.

'Oh dear,' said Esther looking dismayed.

'I won't crash it,' murmured Rebekah, passing a plate of scones to her aunt. 'Just you wait and see. I'll show her.'

'Oh dear,' said her aunt again, putting down her sewing. 'I really do need a bit of peace at my time of life.'

'Sorry,' Rebekah said meekly, and put a scone in her hand. 'I'll change the subject.' She sat and began to talk about Mrs Rimmer and her family.

When Thursday came Rebekah made her way to Lyons cafe with only seconds to spare to seven o'clock. Brigid was not there but someone else was waiting for her.

'I hope you don't mind my coming instead of our Bridie,' said Pat, running a finger round his collar and moving his shoulders awkwardly. 'We'll be sailing soon after all – and she said I had no right to say what I did.'

'She was right.'

'I'm sorry,' he muttered.

Rebekah had been feeling annoyed two seconds ago but his apology changed that. 'I forgive you,' she said with a smile.

He grimaced. 'It's just that I didn't realise what I felt towards you.' He looked down at his well-polished shoes.

'Let's forget about it,' she said, choosing to ignore what he had just said. 'Will we have a cup of tea?'

He lifted his head. 'I thought you might like to go to the pictures?'

'No,' she said hurriedly, considering the cosy intimate darkness inside the picture house. 'Just a cup of tea.'

'OK.' He sighed and stared at her, his brown eyes

reminding her of a pony she had once ridden on her grandma's farm.

They went inside Lyons and she asked him whether the strike was over. He told her that most of the stewards were signing on, with only the chief stewards holding out and talking of forming their own union. Then he fell silent. She forced the conversation, enquiring after his mother and whether Brigid had given him a message for her. 'Ma should be out soon. We're thinking of throwing a party to celebrate. You will come?' he said eagerly. 'Ma thinks a lot of you.'

'Of course I'll come.' She smiled and he placed his hand over hers on the table.

'Mr Green – you and him aren't—?'

She withdrew her hand, feeling irritated again. 'You asked me once whether I was a one man woman – I am! Shall we go now?'

He sighed, nodded and rose. 'I'll see you home.'

'There's no need. Just tell me what Brigid said.' He told her. 'Fine,' she replied, impulsively kissed his cheek, waved a hand and walked away, not looking back, and uncertain as to whether she was relieved or sorry about the way things had changed between them.

The weekend arrived and Rebekah was waiting outside the gate for Joshua to arrive. Her aunt had not made up her mind yet about buying a car but Rebekah was working on her, telling her how useful it would be. They would not have to get groceries and goods delivered but pick up what they wanted themselves. Hannah had grunted that they'd be putting people out of work. Rebekah could not see how just having a car could do that.

There was the tooting of a horn and Joshua drove up. This time they travelled south out of the city. He stopped near some stones. 'They're called calder stones,' he said. 'They're believed to be very old. Probably Neolithic. See the engravings on them.'

Rebekah peered closely at the weird rings and cuplike marks. They remind me of some of the old stones to be seen in Ireland.'

'Probably not as old as these,' he said dismissively and ushered her back to the car.

They travelled a couple more miles and still he did not mention anything about driving lessons so she did.

'I thought you might have changed your mind,' he muttered.

'No. I've mentioned about buying a car to Aunt Esther and she's thinking about it.'

'Hmmph!' He frowned.

She glanced at him and smiled. 'Are you scared of being in the car with me driving, Joshua?'

His expression sharpened. 'Too bloody right I am,' he said, but without any more preamble began to explain to her about steering and gear levers. She listened intently, waiting for the moment when he would move out of the driving seat and let her have a go. Eventually he did so and after a jerky start they were off. At first she went much too slowly because she was nervous about damaging his car. It was *his* car all the time he spoke about it. Be careful of *my* car . . . If you damage *my* car . . . She could understand his feelings but at last she went a bit faster. He did not allow the lesson to go on too long and it came to an end all too swiftly for her.

'Another one tomorrow?' she said.

'We'll see.' He pulled her towards him and kissed her. After a minute she disengaged herself. He laughed but did not persist. He drove back to Liverpool, telling her on the way about the day out they were having for the orphans on the river. 'We're taking them to Eastham on the other side of the Mersey. You must come. You'll enjoy it.'

'What day is it?'

He told her and she agreed to go, and he said that he would give her another lesson after church tomorrow.

On Sunday they went north again, out past Litherland where the smells from a tannery impinged on the country air. They picnicked on the bank of the Leeds-Liverpool canal and afterwards he allowed her to drive round the quiet lanes near the medieval church of Sefton and Ince Woods. He asked her how she was finding her work.

'I enjoy meeting the families.'

'You don't want to be too soft with them,' he said

absently. 'Some of them are up to all kinds of dodges.'

'Perhaps you'd be crafty if you had nothing,' responded Rebekah. She had thought of talking to him about Kitty Dodds, whom she had met a couple of days ago, but changed her mind. It was her problem.

'Just be careful who you recommend. Money doesn't grow on trees,' he murmured, pressing her knee.

She said nothing, only removing his hand and changing the subject.

On Monday she met Brigid. Her friend looked relieved. 'I wasn't sure if yer'd be here,' she said, putting her hand in her arm as they walked towards the cinema. 'Our Pat couldn't make up his mind to whether yer'd said yes or no. He's been real moody and got drunk a couple of times.'

'I'm sorry about that.'

'It's not your fault.' Brigid frowned. 'I'm fed up with him. I have enough on me mind with thinking about Mam coming out of hospital. Did Pat tell yer about the party?'

Rebekah nodded. 'Have you a date?'

'Yeah.' Brigid told her.

Rebekah barely hesitated before saying. 'No problem.' It might be, though, because it was the day of the orphans' outing but she could see no way of saying no to Brigid or Joshua without offending one or the other.

CHAPTER SIXTEEN

The day of the outing dawned bright and clear and Rebekah, wearing a lemon wash frock and a broad-brimmed white hat to keep off the sun, and with a jacket over her arm in case it was cool on the water, met Joshua down at the Pierhead. 'You look stunning,' he murmured, as he took her hand and led her up the gangway and on to a crowded upper deck.

He ruffled several children's hair and one lad said, 'Is she your girl, sir?'

He laughed and said, 'Yes.' He introduced Rebekah to several of the teachers, not mentioning that he was her guardian and giving the impression that they were sweethearts. She was not prepared for events to move so fast and when he pulled her down on a seat beside him and slipped his arm round her waist, she removed his hand.

The Mersey glistened like a sheet of crinkled silver paper. Rebekah only half listened to Joshua. Her thoughts were of Daniel and the time they had spent on the *Samson*. She was betraying what was still in her heart by being with Joshua, and yet her father would have approved. Strangely, that mattered. It was as if by doing what he wished now she was making her peace with him. She thought of how he and Daniel had fought as the ship steamed across the water and only put it out of her mind when she left the ship.

Eastham Woods rang with the children's shouts and Rebekah smiled, finding pleasure in their enjoyment.

'Miss, miss, come and see this!'

'Miss, look at this bird's egg. Can I keep it? Can I, can I?'

'Miss, what's this animal?' A pair of huge dark eyes gazed up at Rebekah.

'It's a squirrel,' answered Rebekah. It eats nuts and hides them away in winter when it goes to sleep.'

It sleeps the whole winter!' exclaimed the boy. 'Bluddy hell, fancy that! I wouldn't mind doing that meself.'

Joshua gave him a clip over the ear. 'You don't use that language in front of ladies, boy! I'll have a word with the matron and see you get your mouth washed out with soap.'

'Sorry, miss,' said the lad cheerfully, following them,

'I forgot meself. But if I was one of them squirrels I wouldn't have to worry about feeling the cold in winter.' He frowned. 'How does it survive if it sleeps for months? What does it do about them nuts?'

'It wakes up now and again when it gets a little warmer and digs them up,' informed Rebekah, aware of Joshua's scowl.

'Bluddy hell! That's clever! How does it know where—' The lad stopped abruptly as Joshua raised his hand, and fled.

Rebekah laughed but Joshua shook his head. 'You shouldn't have encouraged him.'

'He was trying to learn.' She gazed up at the leafy green branches above them and breathed deeply of the woodland smells. Suddenly Joshua's hands gripped her breasts and she gasped. 'What do you think you're doing?'

He looked at her but did not stop. She attempted to slap his hands away but he caught hold of her fingers and said huskily, 'Isn't it what you expected me to do?' He forced her into his arms. 'You girls like to play the temptress and then pretend you're doing nothing of the sort! But I'm on to you, Rebekah. I'm willing to go along with whatever you wish. I want you, you see.' His mouth came down over hers. She struggled but it was no use. He only let her go when she kicked him on the shins.

He rubbed his leg but smiled up at her. 'That was naughty but I forgive you.'

Rebekah touched her throbbing lips, 'I don't care if you forgive me or not,' she said. 'You hurt me.'

'Sorry.' He pulled her hand away from her mouth and pressed his lips lightly against hers. 'There. I've kissed it better. D'you want to kiss my leg?' he said in a teasing tone.

'Certainly not!' She remembered how Daniel had kissed the insides of her thighs and suddenly shivered. Did she really given the impression of being a tease? If so it must be unconsciously because she was lonely for Daniel's arms. She sighed. 'Shouldn't we be going back now? It must be time for the picnic.'

He nodded. 'I suppose so. Besides, there's a couple of children watching us. Put your hand through my arm and smile.'

Rebekah saw the sense in what he suggested and after that the afternoon passed off smoothly. It was only when they reached the Pierhead and he wanted to make an evening of it in town that there was a little unpleasantness. She stated that she was too tired to go gallivanting round the nightspots, and he sulked. She pretended to doze off in the cab and that seemed to convince him that she was definitely too tired to paint the town even a delicate shade of pink.

As soon as he was out of sight, Rebekah stopped waving at the gate, pulled a comb through her hair and then ran up the road in the opposite direction. It was still light.

'You're late,' said Brigid as soon as she opened the door. 'Our Pat said yer weren't coming.'

Rebekah was surprised. 'Why should he think that? I said I'd come.'

Brigid shrugged. 'Come in anyway. The men have gone to the pub. We've done the butties and everything. There's some of the neighbours in, and me aunts and a few cousins.'

'Come in, girl, and have yourself a shandy,' called Ma Maisie, beckoning to her. 'I'm on the tonic wine to build meself up.'

'You should be drinking Guinness,' said Rebekah, fishing a bottle from inside her jacket. She had bought it on the way. 'Best that Ireland can produce.'

'Now there's a good girl!' Ma Maisie's lined face eased into a big smile. 'Get me a glass and we'll drink to the Emerald Island – that her troubles will soon be over and there'll be peace between us.'

'Amen to that,' chorused several of the women.

Kath handed Rebekah a cup of shandy while Brigid forced off the jink from the bottle of Guinness, They all drank to peace in Ireland and afterwards Rebekah told Brigid about the outing with the orphans, without mentioning Joshua. By the time she had finished, the men were filling up the room and one of the woman was coaxing a tune from a concertina. Rebekah caught a glimpse of Pat across the crowded room. He was swaying and there was an idiotic smile on his good-looking face. 'I'll Take You Home Again,

Kat'leen,' he bellowed off-key at the top of his voice.

'Oh, shut up. Uncle Pat, that's terrible,' said Jimmy, appearing from beneath the table with his hands over his ears. 'It's enough to kill the cat.'

'Are yer saying I can't sing, lad?' Pat squinted at him.

Veronica bobbed up beside Jimmy. 'Yeah. It was awful. Yer'd be better letting Becky sing. She sings real gud!'

Pat scowled ferociously. 'She's not here! And she's not one of us! Becky has a fancy man and thinks she's too bloody good for the likes of me.'

'Yer drunk,' said Brigid in disgust. 'Where's the eyes in yer head? Becky's here and she does sing better than you!'

'I'm not singing,' said Rebekah in a low voice to her friend, making up her mind to leave as soon as possible. She didn't know why Pat had said what he had but her feelings were injured at that 'She's not one of us!' Besides, she nurtured healthy suspicion of drunks and having Pat offer to see her home in this condition was the last thing she wanted. As well as that she was tired after her day in the fresh air. She picked up her empty glass from the table and took it into the back kitchen. She rinsed it in the sink and stood for a moment, thinking, and then went out through the back door and down the yard. Explanations could wait until next time she saw Brigid.

Running up the back entry, she was glad that it

was still only dusk. With a bit of luck she would be home before dark.

It was as Rebekah came out into the road that she collided with Pat. 'How did you get here so quickly?' Her pulses were beating in her ears and she was in no mood for a tussle or an argument.

'Why are yer leaving so soon?' he demanded in a slurred voice, seizing her arm.

'I didn't want to stay.'

'Because of me?'

She sighed. 'If the cap fits – I'm not one of you, remember?'

Pat's eyes darkened and his throat moved. 'I saw you with him down at the Pierhead. I'm bloody surprised at you for spending today with him. I thought you'd come early to Ma's do. He's a bloodsucker, living off the backs of the poor. I thought that you and me—'

'It was the orphans' day out,' she interrupted. 'And there's no you and me! I didn't pretend anything different. You're Catholic, remember, and your mam wouldn't like there being anything serious.'

Pat scowled and his fingers tightened on her arm. 'Daniel O'Neill's being Catholic didn't stop you fancying him.'

'Daniel was Daniel and you can never fill his place.' Her voice was low and unsteady.

'Can Mr Bloody Joshua Green fill it?' He attempted to kiss her – a big slobbery kiss.

With all her strength she pushed him off and

backed away. 'I don't want to go out with you any more! You're not my friend! And it's nothing to do with your boss. You've spoilt everything. Goodbye, Pat.' Turning she ran, tears rolling down her cheeks, and did not stop until she was nearly home.

She let herself in with her key as Hannah came charging up the lobby. 'Where hast thee been to this hour?' she demanded.

'It's nothing to do with you,' said Rebekah wearily, pushing past her and entering the sitting room.

'Thou art later than I thought, Rebekah,' said her aunt, struggling to her feet.

'I'm sorry.'

'It's that man, Miss Esther,' put in Hannah. 'He's a bad influence. No meeting house last week and now this! He's leading her astray! She'll be getting a name for herself in the neighbourhood. And we know she drinks.'

'That's enough, Hannah,' snapped Esther. 'Shall we be a little more charitable? It was the orphans' day out. And didn't Paul, in the Bible, say that a little wine is good for the stomach.'

'Always excuses for her,' muttered the maid and went out of the room.

'Oh dear,' said Esther, 'I don't know what to do about her, Becky.'

'Ignore her, and me,' said Rebekah. 'I'm going to bed.' She kissed her aunt and went upstairs. Enough was enough! Pat's mention of Daniel had brought him alive that day for the second time and she wondered what she had been playing at, going out with either of the men. But what was she to do? Shut herself away from male company for ever and turn into another Hannah, frustrated and bad-tempered, because it was obvious her religion didn't give her much joy? She thumped the pillows and that night cried herself to sleep.

Early Monday morning she wrote a letter to Brigid, explaining why she had left the party, and posted it on the way to visit Kitty Dodd for the fourth time.

'You're back, are you?' said Mrs Dodd. She was large, middle-aged, and had her hair in plaited coils about her ears. 'You might as well come in now you're here. Are you going to take them?'

'I've explained, Mrs Dodd.'

The older woman's mouth tightened and she reached for her coat and handbag. 'Well, I'll be leaving you with them, then, and maybe you'll change your mind and they won't be here when I come back.'

Rebekah stared at the four children. There were two sets of twins, three boys and one girl, all under seven, and their parents were dead. Their father had been Mrs Dodd's son. He had been killed, playing football on deck after his ship had docked in Montreal. He had not looked where he was going and fallen down an open cargo hold. His mother wanted his children placed in the orphanage 'You're a stubborn woman, Mrs Dodd. They're lovely children. How can you bear to be parted from them?'

'I can't cope,' she said, not meeting Rebekah's eyes but checking her handbag for her purse, 'I'm over forty. I'm too old. Even with her help next door they're too much of a handful, and it'll get worse.'

'I've told you we'll help out.'

'Financially, girl, but children's needs can't all be met with money. It's time they need, and someone with plenty of energy.' She pulled on black gloves, 'I don't mind keeping the girl.'

'The boys are still too young,' said Rebekah, the tension inside her easing. That was something at least. 'What if I take them just for a while?' she suggested. 'It'll give you time to get your work done or put your feet up.'

Mrs Dodd stared at her and shook her head. A slight smile lightened her stern face. 'You're a right Miss do-gooder, aren't you? Why aren't you married with a baby of your own instead of bothering with other people's?'

'Perhaps I might have been,' Rebekah's voice was low, 'but he went down with his ship last year.'

There was silence except for the noise of the two older children whispering, then Mrs Dodd took off her coat and sat down. She waved Rebekah to the chair opposite hers the other side of the fireplace. 'I lost my man years ago but I had my lad. When the war came I thought I'd lose him, but he came through.' Her throat moved. 'Then for him to be killed in a stupid accident – I just couldn't accept it. It seemed unbelievable.' She drew in a shaky breath and when she spoke again her voice was brisker. 'Well, no use us crying, girl. You're only young and have your life ahead of you. You'll find someone else. Have children. That'll help you over it. Now if you want to take them out, I'll appreciate it, and maybe I'll have a cup of tea for you when you come back.'

Rebekah nodded, emotion making it too difficult for her to speak. She picked up the two younger children, Stanley and Lily, who were three years old. Their grandmother told their five-year-old brothers to stop messing about with chalks and put pullovers on them. Rebekah fastened the others in the large twin perambulator kept in the lobby, and with the elder boys holding on the pram handle, they walked the short distance up Farnworth Street in the direction of Kensington Gardens.

'I felt like I won a battle this week,' said Rebekah as she and Joshua came out of Crane Hall after a Chopin recital.

He pulled her hand through his arm. 'I see the police in London have captured a gang of Sinn Feiners. There were women involved too, carrying revolvers inside their blouses which they handed to the men to fire.'

Rebekah's stare fixed on his satisfied expression. 'Why are you telling me?' She attempted to suppress the annoyance in her voice because he had shown no interest in what she said. 'Perhaps you think I've got a gun up the leg of my knickers?'

'My sweet!' He raised his eyebrows. 'Is there really any need for that kind of talk?'

'I suppose not,' she said stiffly. 'But think why I don't like you telling me things like that! I want to forget about anything to do with the struggle in Ireland. I know there were elections yesterday. That in Belfast the streets were festooned with red, white and blue, and that there was trouble. But I don't *want* to know! Instead why can't you tell me about the hundreds of unemployed who are rushing to sign ships' articles and your taking them on so your ships can sail?' Her tone was disparaging as she remembered Joe's talk a short while ago. She presumed that he and Pat had gone back to their ship. She had not seen them since the night of the party and she had received no reply to her letter and was feeling hurt.

'Rebekah, it's in your interest that my ships sail.' Joshua was frowning down at her. 'And you should be glad that at least some of the unemployed are getting work.'

'I am.' She closed her eyes briefly. 'But I bet you'll be paying them less than you were the chief stewards.'

'That's business, I'm afraid.' He sounded almost

regretful. 'I would have preferred to pay it to the chief stewards. They're better at the job but proving stubborn. They've formed their own guild with some of the higher ratings of the catering staff.' He kissed her lightly on the cheek and smiled into her eyes. 'Let's forget about all these troubles and talk about us.'

'What about us?' Her voice was wary.

'You must know I'm mad about you.'

'Do I?'

'Of course you do.'

She moistened her lips. 'Say that I do?'

'You can't like living with that aunt of yours.'

'She's not so bad,' she said promptly. 'It's Hannah who drives me mad. She'd love to get me out of the house.'

His eyes narrowed. 'It's like that, is it? Can't you persuade your aunt to get rid of her?'

'She's been with her for a long time. Better the devil you know, I suppose.'

He stared into the distance. 'Does your aunt still resent my being your guardian?'

'Yes.' Rebekah glanced at him. 'Understandable, don't you think? She is my closest relative and you were a stranger to me.'

He smiled and patted her hand. 'But not now. I want to marry you, my sweet, but we don't want to alienate your aunt.'

Rebekah's heart had already begun to race

because she had sensed what was coming and wanted to shout, No, no! But all she could say was, 'Marry you?' because it was what her father had wanted and she still felt bad about him, but it was all happening too swiftly.

'Yes, marry,' he murmured, squeezing her arm against his side.

She cleared her throat. 'It isn't a year since Mama and Papa died.'

'I don't want to wait.' His tone was determined.

'I'd need time to get Aunt Esther used to the idea,' she said in a rush. 'She's not going to like it. She might cut me off just like Grandpapa cut Mama off.'

He tapped a nail against his teeth. 'That is a thought. Do you know if she's made a will?'

A small laugh escaped Rebekah. 'It's not something you bring up in everyday conversation! Am I supposed to say, "Dear Aunt, have you left everything to me?"'

He frowned. 'It would make sense for her to tell you, seeing as how you are her next of kin. Anyway, even if she hasn't, everything should come to you, and by my reckoning she's the type who doesn't give business matters the due attention they deserve. I don't think we really have anything to worry about.'

Anger suddenly flared inside her. 'I know that money is important but do you really have to speak about my aunt in such a way? I don't want to think of her dying. Enough people I love have died already.

I'm still mourning although I know I'm not dressed for it. I'd have to wait at least a full year before considering marrying!'

'A year!' He stared at her and she was surprised at how anxious his pleasant face looked as he clutched at her free hand. 'I had hoped – I do love you, Rebekah. I couldn't bear it if you said no.' His tongue stumbled over the words. 'Please do say you'll at least think about us being married?'

Still she hesitated but her heart softened at the sight of this different side to him. 'I'd like to know you a bit longer,' she said warmly, 'and then maybe the answer will be yes.'

His relief was obvious. 'Thank you. You won't regret it if you do decide to marry me.'

She said nothing only smiled. Nothing definite was settled and a year seemed a long way off. But the topic of marriage was to recur a couple of weeks later from a different source.

'Miss Rhoades! Miss Rhoades!' Mr McIntyre waved a newspaper in the air, signalling Rebekah to his doorway.

She was wilting from the heat and wanted nothing more than to get indoors, have a cup of tea, a bath, lie down on her new bed, but she pushed open the gate and went up the path past drooping marigolds. 'What is it, Mr McIntyre?'

'They've declared a truce!' His strong-boned face

was bright. 'It's been signed by General Macready and Michael Collins!' He nodded his head sharply. 'You'll know him? One of the leaders of the Sinn Feiners. Had a price on his head.'

'Ten thousand pounds at one time.' She was relieved and pleased even though she had tried not to care about what was happening in Ireland. 'It's marvellous! When did it happen?'

He grinned. 'Come inside, have a cup of tea, and you can read it for yourself. I reckon it's all down to that Brigadier-General Crozier, who was the leader of the Black and Tans. He resigned because he didn't like what was going on.' Rebekah followed him up the lobby. 'A week or so back he said that you can't outmurder the murderers, and a whole lot more besides. It looks like the High-ups might have taken notice of him.'

'It seems like it.' Rebekah smiled at Edwina.

'So you've come for that cup of tea at last,' she said, returning her smile.

'Yes.' Rebekah took the newspaper thrust under her nose and read quickly of soldiers and civilians discussing peace prospects in Dublin. 'There's still difficulties ahead,' she murmured. 'The Unionists in Ulster have already set up a parliament. They want to stay in the Empire. President De Valera doesn't want any part of it.'

'The North and South will have to agree to differ,' said Mr McIntyre firmly.

Rebekah frowned. 'They might yet. But Lord Midleton is elected as a Unionist in the South, so there's going to be differences of opinion in the Dáil.'

'I wish you two would stop talking politics' chided Edwina, putting the teapot on the hob. 'I'm fed up of hearing about Ireland. Father, go and fetch me a lettuce from the garden so I can chat with Rebekah.' Mr McIntyre protested but was shooed out, and Edwina turned to Rebekah. 'Sit down and tell us about the job.'

Rebekah sat. 'How do you know about that?'

Edwina winked. 'I heard it on the grapevine. Most reckon that you won't be working for long, though.'

'Why do they say that?' she asked as casually as she could.

'Because they reckon you'll be getting married. They're not sure who to, though. Is it the shipowner with the motor or the dark handsome one they don't know much about? They're rooting for the shipowner because he's your guardian and has money. They say your aunt doesn't like either of them.'

'I suppose it's Hannah who's been gossiping.' Rebekah sipped her tea. – The dark one was the brother of a friend but we don't see each other any more. Joshua has asked me to marry him but I haven't said yes. If I do marry him, at least with plenty of money I can be miserable in comfort.'

'Miserable?' Edwina pulled up a chair close to Rebekah. 'Tell Auntie Edwina all your troubles, love.

Is it that you're wanting to get out of that house?'

Rebekah smiled. 'Aunt Esther I can cope with.'

'Is it a lover's tiff with this Pat then? Sounds Catholic. Is it religion?'

'I don't love Pat,' Rebekah said in a low voice. 'There was someone else but he died.'

'You'd only be young in the war,' said Edwina, her brow thoughtful. 'I presume that is—'

'It wasn't the war. He was an engineer on the *Samson* and was lost when it sank.'

Edwina pressed her hand and it was a few moments before Rebekah said, 'I'm not going to spend my life thinking "if only". With plenty of money I can have fun and do some good with it!' She could hear the defiance in her voice. 'I like my work with the Royal Seamen's Orphanage Outdoor Relief. I like children.'

'And you'd like some of your own?'

Rebekah was silent. 'I have thought about it. There's this family I visit. They're orphans but live with their grandmother. I take them out and give her a break sometimes. In their company it's easier not to think of yourself. Otherwise I do think far too much about my future.'

Edwina looked down at the floor. 'I had my daughter adopted,' she said quietly. 'Sometimes I wish I hadn't.' Her mouth tightened. 'My brother went on and on about my having already brought enough shame on the family by having gone to prison. Father had stood by me through all that, although many others would have given up on me. That's what my brother wanted to do.'

'Your brother doesn't believe in women having the vote?'

'Does he hell!' Edwina's eyes glinted. 'His poor wife is right under his heel. And, of course, getting pregnant was all my fault! I must have led the fellow on! You can imagine the type, can't you?'

'Did you love the father? Was he killed in the war?'

'Love?' Edwina shrugged. 'Not enough to want to marry him. He was exciting and all for women having the vote. He knew Bertrand Russell and believed in free love. I did at the time. I never told him about the baby.' She smiled. 'But that's all in the past. I wish you luck with your shipowner.'

'Thanks,' said Rebekah politely.

Over the next few weeks she began to view marriage with Joshua differently – to dream of having a family. She would have several children and take them to the farm in Ireland. She asked Joshua about the farm and the animals as they walked past the Floral Pavilion in New Brighton, a seaside resort across the Mersey.

'I've no idea what animals we have.' His voice was disinterested. 'Father tried his hand at farming, but I put a man in and left him to it. Anyway, I told you, I'll try and sell the place when I know where we are with Ireland.'

'I'd love to visit it one more time before you sell it,' said Rebekah.'

'If that's what you'd like,' he said good-humouredly. 'I'll take you there as part of our honeymoon.'

'I haven't said I'll marry you yet,' she murmured.

The humour vanished from his eyes. 'No, you haven't. But I was presuming you would say yes.' He lifted her hand and kissed her fingers. 'Do say yes now, Rebekah,' he pleaded, 'and we could get engaged on your birthday and married in spring. You'll be wanting a fancy wedding, I suppose?'

'The whole works,' she murmured, trying to imagine what it would be like going to bed with Joshua. He could be passionate, and had it not been for Daniel she might have been able to view marriage with him as exciting and right, because she would be obeying her father's wishes at last. As it was she still had vague doubts, but supposed that since Daniel she would have them about marrying any other man.

'Well?' he said impatiently.

She decided and kissed his cheek. 'Yes. I'll marry you.'

His face creased into a smile. 'In the spring? By then Lloyd George should have sorted out De Valera and you can have your visit.'

Rebekah hoped so because the peace talks had been in danger of breaking down.

There seemed to be unrest everywhere in the

following months. In September there were riots in Liverpool when the growing numbers of unemployed staged a protest and charged the Walker Art Gallery. They came up against the police who used their truncheons. Blood splattered the walls of the foyer but no one was killed. It was horrible, thought Rebekah. Violence did not solve anything. A meeting between leaders of Sinn Fein and the British government took place in October despite there still being disturbances, but at last it seemed that a Free Ireland was in sight.

Rebekah, remembering conversations with Daniel, experienced a deep sadness. But there was something else that was causing her sorrow. She had still heard nothing from Brigid and could only presume that her sympathy was with her brother and therefore she did not wish to see Rebekah. She was too proud to write again or to visit. She did miss the whole family but realised with the changes soon to be made in her own life, the split might well have been inevitable.

In December Joshua bought Rebekah a diamond and ruby ring on her twenty-first birthday and took her to Lyon's State restaurant where they dined and danced.

Her aunt bought her a secondhand car. A Tin Lizzie four-seater, it had side and rear lamps, which frequently went out because they were oil lit. The headlights, though, were electric and ran directly off the engine. When it was revved up they were bright but when it idled they only let out a dull glow. Rebekah loved it and immediately took her aunt for a drive, having a little trouble with the gears. There were two forward ones, bottom and top, operated by a pedal. Neutral was halfway, but she soon learnt she could only stay in neutral if the handbrake was on. Still, it was her very own car. Her aunt enjoyed the drive but was not pleased when Rebekah told her about the engagement and when she was getting married. 'I had hoped you would have stayed with me longer. He's marrying thee for thy money, my dear.' Her voice was agitated.

'He's got money,' responded Rebekah, sitting on the rug in front of the fire. She added in exasperation: 'It's what Papa would have wanted! He mentioned it the last time we spoke. It's the least I can do to make amends for the worry I gave him. I nearly ran away with someone, just like Mama!'

'But he stopped thee?' Her aunt's cherubic mouth pursed. 'He would, the hypocrite! Who was it? What happened?'

'He was a sailor and went down with his ship,' murmured Rebekah briefly, not wanting to go into further explanations.

Esther's hands paused on her knitting and she surprised Rebekah again by saying, 'I loved a sailor once but he was utterly unsuitable. I didn't need my father to tell me that. He came into St Anne's Centre and was different to anybody else I knew. He was a charmer and I thought I might have been able to change him, but he didn't want to be changed and I wasn't going to.' She smiled grimly and started knitting again. 'Sometimes I wonder how it would have been if I hadn't been me but thy mother. Still, that's the past and I can only hope thou won't rue the day thee marries Mr Green.'

She could not hope it any more than Rebekah as the days passed. In January a Free Irish government was set up and the keys of Dublin Castle handed over to the Dáil. A peace treaty was confirmed under a new President, Arthur Griffiths. All seemed to be going well.

As winter turned to spring there was one person in the household happy about the approaching wedding day, although neither her aunt nor Hannah was attending the ceremony because it was in an Anglican church.

'We'll have a bit of peace at last,' said the maid with obvious satisfaction as she wielded the heavy iron on Rebekah's silk underwear.

'I'm not going to America, dear Hannah,' murmured Rebekah, hurriedly removing her knickers.

Hannah gave her an ugly look. 'He'll soon stop thy gallop, miss. A couple of babies and thee'll know what life's about.'

'I already do. Did you ever have any children, Hannah?' asked Rebekah with an innocent air.

Hannah's dark eyes glistened. 'Thee thinks thee's smart. But if thee dies in childbed, I'll have the last laugh.'

Rebekah smiled twistedly. 'You don't pull any punches, do you, Hannah? But I'll survive, just to spite you, and visit often just so we can stay friends.' She blew her a kiss and left the room, wishing the maid did not hate her so much.

Rebekah chose Edwina for her bridesmaid. Her aunt did not approve of the choice. 'She's no maid,' she muttered. 'Surely thou can find someone else more respectable?'

'There is no one else,' said Rebekah, controlling her impatience and thinking that at least once she was married she would be mistress of her own home, though deeply regretted that Brigid was not her bridesmaid and Daniel her groom, but there was no getting out of it now. Joshua had been jilted once before and however nervous she was she could not serve him such a turn. For better or for worse, in a few days' time she would marry him.

CHAPTER SEVENTEEN

Rebekah was feeling faint, unreal, wondering if anyone had ever passed out at their own wedding. That morning she had wanted to run away but Edwina's timely arrival with the bouquet of spring flowers had caused her to pull herself together. Her white-gloved hand tightened on Mr McIntyre's arm, because it was he she had asked to give her away, despite Joshua's disapproval; he had offered an elderly uncle whom she had never met. To her surprise Aunt Esther had changed her mind, almost at the last minute, about coming to the wedding, and now sat as stiff as a poker in a sparsely populated pew as the organ played 'Here comes the Bride'. Some of the older children from the Orphanage – boys in sailor suits and girls in blue dresses and white pinafores – sat a few rows behind her.

It was after all not a splendid social affair because Joshua had come round to mentioning his being left at the altar before. 'I'd rather not have exactly the same crowd,' he had muttered. 'Just a few selected people.' So there were to be only twenty at the Breakfast to be held in his house. Rebekah had considered asking him about his first fiancée but he had frozen her off. She wondered if he had really loved her and was curious enough to want to ask questions but did not care to insist when it was obvious he did not want to talk.

The aisle was longer than Rebekah remembered but still not long enough. A few more seconds and she would reach Joshua, where he stood with his best man, David Beecham, who was prematurely bald, and owned a shipyard. She wondered why he had not asked his cousin, Mr Eaton.

She was there and her knees were knocking. After a brief glance at Joshua, handsome in his morning suit, Rebekah turned and gave her bouquet to Edwina, who winked at her. Suddenly it did not matter what she did or said, she thought vaguely, deep inside she still belonged to Daniel.

Conversation bubbled, hissed and buzzed about Rebekah's ears, as, champagne glass in hand, she circulated among her guests, heedless of the fact that the trailing lace veil she wore was in danger of being trodden on.

A grey kid-gloved hand suddenly gripped her

duchesse satin sleeve, causing her to stop, and she found herself being scrutinised by a pair of reptilian eyes. 'I hope you're not too young.' The voice was gruff. 'The other one seemed sensible enough and able to handle Joshua, but she let me down. It was Emma, no doubt. Their mother was never strong and could behave very strangely. Emma was like her, and one can't blame Joshua for putting her in that place in Formby-by-the-Sea. It was just as well she went the way she did, leaving the field clear for you.'

'What place?' asked Rebekah.

The woman ignored her question. 'Give him a few children and I'm sure he'll be all right. War unsettles men. You read about it in the newspapers all the time.' She patted Rebekah's arm and before she could recover from her astonishment, the elderly woman had crossed over to Esther who was peering curiously at a china statuette.

Edwina suddenly appeared at Rebekah's elbow. 'That was Amelia Green,' she marvelled. 'I never thought of her being related to the shipping Greens.'

Rebekah thoughtfully sipped her champagne and gazed at the old lady and her aunt. 'They're a pair of characters. They'd look good on the mantelshelf if you could shrink them.'

'Shrink your Aunt Esther and Amelia Green!' Edwina grinned. 'She'd knock you out with her umbrella first. She was a suffragette. What advice was she giving you? To stand up to your man?'

Rebekah shook her head and surprised her friend by saying, 'What's at Formby-by-the-Sea besides the sea?'

Edwina shrugged. 'I've seldom been there. There's a village and a lighthouse . . . woods and fields. They grow asparagus. Why? You're not going there on honeymoon, are you?' she said jokingly.

'The honeymoon is a secret,' said Joshua, making them both jump as he came up behind them. He filled both their glasses.

'What's so secret about Ireland?' said Rebekah, raising her glass to him.

'Ireland!' Edwina spluttered out champagne. 'If you heard Father on the subject you wouldn't be talking about going to Ireland. It's still much too dangerous for a honeymoon.'

'My sentiments exactly,' said Joshua, putting the bottle on a convenient occasional table.

Rebekah's smile faded. 'But you promised! You said—'

'My dear, you said when the fighting ends,' he interrupted in a gentle voice. 'The fighting still goes on and it's not just in Belfast, where it broke out first after the truce. It's happening all over the place because North and South can't agree where the borders should be. It could end in civil war because the Dáil is at outs with itself. It's what one expects of amateurs in government. But at least if there's a civil war they'll be killing each other and not British soldiers. My man's already been threatened and we had a fire at the farm.'

'You never told me,' stammered Rebekah, her fingers tightening on the stem of the glass. 'How much of it was destroyed?'

'It's still standing but that's all I know. Now let's change the subject. We'll be leaving soon and I want to have a few words with David.'

He left Rebekah and Edwina staring at each other. 'It's for the best,' said the older woman weakly.

Rebekah swore and downed her drink in one go.

'Where are we?' Rebekah stretched and yawned. Disappointment and doubt had crowded in once she had known there was no Ireland at the end of the journeying and she had drunk too much champagne. Only vaguely did she remember boarding the train.

'Chester, my dear.' Joshua's gaze washed over her. 'I'm sure you'll like it. It's very attractive – medieval in places. The Romans were here, and it has some decent shops. If you're good, I'll let you have some money to spend.'

'If I'm good?' She stared at him.

'Don't look so frightened, darling. I'm sure you will be.' He smiled and took their cases from the luggage rack, leaving the carriage.

Rebekah's throat tightened with nerves but she held her head high, wrapped the white fox fur around her shoulders and concentrated on walking in a straight line as she followed him.

Joshua's choice of honeymoon hotel could not have been more perfect if your taste ran to oak beams and white-painted plaster, luxury and a view of the tree-lined River Dee. She wondered whose money they were spending, his or hers.

As she stood gazing out of the window, steeling herself to make a move to take off her clothes and don the white silk nightdress, he said, 'Come and undress me.'

'What?' Her voice came out as a harsh whisper.

'You heard me, my sweet. Come away from the window and do as I tell you.'

Rebekah turned and looked at him. He had taken off his jacket and was in his shirt sleeves. There was a glass of whisky in his hand. 'I'm tired,' she stammered.

'Of course you are. The sooner you're in bed the better.' He crooked his finger. 'Come, my darling. It's natural that you'll be a little nervous but I'll be good to you.'

Her hands curled into fists. 'Can't I have a drink?'

'You've drunk enough.'

'But it's our wedding night.' She cleared her throat. 'A drink to celebrate?'

Suddenly the smile was wiped from his face. 'I want you to remember this night, not be in a drunken stupor! Now come here, or must I fetch you?' he barked.

Rebekah moved, frightened by Joshua's change of mood. It was all right for him to drink but not her it seemed. There was a glitter in his eyes that reminded her of her father when he had beaten her that day she had walked to the bay with Daniel. She stopped a foot away from him, her eyes fixed on his tie. How she wished he was Daniel.

Suddenly Joshua's arm shot out and his fingers fastened on the front of her peach chiffon blouse, pinching her skin so that she cried out and struggled. Relentlessly he pulled her against him. 'What is the matter with you?' he said through gritted teeth. 'Although your shyness does you credit, it's a bit late. You weren't averse to my attention before. I hope it's for the right reasons, my darling, and that you are a virgin? That O'Neill didn't have you?'

'Why do you have to bring up Daniel now?' said Rebekah unevenly. 'Why won't you let him lie in peace?'

'Because I hate him,' said Joshua, emphasising every word.

'What? Why do you hate him?' Her voice had risen. 'What has he ever done to you?'

'Keep your voice down!' he muttered. 'O'Neill turned against me like the others! Dared to tell me, "You're making a mistake, sir!" Called me a coward!' His chest heaved. 'Rebekah, don't you see what that does to a man?' His pale eyes widened. 'I thought he liked me! Even my father was the same. My brother was first with him, and he spoilt Emma soft. I was sent to Ireland to learn about farming and hated it. I wanted to come back but he said no.'

'You said you knew nothing about the animals on the farm – that you'd spent hardly any time in Ireland.' She was puzzled. 'Why lie?'

His mouth tightened. 'I didn't want to talk about it. The war came and I joined the navy. I'd always loved ships. I met O'Neill when the government requisitioned his ship. We were friendly at first.' He took a deep breath.

'And?' she demanded.

'He questioned my judgement. My knowing what was right. He was as bad as father, not believing I could have done better by Green's than my brother. He made a right mess of everything. It was a good job he died when he did or we'd have been bankrupt. Then I met Muriel and fell in love.' He laughed. 'She left me a note saying that she had only been going to marry me because she thought she needed a man after her fiancé was killed in the war, but at the last minute she couldn't go through with it. If she hadn't gone to Africa as a missionary, I would have cooked her goose.' He smiled. 'Now you're a sensible girl, my darling, so you'll do just what I say, won't you?'

'Will I?' she stammered.

'Of course. Come here.'

She stared at him, suddenly too frightened to move. What had he meant about cooking Muriel's goose? She jumped when he caught hold of her arm and instinctively tried to pull away but he seized her other wrist and, crossing her arms, twisted her round and flung her on to the bed. She rolled over and almost managed to get to her feet but he was too quick for her. He pushed her down on the bed, leaning over her and gripping her with his knees one either side of her. He tore open her blouse and despite her attempts to free herself, dragged it off. 'Joshua, please don't be so rough,' she cried.

'Why? I thought you girls liked being manhandled. You read about it all in *The Sheik*,' he said in a clipped voice, and hit her arm away.

'That's only a book,' she stuttered, on the edge of a scream, as he forced her to part with her chemise with a couple of slaps. 'I don't want to do it,' she stammered. 'I don't—'

'It's too late for that.' His eyes sparkled. 'You're my wife and I can do what I want with you. Fight as much as you like, I quite enjoy a struggle.'

She suddenly remembered how it had been with Daniel and could have screamed. 'I won't fight you.'

'What a pity, but perhaps wise.' He smiled as with one hand he kept both of hers imprisoned over her head. She did not move as he forced up her skirt and took off her cami-knickers. She would lie as still as if she was dead. Her eyes closed as Joshua fondled her breasts and crushed her with his weight. A sob bubbled in her throat as he poked at her down below, was pushing, forcing his way inside her. Her whole body tensed. It hurt! She had not expected it to hurt. Her fingers and toes curled, teeth clenched. She bit back a scream but could not prevent a groan. Dear God, make it be over soon! He ground his way into her. Up down, up down, up down! His stomach slapped against hers and he was moaning. A scream broke from her as he pressed down on her with terrible force. A few minutes later she realised what Daniel must have done to prevent her having a baby, and also that she no longer wanted a child by Joshua.

The breakfast tray had just been taken away. Rebekah had managed half a slice of toast and a cup of tea but Joshua had eaten a full English breakfast. Now he lay back against the pillows, smoking. 'You were a virgin. I'm glad you didn't cheat me,' he murmured, opening the morning paper.

Rebekah wanted to say, Yes, I did, but dare not. 'You hurt me,' she whispered. Down below she throbbed as if that part of her had a pulse of its own. Her nipples were sore and her ribs felt as if they had been crushed in a vice. He had taken her twice more during the night and that morning.

'It was inevitable. I didn't really expect you to enjoy it. Some women don't. Especially at first.' He tapped ash into the ashtray.

She thought how she had enjoyed that very first time with Daniel. 'You made sure I wouldn't enjoy it by mentioning Daniel and treating me like an object for your pleasure,' she could not prevent herself from saying. 'Why tell me that you hated him? Why last night?'

'Because you said you loved him and you've never once said you love me,' he said coldly.

'But that's bloody stupid!' She ran a hand through her short hair. 'You're not going to make me love you by behaving the way you did.'

'Don't swear, darling. It's not ladylike!' There was a sudden seething in Joshua's face as he flung aside the newspaper and grabbed hold of her arm. 'Why did you marry me? One of the reasons I married you was for your money, but you with all your talk of its not being important wouldn't have married me for mine. So why?'

Rebekah suddenly laughed. 'I'm a fool! Aunt Esther said you were marrying me for my money! I should have listened to her but I thought it couldn't be true because you seemed to have plenty of it. I was wrong!'

'The young never listen to their elders the way they should. I'm not broke, my dear, but more money is always useful.' He forced her against him. 'But you still haven't answered my question. Why? If you answer me correctly then we could be happy.'

She stared at him. 'You want me to say that I love

you.' He made no answer, just looked at her, and she experienced a feeling of pity. 'I wish I could say I did. I'm sorry.'

For a moment he was silent then he pushed her back against the pillows. 'Don't be sorry for me, my dear,' he growled. 'Be sorry for yourself. I married you because I knew it would make O'Neill mad.'

She scowled. 'He's dead! Why do you have to behave like this? Couldn't we at least try to please each other?'

Joshua opened his mouth and she waited but he did not speak, only shaking his head before sliding over her. 'I'll make you forget him. By Jove, I will!' She tried not to tense as he crushed her beneath him but could not help herself. He began to bite her throat. Her fists clenched and she started to feel angry. Why did he have to hurt her? 'Hit me,' he mumbled. 'Let's make a fight of it.'

'No!'

He stilled and sat back on his heels, frowning down at her. 'Why won't you? You want to hit me, don't you? Emma often wanted to. She threw things. Hit me twice and cut my head open, the little Madam.'

'It must be the Quaker in me coming out that doesn't like fighting,' she said with an edge to her voice.

'Little Miss Quaker.' He laughed and seizing her shoulders, shook her violently, causing her to bite her tongue. 'Respond my sweet, or else!'

Rebekah wiped blood from her mouth. 'No. You've brought Daniel into this, so I will. You want me to pretend in some twisted way that he can still be hurt by what you do. Well, I can pretend too.'

'What do you mean?'

She smiled. 'You're so clever. Think.'

Joshua did not move but his mouth quivered and she thought for a moment he might cry. She waited for him to say something but he just reached for his cheroot case. He lit up and took deep lungfuls of smoke until the end glowed red. Then, before she realised what he was about, he stubbed the cheroot several times on her shoulder. She reared up, gasping with pain.

'You will never get pleasure imagining that I am him. Never! Never!' He got out of bed. 'I think we'll go home today. Get yourself dressed.'

She stared at him, her breasts heaving as she regained her breath. 'But we've only just come.'

'Now!' he yelled.

Rebekah was out of the bed in a trice, scared in case he burnt her again. She was certain her shoulder was blistering but dare not look at it. What was she going to do? Keep her mouth shut and not provoke him would be the wiser course. Be sweet and nice and a dutiful wife. Oh God! What had she done?

She dressed hurriedly, trying to ignore his watching her as she placed a handkerchief over the burn, and thinking all the time that coping with Hannah had been easy compared with the future she now visualised.

Why hadn't she given it more consideration? Because she had not been thinking realistically, she supposed, believing Joshua madly in love with her and incapable of hurting someone he loved. Money! He had married her for her money. When she looked back on their life in Ireland, when her mother had always seemed to be penny pinching, she felt slightly hysterical. What good had it done her father being thrifty? Suddenly she wanted to laugh and laugh, but instead she jumped when Joshua snapped. 'What are you stopping and smiling at? You've got nothing to be happy about. Last night was only the beginning. Now move or we'll miss the next train.'

Rebekah did not tell him her thoughts, only slipping her arms into her tan and cream dog-tooth checked jacket. She packed her nightdress and soiled underwear, then stood waiting for him to give his next order. At least, she thought, once back in Liverpool, you'll be out all day. But the nights! The thought of all the nights she would have to spend with him made her fearful. Suddenly she remembered what she had said to Edwina about being miserable in comfort and thought how she seemed to go through life saying stupid things. Why had she not foreseen cruelty and fear? It was not as if she hadn't come in contact with them. Little Mrs Rimmer, she had suffered both. 'And survived,' said a little voice in Rebekah's head. 'You'll come through if you use a little commonsense.'

She stared at her husband as he picked up the suitcase, and smiled.

'What are you smiling at now?' he muttered.

She raised her eyebrows. 'You'd rather I went down weeping? I am a bride and so I'm supposed to be happy.'

'Of course you are.' He smiled unexpectedly. 'Perhaps we should stay?'

'That's up to you.'

'What do you want to do?'

'Whatever you want,' she lied.

He put down the case and took off his coat. Still smiling, he unknotted his tie. 'Take off your clothes. This time let's see some activity. You can stroke, bite, suck – anything! If you hurt me, I don't mind. A bit of pain heightens sensations, don't you think?'

She gave him an uncertain look. 'I don't know—'

'My dear, you do. Now don't waste time. And afterwards I'll take you to the Cathedral. You'll enjoy that. And we must get some ointment for the burn tomorrow. I'm sorry about that.'

With a sick feeling in her stomach Rebekah obeyed him, and he seemed to be satisfied with what she did, although he landed her a couple of blows in her ribs for pulling away too soon. Afterwards she would have preferred being alone and suggested that maybe he would like to read the Sunday papers while she went to the Cathedral, but he said certainly not.

As she sat in a pew staring at the intricately

carved stalls in the choir with Joshua beside her, she felt divorced not only from her surroundings but from reality. She was no longer the Rebekah she had been twenty-four hours ago, but felt a poor creature unable to stick up for herself. Surely this could not be what God intended when it had been written 'Wives be subject to your husband?' She was confused, deeply unhappy, and filled with dread.

It was just as bad for her that night but this time Joshua too seemed to be feeling no pleasure. 'You're holding back on me,' he muttered, slapping her face. 'You're thinking of him, aren't you?'

'When you're giving me pain, I can't think of anything but that,' she gasped.

'As long as you're not thinking of him,' he said in a satisfied voice, and carried on hurting her. It was then she began to hate him.

The next day he suggested that he went shopping with her. 'You'll be bored,' said Rebekah, powdering her face where a bruise showed, and desperate to be alone.

'You don't bore me, my sweet,' murmured her husband, putting down the morning paper and picking up a silver-handled cane. 'At least, not yet.'

He pulled her hand through his arm and it would seem to an onlooker that they were in harmony as they strolled in the direction of the medieval Rows that ran along Watergate, Bridge, and Eastgate Streets in the centre of the city. One had to go up steps from the street to walk along the covered arcades with shops running along one side. Rebekah was in no mood for shopping but took the money Joshua handed her. Probably hers, she thought resentfully. She bought a new hat in pink straw with a deep crown and a dipping brim at the sides, a magazine and a bar of Fry's chocolate cream. He did not ask for the change and she did not offer it. She decided then that she would save it for a rainy day.

They stayed two more days in Chester and then went back to Liverpool, Rebekah still suffering from a sense of unreality.

'Welcome home, sir, ma'am.' The maid, a smile on her red-cheeked face, bobbed a brief curtsey. 'There's a fire in the living room. I'll make some tea and bring it in.'

'Thank you, Janet.' At least, thought Rebekah, she is pleased to see me.

And so it proved. Once Joshua went to work the next morning, the maid came in to discuss what was needed that day and to say how nice it was to have a mistress in the house after all these years. 'One can't count Miss Emma, if you don't mind my saying, mam. She was no good at being in charge, always needed looking after. Very highly strung she was.' She smiled. 'I think, though, you and I can work together.'

'I'm sure we can,' said Rebekah, returning her smile. 'First things first – food. I'm going shopping.

You can deal with the clothes we brought home that need washing.'

Janet looked surprised. 'You're not phoning the shops, mam?'

'No, I'll take my car.' Joshua had given her housekeeping money that morning and she planned using Tin Lizzie to go into town and shop at St John's Market, where she had often gone with Brigid. The dinner she planned would not cost as much if she bought there sometimes, and what was saved could be put in her hoard. She thought of Brigid and how she had spoken on the *Samson* of changing husbands characters. Only dynamite, she thought, would change Joshua. At that moment she had every intention of being a dutiful wife and housekeeper but she had vague thoughts about its not being forever.

CHAPTER EIGHTEEN

Rebekah put petrol in the tank of her car and drove away from her husband's house. Strangely, as she passed familiar streets, the feeling of unreality faded. Impulsively she decided to call on her aunt. The sun was shining and she would not be seeing Joshua for hours.

'So thou's back, is thee?' grunted Hannah on opening the door.

Rebekah looked at her with something akin to affection. 'Thanks for the welcome. Is my aunt in?'

'She's in.' Hannah thrust her face close to hers. 'We've been managing fine without thee. So there's no need for thee to be always showing thy face.'

Rebekah drew back, not wanting anyone to look too closely at her. 'I've come to take her out,' she said promptly. 'I thought we'd go to town and then for a trip in the country.'

'Her knee's bad,' said Hannah, folding her arms across her thin breasts. 'Got to rest it.'

'You told me that she should keep on the move,' retorted Rebekah, and pushing past the maid went up the lobby to steal her aunt from Hannah's clutches.

'This really is good of thee, Becky love,' said Esther, holding on to her hat as her niece drove along a road in Formby-on-Sea which led to the coast. 'I've never been this far out of Liverpool.'

'I thought you'd enjoy it.' Rebekah glanced at her. It was curiosity that had taken her in this direction and they would have to be turning back soon if Joshua's meal was to be on the table by the time he returned home. She glanced about her, not sure what she was looking for, and then suddenly saw it. There was a set of imposing wrought iron gates and through them she could make out a large building. There was a notice which read 'Asylum for Mentally Afflicted Gentlefolk'. She went a little further up the road and then turned round.

Rebekah often thought of Emma in the weeks that followed, questioning what Amelia Green had said to her the day of the wedding, not only about Emma and her mother, but Joshua too. War unsettled men, she had said. Had war inflicted on her husband the peculiar fascination he had with pain? There were times when she did not know whether to be glad or sorry that the tweeny slept out and Janet's room was so far from the large bright bedroom overlooking the park that she and Joshua shared.

She did most of what he asked her without comment but she would not use the cat o' nine tails. Something inside her would not allow her to vent her hatred in that way. Perhaps it was because she knew that was exactly what he wanted – for her to show passionate response to his mishandling of her. She suffered his calculated assault on her body without a struggle. Only once did he hit her with the whip and afterwards he astonished her by crying at the sight of her blood and saying he was sorry. She just could not understand him.

There were evenings when they entertained some of his associates and he gave her money for a new dress, telling her just what he expected of her. She would go to Bold Street and buy a new gown, never spending the amount he gave her, and what was over she put away.

If she stayed in, the days seemed endless. Her job had finished when she married but she still went to visit Mrs Dodd. 'You don't look well, girl,' she said, staring at Rebekah. 'Have you been caught?'

'You mean, am I having a baby?' she murmured, bobbing Lily on her knee. 'No.' She would have added, Thank God, but that would have meant explanations and she had no intention of telling anybody what she suffered at Joshua's hands. Not even Edwina, who had been a VAD during the war and was now a member of the Red Cross. She was suggesting that

Rebekah, who had been a junior member in Ireland, should come along to the meetings and be useful.

In the end she agreed to go along, and life seemed very real and earnest during the weeks when spring turned to summer. Civil war was threatening in Ireland. Edwina and her father went on holiday. Her aunt also went away on some peace conference. Joshua mentioned that he might have to go to New York on business. She prayed that he would go but the days passed and he did not mention it again.

One afternoon she was in town, having left the car at home because she wanted to save money on petrol, when she noticed that there was an Ethel M. Dell film on at the cinema. Earlier in the year Ethel had got engaged to a Colonel Savage. The paper had said that her books had made her a fortune. Rebekah wished that she could get her hands on her money so that she could leave Joshua.

The film was guaranteed to melt the stoniest hearts and Rebekah came out of the cinema feeling a little better for it. She paused to pull on her gloves but a poke in the back caused her to stumble. A hand at her elbow prevented her from hitting the ground.

'Are yer all right, luv?'

It was a voice Rebekah recognised. 'Joe?' She turned and saw him with Brigid. Unexpectedly, tears filled her eyes.

For a moment neither of the women spoke. Then Brigid said faintly, 'Yer not going to cry, are yer?

What have you got to cry about? Didn't yer get just what yer wanted when yer married his lordship!'

Rebekah blinked back the tears. 'So you know about that?'

'I saw it in the *Echo*, and I saw it coming anyway.' Brigid squared her shoulders. 'But there wasn't any need for yer to leave Ma's party the way you did without a word of explanation. Although our Pat told us what happened.'

Rebekah's expression froze. 'Your Pat? I suppose that's why you never answered my letter? You took his side.'

'What letter?' said Brigid, frowning.

'The one I sent, saying that Pat was getting too serious and I didn't want that. We'd agreed just to be friends. I supposed he gave his own version of the story so you weren't prepared to believe mine.'

Brigid exchanged glances with Joe, who shrugged. 'Don't look at me. I know nothing about it.'

'I never received any letter,' said Brigid earnestly. 'I would have answered it if I had.'

'Well, I sent one.'

Brigid shook her head. 'I'm sorry I didn't answer it but I thought you'd finished with us because of his lordship.'

Rebekah stared at her. 'We were friends.'

Joe's glance took in Rebekah's expression, then Brigid's. 'Listen, luv, I'll go and have a pint over the road. I think you two have some talking to do. I'll give yer a quarter of an hour and then meet you at the tram stop.'

'All right.' Brigid did not watch him go. Her gaze was fixed on Rebekah. 'Yer can see why I believed our Pat. I knew that his lordship wanted you when we were in New York. When I read about the wedding, I was convinced yer'd chucked Pat and ended our friendship because of him.'

'It's not true!' Rebekah cleared her throat.

There was a short silence before Brigid said fiercely, 'But yer married him! Where does that leave all yer talk about loving Daniel and never forgetting him?'

'I haven't forgotten him! But he's dead.'

Brigid's eyes flashed. 'He's dead but our Veronica thought she saw him the other day.'

'She couldn't have,' said Rebekah, feeling as if her heart had suddenly sunk into her stomach.

'That's what I said. But it's funny all the same.'

'I don't find it funny.' Rebekah suddenly could not bear being still and almost ran across the cobbled road to the tram stop. She turned and stared at Brigid who had followed her. 'I'd like to believe it! If you'd said you'd seen him, I probably would, even though it's impossible.'

'I know.' Brigid sighed. 'I bumped into his brother the other day down at the Pierhead. After all this time I thought that queer. I asked him how he was and whether he'd been living in America. I said how sorry I was about Daniel being drowned and how upset you'd been at the time.'

Rebekah's expression barely concealed her emotions. 'I'm surprised you spared a thought for me if you believed I'd just walk out without a word. Besides, you'd be wasting your time if you expected Shaun to weep for me. He hated me. So you probably made his day!' She dug her fists deep into her jacket pockets. 'What was he doing in Liverpool anyway?'

Brigid shrugged. 'I didn't ask. I presumed he was over here seeing his cousins, but when I mentioned him to Maureen she said that she hadn't seen hide nor tail of him.'

'Probably up to no good,' said Rebekah politely. 'Remember the telegraph wires being cut on the Wirral? They got Sinn Feiners for it? I bet he's been up to something like that! Some Republicans are still at war with the British.'

'You mean – he's a terrorist and was making a quick getaway on the Irish ferry?' Brigid's voice rose to a squeak.

Rebekah stared at her and the hurt that Brigid's words had inflicted caused her to say, 'He's a troublemaker! And for all you know the police might have been watching him and now could be watching you!'

Brigid's mouth fell open and she crossed herself quickly, glancing about her. At the sight of a policeman standing on the other side of the road she darted behind Rebekah. It proved too much for her when she had had nothing to laugh at for ages, and she burst out laughing. 'You idiot! Nobody's going to arrest you!'

For a moment Brigid did not move then she smiled. 'You thing! Yer had me going then!'

Rebekah's eyes still wore a warm expression. 'You hurt my feelings. I do still care for Daniel, but I wanted to please my father and I wanted children. It's all right for you. There's your Pat and your Kath and her kids. Then there's your other sisters and cousins and aunts and uncles. I only have Aunt Esther.'

For a moment Brigid was silent. 'Veronica misses you. Why don't yer come round some time? Our Pat's home at the moment, but he left Green's and does long trips to Australia now. He'll be sailing in a day or so.'

Rebekah's expression softened. 'Thanks. Perhaps I will.'

'Do yer love his lordship?' asked Brigid tentatively.

'Don't ask daft questions.'

Brigid burst out, 'Are you happy?'

'I'm as miserable as sin. If he pops off, I won't grieve.'

Brigid stared at her. 'Yer terrible!' She started to laugh.

'Aren't I just?' Rebekah's laugh was hollow. 'I want to leave him.'

'Yer what?' The laughter died on Brigid's face.

'You heard me. He's a real – monster.'

'What d'yer mean, he's a monster?'

Rebekah shrugged. 'I can't tell you everything now. Joe'll be back in a minute.'

Brigid scrutinised her face. 'We'll have to meet again,' she said. 'Soon.'

Rebekah nodded. 'When does Joe go back?'

'In a couple of days. We can meet on Friday. I have a half day.'

'Right.' Rebekah freed a shaky breath. 'You can't know how glad I am that I went to see Ethel M. Dell.'

'I do,' said Brigid, and hugged her. 'Here's yer tram. I'll meet yer outside the new Palladium on West Derby Road at one.'

Rebekah nodded and caught the tram. Her mood was buoyant as she travelled home.

Joshua was there before her and her spirits sank at the sour expression on his face as he looked up from his newspaper. 'You're late.'

'I went to Cooper's in town to get that special cheese you like.' Impulsively she put her arms around his neck and kissed his cheek. 'How are things in the shipyards now that the engineers have returned to work? Will you be getting that ship converted?'

'Probably.' He looked at her, an arrested expression on his face, then folded the newspaper and put his arm round her waist, squeezing it. 'That trip I mentioned to New York – I've got to go in a couple of days. I could be away for a few weeks.'

For a moment Rebekah could not speak for joy

but she schooled herself not to show her true feelings. 'I'd go with you but I think I'd find it too upsetting still,' she said, infusing a touch of regret in her voice. 'It's only now that I can think of Mama and Papa without it hurting. Memories would come flooding back and we don't want that, do we, just when I think I might be forgetting the past.'

'You're talking about O'Neill?' He pulled her against him and frowned into her eyes.

'Who?' she said lightly.

Joshua smiled. 'I told you I'd make you forget him.' He stroked her shoulder, and his fingers wandered over her breast. 'He could never give you all what you have here with me.'

'No.' She forced herself to press her lips against his. 'You aren't too angry at me staying at home?'

'I understand. Although you'll have to make up for it tonight. Perhaps tonight will be the night. I would have thought you'd have started having a baby by now.'

'I'm not.'

A disgruntled expression settled over his face and she kissed him quickly, knowing that it was going to be difficult because she had a period.

Rebekah closed the door and her dancing footsteps echoed round the hall as she spun round and round with Moggy in her arms. 'He's gone! He's gone!' she whispered in the cat's flickering ear. 'And he won't be back for weeks!' Perhaps she should leave him now before she did start having his baby? She had saved forty pounds and Joshua had left her money to live on. She could get a job. Any job! And if she pawned a few things that would bring in extra money. The white fox furs could go. They reminded her of that honeymoon in Chester. She thought of how Joshua had spoken of his hatred for Daniel and then shook her head to rid herself of the memory, considering instead how Veronica had believed that she had seen Daniel. Perhaps she had mistaken him for Shaun? They were brothers after all and Shaun might have grown more like Daniel over the last couple of years. She would mention that, and about pawning the furs, to Brigid whom she was meeting in an hour's time.

Brigid shook her head uncomprehendingly and stroked the white fox furs. 'I know men can be cruel, but to hit you and want to beat you . . . I don't understand it.'

Rebekah tucked her arm in Brigid's. 'I haven't told you the half of it, and I'm not going to,' she said lightly. 'But you do see why I want to leave him?'

'Yes. Although – don't you think he'll come after you? The law would be on his side, you know? He could make you go back and he'd be mad at yer, wouldn't he?'

'I know.' Rebekah felt cold and sweaty at the thought. 'That's why I have to get away now, before he comes back. Can you pawn the furs for me?'

'Of course I can.' Brigid smiled and her voice

was deliberately cheerful. 'I'll take them to Ol' Solly. He'll give you a good price. He's an old Jew but he's fair. Mam always swore by him in the old days.'

'Good.' Rebekah placed the furs back in the brown paper bag and they began to walk.

There was a short silence before Brigid said, 'Yer know that yer welcome to come and stay with us. The only thing is, he might find you.'

'I know. It's the same with Aunt Esther.' She cleared her throat. 'I could go to Ireland. I doubt if Joshua would follow me there because he hates the plate. He hates Daniel! One of the reasons he married me was because he thought it would hurt Daniel. Ridiculous, when he's dead.'

Brigid dropped her gaze to the pavement. 'Is he, though?' Her voice sounded strained.

Rebekah stared at her. 'Are you saying that you believe Veronica? Because it could have been Shaun she saw.'

'It's not just Veronica.' Brigid lifted her head. 'It's our Pat. *He* says Daniel's alive.'

For several moments Rebekah could not speak while the words penetrated like sharp knives into her brain. Suddenly she was reliving that terrible time after the disaster. It had seemed incredible that Daniel could be dead and she had not believed it. But Shaun had said he was. Why should he lie to her? *Why?* An hysterical laugh burst inside her. *Why!* Shaun had wanted to break up her relationship with

Daniel! And Joshua? She stared at Brigid and her fury exploded into words. 'He lied to me! Joshua must have known Daniel was alive! I could kill him – kill him.' Her fists clenched. 'If I had that Cat now I'd—'

'Shhh!' Brigid dragged on her arm. 'I shouldn't have told you like that.'

Rebekah turned on her. 'When did Pat tell you?'

'Yesterday. I told him about seeing yer and just that yer were unhappy – that his lordship was a bit of a monster. Then I spoke about how besotted yer'd been about Daniel on the ship, and how his death had really broken you up. I mentioned what Veronica had said.' She bit her upper lip. 'He laughed and muttered something about yer making your bed and having to lie on it. That he didn't believe yer cared about anybody but yerself, and that Daniel and him were just pawns in some game you'd played. That he'd seen Daniel last winter in some port or other.'

'He did?' croaked Rebekah. 'Did he say whether Daniel mentioned me?'

'He didn't speak to him. Just caught sight of him in a pub.'

'Oh God!' Rebekah suddenly felt faint. 'Perhaps Pat was imagining things.'

'He seemed pretty definite. What are you going to do?'

Rebekah pulled herself together and was silent for a few seconds. 'You can find out if Daniel is still alive by asking his cousin or aunt. I-I don't mean to sound unkind but I wouldn't put it past your Pat just to make it all up so that you could tell me and hurt me. Does that make sense? Or do I sound completely crazy?'

'I don't think our Pat's lying.'

Rebekah nodded. 'Then ask Daniel's cousin for the truth. She might not have wanted to tell you that Shaun had visited. He's a known rebel. For all we know, Daniel might have been there as well.'

Brigid's eyes narrowed. 'Yer mean she could have thought I'd betray him to the police?'

'Yes!'

Brigid's cheeks puffed and then she blew out a breath. 'That could be it – and yer see what this means? It could have been him that Veronica saw.'

'Yes!' Rebekah's lips quivered. 'Oh, Brigid, I've got to see him.'

'He mightn't want to have anything to do with yer when he knows about his lordship,' said Brigid reluctantly.

'And he might! He loved me! He'll understand,' she stammered. 'I thought he was dead, and he must believe I'm dead or he'd have come looking for me.'

'Not necessarily,' said Brigid. 'Perhaps it was just a shipboard romance on his part. Yer don't know.'

A cold shiver raced through Rebekah and for a moment she could not think, then she said, 'I have to find out. You'll ask his cousin?'

Brigid nodded.

'Thanks!' Rebekah hugged her. 'You're my bestest friend.'

'Hmph!' Brigid smiled. 'Yer using me but I'll find out what I can and tell you tomorrow.'

'Bring the kids to Joshua's house and we can go to the park before having tea in the garden.'

'OK. I'd like to see the house,' said Brigid.

They said no more but parted and went their separate ways.

The sun gleamed on thickly leafed trees and lush grass in Newsham Park. Jimmy had brought a ball with him and was booting it as far as he could with his left foot. Veronica was sent to fetch it every time but did not seem to mind. Rebekah was pleased to see them both but glad to have them out of earshot.

'Well?' she demanded, clutching Brigid's arm. 'I've hardly slept. Tell me – he is alive?'

Her friend nodded. 'He's alive and in Ireland.'

Rebekah felt weak with relief. 'Thank God.'

Brigid shook her head. 'Yer haven't got anything to thank Him for yet. Ireland's a terribly dangerous place at the moment. There's divisions in the Provisional Army and the Dáil. There's already fighting and it's almost certain that there'll be open civil war between the Free Irish troops and the Irregulars soon.'

Rebekah nodded. 'It can't be any more dangerous than when the Black and Tans were there. Where in Ireland is he?'

Brigid sighed. 'Yer still going to go?'

'You know I am.'

'He and Shaun are with the Irregulars in Dublin.'

'Dublin!' Rebekah closed her eyes on sudden tears because she knew that she could find her way around the city. 'Have you an address?'

'They seem to move about a bit but Maureen said something about the Four Courts building.'

Rebekah was surprised. 'What's he doing there? Still, I'll be able to find him.'

Brigid shook her head. 'Yer crazy. Yer could be killed stone dead.'

'I've got to go.'

'I'll come with yer if yer like.' Brigid looked away across parkland.

Rebekah smiled. 'Don't be daft.'

Her friend looked at her and said awkwardly, 'When the *Samson* went down we said we'd stick together. Cross our hearts! I feel bad about his lordship. If I'd have known about that letter you sent, I've a feeling yer'd have never married him.'

Rebekah shrugged. 'We'll never know. I appreciate what you're saying but I'm going it alone. Joe would never forgive me if anything happened to you.'

'He wants to marry me.'

'And will you?'

'Mam likes him. He's a good steady bloke. I'm not crazy for him but he'd do anything for me and I'm fond of him. There's not many like him around.'

'No.' Rebekah squeezed her arm. 'He's a good bloke, as you say. Now let's call the kids and have tea.'

That evening Rebekah informed Janet that she was going away for a few weeks and that she could take some time off on full pay.

The next day Rebekah visited her aunt and took the cat with her. Unexpectedly she felt sad because she had no idea if she would ever see her again. 'I'm taking a little holiday, Aunt Esther,' she murmured, not looking her straight in the eye. 'I wondered if you would look after Moggy for me?'

'Hannah won't like it, but I don't mind,' said Esther, taking the cat on to her knee. It purred as she stroked it. 'Where art thou going?'

'London,' she said quickly. 'I've never been before and I thought it's about time I saw the capital of England.'

Her aunt looked up. 'Will thou be away long?'

'A couple of weeks. Joshua's in America.' She fiddled with her teaspoon. 'I'm going with a friend,' she added, completely perjuring herself. 'I'll write if I'm away longer.'

'Well, look after thyself. Don't overdo it.'

'I won't.' She hugged her aunt before hurrying out.

Hannah followed Rebekah up the lobby. 'London,' she said opening the door for her. 'Right den of iniquity that place is. Thee could fall into all kinds of sin without thy husband.'

'Couldn't I just,' retorted Rebekah, amused. 'And

you could get run over by a tram while I'm away. Stop listening at keyholes, Hannah, and take care of Aunt Esther. Don't be putting arsenic in her tea.'

Hannah flushed. 'The very idea,' she said, and slammed the door.

As Rebekah strode up the road she met Edwina. 'Come in and have a chat and a cuppa,' said the older woman.

'Love to,' said Rebekah, flushed with rushing. 'But I can't. I'm going away and have to pack.'

'Where are you going?'

'Joshua's on his way to New York so I thought I'd go to London.'

'London?' Edwina stared at her and grinned. 'Now if you'd said Ireland I wouldn't have been a bit surprised. But maybe you've grown more sensible since marriage.'

'Maybe.' Rebekah smiled. 'Would it be so daft to go to Ireland? The Red Cross go into such situations with their eyes wide open and some would consider them crazy.'

Edwina eyed her thoughtfully. 'You're not bored, are you, and thinking of playing Florence Nightingale? Because if you do, make sure you have a white flag handy.'

Rebekah laughed. 'Of course! But marriage has completely knocked out of me any daft notions I once had.' She lifted a hand in farewell and ran up the road.

A short while later she was on her way to Ireland.

It was a calm crossing but her insides churned and her emotions were in turmoil. What would Daniel say? What would he think? Would he believe her when she told him that his brother and Joshua had deceived her? Surely the same thing had happened to him? Her nerves were all strung up and she could not keep still. She paced the deck as if her existence depended on her walking all the way to the Emerald Isle. She considered what she would find in a country swiftly dividing against itself. There was the provisional army and government led by the one time newspaper man Arthur Griffiths and Michael Collins, pro-treaty men both. They were up against a growing army of Irregulars, who believed republican principles had been betrayed by still retaining British sovereignty, and who had among their supporters De Valera, Rory O'Connor, Liam Mellows and many others. Why had Daniel joined them? She could understand Shaun doing so but Daniel had wanted peace. Doubts crowded into her mind. Perhaps Brigid would be proved right and he would not be pleased to see her. Maybe she should not have come? She slumped on a seat and gazed with unseeing eyes across the sea.

Her first glimpse of the Irish coast brought memories flooding back. A faint rattle of gunfire came to her across the water and with it, fear. For a moment it was as if she was back in the past and all that happened since had not taken place. Then she squared her shoulders and prepared to disembark.

CHAPTER NINETEEN

As Rebekah walked the streets of Dublin she was conscious of a feverish excitement. A number of the shops were closed and shuttered and Free State troops were stopping and questioning people, while carts were held up and searched. The Customs House had been damaged since she was last in town and O'Connell Street with its many hotels was choked by armoured cars. She had hoped to find a room there but instead made for a hotel she knew overlooking St Stephen's Green, away from the centre of activity. She freshened up, took off her wedding and engagement rings, and dropped them in the pocket of a large canvas bag. She also placed in the bag's depths money and – remembering what Edwina had said – a basic first aid kit, Red Cross armband, and small bottle of brandy. Then she went in search of refreshment while she thought about what she was going to do.

Although apprehension had destroyed Rebekah's appetite she drank two cups of tea and ate a slice of bread and butter. The firing of heavy artillery soon shattered the tinkle of teacups and she jumped to her feet, only to sit down when no notice seemed to be taken of what was happening. She caught the eye of a youngish man sitting at the next table. He looked tired and dishevelled. 'What's happening?'

He stubbed out a cigarette. 'Have you been on a desert island that you don't know?' The accent was English.

'I've just come from Liverpool.'

He grimaced. 'You should have stayed there. Rory O'Connor could be planning on making martyrs out of his Irregular troops. They've occupied the Four Courts building since April but now they've been issued with an ultimatum.'

'The Four Courts?' Rebekah gripped the edge of the table.

He nodded. 'The state troops have them surrounded and are telling them to come out. There's a chance that they could be blown sky high if they don't, because there's a cache of ammunition beneath the building. I've been outside all night. There was a dawn raid. Now there are several breaches in the walls – but the Irregulars are refusing to surrender.'

Rebekah's heart began to pound. 'Are all the Irregulars in Four Courts?'

He shook his head. 'They're all over the place. They've taken over several of the hotels in O'Connell Street, so I'd steer clear of that area if I was you.' His voice was kindly. 'In fact, I'd get out of Dublin.' He drained his cup and rose, picking up his trilby from the table. 'Well, duty calls. My editor will have my guts if I miss out on any of the excitement.'

'You're a reporter?'

He nodded and moved away.

The blood seemed to be rushing to Rebekah's head. What were the odds of Daniel still being inside Four Courts? Even fifty-fifty seemed too high and she raced after the reporter. Her fingers fastened on his arm just as he reached the street. He turned with a frown but she smiled disarmingly! 'Can I come with you? I won't get in the way.' She released her hold on his arm.

He stared at her from weary grey eyes. 'You're crazy. It's no place for a woman. You could see some unpleasant sights.'

She made an impatient noise in her throat. 'I was here during the time of the Black and Tans! Besides, I could help. I've done some Red Cross work.'

He shrugged. 'It's a free country. Just don't get in my way.'

Rebekah had no intention of getting in his way. As it was she had difficulty keeping up with him, and if she had not known Dublin well she might have lost him. As they drew nearer the Liffey, the sound of an enormous explosion tore the air. For a moment they froze. Then they were running.

'Press!' shouted the reporter to a group of soldiers clustered around artillery. They both ran on before any one moved to stop them and crossed the bridge.

The gateway to the Four Courts building was blocked by vehicles, and dust and smoke choked the air. The reporter pounced on one of his colleagues and dragged him to one side. Rebekah waited impatiently, getting her breath back as the sound of fire engines came closer. She went over to the journalist. 'What have you found out?'

'They're arranging a truce so the firemen can have a go at getting the fire under control.' he said quietly.

'They'll be some dead?' She had her emotions firmly under control. He pushed back his trilby and took out a packet of cigarettes. 'Sure. But there's some still alive. Otherwise we wouldn't be having a truce.' He scrutinised her face. 'Do you know somebody in there?'

'I might.'

'Hard luck. But they'll probably allow them to bring the wounded out.'

'Can we go closer now the shooting's stopped?'

He shrugged but they made tracks.

It was pandemonium with soldiers shouting and rushing about. Firemen trailed hosepipes. There were sightseers, as well as several vehicles whose drivers had deserted them to have a closer look. There

342

were also a couple of ambulances, and nurses.

Already there were bodies stretched on the ground and several more bloodied figures were being brought out. At the sound of a voice Rebekah stopped and stared at a young Irregular kneeling beside a man on the ground. Then she ran towards him. When a trooper would have stopped her, she pulled an armband from her bag. 'I'm a Red Cross helper!' she blurted out.

'All right, miss.' He allowed her to go through.

She slithered to a halt and knelt down. The young man looked at her but said nothing as she lowered her gaze to the figure on the ground. Her vision blurred and she had to rub her eyes before being able to see the face properly. It was coated with dust and smeared with dried blood from a gash on the side of the head. His eyes were closed. The left shoulder of his battledress was sticky. It was Daniel. She had to fight the wave of dizziness that passed over her.

'Well! Can you do anything for my brother?'

Rebekah bit back what she would have liked to say and looked at Shaun who appeared not to have recognised her. 'Give me time to think,' she murmured, glancing around. There was a priest in attendance, and nurses and orderlies were seeing to the loading of some of the wounded into ambulances. They all drove off as she watched. She looked at Daniel and brushed his cheek with the back of her hand. 'Help me to get him over to one of those cars,' she said quietly.

'I can't drive,' said Shaun.

'I can.' She slung her bag over her shoulder. 'Now let's move him.'

'We might be stopped.'

'And we might not,' she said impatiently. 'Let's just do it.'

Daniel groaned as they lifted him to his feet, but he did not open his eyes and was a dead weight as they dragged him to the car. Rebekah prayed that the driver of the Morris Oxford four-seater she had her eye on would keep on watching the fire. Water hissed on the flames, causing smoke to billow everywhere. People coughed and blinked their eyes but it was perfect for her plans. 'How the bloody hell am I going to open the door?' gasped Shaun.

'I'll take his weight while you get a hand free,' said Rebekah.

But before Shaun did so, a boy came over and opened the door.

'Thanks,' whispered Rebekah.

They managed with a struggle to get Daniel into the back of the car. She took off her jacket and made a pillow for his head. Shaun got in the front seat and she stared at him in exasperation.

'D'you want me to turn the handle, miss?' asked the boy.

'Yes! Yes!' She smiled and flipped him a florin before getting into the driving seat.

After a couple of false starts the engine came to

life and cautiously she drove off. There was a shout followed by shots. She ducked even though it would have probably been too late if the bullets were on target, but they were not and she did not stop. Soon they were out of range. It was then that she felt cold steel against her neck. 'Don't go to the hospital.'

'What?' Had Shaun recognised her?

'Keep you eyes on the road,' he ordered. 'People die in hospitals. And I don't know where you've come from but you must know that the Free State troops won't be letting me or Danny go free, *if* he gets better.' His voice quivered. 'Head for O'Connell Street.'

'You can't get through. It's blocked with armoured cars.' She glanced at him. 'The hospital would be better. Unless you want you brother to die?'

'Of course I bloody don't!' he snarled. 'But you can help him, can't you?'

'Yes!' She concealed her trepidation. 'But I'm no doctor. His head and shoulder – what happened?'

A bullet went straight through his shoulder. And he was hit by a brick or something when everything seemed to explode.'

Rebekah was relieved that she wouldn't have to be digging out a bullet. 'I'll need water.'

'I'll get you some,' he muttered.

'In that uniform? If we're stopped—'

'I'll shoot the lousy sods.'

'Dear God,' she groaned. 'Is violence the only

way you ever think of dealing with a situation?'

Shaun stared at her. 'Do I know you?'

'Hardly.' She started to slow down despite the barrel of the gun digging in her ribs now. 'I'm not going any further. There's troops ahead.'

'Drive through them,' he ordered. 'I've got our Danny's gun as well as my own.'

She sighed. 'You mean I'm to run them down while you have a gun battle?'

'You've got it.'

'I won't do it.'

'I'll shoot you.'

'Do it then. Then you won't have to explain to your brother why I'm still alive.' Her voice was expressionless.

Shaun's mouth fell open and he scrutinised her carefully before muttering, 'I thought I'd seen you before. It was best for both of you to think the other dead.'

She raised her eyebrows. 'You call the state Daniel's in best for him? You're crazy. I'm turning round.' She spun the wheel and Shaun was flung against the door.

He grappled for a hold. 'You bitch! I'll kill you for this!'

'Save your breath.'

A weak voice behind them said, 'You heard the lady, Shaun. Shut up.'

For a moment Rebekah's muscles seemed to lose

strength and the car skidded across the road before she managed to bring it to a halt with the engine still running. Trembling, she rested her head on the steering wheel for several seconds before pulling herself together and looking over the back of her seat.

'They lied,' said Daniel faintly. 'They bloody lied.' He reached out a hand and she took it.

'As soon as I knew you were alive, I came.'

He nodded and closed his eyes, still holding her hand.

'This is great,' muttered Shaun, hunched up against the door, glowering at her. 'Are we going to sit here all bloody day with you two holding hands?'

'We probably wouldn't be in this mess if it wasn't for you,' said Rebekah, her gaze flickering over him before returning to Daniel's face. 'We've got to find somewhere safe to take him. If I could I'd get him on the first boat back to Liverpool. But I suppose that's out of the question?'

'Too bloody right,' said Shaun, shifting to kneel on the seat and stare over the back. 'How about Lily's place, Danny boy? She's be glad to see you.' He smirked.

Daniel's eyes slowly opened and with difficulty he forced himself into a sitting position. 'Find a quiet street to park in, Becky, and give me time to think.'

She nodded and released his hand.

Shaun swore. 'We can't just—'

'You don't have to *just* do anything,' muttered Daniel. 'You can go and find out what's going on. There's places where you'll be welcomed.'

'You just want me out of the bloody way.'

'Too right,' said Daniel.

Shaun slumped in the seat, staring down at the gun on his lap.

Rebekah was wondering who Lily was and how best to keep Daniel out of sight. 'Help me to get the hood up,' she said to Shaun. He muttered something incomprehensible but did as she told him.

She drove around till she found a quiet street and brought the car to a standstill.

Shaun got out. 'Are you going to wait for me?'

Rebekah remained silent, waiting for Daniel to say something, but at that moment the air was split by an explosion and Shaun tossed Daniel's gun into the car and began to run back the way they had come.

Before Daniel or Rebekah could speak, the door of the house opposite opened and an elderly woman came out. She crossed the street. 'Did you hear it? Loud enough to wake Old Nick himself.'

'Where d'you think it came from?' Rebekah leant against the car, hoping the woman could not see inside.

'It'll be Four Courts.' She shook her head and tightened the shawl about her shoulders, peering round Rebekah. 'I worry about them bullets flying about when my son's coming home from work. And the shells! They're making a terrible mess of Dublin. All the fine buildings getting holes in them.'

'It's a shame.' Rebekah hesitated, 'I wonder if I could bother you for some water?'

The woman stared at her. 'You can have a cup of tea, girlie. Two, if you're wanting one for him in the motor as well?'

Rebekah smiled. 'Two cups of tea and some water would be fine. I can pay you.'

The woman fixed her with a look. 'I'm not after having your money, girlie. I'm not on anybody's side. I just want it all to stop. An Irregular, is he, like the one who ran off?'

Rebekah blurted out, 'He's wounded! That's why I need the water. It's best if it's boiled. Would you mind?'

The woman's face creased. 'Once a woman gave our Lord a drink of water. Sure, and shouldn't I do the same? Would you both like to come in?'

Some of the tension went out of Rebekah. 'Thanks. But I think I'm better not moving him at the moment.'

'That's all right.' The woman went back across the street.

Rebekah opened the back door of the car and slid along the back seat. Daniel's eyelids lifted and he stared at her.

'You look a right mess,' she said. Then her fingers

covered her chin and mouth in an attempt to stop them quivering, but she could not prevent tears filling her eyes and spilling over and a sob sounding in her throat.

'Shhh!' His expression was a mixture of pain and tenderness as he forced his arm up and grasped her fingers. She kissed his palms before rubbing her wet cheek against the back of his hand.

'The swines!' She sniffed and kissed his hand again.

'You mean Shaun and Green?' His voice sounded terribly weary.

She nodded, unable to speak for the tears that continued to well up in her throat, at the back of her nose and in her eyes. Instead she undid the buttons on his uniform with shaking fingers and fought for control of her emotions. 'I don't think I'll ever forgive them.'

'Me neither. What are you doing?'

'I want your jacket off. I need to see the wound.'

With her help he straightened up and she held his head against her breast while peeling off his jacket. Before she could do anything more, there was a knock on the window. Their Good Samaritan had moved fast and was outside with a tray.

Rebekah took it and thanked her. The woman gazed at Daniel. 'You'll need some different clothes, laddie. If you don't mind my dead husband's, I'll get you them.'

'I'd be grateful,' whispered Daniel, looking paler

than before. The woman vanished from his sight.

Rebekah placed the tray on the seat and reached for her bag. She poured two tots of brandy into the tea and held Daniel's cup to his lips while he drank. There were slices of buttered soda bread on a blue and white plate but he could eat no more than two bites.

She downed her tea swiftly, as well as a slice of bread, then set about dampening the bloodied shirt where it was stuck to his skin. To get rid of any dirt as quickly as possible was vital. The wound had to be cleaned and kept clean if septicaemia was not to set in. Knowing that she was hurting him made the task even more difficult.

She talked to try and keep both their minds from the task in hand. 'What are you going to do about Shaun?'

'Can't do anything.' The words were slurred. 'All I care about is us getting out of this alive.' He gritted his teeth as she pulled the fabric away from the wound.

'Sorry,' she whispered. 'I'd get you to Liverpool if I could but I think that's not on at the moment. Out of Dublin will have to do. Somewhere quiet in the country.' She lifted him against her and took off his shirt, letting him rest against her for five minutes or so before going on to the next stage of the treatment which she knew would be difficult for them both.

'Remember me telling you about Grandmama's farm in Wicklow?' She moistened some clean cotton waste as she gazed at the bruised and bloodied skin about the punctured skin.

'Green owns it.' He pressed his lips tightly together as she began to swab the wound.

She kept her head bent. 'He did. But I heard that it was set on fire. It's still standing, though.'

'How d'you know all this?' His voice was faint.

Rebekah hesitated. 'His lordship himself told me. That's what Brigid calls Joshua.'

'So you've been seeing him?' Suddenly his fingers were on her chin, pushing it up so that she had to look into his angry eyes.

'Papa made him my guardian,' she said in clipped tones.

'That explains a few things.' His hand dropped and he leant back, closing his eyes. 'We've got a lot of catching up to do. Where's Green now?'

'America – on business.'

'Good. We'll go to that farm then. I can't think of anywhere else right now.'

She nodded, praying that it would not be too difficult to get out of town if the Good Samaritan came up with those clothes. She put some gentian violet on his back and chest and bandaged him up.

The woman came back with a suitcase. 'I hope they'll fit.'

'I'm grateful,' said Rebekah, holding out a hand, knowing that she dare not offer the woman money again. 'God bless you.'

'And you, girlie. Try and get him to stay out of trouble.'

'I will.' Rebekah smiled and thanked her again.

It was a struggle getting the almost unconscious Daniel out of his uniform trousers and into a tobacco-smelling suit of too large clothes but she managed it, knowing that she would have to move soon because she had noticed several curtains twitching. She got out of the car and turned the starting handle. Her arm ached with the effort and at first the engine would not fire. Then it coughed into life and she raced to her seat.

Rebekah chanced going back to the hotel, paying her bill and picking up her clothes, and it was not so difficult after all.

She smiled brilliantly at whichever troops stopped them on the way out of town and put on a country Irish accent to pass off Daniel, slumped unconscious in the back, as her drunken merchant sailor brother. The fact that he smelt of alcohol gave a realistic touch to her tale.

She did not breathe easy, though, until she reached the top of a hill and paused briefly to ease her taut muscles – to look back on Dublin lying far below them and the Irish Sea beyond. Liverpool seemed a very long way away.

CHAPTER TWENTY

Rebekah's memory was good but even so she would not have remembered the way to the farm if in the past her father had not pointed out, on various trips into the country, the roads and narrow lanes which led to his childhood home.

She stopped at Naas and left Daniel sleeping in the car while she filled the tank and the spare can with petrol, and bought food and some essentials. She was glad that the June evenings were long as she coaxed the car up a steep hill. She had put down the hood and the smell of honeysuckle sweetened the air.

Suddenly Daniel spoke. 'Where are we?'

'Nearly there.' She glanced over her shoulder. 'If you want to pinpoint it, Glendalough is a good few miles the other side of those hills to our right. I reckon we've got about a mile and a half to go.'

'Let's hope we don't have any visitors.'

Rebekah wondered what kind of visitors he meant and was apprehensive. Joshua's man might call. She turned the steering wheel and they went up a narrow rutted lane. They bumped along with leafy branches brushing the sides of the car and she prayed they wouldn't lose a wheel. 'It was pony and cart when I was last here,' she called. 'I hope we can go all the way along.'

They could, but had to leave the car in the lane because the turn into the farmyard was too sharp and steep.

Rebekah had to help Daniel down from the running board. She opened a rickety gate and they stood a moment, with him holding on to her, staring at the neglected vegetable garden and a vista of fields where the grass grew tall. There was a grey stone house and a couple of outhouses.

'There doesn't look like there's been a fire,' said Daniel. 'No smoke on the walls and the windows are intact.'

'Perhaps his man lied. Wanted out,' murmured Rebekah, believing that it was Joshua who had been untruthful. 'It looks empty. I don't remember it being so desolate.'

They went towards the house and she remembered that there were no drains, no piped water. The door was not locked and they stepped straight into a kitchen with an open staircase running up one side. It was almost as she remembered. There was a cavern of a fireplace with chains and a hook for the large blackened cooking pot that still stood there. Placed beside the fireplace was a stack of cobwebby peat, chipped wood and newspapers. There were cupboards and a table and two wooden chairs, as well as a dusty, leaking horsehair leather sofa. A couple of shelves with some crockery and a number of books hung above a stone sink with a single tap. Underneath there was a galvanised bucket.

'It's not Paradise.' Her imagination had painted something better.

'It's not Hell either,' said Daniel. 'And it looks like sometimes it's occupied.'

'I don't think so.' She led him over to the sofa and he slumped down and closed his eyes. 'I won't be a moment.' She went outside remembering that the privy was the outhouse with the rambling pink roses round the door. It looked like it had been some time since it had last been used. She would have to fetch water from the river unless – She looked up at the roof, remembering the tank to catch rainwater, and went back inside the house.

Daniel opened his eyes. 'Lavatory?'

She showed him and wandered through the garden, gazing at the distant hills, shadowy neglected fields and the trees that shifted and whispered in the evening breeze. She thought of Joshua and was glad that he had never brought her here. Not that he would have stayed in this house. It would have had to be his father's mansion.

Daniel came out of the privy in the borrowed trousers and with a blue shirt flapping about his hips. His lean face was drawn with pain. 'We'll have to do something about that,' he said, indicating the building behind him with his head. 'But right now what are we going to do about food?'

'I bought some in Naas when you were asleep. It's in the car.'

'Good girl.' He managed a smile. 'Lights?'

'Grandmama used to have oil lamps but I didn't see any, did you?'

'No.' He drew nearer, holding his left arm awkwardly. 'At least the nights are short at this time of year.'

'And it's not really cold. We can have a go at lighting the fire tomorrow.'

'You remembered matches?'

'Yes. And firewood and a tin opener and a sharp knife. I even brought several newspapers. Are you hungry?'

'A bit.' He leant against the house wall. 'I'd forgotten quiet like this existed.'

'I'm not surprised. Do you want me to help you inside or do you want to look at the view while I fetch some things from the car?'

'I'll watch you.'

She smiled faintly and hurried to the car. Daniel was sitting on the ground when she returned with the box of food. She put it down and went over to him.

'My legs aren't as strong as I'd hoped.' He pulled a face as she bent over him. 'Don't try and lift me! Give me another minute and I'll get up.'

'I'm not a weakling,' she said, picking up the box and taking it inside.

'I never thought you were.' He looked up as she came through the doorway. 'But we'd be stuck if your back went. Give me a hand now and I'll get meself up against the wall.'

Rebekah did as he said, and taking it slowly together, soon had him on his feet. They went inside and over to the sofa once more. This time she ordered him to lie down. There was a back to the sofa but only one arm. She put her jacket under his head. 'Now rest.'

She was aware of him watching her as she opened a tin of beef and cut bread, buttered it, opened a jar of mustard, and made thick sandwiches of the lot. Into two cups she poured a bottle of Guinness. Then she took them over to him and sat on the edge of the sofa. They did not speak while they ate and drank, but kept glancing at each other.

He looks older, thought Rebekah. There were tiny wrinkles round his mouth and eyes. His eyes! She had forgotten they were such a beautiful mahogany brown. And his lashes were dark and thick like paint brush bristles. His hair was still curly despite the grey. No, it was dust, and there was blood making the front bit stick together above his nose. She had always liked his nose. Lovely and straight. And his mouth. She remembered how he had kissed her, and looking was not enough.

'I'm sorry about your father and mother,' he said. 'At least, I presume she's dead if Green's your guardian?'

She nodded and drained her cup. 'I was lucky. I had just gone into the cabin. What happened with Papa?'

He put the plate on the floor and told her, adding, 'I'm sorry.' There was a pause. 'Did Shaun really tell you I was dead?'

'He insinuated it.' She laced her fingers in her lap. 'I presume he told you I was dead too?'

'Green had just told me you were, and when I asked Shaun he made out that it was true.' Daniel stared at her and she stared back.

'Your brother was against us going together from the start.' She looked down at her hands.

'And Green hated me as much as I hated him.'

'I could have killed him when Brigid told me you were still alive. All that time—'

'I know.' His head dropped on to her coat and his throat moved.

Her own constricted and it was a minute before

she could say, 'Brigid and I threw flowers on the Mersey.'

He cleared his throat. 'Thanks.'

'They were chrysanthemums. Yellow for remembrance.'

'That's nice.' He smiled slightly.

Her fingers twisted round each other. 'I stood on that spot at the end of the landing stage where you took me that first time we met in Liverpool. It wasn't nice at all.'

There was a pause before he said, 'I've stood there since.'

'If only we'd seen each other.'

He nodded. 'You've been living in Liverpool with your aunt?'

'I did. Yes!' She smiled with relief. 'And Hannah! Remember Hannah the gorgon?'

'You mentioned her when we first met.' There was a silence.

'It seems a long time ago.'

'We only knew each other for just over a week.' Her breath shivered in her throat. She wanted to hold him and keep on holding him and could not understand what was preventing her from even touching him.

He stared at her from beneath half closed eyelids. 'I often wished I'd known you longer.'

'So there were more memories.' Her voice was quietly meditative. 'It was such a short time we had.'

'Now we have today.' He stifled a yawn.

'I hope we have more than today.'

'Mmm!' His lids closed.

Rebekah watched him, listened to his breathing, then rose and went outside to fetch the suitcases. When she returned, the room was full of shadows. She covered him with an overcoat and then sat at the table, staring through the small sash window at a silver and apricot-streaked sky being overtaken by the purply plum-coloured mantle of night.

Before it was completely dark she went upstairs and found that in one of the two rooms stood the bed that had been her grandparents'. There was also an old oak wardrobe with a large drawer in the bottom. Inside were a couple of well-worn blankets smelling of lemon balm and lavender. Instantly in her mind's eye she saw her grandmother and memories flooded in. She smiled, remembering how she had always been happy in this house.

Rebekah took out the blankets and had to push the drawer hard to make it shut. It made a noise and strangely she half expected the house to come alive then, but the only thing that happened was that flecks of whitewash fell from the ceiling. She bent to pick them up from the wooden floor but they powdered under her fingernails. When she straightened she winced and put a hand to her back. It struck her suddenly just how much she had crammed into one day.

She dropped the blankets onto the bed and went downstairs feeling her way cautiously in the dark. Daniel was still asleep. She placed the back of her hand against his forehead. It was hot but not burning. For a moment she hesitated, considering whether to wake him and help him upstairs where he would probably be more comfortable. Then she decided against it and went to bed.

Rebekah woke early to the chatter and song of birds in the trees, and her name being called. She yawned, stretched, forced her eyelids open and crawled from beneath the blankets.

Daniel was sitting at the table with his shoulders hunched beneath the overcoat. He faced the window but turned at the sound of her footsteps. There was blood on his shirt and smeared down the side of his eye and on his cheekbone. He looked glad to see her. 'I wasn't sure where you were.'

'You shouldn't have got up.' She tried to keep the worry out of her voice as she touched his face and shirt and was glad that the blood was dry. 'I'll have to get some water.'

'You want the fire lighting.'

'Yes. But you can't do it.'

'Can you?'

A smile twisted her mouth. 'I'll get the water.'

She tried the tap but all that came out was a thin brown trickle. 'The tank must be blocked with leaves. I'll have to go to the river.' She reached for the bucket and went outside.

The air was chilly because the sun was having a struggle to break through the mist that still clung to branches of trees and bushes and wove thin ribbons in the tall grass. She went through the gate, wishing she had paused to put on her jacket, and crossed the lane. She found the footpath that led to the river bank, a five-minute walk away, thinking about Daniel.

When she returned he had lit the fire and there was fresh blood on the shirt. 'You're an idjit.'

He raised his eyebrows but said nothing.

'We'll have to get that shirt off, and the bandage.'

He nodded and started to undo buttons. She looked away and into the blackened cooking pot, which was clean. She poured the water into it and went for more.

He was still sitting where she had left him when she returned but the lines about his mouth had deepened. He was in pain and she wished she could bear it for him. She must still love him. She poured half the water into the pot and then went over to him.

They went through almost the same rigmarole as they had yesterday with them both gritting their teeth as she eased lint and bandage away from his skin. Again she talked to try and make it easier. Commonplace things. 'I think it'll be a nice day when the mist lifts completely.'

He nodded, his eyes shut.

'You'll be able to lie outside in the sun.'

'What about you? Are you going to rest?'

'I want to find some sphagnum moss.'

He opened his eyes.

'It's supposed to have antiseptic properties, and it's absorbent,' she explained, starting to clean his face. 'The Red Cross used it in the war.'

'I didn't know you were in the Red Cross.'

'I was a junior recruit. Children helped to gather the moss.'

'You're going to be poking around bogs then? You could get stuck.'

She smiled. 'That reminds me of a conversation we had once.'

'On Seaforth beach.'

'Yes.'

There was a brief silence before he said, 'I'll come with you.'

'You won't!'

'I will.'

She opened her mouth to argue but changed her mind because of the expression on his face, and instead went and made tea.

They had bread and jam and a scalding sweet brew with tinned milk but she planned to make a good nourishing stew for dinner. After she had gathered some moss.

The mist had cleared, and the air was soft and warm. Bees and flies buzzed amid the sweet-smelling flowers and grass that reached Daniel's shoulders and were level with the top of Rebekah's head. Today seemed to belong to a bygone age. A time of innocence before mankind started making its mark on the earth. If it had not been for worrying about his wound she might have relaxed completely, but she was made anxious by the fear of losing him again.

'Why do you think the house still has furniture in it?' she said, swishing the grass with the arm that carried a bag for the moss.

'The occupier left in a hurry and nobody cares about the house or the land.'

She almost said, Joshua certainly doesn't, but had no desire to bring him into the conversation. 'You think he was threatened?'

'Could have been, in these times. Does it matter? Whoever it was has gone, leaving it for us.'

'You don't think he'll come back?'

'We'll worry about that if it happens.'

'There were no clothes in the wardrobe upstairs.'

He looked at her. 'But there was a bed?'

'Yes. You'd better sleep in it tonight.'

A corner of his mouth twitched slightly but he did not say yes or no. She had trouble keeping her colour down and wondered why she should flush like a virgin at the thought of the two of them in bed together. Although she had not suggested that.

They came to the river where it was shallow and wide. The sun slanted down through trees, dappling the water so that it was a deep mysterious green in places and translucent in others. They could see mud, flowing weed and shiny pebbles beneath.

Daniel stopped and drank from his cupped hand where the river rushed white and foaming around rocks. Rebekah slipped off her shoes and trod carefully in boggy ground where the river had once overflowed its banks and washed over the odd large stone. She found what she was looking for and soaked it to rid it of any mud before putting it in the bag.

Daniel had seated himself on a rock and was staring into the water. 'There's fish.'

'I know. Papa used to bring a rod here.' She perched sideways on a few inches of rock beside him, and was immediately conscious of the warmth of his hip. 'There's a rod in the cupboard back at the house, and a reel with line and hooks and a box of flies.'

'Perhaps I'll try my hand.' He turned his head and their faces were only inches apart. 'Can I kiss you?' he said.

'Yes.' She took his face between her hands.

His lips were cool with the water he had just drunk and he was in need of a shave, but it was the kiss she had been wanting and needing for a long time.

They put an arm round each other and carried on kissing, long and leisurely, rousing latent passions.

They could not get enough of each other and desire left them breathing heavily when his mouth lifted from hers.

'Nothing,' he said, holding her close, 'has tasted that good in almost two years.'

'No.' She rested her cheek against his neck. 'This is like a miracle.'

He stroked the back of her head. 'I remember when I first saw you with your hair cut. I'd just been thinking that you'd changed your mind about coming, and it hurt.'

'I remember your face smeared with grease and dirt in the engine room. I wanted to rush over and fling my arms around you – I'd started to believe that I'd never see you again.'

'And now we're here.'

She leant against his arm and laughed.

Daniel grinned. 'What's so funny?'

'Nothing. I'm just happy.'

'Happy, happy, happy!' He tried to swing her over on to his knee but could not.

He grimaced with painful effort and she scolded. 'Give it time!'

'We've lost enough of that.'

Rebekah stood. 'We'll catch up.' She grasped his hand and he came to his feet.

They walked back, arm in arm, enjoying the peace and being in each other's company.

On exploration of the neglected kitchen garden

they found some strawberries and rhubarb. There were potato plants, too, growing among weeds, but they both reckoned it was too early to dig them up yet.

Rebekah put the moss on the windowsill to dry in the sun, then made sandwiches from the remains of the beef. She had a cup of tea and Daniel a bottle of Guinness. 'It's good for you,' she said with a smile.

'So are you.' The kissing this time reminded her of all that was sweet and light. It was honey, sunshine and flowers, and left them both light-headed with joy.

She ordered him to rest in the garden and he told her that she must as well. 'I've got things to do,' she protested, smiling. 'A stew to get ready, and those clothes you were given will need altering. And I'll have to go for some more water and wash a couple of things.

'Later, girl.' He took her hand and led her outside.

They lay in the grass, with his head on her midriff, her arm across him, eyes closed against the sun.

'Less than thirty hours ago I thought you dead,' he murmured. 'I'd been shot in an exchange of gunfire outside Four Courts and by the middle of the morning there was a possibility of my joining you in the great blue yonder. "No surrender", that's what half of them were saying before the explosion.'

'What about you?'

'I was wondering what the hell I was doing there.

Irishmen shooting Irishmen. It's a terrible thing, Becky.'

'Why did you join the Irregulars then?'

'Because I wanted what de Valera wanted: a united Ireland. I'd gone back to sea after the ceasefire, believing it was all over. But it wasn't, and our Shaun got himself involved and went on about me sitting on the fence. He said I had to choose sides. The trouble was I'd been hankering for a fight ever since Green told me you were dead. I wanted to smash his face in because he was crowing, knowing what I was suffering.' The bitterness was in his voice again.

Her arm tightened about him. 'He's not worth thinking about.'

'I know. But that doesn't stop me. Especially now I know he's in charge of your affairs.'

'I can cut the connection. The money doesn't matter.'

There was a pause before he said, 'Was there much?'

She stilled. 'You know, I never asked. He gave me an allowance, but there are the shares in the company too. The trouble is that Papa made it so that I couldn't have control of my affairs until I was twenty-five. I was annoyed about that. Why not twenty-one?'

'What if you married?'

'I don't know, I never asked.'

'I bet it would be different. It could be why he lied to me.'

'He lied to you because he hates you,' she said with a sudden surge of anger. 'It's as you said – he wanted to hurt you. He's that kind of man.' She opened her eyes and pushed herself up on one elbow.

Daniel twisted his head and looked at her. 'You must have got to know him pretty well to have discovered that about him.'

'Pretty well. But I'll never understand him.' She looked across the garden, thinking now was really the time to tell the truth. But suddenly it seemed like the serpent in the Garden of Eden – destructive. 'Can we talk about something else?'

'Suits me.' He closed his eyes. 'Tell me what you've been doing for the last twenty months or so?'

Rebekah breathed easier and lay back. Daniel seemed to have no suspicion about her and Joshua. And why should he? It seemed incredible to her now that she had actually gone and married him, for better or for worse, in sickness and in health, till death do they part. She pushed that thought aside and began to talk about the life she had led in Liverpool that had not involved Joshua.

'This Pat – Brigid's brother,' said Daniel after she had mentioned him several times, 'you went out with him?'

'I was hurting and lonely. It was nothing important. Brigid lost her husband, as you probably know, and it was Pat's way of cheering us up. I never went out with him alone and I stopped seeing him a while ago.' She hesitated before saying, 'What about this Lily Shaun mentioned?'

'Lil has a bike. She was acting as messenger for our units in Dublin.' His head shifted on her stomach.

'That's all?'

'No. Our Shaun told her that there was a woman in my past and that I needed help to get over her.'

'He had a nerve,' said Rebekah indignantly.

'He was never backward in coming forward.' He yawned.

'And?' she prompted.

'And we were friendly.'

'How friendly?'

'Friendly, friendly.'

Rebekah cleared her throat. 'Like we were friendly after a couple of days?'

Daniel turned his head and with difficulty moved to press his face against the fabric covering her breast. She felt the warmth of his breath. 'Never,' he said in a muffled voice.

She wanted to believe him. Then she did not want to believe him. It would lessen her guilt concerning Joshua if he had been with another woman, though she hated the thought. 'I'd better stir myself,' she murmured. 'There's the vegetables to peel.' She sat up and he moved with her.

'You don't believe me.' He stared at her straight in the face.

'Yes I do.'

'You should. It could never be the way it was with you.' His tone was serious.

She swallowed, knowing how true that had been for her. 'I believe you. But I've still got to peel the vegetables.'

There was a short silence, then he smiled. 'Do you want help?'

She shook her head and Daniel pressed his lips against hers briefly, then eased himself down on the grass. When she came back out with some newspaper and the vegetables he appeared to be sleeping. She sat on the step, glancing at him now and again as she peeled potatoes, carrots, onion and turnip, and tried very hard not to think about him and Lil.

'You can cook,' said Daniel in a pleased voice, pushing his empty plate and taking her hand.

She smiled. 'Mama made sure I could. The mutton wasn't too fatty?'

'It wouldn't be your fault if it was – but it was fine.' He kissed her fingers.

'Perhaps we could have fish tomorrow?'

'Sure, if the day's not too sunny I'll take a rod. Will you be coming with me?'

'I might join you after I've been to the village. We'll be needing more bread and I'd like some fresh milk.'

'You'll perhaps need to be careful what you say?'

'I know. You don't have to tell me you're an Irregular on the run,' she said lightly, watching him toy with her fingers.

'A deserter.' His expression was grim. 'The danger in a place you don't know, is not knowing which side people sympathise with.'

'I'll be careful.'

He nodded.

She pulled her hand away. 'I'll wash the dishes. You have a rest.'

Daniel frowned, leaning back in the chair so that all the weight was on the back legs. 'All I've done all day is rest. I'm not used to it.'

'You can fix the fire if you're so desperate to start that shoulder bleeding, or there's yesterday's papers you can read.'

'I know what they'll be saying. Will you get me a paper tomorrow?'

Rebekah agreed and got on with her chores. Afterwards they sat on the sofa together and she would have altered a pair of trousers for him but he took them out of her hand and threw them on a chair. She was pulled against him and his mouth came down on hers. His kisses demanded and she responded with a hungry desire that dissolved all sensible thought. Physically he was just as attractive to her as in the past and she was not going to start worrying about the rights and wrongs of the situation she had got herself into. On the *Samson* she had been ready to do anything to stay with him, and she was ready now. They went upstairs. She had to help him undress and did so carefully, conscious that he was watching her every expression. Her fingers checked his bandage before, trembling slightly, they explored his chest and unbuttoned his trousers. She knew better than to arouse him too quickly and just missed touching the source of his manhood, although it was difficult to avoid and she wanted to please him. She knew, though, that she had to pretend that the only sexual experience she possessed had been in his company. Not easy when her subconscious was telling her where to kiss and caress.

Daniel lay on the bed, watching her undress while the final shafts of evening sunlight played over her body. 'It's the first time I've seen you completely naked,' he said quietly. 'I know you had a good shape because it felt right, but—'

'Shhh!' She clutched her frock in front of her. 'You'll have me blushing.'

He grinned. 'I should hope so. Now come here.'

She went, with that first time that they had made love on the beach in her thoughts. Her need for him took away any inhibitions. He touched and kissed places that Joshua would never have considered. She was high with breathless excitement by the time he finally took her.

Afterwards she worried as her fingers searched the bandages back and front. He had bled a little.

'I'm all right,' he said drowsily, dragging her arm and pulling it across his chest. 'Go to sleep now.'

Unexpectedly, depression spoilt the moment. Joshua had a habit of saying those words when he had finished with her. When was she going to tell Daniel the truth? He would not like it. Wouldn't like it at all! Fear made her feel cold all over. Her arm tightened protectively around him as she tried to shut out a different kind of bedtime memory. She drifted into sleep but the memory followed her and turned it into a nightmare. When she awoke, the decision was made. She was not going to tell Daniel about her marriage.

CHAPTER TWENTY-ONE

Rebekah came through the gate, spilling water in her haste, but Daniel had already got up and was in the garden, gazing at the roof.

'Don't even think it,' she said, putting down the bucket and rubbing a muscle in her arm.

He turned and came over to her. 'Perhaps tomorrow.' His hand reached for the bucket but she gripped the handle before he could touch it.

'Perhaps in a week,' she said severely. He just looked at her. 'Daniel! I don't want you trying to unblock that pipe while I'm in the village. You'll do some gentle fishing.'

'You don't think I'll be using my shoulder for that, woman?'

She sighed. 'I suppose you will, but not to the same extent as getting up on a roof. I'd say rest completely but I've got a feeling you've no intention of doing that.'

'You're getting to know me.'

'I should say I am.' She smiled. 'Is the fire still in?'

'I've seen to that.' His hand fastened on part of the wooden grip of the handle. 'We'll share.' His voice was determined.

'You're a stubborn man.'

'And you're a bossy woman.'

'Only for your own good,' she protested.

The tiny creases at the outer edges of his eyes deepened. 'And don't they all say that before they start trying to change you?'

'There's nothing about you I want to change,' she murmured, eyeing him carefully and putting her tongue in her cheek. 'Except several days' growth of beard, that terrible shirt with blood on it, and your bandages.'

He rasped his chin with a fingernail. 'They might ask awkward questions in the village if you buy a razor.'

She agreed and kissed him. The next moment the bucket was on the ground and they were lying in the grass making love. It was another two hours before she set out, walking to the village to save petrol.

It was set in a narrow valley with most of the houses spread along either side of a single street. There was a church, the priest's house, a small school, a blacksmith's, and a general store that sold everything and had a bar at one end. Rebekah had considered going to the nearest town about six miles away where she had attended church every Sunday when she had stayed with her grandmother, but had changed her mind, thinking it more probably that she would find out more about Joshua's man in the village.

She reckoned on it being reasonably safe for her to admit to who she was or had been to Mary Lochrane, who kept the shop with her husband. She was a large woman with a mass of soft brown hair that she wore tied with a bootlace.

'It's changing times we're living in, Miss Rhoades,' she said as she sliced bacon. 'You must feel it with your granny gone and the land sold to that man in Liverpool. I'm surprised to see you here, I must admit.' Her fine dark eyes were curious.

'You remember my father?'

'Aye! I remember him fine.'

'He died.' Rebekah told her about the accident but said nothing about Joshua's being her guardian. It seemed that it was not known because the woman only tutted and expressed her sympathy.

'I've nearly got over it now,' said Rebekah, 'but I had a yen to see the old place. I was surprised to find the house empty, so I thought I might just stay there a while. Is there someone I should see about it?'

Mrs Lochrane's head drew closer to Rebekah's as she wrapped the bacon in greaseproof paper.

'Nobody'll be minding. Mr Dixon, whose wife died from the appendicitis, lived there after your granny. He got drunk in here one night roundsabout Christmas and spoke up for the Treaty. Next day there's a notice pinned to his front door telling him to get out or else. So he upped and left. Seeing as how there's no Mr Green to check up on people, everything's been left pretty much as it was.'

'You don't see Mr Green here at all?'

'Not him.' She tossed her head. 'Not for years. It's rumoured, though, that there's talk of him selling the place. Let's hope it's true. It's not doing anybody any good for things to be left the way they are.'

Rebekah agreed and asked how much she owed. It seemed reasonable considering all she had learnt.

'Is it on your own you'll be staying there?' asked Mrs Lochrane, handling her change.

Rebekah kept her head down as she put the money in her purse. 'I have my cousin from Liverpool with me.' She picked up her purchases and Mrs Lochrane moved to open to door for her.

'Perhaps we'll be seeing you with your cousin next time?'

'My cousin hasn't been well and needs peace and quiet. Some good Irish country air should do the trick.' She nodded and went on up the street, smiling at anyone who looked her way.

Daniel was not in the house when she arrived

back so she left everything on the table and went in search of him. He had abandoned fishing and was in the river. 'I thought I might as well get myself cleaned up,' he called.

'You've got your bandage wet, idjit.'

'Stop fussing.' His brown eyes wandered slowly over her in the peach cotton frock and his fingers fastened on her bare ankle. 'Get your clothes off and come in.'

'I have no towel and I can't swim very well,' she murmured, eyeing him below the water line.

'It's not deep, and besides I'll look after you.'

She smiled. 'You can't look after yourself, going and getting yourself shot.'

He pulled on her foot and she lowered herself quickly on to the grassy bank. 'All right! But don't rush me. I bet it's cold.'

'It'll take your breath away.'

She pulled a face but began to undo her frock. 'Mr Dixon, who lived in the house, was threatened. He spoke up for the Treaty.'

Daniel frowned and was silent a moment before saying, 'Did you get a paper?'

'They surrendered at Four Courts.'

'I see.' For a moment he looked grim. 'Anything else?'

'The woman who keeps the shop reckons that it'll be all right for us to stay. I told her that I had my cousin from Liverpool with me.'

'So I'll have to put on a Liverpudlian accent?'

'And be Quaker and female, I think,' she said with a mischievous look.'

'Re-bek-ah!' he groaned, shaking his head and so sprinkling her with a myriad drops of water before pulling her into the river.

She gasped with the cold shock and pretended to hit him but he put his arms round her and kissed her long and hard until she actually did strike him.

He loosened his hold. 'This is the life,' he said against her ear.

'You're easily pleased.' She put her arms round him as the current tugged at her legs.

'The simple life. You, me, food to eat and somewhere to lay our heads. What else do we need?' He nuzzled her neck and then lifted his head. 'What's this scar on your shoulder?'

She hesitated before saying. 'It's where the bed fell on me on the *Samson*.'

'It looks like a burn.' He turned her round. 'You've marks on your back as well.'

'Same thing.'

'They look different.' He pulled her close again and rubbed noses. 'Poor love.'

'I survived. But I'm not sure I won't be having pneumonia when I get out of this river,' she said through chattering teeth. 'A hot bath is what I'll be needing, but I'm sure I'm not going to get it.'

'I'll warm you up.' He smiled into her eyes.

'Is that a promise?'

'You bet.' He kissed her, and set about keeping his word.

Daniel slid down from the roof and entered the house where they had lived for ten days. He stared with satisfaction at the brackish-coloured water coming from the tap. 'You can use that water for washing but don't drink it, love.'

'I've no intention.' Rebekah carried a bucket over to the cooking pot and filled it. 'I suppose I should want it to rain so we can have fresh water in the tank.'

'I can't believe we've been so lucky.' He sat on the sofa, gingerly feeling his shoulder, but the bandage and vest were still dry. 'Becky, we'll have to get married.'

Her legs suddenly felt weak and it was several seconds before she turned and looked at him. 'I'm not bothered about getting married. We'd have to talk religion, and as we're already living in sin, what does it matter?'

He stared at her. 'It matters to me. And I never thought I'd hear you talking of living in mortal sin so lightly!'

'I might talk of it lightly, but I don't mean it lightly,' she said, sitting down, 'I was thinking of Adam and Eve the other day and how there was no priest or minister there to marry them. 'When we leave here, who's to know that we're not married?'

He frowned. 'I know you don't want to be a Catholic, love, but I wouldn't force you to go to our church. But if we could just have the priest say the words over us. I want us to be respectable. I don't want our children being bastards.'

'Children!' She got up and began to sort out the washing, thinking how men thought it was so easy to get you with child.

Daniel came up behind her and wrapped his arms about her waist. 'It might have happened already.'

Rebekah turned in his arms and looked at him. 'And it mightn't have.'

'We make love all the time!' he exclaimed, squeezing her.

She looped her arms around his neck. 'You could be making love to me now instead of talking.'

'Later. Now I want to sort this out. Once my shoulder's healed I'm going back to sea.'

She dropped her arms. 'What's the rush? We're safe here and I've still got money.'

'We feel safe,' he said, slackening his hold. 'But feelings can be deceptive. And there's another thing, I don't like living off you.'

'But that's stupid.' She pulled away from him. 'In Liverpool I know women who have to work to keep a family going. I don't suppose the children care who's earning the money.'

'That's different.'

'But in a way it's the same. You can't earn at the moment and the money I have is enough for us to live on for a while longer. I'm not saying for always, just a few more weeks.'

'And then?' he said quietly. 'I go back to sea and you're left on your own? I want a wife to come home to, Becky, not a mistress.'

She flushed. 'When you say that it makes me sound different to how I see myself. I think of myself as your wife already.'

He drew her close again. 'I want to be sure of you and I want you to be secure. If anything were to happen to me—'

'Don't say it!' She clung to him. 'I don't want you to leave me. I couldn't bear it if—'

'Shhh!' He kissed her and for the moment decision-making about marriage was put aside.

It was to come up again a week later when they were walking in the hills.

'Look at that view.' Rebekah forced Daniel to halt. 'Let's rest and have our sandwiches.'

He did as she asked and they sat gazing down the hillside and across a valley to the tree-massed slope on the other side. A rabbit watched them from a few feet away.

'The view won't keep us, Becky. We have to make some decision.' Daniel screwed up his eyes against the sun. 'I met the priest when I was fishing last evening.'

'Did he ask where you were staying?'

'Yes.'

'Did you tell him?'

'I gave him the impression I was sleeping rough, and from my tramp-like appearance and my talk, he drew the conclusion that I was an Irregular on the run. We discussed the Treaty.'

She bit her lip. 'Do you think he'll report you to the constabulary?'

Daniel's brow creased. 'One lone deserter? He asked me what I thought of Father Albert – who was with us at Four Courts – for urging the men to quit to save more bloodshed.'

She sighed. 'What did you say?'

'I said I was out of it but that I would have gone along with him.'

'Sensible man.' She kissed him. 'What do you think has happened to Shaun?'

Daniel shrugged. 'If he was caught he could be in Mountjoy prison.'

'But if he wasn't?' She toyed with a blade of grass. 'Is it possible he could find us?'

'Anything's possible if he really wants to trace us. He has connections and if there's men in the village who sympathise with the cause—' He shrugged. 'We're not that far from Dublin and he knows the car.'

She was dismayed. 'You don't think we should leave now?'

'Not right now, but soon. We'll have to think about where to live.' He lay down, his hands behind his head.

She felt depressed at the thought of being parted from him in an Ireland that was still at war with itself and unexpectedly had a longing to see Liverpool again. At least there she had friends. 'What about Liverpool?'

'Liverpool!' He pushed himself up and his expression had changed. 'Green's there.'

'It's a big city! Besides, we could live just outside. Seaforth, or somewhere like that.' Her voice was eager.

He scowled. 'I don't want you within ten miles of Green. I don't trust him.'

'How's he to know I'm there? You're not thinking, love. When you're away, at least I'll have friends in Liverpool.'

'You're thinking of Brigid, whose brother is Pat. Who's a sailor. Talk gets round. Before you know it Green will know exactly where you are. Or you'll go and visit your aunt or that friend of yours, Edwina, and they'll spill the beans. I don't want him pestering you while I'm away. You don't know him like I do. He's ruthless when he wants his own way.'

'I'm sure you're right.' She felt a strong sense of guilt and apprehension, as if the mere mention of Joshua's name could spoil everything between them. 'I'll have to stay in Ireland.'

He frowned at her. 'You don't have to make it sound like a penance.'

'I'm sorry. It's just that I'm going to miss you when you go.'

'I never told you it would be easy being married to a sailor,' he said, and getting to his feet went on down the hill ahead of her. She followed him slowly, trying to cast off a feeling of gloom.

'Ugh! I got soaked just coming from the car!' Rebekah shook herself, scattering raindrops, as she closed the kitchen door.

'Did you get a newspaper?' Daniel helped her off with her coat.

'And posted my letter.' She took the newspaper from a shopping bag and handed it to him.

He opened it, and after a minute or so said quietly, 'There's been fighting in Limerick and Waterford. It's been going on for days but now both towns have fallen to State troops.'

'That'll mean more Irregulars on the run.' Rebekah stared at him, her breath coming fast.

'And more filling the prisons.'

'Shaun?' She went over to the fire and dipped a ladle in the stew that was simmering in the pot.

'Who knows?' he said shortly. There was a silence.

'I met the priest today,' she said brightly. 'He was very nice. Enquired after your health and asked how much longer we'd be staying.'

'And what did you say?' He placed two bowls on the table.

'I said we'd be leaving at the end of the summer.'

'Why did you say that?' He sat on a chair and drummed his fingers on the table. 'I've got to be earning, Becky. We'll go to Dublin. I know a few people—'

'Lily.' The name came out without Rebekah even thinking about it.

He stared at her. 'If that's a joke, it's not funny.'

'Sorry!' She spooned the stew into the bowls. 'But it seems to me, Daniel, that I'm going to be left alone in a Dublin that's just as dangerous as it was two years ago. I don't believe the Irregulars'll give up on the city. It'll be guerilla warfare again, and woe betide anyone who gets in the way.'

He stirred his stew, frowning down into the bowl. 'You're over-reacting because I've got to leave you. But I did tell you what it would be like married to me.'

'I'm not married to you,' she murmured, hurt because he seemed unable to understand how insecure and scared she felt.

Daniel looked up. 'I did ask you. Is that what this is about?'

'Don't talk stupid,' she said angrily. She sprinkled damp salt on her stew. 'I said the other week I wasn't bothered about being married.'

'So you did. I thought it unlike you.'

'Why?' She met his gaze squarely. 'Did Lily want to marry you?'

'Lily again!' He put down his spoon. 'What the hell's this about? She meant nothing to me!'

'It's easy to say that.' Some devil was driving Rebekah. She dipped her spoon in the stew. 'Did you go to bed with her?'

His eyes hardened. 'I'm not telling you. But I'll say this – she would have been happy to! Perhaps I can still make her happy, the way things are going on!'

'Things!' she banged her spoon down on the table, splattering it with gravy. 'You mean the way *I'm* going on, don't you? Perhaps you'd planned on marrying her? Maybe you're wishing now we'd never met again?'

'Who's talking stupid now?' He stood and rammed his chair against the wall. 'I don't know how you can even think that, never mind say it?' he said vehemently, taking his second-hand coat from a hook on the wall. 'Haven't I asked you to marry me? I'm going for a walk, and perhaps when I come back you'll be talking sense.'

'*Me* talking sense!' Rebekah jumped to her feet, folding her arms across her breast. 'Walking in the pouring rain – you call that sensible?'

Daniel gave her a look and without another word, opened the door and went out.

Rebekah stared after him and burst into tears. She did not know what made her go on about Lily. What would Mama, if she could see her from heaven, be thinking of her now? What was God thinking, her living with Daniel and married to Joshua? She rubbed her wet cheek against her sleeve and tried to control her tears. What was she to do?

A soaked through Daniel returned three hours later. She hurried to help him off with his coat. 'Where've you been? I've been worried sick! I thought you weren't coming back! Come over the fire and get dry.'

He smiled. 'It did me good.' He pulled her towards him and rubbed his wet hair in her face.

She protested but could not help laughing. 'You pig!'

'Grunt, grunt!' He swung her off her feet. 'I'm a selfish swine, Becky love. You've been worrying all the time about us not being married, haven't you?'

'I have?' she stammered.

'Of course you have.' He wrapped his arms round her. 'I went to see the priest. I told him that we'd been living in sin and asked him to marry us as soon as possible.'

'You what?' Rebekah could scarcely believe what she was hearing.

He grinned. 'Don't let's argue religion. I have to make us legal before I go back to sea.'

She swallowed. 'I see.'

'I say you do!' He laughed and swung her around again. 'You will say yes?'

'What about banns?' she said desperately.

'"Tush to that" said Father Donovan, when I told him what Green had done to us in order to get his hands on your money.'

'You said that? Did he believe you?' Rebekah was breathless with the speed of his actions.

'Sure and he believed me! Isn't Green English, a Protestant, and an uncaring landlord to boot?'

'But – but *I'm* Protestant and English. Doesn't he—?'

'But you're half Irish, polite and pretty! And you came back to Ireland in search of me and rescued me from the jaws of death!'

'You didn't say that?' Rebekah was starting to feel peculiar.

'I did. I told him that we loved each other madly.'

'Mad's the operative word,' she said, sagging against him. 'Oh, Daniel, I don't know what to say! I feel sick.'

He looked anxious and ushered her over to the couch. 'Let's sit down. It's the shock! And we didn't eat our dinner. You'll feel better once you've got some food down you.'

'Food. Yes,' she said faintly. 'Let's have some dinner.'

He hurried over to the fire. She watched him filling the bowls and tried to form the words 'I'm already married', but they would not come. Instead she murmured, 'When is this wedding?'

'Soon. Maybe tomorrow. Or the next day.'

'Right,' she said, trying to control the terrible churning in her stomach. 'I'll have to pick out a frock.'

Daniel smiled as he brought her a bowl of stew.

'That pale green crêpe-de-Chine. I like that one.'

She returned his smile and ignored the voice in her head that told her that what she was planning was wrong. 'Dum-dum-de-dum,' she murmured.

'There'll be no music.' he said. 'Just a quiet ceremony.'

'That'll do me.' she said, and ate her stew.

That night Rebekah could not sleep. The words 'Bigamist! Liar! Cheat!' kept running through her mind. She had read of a case in the *Liverpool Echo* only a few months ago. A soldier had been brought to court for having one wife in Liverpool and another in Preston. What was she to do? She could not bear hurting Daniel. She considered all they had been through and how they had found each other again. She smiled. They had been happy. Slowly she relaxed. She slept and dreamt her old dream of being locked in the turret, and was afraid. Someone was coming up the stairs and she could not escape.

It was daylight when she woke. Daniel was out of bed and dragging on a shirt.

'Who do you think it is?' she mouthed.

At that moment there was a knock on the door and a voice said, 'Danny! Are you in there?'

She watched him open the door a few inches to reveal Shaun's face.

'Out!' Daniel pushed his brother before him and closed the door, shutting Rebekah in.

She got out of bed quickly and dragged on

her dressing gown. Downstairs the two brothers confronted each other, one either end of the table.

'I knew she was here.' said Shaun. 'They told me in the village. Miss Rebekah Rhoades is staying in this house with her Liverpool cousin. But nobody has seen the cousin.' He grinned, 'I found that interesting so I came out here.'

Daniel's eyes narrowed. 'How long have you been here?'

'An hour or so. Stirred up the fire. Had a cuppa tea and some bread and jam. Not a bad place but a good bloody walk to find you.'

'How did you find the village?'

'A couple of the lads are from around here. It was one of the mothers who mentioned Miss Rhoades and her motor.' Shaun smirked. 'It was after that I mentioned that I knew her and the cousin might be my brother. They let on that you and her are the talk of the place since yesterday. A wedding in the offering and her getting married in our church. Quite a romantic tale you made out of it, Danny boy, but you're not married to her yet.'

'I will be soon,' said Daniel. 'What d'you want?'

Shaun looked injured. 'You could be a bit more welcoming. I could have been killed. I thought you'd be glad to see me.'

'Why? You're nothing but trouble.'

'Now that's a fine thing to say! There could be state troopers on my tail.'

'So you go and declare yourself to all and sundry in the village?' Daniel's tones were disbelieving. 'Don't make me laugh!'

Shaun sighed heavily. 'It's a fine thing to be calling your brother a liar. And there's me worrying about you.'

'Come off it! You're a liar.'

'Don't believe me then.' Shaun shrugged. 'I was in the fighting at Waterford. I was lucky to get out.'

Daniel stared at him before walking over to the window. 'It's a bloody shame. It says in the newspaper that de Valera wants to talk peace.'

'So he does – but who's listening? Michael Collins and Griffiths sold us down the river. There'll be no peace.' Shaun's expression was ugly. 'What you've got to decide, Danny, is if you're with us or against us.'

'I'm out of it,' said Daniel. 'I'm going back to sea.'

'You can't quit!'

'You're going to stop me?' A grim smile played around Daniel's mouth.

'Danny! You know they won't let you,' insisted Shaun. 'You're either for or—'

'You know what I'm for.' Daniel held his brother's gaze. 'But I'm not going to be fighting my fellow countrymen for it, and that's my final word on the matter.'

There was a silence during which Rebekah felt faint again and lowered herself on to the bottom stair. Shaun glanced at her. 'It's her fault we're arguing!

Mam must be turning in her grave. I tell you, Danny, you could be making a mistake. Guess what I found in that bag over there.'

Involuntarily Daniel looked at Rebekah's canvas bag sitting on the floor in the corner. 'You went nosing in Becky's bag?' he said furiously. 'You've got no right—'

'Hold on,' said Shaun, placing on the table a wedding ring and ruby and diamond engagement ring. 'I found those in it.'

Daniel stared at them and did not speak for a moment. 'So? They're her mother's,' he said at last. 'Aren't they, Rebekah?'

She stood up. 'Yes.' She came over to the table and feeling like an old, old woman, sank on to a chair. She did not look at Daniel.

'There,' he said to his brother. 'Now get out.'

Shaun's gaze went from one to the other. Then without another word, he left the house.

Daniel watched him through the window until he was the other side of the gate, then he turned. 'He could be back with others.'

She stared at him. 'But you haven't done anything wrong.'

'You heard me tell him I've quit. You should know what they're like. I think it's best we do go to Liverpool. You've got friends there.'

There was a silence before she murmured, 'You think I'm going to need friends?'

'We all need friends.'

She felt cold to her stomach. 'Has he actually brought any men with him?'

'You heard what he said.'

She nodded and squared her shoulders but her heart was thumping as she reached for the oats and put a cupful in the frying pan. 'Are we leaving today?'

'Yes.' He picked up the rings. 'I didn't know our Shaun had taken to thieving. Are they your mother's?'

Rebekah stared at him and her throat ached and she felt so sick that she could not answer him immediately. He looked at her with a slight pucker between his brows. 'Well?'

She swallowed. 'I'd hardly take them from her dead hand.'

'Your Grandma's then?'

'No.' A splinter of laughter escaped her. 'The Bible says, "Be sure your sins will find you out!" and that's what's happening to me.'

'Becky!' He went pale and moved over to her. 'What is it? Tell me!'

'You won't love me any more! You'll hate me!' A sob shook her throat.

Tell me!' He shook her.

'I'm married, Daniel!'

She would have found it easier if he had immediately shouted at her but instead he was silent for what seemed an age before his arms slackened and then dropped. There was an expression in his eyes that made her want to cry and cry and when he shouted in a furious voice: 'It's Green, isn't it? It's bloody Green!' she did start crying but he ignored her tears and yelled, 'Why, Rebekah? Why if you loved me?'

'I did love you! I *do* love you!' She scrubbed at the tears on her cheeks and her voice rose, 'But I thought you were *dead,* and he was so persuasive. It was what Papa wanted and I felt so guilty about him because we quarrelled and he died. I wanted to please him even though he was dead! Can you understand that?' Daniel was silent, just staring at her. She continued, 'I realised my mistake as soon as I married him. He changed. It was frightening. He was cruel, calculatingly cruel. That scar on my shoulder you asked about – he did it on our honeymoon with a cigar because I mentioned your name. He knew that I loved you and he told me that one of the reasons he married me was because he hated you.'

'Green told you he hated me on your honeymoon?' His expression was disbelieving.

'Yes!'

'Why?'

'Why on the honeymoon? Or why hate you at all?'

'I know why he hates me.'

Rebekah smiled bitterly. 'You were his friend once. I think he liked you. He kept going on about you. He wanted to know if you'd tried anything on with me. I couldn't understand it, but of course he knew all the time you weren't dead and that I loved you. On our honeymoon I didn't want him to touch me and he raped me. He wanted to be the first with me, but of course he wasn't. You were. Not that I told him that. As it was he hurt me. Since then I've lost count of the times he's hurt me. He has a Cat o' Nine Tails.' She choked on the words and stopped.

'Don't tell me any more.' He was white about the mouth. 'I need to think. I'm going for a walk.' Not bothering with a coat he opened the door and went out.

Rebekah ran after him. 'Daniel, you will come back! You won't—'

He pushed her away. 'Just let me be for a while!'

She watched him go with his hands rammed in his trouser pockets, and had to lean against the door jamb. Her head throbbed and she felt sick.

When he was out of sight she staggered inside and sat down on the sofa. She tried to think what to do but could not. Then she smelt burning. She got to her feet and took the frying pan from the fire. She threw the burnt oats on to the peats, watching them blacken even further. Hell's fire. She had thought it terrible when she believed Daniel dead but now she experienced a different kind of loss. Often she had marvelled that he had loved her, but had believed in that love. Now he might not love her any more. She could not bear the thought. She had to speak to him. And without stopping to think any more, she opened the door and went after him.

CHAPTER TWENTY-TWO

Daniel was striding along the river bank with visions of violence in his mind. He had wanted to hit Rebekah, that was why he had to get out. His white-hot anger had abated somewhat and he was no longer dwelling on her deception but on a childhood memory of his father knocking his mother to the floor, and of her whimpering when her belly was big with Shaun. His brothers had been out and he had put his arms round his father's leg and hung on to prevent him from kicking his mother again. He shuddered even now at the scene. His father had fallen over, and his mother had lumbered to her feet, and grabbing Daniel's hand had fled with him to Old Mary's house.

As he thought of Old Mary, he remembered the day he had walked with Rebekah to the bay. The attraction between them had been strong even then.

Holy Mary, why had he had to love her? He paused and gazed down into the water. It was where he normally fished and they had bathed here once or twice. He remembered the marks on Rebekah's back and shoulder and there was a tightness in his chest. A Cat o' Nine Tails! It was a bad moment as he struggled with his emotions. He was about to turn round when he saw his brother running towards him.

'Troopers,' panted Shaun. 'I told you they were after me and when they realise who you are, they'll be after you too. Although with that beard—'He paused, bending over and resting his hands on his knees, getting his breath back.

'Is this another one of your tricks?' snapped Daniel. 'Because I'm in the mood to biff you one.'

'Don't be like that, Danny,' he protested. 'We've got to get away from here, and quick. You can drive. You can get us out of here.'

'I can what? You're joking if you think I'm going to get involved in anything to do with you! I wouldn't put it past you to be making all this up.'

Shaun laughed. 'I'm not! Why would I do that? I'm telling you, Danny, they'll be up here soon and we've got to get away.'

'We've got to get away!' Daniel's eyes narrowed. 'What about your friends in the village? I bet they've put you up to this to get me back.'

Shaun protested, but Daniel did not believe him.

'Go and put your head in a pot and boil it!' He pushed his brother out of the way and began to walk back to the house.

Shaun followed him. 'Were those rings really her mother's?'

'You heard what she said.'

'Why wasn't she wearing them?'

'Would you wear a ring like that fancy one to do chores?'

'She could have worn the wedding ring. I bet she's been deceiving you.'

Daniel turned and his expression was bleak. 'Don't talk to me about deception. You told me she was dead! Green told us both that the other was dead! Now get out of my sight before I forget that I once cared that you'd been born alive.' Shaun stopped in his tracks and Daniel walked away.

He saw Rebekah half a mile further up the river, running towards him, and when she would have flung herself at him he held her off. He gazed into the drawn face that was blotchy with tears.

'You were coming back to me?' she stammered.

'How should I know? You've got me that way I don't know where I am. Let's go before Shaun catches up with us.'

'He's still around?'

Daniel nodded and hurried her along, making her run to keep up with him.

'What are you going to do?' she asked.

He stared at her unhappy expression and dropped her hand. 'You want me to make you feel better by saying I forgive you?' he said in a seething voice. 'Straight away! Just like that!' He snapped his fingers.

'I don't suppose you'll ever forgive me. You hate Joshua too much for that.' Her voice trembled. 'But I thought you loved me enough to stay with me. After all, I left him to find you and it wasn't easy for me to come to Ireland alone. I was scared, not only of the fighting, but of what I might find out when I met you again.'

'And what did you find out?' he muttered, looking away from her towards the house.

'That I still loved you,' she cried. 'But I soon realised that I'd been living in a fool's paradise thinking that you would understand why I had married Joshua, so I decided not to tell you. I didn't mean to hurt you.'

He looked at her. 'I'll never understand women. You really thought we could carry on without my ever finding out the truth?'

'I didn't want to think,' she said. 'It seemed simpler just living from day to day and pretending Joshua didn't exist. We were happy.'

'Happy? Living in a fool's paradise?' He shook his head and stared down at the ground.

'What are we going to do?'

He looked up. 'Bloody hell, Rebekah, why keep

asking me that? I bloody don't know,' he said savagely. 'Perhaps we should just to go bed and pretend – that – none of this – has happened?' He did not know why he said it.

'Bed?' She stared at him, her eyes twin pools of shock.

Suddenly he wanted to hurt her. 'Do you think it'll be different? Perhaps it will now I know I'm having it with a married woman.'

She flushed. 'You make it sound more sinful.'

'It is more sinful.'

'How can you say that?'

'I just open my mouth—'

'Daniel, don't be cruel.'

'Cruel! Me?' His voice was harsh. 'The way you went on about Lily, and all the time you were married to bloody Green!'

'I know,' she said miserably. 'If you want to know, I was thoroughly ashamed of myself for going on about Lily.'

'You should be.'

'Daniel, I do love you!'

'So you say. You'll have to prove it.'

'I thought I had by leaving Joshua.' She tilted her chin. 'I've given up a lot for you, you know. Perhaps you should think about that.'

For a moment he said nothing, then with some satisfaction he said, 'Green would be bloody mad if he knew we were together. I wonder what he'd say if he found out?' He took hold of her wrist and hurried her into the house. For once he bolted the door before running her up the stairs.

Daniel no longer wanted to strike her but was in no mood to be nice to her. It seemed to him that she had not grieved long for him, but perhaps he would not have minded so much if it had been anyone else but Joshua Green. Then again, he could be kidding himself because he loved and did not want anyone else to have her. He could hazard a guess to how much she had suffered at Joshua's hands and it did occur to him that she had paid for her mistakes. Even so the pain she had inflicted went deep. He wanted to be rough with her but surprisingly she did not seem to mind that and somewhere along the way desire took over and their passion for each other seemed greater than before. He wondered if she believed that this could be the last time they would make love.

'Would you really have gone through with marrying me?' he panted.

'Yes,' she gasped. 'I didn't want to hurt you.'

'Good God!' He was shocked, but incredibly he was flattered at the same time. 'You're more ruthless than I thought.'

'I love you,' she whispered before he kissed her once more.

Afterwards, Rebekah fell into an exhausted sleep and Daniel lay watching her, considering what to do. He was still thinking when he heard someone trying the front door. He got up and looked out of the window. As he did so, Shaun called in a loud whisper, 'Danny, open up! You've got to let me in!'

He opened the window. 'I don't want you in here. Go away!'

'Danny, for God's sake!' called Shaun in desperate tones.

Not wanting Rebekah wakened, he turned from the window and crept downstairs.

His brother almost fell over the step in his haste to get inside. He had a gun in his hand. 'Danny, they're here! The troopers! They're just up the lane! We'll have to fight it out, but we've got a chance in here.'

Daniel stared at him. 'I could kill you!' His voice was harsh. 'Why do you always have to come and muck up my life? D'you think I'd risk a fight in here?'

'I wouldn't have thought you'd have cared where we fought.' Shaun licked his lips. 'You're not worrying about her after the way she deceived you, now?'

Daniel said nothing, only shutting the door and going to look out of the window. 'If they get us, they'll get her,' he murmured. 'They mightn't believe she's not in on it. Where about are they? Near the gate or what?'

'Not that close.' Shaun's eyes shifted away from his brother's. 'Why?'

'Because I want to get them away from here.' He moved swiftly over to Rebekah's bag on the floor and took something from it. 'Come on,' he said to his brother.

'What are you going to do?' stammered Shaun.

'You'll find out.' He opened the door and pushed his brother in front of him. 'Give me the gun and over to the car!'

Shaun stared at him and slowly a smile crossed his face. 'You're gonna run the sods down!'

'Not if I can help it. You'll have to turn the starting handle.' Daniel loped across the ground and through the gateway. He glanced up the lane which curved a few hundred yards down. The men could be just round the bend.

He got in and flung the handle to Shaun, who hurriedly inserted it. The engine coughed into life as Daniel, ears straining, tossed the gun inside. Shaun jumped in, slammed the door and picked up the gun on the seat. He pulled another from his belt, only to be flung back against the seat as the car started up the lane.

Rebekah woke, recalling instantaneously the traumas of the day. She reached out for Daniel but he was not there. A twinge of anxiety made itself felt as she clambered out of bed and dressed. There was no one downstairs and the fire was almost out. How long had she slept? Her stomach rumbled. She had not eaten all day and neither had Daniel. Where was he? Would he have gone fishing? The rod was in the cupboard. A walk?

Opening the door Rebekah went outside. It was quiet except for the sound of birds. She hurried towards the river and walked further than she had ever done until bushes and undergrowth made it impossible to go any further. Her anxiety grew and she felt light-headed with hunger. Had Daniel gone to the village? Retracing her steps she made for the gate and suddenly realised that the car was missing.

For a moment Rebekah just stared at the vacant spot, hardly able to take in the evidence of her eyes. Then she thought of Shaun but remembered he could not drive. Daniel could. Perhaps he had taken his brother to the nearest town? She gnawed at her lip. When? What time? How long would it have taken if he had done so not knowing the roads?

Rebekah meandered along the lane as far as the bend but there was no sign of anyone. She went back to the house and found the fire out. She did not have the heart to attempt to light it again and made do with a slice of bread and jam and a drink of ginger beer. There was a sock to darn so she set to doing that. She checked for Daniel's spare clothing upstairs. It was still there.

She went outside and wandered up the lane again. Her fear was growing. Perhaps he had decided to leave her? Had been so disgusted with her deceit that he had not been able to stand the sight of her any longer. 'Don't be stupid!' She said the words aloud but it did not make her feel any better. She went back to the house. She would light the fire before it became dark because Daniel would want something warm to eat.

It should have been an easy task because she had watched him get the fire going often enough, but it would not light. She could have cried with frustration as the peat smouldered but did not ignore properly. She longed for Daniel to come back but a voice inside her kept saying, 'He's not coming back.'

Again she went outside to the gate. Nothing! It was getting dark and even the birds were silent. Her loneliness was complete. She went back to the house, lay on the couch and pulled a coat over her. It was only just before dawn that she slept.

It was a horse whinnying that roused Rebekah and she sprang up, only to sit down again because everything spun round her. There was a knock on the door but before she could get up, or ask who it was, the door opened.

Joshua, wearing breeches and a tweed jacket, tossed a riding crop down and leant on the table. 'My dear Rebekah, I'm glad to say that you look bloody awful! It serves you right for making me chase after you to this devilish place. You can get your things together. You're coming home.'

'How did you know where to find me?' Rebekah's voice was barely above a whisper.

'It wasn't easy.' He picked up the crop again and toyed with it. 'A gentleman doesn't expect his new bride to be missing when he returns home after weeks away. The house was empty. There was no Janet. I visited your aunt and she said that you were in London but did not know where. I went to see Edwina and she said the same.' He whacked the table with the crop and his voice rose. 'It was very embarrassing not knowing where my wife had gone!' His eyes glinted. 'I waited a week and still there was no word. Edwina called to see if you were home.' He hit the table again. 'She suggested that you might have gone to Ireland. Something about Florence Nightingale and the Red Cross. I remembered how you'd wanted to come here. What were you thinking of? Where you looking for ghosts? O'Neill's perhaps?'

Rebekah's fear was now so great that it took her a full minute to answer. 'Don't be silly. I just had a yen to see the place again,' she stammered, rising to her feet. 'I knew that you were much too busy to bring me so I came alone.' She crossed her fingers behind her back.

'I see.' He touched her chin with the crop. 'It was naughty of you. Anything could have happened. It's a dangerous country and that's why I didn't bring you in the spring.'

'As you can see I'm perfectly all right.' She pushed the crop away but he immediately touched her face with it again.

'Joshua, please!' She moved out of his reach but he followed her.

'No welcoming kiss for your husband, my precious?' His pale blue eyes rebuked her. 'I would have thought that after six weeks apart you would have missed me. I've missed you.' He had forced her into a corner and now reached for her. She would have ducked beneath his arm but he was too quick. He attempted to kiss her but she averted her face and his lips touched her cheek instead. He shook her. 'What's changed you, Rebekah?' His tone had altered, was sharp instead of velvety. 'I'd started to believe that we could rub along quite nicely.'

Rebekah wanted to scream at that but thought it wiser to remain silent.

Her husband's expression turned ugly. 'Nothing to say, my dear! I thought you would have had lots to tell me!' He nuzzled her neck and instinctly she braced herself as his teeth nipped her skin hard. The next moment she was struggling with him but he forced her down on to the floor. He straddled her, painfully prising her fingers away when she sought to keep her skirts down. He gratified himself swiftly.

When he rolled away from her, it was several

minutes before Rebekah could rise but she managed it. She had to rid herself of the stink of him! The door gave beneath her fingers and she was out and stumbling towards the river. She waded in fully clothed, despite the chill water, and tears rolled down her cheeks. Shaun's coming, and now Joshua's arrival, were death to all her dreams.

'You'll get pneumonia like that,' said Joshua from the river bank. 'Come and get dry and put on a clean frock. Pack your case and let's get going.'

Rebekah ignored him.

His lips thinned. 'Rebekah! You're being utterly stupid. Now come on out of there!' He stepped into the water and seizing a fold of her sodden frock, pulled her towards him. 'Now you'll stop this nonsense or you'll be sorry. Being on your own here has affected your mind.'

A muscle moved in her throat but she did not say anything, only doing what he said. She walked stiffly beside him. He was silent and she knew she was in for trouble, but could see no point in trying to run away. It was obvious that Daniel no longer wanted her. What she had done had been terribly wrong and now she was to pay for it.

She changed and then packed her case while Joshua waited downstairs. For that she was grateful, fearing what he would do to her if he saw Daniel's spare clothing. She went downstairs, sick with misery.

Outside, Joshua untethered the horse and told

Rebekah to get on its back. 'I'm too tired to ride,' she said.

'You don't *have* to do anything!' He made a swipe at her bottom with the crop and she moved swiftly. 'That's the ticket.' He smiled. 'Just sit and I'll lead him. We'll fetch my bag from the big house. I'm not staying in this place any longer than I have to. They're a sullen lot and it takes all day to get any information out of them.'

Rebekah made no reply but was relieved that nobody seemed to have mentioned Daniel. When they got to the house she paid little attention to her surroundings because she was so depressed. They stayed only half an hour while a pony trap was brought round. Then they left.

Rebekah was sick on the ferry and Joshua told her that it was all in her mind. She thought of her father and how he had said the same thing to her mother, and how because of him she had married Joshua. In that moment she hated them both.

When the Liver birds came in sight she felt a momentary lifting of her misery. At least Daniel had been right in saying that she had friends here.

CHAPTER TWENTY-THREE

It was to be several weeks before Rebekah saw either of her friends. With having been away there were matters to be seen to and besides she was unwell and felt lethargic, having no interest in anything. Eventually, though, she decided that she should go and see her aunt. On the way she met Edwina.

'So you're home! Did you go to Ireland? It's been ages. You look terrible,' said the older woman.

'Thanks,' said Rebekah drily, not feeling too friendly to Edwina, partly blaming her for mentioning Ireland to Joshua.

'What's up?' Edwina's smile vanished. 'Is it something I've said?'

Rebekah realised that she could hardly tell her the truth. 'Nobody likes being told they look terrible. My tummy's a bit upset and I feel tired since I got back from Ireland.'

'Tougher than you thought, was it?' Edwina put her hand through Rebekah's arm. 'Was Joshua cross?'

'Yes. You know how he feels about Ireland.'

'By the look of you, you saw more unpleasant sights than you planned on?'

'Yes, I did.' Her smile came and went as she remembered her first sight of the wounded Daniel. 'I really don't want to talk about it.'

Edwina nodded. 'I understand that.'

They walked along the road in silence. Rebekah forced herself to ask, 'Have you spoken to my aunt?'

'You're joking! You know her opinion of me.'

'I was on my way to see her.'

'Come and have a cup of tea with me first. Dad's out.'

Rebekah did not really feel like going but said yes. After all, it was not Edwina's fault that everything had fallen apart.

The cup of tea did Rebekah good and so did Edwina's gossip about the neighbourhood, coupled with her talk of the latest films. In return, Rebekah told her a little about Dublin, the house and the village. She had another cup of tea and a couple of scones. Her appetite seemed to have returned and she did not refuse another scone when Edwina attentively offered the plate.

Her friend suddenly blurted out, 'You know, Becky, the more I look at you the more I'm convinced!'

'Convinced about what?' said Rebekah in surprise.

'That you're having a baby!'

'What!'

'You're having a baby,' repeated Edwina. 'There's a look about your face. And you said that your tummy's been upset. Yet you've been tucking into those scones like there's nothing wrong with you. Have you seen your monthlies lately?'

'No!' Rebekah stared at her and a multitude of emotions erupted inside her. 'Are you sure?'

Edwina smiled. 'I can't be sure. I'm not a doctor or a midwife. Would you be pleased?'

'Pleased?' Rebekah pressed a hand to her stomach. Joshua had been going on about a son and heir, but if it was well past two months since her period then . . . Her spirits lifted. 'Yes. I'd be pleased.'

'You'll have to look after yourself. Plenty of good food and rest,' said Edwina.

Rebekah nodded and suddenly wanted to be doing something. It was as if she had suddenly come alive again. 'What should I do?'

'You'll have to see a doctor.' Edwina's eyes twinkled. 'I bet Joshua will be over the moon.'

'Yes.' Rebekah smiled. Hopefully her having a baby would alter matters.

'He'll probably coddle you to death. You'll have to be careful. Lots of babies miscarry in the first few months.'

'I'll tell him that.' Since returning, her husband had taken full advantage of what he called his marital rights. It was very probable that he would consider the child his but she was sure she knew different. Oh Daniel, our baby! There were times when she just could not believe that he had left her without a word. Now she wanted to weep but instead had to smile. 'I'll tell Joshua as soon as I'm sure.'

'You do,' said Edwina. 'The sooner he knows, the sooner you'll be spoilt.'

Rebekah could only hope that was true.

Because she was deep in thought, she would have walked past her aunt's house if Esther had not been leaning on the gate. 'Rebekah!' She pounced on her, seizing her arm. 'Thou must come in. I've missed you so much. Joshua called and didn't seem to know where you were. I didn't tell him about your friend because she told me not to.'

'So Brigid did come to see you?'

Her aunt nodded vigorously. 'She spoke a bit rough but seemed very fond of thee. She told me that thou was well and I wasn't to worry about thee. That you weren't sure when you'd be home. But I have worried, my dear. Hannah kept saying that she knew that thou would just go off and not come back. That thee were kicking thy legs up in London, and giving the men the glad eye.' Her cheeks flushed. 'Thou knows the way she goes on.'

'Who better?' said Rebekah wryly.

'She said it was very odd that thee didn't write to me thyself and I must admit, dear, that I have wondered why.'

'I didn't go to London,' admitted Rebekah. 'I've been in Ireland and I didn't tell you because I knew that would worry you even more.'

Her aunt's look was one of pure disbelief. 'Why on earth did thou go there? So dangerous, Rebekah.'

She shrugged. 'There are lots of places in Ireland that are far more peaceful than Liverpool, Auntie dear. I went to see the farm where Papa was born. I just had a yen. I've been back for weeks but haven't been feeling well. Now shall I come in for that cup of tea or not? I have some news you might be interested in.'

Esther opened the gate and they went inside. Hannah was coming down the stairs as they walked up the lobby and Rebekah was certain she had been spying on them through the upstairs window.

'So thee's back, is thee?' said the maid, giving the shiny knob at the bottom of the stairs a vigorous rub with a duster. 'Just like a bad penny, thou is.'

'I'm pleased to see you, too, Hannah. Killed anybody's character lately?' She smiled.

'What's that?' said the maid, glaring at her. 'I ain't killed nobody. Thee and thee arsenic. Miss Esther's very well.'

'What's this?' said Esther, looking startled.

Rebekah pulled on her arm. 'It's a joke which Hannah didn't get. Let's go and sit down. That knee's still hurting you, I see. I'll have to get you out and about before I won't be able to fit behind the steering wheel.'

'What do you mean?' said her aunt.

Rebekah told her that she could be having a baby.

'But that's lovely!' Esther flung her arms around her. 'I do hope it's a boy.'

Rebekah agreed that a boy would be acceptable.

'Thou'll know thee's born when thee gives birth,' said Hannah, smiling. 'Aye! Thee'll know, me girl.'

Rebekah laughed and wondered just what reception Joshua would give her news.

Startled but pleased, his pale blue eyes fixed on Rebekah's face, and he paused in the act of fastening the last button of his shirt. 'You're having a baby? Well, it's about time! I knew I could do it but I was starting to wonder about you. You've seen the doctor?'

'Yes. It's early days but he's sure I am.' She wished she had the courage to tell him that it was Daniel's child and to wipe the smile off his face.

He sat next to her on the bed, putting his arm round her, and kissed her cheek. 'We'll have to look after you now.'

'Yes. You'll have to be careful,' murmured Rebekah. 'I mean, it might be best – safer – if we don't have relations for a while. I've heard that you can lose a baby that way.' She did her best to infuse regret into her voice.

He frowned. 'Did the doctor say that?'

'Yes.' She smiled and deliberately rested a hand on his trousered thigh. 'I'll need some money.'

His fair brows rose. 'For baby clothes? Don't you think it's a bit early?'

She opened her eyes wide. 'For clothes for me, Joshua. I'm going to grow out of everything I've got and you don't want me looking a frump, do you?'

To her surprise Joshua reddened. 'Of course not. But you won't go buying them in shops,' he said gruffly. 'You'll have them made. There was a woman my sister used to have call. I'll find you her address.' He rose and went over to the walnut dressing table and unlocked a drawer. He came back over to her. She suffered his kiss as he pressed money into her hand and a piece of paper. 'Treat yourself to something nice, Rebekah. Flowers or chocolates. Some new perfume, perhaps? Anything you like.'

She thanked him, although she considered it no more than her due, and planned to save some of it. She would see Brigid, though, and take her out for a slap up meal where she could tell her all her troubles and hope she did not say: 'I told you so!'

'Yer like a bad penny,' said Brigid in a non-nonsense voice but with eyes suspiciously bright. 'Yer keep turning up just when I think I've got rid of yer.' With

419

unnecessary briskness she dusted some non-existent crumbs off the damask cloth on the table between them.

'Hannah said I was a bad penny,' murmured Rebekah. 'I think she still has her eye on my aunt's money.'

Brigid smiled. 'She didn't like me arriving bearing news. She'd rather yer'd just vanished from the face of the earth.'

'I could get a complex,' said Rebekah, looking up from the menu. 'Shaun turned up at the farm after I'd written to you. And, of course, you know how he feels about me.'

'I was wondering when we'd get round to why you're home. Tell me what happened?'

Rebekah told her everything, including what she had not mentioned in the letter.

Brigid's expression was severe. 'Yer're a right pair of sinners and I don't know how many "Hail Marys" yer'd have to say to get yerself forgiveness out of all this.'

'I don't blame you for saying that,' sighed Rebekah. 'Sometimes I wonder if it was really me doing all those things. But I love him and he loved me.'

'And having said that,' said Brigid, 'you think it excuses everything?'

'No. But I'm paying for my sins.'

Brigid shook her head. 'I bet.' She was quiet a moment then said, 'I find it hard to believe that

Daniel would just up and leave yer without a word. Although he had every right to be mad with you for lying through your eye teeth.'

'I didn't lie,' said Rebekah with the smallest of smiles. 'I just didn't tell the truth. It was so difficult because Joshua and Daniel hate each other, and we were so happy.' She leant on one elbow. 'I've thought a lot since being back in Liverpool and wonder now whether Daniel would have come back? Although I can't stop thinking of how he looked when I told him about being married.'

'It's a hard thing for a man to stomach,' said Brigid. 'But I'm inclined to think that it's all down to Shaun, Daniel's going. They must have left together. Weren't there any clues?'

'Clues?'

'Yes! All the best mysteries have clues. Look at Sherlock Holmes and that new writer, Agatha Christie! What was the last thing that Daniel said to yer about Shaun?'

Rebekah considered. 'Not much. Something about him still hanging around, and Daniel not wanting to talk to him.'

Brigid's face brightened. 'There yer are then! He might not have wanted to go with him, but perhaps he had to. You mentioned the troopers—'

Rebekah put down the menu and was silent for several moments. 'I have considered that the troopers or the Irregulars captured him, but I don't like thinking like that. I'd rather he'd just left me than have to start believing all over again that – that he might have been shot by one side or the other.'

Brigid squeezed her hand. 'Don't be thinking of any of it. Yer don't know what's happened. Maybe yer'll see him again?'

Rebekah nervously twisted a strand of hair round her finger. 'I haven't told you all of it – I'm having a baby.'

There was a brief silence before Brigid said, 'Well, there's nothing so surprising about that. Whose do yer think it is?'

'I'm pretty sure it's Daniel's.'

'I wouldn't let his lordship hear yer say that.'

Rebekah gave a tight smile. 'I'm not a complete idiot.' She picked up the menu. 'Now what are we going to have to eat? You can have anything your heart desires.'

Brigid's expression was suddenly upset. 'Oh, Becky, luv, yer really worry me sometimes! Where will it all end?'

She pulled a face. 'I don't know. We'll just have to hope for the best. What are you having?'

Brigid sighed, ordered roast beef and Yorkshire pudding, and changed the subject to talk about Joe and her family, adding that Patrick had been home, had met a girl in Australia and was talking of settling down there. Rebekah was surprised but pleased and wished him all the luck in the world.

The meeting with Brigid made Rebekah feel more settled and although Daniel was never far from her thoughts and she had a continuous aching regret for what might have been, she looked forward to the baby's birth.

Two items of news out of Ireland almost destroyed her determination to get on with life as hopefully as possible. These were the reported deaths of Arthur Griffiths from an apoplexy and the shooting of Michael Collins in an ambush. If Daniel had been captured by the troopers and was in prison, there could be reprisals for the death of such a prominent leader as Collins. For days she fretted, but gradually accepted that she was not doing herself or the baby any good.

The months passed slowly and Joshua, who had been irritable at first due to his enforced celibacy, seemed to grow resigned to Rebekah's unavailability. There were days when he arrived home extremely late but Rebekah asked him no questions. He often talked of 'my son' and of the child inheriting Green's one day.

Just before Christmas the death by firing squad of Liam Mellows, who had been at Four Courts, was reported. His was not the first Irregular's death Rebekah had read about but it affected her deeply as the baby was moving inside her. She did not want to think of death when life was so precious. She wished so many things could have been different and that she knew definitely what had happened to Daniel. The Civil War dragged on despite the Irish gaols being full to overflowing with prisoners.

The New Year came and went and the pile of tiny garments, that Rebekah and her aunt were making grew to ridiculous proportions as April approached.

'There won't be enough days in the week for the poor thing to wear all these,' said Edwina, when Rebekah showed her the deep drawers full.

Rebekah eased her back. 'I'm making sure I'm well prepared. I feel so enormous that I'm sure this baby's twins and they're playing football.'

Edwina sighed. 'All mums-to-be feel huge at the end. Have you decided whether to be confined at home or in hospital? More mums are opting for a hospital birth these days – nice and sanitary.'

'Joshua says home.' Rebekah grimaced. 'I'm to have the doctor and a nurse afterwards. I must admit to feeling more than a bit nervous. Is it as painful as they say? Because the doctor says that I can have an injection of scopolamine and morphine if the pains get bad.'

'Twilight sleep. I've read about it in a brochure.' Edwina sat on the rocking chair and looked up at Rebekah. 'It's said to shorten labour and help with the milk.'

'Then you think it's worth trying?'

Edwina said softly. 'If things get bad, you'll beg for it.'

Rebekah paled and put a hand over her swollen stomach. 'I'll bear anything as long as he doesn't die.'

'Not as many babies do die these days. But you're sure it's going to be a boy?'

Rebekah laughed suddenly. 'Girls don't play football.'

Edwina smiled. 'There'll come a day when nothing will stop us women doing anything we want.'

'I still think you're a suffragette at heart,' said Rebekah, still smiling as she shut the drawer. 'Come and have a cup of tea.'

Edwina rose from the chair and they went downstairs arm in arm.

Two days later Rebekah went into what she called premature labour and there was no time for twilight sleep. She gave birth to a six pound fourteen ounce son, and a smiling Joshua came into the room as the baby was laid in her arms. 'Michaels says it's a boy.'

'He's beautiful!' A sore but not too exhausted Rebekah marvelled as she gazed into the red little face with the screwed up eyes.

'He's ugly and dark-haired!' exclaimed Joshua, his smile fading slightly. 'I thought he'd be fair – and he hasn't the Greens' nose.'

The nurse looked up at him as she folded a towel. 'I've seen babies with hair as dark as dark can be, sir, end up as fair as Goldilocks. First lot of hair often falls out.'

'I see.' He sat on the edge of the bed and touched the baby's cheek. 'He has blue-grey eyes, though?'

'Yes. But eyes can change colour.'

'Good God!' Joshua stared at the baby. 'I hope he doesn't change into a girl,' he said with deliberate humour.

The nurse smiled condescendingly. 'Now that would be a miracle! It's a fine boy you've got there.'

'He's lovely,' said Rebekah, her arms tightening protectively about her son, and hiding her expression from Joshua. 'Thank you, nurse, for everything. And I must thank Doctor Michaels. I didn't have chance to do so before.'

The nurse smiled. 'He said you were a woman of good sense. No screeching, and you did as you were told.'

Joshua looked gratified. 'I should hope no wife of mine would kick up a fuss. But well done, dear.' He kissed Rebekah's forehead.' I'll leave you with nurse now and go and phone the good news to a few people.' He added with unaccustomed consideration, 'If you don't mind, I might need to go out for a while?'

'Don't worry about me,' said Rebekah cheerfully. 'I'll be glad to rest.'

'Of course.' He waggled his fingers in her direction before disappearing behind the open door.

Nurse and Rebekah smiled at each other. 'Best place for husbands, out of the way,' said the nurse.

'Now let me take baby and you have your rest.'

Reluctantly Rebekah handed over her child and relaxed against the pillows. Thank God for nurse! But was it true that eyes could change colour? She did not allow the question to plague her. At least she had been safely delivered of Daniel's son. She wondered what he would do if he knew about his child. For a moment she was sad and then her gaze wanderd to the baby's crib, and turning over carefully, she was asleep in minutes.

CHAPTER TWENTY-FOUR

Rebekah's son was christened Adam Joshua David, and as soon as she was fit and Brigid had a day off, she wheeled him in his pram to call on her friend.

'He's gorgeous,' said Brigid, a dreamy expression on her face as she rocked the wide-eyed baby who was sucking his fist.

Rebekah smiled. 'You'll have to get one of your own.'

Brigid turned pink. 'I'll get married first. What does Joshua think of him?'

'He's as proud as punch.' Rebekah sat in a chair, unbuttoned her blouse and held out her arms for her child. 'Although he still doesn't like David's hair being black. He wants it fair and so it should be fair.' She began to suckle the baby, looking down at him with a gentle expression on her face.

Brigid sat opposite her. 'But David has blue eyes. Isn't he happy with that?'

'They're changing colour,' said Rebekah quietly. 'They're going darker.'

'Oh!' Brigid looked into the baby's face. 'What does he think about that?'

'He hasn't said anything.' She rubbed her cheek against the baby's downy head.

'Perhaps he hasn't noticed?'

'Nurse remarked on it in front of him.'

Brigid's face clouded. 'Do yer think he has any suspicions?'

'If he has, he's keeping them to himself for the moment. Just as I kept quiet my suspicions of his going with prostitutes when I was expecting. I discovered some rubber sheaths inside a pair of his socks and he was often out in the evenings. With that sort of woman, he'd be scared of catching something.'

Her friend frowned. 'He hasn't been violent, has he?'

'Raised his hand and his voice.' Rebekah lifted her head. 'He doesn't like the baby crying. Nor does he like me breast feeding. He goes on about me putting David on the bottle but I have nurse on my side.' A smile lifted her mouth. 'She says mother's breast is best and it really embarrasses him.'

'He's jealous of yer giving all yer attention to the baby. But as long as he doesn't suspect that David is Daniel's.'

Rebekah's arm tightened about her son. 'If he attempts to hurt David, I couldn't stay with him. At the moment I'm resigned to living with him, but there might come a time—'

'Well, yer know what to do if things get tough.'

Rebekah's eyes softened. 'I'm a real trial to you, aren't I, love?'

'Yer a right nuisance,' said Brigid in a gruff voice. 'I'll make us a cup of tea.'

Rebekah smiled and no more was said on the subject of Joshua.

David thrived and Rebekah did most things for him except his washing. She found caring for him a joy, but worried when Joshua played with him. Sometimes her husband would pick David up, gaze into his face, then toss him into the air. She would hold her breath and start forward because he did not put out his arms to catch the child until he almost reached the ground. Twice she spoke to Joshua sharply and he turned on her. 'Do you think I would drop my own son?'

'No,' she said quietly, conscious of the aggression in his voice.

Often Rebekah was aware of Joshua's eyes on her when she was nursing the baby, and she tensed, waiting for him to make some comment but he never did and she could only feel relief when he took himself off somewhere. The weeks passed and she was as happy as she ever could be parted from Daniel.

It was one May day when Rebekah had been to

visit Brigid and was walking home, that Mr McIntyre called to her, waving a newspaper: 'The Civil War's over!'

A smile spread over her face. 'That's good news.'

'Well, everything's been going to pieces, hasn't it?' He leant on the gate. 'They'll have to sort something workable out.'

Rebekah thought of Daniel. 'Peace in Ireland,' she murmured. 'It seems almost unbelievable.'

'Aye, well, people can't be fighting forever.' He grinned. 'Are you coming in for a cup of tea?'

'Thanks but I better hadn't. I want to call in on my aunt and then I'll have to rush home. I've been out all afternoon.'

He looked disappointed. 'Perhaps next time?'

'Yes.' She waved her hand and went on her way.

Esther was pleased to see her and the baby. 'Where's my precious little boy?' she cooed over the pram. 'Can I have a hold of him?'

'Your precious little boy is wet,' said Rebekah promptly. 'I'll have to change him.'

For a moment her aunt's face showed distaste then she smiled. 'He can't help it, the little love. I'll get Hannah to make us a cup of tea. Then I want to talk to thee, Rebekah.'

She looked at her aunt, wondering what Hannah had been up to this time, but Esther's conversation had nothing to do with the maid.

'I've made a will, Rebekah, and I'm leaving all my

431

money to your son. I know thee must be wondering why I haven't left it to thee, but—' Her aunt paused and her mouth tightened. 'I'm not the fool thy husband thinks me. I'm not chancing him getting his hands on it – which he might if I left it to thee. I've tied it up so he won't be able to touch it.'

'Good for you, Aunt Esther!' Rebekah could not be annoyed with her, although expectations of her aunt's money had occasionally figured in her own plans. She balanced her half-naked son on her hip, rose from her seat and kissed her aunt. 'You can't realise how happy it makes me. At least he'll be secure.'

Esther flushed and said unsteadily, 'Thou might have thy faults, Rebekah, but I've watched thee and thou loves the baby and hast the makings of a good mother. Even Hannah has admitted that and she knows about such things. Sarah would have been proud of thee. If only Papa had lived to see this great-grandson of his, he too would have been proud.'

Rebekah did not know what to say, so kissed her aunt again.

She was smiling when she left the house but as she neared the park her expression became sombre. She dreaded facing Joshua. He had started pawing her in bed but she had continued to bind herself underneath, telling him that the bleeding after the birth had not stopped. Surely it would not be long before he realised that she was pretending?

His car was in front of the house but Janet opened the door. 'Mr Green's upstairs,' she answered in response to Rebekah's question.

'Is he in a good mood,' she whispered.

'The cat's in hiding,' muttered Janet. 'That says something.'

Rebekah grimaced. 'Where's Nurse?'

'Gone,' said Janet succinctly.

'Gone where?'

'Gone for good.' Janet jerked her head upwards. 'The master told her to pack her bags and paid her off.'

Rebekah felt a sudden chill. David whimpered. 'Has my husband mentioned anything happening to one of his ships?'

'Never a word. And there's nothing in the *Echo*.'

Rebekah gnawed her lower lip. 'Open the back gate and I'll go into the garden.'

She wheeled the pram round and settled herself in a chair. As she fed David, she gazed unseeingly at the mermaid figurehead, wondering what the dismissal of the nurse meant. Was it money, or was there some deeper reason behind her being sent off?

There was a sound at the french windows and she turned and saw Joshua. He lit a cheroot and came slowly towards her. 'Nurse has gone.'

'Janet told me.'

She determined not to ask why but he answered her unspoken question. 'I didn't see why you needed help with the boy. You spend enough time with him yourself.'

'That's all right.' She flashed him a smile. 'I'll manage. When I was on Outdoor Relief I saw women coping with five and six children without help.'

'Slum children,' he said disparagingly.

Rebekah stared at him. 'I thought you cared about the children and the work of the Seamen's Orphanage?'

His eyes narrowed against the smoke. 'I was taught that it was my duty to show an interest. My father also told me that a man often has to grin and bear things.'

'Men aren't the only ones.' she murmured.

'What's that mean?' He scowled. 'What have you to complain about?'

'Did I complain?'

'It sounded like a complaint.' He looked disgruntled. 'If anyone has cause for complaint, it's me. You're always cuddling that baby. He'll be spoilt. It's not good for children to be picked up all the time.' He moved suddenly and wrenched David out of her arms. The child gave a startled whimper as he was dragged from her breast and she cried with pain and attempted to regain possession of him.

'I'm feeding him,' she said angrily. 'Be careful of that cigar!'

'You're always feeding him,' growled Joshua, pressing David against him and staring at her bared breast. 'There's never any time for me.'

'You'd rather he starved?' She pulled together the edges of her blouse.

'Go on, cover yourself up! Never anything for me these days!'

She looked away from him. 'You wanted a baby.'

'Yes, I did. But I didn't expect it to take you over. Another woman would have been happy to leave it all to the nurse, but not you. You're going to have to learn that I won't put up with it forever. You can put him to bed now and give me some of your time. And by the way, I've moved his crib out of our room.' He offered David to her then feigned dropping him as she put out her arms.

She caught him quickly. 'Why do you do that?' she said in a seething voice. 'One of these days—'

'One of these days I might drop him, were you going to say?' muttered Joshua, stubbing out his cheroot on the place the mermaid would have had a bottom if she did not have a tail. 'Maybe not if you put him on the bottle and give me some of what he's been getting.'

She flushed. 'I want to feed him myself. He's my son!'

'He might be yours but is he mine?' Joshua lit another cheroot.

'What's that supposed to mean?' Rebekah's voice was cool despite her heart's beginning to race.

'His eyes are changing colour. If I believed—'

'Believed what?'

'He doesn't look like me.'

435

'He's only a baby.' She placed David in his pram.

'I've often heard people say "Doesn't he look like his father?" of babies.' His eyes glinted. 'And there's another thing. I don't like you calling him David.'

She was ready for that one. 'I prefer it to Adam. Papa and I weren't always on the best of terms.'

'I suppose you prefer David because it's the nearest you dare get to Daniel?' he snapped.

She stared at him, thinking how often she stopped on the brink of an argument. She did so now, saying in a controlled voice: 'David was the Old Testament hero – and eventually a king. I thought it fitting.'

His face reddened. 'You're pushing your luck, Rebekah. I know my Bible. I'm still king of this castle, not that child. It's something you forget.'

'How could I? You lord it over me whenever you can.'

'I'm your husband! I have rights.' He tossed his cheroot in a flower bed and before she could think of moving away, seized hold of her arms and thrust his face close to hers. 'What were you doing in Ireland last summer? Why did you really go? Did you soothe any rebels' brows? O'Neill's for instance?' It was so sudden that Rebekah could not think what to say for a moment. 'Well?' he demanded.

For a moment she was tempted to fling the truth in his face but common sense asserted itself. She had David's safety to consider. 'Is this some sick joke?

You told me Daniel was dead. Has he suddenly come alive again?'

For a moment he was silent, his anger digging into her upper arms, then he muttered. 'Put the boy to bed. I want some of your attention for a change.'

Rebekah did as she was told, dreading the hours ahead, but it was not as bad as she feared. A business acquaintance of Joshua's called and the men talked shipping and the slump in trade while the level in a bottle of whisky fell. Rebekah slipped away to feed David and stayed in the nursery. She was still there, gazing out of the open window over the moonlit garden, when Joshua came and stood in the doorway.

'Why aren't you in bed? You should be in bed.' His words were slurred.

'I'm coming.' Rebekah tried to inch past him but he took hold of her and pulled her close. Whisky fumes fanned her cheek and she recoiled. 'How much have you drunk?'

'Not enough not to know what to do with you. You should have had a drink with us, my sweet. The alcohol might make you more friendly.'

'I didn't want a drink,' she murmured, trying to free herself. 'But if it's what makes you happy.'

'I'm not happy.' He swayed as he clung to her and said against her ear, 'You could make me happy if you—' He whispered a suggestion.

'No!' She tried to pull away but he kept hold of her.

'You did it when we were first married! You did! You did!' he cried petulantly.

Anger stirred inside her. 'Only because you forced me. I'm not doing it now! Now let me go before you wake the baby.'

'Damn and blast the baby,' he shouted, shaking her. 'I've been patient, staying away from you, and now I want what's my right!'

'Keep your voice down,' stuttered Rebekah. 'Do you want to wake the whole neighbourhood?'

'I damn well don't care!' He slapped her across the face.

Her hand went to her cheek and there was a churning inside her. 'Don't you hit me!'

'And how are you going to stop me?' he sneered.

She kicked his ankle and they began to struggle. He yelled insults at her and she screeched at him, not caring what she said but fighting like one demented, hating him for all he had put her through. The baby's crying brought her back to her senses. 'Now look what you've done,' she panted. 'Let me go to him.'

'No! Let me!' Joshua pushed her against the wall and went over the crib. He snatched up David and went over to the open window and held him out.

Rebekah screamed and darted across the room, hovering around Joshua, terrified to touch him. 'Don't drop him! Please, don't drop him!'

He glanced over his shoulder and there was a

triumphant look on his face. 'What'll you give me if I don't?'

She did not hesitate. 'Anything!'

'What I asked before?'

She nodded.

'Give me your word. I don't trust you.'

'I swear it.'

He brought the baby in and gave him to Rebekah. David's screams turned to whimpers as she hushed and rocked him.

'Just put him in his crib,' ordered Joshua, still smiling.

Rebekah wondered if her husband was quite sane to do such a thing but was still too shocked to attempt further rebellion at the moment.

She performed the act Joshua desired, disliking it and him. She vowed that it was for the last time. The risk to David in staying with Joshua was more than she could cope with. Tomorrow she would leave.

The next morning, Janet asked if she was all right, looking with some concern at the bruising on her face. Rebekah did not want to involve her so she just answered that she felt a little unwell and asked her to do the shopping. With the maid out of the way she hoped that there would be nobody concerned enough about her to notice her leaving.

It was no easy task choosing what to take. When she had left for Ireland it had been a simple matter of packing as suitcase for herself. Now she had all the baby's paraphernalia to think about. She loaded her car. It was a struggle and she could not find room for the crib, but the rest she managed with the help of a couple of boys playing in the park. Then she sat in the driving seat a moment while the enormity of what she was doing overwhelmed her. Then, vividly, like something on a screen she pictured Joshua's face as he held David out of the window and she drove off.

Rebekah arrived at Brigid's home just before noon, not expecting to find her friend in but hoping her sister might be there. Not that she had ever been able to get close to Kath.

'I hope you don't mind but could I come in and wait for Brigid?' Despite all her efforts, Rebekah's voice trembled.

Kath frowned. 'I suppose yer'd better.'

Rebekah felt the colour rise in her cheeks. 'If you'd rather I didn't – I could come back.'

'No. Come in.' Her eyes narrowed as she scrutinised Rebekah's face. 'You look like yer've been in the wars but I'm not going to ask questions. I'm doing the ironing. Our Brigid'll sort yer out.' Her glance passed over the loaded car. 'I'll help yer with the pram and then yer can take it round the back with the baby in.' Rebekah thanked her, hoping that Brigid would not be long.

The children came in first and Veronica fussed over the baby. Brigid was soon after them. 'What is it, Becky luv? I didn't expect to see yer this soon.' She looped her handbag over the door knob and pulled off her gloves. 'Come in the other room and tell me what happened?'

Rebekah told her.

Brigid's mouth tightened. 'The pig! What are yer going to do? Mam'll say that there's a place here as long as yer need it, but it's not what yer used to and I won't always be here.' She toyed with a button on her dress. 'Joe and I have decided to get married at the end of July.'

Rebekah smiled. 'I'm glad for you both. And I'm not planning on staying for ever. Just until I find my feet. I'd have gone to Aunt Esther's only that would be the first place Joshua would look for me. After that it would be Edwina's.'

'He won't think of coming here?' said Brigid.

Rebekah hesitated. 'I don't think he knows that I'm still friends with you.'

'Hmmph! You never know. You'll have to be careful.'

That night David slept in a drawer while Rebekah shared Brigid's double bed. It took some time for Rebekah to sleep as her mind was trying to formulate plans for hers and David's future. The trouble was that there was a great big 'if' over the weeks and months ahead.

The next few days Rebekah discovered what hard work it really was looking after a baby without nurse's help. Dealing with nappies and wet bedding with no running hot water was a never-ending chore, although there was a certain satisfaction in seeing the washing blowing on the line in the yard despite the smuts it collected. But it was not all work, and she enjoyed taking David for his walk. She was often stopped by women in the street who, talking nonsense to her son, made comments about his dark curls. In return he favoured a few with a toothless smile.

Ma Maisie doled her out a share of the household tasks and often asked Rebekah to do the shopping. She had some money of her own and would sometimes buy a special treat for the supper table as well as contributing to expenses. It was while shopping that she came out of a shop about a week after leaving Joshua to find the pram with David in it missing. She tried not to panic, but after scouring the road, shops and sidestreets, her anxiety was pitiful. She ran home to Kath and poured out what had happened. She alerted the neighbours and they joined the search but came back empty-handed.

The local bobby was informed and asked Rebekah some pertinent questions about her married status. When she said that she had left her husband, he proved to be unsympathetic. 'Maybe you should go home, Missus,' he said, closing his book. 'Perhaps the little lad's there.'

The idea that Joshua might have snatched David had been at the back of her mind since she had discovered him missing but the thought of returning to his house had caused her to search every other avenue first. Now she had to face facts. Somehow her husband had guessed where she was hiding. Fearing that he might do something to David and not waiting for Brigid to come home, Rebekah got in the car and drove to her former home.

Joshua opened the door to her. 'I want my son,' she demanded, burning flags of colour high on her cheeks. 'What have you done with him?'

His mouth curved in a smile that did not affect the chill light in his eyes. 'Rebekah! I was expecting you. Do come in?'

'I don't want to come in. I want David!'

He scowled. 'I'm not having a wrangling match with you on the doorstep for the neighbours and passers-by to listen to. Haven't you embarrassed me enough, leaving me the way you did? I won't tell you anything unless you come inside. No! Come round the back first.'

Rebekah glared but accompanied him. 'Is David out in the garden in his pram?'

'You'll see,' he said.

She saw all right. No pram but he had chopped off the head of Andromeda. 'Is this another sick joke of yours?' she demanded after several seconds. 'Where is my baby?'

'You don't like it? I think she looks better. Come and have a drink and I will explain all.' He took her elbow and hustled her inside and into the sitting room. 'Do sit down.' He pushed her on the sofa and went over to the drinks cabinet. 'A brandy for your nerves?'

'There's nothing wrong with my nerves.' she retorted, clasping her hands tightly to stop herself from hitting him.

'A cup of tea, then?' He rang the bell and a maid entered and took his order. She glanced curiously at Rebekah.

'Where's Janet?' asked Rebekah as soon as she was out of the room.

'I decided to dispense with her services.' He opened a cigar box and offered it to her, sighing heavily when she shook her head. 'I'm sorry,' he murmured. 'I forgot that you didn't. I suppose the tea will help to calm you down.'

'Seeing my son will calm me down.' She rose her feet. 'Is he upstairs? I'll go to him.'

Joshua blocked her way. 'A waste of time. He's not there.'

'Let me see.' She tried to go round him but he only moved with her.

'Believe me, Rebekah, he isn't in the house!' His tone was emphatic.

She stared at him. 'How did you find him? Where is he? What have you done to him?'

'A letter from your common friend inside one of your books.' He exhaled a fragrant cloud. 'The boy's in a safe place. An orphanage actually.'

'I don't believe you,' she stammered. 'Why would you—'

Joshua smiled. 'Why indeed? But don't you think his father might still be alive? Or perhaps he's really dead now?'

Rebekah was silent.

Joshua's left eyelid twitched rapidly and the cheroot smouldered between his lips as he spoke jerkily. '*You* might say his father is very much alive. That I am the father! I would like to believe you, my dear, but—' He cleared his throat. 'I'm going to Ireland. Someone in that Godforsaken village must have seen something. I have a photograph of O'Neill. Money talks. If he was there—' He paused expectantly. 'You could save me a journey, Rebekah.'

'And you could tell me the truth.' She was trying her hardest to keep calm. 'Where is my baby?'

Joshua's fist curled and it was obvious that he was struggling for control as much as she was. 'The truth, my sweet, my love, is that you are an adulteress and as such must pay for your sins. Your son, as I said, is in an orphanage.'

Before she could speak there was a knock on the door and Joshua answered it, taking the cup from the maid, shutting the door and turning the key in the lock as Rebekah moved towards the door.

'Joshua, you're crazy!' She clenched her fists. 'Unlock that door. This isn't Victorian times, you know! Let me out!'

He smiled and pocketed the key. 'I'm the king of the castle, remember? You should think before you act.'

She moistened her mouth. 'Joshua, you can't keep me here.'

He said quietly. 'Drink your tea. I'm going to have a brandy.'

'Dear God,' she cried, 'I don't want tea! I don't want brandy! I want my son!'

'The good Lord would agree with what I'm doing,' said her husband, pouring out a generous measure of spirit. 'You're a wicked woman. Drink your tea before it gets cold.'

'You hypocrite! What about you and your prostitutes?'

'It's different for men.'

Her eyes glittered. 'The old excuse! Will you tell me where David is?'

'I might if you calm down and drink your tea.'

She stared at him and then sat down, picking up her cup. 'Well?'

'Well what?' He swirled the brandy, watching her.

'Where's David?' Her mouth was dry so she drank the tea.

'I've told you – I'm not going to have him back here, Rebekah. I'll tell people that he died and that grief turned your brain.'

Suddenly she could not believe that it was all happening. It must be a nightmare. She stared at him as he took a large mouthful of brandy. 'I loved you once, Rebekah. We could have been happy but you turned against me.'

She was starting to feel strange and hysteria rose inside her. 'You caused me to turn against you! You were cruel and you lied to me.'

'Lied to you about what?' He started forward.

'Daniel! You cheated, and cheats never prosper!' She put her hands to hot cheeks. 'This is crazy!'

'No!' Suddenly his face loomed in front of her, large and grotesque. 'It's you that's crazy and I know just the place for you. Only the best asylum for my wife, so it's expensive. If you're good I'll probably let you out in a few months' time. By that time your son will have been put up for adoption.'

'Adoption!' Horror seemed to be paralysing Rebekah's limbs but she managed to fling the cup at him. It hit him on the forehead and then smashed in the fireplace.

'Violence now.' He smiled and tutted. She threw the saucer at his now double image, saw him sidestep before it, too, shattered into pieces. The last words she heard him speak seemed to freeze her mind. 'I think I'll tell the man to bring a straight jacket for you. We didn't need one for poor Emma.'

'She's coming round.' It was a voice Rebekah did not recognise.

She lifted heavy lids and stared up at Joshua

and the stranger. 'There now, Mrs Green, you're all right,' he said with a smile.

'David! Where's David? He said—' Rebekah sat up abruptly. 'Who are you?' She realised that she was lying on top of the bed in the room upstairs. 'Why am I here? Have you taken David away?' she said unsteadily.

'I'm Doctor Gail, and you fainted.'

'I never faint. He must have put something in my tea. My baby!' Her voice broke on a sob. 'Where's my baby?'

The two men exchanged glances and Joshua said in sober tones, 'See what I mean, Doctor, she won't accept the truth.'

Rebekah's eyes sparkled with unshed tears. 'You don't know the meaning of truth! Where's Doctor Michaels?'

'Michaels is away,' said Doctor Gail. 'I'm standing in for him.' He sat on the chair beside the bed and took Rebekah's hand. 'My dear Mrs Green, I'm sorry but your baby is dead.'

'No!' She stared at Joshua. 'My husband stole David from me, to punish me.'

The heavy features of the doctor were sorrowful, 'I've seen your baby. Believe me, he's dead.'

Rebekah had thought she could not feel any worse but she did. 'I don't believe it.' Her mouth quivered. 'Let me see the body.'

'Certainly, Mrs Green, but are you sure this is wise?'

His expression was sympathetic. 'It will upset you.'

Rebekah started to wonder if she was going mad. Surely she could not have imagined what had happened between her and Joshua downstairs? She darted a glance at her husband.

'My sweet, you can see the body if you like,' he said gently.

His words scared her but she slid off the bed, unaided.

Joshua attempted to take her elbow but she pushed him away. 'Show me this baby.'

Joshua shrugged and led the way downstairs. Rebekah followed, accompanied by a grave-faced Doctor Gail. At first sight of the baby in the tiny coffin, Rebekah felt faint. Had her husband killed her son? It was a few moments before she dared take a closer look. 'That's not David,' she stated in a relieved voice. 'This baby has fair hair. My husband is trying to trick you.'

'My dear Mrs Green, why should he do that? You're overwrought.' Doctor Gail put his arm about her shoulders. 'The maid said it's your baby and he's got a look of your husband. Grief has affected your mind and so you refuse to accept the truth.'

Rebekah shrugged off his arm and turned on him. 'How could that maid know? She's never seen my baby! Find Janet or nurse! They'd tell you I'm telling the truth.' She saw that he did not believe her, and despaired. She slammed a hand down on the side of the coffin. 'I don't know where my husband found this child but it is not mine! It is not mine!'

'Calm down, dear,' said Joshua in a soothing voice. 'You're getting hysterical.'

'If I am, you're to blame!' She stared at him with wild eyes. 'Where is David? You told me an orphanage! Which orphanage?'

'I told you nothing of the sort. My dear, you're starting to imagine things.'

Rebekah's fists clenched and she tried to gain control of the anger and fear that was rising, rising, threatening to choke her. 'I am not! You're doing this deliberately, Joshua. You want me to suffer. You want to drive me mad.'

'My love, why should I do that?' His voice had that velvety note that she knew so well. 'I love you. I loved our son. Don't you think I'm upset because David's gone?'

'No! No!' She shook her head vehemently. 'You didn't love him and you've never really loved me. You don't want people you love hurt. Where is David? Where is my son?' On the last two words something snapped inside her and she flew at Joshua, hitting out at him with flailing fists. She wanted to smash his smirking face until there was nothing more of him left. He called the doctor and then she was struggling with both of them. Joshua held her face down on the floor. She felt a stabbing pain in her arm and then was swimming through cotton wool.

CHAPTER TWENTY-FIVE

'It's quite a nice place. I'm sure you'll settle,' said Joshua in conversational tones.

Rebekah made no reply but attempted to free herself from the straitjacket.

'Emma was quite happy here,' he continued. 'The doctor's changed but this one seems quite decent. You'll have lots of sea air . . . nice grounds to wander round once you calm down. You can play tennis. There's a few books and a chapel. You'll be able to confess your sins to Almighty God and perhaps find forgiveness.' He smiled at her and began to peel an orange from the dish on the cream-painted bedside cabinet. 'See, I'm not all bad. I've told them you're to have this private room for a few days – it's costing me a fortune but they would expect it from a man of my position. Then you can go into a general ward. I told them you'd probably like company.'

'I don't want company. I want to get out of here! I want my son.' Her voice shook.

'I notice you always say your son, never our son!' His hand tightened on the orange, and juice and flesh oozed between his fingers.

She tried to get a grip on herself and eased her dry throat and tried a different tack. 'Where did you get the baby from?'

'Baby? What baby?'

'You don't have to pretend with me, Joshua.' Her voice was controlled. 'You've been very crafty but you can tell me the truth.'

There was a silence while he took out a handkerchief and wiped his hand as she waited impatiently for an answer. 'You can get anything if you're willing to pay for it. The mother was unmarried. I have influence in certain circles.'

'And where's David?' she said quietly.

'He became the dead baby, but I'm not going to tell you what its name was or where he is.' He leant back in the chair with his legs stretched out before him. 'If you knew it would make it easier for you. Not knowing is always so much harder to bear. And the fact that you can't do anything makes it even better.'

Rebekah despaired. 'You're evil! Evil!'

His eyebrows rose. 'My dear, it's you who committed adultery, remember?' He leant over and patted her cheek. 'I won't be seeing you for a couple of weeks.

So sweet dreams until then.' And getting up, he left the room.

Rebekah wanted to scream and go on screaming. Her aching breasts were a reminder that somewhere someone else was feeding her son. She had known that Joshua would do something terrible if he ever guessed about her and Daniel, but never anything like this. But at least David was alive. Joshua had not killed him. If only she could get out of this place.

'There now, dear. Are you going to be good?' A buxom middle-aged attendant came in. Her companion, a fresh-faced young girl, smiled in a friendly fashion but Rebekah was too miserable, and also in too much pain, to care.

'My baby. My breasts hurt.'

'Poor lamb. He's in heaven now and as happy as Larry,' said the older attendant. 'You must accept God's will. There'll be other babies.'

'My baby isn't dead,' said Rebekah emphatically. 'And my breasts hurt because of the milk.'

'I know nothing about that,' said the woman. 'Never been married.'

'I do,' said the young girl in a slight Liverpudlian accent. 'My sister had milk fever. Perhaps Mrs Green has it.'

The woman sniffed. 'Have to get one of the nurses. You go, Ada.'

The girl went and returned with a nurse, who

ordered the straightjacket taken off and examined Rebekah's breasts. She told her to express the milk herself and that would give her ease. The straightjacket was to stay off, but of course if she were to get violent again –

Rebekah turned her back on them and wept. They left the room, locking the door.

The next couple of days passed in a peculiar haze. A different doctor visited Rebekah and asked questions which she responded to by telling him that David was alive and in some Orphanage where her husband had put him. He spoke to her in a soothing voice, asking why he should do that? She hesitated to tell him, knowing the truth would probably make them side with Joshua. Her nerves grew so taut that she threw an orange at the doctor. He dodged it expertly and told the nurse to give her cold showers.

Rebekah hated the showers which seemed to numb her brain. She felt trapped as if on a bridge of barbed wire with a waterfall beneath, waiting to sweep her sanity away. Perhaps David really was dead and she was mad? Her thoughts raced like scampering squirrels, causing her to press her hands to her head in an attempt to stop them. She yearned for her baby, and desperately needed Daniel. The war was over. Perhaps he would come. If he still cared. If Brigid could get news about her being missing to him through his cousins. If – if –

if! She wondered what Brigid had thought when she had not returned, and whether Joshua had told her aunt that David was supposedly dead. Dead! No, she did not believe he was dead as they all kept saying. Even though perhaps life would be easier for her if she said that she did believe it. But she could not accept that. Somewhere he was alive and she had to hold on to that thought. To get out and find him.

Rebekah was moved into one of the four general wards, which gave her something else to worry about. Fortunately men and women were kept separate but nearly all the other women patients were older than she, and preconceived ideas of lunacy filled her mind as she watched one approaching.

The woman stared at her, her tongue lolling on her chin like an overheated dog. She asked Rebekah what her name was. She answered in a flat tone and a minute later the woman repeated her question. This went on, interspersed by the singing of hymns and the cackling of laughter, hour after hour. It was maddening.

There was a woman who believed herself to be Queen Victoria, and gave Rebekah orders. 'Fetch me a cushion and be quick about it.' When she did not obey, the woman pushed her. 'Do as you are told, girl. I don't find your behaviour funny. Albert will see to it that you are punished.' Rebekah moved away but the woman followed her, repeating the order. In the end Rebekah pretended to do whatever she asked, even if it meant pouring out invisible tea and handing a cup to her. This, strangely, seemed to pacify her.

There were several younger women who suffered fits. At first these were frightening but Rebekah soon learnt that they were not to be feared and that the orderlies knew how to handle them, without anyone coming to harm. A couple of women of about her own age were suffering from melancholia, so the young Liverpudlian orderly told her. 'It's due to the war,' she said with concern. 'Poor things. They sunk so low into the doldrums that they haven't been able to drag themselves up again.'

Rebekah knew just how they felt. She was having difficulty keeping hope alive. She would never get out and would go mad, like those patients who never met her gaze but directed their conversations to an invisible someone behind her. They became angry when nobody answered them, or they were given wrong answers by real people, and got violent. They went missing for a few days then. She admitted her fears to the young orderly. 'I'm frightened of going mad.'

'Well, if you're only going, then you're not there,' said the girl in bracing tones.

Her words brought a smile to Rebekah's face. 'I'm on the edge. Do you think people can drive you mad?'

'Me mam was always saying that we drove her mad.'

'You live with your mam?'

The girl shook her head. 'I have a room in the village. It's nice and I enjoy having a room to meself.'

Rebekah forced herself to show interest. 'You have brothers and sisters?'

Ada nodded. 'You remind me of one of them. My sister who had milk fever. She was really strange for a while after losing Tommy, her baby. It was the midwife's fault. She came from a sickbed and didn't wash her hands. She's all right now. Had two more babies since. You'll be all right, given time.'

'My baby—' began Rebekah automatically, then stopped at the look in the girl's eyes, and after an inward struggle, continued the conversation. The girl was friendly and she could do with a friend. 'How did you come here?'

'I couldn't get work. Then I saw this advert in the newspaper and decided to have a go at it. I had an interview in Liverpool, and Bob's your uncle, here I am! It's not as bad as I thought – but maybe that's because most of them here aren't what you'd call really dangerous. They have money and because they're a bit soft in the head and can't look after themselves, their families put them in here.'

Rebekah said grimly, 'I don't think all the orderlies think like you. Some of them have no patience.

I've seen Doris smacking some of the older ones.'

Ada's mouth tightened. 'Doris should keep her hands to herself! But you can get that way that you look on them like children who need disciplining.' Her expression softened. 'But you're not like that. You're here just for a rest, really. You've had a shock and you need time to get over it.'

'Is that what the doctor says?' Rebekah's voice was unsteady and for the first time in what felt like months she experienced a glimmer of hope.

Ada smiled. 'That's what I say! Now would you like to have a walk in the gardens? It looks like it's going to be a fine day.'

The fresh air did Rebekah good. The gardens were spacious and the flower beds bloomed. Life was real again. She was not going mad. She would get out and find David.

She kept saying the words to herself but as day slowly followed day with no change, and no visit from Joshua or word from anybody else, she struggled against feelings of panic. She asked for writing materials and wrote letters to her aunt, Brigid and Edwina, telling them what had happened, but they were returned to her without explanation.

Her anxiety became so great that remembering how Emma had escaped she tried to climb the locked iron gates but was spotted by one of the patients who was up a tree calling the birds. The attendants were alerted. Rebekah struggled but she was taken back to the house and confined. It was as if she had committed a crime and was in prison. She screamed to be let out but nobody took any notice of her and eventually she sank on to the floor, weeping.

When she was released, Ada came to speak to her severely. 'You weren't half silly trying to get out. What was it that made you do a thing like that?'

'I'm mad,' said Rebekah, pushing back a strand of lank hair and staring at her. 'Don't you know.'

Ada sat beside her. 'No, you're not.'

Rebekah lifted her head. 'You say that but perhaps I am.' She paused. 'Has there been any news from my husband?'

'No, and they're annoyed about it. Payment's due.'

Rebekah stared at her with a mixture of uncertainty and hope. 'What will they do if he doesn't pay?'

Ada shrugged. 'Not sure. They might move you somewhere else.'

'Somewhere worse? Would you like to see that happen to me, Ada?' She grasped her hand. 'Or would you like to help me get out of here?'

'Help you get out?' Ada stared at her. 'You're not asking me to unlock the gates? I don't—'

'No, I wouldn't get you into trouble.' Rebekah smiled. 'But could you get me paper and an envelope on the sly? If I write a letter to a friend, will you post it?'

Relief slackened Ada's mouth. 'I don't mind doing that.'

'Thanks.' Rebekah laughed and hugged her.

Daniel's eyes scanned the page yet again and then he placed the letter on the table and looked at Brigid, pouring milk into two cups. He had been released from prison two days ago and a headline in a Dublin newspaper had brought him immediately to Liverpool, and Brigid, in the hope that she would help him to find out exactly where Rebekah was. He had not been disappointed because only that morning Brigid had received a letter from her. Such a letter that it made him want to weep. His hand shook slightly as he took the cup of tea from Brigid. 'I'll have to get that doctor.'

'It's terrible! All these weeks believing his lordship had taken her to Ireland when all the time she's been in a place like that!' Brigid hit the letter with her fist. 'Can you believe anyone could be so cruel as to put a dead baby—'

'I can believe anything of Green,' said Daniel, barely able to control his own anger. 'Where do we find this Dr Michaels?'

'Her aunt might have his address. We could try there.'

He nodded, gulped down his tea, impatient to be

on his way. He placed his cup on the table. 'Drink up, Bridie.'

'I'll leave it,' she said with a sigh. 'I can see you're raring to go.' They went.

'Wicked! That's what it is! Wicked!' Rebekah's aunt sat ramrod straight in the armchair next to the fire, gazing up at him. 'Ireland! That's where I was told she was! And all the time—' Words obviously failed her.

'We'll get her out,' said Daniel. 'If you could tell me Dr Michael's address?'

Her mouth trembled. 'I'm sorry, Mr O'Neill, I can't help thee. Reluctant as I am to suggest it, her friend Miss McIntyre might have the address.'

'Thank you.' Daniel held out his hand.

She hesitated and took it. 'Thou will find the boy and bring them both here?'

'I'll find him.'

'She nodded and called Hannah. 'See Mr O'Neill and the young woman out.'

The maid nodded, eyeing Daniel up and down with obvious satisfaction as she went before them up the lobby. 'I knew Miss Becky had someone in Dublin. Sinful, I calls it! And scandalous! But I suppose thee knows what thee's letting thyself in for if thee's known her that long. And I never did like that toffee-nosed husband of hers. Just get that baby back. We miss him.' She opened the door and showed them out.

Daniel's eyebrows went up and Brigid giggled. 'Now yer've met her, yer'll never forget her! Come on. I think Miss McIntyre's house is only a few doors up.'

Edwina answered their knock and Daniel introduced himself.

'You're from Ireland,' she said, gazing at him with obvious interest. 'You'd best come in. Although I can tell you now, if you're looking for Rebekah, I don't know exactly where she is.'

'We know where she is, Miss McIntyre,' said Daniel, turning his hat between his hands. 'It's a doctor we want. A Dr Michaels – do you know where we can find him?'

'Is it a doctor you want for Rebekah because of what's happened to Joshua? I was just reading about his death in the *Daily Post*. I can tell you it gave me quite a shock.'

'I'm sure it did.' The news came as no surprise to Daniel. 'But your paper must have more information than the one I saw in Dublin.'

Edwina opened the door wider. 'Do come in and explain yourself. Even if it's only for a few minutes. You can read the report while I make a cup of tea.'

'No tea for me,' said Daniel, smiling slightly. 'But Bridie would probably like one.'

Edwina shot Brigid a glance. 'Rebekah's spoken of you. It's nice to meet you,' she said politely. 'Do come in.'

They went in and Edwina handed Daniel the newspaper, placing a finger on a front page headline which blazoned: 'Local shipowner's body found in undergrowth on estate in Ireland'.

Brigid read the words over his shoulder in a muted voice. 'It says they think the body's been there a week.'

'He was shot several times,' said Edwina. 'It'll come as a shock to Rebekah. You say you know where she is, Mr O'Neill?'

'Yes.' He folded the paper and handed it back to her. 'She's in an asylum. He placed her there after stealing my son and putting him in an Orphanage.'

Edwina stared at him and then sat down abruptly 'I don't understand! Why *your* son? And Becky – she wasn't mad.'

'No!' exclaimed Brigid fiercely. 'But he was determined to drive her mad!'

Edwina made a helpless gesture. 'You'll have to explain properly. I know she didn't love Joshua but—' She paused and stared at Daniel, who stared back. 'She loved someone else who died—' Her voice trailed off.

'The rumours of my death were greatly exaggerated by Mr Green,' said Daniel, smiling unexpectedly. 'Brigid will explain. You're Becky's friend so I don't think she'll mind you knowing the truth. If you can just tell me where I can find Dr Michaels?'

Edwina drew a long breath. 'Rodney Street. I can't remember the number but his name will be on the brass plate outside.' She stayed him with her hand. 'You said Joshua put your son in an orphanage? You do mean – David?'

He nodded.

'Oh, golly! Which one?'

'We don't know.' His mouth tightened. 'I had thought it might be the Seamen's Orphanage.'

'No,' she said, shaking her head. 'Becky told me that the children have to be at least seven years old.' Daniel swore softly and she gave him a look. 'That won't help. Your best bet is a church organised home. Quite a few run places for unmarried mothers. They take the babies and get them adopted. I—' She stopped and stared at him, and he nodded. 'Golly! Was she with you in Ireland last year? You don't have to answer that! I'll give you the address of the place which, in my opinion, is your best bet. I remember the first time I heard Joshua's name, it was in connection with the orphanage where I placed my baby. I think he was on the board of guardians.' She reached for her handbag and took out a pencil and paper. She wrote down a name and address and handed it to him.

'Thanks,' said Daniel, and left Brigid to do the rest of the talking.

* * *

Rebekah was sitting in the asylum chapel, staring down at her hands. That morning she had done basket weaving and the sides of her fingers were sore from twisting cane. She was in a hopeful mood since Ada had posted her letter but had thought that a prayer or two would not go amiss. She laced her fingers, closed her eyes, and asserted all her will to get God on her side. She promised him all sorts of things if only he would get her out of this place.

There were footsteps and Rebekah turned to see one of the attendants, who looked extremely serious. 'You've got visitors, Mrs Green. The doctor said you were to come to his office at once.'

Rebekah was filled with apprehension but she scrambled to her feet and hurried after the nurse, hoping that Joshua had not returned. The corridors had always seemed long but now they seemed endless. The attendant pushed the door open and Rebekah entered a sunlit room.

Her gaze immediately fell on Daniel. She could scarcely believe that she was really seeing him. The beard was gone and he looked a little older. There really were grey hairs in his mop of curls this time – but it was Daniel! Her legs went weak and she had to put a hand on the back of a chair. He rushed forward and lowered her on to a seat, and his face came close to hers. 'I've come to get you out of here, love,' he murmured. 'I've told them I'm your Irish cousin. Understand?'

'Yes.' she whispered, although she did not, and clung to his hand, only taking her eyes off him when Dr Michaels spoke.

The doctor was looking sombre and came straight to the point. 'I had a talk with Dr Gail this afternoon and his description of the baby that died, that he said was yours, did not match the one I remembered. He was far too young for a start. Also I've been in touch with the nurse who tended you. We had a talk about your husband and his attitude towards your child. She mentioned things that convinced me that your husband was extremely jealous of the attention you gave to the baby, and she believes that this could have led him to act in a way that could cause suffering to you and your baby. I can see no reason for you to be kept here any longer.'

'Thank you,' said Rebekah in a quiet voice. 'But what about my husband? Where is he?'

The resident doctor leant forward. 'Mrs Green, I would hesitate to tell you this news in other circumstances, but as it is, I have to inform you that your husband is dead.'

'Dead!' Rebekah moistened her lips and her gaze switched to Daniel's face for verification, also seeking something else though she did not find it.

His face was expressionless when he said gravely, 'It's true, Becky. He was shot on his estate in Ireland.' I take it that he believed because the civil war was officially over that it was safe for him to visit Ireland, but it wasn't because the fighting hasn't ceased. Some of the Irregulars have sworn to continue the struggle for an united Ireland free from all ties with England. You know that there were such men in that area and that he wasn't liked in the village.'

'Yes, I know,' she whispered, still shocked.

'The police informed us this morning,' said the asylum doctor, toying with an inkstand on his desk. 'We weren't going to tell you yet, but in the light of what has been revealed we think it best you know the truth. You can leave whenever you wish. We'll see that your things are packed.'

She nodded. 'Immediately, please. I have to find my son, you see.'

The doctor flushed and averted his gaze as she thanked Dr Michaels for coming. He offered her and Daniel a lift back to Liverpool and asked if there was anything else he could do. 'I have given Mr O'Neill a letter of explanation and introduction, but if you wish me to go to the orphanage with you, I will.'

'Orphanage! Then you know which one David is in?' Rebekah turned to Daniel. Joy and excitement were suddenly emotions that she could allow herself to indulge in.

He grinned. 'I'm living in hope. Edwina thinks it's a possibility.' He said in a low voice, 'I think we can manage without the good doctor, don't you? We could get the train. There's things we have to say to each other.'

'Yes,' she breathed, wanting nothing more than to be alone with him and to find David.

It was not until they were outside the imposing wrought iron gates that she said in an even voice, 'You didn't kill Joshua, did you?'

He looked amused. 'No. Would you have liked me to?'

She shook her head and said. 'No. He caused us a great deal of suffering, but he was an unhappy man and I'd rather not have his murder hanging over our heads. Tell me how you got here? What happened when you left me? And where've you been all this time?'

He told her as they walked hand in hand to the station. 'I came out of prison a couple of days ago and one of the first people I saw was our Shaun, begging on O'Connell Bridge. He'd lost a leg.' He paused and a muscle moved in his cheek.

She waited a few minutes before saying in a soft voice, 'So you were captured? How did Shaun –?'

'I was getting him as far away from you as possible that last day I saw you. I intended coming back but I crashed the car.'

'You crashed it!' If only she had known. If only. It would have saved her so much heartache. And he had intended coming back.

'I didn't know the roads or the car,' continued Daniel. 'He said there were troopers but there weren't. But after the crash we did meet some. Shaun had broken both legs. I was knocked out and came to in someone's house. They'd called in the troopers because of Shaun's being armed. We were separated and I didn't see him again until yesterday.' He paused and gazed across the road, his expression tight. 'They'd had to amputate one of his legs. Gangrene. But they let him go free. Apparently they didn't consider him a danger any longer.'

'I'm sorry.' She squeezed his hand.

'It's tough on him and at the moment he's blaming me for everything. I brought him to Liverpool to my aunt's because I just couldn't leave him in Ireland.'

'*He's* why you came to Liverpool?' she said lightly.

He looked at her and smiled. 'You know he isn't. After I saw Shaun I read the newspaper headlines about Joshua. I came for you. I went to Brigid thinking she'd know where you were, and she did.'

'You read my letter?'

'Yes. And if Green hadn't already been dead—' He grimaced. 'He must have believed that David was my son.'

'He did.'

'Is he really like me?'

'I think so.'

Daniel took a deep breath. 'Let's go and find him.'

CHAPTER TWENTY-SIX

'We're looking for a baby.' Daniel and Rebekah stood in the open doorway of a large oak-panelled entrance hall, confronting a woman who reminded Rebekah a little of Hannah.

'Go away and come back in the morning,' said Hannah's lookalike.

'No!' Daniel put his foot in the door. 'This is important, Miss.'

She sniffed. 'If you want to adopt you must apply in writing and your situation will be looked into.'

'We're searching for a baby. There was a mix up and we've been directed to you.' Rebekah's tones were haughty. 'Daniel, the note from Dr Michaels.'

He took it from his pocket and handed it to the woman. She opened it, read it, and eyed them with ghoulish interest. 'It says that Mr Green is dead? When? We haven't heard a thing.'

'It's in today's paper,' said Daniel, pushing the door wide and pulling Rebekah inside. 'He was shot in Ireland. So sad about his death. A worthy gentleman.'

'A good man indeed,' said the woman effusively. 'My condolences. He was well thought of, and that must be a consolation to you.'

'Of course,' said Rebekah smoothly. 'He liked children so much. Wanted to help poor mothers.'

'A caring man.' The woman sighed. 'Only a month or so ago he brought the little boy to us. He said it was the child of an unmarried girl – the daughter of one of his sailors washed overboard. We were glad to help and promised to do our best to find the boy a good home.'

Rebekah almost stopped breathing. 'And have you found him one?'

'Not yet.' She sniffed. 'Due to it's being Mr Green's express wishes that we find the boy a home, we've been more particular than usual. Which it seems is just as well in the circumstances. A mix up, Dr Michaels says.' She was obviously curious but they had no intention of enlightening her and causing a scandal.

Daniel squeezed Rebekah's hand. 'Perhaps we can have a look at him?'

The woman hesitated then nodded. 'If you're very quiet you can have a peek. It is late, you understand?'

They said they did and followed her. She led them to a large room with rows of cots and spoke to a nurse who was bottle feeding a baby.

The nurse walked soft-footedly towards them. 'Come with me,' she whispered. 'Jonathan's a lovely baby. He has the most gorgeous curly hair and big brown eyes.'

Rebekah's heartbeat threatened to suffocate her. Brown eyes!

'We had some problems with him at first,' went on the nurse in a low voice. 'Especially feeding him, but he's a good boy now.'

Rebekah remembered her sore breasts and the wasted milk and wanted to cry.

The nurse stopped by a cot which contained a gurgling baby with one of his feet in his mouth. She smiled. 'This is Jonathan.'

Rebekah stared at David and was about to pick him up when something made her look at Daniel. His hand went out and removed the foot from his son's mouth. Immediately the child moved his mouth against the back of his hand and sucked at his knuckle. An indescribable expression crossed Daniel's face and he lifted the baby out of the cot to cradle him awkwardly in his arms.

'You're not supposed to take the babies out of their cots,' said the nurse.

Daniel took no notice, taking a small hand into his own.

'Well?' asked Rebekah, smiling.

'He has a look of our Shaun when he was a baby.'

'Your Shaun!' She groaned. 'You can't mean it! He looks like you. He's a good-looking baby.'

'Please, will you put Jon back?' interrupted the nurse. 'You might think he's yours, sir, but it has to be done legally.'

They both ignored her. 'Our Shaun was OK when he was small,' said Daniel. 'It was only later he got spoilt.'

'I suppose he'd best come and live with us.'

Daniel gave her a look. 'You could both drive each other crazy.'

'Excuse me!' said the nurse in a fierce voice. 'If you don't put that baby back right now I'll have to fetch Matron.'

Daniel took no notice but put his free arm round Rebekah as they walked away from the cot.

'Hey!' Hastily the nurse placed the baby she had been feeding in David's cot. It took only two seconds for it to start screaming.

Rebekah and Daniel passed through an open french window that led on to a terrace. The nurse followed as several more babies started crying.

Rebekah, hearing the noise, turned. 'The other lady will explain. I'm Mrs Green.'

'I don't care if you're Mrs Red, White and Blue,' said the nurse, bristling. 'She didn't say anything about your taking Jon. Only about showing you him. I'll get told off or dismissed!'

'Neither will happen if you do what I say,' insisted Rebekah in a soothing voice.

The nurse stared at her. 'You can't just take a baby like that,' she said weakly. 'Even though him and him have a look of each other. There's rules!'

'They do have a look of each other, don't they?' Rebekah's face lit up. 'Oh, go back, love. Stop those other babies crying! I'll see that you get a great big box of chocolates for being such a help.' She turned and ran to catch up with Daniel and they went out of the gates together.

EPILOGUE

Rebekah came down the steps of the building where Joshua's solicitor's office was situated near Dale Street. She was wearing an eau-de-Nil chiffon frock and a black straw hat with an artificial green gardenia decorating its narrow brim. There was a bounce in her step as she walked. The street sloped downwards towards the river and soon she passed beneath the Overhead Railway, nicknamed the Dockers' Umbrella by Liverpudlians. She narrowly avoided a heavily loaded horse drawn cart.

'Watch it, luv!' The words were accompanied by a wolf whistle. 'Got a date, have yer? I wouldn't mind taking yer on meself.'

Rebekah smiled and felt good.

David was safe with Aunt Esther, who was still in shock after Rebekah had told her that Daniel was David's father and that they were going to get married. Hannah had said with relish: 'Told thee, Miss Esther, she always was one for the men.'

'Men!' Rebekah had retorted. 'There's only ever been one man in my life.'

Now she looked at the man in her life as he gazed over the river at the ships. In the navy pin striped suit, and with his dark brown hair in disarray by the sea breeze, she considered him still the most attractive man she had ever set eyes on. She came up behind him and slipped her hand through his arm. 'Are you wishing yourself on one of them boats?'

'Ships, Becky.' Daniel turned, smiling. 'How did you get on? Did you shock the man in your best green frock?'

'I'm sure I did. He was even more shocked when I told him I was going to a wedding.'

'You're wishing it was your own, perhaps?'

She smiled. 'I thought you might have suggested a double one.'

'I was excommunicated last year.'

Rebekah stared at him. 'You never told me that.'

'Most of us Irregulars were at some time or other. Sure, and I forgot about it in all the excitement. Like you're forgetting to tell me if I was right about Joshua's money.'

'You mean, had he put a clause in his will saying if I married one Daniel O'Neill, then I wasn't to get a penny?' He nodded. 'You were wrong,' she said softly. 'You won't believe this but the shipping line goes to David. Joshua must have made the will after he was born and strangely, considering what he suspected, he never bothered to change it. There's some charitable gifts and a hundred pounds for his cousin. The rest is mine.'

'Odd,' said Daniel, shaking his head. 'I can't understand him. I never could.'

'I don't doubt that he was thinking of his reputation even after death,' murmured Rebekah. 'But after all, what is he giving me? He told me that he married me for my money.'

'It doesn't make sense.' Daniel shook his head.

'Some old aunt of his reckoned there was mental instability from his mother's side of the family.'

Daniel stopped. 'You've had a lucky escape.'

She nodded, remembering. 'What are we going to do about the business? Someone will have to look after it until David is old enough. I know you fought for a free Ireland, but—'

'But it's not the way I dreamt it,' he said quietly.

'Is anywhere?' Her voice softened. 'If you ask me, the pictures of places people carry in their minds have no reality. They're like that Land of the Ever Young you spoke of.'

He shrugged and looked over the river. 'Dreams die hard.'

'You have to dream new dreams. We have to think of David and he has a future here. We'll have to become respectable.'

'Respectable?' he murmured. 'Is Liverpool a city full of respectable people then?'

Her lips twitched. 'It has its share of rogues. But what do you expect? It's a seaport! Its ships go all round the world and you can hear ten different languages in a day!'

He stared at her then smiled. 'You don't have to convince me. I know the place. I thought we might go on a cruise.' He brought out two tickets with all the panache of a magician successfully pulling a donkey from a hat. 'I was thinking that the captain could marry us without any fuss.'

'It sounds a good idea.'

'I thought so. In the morning do?'

She nodded. They kissed, and arm in arm went off to Brigid's wedding.

EPIGRAPH

Set me as a seal upon your heart . . .
for love is strong as death,
jealousy is cruel as the grave . . .
many waters cannot quench love,
neither can the floods drown it.
If a man offered for love
all the wealth of his house,
it would be utterly scorned.

Song of Solomon 8: 6-7

Other Avon Books by
George Turner

BRAIN CHILD

Part I

Fine Upstanding Copper

1

Ostrov: Policeman's Lot

From Commentaries; *Decay of the Family Nexus:*
"The psychological shortcomings and emotional
unrest of 'Harry' Ostrov are echoed today as par-
ents, with the best intentions, strive to rear their
offspring in the straitjacket of their own ideas of
right and wrong. In any culture with rapidly chang-
ing values it cannot be done. The lectured and
pressured children rarely rebel; they simply fail to
conform."

There has been too much stupid talk about what
went on in the Manor in those last days of Beltane's
premiership; there was melodrama enough without the
idiocies propounded by the channels and the amateur
psychologists. I can tell you exactly what happened. I
was there.

I was born into the mid-greenhouse generation, when
the big weather problems were understood, and to some
extent under control. The food situation was easing, and
no more than two thirds of the world's nine billions

3

were undernourished (or starving outright) at any given time. If the population growth could have been halted then, in 2039, we might have come through the century relatively unscathed, but even slowing the growth, so simple in theory, seemed impossible in application.

We kids didn't realize why this should be so until our body's hungers came to plague and exalt adolescence, but we were born with population warnings in the air we breathed and we accepted them as part of life. There were too many people in the world, and we had to put up with them. That they also had to put up with us was their worry, not ours.

Being kids, we played "cull" games. (That word was already being spoken as a prophecy of some distant future but not as a present threat.) In our games one side was picked to be culled and was hunted down by the "real Aussies." Those to be culled were called by the most offensive names we knew—Chinks, Wogs, Nignogs. The names had little real meaning save as denoting outsiders, non-Australians. Our own black, brown, yellow and mixed nationals (about half the population) were "real Aussies," no matter what their origins, but Chinks, Wogs and Nignogs represented the rest of the world, that place somewhere outside, full of people to be got rid of someday. In that way we prepared a chauvinism that bided its time to come home to roost.

All over the world kids played cull games like ours, games dreamed up from odd scraps of parental conversation in the home. Kids, though they may not absorb the words properly, hear the hates and fears behind them very clearly. And sublimate the uneasiness in games. Games keep the fears at bay, trivializing them. We "real Aussies" could never be the culled ones. As we grew older the hardening of familiarity set in, and as adults we didn't talk seriously about the cull at all. At any rate, not in public.

In public we made black jokes about it—

I have begun in the wrong place. Already I am caught up in ends rather than beginnings.

I am a policeman, Detective-Sergeant Harry Ostrov of Melbourne, Australia, a fairly ordinary sort of policeman whose promotions have come through attention to detail rather than through professional brilliance. It may have helped that I never let myself fall into the traps of easy corruption that elevate some to shaky heights and put others into jail with their seducers and victims.

I was brought up the old way, with strict ideas of good and evil, right and wrong—

Another false start, but there has to be some background.

My parents met and married in 2039, at the end of what social historians have dubbed the Dancing Thirties, that last decade of nonsense and thin-ice gaiety before history tightened its grip around the human race.

Perhaps my mother, Arlene, and father, Bill, had reason, along with everybody else, to throw their caps in the air and their brains after them and see life as a ballroom where the dancing would never stop. Everything was on the up-and-up, wasn't it? Man had the greenhouse effect and the ozone holes under an endurable measure of control, had damped down pollution to manageable levels and tamed the environmental vandals, had developed weather forecasting to the point of keeping crops and destructive shortages a step ahead of the brutal fluctuations of rainfall and storms and the complex temperature variations of the oceans. The planet let out the breath it had held for forty years and gave itself a party. (There were doomsayers, but who listened?) That generation seems to have been a

meretricious lot whose gaiety was too often nit-brained inanity, but their party was a wingding while it lasted.

I was two months old when the earthquake that had slept for a century tore Tokyo apart, leveled its stock exchange and destroyed the most powerful financial empire in history—and tossed the dancing planet down to penury in its wake. Overnight the full bellies of the major powers became as close to empty as were the tormented guts of the Third World billions. The world learned, the hard way, what it had always known but refused to face—that shares, investments and IOUs, those computer records and pieces of paper pushed around the world by economists and financiers are not, when all the debts are called in at once, wealth. They may be "money," though even that is doubtful, but they are not wealth. Wealth is what your country can provide to satisfy its people's needs; surplus wealth is what you can trade with. When the spree was over and there were nine billions to provide for, who had surpluses? Money became again the solid stuff you grab and hold; creative exchange of paper promises died for lack of resources to back them.

Australia, that perennially lucky country, as usual suffered less than many others because it was able, by way of a grinding austerity, to feed itself at a borderline sufficiency and by the late sixties was in a condition of penurious stability. We were by then living a good life in comparison with many other nations, but in fact our standard of subsistence would have shocked our grandfathers. Or would it? We had the necessities; what we hungered for were the unattainable extras.

As a child I resented the rich and could not forgive their existence. It takes time and education to learn of the failures of communism, socialism, anarchism, and all the other fantasies based on egalitarian concepts that cannot exist while human IQs vary over a range of more than a hundred points and individual needs

can't be measured on a common scale. So we are stuck with basically capitalist systems with all their faults, and the rich are always with us.

The rich have always been, in one way or another, the rulers of the world, and I had my day among them—which is how this story happened for the telling—though it was a short day and a humiliating one. I didn't ask for it to happen, just as I didn't ask to be a policeman or to be seconded to the Jackson job or even to wear the damnfool name my giddy parents wished on me.

What parents they were, still are! In the thirties they both had jobs, the world was a fun park, and they frolicked with the minor glitterati of their day. They met, married, and raced into having their permitted child (the new procreation laws were a prescient warning that nobody took too seriously, a temporary restriction until the planet sorted itself out) whom they named, with rhythm, rhyme, and a heady giggle, Ian Juan Ivan John. Their friends applauded the whimsy. Tacked on to the family name of Ostrov it made me sound like a multicultural stew.

Even the Ostrov was, if not a whimsy, not quite genuine. Bill's Ukrainian great-grandfather had adopted it for political reasons when he escaped to Australia by the skin of his gritted teeth. It was an anagram of his birthplace, Rostov.

If my parents sound featherheaded they were only reflecting their time, but when the Tokyo crash caught the working world knock-kneed in the face of sudden poverty they showed mettle. From the mild affluence of two jobs they dropped to no jobs and a hungry boy. Arlene, who had been a secretary, found servant work in the households of those who could still afford the hire of status symbols at Scrooge wages. Bill had been an emporium sales supervisor—in his own description, a "superior counter-jumper." He spat on

his hands, bore with his blisters, and made do with sporadic laboring jobs in spite of a slightly crooked spine that had not troubled him until he became a manual worker.

They clung to the fetish of education as the road to success and pushed me down it as far as their tight purses could allow. It was their luck and mine that I was what theatre folk call "a quick study" who could soak up information with minimum effort. That is only a minor talent; it does not equate with high intelligence.

From their thirties gaiety they retained a deliberate, strained cheerfulness that drove me half out of my mind in surroundings that rarely included enough chairs to go round, clothes to wear or food to eat. My four variations of the one name were considered a risible affectation by my school ground peers until at age twelve, in a fury of domestic rebellion (a single outburst, never repeated) I reviled my parents for their unthinking cruelty in a storm of yelling, stamping and foul language.

My mother, instead of smacking my scarlet face, put a hand to her lips and murmured, "Oh, you poor darling." My father, more alive to tactics, asked what name I would like to be called by. I had not planned so far ahead but reached for the first available fantasy and produced the name of a favorite vid cartoon character, Harry the Kung fu Mouse, and Harry I became without further fuss. They really were good people. The kids at school took more convincing, but I grew solid and strong and able to make my decisions stand.

In the middle fifties, when "recession" began to seem a permanent condition, my parents learned the bitter lesson that the world belongs to the young; "too old at forty" was the reality. They stopped pretending that tomorrow would ever come. We became Wardies, the sour-joke word for those who became "wards of the

state," our income the Sustenance Payment, the monthly dole, the Suss. I think that Minders, as a description of the administrative classes whose supposed social responsibility was the welfare of the less fortunate, came into jeering existence at the same time. With use its spiteful edge became dulled and it passed into the language of social description, establishing "us" and "them" and the gulf between.

Then, at sixteen, I passed the Grading Paper of the General Employment examinations. Rejoicings, chez Ostrov! A working son, even an apprentice, would render the logistics of housekeeping less inhuman.

I knew what I wanted to do; age sixteen had it all worked out. When I was given my Career Choice sheet I wrote in the Preferred Training section, "Electrical and computer wiring and installation," confident that my excellent marks in math and manual skills would guarantee acceptance. Installation and wiring cannot be wholly automated even in the age of computerized handling; a specialized manual skill was tantamount to a job for life.

The selection board approved my qualifications. Then it checked my physique, read my genetic print, calculated my ultimate physical development on an optimum diet—and offered me a police training course.

Received Wardie wisdom was that Police Are Bastards. We hated them as Minder menials.

I protested.

The board pointed out that the apprentice lists were crowded with applicants as well equipped manually and intellectually as I (a blow to vanity), whereas my projected strength, physical fitness, learning speed and unusually wide general knowledge (the damnable gift of cultured parents) qualified me for a physically and mentally demanding profession.

The board reminded me, too, of comparatively high wages and a pension entitlement (pensions were a rar-

ity) and of the fact that my parents had made sacrifices,
etc. . . . and didn't I think they were now entitled to my
support?

Yes, sir, but I can support them as well on an elec-
trician's—

The board feared that times of national exigency made
it necessary that capable men and women be allocated
to the niches they could best fill, and that I . . .

Outside the interview room I had the last and worst
crying fit of my adolescence, then went home and told
my Wardie parents that they had a copper in the family.

Bill—I was calling him Bill by then—cried, "Chin up,
Harry boy! You're made!" My mother, closer to social
issues and neighborly attitudes, said little.

The neighbors gave them a rough time for a while.
Cops were bloody lackeys to the bloody Minders; justice was for the wealthy, and Wardies never got a fair go
because the coppers were corrupt and vicious; no good
ever came of associating with . . . then they realized
that some good might be squeezed out of knowing a
rotten bloody copper who just might do you the odd
good turn if you kept on the right side of him. After
all, it wasn't the Ostrovs' fault if they'd reared a bad
'un, was it?

The pressures on Mum and Dad relaxed, and the
unruly natives treated me with expectant civility.

At the Police Training College it was pointed out to me
that my initials were I. J. I. J. and I would not be known
as Harry, so I began with hatred in my heart.

Fate laughed, of course. Manipulated by instructors
who knew just how I felt (hadn't they been through it?)
I walked headfirst into their traps of ego building and
indoctrination. By the end of the first month I and my
whole intake group were in love with the service and
with ourselves, gentled and jollied into proud, elitist,

one-for-all-and-all-for-one police tribesmen, dedicated to the protection of a graceless, ingrate public.

Later I saw that it was not all crafty psychological cat crap. We did become a welded, supportive group; we did learn disciplines, official and social, that gave us small behavioral advantages in a depressed society; we did learn pride in ourselves and our service.

In time we were parceled out to stations to join the rough and tumble of no-nonsense fellow cops who had had street wisdom beaten into their often bloodied heads and now served it back to us good and hard. That, with the sickening and wholly realistic view of the truths a policeman finds behind the facades of bland family lives, refashioned the world for us.

Some of us grew unpleasantly tough, some went rotten, some went under. Most of us grew an extra skin, tried to stay sane and not be the bastards off the job that we often had to be on it; we compensated resentments with a snarling pride and a steadily hardening sheath over the mind. I thought myself an averagely good, honest copper and learned to distance myself from the corrupt (of whom there were enough to tar all of us) and keep to the code of shamed silence that binds men and women whose lives may depend on group loyalty.

I was twice tempted to marry and twice surprised how little heartbreak endured when the romances fell through. I decided on a single life until seniority should lift me out of the daily rottenness and into the calmer air of administration. Time enough then to seek out love and father the child we would be allowed.

I found that I could not talk of my work with my mother. To her it was all "horrors and nastiness." She loved me no less, but what she loved was her conception of me, the "nice" side of me.

I could talk with Bill, who brought me up standing at times with perceptions I had not suspected in my

old-fashioned dad—as when he said, in one private moment, "We're all born bare arsed, boy; it's putting on fancy clothes that dirties our hearts." I knew better than he what lay behind the triteness. A policeman grows away from the public he serves, tends to stand above it, looking down. And a policeman's friends tend to be policemen. Everything conspires to separate him from society and identify him with an official viewpoint that sees moral questions in terms of legal right and wrong.

I could not afford, for my soul's comfort, to admit to myself that I looked forward to the day of retirement when I could be reborn, bare arsed, into the humble world where a man could hold to a morality uncompromised.

I told Bill, long after the Jackson affair was over, that being aware of secrecy, corruption and manipulation is not enough. You deplore it in conversation, tut-tut suitably over the revelations of skulduggery on the vidnews, even play your part in apprehending the despicable and the villainous; but it registers as wickedness only at arm's length, as the rottenness of others—until the day you find your own self trapped in the web of lies and hidden actions, enmeshed without warning or chance of avoidance.

I was thirty when the Jackson job came up, a detective-sergeant with a safe future if I kept my nose clean. (That is harder for detectives than for simple coppers; the temptations are constant and great and the rewards can be breathtaking.)

In December 2068 volunteers were called for a one day special testing stint with the College of Psycho-Biology—testing meaning "guinea pigging." I was doing routine relief in a small, unbusy station on the city perimeter and, in what I took to be the local practice, was chosen to "volunteer."

It was not the local practice. I was sought, pinpointed and chosen, but that was later knowledge.

The test was done in an indoor stadium. I estimated three hundred guinea pigs, male and female, in definable classifications—police, high-IQ students, longtime jobless Wardies, professional athletes, subteen children, over sixties and one lot that appeared to be mentally retarded. Whatever happened, we could be sure of one thing, that the tests would be free of danger or side effects; otherwise criminals would have been used to avoid compensation claims on a bankrupt Treasury.

The psychs and biochemists—there seemed to be a regiment of them—told us, without too much technical fiddle, that we were part of an experiment in hypnotic suggestion.

We police exchanged glances and sighs. The force had discarded hypnotism long ago; its occasional helpfulness was outweighed by complications and opportunities for error. Almost anyone can be hypnotized after a fashion; the problems lie in the questioning. You can't tell, until you have wasted a month chasing false leads, whether you have been eliciting genuine memories, associational responses or mere subliminal garbage.

It seemed, however, that here was something new. What they were about was not hypnosis (so they said) but the effect of a combination of drugs designed to modify selected functions of the brain while sharpening others. There should be a temporary—no more than fifteen minutes—alteration of some facets of the personality, measured by reaction to key words and phrases.

We police at once suspected thought control; if that was in the wind we had better know about it. It sounded like hypnosis no matter what the boffins said, at least a pseudohypnotism, mind management on a measurable basis. It raised spectres of possible use by criminals—but that aspect would have to be weighed

by the lawmakers and only then by us ordered-about lawkeepers.

The usual questionnaire occupied most of the morning until each group was computer sorted into subgroups for the action of the drugs to be observed on variously capable intellects. Not a really significant statistical sample, it was admitted, but a useful initial guide.

In the afternoon we were given our injections and interviewed briefly while "under the influence."

My interviewing psych was of Southeast Asian extraction—Thai, Cambodian, Vietnamese, you can't tell by looking at them. I thought myself culturally unbiased and had a high opinion of the Asians in the force. Outside the force, they were, according to the statisticians, a brainy addition to the cultural mix who did well in the humanities and sciences; according to us they were a brainy addition who created occasional havoc with ingenious variations on old rackets. On the whole they were no better and no worse than the white majority, who could be wicked in anyone's language. This one got down to business without any fake reassuring palaver and for most of the time kept his eyes on a telltale board which he could see but I could not.

The effect of the drug cocktail felt like no effect at all; I thought that perhaps I might be a natural immune. The psych asked seemingly pointless questions while I wondered what the telltale told about my answers. I was not sure that the test had actually started, but it had because the psych said, "That's all; you can go home."

While I was still feeling surprised he raised his voice with a sudden sharpness. "Look at me!" With the habit of responding to command, I stared into his eyes, expectant but unsuspicious. "Do not discuss this test with anyone!"

The tone was to an insulting degree peremptory.

Feeling pretty uptight, I told him that I could accept an instruction without having it screwed into place, but psychs are not impressed by their experimental animals. This one said, "Sorry, but it is important," with his eyes back on the telltale board. He added, as a throwaway, "I don't imagine you will want to discuss it."

I wasn't going to waste ill temper on a state automaton whose attention was on dials and needles and who had no interest in the reactions of a state guinea pig— or so I thought as I got myself out of the building to simmer down in the open air. How wrong you can be.

I crossed the road into the Exhibition Gardens and sat on the lawn as I experienced a moment of light-headedness. Aftereffect of the drugs? (It was in fact a rebalancing of functions as the injected cocktail wore off.) The next moments were disastrous.

I discovered with a slow sickness why the psych had said I would not want to discuss the test.

In his few scrappy minutes he had turned me inside out with drugs that had split my self-awareness into unrelated strata. My ears had taken in what he asked and my mouth had spilled the terrible answers, but in the process my brain had failed to understand what was asked of it; I had been subjected to a pressing of mental buttons and the painless extraction of the secrets of a lifetime. He had taken from me the things that exist in all of us, hidden and suppressed and often unknown to our conscious selves. He had learned, with the ease of breathing, that overt love for my parents overlaid an impatient resentment close to contempt but never admitted to myself, that I had wept in the darkness of my bed when the more obscene pressures of police work became unbearable, that there had been in adolescence—and beyond—episodes of powerful homoerotic feeling endured in frightened silence and shame at the

truth of what passes for hero worship, that I had occasionally stolen unimportant trifles simply because they were available and had not realized that such actions lodged like thorns in the complex mental paths between public and private morality, and that (somehow this seemed infinitely demeaning) I had an inborn fear of spiders and would break out in sweat at the approach of one—

And some other things I don't trust myself even now to put in writing. I don't want to look at them.

Under a hot summer sun I shivered in the horror of exposure, naked as a worm, to the mind of another. That secrets were surely safe in the doctor-patient relationship counted not at all. Were they indeed safe, or would they wait in some "protected" computer file, to be one day resurrected for prurient discussion by the judges of my career, my promotion, my future?

In the end I collapsed into helpless anger—at the man who had unfairly leeched truth out of me, at myself for harboring such meannesses in the corners of my mind and, at last, at the state system which had submitted me to such self-hatred without explanation or pity.

I sat there for two hours before I recalled the end of the interview and the cynicism of the psych's final order. He was right; I could not even discuss self-disgust with my shuddering self.

Nobody, literally nobody, is proof against the secrets of his own heart.

It was late when I made for home, the huddling place, the refuge.

Mum had always made herself deaf to mention of anything more than the routine of my job, refusing to dip her mind into the human sewers, but Bill liked to get me alone and dig for drama; nothing could cure him of the delusion that I must have access to untold

facts behind the cases on the vidnews. This time he asked, innocently enough, about the day's work and my immediate impulse was to unload some of the angry jumble from my mind.

Secrecy provisions are expected to apply to family as well as to all others but in fact are often flouted in the home. It is a commonplace that policemen talk carelessly to their wives and policewomen to their husbands; authority knows this, has always known it and put up with it as a prohibition that cannot be enforced.

My lips were parted for a snarling complaint about invasion of privacy before I realized that complaint would involve giving reasons that I would not, could not give. Just living with self-knowledge is bad enough.

I said, clutching at words, "Nothing much," but I was shaken badly and so, in another way, was Bill who, staring and concerned, cried out, "For God's sake, boy, you're sweating!"

So I was; so would have been anyone so shamefully hurt in secret places.

"Was it that bad, Son?"

My father's worry was acutely shaming to my harshly revealed secret contempt for him. I could only evade. "Was what bad?"

"Whatever it was. Something unpleasant?"

"Nothing unpleasant, Dad. Just a day."

Bill gave me the father-to-son I-know-better grin. "Secret stuff, eh?"

While Mum clung to her fairy floss view of life that ignored and in some fashion sublimated the dreary facts, Bill had buffered shock and disappointment by retreat into romance; he could shunt me into some hypothetical Secret Service with a flip of the mind. For once I was thankful for a father who could invent my lies for me.

At the station next morning I waited uneasily for someone to ask me what the guinea-pig job had been,

but nobody did. I had prepared such a battery of off-handed replies that this was nearly a disappointment though I had no intention of telling anyone of the existence of an interrogation aid that reduced all previous techniques to nursery games. It seeped only slowly into me that the station staff had been warned that the testing carried high order secrecy and that I was not to be questioned.

It followed, then, that high order secrecy was indeed involved, and it might well be that my participation was not finished, that I was on ice until wanted. The idea did nothing for a sullen temper that could not be released; they must have found me hard to bear with until I came to appreciate that this minuscule prohibition made no real difference to my life. There was something purely private that I had to keep to myself. So what?

The ill temper retreated to the back of my mind but did not go away; the sense of unwarrantable invasion persisted like a nagging toothache.

Six weeks later I was called to City Central Station for interview, reason unspecified, and ushered into an interrogation room—chair and table, bare walls—to see again the nameless psych who had tapped my secret mind. He sat across the table from me, and the face that had then been so uninterested surveyed me now with a hint of curiosity.

The duty constable ostentatiously switched off the recording gear and left us; there would be no record of the interview. My buzzer gave no tiny hum in my ear to warn of secondary bugs, so I knew that the psych was not wired. I took immediate advantage to spill stored anger on him. "What do you want now, Peeping Tom?"

It was wrong, childish and did not touch him. He nodded his yellow-brown face gently and in a light,

soft voice commended my restraint. "Some men might have been immediately violent."

"Cracking your skull would only buy me a dishonorable discharge."

The soft voice took on a touch of primness. "I would not dream of laying a charge, whatever action you took. I know your feeling very well; I took the test myself in order to know."

"I hope you suffered."

"If it helps your mood, I did, but the thing is less significant than your anger imagines."

"You speak for yourself."

"For you, too. Are you prepared to listen?"

"To what?"

"Absolution." That was unexpected. As he leaned over the table I saw that he was older than he had at first seemed, age masked by the smooth Asian skin that collapses so suddenly when its time comes. "I promise that it will help."

It seemed that the functionary had a soul of sorts, but I was not prepared to concede much. "Go on."

"Will you take offense if I tell you now that your psychological profile is uninterestingly normal? Many don't care to be told that; they want to be strange, exotic, fascinating. They are usually bores. Your useful variation from the norm—and everybody has some variation—lies in a personal integrity expressed as a strong preference for moral concepts of right and wrong over legal definitions—despite occasional confusions. Does it cause trouble with your superiors?"

"Sometimes. So you're telling me what a good bloke I am. Get on with the rest of it."

The answer seemed to please him. "The rest of it is the clutter pushed out of mental sight as too shameful for contemplation. Your personal clutter is average in about ninety percent of men and women. Even your arachnophobia is common in one form or another.

Snakes and toads are frequent incarnations of inchoate fears, also cats and grubs and even blowflies. I have to force myself to endure the presence of cockroaches. Foolish? You know better. We despise the phobias of others and hide our own, not knowing that so many of our shames are commonplaces. Homoerotic feelings, for instance, are present at some juncture in the majority of both sexes. I feel mild distrust of people who seem to be wholly without them; I sense an inner coldness. Homosexual temptation is common in adolescence, tends to regress in maturity and sometimes returns in middle age. A feeling is not shameful; what you do about it may be—if you act against your nature or experiment stupidly."

He paused for my comment, but I would not help him. He shook his dark head. "It is you I am talking about. I am sure that you know these things intellectually but do not stop to apply them to yourself. Why do we all think ourselves so especially wicked when we are only dithering with juvenile hangovers?"

"Face. You should know about that."

"I do; although I am third generation Australian, I do not pretend to be free of a cultural weakness. That is not as stultifying as fearing it. The matter of your thieving, for instance. A policeman must be aware that all humans are thieves of some kind at some time. Stealing material objects brings punishment, but we also steal time—and knowledge—and the contentment of others—and we plan cunning tricks to steal a march where we may; we are all dishonest where there is no retribution. You deal harshly with those whose departures from the venal norm disturb the public peace, but that does not entitle you to scourge your conscience because you see your peccadillos as reflections of the criminality you punish in others. You are a morally average man. Be content with that; don't try so hard to be an interesting sinner. There, now!"

"Should I cry, Hallelujah, I'm saved? So far it's only words." Then I had to give some grudging fair play. "They may sink in, given time."

"They will because you wish it so. Unnecessary guilt is a station on the road to the psychiatric hospital."

Impassiveness stripped emotion from the words, leaving meaning bare and stark.

"Maybe. Still—" One barb remained embedded, and he would not have forgotten it. Referring to it would cost me a sour effort of will; best let it lie.

"Still?"

It was not to be allowed to lie. "There were questions about my parents."

"Yes. That influence is always paramount, for good or evil. Yours are good people. Good to you."

"Yes."

"And you are a good son." A statement.

To be contradicted? "I try to be." That was the best I could do at that moment.

"But?"

The effort had to be made. "When you questioned my relations with them I was caught in—" I floundered and came up with "—caught between answers."

"It was noticeable, an ambiguity. You resolved it by giving both answers, love and contempt."

"You can't have it both ways."

"Why not? A relationship has many aspects; one does not react equally to all of them."

I was not sure whether that was a placebo or made good sense. "I won't let it make a difference."

"Indeed you will!" He came alive, became a person, emphatic, dictatorial; a man with a mission shone through the professional who measured and weighed. "You will see them with wiser eyes and a better understanding of yourself. All children revolt against their parents but are snared in the culturally inculcated sense of duty; some fight for their identity, others

repress resentment to justify to themselves the role
they feel called upon to play in public. Animals settle
it much better; they turn the cubs out of the lair as soon
as they can hunt. Humans stay together too long and
have to make adjustments. You will make them and
be happier for it. End of lesson, Detective-Sergeant
Ostrov."

This was all possibly good for my mental welfare,
but here was a twist that needed straightening. "Those
questionnaires were coded; where did you learn my
name?"

"Your commissioner told it to me after I had sorted
through several hundred mental profiles to find the
man to match the profile I needed for testing."

"Needed? Why me? What do you want of me?"

"I acted, you might say, as a talent scout. You have
the qualifications for a particular role." His voice, level
again, made nothing special of it. A man had been
required; a man had been found. Yet I felt that this was
not so much coolness as a carefulness with words.

"Role?"

"I cannot tell you much yet; the project is still a
little in the future, but it will involve surveillance and
protection on a high level. A very high level."

"And you selected me that day from all the hundreds
tested?"

"No; I had already chosen you after a more usual
mode of investigation and summation. Your test was
for nailing down what I already knew and for flushing
out anything relevant that I might have missed. The
other test subjects were part of a genuine psychological
comparison of effects on various physical groups."

I felt like a rat in a trap baited with rotten cheese.

"Are you a police psych?"

"No. Let me explain: The work will involve some
training as a ward orderly, really only an extension
of your police first aid capacities, enough to provide

verisimilitude and make you reasonably useful in the hospital where you will begin."

It sounded thoroughly distasteful. "If I begin."

"You have been detailed by your commissioner on my recommendation. You cannot refuse."

"I can, you know. Just like that. It might cost me a little seniority—"

"There are those who would see that it cost you your livelihood." The smooth face showed a real sensibility that might have been distaste for what he was doing. "I had to make a choice, and your professional and psychological profiles suit the requirements. It is an important undertaking. Be complimented."

"Then I'm complimented." I was not; I was afraid. To be tipped out of the force would mean unemployment for life. I could face that in the way you can face anything short of destruction, but Mum and Bill were another matter. More than ever I could not abandon them now that I knew the paradox in my feeling for them. No doubt the psych knew all that. "Tell me about it."

"As much as I am permitted. If all goes well an old man will undergo surgery. His name will be Jackson, an incognito. Your brief will be to see that he comes to no harm, in the hospital or later. It sounds simple. It may not be. In time you will receive detailed instructions from other people."

That sort of thing disgusts a professional. "The 'need to know' principle! It smells of amateurs—people with fancy ideas playing at some stinking little intrigue. What does this one stink of?"

"Would I tell you that? There is another thing." With his eyes on mine he said, "Do not discuss this matter with anyone not already familiar with it."

"How will I know them?"

"They will know you."

"Secret society nonsense. That sort ask for betrayal

with every clumsy cover-up. They make loyalty a burden."

"Your resentment will pass. Have you more to ask?"

"Yes. Boiled down, your requirement is for a man whose total silence can be depended upon, nailed down by a threat of lifetime poverty for himself and his parents. The threat interests me. I smell crime."

He smiled politely. "I have mentioned the highest in the land; do you bracket them with crime?"

"Why not?" I treated him to a touch of Ostrov grim-in-interrogation mode; it had frightened good men before this. "A policeman is coerced into abetting crime. That's what it is, isn't it? Crime?"

If the performance impressed him he did not show it.

"Your part will not be to commit or abet, only to protect an aging man in a position not of his seeking." He stood. "Now I must go. I did not choose a fool for the work; I chose a man of notable moral steadfastness."

Despite his smoothness, the lightest of emphasis made moral steadfastness sound like a weakness which happened, improbably, to fit this special task. He held out his hand. "Good-bye."

"Go to hell."

As though I had not spoken, he said, "One does not choose indiscriminately when singling out a man who will be responsible to the premier of the state and to no other."

Premier? The highest indeed—but it is a truism that real crime starts at the top; what goes on below is, by comparison, a desperate thrashing about.

Within the week I was attending medical orderly classes by night and learning hospital routine, on the job, by day. Three weeks of that saw me shifted to a seventh floor convalescent ward in the State Biophysical Institute which was not, strictly, a hospital but

was rumored, among police as well as others, to carry out work that often required hospitalization—very private hospitalization—of the subjects of biophysical research.

By then my anger had slipped into a habit of mood rather than emotion, an almost token resentment; it did not interfere with my daily life. In fact, my curiosity began to look forward to the appearance of the aging Mr. Jackson who was in a soup not of his own stirring. On the day I first saw my charge, the premier's daughter sat weeping on a bed in a back room in the rundown suburb of Balaclava on the other side of the city. I did not know this at the time and, because he was in Canberra, neither did the premier.

Which, as Bill might have put it, showed that the devil has his own techniques for giving the pure in heart a run for their money.

2

Mrs. Blacker:
Love and Food Coupons

From Commentaries; *The Psychology of Poverty:*
*"This harassed woman, concerned only with the
welfare of her son but beset by untrustworthy
neighbors, pursued by the fear of punishment
and tormented by the cruelty of what she saw as
socially correct behavior on her part, was typical
of the powerless. The mores of hapless masses are
always torn between the commands of law and
the imperatives of survival. There are never clear
solutions."*

I must have been bloody well insane to let that half-
witted bitch into the flat. Sixteen and prissy mannered
up to the neck but with all her Minder schooling she
was ignorant of what a Wardie kid knows that's had
her education in the gutter. I ask her, "How long are
you gone?" and she doesn't know I'm talking about
her belly. She knew enough to get Fred but not a thing
about what happened after the getting. Or so she'd have
you think.

She couldn't stay here. I couldn't keep feeding her on family coupons.

I should have made Fred take her back home and dump her, but if the truth's told I got sentimental and stupid and wanted to protect her, laws or no laws.

No, it was Fred I had to protect. He's all I've got . . . not counting his pisshead father that's a waste of time and good food. . . . Fred's all I'll ever have under these stinking laws.

What if all the women got pregnant at once? What could the Minders do about it? Abort every woman in Australia? We ought to— No. They'd let us bear the kids and then they'd say, "There's no food ration for this outlaw child. Can't issue you any coupons, lady. Sorry and all that." Except it wouldn't be "Sorry"; it'd be, "Chuck it out with the garbage, why doncha?"

What could I do about Fred? In love, poor young bugger. I knew he'd played around before, but this time he'd fallen bad and there was the baby coming and his head full of all the bull about being a father to this wonderful kid.

But I couldn't hide her in just three rooms from all the stickybeaks in the other flats. If I'd told them to stay away, they'd've known I was hiding something and just about busted the doors in to find out what.

It wasn't as if she was just a nobody that I could give a kick up the arse and tell to get out. The premier's daughter, for Christ's sake! There was no Mrs. Premier or whatever they call the wife, so that made her the top lady of the state—at sixteen years old and five months up the duff! And she sat there all day in Fred's room in our falling-down shack of a flat, waiting for him to come home and not game to come out because I'd've cracked her silly mouth if she'd tried it.

How in hell did it happen? Fred was the head gardener's odd-job boy—but he got off with the boss's daughter, for Christ's sake! How did he meet her?

Where did they go for their bit of fun that turned out
serious? He wouldn't have chatted her up; he wouldn't
have been game. It must have been her. He's a good,
solid boy and she took a fancy. That must have been
the way of it.

I couldn't get a thing out of them. Fred carried on
like the lovesick kid he is and she just looked like
she expected me to hit her, which I should've. All I
could find out was that when it got too uncomfortable
to hide any longer she told Daddy. And Daddy Beltane,
the premier of the state, told his daughter she'd have
her bloody abortion like any other careless thickhead,
and so she ran away.

She wanted the kid.

Well, that's natural enough; I would've, too.

The thing was, she didn't give a curse about Fred;
she pretended, but she didn't fool me. She wanted a
kid and she snared a strong, nice-looking boy to give
it to her, but she didn't care what trouble it made for
him. Maybe never thought. I told her the law, and she
looked as if she didn't hear me. He'd get punished
for unauthorized birthing and have his fathering right
taken from him, but she'd keep the kid and Daddy'd fix
it so she got away with it and my Fred would never see
them again.

She said she never let on to Daddy that Fred's the
father, and that had to be true because he still went to
work of a day. He had to or how could we live with
Johnno too sick or too pissed to do even half a job if
it was offered to him?

I didn't know what to do. I should've said no, right
away.

That's why I saw Barney about it. He's a sly old brute,
but he's got some sense.

I didn't give Melissa any warning; I just took Barney
to where she sat on the bed with her legs under her

and said, "Dr. Barney's going to have a look at you."

She squeezed back against the wall, all suspicious I suppose because Barney's part Abo. A good doctor all the same. She said, "What for? I'm not sick."

She was nothing to look at—a bit too big for her age and too podgy for her proper size, but that was an advantage because she was one of those who don't show for months—but you could see she was on the way when she took off the tight corset she had on at first. (These Minder bitches wear corsets for their figures!)

Barney put his old leather bag on the chair while I was telling her, "He'll work out what we got to do about you."

"Do?" she says, silly as they come, and I let out a bit of spite.

"Yes, do! You don't think you're going to drop it on the bed here, do you?" I had to tell Barney, "She's that slow on the uptake it's getting me out of temper. I'll leave youse to it."

I could only go into the kitchen, of course, so I didn't miss any of what went on.

Barney was saying, "Will you please take off that overall?" in his educated voice that could pass for Minder if he wanted. I suppose he is a sort of a Minder though he works amongst us here.

She said, like an idiot, "It's Fred's overall. My dress is being washed."

"So?" says Barney. "Please take it off."

"I'm not sick."

I knew what was upsetting her. Barney always looks dirty. His shoes are never polished (whose are in the Wards?), he wears this old, shabby jacket and his trousers are always rumpled and stained. Add his dark skin to all that and to her it said, *filthy.* In her world doctors look like the dummies in the vidplays; she couldn't recognize a real one.

He says, a bit sharpish, "You're worse than sick, girl you're illegal."

She knew all that and gabbled how Daddy would look after the law side of it. He'd have to when he got over being angry and found she'd run away. When she went back he'd be so glad he'd do anything for her.

Barney put a skewer into that right away, telling her that Daddy mightn't be all that ready to help. He knew who her Daddy was and a by-blow grandchild to the premier of Victoria might be more scandal than enough for him, even if she married Fred. And Daddy mightn't be too pleased about that idea, either.

She sounded a bit guilty, as though she'd thought about it, when she said, "I can't marry Fred. Daddy has people picked out to choose from when I'm a bit older."

If that wasn't cool! Bloody slut, slut, slut!

"With a bastard child for a wedding present?"

"Daddy will find a way. There's always a way. Daddy can do—"

He cut into her like a terrier. "If Daddy has any sense he'll disown you! Now I want to see if abortion is possible, so get that damned overall off."

"Abortion!" She half screamed it. "No!"

She meant it. She didn't want Fred (but when would he wake up to that?), but she wanted his baby. His baby? Anybody's baby as long as it finished up hers. God only knows what had got into her. Besides Fred, that is.

"You want this baby?"

"Yes!"

"Why?"

"My business."

He didn't go on with that; it was a brick wall. "Mrs. Blacker says you're five months pregnant. Correct?"

"About that."

"I'd better check."

"Why?"

I took a peep through the crack of the doorjamb and she was still scrunched back against the wall.

Because, Barney tells her, she obviously knows nothing about motherhood or how to look after herself or how to give the baby a chance to be born healthy. Cunning old Barney! He went on, inventing like mad because she was too ignorant to know it was nonsense. Things can go wrong, he told her, like her mental state could affect the baby's development and so could her change of diet to Wardie food. He couldn't advise unless he knew the state of her pregnancy and her physical condition.

She was quiet for a bit as if she was just about convinced. Then she said, "But you're dirty," and I wished he'd hit the stupid bitch.

Not Barney, though; he'd rather give her a lesson. He told her how Wardie people are suspicious of good clothes and people trying to look better than the rest. You could even get spat on in the street by some of the rougher kids. Then he showed her his hands. "Look! Are they dirty?"

I knew they'd be scrubbed clean, the pink-brown skin almost shining, the nails clean and white tipped. Better than mine. Better than bitch Melissa's, for that matter. His shirt would be clean and when he put on his white coat he would be as presentable as you could want.

He must have got through to her because he said, "Come, come, no tears. A mother has to be strong. Strong enough to lose her child if necessary."

"I won't lose my baby!" It was a bit of a squawl now, mixed with sniffling. "You can look at me and tell me what to do, but I won't lose my baby!" Then she said, as if it was terribly important, "I've never undressed in front of a man before."

What about in front of Fred? Maybe in her world Wardies aren't people. Undressing for them don't count.

It was all quiet for a bit and he must have finished his examination when she said, "What do I have to do?" and he came back to the fight to say, "Get rid of it."

"No!" I peeped again, and she was beating her hands on the bedclothes. "No! No! No!"

"Do you realize what this can do to your father's position?"

"What do you mean? It isn't his baby."

Barney really exploded then, saying he didn't believe anyone like her existed! No premier's daughter could be so ignorant of the facts of political life. Or of sexual life. Or of any damned thing he could ask her or tell her. "Didn't your mother ever talk to you about—" He must have remembered then that the mother had gone off years ago with some boyfriend. "Don't you have a governess of some sort to tell you the things you need to know?"

"I go to boarding school. I have a maid at home at weekends, but she's only a kid."

Kid! Twelve or thirteen, maybe, and pig ignorant.

"Boarding school?" asks Barney. "Nuns?"

"No. We're Protestant."

"Different but not necessarily better. Doesn't your father ever talk to you about intimate things? Sex and boys and the population laws?"

"No. I don't see him that much."

"And do they tell you nothing at school?"

"The girls talk about it. We know all about it."

That was a laugh. They'd have a giggle about the dirty words somebody scribbled on the lavvy wall and that'd be about all.

"In God's name what do they teach you at that place?"

Barney was near to busting, and she couldn't see what was wrong. "Just the usual school things. Why are you so angry?"

"Not with you. With the world for being such a sink of stupidity. Don't they teach anything that matters?"

"You mean dressmaking and hairdressing and those things? Why should they? We aren't people who will have to work. It's an expensive school." Oh, dearie bloody me! Then she thought of something important. "I do bookkeeping because it will be useful when I'm married and running a big house."

I nearly took a fit, laughing. She was hopeless. A Wardie kid of ten knew more about the world.

He said, "You know nothing, but you must understand that your child cannot be born." He tried to make her see that what she wanted didn't count against Fred being punished because of her. Once he'd had a child the law would never give him a second chance. And his parents might serve a jail sentence for harboring her. He finished up, "And it's no bloody use crying."

I could hardly hear her whispering and gulping through the tears, "I'm going to have my baby."

Barney said with a sort of despair, "You'll bring the government down before you're through. For the present, don't leave this room. Nobody must know you are here."

I don't know what she said to that; all I could hear was the sniffling.

Barney came out to me and said, "She has no mother and no effective father and nobody gives a damn about her. What little she knows is just imitation of the brats at her school. She's swinging in midair with only a pregnancy to cling to."

He kept his voice down and we moved over to the outside door, which was as far as we could get from Melissa without being where the neighbors could listen in.

I wasn't going to be taken in by any of his psych stuff and I as good as said so. "She's a born trollop that gets around amongst ladies but doesn't know enough to be one thing or t'other."

He tried to tell me what it is like amongst the Minders where the gap between them and us has got so deep that they go on like a separate kind of people. They have this big idea that they're born to lord it and we're born to put up with it, and they have different manners and a different way of talking and all sorts of things you don't say in front of the children and foolishness like that. Don't they know what kids' minds are like? Little sewers is what they are and what you don't tell them they invent and look what's happened to Melissa. I remember he said something like, "When historical circumstances repeat themselves, the attitudes are repeated, too. They're having a touch of the Victorians up there in cloud land."

That could be, but I didn't know what it meant. Anyway, I wanted to keep to the main thing. "She's got to have the abortion no matter what she wants."

He agreed with that, but said we had to remember who she is. "It has to be kept absolutely quiet; five months is late for a backyard type of abortion and I can't do a clinical abortion in the surgery because I'm not equipped for it. I'm just a Wardie GP, remember, with only the barest means of treatment."

That was bullshit. I knew his real trouble would be getting rid of the evidence. The way they can trace things today you can't just drop it down a drain. You couldn't even boil one down to broth without somebody smelling it and getting curious. But that was his trouble; mine was her.

I said, "She's got to get out of here, then."

Straight away he said, "She's too important to be tossed out like some useless Susser. Keep her for a couple of days while I work something out. I'll try to

get her back home. Keeping Fred's name out of it is the important thing."

I smelt he was up to something. I didn't really want to throw a pregnant girl on the street, but what could I do else? She was all right in the back room so long as nobody saw or heard, but you can't stop accidents. Then there was Fred, up to his ears in calf love and there'd be trouble enough with him, let alone her.

Well, first things first. "I can't keep on feeding her. We've only got the Suss coupons and Fred's wage money's no good there. You can't buy coupons."

That was a try-on and he knew it. He said right away, "I'll bring you some cash-free coupons in the morning." He looked straight at me and said he had a few to spare.

Nobody has coupons to spare, but a lot of whispers said that Barney would take black market coupons from some who couldn't raise cash for treatment and now I knew it was true. He didn't have to be afraid of me letting on; if anybody split on him there would be roundabout ways of seeing they got lumbered for passing illegal tender above their Suss ration.

They talk about honor among thieves, but it comes down to being careful of each other.

So I was going to keep her for a few days and precious few it had better be. I didn't know what Barney was playing at and didn't care so long as I was out of it and my Fred's skin was safe.

3

Ostrov: A Case for Tender, Loving Care

From Commentaries; *The Dilemma of Longevity:* "*Populations supplied with rigidly calculated rations are healthier than those with unlimited quantity and choice. The fact was noted as early as 1942 in an England with food supplies restricted by war; in the twenty-first century it had the unwanted effect of increasing life expectancies, already an embarrassment, to the point where ageing was a greater population growth factor than the birthrate. Outright termination of all on reaching a predetermined age was still emotionally impractical (do not imagine, however, that it was not discussed) but general practitioners were encouraged, at first furtively, then more openly, to deal only cursorily with the elderly or moribund. It was an easy step to active bans on certain life-preserving procedures. . . .*"

Senior Surgeon Cranko took me to the seventh floor (which consisted solely of one-bed wards for reasons

I preferred not to ask about—and wouldn't have been answered if I had) and introduced me to the matron, a jolly-looking woman old enough to be my mother and probably as hard as a boxer's fist.

"Orderly Ostrov," says she brightly. "So you're the silent cop."

I was furious. With no pretense of deference I asked the surgeon, "How many people know I'm under cover here? Half the staff? Or all of them?"

Cranko was conciliatory when he knew he had no real authority to flourish over me. "Only the people who need to know, Harry. Matron here, Jackson's hypnotherapist and myself. Come along to the ward."

We escaped down the passage from a suddenly not-so-pleasant-seeming matron, past closed doors from which no sounds emerged, while he said, "I'm afraid the silent cop joke was mine. It was a kind of traffic regulator in the old days, wasn't it? A sort of hump in the middle of an intersection?"

I had no idea but said yes, to put an end to it.

We stopped at a small room which he called the cubby, the orderly's office. It contained, in the smallest possible space, table and chair, folding bed, sink with running water, first aid cabinet and—

I asked, "What's that doing here?"

"That" was an ordinary tabletop vidscreen with a very unordinary console.

"You know what it is?" He was surprised.

"I know a Spy-eye console when I see it. It's supposed to be secret military equipment." (But the police had a few installed in places where they would frighten the hell out of the occupants if they knew.)

The surgeon, a long streak of a man with large and beautiful hands, answered from an oblique angle. "Haven't you been informed about this institute?"

"I've been told it's a group of experimental laboratories, and that's all. Everything's on a need-to-know

basis, so it's like feeling around in a fog. I don't know what half the departments in this building are for or even where most of them are."

He looked apologetic. "It isn't for me to tell you much more. Take it that we do a lot of regular biophysical research here, stuff that we publish in the usual journals, but also a certain amount better left under wraps. I won't tell you about those and you're better off not knowing."

"More of the same! What about the Spy-eye?"

He chose words with care. "There are, um, operative subjects" (My mind heard "victims" and my imagination turned a little sick.) "who need constant observation but should not be conscious of it. You will find it useful with Jackson. Shall we go in to him?"

The ward was white and bare of all but necessities; the bed stood central against the back wall like an excrescence. Biophysics gave no sign of being a caring discipline.

It is difficult to judge the height of a man in bed, but I guessed him to be about my own height, one of those big-boned men with a narrow frame that renders wrists, knees and knuckles as knobs. He appeared to be in his early sixties, but the forearms exposed on the sheet were smooth fleshed and unwrinkled . . . extremely well preserved sixties. He lay on his back, asleep.

I checked the progress board at the foot of the bed—name, temperature, pulse rate, all the usual . . . "Date of hospitalization isn't entered."

"No, and the board and chart will be destroyed when he leaves. He won't appear in the registrar's records."

"I should have guessed that." Secrets! I listened to his breathing and felt his pulse. "He's not in normal sleep and I don't think he's drugged. What goes on?"

"Hypnotherapy."

"That junk discipline?"

"It has its uses. Drugs can lead to complications where induced-sleep therapy allows normal healing."

"Healing from what?"

"There has been some facial surgery."

"No sign of it. No scars."

"I would be upset if there were. There is art as well as craft in the profession."

"What else? Something internal?"

He asked, "Do you wear a bug alarm?"

"When it seems needed. Not here."

"From now on wear it all the time. There are too many people interested in the work of this institute. This room must be inviolate while this man is in it."

"I really love working in a haze of half truths and evasions. Now—something internal?"

"That's one way of putting it." He turned back the sheet and opened Jackson's pajama coat on the torso of a healthy man. "He is ninety-three years old. A few weeks ago he was in terminal decrepitude, a skeleton in a bag of wrinkles, a shaking, dribbling wreck after twenty-five years of Alzheimer's disease plus general senility."

I let astonishment settle before I said, "Age reversal is supposed to be impossible. Something about compounding of errors in intracell processes as you grow older. Irreversible. I read it somewhere."

"Now you know differently. This building is alive with the unlikely; it exists to test the improbable."

"You have accomplished the illegal—giving extension of life to the terminally ill."

"Quite so. The illegality is fully stated in the Population Containment Act Amendment of forty-seven."

Telling me the institute made its own laws.

"I'm a policeman. I don't condone lawbreaking. I know there's a popular idea that we are all corrupt and buyable, but it isn't so. We know why the laws are how they are and most of us uphold them. I uphold them."

He said to the air, "And I know that you can't do

a damned thing about it, even report it. Best not to worry, Detective-Sergeant. Besides—" he turned a disturbingly speculative gaze on me "—the circumstances are strange; you may find your righteous reservations easing as you learn more about the case. Law and morality can be strange bedfellows."

"I know, but my instinct is against it."

"Does it trouble you?"

"After a dozen years of respecting the law, yes, it troubles me."

"Then I suggest you talk to Nguyen about it."

"Who is he?"

"Dr. Nguyen—Nguyen Donh Minh. He's Jackson's hypnotherapist. He says he has met you."

It seemed I would find little pleasure in this assignment. "That's his name, is it? Yes, we've met. I could do without him around me."

"He's a very good man. Like you, he has reservations, but he knows how to handle them." The air between us was growing steadily cooler. "Is there any more I can tell you?"

"Whatever you can. A great deal, I think."

Cranko spread his hands. "Less than you think, but what there is may abrade your reservations. This man's name is not Jackson; it is Beltane, but to us he is Arthur Jackson. He is the premier's father and he was operated on here at the premier's insistence. Why, I have not been told, but that is something your Spy-eye may discover when the son visits in a day or two. For the rest, he should come to full waking tonight or tomorrow, and not even Nguyen can hazard a guess at what his mental condition will be. Be careful what you say to him. Try not to upset him; the first hours may be crucial in deciding whether he is competent or mentally disturbed past handling."

As he left he said, "Your patient has been fed intra-

venously and there's a catheter in his penis. You won't have any revolting discharges to deal with."

His parting smile regretted that a moralizing copper would not have to dabble in excremental reality.

I studied Beltane's—*Jackson*'s—still face, but faces rarely tell much of the man behind the image. He remained a delicate illegality requiring protection and tender, loving care. I hoped he was worth it.

The premier's father . . . that might explain but did not justify what had been done to me by Nguyen Donh Minh, himself likely a puppet on some other string.

Now I needed some facts to set Jackson in focus, but there was no general information terminal in the ward. I went to the matron's office to ask about reliefs and was told that I would be on call on a twenty-four-hour basis. While I slept Jackson would be checked every quarter hour by the duty nurse and I would be wakened at any change in the patient.

"To do what?"

"Observe. Learn about him." She was brusque.

"Where do I sleep? In the cubby?"

"I'll have a bed shifted into the ward for you."

I had a request, but my welcome had not been promising. "I need information on Jackson, background stuff. Old news files and vidwires would be best, but I can't leave here to track them down. Can you suggest something?"

She surprised me with a smile, forgiving the humble pleader and knowing his need exactly. "I was curious, too, and we have a good library here." From her desk she drew a fat volume and indicated a protruding bookmark.

It was the *Dictionary of National Biography,* compacted edition, and fell open at Beltane G. F., a shortish, single-column entry. "Thank you, Matron. I won't keep it long."

*   *   *

DNB entries for the still living are based on material supplied and approved by the subject. Old Beltane had been miserly with information. (Uninterested, or merely careful to leave no clues?)

Arthur Jackson had been born Gerald Fitzgerald Beltane (what a smell of olde worlde upper class was there!) and had lived what seemed to the prying mind of an ordinary, suspicious copper a dry, almost marginal life. Perhaps the lives of the mighty tended to dryness behind the facade but surely not to the marginal, shy of limelight.

Born 1976—English father and Australian mother of Scottish descent. An only child. Education via state schools and a university scholarship. (What, no money, with that name stinking of lineage?) MA degree.

Became secretary to Melbourne Ports branch of the Labour Party in 2005. (An MA in Labour politics? Well, why not? Socialism had been in a short revival at the turn of the century, despite the Russian upheaval.)

Son, Jeremy, illegitimate, born 2006. His mother, Estelle Lily Broughton, had died in childbirth. (Had birthing still been troublesome then? Mothers did not die save under exceptional circumstances. An odd case, perhaps.) Child reared by foster parents. (Sensible, if no wife or female relatives available.)

Married to Mary Mavis Hogan, 2009. Entered state Parliament as member for new seat of River West, 2010. (Married for that purpose? Electors preferred their members respectably married. Why? Did they think respectability ruled out a possible rat behind the wainscot?)

Long and influential parliamentary career though never achieving ministerial rank. Seemed to have actually preferred the back benches. A "numbers man," a valuable henchman to four state premiers in different administrations. (If valuable why unreward-

ed? Or was he? Check the meaning of "numbers man.")

Claimed son, Jeremy, 2021. (Because no children by wife, Mary?)

Separated from wife, 2022. (One year after claiming. Difference over boy?)

Raised son to be a politician until Jeremy Beltane entered House as member for Melbourne Ports, 2030.

Retired, aged seventy, in 2046, on ground of ill health.

And, of course, the missing entry: *Cheated death by illegal rejuvenation, instigated by son, 2069, after years of Alzheimer degeneration and senility.*

Why?

As a curriculum vitae it was empty space with publicly known tether spots here and there. I needed a more intimate account, but perhaps none existed. Truth, the whole truth, is told only of the dead. There would be journalists and ancient relics of politicians who knew more, but what reason could I advance for prying?

I returned the book to matron and asked her what a numbers man might be. She, being twenty years older, might know the term. She thought it meant someone who continually sounded the ideas of individual party members so that support for or disapproval of proposals of cabinet or premier could be assessed in advance—a very useful man when a spill threatened or a stab in the back was to be averted.

"What they call now a 'weasel'?"

"Something like, but today the faction weasels within the party try to outsmart each other. Politics must be a filthy business."

I asked, on impulse, "And the institute—is this also a filthy business?"

Short-lived goodwill faded. "A policeman will know that there's dirt under every carpet, even his own."

"Score to you, Matron." She did not smile.

*   *   *

Jackson was restless through the afternoon, small movements easing limbs that had lain too long in one position. Once I thought he had opened his eyes, only for a moment, and sunk back into unconsciousness. I called the day nurse who said, "This may happen a few times. Don't call me unless he remains awake, but stay near in case he tries to get out of bed."

My bed was brought in from the cubby and I settled down to read and, when the night nurse came on, to sleep.

I caught two more false wakings before I dozed off and then was myself awakened by a burst of snoring. Jackson lay on his back, fingers twitching in time to his raucous intakes.

I tried the old married-couple remedy of resting my weight gently on his shoulder to trigger a change of position which would roll him off his back. Instead, he sat bolt upright, fighting me off with flailing arms. I slapped the service bell to bring the nurse, folded him against my chest to calm him and laid him back on the pillow. "There, old feller, there. Take it easy. Everything's all right."

His eyes tried to see me, screwing the lids in search of focus. "Who're you?" Voice like a creaking gate.

"I'm looking after you."

"Why? Why?"

The nurse came hurrying, spray hypo ready. "Roll up his sleeve, please."

I pushed up the pajama sleeve as he closed his eyes, said, "I'm sick of bloody nurses," and went back to sleep.

"He won't need that now."

"It's just a relaxant to keep him quiet now he's out of induced sleep." She pressed the nozzle to the skin and squirted the drug through the flesh. "That will hold him for eight hours and Dr. Nguyen will be here by then.

You can get some proper sleep yourself now."

Far from it. I suffered beginner's nerves and dozed in snatches, expecting always to hear the thud of Jackson falling out of bed.

I was in the cubby, eating breakfast with half my attention on Jackson in the Spy-eye and a newscast murmuring in my earplug, when Nguyen came in. He was indeed the man of my test, and I would have to make the best of it. A private war on the other man's ground would be less a running battle than a running defeat.

"Good morning, Sergeant. I see the patient is still sleeping."

You would have thought I had never insulted him. "Yes, Doctor."

"Then I shall wake him. Nurse gave him somnoline at eleven-ten, so it should be fully absorbed by now."

"Do you need me?"

"I think not." He had answered offhandedly, his attention taken by the Spy-eye console. "That is an unusual keyboard. Why are the keys arranged on the faces of a cube?"

"To facilitate finding different points of view from above and from all sides."

"Has it sound also?"

"Yes. Turned off at the moment."

"Turn it on. Watch and listen, but I should not need assistance." He went silently out on soft shoes.

A strictly business association made good sense, but I had a question for him, one better asked this morning than later on.

His dark head moved into the screen, bending over Jackson. I switched the viewpoint until I was watching from the other side of the bed, seeing both faces in profile. Nguyen, satisfied, woke the man gently.

Jackson scowled at him, looked about him and asked

mutinously, "What's this place?" He seemed to be in a poor temper.

"A hospital."

"I can see that! What bloody hospital?"

"The Biophysical Institute."

"Never heard of it."

"It is a recent structure."

Bright, shrewd eyes surveyed Nguyen without grace. "Is it, now? Since when did the government have money for recent structures?"

The question belonged to the circumstances of a past government, but the situation in 2069 was no different. The old brute had wakened with a vengeance, cleareyed, clearheaded and on the ball. I heard Nguyen soothing placidly, "As a politician you will know there is always money for what the government wants."

"Even if nobody else wants it." He was ready to take on the nearest, whether or not they agreed with him. He asked, "What's wrong with me?"

"Very little now. There will be a minor weakness in the legs and arms, needing practice in walking and stretching. A matter of days only."

"Weakness from what?"

Nguyen said with some care, "A form of wasting disease which affected your memory of events."

Jackson peered closely at him. "Wasting? Memory? I remember some things. I remember quite a lot. I remember—" He broke off, rubbing his hands uneasily. As if he had suddenly seen too clearly, he raised them to his mouth in a gesture of shame and shock. Old brute gave way to nervous child.

Nguyen waited, watched, said nothing.

Jackson's hands slipped down to the sheet. He began to say, "I was—" but his voice cracked. Nguyen put a hand to his wrist and had it smacked away. "Don't baby me! I was out of my mind, wasn't I?"

"I would not say that."

"Well, I would and who the hell are you to contradict me? I know how I was."

"It seems so, and I am surprised that you recall even a little." He said casually, "You exhibited mainly the genetic type of Alzheimer's disease. It is mentally debilitating, but we don't class it with the insanities."

That shocked him; it was enough to shock anyone, but his mental resilience was amazing. He asked, with arrogance muted but not gone away, "Am I well now?"

"I see nothing wrong. Your apparent recovery exceeds expectation."

"Apparent, eh? We wait and see, do we?" He was quiet for a while. Nguyen waited silently. A large part of his performance seemed to lie in strategic waiting. Jackson said at last, "It is a disgusting condition."

"But it is over."

"Not recurrent?"

"There is no reason for recurrence. The genetic defect has been corrected."

"And you're my doctor?"

"Not your medical doctor. I am a hypnotherapeutic psychiatrist."

"Ah." Another pause. "I don't think I need you."

"On present evidence, nor do I, but there is always the unexpected."

"Is there? It gives you an excuse to keep sniffing at my mind, I suppose. I could do with some breakfast."

"It will be here fairly soon."

"Good. You can go away; I've things to think about."

To my surprise Nguyen said, "Of course; I'll just look in now and then," and turned away.

Jackson called after him, "Some great ape woke me in the middle of the night. Who was that?"

"When he brings your breakfast you can ask him yourself." Nguyen's smile was faint but relishing.

"I will. And you'd better get a message to my son. Tell him I'm better."

"He knows."

"Then where is he?"

"In Canberra, I believe."

"Why Canberra?"

"For a meeting of state premiers and the PM."

"Premiers? He's state premier?" His narrow face split in something more than a smile, a great, gaping triumph. He bounced gently in the bed, clapping his hands together and chuckling with delight before saying with a wistfulness that had seemed totally absent from such a makeup, "I have been too long gone. I was not here to see it happen."

But Nguyen had left him.

He slipped into the cubby laughing, actually laughing, like a human being. I said, "That wasn't much of a VIP consultation."

"There is nothing urgent to be done, and, as the stage folk say, always leave them laughing."

"You think he's OK mentally?"

"No. Nobody is. Not even you, my little-bit-starchy policeman." That was a new tone from this bland man. "He is an aggressive man, at his best in confrontation; while he questions and distrusts circumstances he will try to ride over them with energy, but other qualities will surface as unpleasant truths come to him. That may be the time for tinkering and adjusting. He spoke of memory. He probably has flashes of recollection rather than continuity. Do you agree?"

"Why ask me? You're the tinker." My surliness disturbed me; I amended, "It sounded bitty."

"Good; we agree. This is important. Alzheimer types lose a great deal of memory, and he was seen to be in mild deterioration for over ten years, followed by severe recession for fifteen. In clinical terms, he has

little right to be alive. A man who has been absent from a changing world for some three decades will need time to establish a place in it."

"An unjustifiable and unlawful place."

"See? Starchy cop! Illegality does not alter facts. We deal with what is. The law is your concern rather than mine since you will be his mentor and guardian."

"After he leaves here? I'm not trained in any but pretty generalized criminal psychology."

"And that is no training at all. For psychotherapy, you will call me; for his safe introduction to present realities, I will depend on you. Who better than the man who will be as close to him as a twin to show him the world? Who better than a policeman to show him what lies behind its self-justifying face?"

That made sense of a kind, but I was suspicious; the psychs have never been popular with the law. "So you only oversee, in standby role?"

"First lesson in therapy, Sergeant: Don't undo what is not knotted. He is what he is, and for that has been brought back. Who will thank us for curing him into somebody different? Now, he wants his breakfast."

"It won't be here for ten minutes or so."

"Then we have time for small talk." He tapped the Spy-eye screen. "Tell me about this, please."

On it Jackson was sitting up, frowning and moving his lips; an indecipherable mutter came from the speaker. He looked like one stripping an enemy for torture. "What do you want to know?"

"Why did my detector not respond to the presence of camera and microphone in the ward?"

"No camera, no microphone, no electronics to detect."

Nguyen was impressed. "Am I permitted to know how it operates?"

The question indicated that he was not a regular member of the institute staff; biophysicists presumably had little use for psychiatrists. "The principles

are on patent file; they can be inspected. Encryption and decoding are the secret stuff. The lens, if you call it that, is a coating of the entire room with a light-gathering varnish of the same color as the walls and ceiling. The light is siphoned to this end by thousands of glass fibers embedded in the plaster; no light is emitted, only gathered, so you can't see them, but the Spy-eye screens their input selectively at this end. The electronics are here, not there."

"And the sound? Without microphone?"

"The optical fibers are fixed loosely and they vibrate to the sound; a computer here measures the vibrations, sorts them, suppresses the noises we don't want and turns what's left back into speech. It's just a high-tech application of available material."

"Now nobody is safe."

"I wouldn't worry. It takes a building team and a gaggle of technicians to install it after they've torn out your walls and ceiling and rebuilt them." There were less wholesale methods, but he didn't need to know them. "Now, I've got a question."

Nguyen's thin smile mocked. "I will make a bet with you. It is a question you should have asked that day in the police station."

"If I hadn't been too angry to think straight."

"But now you have thought of it and you can talk to the psych bastard without wanting to hit him."

You need preparation for these needle-pointed exchanges. I grunted, "Near enough."

"The question is: You know that professional integrity closes your mouth on dangerous knowledge, but what closes mine?"

"You hinted but I didn't follow up. For all I know they simply trust you." I did not believe that; nobody is ever *trusted* with official secrets.

Nguyen had started this hare but now was diffident. "This is difficult for me, but I feel I owe you a tit

for tat. Mine is a pure-blooded Vietnamese family; we have not married outside the—the blood—in our three generations in Australia. We have standing among the unassimilated Asian families—*face,* the word you used to me. Do you understand what it means?"

"Pride? A sort of unsullied appearance? Front?"

"Those and more. The reverse of face is shame and it affects every member of a family. Senior administration understands these things. Listen: I open my mouth, I tell what I know—and my license to practice is withdrawn without reason or notice. My capacity to earn is gone and my family and I are nothing; we are Wardies, eaters of food coupons, anthill dwellers without a future. I am not a tradition-minded man; I could bear it. But for my parents, my wife, my children, the social descent would be ultimate disgrace. Theirs is an artificial and fragile world, but it is the world they live in; I could survive manufactured shame, but they might not, and who am I to destroy those whom I have made what they are? So my tongue is still, and those above me know it. There are pressures other than chemical cocktails."

Emotional blackmail is the most common kind and the most effective; even children practice it. Yet Nguyen's situation had its sardonic aspect and my nursed anger was not about to drown in easy pity. "I'm glad I don't sweat alone in the political steambath."

His mouth grew tight. "I have not used you for jest, Sergeant. I have given an earnest confidence."

I hesitated, conceded, backed down. "OK, I'm sorry; I shouldn't have said it like that. But there's still a question: Who controls us?"

His expression eased a little; it was hard to know his real mind. He gestured at the screen. "The son must be the ultimate controller."

Jackson still sat upright, desultorily exercising his shoulders and arms, staring angrily at the wall.

"The premier? He has probably never heard of either of us."

"Be assured that he has. He knows who we are and what we are."

The screen buzzed an alert. From an ancillary speaker the day nurse called, "Ostrov?"

"Here, Nurse."

"Mr. Jackson's breakfast is ready."

"Coming."

Nguyen walked beside me down the corridor. "You will have noticed that I did not address Jackson by name."

"I noticed."

"It is for you to tell him his new identity."

"Why me?"

"You are the answerer of all questions, his guardian, keeper, nurse and friend. You shelter and protect him. You know his secrets—"

"I don't."

"You will and he will depend on you. Make yourself the one person who understands and cares for him. He was an arrogant man in public life; you must be the one to whose integrity and knowledge he defers. Let him dominate and your position will be impossible. Answer his questions when you know the answers and don't send for me unless he becomes unmanageable. Now, good morning, Sergeant Ostrov. Happy nursing!"

He went quickly round a corner and out of sight.

I took Jackson his breakfast, and he looked murderously at the single bowl on the tray. I asked, "Will you have the tray on your knees or just hold the bowl?"

"The bowl." He lifted the lid. "What's this? Infant gruel? I'm hungry!"

"It's a specially prepared breakfast food with a lot of calories, vitamins and trace elements packed into it."

"Do you always talk like a traveling salesman?"

"No, I can do stand-up comedy and I take off the matron a treat."

"Oh, God, the life of the party and I have to get it!" He waved the bowl at me. "Get me some food! About four times as much as this."

"You wouldn't eat it. You've been on intravenous for weeks and your stomach has shrunk. It does, you know."

He threw the sheet back and opened his pajama coat as I grabbed the bowl from him. He examined his flat stomach, pinching the flesh between his fingers as if testing its genuineness, his face a study in puzzled calculation. Seeing that I watched him he covered himself and reached for the bowl. He spooned up an unwilling mouthful and found it edible, which was as well, for I wouldn't have put it past him to spit it over the bed.

He chose now to ignore me. The way to treat a childish tantrum, as Mum taught me until I learned not to sulk, is to leave it alone to die of inanition.

I left the room and watched him on the Spy-eye.

He wasn't able to finish the gruel. He glared furiously at it, put the bowl down on the side table and looked about for someone to blame. I would not be forgiven for being right. He examined his belly again, threw back the sheet to survey his bony but smooth-skinned legs, pulled back a sleeve to check his forearms and felt his cheeks and jaw.

Then he thought for a long while before he took a last angry look at his unwrinkled skin and banged his hand down on the bell push as though force would bring me like a bullet.

I took my time answering and earned an insult. "I remember you. I saw you last night. You're the ape that woke me up."

It was time to establish the parameters of our relationship. I said conversationally, well below his stand-over level, "And you're an ill-mannered old bugger."

"Oho! The underdog stands up for his rights, eh?"

"Under-ape. Stick with the metaphor."

"Educated under-ape!" He was pleased with me for standing him up to swap punches. "What's your name?"

"Orderly Ostrov while you carry on like a brat, Harry when you're feeling human."

He grinned, though not especially nicely. "All right, truce. But don't make a habit of it."

It had not only gone off better than I had expected, but I was sure now that half his projection was playacting, each role discarded as a more effective one presented itself.

I said, "You rang, sir. You want something?"

"Come off it, man. Unbend."

He didn't do the hearty-fellow persona half as well; it was possibly too distant from his real personality. I wanted to see a genuine reaction, so I said, "If that's what you want, Mr. Jackson."

"You've got your wards mixed, young feller. My name's Beltane."

"No, sir. Your name is Arthur Jackson."

"Some silly mistake—"

"No mistake, sir. Look here." I unhooked the progress board from the foot of the bed and put it in his hands.

"An administrative error. Get it sorted out."

"No error, sir."

He went dead quiet, and the quickly controlled twitch of his mouth was fear. I hadn't wanted quite that, and now it struck me hard how closely he had examined his body and seen that it was not one he remembered. God only knew what fantasies he was beating back.

I said quickly, "It's an alias. I know you are Gerald Beltane, but you must be Arthur Jackson for a while."

"Why?"

"Because as Arthur Jackson you are one more among

the millions of the city, but Gerald Beltane would be an illegality flung in the public's face."

He said harshly, "Explain!" Then he took a deep breath and said, "Please explain."

"I can only tell you what has happened. I can't explain it; I'm not in the confidence of the movers and shakers. You had a terminal disease and have been cured of it some twenty or more years after the onset."

He put up a hand to stop me. "Does the law say the old must be left to die? Have they got round to that while I was—out of the room, so to speak?"

"No, that hasn't happened, but it's more or less what actually occurs. People taking years to die are an unaffordable surplus population; the state can't afford them. We haven't got round to actually killing them yet. Many take a euthanasia option."

(Oh, but we talk tough, don't we! We recognize necessity and try not to recognize that it is a financial necessity, the outcome of something humanity invented for itself. We learn to live with it because we must, to speak of it—when we must—with all emotion tied back and gagged. The aged hope that their final illnesses will be short and painless. The young refuse to think of the day when they will see Mum and Dad dying before their eyes and know there is nothing they can do, although supportive treatments are known—because the supportive treatments will not be given by a Health Service whose funds are cut to the bone and into the marrow, and whose capacities are throttled by cold legislation. We know, endure, talk tough and refuse to think. And yet . . . this was the condition of all humanity throughout most of history. We are reliving the basic facts of existence.)

He said, "You're no sentimentalist, are you? Killing them may be law when your own time comes. Think of that!"

It was all too likely. "But treatment of the terminally

ill is forbidden by law; only analgesics are allowed.
Alzheimer's is recognized as terminal. How you lasted
to be ninety-three I don't know, but I'd guess that your
son's influence had a lot to do with it."

"Ninety-three? So long?" He shifted unhappily as if
easing the body might ease the assaulted mind. "There's
not much memory."

"Not yet, perhaps, but the doctors have got your
brain working again. I guess they've reestablished lost
neurone pathways, but it's only a guess. I think it hasn't
been done before, that you're a first up."

He thrust his plump, unlined hands at me. "More
than that, much more. Look at those! Ninety-three?"

The hands shook badly. I took them in mine and
suddenly he began to cry, all the time glaring fiercely
at me as though I should not observe his weakness, but
he did not pull his hands away.

I told him, "It's rejuvenation, Mr. Jackson. They've
given you back about thirty years." I picked up the
progress board from where he had dropped it. "Look
here—date of birth, twenty-oh-six. Gerald Beltane was
born in nineteen seventy-six. I know; I looked you
up. This is twenty sixty-nine, so Arthur Jackson is
sixty-three years old. And that is about the age he
looks to me."

I didn't have to tell him that rejuvenation techniques
were illegal; that had been so back in his own time of
functioning.

"Your face has been altered a little, too. Not too much,
but enough to be sure no one will look at you and suddenly remember old Beltane who should be dead. That
makes you a sort of secret in full view."

He pulled his hands away. "Harry, get me a mirror." He remembered manners and grinned wickedly.
"Please."

That wasn't an easy commission; a hand mirror
seemed to be an item considered unnecessary in a

ward. In the end I lifted one off the wall of the staff toilet, but when I got back to Jackson he was asleep.

He had been awake for just over one packed hour.

I laid the mirror on the bed table and left him.

He slept through most of the afternoon, and I dozed in the cubby. Policemen catnap when they can. I might have missed his waking if the watching Spy-eye hadn't brought me to with a clatter of something dropped and sounds of frustration from the ward. He had tried to pick up the mirror, but his arms, too long unused, had misjudged the effort and let it slip back onto the bed table.

He cursed unintelligibly and breathed hard as he lugged it back onto his lap, propped it against raised knees and examined his face. It's as well we never see the selves we display when alone; pugnacious old Beltane would never have let anyone observe the startled and petulant child who hated and rejected the face in the mirror.

Compared with the portrait accompanying the bio in the *DNB* it wasn't an unpleasant face, but it wasn't his; I suppose his reaction was natural although there were scraps of the old Beltane to be found, overlaid and redesigned with sharp, bold strokes. Jackson's wrinkles were younger and shallower, less gouged, and his flatter cheeks highlighted the bones to present a hungrier but less forceful character; a narrower jaw had been strongly sculpted and the scraggy fold below the chin had shrunk to a small slackness. The designers—carvers, makeup men—had given him more hair, flatter to the skull than Beltane had worn it and darker than his fading mousiness.

The changes were not sweeping, but they hid him effectively; across a gap of memory no one would make the connection. The doctors had given him back thirty years and done it handsomely but I wondered how

long the glands, hormones and vital cells would labor to preserve the forgery. Years? A month? Days?

And would the new face change the man behind it? That was not psychologically impossible.

He pushed the mirror off his knees and lay back to stare at the ceiling. Once or twice he shuddered and I thought of him confused and doubting and fearing the future in a strange new world. There was anger there, too, but that would be a psyching-up response to new challenge. It was no surprise that he banged the flat of his hand down on the bell as if he would summon hosts to his bidding.

All he got was me, and he squawked in his rusty voice, "Take this thing away!" I smiled, pacifically I thought, as I took up the mirror, but he said, "You grin like that biblical dog that runs about the city!"

Seeking whom it may devour? Old bastard! "The new improved version doesn't please?"

It was the wrong thing and I should have known better, but weeks of battened down annoyance had their day out.

He yelled at me, "Watch your tongue, you hospital flunkey!" and I reacted without thinking about an old and bewildered man not properly in control of himself. At any rate I followed Nguyen's advice to grab the upper hand, and I must have looked as angry as I felt about the whole damned underhanded business (and I haven't the gentlest of faces at any time) because he looked at first surprised and then almost submissive as I laid down the law.

"I am not a hospital orderly or anybody's flunkey. I am a detective-sergeant of Victoria Police assigned to your protection, responsible for your safety and possibly for your life. I may well be all that stands between you and an expedient euthanasia, which is not impossible in the annals of political bastardry. I know you are in a frustrating position and I don't know how to

relieve it any more than you do, so make it easier for both of us by behaving yourself. You are not a human being in trouble—you are a job I could happily be rid of. I would rather deal with someone prepared to watch and wait and not make enemies in a situation he doesn't understand—and which could turn out to be lethal."

Such words to such a man could see my career ended and myself back on the Ward streets, but he had no legal right to complain or even a wholly legal life. Technically, he didn't exist.

To my surprise he apologized, and very persuasively, too, but I hadn't worked off all my ill temper. I said grudgingly, "You politicians turn it on and off like a tap."

Saying it, I reflected with irritation that I had alienated every person I had dealt with in the hospital and had small right to resent another's moods.

Be that as it might, Jackson smiled, not too easily as new muscles creaked in a new face. "We understand each other." It was generous. Then he said, "I have had too many shocks too quickly; I must get used to being sixty-three in a strange land."

That I ought to keep always in mind. I said, "You're taking it better than some might have."

He did not answer that brash guesswork (how we flounder, trying to comfort in another's territory) but went off at a tangent. "It would have to be Jem, wouldn't it?"

"Wouldn't what?"

"All this: face change, rejuvenation, you, all of it. Illegal, you said, so who else could have arranged it?"

That was treacherous ground for a serving copper, and I backed off. "Maybe. How would I know? Nobody tells me Minder business."

"But the real question is, why? What does he want? What is there in me that he needs?"

"Does there have to be something? Down in the Wards they do things for love. Not all the time, because love's like money—never enough to go round—but quite often. Have Minders got rid of love the same way they've got rid of pity for Wardies?"

He answered more gently than I deserved, "We've got rid of nothing, Harry. Jem and I were close, but the most loving son could hardly be expected to carry his affection through decades of senile drooling, could he, now?"

It was a nasty picture. And yet . . . "Perhaps he carried it better than you think. He kept you alive and on prophylactic treatments all that time, didn't he? Otherwise you'd pretty certainly be dead."

That simple reminder raised his spirits amazingly; he really glowed. For a moment I was his dearest friend. Still glowing, he said, "Go away for a while, Harry; I want to think."

Under the circumstances, who wouldn't?

He had half an hour to himself before I was back with his evening meal. He said, "Feeding time, Ape?" but I had determined to shrug off heavy whimsy. His inspection of the food said clearly that it was a bowl of cat crap fit only to poison good relations, but his voice said, "In the name of truce between us, no comment."

This time he got it all down.

When I called back to collect the bowl the afternoon was about over and the evening's twilight storm swept across the windows with its usual tropic suddenness. The short remnant of day vanished in racing cloud; thunder crashed, lightning blazed and the rain came down in waterfall sheets.

Jackson was taken aback by the unheralded violence. "I thought it was summer. Have the weather patterns gone mad again? What time of year is it?"

"Mid-February. Rain month. All that sunshine today was exceptional."

"March used to be the wet time. Floods and storms in from the ocean."

"The pattern is spreading back towards Christmas. Winters are getting drier."

"Is that good or bad?"

"Mostly good. Genetics has come up with some dry-winter cereals not subject to hot weather fungus and UV."

He said, "I must catch up with change," as if that would be as easy as changing his socks.

I waved at the wall screen. "News, current affairs, talk shows."

He seemed not to have noticed it before. There was a selector on the bed table, but he waved it away. "I wouldn't understand half of what I'd see."

"It wouldn't be as bad as that, but I can get you printsheets if you'd rather."

He snorted, "What do they print, news or placebos?"

"News mostly. Was that unusual back then?" Had news dissemination altered in a quarter of a century? There are gradual changes that you scarcely notice.

"Very. Kept up to date, are you? Tell me!"

"News is real because things keep happening that can't be hidden—famine and food chemistry, small wars and big weather disasters. I don't mean that anybody tells all the truth, or even Minders' truth slanted to policy, but facts grow too big to be sat on and bits keep leaking out. I suppose government pretends it's opening its heart by letting us have stuff when it's too late to stop it."

"Wardie cynic! Do you believe that's the way of it?"

"I'm a policeman, Mr. Jackson. I know it's so."

"Then you've told me quite a lot: that the police and public information services are being taken more into official confidence than before, which means that ever so slightly the balance of power has shifted towards the people. Truth has made a small gain. Now, what about

the world scene, the overriding problems?"

"Food again. Or still. Always will be, I suppose. Twelve billion people—"

He broke in, horrified. "Such increase, so quickly!"

People didn't waste good horror on the inevitable; it was hardly worth small talk. I gave him the current catchword: "Sex is the sport of the unemployed, Mr. Jackson. The problems don't change: enough food produced but no knowing just where it will be needed, no knowing what new corruption will steal it or whether the distribution links will stand the strains put on them."

That would be no news to him after twenty-five years or a hundred years. He asked irritably about, "Genetic improvements? Sturdy cereals? Fungus crops?"

I heard myself talking like a vidnews headline reader. "New varieties spawn new ecologies to cope with the unforeseen changes they introduce—insect plagues and insect extinctions and bacterial imbalances. Like the Harmony Cultists say, Man proposes and Gaia disposes. Our grandfathers shook the balance and every correction we make shakes it further. Too many unknowns in the ecology equation. Then there's the sea . . ."

I hesitated because I was venturing on uncertainties there, but he asked, "What about the sea?"

"This is hearsay."

"So is most of history. Go on."

"Fishery police say there's a big increase in poisonous species, down the chain as far as plankton. Survival of the fittest, could be—the best protected. Nobody fishes for poison." It very well could be so; nature (all right, Gaia if you like that sort of thing) uses dirty weapons to hold its own. "It may be we're losing the war. In some parts of the world nutrition levels are falling and that can't be kept quiet. Factory foods look the same and taste the same as ever but don't have the same value; it's faked-up to hide the

shortage of staples. Just not enough arable land per head."

Jackson grunted, "Nothing new in doom and devastation, Ape. We always survive. Tell me a real shocker."

That was the Minder attitude as we saw it from underneath. Bugger you, Jack; I'm all right. So I gave him a shocker. "Global statistics lists the weight of newborn babies as an average eight percent lighter, worldwide, than twenty years ago and the average height is down nearly three centimeters on the last century."

He didn't have a dismissal for that; looked at closely, it wasn't to be dismissed. "Look at me, Mr. Jackson. A hundred and seventy-eight centimeters and ninety-two kilos. I'm no giant, but I'm bigger than most, and I'm ready to bet my kind will go out like the dinosaurs. Dr. Nguyen is the model for tomorrow."

That was one of my personal thoughts about the future. Other species faced famine by ceasing to breed, but humans seemed unable to follow that road; a dozen regimes had tried different forms of restriction and all had failed after initial success. Survival of an overall smaller species would be some sort of stopgap alternative to mass sterilization. Reduction of the biomass would buy time. Men and women were no healthier for being bigger and no less healthy for being smaller. The day was past when sheer size was a survival factor. When you've wiped out the opposition your advantage ceases to matter, becomes a useless property.

Nguyen, now . . . about a hundred and sixty-five centimeters and fifty-five or so kilos, sinewy and trim and limber, neither overbulked nor underdeveloped, capable of doing whatever a man might reasonably need to do. Heavy laborers are often comparatively small men with less brute strength but endless stamina. A race of Nguyens would use less protein, need fewer calories and less of the precious arable land per feeding head. However, starving the hulks and preserving the

lightweights would not be a proposition to lay before the world's Minders; they were themselves apt to fill the tallest and heaviest ends of the population spectrum because they were the best fed and best tended and would have no high-minded desire to eliminate themselves for the greater good.

Their conception of the greater good had long ago refined itself as, Keeping the bastards quiet.

Jackson said, "That's a constructive idea, Ape. All you need is a willing world and a slimming diet."

Back to persiflage. "We might get the diet soon enough without waiting for the willingness."

"True," he said, and closed his eyes.

I took his bowl and left him to sleep again.

Nguyen came through a little later and I told him briefly what had passed. He was happy that the awakened brain operated so well and went through to the ward while I fed my curiosity on the Spy-eye.

Jackson woke and grunted at him, "What do you want?" as if he had been pestered all day.

The Oriental face is as expressive as any other, but that impassivity you hear about came down like a curtain as Nguyen said, "To look at you, to listen and decide."

"Decide what?"

"Whether or not my time is wasted here. Perhaps you have no need of me."

The old playactor heard the warning and became gracefully polite. "Not at the moment, perhaps, but there may be shocks coming to me that will need buffering."

"You have uncertainties?"

"There's no comfort in an illegal existence."

Nguyen smiled thinly and got in a smart rap of common sense. "You would prefer to be dead with your legal standing intact?"

Jackson backtracked. "What's done is done and I'll make the best of it, but I'll remain uneasy until I know where to look for danger."

"For the present leave that to Harry."

"My ape policeman?"

"A trained man who knows the dangers and is better equipped to evade them than you are. Does he answer your questions?"

"Well enough. Are you Vietnamese?"

"No. Why do you ask?"

"I like to place people. It makes them easier to talk to."

Nguyen let his face unfreeze. "Talk? Why not? I am Australian though my grandfather was born in Vietnam."

"Last century? Boat people?"

"Something of the sort; he did not speak of it. It was for him a time to be forgotten. He was a paddy farmer there. He came here that his children might grow up as human beings with room to live."

"Room! My detective nursemaid thinks we should all diet down to your size and take up less space per hungry stomach."

"Don't underestimate him; he has honesty, doggedness and loyalty."

Take a bow, Harry!

"And an untethered tongue."

And now a black mark, Harry!

"Use it! How many tell you the truth at all times?"

"None, praise God. There's a limit to how steadily you can gaze at the facts of a decaying world."

"Asia reached it long ago. Its people are not cheek by jowl but may achieve that any day."

That was a definite subject stopper. Jackson changed tack. "When will Jem be here?"

"Jem?"

"Jeremy. My son."

This seemed to take Nguyen's interest. "I understand that his conference will conclude tonight." He took Jackson's wrist, felt the pulse, consulted his watch. "He may return to Melbourne in the morning; a busy man will not stay away too long."

"I need him."

Nguyen dropped the wrist. "What are you afraid of, Mr. Jackson?"

"I?"

"You control your face with the ease of a lifetime's practice, but your shoulders stiffen slightly, your breathing slows and only an adept can control the pulse. I read tension and anxiety."

Jackson surrendered with a sigh of martyrdom; he couldn't let a word pass without milking it. "My son and I have been very close. Perhaps unusually so."

"Those who remember say so. A team."

"Some do remember?" He allowed himself a flash of satisfaction before making a confession that must have galled his pride, but he did it smartly with no pussyfooting. "I became a burden to him, undependable in the House and in public—and then a fumbling and forgetful nuisance, a relic to be hidden in a back room. I don't remember the worst years, but I can imagine the mumblings and spittings and the smell of incontinent age. Can a son's love survive that?"

"Harry told you it could."

"Oh! You check with him?"

"Naturally."

"He was guessing."

"Guessing well, but he was not to know that your son is as much afraid as you are and with better reason."

That silenced the father with its unexpectedness.

"Consider! You have received treatment so radical that only parts of it have been confirmed in laboratory testing. Your son asks himself will he confront a robot with all memory gone, not knowing so much as its

name? Or a miracle returned to physical competence but with his brain obstructed by a disease which has gone away but left its ruin behind, rusting in disuse? Will his act of love be repaid by empty eyes and a wordless mouth? He has had no communication with the medical staff because no message is safe in an electronic society. He does not know yet whether the end is success or failure. He is the one to be afraid and I know that he is afraid."

All that I should have worked out for myself.

Jackson said, with a pain that rang genuine, "I am a self-centered old man."

"You are a convalescing, youthful sixty-three, gathering together the memories and faculties which I believe will return completely. Until then your first care must be yourself."

"Jem has always been my first care."

"Then be gentle with your frightened son. I must go; I too have a family waiting for me."

Jackson called after him, "What are all the premiers doing in Canberra? What is Jem involved in?"

Nguyen turned his head to say, "In discussion of the population question. That old trip wire: how to restrain birthing. Or perhaps"—his face betrayed nothing at all—"how to expedite dying."

The old politician was at once back in control and making a speech: "Forget the drama. They only talk and make useless proposals and then go home until next talk time. Those unresolvable arguments have circled the globe for seventy years; in the end they throw up their hands and let humanity go to hell at its starving leisure. Any biologist will tell you that no species endures forever, so who's next? That's the real question. Given a million years to heal its wounds and let evolution heave into action like the incompetent old lady it is, Gaia should be able to produce something solidly armored against recurrent fate. Something with

built-in endurance. Something tried and tested. The cockroach?"

Nguyen smiled politely and left him.

That was Wednesday afternoon. On the Thursday Premier Beltane visited his father, so early and at such short notice that I was nearly caught unready.

Matron's voice came from the speaker as I got back to the cubby after giving Jackson his breakfast (besides his gruel, a small peach to keep him happy and help stretch his hungry stomach), telling me that the premier would be here in ten minutes, coming direct from his plane with only barest warning. I was to see that the old devil was shaved, brushed and sweet-smelling for the royal visit.

Matron could not eat me alive as she would another undutiful orderly, so I let Jackson have five minutes to swallow his breakfast undisturbed. He was finishing the peach when I picked up his tray, wearing the grin of a blissful child at a treat and wiping it off as soon as he saw me. "How many days of this sick-kitten diet?"

"A couple. A bit more bulk each day."

"Any news of my son?"

"He should be here in a few minutes."

It was too sudden; he bounced around the bed in desperation, demanding a mirror, clean pajamas, a shave.

"I shaved you only half an hour ago, you silly old bugger. It's only your son, not the pope."

"Only!" As they say, If looks could kill! Then he played his trick of reversing his emotional state in a tick of time. "A mirror, Harry. Please! And a comb."

"It's too late to rip a glass off the toilet wall." I used my pocket comb to smooth his hair for him. "You don't want to look too lively; you're supposed to be sick and in need of sympathy."

"Just go away, Ape." But he remembered to smile.

In the cubby the vid comline was ringing. It was Nguyen. "I'm told the premier will call at the hospital on his way home."

"He's on his way."

"Can you record from that Spy-eye machine?"

"That's what it's for; it's an information gatherer. Sound and picture on wire, every imperishable performance preserved forever."

"Please, this is not a joke. Harry, I want a record of the whole of this father and son meeting, every word and action."

That was certainly no joke; it was more like snooping. "Do you have authority, Doctor?"

"No, Harry, no authority, but I have a patient whose mental welfare is my commission. These two men are dissemblers; little they say or do is without its subtext. If I am to understand them I must take this chance to observe them as it were mentally naked to each other."

He had a point, but there is a limit to prying. I might have demurred if he had not added a rider, "So should you."

I wanted to see for myself what this relationship amounted to, for reasons I told myself were professional, and his were at least as professional as mine.

"OK, I'll make a chip for you."

I switched on the Spy-eye and headed for the main corridor to escort the premier to his father's bedside, but I had used up the ten minutes and a few more. The head of state was already leaving the lift outside matron's office.

He called to her, "I know where he is," which told me that he had visited the comatose man's bedside before my tour of duty began. He passed me as though I was not there and in three paces stopped dead like a parade ground soldier to spin round and ask, "Are you Ostrov?"

Nguyen had been right; he did know. "Yes, sir."

"Good." And he was on his way, not quite running.

He was smartly turned out, trim as a pin and carrying his sixty-odd years with ease, but his face wore the dead expression of a man to whom intense strain was his way of life.

I returned to the cubby. Would he have said *good* if he had known of the Spy-eye?

Perhaps he did know.

What happened in the first minute of that meeting told me that he did not.

The screen lit up on a still life, an unnaturally posed, unpainterly framing of the bed with Beltane at the foot and Jackson upright against his pillows, both under tension like fighters in their corners, urgent to move but held by an invisible timekeeper.

I started Nguyen's recording. What in his psychiatric cookbook would he make of this?

I had time to think that no one would identify them as father and son, and the reason was not only Jackson's facial surgery. The father was narrower in every measurement, a thin man; the son was inches shorter and broad, square skulled and built like a small bull. I recall thinking that his vid appearances must give him extra height by low camera angles and careful placing, and wondering what manner of mother had so impressed her genes on the son as to smother the father's physical characteristics. There are statistical chances about that sort of thing, but I could not remember how they operated.

Beltane moved first, just in time, it seemed to me, before whatever barrier lay between them became impassable. He took two steps and pulled Jackson forward into his arms with a kind of hungry ferocity.

Jackson wept, not quietly as he had done before but noisily, without reserve. In a moment, as if at a signal, they pulled apart, laughing relief at some fear over-

come, then Beltane leaned forward again and kissed his father on the mouth.

It is not easy to convey all my reaction to that. It lasted perhaps two seconds and was over, and it left me feeling voyeurish, intrusive. There are fathers and sons who preserve the kiss of greeting into adult life, habitual to the point of meaninglessness, but it was a gesture I could not imagine myself making. Upon which I at once recalled that when I gave Bill a casual hug after being away for a week or more, he would brush my cheek shyly with his lips and this did not disturb me; it said all the things left unsaid. Mum usually offered only her cheek and I could not remember her kissing me since adolescence save on a birthday or some such occasion.

It may have been that both men being in their sixties—one actually and one apparently—lent incongruity to the action. Surely something did.

Beltane said, "I was afraid," and his father, "So was I," and that was the end of it.

As surprising and unsettling as the kiss was the way in which the greeting was suddenly over, as if so much time had been allotted for sentiment and both had obeyed the stopwatch. Jackson dried his eyes on the sheet with no attempt to hold on to dignity and demanded, as roughly as though a combat signal had sounded, "What the hell do you imagine you've been doing?"

Beltane sat himself on the edge of the bed. "Getting you back into operation."

Jackson watched him evilly, calculating. "You realize what you've done, what will happen to both of us if this becomes known?"

"I have thought about it; that's why we decided on the facial changes."

"We?"

"The senior surgeon and I."

"And?"

"Stop it, Dad! Nobody knows you after thirty years and nobody will know you now. Be glad of stolen time."

"Oh, I am! Did you get tired of having a dribbling scarecrow in the house?"

It was as if they had picked up some ancient quarrel at the word where it had left off.

"No, I didn't." He took Jackson's hand and shook it gently. "Affairs reached a pass where I needed you, need you now, badly." Beltane trying to convince, to make his point, was a more lively man than the one in the corridor with overburdened eyes.

Jackson asked, "For what?"

"Advice. Guidance. Assurance."

"You have a goddamned cabinet for those."

"They're no use to me."

Jackson screwed his face into mixed suspicion and unbelief. "You've alienated your cabinet? They're about to topple you? Is that it?"

"No. They know that the Wardies want me and so do the armed services and the police. Cabinet can put me out—and watch the people put me back in."

"Armed services! Police! This is medieval. Are you dreaming of assuming personal power? Dictatorship?"

"No!" He threw the word out as though the suggestion frightened him. It may have done, because he muttered, "I've enough trouble without blundering into autocracy."

Jackson lay back, watching his son as if for two pins he'd strangle him. "Tell me. Make sense."

"You taught me all I knew. That may have been a mistake."

I had their faces fairly large in the screen and thought that for a quick second Jackson was first insulted and outraged and then alarmed. "Go on."

"While I had you with me, steering and arranging and

bringing off the little coups that kept me in the public eye, everything went well. But I was your puppet."

"No!" Affronted and ferocious.

"Yes, Dad. I thought and so did you, that I was my own man, learning the game. Then you . . . went away . . . and I had to carry on alone. There was momentum; I was on my way up and not to be stopped, but I had to make my own decisions and little by little they became my decisions and not those I knew you would have dictated."

"That's natural."

"I tried to be the one honest man instead of swaying and bending as you taught me."

"Honest! I didn't teach you to be a bloody idiot! Honest, in that cage of snakes!"

Beltane winced, made a small, placating gesture. "It worked, worked very well. It got the people behind me and it got me the premiership. This is my third term. And I'm falling apart. All the tub-thumpers and bureaucrats who came up hanging to my coattails are waiting for the mistake I can't recover from. Oh, I have friends in the House, even amongst the ministers, but I can't talk to them. They tell me either what will suit their own advantage or what they think I want to hear; my friends will topple me for their own purposes as fast as the others will dance on my bones. I have decisions to make and I can't face them and I have no one to talk to, to ask an honest question of, to tell a truth that won't be twisted, misinterpreted and misused."

"In the House," Jackson said, "you rarely did have— you or anybody else. You can have only allies and fellow travelers. Friends are too dangerous; they're up close before you see the knife. What has changed?"

"The nature of the decisions to be made."

Jackson understood an implication that evaded me. "This Canberra conference?"

"Yes. They're closing in. The talking is over."

"Taking sides? Picking the teams?"

"That's done; they're at the tactical stage."

"And you?"

"I can't accept any of it." Now that he had reached his statement Beltane ceased to be upset or confessional; he said, as though exposure had reduced the trouble to a matter of simple planning, "There are actions to be taken, words to be spoken, and I recoil from all of them."

Jackson grimaced; he seemed to grasp exactly what the conversation was about. "What do you want of me?"

"Just that you be here."

A plea for moral support? A confession of dependency? An attempt to shift a load?

He said without emphasis or emotion because it was part of their lives and needed no stress, "You are the only confidant I ever had and I've been lonely long enough."

"And for that you have ruined yourself."

"I shouldn't think so."

Jackson waved his arms. "This—all this! This damned institute and Nguyen and the surgeons and that bloody policeman somewhere down the passage! How many people know what you've been doing with me?"

"Just four—matron, Ostrov, Nguyen, the surgeon. Their mouths are stopped."

He said that as though the stopping of mouths was routine procedure, and I felt a prickle at the nape of my neck. It was the sort of thing the coppers joked about when a case against a Minder collapsed for lack of some item of evidence that we knew had been collected and now was mysteriously missing; it was no longer a joke when I heard corruption spoken aloud by the head of the state, with my own mouth among the stopped.

"Until," Jackson said, "the unthought-of happens and you can't coerce them any longer. Think of this great

ape of a copper with his smarmy conscience aching in his guts—how safe from him will you be?"

"He's safest of them all. Integrity is his conscience and his prison. He does the job given him."

"Without question?"

"In spite of question. A morality wedded to duty. Nguyen found him for me."

At that moment I thought very little of this Beltane who made himself a white knight to the people but who, when trouble loomed, moved heaven and earth, right and wrong and downright criminal, to run to Daddy. And who held trustworthiness in contempt. I felt that Jackson, tantrums and all, was a better man than his son.

Jackson was saying that he would need convincing because the ape ran off at the mouth like a washerless tap.

Ah, well . . . as others see us. Policemen take more abuse than most—and try to pretend that it does not bruise or fester.

Beltane took him—and me—by surprise by bellowing, "Shut up, Dad! You can't guess at the circumstances and there's no time now for long explanations. I have a cabinet meeting at eleven and I need to bathe and change and eat. For God's sake defer making up your mind about anything until—" He seemed to become aware of raucousness and snapped his mouth shut.

They glared at each other, beloved father and beloved son, until Jackson completed the sentence with gimlet spite: "Until my decrepit mind falls into agreement with your errors and flailings."

They observed a half minute's silence.

I can think of no other way of expressing it. They turned their eyes away from each other and sulked at the walls. I supposed it must be some family quiddity, some time-tested custom of stopping before they came to blows, comparable with Mum's stamping out and

slamming the kitchen door or Bill's dealing himself a hand of patience while he spilled the cards in shaking rage.

How they judged the moment I could not tell but Beltane said, in high good humor, "You'll be coming home tomorrow night. There will be a car for you and Ostrov—after dark; you'll have to be smuggled out. Try not to quarrel with him; he was chosen with care."

My precious charge told him, "We bicker amicably, but I do as I am ordered and he hasn't actually struck me yet."

Amicably . . .

Beltane stood up to go and Jackson grasped his wrist. "There are gaps in my memory, Jem. Big gaps. More gaps than memory. I see . . . ." He ran down like an exhausted clockwork, groping for something that escaped him. It was in fact a name. "She is only four or five. And sometimes she is older. There are sequences like scraps of film and I know she is my granddaughter but her name has gone right away from me."

For the first time I found some pity for him, as distinct from understanding of his plight; I slipped a little distance into his confusion and grasping at what might be memories or might be imaginings, inventions of a mind sliced into glimpses of its fragmented past.

"Melissa, Dad."

"Yes! I think somebody else told me, but things come and go."

"She will be home to meet you."

Jackson simpered like a doting old fool, an expression I wouldn't have believed possible to him. "She won't know me."

"No, she won't. But she isn't a silly girl; she will understand. After all, she's sixteen."

"So old?"

"They grow, Dad. Now I have to go."

I half expected another scene of family sentiment, but

Jackson only nodded, swinging from past to present in the flick of an idea. "Till tomorrow night, then."

Beltane gave him a smile and a sketch of a wave and walked off. I had never met two people like them.

Prescience—it can have been nothing less—made me cut off the Spy-eye, switch in a news program, whip Nguyen's chip out of the recording slot and slip it into my pocket.

The premier tapped on the cubby door and walked in.

I got to my feet as he said, "You will be leaving here with Mr. Jackson tomorrow night. A car will be provided. I don't know how long your tour of duty will be; it will depend on circumstances."

"I understand that, sir."

His eyes were on the screen where a newsclip showed highlights from a soccer match of the previous afternoon, then they slipped past it to the distinctive box-shaped console. I was sure he knew what it was though his square, still face gave nothing away. He asked, "Is that the news? What did you think of that stupid riot in Paris?"

Riot? Paris? A trick question if ever I smelled one. I said, "I haven't seen that. I just switched on."

"Ah."

He came right into the cubby and placed his hand casually on the frame of the screen. "Warms quickly, doesn't it?"

I said nothing. You can only lose by protesting when you are already in the idiot seat. He flicked off the news program and cut in the Spy-eye, to see his father scrabbling for something in the drawer of the bed table. He switched it off again. "I'm not sure I approve of these things, but what the security services want they usually get." He moved to the door, turned and gave me the uncommunicative stare of a man confident of his

power. "Never lie to me, Sergeant Ostrov, and never be afraid to tell me anything—anything at all. There must be trust."

He had delivered himself up to my resentment. "Trust, sir? Why, then, there is something else I will never do: I will never forgive you."

He appeared at first not to understand; it was some small thing that had slipped his mind. When he grasped the point his eyes livened with interest and I knew that on impulse I had said something right which had been absorbed and evaluated.

He said, "I ask your pardon for the action of a frightened man who sees too much betrayal and loose talk. I had to be sure of you. You must have heard it said that it's lonely at the top; it can also be terrifying. That is why I brought my father back."

"It was unwise."

"A wiser man might not have needed him."

He left me to think over what I had seen and heard, to see that all of it amounted to confessions of private weakness, that mine field area of the soul where defenses do not exist and which brings us all down in the end. I liked this secondment less than ever.

The Canberra conference had been on population control; that much was common vidnews.

It is disquieting now to recall the jokes about the Big Squeeze, dreary jokes without humor, betraying the underlying anxiety: "They've passed a law banning sex." "Great! I've always fancied a life of crime."

We made jokes about everything in a gray world recovering from the greenhouse onslaught only to be faced with unstoppable fecundity.

Many refused to think of the squeeze at all because the prognosis was the stuff of nightmares; they joked about the food problem instead—but not, I reckon, in Asia or Africa or South America where the nightmare

was already a dreadful century old. "Did you know that all the basics for protein can be drawn from the atmosphere?" "Fine, but what happens when they've recycled all the air?" "They recycle our shit into atmosphere."

Soggy and sad and sick.

I was no better than most others, no more overtly concerned, preferring to get on with living while the good times rolled. (Good times! Our grandparents would have been horrified.) After that curious father-son dialogue, however, I chased round the vid channels to discover what the newscasts had to say about the Canberra meeting of premiers.

They had little to say beyond the official handouts indicating that they had discussed peripheral subjects, mainly a rehash of a topic that rose every so often—the creation of forced-food farms on floating islands of vegetation in the Indian and Pacific oceans—but this time covering a slew of new techniques for holding such fragile constructs together in the teeth of subtropical storms and for recycling pollutants to maintain the purity of the seas. (If you can't stop the birthing, at least feed the bastards!)

As usual the meeting had come to no firm conclusion; further reports had been called for from the Solomon Islands base; CSIRO had been asked for a more searching analysis of nutritive value per square meter deliverable as food for immediate consumption. . . .

I could have written the handout myself from a lifetime of hearing that further investigation was required, that imprecise items needed clarification . . . that, in fact, the scheme was just another carrot dangled a finger's width from the donkey's nose.

What interested me more was the presence of observers from Canada and the United States and Israel. Observers at a meeting of state premiers? Observers commonly attended only major power conferences.

Had they been scientists their attendance would have made some sense, but the United States man was the president's personal aide, and I remembered one of the Israelis as having high military rank. Reasons for their interest might be plain to the newshounds and pollie watchers but not at all to a simple copper who badly wanted to know just what brand of decision making Beltane found intolerable.

I didn't know until later that something was happening elsewhere, something that would influence events. I insert it here to keep the timing in order.

Some seven kilometers on the other side of the city, in the run-down suburb of Balaclava, a down-classified doctor named Barney Fielding had decided to take a fling at rehabilitating himself by turning the criminal stupidity of a couple of kids into political blackmail.

4

Barnabas Fielding:
The Social Ladder

From Commentaries; *The Political Scene: "The
sheer blatancy of the political machinations of the
period is an indication of the moral breakdown of
the Minders and of that indifference of the masses
which amounted to a malaise, an absence of concern in a future without hope. The self became
paramount.* Now *mattered; tomorrow was of little
interest."*

I have never been a schemer, a maker of plots. From
the beginning of my meddling I muddled, fell into
error.

I should never have left the girl in the care of that
inconstant woman, should have known that the moment
I turned my back she would have second thoughts and
third thoughts until fear of the clacking tongues of
neighbors rattled alarms in her head and every step
on the broken cement outside her door became squads
and posses of police seeking her arrest. She would be
taken for a dozen dire offenses . . . harboring criminals,

implication in birthing fraud, concealing knowledge of a crime, food coupon malfeasance, conspiracy against the public welfare. . . . These people, whose minds are so acute in their daily encounters with embattled neighbors and the exigencies of remaining bearably alive, fall into confusions of guilt and punishment when they contemplate the admittedly loaded scales of justice.

Still, that block of flats is a festering snake hole of prying eyes and poison, sheltering at least two known criminals, one of whom doubles as a police nark (God help him if the others ever suspect) and one psalm-singing cult family who would shop Jesus himself in the name of righteousness. She had cause to worry.

I should have smuggled Melissa away after dark of the same day and kept her in the storeroom behind the surgery while I made up my mind.

But—there would have been trouble from Fred. He would have been in and out, cow eyed and putty souled over the Minder mistress who had dropped into his life to make an everlasting summer day. More like an eternity of sour regret, had his brain been geared to thought.

She didn't give a tinker's curse for him. She wanted a baby and Fred was handy. It happens that Fred is good breeding stock—if he harbors no inimical genetic recessives, which I am not in a position to determine—well-shaped, strong and sensible enough if only some crisis would stir his brain out of its peer group somnolence. But, to be "one of them clever bastards" is a social sin in the Wards, matter for ostracism and the odd beating up just for the hell of it.

By what criterion Melissa chose Fred was unimportant; she wanted a baby and the mystery was, why? I felt, more by intuition than deduction, that she was not motivated by any premature maternal compulsion but that for some reason she *needed* a baby. Her determi-

nation was combative rather than helplessly emotional. She needed a baby as a fanatical philatelist will all but kill to possess the one stamp coveted to complete a set.

When I left the Blacker flat on the Wednesday morning I had it in mind to probe this peculiar need, but that was secondary to another project sprung full-born into my head. Melissa Beltane, here under my hand, out of the reach of father and protective security personnel, was a uniquely valuable property for disposal in a civilized but gainful fashion. I was not the fool to dream of a ransom demand, which is a sure way to deadly pursuit and ultimate destruction; I did not dream of rolling in Minder money and the wasteful stupidity of wealth. I longed for, and still long for the only thing worth coveting in an unstable world: personal security, that syndrome of small things—a respectable position in Minder territory, if only on the outskirts, an income sufficiently greater than the statistical average to keep want at arm's length, with access to good music and sophisticated company. These do not demand great wealth, only the trifle more than is needed for decent survival.

My problem in disposal of the goods was, how to obtain a reasonably payable price without resorting to blackmail or major crime. Minor infringements there had already been and more were inevitable; therefore the purchaser should be one with influence to protect me as well as himself. He or she must protect me as part of our common interest in freedom; it would be better still if we shared some other interest, some ambition or other trait demanding solidarity . . . other trait . . .

There the obvious rose up and smiled at me.

We mixed breeds do not love each other with any racial closeness but neither do we betray each other lightly. Our instinct is to protect where possible, swinging as we do between worlds, regarded as

doubtful allies by both in spite of a century or so of multiculturalism. Black and white lie down together more readily than the olive brown with either.

Therefore I thought of Dick Kenney, Richard James Kenney, one quarter white Australian and three-quarters Koori, not pale enough to "pass" and not dark enough to disguise his white heritage. His mother had been a black poet and a good one, his half-caste father an Anglican clergyman. His parents had given a good education to a smart brain, and the issue of their love was a son who had cared for them dutifully in their old age but in his heart resented the accident of birth that left him generally respected but finally close to no one. That, at any rate, was the summing up of the mixed-blood population; as one of the few of us among the Minders he has done well, but the outward success decorates an achievement that leans, on the surface, neither to black nor white. Leaving only his own kind . . .

He was known for a very astute man though too honest to be a wealthy one. He was also, then, the shadow minister for Internal Affairs on the Opposition benches of the state Parliament, and that was what mattered to me. I had never met him. At my most affluent, before my trouble (an illegal birthing that went unpleasantly wrong) I had not moved in his circle, nor could have—but he was human and fallible and a politician. The politician is doubly fallible. Honest or not, he would pawn his Liberal soul for knowledge that would spread an oil slick under the feet of Labour's Beltane.

There is nothing like a sex scandal to start parliamentary skeletons rattling—with fright.

I followed the habit of a lifetime in taking a day for consideration before acting in so delicate a matter. On the Thursday morning I set the affair moving.

In an age when no electronic communication is entirely safe and every politician's words are subject to

eavesdropping by interested professionals as well as by merely mischief-making amateurs, there is a recognized method of doing what I was about. I called the Liberal party headquarters and told the answering voice that I possessed some 062 information. The voice replied, as I had feared it might, "You are not oh-six- two."

"Of course not, but she will vouch."

"Arrange it, then call again."

I had hoped to manage without dragging the woman into it. 062 was then a prostitute who once, in the pursuit of her calling (she was no street drab but a cultured "home entertainer") received, as part of the attentions of a South American diplomat, a mutated worm infestation which could multiply furiously under the skin and create a spreading nuisance difficult to control in its ease of transmission. It was more a pest than a danger, but it brought her by circuitous ways to my Ward surgery rather than to her Minder physician, whom she did not trust to preserve a still tongue.

From my surgery she took the first vidcall step towards relaying to a relevant contact the news of the diplomat's infection, which in his homeland would be regarded as proof of his association with the diseased peonage of his country. It was blackmail material and was at once used as such in the polite world of international pressures.

She did not care that I, a disgraced and demoted doctor, could identify her as a "party tattler"; my opinions would not be canvassed by Minders. She was amused when, instead of charging her for the visit, I asked that she pay the debt in kind if someday I should call on her. That is a common enough arrangement for communication between the Minders and twilight dwellers like myself, who are socially neither one thing nor the other but try (in general, hopelessly) to keep lines open. Throughout history the flesh trade has been a useful linking duct.

The time had come to call her and, when she answered with her screen dark, I let my face flash for a second or two before I cut the visual. Her voice was wary as she said, "I remember you," and waited. She understood at once that no names were to be used between us.

"I have used your number to make a contact."

A moment stretched in a hiss of breath and an arctic silence before she spoke again. "That was an impertinence."

"Had I asked, you would have refused permission."

"Surely."

"So I used it and now I tell you."

She thought about it. "The contact refused a man's voice?"

"I told them you would vouch."

"So sure of yourself! And of me!"

"I am sure of my material. And you owe me."

"I don't need reminding. Have you thought that you may compromise my status? I may agree to vouch—after I have considered the material."

Nothing for nothing in this world where the payment of a debt can be made ground for further extortion. "Time is short."

"Meet me for lunch." She named a city restaurant, a civil service rendezvous. "Have you suitable clothes?"

Bitch! Yes, a closetful, unworn for years. "Enough, but I can't afford that place."

She succeeded in injecting a smile into her voice. "I can. Information is worth paying for."

She cut off. Now I had the thankless task of explaining to my half-trained, semiofficial assistants that they must cope, for a few hours, alone and as best they might, with the odorous queue in the waiting room.

Dressed for once in clothing that could attract unwelcome attention in these pitiless streets, I slipped out through the rear laneway gate and drew only a few

more or less friendly catcalls from old patients.

In the restaurant the lady called for a Privatent, and so we dined and talked in the safety of an electronic screen which, so far as I know (but who really knows these things?) can be pierced only by a powerful array too obviously visible for use in a public place.

Over lamb cutlets whose bone proclaimed them farm grown rather than sliced from the monstrous protein mass in the Yarraville factory, I told her what I proposed to do. At first she thought it dangerous, an adventure into territory where Dick Kenney's vaunted probity was a hazardous unknown. I had to convince her that political power is a greater magnet than money and that probity is to be measured by its breaking strain; also, that if the move paid off, the status of 062 would be enhanced while, if it did not, she could disown me as a paranoid fake. In the end she agreed to vouch for me and did so over the vid while I listened at her elbow.

Complex arrangements for the meeting were made; I had only to do as I was told and be spirited from point to point as possible observation was circumvented.

And so a chance infestation by an exotic worm entered history, but the lady's name must remain out of it. She has sharpened her skills to become a discreet, almost "society" madam whose establishment is noted for the outrageous accomplishments of a gifted staff.

I met the shadow minister that night, not at his home but in the home of friends of his family, people unconnected with politics, ideal cover for a casual encounter. How I reached the house is his business and mine. With newsbugs and scandalcats sniffing after every public figure, it would be graceless of me to reveal how these simple objectives are so simply achieved.

I was ushered into a library and told to wait. I waited for quite a while, sure that my public and private files were under examination and discussion.

This was a rich library, a collector's library; many of the books were old, leather bound, gilt embossed and locked behind glass. There were paintings also, minor works from the Impressionist period. That they were minor did not mean that their value was small, and it seemed to me that such works should be in the public galleries, that this private hugging of wealth is more reprehensible than vulgarly open display. Do not misunderstand if I say that I took little pleasure in examining these things; I was merely murderously jealous of their unknown owner, as though I were personally denied so that he might wallow in possessions. The class war had long been a dead issue in the face of global necessity, but I could have fought it afresh that night, face-to-face with the private sequestering of a planet's heritage. Despite the silliness of old Marx, there are circumstances in which property is theft.

Behind me a voice said, "You are Barnabas Fielding, a registered medico of the third grade?"

That was only a warning that my background had been inspected. I corrected, "Second grade."

"Third," the voice repeated, politely, "after demotion for professional infringement."

"I am still a qualified second."

"Yes, yes, we have our pride. What is the nature of your information?"

"I will tell the shadow minister. You are not he."

The man moved round in front of me. Well dressed and well spoken, he was yet no secretary or confidant; he was a hundred kilos of broken-nosed thug. "We like to guard the shadow minister against wasting his time. Just a general idea, please."

"Ask him does he know where Melissa Beltane is."

The heavy face brooded over me. "Should he care?"

"He will care greatly when he knows where and in what condition."

"She is not at home?"

"Far from home."

He meditated. "You are a doctor and you mentioned 'condition.' Two and two make—what?"

"Between three and five. That is enough."

Without ceremony he hauled me upright with great butcher's fingers clutching my shoulder, holding me one-handed while he searched me with an expertise that spared no privacies.

"My apologies, Doctor, but there are many methods of deceiving the doorway detectors. I will tell the shadow minister what you have said."

Kenney did not keep me waiting. He came quickly into the library, shut the door behind him, skirted the large desk, sat down across from me and said, not making a great declaration of it, "Remember that above all considerations of race and color I am an Australian. The part-Koori bond takes no precedence."

That was unpromising, even menacing, but I had not come all this twisted way to have the initiative stolen from me in a few words. I replied as casually, "You are a shadow minister of the Opposition. I favor the Opposition or my information would go elsewhere."

He said as though he had not heard, "You hint that the premier's daughter is missing."

"Yes."

"Where is she?"

A haggler's bargain must be struck before information is divulged, but I fancied that huckstering would not go far with Kenney. He was a thinnish man, lighter colored than I despite his extra quarter of Koori blood, but still carrying his heritage plainly. He was also a man of palpable self-assurance, no simple fish to be played on a line.

I fenced carefully. "She is in private quarters not far from my surgery in Balaclava."

"Not actually in your charge?"

"Effectively, she is. Her hostess will be relieved to be rid of her."

He gave a short, startling neigh of amusement. "I can imagine it. Balaclava tramp society entertaining a princess! A featherbrained princess, as I remember her." The merriment ceased abruptly. "To Belcher you mentioned her condition. What condition?"

"She is five months pregnant."

"Stupid of her. How old is she?"

"Sixteen."

"And the father?"

"Seventeen. One of the premier's Wardie gardeners."

"Holy God! And the premier knows?"

"The boy's identity? No. But she confessed her pregnancy to her father and he behaved ferociously. Unreasonably so, I gather. So she ran away from home."

"To her boy-love's slum?"

"It isn't quite a slum. A seedy block of flats—"

"I don't want the address; the family need not be involved. You plan to perform a clinical abortion?"

"No. She wants to bear the child."

His sallow face lighted in comprehension. "So that's why she flew the coop. When?"

"Last Sunday night."

"Yet Beltane took off for Canberra that same night."

"He may not know yet that she is gone."

He smacked his hand lightly on the desk. "Now, there's a situation for you!" My doubts eased; he was eyeing the bait, no matter what his scale of honorable commitment. "Can you bring her here?"

"I can remove her from the boy's family. Bringing her here unseen might be more difficult."

"Arrange it through that grubby underground woman, once you have the girl. Tomorrow morning?"

"It can be managed."

"Good. I shall expect her in the course of the day."

All this had passed in the manner of cronies talk-

ing over inconsequentials. I had expected if not drama at least some of the tension with which romance invests intrigue in high places, but I might as well have been selling him a bag of potatoes. Skulduggery seemed unnaturally dull—and still my side of the exchange had not been mentioned.

I asked, "What do you propose to do with her?"

Kenney pursed his lips, spread his hands, made a spectacle of playacting indecision. "A Minder child cannot be left unprotected in the Wards."

Rubbish; many visited there for the frisson of mildly perilous dirt. "A population law breach could be a scandal loud enough to unseat the premier."

"Grossly handled, it might." His manner was still gossipy, but now he spread his hands again, the pink-brown palms towards me. "Look, Dr. Fielding, clean hands!"

I think I preserved dignity in spite of the blow. I had misread him, found for myself the one incorruptible politician. Kenney would do no more than see the girl safely home. I was trapped; there could be no shopping for a more amenable schemer, for I would be under watch to head off such a move. It remained only to put a courteous face on defeat and leave politely.

Kenney said mildly, "You should have taken her home, shouldn't you? There would have been some reward, I think." His face changed to a startling likeness of an animal, teeth bared and lips snarling. "What do you want, you filthy thing? Money?"

To the pure in heart all things are filthy. I said, and I think I managed it equably enough, "Gifts of money are for wastrels. I can earn money. I want my grade two surgeon-physician rating restored."

"A thinking criminal, eh? Not just a greedy grabber. But what you want is not easily given. There must be evident reasons for such action on my part, and what

reasons are there for elevating such as you? Money is a more transient but more certain reward."

"No."

He stood, frowning and angry, then strode round the desk and past me towards the door. He spoke from behind me. "I suppose there must be baksheesh of some kind to shut your mouth, but I make no promise of what you ask—only that I will see what can be done." I heard his hand on the doorknob. "Don't make the amateur's error of not bringing her; there will be no alternative market for your goods."

He slammed the door behind him.

In a few minutes Belcher came to guide me through the sly passage out of there and on my way home.

I spent a bad night. Kenney's contempt had bitten, but some things cannot be bought with money and if my return to grade two had to be paid for in private shame, so be it. Blameless morality is for those who can afford it.

Friday dawned gray and drizzling. It was the season of hot, humid rain, of ill temper and restlessness and short-fused violence amongst the youngsters on the streets; for me, too old and slack muscled to break knuckles on some unoffending jaw, it was the season of sour depression.

I rose early because Kenney had murdered my sleep, and so I heard the vidnews at dawn. No studio screamer made vocal headlines of Melissa Beltane. The premier was home by now, so the matter was being hushed up. If he was bending before the potential fallout of a birthing scandal, then bargaining might yet bear fruit; surely he would act in my favor, guilt calling to guilt.

I could not get the girl from the Blacker flat until young Fred had gone to work; a scene with the worshipping lover would be unbearable. I listened to commentators driveling about the Canberra meeting of

state premiers, praising some food initiative and deploring lack of progress on the planetary population level while I drank cups of the disgusting factory-spewed tea which is the only kind covered by the coupon issue. I remembered real tea, but today's Asia has no room to devote hectares of precious hillside to a luxury plant. The Minders—and not all of those—have what little leaf tea there is.

At eight o'clock I went out into the dreary day and trudged round to Inkerman Street. Strangely, the Blacker flat was silent while all the others were yelling music or talk shows as breakfast was cleared away and the drudgery of housecleaning begun.

Putting my head inside the kitchen door, I saw Mrs. Blacker disconsolate at an uncleared table, drinking the same rubbish as I had done and staring, by habit, at a cracked and dark vidscreen. When she saw me she began to cry, silently, without so much as screwing up her face; tears trickled from wide eyes while mechanically she lifted the cup and sipped at it.

The misery of the hopeless is as real as cruelty; they deny it, refuse to speak of it, but it cannot be hidden. The only kindness is to stick to practicalities, to not intrude too far, so I nodded at the wrecked screen and asked, "Your husband again?" He was alcoholic, prone to destructive hysteria, but he seemed not to be home. He was not one to stay with another's grief.

She put down her cup and said, "It was Fred."

That was hard to believe. Fred, for all his intellectual nonentity, was the quiet, dependable one of the family, the center of what stability existed there. He was a fighting man because in that neighborhood he had to be, but he was never hot without reason, and a fortglass vidscreen is not easily smashed.

"Drunk?"

"You know he don't drink."

"Something to do with the girl?"

Defensiveness burgeoned into a deliberate, worked-up hostility. "It was your fault!"

She needed a whipping boy, and there was I. "How so?"

"You said you'd bring coupons and you never come."

Yes, I had promised and, fizzing with my own plans, had forgotten. "I'm sorry. I'll bring them this afternoon. That's a promise."

She was not listening, bent on my damnation. "You never brought them and I got worried because we're nearly out, what with her to look after and a week to go yet. You don't know what it's like with two men to feed and I was frightened we'd finish up with scenes and noise and the other flats listening to everything. Me old man can't control his drunk's tongue, he'll say anything and soon everybody'd know we'd got Fred's bitch here and then the trouble'd really start."

It would indeed. She broke off to wipe her eyes, but kept her blaming gaze on me. "So I said she had to go, I wouldn't have her no longer, and Fred blew up. The way he yelled at me you'd never think I was his mother. Then that old slag next door has to poke her head in to see what's going on and I just had time to push the girl into the back room before Fred abused next door for a muckraking slut. Next thing her husband's here saying Fred has to apologize, and Fred pushed him through the vidscreen." She said, with incongruous satisfaction, "He's a good protector, my Fred. But I couldn't have her here anymore. You can see that!"

Her tone said that I'd better see it or be the focus of another yelling scene.

"So I said to Fred he had to send her back home and she heard me and started crying. He just looked at me and went in to cuddle her and calm her down. And when I got up this morning they was both gone."

She pushed a scrap of paper at me, the wrapping of a soap packet carrying Fred's farewell on the back of it

in careful schoolboy hand. *Dear Mum Good-bye Sorry Fred xxxx*

She said, weeping again, "Now see what you've done!"

No use protesting; she had her scapegoat and reason would not shift her. I strove helplessly to think where he might have taken Melissa. Home? No; he wouldn't dare. They had gone secretly because Fred did not intend to be found and it is easy to become "lost" in a city of ten million people, of whom a million or more are street kids or vagrants or addressless petty crims.

I don't think I said good-bye to her; all I had in mind in that sweaty, overcast morning was Kenney's face, moving from contempt to rage and vengefulness when he found that I could not produce the girl. Almost worse was the dread of confessing the failure, but it had to be done; I could not hide in shame only to have Belcher or some other remorseless brute hammering on the surgery door, demanding that I make good my word or suffer the reward of a fool.

I thought of 062 because I could not bear to face Kenney as a cheap schemer and a bungler. I told her what had happened and left her to do what had to be done. She was unpleasant about my having smirched the dependability of her number, and that was quite bad enough. This world offers no sympathy to the luckless.

There was worse to come, when Kenney had me hauled forcibly to the Manor to face Beltane.

Part II

The Private Life
of Politics

5

Ostrov: The Players
in the Game

Nguyen came in on the Thursday afternoon, ostensibly to check Jackson's mental condition, actually to collect his chip. I told him that it would replay on any commercial vid and for God's sake not to let it out of his hands; it would be best if he viewed and erased.

"I will view and consider."

"It's my head that will roll if you're caught with it. Beltane knows I watched but not that I chipped him."

"He was angry?"

"Maybe, but he made the best of it. You'll see that he has other worries."

"His daughter?"

"Why her? Jackson driveled about her, but there was no fuss."

"She has disappeared."

"Nothing on the vid about it." Teenagers deserted home every day and made nuisances and often criminals of themselves on the streets. Only the police cared greatly, but Beltane's name would have the newsbugs circling for honey.

"There will not be. Police have been informed but nobody else. They are combing the city for her."

I said that combing the Melbourne labyrinth would take an army. Nguyen agreed and said that the thing had to be kept quiet because the kid was pregnant and even the police had not been told that bit.

That certainly made it more newsworthy. "Did Beltane know about it this morning when he visited the ward?"

"No. That news greeted him when he reached the Manor. He collapsed."

"That wasn't reported either. How do you come to know about it?"

"I was sent for. I am his psychiatrist."

"The hell you are!" I should have guessed as much. "You seem to have some connection with every little thing that happens."

"That is fortuitous; I am nobody. Like you I am caught in a web. We must keep this from Jackson; meeting his son was disturbance enough."

"He and I move to the Manor tomorrow night. He asked after the girl, so he'll have to be told."

"Perhaps. We may concoct a story—a short holiday. Or, she may be found by then. Either way, the premier now has another secret operation to manage and another group of mouths to close. He is beset on every hand."

"He bought it; let him worry. What's the story about the girl?"

"Last Sunday evening, before he went to Canberra, she told him she is pregnant and he lost his temper with her. His self-control has been uncertain for some months and her confession triggered an outburst. He admits he was unreasonable, that he yelled at her and threatened her and she ran out of the room. Later, she could not be found. The housekeeper thought she had returned to school as she always did on Sunday

evening. She attends boarding school during the week and returns home each Friday afternoon. The school seems to have thought nothing of a short absence— some minor indisposition, not worth bothering the premier about—but when she failed to appear on the Wednesday a class mistress rang the home and started a stampede. She had walked out of the house and vanished in circumstances guaranteed to prevent anybody noticing anything unusual."

"Who's the snake in the cradle?"

"The boy? Nobody knows. Beltane says she refused to tell him. I'm not sure that he actually asked her; he seems to have behaved like a madman."

"There goes the only good clue, already out of reach. Just searching the Minders' homes is a near impossibility with a limited force."

Nguyen had a small, reserved smile which came and went as he contemplated disaster; it came and went now. "Why only the Minders' houses, Harry? Sex is classless."

"If she's run away with the butcher's boy, God help them both. And God help Beltane when the Opposition gets its teeth into the story. They'll blow it up until it looks as though he threw his pregnant daughter out of the house when the housekeeper could have fixed the girl with a knitting needle."

"Not at five months."

"Five months and nobody knew?"

"That is possible, given the girl's tubby build and a corset."

It seemed that on Friday night I would be guarding Jackson in a madhouse.

I began to wonder what the arrangements for leaving the institute might be. Beltane had said only that a car would be sent, and that might be as far as he had thought. He was a man removed from gross detail, in a position to say, *Do this,* with no need to think how

it could or should be done—somebody would see to it. We police were competent to carry out such moves, were we not? What, he might ask, did I think I was there for?

I checked with matron, but she had not then been notified of the imminent discharge and it took several minutes of argument to convince her that I should be allowed to speak to the senior surgeon.

He knew but had given the matter no further thought. Why, he asked, should he?

Because, I told him, we had to get Jackson into his home without any not-so-innocent bystander asking himself why the premier's limousine, with state insignia, should be collecting someone from an institute which the general public regarded as a place where unspeakable experiments were carried out. It would be a question worth repeating to the news channels for a small gratuity.

I might have known he would say, "You will have had more experience than I at this sort of planning."

I snarled that my job was arresting criminals, not planning their getaways. We parted without warmth.

I scouted round the entrances and goods delivery intakes of the building, decided how the removal should be made and told the surgeon I wanted Jackson taken out in an ambulance. Since I had the premier's authority to appeal to, he agreed that an ambulance would be provided and even suggested that he drive it himself rather than make a regular driver privy to secrets of state. I thought he saw himself, like my dad, as an intriguer in high places, a cloak-and-dagger type.

Next came the business of making contact with Beltane. He was still at home, preparing to leave for the previous day's postponed cabinet meeting, but the name of Ostrov cut no ice with his staff of secretaries until in desperation I howled into the screen that I had word

of his daughter. That brought him smartly, stuttering in my ear.

I had to explain that the lie had been a necessary stratagem to get his attention. He was furious and so would I have been. When he had done with telling me that the ruse had been an indecency practiced on a distraught father (true enough) he came round to the idea that I had done it for a reason, perhaps a good reason. I explained why the Jackson transfer should be done my way and why he should order affairs at his end as I suggested. Once he grasped the idea that he had to do a little more than toss orders in the air for others to catch, he became apologetic and willing.

That accomplished, the next thing was to get Jackson on his feet and moderately mobile. He should be capable, in emergency, of some degree of self-help.

Jackson had decided this for himself. I found him sitting on his tail in the middle of the ward, halfway between the bed and the window, while the day nurse tried ineffectually to help him to his feet and he cursed her between bouts of telling her to "Call the ape! Get Harry! Get a bloody man on the job!"

I told him to shut up, lifted him over my shoulder and dumped him on the bed. "Now apologize to the nurse."

And so he did, charmingly, making me look like a musclebound thug who did not appreciate the emotional stress on a sick, confused old gentleman.

Life among the Beltanes might be criminal, noisy and passing the understanding of a bedeviled cop, but it would not be dull.

Jackson's trouble was partly stiffness, partly inability to manage the growth of new muscle and partly a fear of making a doddering fool of himself—which he had done on his first attempt to walk unaided, collapsing

flat on his behind and alarming the day nurse, who had come running and scolding.

She thought he should stay in bed for at least another day, and I was less than tactful in putting her right about that. She vanished in the direction of matron's office, hissing that I had too damned big an opinion of myself. What happened down there I don't know, but there was no further opposition to my arrangements.

Jackson, entering into the memory of his old public persona, which involved acute consciousness of dignity, wanted me out of the ward so that he could practice stumbling alone until he mastered the new art.

"Arthur!" I had not used the first name before and he glowered at the impertinence. "We're going to be too close to be suckered by each other's pretensions."

That hadn't occurred to him, living as he did in the instant minute while trying to assemble a coherent life. He snorted and cursed and accepted the idea and clutched my arm to slide off the bed and stand up.

"Now, listen. A person loses about a third of his musculature in old age by failure of cell replacement; you lost nearly all of it in years of inactivity, but the bio boys here have given you a new lot, modeled on the old physique but only guess accurate, so you'll have to experiment to discover what the muscles do and how well they do it. You'll have to assess what is a comfortable pace and what your energy expenditure limits are, like getting down on your knees and deciding just how to go about lifting your weight upright again—"

"Or punching your impudent jaw to see whether or not you fall down."

That was only repartee; he was inspecting the idea of interdependence with someone other than his son and seeing some advantages in it.

We started off across the floor, a matter of four or five meters from bed to window, with him leaning very lightly on my arm, just heavily enough to ensure balance, too obstinate to let me see that he really needed me. He muttered, "I was dizzy the first time." That excused the bruises on his behind, but he knew what was required and set himself to do it and established a fair amount of muscular control in the short stretch.

At the window he leaned on the sill and looked out over the city. The institute had been built on the triangular block just across from State Parliament House, so his view was from the northeast corner of City Center, that square mile that had once been the commercial heart of Melbourne, with towers and canyon streets funneling the wind.

"Nothing different," he said.

This was true. The tall buildings, empty and useless in the long collapse of trade and finance, had been torn down while he was still a functioning MP and replaced by the low, energy-saving structures of a culture governed by thrift. He could see across the Yarra and the Botanical Gardens to the square-cut landmark of the Shrine of Remembrance (we had lost any real idea of the war it commemorated, over a century away in dimness) and over the suburban roofs to the waters of the bay, gray under the seasonal rainclouds.

"Except this. This building." He made the institute sound like an eyesore. "We must be five or six floors up." Such height, he implied, was reprehensible.

"Seven," I told him, "with more above."

"Why? What's gained? What are the running costs in lifts and ducting and maintenance?"

"I don't know."

"What did people say when it was built?"

"Nothing. Since when was government accountable to the people?" I had shocked him. He leaned on the sill, sucking at his lower lip.

"So it's come to that, has it? How long since?"

It was an impossible question. We are aware of big changes that offend and discomfort us but only vaguely of the small ones imposed gently over a long period until another right, another freedom has gone as though it had never been. I did not know when the relationship between government and governed had changed its face. It would have been happening gently from some time in my youth. It could be that even Jackson, at the heart of things, had not noticed the insidious creep.

"I was still a kid when you were bowing out, Arthur; I don't remember a time when government explained itself. Did it ever?"

He surveyed me with troubled eyes before he turned and stepped out in the direction of the bed. I grabbed his elbow, but he pushed me away, fueling his progress with anger. "Of course it did, Harry! If it didn't, the people had their own ways of forcing explanation from it and secretive governments tended to have short lives. Have the people forgotten how to be individuals? Don't they care?"

It seemed to me that we didn't care very much but that we remained individual. Individuality was the big policing problem, the me-first syndrome behind nine tenths of crime; it was individuality in the struggle to exist in a world of shortages and small opportunity that kept the eyes on the self and regarded government only as a source of regulations and laws to be paid lip service but evaded, flouted or, in the last choice, sullenly obeyed. We didn't think much about government; like night and day and food coupons, it was there.

I tried to explain this to him, haltingly because I had never tried to sum up the situation in a few words and was now looking at the citizenry—and myself—from a fresh angle.

He said, "Your lives must be very gray."

"For most, yes." I was not sure about my own; a copper's life is lively but not on that account colorful or lovable.

At last he said, "My legs are trembling," and sat down. "Let me have a spell and we'll try again."

I found some thin oil in the cabinet and, failing anything better, gave him a rubdown with that. The new muscles were stiffer than I had counted on. We tried another walk in the evening after the meal and did appreciably better. I made up some simple exercises for him and checked with the nurse for her approval. She looked me over, stone faced, and said, "Just don't tire him out." I gathered that she no longer cared what I did so long as she was not called on to clean up the mess.

In the evening Nguyen came for another check on Jackson but stopped at the cubby to ask my question a fraction before I could voice it: "What do you make of them?"

In truth I made very little. "People who understand each other so well that they don't have to explain themselves. One starts a line of thought and the other answers as though all the spaces had been filled in."

"Good. And the kiss?"

"Not my line of country. Did you notice that it wasn't sentimental yet it wasn't perfunctory?"

"Yes. Well?"

"It was like recognizing something that needed no words. It made me uneasy. It was—" I cast about for a word and found only a poor one. "—unhealthy."

That caught his interest. "Do you know that a century ago people called relationships 'unhealthy' when they were too genteel to refer to sexual deviation?"

I hadn't known and deviation had not crossed my mind, nor did it impress me now. "No, but it was just a salutation and they went straight into business after it. In fact they went into a quarrel."

It was my turn to ask what he had made of it.

"No more than you, but a psychiatrist's reactions are apt to be clinical and your gut reaction might have shown me a fresh one. It did not. What about Beltane's reason for having his father cured and returned to normal life?"

"Genuine. Their father and son thing had been so strong all their lives that there must have been an almighty big hole left in Beltane's existence when he had to carry on alone. I can imagine that."

"You feel sympathy for Beltane?"

Was it the moment to be outspoken? I thought it was. "None at all. He's as weak as piss. Jackson's worth six of him, temper and all thrown in."

Nguyen smiled at that with his fleeting, semisecret flicker of the lips that might be mockery or might be approval; it was most likely satisfaction that I had formed a positive attitude towards Jackson. I took the opportunity to tell him of the arrangements for Friday night and he said only that it was as well that I had taken the planning on myself and that I should not push Jackson's new musculature too hard. Then he asked, "What about Canberra?"

I hadn't thought about it; that was Beltane's mess, not mine. "He sounds as if they want an agreement or a concession he isn't willing to give. Perhaps the other premiers ganged up on him and he's stalling for time."

"He has weathered that storm before without crying for his father. The subject was population control."

"The newscasts say they talked about food. There are a dozen conferences around the world every year and they never come up with a useful control idea. The range is pretty limited, and they've all been picked over like a lousy singlet, so they concentrate on feeding us until next time."

Nguyen said thoughtfully, "Limiting family size was the first consideration, back in the nineteen seventies."

"Didn't work then and won't work now. People want children, particularly when they're told they mustn't have them. As well as the biological urge, it rouses defiance in them. Besides, the need is to reduce the population of the planet, not to only stall it."

"Deliberate neglect of the old, the useless and the terminally ill."

"That goes on, but it's a drop in the bucket. No effect worth counting."

"Why, then, something more basic, like contraceptives in the drinking water."

"Scuttlebutt says it's been tried, but I don't believe it. Some strains have to be preserved and wholesale sterilization isn't selective."

"So we come to selectivity. Preservation of an elite, eh? A meritocracy ploy."

"How do you decide merit? It would turn out to be preservation of the rich and powerful—sure to be the most useless in a world reduced to basics."

"So a plague would be unsatisfactory?"

He was homing in on something, so I played along. "Too hard to put boundaries on a plague, even if modern techniques weren't good enough to stop most plagues in their tracks."

"Here, yes, but how about in Africa and Asia and parts of South America? Those couldn't stop an outbreak of stomachache."

"Still too risky. They'd know the big powers were doing it to them and they'd loose off some of the nukes they've got stowed away against the day somebody thinks they can be taken off the board. Then we'd all go in a nuclear winter."

He suggested, "Efficient diplomatic meddling could start brushfire wars and keep them fanned."

"Hot enough to kill five billions or so? Nothing much less would be of any use. Out of the question. And unselective."

"Back to that. Do we really think in terms of 'us' and 'them,' of who is to be hit and who spared?"

"Of course we do. Everybody does. When it comes down to bared souls it's always, how will we do it to them? not, we all have to take our chances. Hell, Doctor, we know all the answers to all the questions. Why should Beltane go to water over it?"

"Something new, perhaps?"

"Such as?"

"How should I know, Harry? But I would very much like to know what sort of decision is too repellent for him to embrace."

He did not add, *And you will be next to him and his, in a fine position to find out,* but the thought was clear behind the bland eyes.

He changed the subject abruptly. "He feels he holds the Wards, the army and the police. If the Wards knew about Jackson, about their well-beloved premier breaking some of the most emotion-rousing laws for his personal benefit, would they continue to support him?"

That was tricky; I had to sort out the probabilities before I spoke. "They might. If the rabble-rousers got to them with the idea that Beltane's example gave them the right to demand easing of the population laws, they might stick with him to make him do what they wanted."

"Demonstrations, marches, mobs in the streets, anarchy and unnecessary bloodshed!"

"They always finish up killing some poor harmless bastards."

"And the police?"

"Would do nothing if it got too big. We couldn't handle demonstrators by the millions; we'd be dead if we tried. We'd be guarding special people, I suppose, and keeping communications open."

"The army?"

That was not so easy. "I'm guessing, but I think the

federal corps, the permanent army, would fire on the Wardies if they were ordered, but the duty men doing their obligatory two years might jack up. They aren't real soldiers, they're Wardies in uniform; they might stick with their civilian families and friends."

"So, soldiers fighting soldiers might be the end of it. I think, Harry, that the premier's secret had better be well kept."

With that he went to pay his pointless visit to Jackson. I didn't bother to switch on the Spy-eye; I was too much concerned with a mental queasiness over the monstrous ramifications emanating from a son's act of love for his father.

Or, had it been a purely selfish act, the instant soothing of a need, a desire, a comfort?

All love is touched with selfishness. It is the lover, not the beloved, who races to embrace his obsession.

On Friday morning Barney Fielding's plan had fallen apart and my own worst mistake of the entire affair had already been made when I took it on myself to arrange the Jackson transfer in orderly fashion. There's no profit in asking now, what if? By Friday the chaos effects were unstoppable.

In the morning Arthur was early out of bed, stretching his legs while he clung to the bed table, making tentative forays and at last walking fairly steadily to the window. The doctors had given his comatose body the usual course of isometric exercises so that he was, you might say, factory-fresh for normal usage and needed only a short running in. He should be reasonably capable by nightfall.

When I took in his breakfast he told me of his exploit, peacock proud, passing it off as a mere nothing to a determined man. I congratulated him with a straight face, and he passed the day wandering round the

ward and then the corridors, making longer and longer
expeditions and complaining of the silence and the
locked doors.

The arrangement was that we would leave in the
ambulance at ten o'clock that night, not only because
it would be full dark but because there would be few
pedestrians around the area, which was mostly gardens
and public service buildings; even the small risk of a
passing observer was not worth taking while newsbugs
were a questioning pestilence in the city. I would ride
in the back with Jackson, wearing a gun under my
white orderly's coat. The rest of my gear fitted into
a suitcase; I had not brought a police uniform to the
job.

Going to collect and pack Arthur's gear, I found that
he had none, none at all; not so much as the toothbrush
was his own. Matron said he had been brought in by
ambulance, wearing only a pair of pajamas which had
been burned at once because of his incontinence on
the trip. "His home is only three kilometers away but
you can't outguess their bowels when they're in that
condition."

In the event of an emergency he should be fully
dressed, but matron could not supply clothing. There
was nothing for it but to call the senior surgeon, who
hemmed and hawed and would see what he could do
and I should come down to his office in half an hour.

I had not paid much attention to Hugh Cranko. Senior surgeon or not, to me he was just another doctor
around the place, but his appreciation of the necessity of having an insider drive the ambulance had displayed a little personality, though the impulse had
been romantic rather than realistic. He was a nondescript, fair man of early middle age whose conversation seemed always a touch vague minded, but he
had a public reputation for brilliance on the job and
could afford an affectation (if it was that) of offhanded-

ness. Perhaps I should have taken more interest in him, but my general dislike of the whole Beltane business stopped me bothering with anyone who did not actually get under my feet.

When I went down to him he gave me a clean overall which should fit Arthur, a singlet, underpants and a pair of old sandals. "The best I could do, Sergeant." His best was good enough.

He said, "It's only a short trip. Where will we make the changeover?"

"Not all that short. We'll move right out of the city for the swap."

In a city of ten millions, especially in summer, islands of privacy can be hard to find. My plan was to move right out of city limits, along the Ballarat Road and past Digger's Rest, a few kilometers into the forced-pasture country where there were still empty stretches and little-used side roads and not much night traffic. There Beltane's car would meet us.

I showed Cranko the spot on a road map and he said the job made a nice change from the humdrum. A surgeon's life had not occurred to me as humdrum, but I supposed that after a while one sliced-up interior would look much like another. To a butcher a carcass is only meat.

During the evening I gave Arthur his clothes and would have assisted him to dress but he waved me away. He seemed to have taken fairly good control of his body though he swayed and made two attempts at standing on one foot while he lifted the other to get his leg into the overall, but I was satisfied that he could make a quickish move if he was pushed to it.

After that we could only wait. At some stage he asked, "What the devil is biophysics? Some new branch of biology?" I had never heard of it before entering the institute and I still did not know. "Do you mean you haven't asked?"

"Why should I?" If I sounded surly it was with myself for not having done so. I had accepted the term as indicating some special area of biology with which I was unlikely to come into contact.

Arthur said, "You could translate the word roughly as life measurement. Does that make sense?"

"Why not? Exercise factors, relation of muscle mass to stress positions, effects of internal and external temperatures—all that sort of thing."

"Nothing new in that."

"No."

"So why a special institute?"

"I don't know. Let's do what we have to do tonight and ask questions later."

We were fidgety by the time Cranko called us down to the parking bay. There he was, posing by the white vehicle in an ambulance service uniform and hugely pleased with himself.

I was not so pleased. "Is that getup from the institute store?"

"Of course not; we don't supply the ambulance people. I had to chit them for it."

"On indent?" In my mind's eye I saw a trail of documentation as evidence of our movements.

"No. Does it matter?"

"Do you mean that you asked the ambulance service for one of their uniforms and they just passed it over?"

He gave me a smiling, incredulous stare as if I were ignorant of the facts of life. "I *asked* for the correct size; I *demanded* the use of the uniform. You're a jewel, Harry; you really don't know what authority the institute wields, do you? I suppose not many outside our senior staff do know and we don't keep the police force informed of our daily despotisms. Life is easier that way."

Jackson, leaning against the open rear door of the

ambulance, listened with plain dislike. "The premier will be interested in the arrogance of privilege."

Cranko's amusement did not falter. "He knows, Mr. Jackson, he knows. Shouldn't we start?"

He settled himself into the driver's cabin and I helped Arthur into the back, where he lay on a stretcher. I sat up; anyone looking through the rear window would see only a paramedic in a white coat.

At exactly ten o'clock Cranko lifted us on the air cushion and backed out of the garage.

Jackson was interested. "A hovercraft ambulance! It doesn't sound economical."

"It comes cheaper than maintaining good surfaces over thousands of kilometers of country roads."

That shocked him. "Is the country so poor?"

"Every country is poor. There are too many people to feed and clothe and house and too much necessity to conserve all natural resources. And I mean all, Arthur. We don't have anything we don't need."

He fell silent. Cranko took us around the northern end of City Center, through the decaying western suburbs and on to the Ballarat Road. There he cut in the turbobooster and the screeching siren and we belted up the highway, an ambulance on its mission of mercy to some call from the countryside, its balance system holding it level on a road so neglected that it would soon have wrecked the suspension of a wheeled car at any decent speed.

He drove fast and when he slowed and stopped, still suspended on the air cushion, I checked my watch and opened the sliding hatch to the driver's cabin. "You're three minutes early."

"Doesn't matter," he said, "because they're here."

They were indeed. Looking slantwise through the hatch I could see the red nose of a car alongside us and heard the doors slam as people got out of it. It was a wheeled vehicle and I thought they must have

started very early, driving slowly and carefully on the ruined road, to keep the appointment. It would be a slow trip from here on, but at least Beltane had had the wit not to send one of his official, blatantly identifiable hovercars.

I helped Arthur to his feet and was reaching for my suitcases when somebody hammered on the rear door and yelled for us to hurry up and come out.

What prompted me to murmur to Jackson, "Answer him," while I shifted the gun from its belt holster to the right-hand pocket of my white coat is not easily pinned; the mind works faster than it can trace its movements. The sense of wrongness could have been born of the thought that staff from the Manor would not hammer and bawl but be discreet and polite. Be that right or wrong, I was alerted and it is a firm memory that I recognized at once what the wrongness might portend and whose would be the responsibility.

Jackson called, "Coming!" and undid the double door. As he pushed one wing open I hissed, "Stand aside," but he either did not understand me or was bewildered. I caught a glimpse of an orderly's white coat like my own, but the rest of the man was obscured as Jackson hesitated on the sill, hesitating because he saw what I could not, that the man held a gun.

The gunman yelled at him, "Come out of it, quick!" and gestured with his gun hand so that now I glimpsed the weapon, too.

I dragged Jackson out of the way with my left hand and shot at the gunman through the pocket of my coat. I did not expect to hit him with a hurried, half-aimed round, only to surprise him for a second while I freed my gun—but hit him I did. He stepped back, clutching his side, tripped on the rough road surface and sat down hard, dropping his gun.

There was no time to think because he was not alone and the second man was moving to get a shot at me

through the open door. The luck went my way; my gun was free and firing before he was sure of me, and that shot was better aimed. It took him in the throat, in the artery.

I jumped down to the road and kicked the first thug's gun away from his scrabbling fingers before I peeped cautiously round the side of the ambulance to see Cranko sidling the length of the bus towards me.

Behind me Jackson said, with no sign of panic, "I'll get that gun, Harry. You carry on." A tough old bird in every way.

I called to Cranko, giving nothing away, I hoped, "It's all right, Doc. Enemy dispersed."

In the light from the ambulance he was white to the gills and had every right to be. He glanced at the dead man, saw there was nothing to be done for him and looked to the other who sat glaring at his own weapon as Jackson covered him.

"Kidnap job," I said.

He answered shakily, "Yes."

"Incompetent. They should have sent you to open the doors."

"Me?"

"Their bad manners made me suspicious."

He breathed deeply and some color seeped back into his face. "I'd better see to this one."

"Do. Keep him alive to regret it."

The ambulance had been, through all of this, resting on its hoverjets. Now, without warning, it moved sharply away, gathered speed and shot down the road, leaving me to gaze after it like a slack-jawed nitwit and howl, "Christ! There were three of them!"

Cranko had known it. And knew now that in failure the driver had abandoned him.

The runaway lifted the hovercar over the post-and-wire fence and into the empty field where the wheeled car could not follow. I put three useless shots through

the windscreen as it swung past me but probably hit nobody; the resilient glass would show only little round holes, no impediment to the driver's vision. The ambulance headlights vanished round the hump of a low rise and that was the end of the snatch.

Cranko spoke, in the tentative voice of a man who must speak though he has nothing useful to say. "Did you think of the possibility of this, Harry?"

"Of a planned hijack? No." I had nothing to say to Cranko just yet; later, a great deal. I noted the registration number of the red car though I did not imagine that its owner's name would tell us anything save perhaps that it had no history. I asked Cranko, "Can you drive this thing?"

"I don't know. It's one of the old hydrogen burners with a gearbox. I don't think so."

I wasn't sure that I could drive it either.

Jackson said he had driven the same type in his younger days but never on a road surface like the mess we were stranded on. He wondered about the ambulance: "A very distinctive vehicle for a getaway bus."

It was perfect for the job; it could go almost anywhere unquestioned; the driver could dump it outside a hospital and simply walk away. "And the doctor here will have to account to the ambulance service for it."

Cranko looked round from his bandaging of the wounded man's side. "Beltane's responsibility, I'd think. This man may have a broken rib."

I said, "You can be lucky," meaning my shooting as much as the victim of it. He was a smallish ratface of the typically undernourished breed that swarms in some areas as though the state's balanced diet did not work with particular people. He made no attempt to protest or complain; he would be most conscious of his duty to his employers, who might well be far more fearsome than we. He would know little of any use,

would have been hired for the job and told only what he needed to know—almost nothing—and was philosophical as Cranko ripped his shirt off his back and tore it into a pad and bandage. After all, my wild shot could have killed him as surely as the next round had slaughtered his mate.

Then a brilliance of headlights swept out of the distance and in a few minutes the premier's distinctive hovercar (he had not been so longsighted after all) pulled alongside us with two men peering from the cabin. The driver called out, "Have you seen an ambulance anywhere along here?"

Jackson's tensions erupted in temper. "Yes, and so would you if you'd been on time!"

The driver was indignant. "A couple of bloody minutes is all! Who the hell are you, anyway?" Then he spotted the two hijackers laid out behind us and dug furiously at his mate's ribs. "Look, Gus! Look there!" He yelled at us, "What's been goin' on?"

That was the panic sound of a peaceable man confronted by violence and wanting no part in it. A wounded man and another with his blood spreading black in the headlights, fronted by two men with guns, was enough to unnerve a quiet citizen. He told his offsider, "We're gettin' outa here, Gus," and the car edged backwards.

The headlights dazzled vision, but I thought that the offsider hit him with a swinging open hand and reached for the controls. The hovercar settled to the roadway with a sigh of failing air. The offsider jumped down and came towards me, watching the gun rather than myself.

He was a tall man, fortyish, wide in the shoulders but flat chested and stringy, one of the long-boned types with no fat and little flesh. The immediately noticeable thing about him was the gentleness, verging on sweetness, of his narrow, bony face. It sat poorly

with the gray uniform of a private security firm with a reputation for toughness.

He stopped two meters away. "That's a police issue gun you got there. What's your name?"

"Detective-Sergeant Ostrov."

"ID?"

I showed him and he called back to the car, "Come out, Willy; they're on our side." He counted us and looked round to see there were no more. "We got to pick up two. Who's the freeloaders?"

The driver came cautiously near. "Is one of you Mr. Jackson?"

"I am and I have no documents. I can't prove it."

I said, "I vouch for him." The Jackson face wakened no recognition in the Manor servant. "You can take us all to the Manor."

"Mr. Beltane said two."

"And the copper says all of us."

He looked sideways at the dead man. "Not him."

"He can go in the boot."

"Not in my boot! You don't have to clean up after."

A spasm of glee took the gentleness from the face of the security man; the reverse side of his nature was enjoying itself. He returned to benignity to ask what had happened and I told him, briefly. He stared at Jackson. "What'd they want him for?"

"Tell me and we'll both know."

His face flickered to hard suspicion; he did not believe me. He was not your usual eight-hour shift, disinterested operative. "Not my business, eh?"

"Not yet," I said. It sounded like a half promise of confidences later on, enough to soothe for the moment. "Give me a hand with this bloke."

He took the dead man's feet and I the shoulders, letting the blood stain my coat rather than his uniform. As we dumped him in the boot we could hear the driver complaining that he was a chauffeur, not

a bloody commando. Gus, the security man, winked happily. "You ought to see the blood 'n' guts vids he watches."

"Home, James," I told the driver as we climbed into the passenger compartment. He slew me with a look but got into the cabin and started to lift.

We had a superbly comfortable ride, all of us but Ratface. Cranko's bandaging was less efficient than his surgery and the stripped shirt leaked blood onto the upholstery. Poor Willy!

The hovercar was a work-on-the-run model with folding seats and tables for conference, a panel vid with a capacity for direct communication worldwide and a soundproof glass shield between the driver's cabin and the passenger compartment. Willy was competent once his mouth was shut; apparently holding the map in his head, he went cross-country to hit the city limit in ten minutes, then ran us sedately along the urban roads.

I thought it best not to challenge Cranko immediately; if he had a gun concealed and was fool enough to use it, the results could be disastrous for all in a moving vehicle. He sat still and silent; for a man who must know that he was now a sacrificial goat he was remarkably calm. I watched for recognition between him and Ratface, but there was none. In good planning it was unlikely that they would know each other.

I asked him, as much to end the silence as from curiosity, "What is biophysics?"

The question surprised him; he had been expecting anything but chitchat and he had to think himself into the sociable mode. "The application of the laws of physics to biology. You gave a couple of basic examples to Jackson."

I had forgotten that an ambulance driver's cabin has microphone connection with the casualty compartment. "So it's nothing new?"

"Quite old, a nearly useless term not often heard."

"Good for naming an institute. Yet who needs a ten-storey tower to measure muscle tension or heat dilation?"

"Nobody, Harry, I'm sure."

All right, I was being laughed at. "So?"

"That's privileged information which I won't give you." His smile was frankly malicious.

Jackson listened but kept blessedly quiet.

The hovercar slowed and turned left into Royal Park. We were within minutes of the Manor, and now Cranko made a last show of impudence. He snapped on the intercom mike and said, "You can put me down here, driver. I'll pick up public transport. The premier is not expecting me."

My turn to smile. "No! Dr. Cranko will stay with us."

"Mr. Cranko," he corrected gently. "I am a surgeon."

"Mr. Cranko knows he is needed."

He sighed elaborately, "One has to try." He looked out to the lights of the Manor. "Do you know," he asked, "that once the state premiers lived in their own homes instead of in these high-tech palaces?"

I did not know. He carried on: "The rise of ultra-sophisticated electronic eavesdropping techniques and the consequent employment of ever more expensive countering equipment made the protection of private homes impossibly costly, so each state built itself a single high-tech luxury prison for its premier and congratulated itself that the secrets of official intrigue, corruption and skulduggery were safe from newsbugs and Wardies."

He cocked an eyebrow. To a born playactor I could only feed his next cue. "And the moral of that is?"

"That nobody and nothing can protect the man with a death wish. All the wizardry of the world's protective devices could not save Beltane once he set a course no technology could smother or disguise. Brain or no

brain, he's a born idiot. The question for all of us is: How many will he drag to destruction with him? And you, his faithful hound, can't do a damned thing to help him."

"Mr. Jackson's faithful hound, not Beltane's."

"Of course, Jackson's. That could be worse. Don't let loyalty hobble your feet when it's time to run."

No tour of duty had ever taken me to the Manor, and in the night I gained only an impression of extravagant spaciousness with few lighted windows in long, low walls. The wide lawns were floodlit, but the lights were strategically aimed to dazzle the incomer rather than to reveal the building. All there was to see amounted to dimness and size.

The car swung round the house and halted at a back entrance. The driver's offsider came to open my door. I said to Cranko, "It is not yet time for you to run. Don't do anything to alarm me. I'd enjoy shooting you—in the knee."

He came cautiously after me, keeping his hands in sight, but made an effort at jauntiness. "I didn't really need to escape. Nobody in this fool's paradise can harm me."

He was wrong about that; I was capable of harming him very badly if it could gain me anything. We have good policemen and bad ones, talented men and misfits, the overrighteous and the corrupt, but we all respond identically to an insult to our professionalism, and Cranko had no idea of the illwill I bore his treachery.

Jackson came out behind him and murmured to me, "First time I've ever seen the back door—that I remember."

I told glum Willy to leave the corpse in the boot until we had decided how to deal with it. "And both of you keep your mouths shut to the rest of the staff. Not one word. Not one!"

Willy shepherded us through the Manor passages,

radiating sulky resentment, and ushered us into a large room, part lounge and part office. I glimpsed a sound-screen strip in the lintel and felt the familiar *cluck* in the ears as we passed through the door. Premier Jeremy Beltane sat morosely behind a desk, facing two mixed bloods, both of whom I recognized.

The driver grasped at his moment of safe spite. "There's four of 'em, sir, not two. And there's another one, dead. The copper shot 'im."

The mixed bloods stared, not understanding, while I silently cursed the gabbling ass.

Beltane gave no sign of hearing him. His dull eyes livened as he surveyed his disheveled father; he smiled and nodded, then controlled himself and turned to Willy, as if the chauffeur had said nothing untoward. "Very well. Good night." To the security man he was more civil. "Thank you for your assistance. You can return to your duties."

6

Ostrov: All Through
the Night—

The three-parts Koori, Richard Kenney, a shadow minister in the Opposition, I knew only from print photos and the occasional vid talk show; he was best known for his moral integrity and his political antipathy for Beltane, whom he had once described as "not worth the snot of his father's sneeze." The speaker had suspended him when he refused to withdraw the remark. So, what was he doing in the premier's home? Labour and Liberal members were said to drink together in the House bar after sessions of invective that would disgrace a gay whore's pimp, but I could not imagine it of Kenney and Beltane.

More peculiarly, what was either doing in the company of Barney Fielding? Fielding I had run across three, four years earlier when attached for a while to the Balaclava station, and I knew him for one of those fakes with so many false faces that he no longer knew which was real. He was a doctor, downgraded for malpractice, who worked now (and, admittedly, worked well for a dog's income) among the Wardies, looked

and dressed like a Wardie, talked like a Minder and dealt industriously in forged food and clothing coupons. The local coppers knew it but left him alone as long as he did not exceed a reasonable limit of criminality and because he was often good for useful information with a minimum of arm twisting. He was, at bottom, a self-important twit with little nerve.

Strangely Kenney, with a much greater inheritance of Koori blood, was the lighter skinned of the two; you had to look twice to see the legacy alive there. Fielding, much darker, showed his one-quarter heritage more plainly. The genetic dance plays tricks.

Accepted wisdom says that the mixed breeds stick together, having little feeling for black or white but much sorrow for themselves as swimmers in limbo. Like most accepted wisdom it is only half true, but I could think of no other reason why these two should be together; Kenney's ferocious honesty would not waste spit on the dishonored doctor.

I had to wait a little while for answers, because Beltane asked them to excuse him while he dealt with an emergency, meaning us, and summoned a Manor security man to escort them to another room.

If they were a puzzle, Beltane was a disaster; he crouched at his desk, arms flat on the surface, fingers rigidly bent as if to claw the wood, shoulders drooping and startled eyes crying out bewilderment and despair. There was nothing of the little bull in him that night.

He gestured to all of us to sit down and asked Jackson, "Are you all right?" At Jackson's "Yes," he turned to me. "What happened?"

When I had finished he swung like a dead-weary man between thankfulness and anger. "I appreciate your quick action, Sergeant, but there was a lack of forethought—"

Jackson broke in on him, an outraged father berating his son. "You are ungrateful and ignorant!"

"Am I? If you say so, Dad. Perhaps I am. I am also harassed by human rats."

I told him, "You had one right in your nest." I indicated Cranko. "Him."

Cranko had been tense; now he relaxed, with the first and greatest revelation over.

"Dr. Cranko? But he has—" He shut off whatever had been on his tongue and shook with a psychic fever, clutched his arms across his chest like a man about to crumble in bitter cold, but fell suddenly calm to say in a wondering voice, "My father taught me that betrayal always comes from a friend. I should have remembered."

Cranko said coldly, "Indeed you should," and there was nothing vague or offhanded about him now.

Beltane asked, "How do you know, Sergeant?" and I told him how Cranko and only Cranko had known our route plan and known it early enough to alert an ambush.

Cranko grinned at me, not as a friend. "And who gave me the knowledge, Harry? I wouldn't be in your smugly virtuous shoes for a fortune."

He would keep; his score was mounting for payment.

Beltane said to him, "Shut your trap until I want you to talk," but he was out of his depth. He asked me, "What must I do with him?"

"Hold him here. He has questions to answer."

"Hold him? That is for the police."

"I am the police."

"Yes. But—"

"You have a private security force here. And rooms with locks, surely? Realize, sir, that you have had a secret stolen from under you and Cranko is a link in a chain of thieves. Also, there's a dead man to be accounted for. We must control damage as much as possible by letting no word escape from the Manor.

These two may earn their food as hostages to keep wagging tongues outside from giving you away. So keep them!"

Beltane turned to wounded Ratface for the first time. "Who are you?"

Ratface, whose side must have been an aching torment, pulled his jacket gently round his shoulders. "Name don't matter."

"He'll tell me," I said, "when I'm ready to ask him. Won't you, son?"

" 'Spose so. Lotta good it'll do yers."

True; he was a nobody, probably a stray gun picked up for the job.

"Lock him up, too, sir, but keep them apart."

Beltane said into his desk console, "Will the chief security officer please report to the Small Office."

Through all of this Jackson had sprawled on a sofa, gaze darting like a hunting wasp from face to face. Now he said, "I gather my incognito is broken to some person or group, but what are those two Koori doing here?" To Beltane's stare of helplessness he persisted, "You're open to political blackmail now, aren't you?"

"Yes."

Cranko laughed.

"Well?"

Beltane said slowly, "Nothing is well. I've had two severe blows and my brain has slowed to a halt. Dad, please do something for me."

"Isn't that what I'm here for?"

"Then go to bed, Dad. Please!"

Jackson bristled like an enraged terrier; I fancied the hair rising behind his ears. "To bed, is it? Knowing nothing! Your plans fall apart and you tell me to go to bed!"

"When I can, I'll tell you everything I know. Just now I'm not sure what is truth and what is confusion. Please, Dad!"

Something of the implicit understanding I had observed at the institute seeped into the angry space between them, and Jackson quieted, accepting a need for him to shut up and agree. He gave a surly, "Very well, then," and to me, "How much do you know, Harry?"

"Not a lot."

"Your job involves keeping me informed, doesn't it?"

Sneaky old devil. "Where necessary."

"When you feel like it, eh? Do you also want me in bed and out of the way?"

"Yes, sir."

"Bloody Ape!"

I recognized Beltane's chief of security when she came in. Like so many private security people she was ex-police, working for better wages and conditions than the regular service could earn her, and I remembered seeing her here and there in the past. Jeanette somebody or other; I had forgotten the surname.

Beltane asked was Jackson's room prepared and she said it was. "Then please escort him to it."

I said, "Seeing what has happened tonight, he had better have a guard on his quarters."

"Besides yourself?"

"I also have to sleep sometime."

He told Jeanette, "See to it, please. Also, I want these other two locked in and guarded—most securely guarded. Separately."

Escorting Jackson out, she paused by me, scowling. "So you're the undercover man. I remember you." She said to me what she could not say to Beltane: "Please keep in mind that my manpower is limited, fully employed and entitled to be paid overtime for additional work."

I didn't bother to answer. Overtime might be written into their contracts, but they would be lucky ever to see the cash; their jobs could be filled too easily.

Beltane called to her retreating back, "On your way, please ask the two Koori gentlemen to step back in here."

She sent two standard issue plug-uglies to take Cranko and Ratface away. Cranko went with the insouciance of one who thinks himself untouchable, Ratface with the resignation of the recidivist who has seen it all before.

When we were alone Beltane said, "I apologize for trying to put blame on you. You had no choice but to depend on Cranko." The words came slowly, as sad discoveries. "You could not have suspected him."

Rankling, I said, "I should have suspected every-one."

"Don't beat your breast; there's no time for it. And it smacks of self-righteousness."

That again. And here it was surely unjust. (Or was it? Later. To be thought about later.)

He asked, "What sort of man are you?"

How do you answer such a question? "I do my work."

"Including killing?"

"Tonight? That was unusual. I had to act. Your father's life and perhaps my own . . ."

"It worried you?"

"No time for worry, sir. I just did it."

"I did not mean the risk to your life; I meant the act of killing. Did that worry you?"

That one certainly hadn't. "No, sir. Should it?"

"A life snuffed out, by your hand, and there is no reason for you to be concerned?"

"No, sir." He expected a specific response, but what? I plucked a rationalization out of memory. "My father tells me that when he was young there was talk of the sacredness of life, as if it was to be treated as a . . . as a precious thing . . . like a work of art perhaps. But the fact is, it's more like a disease on the planet. With five times too many of us now, what does one less matter?

It matters to me if I'm the one to be made less, or my mum and dad, but who else cares? So what does it matter if one gets knocked off? There's twelve billion more infesting the place."

He had listened with close interest. "Do all the Ward people think like that?"

"They don't think about it at all. Death is just something that happens, so they make the best of what little life they have and don't give a bugger about the people next door! I'd think the Minders are much the same. Life's basically selfish."

He did not answer but explored my face with an unsettling intentness, as if from within him a Martian was examining his first Earth human.

When he had done surveying me—or perhaps himself—Beltane said, "First things first. My daughter has disappeared and I must find her quickly. Very quickly. Last Sunday—"

"I know. Nguyen told me."

"Did he, indeed? I wonder why."

"So that I might not work in a vacuum. And perhaps he thought finding her might be a job for me."

Kenney and Fielding came quietly in and sat down.

He nodded aimlessly at his hands stretched across the desk. "Why not? This man—" he nodded at Fielding "—had her and lost her. He is a doctor."

"I know him. He is also a manipulator of forged coupons and an occasional police informer. Poor stuff."

Fielding looked through me as if I were not there.

Beltane was unsurprised. "Then he has manipulated beyond his capacity. Mr. Kenney here is a member of the state parliamentary Opposition. He is, within his limits, an honest man. He is also a politician who sees an opportunity to apply pressure—but his lever has vanished into the Wards and his conscience is restless."

Kenney said mildly, "I would have brought her to

you, J.B.; I am not a hostage taker. The weapon was my knowledge of her condition, not the girl herself."

"Don't expect understanding and fair play from me, Dick, while I suffer abduction, treachery and blackmail. Sergeant Ostrov, I need my daughter back in this house; these two are all the information I have and I do not know how to use them." He added in a meandering tone, "You come highly recommended."

He threw himself back in the chair, folding his hands in his lap and watching me as though I might answer with a blaze of Holmesian deduction. Feeling like an actor pushed on camera without a script, I delivered the first apposite line to come to my head: "Who is your daughter's boyfriend?"

The three of them said together, in varying degrees of disapproval and prurience, "Fred Blacker." Fielding pursued with a small man's malice, "The gardener's boy."

"Your gardener, sir?"

Beltane smiled sourly. "A junior in the vegetable section. I can't say I have ever seen him."

Why should he have? Every home has its vegetable patch as a matter of necessity, but I didn't imagine the premier helped with the watering and weeding.

"Where does he live? In your area, Barney?"

"Yes, but he's gone off with the girl. And just remember, Sergeant, I haven't done anything wrong." He reconsidered. "Nothing criminal. I'm not going to be held responsible for any of this."

"Not if you can wriggle round it. What did you do?"

His account was probably truthful in pinpointing Mrs. Blacker as the silly complicating force . . . but not so silly when you know Wardie life. You have to live in that condition of tribal, hand-to-mouth wretchedness, knowing there will be no improvement in your lifetime, before you can understand and condone the wrenching tug of loyalty versus self-preservation that

bedevils their actions, in eternal fear of the mindless, pitiless law.

The most revealing thing he said was that Melissa didn't give a damn for the love-blind Fred but was hell-bent on preserving his baby. No, *her* baby; the father didn't come into it. Barney thought she had got all her sex knowledge from the other girls at school—and knew just enough to fall into trouble without knowing how to avoid it or enjoy it.

"Where do you think she went, Barney?"

"If I knew where I'd be chasing her myself."

"How old is the boy?"

"Seventeen."

"Does he run with a gang?"

"You know better than that. They push 'em out when they take a job."

True. A working man's responsibilities make him undependable.

"How long has he been working?"

"A year or so."

"And before that?"

"He ran with the Handspikes for a while."

I had to think quickly over what little I remembered of the Handspikes while keeping Barney thinking I was a jump ahead of him. "They ran a bunch of teenage prostitutes. Headquarters in the disused railway cutting through Alma Park. Good place for a pregnant girl to hide out. You would have thought of that." A tiny facial tic flickered and twitched as he considered denying contact with the local gangies. "You would, wouldn't you?"

He caved in resentfully. "They said they don't see Fred and they've never heard of Melissa."

"They wouldn't tell you if they had, particularly if she offered them money—real Minder money that buys things coupons can't get."

He had been stupid to go near them and knew it. "Maybe."

"Did she have money?"

"How should I know? If she did, Ma Blacker would have had it off her quick smart."

Possibly, but I guessed that Ma Blacker would have thought twice about rough-handling her son's beloved. He was the family provider, by Barney's account.

I thought the Handspikes might be worth another visit.

I turned to Kenney, more from curiosity than with any expectation of extracting a clue from him. "Tell me about your end of the transaction, Mr. Kenney."

Kenney rounded on Beltane. "Is he really a policeman, J.B.? Are you out of your mind? Why not make the girl's condition public while you are about it?"

Beltane said, "I thought that was your intention; I want to forestall it. The police are searching for her and for young Blacker but do not know of the pregnancy. Sergeant Ostrov knows but will not betray a confidence."

"Can't," I said, reminding him that loyalty can be an artificial condition.

Kenney did not understand the subtext but needled where he could. "A private commission, J.B.? Your own personal copper, bodyguard, hatchet man? Have you come to that?"

Beltane sounded tired to death. "Please, Dick, just tell him what you can."

So now I heard how bumbling Barney tried to barter the premier's daughter for respectability and how Kenney dragged him to the Manor to confess that his ineptitude had lost her.

Barney opened up his store of spite. "You meant to blackmail the premier by threatening to expose the pregnancy. Premier trying to cover up a birth! It'll sound fine on the vid and in the House, won't it? And fine in the Wards, too, where a concealed birth brings jail sentences and a dead child! The Wardies'll love

finding out that their hero thinks he's above the law."

Beltane seemed unmoved, but Kenney observed him with a faint contempt.

I said, "I think they'll sympathize." There was an almost physical sensation of Kenney switching his attention to me. Which was what I had wanted.

Barney sneered, "Then you don't know the Wards."

"I was born and raised in them."

Kenney asked, "Are you saying, Sergeant, that the Wards will not turn against the premier if they see him as conniving at an illegal birth?"

"Wardies live on emotion more than reason. They like a premier who has diverted funds to their food and clothing instead of setting up projects that mean nothing to them—scientific research, road repair, higher education—the things they regard as Minders' perks. They see him on their side, giving them something, so they'll forgive him for getting into the kind of human trouble they get into themselves. If they didn't like him they'd call it a Minder crime and yell for his blood; but he's a mate, so it will be just a peccadillo."

"Interesting." Kenney, frowning and thoughtful, became suddenly all Koori, remote and concentrated, "thinking black" as the Wardies call it. Then the white politician in him returned. "I was born Minder; we don't understand the Wardie thinking as well as we should."

"How can you if you don't talk to them?" I knew the conventional answer to that: Give the Wardies a decision-making responsibility, and in the ten million–voiced argument nothing will ever get done. It might have been the right answer, but historically democracy has been successful. I suppose each age has its own givens.

"So you think I have nothing to bargain with?"

"You might make it stick in the House, but I think

not in the Wards. There you might get demonstrations and blood in the gutters." I decided to lean on him a little. "Besides, you weren't bargaining with the premier, were you? It was blackmail, wasn't it? What did you want as the price of your silence?"

He said only, "Prove it."

"I will if I'm pushed to it."

"Manufactured evidence?"

"If the premier agrees that it was moral blackmail, some form of proof can be found."

"Do you think you can frighten me?"

"Yes."

He turned to Beltane. "J.B., will you get your leech off my back?"

"No. Why should I? He's right." The unexpected support had enlivened him. Kenney retired into his Koori fastness to consider his position as attacker under attack, while Beltane called again for Jeanette.

He told her to take Fielding away and see that he was watched. "Not with Cranko," I interjected. "We don't want him picking up clues about the hijack; he talks too freely."

Barney put on his Minder front as an insulted gentleman but had more sense than to object. She shepherded his dignity briskly out, raging at her multiplying surveillance problems.

Kenney returned from his far country. "I agree that the less that fumbler knows the better for everybody."

I pointed out that I also had no true knowledge of the situation between himself and the premier.

"Better that you don't, Sergeant."

Beltane disagreed. "He needs to know a little. I have to make a decision, to throw my weight for or against a certain proposition. Mr. Kenney thinks to control my decision by holding my daughter's pregnancy over me. Be sure that he will not do so, one way or the other. It is a decision which will affect . . . people . . . outside as

well as inside Australia." He paused before he added, with a stolid refusal of emotion, "It is more than should be required of one man."

Remembering his conversation with Jackson at the institute, I had a hazy and unpleasant idea of the scope of the decision but not its precise nature. I did not want to know that; I did not want to be locked with Beltane in some secret that ate at the roots of nations.

Kenney said, "I think you will live through it, J.B."

I was less sure. Beltane needed his father, that old pragmatist who would return the world snarl for snarl and carry the son with him. He asked, "Would it be of any use to inquire, Dick, where you obtained your information on the subjects discussed at Canberra?"

"Just ask who wants your job."

"All of them, even the talentless."

"And treachery begins at the top, as usual."

"Don't offer me pity, Dick."

"That I will not. The Koori, to whom I should belong if I did not carry a white smell with me, are not a pitying people. In their universe all things have their place and proper behavior; a man fails because of something less than a full recognition of his place in the scheme. That does not command pity."

I found that less than comprehensible, but Beltane seemed interested. He said to me, "Go and talk to Cranko, Sergeant; see what you can get out of him."

"If you insist, but he wouldn't have been left behind if he knew anything useful. I'd rather take a turn round the house; I need to know the layout if I'm to guard Mr. Jackson."

"Do what you need to do." He had more on his mind than the routines of a Wardie copper.

I looked in at nearby rooms to find Cranko placidly reading a book, Fielding sulking and frightened

as imagination magnified brutal possibilities, Ratface asleep and comfortably snoring. One of Jeanette's men sat, bored stiff, outside each door.

The huge house was quiet as a museum, but in a sort of communication-center-cum-armory that they called the wardroom I found some off-duty security guards playing poker for food coupons—probably forgeries but, under the circumstances, not worth making a police fuss about. I introduced myself; they were all retired coppers or time-served soldiers and received me with resignation. Private security groups have their extralegal methods just as police have theirs, and the private men have no wish to be dogged by the force with bigger boots.

Only Willy's hovercar offsider did not sourly resent me, so I asked him to give me a guided tour of the Manor, and he threw in his hand without complaining. Just then, Jeanette returned from settling Jackson for the night, and she was furious. "I have exactly four men for each operating shift, Sergeant, and you now have one complete shift looking after your police affairs! If you need more, call on your own department."

You can't argue with an angry woman, especially when she is in the right. I took my guide and escaped.

First I wanted to know where Jackson was, and he led me straight there. "He's asleep," said the security man at the door. I looked in to note the relevant details of the room, but there was nothing to query or object to, so we moved on.

Kostakis (like half the population, he was second- or third-generation European) knew what I wanted and led me very efficiently round the doors, windows and ducts. There were, he told me, sixteen security men on six-hour shifts of four, one indoors on each shift and three patrolling outdoors; all doors were fitted with metal and explosive detectors, all windows shielded against high-frequency radiation and sound-snooping. . . . "All

the usual junk," he said. "Only better quality and more of it."

His threatening, gravel voice contrasted coarsely with his peaceable, kindly face.

I had expected the Manor to be expensively appointed, luxurious as one of the "great homes" preserved by the National Trust but, save for its size and the proliferation of communication gear and computerware, it was little more impressive than any average Minder home. When you stop to think about it, the difference between a Minder home and a Wardie tenement is that one has enough of everything and it is all in good condition, while the other has just enough to get by on and the place is usually falling down around its dwellers. Nobody these days is really loaded with treasure on Earth, but Beltane seemed to do with less than he could easily have had.

The only relief in all the functional blandness was the pictures on the walls. The corridors and rooms were hung with them, not in great numbers but with enough to bring a fresh one into view at every turning. I found Beltane's taste frustrating and dully modish.

"Does Beltane own all these or do they go with the Manor?"

"They're his. All the regular Manor stuff went back to the art galleries that lent them."

"So there's an expensive private investment in this lot?"

"Nah! I don't reckon he's got much to spare while he's keeping an absent wife in style. She lives better than him. These are all repros. Good repros, though."

He spoke as though he appreciated the stuff; to me it was wholly uninteresting. I have never been able to whip up a taste for collages of scraps of cloth and paper or infinitely receding depictions of a hand drawing a hand drawing a hand down to a microscopic blot,

or even the surreal, cubist and impenetrable works of the previous century. My taste comes to a dead stop somewhere about nineteen hundred, in the recognizable world.

I said, "They mean nothing to me."

"They didn't to me at first."

"Now they do?"

"Some of 'em. You see 'em every day and they start to get meaning. It's—what's a word for it? It's elusive, as if it was peeping from behind a door and would duck back if you didn't cop it right away."

The grass-roots Wardie art critic is a satirist's commonplace, but Kostakis's language struggled for expression without pretending to knowledge.

In a long corridor hung with a dozen of the irritating things but otherwise unfurnished, I stopped at a fan of graded blue tints, all anchored to a single yellow eye from which a drop of blood fell infuriatingly upward. "Does that mean anything to you?"

"Yersss. I don't like it much but it means."

"What?"

"Nah, you have to see for yourself. It'll mean something different for you because you aren't me; you're somebody else. You've got different eyes in your soul— or whatever."

I began to warm to Kostakis; I have a soft spot for the oddities that turn up in commonplace exteriors. "Doesn't he have any ordinary pictures—paintings of scenes of people or such?"

"You mean representational?" I was sure he had discovered and polished up that word for use on the occasional willing listener. "Have a look in his bedroom, right here."

Bedrooms breathe in personality from their users, but this had none, unless you count plain utility as a positive statement. The furnishings were a three-quarter bed, a desk, a chair and a small vidscreen. Opposite

the door was the bed; the other two walls were glass-fronted cupboards—one a wardrobe, the other a repository of massive bound books.

Kostakis pivoted heel-and-toe in the middle of the room, playing the tourist guide. "The whole man's here. This is what he is. Start with the bed."

"Three-quarter. Nothing unusual."

"Single bed for loner, double bed for married man, but three-quarter bed for a lonely bloke with an occasional short-time visitor. In, out, see yer later!"

Crude psychology, but probably near enough for a man deserted long ago. The library cupboard was daunting—Hansard, law, sociology, legal history and philosophy, the sciences—and, in the bottom right-hand corner as if ashamed of its frivolity, a complete Shakespeare in single annotated volumes.

"Works here at night. Gets up all hours and plows into it at the desk there. Doesn't sleep enough."

Yes, this was part of the man who had come to the institute in the early morning; he could be equated with this. I said, "No pictures."

The gravel voice chided, "Should be ashamed of yourself, Sergeant, not noticin'. Black mark!"

Indeed I should have noticed what was not a normal fitting, the rectangular outline of a flap flush with the wall and the same color, some three meters long and twenty centimeters high. Only hairlines betrayed it but I should have noticed.

Kostakis lifted it up and small lights came on, one for each of the fifteen small pictures revealed. I recognized the subject because van Gogh is one of the few artists whose peculiar techniques seem not at all peculiar to me, whose despairing expressions of himself call as loudly across a couple of centuries as on the day he rammed the thick paint onto canvas or board or card or whatever he could afford.

They were fifteen self-portraits reproduced as small,

cheap prints and hidden in a premier's bedroom. I knew them all, knew them well; they told me how Vincent felt, lost in a world with no understanding of him. They spoke to me because I sometimes woke in the night with all my misapprehensions of the world astride my chest like a black dog, reminding me that all I knew of life was its visible face, while the deep truth of it lay in signs I could not translate, perhaps not perceive.

These were all painted during the tormented last two years of his life, when insanity came and went, and unhappy clear hours alternated with the furious times of power and twisted vision, so that he painted Vincent normal and gentle and almost colorless in his sane self, and Vincent flame haired and bare boned and brute eyed in his insanity. The degrees of his madness can be traced in the swirling-flame backgrounds to his haunted heads, at its worst when the flames flow out of the background to eat at his face and clothes.

This was what Beltane hid in his bedroom as others hide the pornographic wishes of easier needs.

"That's the boss," Kostakis said. "That's him all right. I've been five years here, watchin' him as things go right and go wrong, and that's him."

"You think he's mad?"

"Nah! Not him, never that. Just lost. I reckon it's all too much for him."

That was surely true of the crisis of the moment; perhaps he shouldn't be blamed for wanting to throw himself in Daddy's lap.

I had seen enough; I had a diagrammatic idea of the Manor's exits, entrances and defenses. "Let's go back to the office area." On impulse, perhaps because the man showed a quirky brand of insight, I asked Kostakis, "Would you like to help me with an interrogation?"

He was wary. "You mean the two-clowns act—you nasty copper, me good bloke?"

"No. Just be there and put in your coupon's worth if anything suggests itself."

"Anything you say, but I'm just professional muscle; I'm not up on political shit."

I could not picture his skinniness as a strong-arm bouncer, but there can be deflating surprises in these gangling types. "Who mentioned politics?"

"That's all there is in this morgue."

Perhaps, but they were entwined with more mundane matters of which I needed independent opinion. We moved into the corridor, where I could see anyone approaching, and I asked, "What sort of a lad is Fred Blacker?"

"Why him? What's about him? All right, all right, it's your business. Young Fred—gardener's assistant, good build on him, good manners—surprise, surprise—easygoing but not a lot of brains, not so they show, anyway. Good kid if he can keep out of trouble."

"What sort of trouble?"

He hesitated a split second too long; his answer was relevant but not the answer he first thought of. "Fred's just out of the teen-gang stage, and they can call on old members if they need them for something—like a big gang stoush or special talents or whatever. You know what it's like in the Wards—don't let your old mates down, remember they looked after you, you may be off strength because you're workin', but you still live here, you're still a gangie at heart, Freddo. It's a load of shit, but it gets to them."

"Did he tell you he was a gangie?"

"You know they don't tell. They swear an oath on the arsehole of a dead chook or some stupid thing and never to break it, so strike me dead. But when a sweaty boy wears a shirt in the sun instead of UV barrier grease it's because he's hiding something—like, say, the gut

tattoo some Wardie gangs wear round the navel."

"What else would get him into trouble?"

"How do you mean?"

"What were you going to tell me before you changed your mind?"

"Clever bastard, aren't you?"

"Not very; just well trained." I had no idea how much was known by the Manor staff, but experience suggested that they kept a gossipy eye on more private matters than their employer imagined. I asked, "Would it be possible for Fred to be having it off with Melissa Beltane?"

Kostakis did not pretend surprise. "Having it off? I didn't know coppers used nice language for common habits. That pair have been fuckin' like rattlesnakes for half a year. Talk about little innocents! They thought nobody knew what they were at down behind the vine trellises. Everybody knew, even the bloody cook's offsider."

"Everybody except the girl's father."

"If you was a servant here, would you have put him wise?"

"I suppose not, but why didn't he see what everybody else could?"

"Because he's no sort of a father. Sees the girl at mealtimes of a weekend, lets her have what she wants, sends her to visit her mother on Sunday and gives her a kiss for hello and good-bye. And that's it. It isn't only her; he's the same with all of us. He doesn't know the names of half the staff; he's a working politician and that's all he is. He's got eight gardeners here and he never walks in the garden; there's an orchard and he wouldn't know a tree in it. He's got a daughter and doesn't realize she's growing up. Or he didn't until a couple of days ago."

"He certainly knows now. He was told about Fred tonight."

That upset Kostakis. "Poor bloody kid, that'll be the finish of him. He could stay jobless for life because the boss can't spare time to look after his daughter."

"I think the premier may see reason before it's all over."

"Reason!" He shook a bony finger at me as though I had offended him. "The Wardies say Beltane's a good bloke, but I tell you that all he ever sees is what goes on inside his own head."

It began to seem that quite a number of Jeremy Beltanes found shelter in that single skull.

"Come on; we'll talk to Cranko."

"That's the doctor?"

I should have known that the security crew would have been sniffing around the prisoners; they had the excuse that strangers were their responsibility. "Yes."

"You going to fill me in?"

"I can't tell you anything about him."

He misunderstood me in the true spirit of a vidscreen copshow. "We play it by ear? OK by me."

We walked into the room, and I told the guard, "We won't need you for a while. I'll call you."

He shrugged, holstered his gun slowly and marched out with the clear implication that his prisoner had been in good hands and coppers weren't needed round the Manor.

Cranko laid down the book he had been reading (it had a large gold crucifix embossed on the cover) and asked pleasantly, "Would you agree that the doctrine of the transubstantiation of the host has a genuine psychic attraction for the worshiper?"

Aside from its being a pretty clumsy demonstration of cockiness, I had no idea what he was talking about.

Kostakis had. He grunted, "Only for a cannibal."

The instant put-down flustered Cranko unreasonably. Snide intellectualism cut from under him by an obvious product of the Wards left him mentally

flat-footed, and I moved straight in on his disheveled thinking.

"Some questions, Mr. Cranko. We aren't interested in crossed identities, so—"

"So why should I answer at all?"

I had expected that. He had taken the point that Jackson's identity was not to be revealed to Kostakis, and of course, he wouldn't reveal it. It was his ace in the hole for bargaining with Beltane, but he had had to try the gambit. I carried on as though I had not heard; persistence is a good eroder of confidence.

"What did they offer for delivery of the man? What coin do they pay in? What does a high-tech Minder want that has to be cheated and betrayed for?"

He protested raggedly, "I'm not some cheap informer, Harry! I'm not for sale."

I was about to ask was he playing for some holy personal conviction when Kostakis took two quick paces and leaned over him like an avenging fury, his gentle face twisted with a viciousness that seemed to rise out of his depths. "All Minders are for sale, 'specially the brainy ones. They're the ones that want things different from other people and twice as much of it."

Cranko flinched away from him, appealing to me, "Who's this animal, Harry? This isn't right."

Kostakis slapped him hard and painfully across the mouth and bent closer until he could have spat down the man's throat, and screamed at him, "Don't call me names or I'll tear the fuckin' face off you! What was the price? A big promotion? Or maybe permission to do a really nasty experiment? How about that? Or won't some Minder woman say yes till they twist her arm for you, eh? Or maybe little boys! How about little boys?"

Accusations beaten in with brute force don't have to be true, only terrifying; they frighten because the rattled mind has been jolted out of reality into a void

where innocence has no force. Cranko's resistance collapsed in shock. He pleaded, "Harry, you can't allow this! I'm not that sort of—"

Kostakis cut him short. "Sort of what? Forget Harry; it's me you're answerin' to!" He clutched Cranko by the shirtfront and with one hand lifted him clear of the ground and shook him. I would have counted myself as having twice Kostakis's strength, but I could not have done that; the man grew more extraordinary by the minute. Now he kept needling murderously into the frightened face held level with his own. "Picked it right, didn't I? Little boys, eh? You turn over the bloke they want and they keep up the supply for you!"

Cranko must have thought he was in the grip of a maniac; he whined, "Harry, please!"

I gave him a cunning, amused grin, and he howled.

Kostakis hissed, "You want Harry, do you? Do you? Well, I'll give you to him, you bastard!"

Still holding with one hand he turned on his heel and threw Cranko at me. From two meters the surgeon struck me hard enough to stagger me and then nearly brought me down by clinging for protection. Over his head I saw Kostakis breathing hard as he collapsed onto the couch where Cranko had sat. He gave me a shattered, conspiratiorial wink, and I sensed vaguely the nature of the exhibition I had seen. He might be useless for the next ten minutes.

I pushed Cranko into a chair where Kostakis was out of his line of sight. He looked round at him once and did not turn his head gain. I had seen police violence often enough but never anything as fast and effective as Kostakis with homicidal mania in his eyes. Nor had I ever seen the miracle of the total strength of a narrow, lanky body channeled into a single, limited effort. Kostakis was an unsettling phenomenon.

I said, "Tell me about it, Doctor. Who, how, why."

"I don't know who." Cranko looked fearfully into my

eyes, willing me to believe. "It's true, Harry; I don't know who the people are."

It took me half an hour to turn him inside out and discover that he knew almost nothing of any use. Once, when he verged on indiscretion, I had to steer him away from revealing Jackson's identity, and he stammered in the knowledge that Kostakis could have it out of him in two seconds flat. He clung closer to dependence on me, ready to spew his whole brain up if I asked for it.

None of what he told me seemed to be of the slightest use in identifying the kidnappers; he was a pawn, bought at second remove and told nothing. His motive seemed to be sympathy with the political Opposition.

Towards the finish he regained some confidence, enough to remind me obliquely that the premier would protect him rather than have Jackson's identity made public.

Behind him Kostakis made his first statement since he had sat on the couch. "It's my curiosity you've got to worry about, Doc. What if I want to know sometime when Harry's not around?"

That possibility had to be scotched. I said, "Come on, Cranko; we have to talk to the premier."

Kostakis would have come with us, and I had to tell him, "Not this time. This is between the premier and us alone."

Another aspect of the man surfaced. He gazed down while his foot scuffed the carpet, the picture of a disappointed child, protruding lip and all. He muttered, "I reckon you owe me."

He didn't mean money and, uncomfortably, I reckoned so, too; that daunting exhibition had earned a payout. I reckoned also that I did not want that sharp man prying into dangerous matters, for his own sake and mine.

Playing for time, I said, "We'll talk about it in the

morning." He lifted a face full of suspicion that I was only fending him off. Which I was. "I mean it."

I would think of something by morning. And so, as it happened, I did.

Kenney was gone from the premier's office; Beltane sprawled behind his desk, one hand at his lips, eyes blankly on the ceiling, away in his thoughts. I coughed and he straightened with an expression of ambushed guilt. I'll swear he had been sucking his thumb.

He nodded to us to be seated and said to Cranko, with more disappointment than contempt, "What a reptile you've made of yourself."

"I think not." Free of Kostakis, Cranko came rapidly into form, smoothing his clothes, adjusting his face to remote superiority and making a fair attempt at a steady voice. "You have your loyalties; I have mine."

"I persuaded cabinet to approve the backing that had already been refused for your work at the institute." So one item in Kostakis's mad accusations had been near the mark. "You accepted it as payment for your silence."

"Not so; my silence was never mentioned. There was a most gentlemanly agreement between us; my response was taken as read, but it was not spelled out. You understood it so; I did not."

"I see: It was not written in the bond."

That stirred a memory of home, of Bill reciting scenes from the plays—and of the Shakespeare in the premier's bedroom along with the van Gogh portraits. Beltane was a man of moods, secret affinities and solitary fears.

"Not written," Cranko agreed.

"And if it had been?"

The surgeon laughed. "Then I should have had to betray your trust."

I said, "He'll play word games all night, Mr. Beltane. Let me tell it."

What had taken half an hour to extract, check and recheck from Cranko I told in minutes. Most of it was, anyway, common gossip in the slandering streets.

The network of informers (such as that 062 mentioned by Barney Fielding) had developed from casual fellow-traveling contacts and sources into something similar to the police system of informers, where each constable or detective knows and deals with his own snouts and there is no poaching by other coppers; it is the only way to preserve the essential secrecy.

In politics the criminal element, alerted more than once by House members themselves (once again: Corruption begins at the top) moved in to take charge of the sources and through them to squeeze the members, who paid through their two-timing noses for the information that could turn parliamentary debate into hucksters' trading. The crims covered themselves by the ancient and effective "switch" system whereby contacts were made anonymously and the same contact man was never used twice between source and buyer. The member got his information and paid for it without knowing whom he paid. He knew of but rarely met his informant, and everyone beyond that point was a shadow.

The system had pinpointed Cranko as malleable material. Somebody else, he assumed, had alerted Beltane that the surgeon was his man for clandestine work.

Cranko had not appreciated the full scope of the plan until "they" told him they wanted not only the information but also the rehandled man; they wanted the flesh to parade before the vid cameras. Snatching Jackson from the institute had been the most ticklish part of the operation until my too cunning caution gave them our route and the spot for exchange several hours before we set out; "they" had had all the time

in the world to set up their hijack of the ambulance. Beltane, they knew, would not dare any move against them that might reach the public ear; his staunchest party supporters would run for cover if a population law scandal broke around him.

There Cranko's knowledge ran out, but I had little doubt as to who had "alerted" the premier; he might also have suggested the reconstitution of the decaying father in the first place. Beltane had been trapped through the old man; Melissa was an unplanned complication, but one that could be dangerous in its own right.

(But—what was the nature of the swinging decision required of Beltane? Required by whom?)

Beltane held his head for a moment with both hands. "I should sleep, but I don't think I can."

Cranko gave a small, satisfied grunt. He would have done better to have sat quiet.

Beltane asked. "Is there more to be got from him?"

"Not immediately. He had a good squeezing; it ran out of him like juice."

Beltane grimaced a decent man's disgust at what he conceived to be police methods but could not forbear asking, "What did you do to him?"

"I, sir? Nothing at all. He begged me to listen to him." Quite true.

Cranko's professionally superior air slipped away, or it may have been delayed shock that set him squalling, between a stutter and a howl, that I was a liar and a monster who had set a homicidal sadist at him and had stood by enjoying the show.

Beltane, perplexed, doubted that I had so easily procured a homicidal sadist at that hour of night.

To enlighten him as to his ignorance of the world of his own home, I said, "One of your security men."

He was hard to convince. "They've all been screened and found thoroughly steady types. Highly dependable."

Cranko hissed, "Oh, Christ!"

"Name of Kostakis; a rather gentle bloke who claims to understand modern art."

Cranko insisted, "A raving maniac!"

Beltane was no longer interested in Cranko; he was affronted by the idea of such an anomaly on his staff and grumbling that he saw them around the Manor but did not know their names. Why should he? The secretaries dealt with them. I gathered that someone would pay for this. He saw my incredulity at his isolated incomprehension of his surroundings and only half understood it. "These people are here to look after me. That's what a staff is for, man! For God's sake, do I have to be aware of individuals every time a foot falls or a door opens? I delegate. Others are my hands and eyes and ears. I have a state to run, not a bloody household."

No doubt there was reason in that, but it was hard to believe in a man who could not call his staff by name. He said, still fuming over this new upset, "Can't we let Cranko go? I don't want him around me."

"Not yet, I think. Let your security men look after him for the night."

He did not contest my decision nor ask a question; he was used to being looked after. He fingered his desk console and ordered, "Send a guard to the Small Office."

It was not Kostakis who arrived, which was just as well; Cranko might have collapsed and I would not have blamed him. Beltane said nothing, waiting for me to give the orders; when he delegated, he delegated completely.

"Put him somewhere for the night. Lock him in and see that he doesn't get out."

The security man shot a querying glance at Beltane, who nodded slightly. My standing was established.

When we were alone I prodded him for action. "Your

daughter, now. I've no Jackson to guard, so I'm free."

"The police—"

"Forget the police. If they find her they'll get more truth out of her than you want. Let me do it."

"My father—"

"Your father is safe, asleep, locked in and guarded. Your daughter matters more, surely!"

For an unguarded instant his face told me I was wrong, that the priority was otherwise. I saw and he knew what I saw. The instant passed and the blandness returned, but he had made a decision.

He climbed out of the chair like an old man and came round the end of the desk to plant himself squarely before me and say, "I'm assured you won't repeat what you hear in this house. Is it true?"

"Yes, under moral and emotional blackmail. I promised you I would never forgive you for it." Let him keep it in mind!

"So I can't depend on you either."

"You can. How I feel doesn't matter. I am a policeman and I will do the job that was handed me."

"Yes, there was something like that in your profile— loyalty before self. I suppose it's rare enough."

Somewhere in my mind a small voice murmured, *Self-righteous?*

Beltane went back to his chair. "So I can tell you the truth and in effect be talking only to myself."

It was an aspect that had not occurred to me, the role of confidant and emotional shock absorber; it might not be an appealing role, as such, but the opportunity was too valuable to pass up.

"You could say that." And what a two-faced form of assent that was.

"Then here it is: I need Dad badly, badly. I need him here, to know that he is safe, unharmed. I need his advice, his decision. I need him."

God forbid that I should ever suffer such a binding relationship; love is enough without groveling. I
said, "But you must have your daughter home first,
because you neglected her and abused her for a trollop and because of it she ran away. Can you live with
that?"

I thought he could, but, "No. She must be found."
It was a dismal and dishonest admission, but even
heads of state must bow to conventional moral imperatives. He added, "You may regret too much freedom of
speech before you're through."

"Then I'll regret it when the time comes. Until then,
a question or two. One—Was it Nguyen who suggested
you put your father in Cranko's hands?"

He mulled over that as though the answer was
unclear. I had to prod him. "Who beside Nguyen
knew how much you missed that dribbling old man
in the back room?"

"Nobody. Nor did I ever confide in him."

"You didn't know you confided. He would have built
up the picture piece by piece from stray remarks and
simple deductions. And maybe some hypnotherapy.
He set you up."

That must have hurt him badly. A patient places
great trust in his psychotherapist; that's the strongest
weapon in the rat's armory.

He said tightly, "You have another question?"

"Why is the institute the tallest building in the city?"

It was not the change of direction that caused him to
hesitate. Secret information is still secret even from a
mute. I think he decided on a half answer that would
keep the other half hidden. "Because it is built around
a central shaft ten meters or so in diameter and forty
deep. It is a simulation chamber which can model,
on a small scale, atmospheric conditions in graduated
mixtures of temperature, pressure, wind speed and the
rest of it. Now are you any wiser?"

I thought I might be. "That's the shaft that puts the physics into their biophysics."

"More or less."

"So if I have a shaft set up for all sorts of conditions for different heights, like simulating what happens in the air between the top of Mount Everest and sea level . . . Can it do that?"

"I'm no scientist to understand completely." He had decided already that he had said too much even to his mute. He watched me as though I had sprouted a third eye and seen too clearly.

"Then you could drop a handful of very special bugs in at the top and monitor what happens to them all the way down—how long it takes, how many die, that sort of thing. And especially, how wide an area they would disperse over. Like that?"

He chose to laugh it off as if pleased with the toy confessional that could actually talk back to him. "I wouldn't know. Science is not a politician's field."

"But the results are, and I think I know what you were really talking about in Canberra."

The laughter broke up in harsh, hurtful breaths, and he bent over with his hands at his chest as if to quiet it by force. When he had calmed a little, he said, "Oh, no, you don't. You don't know that at all."

He lifted his face and he was crying. "Leave me alone! Go after Melissa, go to bed, go to hell if you like but leave me alone! You don't know a damned thing!"

7

Ostrov:
—And into the Morning

A man in decay becomes confused between trust and discretion. Beltane could tell his mute about the shaft in the institute, which was dangerous enough knowledge, but not about the Canberra discussion, though that was equally safe with me.

They had talked life and death in Canberra, no two ways about that. The institute might be at the crux with its plotting of place, time and dispersion areas.

A reasonable guess: The other six state premiers had agreed to trials, and Beltane had shuddered away from them. Now they were pressuring him to say yes because he had the institute and the bug—bacterium, virus, whatever it might be—and time was running out in a planetary flood of birthing. The prime minister also must be waiting uneasily for this decision.

I could think about this coldly; most people could. The apprehension of some manner of cull had been with us for generations, until familiarity accorded it the mental equivalent of a shrug and a philosophic, *But not just yet.* Given time, human beings can get used to any obscenity that doesn't have to be faced up to right

at this terrible minute or may, with luck, be deferred until someone else will have to do the facing.

Beltane had become suddenly the someone else, and he was not strong enough. In the same case, would I be? Nobody knows what his brain can bear. I had lived too long with the idea as part of the fabric of the world; it had lost the terror of nearness.

Or, was I wholly mistaken? Had I misjudged what had taken place in Canberra? Those overseas observers had been present. Why? What was in it for them? A watching brief for the experimental run?

Or had my guessing fallen short of something beyond the old, waiting fears?

Now, about Melissa . . .

I went back to the office, and Beltane sat there yet, hands clasped behind his head, his short bull body painfully vulnerable as he gazed at nothing. He spoke without moving: "I told you to leave me alone."

"I'm sorry, but I have work to do that won't wait and there are two things I need from you." I rode over his gesture of impatience. "First, we need a line on your father's would-be kidnappers, so can you get Mr. Kenney back here by nine o'clock?"

He straightened as though he saw me whole for the first time. "You begin to sound genuinely sure of yourself. By tomorrow morning?"

"This morning. It's been a long night." It was in fact after 2 A.M.

"That will need arranging. He is of the Opposition party; he can't risk being seen to enter the Manor."

"He did it last night; he can do it again."

He thought about it, turned it over, sighed and said, "I can't command him, but I'll manage."

"Impress him with urgency. The other thing: I want one of your security crew as a personal assistant to help me find your daughter."

"Take whoever you like. See their supervisor."

Such things, his attitude said, arrange themselves. It was hard to accept that anyone could live on so remote a plane. I had to insist that he call Jeanette from his desk console.

"A particular man," I said. "Kostakis."

He ordered it and asked, "Is that all?"

"Yes, sir. Good night."

"Good night, Sergeant."

In the security common room I received no welcome at all. Jeanette had been hauled out of bed by Beltane's call and was not friendly. I remembered her as a tough, unmotherly type.

She complained that her men were privately employed. "We aren't government goons; you've no right over us."

"Tell it to the premier."

"I will." She might—and he would tell her to see one of the secretaries.

"Where's Kostakis?"

"For Christ's sake, you don't want him right away, do you? He's gone to bed."

"Then I'll get him out. Where is he?"

She gave me terse directions to the warren of staff quarters, then relented enough to shout after me, "Gus doesn't wake happy."

"Touchy?"

"Call it looney."

"Then why is he on a high-trust watching job?"

"Because any prowler that runs into him will come out of it near dead. He breaks bones."

"That could be a virtue." She grinned nastily, seeing my bones splinter. I asked, "What does Gus stand for?"

"Gustav. Norwegian mother. That makes him a good Australian mongrel." Greek-Norwegian. Mother might account for his paleness.

I found his room, knocked gently and called his name but heard no sound. The door was not locked; I pushed it open quietly, felt for the lightpress and lit the room. Kostakis had been in bed but the sheet was turned right back as though he had risen quickly in a single coordinated move. The sheet was still warm, so I stood still and spread my empty hands out from my body.

From behind the door he said, "Good boy; you learn fast. I had to break a couple of fingers to teach the fellers not to play jokes, but some never wake up to theirselves."

"I was warned."

"I'd think twice about wreckin' a cop, anyway." It sounded more like soothing syrup than truth.

He was birthday naked, and without his clothes he was cat skinny, too finely built for the lift and throw he had used on Cranko. At a closer look he carried a fair amount of muscle on slender bones, which can be a deceptive mixture, but it did not explain his lifting some ninety kilos, one-handed, by the shirtfront. I was not sure I could do it myself and then throw it away.

He sat on the bed and waved me to the only chair. "What now?"

"Get dressed. You're seconded to me and there's work to do."

He did not question the secondment, merely looked slyly pleased as though he had forced payment from me. He was a clothes-on-the-floor type and found his singlet and shirt by stretching an arm down for them. He was half dressed before he checked his watch. "At this hour!"

"The best hour for where we're going."

"Such being?"

"Where young Melissa is."

"You know?"

"I've got a line."

"Like?"

"Handspike."

"Gangies?"

"It's probably what young Fred has tattooed on his belly. It's the brat gang that hunts the Balaclava district."

"I've never worked that side. That Fielding rabbit thought Melissa might be with them."

"How do you know about that?"

"The boys have got him on ice in one of the bedrooms, and they get curious—you know. It took about two minutes for them to get the story out of him, and they told me all about it when you went in to the boss. Do you know she's up the duff?"

"Is she, now? Tell about that."

And so he told me all Dr. Barney's stupid tale and freed my tongue to discuss it with him. There was a way round the information embargo by nudging the listener's ideas until he revealed how much he knew. If he knew enough, my freedom to talk was that much enlarged.

I told him, "Barney Fielding is a self-satisfied piker and as sloppy minded as they come. Of course Fred took her to the Handspikes. Who could do a better job of hiding her than a brat gang that knows every hole in the Ward? What other friends would hide her just for the hell of it, to cock a snook at the law? Everybody else would be yelling that they didn't want to be involved. Barney knew that and tried to get them to admit they had her, because as a doctor he looks after their bruises and breaks and has a little bit of privilege with them. But—he'd already threatened her with abortion, the idiot bastard, and of course their first loyalty was to Fred, so they denied all knowledge."

Kostakis stood up, fully dressed and gentle eyed, incapable of hurting a fly. "And you reckon she's still with them?"

"It's a place to start."

"The only place you've got. But will they truck with a copper?"

"Maybe, maybe not. Some of the older ones might remember me from three years back; I always gave them a fair go. The thing is, she'll know you and perhaps be willing to talk."

"Could be." I thought I detected a sudden uneasiness there, but he covered it quickly. "What then? What if she won't come home?"

"We play it by ear. Ready?"

"Sure." He patted his shoulder holster. "You got transport?"

"No problem."

I vidded the CIB at City Center, identified myself and asked for a car to be sent to the Manor; I didn't want an all too identifiable Manor monster. The super complained, mainly for effect and, knowing I was on a Manor job, tried to wheedle out of me why I wanted it; failing, he cursed the premier's inconsiderate use of privilege and sent the car.

The hovercar arrived at ten to four. By ten past we were as close to the Handspike hangout as innocent parties could get without raising the bratpack alarm. The police driver whooshed off into the night, leaving us alone in the not-quite-silence of a city never wholly still; streetlights were doused to conserve power in the early hours, but the sense of eyes and covert movement was never doused. Kostakis and I headed for Alma Park and the railway cutting.

The signs are that Alma Park was once a recreational area with a cricket ground, but now it was grass grown and weed grown under shrubs and trees, with ragged outcrops of asphalt where paths once had been. It was, like all the neglected old parks around the city, a place to skirt by day and stay well away from by night, a haunt of fugitives, thieves and violence. Its only decent

use was as a refuge for the city's small birds and animals; even teenage gangies had had enough ecological sense thumped into their arrogant skulls to let the wildlife alone. The park's attraction for the Handspikes was the ancient railway cutting that ran through the middle of it, thirty feet deep and overgrown, the rails long ago torn up and recycled for more urgent use. Somewhere in its three hundred meters the gangies would be gathered, most of them sleeping but with sentries posted.

The rule is: If you must go into a park at night, go in as if you mean it, standing upright and walking a direct line. Weave and dodge and try to avoid detection and the night life will be all over you from sheer need to know what you are being careful about. We marched straight along the line of fence posts, most of them broken and rusted, that still guarded the edge of the cutting though the protective wire had been stripped for reuse long ago.

After twenty meters or so I said to Kostakis, "Talk. We aren't skulking; we want to be seen and heard."

Said a young voice from the shrubbery ahead, "Well, I seen yers." And so he should have; the moon was bright enough through the cloud cover. "So stop right there."

From behind us another voice, female, said, "An' no reachin' for the pockets, neether."

The first one carried on, "Yers wantin' somethin'?"

"Some talk," I said, "with the Big Spike."

"Who are youse?"

"Tell the Big Spike that Harry Ostrov's here. Someone ought to remember me."

Beside me Kostakis giggled softly. "Big Spike! Fancies himself, that one."

The sentry whistled and someone came grunting and stumbling up the steep side of the cutting; after a short, whispered colloquy he snorted and stumbled down again. Then there was more scrambling as a group

climbed to ground level. Four or five, I thought; the Big Spike was taking no chances.

With increased numbers the air smelled of sweat and unwashed flesh. They were a scruffy lot, clad in the usual unimaginative junk they thought set them apart from and superior to the law-abiding "shitheads"; narrow chests pretended breadth and depth under the cover of fluffed-up imitation fur shirts, knobbly teen-age knees peeked from patchwork kilts; shaven scalps, painted black, made the latest in terror announcement. They all looked as though they could do with a good meal, which they probably could; most of them were, after all, street kids, whether or not they had homes to retreat to as a last resort. These stupidities made them no less dangerous when reason, never their strong point, snapped. They could be hysterically vicious, murderous.

The Big Spike pushed past the sentry and came right up to us, making a show of bravado for his watching gangies, and he had a gun in his hand. He was about fifteen. Before he could speak, I said, "I reckoned Ronnie'd be the Big Spike by now." That stamped me as familiar enough with the gang to be worth a hearing.

"Ronnie's copped it." Somebody had probably slit him up and left a vacancy for an up-and-coming young vandal.

One of the retinue said, "That's 'Arry, all right. 'E wasn't bad for copper shit. Don't know the other one."

The Big Spike asked, "Who's yer mate?"

"Name's Gus. Not a copper. I'm not a copper now, either." All right, omnipresent listening God! So I was detached on a civvy job, wasn't I?

"So what yer want?"

"Fred Blacker and his girl."

"Never 'eard of 'em."

"So you told Barney."

"That old shit! Wouldn't tell 'im nothin' anytime."

"But tell me. Fred's your old gangie. You'd help him out."

"Maybe we would, maybe not." After an impressive silence while the great man pretended to consider all sides of the matter, curiosity won out. "All right, they're 'ere, but they got sankcherry."

"Let me talk to Fred. He's in trouble and maybe I can get him out of it."

A runner was sent for Fred. More stumbling and slipping.

The Big Spike shoved his gun into his rope belt, a swagger to let us know he had no fear of us, but other guns glinted in the moonlight, keeping us covered. (Their guns were mostly for show; half of them would be jammed for lack of proper care or useless for lack of the ammunition so hard to get in a world largely stripped of small arms. But which half?) Big Spike asked, "You got guns?"

He should have thought of that earlier; he was new in the hot seat. "Think I'd tread the park without?"

He didn't try to take them from us; that could have been for him a bad move in the shadows and half light. "Then both of yers put yer hands up an' keep 'em there."

We did as told and stood in silence, feeling foolish for an age before Fred came.

He was a big lad, strongly made and not at all bad looking as the popular models went; he would have had a successful pick-and-choose sex life before Melissa hooked him to destruction. I recalled him as a one-time nuisance in the area, steadier looking now.

He studied me closely. "Harry Ostrov. I don't owe you."

"I wouldn't say that. I've kicked your arse and sent you home when I could have slammed you in the nick."

"All right, then, what do you want?"

"To take Melissa somewhere safe."

"She's not leaving me." He said it as something settled, inarguable; she was his responsibility and he had
accepted it. This was rite of passage time for Fred when
he was growing up too fast to see reason outside his
protective manhood. And, if Barney's observation was
correct, too besotted to be frightened by his situation.

I made up my mind on the spot. "You can come with
her." Beltane might rave and call down the lightning
but a concession would be in order.

"Where to?"

"To her home." I did not name the Manor, hoping
that Fred had retained sufficient sense not to reveal the
girl's true background. Apparently he had.

"She won't go there. Her father called her names.
And he'd make her have an abortion. And what do
you think he'd do to me?"

"To you, nothing. He has his own troubles. He'll be
glad just to have her back."

"She won't go home."

"I tell you she has nothing to fear from her father."

He said morosely, "I still think I have. And what
about the pop laws? She wants her kid and so do I;
it's my kid, too. That bastard, Barney, frightened her
with abortion talk like her old man. She won't go."

"Will you let me talk to her?"

"Does she know you?"

"No."

"Then what's the good?"

Playing by ear was getting me nowhere. Fred was not
belligerent, merely stubborn, while the Big Spike and
his train were showing signs of boredom.

Into the pool of silence Kostakis dropped the coupon's worth I had hoped from him. "Fred, boy, tell
her Gus from the house is here. She might talk to
me."

Fred came closer to examine him. "Gus! I couldn't see you properly in the dark. What are you doing here?"

"Just friendly interest, boy. And I got an idea where she can go instead of home."

"Where?"

"Not so fast. That's for her to hear."

"Why would she listen to you?" I heard suspicion and jealousy; this was love on a quick trigger. Poor kid.

"Because she knows something you don't, but I'll tell you now. She knows I was awake up to you two all along, but I kept it to myself and I reckon that was friendly of me. She ought to give me a hearing."

Would that bring her? Had she, perhaps, a secret with Kostakis, a debt he could call in? A policeman's suspicions don't exempt his allies.

Fred said reluctantly, "All right," and started down the cutting.

Time dragged and my arms ached; I locked the fingers behind my head and that helped a little but I felt uncomfortable and silly, bailed up like any sucker by a pack of brats. But they were murderous brats and Gus and I were the weak force. I noticed that Gus's hands were raised as high as mine but did not touch his head; he kept them there, unsupported, and still seemed at ease.

After an age of silent stress the girl came through the shrubbery. She was a big girl, nearly as tall as Fred, and she had nothing in the way of a figure. She was not dumpy in the rolls-of-fat sense, just straight up and down, shapeless, with nothing much wrong that exercise and some mealtime restraint wouldn't cure, but her face was sullen and short of the signs of burgeoning character that should be visible at sixteen years old. My immediate thought was, What did the boy see in her to land himself in this mess?

The possessiveness in his bearing as he led her towards us said he saw much that I could not. In a

less fraught situation it would have been touching.

She said with only a touch of suspicion, "Gus," and stood still, gazing and puzzled. "Why did he send you?"

"He didn't. Daddy doesn't know about this little jaunt."

She took a half pace back into the safety of Fred's solid presence. "Then what are you here for?"

"To get you out of trouble."

"I'm not in any trouble."

"Not yet, but your boyfriend is."

"Fred?" She turned to look closely at him in the half dark as if he might be a fresh complication. "Fred isn't afraid."

That was a shocker. To her it was a matter of plain fact, needing no discussion; almost certainly she had never seriously considered the danger to him of his involvement. Barney Fielding had been right; to her Fred was just a useful appendage, a bodyguard and comforter.

Kostakis said slowly, clearly, as to a child, "Then Fred can start being afraid right now."

The boy answered him, loudly and aggressively, "I can take care of Melly."

"Like hell you can! Listen, you two! Barney Fielding will be squealing to the coppers by morning to save his own skin for not reporting a pop law evasion. What happens to Fred then? And to his mum and dad that harbored his girl? What about them, Fred?"

Fred, stupid with love and gallantry, said, "I stick with Melly."

"She'll be all right; Daddy will see she doesn't cop a penalty." Then Gus shot the bolt he had saved for last. "But who'll look after the Handspikes?"

The Big Spike and his sentries had been acting sophisticated boredom, above all this shop talk, but suddenly they were in the middle of the exchange.

The Big Spike said quickly, "Nobody knows she's 'ere."

"That's what you told Barney and what he told us, but me and Harry came straight here just the same. You know why? Just in case you didn't trust Barney any more than anybody else would, is why. And the coppers will think exactly the same way. Eh, Harry?"

"That's right," I said, and picked up his lead. "And all you Handspikes won't last ten minutes with your little pistols if the cops decide to clean you out. They'll gas the cutting and pick you out with copter claws, and don't you know it!"

The Big Spike was not slow on the uptake when his skin was in question. "You reckon they'll care that much? About her?" He believed; danger is always believable when you live on the thin edge. He turned on Fred. "Who is this bitch of yours? Maybe she isn't just a Minder bitch lookin' for a Wardie thrill." He shoved his face into Melissa's in the half light, and her eyes were frightened as he accused her of the worst thing he knew. "Is your dad a copper, is he?"

I put in quickly, "You could call him the head man of all the coppers."

The Big Spike pulled Melissa out of the way and confronted Fred in fury. "You never said that! You never told me! You never said her dad was the top copper!" I have to say for Fred that he stood his ground although he was as close to a gangie payoff as anyone would ever want to be. He grabbed the terrified Melissa and held her close while the Big Spike howled in near hysteria, "I oughta spill yer rotten guts on the grass, yer bastard! Yer put the whole gang in the shit!"

Kostakis raised his voice. "Not if we take her away with us."

Melissa became hysterically noisy. "I won't go to Daddy! He'll take my baby away!"

"Shut up, yer stupid bitch! I don't give a fuck about yer baby. I got my gangies to look after, an' you don't mean nothin'!"

Kostakis said before she could start squalling again, " 'Course you can't go to your daddy. We'll take you to your mum's place."

"She'll only tell him."

"You reckon? She doesn't like him all that much and she'll listen to us when we explain. She'll look after you just to spite him. I know your mum; she'll listen to me." Melissa also seemed to listen to him; he added, for good measure, "She'll look after Fred, too."

At last Fred was interested.

The Big Spike strode close to Kostakis. "You dinkum?"

"I'll get 'em off your hands, and Harry'll stop the coppers looking. That's all you got to worry about. Right, Harry?"

"Right. I can stop them; I've still got contacts."

"Then get 'em outta here!" He turned to Fred and Melissa. "Get goin', the pair o' yers! And don't you never come near us again, Fred. Brother'ood's cut, right now!"

Because my shoulders were now aching like centers of rheumatism, I said, "For Christ's sake, let's go. Come on, you two."

We backed away a good twenty paces, the gangies watching us with guns up and ready. Fred came after us, half dragging a crying Melissa who seemed now to have believed nothing said by anybody. When the gangies at last took a couple of backward paces and vanished behind the shrubs I was able to lower my arms, with shoulder joints grinding.

We reached the comparative safety of Alma Road before Fred asked, "What about my mum and dad?"

"They won't be touched."

"How do you know that?"

"Because I'm not an ex-copper; I'm a serving detective-sergeant, and I'll see they aren't pulled in."

"Jesus!" said Fred and I don't know whether he was awed, gratified or dismayed. He asked, "What about you, Gus? Are you something else besides a security guard?"

"Not me, boy. What you see is what you get."

Privately I doubted that.

Melissa, still full of a fugitive's suspicions, asked, "How would a man like you know my mother?" and seemed unaware of insult. That school of hers must have been an outpost of aristocracy operating on a closed circuit.

Kostakis was cheerfully uninsulted. "Never seen her in my life. Now don't start bawling again; if she won't play we'll find someone else."

And so, I thought, he probably would. Choosing him had been a stroke of idiot genius.

At 5:15 the streaks of dawn were livening in the east and the Balaclava police station was within ten minutes' walking distance. There we picked up another car after a reference to the Manor stopped protest in its teeth. I hoped it might be possible to fit in a short nap before the morning conference with Kenney and Cranko.

Mrs. Ivy Beltane lived in the Dandenong foothills, which meant either that she had private means or that Beltane could afford to keep her in lush style; it also meant a longish trip, with my short nap as a casualty. From the Balaclava station I vidded her home and waited while she failed to hear or was slow getting out of bed. Then a male voice answered without clearing the screen at his end; he sounded very much at home and out of temper.

Melissa said crossly, "That's Val. I don't like him." She pushed past me to the microphone and said, "It's me, Val. Get Mummy!"

"Melissa? At this hour? What the devil's up with you?" I thought he didn't care much for her, either.

She repeated, "Get Mummy. I'm in trouble."

"You could have picked a better time for it. Hang on."

I asked, "Who's Val?"

"Oh, you know . . . he lives there."

One of the consolations of loneliness.

A woman's voice spoke, still without clearing the screen. "What's wrong, Melissa? Is it something serious?" It was a pleasant voice, concerned but not flustered.

I butted in. "Police here! I have your daughter with me and I want to take her to you right away."

"What trouble is she in?" No panic there.

"Not very much, Mrs. Beltane; I think we've cleaned up most of it. Could you let the details wait until we get there? She hasn't been harmed. I'm ringing to make certain she will be welcome."

"Welcome? My daughter? Are you out of your mind? Of course she must come here. Why should you think I might not want her?"

Best to make it short and sharp, because Melissa's time of secrecy was over. "She is pregnant."

Melissa began to cry again and Fred whispered in her ear. The mother was silent for a while, but we could hear Val muttering in the background, sounding like a spate of objections delivered at speed. She hissed at him to shut up and spoke to the vid again. "Why can't she go to her father?"

"Best to keep him out of it for a while, I think."

Her tone changed. "That I can imagine! It would make demands on his time, keeping it out of the news. Bring her here." She was no Jeremy fan.

"And the boy, the father? I have him, too."

"My God, you've got a nerve!"

"It may seem so to you, ma'am, but I'm sure you realize the political implications. It would be best to have both of them out of sight until other arrangements can be made."

Ivy Beltane began to say, "She'll have to be abort—" and Melissa shouted over her, "I won't! I won't! I want my baby."

There was desperation in her voice, but somehow not the urgency of a mother fighting for her child; the determination was loud and clear, but something other than maternal love gave it strength. I saw that Kostakis watched her with head cocked and teeth closed over his lower lip. Only Fred seemed in his normal state of unquestioning devotion.

The mother said in no motherly tone, "We'll discuss that when you get here. I will be waiting for you, Officer."

"About half an hour," I said, and she cut the connection while Val still argued in the background.

Melissa returned promptly to hysteria, and we left her to Fred to deal with; his loving patience cared beyond any sympathy I could feel for her just then. It took him ten minutes to calm her to the point where we were ready to leave in the police hovercar.

I put the pair of them in the front with the police driver and switched off the communicator so that Kostakis and I could talk privately in the rear. As we slipped over the road to the Dandenongs I told him that I felt I owed him a debt for his performance in Alma Park.

He said, "Reckon I'm paid."

"How?"

"Workin' with you. That's what I wanted."

Another romantic? They come in all shapes and sizes. "Do you think police work is all like tonight's game with a bratpack? It isn't."

"Better than walking the Manor grounds six hours a day fighting off intruders that never come."

"Makes a nice change, does it? You earned it, thinking of the mother."

"Should have thought of her yourself."

So I should have. "The truth is that Melissa is a side issue. All the time I'm thinking of something much more important than her."

"About the one who nearly got pinched off you?"

"What do you know about him?"

"Nothing really."

"You and your mates deviled a story out of Fielding; what did you get out of Cranko?"

He put his hands up defensively. "Fielding's only shit, but Cranko's got status and influence. Nobody was going to put the scares up him. That was all right while you was backing me but he could be real bad news afterwards if security tried it on."

"Is that all you know?"

"That's all."

"Sure?"

He was upset. "You'll learn I tell the truth, Harry."

"Except when a lie smooths the way, as in telling Melissa you know her mother."

"That wasn't a lie, Harry; that was a stratagem."

Mockery was barely audible. My father would love this one; I would have to take him home someday. "Gus, do you think she'll make a good mother?"

"Melly? She wouldn't know which end pisses. These Minder girls are brought up pig ignorant. They learn how to be society hostesses and that's about it."

"She knew enough to get Fred."

"They learn that off secret porn vids and lavatory walls and think they know it all. Then the real thing knocks 'em for a screaming loop because it wasn't like that in the vidplay." He eyed me distrustfully, having more to say and weighing my acceptance of it. "She

got me before young Fred. And I wasn't the first."

That was not the surprise it might have been for some. In my years in the force I had seen too much of sexual ignorance displaying itself as easy access. "Who started it? You?"

"Fair go, Harry! I'm not in the kiddy market."

He sounded honest rather than outraged—within his uncertain definition of honesty. "So?"

"She just walked up one day and put her hand on it and said she'd yell for help if I didn't give it to her. She might've. I wasn't going to risk her doing it."

"That from a sixteen-year-old?"

"Fifteen then. And she was no virgin."

A fresh and unlovely portrait of Melissa emerged; Beltane's lack of interest in his daughter could be a political rope to hang him. I was haunted by the false note I had heard in the girl's voice. "Do you think she might have been trying to get a child by no matter who?"

"I think so now, but it wasn't me that filled her up. I take the pills."

"You think so now? You think she doesn't sound like a loving mother-to-be?"

He concentrated, frowned and said, "You know what she sounds like when she starts yelling about having the kid? She sounds like someone seeing all her hard work go for nothing. It's got nothing to do with Fred; she don't give him a thought unless she wants something."

Similes are never quite right but this one had a homing-in ring to it. She could not bear the thought of the prize being snatched from her.

Mrs. Beltane was dark, much younger than her husband—say, forty-fiveish—and good looking without being a beauty; her figure was what Melissa's should have been with attention to exercise and diet. She was

also self-possessed, direct and intelligent; Beltane had been a fool to lose her.

To Melissa she said, without preamble, "It was deliberate, wasn't it? I saw it coming and gave you preventive pills, but you didn't use them. Later you will tell me why; for the moment we must think what to do."

Melissa said nothing at all and for once did not crowd poor Fred for comfort; he seemed overwhelmed by his surroundings and afraid to move. Mrs. Beltane assessed him in a deliberate, slow summation and seemed to decide that her daughter might have done much worse. "I suppose that the rule is: If you must throw yourself at a Wardie, pick a good-looking one and hope to God." After that she paid no attention to him though he flamed lobster red down to the chest. "Still, there's a price to be paid for stupidity. The two of you can sit in the kitchen while I talk to these gentlemen."

Being treated as children, as a problem to be solved by responsible adults, had an effect. There was not a peep out of Melissa, who showed a wary respect for her mother; she went in silence with a dazed Fred trailing behind, surprised eyes trying to take in his surroundings with a sort of cowed envy. Ivy Beltane's house was nothing special as Minder houses go, though a dozen times better than anything I was likely ever to live in. Like all Minder places, it had too much of everything—or so it seemed to me—too many pieces of furniture serving only to fill up space, too many decorations on walls and shelves, too many hangings where a single blind or curtain would have done, so much of everything that it looked like an exhibition of what can be got for money. Don't think I was contemptuous; I would have given a slice of my life to live under conditions as clean and convenient and easy to look at, but it would have taken me years to get used

to them. Fred was shaken and a bit frightened by what may have appeared to him real grandeur; he had probably never been so far as inside the back door of the Manor. Though I knew this was only what they call middle class, it left me uncomfortable, too.

When they were gone, Mrs. Beltane said, "I knew she had hot pants and God knows I lectured her enough, yet she even made a play for Val."

Val, a little middle-aged and a little portly and not wholly at ease in his role as man of the house, said, "It was embarrassing. One did not know what one should do."

"You knew exactly what; you told me before worse happened."

There was no doubt who wore the trousers, but Val had his eye on legal safety as well as on his lady's love. "She must go back to her father, Ivy. She can't stay here. You lay yourself open to a harboring charge."

"Harboring? I'm her mother! You'll go before she does. In any case, Sergeant Ostrov is the police and he brought her here for me to harbor."

I said, "Temporarily, ma'am. Until the premier gets his affairs sorted out. I assure you that he has matters on his mind more urgent than an illegal birthing. Your daughter is better out of the way for a while."

Val gave an I-have-done-my-best shrug and contented himself with listening. Mrs. Beltane was more upset than she allowed us to see. "She would have been better off with me all the time, but I agreed to let him have her while I took the blame for our separation in order not to foul his political career. The honorable member had to be stainless in the eyes of the electorate! I could tell them a tale! Do you know why I left him?"

"No, ma'am; it's no business of mine."

"I have sometimes wondered if the police knew—or the secret service, whatever that may be." She pressed

a bell push. "You could do with a cup of tea, I suppose? Real tea from New Guinea?"

A nondescript male servant appeared and she ordered, "Tea for four. And give the children something in the kitchen; at their age they'll want breakfast." He disappeared and she continued with no change of tone, "I could throw Jeremy to the dogs if I opened my mouth—and his disgusting father after him."

Then she switched to small talk with no sound of social gears changing. The business session was over. We drank our tea from ridiculously flimsy china, feeling like clumsy gutterbums, and left.

Minders also, it seemed, had their home dramas— just like the sillier vidplays.

The police hovercraft dropped us at the Manor just before seven o'clock. It had been a long night and the new day was no tonic for me.

Gus, insultingly fresh, asked, "What now?"

"Breakfast. A quiet nap. I've a meeting at nine o'clock."

"Do I come to it?"

"Not this one." Perhaps my subconscious was performing better than my tired, rest-needing forebrain, because I changed my mind. "Yes, you can be in on it. I'll pick you up when we're ready."

His gentle, infinitely deceitful face lit up with unspoken thanks.

Beltane was not in the Small Office. Asleep at last, perhaps, despite his cares. Or because of them. I needed an hour on the spine for myself; thirty-six-hour stretches were not unusual on intensive cases and I had learned to snatch at opportunity.

I told security that I would be on the couch in the Small Office and that I should be wakened at 8:15.

They accepted my authority with resignation.

I fell asleep in the middle of a thought that I stank of a night's sweat and tension.

A guard woke me on time and told me where my own bedroom had been prepared. He said, straightfaced, "Chauffeur Willy's having fits over a body in the boot of the limo. Did you forget a little thing like that?"

Yes, I had forgotten the damned thing in the piling up of events. "Tell him to ferry it to the police morgue in City Center for identification and to tell them I'll make a full report later in the morning."

"Your job, I'd think."

"You an ex-cop?"

"So what?"

"So for Christ's sake try to help instead of standing on your civil rights. The Manor's in crisis."

He eyed me with personal hostility. Crisis in the Manor was a security affair, in his book, but he hadn't the nerve to carry it through. "OK. I'll do it."

My case had been taken to my room. There was a shower recess; by eight-thirty I was in clean clothes and looking for Kostakis.

Whether he had slept or not, he looked daisy fresh. I asked, "What time's breakfast?" and he told me, "When you want it. This is the ever-flowing trough."

"Now?"

"Me, too."

He took me to the security wardroom, which was for once empty, and buzzed the kitchen for food.

While we waited, I quizzed him. "You'd be a bad man in a brawl, I'd think."

He became at once reserved, noncommittal. "Can be."

"And stronger than you look."

"No. Just ordinary."

"I'd put Cranko at ninety kilos. You don't throw that around 'just ordinary.' "

"Some special training." The peculiar man was bashful.

"As in how to concentrate and coordinate mind and muscle to get the effect of hysterical strength."

"Something like that."

"Tell me about it, Gus. Give out."

He mumbled as if it was all a terrible embarrassment, "Can't keep it up, of course. A big effort, then I have to rest up. You can only use what's there, but all at once instead of a bit at a time."

"The energy equation is conserved."

"Eh? What's that?"

Gus was purely a practical man, without theory. I suggested, "Oriental stuff?"

"In a way." He capitulated. "Look, Harry, I had to have some self-respect. Physically, I mean. Better than the next bloke."

"Why?"

"Well . . . because I don't love this security work, but I'm not much good for anything else. And who wants to be a Wardie on Suss? I wanted to be an artist, but I got no talent, only thought I had. I like poetry, but I can't even remember to speak proper English. So I got this job where you don't need to know much except what you're told, and still I was with blokes who could run rings round me when a brawl come up. I felt useless. Then this Asian psychiatrist spotted me as delivering less than a full dollar on the job and got to work teaching me how to use what I've got instead of whining about it. Lot of concentration and pinpointing your intention and all that, but it works."

Kostakis as a bruised soul! I didn't dare laugh. "From what I've seen, it surely does. Nguyen?"

"Yes, but why'd you pick him?"

"He turns up in everything connected with my job here, and I don't trust him."

"No?" He reached across the table to grab my hand. "I don't trust anybody all the way. Not even you."

I pulled my hand back. "What's against me?"

"Nothing. We're just different people. There's always some point where nobody can trust another person."

There seemed no end to his oddities. "For example?"

"You killed a man last night."

"If you'd been me, so would have you."

"But I would have been sick all night afterwards."

"Why? He would have shot me."

"It isn't about right or wrong; it's about feeling. There's no way you can feel right about killing someone. A man's alive and then, all of a sudden, nothing. Think of it happening to you!"

I had had this conversation during the past night; Kostakis was carrying on with the things Beltane had left unsaid, as though I were under fire for . . . for what? Righteousness? "Thinking about it wouldn't help. It might make me hesitate and then I'd be dead instead of him. And once I was dead it wouldn't mean anything at all to me, would it?"

"But you shoot first to stay alive, don't you?"

"You mean life is precious? Mine is—to me."

"And the other bloke's isn't?"

That was the stopper. *No* would have been a not quite true answer, but the other man's life wouldn't bother me too much. Kostakis had a point, but it was in fact a matter of right and wrong. Getting sick over death was meaningless. When a thing was done, what did regret achieve?

Kostakis was saying, "Jeanette says you're hard in the head, a right-and-wrong man. But nobody's hard all the way through."

His persistence became an irritation. "For Christ's sake, Gus, everybody needs somebody else, but he doesn't have to need the whole goddamned population!

You're like Beltane—" I stopped dead there because I began to see the nature of Beltane's problem—not the problem itself but the idea of intractable choice. I saw why I had put it aside as one I did not want to share. Now my moral ground was in question as a right-and-wrong man.

Instant psychology was averted by Jackson in dressing gown and slippers and a full morning grouch.

"I've been looking everywhere for you! What's been going on all night, Harry? Why am I shut out of what's happening?"

"You aren't shut out, Mr. Jackson; you're a linch-pin—"

The PA system shouted suddenly, "Vid for Detective Sergeant Ostrov."

There was a screen in the room, but I could not guess who might be calling. I said into the mike, "I'll take it in the Small Office."

The Small Office was empty, and the miniature desk screen was alight with Ivy Beltane, both frightened and angry. She cried out, "Val's gone! We went back to bed, but he got up again when I slept."

I did not jump to the connection that was obvious to her, and she shrieked into the screen, "He was afraid. You saw that! He was afraid of a harboring charge!"

"He'll go to the police? I can fix that."

"Not them! He's taken his clothes, so he isn't coming back. He's a mean spirit, and he'll want money. It's all he ever wants. He'll sell the story to the channels. They'll pay a lot for it."

They surely would! I had a vision of her home invaded by the merciless vidpress; there would be no right of privacy, no pity or mercy. "How long has he been gone?"

"I can't tell. At least an hour. Maybe more."

"Pack a bag. I'll send a car for you and the kids. Quarter of an hour, so be ready! You've got to be out of

there before the newsbugs get their claws into you."

"Where to?"

"The Manor, of course. They can't get in here."

She seemed distraught. "Jem won't have me in the place—"

"Oh, yes, he will! Get moving!"

I cut the connection before she could waste time with protests and uncertainties, and put out a PA call for Jeanette, who answered at once. "Do you have a security car available? Not a Manor car."

"Yes." She sounded, like her men, resigned.

"Please, this is mad urgent. Get Kostakis to pick up Mrs. Beltane and bring her here with Melissa and Fred."

"And Fred? You said Fred?"

"Explanations later. He has to get there before the newsbugs find them." She began to say something but I talked over her. "Gus is in the wardroom. Please, just do it!"

By the time I reached the wardroom Kostakis was already gone, my breakfast was on the table and Jackson was drinking tea—real tea in the Manor.

"Is it any use asking questions, Ape?"

I checked the time. "In just seven minutes we'll get the nine o'clock news and perhaps more answers than anybody wants." They would work as fast as that to get a hot scoop on the air before others smelled it out.

I switched on the room screen, and we were at once in the middle of a brutal lead-up. Third Channel had it; it had been my guess that hungry Val would go for their standing "story of the week" offer and the channel had seen it as good enough to deserve a promo.

The little cartoon, Snoop Monkey, was parting the bushes with lickerish expectation and swinging his camera up to catch something just out of view, while the voice-over belted out a promise of titillation to come: "Have we got something for you on the *Nine*

O'clock News or have we got it! Just a hint to whet your attention so you can grab your crotches and hold on for the porno feature of the century! What you like in the Wards is just the same as what they like up in the society lovenests, and this item is as high up as you can get! Just five and a half minutes left for drooling until Third Channel brings you the hottest love story since Samson trashed the temple—and maybe there'll be somebody important rocking under the pressure when this roof falls in on him."

Jackson heard it with glowering distaste, unaware of worse to come. He exploded, "And those disgusting animals squawk about the 'public right to know'! Bedroom crawlers! In my day that snake would have been sacked on the spot for such a performance!"

Would he? Had vidcasts changed so much in a couple of decades? Overseasoned hype had become so common that we scarcely heard it; it was just noise preluding a story that nine times in ten would be an innocuous beat-up. But this was the tenth time. I hoped, felt like praying, that Kostakis was a criminally fast driver.

Then I realized what Jackson had said.

"Please remember not to say things like 'in my day.' Say it a few times and people will be puzzled, and puzzled people ask questions."

He snapped, "We're alone, aren't we?" then conceded ungraciously, "I'll remember." The screen was now displaying some harmless fill-in oddment, but he continued to glare. "Has public taste found its level in the gutter at last?"

"It was never far above it."

"There are limits to public barbarism. Jeremy should have it stopped. Does nobody complain?"

"Those that don't like the mass communicators tune to First Channel. That's the one for propriety and art shows and good English grammar."

"Then shift to First Channel."

"I think you should listen to this news; this may be the only channel to carry it."

"Why should I?"

For all his abrasiveness he was at bottom an old man, lost and afraid and covering fear with pugnacity—and due for a considerable shock. I thought of my own dad, never quite recovered from the collapse of his world, and had no courage to brief Jackson beforehand. Besides—and it was true that I could never forget being a cop who wanted every scrap of information—it was necessary to know exactly what had been told to this squawking public vidmouth.

The Third Channel fanfare blared over the logo, and the screen faded it out as it faded in the head and shoulders of Ivy Beltane's decamped lover, Val. He stared doggedly into the camera, unhappy with the publicity (had he imagined the channel would let him get away with anonymity?) but seeing it through because Albie Aldridge, the "Wardies' communicator and great good mate," allowed him no choice. Albie's face appeared, with its soundtrack *ta-da,* in the top right corner as he gave the wink that meant "all the news that's fit to tell and just a whisker more," and launched into his spiel.

"See this gentleman, all you good citizens, and be glad there are still a few like him—men who will stand for the truth when truth needs to be told. This is a pop law story and a political story and a sex story, and I can tell you right now that Mr. Val Frewby is the top contender for our regular bonus for breaking the story of the week. A bigger story would have to be a war."

Beside me Jackson snorted disgust. The screen switched to a view of a big, rambling, old-style house set among trees and lawns. "This is the Fitzhugh Ladies' College and School of Culture, where the girl children of the wealthier Minders—the super-Minders you might say—go to be educated. Educated? Curious word, that.

They go to learn how to make polite conversation and do the old-time waltz with icy elegance and choose the right spoon for oysters—or is it a fork for oysters? But it seems they also learn a few things not on the ostensible curriculum. Like, for instance, sexual behavior. You see, one of these highborn young ladies has got herself pregnant—or, as they say in the Wards, up the duff!"

Val's head and shoulders surfaced again. "Tell us about it, Val." *Sing for your supper, Val.* "When did you see the little lady, Val?"

"This morning. The police got us out of bed, saying they had these two kids and the girl was pregnant."

"Cops? Why the cops?"

"Because she'd run away and they'd been put on to finding her."

"And find her they did, pregnant and all. But what's unusual about that? The little lady takes her blue pill and it's all over. So what's different here, Val?"

"She didn't take the pill when she should have."

"And so?"

"So she's five months gone and swearing she won't have an abortion. And her mother's on the girl's side. She's taken her in to look after her."

A rat and a half, Ivy's Val. He'd run like a rabbit from the mere suggestion of harboring and run straight for the money.

Albie said sweetly, "The little lady is just sixteen, not married or engaged to be married and so has no legal right to birthing. Correct, Val?"

"Correct, sir."

"Well, there's still time to fix it all up—but both mother and daughter say, No abortion!" With a wild change of emphasis he screamed, "Who the hell do they think they are!" His face expanded to fill the screen, the face of the fighter for right and truth and the underdog! "Who are these Minders who think they are above the law, think they can assume the

sacred privilege of parenthood at their own arrogant wish and thumb their high-class noses at decency and deprivation? Would you like to know who, you Wardie millions? What would happen to you if *your* daughter was illicitly pregnant and you parents were not merely harboring but conniving? Doesn't bear thinking about, does it? So, who are they? Well, here's the daughter."

On the screen appeared a street snap of Melissa, taken a couple of years earlier and not easily recognizable. Jackson, at any rate, did not recognize her as the tiny girl he remembered in flashes.

"Know her? Of course you don't. You Wardies aren't society; you don't get to meet such people. But some of you may remember Mama."

He had a fairly recent picture of Ivy Beltane. Jackson made a sound of glottal shock, and I put out a hand to steady him. He trembled violently.

"This is Mrs. Ivy Beltane, wife of our much-respected premier, Jeremy Beltane, from whom she separated—amicably, so it is said—well, so it is said—a dozen years ago. And the daughter is Melissa Beltane, their one and only child. And Daddy is liable to be granddaddy pretty soon unless justice is done. But will justice be done? Well, now . . . if Val Frewby hadn't done the honorable thing and blown the whistle on this family setup, and if your Third Channel watchdog, old Albie, hadn't seen at once that you had a right to know of these top-flight shenanigans, justice might well have been thwarted. If you have money and position you can get away with most things—until you are found out!"

With an obscene switch to virtue (and an escape route) he carried on, "Don't think I am maligning Premier Beltane, the people's premier. We don't know yet what he has to say, or even if in some fashion this has been kept from him." Yes, old Albie's arse was kept clear of the firing line. "You can be sure we will be seeking comment from the premier as soon as he

is available. In the meantime one question remains unanswered. Who is the father? Do you know, Val?"

Val reappeared, more confident now. "I've seen him, Albie. I don't know his name, but I could tell by his speech that he's a Wardie kid."

Albie exulted, "A Wardie kid; people! The princess and the pauper, eh? There's a phrase the girls learn in their highfalutin finishing schools—*nostalgie de la boue.* I looked it up only just now. It's French so maybe my accent isn't quite right, but I can tell you what it means. It means, they still like rolling in the mud! Well, the princess may come out of it smelling like a rose, but God help the boy from the mud!"

Jackson pawed helplessly at my arm. "Take me to my room, Harry. Please, Harry." He couldn't see for tears.

"I can tell you the premier didn't know. She managed to hide it." A kind lie, I hoped.

He whispered, "It will be the finish of Jeremy. A pop law scandal is the end."

Perhaps, but I saw worse to come. As I guided him through the passages I tried to explain to him why, in spite of the trash-stirring Albie and his like, Jeremy might still come through.

He shook his head. "Somebody knows about me, too."

"I think we can head that scheme off."

That is, I hoped we could.

I got him into his room and onto the bed before I recalled that I was late for the meeting I had set up myself.

Kenney was there, calm and neat and collected. So was Fielding; I hadn't asked for him, but he might be useful.

Beltane waved me to a chair. "I know why you're late. We've seen it."

He was unbelievably sprightly, nothing like the man who had been up most of the night, bowed under shock and strain. He was the kind, perhaps, who faced up poorly to the gathering storm but came together as a fighter when it broke.

Kenney nodded coolly to me; Fielding stared at the carpet.

"I'm told you have sent for my wife and Melissa and the boy. Thank you for moving quickly, but you should have brought the youngsters here in the first place."

"She needed sympathetic understanding."

His face became very still. At length he said, "Yes," and after another pause, "that was proper thinking. We'll deal with the situation when they get here. You will have heard that vidlouse say he would try to get a statement from me. He'd better have one or he'll speculate worse things. He's survived enough defamation actions to know his limits, but he still spits poison."

Kenney said, looking at me, "The truth should do. Why be complicated?"

I could only agree. "Your daughter was not pregnant to the eye; you knew nothing of it until, say—late last night. She left home under pretense of going to school and the police have been searching for her. You will see her later this morning. That's enough."

"And what then?"

I had no ideas but Kenney had. "Wait until your statement has been vidcast, then get the First Channel pollsters into the Wards to sift opinions. The analysis the sergeant gave last night may be correct. At least you'll know, one way or the other."

"Thank you. I wasn't expecting help from you, Dick."

"Just a suggestion. And that Aldridge disgusts me. Besides, I also need to know."

How to fight dirty while maintaining decency.

Barney Fielding was still rancorous over his own stupidities, still wanting to hurt someone, anyone, if

he could do it safely. "Albie told the truth, didn't he? He told it in the people's language. They like him."

Kenney said, "The people are sheep."

That stirred a little venom in me. "Of course they are because that's what you and your kind have made them. They're bound up in their personal affairs because just staying decently alive takes all their attention; they've none to spare for your political caperings until you do something that hurts them. Then see how sheeplike they are! The people have a nasty way of looking straight at the truth while you argue ideology. Treat them like sheep and you'll finish up trampled by bulls."

Fielding grinned. "Sergeant Ostrov for the grimy people! All red and bothered about them."

Beltane's console buzzed, and he picked up the earpiece, listened and grimaced. "The channel. Put them on. On the big screen." On the left wall of the Small Office a painted hanging rolled up to uncover a wall screen, already lighting to show a half-length of a smallish, bald-headed man in shirt sleeves sitting at a desk. His eyes were furious, but his voice under control as he said, "Good morning, Premier."

"Good morning." Not frigid but barely interested.

"I am the chief news editor for Third Channel, and I offer the apologies of the channel and myself for the embarrassing news release concerning your daughter and yourself on the nine o'clock roundup."

He paused expectantly. Careful people, even premiers, treated the channels with respect and kid gloves. Beltane said, "Rubbish! Get on with it."

The news editor's eyes were feral, but he was under orders to placate. "I am instructed to ask if you have any statement to make for the ten o'clock 'cast. This should have been asked of you before the original announcement was made. It certainly would have changed the nature of Mr. Aldridge's delivery."

"Would it? Can you teach an old hyena new tricks?" The editor waited, hating. "Well, yes, I have a statement. You will notice that I deliver it in the presence of Mr. Dick Kenney, a shadow minister from the Opposition benches. He will, I think, vouch for my honesty."

So much for the secrecy of Kenney's visit. Beltane was not above taking advantage, and Kenney could explain to his party as best he might. Beltane gave his statement much in the words I had suggested. To the editor's questions he replied that he had nothing to add until he had seen his daughter, who had not yet arrived home.

The editor had a final message. "Your statement will be on air at ten o'clock. I am instructed to tell you also that Mr. Aldridge is to be severely disciplined for gross violation of news channel ethics in not contacting you before his 'cast. Good morning, sir."

The screen blanked. Beltane asked the air, "Now what was that disciplinary nonsense about?"

"Reassuring you," Kenney suggested. "Letting you think the channel will soft-pedal from now on."

"Which it won't, if that man's eyes give a straight message. But why take it out on Aldridge?"

I had an idea about that. "Somebody high up in the channel administration is venting spite. A bigger blast was being readied, but Aldridge hadn't been consulted and he got in first with the wrong story. Now they're committed to testing the wind on the premier's popularity before they let loose with the big one."

Fielding asked, "What big one?"

I said, "Get him out of here. He's not in this." A security man was summoned to march Fielding out.

Kenney mused, "I am in this, am I? Well, then, what big one?"

Beltane told him: "About twelve hours ago the kidnap failed. I am sure that by now the Opposition network will have got round to telling so senior a member

as yourself that the Cranko ploy had gone astray."

Kenney played at thinking it through, pursing his lips, shaking his head, crossing and uncrossing his legs, enjoying the stretched-out moment. When he was ready he said, "Yes, J.B., I would like to see your father in his new guise. Last night's 'Mr. Jackson,' I take it?"

His imperturbability needed shaking. "Presume what you like, but you can't see him. He's in distress." Beltane cocked an eye at me, considering how much of me he would continue to put up with, and I said to him, "Jackson's my responsibility, and I want him properly recovered. It's him we have to discuss—and not to his face while half of his knowledge is still unrecovered. From what I hear of you, Mr. Kenney, you wouldn't dirty your political fingers with kidnapping for blackmail, so just when did you hear of the kidnap plan?"

"Do you propose to arrest me?"

"Whatever for?"

"Then I will not answer questions."

"You will, Mr. Kenney, if I have to beat answers out of you."

Beltane made some horrified interjection that passed me by, and Kenney sat up straight in his chair. Beyond that he did not seem too greatly disturbed. He said, "You wouldn't be such a fool."

"Jackson is in my care and your loyal and honorable Opposition threatens him. In turn I threaten you—with personal violence."

"You won't dare."

"I will dare, and you will tell me what is necessary and you won't do a solitary thing about it because to do so would entail explaining publicly your party's involvement in criminal activity."

"Then both sides of the House would fall together."

"If the public has to choose between a sentimentally foolish premier and an Opposition that calls on crooks for its dirty work, which will it prefer?"

I didn't dare look at Beltane. Aside from the personal criticism, this was politics at sewer level. Kenney retired into thought, made his decision and said, "About three hours ago I was given a bare outline of what had occurred. I knew nothing of the plan until that moment. I strongly disapprove of the whole affair."

"Your reputation says I should believe you. What matters is: Who told you?"

"I don't know."

"I suppose that's true in a way. We know how the system works and your network contact would be that lady, oh-six-two."

"Whom I would not recognize if I saw her."

"No matter. Fielding knows her and will talk like a gusher. Then there are Cranko and Ratface, still here and with no convictions to have the courage of. They will talk. The system being what it is, none will know very much, but in total they'll supply unrelated driblets of fact and guesswork that will eventually add up to a picture of sorts. We'll get there in the end, Mr. Kenney. Then, there's the evidence of the man I shot."

"You don't imagine I know his name, do you?"

"No, but the morgue will identify him, and that will give us the network of his immediate associates. And so on. You see how it builds."

He said nothing.

I turned to Beltane. "You might as well send him home now. His knowledge of Melissa has been pre-empted by the Third Channel, and his immediate business will be to stop his party making any move against you while we hold Cranko and Ratface."

Beltane said to him, "Yes, go away." Like sending a bad child to bed.

Kenney stood. "You've come down to taking orders from your hired gun."

"In his area of competence."

"He's a hoodlum at heart. Be wary of him."

"I know it and I am."

That rankled but did not surprise. Beltane trusted me within certain limits but did not approve of me as a human being. I, for that matter, thought little of him. We moved in different worlds. I preferred mine.

Kenney said, "Good morning to you, Premier. Happy grandfatherhood," and as he passed me, "Your kind wins police medals. The citation: He gave his wasted life to brutishly insensitive loyalty to a myth."

I would not give my life willingly for any loyalty. People build too much on a personal impression.

In the silence of his going there seemed little to discuss. Beltane fiddled with papers on his desk. After a while I caught him looking at me.

"Thank you," he said.

For all the grudging tone, it was more than a copper usually gets for making a bastard of himself to a mixed-blood gentleman who I suspected was basically worth more, in human qualities, than either of us.

When Ivy Beltane came, she came with banners flying, followed by a grinning Kostakis. She stormed in, crying, "Your damned driver should have his license canceled!"

Kostakis mimed apologetic grief. "The boss said to hurry. Had to hop a few fences."

Behind him Melissa and Fred crept in like frightened mice, whether overwhelmed by circumstances or simply terrified by Kostakis's driving was hard to say. Corner cutting by hopping fences is one of the few maneuvers capable of overturning a hovercar.

Beltane faced his wife—for the first time in years if the gossip was true—with a blank stare, but she, thoroughly upset, was ready to hit out at anyone and he was a given target.

"I didn't ask to come here! I don't want to be here, and it's certain that Melissa has lived here too long. You are not a fit father!"

Beltane answered like a statue giving voice, with honesty but without heart. "I don't want you here but for your own sake it is necessary that you remain. Unless you prefer to be thrown to the vidhounds. I bow to your judgment about Melissa and my fitness as a father; my neglect has brought this situation about. Now, if you will sit down and we can cease quarreling, we may be able to decide what's next."

The sheer bloodlessness of his answer took the hostility out of her. Besides, she was in my view an intelligent woman who could have her moment of spitefulness and at once retire into firm sense. She sat on the nearest chair and said bitterly, "Not quite all your fault. I hadn't many illusions about Val, but I didn't think he was quite such a cowardly bastard."

Kostakis explained, "There's a miniscreen in the security bus, and they saw the vidcast. We only made it out just in time, Harry. The channel copters were coming in all angles, so they know we headed for here."

Beltane was unmoved. "This place is safe from bugging. Any channel attempting it will be put off the air. The important thing is that no public statements be made by anyone but myself." He looked at last with tightening lips at Melissa, then surveyed Fred with a frankly inquisitive stare before nodding obscurely to himself. Perhaps he approved of the look of the boy. He waved them to the couch.

They sat down gingerly and Fred put out a hand to hold the girl's, but she pulled away.

Mrs. Beltane asked, "And what position do you propose to take?"

"We must decide that here and now."

"In front of strangers? This is a family matter."

"No longer. It may be a national scandal before it's over. And these two strangers have so far been our staunchest helpers. What they know is safe with them."

That was handsome; at least he didn't waver over a decision once made. He turned to Kostakis. "You must not confide these affairs to your colleagues or to anyone else at all."

"Understood, Boss . . . sir."

The premier returned his attention to the couch. "You are Fred Blacker?"

"Yes, sir." His voice was strong but strained, a touch too determined not to be overawed.

"And you wish to marry my daughter?"

"Yes, sir!" No strain about that.

Melissa said, "No!"

Fred regarded her with astonishment, not quite believing . . . some error . . . some misapprehension . . .

Beltane, faced with the unexpected, waited. His wife, better prepared, said quietly, "You have two choices, Melissa: You marry the child's father or—" She checked and asked the obvious question, "This boy is the child's father, is he? Are you sure?"

The implication brought Beltane's head sharply up.

Melissa said, "Yes."

Her mother asked, "How can you be sure?" and Beltane's expression I can describe only by a word you don't often hear these days—scandalized.

There is a phenomenon you come across occasionally in kids in their mid-teens, a vacillation between the grotesque ignorance that leads to so much of their idiot behavior and an uncanny assumption of adulthood and dignity. It is as though in the midst of juvenile chaos some promise of the man- or woman-to-be shines through, and for a moment you are dealing on an equal footing. I had seen Melissa, up to this instant, as a plump, self-absorbed, sulky little bitch; now, suddenly, she was a woman facing unpleasant facts and ready to

deal with them, older and gravely sure of herself.

She said, "I got frightened with the others and took those pills. Then I saw I had to go through with it and didn't take them after Fred. So it's Fred's."

Fred's baffled, horrified gaze was fixed on a stranger, someone he had not dreamed existed. Beltane retreated into stony blankness, his politician's tactic for covering fast reappraisal. Then he asked what seemed to me the wrong question because shock overtook thought. He asked, in startlement, "Others?"

"Three others." She made it a fact, not a confession.

I stole a glance at Kostakis, standing close by me, and he was in a petrified funk, eyes helplessly on the girl, waiting for the moment when she would turn her head and identify him with a collusive smile. Melissa looked only at her father; she was intent on the matter in hand, not on her incidental diversions.

Beltane remarked aimlessly, "Three!" He pulled himself back into the immediate scene. "Melissa, you have two choices: You marry Fred Blacker or you have the child aborted."

She responded with a calm precision that cried aloud of her Ladies' College training. "I can't marry Fred. It wouldn't be suitable. He will realize that when he goes home and thinks about it. Besides, Daddy, I've been thinking about those boys we discussed as possible husbands and I think we should settle on Jimmy Sinclair. He's quite nice, and his people have a lot of money."

I had never heard anything quite like the cool delivery. It pinpointed what was often said of the finishing schools: that they turned out girls who understood every twist of the social maze but not a solitary fact about the pity of the human heart. It was not the girl's fault; it was the outcome of parental neglect and an education that equated social requirement with emotional reality. She was not deliberately cruel to Fred;

she did not consider him because he was, aside from the usefulness expected of Wardie workers, outside the ambit of her consideration. One considered one's equals; others recognized their places. The old joke says that sexual congress does not constitute a formal introduction. I had seen it come true.

Ivy Beltane, more aware than the rest of us of the forces at work in her daughter's mind, recovered first. "You will present this Jimmy Sinclair with a ready-made infant? He might not be willing to forgo his right."

"I've thought about that. He doesn't have to know. Once it is born the baby can be given to some barren couple who can't have their own child."

Beltane's face was unreadable. He said slowly, "That will not entitle you to a second conception. Also, the law does not concede the right of adoption to barren couples save on the death of both natural parents of the child. It would leave the way open to concealment and illegal birthings."

Melissa shrugged. "Oh, the law, the law!"

"It decides."

Fred rose to sudden outrage. "It's my kid, too! It's my baby you're all talking about!"

Melissa half turned to him. "You can have it if you insist, but I would prefer a better home for it."

She was merely practical, in her view, unconscious of insult; she was the one talking sense in a welter of adult obstructionism.

Her mother tried to close some understanding around the girl. "You still will have used up the single permission you have in fact not yet been given. You won't be able to give your husband his own child."

Melissa's adult calm deserted her as she turned on her mother in an exasperated tantrum. "All you talk about is the law! Well, Daddy can change the law."

Beltane said, "He can't."

"Of course you can! It's only a little thing."

"It is not a little thing. Even if it were, I could not do it and I would not."

The girl did not believe him. "But you're the premier! You're the one who tells them what laws to make."

"Where did you hear that?"

She began to cry, not in breakdown but in frustrated rage. "Everybody knows that! The girls at school all know; their people know. They know you can do anything if you want to." Her voice rose to a thin squeal. "Otherwise what's the good? What are you premier *for*?"

A sickness passed over Beltane's face, and I wondered was he thinking of the disgraceful truth that had thrust itself into the open: That our society of oligarch administrators striving to maintain themselves in position had created so corrupt a system that their children saw corruption as the way of life, the norm, and never realized more than dimly what "corruption" meant. To them it represented the perks of position. They grew up knowing the true purpose of power.

Beltane said softly, knowing he would not be understood but that the beginning must be made, "Your pregnancy has become public knowledge. It is no longer possible for me to bend the law without the entire nation observing me at it. It cannot be done."

Melissa retreated directly from rage into hysteria. She threw herself screaming to the floor, beating at the carpet. The hapless Fred, still incredulous of his utter rejection, lifted her up, and she battered his face with closed fists, drawing blood. In the end I had to take her from him, clasping her arms to her sides while she squalled and hacked at me with her heels.

Beltane used the console to call for a first aid attendant, and it was Jeanette who appeared with a ready syringe. With her came a security man who carried a quiescent Melissa to her room.

When they had gone, Beltane sat still in his chair, but his hands shook. His wife tried to comfort the shattered Fred; she put an arm round his shoulders and murmured to him while with a handkerchief she dabbed at his ignominiously bleeding nose. He listened dully, saying nothing. Or, perhaps, he didn't listen at all.

Beltane said, "Now a word with you, young fellow!"

Ivy stood to face him. "You'll leave him alone. He may be the greatest loser in this unpleasantness, and you are not blameless."

They confronted each other in silent thoughtfulness. A bitter and demeaning personal battle was brewing and that was better left to them alone. I took Fred's arm and urged him out of the room. Kostakis came after us, happy to escape unscathed.

We went to the wardroom, empty while poor Jeanette scratched for men to fulfill my unreasonable calls upon her small command. I commented to Kostakis on the thing uppermost in my mind. "I've never realized the extent to which these Minder kids grow up thinking that power is the right to do as you like."

Kostakis pretended surprise. "Isn't it that? Even you believe it—a bit—in your own way."

"I don't think so."

"Every copper believes it. He knows he can get away with bribe taking and violence and that's just what he does."

"Not all of us, Gus."

"Too many of you, anyway. And you all get funny ideas, like the kids at that school of hers."

Kostakis had the mischief-making instinct of the cunning. He was fumbling for a blade to prick me with, so I thought he might as well unload what bothered him.

"Such as?"

"Such as that the law is right. And if it's right, then law and right are the same thing. But they aren't, are they? Then there's justice. That gets mixed up with law

and right, but it's really something else; and between
the lot you can always find a moral reason for what you
want to do—just the way those kids see power is right
and don't worry about who gets hurt. You get that way
it seems every thought a man has should be questioned
because it's hiding something else."

Maybe, maybe, but I was too tired for abstractions.
"And what do you believe in, Gus, that should be
questioned?"

"Me? I'm silly—I believe that having a good heart
gets you further than worrying about right and wrong."

Fred lifted his head from his hands to say, "Bugger
that for a sod's idea." He looked from Gus to me with
tears in his eyes. "What the hell does she want the kid
for? Just to give it away! What for?"

That question, lost in the crossfire, still needed
answering. But not now. . . . I needed sleep.

Part III

The View
from the Gutter

8

Ostrov: A Place for Jackson

I had counted on five hours sleep, but Kostakis shook me awake shortly after midday.

Spitting and snarling as though the whole news service was an outrage, he told me how the midday 'cast had carried the premier's bald statement and followed it with reactions to street interviews. I stopped him there. "What reactions? What did they get?"

"Thumbs up for Daddy, not one lousy crocodile tear for the girl."

"That could be a matter of how the questions were asked; Third Channel is only a garbage hunter. We'll get First Channel opinion later in the day; they'll ask the right questions in the right way."

"So what? Wardies don't watch First Channel; that's for snobs and arty types."

That was unfortunately true; public opinion was molded by the loudmouths. In the Wards, Melissa would remain Bitch of the Season.

"There's more," Kostakis said. "They got on to Fred's parents."

Bastards! "How?"

"That's my question, too. Only Fred and Fielding knew about them, and they've never left the Manor to be able to talk to anyone."

The world wouldn't wobble on its axis if the Blackers served jail terms. Leakage of information was the irritant. I suggested, "Your security group?"

"No chance. Beltane ordered that nobody leave the grounds or make private calls without supervision. Everything goes through Jeanette."

"Then security's tight. I know Jeanette."

"Nobody else knows about the Blackers."

"Somebody does; somebody outside. Miss oh-six-two, whoever she is."

Kostakis was glum. "The Opposition link. Kenney's. No name, so we can't find her."

"Fielding knows her, so she's a pipeline to—" I became uncertain of how much I could say and finished lamely, "the enemy."

"What enemy?"

"We'd better talk to the premier."

"What's this about an enemy? Aren't I supposed to know?" He sounded like a child told he can't be trusted with grown-up matters. This peculiar man—part lunatic actor, part failed artist, part efficient operative and wholly romantic—was readying himself to sulk. "Why won't you tell me?"

I said, "Classified. I'll pick you up in the wardroom in ten minutes."

He slouched out, convinced that I hid things from him in sheer capriciousness.

This raised the question of whether or not he could be trusted with knowledge of Jackson's identity. I saw him as one who would guard a secret to the death while he fancied himself a masterminding spider in the web, but romance can make an unmanageable hash of reality. Yet, my effectiveness could be enormously

increased by an offsider who knew enough of the facts to act in an emergency without consulting me.

Beltane's morning recovery had come and gone; we found him alone but harassed and gray and tired out.

He told us to sit down and had to tell Kostakis twice, at which Gus perched on the edge of a chair like a small boy wary of taking some disastrous liberty. Delivering the family had been one thing, but inclusion in planning at the highest level of state was more than a Wardie soul had dreamed of.

Beltane asked had I seen the midday news on three.

"No, but Mr. Kostakis has told me about it."

He looked at Kostakis as though aware of him for the first time as an individual with a face as well as a function. "Are you co-opting this man as a permanent assistant?"

"With, I hope, your approval."

"I have other work for Mr. Kostakis. Your task is to look after Mr. Jackson and you should not need an assistant for that."

The next few minutes might be difficult and were best broached head-on. "There is the complication of your wife and daughter."

"He is a stranger to them. People stay in the Manor for short periods—politicians, diplomats, persons of influence in civil sectors. Mr. Jackson is known as a visiting political aide. That is enough."

"Perhaps not, sir." I had been thinking over an aspect of Mr. Jackson's disguise that could be difficult to deal with. I tried a shot in the dark. "Let me ask Mr. Kostakis a question. Gus, has Mr. Jackson ever put you in mind of somebody else?"

Beltane was in immediate fury but contained it.

Kostakis, who had been following or failing to follow the conversation blank faced, said, "I was meaning to ask you if he was a relation of the old man—old Mr.

Gerald I mean, the one resting up country."

I didn't care to look just then at Beltane. "What makes you think that?"

"This morning I saw him in a dressing gown and slippers like the old—Mr. Gerald I mean—used to do on his good days when he could get around a bit. It was just for a minute when he had his back to me I thought if he hunched down and shuffled a bit he could be old Mr. Gerald to the life. When you've seen people a lot you recognize them from the back as much as the front. Would he be a nephew or some such?"

Beltane said sharply, "No!"

I told him as gently as I could, "You do recognize back views. The person turns round and you see it is someone else, but the confusion lingers. Members of the household remark on it to each other and ask questions—about relatives, for instance. If they don't get answers they start to make them up, and sometimes they finish with something worse than the truth. We should—"

He stopped me with a gesture. "What have you told this man, Sergeant?"

"Nothing, sir. How should I?"

"Indeed, how should you! Yet here and now you are feeding his curiosity to a point where it must be satisfied." In anger his battered weariness had fallen away. "Are you trying to force my hand?"

Nothing for it now but boldness. "Yes, sir. We must get Jackson out of the Manor before your wife and daughter feel the first prickles of familiarity. We don't want questions—and there is altogether too much vid interest centered on the place."

He tried to stare me down as though rage might wilt me, then roared like a tormented bull, "He was brought here because I need him here! Here! He's of no damned use to me somewhere out of reach!"

I could see Kostakis relaxing, enjoying himself now,

at the heart of affairs and loving it. I wondered was I risking a gun in the hands of a big child.

Beltane needed pushing. "You depend on me—or say you do—but every twist makes my job harder to do. I'm not equipped to outthink fate and accidents. If I ask for something it's because I need it." He listened with stiff patience, preparing more anger; I needed to jolt him. "This whole Jackson affair has been a blunder from the beginning."

He said, pleasantly and dangerously, "I think otherwise," but I sensed a willingness to listen. He was not so sure of his planning as he had been. Then he surprised me by saying, casually, to Kostakis, "Would you call yourself an honest man?"

Kostakis looked helplessly at me, found no answer there and settled for truth. " 'Course I would. Only a nit'd say different of hisself."

"And what would you be prepared to die for?"

"Me?" His tone said this was unfair; a man shouldn't be pelted with thought stoppers. "I'd die fighting for me life, but I don't go for any guff about dying for me mates; that only swaps one waste for another. And I don't think much of dying for a cause, neither. You have to live for it. You don't train a soldier to die for his country; you train him to stay alive so he can make some other silly prick die for his."

Years might have passed since Beltane had heard the like; he was fascinated. He asked me, "Do you trust him?"

"Yes."

"Why?"

There's no answer to that, no matter how well you know the one in question. I could only shrug and say, "You do or you don't. If you trust a man it lifts his opinion of himself and he tries to justify it."

Beltane disregarded that nonsense and asked, "Do you feel important, Mr. Kostakis?"

"I feel I'm being suckered by experts."

"Take my word, you are not. Sergeant, tell him who Mr. Jackson is."

I said, "Think twice."

"You urge me, then you caution me."

"It's your risk, not mine."

He corrected me, "Yours, I think. You will be responsible for seeing that he does not betray knowledge carelessly. If he does, what will you do? Shoot him?"

Perhaps he was testing me, perhaps only laughing at the bind I had got myself into. "Maybe. Maybe not. I don't know." I really did not know; the question had taken me by surprise. Calling yourself a pragmatist is a far cry from bringing a life-or-death decision immediately home to roost.

Kostakis said, "He would, you know. He's one of those bastards who thinks he knows right from wrong and which poor sap ought to suffer for it."

Beltane nodded companionably. "I know. But how about you? Do you want such dangerous knowledge?"

"Of course I do. I want to know what I'm doing and why I'm doing it."

He wanted it for the fluff-headed reason that he was having a ball and wanted every dance. And he was all too sure that he knew what made me tick. So was Beltane. Parlor shrinks should remember that a man is many men.

"Then listen carefully. My father is not, as you think, in a country retreat. He is here, in the Manor, as Mr. Jackson, rejuvenated and restructured."

Kostakis swallowed that whole—the miracles of science are, after all, only two-hour vidcast wonders—but applied a cautious test. "But the old feller—your father that is—was off his—got senile."

"Off his head? Out of it, perhaps." Quickly he told the whole demeaning story while Kostakis listened like a bright lad to a cloak-and-dagger yarn, and I wondered,

with a sick feeling of having jumped off a cliff, if I had not acted with more instinct than judgment.

He told how an increasing inability to deal with some decisions (carefully he did not specify which) had caused him to consider and in the end connive at the cure and rejuvenation of his father. He needed a crutch and knew no other than the one he had been taught and disciplined by. He spoke of Nguyen selecting a bodyguard of total integrity—at which Kostakis shot me a glance of curious wonder. Or was it doubt? Finally Beltane spoke of a momentous decision he must make and deliver to a meeting of the prime minister and state premiers in the next forty-eight hours. He needed, could not do without his father's advice. He made no bones about his position of emotional dependence. At the end he said, "There you have it. No more mystery."

He mistook his man. "Beg to differ, Boss. Two mysteries still."

"The nature of the decision to be made? That remains my affair. The other?"

"Why trust me?"

"Do I? I trust Sergeant Ostrov. You are the only other person capable of betraying what I have said. If the word leaks you must be the informant, but you can easily be discountenanced as an eccentric with romantic ideas and a rich imagination. Your supervisor's description was vivid."

So he had had his own reasons for checking on Kostakis, but he was Minder clumsy with people outside his class; I saw the flash of anger on Kostakis's face, instantly hidden but undercutting his apparent gentleness in unnerving fashion. It was not something to become easily used to.

Beltane asked, frowning, "Do I wrong you?"

"No." I chalked up a plus for honesty; no man enjoys

having truth fired at him. "But I got more going for me than just some private beliefs."

"She said that also." Jeanette, I feared, would hear more about that, but I would back her to return as good as she got.

Kostakis took hold now to point out that Cranko and his connections could tell of the hospital treatments.

"Not while I can prove their association with professional crime."

"So where do I come in? What do I have to do?"

"Be my personal bodyguard, unnoticeable in a crowd."

I had to protest, "You surely don't mean to show yourself outside the Manor!"

"I am a public person, almost public property, and I have appointments to keep. I must not be seen to hide or to enter by back doors or to disappear for no good reason or to appear suddenly with an augmented police guard. So I am recruiting Mr. Kostakis on his supervisor's commendation of him as a man with fast reflexes and some unexpected physical capacities."

Kostakis didn't actually preen, but his resentments began to cancel out. He asked, "What do you reckon might happen?"

Beltane smiled, all good fellowship. "They should try to kill me. In their place that is what I would consider. Wouldn't you?"

Kostakis matched him grin for grin. "Not with me guarding you, I wouldn't."

He meant just that. Nguyen had certainly given him self-confidence.

Beltane asked me, "Where will you hide my father? With the police?"

"Good God, no! Give them a mystery and they'll drive him mad with snooping. I wouldn't put it past some of them to try drugging the info out of him."

He said something foul about police methods, and I

pointed out that people had been saying that for two centuries. "But, for better or worse, they're all you've got. Can't live with 'em and can't live without 'em."

"Where, then?"

"In my home, with my parents."

"Telling them what?"

"That they have a guest. Big secret! My father will be awed but delighted; my mother will disapprove but say nothing. She's the kind that slams doors and stays tight-lipped for a week."

He smiled grimly, admitted that he must trust my judgment and asked, "What sort of place is it?"

It was a fair question, but it scratched the class consciousness I pretended was not in me. "Poor but honest. Mr. Jackson will have a chair to sit on and a bed to lie in."

He said, "Don't be so touchy," but he looked away.

"Now I'll have to think how to get him out of here unseen. The newsbugs are swarming."

"In darkness, I presume. You can have him after midnight."

"So late?" I had already been up all one night.

The charging bull expression returned. "I brought him back for a purpose and I haven't had ten minutes alone with him! Midnight—or later if we're not through by then." He stood up. "Mr. Kostakis, be ready to accompany me into City Center at three o'clock. Afternoon suit and brimmed hat. If you have nothing suitable, see my chief secretary. His name is Collins."

He walked out of the Small Office as though he had already forgotten us. Perhaps he had.

Kostakis made a grimace of distaste. "Under all the acting he's as weak as piss. Would you believe it, hanging on to Daddy's hand!"

"I believe it, but I don't really understand."

"That's another little mystery to put with why Melissa wants a baby. It's a real hang-up of a family."

* * *

Kostakis went in search of Collins for clothes suitable to a gentleman mingling in the crowd round the premier. I thought he would pass so long as he kept his mouth shut.

Going to my room, which was next to Jackson's, I was hailed peremptorily by the voice of Mrs. Beltane coming up behind me. She asked without preliminary frills, "Who is the man occupying old Gerald's room?"

I told her I had no idea which had been old Gerald's room, while silently I cursed the premier's idiocy. Whatever tales he told the staff to account for the old man's absence, he should have had better sense than to allow a stranger to be put into his father's room.

"That one," she said, pointing. "You have just passed it."

"Mr. Jackson is in there. A political aide from interstate, I'm told."

"So Gerald will not be returning?" More than curiosity loaded the question—suspicion and something nasty, an almost prurient nuzzling after information. Her animus against the old man ran deep.

"I couldn't say. I'm told he is under treatment."

"Do you believe that? He has been in senile decay for over twenty years. No doctor will treat the moribund and no hospital would accept him."

I could only say that in that case I didn't know where he might be.

"Nobody knows or cares," she said. "I would not have known he was away if Melissa didn't have a soft spot for the old wreck. Thinking he might be back from wherever they took him she went to this room and was shooed away by a stranger."

"I can't help you. I've been here only a few hours."

She regarded me closely as if wondering would I respond to a blatant pass (and I might have done despite her being some fifteen years older) but instead asked, as

if for a favor, "Would you please ask my husband where Gerald is? Melissa wants to know."

"Can't you ask him?"

She became harsh. "Only if I must. We speak when speech can't be avoided."

It would have been interesting then to have known what lay behind their estrangement or what in fact powered the whole unbalanced family. "Very well; I'll ask him."

"Thank you."

She would have gone on past me if I had not said, "In return, can you tell me something?"

"What is it?"

"Why your daughter insists on having her baby."

She could have told me to mind my own affairs, but perhaps she considered that Melissa's rescue from the Handspikes constituted a debt to be paid. "She no longer insists. She will submit to a clinical abortion."

After all the squalling hysteria that was anticlimax. "That will calm the public airwaves for the premier, at any rate."

"Him? Who gives a damn for him except those precious Wardies he placates with tiny concessions? My thought is for the man she will eventually marry and who will want his own child."

"And Fred Blacker?"

She bit her lip, looked undecided and then guilty, and settled for an unconvincing hardness. "A good enough boy of his kind, but he doesn't count. He'll father his own legal child when his time comes. He's been sent home. Big-hearted Jem, instead of kicking him out, has arranged to transfer him to City Parks. That will have to satisfy him."

Power solves its problems easily—a new job to massage heartbreak. *That's it, son; like it or lump it! Could have chucked you on the junk heap, you know!*

She mistook my brooding on Fred for unsatisfied curiosity. "How did I get her to agree? I pointed out that she can't go back to her Fitzhugh school after all the public foofaraw; she'll have to be tutored at home until the noise dies down, and in any case she'll be social poison to the rich bitches with daughters at the school. It took her about ten seconds to decide to get rid of it when she saw that she wouldn't have to face up to the girls at school. She said they'd know she'd won her bet anyway because of the Aldridge vidcast."

"Bet?"

She echoed flatly, "Bet. Never underestimate peer group inanity among teenagers. Our rich little sluts-in-the-making talk smut just like Wardie sluts-in-the-making but without the firsthand observation. Because ours are kept in ladylike ignorance of the obligations of the sexual contract, they fantasize on the basis of girl-ish scurrilities whispered behind their hands. Melissa has had, as well, a savagely deprived home life, for which I have to accept blame for not seeing just how deprived. She strives for attention. I've known that she exaggerates to make herself interesting, but her dormitory fancies have been more unrestrained than I imagined. She boasted to the girls that she had had sex with a man. They know her too well to believe her so she vowed to prove it by having a baby. So— three men, three failures, and up and over with the gardener's boy!"

On that savage sentence her voice broke and she wept.

In the helplessness that tears bring to a man I mumbled, "You must get Beltane to let her go."

"Let her go!" She moved from tears to ferocity. "I'll take her from here if I have to shoot him! And I hope the other old animal is dead, too. I hope they took him away to kill him."

She pushed past me, turned the corner and vanished.

Kostakis's "hell of a family" didn't cover the half of it.

I lay on my bed in preparation for another long night and drifted into sleep while pondering on Ivy Beltane's hatred of old Beltane . . . and on where Nguyen fitted into the big pattern.

The premier's appointment had not been a lengthy one because Kostakis woke me a little after five. The change in him was enough to make me say, "Clothes make the man!", and indeed he was Gus transformed into an estimable Mr. Gustav Kostakis by the outfit Collins had found for him. It was by Minder standards a simple afternoon suit, but it fitted him like a sheath and would have been the nearest thing to finery he had worn in his life. "What was the job?"

"Opening a science history exhibition. Waste of time for a top man."

"He has to keep the scientists on his side; they're a strong lobby. No suspicious characters all gunned up and aiming to kill?"

"Don't laugh. You just try personnel protection in a crowd and see how you go. We got a drill for sifting groups and vantage spots, but it isn't perfect; it's hard to sniff out a bloke who might risk a shot from twenty or thirty paces." He sat himself on the end of the bed. "Finished with the gossip? Now—there's a new twist in the story."

"Christ, what now?" I reached automatically for trousers and shirt for instant action; the job had me on tenterhooks.

"Newsbugs. Fourth Channel this time, looking for something to match Albie A.'s beat-up this morning. And it stinks."

"Tell me."

"I can show you. Did you know all news releases are recorded here for study by the secretaries? We can get a playback on the Small Office screen."

In the Small Office he fiddled with Beltane's desk controls as to the Manor born. "Boss showed me hisself!" Peacock vain but no less effective for that.

On the screen some idiot crowd idol asked with a more-in-this-than-meets-the-eye wink, "Who's heard of old Gerald Beltane lately? You oldies will remember the premier's father, battle-weight loudmouth of the House of Reps for thirty years, the numbers man who just about ran the state by conniving behind the scenes and rode his son to victory as member, minister and deputy premier and had him on the way to the premiership before he— Before he what? Disappeared from politics, that's what. Went away with no farewells, no tears, no nothing at all. Well, it's no secret what happened, but folks do forget. The old man went home to live with the genetic form of Alzheimer's disease and no memory of what happened yesterday or two minutes ago—complicated by a type of stutter-and-dribble senility. Something nasty in the family chromosomes, it seems."

The yammering icon made a meal of it, a tattler's banquet. "The old man has lived close on thirty years with a disease that usually kills much faster than that. So—has he been receiving unauthorized care, taking up medical time and talent for the dying rather than for the living? The system is plain, folks, with no room for sentiment: When you've had it, you've had it and you don't snaffle the services needed by the useful young.

"It's possible for Alzheimer sufferers to live a long time, but wouldn't you think they'd be better off dead? Staying alive could be torture. And should the useless old occupy population space on a planet that can hardly feed itself? Some people think we should stop being po-faced about euthanasia and make a law. . . .

"Well, some weeks ago the old boy was transferred from the Manor to a rest cottage in the countryside. So we were told, though in fact nobody gave a damn where he was; he was history. But was he transferred? And if so, where to? You know the public record system—cradle to grave, every move, everything except how many craps a day you have—but we can't locate old Gerald. No rest home or cottage has him, even under an assumed name. And Jeremy Beltane owns no secret properties, being a more honest man than some of his confreres.

"But how honest? Where is old Gerald, why is truth covered up, why can't an old, sick man be traced? And why make a secret of it? After this morning's keyhole peep at the premier's daughter we find some intriguing questions about her father and grandfather. What goes on in the Manor, eh? What goes on?"

It was classic smut, delivered with loads of "honest puzzlement," scratching a story out of nothing . . . save that it came out of something deadly.

"What did the boss say?"

"They jammed a mike in his face as we left the exhibition and asked where his father was. Resting in the country, says he. 'So why can't we find him?' squawks the bug, and the boss says, 'Bad staff work I reckon,' and clams up on him."

It had been the only possible spur-of-the-moment tactic. "Did the question upset him?"

"No. He just treated it like bad manners. These public men learn to handle theirselves."

In public, yes; in private this one was less impressive. "Did he comment about it to you?"

"No, but when I got a chance I said to him it was as well the old man was getting out because the bugs would be sniffing at the Manor fences to see who went in and out or even blew his nose. He just nodded."

"I'd better talk to him."

"You can't. He's with his father and said not to interrupt him for anything short of murder. You can see him maybe at midnight, not before."

"Then how the hell can I spirit the old man away without planning? There's a gauntlet of eyes to run—a skyful of them."

Kostakis said, "I've got that arranged."

I didn't believe him. "He told you to see to it?"

"He said he wondered how it could be done, and I told him how and he said, 'Hop to it.' "

" 'Hop to it'?"

"Well, words to that effect."

"So tell me how."

He did, and his method was as complex as his own personality but as nearly flawless as shooting in the dark can be. I had to pay his ingenuity; he remained my one piece of good fortune in this business.

After that I could only cool my heels until he should decide it was time for us to move. He loved having me under orders, and I was too amused—and too pleased—to resent it.

The channel copters, five of them, circled at low altitude, searching the area for persons entering or leaving. The Manor was protected against electronic bugging but "news observation" (an elastic term) had to be permitted. Beltane could have had the police minister shepherd them off as constituting a nuisance, but that would only have brought vidhowls of "What has the Manor to hide? The public has a right to know what happens at the residence maintained by public money."

What they hoped to find they could not have said, but they had started two hares and hoped to catch one or both. As people moved in and out, the copters dropped a camera or two on extension lines, taking full-face pictures to vid to their head offices for identi-

fication. They bagged a score of deliverymen, political secretaries, gardeners and outside security men—and one channel lost an expensive camera when it swung too close to a sturdy old Moreton Bay fig tree.

At sundown they switched in the infrareds, tuned to body heat. That gained them nothing. Any more than my attempts to sleep gained me anything. A broken sleep pattern upsets my rhythms completely; I drop off at wrong moments when I should be alert, then fail to drop off when there is time to relax.

That night I read and dozed and read again and squirmed on the bed until, a little before midnight, I began walking the corridors because I could not keep still.

So it was that I walked down a corridor and round the corner into the main reception hall, to find father and son alone in the huge space and at a furiously hostile end to the meeting the son had moved science, law and love to bring to pass.

They saw me and fell silent.

Beltane, for the instant before he controlled himself, blazed with anger and hurt, not at me but at his father; he presented, for the unforgettable second, a picture of a man insulted and goaded beyond bearing. Yet with it he was a son, a small boy who had been shamed and humiliated where he had sought guidance and love.

The tableau broke at once. Beltane pushed silently past me as though he would as soon have run me down. I doubt that he recognized me, that he saw more than an interruption closing off an intolerable scene. His breathing hard and hoarse, he went in the direction of the Small Office without a further word.

Jackson gazed after the retreating back with an expression of acute disappointment and distress, as if he had picked up some familiar thing to find it tainted and decayed. Then, slowly, his face fell apart into lines of regret and grief. For the second time I saw him cry

slow tears that gathered at the corners of his eyes and hung there before they slid to his cheeks and he raised a hand to brush them away.

I asked, if only to cover the embarrassment of intrusion, "What's wrong, Arthur?"

I thought he might snap at me, but he replied only, "This is outside your brief, Ape." I stood there, discomfited and helpless, until he said, closing off the scene, "I understand I am to be shipped out to other quarters."

"Yes."

"In your care."

"Yes."

"That may be best; there's nothing left here." He put a hand on my arm. "I need rest."

Leaning heavily as I took him to his room, he was near to emotional collapse. As I laid him on the bed and pulled the slippers off his feet, I told him, "We leave in three hours or so."

"Well enough." After a moment he said, "He didn't need me; he only thought he did." He sounded like a man speaking from the far end of an echoing hall. "He needed someone to agree with him, to assure him he hadn't got it wrong. And now he is in his office, rearranging destiny after bringing his own disasters upon himself. And this damned resurrection has been a total waste."

He closed his eyes, and I left him, feeling that what I had seen in the reception hall had been something more than the end of a lifetime's affection, the recognition that the affection had in fact died long ago. It had been the kind of falling out that occurs when each sees the other—and himself—for the first time whole and undistorted by love.

That can be terrifying. As you will discover, I know what I am talking about.

Strangely, I slept easily and woke, as I had timed myself (it's something you learn to do) at 3:30.

*   *   *

I wakened Jackson and at first tried to help him dress, but he pushed me away with a mulish determination to look after himself. "That's all done with," he said and half snarled, " 'Richard is himself again.' "

We went down to the wardroom to find not only security but staff from all areas of the Manor gathering there.

The prelude to the movement was something close to a yelling tantrum from Jeanette, who was threatening to throw in the job. It seemed that on discovering what Kostakis intended she had taken the risk of confronting Beltane in the early hours of the morning, only to be told that the bodyguard's orders were to be followed. For once tough Jeanette had been near tears of fury and had vented some loud, unwholesome truths about hours of work and the state's unwillingness to pay overtime. She was appeased only by a rattled premier's promise that every due cent would be paid. (From whose purse?) It had probably been the only way he could struggle free of her.

I asked her what condition he had been in, and she screamed at me, "In his bloody pajamas, of course!"

"I meant mental condition, mood."

She didn't know and didn't care, and sat herself in a corner of the wardroom in shrewish silence. Who could blame her?

What Kostakis had done was, co-opt every available member of staff in the Manor, including two affronted but press-ganged junior secretaries, to form a night search party which would spread in an expanding circle from the house (and let the ambushing spycraft make of it what they cared to) until, at a covered point, some of the thirty-two pieces would vanish from the board while the others continued their scouring of the Royal Park gardens and sports grounds. The channels would receive a garbled account of perimeter alarms being

set off, necessitating an area search, though triggering had possibly been caused by a straying cat or dog or a failed circuit. An inspection would be "proceeding." They wouldn't believe a word, but they would have to swallow it.

Beltane did not put in an appearance.

As we waited, Jackson asked, almost in his old form, "Have you prepared your family for a curmudgeonly old bastard?"

"I haven't had opportunity to prepare anything, but they'll accept you as my friend."

"Friend, Ape? You? Irritant and tyrant! If father is like son I can expect a rough passage. Do you know that in all my years I have never experienced at firsthand how the other half lives?"

"You will find your needs provided but little to spare and not as much space as you are used to."

"I shall suffer cheerfully."

If his mood required me to match his own sour friendliness, it was best to oblige him. "You will find these particular slum dwellers as cultured as yourself though their interests may not be yours."

"Then they shall teach me survival philosophy and I'll teach them opportunist politics."

Which might well be how it would work out.

Kostakis came and called for silence from the chattering crew. That earned him a few catcalls, some laughter and a glance of lacerating hatred from Jeanette, but the briefing went well. He knew what he wanted and had reduced his orders to simplicity. The thirty-two of us were to work in pairs, fanning out from the perimeter on compass bearings, examining obstacles and possible points of cover as if in a genuine search. The object was to smuggle two people out undetected. He did not say whom.

"Keep search speed; that's about thirty meters a minute in open country. If a copter drops a camera, cover

your face and don't get photographed. Don't talk too much and for Christ's sake don't say anything to let the channels think it's a fake exercise; there's sound pickups on the cameras. You spread out for an hour and come back when you get the call on your personal coms; otherwise, radio silence. Groups four, five, six and seven will rendezvous with me at the old Royal Park railway station on the outward move. Start time, oh-four-hundred. Questions?"

No questions. Jackson and I were group six. Kostakis came for a quiet word. "I better have your home address, Harry. Just in case."

True. I wrote it down for him. He whistled softly. "Port Melbourne, eh? Flash!"

That told me much about his own background. Port Melbourne is run-down and shabby, not as mildewed and neglected as the Handspike-infested tenements of Balaclava but in no way flash.

At four o'clock we poured out through the rear exits and the noise of circling copters was an instant insult to the ears. They saw only an erupting mob sorting itself into pairs and shaking out into a search pattern.

Their frustration would have begun immediately as they made hurried vid-links with the Manor, shouting each other down until Jeanette, sole remaining security representative, sorted them out. I could imagine it:

Why the search, lady?

Perimeter alarms blew.

But thirty-two bodies! You got that many?

Staff helping; alarm is alarm is alarm.

Looks like a prearranged search pattern.

It is. Standard security pattern.

What blew the alarms?

No guesses.

Keep your line open for us.

Too busy.

Aw, now, listen . . .

Silence. From Jeanette they wouldn't get enough for even a beat-up. In the end it turned out to be a false alarm, a technical fault. Or so they were told.

We fanned out across the park in near darkness. Cloud cover was normal for this rainy time of year, and the moon penetrated just sufficiently to plot the bumps and furrows before we stumbled over them, so I kept one eye on the old man for fear of him falling on his face. He was aware of his convalescent clumsiness and moved with care. The slow search pace helped.

A couple of copters dropped cameras on carbon polymer ribbons, but the odd shrubs and lone trees prevented them getting to face level. Losing a camera could be a heavy setback in a ready-cash economy and a few recorded scrappy grunts and curses were not worth the risk. Jackson spoke only once, to say loudly, "Shit!" and massage his ankle.

It was about six hundred meters to the old railway station, and we covered it in twenty minutes. Four, five and seven came curving in just after us. The copters gathered to see what came of our search of the building.

The eight of us scrambled onto the platform and under the ancient, rusting, galvanized iron roof. Kostakis, with seven, herded us at once into the ticket box. The copter cameras could not see us because the box faced the length of the station platform and had no side windows; they could not peek from any angle. We were safe there from any but ground-based surveillance, and they could not risk landing a man who might be taken for one of the searched-for intruders, and perhaps shot; they could only buzz in a balked swarm. Still, we kept our voices down while he outlined our way of escape under the noses of the newsbugs.

It was very simple. The disused rails had long ago been removed and recycled and the resulting bare

paths had been disguised cheaply by planting shade trees on either side of them, forming covered walks and picnic spots for the gentle weeks of autumn and early spring.

So there were four totally covered ways out of the station, two running northeast to Brunswick and two southwest to Flemington Road. At five o'clock the four groups would leave the station together, four and five to move towards Brunswick, ourselves and the Kostakis pair towards the road, under tree cover all the way to the public transport hoverbus route, where the first dayshift engineers and service staffs would be commuting and cycling to City Center.

The copters would soon discover what we did but not who we were.

When the time came we all moved together. Jackson and I went a little faster now, with Kostakis and his offsider keeping pace under the trees of the other track. Our only punishment for deception was the rain. After holding off all night in this, the wettest season of the year, it came down without warning in the proverbial buckets. The trees could not keep it off nor capes save us being drenched to the knees or wincing at cold trickles down our necks. It was a small price for escape, though Jackson tired quickly on the rough footing and had to take my arm.

Otherwise, the escape went without a hitch. At Flemington Road we hailed the first hoverbus for City Center and all four of us boarded. It was, as we had known it would be, crowded; we were lost among the early workers. The copters could pack up and go home.

I was given a glimpse of Kostakis's thoroughness when Jackson pointed out, softly, that four searchers vanishing into the city instead of returning to the Manor would cause comment. Kostakis only beamed at him. "I must of forgot to say how the Manor called

on the com and said since the night was over and the
search was called off, us four could go straight off on
our rostered Sunday leave. And so we did."

We left the bus at Center Terminus, all hundred or
so of us, indistinguishable in raincapes, moving off to
workplaces. For farewell Kostakis said, "Call if you
need me, night or day." I assured his enthusiasm that
I would. His companion gave us a fed-up grin, and they
wandered off to find their way back to the Manor and
breakfast.

Under the footpath verandah Jackson insisted on
pausing to peer up and down the street through the
curtain of rain. He grumbled, "There would have been
a few cars still."

He was looking back thirty years. "Not now, Arthur.
Nobody makes them; nobody keeps up the roads. Public transport is good and we use bikes a lot; they're just
as good."

There were, in fact, quite a few bikes on the street.

He asked, "Is that what they teach you? Still rewrit-
ing history, are they? There's more to life than making
do within the circle of walking distance."

I tried to see with his eyes; memory did add a time,
back in the forties when I was a kid, when private cars
still threaded among the streams of buses and bikes.
They had been on their way out even then, part of
the guzzling consumption a bankrupt planet had had
to sacrifice if it wanted to eat.

As if he heard my thought, Jackson said, "I'm hungry,
Ape."

"You'll have to wait till we get home."

"No!" He stopped dead, a small rock of stubbornness
in the flow of a city going about its business. "Your job
is to look after me. I'm hungry and I expect you to earn
your pay."

Undercover work is often as petty as it can be bracing. Wind swept fresh rain in on us half-drowned rats

while we argued a triviality. I asked, "Have you money?"

"How should I? Never thought of it."

"And I won't have any till I get home. And your food coupons and mine were lodged with the Manor catering staff. What will you have? Rainwater?"

He jeered, "You didn't think ahead."

How right he was; the police mentality wasn't coming well out of this confusing exercise. "I'll see what I can do." Like Nguyen, I had face to preserve.

I took him to the City Central police canteen, where I could get tea and toast without coupons and charge them to my account. He complained that the tea was tasteless and the toast like straw. Since both were ersatz, he was right. Nobody queried his presence; he could be a witness or a nark being buttered up for questioning.

While there, I told a few lies and was able to sign for a week's supply of emergency food coupons—which would have to be repaid.

We arrived in Port Melbourne about nine o'clock. The rain had stopped and the footpaths steamed. As in the city, Jackson looked about him. There were few people around; those with nothing to do began Sunday when it suited them.

Our street was considered "class" because it had not been overbuilt with apartment blocks. Shabby and ancient though the dwellings were, a faint social clout clung to the possession—well, rental—of a family home with a patch of garden, some vegetable beds at the back and a fence dividing neighbor from neighbor. If the gardens were ill kept and the fences unmended and the walls weatherbeaten because paint was expensive and hard to get, the house dweller was still immeasurably better off than the apartment dweller; simple privacy was an enormous and envied advantage.

I asked, "Better? Worse?"

"Much the same. Years pass and nothing is achieved."

"I wouldn't say that."

"Nothing that matters. It will be so until we learn to live within the planet's means. We can't continue maintaining billions on the resources of millions."

Nothing new or memorable there, but it gave me an opening. "Is that what the all-night dialogue was about? All the long, long thoughts of political world minders?"

He snapped at me, "Yes! Need we stand here? I want to sit down. I want to think."

When Dad answered the door I pushed Jackson in ahead of me and said, "I don't want anyone knowing he's here."

Dad brightened at drama landing on his doorstep. He pulled Jackson in, nearly shut the door in my face, then threw his arms around me in the ritual hug. "Three weeks! We thought you'd never come."

Jackson mimed stunned surprise. "Somebody loves my Ape! I thought I'd be the only one."

From down the passage Mum's voice floated with an edge. "Who called my boy an ape? Mind your manners, whoever you are!"

The old brute only said, "Protect me, Harry! I'm new around here."

So my first necessity was to excuse what the cat had dragged in.

With four persons in it the lounge room seemed crowded as never before; after the spaciousness of the Manor salons it was a cupboard.

I introduced old Beltane as Arthur Jackson, and he chose to revert to his best behavior. Dad, old romantic, received him with the courtesy of a father taking pride in his professional son (a middle-ranking copper, for God's sake!), but Mum preferred cool reserve, conveying a we-are-something-better-than-nobodies impression and not quite ready to forgive the "Ape."

My mind was busy with contrasts. Ours was a semi-detached, five-room weatherboard dwelling a hundred or more years old and typical of the suburban houses of its period; it was also becoming typical of the centennial state of decay. The floorboards creaked with warps and shrinkages past curing, and the second grade paint which was all we could obtain was peeling from the inner walls as my last inept attempt at plastering crumbled under it. We had the furniture to be able to entertain friends but my Manor-fed eyes were conscious of coverings that looked like brocade but felt like what they were, stamped plastic.

One raucous putdown from Jackson and I would have been tempted to hit him, forgetting that he knew more than I ever would about being all things to all men. With introductions over I said, "I'd like you to take Mr. Jackson as a boarder for a little while."

The word confused them momentarily. The idea of boarding was by then almost extinct in the Wards; you either mucked in—share and share alike in everything—or you found yourself a solitary hutch. Mum repeated uncertainly, "Boarder?" and I told her it would be for only a few days. That meant immediate creation of fictional explanations. I drummed up a tale of interstate conferences which required participants being kept out of public view.

Dad was only too willing to be convinced; Mum wasn't. She gave me the look that promised inquisition later but said, like a careful housewife, that she hoped Mr. Jackson had been provided with state coupons. I gave her enough for three days for both of us, and she said at once, "These are police issue."

"Yes."

Politics? asked her eyes. *Police business, rather, and I do not want to know.* But she put the coupons safely away.

Jackson said, very gently, "I doubt if even three days

will be required," and the trouble in his voice told at last that he was desperately worried and trying to find resignation.

"Or maybe a week," I said.

He shook his head slightly. "Harry, you must know it is all over with him. The vultures have him trapped."

I had thought so from the moment of the failed kidnap; any observer would have thought so. If Jackson crumpled I would have to deal with it, knowing there would be no fresh miracle of rescue, and to plan for disaster.

My parents heard this exchange with the pained good manners of unintentional eavesdroppers. Mum solved her social problem by vanishing into the kitchen to make tea.

Jackson, playing his game of quick-change moods, sent a malicious half smile after her. "The housewife's unfailing panacea . . ." He let it die away.

I finished it for him, determined to allow no snide jibes, "and the perpetual poultice of the common people."

He didn't like that and shot me a look like the crossing of swords, but Dad moved in on us with gentle reproof. "There are no common people, Son, as I am sure Mr. Jackson would agree; there are only those less well equipped than the uncommonly fortunate."

That set both of us in our places. Dad was in his early fifties then, a spare, graying stick of stubbornness he could disguise with wounding politeness. Jackson, old politician and old socialite both, read the signs and capitulated; he made one of his rare, totally honest speeches uncontaminated by bile or guile.

"Mr. Ostrov, I apologize for my behavior, now and to come. I am under stress and unaccustomed to restraint on my tongue." Dad listened with the encouraging gaze of a schoolmaster with a talented pupil. "I was born to be a Minder, though the word had not its present mean-

ing then, and I have never known any other existence. Simply entering your home has for me an element of adventure, of new experience. I am uncomfortable not only for that but because I am unable fully to explain my presence."

Mum (not one to miss a word simply through being in another room) said from the kitchen door, "I'm sure Harry will make it plain."

"Harry won't," I said, "because he can't."

"But you said—"

"I said as little as possible. I suspect that what I said is more or less true, but I don't know. And, Arthur, please don't create unnecessary mysteries."

"Mysteries!" Mum said. "We are not children, Harry."

Jackson rescued me. "Allow me, Mrs. Ostrov." He became the complete gentleman, communicating with an equal, solving her problem with courteous dispatch. "Harry has in the course of his duties been subjected to a threat which inhibits his speaking of certain matters. It was done to ensure his silence."

My parents' most notable reaction was that they did not at once question the validity of such nastiness. In sensibility they belonged to an earlier convention, but they had few illusions about this one. My father's comment was typically practical. "It would ensure Harry's enmity, if I know my son, and strain his loyalty rather than preserve it."

He had that dead right. Mum said, "I never did approve of his police work; there's something inhuman about it." And retreated to the kitchen.

No, Mum, it's all too human—at the lowest level of self-preservation.

Jackson stared after her as he told Dad, "You should be horrified, not acceptant."

"Horrified by some mean-minded expedient of power? This is the age of stopgap crudities."

"At the use to which it has been put."

Dad sat up straight in his chair. "A corrupt and cruel use?" His voice did not rise a decibel above its usual placid level. "You must be a full decade older than I as well as Minder born and bred; you must know more of immoral expediency than I who can only deduce and suspect, yet you ask me to expend emotion on futile resentment. At this lower end of the financial tree—and this house lives more comfortably than most—we see that the individual is the unit and that existence is hand-to-mouth, while the international plottings of the monkeys in the higher branches make good tribal gossip but are nearly irrelevant as fact. Premier Beltane preserves a sort of status quo in Victoria, yet still we are driven to concentrate on essentials—food and shelter. On this planet dog eats dog without gagging; our last pretense at civilization is to refrain from overt cannibalism until the alternatives run out."

Jackson was getting his fill of the Wardie philosophy he had joked about. "You can't speak for all people, Mr. Ostrov."

"Can I not? Shall I remind you of Africa and South America where sixty years ago the Western world forgave their unpayable debts and poured billions of dollars into feeding and healing and maintaining them so that they could cease destroying their environments in order to clear arable land? The debtor nations were expected to develop internally, to produce individual stability and justify the forgiveness of debts by buying from the donor countries. That was the catch in their generosity. You cease deforestation, we give you money and you return it to us in payment for our cheap goods with inbuilt obsolescence, our luxuries that you don't need but must be taught to want and the suspect pharmaceuticals banned from the shelves of our own stores! The big dogs, slavering with generosity, had the little dogs halfway down their throats! But the

little dogs had learned hard lessons about subsistence; they refused to buy. They employed the largess to produce their own necessities and shut out unnecessary imports; the financial dominance of the West shrank for lack of the markets it had sought to perpetuate. The little dogs were eating the paws and tails of the big dogs because they knew all about subsistence living, while the big dogs couldn't stand tight belts and long fasts. Once there would have been a war (remember how 'all wars were trade wars'?) but that was no longer a response in a world terrorized by its own destructiveness. The choice lay between knuckling down and nuclear winter, and the outcome was that we all live in an approximation of poverty, in what I would guess has been the lot of the average citizen throughout most historical times. The world's wealth has become fairly evenly spread and, as the economists foretold, there isn't enough to go round. Among twelve billions there never will be—except, of course, among our Minders, who are 'more equal than others.'"

Mum, who had heard it a hundred times, brought in the tea tray and set out the cups. Jackson said, as if prodding a sore spot, "I fear you can't do without Minders in some form."

Mum asked, "Who can't?" but Dad said, "We're so accustomed to elitist administration that we've lost the power to imagine any other."

"At least we don't eat you."

"Only enough off each one to supply the comforts due to an intelligent and hard-worked government. One grants your necessity, with a permanent ruffling of resentment."

"So there is no cure?"

Jackson was obviously enjoying himself, but Dad surveyed him incredulously. "Of course there is a cure: Curb population growth until there are once again enough natural resources to sustain a human

culture and its ecological support. That is, to allow rational behavior back into life."

Mum said as she poured, "This is artificial milk, but it's drinkable."

Jackson seemed never to have heard of such a thing, but he kept his attention on Dad. "Curb?"

Dad smiled gently. "Reduce."

"To what level?"

Dad stirred his tea and kept his eye on the cup as he answered, "Two billions? Perhaps fewer? A figure low enough to give us time to learn how to conserve population increase before it happens all over again. There will be psychological processes to learn and disseminate, all manner of cultural profit and loss accounts to be exposed and balanced. Basic biological processes are not throttled back without payment in unpredictable traumas. Two centuries, perhaps, for learning and training?"

There could be nothing new to Jackson in all this, but he thought about it and what he asked was, "Do the Wardies think on such lines?"

"Those who bother to think. Most are concerned with shelter and the next meal."

"But you—?"

"Thanks to my son's career I have leisure to think."

Career, he called it, with a straight face.

Jackson tasted his tea and nodded appreciation to Mum. "This is not substitute."

"I keep real tea for visitors." Her smile challenged him. "Snobbery from a uselessly educated background."

He said, deadpan, "But culture is preserved," and then, without change of tone, "How, Mr. Ostrov, do you propose to reduce the population so drastically?"

Dad was ready for him. "Murder."

For the first time I saw Jackson's brio stopped cold. He picked up his cup and put it down, loured furi-

ously at Dad and said, "You're blunt—or you're not serious."

"Why should I not be? Politicians speak of it—behind their hands."

"Why should you think that?"

"If they don't, then they're fools with their heads in the sand. Even Wardies talk about it—only occasionally but not behind their hands—as something that has to happen. In husbandry it's called culling the herd."

"They talk about it?"

"Why be surprised? Subsistence living sharpens the wits to accept the obvious instead of intellectualizing it. They make jokes about it, think up wilder and wickeder ways of going about it."

Jackson set his cup down carefully. "That makes for jokes?"

"Like sitting under an axe and making good-humored bets about whose neck will get the chop."

Mum said, "I find it hard to believe that the administration is unaware of these feelings in the Wards."

Jackson twinkled at her. "It is not unaware. Nor was I. I was in some degree checking that nothing has changed radically during my absence."

"You have been away?"

"I have been . . . shall we say, absent from the public scene for many years."

He might as well have said he'd been in jail; there were few other modes of being "away" in a computer-recorded culture. Good manners triumphed over the tiny hiatus as Mum (always quicker than Dad at these recoveries) asked, "And how do the administrative classes feel about such Ward joking?"

"There is an intellectual element that abstractualizes fear, treats it as a specimen for examination. Wardies make jokes, Minders play mind games. Same thing, different expression."

Mum said, with an air of closing off discussion, "And then there are those of us who rarely think of it at all. One lives in the present, having no other time."

Dear Mum, saying in effect, Under the falling axe we preserve the dignity of life. Her flag would fly, come what might.

Foolish? Maybe, but no indomitability of spirit can erase fact, and for a moment she looked all of her years, weary with the disappointment of talent denied and the dull ennui of living just to be alive. She pulled herself together and fussed with the tea things, but Jackson observed and diagnosed. "I agree that this century will not bear much thought except as an object lesson to those who come after us."

"The survivors?" Dad asked, and there didn't seem much more to say about it.

Jackson purred at me, reminding me of duty. "Harry, I have been awake since the devil was pupped and wasted six hours in exhausting quarreling with my son. And I am still convalescent."

Quarreling about what? "You want to be tucked in and sung a lullaby?"

"So long as there's sleep at the end of it."

I put him into my own bed in the sleepout at the back of the house. He fell asleep in the middle of undressing and scarcely rallied to my rough removal of his trousers and socks.

Back in the lounge room I asked Dad if he had been trying to shock our visiting politician. He was smug. "Succeeded, didn't I? What's the story, son? What's he hiding from?"

Only professional steadiness prevented me from telling him; it would have been a relief from the endless crises arising from a weak premier's multiplying error.

The urge was still between my teeth when the front doorbell rang and Mum said, "I'll get it."

She returned almost at once, saying, "A gentleman for you, Harry."

Behind her, Dr. Nguyen entered the room. He did not wait on civilities but said, "You must get back to the Manor, Harry; the premier is in a—a very odd mental condition and is asking for you. In fact, demanding."

"Mr. Jackson—"

"Will be safe here, will he not?"

At "Manor" and "premier" all Dad's dreams of my involvement in great matters came true. He said steadily, "Perfectly safe; no one will know he is here. You run along, Harry, and leave us to look after our guest."

Dependable Bill Ostrov—the smooth, suave, secret agent with never a mental hair out of place!

So dear old Dad sent me off with his blessing to the most terrible moment of my life.

9

Ostrov:
The Political Madhouse

Waiting for us outside the house was no opulent Manor luxury body but a dirty dump-tray utility with no identification—a service truck the outside staff might use to ferry waste to the recycling points. Beltane had learned common sense. Or had he?

"Did the premier allocate you this truck?"

"No; I commandeered it. It was the nearest to hand."

"And unlikely to cause comment in the street outside our house."

"That, too."

He started up, swung the truck in an inept U-turn and moved too fast towards City Center.

I yelled at him, "Slow down, man; you'll kill someone!" There were children in the streets now, always in evidence long before their parents and as likely to play on the roadway as on the footpaths. "You're a lousy driver. Why didn't you send someone with a message?"

"Would you have obeyed it? Or would you have niggled that your commission is to accompany the old man, wasted time in argument? Perhaps sent the driver

back for confirmation? And would I tell a servant that the premier is unbalanced? For me you would come at once."

The speedometer was creeping up again already. "Slower, man! You're all nerves. Frightened?"

His brown eyes slanted towards me and away, but his expression did not change. "You must not try your interrogation tricks on me, Harry. Still, I am excited and a little concerned. The man whose mental welfare was my watching brief has become, overnight, my patient."

"Unexpectedly?"

He took his time answering. "Not altogether."

So he was prepared to be truthful, at least up to a point. "Did he in fact send for me or is this your idea?"

"He sent for you."

"Why?"

We were approaching City Center as he answered, "He said—and I quote without fully understanding— that he wants truth from the gutter."

He took his eyes from the road to watch my reaction and I said, "Pull in to the curb. I wonder you got to Port without an accident. Let me drive."

We changed over and he sat in the offsider's seat, sweating. With excitement and concern?

There was commercial traffic in the streets now and the usual amount of irresponsible driving of vehicles that do not respond well to turning and deceleration and are, after all, owned by the state rather than by their unconcerned drivers. I stayed in the road center with minimum ground clearance and pondered "gutter." My status was now clearer than it had been. I could be trusted, even allowed some small impertinence—but there was a gulf fixed.

Police bear with the enmity of those they serve but not easily with their contempt.

I tried a shot in the dark: "A truth to oppose the different truth his father gave him last night? A sugary truth that doesn't put action into the too-hard basket?"

He turned his head to look full at me and I'll swear the brown eyes were wide with a sort of anticipation. He asked, "What did the old man tell him?"

"How should I know? I only saw that filial affection seemed to have sprained its smile."

His disappointment was palpable. "I had hoped . . . well, we shall learn soon enough."

"The whole Jackson operation was stupid."

"Indeed, yes. Beltane raised his decrepit oracle to advise him and now wishes he had let it lie."

"But you pushed him into it, didn't you?"

"No!" Even the supposedly inscrutable East can be startled into truth when the insult is straight enough. "I am not a manipulator of shaking wills."

"You manipulated mine and it was not even shaking."

"I showed yourself to you, no more than that."

He did not claim that he had only been working under orders; that was one sign of a fairly honest man.

"As for Beltane," he said, "I did not dissuade him from foolishness."

"Such being not your brief?"

"Don't sneer, Harry. I explained foolishness to him; further than that I could not go."

"He ignored you. He was desperate."

"Of course."

"And you couldn't calm his desperation?"

He waited a half second too long to say, "There was no point of entry; it was a response to ongoing circumstances."

That was at best an evasion. I guessed that though he may not have prompted Beltane towards Cranko he had also not attempted to check the foolishness. He was at least an enemy by default.

I would get no more from him on that line. I changed direction. "Did he let me take the old man away because he no longer cares a damn what happens to him? Does a lifetime's dependence reverse itself so easily?"

"Given the right disappointment, yes. The dependant suddenly sees his shackle for what it is—the tie of his own weakness. At once he is free. And raging."

"Free forever?"

"For perhaps a day or two. The anger passes. Dependence is a most persistent emotional trauma."

"Trauma?"

"Certainly. An undercutting of the will to act, as ultimately disabling as a lost limb."

Before that, I would have called it a weakness to be overcome by an act of will. That's the sort of loose thinking a man will carry with him throughout his life, never considering closely, dismissing weakness with contempt until someone like Nguyen lifts it suddenly into a new perspective that fits all the parameters with fresh understanding. "That makes him a cripple."

"Yes." He glanced at me again, smiling this time. "And you snatched his crutch away to Port Melbourne."

It seemed that every decision I had made during these two nights and a day had brought disaster, because in each case I had lacked essential knowledge. But this disaster, this leaving of Beltane alone and unbalanced, could have been retrieved.

I said to Nguyen, "We could have brought Jackson back with us."

His smile did not waver. "The premier is my patient; I make the choices."

There was obscurity in that, but he would have blinded protest with psychological science. To cap it, he had another development to throw to me: "Beltane has sent for Kenney. An Opposition member! Expect entanglements."

That sounded like a friendly warning. I would be fumbling in the dark to discover what role Nguyen played behind his knowing efficiency.

As we pulled in at the rear of the servants quarters he asked, with an expression of one contemplating a splattered egg, had I ever noticed the outward serenity and peace of a mental hospital. "Flowers, lawns, spick-and-span walkways! Then you enter the wards . . . the Manor differs only in degree."

As we passed the wardroom he called to Jeanette, asking if Kenney had arrived.

"Somebody in a flesh-mask," she told him, "wearing white gloves. Could have been hiding Koori skin."

"Most likely."

I asked, "How is he smuggled in? In a closed van with a load of vegetables for the kitchen?"

"Why not? It's simple and it works."

Jeanette said, "Try the Small Office. He's got Cranko in there. Have you seen the channels?"

"Something fresh?"

"On the face of it just trouble stirring. A rumor story about old Gerald being shanghaied into the Biophysical Institute. All nudge, wink and further revelations in the next installment of our muckrake saga."

Somebody in the political network had talked. Black-mail would be in full squeeze by now. I wanted to think about it, but Nguyen hurried me on.

Then Ivy Beltane swept out of a corridor a few meters ahead, not seeing us and moving ahead of us to the Small Office with the determined stride of one with body and mind concentrated on a thing to be done. In her own home I had seen her roused from bed by police, hurriedly dressed and yet presented flawless-ly for the day. Now I saw her close to bedraggled in slippers and kimono with hair hanging wild as though she had lunged from the bed after a night of furious

thinking, caught up a wrap and moved into action before procrastination should disarm her.

At the door of the Small Office she shouted Beltane's name, really shouted it in a full female baritone of hoarse anger. She found herself in the middle of a room where her husband was not alone.

Either she had immense self-possession or her anger carried her, because she launched her tirade as though she and he were solitary and private.

I would have hesitated at the door, but Nguyen muttered excitedly and stepped through. If he could count on his profession to allow intrusion, so could I.

Kenney was there, unperturbed, observing and hearing Mrs. Beltane with the well-bred, polite interest of the perfect guest. He was not inwardly calm, though; between his fingers he crumpled and smoothed the flesh-mask.

Cranko lounged across the room from him, acting insouciance but looking seedy and tired after two nights of wondering what was to become of him. Kostakis, leaning against the wall behind him, saintly faced and thoroughly alert, did not help his role-playing.

Beltane stood at one end of the desk, blindingly enraged, while his wife played virago at the other. They did not see us enter; they were intent on each other.

I caught the tail end of Mrs. Beltane's yelling that she would do just as she bloody well pleased, that Melissa was her daughter and she'd not leave her in this cesspit a day longer. "Cesspit" was the word she used.

Beltane bellowed back at her, with the unnerving resonance of the public speaker, that she should leave well alone and add no further scandal to the scum already clogging the channels. "Don't you realize what will be said if you take her away? That the abortion talk is only talk and you are conniving at secret birthing!"

She was in no mood to listen to reason. "Let them say! I'll take her interstate and put her into a school where they train girls to be women instead of bird-brained harlots by default! As her mother I'll teach her what she was never able to learn in the perverted household of her disgusting father!"

I could not see Nguyen's face because he stood a little in front of me, but Cranko's eyes popped and perhaps mine did; Kenney's wrecking of his flesh-mask halted in amazement. Only Kostakis listened placidly as though human beings could not surprise him.

Beltane stiffened as if she had struck him, but he said only, "You'll take her when I'm dead and not an hour sooner."

"Then die and let her live in a normal world!"

Simultaneously they became aware that the number of the company had grown. Beltane yelled at us, "Get out of here, all of you!"

His wife said, very coolly now, "All their ears are burning. Safer to let them stay while you think fast, Jeremy. Is that little gray-yellow man the psychiatrist Melissa talks about? What does he make of the family history? It should be good for a scurrilous thesis."

Her coolness was venom; she had stepped over the safe mark and could no longer retreat if she would. I saw, with some shock, that Beltane's bull roaring was done with also. She had returned him brutally to a here and now in which he was afraid. His eyes sought escape; for a moment all he wanted was to run and hide.

The skills of a drilled lifetime returned. He stood straight, dredging up the outlines of the practiced smile. "You go too far, Ivy. These gentlemen do not know the family history. I am surprised that you do. Or do you?"

She refused the cue, turned it against him. "Your creatures don't know? They are your creatures, aren't

they? All except the snotty Koori double-dealer from the Opposition, and he'll be here only to bid for some rottenness. But the sly little Veet and the big macho copper belong to you, don't they? What does it matter how much your creatures know?"

Nguyen cocked his head. "What indeed, madam? In my profession all communication is confessional sacred."

"Until someone pillages your files! But poor old Ostrov does what he's damned well told—or else. Why should a young girl have to live in a house of dirty secrets? What do you say, psychiatrist?"

"Knowing nothing, madam, I say nothing."

"Then what about this: two perverted old men protected by their professional lapdogs! A proper setting for a teenage girl?"

A change came over Beltane. He had heard the doors of escape slam shut around him, and he was one of those who can conduct themselves coolly enough when there is nowhere left to run. He moved round and behind the desk, settled into his chair and lay back with hands behind his head. With deliberation he set his feet on the blotting pad and said, "Go on, Ivy. To stop now would be ungracious to your audience. It would create speculation beyond the facts."

She made an exaggerated double take of unbelieving amazement. "Beyond? How, beyond? Then tell all of us, where's the dribbling old pederast you call your father?"

Easy now as a man with nothing more to lose, he did not change position. "He's elsewhere, safe from your poison, Ivy. And 'pederast' is not a proper word for him. I was an aberration, a behavioral sport."

"I don't know the sporting term for it. Boy-lover? Will that do?" She turned a little to face me. "How about that, policeman? What's the official charge?"

I schooled my voice to flat indifference. "If supported

it might refer to corruption of a minor. But that must have occurred many years ago."

"Oh, our cold-blooded Ostrov! The law names the crime without emotion. Do you reckon only by the scale of sentences and have no moral attitude to the criminal?"

"Moral attitudes can be as evil as the crimes they affect to despise."

Before the morning was out I was to remember that reply and taste it like poison on the tongue.

Now I added, trying to play down in advance the nastiness that surely must come, "After so long a time, who would care?"

Ivy Beltane hissed at me as though I had become the object of her rage, "I care, policeman! I care for my daughter caged in a moral pigsty."

Beltane said with sudden exasperation, "Get on with it, you unpleasant woman."

It sounded like simple impatience, but his voice was tensely off-key. He half raised himself to glance at Nguyen and myself, and I saw his eyes. He was running to destruction, staring into it without welcome but also without avoidance, not mad in any clinical sense but moved aside from common perception to view himself and the world from an angle denied to the rest of us. Is that madness? Close to it, I think.

Nguyen straightened his shoulders with a tiny, almost imperceptible shrug, and his head poked minutely forward. In him that was a strong sign of interested calculation.

I looked back to Beltane. He had relaxed again, but I saw him now at the edge of a high place, feeling that curious urge to leap that makes you shudder and step back before it takes over. But he had decided to leap.

I thought Nguyen should interfere professionally, but he did nothing.

Ivy Beltane, with the challenge leveled at her, became more subdued, less certain of rightness. Her peak of anger had begun to ebb. She said without heat, trying to get the thing done with, "Old Gerald is not Jeremy's father. He is his lover. That's all."

The dart fell curiously short. Perhaps the others felt, as I did, only that puzzling aspects of a long public relationship had been satisfactorily explained. It may have seemed less important, now that it was aired, to Mrs. Beltane; after all, her interest was in prying Melissa loose from an old agreement to allow her father to keep her. The rest had been dragged in on the tide of intemperate determination to have her way.

Beltane, almost lying in his chair, spoke to the ceiling, correcting her on a point of fact. "That was true forty-eight years ago but not now. He picked me out of an orphanage when he was on the edge of middle age, and Dr. Nguyen will tell you that the middle period can give rise to aberrant behavior in otherwise normal men. I think that is true of Dad. I think of him as Dad because I don't know any other. He was married for reasons of political advancement to a woman who could not give him children and refused surrogacy. He wanted a child, was obsessive in his wanting; obsession and his wife's obduracy may have combined to tangle his emotions. On a Charities Commission visit to an orphanage he saw a fifteen-year-old and fell in love. Those are his words, not mine. Do you follow, Dr. Nguyen?"

"You make the matter psychologically simpler than is probably the case, but such midlife disturbances are documented. As a case observation, did sexual advances begin at once?"

"No. He claimed me as his illegitimate son by an old liaison and was able to carry on the imposture because the shift to total registration of the population in a central data library was still in progress, with all the usual errors and stumblings and bureaucratic bumbling. In

the muddle he was able to arrange a false genealogy.
I doubt that it could be done today."

It certainly could not. There had been wild tamper-
ings at that time; some were still coming to light as
anomalies emerged, but nobody cared enough to make
legal fuss over ancient villainies unless inheritance was
involved.

"He separated from his wife, amicably he told me.
And why not? I, an impressionable fifteen-year-old,
was to be brought up by a personable pseudofather
who very quickly claimed my gratitude and affection.
He wanted a son to attain the political heights he could
not. He got what he wanted."

He said it all smoothly and easily, but he would not
look at us.

Nguyen asked, "May I guess that sexual advances
began when he and his wife separated?"

"Before that. It was why they separated. She was
quieted by money; she kept him comparatively poor."

"And pederastic contact persisted?"

"For two or three years."

"And ceased suddenly?"

"I think he lost interest. I've read that pederasty rarely persists with late-teen objects. Perhaps I turned him
off; I was more acquiescent than interested. Don't imagine that affection was lost. He became a father; I became
a son. The aberration was over."

Ivy Beltane said, "You're a liar. I've seen you kissing."

Nguyen interfered quickly. "So has Harry; so have
I. It was not an overtly sexual kiss, yet more than
filial."

Beltane became testy as though we were all missing the point. "I did not say we ceased to love, only
that affection changed its nature. It remained strong; it
became, also, habitual. Dad was a dominant personality; he said and I did what he said. Willingly. Note that:

willingly. He wanted me to achieve the political leadership that was beyond his purely manipulative talents, and I wanted it because he wanted it of me. It was not simple submission to a more powerful will; I loved him and I also wanted what he planned for me."

Nguyen said, "Past tense."

Beltane was silent as though he had not heard. Then he lifted his feet from the desk and sat up. "Past tense," he agreed. "It's all over."

"Since last night," I suggested.

"Good Sergeant Harry, who sees all and says nothing! Yes, since last night. I called Dad back from the edge of dissolution because I needed him. I told myself I needed his vision and advice, but what I really wanted was his paternalism to shelter me. I recognized that as soon as it failed me. Last night I told him the problem that troubles me, and all he saw was incompetence and cowardice. He found that he hadn't trained a brilliant talent; he had only created a robot that jerked to his commands and coasted to success on a slowing momentum until the commands died out. It's true; I coasted on popularity until the test came and I couldn't face it. That shocked him out of all restraint. For my part, I saw a selfish old man realizing that his whole life with me had been wasted effort and unable to forgive me for it. Love is the most demanding emotion and the most unforgiving."

Nguyen asked with clinical coldness, "What love? You had twin illusions complementing each other and crumbling at a touch of reality."

"You aren't usually facile, Doctor."

"Facile? The relationship died when the falsity of its premises became clear." He turned to Mrs. Beltane. "Basically, madam, you had nothing to fear."

She said, stubbornly, "I saw him kiss the old beast. They didn't know, but I saw them, several times. That was before old Gerald became altogether irrational.

Melissa was newborn and I may have been irrational myself; but I knew that Gerald's wife was still alive and I found her and told her what I'd seen. She told me about the adoption and how she found them out and what she did about it. I did the same to Jeremy."

She might have left it at that if an aspect of callousness had not tripped my tongue. "And you left your daughter behind!"

She would take no criticism from me. "I thought the police were beyond surprise at what human beings will do. Are you also bereft of any kind of understanding?"

Jeanette used to say, *If a man hits a woman he's contemptible; if he argues with her he's a fool. We'd run the world if we didn't pity the poor dupes.*

I backed off as gracefully as I might. "I hope not, Mrs. Beltane."

"I was out of love and I loathed Melissa as the issue of such a father, though in time that passed. In return for freedom and money I made promises that were easy then; he didn't want a scandal in what happened to be an election year and I wanted above all to get away from him and all contact with the marriage; so I agreed to conditions that I knew later I never should have. It seemed easier because I had met another man. . . ." Her voice faded away until she picked up again, talking to herself. "There have been other men. They pass the time." She looked up. "Time catches up with us, doesn't it, Jeremy? The actions of years ago erupt today."

His answer held an incongruous touch of pity, as though only she needed support. "Don't blame your own humanity, Ivy. We build ourselves social systems fit only for saints and are forced to live lives of deceit to preserve them." He had calmed himself into a gentle amiability. "We are sufficiently civilized to know what we should be; our problem is what we are."

Mrs. Beltane gave a faint, sour smile. "I won't be patted into acquiescence. I mean to take Melissa away."

"With one cat out of the bag and others waiting, she has served her turn of damage. You may as well take her and go. Her belongings can be sent after her. Get her away within the hour."

"Good God, but you make it sound like an eviction order!"

"It is. Go quickly, Ivy. There will be disturbances here this morning, and you will want nothing to do with them."

I wonder now if that was the point at which he finally made up his mind. I felt the tenseness of climax waiting.

Mrs. Beltane hesitated, with questions unasked, then saw that she would get no answers. She said, "Goodbye, Jeremy. We need not meet again. There can be some arrangement for you to visit Melissa. If you wish."

He did not answer that, said only, "Good-bye, Ivy."

She turned, with all of us watching her, pulled the kimono round her, said, "I must look a fright," and went.

She was given a brutal time by the newsbugs when all the stories finally broke, but she dealt stolidly with them, conceding nothing; she was one with unused reserves to fall back on. She had made her mistakes, neglected her daughter and played courtesan with more energy than careful taste, but she had my respect. Not many women or men had that.

Beltane motioned Nguyen and myself to sit down. I chose a seat within easy reach of Cranko, perhaps because I would have welcomed a reason to do him harm for the treachery that had spread like a running sore. He grinned at me as though he knew it and mocked my chances.

Nguyen said, "You are clearing your decks, sir, setting your affairs in order."

"Yes."

"You have thrown in your hand." Smooth as silk, stating without accusing.

"By no means. It will be played out this morning and I'll take the last trick."

Nguyen let him have his little mystery and asked instead, "Why have you brought Mr. Kenney back here?"

Beltane answered at once, "So that he may witness the end of his and his party's meddling." He made a small gesture towards Cranko. "This rubbish also."

Cranko said sourly, "I have my beliefs to act on; you are helpless without the strength of others."

"I'll not swap spite with you; I have news to interest all of you." He was suddenly bright, brisk, purposeful. "Those of you who pay more than minimal attention to the newscasts will know that the Canberra conference of premiers held earlier in the week was attended by overseas observers. So-called. In fact, they had their own irons in our fire, axes to grind, what you will— meaning, a contributing interest in secret deliberations which were not open to the channels or to anyone else. Circumstances have so fallen out that my decision on the matter discussed will determine the outcome. My decision will be known in Canberra today."

He was blandly cool with every word predetermined and exact, in character as premier in session. The political mask covered completely the desperate and driven man. Old Gerald's training had its uses.

"One of the observers called me, at the barbarous hour of five-thirty this morning, on the direct, personally encrypted line." He flicked a glance at Kenney. "How he gained such access becomes a minor question; I will not pursue it." Kenney showed no reaction, only an intelligent interest in Beltane's speech. "The caller's purpose was political blackmail. He insisted that my decision should be the one desired by his country. His weapon was knowledge of my—of Gerald's—oh, call

him my father—of my father's recent treatment in the Biophysical Institute. He threatened to make the matter public. Something of the sort has been inevitable since Mr. Cranko chose treason, but I had hoped it would be delayed a few days while the sale-of-secrets network haggled in its dirty marketplace."

Cranko made a contemptuous, dismissive sound, ending in a hiss of pain as Gus slapped him with his open hand.

Beltane said, "Leave him alone, Mr. Kostakis, unless some purpose is served. The political weapon is powerful despite Sergeant Ostrov's confidence in the sentimentality of the people but the—foreign observer—had another, to be used in case I should attempt to bank on that popularity to stand firm against his requirement. And I assure you that I will stand firm against it. His more personal weapon is knowledge of the genealogical matters and falsified data my wife has just made so unpleasantly plain to you. Add Melissa's regrettable escapade, already public knowledge, and nothing could preserve me against such an avalanche of scandal. The observer—it's best you should not know his country—will call for my capitulation at one-thirty today. He will not get it."

Like puppets on a single string we all looked at our watches. It was a few minutes after eleven.

Kenney asked, "And you?"

"No matter what public revelations ensue, my decision will be made plain at one-thirty. I imagine tomorrow's Canberra meeting will be abandoned."

Kenney showed an emotion now, curiosity. "You will go public?"

"Very public. You might say, most noisily public." The idea seemed to please him; he returned to humanity in a smile close to smugness.

Gus had been frowning over his own thoughts and asked a question as though the fact of his presence

gave him as much purchase in the affair as the rest
of us. Perhaps it did. "How would this observer know
about the adoption thing?"

"My question also, Mr. Kostakis—how? Not, I am
sure, through my wife."

Kenney said, "I have known for several days of the
data falsification."

That succeeded in rocking Beltane. "The hell you
have!"

"Indeed so. It was whispered to me by the administrator of records in an attempt to cover his own position if the news leaked to the channels and he might
then be charged with failure to protect the security of
the Limited Access files. The matter had been uncov-
ered accidentally, he said, during a routine information
search for something else. I am not one to use such
underhand information, but I promised to stand by him
on condition that he kept his mouth shut. Apparently
he did not. I suppose he wanted money."

That was in my field. I said, "Not necessarily the
administrator; more likely the search clerk who stumbled on the data."

"Possibly; I did not think of him; I'm not familiar
with the internal procedures of that department. Are
you, Sergeant?"

"Fairly well. These chance discoveries sometimes
call for police involvement; they're more common than
you'd think."

Beltane said, "Perhaps you can tell us how it might
happen."

"I can make a rough guess at it since it involves old
Gerald faking an entry fifty years back. Something like
this: The search clerk is perhaps doing a legal job, such
as a land inheritance claim that may get into equity
and division questions that go back generations. In the
2020s he comes on an anomaly. The line he is tracing
suddenly expands to take in a boy named Beltane who

makes no relationship sense. Peculiar. He traces further back and finds the kid's birth certificate faked to Gerald and a woman who seems to have no other existence, before or after the birth. He's onto something. Who really is Premier Beltane and why did old Gerald pretend to be his father and who doctored the data? He smells money. He tells the administrator in order to protect his arse and make him equally culpable in secret knowledge. The administrator uses the network to contact Mr. Kenney because he thinks the Opposition will welcome the information. But he's picked the wrong man; he's told to shut up and stay shut. Meanwhile, the search clerk is looking round for a customer. We believe the political information networks reach into Limited Access as they do everywhere else, and that particular piece of dirt would fetch a high price."

Kenney grunted, "Corruption everywhere."

I told him, "You can't afford to be both honest and ignorant, Mr. Kenney. The rats will gnaw your feet before you can get your shoes on."

He said nothing to that. Who the hell was some upstart cop to tell him his business? Irritated by his refusal to acknowledge, I pushed a little harder. "My advice comes from service in the Wards, Mr. Kenney. After all, I was brought back here this morning to give the premier an opinion from the gutter."

Beltane asked sharply, "Did you repeat that to him, Nguyen? Why?"

Nguyen answered with no respect at all, "At this juncture he's as entitled to truth as anyone else."

Beltane controlled anger. I know now that he was saving Nguyen for shredding later. He looked at his watch. "Perhaps. There's time for more truth than any of you will enjoy, time enough to tell you just what was discussed at the Canberra meeting."

I found myself sick of revelations wriggling out as each stone was turned. I said, "You talked about the

bloody cull. You always do, here and everywhere."

He nodded. "The cull that everybody holds in mind and tries not to believe in. Not me and not today—somebody else, somewhere else, some other time."

I told him, "You don't really know how people think."

"You and Mr. Kostakis can teach me."

Kostakis, forever unexpected, put in an indignant oar. "You shouldn't've called Harry a gutter man. To me he's class." His gentle face did not change as he gave a complacently matter-of-fact datum: "I'm gutter, the real thing; I was actually born on a scrap dump. Or so me mum told me. Sometimes I think I've never got off it."

Nguyen smoothed ruffled feathers. "You've reached the Manor; that is something."

Gus grinned at him, and the effect was ferocious. "That's what I meant."

Only Cranko laughed outright. "How does opinion from the gutter smell at close range, Mr. Premier?"

Nobody answered him. Nguyen looked Gus over with an interest close to whimsical, while Kenney smiled for the first time, as if he had found a man he could do honest business with.

I wished I could have spoken as forthrightly, but constraints of duty, of respect for superiors and of the policeman's eternal need to keep his thinking to himself, kept warning my tongue. I had already thrown away strategic advantage by letting anger show.

These Minders of the fates of millions had made game of me in the last two days and nights and of my ideas of right and wrong. They could not or would not understand that my situation as a man bound by oath to carry out the duties given me had forced, the whole time, my connivance with actions that clashed with common morality. They had shown contempt for morality more than once. I had done my share of evil in this life—and writhed for it afterwards—but never with

the cold disdain for right and wrong that invested these men of power. They did not glory in their activities like driven psychopaths; they transgressed against decency and justice like intelligent men whose pragmatism paid full respect to facts and none to humanity. Their disagreements were over comparative degrees of rottenness. Even Kenney's pretenses balanced on knife-edged quibbling as to how dirty he would allow his hands to get.

It would have been a pleasure to walk out on them, taking simple Gus with me, but I was a man under authority, as the Bible has it, learning to what dirty ends an oath of loyalty and obedience can bind.

The real monstrousness was still to come, and Beltane was about to deliver it. "These asides have their interest, but I must keep to the point. I have something to tell you and something to show you, beginning with the cull. It is indeed what was discussed in private session in Canberra and not for the first time. It has been discussed at the highest levels—as a possibility, that is—for half a century, all over the world, by different combinations of powers with different ends in view. The ends can be described simply as variations on, How can we kill off half the planet without ourselves becoming victims? That can be translated as a universal desire to rule the ruins."

His bluntness shocked none of us. We have grown up with the bogey in the cupboards of our minds; having it brought into the light for open survey was perhaps equivalent to being told that your pet dog could destroy you if it ran mad with hydrophobia. Well, you know that, but you don't worry about it, do you?

"There are twelve billions of human beings on this earth. We can feed them at a reasonably healthy subsistence level and for the most part we do, but that level is now strained to its limit. Bulk additives are being introduced into mass-distributed foods. Reafforestation

after the greenhouse debacle still must be balanced
against arable necessity—and half the planet's topsoil
was blown into the oceans a century ago; only God
knows how long is needed to replace it by husbandry.
The sheer processing of human waste, personal and
artificial, is a problem of endless ramification as each
solution breeds a new crisis. Do I have to run down the
list of resources vanished or in short supply, of food
plants whose basic genomes have been lost in decades
of breeding for special environments, and all the rest?
You know that resources are not the true problem;
numbers are. Present demographic opinion—" here he
actually smiled as if his punch line would bring down
the house "—is that a practical cull, designed not for
human well-being but to allow the planet a couple
of centuries to recover at least in part, would reduce
the human population to a maximum of one billion—
a single thousand million."

Someone, I didn't notice who, muttered, "Eleven of
twelve to be—"

He stopped, whoever he was, and into the hiatus
Beltane dropped his one word with the coolness that
comes of having lived too long with an idea. "Killed,"
he said. Then he reconsidered. "Or, perhaps, prevented
from being born."

At the back of all our simple calculations had been
ideas of ruthless enforcement of birth control for half a
dozen generations, of placing limits on life expectancy
with euthanasia at sixty or so, of denying treatment
to the mortally injured or terminally ill, of by these
means slowing population increase until the birthrate
showed actual decline. These stringencies could be
maintained while we husbanded the ruined earth back
to a sane ecology. There would be an era of appalling
harshness, one in which all concepts of sentiment and
moral philosophy would be adjusted, not to the greatest immediate good for the greatest number but to the

rehabilitation of the planet as a total environment.

Despite all statistical demonstrations of the shallowness of this approach, it was the comforting, seemingly desirable outcome—because beyond it lay the obscenity of the cull and nobody wanted to look directly at that.

Yet here was Beltane telling us that our Minders, our balancers of need against bounty, our shepherds through the valley of the shadow of want, had stared it in the teeth for years past. But why should that shock? Deep down we had known what we refused to face. *Don't look, and it will go away.* It hadn't gone away; it had gathered strength to pounce.

Beltane continued in the manner of a general laying out his staff appreciation before announcing the battle order. "Consultation always foundered on determination of method. Simple reversal of population trends by strict control was always out of the question; it could not halt the continuing ruin of the planet. Already some ninety-five percent of all known species exist only in DNA banks against the day when an emerging habitat can welcome them back. Humanity is a disease that slaughters everything in its ambit; now it must slaughter its own flesh in order to preserve a viable core. Are you with me, gentlemen?"

Kenney snapped at him, "To the point, man!"

"The point? Method is the point. Several ways have been suggested. The obvious stupidity of nuclear raids on swollen cities was discarded without discussion. Even with its back to the wall of decision, the race can do without a nuclear winter. Conventional warfare leading to mass annihilation in densely populated areas, reducing millions at a stroke, is wholly impracticable for a variety of reasons, including the fantastic outpouring of scarce resources to achieve a measurable effect. But the real argument against war of attrition is the inevitability of the killers declaring themselves.

Once the attacker is known, even the unattacked take fright; sides are chosen, alliances are made, the attacker becomes the attacked and all plans collapse in chaos. Nobody wants to leave the outcome to chance; everybody wants to be one of the victors. But how do you guarantee survival when every man's hand is against his brother? Warfare is wholly impractical. It might be said that only the need for self-preservation has kept us from each other's throats for the last half century.

"It became necessary to decide who should be preserved and who wiped out, even if the method was still to be found. Of course each alliance had different ideas about that. Blacks would dispose of whites with some sense of justice done, and who would blame them? Islam would have little mercy for the non-Mohammedan, while Hindus and a few others would cheerfully see Islam to the devil. Religion and race are only part of the problem; political persuasions enter, too, likewise possession of mineral resources and arable land—and who you can trust when it comes to carving the turkey afterwards.

"Then there's this: How do you preserve the scientifically and politically competent, or make certain of preserving people with essential primitive skills in farming, hunting, building, weaving and cottage industries? Such skills will be in demand as technology shrinks for lack of use. It will be a pauper planet until it devises new philosophies of living. So the cull is fraught with difficulties, to be undertaken only with absolute certainty of the outcome.

"Disease was an option discarded. Bacteriological warfare directed against food supplies would become a two-edged weapon. It might starve friend as well as foe because bacteria do not recognize boundaries and checkpoints, particularly when mutation occurs. Direct infection of human populations was ruled out for similar reasons; in so crowded a world area control

is impossible. Even oceans are not barriers to disease vectors—insects, personnel, freight. So—stalemate.

"Until now."

He scanned each of us in turn, seeking reaction and getting little. Everything he had said had been discussed to the point of boredom by theorists from the gutter upwards. Until the last two words. His audience was attentive.

He asked, "Do I make myself clear? The difficulties attendant on direct assault have been eliminated." He paused before he added without emphasis or feeling. "The way to global holocaust is open, thanks to the Biophysical Institute."

Only that egomaniac, Cranko, had the stupidity to comment. "Ten for content, only five for delivery. The crowd failed to applaud."

From behind, Gus reached a long arm to take him under the chin, turn his face up and half around, and say, "You'll be one of the first off the drop. I promise it."

"Enough, Mr. Kostakis. I still have use for him." Beltane was amused.

Gus stepped back. Cranko had gone corpse white; Gus's face had imprinted in him a fear of hellfire—in *this* life.

Beltane continued, "I am not highly educated in the technology of mass murder, so Mr. Cranko can earn the price of his meals this weekend by giving us a clear, not too technical account of the work of the institute."

"What's this? Revenge?"

"Why not?"

"An attempt to off-load blame! You knew why the place was built."

Gus leaned over him. "Get on with it, shithead!"

Beltane signaled, *no more,* but Cranko was already in spate. "The biggest problem of the greenhouse years

has been weather forecasting. With help from specialists in the mathematics of chaos it was determined that
greater understanding of the effects of minor fluctuations could bring meteorology close to zero accuracy for periods of up to twenty-four hours with point
predictions possible for areas as small as a couple of
hectares. This meant that conditions might be safely
predicted for the immediate environment of a village
or a city."

It had been almost a gabble, but the gabble of a man
who knew the order of the subject and the simplifi-
cation of its ideas. He had given this talk before, but
not to scientists. To military staff, perhaps, or satellite
operation groups?

"The operational difficulty was in testing the efficiency of microcondition measurements and of the
deductions drawn from them. An experimental method was projected and shown on paper to be feasible.
It was costed at something like forty times the state of
Victoria's annual budget." He dropped suddenly into
the venom that seemed natural to him. "Your tough
premier, the friend of the Wardies, took fright, didn't
want any part of it, saw what the knowledge could be
used for and turned his compassionate back on it."

"True," Beltane said. "I saw that in tandem with
another line of research the physical uncertainties of
a deliberate cull could be almost eliminated. I did not
care to have that on my head."

"As gutter opinion would phrase it, the premier
dogged out on the big decision. But interested people
made sure that members of his cabinet knew the facts,
and cabinet threatened to roll him if he didn't give
the go-ahead. So he said, 'Yes, boys, have it your way,
boys,' and saved his job. So much for his sentimental
conscience. Since it was all done in cabinet session,
the story never reached the channels. The Wards never
knew that their champion could back down."

Beltane said mildly, "Cabinet would have elected a leader who would do whatever they wanted; it was better for me to stay in office and try to control events."

"But you did nothing. You *could* do nothing."

Beltane looked at his watch. "That is to be seen. Get on with it, Mr. Cranko. It is midday and we have still to hear from the Wardies present."

"What can they—" He scowled suspiciously at me. "All right, Mr. Premier, play your game out; it's all you've done for eight years. You took fright when your cabinet showed a will of its own, and you've never been sure of yourself since. It ended in crying for Daddy. Or whatever he is to you."

"You've lost the thread of your discourse, Mr. Cranko."

Cranko took a long breath and said in his platform voice, "Money was a stumbling block, so was a lack of top-level weather scientists to pinpoint the precise structures for microexperimentation. It was necessary to put out feelers in the larger world, and for once the idiotic secret service agencies were able to locate and confirm the necessary contacts without alerting the rest of the planet in their usual ham-fisted way. We were able to gather expertise and a large amount of impossibly expensive equipment from Britain, Canada and the United States. Unfortunately we had to take a scientist from Israel; he was the sole practitioner of some essential techniques."

Kenney observed gently, "A touch of racism, Mr. Cranko?"

"I'm white Australian and I know where my priorities lie."

"You're white but not Australian. Even I am only partly Australian. We are interlopers on a forty-thousand-year-old culture. But that is the condition of the world. My best friend is a Jew."

"Your taste in company is your own."

Beltane tapped the desk. "Twelve-oh-three and time flies. So the institute was built. But what is it?"

"It is a laboratory. The empty cylinder in the center is the meteorological testing ground; most of the rest of the building is devoted to bacteriological experiment; the hospital wards are for the most part occupied by patients playing their patriotic roles in these experiments. Rejuvenation procedures and other dubious favors for the powerful are an optional extra."

"Please confine yourself to explanation, to facts."

"None of you would understand them; I'll make do with approximations. The cylinder at the heart of the building is a well of empty air, but the instruments and activators built into its walls can render it a microreplica of any set of meteorological conditions the operators wish to study—conditions at the edge flows of major air currents, long-distance effects of storm turbulence, ground-air turbulence, moment-to-moment operations of heat gradients, interference by gusts and eddies . . . a thousand interacting forces not in my field of expertise. Measured and computed, they allow such exact knowledge of the behavior of a column of air that an aerodynamic missile of thin plastic, a few centimeters in length, can be launched from an orbiting satellite and landed, without guidance, within a hundred meters of its designed point of arrival. Guidance, you see, is detectable. The satellite records its regular weather observation of the target area and passes it to the institute's computers, which factor in all the variables common to such conditions and instruct the satellite when and where to release its tiny, fragile, buffetable load. The missile will strike where desired, split open on contact and discharge its contents, with a precalculated favorable wind to waft them to their point of operation. No one will know where the cloud of plague came from, save that it was carried on an ill wind. And who will connect it

with a scrap of crumpled plastic rotting in a field some distance outside the city?"

It sounded disgustingly practical, and Beltane was watching us for reactions. Nguyen had retreated into his charlatan's shell of impassivity, and Gus seemed puzzled by the complexities. Kenney said thoughtfully, "In a column of air the full depth of the atmosphere and probably two hundred square kilometers in upper area, and allowing for a slanting and erratic descent, the chaos effects would be too many to formulate."

"Chaos mathematics deals with precisely that probability, and chaos effects themselves usually add up to a total observable overeffect. In practice, the accuracy is about sixty percent of effective drops, with the remainder close enough to guard against the possibility of bombarding a friend a thousand kilometers away by mistake."

"It has been tested?"

"Several hundred drops have been made. None has been detected. Why should they be? Scraps of rotting plastic!"

"Filled with?"

"So far, water."

We have become used to technological solutions to unlikely problems; Cranko was wholly believable. What was hard to believe in that moment was that we ill-assorted six sat together in a comfortable room and discussed—fairly quietly, all things considered—the fate of the human race.

Beltane asked, "Didn't you know any of this, Dick?"

"No. I suppose the party leader has it all, but it has been kept from the rest of us. Network security is strict and effective until some vainglorious ass like Fielding blunders into it. What will be the active filling of these scraps of plastic?"

"A product of Mr. Cranko's busy genius. Don't let me steal his thunder."

Cranko said with the judicious air of a judge at a cat show, "There are several possibilities. I favor a strain of nasal-infective bacteria developed in my own research area. It is airborne and therefore aerobic but can also extract its oxygen from body fluids. Its symptoms are those of the common cold, save for a slight drop in body temperature. It invades both sexes but leaves the males irreversibly infertile. Any community exposed to it in large force should see its numbers halved in fifty years and be extinct within a century."

"The common cold," Kenney observed, "shows no respect for international boundaries. It could sterilize the planet."

"Perhaps this is after all not so common a cold; it is one strain of a family designed with inbuilt instability leading to quick mutation to a harmless form. It does its work on the body in a few hours, mutates with a reduced reproductive capacity and is then easily dealt with by the human immune system. It can be spread by a sneeze or a kiss in the first few hours but not thereafter. I take some pride in such fine tailoring for its purpose."

I think Gus might have hit him again if Beltane had not caught his eye and mouthed a silent order to be still. "Whole cities!" Gus said with a child's wonderment. "He'd kill off whole cities!"

Cranko cringed away from him but in vanity could not stay silent. "Cities! Whole countries! The whole planet if they're stupid enough!"

Kenney asked, "If who are stupid enough?"

"The people waiting for the premier's decision. I don't know who they are. That is not my business."

He was resentful; genius surely deserved a seat on the councils of the great.

"You have heard who they are: Australia, New Zealand, Britain, America, Canada and Israel. All

English-speaking countries except Israel, who entered the club perforce. The smell of racism rises to a stench."

Beltane said, "That brings us to the decision-making process. Thirteen minutes past twelve and time does not slow down. Let me bring you to the nub of the matter, which is that we have a capacity to act. The question debated in Canberra is not whether we should act, but how. The situation has degenerated to that. There are several possibilities."

At this point I was not sure how to interpret what went on here. It occurred to me that Beltane was, however gently, quite mad because only a madman could discuss the sterilization of millions with such placid lack of commitment. Then, too, I was acutely conscious of his reason for having recalled me; I was a piece in a game that had turned disgusting.

Kenney addressed him now like someone gentling a confused child. "Is it wise, Jem, to speak so freely? Why not—"

"What has wisdom to do with what we speak of here?"

Nguyen stood. "I agree with Mr. Kenney. You are in a euphoric mood and present decisions may be regretted later. I recommend a mild sedative."

Beltane's gaze on him was quizzical, whimsical, the gaze of a player in control of the board.

Nguyen turned towards the door. "There are medications in the security wardroom."

Beltane said mildly, "I can do without them," and then, without raising his voice, "If you quit this room, Doctor, you will be arrested before you can leave the Manor. The only equipment you need is the instrument I asked you to bring. You have it?"

Nguyen remained calm. "I have it." He returned to his chair and seemed attentive to what the premier might say next.

So I had got one thing right in these sorry couple of days—Nguyen was no innocent consultant. The threat of arrest indicated activity more serious than mere urging.

"I was saying that there are several possible views of the uses of the culling tool—how it should be used and to what numerical effect, but more importantly, on whom. These questions are neither new nor recent; they are what many have considered but few voiced until the Biophysical Institute made discussion mandatory. You don't create a weapon just to mothball it.

"The first suggestion was that our possession of a practical culling weapon should be made secretly known to all governments, with the recommendation that they take harsh, effective birth control measures or have measures forced upon them. This was voted down. Knowledge of the weapon would concentrate scientific effort and the attention of a swarm of intelligence services upon it; very soon it would be duplicated by other powers and an outbreak of racial stupidity might sterilize the planet. There are times when I contemplate humanity and conclude that this might be a proper solution, allowing evolution to turn to the development of a less truculent species."

Gus said, "Balls!"

"It's an opinion and I am not alone in it. The next suggestion was that it should be used heavily on the most congested areas, less heavily on more lightly populated countries, maintaining a rough parity of ratios with today's figures. This I take to have been the last gasp of the once-British ethic of fair play—to give all poor benighted beggars an equal chance, as it were, with all still on the same footing as at present when it was over. At this juncture the real nature of the discussion became apparent. Fair play was not on the agenda, not on anybody's agenda. The question, the only question was, Who's to rule the ruins? It was an exercise in power."

"Of course." Kenney ticked off his fingers. "Attila, Batu Khan, smallpox for Red Indians, Imperial Britain, Auschwitz, Babi Yar. Nothing changes."

"Quite so. It would be expedient—now there's a word that explains most of parliamentary history—to open up for rescue and redevelopment the most fertile but overused and choked ecological areas of the planet. That pinpoints half of Asia, half of Africa and the bulk of South and Central America. Also, of course, all of Western Europe and the Ukraine—save that nobody seriously considered striking Western Europe and the Ukraine. Those were civilized areas, preservers of the great Western traditions of art and science and philosophy. To be conserved at all costs. Just a light touch of the cull, perhaps, to thin them out a little."

"Besides," Nguyen said with only the gentlest of sneers, "they are homes of the white races."

"Yes. I was surprised by how long it took for anyone to say, *Why not a white man's world?*—but once the dam was broken it became easy to speak the unspeakable. There was some talk of preserving carefully monitored numbers of nonwhites for the sake of the gene pool, but it seems that most Western societies have been so infiltrated through migration that this is not a factor. A more useful suggestion was that reasonable numbers be preserved to form a serving and laboring caste."

"That happened," Kenney said, "to the black branch of my ancestry; they are only recently out of repression. Hitler had a similar idea in the early years of the last century. Others have shared it. Ah, well, power corrupts. What did *you* say, Jem?"

"I said nothing at all; I took the coward's way and cried for my father. I got him, too. All for nothing. You'd never believe what he said to me."

Gus cackled like a delighted schoolboy. "What if he said to scrap the whole lousy idea and let the world rot

any way it likes. That'd stop you with a bloody nose, wouldn't it?"

Beltane seemed astonished, eyeing the innocent face and possibly wondering what he had chosen for a bodyguard. "You are an extraordinary man. It is very much what he said, and it made the first crack in our relationship. When I ask advice on how to act I don't care to be told to do nothing. Think of this: There are seven nations involved; three favor one plan and three another. Australia has the casting vote. Our seven states are also three and three on each plan, which leaves me to come down one way or the other. It is my privilege to decide who breeds and who is never born. No small decision, I think. That old man whom I returned to life treated me with contempt for being unable to make it. So much trouble and nothing for it. So, this morning we will do what no politician in his right mind would dream of doing—we will put the question to the people. We have only two here but they must suffice. Mr. Kostakis, on his own admission represents the gutter; Detective-Sergeant Ostrov possibly imagines he represents the thinking stratum of the masses, all astir with morality and good sense. We will discover what they think. Or what they think they think."

Kenney murmured, "For Christ's sake, Jem, are you out of your mind?"

"Possibly. Or at last in it."

"You can't possibly mean that you will make your response contingent on the ideas of people without . . ."

Beltane topped him while he searched for expression. "You mean, without political sophistication? Why not? They elect us and we treat them thereafter as vote fodder. Let them for once have a say in their own destinies."

Kenney relaxed with a fresh thought. "You talk like an autocrat, but cabinet will decide what answer you take to Canberra."

"That would be proper? Parliamentary? According to the rules? Wait and see, Dick. Mr. Kostakis!" Gus cocked his head, all interest and expectation. "Which of the programs I have outlined would you suggest be implemented?"

Gus eased himself off the wall. "You mean, like speaking for the gutter?"

"For yourself."

"You think that's the same thing, don't you? It may be, but no gentleman would have said it."

"I apologize. Are you angry?"

"A bit, maybe, but you're the top man that can say what he likes."

"Then now's your chance to say what *you* like."

"Then I reckon you're shit. No mind of your own."

Even with permission to speak, that was pushing directness too far, and I was surprised that Kenney laughed aloud. "Oh, Jem, you cried out for it!"

Parliamentarians are remote from us, pictures on a vidscreen, open mouths delivering ghost-written speeches; at close range their lapses into common humanity smell of deceit, as though the screen figure is truth and the real man a poorly made fake. Respect is hard to maintain. Yet, although I had traded some blunt words with the premier, Gus's open insult was more than a sense of fitness could approve.

Yet Beltane ignored Kenney and said to Gus, "That's straight speech and whether I like it or not it's what I require of you. Now, please, your opinion on the cull weapon options."

Gus looked peculiarly gangling and helpless, but I knew better than to think he was rattled, and after a moment he asked, "Didn't nobody suggest a killing bug instead of the sterilizing thing?"

"No. Sudden plagues striking certain areas and not spreading to others would identify plague-free countries

as the aggressors. Sterilization, carefully administered
would delay identification for a long period, and
small leakage of the bacterium into the aggressor area
would make positive identification difficult. Propa
ganda would be used to suggest equivalent sufferin
all round. You couldn't count the victims because the
would show no symptoms, for many years, beyond
forgotten cold."

"You bastards have got it set up right, eh?"

"Planned, yes. Your opinion?"

"Dump it. Don't do anything except close the insti
tute and destroy the bugs. Drown them in acid or what
ever."

"And let the planet rot under its rising heap of livin
bodies?"

"Yeah. Let it rot."

Beltane seemed not to believe him, but Kenne
appeared charmed by this oddity; only Nguyen smile
like an idol with a secret.

"Your profile identifies you as a sentimentalist, bu
your suggestion is for long-drawn suffering over de
cades, perhaps centuries of starvation and squalor."

"I'm not all that sentimental, but I like seeing every
body get a fair go; none of this pickin' off the shit an
keepin' the chosen people. The people have to suffe
whatever way it goes, so they ought to choose their ow
way. You blokes with power are always itching to us
it instead of watching which direction the fair chance
point. But when the people start fighting for space t
breathe you'll be some of the first to go, because you'l
be useless then. How's that for an answer?"

Beltane shook his head, I couldn't decide whethe
in admiration or disbelief. He said, "A good answe
but simpleminded, off the point and loaded with clas
contempt. We should test it for truthfulness."

Gus bridled like a good boy accused of dirty habits
"How's that? I don't tell lies."

"We all say less or more than we mean. Dr. Nguyen?"

Nguyen produced from an inner pocket an instrument I had seen before, shaped like a small handgun, blunt nosed to rest against the skin and force a drug clear through it to vein or area as desired. A transcutaneous injection syringe.

I said, "Don't let him, Gus!"

Nguyen grimaced irritably at me, and Beltane said, "It's a truth drug and quite harmless. Hundreds of people have taken it in clinical tests."

"I'm one of them, Gus, and I say don't let him."

Nguyen said, "The sergeant was caught in untruth."

Gus was puzzled, undecided; he had trust in Nguyen and his probity had been challenged. Nguyen said, "It ensures only the telling of truth, Gus."

I said as forcibly as I could, "Too much bloody truth! Truth right out of your guts!"

I couldn't have chosen a clumsier warning, delivering a straight jab to his pride, but my thinking was cluttered with personal resentment. Gus colored with very real anger and protested, "I'm honest. I don't have to be afraid."

It left in the air an unspoken, *Even if you do.*

Nguyen told him to open his shirt and, when he did so, pressed the injector nozzle under his sternum to deliver the dose into the main artery from the heart. "Four minutes," he said to Beltane. "Then ask again."

The surface of my mind was muttering murderously that I would not let this be done to me again, that under no circumstances would I permit a second humiliation at Nguyen's hands. Behind that was a curiosity, almost an eagerness to hear what belched out of Gus when his defenses melted away; Nguyen, who had given him self-respect with his training, would leave him with a new wound in his vision of himself. I had had the mental strength to withstand and absorb the new truth of my feelings, to rock back to an even keel, but I

doubted that Gus's grasshopper mind would be ab
to bear with himself stripped mentally naked.

The minutes passed in expectant silence save whe
Gus said, "I'll be all right, Harry." He was trying t
make peace with me, so I nodded, OK.

Time ticked by.

Nguyen gestured to Beltane, and the premier aske
his question.

Gus said, "Like I told you, the proper way to go is t
close up that institute and kill all the bugs. Let thing
go their way. When life gets too hard to handle, th
poor buggers that have to live it will look for their ow
answers. It won't be nice but it'll be fair."

Nguyen's eyes were on mine and he was stiflin
laughter. He turned to tell Beltane, "A man hones
on two levels. A rarity. Simplicity of mind or dee
self-knowledge? It is something to be investigated."

Gus winked at me and I couldn't respond.

Nguyen said, "There are greater depths of truth—th
reasons behind the truth."

He gestured with the injector and Gus said, "Tr
me!" walking proud on the edge of the pit.

The dose went into his midriff and we waited.

There was physical change this time. His eyelids na
rowed and his shoulders drooped; he leaned heavily o
the back of Cranko's chair, and the surgeon squirme
nervously away from him. Gus's eyes roamed throug
slits as if seeking a target, but I knew from experienc
that his conscious mind was out of contact with it
depths; the surface man knew nothing of what stirre
down there.

The minutes passed as though time had slowed. W
were silent before the unusual and bizarre. Only Nguye
had any idea of what might be expected from the dreg
of the mind, from areas that I guessed might touc
on intuition, self-preservation and the snake's nest o

repressions. At last I warned, "He could be violent," but Nguyen shook his head.

"His attention will be wholly fixed on the questions asked."

We waited.

It was almost shocking when Nguyen broke silence again. "Mr. Kostakis, what use should be made of the cull weapon?"

Gus's head moved on the pivot of his neck as though he looked for the source of the sound.

He said, with a faint blurring, "Kill them all. Don't sterilize. Don't wait. Kill them all."

The tone was at odds with all my idea of him—harsh, vicious, vengeful.

"Kill which people?"

"All of them. Everybody. What good are they? Selfish. Who cares what happens to anybody else?"

"Why do you say that?"

"Because and because. I know." The next words rushed up like vomit, fast and sour. "Who's killing the world? People. Can't stop eating, can't stop fucking, can't stop living, can't stop anything. Everyone says it's the other man's fault so kill *him* but leave *me* alone to do as I like. You got to get people out of the world to let it live." His voice changed to a saccharine whine as sickening as his hatred. "Let the wild things live— the tigers and eagles and sharks and all the beautiful strong shapes."

His subjects of beauty were startling.

Nguyen asked, "Should you die with the rest?"

Gus's face fell apart, out of control. Tears rolled down and splashed on Cranko, who heaved himself out of the chair to sit on the floor, refusing to look round.

Gus said in the cracked voice of a lonely boy, "I want to die."

"Why?"

"Why live? Who wants me? I try to do the right things, and they think I'm mad. I'm not mad, I'm just lonely. I want to die."

I had a moment's shamed vision of all the world of the lonely, the retarded, the God lovers, the deviates, the bearers of private internal visions and all the unwanted whom we try not to see or accept or understand.

Nguyen asked, "Because you want to die the world must die with you. Is that it?"

"No. Nobody dies with anybody. Everybody dies alone. Nobody cares."

It was eerie. I saw him in the prison of his mind, naked and skinny and shivering in an unrelenting cold, solitary in a vast echo chamber clanging with his own sad thoughts.

Nguyen broke the spell in the practical tones of a lecturer. "His conscious mind is not aware of these miseries save in flashes which it buries to save itself. It is not easy to will yourself to die. The need surfaces also in dreams, calming itself with symbols disguised and unrecognized. Sergeant, would you seat him in a chair? He will experience a certain shock as he recovers." He flashed me a smile. "Remember?"

I remembered. I approached Gus cautiously, not wishing to encounter a sudden outbreak of total muscular concentration. Nguyen understood, said, "He will not be aware of being handled."

He was no more than a heavy doll to be plumped into place.

Kenney said, "The voice of the gutter doesn't help, Jem. You've picked a solitary, a psycho sport, not the voice of the people."

"Did you expect that?" Nguyen asked. "The premier asked me to provide gut reactions and I am doing so, but there will be no consensus from the gutter. In spite of the good John Donne, every man is an island."

I don't think Beltane listened to him. "I want to hear from the sergeant."

It was the moment, and I was prepared for it. I stood up, ready to move. "My opinion is the same as that of Kostakis. The entire setup should be destroyed and the world left to worry its own way out of starvation and failing resources. Other species face drought and famine and survive; so shall we. I suggest also that these secret political talks be made public so that the rubbish in the gutter may experience at firsthand the care and solicitude of the guardians of its well-being."

I tried to say it in the level tone I used when giving evidence in the courts, but my voice shook a little with anger and disgust.

Beltane seemed pleased. "I incline to agree, but I wonder what basic drives lie behind the conscious thought."

I told him, "Wonder and be damned." I could no longer pretend respect for him or his game playing when my inner integrity was at stake. "I've had Nguyen's treatment before and I'm not playing a second round. I'm not baring my belly for him. Good morning, sir."

There's no fool like a dramatizing fool seeking to make a big exit. To walk from the room like a self-respecting police officer, I turned my back, confident that Nguyen would not be able to reach the main artery without my concurrence. He must have come after me like a slender cat because I felt the cold shot in the side of my neck.

Raging at him and at myself I turned about, took the injector from him and threw it onto Beltane's desk, grabbed his right forearm and broke it across my own.

He reeled back, gasping and pale. Resting the arm in his left hand, he retreated until a chair caught his legs and he sat heavily down.

He spoke, and I felt a kind of involuntary admiration for his fortitude and control, "There's no point

in trying to leave now, Harry. The cocktail will be a
little longer taking effect from random injection, but
you would not want to be roaming outside with the
levels of your mind disconnected, would you? Who
knows what might be asked of you and what you might
reply?"

I could not argue with that. I sat down again, miserable and frightened. "Nguyen, you said that this procedure was useless to the premier. So why did you do
this to me?"

"Curiosity. I am a scientist." He let the words hang
like an echo in the air before he continued, "I am
also a human being. I know your mask of self-inflicted
rectitude and I know the welter of unimportant little
shames that makes it necessary to you. It is almost
worth this—" he moved the broken arm slightly "—to
know what at bottom fuels the pride of such a counter-
feit of virtue." He turned to Beltane. "Would you please
use your vid to summon a doctor?"

Beltane said bluntly, "You will have to wait. Keep
the arm still and no harm will come to it."

That was heartless enough to penetrate my self-
absorption and panic at what was to come to me.
Come *from* me.

Beltane continued, "I don't give a damn for your
suffering, Nguyen. When you leave here it will be for
a prison cell, along with Cranko. Each of you knows
why. You will be able to go fairly soon, but you must
see the play out first since both of you had a part in
setting it up. If you try to leave before I permit it you—
or any of you—will be apprehended in the corridor and
returned to this room."

The Small Office seemed to brace itself against further surprise. Or, perhaps, that was an illusion of my
wandering senses as the cocktail began to take its first
effect. I recall staring at Kenney and wondering how
all this affected his consciousness of racial past and

divided present. Then I heard Beltane ask a question and my mouth started to open and shut and make sounds that had nothing to do with my awareness of self. . . .

10

Kostakis:
The Facts of Life

From Commentaries; *The Social Complex: "It is
difficult to refrain from conjecture, admittedly
futile, as to what manner of man Kostakis might
have been, given education and guidance. The
twenty-first century must surely have seen, in its
unregarded masses, the greatest waste of human
potential in historical time."*

For quite a bit I didn't know what they were talking
about, it was that much mixed up with stuff about
satellites and experiments, all over my head. Truth
is, I wasn't listening too hard because I was thinking
about the things Beltane had said about him and old
Gerald.

I know a few blokes—some women, too—who get
their kicks doing things that to me just don't seem
interesting. I don't have any moral ideas about off-
course sex, except for pederasty because that can leave
a kid bleeding and damaged. So I was knocked sideways when I heard Beltane talking about pederasty

like a love affair. As if there were kinds of love I knew nothing about.

It started me thinking about love on my own account, as if he had opened up a whole country I never knew existed, where perhaps everybody had his own ideas about it and two people getting it right together might be . . .

I knew, just like somebody hitting me with it, why love and Gus had never really worked together. It was because I thought my loving was the only kind and when people didn't respond to it I got puzzled and thought there was something wrong with them.

I knew my wife thought I was some sort of a clown. When we got married she thought I was a real breakup, a joker to make life one long laugh. Somewhere she stopped laughing. Got tired of laughing. She changed.

That's how it seemed to me.

And the kid, the little boy . . . When he was little we was the greatest friends. We played together as if the laughing would never stop. But it did. He changed as he got bigger. He started to think I was a ratbag, and wouldn't bring his friends around when I was home.

I loved Belle and the boy, but I couldn't get close to them any more. And I'd been thinking all this time that it wasn't my fault, but it was. Beltane had been saying, under all his stupid confessing, that there are different kinds of love, and all the time I'd been satisfied mine was the only kind. My family . . . I thought they loved me still, or they wanted to, only I wouldn't go their way about living and behaving and I blamed them for handing me off.

What it come down to was, I'm selfish, too selfish to see I had to make the effort to meet them, to be what they called "normal" instead of chasing interests and ambitions that couldn't come to anything because I haven't got the knowledge or the talent or what it takes.

I felt as if my whole life had been wasted in the lies I told myself. Worse than that, I didn't know how to change . . . or which part was the lies. . . .

I had to stop muddling about in my head and try to make sense of what was going on. It come through to me slowly that they were talking about the cull, as if it was something real. They were dead serious about it and had got round to working out who had to go. At first I couldn't believe they could sit there talking it over like a club fixture the boys had to agree on.

But they could. They did.

Harry got hot about being called "gutter," but Harry has a big opinion of hisself. It didn't worry me much because I always knew what Minders thought about Wardies; still, I gave Beltane a serve when my turn came. He had no call to look down on anyone; I come off of a scrap heap and knew it, but he wouldn't know if old Gerald had picked him off of a trash recycler.

When he asked me what to do about the cull, I told him just what I thought and he seemed to like it. His trouble was that it didn't matter what he liked; in the finish he'd do what the strongest told him. I wasn't joking when I said he had no mind of his own; I thought it might put a bit of starch in his spine, but that Kenney only laughed like I'd scored a bull's-eye, and I knew it was only chitchat like a couple of comics on the vid.

Then they got on to this business with the truth drug and that was insulting. Harry tried to warn me off, but I know he's got a weak streak under that copper's hide and I felt like showing them how an honest man doesn't shift his ground, so I let Dr. Nguyen use his little drug gun. I know I answered the same under the detector because that was how I saw it and it was a better idea than their cold-blooded picking over the heap. I felt a bit vague about then, but I'm dead sure the words come out right. They must have because Dr.

Nguyen wanted to go deeper and I didn't see no reason to stop him; he'd only get more of the same.

But this time was nasty. It was like being split in two or like one of those dreams when you're outside yourself but can't hear what you are saying. You know you've got to find out, but you can't and you get that frightened that you wake up.

Then it *was* like waking up because I was sitting in a chair, when I knew I had been leaning over that bastard Cranko. I couldn't remember anything about being questioned, but that didn't worry me right then because it was Harry's turn, and he acted up bad and I was concerned about him. Apparently he'd had the gun before and got caught out in some way and didn't want a second lot. There was things I liked about Harry and I didn't want to find out that he's a liar. Still, I supposed, police have to keep some things to theirselves.

But first he said the same as me but with more reasons, but he tried to run out on the check test and Nguyen sapped the back of his neck and paid for it with a busted forearm, too fast for me to interfere. I wasn't ready, pumped up for rough stuff. It needs warning.

Once he knew the shot had gone in Harry didn't try anything else after that one bit of temper but just sat down and waited. I had time to think then and was trying to remember the dream, if that's what it was after I took the second shot; it was important if only I could place it. Maybe I had said something different the third time. I might have dug a better idea out of my deep mind and told them that; if the drug freed your brain up for truth, that was just what might have happened.

I was really shocked when they asked Harry the question for the second time and he went right away from his first idea. He talked in an ordinary voice as if he was talking about the weather or whatever, but what he said was, "We should make a white man's world.

No slaves, no servants; just us. We can talk to each other; we understand the same things."

Mr. Kenney said, "Listen to the racist behind the mask of professional virtue!"

Harry said, "No, no; I don't care what color they are. Not even dirt-digging Minder shit like you. It's just that there's no peace because Asiatics and black Africans and the South Americans that seem to come all colors don't have the same ideas we have or the same ideas as each other." He sounded so reasonable, as if this was obvious stuff anybody could follow. I suppose it was, really. "They're troublemakers, all of them, always wanting what they haven't got as though we should give it to them. That means trouble, all the way into the future, so why not stop it now? The future's for the fittest. One world, one white world of people that get on together. Dick Kenney, here, he's all right. He lives like a white man and he thinks like us. We don't have to be, to be—what? We don't have to be indiscriminate. We can keep a few good ones. See what I mean?"

Nguyen said, "I see very well," and Harry tried to spit at him, but his body seemed to be out of control and the gobbet dribbled on his chin. He looked nasty.

I got worried then whether I'd said what I thought I'd said. Harry had said, first up, what he thought fitted the picture of him he wanted the world to see, the good bloke all for fair play; now it sounded like he was saying what he really thought, how he felt about the world. What really made his idea stink was the way he invented a sort of reason for wanting it that way. Then I wondered, Did he invent the reason? After all, this was like having truth dug out of him like the muck out of a cesspit and this could be what he believed.

I got really scared then about what I couldn't remember.

Mr. Kenney said, "My maternal ancestors could teach you a thing or two about how well white men get

on together. The greatest wars in history have been yours."

Harry waved a finger at him, admonishing. "That was the fault of different languages. Take them out, too. A white, English-speaking world is what we should have."

The premier had been watching and listening with a sort of disgusted fascination as if he was cornered by a snake. Now he said, "Three nations and three Australian states agree with that plan. Some of them follow the sergeant's reasoning, some find other justifications; only one is honest enough to hate what he calls the black and yellow scum. Scratch an educated man and find his ignorance; scratch a logician and find a sophist. On the whole I prefer Mr. Kostakis, whatever hell he lives in."

That frightened me, because I didn't know what he meant about me and hell.

He picked up the drug gun that Harry had tossed on his desk. "We'll have to excuse Dr. Nguyen on ground of incapacity." He held out the gun. "You, Dick? I feel we should know what lies behind the sergeant's nonsense."

Mr. Kenney said, like the gentleman he seemed to be, "Not I. The whole business is repellent. I don't know what has got into you, Jem. All this playacting!"

The premier came round to the front of the desk. "Then I must do it myself. The purpose is to look at some aspects of the world as they are, in spite of what we may imagine they are. Do you think any of us would emerge from the test smelling any sweeter than these two? Different, perhaps, but scarcely better. And if one of us turned out to have the mind of Christ himself, how we would hate him!"

He hefted the little gun and asked Dr. Nguyen, "Under the sternum, dead center, and squeeze the trigger?"

The doctor said like an automaton, still supporting

his arm, "Squeeze once. It delivers a metered dose." He must have been in horrible pain.

The premier moved up to Harry, who didn't look at him, and stood there, unsure of what to do next. The doctor said, "Sergeant Ostrov, open the front of your shirt."

Harry did what he was told like a vidplay zombie, and the premier jammed the gun into his middle and shot in the dose.

We waited for the longest minutes of my life while I tried and tried to think of what I said under the second dose. It began to seem it must have been something pretty bad that I didn't want to remember, the sort of thing that makes you afraid ever to look in a mirror again. Yet I had to find out.

When the time was up the premier asked, "Sergeant, what use should we make of the cull weapon?"

And Harry said, "Forget about it for now. Keep it for later. Clean our house first."

He had slumped forwards on his chair with his head just about on his knees, and his voice was hard to hear because he was talking somewhere down between his legs.

"Old people," he said. "You know how many old people there are, useless old buggers like old Gerald? No, not him. He's got some life in him. I like old Gerald. But the rest! Forty percent of the population over fifty! No jobs, no use to anyone. Eat and take up space and cost money and give nothing back. Start up euthanasia! You've talked about it enough, haven't you? Think the Wardies don't know what you talk about behind the doors? We know. Do it. Off at fifty! Knock off two-fifths of the world at one smack! No waiting!"

He slipped further forwards till he was nearly off the chair. The premier said, "That would have me pronouncing my own death warrant."

"You? Who'd care? No guts to do the wrong thing

and no guts to do the right thing! Tell me what to do, Daddy, but make it something nice that won't frighten me! It needs people who see straight to take hard decisions."

That should've busted Beltane, because it was true and he knew it was true, but he didn't show anything. I could see Kenney was hating it, but Dr. Nguyen was laughing fit to kill, without any noise, bending over his broken arm and shaking with the joke. It was the first time I ever seen him laugh and it wasn't nice. He was having some sort of revenge by digging the dregs out of Harry.

Beltane asked, as if this was a real king-hit of a question, "How old are your father and mother, Harry?" and Dr. Nguyen made a little clapping noise with his good hand on his knee, as if he knew what was coming and couldn't wait for it.

Harry made a chuckling sound, then I thought it was more like a snarl. "Old enough! Get them first. Get them out of my way."

That stumped the premier, but Nguyen asked, "How are they in your way, Harry?"

Harry slipped off the chair onto his hands and knees. I think this disconnection thing wasn't letting him have any physical control and his body couldn't hold itself up. (Holy Jesus, had I been like that, spilling all my deep dirt onto the carpet?)

Harry said with the sort of contempt you'd give to a queer's pimp, "You know that, Nguyen. Ian Juan Ivan John! I told you before. Ian! Know right from wrong! Juan! Always respect the law! Ivan! Obey your lawful superiors without question! John! Be upstanding for truth! Little boy being prepared to face the world foursquare for the right! But what for Harry? What is there for Harry? Them and their damned love round his neck like a rope till Harry's too old himself and it's too late for Harry. I wanted to kill them but I couldn't. You

can't kill love. It hounds you. Besides, murder's wrong and Harry knows right from wrong. The law says no and Harry is the law! Make a law that says, *Kill them,* and set us all free."

He fell flat on his face as his hands slid away from under him. He kept saying into the carpet, "Ian Juan Ivan John," like a nursery rhyme and made gulping noises trying to be sick.

Beltane ran out of being stone faced. "That's enough, for God's sake!" He said to me, "Are you sufficiently recovered to pick him up, Mr. Kostakis?"

Yes, sir, of course, sir. He couldn't ask another Minder to do it, could he? Bad protocol!

I picked him up and shoved him back into the chair. It wasn't easy because he's a big man and I'm not all that strong when I'm not pumped up to it. I felt sorry for him with all that childhood stuff standing between him and all his natural feelings. Whatever they were. Most natural feelings need a bit of reining in, but his were plain stuffed up.

I heard Dr. Nguyen saying, "Note the essential dichotomy at the heart of mankind. He loves his parents dearly, otherwise their prohibitions would not be so supinely obeyed. His righteousness is simple fear of offending the adored, just as his vengefulness is his inability to free himself from a beloved constraint."

Kenney said, "What an unpleasant calling yours must be," and then I wasn't paying attention to anyone but myself because all my questions were getting answered in my head. The drug must have worked off because I started to remember those missing minutes, a little at a time, like a fog lifting from this bit and that bit until the whole thing was clear.

It didn't matter about wanting to die; that come up like something I always knew but never come to grips with because I never let myself look straight at it. What hit me was sick shame at being naked right through to

the bone in front of these heartless bastards that pawed through my skull just to make points in a frightened game the premier played with hisself.

Then there was another shame, at how the world saw me, at what other people thought about me, at what I knew all the time but pretended that I was proud to be just what I was and to hell with what the world thought . . . when all the time I cared and cared, ashamed because my wife had married somebody that didn't fit the world properly and my kid put up with me and wished he didn't have to—and what really drove me all the time was wanting to be things I never could be. Like that one that challenged the god to music and all he got was the skin stripped off him. That's really having nothing to live for.

I don't know how long I sat there like a sick dog, thinking I would never be the same again and wishing I didn't know about what drove me. The next thing I remember clearly is Dr. Nguyen standing over me, still holding his arm, and saying, "Don't worry too much, Gus. The mind has its defenses. In a little while it will heal over revelation like a scab over a wound and you will draw new strength from the knowledge of weakness."

That sounded preachy, and I was nearly crying when I said, "What about you? What goes on behind your yellow face?"

I shouldn't have insulted him, but I was upset. He only shook a bit and said, "Some fear goes on there because I am found out."

Beltane interrupted, with anger boring like a gimlet, "You surely are, Doctor, and I have to thank Sergeant Ostrov for that. He alerted me to a possibly sinister interpretation of your guidance of my mental welfare; it took the combined intelligence services just twenty-four hours, once the suspicion was voiced, to pinpoint you as a source for field agents of the Southeast Asian

Federation. It remains only to be discovered what you
have reported and when and to whom. Your own drug
will tell us."

Dr. Nguyen said, "At least the police will give me
the medical attention you deny me. I am safe from
interrogation; biochemistry has its uses and it has been
seen to that a truth drug will kill me quickly. That will
leave your decision makers in Canberra with a dilemma
on their minds: Does the enemy know what you have
or does he not?"

Beltane seemed to have cards in his hand that he
kept to hisself. He said, "It won't come to that. In any
case, Cranko probably spilled what beans he possessed
some weeks ago; the network that snared him would
certainly have contacts among enemy agents."

Cranko didn't like that and tried to protest that he
was only locally political. Kenney gave him a tired
smile, the sort you give to a kid who hasn't cottoned
on yet to what the old folks do in bed.

Beltane checked the time and said, "It doesn't matter." He went back to the desk console and killed the
room's sound screen. It was like being put back into a
suddenly bigger world as all the noises of the Manor
spattered into the room. I heard a big laugh raised up
in the wardroom and wondered what the joke was.

Then all the insulated windows went up and the
noise of the whole world burst in. Most of it was the
racket of copters overhead, as if there was dozens of
them up there.

Kenney thought they'd be channel copters and asked
couldn't they be kept out of close range?

Beltane said, "The Air Force shepherded the channel machines away an hour ago. Those are Air Force
fliers."

"For what?"

"Like me, they are waiting for one-thirty."

Kenney opened his mouth, ready to be indignant

then must have decided he was dealing with a man off his balance. He shut up.

There was five minutes to go. I watched Harry come to life. He looked across to me and nodded without meaning anything and put on a smile without any fun in it. I reckoned he hadn't started remembering yet and his bad time was still to come. I felt better about Harry now than I had felt about anyone since I asked Belle to marry me and she buggered her life by saying yes. It was the feeling of recognizing somebody else's rock bottom is just as hard as your own.

The copters must've been circling because they began to fade away towards City Center. They got fainter and fainter and then stayed at the same level of sound as if they had gathered over one spot.

Cranko woke to it first. He screeched—really screeched—"You bastard, there are hundreds of people in there!"

"There are none. They were herded out an hour ago on pretense of a bomb scare. Not altogether a pretense."

Cranko stammered and made no sense for a bit. Then he was crying out about, "Years of work! Brilliant work by brilliant people. Irreplaceable records. Elegant, beautiful experimental procedures . . ."

Beltane pretended to clap. "So much beauty for such beautiful ends! At last I hear you concerned for something other than yourself."

Then the bombing began.

It lasted maybe a minute, in patches as if a pattern was being worked out.

Then it stopped, and it was as if silence had dropped on the world except for a long, long rumble that went on and on as if the institute would never stop falling. Then it did stop, and for a bit we were all quiet.

I didn't really give a bugger about the institute because somebody was sniveling out his self-pity, and it was me.

11

Ostrov: Coming to Terms

This drugging had been different from that first large-scale experiment; I wasn't sure, but I thought so. I thought that this time there had been a second shot, a booster, because there was a definite hiatus wherein I didn't remember talking or being questioned, much less what I had said or if I had said anything.

I felt sick and sore throated as though I had been retching, but there was no stinking mess on the carpet. The first thing I heard was Nguyen speaking of dichotomy and then, quite clearly, "He loves his parents dearly, otherwise their prohibitions would not be so supinely obeyed. His righteousness is simple fear of offending the adored; just as his vengefulness is his inability to free himself from a beloved constraint."

He was talking about me and he was saying something profoundly right, something I knew to be true though I had never thought about it—at any rate, not in those terms—in all my life. Or had I? Had it floated in my mind like a fact unnoticed? Or avoided?

He was trying to be kind. He was like most of us—repellent and remote or kindly and forthcoming by

turns, with no knowing which turn would come next.

I saw Gus, in Cranko's chair still and looking like death, shaking slightly and paying attention to no one, wholly lost in himself and sniffing to hold back tears. I had a fair idea what was happening to him and could do nothing about it. Each man is indeed an island . . . consciousness is a desperate reaching for each other against ultimate loneliness, a need of community to hold at bay the territorial wild beast unexorcised from the foundations of the mind.

I lost track of passing time, self-absorbed to the point of seeing and hearing the people in the Small Office only when some word or movement caught my fleeting attention. I was absorbed in sickness and fear of the unrecovered minutes. A man should not be hit twice with terror of his true self. The mind suppresses with good reason. . . .

There was talk of Nguyen as a spy, seeming so obvious as to be irrelevant. I had known it. Or had I? Had it been one of those mental notes of possibility waiting for me to attend to it when there was time?

There was noise from outside the Manor as somebody cut the room's sound screen. Copters. A swarm, as if all the channels had converged on their prey at once. Somebody, Beltane I think, said "Air Force" and they went away. I heard the bombs—you can't mistake that sound—and thought at once that the advice of the gutter had been taken and the plague spot destroyed.

Then the gap cleared from my memory with smooth menace and the continuity was complete.

I stood aside from me while the bombs fell on Bill and Arlene, burying them and setting me free to blow with the wind, to be Harry at last and never again Ian Juan Ivan John, the puppet of a rhyme. Simultaneously my heart burst with grief and longing and a horror of unfettered hatred, and the bombs fell between the two halves of me.

They stopped and the world stopped with them.

I remembered what Nguyen had told my returning mind and knew that all my contradictions and
brutalities could be resolved—not now but later, in
solitude. In the grateful silence I thought of the fool
who said that to understand all is to forgive all. I wasn't
going to forgive myself anything, only to . . . what? Look
about me with new knowledge?

Only minutes before, I had felt an almost hysterical
ecstasy as I broke Nguyen's arm. Yet he had begun
setting me free while he stifled his pain. Who knows
what hides in us, for good and bad, waiting to get out,
obeying no morality, only need?

I felt a pang for Kostakis whom I had taken up as
a useful oddity and delivered to the torturers. There
something must be done. . . .

I set myself, for sweet sanity's sake, to attend to what
went on around me.

"You have seen that I followed my father's advice
after all—and anticipated the voices of the gutter."
That was Beltane explaining, like a teacher to his class.
"With the institute sitting on the edge of City Center
and close to several National Heritage buildings, the
drop required delicate preparation. The tubular con-
struction of the institute allowed a pattern of drops
causing the whole structure to collapse inwards into
its own central space in a pyramid of rubble. Followed by high-temperature incendiaries. What's left,
Mr. Cranko, will be a pool of lava. Think of it! All
your finely manufactured mutating bacteria boiled and
incinerated in their culture media! All those minutely
calculated chaos-ordered records reduced to ash and
atoms! That's payment for treachery."

Cranko was stunned speechless, and I think it was
the scientist in him that mourned for what he would
have seen as great art destroyed.

But Kenney exploded, "Jem! You couldn't order the

destruction of a state building on your own authority!
You haven't the power for that."

"I haven't and I didn't order it. In the small hours of
this morning I told the Southern Area Services commander what was in there and why and what I felt
could be done about it. He agreed with me on the score
of necessity. Have you ever noticed that the armed
services don't favor cold-blooded genocide? It takes
politicians to order that. So he saw to the action, and
it would be interesting to see, once the tale is told, if
any fool tries to have him disciplined for it."

"You're going public to the country, Jem?"

"To the world. Names, dates, plans, arguments, every
little nastiness, every monstrous selfishness."

Can you imagine manic serenity? We were hearing
it.

On his desk a crypter beeped, and he picked up
the strip of extruded paper. "I usually leave encrypted
messages to the secretarial staff, but I can decode this
one for you. It is from Southern Area Command. It says,
*One hundred percent evacuation; one hundred percent
demolition.* There you have it—not a life lost, not a bug
spared."

Kenney had seen the wastefulness and the weakness
at once. "Now it all remains to be done again. You have
settled nothing, simply deferred decision."

"Referred it to the people."

"My ancestral *kadaitja* man would have known better. Do you expect rational discussion? You'll get panic,
fear, terrorism, war, revolution."

Beltane frowned at him like a thwarted boy, and
barked suddenly at me, "Ostrov! What will the people do?"

I had to shake myself together though it didn't much
matter what I said. "You mean, what will the gutter
vote be? Will the sewers drown in apathy or run with

blood? Either. Both. How would anybody know? But in the long run you haven't killed knowledge; it's all there in scientists' heads, waiting for reassembly."

That didn't disturb him. "Reassembling the weather column will take years; its microcircuitry was unique. By the time another can be ready the future will have been discussed, weighed, thrashed out round the planet. It will be a time for fresh ideas, new alternatives."

What can you say to a man who wishes on the world an atmosphere of terror in the hope that fear will generate a miracle? I said, "Here's one humane idea: Get some help for Nguyen."

The bland Asiatic face relaxed in brief acknowledgment. Of what? A kindness, a relief, a gratitude?

Beltane told him, with no kindness at all, to get out. "The security chief has her orders; she will attend to you."

Nguyen bowed slightly, courteously, to Gus and myself. "Knowledge sets you free to think real thoughts; it removes basic contamination." He nodded to Kenney. "You will find that the way of the honest man is impossible; it leads to the nuthouse." The word was strange in his usually precise mouth. "You, Mr. Premier, have spent your life in a nuthouse created for you by a confused and selfish man, and now you want to bring the whole of humanity inside with you. Bring their repressed fear of the cull to immediate reality and you will see the planet go down in blood as each nation seeks to inherit the ruin. Do not make your confession to the nation; stop the mouth of the area commander; invent any fiction you please but do not broadcast the truth about the institute and its contents."

He went to the door, and Beltane called after him, "The truth will be told."

Nguyen paused, looked back. "I am in no condition to kill you. I hope one of these capable gentlemen will

do it before your stupidity sets the nations at each other's throats."

Beltane said in the calm voice of reason, "My speech was dispatched by courier to all channels as soon as the bombing began. It could be on the air by now. It possibly is. My blackmailer has not called for his answer; I suspect he is hearing it in the public domain."

Nguyen's face showed his pain. "I'm told that a butterfly beats its wings in the jungle and originates a train of effect that may burst in a typhoon in the China Sea. A sexually aberrant man is enthralled by a boy's face and half a century later the planet is given the conditions for a bloodbath."

Holding his arm, he went down the corridor to the wardroom and arrest.

Beltane stabbed at his console. "Listen to my own chip of the speech. You have earned the hearing."

His voice—calm, ministerial, practiced—came like political cream into the room. He addressed the country—in fact the world—as smoothly as he had for years addressed the House. The world knows what he said, is sick of hearing the farrago of confession run and rerun and analyzed. We four—Kenney and Cranko, Gus and myself—would have been the first to realize that we listened to the unemphatic, matter-of-fact, precise words of a man who if not actually insane was, at best, beyond rational thinking.

The hair-raising opening, "The seeds of this speech were planted half a century ago," warned us that he was about to shred his private history on the airwaves, and we listened in dumb, astonished discomfort as he made public the story of his relationship with Gerald, the medical and surgical dealings with Cranko (sitting there like a statue, with a rictus grin) and the previous night's appeal to the father who berated and disowned him. Having stripped his own life naked, he spared nobody, exposing the political information networks

with a completeness that made a joke of the simple
popular suspicions, naming names on both sides of the
House and in the public service (including the police
force) and naming go-betweens who ferried knowledge,
threats and deals for money. He told the story of the
Canberra discussions, naming this time not only people
but countries (and setting the planet's communications
in an electronic jam of denial, excuse and accusation)
and at last of the destruction of the institute. His final
words were as elegantly political as the people were
accustomed to hear from him, and they were designed
to set a match to the pyre: "It was not to be thought of
that decision in such a matter should be forced upon
us by racists, elitists and selfish men. Now the people
will see their leaders as they are and will be able in
future to do their own thinking in spite of them."

There was nothing for any of us to do; Beltane had
upset the board and tossed the pieces to the Wardies
of the world for rending and destruction.

It was Cranko, on his way to arrest and imprisonment,
who had the last word of the morning. "You'll see
democracy in action, Mr. Premier—just for a moment
as its boots smash your face."

Beltane did not answer him. Alone at the desk as we
retreated, his lip jutted in petulance. Misunderstood,
misunderstood . . .

We left him there. The secretaries would have to set
in motion whatever was to be done with him. Kenney
walked swiftly ahead of us, wanting only to be spirited
out as he had been spirited in and not be connected
with the debacle; Beltane had, for whatever reason (recognition of basic political honesty?) left his name out of
the listing of the damned.

The last I saw of him, he was being escorted towards
the parking area by a security man for an undignified
exit in some anonymous van. But who around here had
any dignity left to flaunt?

Gus plucked at my sleeve to hold me back while Cranko went on to the police waiting for him with a Secrecy Act warrant.

I'm not psychologist enough to guess at Gus's state of mind; it must have been damnable, even with Nguyen's word of encouragement. He looked shocking. The innocent face that could ape manic rage had little capacity for the reality of puzzled misery; he looked unpleasantly like a beaten child, and what he wanted to ask was whether or not I considered suicide wrong—as though my trust in right and wrong had come through the morning unscathed.

I could only regurgitate old convictions. I told him, "It would be wrong for you."

"Why for me?"

"It would be cowardice, fear to face facts."

He stopped dead, mouth open and jaw dropped, again like a kid but with the beginning of the raging mask that had terrified Cranko, and this time it was real. He screamed at me like a drunk who sees a single mad vision of all his hatreds and failures, "You sanctimonious bastard! How you fuckin' love yourself!"

I had heard that so often, spoken in cold blood in the past few days, that it had lost power to wound, and now, hurled at me in howling outrage, it started me on a bout of helpless laughter. I suppose I was, at bottom, as worked up as he but more practiced at suppressing feeling; what caught me was probably deep hysteria forcing itself into the light. I know I leaned against the wall and choked and hawked and spat with laughter.

In anyone's logic that should have driven Gus to mania, but it could be that both of us had taken the sort of beating you want to leave behind you; the mental first aid is to grasp at any attitude that frees you from pain. I didn't know what he might do; I was shaking and helpless and gasping for air, and I knew he was looming over me though I couldn't get my

head up to see his face. I expected to be hit by a
madman.

Instead, he slapped me sharply on the cheeks, saying,
"Stand up, Harry; snap out of it, man!" Then, like an
exasperated nanny, "You'll make yourself sick."

He waited while I shuddered back to normal, and we
continued to the wardroom.

I must have got something right, however much by
accident, because I have known Gus for many years
now and I have never again heard him mention suicide.

In the wardroom was the quiet of stunned unbelief. Nguyen and Cranko sat apart, nobody speaking to
them. Treachery has no friends. In that stillness there
could be no privacy, but I had a question for Nguyen.

"Why did you give me that cruel second shot instead
of letting me walk out of the room?"

He said steadily, "Because, like you, I am a professional with a conscience. It was necessary that your
crux problem be resolved."

"Conscience brought you a broken arm."

"It brought you some understanding. As for the arm,
that will be superseded by bullets against a wall. Old-
fashioned but final."

"You did spy?"

"The premier used my name in his foolish broadcast and in the public mind that will be sufficient
evidence. The intelligence agencies will surely find
an execution expedient to help quiet Ward discontent."

That was pretty certainly how it would go. No comment could be adequate. I mumbled that I was sorry
about his arm. He had done what he could for me in
lunatic circumstances.

He said, "I should have taken more care."

That sounded like forgiveness.

* * *

Nguyen was a good man; his tenets were not mine but I could recognize and respect them. But—can a good man be a traitor? Or can a traitor be a good man? Is it honorable to recognize a loyalty higher than the one you have served all your life and which has, as your country, served you? Has a person the right to a judgment beyond the loyalty that supported him while he grew to a mature capacity for judgment?

Would not, for instance, loyalty to the planet's future take precedence over all others?

Or, was loyalty itself a political ploy, a trap to bind the sucker hand and foot and turn thought into a despicable treason?

My country, right or wrong?

Round and round, yes and no. Self-confidence had been sheared from under me. The vision of oneself as a quarreling dichotomy leaves few certainties, but I clung to the thought that Nguyen was, at base, a good man—he did duty as he saw it and in the welter of loyalties found a moment to attend to me whom he owed nothing.

It is not easy to pin down my state of mind just then, but there is a placidity, a sense of relief in seeing all the rigid structures of morality crumble and vanish.

Gus was nudging my ribs. "Here's Mrs. Beltane, Harry." Mrs. Beltane and Melissa stood in the wardroom doorway, dressed for the street and ready to leave, but Jeanette was expostulating with Ivy, trying to make her understand that security took orders only from the first secretary or from the premier himself.

Mrs. Beltane tried to push past her, and Jeanette stood in her way, physically capable of dealing with three like her but not sure that she dared risk using force.

Melissa stood back, puzzled and frightened by the

reality of anger between adults who were, according to her training, supposed to control their emotions.

Her mother called out to me, "Sergeant! Get this woman away from me!"

I had to explain as peaceably as I could, "This is her area of command, ma'am."

"To hell with her and her command! I want to know what I am to do. Now that Jeremy has made a publicly criminal fool of himself, am I to be pushed off home to face four damned channels interrogating and snooping until they are in possession of every secret of our lives? What's to be done?"

I made a spur-of-the-moment decision. "You'll have to stay a while longer. The channels can be stood off here. Later we'll find some out-of-the-way place for you."

Jeanette was stubborn. "It has been arranged that Mrs. Beltane and her daughter will leave the Manor. Only the premier can countermand that."

"Very well, I'll talk to him."

"Not yet you won't." She waved at the com-board where the green light was steady in the top right-hand corner. "He's reinstituted the sound screen. That means no interruption until he signals for it."

"Can't he be interrupted for emergency?"

"Not by you." She meant it. She had had enough of her command being pushed and stretched and ignored. I wasn't going to put her out of my way, physically, in order to reach the com override, damaging her dignity while her men looked on. In that case they might have ganged up on me.

I said to Mrs. Beltane, "I'll go to him," and started down the corridor with mother and daughter hurrying behind me and Jeanette yelling, "You go too damned far, Harry!" But she wouldn't risk physical arrest with all its administrative investigation and snarling any more than I would. She called to Gus, "Go after him

and see what happens. Report every word. I'll not be blamed for this."

The door of the Small Office was still open, which was peculiar in itself when the green privacy light was still showing. I could see without going in that the soundproof windows had been closed.

Beltane was not in sight and there seemed to be nobody else in the room. The strong social taboo against breaking a sound screen held me in doubt (though all you need do is walk through it) until the black splotches on the gold curtain behind the desk decided me.

He was flat on his back behind the desk. He had stood up to do it, and the force of the old, large-bore round had flung him back and down like a doll. He had done it the dramatic, senseless, disgusting way with the muzzle in his mouth to blow brains, blood and shards of skull over everything behind him.

I heard Melissa tiptoeing behind me and saying faintly, "Daddy!" and her mother telling her to go out of the room.

Gus came to shake his head over the corpse, brooding and angry. "What good does that do? He's out of it and everybody else is left to swim in the shit."

I had another puzzlement. "Why did he do it? He could have made himself the hero of the affair, played the one honest man in a dirty world, standing up for his Wardies. He had a life to live."

Gus had found something on the desk. "Look here."

"What is it? Not poetry, for God's sake!" The note was scrawled in short, single lines, like verse.

"No. Well, a sort of a prose poem, maybe."

He remembered not to touch it, and we bent over it together with Mrs. Beltane peering between us.

> *I am nothing, I am nobody.*
> *I am a construct.*

> *I am a botched artifact, another man's*
> *desire for creation.*
> *I am nobody, I am nothing.*

"Lousy verse," I said because the silence was too holy for the idiotic event. "Not even a good reason."

Gus disagreed. "I don't know about that. Old Gerald gave him the emotional heave-ho last night, told him he didn't have a mind to think with or something like that. You and me didn't make things any better. Maybe worse. So he did what we all said and blew the institute to stop the politicking and then took himself off."

"After talking his head off to the channels and telling things he should have kept to himself."

"I reckon he wasn't responsible by then."

I had forgotten Mrs. Beltane. She said sharply, "If I understood that horrible speech correctly, he never was. He was a puppet until the doll master became senile; then he was left dangling on the strings." She turned her back on the desk and the mess behind it. "I make no concessions to deviance, but Jeremy was seduced in adolescence and badly treated by his monitor. That paper says it: 'I am a botched artifact, another man's desire for creation.' So what did he have to live for? He had been discarded and derided."

Jeanette came, asking what nonsense Melissa was crying about, and stopping short, knuckles to lips, when she saw what the nonsense was.

Mrs. Beltane said, "I wonder if he left a will," and we stared at her, thinking, *So hard, so selfish, so soon.* "You think I'm heartless? I have Melissa to think of besides myself. The lord of the Manor is dead in a Manor he inhabited only by courtesy of the state, so this is no longer his or my home."

Gus snorted at her, "You got your own house."

"The house, yes, but no money of my own. House and I were supported by an allowance paid monthly.

That has, I'd say, just ceased, so I am interested to discover if there is any provision in a will."

I wasn't sure of the protocol but I said, "You'll have to stay here a while. There'll be a period of grace while things are sorted out."

Jeanette said, "The first secretary is the man for this," and made for the desk console.

Mrs. Beltane collapsed without signal or warning. She did not fall but shrank. Abruptly her clothes no longer fitted as she dwindled within them; the lines of her face, so fine and unnoticed, became in a moment lines of age; her mouth relaxed in helplessness. She sat slowly down on the couch where Kenney had sat through the morning and her voice murmured in a fog, "I hated him but I wouldn't have wished his awful death on him. Or his awful life."

Jeanette came from the desk to sit beside her, and her glance told us to get out of the place. We left, shepherding Melissa from her spellbound post by the threshold. In the passage she took Gus's hand, like a child, and he was terrified, but by then he had become part of a past in which she was no longer interested.

The first secretary came bustling along, a harassed official to whom emergencies were tantamount to lèse-majesté, and she flung herself on him, crying out, "Oh, Phil, Daddy's shot himself!"

Phil protested, before he took it in, "Don't be silly, girl!" and then, "Oh, sweet Jesus!" and began to run.

12

Ostrov: The Last Loose End

From Commentaries; *Ostrov: "For all of his vague conversion to emotional values, which may have been little improvement on his 'righteousness,' he was in the last analysis only a man of his time, little interested in the great questions to which he gave lip service but wholly immersed in the narrow ambit of family and friends. 'That's how the world became the way it is,' he wrote. Quite so."*

That seemed to be the end of my commitment to the Manor, with the paymaster lying dead. Of course it was not. My secondment was to old Gerald, to Jackson. And he was sitting at home with my parents, who would only minutes ago have listened to Jeremy Beltane's cold-blooded relation of the obscenities of his political life. I would have to take him out of there before accident or deduction announced to them who he was.

I would have commandeered the most easily available work truck in the garages if two detectives from

Center Station had not come through the back door as I reached it. I knew them both.

They had come for Nguyen and Cranko, so I took them to the wardroom where they solemnly charged them with enough crimes against the state to be sure of catching them on some of them.

One of them said to me, "The super says you're in charge of old man Beltane. Right?"

"So?"

"So you bring him along to the station and come in with us."

What charge could be laid on him? Burglary of time? Larceny of youthfulness? "He isn't here."

"Where is he?"

"I'll tell the super where."

They didn't like that, but I outranked both of them and so I sat in the back of the paddy wagon with Nguyen and Cranko and left the Manor without farewell or regret.

In the parkland surrounding the house some kids played football. I said to Nguyen, "The world's troubles don't concern them. They can't alter anything so they keep on playing. Sensible."

"The troubles concern you, Harry?"

"I'll have to help control our corner of them when the rioting starts. If it hasn't already started."

"I think not. There will be small outbursts and then a vast, uneasy calm, a placid film over alarm and despair and hatred of government everywhere."

"That pleases you?"

"No."

"But you did your bit to create this situation."

Unwillingly, he agreed. "But who could know that the disordered man would make public confession?"

"He was beyond reason."

I recited to him the lines left on the premier's desk, and he saw them as a plea for sympathy. "A vidplayer

to the end. The actor believes in his histrionics and the histrionics become the man. 'A botched artifact,' indeed! Still, the old man must have wounded him unbearably to cause such an outburst of public pleading—crying out, 'It wasn't my fault; I was driven to it.' "

"Yet he spared the old man. He told secrets galore but not where Gerald is hiding."

Nguyen glanced at the detectives in front, shook his head very slightly and with his lips formed unspoken words: I will not tell them.

Oh, yes, he would when they took to him! I hoped to have the problem of Gerald under control before some fool photographer made his new face public. He was illegality incarnate as well as a sure subject of sniggering jokes and political grandstanding from the Opposition.

We left the park and moved along the road to City Center. This was not a residential area and at this hour only bicycle traffic moved; nothing attested strong reaction to a world-shaking revelation.

We moved into the top of Elizabeth Street, at the Center's edge, and at last there were people on the footpaths. They stood around in gesturing, excited groups, but I could see no hint of rising ugliness; there would have been more animation for a football final.

"I expected more reaction."

"It will be slow at first," Nguyen said. "It is, after all, only an old fear breaking the surface of reality at last. Later there will be gatherings and outbursts. Politicians might do well to leave town."

Cranko gave a barking laugh but did not speak.

A few weeks later, law and vengeance shot both of them. As though it mattered any longer.

The station superintendent was grim, his mind fixed on immediate duties, keeping the impact of world shock at a distance. "Your Manor secondment will be over

when you have turned Gerald Beltane in to us. Where is he?"

I suppose it was the habit of obedience that made me answer automatically to a direct question, "In my home." Yet I was wondering whether I *should* hand the old devil over. He needed protection, not bullying. As a delaying tactic, I said, "He's done nothing wrong; what was done to him was not by his will."

"With the premier dead"—Jeanette had been in duty bound to pass that information to the police—"the older Beltane becomes an essential witness. And his own legal position is uncertain." For a moment he looked human, even likable. "I'm surprised that you should have involved yourself personally—and your parents— when you could have stowed him safely in a police cell. It isn't like you."

"My brief was to protect him, sir."

"Against the police? Definitely not like you. I've always thought you too cool for compassion." His moment of humanity passed. "You can have a car. Get him."

When I commented on the orderliness of the streets the constable driver said, "We won't get much trouble in Center. It's the Wardies'll kick up." He homed in on his own particular puzzlement. "I don't know what to make of the racist stuff. How can we be like that when three Australians in four are brown or yellow or black or some sort of brindle?"

"Old ties. They dangle down the generations."

"Bloody stupid. The people don't think like that."

"Politicians do when they're looking for overseas friends."

In Port Melbourne, that warren of apartment blocks and lodging houses and dwellings crammed with aging, extending families with no space to spread, the people were in the streets. Where else to go? Yet the

air was not tense. There were groups, a few arguments, even a couple of loudmouths trying to be rabble-rousers, but no sign of mob instinct. They had come into the daylight to see each other, feel each other's nearness and be not alone in anger and apprehension.

They had lived so long with the cull threat as an undercurrent to life that the sudden reality struck no sparks from old fears. After all my tensions of the past forty or so hours (all that had elapsed since I set out for the Manor on Friday night!) it was hard to credit an atmosphere of simple talkative concern. I felt there should be mobs marching and burning, blood warnings flashing across the world, murder in the air.

Well, there would be time for those while the race bred like maggots across the carcass of the earth.

At the house I told the driver to wait while I went inside.

Gerald was not in sight. Dad put down his book and looked questioning but not disturbed; Mum put her head out from the kitchen to say, "I didn't know when to expect you back."

"I didn't know either. I'm hungry."

She did the housewife's split-second calculation of food. "I'm saving the meat for tonight. There's cereal and some fruit."

"Anything. Is Jackson still asleep?"

Dad supposed he was, since they had heard nothing from him. I waited until Mum put the food on the table before I asked, "Didn't you hear the premier's speech at one-thirty?"

Dad nodded. Mum said as she poured the tea (whenever I saw her she seemed to be pouring tea), "How could we miss it? The channels used the priority flash signal." She passed me my cup. "Even if all the things the premier said are true, he should have been prevented from saying them. Couldn't you have stopped such foolishness?"

"The speech was recorded long before I got back to the Manor. Neither of you seems much bothered by it."

Dad asked, "Should we be? What good would agitation serve? A pack of fools was set to be more than usually inhuman, and the premier blocked them, but he should have kept his good deed to himself. The world was reasonably balanced in misery; now there will be enmity and suspicion."

Mum took over. They seemed often to work as a double act. "The dark peoples of Asia and Africa and South America will not forgive that Anglophone alliance. Their share of the land surface is far too small for their numbers and now they have a fine reason for pushing harder into the European and American territories. One can't blame them, but it will be brutal and unpleasant."

The primness of her speech was the telltale sign; she was appalled by events. She was as artificial as any Minder, but at that moment I loved her for it, for keeping feeling at bay while she got on with feeding her son. Her behavior made sense of Nguyen's human dichotomy.

Dad's secret service fantasy peeped out in an eagerness he could not quite suppress. "Why did the premier call you back? Are we allowed to know?"

A day earlier I would have ducked around the question; today I didn't give a damn for discretion or the closed mouth of responsibility. Like suicidal Beltane, I felt free to do and say as suited me. "He wanted to lay truth on the table, no matter who got hurt, and watch it throb. He wanted to speak his own unaided mind for the first time in his adult life. He was mad."

Mum reproved, "You shouldn't speak like that. He was unwise, certainly."

"I mean mad. Insane. Out of his mind. Trash for the looney bin. And when he'd finished doing maximum

damage he shot the back of his head out. He's dead. I found the body."

They were suitably horrified for the moment that horror lasts in a violent world, until Dad said, "There's been no vid announcement."

"They'll hold it until they set the deputy premier in control and work out a smart lie to cover the facts. They'll say he was out of his mind and spouting garbage, but too many people around the world know that he told truth. Including the Southeast Asia Federation. Still, don't go putting it round the neighborhood yet."

Mum said, "You know I don't gossip," and Dad, "We know how to keep quiet."

Their awful equanimity pierced my calm. "Don't you care? Aren't you afraid of the future?"

Dad said, "We have always been afraid of the future. Our world fell apart in the thirties, but we survived. Life became less livable, but it still went on."

"Perhaps not this time."

Mum was admitting nothing. "You worry too much. I suppose it's in the nature of your work."

If the hordes of Asia poured in overnight they would find my parents drinking tea, quietly affronted by noisy invasion manners, preserving the masks that helped make empty existences bearable.

I told them that I had returned for Jackson. "I have to put him under arrest and take him in."

Dad wanted to know what he had done. "Or should I not ask?"

"Protective custody only."

"He has enemies? In the Manor?" For once in his life his romantic notions paid a dividend as he made the intuitive leap: "Visiting politician? With the new face the premier spoke of? That one?"

"Yes. I'll get him out of here. You won't want him hanging around."

Mum surprised me. "Do I hear morality speaking? Be gentle with him."

I marveled, "Nothing shakes you two, does it?"

They made that lightning communication of eyes that comes with time and love, and Dad said, "Many things shake us, but even fear becomes commonplace, like noises in the street. Small compensations are one's life, not the large despairs. So do what you have to do with the man and come back to us when you can."

It had never before occurred to me that they missed me during my absences, that their son was one of the compensations for despair. I thought of Nguyen leaving his family without farewell and of Gus unable to be at one with his, and was ashamed.

Gerald (there was no point now in thinking rigorously of him as Jackson) rose a little from the pillow when I entered. He was in glaring mood, bear savage.

I tried with, "Were you able to sleep?"

"With that damned thing squawking in my ear?" He jerked his head at the tabletop vid I kept for long nights when shift rotation left me awake while my parents slept. "It nagged at me to listen to a special bulletin."

"So you don't need me to tell you what has happened."

He snarled at me, "Were you looking forward to telling me?"

"No." I had dreaded it.

"Don't pity me!"

"I must. I'm human."

"You are? What other wonders do you bring?"

He was hiding behind his game of get the copper's goat, and I had no urge to explain my changing heart to him.

He sat up and put his feet to the floor. "Made a fool of himself, didn't he?"

"Of you, I think. You taught him and wrecked him."

That was cruel, but there had to be an end of his playacting. He folded his hands between his knees and bowed his head and said quietly, without any tremor, "Leave me a little dignity, Harry. Last night my disappointment and wounded vanity exposed the fact that love had foundered long before. Can you listen— before the psychiatrists get at me and tear motive and intention to falsified pieces?" He fumbled at openings until, baldly, "Are child molesters still hated?"

"Yes. People don't give a pimp's curse about sexual preferences—I don't think most ever did—but pederasty has always been the unendurable perversion."

He said in a wondering tone, "Pederasty? I never thought of it like that. Jem was the only time for me. I bedded women all my life but never loved them as I loved the boy. I wanted a son, but there was a congenital defect and the new laws banned IVF; if you couldn't, you didn't. Do you know why I wanted a son?"

He needed an answer, to be comforted that another could understand him. I made a stab at it: "To carry on when you would have to leave off. To leave a continuing mark on our history."

He was pleased with me. "Yes!"

"Well, you've surely done that." There was no point in letting him wander among his dreams.

"I know I spoiled it, Harry. Or did I? Was it just the luck that ran against me, the senility and the Alzheimer years? You can't say I didn't train him well; he went up through the ranks like a bullet. Oh, I was proud! And then there was a more personal pleasure . . ."

He paused to consider that. I suggested, "Of running the show from behind the curtain. Dealing and manipulating."

"Yes, Harry—the vanity. It clouds the vision more than hate or love or despair; nothing warns you when to stop or to try to see straightly what you are about.

Jem and I didn't last long as lovers. That was a side issue, an excuse I made to myself for choosing this intelligent, malleable son. I never did such a thing again. Truth is, I suppose, that I gave all my love to myself. No matter. I taught him well, and when I faded out he went on to become premier, without me. I came back from the dimness to find him head of the state, and that was some justification for it all. If I had been there to steer and advise he wouldn't have been premier of Victoria but prime minister of Australia.

"I knew something was wrong when he visited the ward. An uncertainty. A lack of strength. I didn't see yet that all his certainty and strength in the past had been my certainty and strength. If he had had any of his own I had knocked them down and imposed mine. I failed to see that he became only a speech-making extension of myself. Then I retired into incompetence, and he ran for years on borrowed impetus until he came to the problem he couldn't solve. He skidded to a helpless halt, crying for the father who had deserted him. So he called me back, and last night he told me how he had let himself be maneuvered into the hands of political blackmailers and a spy. You know all that."

"Yes."

"I let myself be disgusted with him. Vanity ruled. He had broken the first rule of confrontational politics: Trust nobody! Now he was in an impossible position that he wanted me to see him out of. That's where the end began."

He stood to stretch his arms and legs as though he ironed out creases in himself, but I have the impression that he needed to be on his feet to say the rest without whining.

He bared his teeth in what should have been mockery, but there was no mirth there. "Two lifetimes of devotion ended where every divorce begins, in recrimi-

nation and name-calling and the exposure of feelings concealed under years of habit. I raged at his stupidity and found myself berating an empty vessel labeled premier, while he resented being talked down to by an old fool he had rescued from doddering senility. He wanted a comforter and got a contemptuous scold. I wanted pride in my creation and got a puppet that had lost its strings. At some stage he yelled that all his mistakes were mine, that he was what I had made him—and that was where both of us realized that true affection had died when we had become a ruthless team where I planned the strategies and he kicked the goals. The end of love is cold dislike on both sides.

"At some stage I told him that any fool could see that the institute must be destroyed and the whole situation brought to a halt. He said that would finish nothing, but I made him see that it would get them all a breathing space. Some fool said that politics is the art of the possible. It isn't; it's the art of the stopgap. We parted in anger, but at least he did what I told him; he had the foul place destroyed. I suppose he could think of nothing better. Then he had to tell the world about it! He must have been out of his mind."

"He was. He shot himself. He is dead."

He looked at me for a long time without speaking. His face changed gradually, rumpling like paper crushed between the hands, and silent tears edged out of his eyes and down the wasted reconstruction of his cheeks.

He felt aimlessly at his pockets for a handkerchief, then took the one I offered him to scrub at his face like an angry child. He said in a voice like stone grinding, "Pay no attention. It's only self-pity."

He sat back on the bed, all pride gone out of him.

Someone knocked.

Mum called through the door, "Your driver is asking how long you will be. He says the station keeps vidding him."

I opened the door a little way. "I'll be with him in a few minutes."

She peered past me to Gerald with frank curiosity in a sudden celebrity, however tarnished.

Gerald recovered aplomb with a public performer's agility and closed one eye to her in a conspiratorial, meaningless wink. She giggled like a schoolgirl as she shut the door, and I reflected that I had never before heard my well-conducted mother giggle. Or, perhaps, I hadn't noticed. In God's name, where had my eyes been all these years? Fixed on myself?

I said, "We'd better go," and opened the wardrobe to get my uniform. It was time again for professional harness; secondment really was over.

"Go where?"

As I laid out the jacket, shirt and trousers I told him I had to take him in.

"I thought I was to stay here."

"That was a good idea, but a dead man's orders no longer run. The commissioner wants you and I have to deliver you. I'm sorry." I meant it; I saw no humane future for him.

"I have committed no crime."

"Not recently, but there was once a falsification of records, contribution to the delinquency of a minor and later on a fraudulent imposition on Parliament. If they want to get you they'll rake up charges from history if they must."

"From half a century ago!"

"But with ongoing consequences. And your right to life will be questioned."

He sat back on the bed. "That's a poor ending."

They might, I thought, find some circuitously legal way to invoke the euthanasia provisions. That would be kind though kindness would not be the object. I picked up the braided cap and shepherded him before me into the lounge room. The mid-afternoon was bril-

liant in the front window and Gerald gestured angrily at it.

"Look there! I've scarcely had opportunity to see the daylight and they're ready to close me in." He swung on me. "Is an old man's detention so urgent as to deny him an hour's walk in the sun?"

I started to tell him not to be so damned silly and in mid-sentence changed my mind. Without thinking it through I said, "Walk in the sun if you want to. The commissioner can wait that long."

He hadn't really expected that. "Do you mean it?"

"Why not?"

At this late hour in his affairs he still couldn't resist a dig. "Where's my Ape, my dutiful orders man?"

"It's a day of changes for me, too." He could make what he wished of that. "My father might like to take the walk with you."

Dad looked suitably startled until he decided that subtle planning lay behind my words and was at once ready to take his part in intrigue.

Gerald asked, "To keep an eye on me?"

"Company. Where could you run to?"

He shrugged and said to Dad, "It will be a pleasure to spend an hour with a cultured gentleman." So composure was to be the stage direction; he would carry it well. "I recall that as a boy I used to walk out along the jetties on the beachfront. Some were dismantled when the water level rose. Do any remain?"

Dad said, "There is one, preserved by the National Heritage Foundation."

"Good. I should like to stand there in sunlight and look over the sea. It should be not too far from here."

Dad matched him, olde worlde hospitality for total self-control: "Some ten minutes, but the UV is strong and you have no hat. Allow me to loan you one."

"A kind thought. Thank you."

The exchange of gents' club courtesies had to be

brought back to this day and age; I told them, "Go out the back way; there's a policeman in front."

From the back door Gerald said to me, "Thank you, Harry. I trust this will cause you no embarrassment."

"Who cares?"

He permitted himself a theatrical raised eyebrow. *Is my Ape a human in disguise?* At the laneway he put on Dad's hat, which was a trifle too big for him, and gave a brief wave. The expression on his face was pure mischief; we two had made our deal. The pair of them ambled away together.

Mum said, "I hope you know what you are doing?"

"What am I doing?"

"Risking your career."

My career. She did not mention the consequent descent into poverty for herself and Dad. I didn't deserve them.

She asked, "What's come over you? Why did you send your father with him?"

"To be a witness." That is, if Gerald's nerve held.

She began to gather up the cups and saucers. "You've changed overnight, become somebody else. What has happened?"

"I was given my life to look at and I didn't like it."

I went out to the driver and told him to take the patrol car back to the station.

"What about the prisoner we had to pick up?"

"He isn't here."

"Is that all I tell the super?"

"That's all. I'll see him later."

I watched the time edge slowly by until, after just fifty-three minutes, Dad came back, alone and shaken but still buoyed at having played his little part on the fringe of great events and asking wonderingly, "Did you know what he intended?"

"More or less."

"You should have warned me."

"And spoiled it for him? He liked an unexpected twist. How did he do it?"

Dad searched for a word. "Formally. Like the gentleman he seems never to have been in fact. We walked to the end of the pier while he expounded his rather cynical view of the immediate future; then he said, apropos of nothing, 'Tell Harry: *Vanitas vanitatum*— and there's an end of it.' He handed me my hat, thanked me for the loan and stepped off into six or seven meters of water. I watched the bubbles rise as he emptied his lungs. I imagine he gulped water and drowned at once." He gave me the undercover look of a back room boy making his report. "There was no one near us to help and, as I told the desk officer when I reported the accident, I can't swim."

Dad must have done some thinking on the end of the pier; he swims better than I do. However, in these days we don't interfere gratuitously with the choice of life or death. You don't get thanked for it.

Later in the evening I told the superintendent what I had done and even gave a nonsensical account of feeling sorry for the old man (which may have been the truth, or some of it) as a reason for my action.

He heard me out in grim disbelief and vidded the commissioner. He believed still less in the texture of reality when the commissioner called me to the screen, dressed me down very mildly for taking the case into my own hands and decided that under the circumstances it was as useful an outcome as any. The deputy premier had got to him, I guessed.

The super, balked of a hapless victim, could only order me to report for duty to my suburban station in the morning.

I went home.

*   *   *

Public numbness wore off quickly; there were mob-
bings and manhunts and street brawls in the night,
fired by the cynical outrage of the vid releases from the
colored nations who saw whitey delivered into their
insulted hands.

I was called out to do my professional job of mob control in the streets, but my thoughts were elsewhere—
with my empty mind, shorn of easy morality and stupid certainties and the thoughtless habit of belief in my
own probity . . .

With Gus, who needed someone to stick by him while
he struggled for balance . . .

With my father and mother and the long, long job of
getting to know them . . .

The horrors to come meant little while I battled with
the problems of the here and now.

That's the human fashion. Tomorrow is always a
long way off. Something will turn up, won't it? We'll
muddle through.

Won't we?

Won't we?

That's how the world became the way it is.

Contents

For
Russell and Jenny Blackford
who have done so much
for Australian
science fiction

THE DESTINY MAKERS is an original publication of Avon Books. This work has never before appeared in book form. This work is a novel. Any similarity to actual persons or events is purely coincidental.

AVON BOOKS
A division of
The Hearst Corporation
1350 Avenue of the Americas
New York, New York 10019

Copyright © 1993 by George Turner
Cover illustration by Dorian Vallejo
Published by arrangement with the author
Library of Congress Catalog Card Number: 92-2414
ISBN: 0-380-71887-1

First AvoNova Printing: November 1993
First Morrow/AvoNova Hardcover Printing: February 1993

AVON TRADEMARK REG. U.S. PAT. OFF. AND IN OTHER COUNTRIES, MARCA REGISTRADA, HECHO EN U.S.A.

Printed in the U.S.A.

RA 10 9 8 7 6 5 4 3 2 1

KT-562-658

THE DESTINY MAKERS

GEORGE TURNER

AVON BOOKS • NEW YORK

My Age of Anxiety

Fear, Hope, Dread and the Search for Peace of Mind

S<small>COTT</small> S<small>TOSSEL</small>

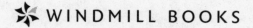

Published by Windmill Books 2014

4 6 8 10 9 7 5

Copyright © Scott Stossel 2014

Scott Stossel has asserted his right under the Copyright, Designs and
Patents Act, 1988, to be identified as the author of this work.

First published in Great Britain in 2014 by William Heinemann

Windmill Books
The Random House Group Limited
20 Vauxhall Bridge Road, London SW1V 2SA

Addresses for companies within The Random House Group Limited can be found at:
www.randomhouse.co.uk/offices.htm

The Random House Group Limited Reg. No. 954009

www.randomhouse.co.uk

A CIP catalogue record for this book
is available from the British Library

ISBN 9780099592068

Printed and bound by CPI Group (UK) Ltd, Croydon, CR0 4YY

For Maren and Nathaniel—
may you be spared.

Contents

PART V
Redemption and Resilience

PART I

The Riddle of Anxiety

The Nature of Anxiety

And no Grand Inquisitor has in readiness such terrible tortures as has anxiety, and no spy knows how to attack more artfully the man he suspects, choosing the instant when he is weakest, nor knows how to lay traps where he will be caught and ensnared, as anxiety knows how, and no sharpwitted judge knows how to interrogate, to examine the accused as anxiety does, which never lets him escape, neither by diversion nor by noise, neither at work nor at play, neither by day nor by night.

—SØREN KIERKEGAARD, *The Concept of Anxiety* (1844)

There is no question that the problem of anxiety is a nodal point at which the most various and important questions converge, a riddle whose solution would be bound to throw a flood of light on our whole mental existence.

—SIGMUND FREUD,
Introductory Lectures on Psycho-Analysis (1933)

I have an unfortunate tendency to falter at crucial moments.

For instance, standing at the altar in a church in Vermont, waiting for my wife-to-be to come down the aisle to marry me, I start to feel horribly ill. Not just vaguely queasy, but severely nauseated and shaky—and, most of all, sweaty. The church is hot that day—it's early July—and many people are perspiring in their summer suits and sundresses. But not like I am. As the processional plays, sweat begins to bead on my forehead and above my upper lip. In wedding photos, you can see me standing tensely at the altar, a grim half smile on my face, as I watch my fiancée come down the aisle on the arm of her father: in the photos, Susanna is glowing; I am glistening. By the time she joins me in the front of the church, rivulets of sweat are running into my eyes and dripping down my collar. We turn to face the minister. Behind him are the friends we have asked to give readings, and I see them looking at me with manifest concern. *What's wrong with him?* I imagine they are thinking. *Is he going to pass out?* Merely imagining these thoughts makes me sweat even more. My best man, standing a few feet behind me, taps me on the shoulder and hands me a tissue to mop my brow. My friend Cathy, sitting many rows back in the church, will tell me later that she had a strong urge to bring me a glass of water; it looked, she said, as if I had just run a marathon.

The wedding readers' facial expressions have gone from registering mild concern to what appears to me to be unconcealed horror: *Is he going to die?* I'm beginning to wonder that myself. For I have started to shake. I don't mean slight trembling, the sort of subtle tremor that would be evident only if I were holding a piece of paper—I feel like I'm on the verge of convulsing. I am concentrating on keeping my legs from flying out from under me like an epileptic's and am hoping that my pants are baggy enough to keep the trembling from being too visible. I'm now leaning on my almost wife—there is no hiding the trembling from her—and she is doing her best to hold me up.

The minister is droning on; I have no idea what he's saying. (I am not, as they say, present in the moment.) I'm praying for him to hurry up so I can escape this torment. He pauses and looks down at my betrothed and me. Seeing me—the sheen of flop sweat, the panic in my eyes—he is alarmed. "Are you okay?" he mouths silently. Helplessly, I nod that I am. (Because what would he do if I said that I wasn't? Clear the church? The mortification would be unbearable.)

As the minister resumes his sermon, here are three things I am actively fighting: the shaking of my limbs; the urge to vomit; and unconsciousness. And this is what I am thinking: *Get me out of here.* Why? Because there are nearly three hundred people—friends and family and colleagues—watching us get married, and I am about to collapse. I have lost control of my body. This is supposed to be one of the happiest, most significant moments of my life, and I am miserable. I worry I will not survive.

As I sweat and swoon and shake, struggling to carry out the wedding ritual (saying "I do," putting the rings on, kissing the bride), I am worrying wretchedly about what everyone (my wife's parents, her friends, my colleagues) must be thinking as they look at me: *Is he having second thoughts about getting married? Is this evidence of his essential weakness? His cowardice? His spousal unsuitability?* Any doubt that any friend of my wife's had, I fear, is being confirmed. *I knew it,* I imagine those friends thinking. *This* proves *he's not worthy of marrying her.* I look as though I've taken a shower with my clothes on. My sweat glands—my physical frailty, my weak moral fiber—have been revealed to the world. The unworthiness of my very existence has been exposed.

Mercifully, the ceremony ends. Drenched in sweat, I walk down the aisle, clinging gratefully to my new wife, and when we get outside the church, the acute physical symptoms recede. I'm not going to have convulsions. I'm not going to pass out. But as I stand in the reception line, and then drink and dance at the reception, I'm pantomiming happiness. I'm smiling for the camera, shaking hands—and wanting to die. And why not? I have failed at one of the most elemental of male jobs: getting married. How have I managed to cock this up, too? For the next seventy-two hours, I endure a brutal, self-lacerating despair.

Anxiety kills relatively few people, but many more would welcome death as an alternative to the paralysis and suffering resulting from anxiety in its severe forms.
—DAVID H. BARLOW, *Anxiety and Its Disorders* (2004)

My wedding was not the first time I'd broken down, nor was it the last. At the birth of our first child, the nurses had to briefly stop ministering to my wife, who was in the throes of labor, to attend to me as I turned pale and keeled over. I've frozen, mortifyingly, onstage at public lectures and presentations, and on several occasions I have been compelled to run offstage. I've abandoned dates, walked out of exams, and had breakdowns during job interviews, on plane flights, train trips, and car rides, and simply walking down the street. On ordinary days, doing ordinary things—reading a book, lying in bed, talking on the phone, sitting in a meeting, playing tennis—I have thousands of times been stricken by a pervasive sense of existential dread and been beset by nausea, vertigo, shaking, and a panoply of other physical symptoms. In these instances, I have sometimes been convinced that death, or something somehow worse, was imminent.

Even when not actively afflicted by such acute episodes, I am buffeted by worry: about my health and my family members' health; about finances; about work; about the rattle in my car and the dripping in my basement; about the encroachment of old age and the inevitability of death; about everything and nothing. Sometimes this worry gets transmuted into low-grade physical discomfort—stomachaches, headaches, dizziness, pains in my arms and legs—or a general malaise, as though I have mononucleosis or the flu. At various times, I have developed anxiety-induced difficulties breathing, swallowing, even walking; these difficulties then become obsessions, consuming all of my thinking.

I also suffer from a number of specific fears or phobias. To name a few: enclosed spaces (claustrophobia); heights (acrophobia); fainting (asthenophobia); being trapped far from home (a species of agoraphobia); germs (bacillophobia); cheese (turophobia); speaking in public (a subcategory of social phobia); flying (aerophobia); vomiting (emetophobia); and, naturally, vomiting on airplanes (aeronausiphobia).

When I was a child and my mother was attending law school at night, I spent evenings at home with a babysitter, abjectly terrified that my parents had died in a car crash or had abandoned me (the clinical term for this is "separation anxiety"); by age seven I had worn grooves in the carpet of my bedroom with my relentless pacing, trying to will my parents to come home. During first grade, I spent nearly every afternoon for months in the school nurse's office, sick with psychosomatic headaches, begging to go home; by third grade, stomachaches had replaced headaches, but my daily trudge to the infirmary remained the same. During high school, I would purposely lose tennis and squash matches to escape the agony of anxiety that competitive situations would provoke in me. On the one—the only one—date I had in high school, when the young lady leaned in for a kiss during a romantic moment (we were outside, gazing at constellations through her telescope), I was overcome by anxiety and had to pull away for fear that I would vomit. My embarrassment was such that I stopped returning her phone calls.

In short, I have since the age of about two been a twitchy bundle of phobias, fears, and neuroses. And I have, since the age of ten, when I was first taken to a mental hospital for evaluation and then referred to a psychiatrist for treatment, tried in various ways to overcome my anxiety.

Here's what I've tried: individual psychotherapy (three decades of it), family therapy, group therapy, cognitive-behavioral therapy (CBT), rational emotive therapy (RET), acceptance and commitment therapy (ACT), hypnosis, meditation, role-playing, interoceptive exposure therapy, in vivo exposure therapy, supportive-expressive therapy, eye movement desensitization and reprocessing (EMDR), self-help workbooks, massage therapy, prayer, acupuncture, yoga, Stoic philosophy, and audiotapes I ordered off a late-night TV infomercial.

And medication. Lots of medication. Thorazine. Imipramine. Desipramine. Chlorpheniramine. Nardil. BuSpar. Prozac. Zoloft. Paxil. Wellbutrin. Effexor. Celexa. Lexapro. Cymbalta. Luvox. Trazodone. Levoxyl. Propranolol. Tranxene. Serax. Centrax. St. John's wort. Zolpidem. Valium. Librium. Ativan. Xanax. Klonopin.

Also: beer, wine, gin, bourbon, vodka, and scotch.

Here's what's worked: nothing.

Actually, that's not entirely true. Some drugs have helped a little, for finite periods of time. Thorazine (an antipsychotic, which used to be classified as a major sedative) and imipramine (a tricyclic antidepressant) combined to help keep me out of the psychiatric hospital in the early 1980s, when I was in middle school and ravaged by anxiety. Desipramine, another tricyclic, got me through my early twenties. Paxil (a selective serotonin reuptake inhibitor, or SSRI) gave me about six months of significantly reduced anxiety in my late twenties before the fear broke through again. Ample quantities of Xanax, propranolol, and vodka got me (barely) through a book tour and various public lectures and TV appearances in my early thirties. A double scotch plus a Xanax and a Dramamine can sometimes, when administered before takeoff, make flying tolerable—and two double scotches, when administered in quick enough succession, can obscure existential dread, making it seem fuzzier and further away.

But none of these treatments have fundamentally reduced the underlying anxiety that seems woven into my soul and hardwired into my body and that at times makes my life a misery. As the years pass, the hope of being cured of my anxiety has faded into a resigned desire to come to terms with it, to find some redemptive quality or mitigating benefit to my being, too often, a quivering, quaking, neurotic wreck.

Anxiety is the most prominent mental characteristic of Occidental civilization.
— R. R. WILLOUGHBY, *Magic and Cognate Phenomena* (1935)

Anxiety and its associated disorders represent the most common form of officially classified mental illness in the United States today, more common even than depression and other mood disorders. According to the National Institute of Mental Health, some forty million Americans, nearly one in seven of us, are suffering from some kind of anxiety disorder at any given time, accounting for 31 percent of the expenditures on mental health care in the United States. According to recent epidemiological data, the "lifetime incidence" of anxiety disorder is more than 25 percent—which, if true, means that one in four of us can expect to be stricken by debilitating anxiety at some point in our lifetimes. And it *is* debilitating: Recent academic papers have argued that the psychic and physical impairment tied to living with an anxiety disorder is equivalent to living with diabetes—usually manageable, sometimes fatal, and always a pain to deal with. A study published in *The American Journal of Psychiatry* in 2006 found that Americans lose a collective 321 million days of work because of anxiety and depression each year, costing the economy $50 billion annually; a 2001 paper published by the U.S. Bureau of Labor Statistics once estimated that the median number of days missed each year by American workers who suffer from anxiety or stress disorders is twenty-five. In 2005—three years before the recent economic crisis hit—Americans filled fifty-three million prescriptions for just two antianxiety drugs: Ativan and Xanax. (In the weeks after 9/11, Xanax prescriptions jumped 9 percent nationally— and by 22 percent in New York City.) In September 2008, the economic crash caused prescriptions in New York City to spike: as banks went belly up and the stock market went into free fall, prescriptions for antidepressant and antianxiety medications increased 9 percent over the year before, while prescriptions for sleeping pills increased 11 percent.

Though some have argued that anxiety is a particularly American affliction, it's not just Americans who suffer from it. A report published in 2009 by the Mental Health Foundation in England found that fifteen percent of people living in the United Kingdom are currently suffering from an anxiety disorder and that rates are increasing: 37 percent of British people report feeling more frightened than they used to. A recent paper in *The Journal of the American Medical Association* observed that clinical anxiety is the most common emotional disorder in many countries. A comprehensive global review of anxiety studies published in 2006 in *The Canadian Journal of Psychiatry* concluded that as many as one in six people worldwide will be afflicted with an anxiety disorder for at least a year during some point in their lifetimes; other studies have reported similar findings.

Of course, these figures refer only to people, like me, who are, according to the somewhat arbitrary diagnostic criteria established by the American Psychiatric Association, technically classifiable as *clinically* anxious. But anxiety extends far beyond the population of the officially mentally ill. Primary care physicians report that anxiety is one of the most frequent complaints driving patients to their offices—more frequent, by some accounts, than the common cold. One large-scale study from 1985 found that anxiety prompted more than 11 percent of all visits to family doctors; a study the following year reported that as many as one in three patients complained to their family physicians of "severe anxiety." (Other studies have reported that 20 percent of primary care patients in America are taking a benzodiazepine such as Valium or Xanax.) And almost everyone alive has at some point experienced the torments of anxiety—or of fear or of stress or of worry, which are distinct but related phenomena. (Those who are unable to experience anxiety are, generally speaking, more deeply pathological—and more dangerous to society—than those who experience it acutely or irrationally; they're sociopaths.)

Few people today would dispute that chronic stress is a hallmark of our times or that anxiety has become a kind of cultural condition of modernity. We live, as has been said many times since the dawn of the atomic era, in an age of anxiety—and that, cliché though it may be, seems only to have become more true in recent years as America has been assaulted in short order by terrorism, economic calamity and disruption, and widespread social transformation.

And yet, as recently as thirty years ago, anxiety per se did not exist as a clinical category. In 1950, when the psychoanalyst Rollo May published *The Meaning of Anxiety,* he observed that at that point only two others, Søren Kierkegaard and Sigmund Freud, had undertaken book-length treatments of the idea of anxiety. In 1927, according to the listing in *Psychological Abstracts,* only three academic papers on anxiety were published; in 1941, there were only fourteen; and as late as 1950, there were only thirty-seven. The first-ever academic conference dedicated solely to the topic of anxiety didn't take place until June 1949. Only in 1980—after new drugs designed to treat anxiety had been developed and brought to market—were the anxiety disorders finally introduced into the third edition of the American Psychiatric Association's *Diagnostic and Statistical Manual of Mental Disorders,* displacing the Freudian neuroses. In an important sense, the treatment predated the diagnosis—that is, the discovery of antianxiety drugs drove the creation of anxiety as a diagnostic category.

Today, thousands of papers about anxiety are published each year; several academic journals are wholly dedicated to it. Anxiety research is constantly yielding new discoveries and insights not only about the causes of and treatments for anxiety but also, more generally, about how the mind works—about the relationships between mind and body, between genes and behavior, and between molecules and emotion. Using functional magnetic resonance imaging (fMRI) technology, we can now map various subjectively experienced emotions onto specific parts of the brain and can even distinguish various types of anxiety based on their visible effect on brain function. For instance, generalized worry about future events (my concern about whether the publishing industry will survive long enough for this book to come out, say, or about whether my kids will be able to afford to go to college) tends to appear as hyperactivity in the frontal lobes of the cerebral cortex.

The severe anxiety that some people experience while speaking in public (like the sheer terror—dulled by drugs and alcohol—that I experienced while giving a lecture the other day) or that some extremely shy people experience in socializing tends to show up as excessive activity in what's called the anterior cingulate. Obsessive-compulsive anxiety, meanwhile, can manifest itself on a brain scan as a disturbance in the circuit linking the frontal lobes with the lower brain centers within the basal ganglia. We now know, thanks to pioneering research by the neuroscientist Joseph LeDoux in the 1980s, that most fearful emotions and behaviors are in one way or another produced by, or at least processed through, the amygdala, a tiny almond-shaped organ at the base of the brain that has become the target of much of the neuroscientific research on anxiety over the last fifteen years.

We also know far more than Freud or Kierkegaard did about how different neurotransmitters—such as serotonin, dopamine, gamma-aminobutyric acid, norepinephrine, and neuropeptide Y—reduce or increase anxiety. And we know there is a strong genetic component to anxiety; we are even starting to learn in some detail what that component consists of. In 2002, to cite just one example among many hundreds, researchers at Harvard University identified what the media called the "Woody Allen gene" because it activates a specific group of neurons in the amygdala and elsewhere in the crucial parts of the neural circuit governing fearful behavior. Today, researchers are homing in on numerous such "candidate genes," measuring the statistical association between certain genetic variations and certain anxiety disorders and exploring the chemical and neuroanatomical mechanisms that "mediate" this association, trying to discover precisely what it is that converts a genetic predisposition into an actual anxious emotion or disorder.

"The real excitement here, both in the study of anxiety as an emotion and in the class of disorders," says Dr. Thomas Insel, the head of the National Institute of Mental Health, "is that it's one of the places where we can begin to make the transition between understanding the molecules, the cells, and the system right to the emotion and behavior. We are now finally able to draw the lines between the genes, the cells, and the brain and brain systems."

*Fear arises from a weakness of mind and therefore does not apper-
tain to the use of reason.*
        —BARUCH SPINOZA (CIRCA 1670)

And yet for all the advances brought by the study of neurochemistry and neuroanatomy, my own experience suggests that the psychological field remains riven by disputes over what causes anxiety and how to
treat it. The psychopharmacologists and psychiatrists I've consulted tell
me that drugs are a *treatment* for my anxiety; the cognitive-behavioral
therapists I've consulted sometimes tell me that drugs are partly a *cause*
of it.

The clash between cognitive-behavioral therapy and psychopharmacology is merely the latest iteration of a debate that is several millennia old. Molecular biology, biochemistry, regression analysis, and
functional magnetic resonance imaging—all of these developments
have made possible discoveries and scientific rigor, as well as courses
of treatment, that Freud and his intellectual forebears could scarcely
have dreamed of. Yet while what Thomas Insel of the NIMH says
about anxiety research being at the cutting edge of scientific inquiry
into human psychology is true, it is also true that in an important sense
there is nothing new under the sun.

The cognitive-behavioral therapists' antecedents can be traced to
the seventeenth-century Jewish-Dutch philosopher Baruch Spinoza,
who believed anxiety was a mere problem of logic. Faulty thinking
causes us to fear things we cannot control, Spinoza argued, presag-
ing by more than three hundred years the cognitive-behavioral therapists' arguments about faulty cognitions. (If we can't control something,
there's no value in fearing it, since the fear accomplishes nothing.) Spinoza's philosophy seemed to have worked for him; biographies report
him to have been a notably serene individual. Some sixteen hundred
years before Spinoza, the Stoic philosopher Epictetus anticipated the
same idea about faulty cognitions. "People are not disturbed by things
but by the view they take of them," he wrote in the first century; for
Epictetus, the roots of anxiety lay not in our biology but in how we
apprehend reality. Alleviating anxiety is a matter of "correcting errone-

ous perceptions" (as the cognitive-behavioral therapists say). The Stoics, in fact, may be the true progenitors of cognitive-behavioral therapy. When Seneca, a contemporary of Epictetus, wrote, "There are more things to alarm us than to harm us, and we suffer more in apprehension than in reality," he was prefiguring by twenty centuries what Aaron Beck, the official founder of CBT, would say in the 1950s.*

The intellectual antecedents of modern psychopharmacology lie even further in the past. Hippocrates, the ancient Greek doctor, concluded in the fourth century B.C. that pathological anxiety was a straightforward biological and medical problem. "If you cut open the head [of a mentally ill individual]," Hippocrates wrote, "you will find the brain humid, full of sweat and smelling badly." For Hippocrates, "body juices" were the cause of madness; a sudden flood of bile to the brain would produce anxiety. (Following Hippocrates, Aristotle placed great weight on the temperature of bile: warm bile generated warmth and enthusiasm; cold bile produced anxiety and cowardice.) In Hippocrates's view, anxiety and other psychiatric disorders were a medical-biological problem best treated by getting the humors back into proper equilibrium.†

But Plato and his adherents, for their part, believed that psychic life was autonomous from physiology and disagreed with the idea that anxiety or melancholy had an organic basis in the body; the biological model of mental illness was, as one ancient Greek philosopher put it, "as vain as a child's story." In Plato's view, while physicians could sometimes provide relief for minor psychological ailments (because sometimes emotional problems are refracted into the body), deep-seated emotional problems could be addressed only by philosophers. Anxiety

---

* Seneca was also in some sense anticipating FDR's famous formulation: "The only thing we have to fear is fear itself."

† Hippocrates believed that staying in good physical and mental health required maintaining the right balance of what he called the four humors, or bodily fluids: blood, phlegm, black bile, and yellow bile. A person's relative humoral balance accounted for his temperament: whereas someone with relatively more blood might have a fiery complexion and a lively or "sanguine" temperament and be given to hot-blooded explosions of temper, someone with relatively more black bile might have swarthy skin and a melancholic temperament. An optimal mixture of the humors (*eucrasia*) produced a state of health; when the humors fell into disequilibrium (*dyscrasia*), the result was disease. Though Hippocrates's humoral theory of mind is now discredited, it persisted for two thousand years, until the 1700s, and it lives on still in our use of words like "bilious" and "phlegmatic" to describe people's personalities—and in the biomedical approach to anxiety and mental illness generally.

and other mental discomfort arose not from physiological imbalances but from disharmony of the soul; recovery demanded deeper self-knowledge, more self-control, and a way of life guided by philosophy. Plato believed that (as one historian of science has put it) "if one's body and mind are in generally good shape, a doctor can come along and put minor ills to right just as one might call in a plumber; but if the general fabric is impaired, a physician is useless." Philosophy, in this view, was the only proper method for treating the soul.

Poppycock, said Hippocrates: "All that philosophers have written on natural science no more pertains to medicine than to painting," he declared.*

Is pathological anxiety a medical illness, as Hippocrates and Aristotle and modern pharmacologists would have it? Or is it a philosophical problem, as Plato and Spinoza and the cognitive-behavioral therapists would have it? Is it a psychological problem, a product of childhood trauma and sexual inhibition, as Freud and his acolytes would have it? Or is it a spiritual condition, as Søren Kierkegaard and his existentialist descendants claimed? Or, finally, is it—as W. H. Auden and David Riesman and Erich Fromm and Albert Camus and scores of modern commentators have declared—a cultural condition, a function of the times we live in and the structure of our society?

The truth is that anxiety is at once a function of biology and philosophy, body and mind, instinct and reason, personality and culture. Even as anxiety is experienced at a spiritual and psychological level, it is scientifically measurable at the molecular level and the physiological level. It is produced by nature and it is produced by nurture. It's a psychological phenomenon and a sociological phenomenon. In computer terms, it's both a hardware problem (I'm wired badly) and a software problem (I run faulty logic programs that make me think anxious thoughts). The origins of a temperament are many faceted; emotional dispositions that may seem to have a simple, single source—a bad gene, say, or a child-

---

* Or someone who followed him declared. Most historians believe that what have come down to us as the so-called Hippocratic writings were in fact produced by a number of doctors who were followers of Hippocrates. Some of the writings in the corpus seem to date from after his death and are believed to have been written by his son-in-law Polybus; Hippocrates's sons Draco and Thessalus also became famous doctors. For simplicity's sake, I treat Hippocrates's writing as the work of one man, since the mode of thinking that the writings represent derives from him.

hood trauma—may not. After all, who's to say that Spinoza's vaunted equanimity didn't derive less from his philosophy than from his biology? Mightn't a genetically programmed low level of autonomic arousal have produced his serene philosophy, rather than the other way around?

> *Neuroses are generated not only by incidental individual experiences, but also by the specific cultural conditions under which we live.... It is an individual fate, for example, to have a domineering or a "self-sacrificing" mother, but it is only under definite cultural conditions that we find domineering or self-sacrificing mothers.*
> —KAREN HORNEY, *The Neurotic Personality of Our Time* (1937)

I don't have to look far to find evidence of anxiety as a family trait. My great-grandfather Chester Hanford, for many years the dean of Harvard College, was in the late 1940s admitted to McLean Hospital, the famous mental institution in Belmont, Massachusetts, suffering from acute anxiety. The last thirty years of his life were often agony. Though medication and electroshock treatments would occasionally bring about remissions in his suffering, such respites were temporary, and in his darkest moments in the 1960s he was reduced to a fetal ball in his bedroom, producing an inhuman-sounding moaning. Perhaps wearied by the responsibility of caring for him, his wife, my great-grandmother, a formidable and brilliant woman, died from an overdose of scotch and sleeping pills in 1969, after Chester had been confined to a nursing home.

Chester Hanford's son is my maternal grandfather. Now ninety-three years old, he is an extremely accomplished and, to outward appearances, confident man. But he has a worry-prone temperament and for much of his life has been burdened by a collection of rituals typical of obsessive-compulsive disorder (OCD), which is officially classified as a species of anxiety disorder. For instance, he will never leave a building other than through the door he came in, a superstition that sometimes leads to complex logistical maneuverings. My mother, in turn, is a high-strung and inveterate worrier and suffers from many of the same phobias and neuroses that I do. She assiduously avoids heights (glass elevators, chairlifts), public speaking, and risk taking of most kinds. Like me, she is also mortally terrified of vomiting. As a young woman, she suffered from frequent and severe panic attacks. At her most anxious (or so my father, her ex-husband, insists), her fears verged on paranoia: while pregnant with me, my father says, she became convinced that a serial killer in a yellow Volkswagen was watching our apartment.* My only sibling, a younger sister, struggles with anxiety that is different from mine but nonetheless intense. She, too, has taken Celexa—and also Prozac and Wellbutrin and Nardil and Neurontin and BuSpar. None of them worked for her, and today she may be one of the few adult members of my mother's side of the family not currently taking a psychiatric medication. (Various other relatives on my mother's side have also relied on antidepressants and antianxiety medications continuously for many years.)

On the evidence of just these four generations on my mother's side (and there is a separate complement of psychopathology coming down to me on the side of my father, who drank himself into unconsciousness five nights out of every seven throughout much of my later childhood), it is not outlandish to conclude that I possess a genetic predisposition to anxiety and depression.

But these facts, by themselves, are not dispositive—because is it not possible that the bequeathing of anxiety from one generation to the next on my mother's side had nothing to do with genes and everything to do with the environment? In the 1920s, my great-grandparents had a young child who died of an infection. This was devastating to them. Perhaps this trauma, combined with the later trauma of having many of his students die in World War II, cracked something in my great-grandfather's psyche—and, for that matter, in my grandfather's. My grandfather was in elementary school at the time of his brother's death and can remember sitting alongside the tiny casket as the hearse drove to the cemetery. Perhaps my mother, in turn, acquired her own anxieties by witnessing the superstitions and obsessions of her father and the emotional anguish of her grandfather (not to mention the anxious ministrations of her worrywart mother); the psychological term

---

* Today, my mother and father, now divorced fifteen years, disagree about the severity of the paranoia: my father insists it was considerable; my mother says it was minor (and that, for that matter, there was actually a serial killer afoot at the time).

for this is "modeling." And perhaps I, observing my mother's phobias, adopted them as my own. While there is substantial evidence that specific phobias—particularly those based on fears that would have been adaptive in the state of nature, like phobias of heights or snakes or rodents—are genetically transmittable, or "evolutionarily conserved," isn't it just as plausible, if not more so, to conclude that I learned to be fearful by watching my mother be fearful? Or that the generally unsettled nature of my childhood psychological environment—my mother's constant anxious buzzing, my father's alcoholic absence, the sometimes unhappy tumult of their marriage that would eventually end in divorce—produced in me a comparably unsettled sensibility? Or that my mother's paranoia and panic while pregnant with me produced such hormonal Sturm und Drang in the womb that I was doomed to be born nervous? Research suggests that mothers who suffer stress while pregnant are more likely to produce anxious children.* Thomas Hobbes, the political philosopher, was born prematurely when his mother, terrified by the news that the Spanish Armada was advancing toward English shores, went into labor early in April 1588. "Myself and fear were born twins," Hobbes wrote, and he attributed his own anxious temperament to his mother's terror-induced premature labor. Perhaps Hobbes's view that a powerful state needs to protect citizens from the violence and misery they naturally inflict on one another (life, he famously said, is nasty, brutish, and short) was founded on the anxious temperament imbued in him in utero by his mother's stress hormones.

Or do the roots of my anxiety lie deeper and broader than the things I've experienced and the genes I've inherited—that is, in history and in culture? My father's parents were Jews who fled the Nazis in the 1930s. My father's mother became a nastily anti-Semitic Jew—she renounced her Jewishness out of fear that she would someday be persecuted for it. My younger sister and I were raised in the Episcopal Church, our Jewish background hidden from us until I was in high school. My father, for his part, has had a lifelong fascination with World War II, and spe-

---

* One study found that children whose mothers were pregnant with them on September 11, 2001, still had elevated levels of stress hormones in their blood at six months. Similar findings—showing as-yet-unborn children acquiring higher lifetime baseline levels of stressed-out physiology—have been reported during war and other chaotic times.

cifically with the Nazis; he watched the television series *The World at War* again and again. In my memory, that program, with its stentorian music accompanying the Nazi advance on Paris, is the running sound track to my early childhood.* The long-persecuted Jews, of course, have millennia of experience in having reason to be scared—which perhaps explains why some studies have shown that Jewish men suffer from depression and anxiety at rates higher than men in other ethnic groups.†

My mother's cultural heritage, on the other hand, was heavily WASP; she is a proud *Mayflower* descendant who until recently subscribed wholeheartedly to the notion that there is no emotion and no family issue that should not be suppressed.

Thus, me: a mixture of Jewish and WASP pathology—a neurotic and histrionic Jew suppressed inside a neurotic and repressed WASP. No wonder I'm anxious: I'm like Woody Allen trapped in John Calvin.

Or is my anxiety, after all, "normal"—a natural response to the times we live in? I was in middle school when *The Day After*, about the dystopian aftermath of a nuclear attack, aired on network television. As an adolescent, I regularly had dreams that ended with a missile streaking across the sky. Were these dreams evidence of anxious psychopathology? Or a reasonable reaction to the conditions I perceived—which were, after all, the same conditions that preoccupied defense policy analysts through the 1980s? The Cold War, of course, has now long since ended—but it has been replaced by the threat of hijacked airplanes, dirty bombs, underwear bombers, chemical attacks, and anthrax, not to mention SARS, swine flu, drug-resistant tuberculosis, the prospect of climate-change-induced global apocalypse, and the abiding stresses of a worldwide economic slowdown and of a global economy undergoing seemingly constant upheaval. Insofar as it's possible to measure such things, eras of social transformation seem to produce a quantum

---

* When my mother was attending law school at night, my sister and I would spend evenings moping around the house while my father played Bach fugues on the piano and then parked himself with a bowl of popcorn and a bottle of gin in front of *The World at War*.

† There's also evidence that the high IQ scores of Ashkenazi Jews are attached somehow to the high anxiety rates of that same group, and there are plausible evolutionary explanations for why both intelligence and imagination tend to be allied with anxiety. (Various studies have found that the average IQ of Ashkenazi Jews is eight points higher than that of the next highest ethnic group, Northeast Asians, and close to a full standard deviation higher than other European groups.)

increase in the anxiety of the population. In our postindustrial era of economic uncertainty, where social structures are undergoing continuous disruption and where professional and gender roles are constantly changing, is it not normal—adaptive even—to be anxious?

At some level, yes, it is—at least to the extent that it is always, or often, adaptive to be reasonably anxious. According to Charles Darwin (who himself suffered from crippling agoraphobia that left him housebound for years after his voyage on the *Beagle*), species that "fear rightly" increase their chances of survival. We anxious people are less likely to remove ourselves from the gene pool by, say, frolicking on the edge of cliffs or becoming fighter pilots.

An influential study conducted a hundred years ago by two Harvard psychologists, Robert M. Yerkes and John Dillingham Dodson, demonstrated that moderate levels of anxiety *improve* performance in humans and animals: too much anxiety, obviously, and performance is impaired, but too *little* anxiety also impairs performance. When the use of antianxiety drugs exploded in the 1950s, some psychiatrists warned about the dangers presented by a society that was not anxious enough. "We then face the prospect of developing a falsely flaccid race of people which might not be too good for our future," one wrote. Another psychiatrist averred that "Van Gogh, Isaac Newton: most of the geniuses and great creators were not tranquil. They were nervous, ego-driven men pushed on by a relentless inner force and beset by anxieties."

Is muting such genius a price society would have to pay for drastically reducing anxiety, pharmacologically or otherwise? And would that cost be worthwhile?

"Without anxiety, little would be accomplished," says David Barlow, the founder and director emeritus of the Center for Anxiety and Related Disorders at Boston University. "The performance of athletes, entertainers, executives, artisans, and students would suffer; creativity would diminish; crops might not be planted. And we would all achieve that idyllic state long sought after in our fast-paced society of whiling away our lives under a shade tree. This would be as deadly for the species as nuclear war."

I have come to believe that anxiety accompanies intellectual activity as its shadow and that the more we know of the nature of anxiety, the more we will know of intellect.
—HOWARD LIDDELL, "THE ROLE OF VIGILANCE IN THE
DEVELOPMENT OF ANIMAL NEUROSIS" (1949)

Some eighty years ago, Freud proposed that anxiety was "a riddle whose solution would be bound to throw a flood of light on our whole mental existence." Unlocking the mysteries of anxiety, he believed, would go far in helping us to unravel the mysteries of the mind: consciousness, the self, identity, intellect, imagination, creativity—not to mention pain, suffering, hope, and regret. To grapple with and understand anxiety is, in some sense, to grapple with and understand the human condition.

The differences in how various cultures and eras have perceived and understood anxiety can tell us a lot about those cultures and eras. Why did the ancient Greeks of the Hippocratic school see anxiety mainly as a medical condition, while the Enlightenment philosophers saw it as an intellectual problem? Why did the early existentialists see anxiety as a spiritual condition, while Gilded Age doctors saw it as a specifically Anglo-Saxon stress response—a response that they believed spared Catholic societies—to the Industrial Revolution? Why did the early Freudians see anxiety as a psychological condition emanating from sexual inhibition, whereas our own age tends to see it, once again, as a medical and neurochemical condition, a problem of malfunctioning biomechanics?

Do these shifting interpretations represent the forward march of progress and science? Or simply the changing, and often cyclical, ways in which cultures work? What does it say about the societies in question that Americans showing up in emergency rooms with panic attacks tend to believe they're having heart attacks, whereas Japanese tend to be afraid they're going to faint? Are the Iranians who complain of what they call "heart distress" suffering what Western psychiatrists would call panic attacks? Are the *ataques de nervios* experienced by South Americans simply panic attacks with a Latino inflection—or are they, as modern researchers now believe, a distinct cultural and medical syndrome? Why do drug treatments for anxiety that work so well on Americans and the French seem not to work effectively on the Chinese?

As fascinating and multifarious as these cultural idiosyncrasies are, the underlying consistency of experience across time and cultures speaks to the universality of anxiety as a human trait. Even filtered through the distinctive cultural practices and beliefs of the Greenland Inuit a hundred years ago, the syndrome the Inuit called "kayak angst" (those afflicted by it were afraid to go out seal hunting alone) appears to be little different from what we today call agoraphobia. In Hippocrates's ancient writings can be found clinical descriptions of pathological anxiety that sound quite modern. One of his patients was terrified of cats (simple phobia, which today would be coded 300.29 for insurance purposes, according to the classifications of the fifth edition of the *Diagnostic and Statistical Manual,* the *DSM-V*) and another of nightfall; a third, Hippocrates reported, was "beset by terror" whenever he heard a flute; a fourth could not walk alongside "even the shallowest ditch," though he had no problem walking *inside* the ditch—evidence of what we would today call acrophobia, the fear of heights. Hippocrates also describes a patient suffering what would likely be called, in modern diagnostic terminology, panic disorder with agoraphobia (*DSM-V* code 300.22): the condition, as Hippocrates described it, "usually attacks abroad, if a person is travelling a lonely road somewhere, and fear seizes him." The syndromes described by Hippocrates are recognizably the same clinical phenomena described in the latest issues of the *Archives of General Psychiatry* and *Bulletin of the Menninger Clinic.*

Their similarities bridge the yawning gap of millennia and circumstances that separate them, providing a sense of how, for all the differences in culture and setting, the physiologically anxious aspects of human experience may be universal.

In this book, I have set out to explore the "riddle" of anxiety. I am not a doctor, a psychologist, a sociologist, or a historian of science—any one of whom would bring more scholarly authority to a treatise on anxiety than I do. This is a work of synthesis and reportage, yoking together explorations of the idea of anxiety from history, literature, philosophy, religion, popular culture, and the latest scientific research—all of that woven through something about which I can, alas, claim extensive expertise: my own experience with anxiety. Examining the depths of my own neuroses may seem the height of narcissism (and studies do show that self-preoccupation tends to be tied to anxiety), but it's an exercise with worthy antecedents. In 1621, the Oxford scholar Robert Burton published his canonical *The Anatomy of Melancholy*, a staggering thirteen-hundred-page work of synthesis, whose torrents of scholarly exegesis only partially obscure what it really is: a massive litany of anxious, depressive complaint. In 1733, George Cheyne, a prominent London physician and one of the most influential psychological thinkers of the eighteenth century, published *The English Malady*, which includes the forty-page chapter "The Case of the Author" (dedicated to "my fellow sufferers"), in which he reports in minute detail on his neuroses (including "Fright, Anxiety, Dread, and Terror" and "a melancholy Fright and Panick, where my Reason was of no Use to me") and physical symptoms (including "a sudden violent Head-ach," "extream Sickness in my Stomach," and "a constant Colick, and an ill Taste and Savour in my Mouth") over the years. More recently, the intellectual odysseys of Charles Darwin, Sigmund Freud, and William James were powerfully driven by their curiosity about, and the desire to find relief from, their own anxious suffering. Freud used his acute train phobia and his hypochondria, among other things, to construct his theory of psychoanalysis; Darwin was effectively housebound by stress-related illnesses after the voyage of the *Beagle*—he spent years in pursuit of relief from his anxiety, visiting spas and, on the advice of one doctor, encasing himself in ice. James tried to keep his phobias hidden from the public but was often quietly terrified. "I awoke morning after morning with a horrible dread in the pit of my stomach and with a sense of insecurity of life that I never knew before," he wrote in 1902 of the onset of his anxiety. "For months, I was unable to go out in the dark alone."

Unlike Darwin, Freud, and James, I'm not out to adumbrate a whole new theory of mind or of human nature. Rather, this book is motivated by a quest to understand, and to find relief from or redemption in, anxious suffering. This quest has taken me both backward, into history, and forward, to the frontiers of modern scientific research. I have spent much of the past eight years reading through hundreds of thousands of the pages that have been written about anxiety over the last three thousand years.

My life has, thankfully, lacked great tragedy or melodrama. I haven't served any jail time. I haven't been to rehab. I haven't assaulted anyone or carried out a suicide attempt. I haven't woken up naked in the middle of a field, sojourned in a crack house, or been fired from a job for erratic behavior. As psychopathologies go, mine has been—so far, most of the time, to outward appearances—quiet. Robert Downey Jr. will not be starring in the movie of my life. I am, as they say in the clinical literature, "high functioning" for someone with an anxiety disorder or a mental illness; I'm usually quite good at hiding it. More than a few people, some of whom think they know me quite well, have remarked that they are struck that I, who can seem so even-keeled and imperturbable, would choose to write a book about anxiety. I smile gently while churning inside and thinking about what I've learned is a signature characteristic of the phobic personality: "the need and ability"—as described in the self-help book *Your Phobia*—"to present a relatively placid, untroubled appearance to others, while suffering extreme distress on the inside."*

To some people, I may seem calm. But if you could peer beneath the surface, you would see that I'm like a duck—paddling, paddling, paddling.

The chief patient I am preoccupied with is myself.
　—SIGMUND FREUD TO WILHELM FLIESS (AUGUST 1897)

It has occurred to me that writing this book might be a terrible idea: if it's relief from nervous suffering that I crave, then burrowing into the history and science of anxiety, and into my own psyche, is perhaps not the best way to achieve it.

---

* "For many, many people who have anxiety disorders—particularly agoraphobia and panic disorder—people would be surprised to find out that they have problems with anxiety because they seem so 'together' and in control," says Paul Foxman, a psychologist who heads the Center for Anxiety Disorders in Burlington, Vermont. "They seem to be comfortable, but there's a disconnection between the public self and the private self."

In my travels through the historical literature on anxiety, I came across a little self-help book by a British army veteran named Wilfrid Northfield, who suffered nervous prostration during the First World War and then spent ten years largely incapacitated by anxiety before successfully convalescing and writing his guide to recovery. Published in 1933, *Conquest of Nerves: The Inspiring Record of a Personal Triumph over Neurasthenia*, became a best seller; the copy I have is from the sixth printing, in 1934. In his last chapter, "A Few Final Words," Northfield writes: "There is one thing the neurasthenic must guard against very strongly, and that is talking about his troubles. He can get no comfort or assistance in so doing." Northfield goes on: "To talk of troubles in a voluble, despairing way, merely piles on the agony and 'plays-up' the emotions. Not only so, but it is selfish." Citing another author, he concludes: "'Never display a wound, except to a physician.'"

Never display a wound. Well, after more than thirty years of endeavoring—successfully much of the time—to conceal my anxiety from people, here I am putting it on protracted exhibition for acquaintances and strangers alike. If Northfield is correct (and my worried mother agrees with him), this project can hardly be auspicious for my mental health. Elements of modern research lend support to Northfield's warning: anxious people have a pathological tendency to focus their attention inward, on themselves, in a way that suggests a book-length dwelling on one's own anxiety is hardly the best way to escape it.*

Moreover, one concern I've had about writing this book is that I've subsisted professionally on my ability to project calmness and control; my anxiety makes me conscientious (I'm afraid of screwing things up), and my shame can make me seem poised (I need to hide that I'm anxious). A former colleague once described me as "human Xanax," telling me, as I chuckled inwardly, that I project such equanimity that my mere presence can be calming to others: simply to walk into a room full of

---

* David Barlow, one of the preeminent researchers in the field, notes (in the jargon-intensive terminology of the specialist) that pathological, negative self-focus "seems to be an integral part of the cognitive-affective structure of anxiety. This negative self-evaluative focus and disruption of attention is in large part responsible for decreases in performance. This attention shift in turn contributes to a vicious cycle of anxious apprehension, in which increasing anxiety leads to further attentional shifts, increased performance deficits, and subsequent spiraling of arousal."

agitated people is to administer my soothing balm; people relax in my
wake. If only she knew! By revealing the fraudulence of my putative
calm, am I forfeiting my ability to soothe others and thereby compro-
mising my professional standing?

My current therapist, Dr. W., says there is always the possibility
that revealing my anxiety will lift the burden of shame and reduce the
isolation of solitary suffering. When I get skittish about airing my psychiatric issues in a book, Dr. W. says: "You've been keeping your anxiety
a secret for years, right? How's that working out for you?"

Point taken. And there is a rich and convincing literature about
how—contrary to the admonitions of Wilfrid Northfield (and my
mother)—hiding or suppressing anxiety actually produces *more* anxiety.* But there is no escaping my concern that this exercise is not only
self-absorbed and shameful but risky—that it will prove the Wile E.
Coyote moment when I look down to discover that, instead of inner
strengths or outer buttresses to support me, there is in fact nothing to
stop me from falling a long way down.

> *I know how indecent and shocking Egotism is, and for an Author
> to make himself the Subject of his Words or Works, especially in so
> tedious and circumstantiated a Detail: But . . . I thought . . . perhaps
> it may not be quite useless to some low desponding valetudinary,
> over-grown Person, whose Case may have some Resemblance to
> mine.*
>
> —GEORGE CHEYNE, *The English Malady* (1733)

"Why," Dr. W. asks, "do you think writing about your anxiety in a
book would be so shameful?"

Because stigma still attaches to mental illness. Because anxiety is
seen as weakness. Because, as the signs posted on Allied gun installa-
tions in Malta during World War II so bluntly put it, "if you are a man
you will not permit your self-respect to admit an anxiety neurosis or to
show fear." Because I worry that this book, with its revelations of anxi-

---

* On the desk in front of me is a 1997 article from the *Journal of Abnormal Psychology* called "Hiding
Feelings: The Acute Effects of Inhibiting Negative and Positive Emotions."

ety and struggle, will be a litany of Too Much Information, a violation of basic standards of restraint and decorum.*

When I explain this to Dr. W., he says that the very act of working on this book, and of publishing it, could be therapeutic. In presenting my anxiety to the world, he says, I will be "coming out." The implication is that this will be liberating, as though I were gay and coming out of the closet. But being gay—we now finally know (homosexuality was classified as a mental disorder by the American Psychiatric Association until 1973)—is not a weakness or a defect or an illness. Being excessively nervous is.

For a long time, governed by reticence and shame, I had told people who inquired about my book that it was "a cultural and intellectual history of anxiety"—true, as far as it goes—without revealing its personal aspects. But a little while ago, in an effort to test the effects of "coming out" as anxious, I began gingerly to speak more forthrightly about what the book was about: "a cultural and intellectual history of anxiety, *woven together by my own experiences with anxiety*."

The effect was striking. When I had spoken about the book as arid history, people would nod politely, and a few would buttonhole me privately later to ask me specific questions about this or that aspect of anxiety. But as I started to acknowledge the personal parts of the book, I found myself surrounded by avid listeners, eager to tell me about their own, or their family members', anxiety.

One night I attended a dinner with a bunch of writers and artists. Someone asked what I was working on, and I delivered my new spiel ("a cultural and intellectual history of anxiety, *woven together and animated by my own experiences with anxiety*"), talking about some of my experiences with various antianxiety and antidepressant medications. To my astonishment, *each of the other nine people within earshot* responded by telling me a story about his or her own experience with

* As I write this, I can hear the strains of what may be my better judgment: *Even if you are so unfortunate as to be excessively anxious, at least have the dignity not to prattle on about it publicly. Keep a stiff upper lip, and keep it to yourself.*

anxiety and medication.* Around the table we went, sharing our tales of neurotic woe.†

I was struck that admitting my own anxiety over dinner had dislodged such an avalanche of personal confessions of anxiety and pharmacotherapy. Granted, I was with a bunch of writers and artists, a population ostensibly more prone, as observers since Aristotle have noted, to various forms of mental illness than other people. So maybe these stories simply provide evidence that writers are crazy. Or maybe the stories are evidence that the pharmaceutical companies have succeeded in medicalizing a normal human experience and marketing drugs to "treat" it.‡ But maybe more people than I thought are struggling with anxiety.

"Yes!" said Dr. W. when I ventured this proposition at my next session with him. Then he told me a story of his own: "My brother used to host regular salon evenings, where people would be invited in to lecture on various topics. I was asked to give a talk on phobias. After my lec-

---

* For instance, S., a nonfiction writer in her midthirties, told of taking Xanax and Klonopin for her anxiety and about how she switched from Prozac to Lexapro because Prozac had killed her libido. C., a poet in his midforties, said that he'd had to take the antidepressant Zoloft for panic attacks. (C.'s first panic attack had landed him in the emergency room, convinced he was having a heart attack. Subsequent attacks, he said, "were not so bad because you know what they are—but they're still scary because you always wonder, *Maybe this time I really* am *having a heart attack.*" Some epidemiological surveys have found that one-third of adults suffering their first panic attack end up in the emergency room.) K., a novelist, said that while she was trying to finish her last book, her anxiety got so bad that she couldn't work. Fearing she was going crazy, she went to her psychiatrist, who prescribed her Zoloft, which made her fat, and then Lexapro, which increased her anxiety so much that she could no longer even bear to pick her children up at school.

† After dinner, yet another writer approached me. The woman—let's call her E.—is a globe-trotting war correspondent and best-selling author in her late thirties who suffers, she told me, from a litany of depressive, anxious symptoms (including trichotillomania, a disorder that causes people, mainly women, to compulsively pull their hair out when under stress), for which a doctor had prescribed her the antidepressant Lexapro. I marveled that E., despite her anxiety and depression, had managed to travel all around Africa and the Middle East, filing dispatches from war-ravaged countries, often at great risk to her personal safety; for me, simply traveling more than a few miles from home can be miserably anxiety producing and bowel loosening. "I feel calmer in war zones," she said. "I know it's perverse, but I feel more calm while being shelled; it's one of the few times I *don't* feel anxiety." Waiting for an editor to make a judgment about an article she's submitted, however, can send her spiraling into anxiety and depression. (Freud observed that threats to our self-esteem or self-conception can often cause far more anxiety than threats to our physical well-being.)

‡ There is definitely some truth to that, and I will have a lot to say about the topic in part 3 of this book.

ture, every single one of the people there came up to tell me about their phobias. I think the official numbers, as high as they are, underreport."

After he told me this, I thought about Ben, my best friend from college, a rich and successful writer (he regularly graces the best-seller lists and box-office charts), whose doctor had recently prescribed him Ativan, a benzodiazepine, to combat the anxious tightness in his chest that had him convinced he was suffering a heart attack.* And I thought of Ben's neighbor M., a multimillionaire hedge fund manager, who takes Xanax constantly for his panic attacks. And of my former colleague G., an eminent political journalist, who in the years since ending up in an emergency room after a panic episode has been taking various benzodiazepines to prevent further attacks. And of another former colleague, B., whose anxiety left him stammering in meetings and unable to complete work projects until he went on Lexapro.

No, not everyone gets overwhelmed by anxiety. My wife, for one, does not. (Thank God.) Barack Obama, by all accounts, does not. Nor, evidently, does David Petraeus, the former commander of U.S. forces in Afghanistan and former director of the CIA: he once told a reporter that despite being in jobs where the day-to-day stakes are a matter of life and death, he "rarely feels stress at all."† All-Pro quarterbacks like Tom Brady and Peyton Manning manifestly do not, at least not on the field.‡ One of the things I explore in this book is why some people are preternaturally calm, exhibiting grace even under tremendous pressure, while others of us succumb to panic at the mildest hint of stress.

Yet enough of us do suffer from anxiety that perhaps writing about

---

* Even though Ben now travels the world and walks red carpets and commands tens of thousands of dollars for a speech, I can still remember the times, in the lean years before his first book came out, when he would get overwhelmed by panic attacks if we strayed too far from his apartment and when the prospect of socializing at a party would leave him so nervous he'd vomit into the bushes outside beforehand.

† Perhaps he would have been better off feeling more stress—a greater intensity of worry about consequences might have prevented the adulterous misadventure that led to his downfall.

‡ Not that coolness and toughness on the field are guarantees of equanimity off of it. Terry Bradshaw, the Steelers Hall of Fame quarterback from the late 1970s, was a fearless gladiator who went on to be debilitated by depression and panic attacks. Earl Campbell, the burly, fearsome Houston Oilers running back from the 1970s, found himself, a decade later, housebound by panic attacks.

my own ought not to be an occasion for shame but an opportunity to provide solace to some of the millions of others who share this affliction. And maybe, as Dr. W. often reminds me, the exercise will be therapeutic. "You can write yourself to health," he says.

Still, I worry. A lot. It's my nature. (Besides, as many people have said to me, how can you *not* be anxious writing a book about anxiety?)

Dr. W., for his part, says: "Put your anxiety about the book into the book."

The planning function of the nervous system, in the course of evolution, has culminated in the appearance of ideas, values, and pleasures—the unique manifestations of man's social living. Man, alone, can plan for the distant future, and can experience the retrospective pleasures of achievement. Man, alone, can be happy. But man, alone, can be worried and anxious.

—HOWARD LIDDELL, "THE ROLE OF VIGILANCE IN THE
DEVELOPMENT OF ANIMAL NEUROSIS" (1949)

In all the insights into history and culture that a study of anxiety might produce, is there anything that can help the individual anxiety sufferer? Can we—can I—reduce anxiety, or come to terms with it, by understanding the value and meaning of it?

I hope so. But when I have a panic attack, there is nothing interesting about it. I try to think about it analytically and I can't—it's just miserably unpleasant and I want it to stop. A panic attack is interesting the way a broken leg or a kidney stone is interesting—a pain that you want to end.

Some years ago, before embarking on the research for this project in earnest, I picked up an academic book about the physiology of anxiety to read while on a flight from San Francisco to Washington, D.C. As we flew smoothly over the West, I was immersed in the book and felt like I was gaining an intellectual understanding of the phenomenon. *So,* I thought as I read, *it's simply a flurry of activity in my amygdala that produces that acutely miserable emotion I sometimes feel? Those feelings of doom and terror are just the bubbling of neurotransmitters in my brain? That doesn't seem so intimidating.* Armed with this perspective, I continued thinking: *I can exert mind over matter and reduce the physical symptoms of anxiety to their proper place—mere routine physiology—and live more calmly in the world. Here I am, hurtling along at thirty-eight thousand feet, and I'm not even that nervous.*

Then the turbulence started. It wasn't particularly severe, but as we bumped along above the Rockies, any perspective or understanding I thought I had gained was rendered instantly useless; my fear response revved up, and despite gulping Xanax and Dramamine, I was terrified and miserable until we landed several hours later.

My anxiety is a reminder that I am governed by my physiology— that what happens in the body may do more to determine what happens in the mind than the other way around. Though thinkers from Aristotle to William James to the researchers who publish today in the journal *Psychosomatic Medicine* have recognized this fact, it runs counter to one of the basic Platonic-Cartesian tenets of Western thought—the idea that who we are, the way we think and perceive, is a product of our disembodied souls or intellects. The brute biological factness of anxiety challenges our sense of who we are: anxiety reminds us that we are, like animals, prisoners of our bodies, which will decline and die and cease to be. (No wonder we're anxious.)

And yet even as anxiety throws us back into our most primitive, fight-or-flight-driven reptilian selves, it is also what makes us more than mere animals. "If man were a beast or an angel," Kierkegaard wrote in 1844, "he would not be able to be in anxiety. Since he is both beast and angel, he can be in anxiety, and the greater the anxiety, the greater the man." The ability to worry about the future goes hand in hand with the ability to plan for the future—and planning for the future (along with remembering the past) is what gives rise to culture and separates us from other animals.

For Kierkegaard, as for Freud, the most anxiety-producing threats lay not in the world around us but rather deep inside us—in our uncertainty about the existential choices we make and in our fear of death. Confronting this fear, and risking the dissolution of one's identity, expands the soul and fulfills the self. "Learning to know anxiety is an adventure which every man has to affront if he would not go to perdition either by not having known anxiety or by sinking under it," Kierkegaard wrote. "He therefore who has learned rightly to be in anxiety has learned the most important thing."

Learning rightly to be in anxiety. Well, I'm trying. This book is part of that effort.

CHAPTER 2

What Do We Talk About
When We Talk About Anxiety?

Although it is widely recognized that anxiety is the most pervasive psychological phenomenon of our time . . . there has been little or no agreement on its definition, and very little, if any, progress on its measurement.

—PAUL HOCH, PRESIDENT, AMERICAN
PSYCHOPATHOLOGICAL ASSOCIATION, IN AN ADDRESS
TO THE FIRST-EVER ACADEMIC CONFERENCE
ON ANXIETY (1949)

For researchers as well as laymen, this is the age of anxiety. . . . [But] can we honestly claim that our understanding of anxiety has increased in proportion to the huge research effort expended or even increased perceptibility?
We think not.

—"THE NATURE OF ANXIETY: A REVIEW OF THIRTEEN
MULTIVARIATE ANALYSES COMPRISING 814 VARIABLES,"
Psychiatric Reports (DECEMBER 1958)

Anxiety is not a simple thing to grasp.
—SIGMUND FREUD, *The Problem of Anxiety* (1926)

On February 16, 1948, at 3:45 in the afternoon, my great-grandfather Chester Hanford, who had recently stepped down after twenty years as the dean of Harvard College to concentrate full-time on his academic work as a professor of government ("with a focus on local and munici-pal government," as he liked to say), was admitted to McLean Hospital with a provisional diagnosis of "psychoneurosis" and "reactive depres-sion." Fifty-six years old at the time of his admission, Chester reported that his primary complaints were insomnia, "feelings of anxiety and tension," and "fears as to the future." Described by the hospital director as a "conscientious and usually very effective man," Chester had been in a state of "anxiety of a rather severe degree" for five months. The night before presenting himself at McLean, he had told his wife that he wanted to commit suicide.

Thirty-one years later, on October 3, 1979, at 8:30 in the morning, my parents—worried that I, ten years old and in the fifth grade, had of late been piling various alarming new tics and behavioral oddities on top of my already obsessive germ avoidance and acute separation anxiety and phobia of vomiting—took me to the same psychiatric hos-pital to be evaluated. A team of experts (a psychiatrist, a psychologist, a social worker, and several young psychiatric residents who sat hidden behind a two-way mirror and watched me get interviewed and take a Rorschach test) diagnosed me with "phobic neurosis" and "overanxious reaction disorder of childhood" and observed that I would be at signifi-cant risk of developing "anxiety neurosis" and "neurotic depression" as I got older if I wasn't treated.

Twenty-five years after *that*, on April 13, 2004, at two o'clock in the afternoon, I, now thirty-four years old and working as a senior edi-tor at *The Atlantic* magazine and dreading the publication of my first book, presented myself at the nationally renowned Center for Anxiety and Related Disorders at Boston University. After meeting for sev-eral hours with a psychologist and two graduate students and filling out dozens of pages of questionnaires (including, I later learned, the Depression Anxiety Stress Scales and the Social Interaction Anxiety Scale and the Penn State Worry Questionnaire and the Anxiety Sensi-tivity Index), I was given a principal diagnosis of "panic disorder with agoraphobia" and additional diagnoses of "specific phobia" and "social phobia." The clinicians also noted in their report that my questionnaire scores indicated "mild levels of depression," "strong levels of anxiety," and "strong levels of worry."

Why so many different diagnoses? Did the nature of my anxiety change so much between 1979 and 2004? And why didn't my great-grandfather and I receive the same diagnoses? As described in his case files, the general scope of Chester Hanford's syndrome was awfully similar to mine. Were my "strong levels of anxiety" really so different from the "feelings of anxiety and tension" and "fears as to the future" that afflicted my great-grandfather? And anyway, who, aside from the most well adjusted or sociopathic among us, *doesn't* have "fears as to the future" or suffer "feelings of anxiety and tension"? What, if anything, separates the ostensibly "clinically" anxious, like my great-grandfather and me, from the "normally" anxious? Aren't we all, consumed by the getting and striving of modern capitalist society—indeed, as a consequence of being alive, subject always to the caprice and violence of nature and each other and to the inevitability of death—at some level "psychoneurotic"?

Technically, no; in fact, no one is anymore. The diagnoses that Chester Hanford received in 1948 no longer existed by 1980. And the diagnoses that I received in 1979 no longer exist today.

In 1948, "psychoneurosis" was the American Psychiatric Association's term for what that organization would, with the introduction in 1968 of the second edition of psychiatry's bible, the *Diagnostic and Statistical Manual* (*DSM-II*), officially designate as simply "neurosis" and what it has, since the introduction of the third edition (*DSM-III*) in 1980, called "anxiety disorder."*

This evolving terminology matters because the definitions—as well as the symptoms, the rates of incidence, the presumed causes, the cultural meanings, and the recommended treatments—associated with these diagnoses have changed along with their names over the years. The species of unpleasant emotion that twenty-five hundred years ago was associated with *melaina chole* (ancient Greek for "black bile") has since also been described, in sometimes overlapping succession, as "melancholy," "angst," "hypochondria," "hysteria," "vapors," "spleen," "neurasthenia," "neurosis," "psychoneurosis," "depression," "phobia," "anxiety," and "anxiety disorder"—and that's leaving aside such colloquial terms as "panic," "worry," "dread," "fright," "apprehension,"

---

* The anxiety disorders have persisted through the publication of the *DSM-III-R* (in 1987), the *DSM-IV* (in 1994), the *DSM-IV-TR* (in 2000), and the *DSM-V* (in 2013).

"nerves," "nervousness," "edginess," "wariness," "trepidation," "jitters," "willies," "obsession," "stress," and plain old "fear." And that's just in English, where the word "anxiety" was rarely found in standard psychological or medical textbooks in English before the 1930s, when translators began rendering the German *Angst* (as deployed in the works of Sigmund Freud) as "anxiety."*

Which raises the question: What are we talking about when we talk about anxiety?

The answer is not straightforward—or, rather, it depends on whom you ask. For Søren Kierkegaard, writing in the mid-nineteenth century, anxiety (*angst* in Danish) was a spiritual and philosophical problem, a vague yet inescapable uneasiness with no obvious direct cause.† For Karl Jaspers, the German philosopher and psychiatrist who wrote the influential 1913 textbook *General Psychopathology,* it was "usually linked with a strong *feeling of restlessness* . . . a feeling that one has . . . not finished something; or . . . that one has to look for something or . . . come

---

* There are long-running debates among psychologists and philologists about the differences between, say, *angoisse* and *anxiété* (not to mention *inquiétude, peur, terreur,* and *effroi*) in French and between *Angst* and *Furcht* (and *Angstpsychosen* and *Ängstlichkeit*) in German.

† Kierkegaard, the son of a Danish wool merchant, was the first nonphysician to write a serious book-length treatment of anxiety. Some fifty years before Freud, Kierkegaard distinguished anxiety from fear, defining the former as a vague, diffuse uneasiness produced by no concrete or "real" danger. Kierkegaard's father had renounced God (cursed him, in fact), and so young Søren was much preoccupied with whether to believe in or to reject Christ; the freedom to choose between these two options—and the inability to know for certain which one was correct—was what Kierkegaard believed to be the principal wellspring of anxiety. In this, Kierkegaard was arguing in the vein of Blaise Pascal, his seventeenth-century philosophical predecessor and fellow anxiety sufferer. Kierkegaard was also giving birth, more or less, to existentialism; twentieth-century successors like the psychiatrist Karl Jaspers and the philosopher-novelist Jean-Paul Sartre, among others, would take up similar questions about choice, suicide, engagement, and anxiety.

When man lost his faith in God and in reason, existentialists like Kierkegaard and Sartre believed, he found himself adrift in the universe and therefore adrift in anxiety. But for the existentialists, what generated anxiety was not the godlessness of the world, per se, but rather the freedom to choose between God and godlessness. Though freedom is something we actively seek, the freedom to choose generates anxiety. "When I behold my possibilities," Kierkegaard wrote, "I experience that dread which is the dizziness of freedom, and my choice is made in fear and trembling."

Many people try to flee anxiety by fleeing choice. This helps explain the perverse-seeming appeal of authoritarian societies—the certainties of a rigid, choiceless society can be very reassuring—and why times of upheaval so often produce extremist leaders and movements: Hitler in Weimar Germany, Father Coughlin in Depression-era America, or Jean-Marie Le Pen in France and Vladimir Putin in Russia today. But running from anxiety, Kierkegaard believed, was a mistake because anxiety was a "school" that taught people to come to terms with the human condition.

into the clear about something." Harry Stack Sullivan, one of the most prominent American psychiatrists of the first half of the twentieth century, wrote that anxiety was "that which one experiences when one's self-esteem is threatened"; Robert Jay Lifton, one of the most influential psychiatrists of the second half of the twentieth century, similarly defines anxiety as "a sense of foreboding stemming from a threat to the vitality of the self, or, more severely, from the anticipation of fragmentation of the self." For Reinhold Niebuhr, the Cold War–era theologian, anxiety was a religious concept—"the internal precondition of sin . . . the internal description of the state of temptation." For their part, many physicians—starting with Hippocrates (in the fourth century B.C.) and Galen (in the second century A.D.)—have argued that clinical anxiety is a straightforward medical condition, an organic disease with biological causes as clear, or nearly so, as those of strep throat or diabetes.

Then there are those who say that anxiety is useless as a scientific concept—that it is an imprecise metaphor straining to describe a spectrum of human experience too broad to be captured with a single word. In 1949, at the first-ever academic conference dedicated to anxiety, the president of the American Psychopathological Association opened the proceedings by conceding that although everyone knew that anxiety was "the most pervasive psychological phenomenon of our time," nobody could agree on exactly what it was or how to measure it. Fifteen years later, at the annual conference of the American Psychiatric Association, Theodore Sarbin, an eminent psychologist, suggested that "anxiety" should be retired from clinical use. "The mentalistic and multi-referenced term 'anxiety' has outlived its usefulness," he declared. (Since then, of course, the use of the term has only proliferated.) More recently, Jerome Kagan, a psychologist at Harvard who is perhaps the world's leading expert on anxiety as a temperamental trait, has argued that applying the same word—"anxiety"—"to feelings (the sensation of a racing heart or tense muscles before entering a crowd of strangers), semantic descriptions (a report of worry over meeting strangers), behaviors (tense facial expressions in a social situation), brain states (activation of the amygdala to angry faces), or a chronic mood of worry (general anxiety disorder) is retarding progress."

How can we make scientific, or therapeutic, progress if we can't agree on what anxiety is?

Even Sigmund Freud, the inventor, more or less, of the modern idea of neurosis—a man for whom anxiety was a key, if not *the* key, foundational concept of his theory of psychopathology—contradicted himself repeatedly over the course of his career. Early on, he said that anxiety arose from sublimated sexual impulses (repressed libido, he wrote, was transformed into anxiety "as wine to vinegar").* Later in his career, he argued that anxiety arose from unconscious psychic conflicts.† Late in his life, in *The Problem of Anxiety,* Freud wrote: "It is almost disgraceful that after so much labor we should still find difficulty in conceiving of the most fundamental matters."

If Freud himself, anxiety's patron saint, couldn't define the concept, how am I supposed to?

Fear sharpens the senses. Anxiety paralyzes them.
— KURT GOLDSTEIN, *The Organism:*
A Holistic Approach to Biology (1939)

Standard dictionary definitions make fear ("an unpleasant emotion caused by the belief that someone or something is dangerous, likely to cause pain, or a threat") and anxiety ("a feeling of worry, nervousness, and unease, typically about an event or something with an uncertain outcome") seem relatively synonymous. But for Freud, whereas fear (*Furcht* in German) has a concrete object—the lion that's chasing you, the enemy sniper that's got you pinned to your position in battle, or even your knowledge of the consequences of missing the crucial free

---

* Some of Freud's first writings on the subject boil anxiety down to pure biomechanics: neurotic anxiety, he theorized, was mainly the result of repressed sexual energy. Trained as a neurologist (his early research was on the nervous system of eels), Freud subscribed to the principle of constancy, which held that the human nervous system tends to try to reduce, or at least hold constant, the quantity of "excitation" it contains. Sexual activity—orgasm—was a principal means by which the body discharged excess tension.

Such beliefs about the relation between sexual tension and anxiety had ancient precedent. The Roman physician Galen describes treating a patient, whose brain he believed was affected by the rotting of her unreleased sexual fluids, "with a manual stimulation of the vagina and of the clitoris." The patient "took great pleasure from this," Galen reports, "and much liquid came out, and she was cured."
† His acolytes and would-be successors then spent a generation arguing over what those conflicts might be about: Karen Horney said "dependency needs," Erich Fromm said "security needs," and Alfred Adler said "the need for power."

throw you're about to shoot in the closing moments of an important basketball game—anxiety (*Angst*) does not. According to this view, fear, properly occasioned, is healthy; anxiety, which is often "irrational" or "free-floating," is not.*

"When a mother is afraid that her child will die when it has only a pimple or a slight cold we speak of anxiety; but if she is afraid when the child has a serious illness we call her reaction fear," Karen Horney wrote in 1937. "If someone is afraid whenever he stands on a height or when he has to discuss a topic he knows well, we call his reaction anxiety; if someone is afraid when he loses his way high up in the mountains during a heavy thunderstorm we would speak of fear." (Horney further elaborated her distinction by saying that while you always know when you are afraid, you can be anxious without knowing it.)

In Freud's later writings, he replaced his distinction between fear and anxiety with a distinction instead between "normal anxiety" (defined as anxiety about a legitimate threat, which can be productive) and "neurotic anxiety" (anxiety produced by unresolved sexual issues or internal psychic conflicts, which is pathological and counterproductive).

So am I, with my phobias and worries and general twitchiness, "neurotically" anxious? Or just "normally" so? What's the difference between "normal" anxiety and anxiety as a clinical problem? What differentiates the appropriate and even helpful nervousness that, say, a law student feels before taking the bar exam or that a Little Leaguer feels before stepping into the batters' box from the distressing cognitive and physical symptoms that attend the official anxiety disorders as defined by modern psychiatry since 1980: panic disorder, post-traumatic stress disorder (PTSD), specific phobia, obsessive-compulsive disorder (OCD), social anxiety disorder, agoraphobia, and generalized anxiety disorder?

To distinguish the "normal" from the "clinical," and the different clinical syndromes from one another, pretty much everyone in the entire wide-ranging field of mental health care relies on the American Psychiatric Association's *Diagnostic and Statistical Manual* (now in its just-published fifth edition, *DSM-V*). The *DSM* defines hundreds of

---

* This Freudian view of *Angst* has a Kierkegaardian "quality of indefiniteness and lack of object."

mental disorders, classifies them by type, and lists, in levels of detail that can seem both absurdly precise and completely random, the symptoms (how many, how often, and with what severity) a patient must display in order to receive a given psychiatric diagnosis. All of which lends the appearance of scientific validity to the diagnosing of an anxiety disorder. But the reality is that there is a large quotient of subjectivity here (both on the part of patients, in describing their symptoms, and of clinicians, in interpreting them). Studies in the 1950s found that when two psychiatrists evaluated the same patient, they gave the same *DSM* diagnosis only about 40 percent of the time. Rates of consistency have improved since then, but the diagnosis of many mental disorders remains, despite pretensions to the contrary, more art than science.*

Consider the relationship between clinical anxiety and clinical depression. The physiological similarities between certain forms of clinical anxiety (especially generalized anxiety disorder) and clinical depression are substantial: both depression and anxiety are associated with elevated levels of the stress hormone cortisol, and they share some neuroanatomical features, including shrinkage of the hippocampus and other parts of the brain. They share genetic roots, most notably in the genes associated with the production of certain neurotransmitters, such as serotonin and dopamine. (Some geneticists say they can find no distinction between major depression and generalized anxiety disorder.) Anxiety and depression also have a shared basis in a feeling of a lack of self-esteem or self-efficacy. (Feeling like you have no control over your life is a common route to both anxiety and depression.) Moreover, reams of studies show that stress—ranging from job worries to divorce to bereavement to combat trauma—is a huge contributor to rates of both anxiety disorders and depression, as well as to hypertension, diabetes, and other medical conditions.

If anxiety disorders and depression are so similar, why do we distinguish between them? Actually, for a few thousand years, we didn't:

---

* The bitter fights over revisions for the *DSM-V*—which have included public denunciations of it by the chairmen of the task forces that produced the *DSM-III* and *DSM-IV*, respectively—suggest that psychiatric diagnosis may be more a matter of politics and marketing than either art or science.

doctors tended to group anxiety and depression together under the umbrella terms "melancholia" or "hysteria."* The symptoms that Hippocrates attributed to *melaina chole* in the fourth century B.C. included those we would today associate with both depression ("sadness," "moral dejection," and "tendency to suicide") and anxiety ("prolonged fear"). In 1621, in *The Anatomy of Melancholy*, Robert Burton wrote, with a clinical accuracy that modern research supports, that anxiety was to sorrow "a sister, *fidus Achates* [trusty squire], and continual companion, an assistant and a principal agent in the procuring of this mischief; a cause and symptom as the other."† It is a fact—I say this from experience—that being severely anxious is depressing. Anxiety can impede your relationships, impair your performance, constrict your life, and limit your possibilities.

The dividing line between the set of disorders the American Psychiatric Association lumps under "depression" and the set of disorders it lumps under "anxiety disorders"—and, for that matter, the line between mental health and mental illness—seems to be an artifact as much of politics and culture (and marketing) as of science. Every time the scope of a given psychiatric disorder grows or shrinks in the *DSM*'s definition, it has powerfully ramifying effects on everything from insurance reimbursements to drug company profits to the career prospects of therapists in different fields and subspecialties. Quite a few psychiatrists and drug industry critics will tell you that anxiety disorders do not exist in nature but rather were invented by the pharmaceutical-industrial complex in order to extract money from patients and insurance companies. Diagnoses such as social anxiety disorder or general anxiety disorder, these critics say, turn normal human emotions into pathologies, diseases for which medication can be profitably dispensed. "Don't allow the sum total of your life to be reduced to phrases like clinical depression, bipo-

---

* Some historians of science lump all the syndromes with this "matrix of distress symptoms"—psychological symptoms like worry and sadness and malaise, as well as physical ones like headaches, fatigue, back pain, sleeplessness, and stomach trouble—under the broad category of the "stress tradition." "Stress" can refer to both psychological stresses and physical ones, in the form of the "stress" placed on the biological nervous system that doctors since the eighteenth century believed caused "nervous disease."

† Burton wrote that in the daytime melancholics "are affrighted still by some terrible object, and torn in pieces with suspicion, fear, sorrow, discontents, cares, shames, anguish, etc., as so many wild horses, that they cannot be quiet an hour, a minute of the time."

lar disorder, or anxiety disorder," says Peter Breggin, a Harvard-trained psychiatrist who has become a fierce antagonist of the pharmaceutical industry.

As someone who has been diagnosed with some of these disorders, I can tell you the distress they cause is not invented; my anxiety, which can at times be debilitating, is real. But are my nervous symptoms necessarily constitutive of an *illness*, of a *psychiatric disorder*, as the *DSM* and the pharmaceutical companies would have it? Mightn't my anxiety be just a normal human emotional response to life, even if the response is perhaps somewhat more severe for me than for others? How do you draw the distinction between "normal" and "clinical"?

You might expect that recent scientific advances would make the distinction between normal and clinical anxiety more precise and objective—and certainly in some ways they have. Neuroscientists, working with functional magnetic resonance imaging (fMRI) technology that enables them to observe mental activity in real time by measuring oxygenated blood flow to different regions of the brain, have produced hundreds of studies demonstrating associations between specific subjectively experienced emotions and specific kinds of physiological activity that can be seen on a brain scan. For instance, acute anxiety generally appears on fMRI scans as hyperactivity in the amygdala, that tiny almond-shaped structure located deep in the medial temporal lobes near the base of the skull. Reductions in anxiety are associated with diminished activity in the amygdala and with heightened activity in the frontal cortex.*

All of which makes it sound like you should be able to identify anxiety, and gauge its intensity, on the basis of something akin to an X-ray—that you could differentiate between normal and clinical anxiety in the way X-rays can differentiate between a broken ankle and a sprained one.

Except you can't. There are people who exhibit telltale physiological signs of anxiety on a brain scan (their amygdalae light up colorfully in response to stress-inducing stimuli) but who will tell you they are not

---

* I'm oversimplifying—the full neuroscientific picture is more complex and detailed—but this is the gist of what research has found. During intensely anxious moments, the primitive effusions of the amygdala overpower the more rational thinking of the cortex.

feeling anxious. Moreover, the brain of a research subject who is sexually aroused by a pornographic movie will light up on an MRI scan in much the same way it does in response to a fear-inducing event; the same interconnected brain components—the amygdala, the insular cortex, and the anterior cingulate—will be activated in both cases. A researcher looking at the two brain scans without knowing their context might be unable to determine which image is a response to fear and which is to sexual arousal.

When an X-ray shows a fractured femur but the patient reports no pain, the medical diagnosis is still a broken leg. When an fMRI exhibits intense activity in the amygdala and basal ganglia and the patient reports no anxiety, the diagnosis is . . . nothing.

> *When it comes to detecting and responding to danger, the [verte-brate] brain just hasn't changed much. In some ways we are emotional lizards.*
> —JOSEPH LEDOUX, *The Emotional Brain* (1996)

Researchers since Aristotle have made frequent recourse to "animal models" of emotion, and the many thousands of animal studies conducted each year are predicated on the notion that the behaviors, genetics, and neurocircuitry of a rat or a chimpanzee are similar enough to our own that we can glean relevant insight from them. Writing in *The Expression of the Emotions in Man and Animals* in 1872, Charles Darwin observed that fear reactions are fairly universal across species: all mammals, including humans, exhibit readily observable fear responses. In the presence of perceived danger, rats, like people, instinctively run, freeze, or defecate.* When threatened, the congenitally "anxious" rat trembles, avoids open spaces, prefers familiar places, stops in its tracks if encountering anything potentially threatening, and emits ultrasonic distress calls. Humans don't issue ultrasonic distress calls—but when

---

* Defecation rate—the number of pellets dropped per minute—is a standard measure of fearfulness in rodents. In the 1960s, scientists at a psychiatric hospital in London bred the famous Maudsley strain of reactive rats by pairing animals with similar poop frequencies.

we get nervous, we do tremble, shy away from unfamiliar situations, withdraw from social contact, and prefer to stay close to home. (Some agoraphobics never leave their houses.) Rats that have had their amygdalae removed (or whose genes have been altered so that their amygdalae are not working properly) are incapable of expressing fear; the same is true of humans whose amygdalae get damaged. (Researchers at the University of Iowa have for years been studying a woman, known in the literature as S.M., whose amygdala was destroyed by a rare disease— and who cannot, as a consequence, experience fear.) Moreover, if continuously exposed to stressful situations, animals will develop some of the same stress-related medical conditions that humans do: high blood pressure, heart disease, ulcers, and so forth.

"With all or almost all animals, even with birds," Darwin wrote, "terror causes the body to tremble. The skin becomes pale, sweat breaks out, and hair bristles. The secretions of the alimentary canal and of the kidneys are increased, and they are involuntarily voided, owing to the relaxation of the sphincter muscles as is known to be the case with man, and as I have seen with cattle, dogs, cats, and monkeys. The breathing is hurried. The heart beats quickly, wildly, and violently. . . . The mental faculties are much disturbed. Utter prostration soon follows, and even fainting."

Darwin pointed out that this automatic physical response to threat is evolutionarily adaptive. Organisms that respond to danger in this way—by being physiologically primed to fight or flee, or to faint—are more likely to survive and reproduce than organisms that don't. In 1915, Walter Cannon, the chair of the physiology department at Harvard Medical School, coined the term "fight or flight" to describe Darwin's idea of an "alarm reaction." As Cannon was the first to document systematically, when the fight-or-flight response is activated, peripheral blood vessels constrict, directing blood away from the extremities to the skeletal muscles, so the animal will be better prepared to fight or run. (This streaming of blood away from the skin is what makes a frightened person appear pale.) Breathing becomes faster and deeper to keep the blood supplied with oxygen. The liver secretes an increased amount of glucose, which energizes various muscles and organs. The pupils of the eyes dilate and hearing becomes more acute so that the animal can better appraise the situation. Blood flows away from the alimentary canal and digestive processes stop—saliva flow decreases (causing that anxious feeling of a dry mouth), and there is often an urge to defecate, urinate, or vomit. (Expelling waste material allows the animal's internal systems to focus on survival needs more immediate than digestion.) In his 1915 book, *Bodily Changes in Pain, Hunger, Fear and Rage,* Cannon provided a couple of simple early illustrations of the way the experience of emotion translates concretely into chemical changes in the body. In one experiment, he examined the urine of nine college students after they had taken a hard exam and after they had taken an easy one: after the hard exam, four of the nine students had sugar in their urine; after the easy exam, only one of them did. In the other experiment, Cannon examined the urine of the Harvard football team after "the final and most exciting contest" of 1913 and found that twelve of the twenty-five samples had positive traces of sugar.

The physiological response that produces fainting is different from the one that primes the organism for fighting or fleeing, but it can be equally adaptive: animals that respond to bleeding injuries with a sharp drop in blood pressure suffer less blood loss; also, fainting is an involuntary way for animals to feign death, which in certain circumstances might be protective.*

When the fight-or-flight reaction is activated appropriately, in response to a legitimate physical danger, it enhances an animal's chances of survival. But what happens when the response is activated inappropriately? The result of a physiological fear response that has no legitimate object, or that is disproportionate to the size of the threat, can be pathological anxiety—an evolutionary impulse gone awry. William

---

* Here's another way in which writing this book has been bad for me: before I started researching it, I wasn't familiar with blood-injury phobia—a condition that causes the estimated 4.5 percent of people it afflicts to get extremely anxious and sometimes, because of a drop in blood pressure, to faint when injected with needles or at the sight of blood—and was therefore able to get shots and have my blood drawn without distress, a rare area of relative noncowardice for me. Now, having learned about the physiology that produces this phenomenon, I have become phobic about fainting in these situations and have, by the power of autosuggestion, nearly done so several times.

"For God's sake, Scott," Dr. W. says when I tell him about this. "You've given yourself a new phobia." (He advises that I practice getting injected by a physician soon—a form of exposure therapy—before the phobia becomes a serious problem.)

James, the psychologist and philosopher, surmised that the cause of severe anxiety, and of what we would today call panic attacks, might be modernity itself—specifically, the fact that our primitive fight-or-flight responses are not suited to modern civilization. "The progress from brute to man is characterized by nothing so much as by the decrease in frequency of proper occasions for fear," James observed in 1884. "In civilized life, in particular, it has at last become possible for large numbers of people to pass from the cradle to the grave without ever having had a pang of genuine fear."*

In modern life, occasions for what James called "genuine" human fear of the sort occasioned in the state of nature—being chased by a saber-toothed tiger, say, or encountering members of an enemy tribe— are relatively rare, at least most of the time. The threats that today tend to activate fight-or-flight physiology—the disapproving look from the boss, the mysterious letter your wife got from her old boyfriend, the college application process, the crumbling of the economy, the abiding threat of terrorism, the plummeting of your retirement fund—are not the sorts of threats the response is designed to help with. Yet because the emergency biological response gets triggered anyway, especially in clinically anxious people, we end up marinating in a stew of stress hormones that is damaging to our health. This is because whether you are in the throes of neurotic anxiety or responding to a real threat like a mugging or a house fire, the autonomic activity of your nervous system is roughly the same. The hypothalamus, a small part of the brain located just above the brain stem, releases a hormone called corticotropin-releasing factor (CRF), which in turn induces the pituitary gland, a pea-size organ protruding from the bottom of the hypothalamus, to release adrenocorticotropin hormone (ACTH), which travels through

---

* William (along with his brother Henry and sister Alice and several other siblings) seems to have inherited his own anxious, hypochondriacal tendencies from his father, Henry James Sr., an eccentric Swedenborgian philosopher who, in an 1884 letter to William, provided a description of an experience easily recognizable to the modern clinician as a panic attack: "One day . . . toward the close of May, having eaten a comfortable dinner, I remained sitting at the table after the family had dispersed, idly gazing at the embers in the grate, thinking of nothing . . . when suddenly—in a lightning-flash as it were—'fear came upon me, and trembling, which made all my bones to shake' [he's quoting Job here]. . . . The thing had not lasted ten seconds before I felt myself a wreck; that is, reduced from a state of firm, vigorous, joyful manhood to one of almost helpless infancy."

the bloodstream to the kidneys, instructing the adrenal glands sitting atop them to release adrenaline (also known as norepinephrine) and cortisol, which cause more glucose to be released into the bloodstream, which increases heart and breathing rates and produces the state of heightened arousal that can be so useful in the case of actual danger and so misery inducing in the case of a panic attack or of chronic worrying. A large body of evidence suggests that having elevated levels of cortisol for an extended period of time produces a host of deleterious health effects, ranging from high blood pressure to a compromised immune system to the shrinking of the hippocampus, a part of the brain crucial to memory formation. An anxious physiological response deployed at the right time can help keep you alive; that same response deployed too often and at the wrong times can lead to an early death.

Like animals, humans can easily be trained to exhibit conditioned fear responses—that is, to associate objectively nonfrightening objects or situations with real threats. In 1920, the psychologist John Watson famously used classical conditioning to produce phobic anxiety in an eleven-month-old boy he called Little Albert. After Watson repeatedly paired a loud noise—which provoked crying and trembling in the boy—with the presence of a white rat (the "neutral stimulus"), he was able to elicit an acute fear response in the boy simply by presenting the rat alone, without the noise. (Before the conditioning, Little Albert had happily played with the rat on his bed.) Soon the boy had developed a full-blown phobia not only of rats and other small furry animals but also of white beards. (Santa Claus terrified Little Albert.) Watson concluded that Little Albert's phobia demonstrated the power of classical conditioning. For the early behaviorists, phobic anxiety in both animals and humans was reducible to straightforward fear conditioning; clinical anxiety, in this view, was a learned response.*

For evolutionary biologists, anxiety is merely an atavistic fear

---

* The pure behaviorist view of fear conditioning is complicated, if not largely undermined, by the fact that humans and other mammals seem genetically hardwired to develop phobias of certain things but not others. Today, evolutionary psychologists say Watson misinterpreted his Little Albert experiment: the real reason Albert developed such a profound phobia of rats was not because behavioral conditioning is so intrinsically potent but because the human brain has a natural—and evolutionarily adaptive—predisposition to fear small furry things on the basis of the diseases they carry. (I explore this at greater length in chapter 9.)

response, a hardwired animal instinct triggered at the wrong time or for the wrong reasons. For behaviorists, anxiety is a learned response acquired, like Pavlov's dogs' propensity for salivating at the sound of a bell, through simple conditioning. According to both, anxiety is as much an animal trait as a human one. "Contrary to the view of some humanists, I believe that emotions are anything but uniquely human traits," the neuroscientist Joseph LeDoux writes, "and, in fact, that some emotional systems in the brain are essentially the same in . . . mammals, reptiles, and birds, and possibly amphibians and fishes as well."

But is the sort of instinctive, mechanistic response that a mouse displays in the presence of a cat, or when it hears the bell associated with a shock—or even that Little Albert displayed after he'd been trained to fear the rat—really anxiety of the sort that I feel when boarding an airplane or obsessing about my family's finances or about the mole on my forearm?

Or consider this: Even *Aplysia californica,* a marine snail with a primitive brain and no spine, can demonstrate a physiological and behavioral response that would, if exhibited by a human, be biologically equivalent (more or less) to anxiety. Touch its gill and the snail will recoil, its blood pressure will rise, and its heart rate will increase. Is *that* anxiety?

Or what about this: Even brainless, nerveless single-celled bacteria can exhibit a learned response and display what psychiatrists call avoidant behavior. When the pond-dwelling paramecium encounters a shock by an electric buzzer—an aversive stimulus—it will retreat and thenceforth seek to avoid the buzzer by swimming away from it. Is *that* anxiety? By some definitions, it is: according to the *Diagnostic and Statistical Manual,* "avoidance" of fearful stimuli is one of the hallmarks of almost all the anxiety disorders.

Other experts say that the presumed analogies between animal and human behavioral response are risibly overextended. "It is not obvious that a rat's display of an enhanced startle reaction . . . [is a] fruitful model for all human anxiety states," says Jerome Kagan. David Barlow of Boston University's Center for Anxiety and Related Disorders asks whether "entering a seemingly involuntary state of paralysis when under attack"—the sort of animal behavior that clearly does have a strong evolutionary and physiological parallel in humans—"really [has] anything in common with the forebodings concerning the welfare of our family, our occupation, or our finances?"

"How many hippos worry about whether Social Security is going to last as long as they will," asks Robert Sapolsky, a neuroscientist at Stanford University, "or what they are going to say on a first date?"

"A rat can't worry about the stock market crashing," Joseph LeDoux concedes. "We can."

Can anxiety be reduced to a purely biological or mechanical process—the instinctive behavioral response of the rat or the marine snail retreating mindlessly from the electric shock or of Little Albert conditioned, like Pavlov's dogs, to recoil and tremble in the presence of furry things? Or does anxiety require a sense of time, an awareness of prospective threats, an anticipation of future suffering—the debilitating "fears as to the future" that brought my great-grandfather, and me, to the mental hospital?

Is anxiety an animal instinct, something we share with rats and lizards and amoebas? Is it a learned behavior, something acquirable through mechanical conditioning? Or is it, after all, a uniquely human experience, dependent on consciousness of, among other things, a sense of self and the idea of death?

The physician and the philosopher have different ways of defining the diseases of the soul. For instance anger for the philosopher is a sentiment born of the desire to return an offense, whereas for the physician it is a surging of blood around the heart.
—ARISTOTLE, *De Anima* (FOURTH CENTURY B.C.)

One morning, after months of wrestling in frustration with these questions, I dump myself on my therapist's couch in a heap of worry and self-loathing.

"What's wrong?" Dr. W. asks.

"I'm supposed to be writing a book about anxiety and I can't even work out what the basic definition of anxiety is. In all these thousands of pages I've pored through, I've come across hundreds of definitions.

Many of them are similar to one another, but many others contradict each other. I don't know which one to use."

"Use the *DSM* definitions," he suggests.

"But those aren't *definitions*, just a list of associated symptoms," I say.* "And anyway, even that's not straightforward, since the *DSM* is in the process of being revised for the *DSM-V*!"†

"I know," Dr. W. says ruefully. He laments that the mandarins of psychiatry had recently considered dropping obsessive-compulsive disorder (OCD) from the anxiety disorders category in the new *DSM*, placing it instead into a new category of "impulsive disorders," on a spectrum alongside ailments like Tourette's syndrome. He thinks this is wrong. "In all my decades of clinical work," he says, "OCD patients are *always* anxious; they worry about their obsessions."

I mention that at a conference I'd attended a few weeks earlier, one of the rationales given for why OCD might be reclassified as something other than an anxiety disorder was that its genetics and its neurocircuitry seem to be substantially different from that of the other anxiety disorders.

"Goddamned biomedical psychiatry!" he blurts. Dr. W. is ordinarily a gentle, even-keeled guy, and he is aggressively ecumenical in his approach to psychotherapy; he has tried, in his writing and in his clinical practice, to assimilate the best of all the different therapeutic modes into what he calls an "integrative approach to healing the wounded self." (He is also, I should say here, the Best Therapist Ever.) But he believes strongly that over the last several decades the claims of the biomedical model generally, and of neuroscience particularly, have become increasingly arrogant and reductionist, pushing other avenues

---

* For example, here's how the *DSM-IV* defines generalized anxiety disorder: "Excessive anxiety about a number of events or activities, occurring more days than not, for at least 6 months. The person finds it difficult to control the worry. The anxiety and worry are associated with at least three of the following six symptoms (with at least some symptoms present for more days than not, for the past 6 months): Restlessness or feeling keyed up or on edge; Being easily fatigued; Difficulty concentrating or mind going blank; Irritability; Muscle tension; Sleep disturbance." (The *DSM-IV* does in one place provide a general definition of anxiety that I think is, although both generic and technical, fairly accurate: "The apprehensive anticipation of future danger of misfortune accompanied by a feeling of dysphoria or somatic feelings of tension. The focus of anticipated danger may be internal or external.")

† I had this conversation with him before the new *DSM-V* was published in 2013.

of research inquiry to the margins and distorting the practice of psychotherapy. Some of the more hard-core neuroscientists and psychopharmacologists, he feels, would boil all mental processes down to their smallest molecular components, without any sense of the existential dimensions of human suffering or of the *meaning* of anxious or depressive symptoms. At conferences on anxiety, he laments, symposia on drugs and neurochemistry—many of them sponsored by pharmaceutical companies—have started to crowd out everything else.

I tell Dr. W. I'm on the verge of abandoning the project. "I told you I was a failure," I say.

"Look," he says. "That's your anxiety talking. It makes you excessively anxious about, among other things, finding the correct definition of anxiety. And it makes you worry relentlessly about outcomes"— about whether my definition of anxiety will be "wrong"—"instead of concentrating on the work itself. You need to focus your attention. Stay on task!"

"But I still don't know what basic definition of anxiety to use," I say.

"Use mine," he says.

No one who has ever been tormented by prolonged bouts of anxiety doubts its power to paralyze action, promote flight, eviscerate pleasure, and skew thinking toward the catastrophic. None would deny how terribly painful the experience of anxiety can be. The experience of chronic or intense anxiety is above all else a profound and perplexing confrontation with pain.
—BARRY E. WOLFE, *Understanding and Treating Anxiety Disorders* (2005)

As it happens, I had chosen Dr. W. as a therapist a few years earlier precisely because I found his conception of anxiety interesting and his approach to treatment less rigid or ideological than previous therapists I'd worked with. (Also, I thought the author photo on his book jacket made him look kindly.)

I discovered Dr. W.'s work when, while in Miami attending an academic conference on anxiety, I stumbled across a book he had recently published on a display table outside a hotel ballroom. Though the book, a guide to treating anxiety disorders, was geared toward professional psychotherapists, his "integrative" conception of anxiety appealed to me. Also, after reading so many specialized books on the neuroscience of anxiety that featured sentences like "Theta activity is a rhythmic burst firing pattern of neurons in the hippocampus and related structures which, because it is synchronous across very large numbers of cells, often gives rise to a high-voltage quasi-sinusoidal electrographic slow 'theta rhythm' (approximately 5–10 Hz in the unanesthetized rat) that can be recorded from the hippocampal formation under a variety of behavioural conditions," I found his writing to be clear and nontechnical and his approach to his patients refreshingly humanistic. I recognized my own issues—the panic attacks, the dependency problems, the sublimated fear of death masked as anxiety about more trivial things—in many of the case studies in his book.

I had recently moved from Boston to Washington, D.C., and found myself for the first time in a quarter century without a regular psychotherapist. So when I read in Dr. W.'s author's note that he had a practice in the Washington area, I e-mailed him to ask if he was accepting new patients.

Dr. W. has not cured me of my anxiety. But he continues to insist that he will, and in my more hopeful moments I even sort of think he might. In the meantime, he has provided me with useful tools for trying to manage it, good and steady practical advice, and, perhaps most important, a usable definition—or a taxonomy of definitions—of anxiety.

According to Dr. W., the competing theories of and treatment approaches to anxiety can be grouped into four basic categories: the psychoanalytic, the behavioral and cognitive-behavioral, the biomedical, and the experiential.*

The psychoanalytic approach—crucial aspects of which, though

---

* This schematic overview of the different theoretical approaches to anxiety is necessarily somewhat oversimplified.

Freudianism has been widely repudiated in most scientific circles, still permeate modern talk therapy—holds that the repression of taboo thoughts and ideas (often of a sexual nature) or of inner psychic conflicts leads to anxiety. Treatment involves bringing these repressed conflicts into conscious awareness and addressing them through psychodynamic psychotherapy and the pursuit of "insight."

Behaviorists believe, like John Watson did, that anxiety is a conditioned fear response. Anxiety disorders arise when we learn—often through unconscious conditioning—to fear objectively nonthreatening things or to fear mildly threatening things too intensely. Treatment involves correcting faulty thinking through various combinations of exposure therapy (exposing yourself to the fear and acclimating to it so your fear response diminishes) and cognitive restructuring (changing your thinking) in order to "extinguish" phobias and to "decatastrophize" panic attacks and obsessional worrying. Many studies are now finding that cognitive-behavioral therapy, or CBT, is the safest and most effective treatment for many forms of depression and anxiety disorders.

The biomedical approach (where research has exploded over the last sixty years) has focused on the biological mechanisms of anxiety—on brain structures like the amygdala, hippocampus, locus coeruleus, anterior cingulate, and insula, and on neurotransmitters like serotonin, norepinephrine, dopamine, glutamate, gamma-aminobutyric acid (GABA), and neuropeptide Y (NPY)—and on the genetics that underlie that biology. Treatment often involves the use of medication.

Finally, what Dr. W. calls the experiential approach to anxiety disorders takes a more existential perspective, considering things like panic attacks and obsessional worrying to be coping mechanisms produced by the psyche in response to threats to its integrity or to self-esteem. The experiential approach, like the psychoanalytic, places great weight on the *content* and *meaning* of anxiety—rather than on the *mechanisms* of anxiety, which is where the biomedical and behavioral approaches concentrate—believing these can be clues to unlocking hidden psychic traumas or convictions about the worthlessness of one's existence. Treatment tends to involve guided relaxation to reduce anxiety symptoms and helping the patient to burrow into the anxieties to address the existential issues that lie beneath them.

The conflicts between these different perspectives—and between the psychiatrists (MDs) and the psychologists (PhDs), between the drug proponents and the drug critics, between the cognitive-behaviorists and the psychoanalysts, between Freudians and Jungians, between the molecular neuroscientists and the holistic therapists—can sometimes be bitter. The stakes are high—the future stability of large professional infrastructures rides on one theory or another predominating. And the fundamental conflict—whether anxiety is a medical disease or a spiritual problem, a problem of the body or a problem of the mind—is age-old, dating back to the clashes between Hippocrates and Plato and their followers.*

But while in many places these competing theoretical perspectives conflict with one another, they are not mutually exclusive. Often they overlap. Cutting-edge cognitive-behavioral therapy borrows from the biomedical model, using pharmacology to enhance exposure therapy. (Studies show that a drug called D-cycloserine, which was originally developed as an antibiotic, causes new memories to be more powerfully consolidated in the hippocampus and the amygdala, augmenting the potency of exposure to extinguish phobias by intensifying the power of the new, nonfearful associations to override the fearful ones.) The biomedical view, for its part, increasingly recognizes the power of things like meditation and traditional talk therapy to render concrete structural changes in brain physiology that are every bit as "real" as the changes wrought by pills or electroshock therapy. A study published

* Modern science has eventually shown Hippocrates to be the more correct—the mind *does* arise from the physical brain and, in fact, from the whole body—but Plato's influence on the study of psychology has nevertheless remained powerful and enduring, in part because of his influence on Freud. In the *Phaedrus*, Plato describes the soul as a team of two horses and a charioteer: one horse is powerful but obedient, the other is violent and ill behaved, and the charioteer must wrestle mightily to make them work together to move ahead. This view of the human psyche as divided into three parts—the spiritual, the libidinal, and the rational—presages the Freudian mind, with its id, ego, and superego. For Plato, even more than for Freud, successful psychological adjustment depended on the rational soul (*logistikon*) keeping the libidinal soul (*epithumetikon*) in check. This passage from Plato's *Republic* uncannily prefigures Freud's Oedipus complex: "All our desires are aroused when . . . the rational parts of our soul, all our civilized and controlling thoughts, are asleep. Then the wild animal in us rises up, perhaps encouraged by alcohol, and pushes away our rational thoughts: in such states, men will do anything, will dream of sleeping with their mothers and murdering people." (When Wilfred Trotter, an influential British neurosurgeon of the early twentieth century, came across this passage, he declared, "This remark of Plato makes Freud respectable.")

by researchers at Massachusetts General Hospital in 2011 found that subjects who practiced meditation for an average of just twenty-seven minutes a day over a period of eight weeks produced visible changes in brain structure. Meditation led to decreased density of the amygdala, a physical change that was correlated with subjects' self-reported stress levels—as their amygdalae got less dense, the subjects felt less stressed. Other studies have found that Buddhist monks who are especially good at meditating show much greater activity in their frontal cortices, and much less in their amygdalae, than normal people.* Meditation and deep-breathing exercises work for similar reasons as psychiatric medications do, exerting their effects not just on some abstract concept of mind but concretely on our bodies, on the somatic correlates of our feelings. Recent research has shown that even old-fashioned talk therapy can have tangible, physical effects on the shape of our brains. Perhaps Kierkegaard was wrong to say that the man who has learned to be in anxiety has learned the most important, or the most existentially meaningful, thing—perhaps the man has only learned the right techniques for controlling his hyperactive amygdala.†

---

* The very best meditators seem even to be able to suppress their startle response, a rudimentary physiological reaction to loud noises or other sudden stimuli that is mediated through the amygdala. (The strength of one's startle response—whether measured in infancy or adulthood—has been shown to be highly correlated with the propensity to develop anxiety disorders and depression.)

† For his part, William James, like Darwin, believed that purely physical, instinctive processes *preceded* awareness of an emotion—and, in fact, preceded the existence of a given brain state. In the 1890s, he and Carl Lange, a Danish physician, proposed that emotions were produced by automatic physical reactions in the body, rather than the other way around. According to what became known as the James-Lange theory, visceral changes generated by the autonomic nervous system, operating beneath the level of our conscious awareness, lead to such effects as changes in heart rate, respiration, adrenaline secretion, and dilation of the blood vessels to the skeletal muscles. Those purely physical effects occur first—and then it is only our subsequent *interpretation* of those effects that produces emotions like joy or anxiety. A fearful or angering situation produces a series of physiological reactions in the body—and then it is only the conscious mind's becoming aware of those reactions, and appraising and interpreting them, that produces anxiety or anger. According to James-Lange, no purely cognitive or psychological experience of anything like anxiety can be divorced from the autonomic changes in the viscera. The physical changes come first, then the emotion.

This suggests that anxiety is primarily a physical phenomenon and only secondarily a psychological one. "My theory," James wrote, "is that the bodily changes follow directly the perception of the exciting fact, and that our feeling of the same changes as they occur is the emotion. Common sense says, we lose our fortune, are sorry and weep; we meet a bear, are frightened and run; we are insulted by a rival, are angry and strike. The hypothesis here to be defended says that this order of sequence is incorrect . . . and that the more rational statement is that we feel sorry because we cry, angry because we strike, afraid because we tremble." Physical states create psychic ones and not vice-versa.

Darwin observed that the equipment that produces panic anxiety in humans derives from the same evolutionary roots as the fight-or-flight reaction of a rat or the aversive maneuvering of a marine snail. Which means that anxiety, for all the philosophizing and psychologizing we've attached to it, may be an irreducibly biological phenomenon that is not so different in humans than in animals.

What, if anything, do we lose when our anxiety is reduced to the stuff of its physiological components—to deficiencies in serotonin and dopamine or to an excess of activity in the amygdala and basal ganglia? The theologian Paul Tillich, writing in 1944, suggested that *Angst* was the natural reaction of man to "fear of death, conscience, guilt, despair, daily life, etc." For Tillich, the crucial question of life was: Are we safe in some deity's care, or are we trudging along pointlessly toward death in a cold, mechanical, and indifferent universe? Is finding serenity mainly a matter of coming to terms with that question? Or is it, rather more mundanely, a matter of properly calibrating levels of serotonin in the synapses? Or are these somehow, after all, the same thing?

The James-Lange theory was later undermined by research on patients with spinal cord injuries that prevented them from receiving *any* somatic information from their viscera—people who literally could not feel muscle tension or stomach discomfort; people who were, in effect, brains without bodies—yet who still reported experiencing the unpleasant psychological sensations of dread or anxiety. This suggested that the James-Lange theory was, if not wholly wrong, at least incomplete. If patients unable to receive information about the state of their bodies can still experience anxiety, then maybe anxiety *is* primarily a mental state, one that doesn't require input from the rest of the body.

But various studies conducted since the early 1960s suggest that the James-Lange theory was not, after all, completely wrong. When researchers at Columbia gave study subjects an injection of adrenaline, the heart rate and breathing rate of all the subjects increased, and they all experienced an intensification of emotion—but the researchers could manipulate what emotion the subjects felt by changing the context. Those subjects given reason to feel positive emotions felt happy, while those given reason to feel negative emotions felt angry or anxious—and in every case they felt the respective emotion (whatever it happened to be) more powerfully than those subjects who had been given a placebo injection. The injection of adrenaline increased the *intensity* of emotion, but it did not determine *what emotion that would be;* the experimental context supplied that. This suggests that the autonomic systems of the body supply the mechanics of the emotion—but the mind's interpretation of the outside environment supplies the valence.

Other recent research suggests that James and Lange were right in observing that physiological processes in the body are crucial to driving emotions and determining their intensity. For instance, a growing number of studies show that facial expressions can *produce*—rather than just reflect—the emotions associated with them. Smile and you will be happy; tremble, as James said, and you will be afraid.

Perhaps man is one of the most fearful creatures, since added to the
basic fears of predators and hostile conspecifics come intellectually
based existential fears.
—IRENÄUS EIBL-EIBESFELDT, "FEAR, DEFENCE AND AGGRESSION
IN ANIMALS AND MAN: SOME ETHOLOGICAL PERSPECTIVES" (1990)

Not long ago, I e-mailed Dr. W., who has specialized in treating
anxiety for forty years, to ask him to boil his definition of it down to a
single sentence.

"Anxiety," he wrote, "is apprehension about future suffering—the
fearful anticipation of an unbearable catastrophe one is hopeless to prevent." For Dr. W., the defining signature of anxiety, and what makes it
more than a pure animal instinct, is its orientation toward the future. In
this, Dr. W.'s thinking is in line with that of many leading theorists of
the emotions (for instance, Robert Plutchik, a physician and psychologist who was one of the twentieth century's most influential scholars
of the emotions, defined anxiety as the "combination of anticipation
and fear"), and he points out that Darwin, for all his emphasis on the
behavioral similarities between animals and humans, believed the same.
("If we expect to suffer, we are anxious," Darwin wrote in *The Expression of the Emotions in Man and Animals.* "If we have no hope of relief,
we despair.") Animals have no abstract concept of the future; they also
have no abstract concept of anxiety, no ability to worry about their
fears. An animal may experience stress-induced "difficulty in breathing"
or "spasms of the heart" (as Freud put it)—but no animal can *worry*
about that symptom or *interpret* it in any way. An animal cannot be a
hypochondriac.

Also, an animal cannot fear death. Rats and marine snails are not
abstractly aware of the prospect of a car accident, or a plane crash,
or a terrorist attack, or nuclear annihilation—or of social rejection,
or diminishment of status, or professional humiliation, or the inevitable loss of people we love, or the finitude of corporeal existence.
This, along with our capacity to be consciously aware of the sensations of fear, and to cogitate about them, gives the human experience of anxiety an existential dimension that the "alarm response" of

a marine snail utterly lacks. For Dr. W., this existential dimension is crucial.

Dr. W., echoing Freud, says that while *fear* is produced by "real" threats from the world, *anxiety* is produced by threats from within our selves. Anxiety is, as Dr. W. puts it, "a signal that the usual defenses against unbearably painful views of the self are failing." Rather than confronting the reality that your marriage is failing, or that your career has not panned out, or that you are declining into geriatric decrepitude, or that you are going to die—hard existential truths to reckon with—your mind sometimes instead produces distracting and defensive anxiety symptoms, transmuting psychic distress into panic attacks or free-floating general anxiety or developing phobias onto which you project your inner turmoil. Interestingly, a number of recent studies have found that at the moment an anxious patient begins to reckon consciously with a previously hidden psychic conflict, lifting it from the murk of the unconscious into the light of awareness, a slew of physiological measurements change markedly: blood pressure and heart rate drop, skin conductance decreases, levels of stress hormones in the blood decline. Chronic physical symptoms—backaches, stomachaches, headaches—often dissipate spontaneously as emotional troubles that had previously been "somaticized," or converted into physical symptoms, get brought into conscious awareness.*

But in believing that anxiety disorders typically arise from failed efforts to resolve basic existential dilemmas, Dr. W. is, as we will see, running against the grain of modern psychopharmacology (which proffers the evidence of sixty years of drug studies to argue that anxiety and depression are based on "chemical imbalances"), neuroscience (whose emergence has demonstrated not only the brain activity associated with various emotional states but also, in some cases, the specific structural abnormalities associated with mental illness), and temperament studies and molecular genetics (which suggest, rather convincingly, a powerful role for heredity in the determination of one's baseline level of anxiety and susceptibility to psychiatric illness).

Dr. W. doesn't dispute the findings from any of those modes of

---

* Even as much of Freudianism has been substantially discredited, elements of Freud's theories have gained empirical support in the recent findings of research like this.

inquiry. He believes medication can be an effective treatment for the symptoms of anxiety. But his view, based on thirty years of clinical work with hundreds of anxious patients, is that at the root of almost all clinical anxiety is some kind of existential crisis about what he calls the "ontological givens"—that we will grow old, that we will die, that we will lose people we love, that we will likely endure identity-shaking professional failures and personal humiliations, that we must struggle to find meaning and purpose in our lives, and that we must make trade-offs between personal freedom and emotional security and between our desires and the constraints of our relationships and our communities. In this view, our phobias of rats or snakes or cheese or honey (yes, honey; the actor Richard Burton could not bear to be in a room with honey, even if it was sealed in a jar, even if the jar was closed in a drawer) are displacements of our deeper existential concerns projected onto outward things.

Early in his career, Dr. W. treated a college sophomore who had trained his entire life to become a professional concert pianist. When the patient's professors told him that he wasn't talented enough to realize his dream, he was beset by terrible panic attacks. In Dr. W.'s view, the panic was a symptom produced by the patient's inability to reckon with the underlying existential loss here: the end of his professional aspirations, the demise of his self-conception as a concert pianist. Treating the panic allowed the student to experience his despair at this loss—and then begin to construct a new identity. Another patient, a forty-three-year-old physician with a thriving medical practice, developed panic disorder when, right around the time his older son went off to college, he began getting injuries playing tennis, a sport at which he had formerly excelled. The panic, Dr. W. concluded, was precipitated by these dual losses (of his son's childhood, of his own athletic vigor), which in combination aroused existential concerns about decline into decrepitude and death. By helping the physician come to terms with these losses, and to accept the "ontological" reality of his eventual decline and mortality, Dr. W. enabled him to shake free of the anxiety and depression.*

---

* I should say here that I am not betraying any confidentiality in writing about these patients; Dr. W. has published (anonymous) case histories of them in various places.

In Dr. W.'s view, anxiety and panic symptoms serve as what he calls a "protective screen" (what Freud called a "neurotic defense") against the searing pain associated with confronting loss or mortality or threats to one's self-esteem (roughly what Freud called the ego). In some cases, the intense anxiety or panic symptoms patients experience are neurotic distractions from, or a way of coping with, negative self-images or feelings of inadequacy—what Dr. W. calls "self-wounds."

I find Dr. W.'s existential-meaning-based interpretations of anxiety symptoms to be in some ways more interesting than the prevailing biomedical ones. But for a long time, I found the modern research literature on anxiety—which has much more to do with "neuronal firing rates in the amygdala and locus coeruleus" (as the neuroscientists put it) and with "boosting the serotonergic system" and "inhibiting the glutamate system" (as the psychopharmacologists put it) and with identifying the specific "single-nucleotide polymorphisms" on various genes that predict an anxious temperament (as the behavioral geneticists put it) than with existential issues—to be more scientific, and more convincing, than Dr. W.'s theory of anxiety. I still do. But less so than I did before.

Not long ago in my own therapy with Dr. W., we moved gingerly into "imaginal" exposure for my phobias.* Dr. W. and I established a hierarchy of frightening situations and then did a gentle "staged deconditioning," in which I was supposed to picture certain distressing images while doing deep-breathing relaxation exercises, hoping to reduce the anxiety these images stimulated. Once I'd conjured an image and was trying to hold it in my mind without panicking, Dr. W. would ask me what I was feeling.

This proved to be surprisingly hard. Although I was sitting safely in the consulting room of Dr. W.'s suburban home and was free to stop the exercise at any time, merely imagining frightening scenarios became an agony of anxiety. The smallest, most unlikely-seeming cues—seeing myself riding on a chairlift or a turbulence-racked airplane; picturing the green bucket that would be placed by my bed when I had an upset

---

* This therapy draws on a technique called systematic desensitization, which was pioneered in the 1960s by Joseph Wolpe, an influential behavioral psychologist, whose initial research was on how to eliminate fear responses in cats.

stomach as a young boy—set me to sweating and hyperventilating. So intense was my anxious response to these purely mental images that several times I had to leave Dr. W.'s office to walk around in his backyard and calm down.

In these deconditioning sessions, Dr. W. has tried to get me to focus on what, precisely, I'm anxious about.

I have a hard time answering this question. During the imaginal exposure—let alone when I'm actually confronted with a "phobic stimulus"—I cannot focus at all on answering the question. I just feel complete, all-consuming dread, and all I want is to escape—from terror, from consciousness, from my body, from my life.*

Over the course of several sessions, something unexpected happened. When I tried to engage with the phobia, I'd get derailed by sadness. I'd sit on the couch in Dr. W.'s office, doing deep breathing and trying to picture the scene from my "deconditioning hierarchy," and my mind would start to wander.

"Tell me what you're feeling," Dr. W. would say.

"A little sad," I would say.

"Go with that," he would say.

And then seconds later I'd be racked by sobs.

I am embarrassed to recount this little tale. For one thing, how unmanly can I be? For another, I am not a believer in the magical emotional breakthrough or the cathartic release. But I confess that I did feel some kind of relief as I sat there shuddering with sobs.

This outburst of sadness occurred each time we tried the exercise.

"What's going on?" I asked Dr. W. "What does this mean?"

"It means we're onto something," he said, handing me a tissue to dry my tears.

Yes, I know, everything about this scene makes me cringe, too. But at the time, as I sobbed there on the couch, Dr. W.'s statement felt like a wonderfully supportive and authentic gesture—which touched me and made me cry even harder.

"You're in the heart of the wound now," he said.

---

* I once suggested to Dr. W. that if I had a gun and knew that I at least had the option of escaping phobic terror, then maybe my anxiety would subside, since having the *option* of escape would give me the feeling of some control.

"Perhaps," he conceded. "But it would also increase the chances of you offing yourself."

Dr. W. believes, as Freud did, that anxiety could be an adaptation meant to shield the psyche from some other source of sadness or pain. I ask him why, if that's the case, the anxiety often feels much more intense than the sadness. As hard as it's making me cry, this "wound" that I'm supposedly in feels less unpleasant than the terror I feel when I'm on a turbulent flight, or when I'm feeling nauseated, or when I was enduring separation anxiety as a child.

"That's often the case," Dr. W. says.

I'm not sure what to make of this. Why do I feel so much better—happier and relatively less anxious—after swimming around in my putative "wound"?*

"We don't know yet," Dr. W. says. "But we're getting somewhere."

---

* In their early work developing psychoanalytic techniques together during the 1890s, Sigmund Freud and his mentor Josef Breuer called this cathartic dredging up of suppressed thoughts and emotions "chimney sweeping."

PART II

A History of My Nervous Stomach

CHAPTER 3

A Rumbling in the Belly

Anxiousness—a difficult disease. The patient thinks he has something like a thorn, something pricking him in his viscera, and nausea torments him.

—HIPPOCRATES, *On Diseases* (FOURTH CENTURY B.C.)

I have this recurring nightmare of being ill as a bride, running out of the church and abandoning my husband at the altar.

—EMMA PELLING, QUOTED IN THE JUNE 5, 2008,
UNITED PRESS INTERNATIONAL ARTICLE "BRIDE'S VOMIT
FEAR DELAYS WEDDING"

I struggle with emetophobia, a pathological fear of vomiting, but it's been a little while since I last vomited. More than a little while, actually: as I type this, it's been, to be precise, thirty-five years, two months, four days, twenty-two hours, and forty-nine minutes. Meaning that more than 83 percent of my days on earth have transpired in the time since I last threw up, during the early evening of March 17, 1977. I didn't vomit in the 1980s. I didn't vomit in the 1990s. I haven't vomited in the new millennium. And needless to say, I hope to make it through the balance of my life without having that streak disrupted. (Naturally, I was reluctant even to type this paragraph, and particularly that last sentence, for fear of jinxing myself or inviting cosmic rebuke, and I am knocking wood and offering up prayers to various gods and Fates as I write this.)

What this means is that I have spent, by rough calculation, at least 60 percent of my waking life thinking about and worrying about something that I have spent 0 percent of the last three-plus decades doing. This is irrational.

A part of me protests instantly: *But wait, what if it's not irrational? What if, in fact, there's a causal relationship between my worrying about vomiting and my not doing it? What if my eternal vigilance is what protects me—through magic or through neurotic enhancement of my immune system or through sheer obsessive germ avoidance—from food poisoning and stomach viruses?*

When I've made this argument to various psychotherapists over the years, they respond: "Let's say you're right about the causal relation—your behavior is still irrational. Look how much time you waste, and what you've done to your quality of life, worrying about something that, while unpleasant, is generally rare and almost always medically insignificant." Even if the cost of relaxing my vigilance was a stomach virus or bout of food poisoning every so often, the therapists say, wouldn't that be worthwhile for what I'd gain in getting so much of my life back?

I suppose a rational, nonphobic person would answer yes. And they'd surely be right. But for me the answer remains, emphatically, no.

An astonishing portion of my life is built around trying to evade vomiting and preparing for the eventuality that I might. Some of my behavior is standard germophobic stuff: avoiding hospitals and public restrooms, giving wide berth to sick people, obsessively washing my hands, paying careful attention to the provenance of everything I eat.

But other behavior is more extreme, given the statistical unlikelihood of my vomiting at any given moment. I stash motion sickness bags, purloined from airplanes, all over my home and office and car in case I'm suddenly overtaken by the need to vomit. I carry Pepto-Bismol and Dramamine and other antiemetic medications with me at all times. Like a general monitoring the enemy's advance, I keep a detailed mental map of recorded incidences of norovirus (the most common strain of stomach virus) and other forms of gastroenteritis, using the Internet to track outbreaks in the United States and around the world. Such is the nature of my obsession that I can tell you at any given moment exactly which nursing homes in New Zealand, cruise ships in the Mediterranean, and elementary schools in Virginia are contending with outbreaks. Once, when I was lamenting to my father that there is no central clearinghouse for information about norovirus outbreaks the way there is for influenza, my wife interjected. "Yes, there is," she said. We looked at her quizzically. "You," she said, and she had a point.

Emetophobia has governed my life, with a fluctuating intensity of tyranny, for some thirty-five years. Nothing—not the thousands of psychotherapy appointments I've sat through, not the dozens of medications I've taken, not the hypnosis I underwent when I was eighteen, not the stomach viruses I've contracted and withstood without vomiting— has succeeded in stamping it out.

For several years, I worked with a therapist named Dr. M., a young psychologist who had a practice at Boston University's Center for Anxiety and Related Disorders. I had originally sought treatment for my public speaking anxiety, but after several months of consultations Dr. M. proposed that we also try applying the principles of what's known as exposure therapy toward extinguishing my emetophobia.

Which is how I came to find myself not long ago at the center of an absurdist tableau.

I'm giving a speech about the founding of the Peace Corps—which feels a little artificial and awkward to begin with, because the venue is a small conference room off a hallway in the Center for Anxiety and Related Disorders. My audience consists of Dr. M. and three graduate students she's corralled at a moment's notice from around the building. Meanwhile, in the corner of the room, a large television is showing a video loop of a series of people throwing up.

"Originally, President Kennedy's plan was to house the Peace Corps inside the Agency for International Development," I'm saying as a man on the screen to my right retches loudly. "But Lyndon Johnson had been convinced by Kennedy's brother-in-law Sargent Shriver that stuffing the Peace Corps inside an existing government bureaucracy would stifle its effectiveness and end up neutering it." On the screen, vomit spatters onto the floor.

A device attached to my finger is monitoring my heart rate and levels of blood oxygen. Every few minutes, Dr. M. interrupts my speech to say: "Give me your anxiety rating now." I'm to respond by giving her an assessment of my anxiety at that moment on a scale of 1 to 10, with 1 being completely calm and 10 being unalloyed terror. "About a six," I say truthfully. I'm less anxious than embarrassed and grossed out.

"Go on," she says, and I resume my lecture as the cacophony of puking continues on the screen. When I glance up, I can see that the graduate students, two young women and a young man, are trying to pay attention to what I'm saying, but they're clearly distracted by all the literal upheaval in the background. The male student is looking green; his Adam's apple is twitching. I can tell he's fighting his gag reflex.

I'm feeling a little anxious, yes, but also frankly ridiculous. How is giving a fake speech to a fake audience amid cascading images of vomiting going to cure me of my phobia of public speaking or of throwing up?

As bizarre as this scene was, the therapeutic principles underlying it are well established. Exposure therapy—in essence, exposure to whatever's causing the pathological fear, whether that's rats or snakes or airplanes or heights or throwing up—has for dozens of years been a standard treatment for phobias, and it is now an important component of cognitive-behavioral therapy. The logic of this approach—which has lately been undergirded by neuroscience research—is that extended exposure to the object of fear, under the guidance of a therapist, makes that object less frightening. Someone with fear of heights would, accompanied by a therapist, walk farther and farther out onto the balconies of higher and higher buildings. Someone with siderodromophobia (train phobia) would take a short subway ride, and then a longer one, and then a still-longer one, until the fear diminished and was gradually extinguished completely. A more aggressive form of exposure, known as flooding, calls for a more intense experience. To treat, say, airplane phobia using the standard exposure technique, a fearful flier might be started off with visits to the airport to watch airplanes take off and land until his anxiety level comes down. He would progress to actually walking onto an airplane and getting acclimated to being on it, allowing the intensity of physical responses and fearful emotions to crest and fall, and then advance to taking a short commercial flight in the company of a therapist. Ultimately, he would graduate to taking longer flights alone. Applying flooding to aerophobia might entail, instead, starting the patient out on a tiny twin-engine plane, flying him up into the sky, and subjecting him to stomach-churning aeronautical gymnastics. According to the theory, the patient's anxiety will spike initially but will then subside as he learns quickly that he can survive both the flying and the experience of his own anxiety. Some therapists maintain relationships with local pilots so they can offer this sort of therapy. (Dr. M. offered it to me; I declined.)

David Barlow, the former head of the Center for Anxiety and Related Disorders, says the goal of exposure therapy is to "scare the hell out of the patient" in order to teach him that he can handle the fear. Barlow's exposure techniques may sound cruel and unusual, but he claims a phobia cure rate of up to 85 percent (often within a week or less), and an ample number of studies support this claim.*

The idea behind Dr. M.'s notion of trying to combine my exposures to public speaking and to vomiting was to ratchet up my anxiety as high as possible—the better to "expose" me to it, and to the things that I feared, so that I could begin the process of "extinguishing" those fears. The problem was that these simulations were too artificial to generate the requisite level of anxiety in me. Speaking to a few graduate students in Dr. M.'s office made me nervous and uncomfortable, but it never generated anything like the all-consuming dread that a real public speaking engagement does—especially since I knew that the graduate students were all studying anxiety disorders. I didn't feel compelled, as I usually do, to try to hide my anxiety; I already assumed Dr. M.'s colleagues saw me as damaged, and therefore I didn't have to go to such anxiety-producing lengths to hide my damagedness. So although even small meetings at work could still throw me into an agony of panic—to say nothing of the large-scale public speaking engagements that I would dread for months in advance—the faux presentations I'd make in my weekly sessions with Dr. M. felt like clammy facsimiles of the real thing. Awkward and unpleasant, yes, but not sufficiently anxiety provoking to be effective exposure therapy.

Similarly, while the experience of watching the vomit videos was discomfiting and unpleasant, it produced nothing close to the level of limb-trembling, soul-shaking horror that feeling about to vomit does; I knew the videos couldn't infect me, and I knew I could always sim-

---

* On the other hand, a lot of the evidence suggests that phobic anxiety is much more easily formed than extinguished. Barlow himself has a phobia of heights that he admits he has been unable to cure himself of.

ply look away, or turn them off, if my anxiety became too much to bear. Crucially—and fatally, as far as effective exposure therapy went—escape was always possible.*

Determining—as a number of other therapists, before and since, also have—that my fear of vomiting lay at the core of my other fears (for instance, I'm afraid of airplanes partly because I might get airsick), Dr. M. proposed that we concentrate on that.

"Makes sense to me," I concurred.

"There's only one way to do that properly," she said. "You need to confront the phobia head-on, to expose yourself to that which you fear the most."

Uh-oh.

"We have to make you throw up."

No. No way. Absolutely not.

She explained that a colleague had just successfully treated an emetophobe by giving her ipecac syrup, which induces vomiting. The patient, a female executive who had flown in from New York to be treated, had spent a week visiting the Center for Anxiety and Related Disorders. Each day she'd take ipecac administered by a nurse, vomit, and then process the experience with the therapist—"decatastrophizing" it, as the cognitive-behavioral therapists say. After a week, she flew back to New York—cured, Dr. M. reported, of her phobia.

I remained skeptical. Dr. M. gave me an academic journal article reporting on a clinical case of emetophobia successfully treated with the ipecac exposure method.

"This is just a single case," I said. "It's from 1979."

"There have been lots of others," she said, and reminded me again of her colleague's patient.

"I can't do it."

---

* Incidentally, the very existence of these vomit videos—and I've now seen several—is evidence of how common emetophobia is; using them has become common practice in treating phobics. Some therapists also try to gradually decondition their emetophobic patients by exposing them to fake vomit. (In case you're interested, here's a recipe recommended by two Emory University psychologists I met at a conference in 2008: Mix one can of beef and barley soup with one can of cream of mushroom soup. Add small quantities of sweet relish and vinegar. Pour into a glass jar, seal, and leave on a windowsill for one week.)

"You don't have to do anything you don't want to do," Dr. M. said. "I'll never force you to do anything. But the only way to overcome this phobia is to confront it. And the only way to confront it is to throw up."

We had many versions of this conversation over the course of several months. I trusted Dr. M. despite the inane-seeming exposures she cooked up for me. (She was kind and pretty and smart.) So one autumn day I surprised her by saying I was open to thinking about the idea. Gently, reassuringly, she talked me through how the process would work. She and the staff nurse would reserve a lab upstairs for my privacy and would be with me the whole time. I'd eat something, take the ipecac, and vomit in short order (and I would survive just fine, she said). Then we would work on "reframing my cognitions" about throwing up. I'd learn that it wasn't something to be terrified of, and I'd be liberated.

She took me upstairs to meet the nurse. Nurse R. showed me the lab and told me that taking ipecac was a standard form of exposure therapy; she said she'd helped preside over a number of exposures for erstwhile emetophobes. "Just the other week, we had a guy in here," she said. "He was very nervous, but it worked out just fine."

We went back downstairs to Dr. M.'s office.

"Okay," I said. "I'll do it. Maybe."

Over the next few weeks, we'd keep scheduling the exposure—and then I'd show up on the appointed day and demur, saying I couldn't go through with it. I did this enough times that I shocked Dr. M. when, on an unseasonably warm Thursday in early December, I presented myself at her office for my regular appointment and said, "Okay. I'm ready."

The exercise was star-crossed from the beginning. Nurse R. was out of ipecac, so she had to run to the pharmacy to get some more while I waited for an hour in Dr. M.'s office. Then it turned out that the upstairs lab was booked, so the exposure would have to take place in a small public restroom in the basement. I was constantly on the verge of backing out; probably the only reason I didn't was that I knew I could.

What follows is an edited excerpt drawn from the dispassionate-as-possible account I wrote up afterward on Dr. M.'s recommendation. (Writing an emotionally neutral account is a commonly prescribed way of trying to forestall post-traumatic stress disorder after a traumatic experience.) If you're emetophobic yourself, or even just a little squeamish, you might want to skip over it.

We met up with Nurse R. in the basement restroom. After some discussion, I took the ipecac.

Having passed the point of no return, I felt my anxiety surge considerably. I began to shake a little. Still, I was hopeful that sickness would strike quickly and be over fast and that I would discover the experience was not as bad as I'd feared.

Dr. M. had attached a pulse and oxygen-level monitor to my finger. As we waited for the nausea to hit, she asked me to state my anxiety level on a scale of 1 to 10. "About a nine," I said.

By now I was starting to feel a little nauseated. Suddenly I was struck by heaving and I turned to the toilet. I retched twice—but nothing felt like it was coming up. I knelt on the floor and waited, still hoping the event would come quickly and then be over with. The monitor on my finger felt like an encumbrance, so I took it off.

After a time, I heaved again, my diaphragm convulsing. Nurse R. explained that dry-heaving precedes the main event. I was now desperate for this to be over.

The nausea began coming in intense waves, crashing over me and then receding. I kept feeling like I was going to vomit, but then I would heave noisily again and nothing would come up. Several times I could actually feel my stomach convulse. But I would heave and . . . nothing would happen.

My sense of time at this point gets blurry. During each bout of retching, I would begin perspiring profusely, and when the nausea would pass, I would be dripping with sweat. I felt faint, and I worried that I would pass out and vomit and aspirate and die. When I mentioned feeling light-headed, Nurse R. said that my color looked good. But I thought she and Dr. M. seemed slightly alarmed. This increased my anxiety—because if *they* were worried, then I should really be scared, I thought. (On the other hand, at some level I *wanted* to pass out, even if that meant dying.)

After about forty minutes and several more bouts of retching, Dr. M. and Nurse R. suggested I take more ipecac. But I feared a second dose would subject me to worse nausea for a longer period of time. I worried I might just keep dry-heaving for hours or days. At some point, I switched from hoping that I would vomit quickly and have the ordeal over with to thinking that maybe I could fight the ipecac and simply wait for the nausea to wear off. I was exhausted, horribly nauseated, and utterly miserable. In between bouts of retching, I lay on the bathroom tiles, shaking.

A long period passed. Nurse R. and Dr. M. kept trying to convince me to take more ipecac, but by now I just wanted to avoid vomiting. I hadn't retched for a while, so I was surprised to be stricken by another bout of violent heaving. I could feel my stomach turning over, and I thought for sure that this time something would happen. It didn't. I choked down some secondary waves, and then the nausea eased significantly. This was the point when I began to feel hopeful that I would manage to escape the ordeal without throwing up.

Nurse R. seemed angry. "Man, you have more control than anyone I've ever seen," she said. (At one point, she asked peevishly if I was resisting because I wasn't prepared to terminate treatment yet. Dr. M. interjected that this was clearly not the case—I'd taken the ipecac, for God's sake.) Eventually—several hours had now elapsed since I ingested the ipecac—Nurse R. left, saying she had never seen someone take ipecac and not vomit.*

After some more time passed, and some more encouragement from Dr. M. to try to "complete the exposure," we decided to "end the attempt." I still felt nauseated, but less so than before. We talked briefly in her office, and then I left.

Driving home, I became extremely anxious that I would vomit and crash. I waited at red lights in terror.

When I got home, I crawled into bed and slept for several hours. I felt better when I woke up; the nausea was gone. But

---

* I've since read that up to 15 percent of people—a disproportionate number of them emetophobes—don't vomit from a single dose of ipecac.

that night I had recurring nightmares of retching in the bathroom in the basement of the center.

The next morning I managed to get to work for a meeting—but then panic surged and I had to go home. For the next several days, I was too anxious to leave the house.

Dr. M. called the next day to make sure I was okay. She clearly felt bad about having subjected me to such a miserable experience. Though I was traumatized by the whole episode, her sense of guilt was so palpable that I felt sympathetic toward her. At the end of the account I composed at her request, which was accurate as far as it went, I masked the emotional reality of what I thought (which was that the exposure had been an abject disaster and that Nurse R. was a fatuous bitch) with an antiseptic clinical tone. "Given my history, I was brave to take the ipecac," I wrote. "I wish that I had vomited quickly. But the whole experience was traumatic, and my general anxiety levels—and my phobia of vomiting—are more intense than they were before the exposure. I also, however, recognize that, based on this experience in resisting the effects of the ipecac, my power to prevent myself from vomiting is quite strong."

Stronger, it seems, than Dr. M.'s. She told me she had to cancel all of her afternoon appointments on the day of the exposure—watching me gagging and fighting with the ipecac evidently had made her so nauseated that she spent the afternoon at home, throwing up. I confess I took some perverse pleasure from the irony here—the ipecac *I* took made *someone else* vomit—but mainly I felt traumatized and intensely anxious. It seems I'm not very good at getting over my phobias but quite good at making my therapists and their associates sick.

I continued seeing Dr. M. for a few more months—we "processed" the botched exposure and then, both of us wanting to forget the whole thing, turned from emetophobia to various other phobias and neuroses—but the sessions now had an elegiac, desultory feel. We both knew it was over.*

---

* Eventually, she moved away, accepting a tenure-track faculty position at a university in the Southwest. I run into her occasionally at academic conferences on anxiety. Despite everything, I like her. But I always wonder: does it feel weird to her to be talking to a former patient who's now at these conferences with a notebook, posing as a journalist and a kind of lay expert on anxiety? How often does she

That sphincter which serves to discharge our stomachs has dilations and contractions proper to itself, independent of our wishes, and even opposed to them.

—MICHEL DE MONTAIGNE,
"ON THE POWER OF THE IMAGINATION" (1574)

The mind, as the neurophilosophers say, is fully embodied; it is, as Aristotle put it, "enmattered." The bodily clichés of nervous excitement ("butterflies in the stomach"), anxious anticipation ("a loosening of the bowels," "scared shitless"), or dread (felt "in the pit of the stomach") are not in fact clichés or even metaphors but truisms—accurate descriptions of the physiological correlates of anxious emotion. Doctors and philosophers have observed for millennia the potency of what the medical journals call the brain-gut axis. "There may even be some connection between a phobia and a beef-steak, so intimately related are the stomach and the brain," Wilfred Northfield wrote in 1934.

Nerve-disordered bellies are a bane of modern existence. According to a Harvard Medical School report, as many as 12 percent of all patient visits to primary care physicians in the United States are for irritable bowel syndrome, or IBS, a condition characterized by stomach pain and alternating bouts of constipation and diarrhea that most experts believe to be wholly or partly caused by stress or anxiety. First identified in 1830 by the British physician John Howship, IBS has since then been referred to as "spastic colon," "spastic bowel," "colitis," and "functional bowel disease," among other names. (Physicians in the Middle Ages and Renaissance referred to it as "windy melancholy" and "hypochondriache flatulence.") Because no one has ever definitively identified an organic cause of IBS, most doctors attribute its appearance to stress, emotional conflict, or some other psychological source. In the absence of a clear malfunction in the nerves and muscles of the gut, doctors tend to assume a malfunction in the brain—perhaps a hypersensitized awareness of sensations in the intestine. In one well-known set

think, *That's the guy I gave ipecac to, the guy I watched retching and weeping and shaking on the floor of a public restroom for hours?*

of experiments, when balloons were inflated in the colons of both IBS patients and healthy control subjects, the IBS patients reported a much lower threshold for pain, suggesting that the viscera–brain connection may be more sensitive in patients with irritable bowels.

This is consistent with a trait called anxiety sensitivity, which research has shown to be strongly correlated with panic disorder. Individuals who rate high on the so-called Anxiety Sensitivity Index, or ASI, have a high degree of what's known as interoceptive awareness, meaning they are highly attuned to the inner workings of their bodies, to the beepings and bleatings, the blips and burps, of their physiologies; they are more conscious of their heart rate, blood pressure, body temperature, breathing rates, digestive burblings, and so forth than other people are. This hyperawareness of physiological activity makes such people more prone to "internally cued panic attacks": the individual with a high ASI rating picks up on a subtle increase in heart rate or a slight sensation of dizziness or a vague, unidentifiable fluttering in the chest; this perception, in turn, produces a frisson of conscious anxiety (*Am I having a heart attack?*), which causes those physical sensations to intensify. The individual immediately perceives this intensification of sensation—which in turn generates more anxiety, which produces still more intensified sensations, and before long the individual is in the throes of panic. A number of recent studies published in periodicals like the *Journal of Psychosomatic Research* have found a powerful interrelationship among anxiety sensitivity, irritable bowel syndrome, worry, and a personality trait known as neuroticism, which psychologists define as you would expect—a tendency to dwell on the negative; a high susceptibility to excessive feelings of anxiety, guilt, and depression; and a predisposition to overreact to minor stress. Unsurprisingly, people who score high on cognitive measures of neuroticism are disproportionately prone to developing phobias, panic disorder, and depression. (People who score low on the neuroticism scale are disproportionately resistant to those disorders.)

Evidence suggests that people with irritable bowels have bodies that are more physically reactive to stress. I recently came across an article in the medical journal *Gut* that explained the circular relationship between cognition (your conscious thought) and physiological correlates (what your body does in response to that thought): people who are less anxious tend to have minds that don't overreact to stress and bodies that don't overreact to stress when their minds experience it, while clinically anxious people tend to have sensitive minds in sensitive bodies—small amounts of stress set them to worrying, and small amounts of worrying set their bodies to malfunctioning. People with nervous stomachs are also more likely than people with settled stomachs to complain of headaches, palpitations, shortness of breath, and general fatigue. Some evidence suggests that people with irritable bowel syndrome have greater sensitivity to pain, are more likely to complain about minor ailments like colds, and are more likely to consider themselves sick than other people.

Most cases of stomach upset, the physiologist Walter Cannon wrote back in 1909, are "nervous in origin." In his article "The Influence of Emotional States on the Functions of the Alimentary Canal," Cannon concluded that anxious thoughts had direct effects—through the nerves of the sympathetic nervous system—on both the physical movements of the stomach (that is, on peristalsis, the process by which the digestive system moves food through the alimentary canal) and gastric secretions. Cannon's theory has been borne out by modern surveys conducted at primary care centers, which find that most routine stomach trouble emanates from mental distress: between 42 and 61 percent of all patients with functional bowel disorders have also been given an official psychiatric diagnosis, most often anxiety or depression; one study has found a 40 percent overlap between patients with panic disorder and functional GI disease.*

---

* As further evidence that a great deal of stomach trouble starts in the brain, not in the gut, no stomach medication has yet been proved consistently effective against the symptoms of irritable bowel syndrome—but substantial evidence suggests that certain antidepressant medications can be effective. (Before the 1960s, one of the most frequent prescriptions for IBS was a cocktail of morphine and barbiturates.) In a recent study, IBS patients injected with the SSRI antidepressant Celexa reported reduced "visceral hypersensitivity."

Michael Gershon, a professor of pathology and cell biology at Columbia University, says that the reason antidepressants reduce IBS symptoms is not that they affect neurotransmitters in the brain but that they affect neurotransmitters in the stomach. Some 95 percent of the serotonin in our bodies can be found in our stomachs. (When serotonin was discovered in the 1930s, it was originally called enteramine because of its high concentration in the gut.) Gershon calls the stomach "the second brain" and observes that stomach trouble is as likely to beget anxiety as the other way around. "The brain in

"Fear brings about diarrhea," Aristotle wrote, "because the emotion causes an augmenting of heat in the belly." Hippocrates attributed both bowel trouble and anxiety (not to mention hemorrhoids and acne) to a surplus of black bile. Galen, the ancient Roman physician, blamed yellow bile. "People attacked by fear experience no slight inflow of yellow bile into the stomach," he observed, "which makes them feel a gnawing sensation, and they do not cease feeling both distress of mind and the gnawing until they have vomited up the bile."

But it was only in 1833, with the publication of a monograph called *Experiments and Observations on the Gastric Juice and the Physiology of Digestion*, that the link between emotional states and indigestion began to be understood with any kind of scientific precision. On June 6, 1822, Alexis St. Martin, a hunter employed by the American Fur Company, was accidentally shot in the stomach at close range by a musket loaded with buck shot. He was expected to die—but under the care of William Beaumont, a physician in upstate New York, he survived, albeit with an unusual condition: an unhealed open hole, or fistula, in his stomach. Beaumont realized that the hunter's fistula provided a remarkable opportunity for scientific observation: he could literally see into St. Martin's stomach. Over the next decade, Beaumont conducted many experiments using the hunter's fistula as a window into his digestive workings.

Beaumont noticed that St. Martin's emotional states had a powerful effect on his stomach, one readily observable to the naked eye: the mucosal lining of the hunter's stomach would change color dramatically, like a mood ring, in tandem with his emotional states. Sometimes the stomach lining was bright red; at other times, such as when St. Martin was anxious, it turned pale.

"I have availed myself of the opportunity afforded by an occurrence of circumstances which can probably never occur again," Beaumont wrote. But he was wrong. Medical literature records at least two subsequent instances of digestion research conducted on patients with holes in their stomachs over the course of the next century. And then, in 1941,

---

the bowel has got to work right or no one will have the luxury to think at all," he says. "No one thinks straight when his mind is focused on the toilet."

Stewart Wolf and Harold Wolff, physicians at New York Hospital in Manhattan, discovered Tom.

One day in 1904, when Tom was nine years old, he took a swig of what he thought was beer (it was in his father's beer pail) but turned out to be boiling hot clam chowder. The chowder seared his upper digestive tract and knocked him unconscious. By the time his mother delivered him to the hospital, his esophagus had fused shut. For the rest of his life, the only way for him to receive nourishment was through a surgically opened hole in the stomach wall. The hole was ringed on the outside by a segment of his stomach lining. He fed himself by chewing his food and then inserting it directly into his stomach through a funnel placed in the hole in his abdomen.

Tom came to the attention of Drs. Wolf and Wolff in 1941, when, while working as a sewer laborer, he was compelled to seek medical assistance after his wound became irritated. Recognizing the unusual research opportunity represented by Tom's condition, the doctors hired him as a lab assistant and conducted multiple experiments on him over the course of seven months. The results were published in their 1943 book, *Human Gastric Function*, a landmark of psychosomatic research.

Building on Beaumont's findings, the doctors observed that the lining of Tom's stomach varied significantly in color based on its level of activity—from "faint yellowish red to a deep cardinal shade." Greater levels of digestive activity tended to correlate with deeper shades of red (suggesting increased blood flow to the stomach), while lesser levels, including those induced by anxiety, correlated with paler colors (suggesting the flow of blood away from the stomach).

The doctors were able to chart correlations that had long been assumed but were never scientifically proved. One afternoon another doctor barged into the lab, swearing to himself and rapidly opening and closing drawers, looking for documents that had been mislaid. Tom, whose job it was to keep the lab tidy, became alarmed—he feared he would lose his job. The lining of his stomach went instantly pale, dropping from "90 percent redness" on the color scale to 20 percent. Acid secretion nearly stopped. When the doctor found the missing papers a few minutes later, acid secretion resumed and the color gradually returned to Tom's stomach.

At some level, all this is unsurprising; everyone knows that anxiety can cause gastrointestinal distress. (My friend Anne says that the most effective weight-loss program she ever tried was the Stressful Divorce Diet.) But *Human Gastric Function* represented the first time that the connections had been charted in such precise and systematic detail. The relationship between Tom's mental state and his digestion was not vague and diffuse; his stomach was a concrete and direct register of his psychology. Summing up their observations, Wolf and Wolff concluded that there was a strong inverse correlation between what they called "emotional security" and stomach discomfort.

That's certainly true in my case. Being anxious makes my stomach hurt and my bowels loosen. My stomach hurting and my bowels loosening makes me *more* anxious, which makes my stomach hurt more and my bowels even looser, and so nearly every trip of any significant distance from home ends up the same way: with me scurrying frantically from restroom to restroom on a kind of grand tour of the local latrines. For instance, I don't have terribly vivid recollections of the Vatican or the Colosseum or the Italian rail system. I do, however, have searing memories of the public restrooms in the Vatican and at the Colosseum and in various Italian train stations. One day, I visited the Trevi Fountain—or, rather, my wife and her family visited the Trevi Fountain. I visited the restroom of a nearby *gelateria*, where a series of impatient Italians banged on the door while I bivouacked there. The next day, when the family drove to Pompeii, I gave up and stayed in bed, a reassuringly short distance from the bathroom.

Some years earlier, following the fall of the Berlin Wall and the dissolution of the Warsaw Pact, I traveled to Eastern Europe to visit a girlfriend, Ann, who was studying in Poland. She had been there for six months by the time I visited; I had planned and aborted (because of anxiety) several previous trips, and only the fear that Ann would finally break up with me if I didn't visit her impelled me to fight through my tremendous dread of a transatlantic flight to meet her in Warsaw. Drugged to near unconsciousness, I flew from Boston to London and then to Warsaw. Befogged by sedatives, antiemetic medications, and jet lag, I stumbled through our first day and a half together. My bowels percolated to life about the time the rest of me did, when the Dramamine and Xanax wore off. We ended up traipsing around Eastern Europe from restroom to restroom. This was frustrating for her and harrowing for me—because, among other reasons, many Eastern European public commodes were at that time rather primitive; you often had to pay an attendant in advance on a per sheet basis for scratchy, ill-constructed toilet paper. By the end of the trip, I'd given up; Ann went sightseeing while I retreated to our hotel room, where at least I didn't have to gauge my toilet tissue use in advance.

Ann, understandably, grew peevish about this. After visiting the home of Franz Kafka (who, I note, suffered from chronic bowel trouble), we walked across Wenceslas Square in Prague while I griped about my aching belly. Ann could no longer contain her exasperation. "Maybe you should write a dissertation about your stomach," she said, mocking my preoccupation. A preoccupation, you may have noticed, that I have yet to overcome.

But when your stomach governs your existence, it's hard not to be preoccupied with it. A few searing experiences—soiling yourself on an airplane, say, or on a date—will focus you passionately on your gastrointestinal tract. You need to devote effort to planning around it—because it will not always plan around you.

Case in point: Fifteen years ago, while researching my first book, I spent part of the summer living with the extended Kennedy family on Cape Cod. One weekend, then–president Bill Clinton, who was vacationing on Martha's Vineyard, came across Nantucket Sound to go sailing with Ted Kennedy. Hyannis Port, where the Kennedys have their vacation homes, was crawling with presidential aides and Secret Service agents. With some time to kill before dinner, I decided to walk around town to take in the scene.

Bad idea. As is so often the case with irritable bowel syndrome, it was at precisely the moment I passed beyond Easily Accessible Bathroom Range that my clogged plumbing came unglued. Sprinting back to the house where I was staying, I was several times convinced I would not make it and—teeth gritted, sweating voluminously—was reduced to evaluating various bushes and storage sheds along the way for their potential as ersatz outhouses. Imagining what might ensue if a Secret Service agent were to happen upon me crouched in the shrubbery lent a kind of panicked, otherworldly strength to my efforts at self-possession.

As I approached the entrance, I was simultaneously reviewing the floor plan in my head (*Which of the many bathrooms in the mansion is closest to the front door? Can I make it all the way upstairs to my room?*) and praying that I wouldn't be fatally waylaid by a stray Kennedy or celebrity (Arnold Schwarzenegger, Liza Minnelli, and the secretary of the navy, among others, were visiting that weekend).

Fortunately, I made it into the house unaccosted. Then a quick calculation: *Can I make it all the way upstairs and down the hall to my suite in time? Or should I duck into the bathroom in the front hall?* Hearing footsteps above and fearing a protracted encounter, I opted for the latter and slipped into the bathroom, which was separated from the front hall by an anteroom and two separate doors. I scampered through the anteroom and flung myself onto the toilet.

My relief was extravagant and almost metaphysical.

But then I flushed and . . . something happened. My feet were getting wet. I looked down and saw to my horror that water was flowing out from the base of the toilet. Something seemed to have exploded. The floor—along with my shoes and pants and underwear—was covered in sewage. The water level was rising.

Instinctively, I stood up and turned around. Could the flooding be stopped? I removed the porcelain top of the toilet tank, scattering the flowers and potpourri that sat atop it, and frantically began fiddling with its innards. I tried things blindly, raising this and lowering that, jiggling this and wiggling that, fishing around in the water for something that might stem the swelling tide.

Somehow, whether of its own accord or as a result of my haphazard fiddling, the flooding slowed and then stopped. I surveyed the scene. My clothes were drenched and soiled. So was the bathroom rug. Without thinking, I slipped out of my pants and boxer shorts, wrapped them in the waterlogged rug, and jammed the whole mess into the wastebasket, which I stashed in the cupboard under the sink. *Have to deal with this later,* I thought to myself.

It was at this unpropitious moment that the dinner bell rang, signaling that it was time to muster for cocktails in the living room.

Which was right across the hall from the bathroom.

Where I was standing ankle-deep in sewage.

I pulled all the hand towels off the wall and dropped them on the ground to start sopping up some of the toilet water. I got down on my hands and knees and, unraveling the whole roll of toilet paper, began dabbing frenziedly at the water around me. It was like trying to dry a lake with a kitchen sponge.

What I was feeling at that point was not, strictly speaking, anxiety; rather, it was a resigned sense that the jig was up, that my humiliation would be complete and total. I'd soiled myself, destroyed the estate's septic system, and might soon be standing half naked before God knows how many members of the political and Hollywood elite.

In the distance, voices were moving closer. It occurred to me that I had two choices. I could hunker down in the bathroom, hiding and waiting out the cocktail party and dinner—at the risk of having to fend off anyone who might start banging on the door—and use the time to try to clean up the wreckage before slipping up to my bedroom after everyone had gone to bed. Or I could try to make a break for it.

I took all of the soiled towels and toilet paper and shoved them into the cupboard, then set about preparing my escape. I retrieved the least soiled towel (which was nonetheless dirty and sodden) and wrapped it gingerly around my waist. I crept to the door and listened for voices and footsteps, trying to gauge distance and speed of approach. Knowing I had scarcely any time before everyone converged on the center of the house, I slipped out the bathroom door and through the anteroom, sprint-walked across the hallway, and darted up the stairs. I hit the first landing, made a hairpin turn, and headed up the next flight to the second floor—where I nearly ran headlong into John F. Kennedy Jr. and another man.

"Hi, Scott," Kennedy said.*

"Uh, hi," I said, racking my brain for a plausible explanation for why I might be running through the house at cocktail hour with no pants on, drenched in sweat, swaddled in a soiled and reeking towel. But he and his friend appeared utterly unfazed—as though half-naked

---

* I'd just met him for the first time the day before. "I'm John Kennedy," he had said when he extended his hand in introduction. *I know*, I had thought as I extended mine, thinking it funny that he had to pretend courteously that people might not know his name, when in fact only a hermit or a Martian wouldn't have known who he was, so ubiquitous was his face on the cover of checkout counter magazines.

houseguests covered in their own excrement were frequent occurrences here—and walked past me down the stairs.

I scrambled down the hallway to my room, where I showered vigorously, changed, and generally tried to compose myself as best I could—which was not easy because I was continuing to sweat terribly, right through my blazer, the result of anxiety, exertion, and summer humidity.

If someone had snapped a photo of the scene at cocktails that evening, here's what it would show: various celebrities and politicians and priests all glowing with grace and easy bonhomie as they mingle effortlessly on the veranda overlooking the Atlantic—while, just off to the side, a sweaty young writer stands awkwardly gulping gin and tonics and thinking about how far he is from fitting in with this illustrious crowd and about how not only is he not rich or famous or accomplished or particularly good-looking but he cannot even control his own bowels and therefore is better suited for the company of animals or infants than of adults, let alone adults as luminous and significant as these.

The sweaty young writer is also worrying about what will happen when someone tries to use the hallway bathroom.

Late that night, after everyone had gone off to bed, I sneaked back down to the bathroom with a garbage bag and paper towels and cleaning detergent I'd purloined from the pantry. I couldn't tell whether anyone had been there since I left, but I tried not to worry about that and concentrated on stuffing the soiled rug and towels and clothes and toilet paper I'd stashed under the sink into the trash bag. Then I used the paper towels to scrub the floors, and I put those into the trash bag as well.

Outside the kitchen, between the main house and an outbuilding, was a Dumpster. My plan was to dispose of everything there. Naturally, I was terrified of getting caught. What, exactly, would a houseguest be doing disposing of a large trash bag outside in the middle of the night? (I worried that there might still be Secret Service afoot, who might shoot me before allowing me to plant what looked like a bomb or a body in the Dumpster.) But what choice did I have? I slunk through the house and out to the Dumpster, where I deposited the trash bag. Then I went back upstairs to bed.

No one ever said anything to me about the hallway bathroom or about the missing rug and towels. But for the rest of the weekend, and on my subsequent visits there, I was convinced that the household staff were glaring at me and whispering. "That's him," I imagined they were saying in disgust. "The one who broke the toilet and ruined our towels. The one who can't control his own bodily functions."*

> *Most persons with a sore colon are of a tense, sensitive, nervous temperament. They may be calm externally, but they usually seethe internally.*
>
> —WALTER C. ALVAREZ, *Nervousness, Indigestion, and Pain* (1943)

Of course, I know that such shame should not attach to what is, officially, a medical condition. Irritable bowel syndrome is a common gastrointestinal complaint frequently associated with mood and anxiety disorders, as has been observed since ancient times. In 1943, the eminent gastroenterologist Walter Alvarez noted in his delightfully titled *Nervousness, Indigestion, and Pain* that there is no more reason a person should feel ashamed about a nervous stomach than someone should feel ashamed at blushing at a compliment or weeping at a sad play. The nervousness and hypersensitivity that such physical reactions produce, Alvarez wrote, are associated with personality traits that, if "properly used and controlled," can "do much to help a man succeed."†

---

* As bad as my own agoraphobic belly sometimes seems to me, others have it worse. One of the more alarming case studies I've come across was of a forty-five-year-old man who showed up at a mental health clinic in Kalamazoo, Michigan, in 2007. He had been suffering from acute travel anxiety for twenty years, ever since the time a panic attack caused him to vomit and lose control of his bowels. Since then, the man had not been able to travel more than ten miles from home without experiencing uncontrollable vomiting and diarrhea. Clinicians later mapped his comfort zone by his symptoms: the farther from home he went, the more dramatic his eruptions. So violent were his gastrointestinal reactions that on several occasions he had to be rushed to emergency rooms because he was vomiting blood. After physicians ruled out ulcers and stomach cancer, he was finally referred to the psychology clinic, and he was, his therapist told me when I met him at a conference in 2008, successfully treated with a combination of exposure therapy and cognitive-behavioral therapy.

† Alvarez observed that the most common source of his patients' chronic stomach discomfort was the "challenges of modern living": "The stomach specialist has to be a psychiatrist of sorts," he wrote. "He must spend hours each week trying to teach neurotic persons to live more sensibly."

One young woman was referred to Alvarez after vomiting "day and night for a week." When he learned that she had recently received an ominous letter from the Internal Revenue Service, he

But a nervous stomach is bad enough—what's most disabling to me is that my nervous stomach itself makes me nervous. That's the infernal thing about being an anxious emetophobe: the very fact of one's stomach hurting is itself often the most acute source of fear. Any time your stomach hurts, you worry you might vomit. Thus being anxious makes your stomach hurt, and your stomach hurting makes you anxious—which in turn makes your stomach hurt more, which makes you more anxious, and so on and so forth in a vicious cycle that hurtles rapidly toward panic. The lives of emetophobes are largely built around their phobia—some have not worked or left their houses for years because of their fears and cannot bear even to say or write "vomit" or related words. (Online emetophobia communities usually have rules requiring that such words be rendered as, for instance, "v**.")

Until recent years, emetophobia rarely appeared in the clinical literature. But the arrival of the Internet provided a means for emetophobes, many of whom had previously believed they were alone in their affliction, to find one other.* Online communities and support groups sprouted. The appearance of these virtual communities, some of which are quite large (by one estimate, the forum of the International Emetophobia Society has five times as many members as the largest flying phobia forum), came to the attention of anxiety researchers, who have started to study this phobia more systematically.

Like all anxiety disorders, emetophobia presents with elevated levels of physiological arousal, avoidance behavior (and also what experts call safety, or neutralizing, behavior, by which they mean doing what I

---

treated her by paying her back taxes—it turned out she owed only $3.85—and she was instantly cured. Another patient, whom Alvarez described as "a tense, high-pressure type of sales manager," came to him because he loved poker but couldn't play it: If he got a good hand, he would become "nauseated and chilly" and his face would turn red. Bluffing was impossible because any time he was dealt a full house or better, he would immediately have to get up and vomit. But "the cruelest prank of nature" Alvarez ever saw was the way nervous stomachs could destroy the love lives of the anxious. He treated one woman who would get stomach cramps and have to move her bowels whenever she was touched by a man, another who belched uncontrollably whenever a date became intimate, and numerous others who would break wind or vomit in romantic moments. (In his memoirs, the legendary lover Casanova reported on his escapades with a woman who, whenever she became sexually excited, would pass large quantities of gas.) Alvarez also treated "several men who were divorced by outraged wives because of their having to stop and run to the toilet whenever they became sexually excited."

* Among celebrities who have reported themselves to be emetophobic are the actress Nicole Kidman, the musician Joan Baez, and Matt Lauer, the host of the *Today* show.

do: carrying stomach remedies and antianxiety medications in case of emergency), attention disruption (meaning that in the presence of a phobic stimulus, such as a virus going around the office or through the family, we can concentrate on little else), and, typically, problems with self-esteem and self-efficacy. We emetophobes tend to think poorly of ourselves and to believe we have trouble coping with the world, and especially with something as catastrophic-seeming as vomiting.*

As we've seen, both patients with panic disorder and patients with irritable bowel syndrome (who much of the time are the *same* patients) have what mental health experts call "high somatization vulnerability" (that is, a tendency to convert emotional distress into physical symptoms) and "cognitive biases in the discrimination and interpretation of bodily symptoms" (that is, they are especially conscious of even minor changes in physiology and have an attendant predisposition to interpret those symptoms in a catastrophic, worst-case-scenario way). But whereas the primary concern for most panic patients tends to be that anxious bodily symptoms augur a heart attack or suffocation or insanity or death, emetophobes are afraid that the symptoms foretell imminent vomiting (and also insanity and death). And whereas the fears of the panic patients are, except in rare cases of anxiety-induced sudden cardiac death, extremely unlikely to be realized, emetophobes are quite capable of bringing on, through their anxious symptoms, the very thing they fear most. Which, of course, is another reason to be constantly afraid of being constantly afraid. Is it any wonder that sometimes I feel like my brain is turning inside out?

Psychologists have developed several standardized scales for measuring control-freakiness—there is, for instance, Rotter's Locus of Control Scale and also the Health Locus of Control Scale. That anxiety and depression are bound up tightly not only with self-esteem issues but with control issues (anxiety disorder patients tend both to feel like they don't have much control over their lives and to be afraid of losing control of their bodies or their minds) has been thoroughly established by generations of researchers—but that connection seems to be especially pronounced in people with emetophobia. A study published in

---

* According to emerging research data, emetophobes also tend to demonstrate "a heightened sensitivity to the opinions of others."

the *Journal of Clinical Psychology* observed that "emetophobics appear completely unable to negate their insatiable desire for the maintenance of control."*

Dr. W. has pointed out what he believes is the obvious multilayered symbolism of my emetophobia. Vomiting represents a loss of control and also my fear of letting my insides out, of revealing what's inside me. Most of all, he says, it represents my fear of death. Vomiting, and my unruly nervous stomach generally, are inarguable evidence of my embodiedness—and consequently of my mortality.†

Someday I'm going to vomit; someday I'm going to die.

Am I wrong to live in quivering terror of both?

---

* I once dated a woman whose aunt had for decades been a full-blown bulimic. From her teens into sometime in her thirties, my girlfriend's aunt had made herself vomit after most meals. To me, this was as fascinating as it was unfathomable. *Someone would actually choose to make herself vomit?* I had known about anorexia and bulimia since junior high, when I'd watched after-school specials about them on TV, but hadn't to my knowledge ever met anyone who voluntarily regurgitated on a regular basis. My whole life was built around trying *not* to vomit—and here was someone who vomited, all the time, by *choice?* True, this person was mentally ill, easily diagnosable according to the *DSM:* "Bulimia: Eating, in a discrete period of time, an amount of food that is definitely larger than most people would eat during a similar period of time and under similar circumstances [combined with] recurrent inappropriate compensatory behavior to prevent weight gain [such as] 1. Self-induced vomiting." But wasn't I also, according to the very same authority, ill? "Phobia: A. Marked and persistent fear that is excessive or unreasonable, cued by the presence or anticipation of a specific object or situation. B. Exposure to the phobic stimulus almost invariably provokes an immediate anxiety response, which may take the form of a situationally bound or situationally predisposed panic attack."

Even at the time, it struck me that our disorders were oddly self-canceling. If I could get my mind to embrace the idea that some people vomited by choice to make themselves feel *better*, could that maybe lead me to accept that vomiting was not so catastrophic? And if bulimics could assimilate some of my horrified aversion to vomiting, mightn't that help to decondition them away from the practice?

A modest proposal: Why not fill a group home with bulimics and emetophobes and hope that they model themselves out of their pathologies? The emetophobes, watching the bulimics make themselves vomit routinely, will learn that throwing up is not that big a deal; the bulimics, seeing the terror and disgust of the emetophobes, might be conditioned against such casual regurgitation.

And anyway, aren't we fundamentally both, bulimics and emetophobes alike, afraid of the same thing: the loss of control? It's not so much being fat that anorexics fear—it's feeling out of control, a feeling that purging helps them perversely to combat. They binge and then, not feeling in control of their own appetites, seek to exert dominion over their bodies by purging. But locked into this cycle of binge and purge, they are not really in control at all.

† As the British physician and philosopher Raymond Tallis has put it, "One sure-fire cure for . . . any whimsical or philosophical stance on one's own body . . . is vomiting. . . . Your body has you in its entire grip. . . . There is a kind of terror in vomiting: it is a shouted reminder that we are embodied in an organism that has its own agenda."

I find the noodle and the stomach are antagonistic powers. What thought has to do with digesting roast beef, I cannot say, but they are brother faculties.

—CHARLES DARWIN TO HIS SISTER CAROLINE (1838)

I try to draw solace from the knowledge that I am hardly alone in having both a mind and a belly so easily perturbed by anxiety. Observers going back to Aristotle have noted that nervous dyspepsia and intellectual accomplishment often go hand in hand. Sigmund Freud's trip to the United States in 1909, which introduced psychoanalysis to this country, was marred (as he would later frequently complain) by his nervous stomach and bouts of diarrhea. Many of the letters between William and Henry James, first-class neurotics both, consist mainly of the exchange of various remedies for their stomach trouble.

But for debilitating nervous stomach complaints, nothing compares to that which afflicted poor Charles Darwin, who spent decades of his life prostrated by his upset stomach.

In 1865, he wrote a desperate letter to a physician named John Chapman, listing the array of symptoms that had plagued him for nearly thirty years:

Age 56–57.—For 25 years extreme spasmodic daily & nightly flatulence: occasional vomiting, on two occasions prolonged during months. Vomiting preceded by shivering, hysterical crying[,] dying sensations or half-faint. & copious very palid urine. Now vomiting & every passage of flatulence preceded by ringing of ears, treading on air & vision. . . . Nervousness when E[mma Darwin, his wife] leaves me.

Even this list of symptoms is incomplete. At the urging of another doctor, Darwin had from July 1, 1849, to January 16, 1855, kept a "Diary of Health," which eventually ran to dozens of pages and listed such complaints as chronic fatigue, severe stomach pain and flatulence, frequent vomiting, dizziness ("swimming head," as Darwin described it), trembling, insomnia, rashes, eczema, boils, heart palpitations and pain, and melancholy.

Darwin was frustrated that dozens of physicians, beginning with his own father, had failed to cure him. By the time he wrote to Dr. Chapman, Darwin had spent most of the past three decades—during which time he'd struggled heroically to write *On the Origin of Species*—housebound by general invalidism. Based on his diaries and letters, it's fair to say he spent a full third of his daytime hours since the age of twenty-eight either vomiting or lying in bed.

Chapman had treated many prominent Victorian intellectuals who were "knocked up" with anxiety at one time or another; he specialized in, as he put it, those high-strung neurotics "whose minds are highly cultivated and developed, and often complicated, modified, and dominated by subtle psychical influences, whose intensity and bearing on the physical malady it is difficult to apprehend." He prescribed the application of ice to the spinal cord for almost all diseases of nervous origin.

Chapman came out to Darwin's country estate in late May 1865, and Darwin spent several hours each day over the next several months encased in ice; he composed crucial sections of *The Variation of Animals and Plants Under Domestication* with ice bags packed around his spine.

The treatment didn't work. The "incessant vomiting" continued. So while Darwin and his family enjoyed Chapman's company ("We liked Dr. Chapman so very much we were quite sorry the ice failed for his sake as well as ours," Darwin's wife wrote), by July they had abandoned the treatment and sent the doctor back to London.

Chapman was not the first doctor to fail to cure Darwin, and he would not be the last. To read Darwin's diaries and correspondence is to marvel at the more or less constant debilitation he endured after he returned from the famous voyage of the *Beagle* in 1836. The medical debate about what, exactly, was wrong with Darwin has raged for 150 years. The list proposed during his life and after his death is long: amoebic infection, appendicitis, duodenal ulcer, peptic ulcer, migraines, chronic cholecystitis, "smouldering hepatitis," malaria, catarrhal dyspepsia, arsenic poisoning, porphyria, narcolepsy, "diabetogenic hyperinsulism," gout, "suppressed gout,"* chronic brucellosis (endemic to Argentina, which the *Beagle* had visited), Chagas' disease (possibly contracted from a bug bite in Argentina), allergic reactions to the pigeons he worked with, complications from the protracted seasickness he experienced on the *Beagle,* and "refractive anomaly of the eyes." I've just read an article, "Darwin's Illness Revealed," published in a British academic journal in 2005, that attributes Darwin's ailments to lactose intolerance.[†]

But a careful reading of Darwin's life suggests that the precipitating factor in every one of his most acute attacks of illness was anxiety. According to Ralph Colp, a psychiatrist and historian who in the 1970s combed through all the available Darwin journals, letters, and medical accounts, the worst periods of illness corresponded with stress either about his work on the theory of evolution or about his family. (The anticipation of his wedding produced a "bad headache, which continues two days and two nights, so that I doubted whether it ever meant to allow me to be married.") In a 1997 article from *The Journal of the American Medical Association* called "Charles Darwin and Panic Disorder," two doctors argue that, according to his own account of his symptoms, Darwin would easily qualify for the *DSM-IV*'s diagnosis of panic disorder with agoraphobia since he demonstrated nine of the thirteen symptoms associated with it. (Only four symptoms are required to receive the diagnosis.)[‡]

The voyage of the *Beagle,* four years and nine months long, was

---

* "What the devil is this 'suppressed gout' upon which doctors fasten every ill they cannot name," Darwin's friend Joseph Hooker wrote to him when informed of this diagnosis. "If it is *suppressed* how do they know it is gout? If it is apparent, why the devil do they call it *suppressed*?"

† The authors, two Welsh biochemists, studied Darwin's journals and health diary to draw correlations between his diet and his bouts of upset stomach.

‡ In 1918, Edward J. Kempf, an early American psychoanalyst, suggested in *The Psychoanalytic Review* that the trembling and eczema that afflicted Darwin's hands were evidence of "neurotic hands"—which would, Kempf concluded, "lead one strongly to suspect an auto-erotic difficulty that had not been completely mastered." Less outlandish psychological explanations ventured in the years since include hypochondriasis, depression, repressed feelings of guilt about his hostility toward his father, "severe anxiety neurosis in an obsessional character, certainly much complicated by genius," and "bereavement syndrome" produced by the loss of his mother at a very young age. (Creationists have seized upon all this with zealous aplomb, implying in one pseudoscholarly paper I came across that the evidence of mental illness suggests Darwin was "psychotic" and that therefore his theory of evolution was the product of delusion.)

a pivotal experience, enabling Darwin to develop his scientific work.* The months in port prior to the launch of the *Beagle* were, as Darwin would write in his old age, "the most miserable which I ever spent"—and that's saying something, given the terrible physical suffering he would later endure.

"I was out of spirits at the thought of leaving all my family and friends for so long a time, and the weather seemed to me inexpressibly gloomy," he recalled. "I was also troubled with palpitations and pain about the heart, and like many a young ignorant man, especially one with a smattering of medical knowledge, was convinced I had heart disease." He also suffered from faintness and tingling in his fingers. These are all symptoms of anxiety—and in particular of the hyperventilation associated with panic disorder.

Darwin forced himself to overcome his low spirits and embark on the voyage, and though he was beset by both claustrophobia (which put him in "continual fear") and grievous seasickness, he was mostly healthy on the trip, gathering the evidence on which he would make his name and build his life's work. But after the *Beagle* docked in Falmouth, England, on October 2, 1836, Darwin would never again set foot outside England. After nearly five years of traveling, Darwin found his geographical ambit increasingly circumscribed. "I dread going anywhere, on account of my stomach so easily failing under any excitement," he told his cousin.

It's remarkable that *On the Origin of Species* ever got written. Soon after his marriage, when Darwin was beginning in earnest his work on evolution, he suffered the first of his many episodes of "periodic vomiting," stretches where he would vomit multiple times daily and be bedridden for weeks—or, in several cases, years—on end. Excitement or socializing of any kind could throw him into great physical upheaval. Parties or meetings would leave him "knocked up" with anxiety, bringing on "violent shivering and vomiting attacks." ("I have therefore been compelled for many years to give up all dinner-parties," he wrote.) He

---

* Darwin's discovery of variant species of finches in the Galápagos Islands would eventually prompt his realization that species were not fixed for all time but rather transmuted—or, as he would later say, evolved—over time.

installed a mirror outside his study window so he could see guests coming up the drive before they saw him, allowing him time to brace himself or to hide.

In addition to Dr. Chapman's ice treatment, Darwin tried the "water cure" of the famous Dr. James Gully (who also treated Alfred Tennyson, Thomas Carlyle, and Charles Dickens around this time), exercise, a sugar-free diet, brandy and "Indian ale," chemical concoctions (scores of them), metal plates strapped to his torso meant to galvanize his insides and "electric chains" (made of brass and zinc wires) meant to electrify him, and drenching his skin with vinegar. Whether the result of the placebo effect, distraction, or actual efficacy, some of these sort of worked some of the time. But always the illness returned. A day trip to London or any mild disturbance in his well-ordered routine would bring on "a very bad form of vomiting" that would send him to bed for days or weeks. Any work, especially on *Origin*—"my abominable volume," as Darwin called it—could lay him low for months. "I have been bad, having two days of bad vomiting owing to the accursed Proofs," he wrote to a friend in early 1859 while going over printer's corrections. He installed a special lavatory in his study where he could vomit behind a curtain. He finished with the proofs amid fits of vomiting on October 1, 1859, ending a fifteen-month period during which he had rarely been able to work free of stomach discomfort for more than twenty minutes at a time.

When *On the Origin of Species,* more than twenty years in gestation, was finally published in November 1859, Darwin was laid up in bed at a hydropathy spa in Yorkshire, his stomach in as much tumult as ever, his skin aflame. "I have been very bad lately," he wrote. "Had an awful 'crisis'—one leg swelled up like elephantiasis—eyes almost closed up—covered with a rash and fiery Boils . . . it was like living in Hell."*

Darwin continued in poor health even after the book's publication. "I shall go to my grave, I suppose, grumbling and growling with daily,

---

* One of Darwin's biographers, the British psychoanalyst John Bowlby, noted in the 1980s that the sorts of eruptions of boils and rashes that Darwin endured were thought by dermatologists to be associated with people who "strive to suppress their feelings and who are given to low self-esteem and overwork." Bowlby, like other biographers, also observed that any stress or "increase in arousal, however trivial," would produce physical symptoms in Darwin.

almost hourly, discomfort," he wrote in 1860. Those who argue that Darwin suffered from some germ-based or structural disease point to the severity and duration of his symptoms. ("I must tell you how ill Charles has been," his wife wrote to a family friend in May 1864. "He has had almost daily vomiting for 6 months.") But in rebuttal there is this: When Darwin would stop working and go riding or walking in the Scottish Highlands or North Wales, his health would be restored.

Charles is too much given to anxiety, as you know.
—EMMA DARWIN TO A FRIEND (1851)

If I seem unduly preoccupied with Darwin's stomach, perhaps you can understand why. It seems both apt and ironic that the man responsible for launching the modern study of fear—and for identifying it as an emotion with concrete physiological, and especially gastrointestinal, effects—was himself so miserably afflicted by a nervous stomach.

Then there is the matter of his excessive dependence on his wife, Emma. "Without you, when I feel sick I feel most desolate," he wrote to her at one point. "O Mammy I do long to be with you & under your protection and then I feel safe," he wrote at another.

Mammy? No wonder some Freudians would later argue that Darwin had dependency issues, as well as Oedipal ones. I suppose this is the place to say that—based on my burdensome overreliance on my wife and, before that, on my parents—Dr. W. has diagnosed me with dependent personality disorder, which is, according to the *DSM-V*, characterized by excessive psychological dependence on other people (most often a loved one or caretaker) and the belief that one is inadequate and helpless to cope on one's own.

Finally, of course, there is the matter of Darwin's decades of constant vomiting. For an emetophobe like me, this holds a morbid fascination. His anxiety produced vomiting, yet his vomiting did not (or so it seems) produce additional anxiety. Moreover, Darwin lived, despite his years of vomiting, to the old-for-the-time age of seventy-three. Shouldn't Darwin's accomplishments in defiance of such a debilitating gastrointestinal affliction provide reassurance that if, say, I were to throw up just once, or even five times, or even five times in a day—or even, like Darwin, five times a day for years on end—I might not only survive but perhaps even remain productive?

If you're not an emetophobe, this question surely seems impossibly strange—patent evidence of the irrational obsession at the core of my mental illness. And you're right. But if you *are* an emetophobe—well, then, you know exactly what I'm talking about.

CHAPTER 4

Performance Anxiety

Many lamentable effects this fear causeth in men, as to be red, pale, tremble, sweat; it makes sudden cold and heat to come over all the body, palpitation of the heart, syncope, etc. It amazeth many men that are to speak or show themselves in public assemblies, or before some great personages; as Tully confessed of himself, that he trembled still at the beginning of his speech; and Demosthenes, that great orator of Greece, before Philippus.
— ROBERT BURTON, *The Anatomy of Melancholy* (1621)

All public speaking of merit is characterized by nervousness.
— CICERO (FIRST CENTURY A.D.)

I've finally settled on a pretalk regimen that enables me to avoid the weeks of anticipatory misery that the approach of a public speaking engagement would otherwise produce.

Let's say I'm speaking to you at some sort of public event. Here's what I've likely done to prepare. Four hours or so ago, I took my first half milligram of Xanax. (I've learned that if I wait too long to take it, my sympathetic nervous system goes so far into overdrive that medication is not enough to yank it back.) Then, about an hour ago, I took my second half milligram of Xanax and perhaps twenty milligrams of Inderal. (I need the whole milligram of Xanax plus the Inderal, which is a blood pressure medication, or beta-blocker, that dampens the response of the sympathetic nervous system, to keep my physiological responses to the anxious stimulus of standing in front of you—the sweating, trembling, nausea, burping, stomach cramps, and constriction in my throat and chest—from overwhelming me.) I likely washed those pills down with a shot of scotch or, more likely, of vodka. Even two Xanax and an Inderal are not enough to calm my racing thoughts and to keep my chest and throat from constricting to the point where I cannot speak; I need the alcohol to slow things down and to dampen the residual physiological eruptions that the drugs are inadequate to contain. In fact, I probably drank my second shot—yes, even though I might be speaking to you at, say, nine in the morning—between fifteen and thirty minutes ago, assuming the pretalk proceedings allowed me a moment to sneak away for a quaff. And depending on how intimidating an audience I anticipated you would be, I might have made that second shot a double or a triple. If the usual pattern has held, as I stand up here talking to you now, I've got some Xanax in one pocket (in case I felt the need to pop another one before being introduced) and a minibar-size bottle or two of vodka in the other. I have been known to take a discreet last-second swig while walking onstage—because even as I'm still experiencing the anxiety that makes me want to drink more, my inhibition has been lowered, and my judgment impaired, by the liquor and benzodiazepines I've already consumed. If I've managed to hit the sweet spot—that perfect combination of timing and dosage where the cognitive and psychomotor sedating effect of the drugs and alcohol balances out the physiological hyperarousal of the anxiety—then I'm probably doing okay up here: nervous but not miserable; a little fuzzy but still able to convey clarity; the anxiogenic effects of this situation (me, speaking in front of people) counteracted by the anxiolytic effects of what I've consumed.* But if I've overshot on the medication—too much Xanax or liquor—I may seem loopy or slurring or otherwise impaired. And if I didn't self-medicate enough? Well, then, either I'm miserable and probably sweating profusely, with my voice quavering weakly and my attention folding in upon itself, or, more likely, I ran offstage before I got this far.

I know. My method of dealing with my public speaking anxiety is not healthy. It's evidence of alcoholism; it's dangerous. But it works.

---

* Together, the alcohol and the benzodiazepines slow the firing of neurons in my amygdala, increase transmission of dopamine and gamma-aminobutyric acid, boost production of beta-endorphins in my hypothalamus, and decrease transmission of acetylcholine.

Only when I am sedated to near stupefaction by a combination of benzodiazepines and alcohol do I feel (relatively) confident in my ability to speak in public effectively and without misery. As long as I know that I'll have access to my Xanax and liquor, I'll suffer only moderate anxiety for days before a speech, rather than miserable, sleepless dread for months.

Self-medicating, sometimes dangerously so, is a time-honored way of warding off performance anxiety. Starting when he was thirty, William Gladstone, the long-serving British prime minister, would drink laudanum—opium dissolved in alcohol—with his coffee before speeches in Parliament. (Once, he accidentally overdosed and had to go to a sanatorium to recover.) William Wilberforce, the famous eighteenth-century British antislavery politician, took opium as a "calmer of nerves" before all his speeches in Parliament. "To that," Wilberforce said of his prespeech opium regimen, "I owe my success as a public speaker."* Laurence Olivier, convinced that he was about to be driven to what he was sure would be reported as a "mystifying and scandalously sudden retirement" by his stage fright, finally confided his distress to the actress Dame Sybil Thorndike and her husband.

"Take drugs, darling," Thorndike told him. "We do."†

I try to draw solace from what I have learned about Gladstone, Olivier, and other successful and exalted people who have been debilitated by their stage fright.

Demosthenes, a Greek statesman renowned for his oratorical skills, was, early in his career, jeered for his anxious, stammering performances. Cicero, the great Roman statesman and philosopher, once froze while speaking during an important trial in the Forum and ran offstage. "I turn pale at the outset of a speech and quake in every limb and in all my soul," he wrote. Moses, according to various interpretations of Exodus

---

* Of course, to opium Wilberforce likely owed many other things, too, among them his horrible depression and a host of physical problems. After initially being prescribed the drug for bowel troubles, he became addicted, taking it every day for forty-five years straight.

† Actually, Olivier seems not to have resorted to drugs. "There was no other treatment than the well-worn practice of wearing *it*—the terror—out," he wrote in his autobiography, "and it was in that determined spirit that I got on with the job." But he did quit the stage for five years to escape his anxiety.

4:10, had a fear of public speaking or was a stutterer; he overcame this to become the voice of his people.

Every era of history seems to offer up examples of prominent, accomplished figures who managed—or didn't manage—to overcome crippling public speaking anxiety. On the morning before William Cowper, the eighteenth-century British poet, was to appear before the House of Lords to discuss his qualifications for a government position, he tried to hang himself, preferring to die rather than endure a public appearance. (The suicide attempt failed, and the interview was postponed.) "They ... to whom a public examination of themselves on any occasion is mortal poison may have some idea of the horrors of my situation," Cowper wrote. "Others can have none."

In 1889, a young Indian lawyer froze during his first case before a judge and ran from the courtroom in humiliation. "My head was reeling and I felt as though the whole court was doing likewise," the lawyer would write later, after he had become known as Mahatma Gandhi. "I could think of no question to ask." Another time, when Gandhi stood up to read remarks he had prepared for a small gathering of a local vegetarian society, he found he could not speak. "My vision became blurred and I trembled, though the speech hardly covered a sheet of foolscap," he recounted. What Gandhi called "the awful strain of public speaking" prevented him for years from speaking up even at friendly dinner parties and nearly deterred him from developing into the spiritual leader he ultimately became. Thomas Jefferson, too, had his law career disrupted by a fear of public speaking. One of his biographers notes that if he tried to declaim loudly, his voice would "sink in his throat." He never spoke during the deliberations of the Second Continental Congress and, remarkably, he gave only two public speeches—his inaugural addresses—during his years as President. After reviewing Jefferson's biographies, psychiatrists at Duke University, writing in the *Journal of Nervous and Mental Disease*, diagnosed him posthumously with social phobia.

The novelist Henry James dropped out of law school after giving what he felt was an embarrassing performance in a moot court competition in which he "quavered and collapsed into silence"; thereafter, he avoided making formal public presentations, despite being known for his witty dinner party repartee. Vladimir Horowitz, perhaps the most talented concert pianist of the twentieth century, developed stage fright so acute that for fifteen years he refused to perform in public. When he finally returned to the stage, he did so only on the condition that he could clearly see his personal physician sitting in the front row of the audience at all times.

Barbra Streisand developed overwhelming performance anxiety at the height of her career; for twenty-seven years she refused to perform for money, appearing live only at charity events, where she believed the pressure on her was less intense. Carly Simon abandoned the stage for seven years after collapsing from nerves before a concert in front of ten thousand people in Pittsburgh in 1981. When she resumed performing, she would sometimes drive needles into her skin or ask her band to spank her before going onstage to distract her from her anxiety. The singer Donny Osmond quit performing for a number of years because of panic attacks. (He is now a spokesman for the Anxiety and Depression Association of America.) The comedian Jay Mohr tells a story about frantically trying to pop a Klonopin on live television to stave off what he feared would be a career-ending panic attack while performing a skit on *Saturday Night Live*. (What saved Mohr on that occasion was not the Klonopin but the distracting hilarity of his sketch mate Chris Farley.) A few years ago, Hugh Grant announced his semiretirement from acting because of the panic attacks he'd get when the cameras started rolling. He survived one film only by filling himself "full of lorazepam," the short-acting benzodiazepine with the trade name Ativan. "I had all these panic attacks," he said. "They're awful. I freeze like a rabbit. Can't speak, can't think, sweating like a bull. When I got home from doing that job, I said to myself, 'No more acting. End of films.'" Ricky Williams, who won the Heisman Trophy in 1998, retired from the National Football League for several years because of his anxiety; social interactions made him so nervous that he would give interviews only while wearing his football helmet.* Elfriede Jelinek, the Austrian novelist who won the Nobel Prize in Literature in 2004, refused to

---

* For a time, Williams took Paxil for his anxiety, and he briefly became a pitchman for SmithKline Beechman—though he later told *The Miami Herald* that marijuana "worked 10 times better for me than Paxil."

accept her award in person because her acute social phobia made it impossible to bear being looked at in public.

Cicero, Demosthenes, Gladstone. Olivier, Streisand, Wilberforce. Physicians and scientists and statesmen. Oscar winners and Heisman winners and Nobel laureates. Gandhi and Jefferson and Moses. Shouldn't I draw consolation from the knowledge that so many people so much greater than I am have been, at times, undone by their stage fright? And shouldn't their ability to persevere and, in some cases, to overcome their anxiety give me hope and inspiration?

> *Why should the thought that others are thinking about us affect our capillary circulation?*
> —CHARLES DARWIN, *The Expression of the Emotions in Man and Animals* (1872)

> *The symptoms of performance anxiety can sometimes take the form of what seems to be a terrible joke custom-designed to humiliate.*
> —JOHN MARSHALL, *Social Phobia* (1994)

The *DSM* officially divides social anxiety disorder into two subtypes: specific and general. Those patients diagnosed with specific social anxiety disorder have anxiety attached to very particular circumstances, almost always relating to some form of public performance. By far the most common specific social phobia is the fear of public speaking, but others include the fear of eating in public, the fear of writing in public, and the fear of urinating in a public restroom. A startlingly large number of people arrange their lives around not eating in front of people, or are filled with dread at the prospect of having to sign a check in front of other people, or suffer what's known as paruresis when standing at a urinal.

Patients suffering from the general subtype of social anxiety disorder feel distress in any social context. Routine events such as cocktail parties, business meetings, job interviews, and dinner dates can be occasion for significant emotional anguish and physical symptoms. For the more severely afflicted, life can be an unremitting misery. The most mundane social interaction—talking to a store clerk or engaging in watercooler chitchat—induces a kind of terror. Many social phobics endure lives of terrible loneliness and professional impairment. Studies find strong links between social phobia and both depression and suicide. Social phobics are also, unsurprisingly, highly prone to alcoholism and drug abuse.*

The terrible irony of social phobia is that one of the things people suffering from it fear most is having their anxiety exposed—which is precisely what the symptoms of this anxiety serve to do. Social phobics worry that their interpersonal awkwardness or the physical manifestations of anxiety—their blushing and shaking and stammering and sweating—will somehow reveal them to be weak or incompetent. So they get nervous, and then they stammer or blush, which makes them more nervous, which makes them stammer and blush more, which propels them into a vicious cycle of increasing anxiety and deteriorating performance.

Blushing is infernal in this regard. The first case study of erythrophobia (the fear of blushing in public) was published in 1846 by a German physician who described a twenty-one-year-old medical student driven to suicide by shame over his uncontrolled blushing. A few years later, Darwin would dedicate a full chapter of *The Expression of the Emotions in Man and Animals* to his theory of blushing, observing how at the moment of most wanting to hide one's anxiety, blushing betrays it. "It is not a simple act of reflecting on our own appearance but the thinking of others thinking of us which excites a blush," Darwin wrote. "It is notorious that nothing makes a shy person blush so much as any remark, however slight, on his personal appearance."

Darwin was right: I've had colleagues prone to nervous blushing, and nothing makes them glow redder than to have their blushing publicly remarked upon. Before her wedding, one such colleague tried multiple combinations of drug treatments, and even contemplated surgery, in hopes of sparing herself what she believed would be intolerable humiliation. (Every year thousands of nervous blushers undergo an endoscopic transthoracic sympathectomy, which involves destroying the ganglion of a sympathetic nerve located near the rib cage.)

---

* Early in his career, Sigmund Freud took cocaine to medicate his social anxiety before salons at the home of one of his mentors.

I, who am fortunate not to count blushing among one of my regular nervous symptoms, observe her and think how silly she is to believe that blushing at her wedding would be humiliating. And then I think how ashamed I was of sweating and trembling at my own wedding and wonder if I am not any less silly than she.

Shame, perhaps, is the operative emotion here—the engine that underlies both the anxiety and the blushing. In 1839, Thomas Burgess, a British physician, argued in *The Physiology or Mechanism of Blushing* that God had designed blushing so that "the soul might have sovereign power of displaying in the cheeks the various internal emotions of the moral feelings." Blushing, he wrote, can "serve as a check on ourselves, and as a sign to others that [we're] violating rules which ought to be held sacred." For Burgess as for Darwin, blushing is physiological evidence of both our self-consciousness and our sociability—a manifestation of not only our awareness of ourselves but our sensitivity to how others perceive us.

Later work by Darwin, as well as by modern evolutionary biologists, posits that blushing is not only a signal from our bodies to ourselves that we're committing some kind of shameful social transgression (you can feel yourself blush by the warming of your skin) but also a signal to others that we are feeling modest and self-conscious. It's a way of showing social deference to higher-ranking members of the species—and it is, as Burgess would have it, a check on our antisocial impulses, keeping us from deviating from prevailing social norms. Social anxiety and the blushing it produces can be evolutionarily adaptive—the behavior it promotes can preserve social comity and can keep us from being ostracized from the tribe.

Though social anxiety disorder as an official diagnosis is relatively new in the history of psychiatry—it was born in 1980, when the disease was one of the new anxiety disorders carved out of the old Freudian neuroses by the third edition of the *DSM*—the syndrome it describes is age-old, and the symptoms are consistent from age to age.* Writing in 1901, Paul Hartenberg, a French novelist and psychiatrist, described a

---

* The term "social phobia" first appeared in 1903, when Pierre Janet, an influential French psychiatrist who was a contemporary and rival of Freud, published a taxonomy of mental illnesses that classified erythrophobia among what he called *phobies sociales* or *phobies de la société*.

syndrome whose constellation of physical and emotional symptoms corresponds remarkably to the *DSM-V* definition of social anxiety disorder. The social phobic (*timide*) fears other people, lacks self-confidence, and eschews social interactions, Hartenberg wrote in *Les timides et la timidité*. In anticipation of social situations, Hartenberg's social phobic experiences physical symptoms such as a racing heart, chills, hyperventilation, sweating, nausea, vomiting, diarrhea, trembling, difficulty speaking, choking, and shortness of breath, plus a dulling of the senses and "mental confusion." The social phobic also always feels ashamed. Hartenberg even anticipates the modern distinction between people who feel anxious in all social situations and those who experience anxiety only before public performances—a particularized emotional experience he called *trac*, which he described as afflicting many academics, musicians, and actors before a lecture or performance. (This experience, Hartenberg writes, is like vertigo or seasickness—it descends suddenly, often without warning.)

Yet despite what seems to be the consistency in descriptions of social anxiety across the millennia, the diagnosis of social anxiety disorder remains controversial in some quarters. Even after the syndrome was formally inscribed in the *DSM* in 1980, diagnoses of social phobia remained rare for a number of years. Western psychotherapists tended to see it as a predominantly "Asian disorder"—a condition that flourished in the "shame-based cultures" (as anthropologists describe them) of Japan and South Korea, where correct social behavior is highly valued. (In Japanese psychiatry, a condition called *Taijin-Kyofu-Sho*, roughly comparable to what we call social anxiety disorder, has long been one of the most frequent diagnoses.) A cross-cultural comparison conducted in 1994 suggested that the relative prevalence of social phobia symptoms in Japan could be related to "the socially promoted show of shame among Japanese people." Japanese society itself, the lead researcher of the survey argued, could be considered "pseudo-sociophobic" because feelings and behaviors that in the West would be considered psychiatric symptoms—excessive shame, avoidance of eye contact, elaborate displays of deference—are cultural norms in Japan.*

---

* If nothing else, this demonstrates the complex ways in which culture and medicine interact: what's normal, even valorized, in one culture is considered pathological in another.

In the United States, social anxiety disorder found an early champion in Michael Liebowitz, a psychiatrist at Columbia University who had served on the *DSM* subcommittee that brought the disease into official existence. In 1985, Liebowitz published an article in the *Archives of General Psychiatry* called "Social Anxiety—the Neglected Disorder," in which he argued that the disease was woefully underdiagnosed and undertreated.* After the article appeared, research on social phobia began to accrete slowly. As recently as 1994, the term "social anxiety disorder" had appeared only fifty times in the popular press; five years later, it had appeared hundreds of thousands of times. What accounts for the disorder's colonization of the popular imagination? Largely this single event: the Food and Drug Administration's approval of Paxil for the treatment of social anxiety disorder in 1999.† SmithKline Beecham quickly launched a multimillion-dollar advertising campaign aimed at both psychiatrists and the general public.

"Imagine you were allergic to people," went the text of one widely distributed Paxil ad. "You blush, sweat, shake—even find it hard to breathe. That's what social anxiety disorder feels like." Propelled by the sudden cultural currency of the disease—that same ad claimed that "over ten million Americans" were suffering from social anxiety disorder—prescriptions of Paxil exploded. The drug passed Prozac and Zoloft to become the nation's best-selling SSRI antidepressant medication.

Before 1980, no one had ever been diagnosed with social anxiety disorder; twenty years later, studies were estimating that some ten million to twenty million Americans qualified for the diagnosis. Today, the official statistics from the National Institute of Mental Health say that more than 10 percent of Americans will suffer from social anxiety disorder at some point in their lifetimes—and that some 30 percent of these people will suffer acute forms of it. (Studies in reputable medical journals present similar statistics.)

No wonder there's controversy: from zero patients to tens of millions of them in the course of less than twenty years. It's easy to lay out the cynical plot: A squishy new psychiatric diagnosis is invented;

* Liebowitz also developed what became the standard psychological rating scale for measuring a patient's degree of social anxiety.

† Paxil had earlier been approved for the treatment of depression, obsessive-compulsive disorder, and generalized anxiety disorder.

initially very few patients are deemed to be ill with it. Then a drug is approved to treat it. Suddenly diagnoses explode. The pharmaceutical industry reaps billions of dollars in profit.

Moreover, these critics say, there's another name for the syndrome ostensibly afflicting those with social anxiety disorder. It's called shyness, a common temperamental disposition that should hardly be considered a mental illness. In 2007, Christopher Lane, a professor of English at Northwestern University, published a book-length version of this argument, *Shyness: How Normal Behavior Became a Sickness,* claiming that psychiatrists, in cahoots with the pharmaceutical industry, had succeeded in pathologizing an ordinary character trait.*

On the one hand, the sudden explosion in diagnoses of social anxiety disorder surely does speak to the power of the pharmaceutical industry's marketing efforts to manufacture demand for a product. Besides, some quotient of nervousness about social interactions is normal. How many of us *don't* feel some discomfort at the prospect of having to make small talk with strangers at a party? Who *doesn't* feel some measure of anxiety at having to perform in public or to be judged by an audience? Such anxiety is healthy, even adaptive. To define such discomfort as something that needs to be treated with pills is to medicalize what is merely human. All of which lends weight to the idea of social anxiety disorder as nothing more than a profit-seeking concoction of the pharmaceutical industry.

On the other hand, I can tell you, both from extensive research and from firsthand experience, that as convincing as the case made by Lane and his fellow antipharma critics can be, the distress felt by some social phobics is real and intense. Are there some "normally" shy people, not mentally ill or in need of psychiatric attention, who get swept up in the broad diagnostic category of social anxiety disorder, which has been swollen by the profit-seeking imperatives of the drug companies? Surely. But are there also socially anxious people who can legitimately benefit from medication and other forms of psychiatric treatment—

---

* Lane's book is representative of a substantial and ever-growing literature that accuses the pharmaceutical-industrial complex of creating new disease categories for profit. I will have more to say about this in part 3.

who in some cases are saved by medication from alcoholism, despair, and suicide? I think there are.

A few years ago, the magazine I work for published an essay about the challenges of being an introvert. Not long after that, this letter arrived at my office:

> I just read your article on introversion. A year ago my 26-year-old son bemoaned the fact he was an introvert. I assured him he was fine, we are all quiet introverts in our family. Three months ago he left us a note, bought a shotgun, and killed himself. In his note he said he wasn't wired right. . . . He felt anxious and awkward around people and he couldn't go on. . . . He was smart, gentle and very educated. He had just started an internship dealing with the public and I think it pushed him over the edge. I wish he had said something before he bought the gun. It seems he thought it was his only option. This was a guy who got nervous before getting his blood drawn. You can't imagine how horrible it has been.

One study has found that up to 23 percent of patients diagnosed with social anxiety disorder attempt suicide at some point. Who wants to argue that they are just shy or that a drug that might have mitigated their suffering was purely a play for profit?

No passion so effectively robs the mind of acting and reasoning as fear.
—EDMUND BURKE, *A Philosophical Inquiry into the Origin of Our Ideas of the Sublime and Beautiful* (1756)

As best I can recall, my performance anxiety blossomed when I was eleven. Before then, I had made presentations in class and in front of school assemblies and had experienced only nervous excitement. So I was blindsided when, standing onstage in the starring role in my sixth-grade class's holiday performance of *Saint George and the Dragon*, I suddenly found I could not speak.

It was an evening in mid-December, and the auditorium was filled with a few dozen parents, siblings, and teachers. I remember standing backstage beforehand, awaiting my cue to enter stage left, and feeling only mildly nervous. Though it's hard for me to imagine now, I think I was even enjoying myself, looking forward to the attention I would receive as star of the play. But when I walked to center stage and looked out into the auditorium to see all those eyes upon me, my chest constricted.* After a few seconds, I found myself in the grip of both physical and emotional panic, and I could barely speak. I eked out a few quavering lines with a diminishing voice—and then arrived at a point where I could make no more words emerge. I stopped, midsentence, feeling that I was about to vomit. A few agonizing seconds of silence ticked by until my friend Peter, who was playing my valet, bailed me out by saying his next line.† This surely seemed to the audience like a non sequitur, but it moved the scene to its conclusion and mercifully got me off the stage. By my next scene, the physical symptoms of my anxiety had abated a little; at the end of the play I slew the dragon as directed. Afterward, people said they had liked my fight scene, and (out of politeness, I was sure) nobody remarked on my first scene, where it must have looked, at best, like I had forgotten my line or, at worst, like I had frozen in terror.

A trapdoor opened beneath me that night. After that, public performances were never the same. At the time, I was singing in a professional boys' choir that appeared in churches and auditoriums all over New England. Concerts were torture. I was not one of the better singers, so I never had solos; I was just one of twenty-four prepubescent boys standing anonymously onstage. But every moment was misery. I'd hold my score in front of my face so the audience couldn't see me and mouth the words silently. I'd have that horrible choking feeling, and

---

* Research has shown that being the object of another's direct gaze is highly emotionally and physiologically arousing. One of the surest ways to cause the neurons in the amygdala of a human test subject to fire is simply to have someone stare at the subject. Many studies have demonstrated that the amygdalae of those diagnosed with social anxiety disorder tend to be consistently more reactive to the human gaze than those of healthy control subjects.

† Peter, I can only assume, felt no such anxiety. He went on to become a member of President Barack Obama's first-term cabinet.

my stomach would hurt, and I would fear that if I made any sound, I'd vomit.*

I quit the choir, but I couldn't completely avoid public performances—especially as my anxieties worsened and my definition of public got broader. The next year, I was making a presentation in Mr. Hunt's seventh-grade science class. True to my phobic preoccupations, I had chosen to do a report on the biology of food poisoning. Standing at the front of the class, I became overwhelmed by dizziness and nausea. I made it only a few halting sentences into my presentation before pausing and then squeaking plaintively, "I don't feel well." Mr. Hunt told me to go sit down. "Maybe he's got food poisoning!" a classmate joked. Everyone laughed while I burned with humiliation.

A couple of years later, I won a junior tennis tournament at a local club. Afterward, there was a luncheon banquet, where trophies were to be given out. All that was required of me was to walk onto the dais when my name was called, shake the hand of the tournament director, smile for the camera, and walk off the dais again. I wouldn't even have to speak.

But as the tournament organizers proceeded down through the different age groups, I started to tremble and sweat. The prospect of having all those eyes upon me was terrifying—I was sure I would humiliate myself in some indeterminate way. Several minutes before my name was announced, I slipped out the back door and ran down to a basement restroom to hide, emerging only several hours later, when I was sure the luncheon had ended. (This sort of extreme avoidant behavior is common among social phobics. I once came across a report in the clinical literature of a woman who, feigning illness, skipped a company banquet where she was to be given an award for outstanding performance, because the prospect of being the center of attention made her so nervous. After she missed the dinner, a small group of colleagues planned a more intimate reception in her honor. She quit her job rather than attend.)

---

* It didn't help that the choir director was a strange and tyrannical man who lived with his parents and had a horrific stutter. He'd start screaming at you during choir practice and would get stuck on a word, his face contorted into a paroxysm of anger and frustration, and you would have to wait many seconds for whatever expletive he was trying to direct at you to finally burst out.

Once, in college, I applied for a fellowship that required me to sit for an interview with a committee of half a dozen faculty members, most of whom I was already friendly with. We bantered easily before the official proceedings began. But when the interview started and they asked me the first formal question, my chest constricted and I could make no sound emerge from my trachea. I sat there, mouth silently gaping open and then shutting like some kind of fish or suckling mammal. When finally I was able to get my voice to work, I excused myself and scurried out, feeling the committee's befuddled eyes on my back, and that was that.

The problem, alas, has persisted into adulthood. There have been humiliating minor catastrophes (walking offstage midsentence during public presentations) and scores of near misses (television shows where I've felt the chest constriction begin; lectures and interviews where the room started to swim, nausea rose in my gullet, and my voice diminished to a sickly warble). Somehow, in many of those near-miss instances, I've managed to fight through and continue. But in all these situations, even when they're apparently going well, I feel I am living on the razor's edge between success and failure, adulation and humiliation—between justifying my existence and revealing my unworthiness to be alive.

People are not disturbed by things but by the view they take of them.
—EPICTETUS, "ON ANXIETY" (FIRST CENTURY A.D.)

Why does my body betray me in these situations?

Performance anxiety is not some ethereal feeling but rather a vivid mental state with concrete physical aspects that are measurable in a laboratory: accelerated heart rate, heart palpitations, increased levels of epinephrine and norepinephrine in the bloodstream, decreased gastric motility, and elevated blood pressure. Almost everyone experiences a measurable autonomic nervous response while performing in public: most people register a two- to threefold increase in the level of norepinephrine in their bloodstream at the beginning of a lecture, a rush of adrenaline that can improve performance—but in social phobics this autonomic response tends to be more acute, and it translates into debilitating physical symptoms and emotional distress. Studies at the University of Wisconsin have found that in the run-up to a speech, socially anxious individuals show high activation of their right cerebral hemispheres, which seems to interfere with both their logical processing and their verbal abilities—the sort of brain freeze that young Gandhi experienced in the courtroom. The experience of struggling to think or speak clearly in moments of social stress has clear biological substrates.

Cognitive-behavioral therapists argue that social anxiety disorder is a problem of disordered logic, or faulty thinking. If we can correct our false beliefs and maladaptive attitudes—our "cognitions" or "schema," as they say—we can cure the anxiety. Epictetus, a Greek slave and Stoic philosopher living in Rome in the first century A.D., was the prototype of the cognitive-behavioral therapist. His essay "On Anxiety," in addition to being one of the earliest contributions to the literature of self-help, seems to be the first attempt to connect performance anxiety to what we would today call issues of self-esteem.

"When I see anyone anxious, I say, 'what does this man want?'" Epictetus writes. "Unless he wanted something or other not in his own power, how could he still be anxious? A musician, for instance, feels no anxiety while he is singing by himself; but when he appears upon the stage he does, even if his voice be ever so good, or he plays ever so well. For what he wishes is not only to sing well but likewise to gain applause. But this is not in his own power. In short, where his skill lies, there is his courage." In other words, you can't ultimately control whether the audience applauds or not, so what use is there in worrying about it? For Epictetus, anxiety was a disorder of desire and emotion to be overcome by logic. If you can train your mind to perform the same way whether you're alone or being observed, you'll not get derailed by stage fright.

Two influential twentieth-century psychotherapists, Albert Ellis and Aaron Beck, the founders of rational emotive behavioral therapy (REBT) and cognitive-behavioral therapy (CBT) respectively, each argued that the treatment of social anxiety boils down to overcoming fear of disapproval. To overcome social anxiety, they say, you need to inure yourself to needless shame.

To this end, when Dr. M., a practitioner in the CBT mold, was treating me at Boston University's Center for Anxiety and Related Disorders, she aimed, as a therapeutic exercise, to intentionally embarrass me. She would escort me to the university bookstore next door to the Center and lurk discreetly nearby while I asked purposely dumb questions of the clerks or told them I needed a bathroom because I was going to throw up. I found this excruciatingly awkward and embarrassing (which was the whole point), and it didn't really help. But this is standard exposure therapy for social phobics; a growing body of controlled studies support its effectiveness. The idea, in part, is to demonstrate to the patient that revealing imperfection, or doing something stupid, need not mean the end of the world or the unraveling of the self.*

Therapists of a more psychoanalytic bent tend to focus on the social phobic's firmly held view of himself as a deeply flawed or disgusting human being devoid of intrinsic value. Kathryn Zerbe, a psychiatrist in Portland, Oregon, has written that the social phobic's biggest fear is that other people will perceive his true—and inadequate—self. For the social phobic, any kind of performance—musical, sporting, public speaking—can be terrifying because failure will reveal the weakness and inadequacy within. This in turn means constantly projecting an image that feels false—an image of confidence, competence, even perfection. Dr. W. calls this impression management, and he observes that while it can be a *symptom* of social anxiety, it's an even bigger *cause*. Once you've invested in the perpetuation of a public image that feels untrue to your core self, you feel always in danger of being exposed as a fraud: one mistake, one revelation of anxiety or weakness, and the façade of competence and accomplishment is exposed for what it is—an artificial persona designed to hide the vulnerable self that lies within. Thus the stakes for any given performance become excruciatingly high: success means preserving the perception of value and esteem; failure means exposure of the shameful self one is trying so hard to hide. Impression management is exhausting and stressful—you live in constant fear that, as Dr. W. puts it, the house of cards that is your projected self will come crashing down around you.

---

* On a number of occasions, I saw other therapists from the center putting their patients through similar exposures at the same store, forcing them to ask strange questions or to make obvious and embarrassing mistakes. The store employees must have wondered why they had so many weird interactions with apparently deranged customers every day.

A stammering man is never a worthless one. Physiology can tell you why. It is an excess of sensibility to the presence of his fellow creature, that makes him stammer.

—THOMAS CARLYLE, FROM A LETTER TO
RALPH WALDO EMERSON (NOVEMBER 17, 1843)

As early as 1901, Paul Hartenberg anticipated one of the key findings of modern research on social phobics. While social phobics are unusually attentive to other people's feelings, he wrote in *Les timides et la timidité*, scrutinizing the verbal intonations, facial expressions, and body language of their interlocutors for signs of how people are reacting to them, they are also unduly confident about the conclusions they draw based on those observations—and specifically about the *negative* conclusions they draw. That is, social phobics are better at picking up on subtle social cues than other people are—but they tend to overinterpret anything that could be construed as a negative reaction. Since they are predisposed to believe that people won't like them or will react badly to them (they tend to have obsessive thoughts like *I'm boring* or *I'm going to make a fool of myself by saying something stupid*), they're always seeking confirmation of this belief by interpreting, say, a suppressed yawn or a slight twitch of the mouth as disapproval. "Highly anxious people read facial expressions faster than less anxious people," says R. Chris Fraley, a professor of psychology at the University of Illinois, Urbana-Champaign, "but they are also more likely to misread them." Alexander Bystritsky, the director of the Anxiety Disorders Program at UCLA, says that while anxious people do have "a sensitive emotional barometer" that allows them to detect subtle changes in emotion, "this barometer can cause them to read too much into an expression."

Social phobics are, in at least this one respect, gifted—faster and better at picking up behavioral cues from other people, with social antennae so sensitive that they receive transmissions that "normal" people can't. Put the other way around, the perception of healthy people may be adaptively blunted; they may not pick up on the negative cues—that yawn of boredom or twitch of disdain—that are in fact present.

Arne Öhman, a Swedish neuroscientist at Uppsala University who has written extensively about the evolutionary biology of phobic behavior, believes that oversensitive emotional barometers are genetically hardwired into social phobics, causing them to be acutely aware of social status in interpersonal interactions. Consider the case of Ned, a fifty-six-year-old dentist who had been in practice for three decades. To outward appearances, Ned was successful. But when he showed up in a psychiatrist's office, Ned said his career had been destroyed by his fear of "doing something foolish."* Anxiety about doing something wrong that will lead to social humiliation is quite common. But Ned's fear was interestingly specific: his performance anxiety was only acute when working on patients whom he perceived—based on the kind of insurance they carried—to have social status greater than he did. While he worked on Medicaid patients or those without insurance, his anxiety was negligible. But while treating patients with fancy insurance indicative of a high-status job, Ned was terrified that his hands would shake visibly or that he would sweat excessively, revealing his anxiety to his patients, who he believed were immune to anxiety and (as he put it) "completely at home in the world" and therefore prone to judge and even to ridicule him for his weakness.

Symptoms of this kind of status-based social anxiety—and particularly the fear of being exposed as "weak" relative to one's peers—appear regularly in the psychiatric literature going back a century. And lots of evidence supports Öhman's proposition that people like Ned have an awareness of social status, and of social slights, that is too finely calibrated. A National Institute of Mental Health study published in 2008 found that the brains of people with generalized social phobia responded differently to criticism than the brains of other people. When social phobics and healthy control subjects read neutral comments about themselves, their brain activity looked the same. But when the two groups read *negative* comments about themselves, those diagnosed with social anxiety disorder had markedly increased blood flow to the amygdala and the medial prefrontal cortex—two parts of the brain associated with anxiety and the stress response. The brains of

* Ned's case is drawn from John Marshall's book, *Social Phobia*.

social phobics appear physiologically primed to be hyperresponsive to negative comments.

This finding aligns with the many studies showing that social phobics demonstrate a more hyperreactive amygdala response to negative facial expressions. When social phobics see faces that appear angry, frightened, or disapproving, the neurons in their amygdalae fire faster and more intensively than those of healthy control subjects. As the NIMH researchers put it, "Generalized-social-phobia-related dysfunction may at least partly reflect a negative attitude toward the self, particularly in response to social stimuli, as instantiated in the medial prefrontal cortex." What this means, in plain English, is that shame and low self-esteem have a biological address: they reside, evidently, in the interconnections between the amygdala and the medial prefrontal cortex.

There's now a whole subgenre of fMRI studies that demonstrate that the amygdala reacts vividly to social stimuli not perceived by the conscious mind. When individuals are placed in an fMRI machine and shown images of faces displaying fear or anger, their amygdalae flare with activity. This is not surprising: we know that the amygdala is the seat of the fear response. It's also not surprising that neurons in the amygdalae of diagnosed social phobics tend to fire more frequently and intensively than those of other people in response to frightened or angry faces. What is surprising is that all people—social phobics and healthy control subjects alike—show a marked amygdala response to photos they are not consciously aware of seeing. That is, if you watch a slide show of innocuous images of flowers interspersed with pictures of scared or angry faces flashed so quickly you are not consciously aware of seeing them, your amygdala will flare in response to the emotional faces—even though you don't know you saw them. Ask the test subjects in these experiments whether they saw the scared or angry faces and they will say they did not; the images flashed by too quickly for the conscious brain to register them. But the amygdala, operating with lightning-fast acuity beneath the level of conscious awareness, perceives the distressing faces and flares in the fMRI. Some subjects report feeling anxiety at these moments—but they can't identify its source. This would seem to be neuroscientific evidence that Freud was right about the existence of the unconscious: the brain reacts powerfully to stimuli that we are not explicitly aware of.

Hundreds of studies reveal an unconscious neurobiological stress response to social stimuli. To cite just one, a 2008 study published in the *Journal of Cognitive Neuroscience* found that people shown images of emotional faces for thirty milliseconds—faster than the conscious mind can perceive them—demonstrated "marked" brain responses. (The socially anxious had the strongest brain responses.) Fascinatingly, when test subjects were asked to judge whether images of surprised faces were positive or negative, their judgments were powerfully affected by the subliminal images flashed just beforehand: when the image of the surprised face was preceded by a subliminal image of an angry or scared face, subjects were much more likely to say that the surprised face they were looking at was negative, expressing fear or anger; when the image of the same surprised face was preceded by a flashed happy face, the test subjects were more likely to say the same surprised face was expressing joy. As one of the researchers put it, "Unconsciously perceived signals of threat . . . bubble up and unwittingly influence social judgments."

What's the point of having such finely tuned social perception equipment? Why do our brains make judgments we're not consciously aware of?

One theory is that such "quick social judging" historically enhanced our odds of survival. In a baboon troop or a tribe of hunter-gatherers, you don't want to make social impressions that will invite attacks from your peers or cause you to be banished. For baboons, being kicked out of the troop is often tantamount to death: a lone monkey found by another group is likely to be set upon and killed. To be an early human banished from the tribe was to be both denied access to communal food supplies and rendered vulnerable to animal predators. Thus a certain social sensitivity—a keen attunement to what group norms demand, an awareness of social threats, a sense of how to signal the deference that will keep you from getting pummeled by a higher-status member of your troop or banished from your tribe—is adaptive. (This is where blushing can be helpful as an automatic signal of deference to others.) Being aware of how your social behavior—your "performance"—is being perceived by others can help you stay alive. Calling attention to yourself and being judged negatively is always risky: you're in danger of having your status challenged or of being kicked out of the tribe for making a bad impression.*

Murray Stein, a psychiatrist at the University of California, San Diego, has observed that social submissiveness in baboons and other primates has striking parallels with social phobia in humans. The stress that social phobics feel in anticipation of normal human interactions, and especially of public performances, Stein says, produces the same hypercortisolism—an elevation in the levels of stress hormones and an activation of the hypothalamic-pituitary-adrenal (HPA) axis—that subordinate status does in baboons. Hypercortisolism, in turn, kindles the amygdala, which has the effect of both intensifying anxiety in the moment and tying social interactions more deeply to a stress response in the future.†

Stein's research builds on the work of Robert Sapolsky, a neurobiologist at Stanford who has done fascinating research showing a direct correlation between a baboon's status in his troop and the quantity of stress hormones in his blood. Baboon populations have strictly ordered male hierarchies: there is the alpha male, who is usually the biggest and strongest and has the most access to food and females and is deferred to by all the other male monkeys, then there is the second-highest-ranking monkey, who is deferred to by all the other monkeys except for the alpha male—and so on, all the way down to the lowest-ranking male at the bottom of the social ladder. If a fight breaks out between two baboons and the higher-ranking one wins, the social order is preserved; if the lower-ranking one wins, there is a re-sorting, with the victorious baboon moving up the social ladder. Through careful obser-

---

* Some social phobics find even positive attention to be aversive. Think of the young child who bursts into tears when guests sing "Happy Birthday" to her at a party—or of Elfriede Jelinek afraid to pick up her Nobel Prize. Social attention—even positive, supportive attention—activates the neurocircuitry of fear. This makes sense from an evolutionary perspective. Calling positive attention to yourself can incite jealousy or generate new rivalries.

† The phobic response gets deeply consolidated in the neurons of the amygdala and the hippocampus—which is in part what makes it so hard to stamp out phobias. In this way, anxiety can be wretchedly self-reinforcing: stress activates the amygdala, which increases anxiety; increased anxiety stimulates the HPA axis, which makes the amygdala twitchier still—and all of this neural activity deepens the association of anxiety with the phobic stimulus, whether that's social interaction or a turbulent plane flight. In short, being anxious conditions you to be more anxious in the future.

vation, Sapolsky's team has been able to determine the social hierarchies of particular baboon populations. Using blood tests from these primates, Sapolsky has found that testosterone levels correlate directly with social standing: the higher ranking the baboon, the more testosterone he'll have. Moreover, when a baboon rises in the social hierarchy, the amount of testosterone he produces increases; when a baboon declines in status, his testosterone levels fall. (The causation seems to work in both directions: testosterone produces dominance, and dominance produces testosterone.)

But just as higher rank is associated with testosterone, lower rank is associated with stress hormones like cortisol: the lower a baboon's standing in the hierarchy, the greater the concentration of stress hormones in his blood. A subordinate male not only has to work harder to procure food and access to females but also has to tread carefully so as not to get beaten up by a dominant animal. It's unclear whether high levels of cortisol cause a baboon to become submissive or whether the stress of being low status causes cortisol levels to rise. Most likely it's both—the physical and psychological pressures of being a subordinate baboon lead to elevated levels of stress hormones, which produce more anxiety, which produces more stress hormones, which produce more submissiveness and general ill health.

While findings from animal studies can be applied to our understanding of human nature only indirectly (we can reason in ways other primates cannot), Ned's anxious response to practicing dentistry on "higher-status" patients may well have its roots in primitive concerns about overstepping bounds in the status hierarchy. Low-ranking baboons and orangutans that fail to lower their eyes—to signal their submissiveness—in the presence of higher-ranking ones risk inviting attack. A baboon's status in the social hierarchy—and, beyond that, his skillfulness at behaving in accord with his rank, whatever that may be—does a lot to determine his physical well-being.*

Both low-ranking baboons and humans with social anxiety dis-

---

* Interestingly, recent studies have found that the happiest-seeming and least stressed monkeys are what we might call the beta males—those monkeys near the top of the hierarchy, who tend to be easygoing and socially skillful. Being the highest-ranking male is a lot healthier and less stressful than being the lowest-ranking male—but being a *high*-ranking male who is not the *highest*-ranking male is

order resort easily to submissive behavior. Like low-ranking animals, people with the general subtype of social anxiety disorder tend to look downward, avoid eye contact, blush, and engage in behaviors that advertise their submissiveness, eagerly seeking to please their peers and superiors and actively deferring to others to avoid conflict. For low-ranking baboons, this behavior is a protective adaptation. It can be adaptive in humans, too—but in social phobics it is more often self-defeating.

Low-status monkeys and socially phobic humans also tend to have notable irregularities in the processing of certain neurotransmitters. Studies have found that monkeys with enhanced serotonergic function (in essence, higher levels of serotonin in their brain synapses) tend to be more dominant, more friendly, and more likely than those with normal serotonin levels to bond with their peers. In contrast, monkeys with unusually low serotonin levels are more likely to display avoidant behavior: they keep to themselves and avoid social interactions. Recent studies of humans have found altered serotonin function in certain brain regions of patients diagnosed with social anxiety disorder. These findings help explain why selective serotonin reuptake inhibitors like Prozac and Paxil can be effective in treating social anxiety. (Studies have also found that when nonanxious, nondepressed people take SSRIs, they become more friendly.)

Dopamine has also been implicated in shaping social behavior. When monkeys who have been housed alone are taken from their cages and placed into a group setting, the monkeys that rise the highest in the dominance hierarchy tend to have more dopamine in their brains— which is interesting in light of studies finding that people diagnosed with social anxiety disorder tend to have *lower*-than-average dopamine levels. Some studies have found striking correlations between social anxiety and Parkinson's disease, a neurological condition associated with a deficit of dopamine in the brain. One 2008 study found that half of Parkinson's patients scored high enough on the Liebowitz Social Anxiety Scale to be diagnosed with social phobia. Multiple recent stud-

---

even more healthy and less stressful, because you're not always having to worry about the palace coup that threatens to topple you.

ies have found "altered dopamine binding potential" in the brains of the socially anxious.* Murray Stein, among others, has hypothesized that the awkwardness and interpersonal clumsiness of social phobics are directly connected to problems in dopamine functioning; the dopamine "reinforcement/reward" pathways that help guide correct social behavior in healthy people may somehow be askew in the brains of social phobics.

My sister, who has for years suffered from social anxiety, strongly endorses this view. Without knowing anything about neurobiology, she has long insisted that her brain is "wired wrong."

"Social situations that normal people breeze through unthinkingly cause my brain to shut down," she says. "I can never think of what to say."

Though her brain otherwise functions well (she's a successful cartoonist, editor, and children's book author who graduated from Harvard), she has, ever since junior high, wrestled with what she calls her "talking problem." Neither decades of psychotherapy nor dozens of drug combinations have much alleviated it. She has been evaluated for Asperger's syndrome and other disorders on the autism spectrum, but she doesn't lack empathy the way Asperger's patients do.†

The association of dopamine and serotonin with social phobia doesn't prove that neurotransmitter deficits *cause* social anxiety—those irregularities could be the *effects* of social anxiety, the neurochemical "scars" that develop when a brain becomes overstressed from having to be so vigilant all the time, constantly scanning the environment for social threats. But emerging research suggests that the efficiency with which dopamine and serotonin get ferried across the synapses is genetically determined. Researchers have found that which variant of the serotonin transporter gene you have determines the density of serotonin receptors in your neurons—and that the relative density of your

---

* All drugs of abuse elevate dopamine levels in the basal ganglia—an area of the brain where dopamine is low in socially anxious patients. A chronic dopamine deficit may help account for why social phobics are more likely than others to struggle with addiction.

† Although Asperger's patients and social phobics in some ways suffer from a similar problem—a difficulty in managing social interactions that puts off others—they arrive at it from more or less opposite directions: whereas the Asperger's patient is no good at imagining what's in other people's minds, the social phobic is *too* good at it.

serotonin receptors helps determine where you fall on the spectrum between shy and extroverted.*

The introduction of social uncertainty into a group of baboons does interesting things to rates of anxiety. Low-ranking baboons are always stressed. But Robert Sapolsky has found that whenever a new male joins the troop, the glucocorticoid levels of *all* the baboons—not just the low-ranking ones—become elevated. With the introduction of new members into a social hierarchy, appropriate rules of conduct, such as who should defer to whom, become unclear; there are more fights and general agitation. Once the new baboon has been assimilated into the tribe, stress levels and glucocorticoid concentrations decline, and social behavior returns to normal.

This also happens in humans. In the late 1990s, Dirk Hellhammer, a German psychobiologist, coded sixty-three army recruits at boot camp according to their relative position in the social hierarchy (as determined by anthropological observation) and then measured their cortisol levels every week. During stable periods, the more dominant recruits had lower baseline levels of salivary cortisol than the subordinate ones—just like baboons. But during periods of experimentally induced psychological and physical stress, cortisol levels increased in all the soldiers—markedly in the dominant subjects and modestly in the subordinate ones. While it's always stressful being a low-ranking member of the tribe, disruptions to the social order seem to make everyone, even the high-ranking members, stressed.†

---

* I will discuss the relation between genes and anxiety in greater depth in chapter 9.

† One of the hallmarks of modernity is an abiding uncertainty about status. Hunter-gatherer societies tended not to be very socially stratified; for most of human history, people lived in fairly egalitarian groups. That changed during the Middle Ages. From the twelfth century or so all the way through the American Revolution, society was highly stratified—but also largely fixed: people didn't move between feudal castes. Modern society, in contrast, is both highly stratified (there's a high degree of income inequality in many countries) and highly fluid. The notion that anyone can, with luck and pluck, rise from poverty to the middle class, or from the middle class to great wealth, is integral to our idea of success. But not all mobility is upward. Unlike in a society with more fixed socioeconomic strata, there is always the fear of falling—a fear that is heightened in economic times like these. The many forces bearing down on the American worker—the creative destruction of free-market capitalism; the disruptions to the labor force caused by technology; the changing and uncertain relations between the sexes and the accompanying confusion about gender roles—combine to produce constant uncertainty. People naturally worry: *Am I being overtaken by other people with more relevant job skills? Will I lose my job and fall out of the middle class?* Some have argued that this chronic uncertainty is physically rewiring our brains to be more anxious.

Many of us have strived for perfection in order to try to control our world. . . . There is generally a deep-seated feeling of not being good enough, of being deficient or defective in some way, or of being different from others in a way that will not be accepted by others. This creates a feeling of shame and a fear of embarrassment and humiliation in exposing your true self in front of others.
—JANET ESPOSITO, *In the Spotlight* (2000)

Recently, while sifting through the records from my treatment with Dr. M. nearly a decade ago, I came across a document I'd written at her request. She had asked me to write down what the outcome of a worst-case-scenario public speaking catastrophe would be for me. The idea behind this sort of exercise is to fully imagine the worst thing that could happen (total failure, complete humiliation) and then, once you've really thought about it, to conclude that, first, the worst-case scenario was unlikely to unfold and, second, even if it did, maybe it would not be so shatteringly catastrophic. Reaching that conclusion, and assimilating it intellectually and emotionally, is supposed to lower the stakes of the performance and therefore diminish anxiety.

That's the theory anyway. But when I showed up at my lunchtime appointment one Thursday after having e-mailed her my imagined worst-case public speaking scenario (humiliation and physical collapse followed by unemployment, divorce, and ostracism from society), Dr. M. looked stricken.

"Your write-up," she said. "It's the most negative thing I've ever read." She told me she had been horrified at what I'd written and had felt compelled to show my account to her department supervisor in search of more experienced counsel. As she looked at me with sympathy, concern, and, I believe, no small alarm, I suspected she'd raised the question of whether I might be gravely depressed and possibly psychotic.

Perhaps I have an overactive imagination; perhaps I'm unduly pessimistic. But I now know that negativity and poor self-image—along with a desperate desire to conceal that poor self-image—are textbook for a social phobic. Nearly every book on the subject, both popular and academic, observes that social anxiety disorder is associated with feelings of inferiority and with extreme sensitivity to any kind of criticism or negative evaluation.*

"Jeez," Dr. W. said to me one day when I was explaining to him the high stakes I ascribed to an upcoming public event and how important I thought it was to maintain my façade of efficacy and to hide my sense of fraudulence and weakness. "Do you realize how potently your sense of shame contributes to your anxiety?"

Both Dr. M. and Dr. W.—not to mention Epictetus—would say that the best cure for this kind of social anxiety is to diminish the power of shame. The embarrassing exposures that Dr. M. subjected me to were designed to inure me somewhat to feelings of shame.

"Go ahead, put it out there," Dr. W. says, speaking of my anxiety. "You may be surprised by how people respond.

"Stop caring so much about what other people think," he says, echoing the advice of a hundred self-help books.

If only it were that easy.

The day I'm not nervous is the day I quit. To me, nerves are great. That means you care, and I care about what I do.
—TIGER WOODS, AT A PRESS CONFERENCE BEFORE THE 2009
WGC-ACCENTURE MATCH PLAY CHAMPIONSHIP

I don't give a shit what you say. If I go out there and miss game winners and people say, "Kobe choked" or "Kobe is seven for whatever in pressure situations," well, fuck you. Because I don't play for your fucking approval. I play for my own love and enjoyment of the

---

* Even, and perhaps especially, psychotherapists are not immune. Because they feel patients and peers look to them to be in control of their emotions, the pressure psychotherapists put on themselves not to appear anxious or agitated can be great—and can perversely make them feel more anxious and out of control. I have on my shelf several books by therapists who have at times felt handicapped and humiliated by their own anxiety. *The Anxiety Expert: A Psychiatrist's Story of Panic* (2004) was written by Marjorie Raskin, a psychiatrist specializing in anxiety who was tortured by panic attacks brought on by public speaking. She went to great lengths to hide her anxiety and, like me, medicated herself heavily with benzodiazepines. *Painfully Shy: How to Overcome Social Anxiety and Reclaim your Life* (2001) was cowritten by a psychologist, Barbara Markway, who concedes that she herself has not, in fact, ever fully "overcome her social anxiety or reclaimed her life."

*game. And to win. That's what I play for. Most of the time, when
guys feel the pressure, they're worried about what people might say
about them. I don't have that fear, and it enables me to forget bad
plays and to take shots and play my game.*

   —KOBE BRYANT, DURING AN INTERVIEW FOLLOWING GAME 3
   OF THE 2012 NBA WESTERN CONFERENCE SEMIFINALS

One day in seventh grade, while playing my classmate Paul in a
tennis match, I become overwhelmed with anxiety. My stomach is
distended; I am burping uncontrollably. Before the match started, the
most important thing was that I win. But now that I am in the middle
of the match and my stomach hurts and I am afraid of throwing up, the
most important thing is that I get off the court as quickly as possible.
And the quickest way to do that is to lose. And so I hit balls out. I hit
them into the net. I double-fault. I lose 6–1, 6–0, and when I shake
hands and get off the court, the first thing I feel is relief. My stomach
settles. My anxiety relents.

And the next thing I feel is self-loathing. Because I have lost to the
overweight and oleaginous Paul, who is now strutting around proudly,
crowing about how badly he has beaten me. The stakes are low: it is a
challenge match for one of the lower ladder positions on the middle-
school junior varsity. But to me they feel existentially high. I have lost
to Paul, who is not a particularly good player—his skills, his quickness,
his fitness are manifestly worse than mine—and the result is there on
the score sheet and on the ladder hanging on the locker room wall
and radiating from Paul's puffed-out chest, for all to see: he has won,
so he is superior to me. I have lost; I am therefore, by definition, a
loser.

This sort of thing—purposely losing matches to escape intolerable anxiety—happened dozens of times throughout my school sports
career. Not every thrown match was as egregious as the one against
Paul (whose name, by the way, I have changed here)—I often tanked
matches against players who would likely have beaten me even if I
hadn't suffered an anxious meltdown—but some of them were. My
coaches were baffled. How could it be, they wondered, that I could look
so skillful in practice and yet so rarely win a significant match?

The exception was tenth grade, when I played for the junior varsity squash team and went undefeated: 17–0 or something. What, you might ask, accounts for that?

Valium.

Squash matches, even squash practices, were making me so miserable that the child psychiatrist I was seeing then, Dr. L., prescribed a small dose of the benzodiazepine. Every day during squash season that year, I took the pill surreptitiously with my peanut butter sandwich at lunch. And I didn't lose a match. I was still unhappy during squash season: my agoraphobia and separation anxiety made me hate traveling to matches, and my competitive anxieties still made me hate playing in them. But the Valium took enough of the physical edge off my nerves that I could focus on trying to play well instead of on trying to get off the court as quickly as possible. I didn't feel compelled to lose matches on purpose anymore. Drugs got me into the zone of performance where anxiety is beneficial.

In 1908, two psychologists, Robert M. Yerkes and John Dillingham Dodson, published an article in *The Journal of Comparative Neurology and Psychology* demonstrating that animals trained to perform a task performed it slightly better if they were made "moderately anxious" beforehand. This led to what has become known as the Yerkes-Dodson law, whose principles have been experimentally demonstrated in both animals and humans many times since then. It's kind of a Goldilocks law: too little anxiety and you will not perform at your peak, whether on a test or in a squash match; too much anxiety and you will not perform well; but with just the right amount of anxiety—enough to elevate your physiological arousal and to focus your attention intensely on the task, but not so much that you are distracted by how nervous you are—you'll be more likely to deliver a peak performance. For me, evidently, getting from the too-anxious part of the curve to the optimum-performance part required a small dose of Valium.*

---

* There have been elite athletes for whom this has been the case, too. Reno Bertoia, to name just one, was a young third baseman for the Detroit Tigers who once seemed to have a bright future in the major leagues—until, in 1957, he became so overwhelmed by anxiety that, as the Tigers' trainer observed, he "couldn't hit and sometimes bobbled fielding plays that should have been easy." The more nervous Bertoia got, the worse he played; the worse he played, the more nervous he got—a

I wish I could say competitive anxiety was merely an adolescent phase. But about ten years ago, I found myself playing in the finals of a squash tournament against my friend Jay, a personable young physician. It was championship night at the squash club, and a couple of dozen people had turned out to watch. We were two just-better-than-average club players; absolutely nothing of significance (no money, hardly a trophy to speak of) was on the line.

In this tournament, matches were best of five games; to win a game you needed nine points. I jumped out confidently to an early lead in the first game, but I let it slip away. I won the second game; Jay won the third. My back against the wall, I won the fourth, and Jay sagged visibly. I could see that he was tired—more tired than I was. In the fifth and deciding game, I pulled steadily ahead and got to 7–3, two points away from victory. Jay looked defeated. Victory was mine.

Except it wasn't.

The prospect of imminent victory sent anxiety cascading through my body. My mouth went dry. My limbs grew impossibly heavy. Worst of all, my stomach betrayed me. Overwhelmed with nausea and panic, I hit weak shots, desperate shots. Jay, moments earlier disconsolate and resigned to losing, perked up. I'd given him a ray of hope. He gained momentum. My anxiety mounted, and suddenly it was like I was back in seventh grade, playing tennis against Paul: all I want is out. I withered before everyone's eyes. I began, on purpose, to lose.

Jay seized his opportunity, Lazarus from the grave, and beat me. Afterward, I tried to be gracious in defeat, but when everyone inevitably commented on how dramatically I had blown my near victory, I attributed my collapse to back trouble. My back did hurt—but it was

---

classic vicious cycle of ever-increasing anxiety and ever-decreasing performance. Soon, his play had so deteriorated that Tigers management was on the verge of dropping him from the team. Desperate and unhappy, Bertoia resorted to taking Miltown, an early, pre-Valium tranquilizer. The transformation was astounding. Bertoia "stopped holding himself in," the trainer reported. "He's a different man on the bench—talking and joking—and much more relaxed." On the field, meanwhile, he started "pounding the ball in tremendous fashion." His batting average rose a hundred points.

not why I lost. I had the championship in my clutches, and I let it slip away because I was too anxious to compete.

I choked.

Just about the worst epithet one can sling at an athlete—worse, in some ways, than "cheater"—is "choker": to choke is to wilt under pressure, to fail to perform at the moment of greatest importance. (A technical definition, as laid out by Sian Beilock, a University of Chicago cognitive psychologist who specializes in the topic, is "suboptimal performance—worse performance than expected given what a performer is capable of doing and what this performer has done in the past.") The etymological stem of "anxious"—*anx*—comes from the Latin *angere,* which means "to choke"; the Latin word *anxius* probably referred to the feeling of chest constriction experienced during a panic attack. To choke, in an athletic or any other kind of performance context, implies an absence of fortitude, a weakness of character. The most common explanation for choking in a sporting event is, in the shorthand of the sports reporter, "nerves." Choking, in other words, is produced by anxiety—and in the sporting arena, as well as on the field of battle or in the workplace, anxiety is ipso facto a sign of weakness.

Since my collapse in the club finals that year, I have learned the beneficial effects of prematch meditation and have gotten better at titrating my dosages of prophylactic antianxiety medication. My wife has also borne us two children, which should have put into perspective the existential insignificance of a recreational sporting event. And yet the problem persists.

Not long ago, I found myself in the semifinals of another squash tournament.

"Why do you play in these tournaments if they make you so miserable?" Dr. W. had asked me several years earlier. "If you can't learn to enjoy them, stop torturing yourself by playing in them!"

And so I had stopped for a while. And when I started again, I did so with a conscious lack of emotional investment. *I'm just doing it for the exercise,* I tell myself. *I can enjoy the competition without making myself anxious and miserable about the outcome.* And through the first rounds of this tournament, I do. Sure, there are tense moments; at times I feel pressure, which fatigues me and diminishes the quality of my play. But that's normal, the vicissitudes of competition; it doesn't debilitate me. And I keep winning.

So when I step out onto the court for the semifinals, I tell myself, *I still do not care.* Only five people are watching. I lose a close first game. But it's fun. *No big deal. I don't care. My opponent is good. I* should *lose this match. No expectations, no pressure.*

But then I win the next game. *Wait a minute,* I think. *I'm in this match. I could win it.* The moment my competitive impulse surges, the familiar heaviness descends and my stomach inflates with air.

C'mon, Scott, I tell myself. *Have fun. Who cares who wins?*

I try to relax but my breathing is getting heavier. I'm sweating more profusely. And as word spreads that the match is a close one, more people begin gathering behind the court to watch.

I try to slow everything down—my breathing, the pace of my play. As my anxiety rises, the quality of my game deteriorates. But I am still, for the moment anyway, focusing on trying to play well, on trying to win. To my surprise, my slowing-the-pace-down strategy works: I come from behind to win the third game. One more game and I will be in the championship.

At which point I find I am so enervated by my anxiety that I can no longer play. My opponent wins the next game quickly, evening the match at 2–2. Whoever wins the next game will be into the finals.

I use the allotted two-minute break between games to retreat to the men's room to try to collect myself. I am pale and shaking—and, most terrifying to me, nauseated. As I walk back out on the court, the referee asks if I am okay. (I clearly do not look well.) I mumble that I am. The fifth game begins, and I no longer care at all about winning; as in my match against Paul thirty years earlier, I care only about getting off the court without vomiting. Once again, I start trying to lose as quickly as possible: I stop running for the ball; I shank balls on purpose. My opponent is puzzled. After I fail to run for an easy drop shot, he turns and asks me if I'm okay. Mortified, I nod that I am.

But I am not okay. I am terrified that I will not be able to lose enough points quickly enough to get off the court before retching and humiliating myself. In seventh grade, at least, I had been able to stay on the court until the end of the match with Paul; this time, with so many eyes upon me and my gorge rising, I cannot do even that. Two points later, with the match many points from conclusion, I raise my hand in defeat.

"I concede," I say to my opponent. "I'm sick." And I scurry off the court in defeat.

I have not just lost. I have given up. Folded like a cheap lawn chair. I feel mortified and pathetic.

Friends in the audience murmur words of consolation in my direction. "We could tell you weren't feeling well," they say. "Something wasn't right." I shake them off ("Bad fish for lunch," I mumble) and retreat to the locker room. As ever, once I am out of the competitive moment, and out of public view, my anxiety recedes.

But I have lost to another opponent I might well have beaten. In truth, I don't really care about the losing. What bothers me is that, yet again, my anxiety has defeated me, reduced me to a helpless mass of quivering jelly and exposed me to what feels like minor public embarrassment.

I know: the reality is that no one cares. Which somehow just makes this all the more pathetic.

Never in my career have I experienced anything like what happened. I was totally out of control. And I couldn't understand it.
—GREG NORMAN, TO *GOLF MAGAZINE* ON BLOWING A LARGE
LEAD AT THE 1996 MASTERS

The list of elite athletes who have choked spectacularly, or who have developed bizarre and crippling performance anxieties, is extensive.

Greg Norman, the Australian golfer, came unglued at the 1996 Masters, nervously frittering away a seemingly insurmountable lead over the final few holes; he ended up sobbing in the arms of the man who beat him, Nick Faldo. Jana Novotna, the Czech tennis star, was five points away from winning Wimbledon in 1993 when she disintegrated under pressure and blew a huge lead over Steffi Graf; she ended up sobbing in the arms of the Duchess of Kent. On November 25, 1980, Roberto Durán, then the reigning world welterweight boxing champion, squared off against Sugar Ray Leonard in one of the most famous bouts ever. With sixteen seconds left in the eighth round—and millions of dollars on the line—Durán turned to the referee, raised his hands in surrender, and pleaded, "*No más, no más* [No more, no more]. No more box." He would later say his stomach hurt. Until that moment, Durán was perceived to be invincible, the epitome of Latino machismo. Since then, he has lived in infamy—considered one of the greatest quitters and cowards in sports history.

These are all classic chokes—mental and physical collapses in isolated moments of high anxiety. More puzzling are those professional athletes who, in an excruciatingly public manifestation of performance anxiety, go into a kind of chronic choke. In the mid-1990s, Nick Anderson was a guard for the Orlando Magic. He entered the 1995 NBA finals as a solid free-throw shooter, having made about 70 percent of his foul shots throughout his career. But in the first game of the championship series against the Houston Rockets that year, Anderson had four consecutive opportunities to secure a victory for Orlando with a foul shot in the final seconds of regulation time: all he had to do was hit one shot.

He missed all four. The Magic went on to lose that game in overtime, and then to lose the series in a four-game sweep. After that, Anderson's free-throw percentage plummeted; for the remainder of his career, he was a disaster at the foul line. This caused him to play less aggressively on offense because he was afraid he'd get fouled and have to shoot free throws. The missed championship free throws, Anderson recalled later, were "like a song that got in my head, playing over and over and over." He was driven to early retirement.

In 1999, Chuck Knoblauch lost the ability to throw a baseball from second to first base. This would not have been a problem had he not happened to be, at the time, the starting second baseman for the New York Yankees. Knoblauch had no physical injury that would have impeded him—he could throw to first just fine during practice. During games, however, with forty thousand fans watching him in the stadium and millions more watching him on television, he repeatedly overthrew the base, launching the ball into the stands.

Two decades earlier, just a year removed from being named the National League's rookie of the year, Steve Sax, the second baseman for the Los Angeles Dodgers, developed the same affliction as Knoblauch. He had no trouble in practice, though, even successfully throwing blindfolded in an effort to break the habit.

Most infamously there is Steve Blass, an All-Star pitcher for the Pittsburgh Pirates who, in June 1973, following a stretch when he was perhaps the best pitcher in baseball, was suddenly unable to throw the ball through the strike zone. In practice, he could throw as well as ever. But during games, he couldn't control where the ball was going. After psychotherapy, meditation, hypnotism, and all manner of cockeyed home remedies (including wearing looser underwear) failed to cure him, he retired.

Odder still are the examples of Mike Ivie and Mackey Sasser, catchers for the San Diego Padres and New York Mets, respectively. Both became so phobic about throwing the ball back to the pitcher—the sort of thing Little Leaguers do without trouble—that they ended up having to leave their positions. (The sports psychiatrist Allan Lans half jokingly coined the term "disreturnophobia" to describe this affliction.)

The explicit monitoring theory of choking, derived from recent findings in cognitive psychology and neuroscience, holds that performance falters when athletes concentrate too much attention on it. Thinking *too much* about what you are doing actually impairs performance. This would seem to run counter to all the standard bromides about how the quality of your performance is tied to the intensity of your focus. But what seems to matter is the type of focus you have. Sian Beilock, who studies the psychology of choking at her lab at the University of Chicago, says that actively worrying about screwing up makes you more likely to screw up. To achieve optimal performance—what some psychologists call flow—parts of your brain should be on automatic pilot, not actively thinking about (or "explicitly monitoring") what you are doing. By this logic, the reason Ivie's and Sasser's "disreturnophobia" became so severe was that they were thinking too much about what should have been the mindless mechanics of throwing the ball back to the pitcher. (*Am I gripping the ball right? Am I following through in the right arm position? Do I look funny? Am I going to screw this up again? What's wrong with me?*) Beilock has found that she can dramatically improve athletes' performance (at least in experimental situations) by getting them to focus on something other than the mechanics of their stroke or swing; having them recite a poem or sing a song in their head, distracting their *conscious* attention from the physical task, can rapidly improve performance.

But anxious people generally can't stop thinking about everything, all the time, in all the wrong ways. *What if this? What if that? Am I doing this right? Do I look stupid? What if I make a fool of myself? What if I throw it into the stands again? Am I blushing visibly? Can people see me trembling? Can they hear my voice quavering? Am I going to lose my job or get demoted to the minors?*

When you look at brain scans of athletes pre- or midchoke, says the sports psychologist Bradley Hatfield, you see a neural "traffic jam" of worry and self-monitoring. Brain scans of nonchokers, on the other hand—the Tom Bradys and Peyton Mannings of the world, who exude grace under pressure—reveal neural activity that is "efficient and streamlined," using only those parts of the brain relevant to efficient performance.

In a sense, the anxiety exhibited by all these choking athletes is a version of the blushing problem: their fear of embarrassing themselves in public leads them to embarrass themselves in public. Their anxiety drives them to do the very thing they most fear. The more self-conscious you are—the more susceptible to shame—the worse you will perform.

If you are a man you will not permit your self-respect to admit an anxiety neurosis or to show fear.
          —SIGNS POSTED ON ALLIED GUN SITES IN MALTA
                    DURING WORLD WAR II

In 1830, Colonel R. Taylor, the British consul in Baghdad, was exploring an archaeological excavation on the site of an ancient Assyrian palace when he came across a six-sided clay prism covered with cuneiform. The Taylor prism, which today is housed in the British Museum, tells of the military campaigns of King Sennacherib, who ruled Assyria in the eighth century B.C. The prism has been of great value to historians and theologians because of the contemporaneous accounts it provides of events described in the Old Testament. To me, however, the most interesting passage on the prism describes Assyria's battle with two young kings of Elam (southwestern Iran on a modern map).

"To save their lives they trampled over the bodies of their soldiers and fled," the prism reads, recounting what happened when Sennacherib's army overwhelmed them. "Like young captured birds they lost their courage. With their urine they defiled their chariots and let fall their excrements."

Here, in one of the earliest written records ever discovered, is the damning judgment cast on the weak stomach and moral character of the anxious warrior.

Many of the sports tropes about heroism, courage, and "grace under pressure" are also applied to war. But the stakes attending a sporting performance pale beside those attending performance in war, where the difference between success and failure is often the difference between life and death.

Societies grant the highest approbation to soldiers (and athletes) who display grace under pressure—and harshly disparage those who falter under it. The anxious are inconstant and weak; the brave are stolid and strong. Cowards are governed by their fears; heroes are unperturbed by them. In his *Histories,* Herodotus tells of Aristodemus, an elite Spartan warrior whose "heart failed him" at the Battle of Thermopylae in 480 B.C.; he remained in the rear guard and did not join the fight. Thenceforth Aristodemus became known as the Trembler, and he "found himself in such disgrace that he hanged himself."

Militaries have always gone to considerable length to inure their soldiers to anxiety. The Vikings used stimulants made from deer urine to provide chemical resistance to fear. British military commanders historically girded their soldiers with rum; the Russian army used vodka (and also valerian, a mild tranquilizer). The Pentagon has been researching pharmacological means of shutting down the fight-or-flight response, with an eye toward eradicating battlefield fear. Researchers at Johns Hopkins University recently designed a system that would allow commanders to monitor their soldiers' stress levels in real time by measuring the hormone hydrocortisone—the idea being that if a soldier's stress hormones exceed a certain level, he should be removed from battle.

Militaries denigrate fearful behavior for good reason: anxiety can be devastating to the soldier and to the army he fights in. The *Anglo-Saxon Chronicle* recounts the battle between England and Denmark that took place in 1003, in which Ælfric, the English commander, became so anxious that he began to vomit and could no longer command his men, who ended up being slaughtered by the Danes.

Anxiety can spread by contagion, so armies seek aggressively to contain it. During the Civil War, the Union army tattooed or branded soldiers found guilty of cowardice. During World War I, any British soldier who developed neurosis as a result of war trauma was declared to be "at best a constitutionally inferior human being, at worst a malingerer and a coward." Medical writers of the time described anxious soldiers as "moral invalids." (Some progressive doctors—including W. H. R. Rivers, who treated the poet Siegfried Sassoon, among others—argued that combat neurosis was a medical condition that could affect even soldiers of stern moral stuff, but such doctors were in the minority.) A 1914 article in *The American Review of Reviews* argued that "panic may be checked by officers firing on their own men." Until the Second World War, the British army punished deserters with death.

The Second World War was the first conflict in which psychiatrists played a significant role, both as screeners of soldiers before combat and as healers of their psychic wounds afterward. More than a million U.S. soldiers were admitted to hospitals for psychiatric treatment of battle fatigue. But some senior officers fretted about what this more humane treatment of soldiers meant for combat effectiveness. George Marshall, the U.S. Army general who later became secretary of state, lamented that soldiers who on the front lines would be considered cowards and malingerers were considered by psychiatrists to be patients. The "hyperconsiderate professional attitude" of the psychiatrist, Marshall complained, would lead to an army of cosseted cowards. British generals stated in reputable medical journals that men who panicked during combat should be sterilized "because only such a measure would prevent men from showing fear and passing on to another generation their mental weakness." High-ranking officers on both sides of the Atlantic argued that soldiers diagnosed with "war neurosis" should not be allowed to poison the gene pool with their cowardice. "It is now time that our country stopped being soft," one British colonel declared, "and abandoned its program of mollycoddling no-goods." For his part, General George Patton of the U.S. Army denied there was such a thing as war neurosis. He preferred the term "combat exhaustion" and said it was a mere "problem of the will." In order to prevent combat exhaustion from spreading, Patton proposed to the commanding general, Dwight Eisenhower, that it be punishable by death. (Eisenhower declined to implement the suggestion.)

Modern armies still struggle with what to do about soldiers undone by their combat-shattered nerves. During the Iraq war, *The New York Times* reported on an American soldier who had been dishonorably discharged for cowardice. The soldier contested his discharge, arguing it should have been an honorable one. He was not a coward, he said, but rather a medical patient suffering from a psychiatric illness: the stress of war had given him panic disorder, which caused him debilitating anxiety attacks. He was sick, his lawyers argued, not cowardly. The military, in this instance, initially refused to recognize the distinction—though Army officials later dropped the cowardice charges, reducing them to the lesser offense of dereliction of duty.

Throughout history there have always been anxious soldiers, men whose nerve failed them and whose bodies betrayed them in crucial moments. After his first experience with combat, in 1862, William Henry, a young Union soldier of the Sixty-Eighth Pennsylvania Volunteers, suffered horrible stomach pains and diarrhea. Deemed by his doctors to be in otherwise good physical health, Henry was the first person to be formally diagnosed with "soldier's heart," a syndrome brought on by the stress of combat.* Studies of "self-soiling rates" among U.S. soldiers during World War II consistently found that 5 to 6 percent of combatants lost control of their bowels, with rates in some combat divisions exceeding 20 percent. Before landing on Iwo Jima in June 1945, American troops suffered rampant diarrhea; some soldiers used this as an excuse to avoid combat. A survey of one U.S. combat division in

---

* This diagnosis had been applied informally since the French Revolution to men who broke down during combat, but it was only in 1871, when a physician named Jacob Mendes Da Costa wrote up a case study on Henry for *The American Journal of the Medical Sciences,* that the condition was formally inscribed in the scientific literature as soldier's heart or irritable heart or Da Costa's syndrome. Historians of psychiatry often identify this article as the first in the medical literature to describe the conditions we would today call panic disorder and post-traumatic stress disorder.

France in 1944 revealed that more than half of the soldiers broke out in cold sweats, felt faint, or lost control of their bowels during battle. Another survey of World War II infantrymen found that only 7 percent said they never felt fear—whereas 75 percent said their hands trembled, 85 percent said they got sweaty palms, 12 percent said they lost bowel control, and 25 percent said they lost bladder control. (Upon hearing that a quarter of survey respondents admitted to losing control of their bladders during battle, one army colonel said, "Hell . . . all that proves is that three out of four are damned liars!") Recent findings issued by the Pentagon revealed that a high number of soldiers deployed in Iraq vomited from anxiety before going out on patrol in combat areas.

William Manchester, who would go on to become an eminent American historian, fought at Okinawa during the Second World War. "I could feel a twitching in my jaw, coming and going like a winky light signaling some disorder," he wrote, recalling his first experience of direct combat, in which he approached a Japanese sniper hiding out in a shack. "Various valves were opening and closing in my stomach. My mouth was dry, my legs quaking, and my eyes out of focus." Manchester shot and killed the sniper—and then vomited and urinated on himself. "Is this what they mean by 'conspicuous gallantry'?" he wondered.

I would argue that Manchester's anxious physiological reaction had an almost moral quality to it, a sensitivity to the existential gravity of the situation. Anxiety, as observers since Augustine have noted, can be usefully allied to morality; people who have no physiological reaction in these situations are the proverbial cold-blooded killers. As the writer Christopher Hitchens—no one's idea of a coward—once put it, "Now, those who fail to register emotion under pressure are often apparently good officer material, but that very stoicism can also conceal—as with officers who don't suffer from battle fatigue or post-traumatic stress—a psychopathic calm that sends the whole platoon into a ditch full of barbed wire and sheds no tears."

Nevertheless, there is a culturally accepted connection stretching back to ancient times between courage and manliness, as well as an approbative moral quality assigned to the ability to control one's bodily functions when in extremis. Legend has it that when Napoleon needed a man "with iron nerve" for a dangerous mission, he ordered several volunteers before a fake firing squad and chose the one who "showed no tendency to move his bowels" when fired upon with blanks.

My colleague Jeff, a journalist who has reported from war zones all over the world and has been kidnapped by terrorist organizations, says that neophyte war correspondents always wonder about what will happen the first time they find themselves pinned down by gunfire. "Until you've been under fire," he says, "the question you ask yourself is, Will I shit my pants? Some do; some don't. I didn't—and I knew from then on I would be fine. But until it happens, you just don't know."

Happily, I've never been fired upon. But I suspect I know into which category I would fall.

> *A coward changes color all the time, and cannot sit still for nervousness, but squats down, first on one heel, then on the other; his heart thumps in his breast as he thinks of death in all its forms, and one can hear the chattering of his teeth. But the brave man never changes color at all and is not unduly perturbed, from the moment when he takes his seat in ambush with the rest.*
>
> —HOMER, *THE ILIAD* (CIRCA EIGHTH CENTURY B.C.)

Why do some people exhibit grace under fire while others fall so readily to pieces? Studies show that almost everyone—all but the most resilient and the most sociopathic—has a breaking point, a psychic threshold beyond which he or she can bear no more combat stress without emotional and physical deterioration or collapse. But some people can withstand lots of stress before breaking down and can recover from combat exhaustion quickly; others break down easily and recover slowly and with difficulty—if they recover at all.

There seems to be remarkable consistency across human populations: a fixed percentage of individuals will crack under pressure, and another fixed percentage will remain largely immune to it. Comprehensive studies conducted during World War II found that in the typical combat unit, a fairly constant proportion of men will emotionally collapse early on, usually even before getting to the battlefield; another relatively fixed proportion (some of them sociopathic) will be able to withstand extraordinary amounts of stress without ill effect; and the majority of men will fall somewhere between these extremes.

John Leach, a British psychologist who studies cognition under extreme stress, has observed that, on average, 10 to 20 percent of people will remain cool and composed in combat situations. "These people will be able to collect their thoughts quickly," he writes in *Survival Psychology*. "Their awareness of the situation will be intact and their judgment and reasoning abilities will not be impaired to any significant extent." At the other extreme, 10 to 15 percent of people will react with "uncontrolled weeping, confusion, screaming and paralyzing anxiety." But most people, Leach says, up to 80 percent of them, will in high-stress lethal conditions become lethargic and confused, waiting for direction. (This perhaps helps account for why so many people submit so readily to authoritarianism in periods of extreme stress or disruption.)

On the other hand, British psychiatrists observed that during World War II, as the Luftwaffe rained bombs on London, civilians with pre-existing neurotic disorders found that their general levels of anxiety actually *declined.* As one historian has written, "Neurotics turned out to be remarkably calm about being threatened from the skies"—probably because they felt reassured to discover that "normal" people shared their fears during the Blitz. One psychiatrist speculated that neurotics felt reassured by the sight of other people "looking as worried as they have felt over the years." When it's acceptable to feel anxious, neurotics feel less anxious.

One fascinating study of stress during wartime was conducted by V. A. Kral, a doctor who was held in the concentration camp Theresienstadt during World War II. In 1951, he published an article in *The American Journal of Psychiatry* reporting that although thirty-three thousand people died at Theresienstadt—and another eighty-seven thousand were transferred to other Nazi concentration camps to be killed—no new cases of phobia, neurosis, or pathological anxiety developed there. In fact, Kral, who worked at the camp hospital, noted that while most detainees became depressed, few experienced clinical anxiety. He wrote that those who had before the war suffered from "severe and long-lasting psychoneuroses such as phobias and compulsive obsessive neuroses" found that their ailments had gone into remission. "[Patients'] neuroses either disappeared completely in Theresienstadt or improved to such a degree that patients would work and did not have to seek medical aid." Interestingly, those patients who survived the war relapsed into their old neurotic patterns afterward. It was as though real fear crowded out their neurotic anxiety; when the fear relented, the anxiety crept back.

Military psychiatrists have collected a lot of data on what kinds of situations cause soldiers the greatest anxiety. Many studies have shown that the amount of control a soldier feels he has strongly determines how much anxiety he experiences. As Roy Grinker and his colleagues first described in *Men Under Stress*, the classic study of combat neuroses during World War II, while fighter pilots were terrified of flak shot from the ground, they found fighting with enemy planes to be exhilarating.*

Combat trauma is a powerful psychic destroyer: many soldiers break down emotionally during war; still more break down afterward. Vietnam produced thousands of traumatized soldiers, many of whom ended up homeless and addicted to drugs. Some fifty-eight thousand U.S. soldiers died during active combat in Vietnam between 1965 and 1975—but an even greater number have committed suicide since then. Suicide is also rampant among veterans of our recent wars in Iraq and Afghanistan. According to numbers from the Army Behavioral Health Integrated Data Environment, the suicide rate among active-duty soldiers increased 80 percent between 2004 and 2008; a 2012 study published in *Injury Prevention* reported that the number of suicides is "unprecedented in over 30 years of U.S. Army records." A study in *The Journal of the American Medical Association* concluded that more than 10 percent of Afghanistan veterans and nearly 20 percent of Iraq veterans suffer from anxiety or depression. Other studies have found massive rates of antidepressant and tranquilizer consumption among Iraq veterans; ABC News reports that one in three soldiers is now taking psychiatric medication. The mortality rates for those who break down under combat stress are much higher than for those who don't: a

---

* The relationship between lack of control and anxiety has been demonstrated many times over the years in noncombat situations, too. Researchers have produced ulcers in mice simply by depriving them of control over their environment, and a raft of studies have demonstrated that people in jobs where they don't perceive themselves to have a lot of control are much more susceptible to developing clinical anxiety and depression, as well as stress-related medical conditions like ulcers and diabetes.

recent study published in the *Annals of Epidemiology* showed that army veterans diagnosed with post-traumatic stress disorder have twice the premature death rate of their unafflicted peers. The rates of postcombat suicide have become so high in recent years that the U.S. military has made providing prophylactic treatment for post-traumatic stress disorder a high priority. In 2012, the suicide rate reached a ten-year high—a staggering eighteen current and former servicemen are killing themselves every day in the United States, according to Admiral Mike Mullen, the former chairman of the Joint Chiefs of Staff.

Of course, until 1980, when the diagnosis was decreed into existence alongside the other anxiety disorders with the publication of the *DSM-III,* there was officially no such thing as PTSD.* As with social anxiety disorder, there remains some controversy over whether such a thing as post-traumatic stress disorder really exists in nature—and over whether, if it does, how broadly it should be defined. These debates inevitably get politicized because of the billions of dollars at stake in veterans' medical benefits and drug company revenues and because of abiding tensions over the distinction between moral cowardice and a medical condition. For its part, the U.S. military today views PTSD as a real and serious problem and is dedicating considerable resources to researching its causes, treatment, and prevention. The Pentagon underwrites many studies of Navy SEALs, generally the toughest, most resilient soldiers in the military, to uncover what combination of genes, neurochemistry, and—especially—training makes them so mentally formidable. Experiments have consistently found that SEALs think more clearly, and make faster and better decisions, than other soldiers in chaotic or stressful situations.

As important as the nature of the combat stress a soldier experiences is, recent findings in neuroscience and genetics suggest that the nature of the soldier may be more important in contributing to the likelihood of a nervous breakdown. Whether you are more likely to break down under modest combat stress or to remain implacable even under

---

* PTSD is the successor to soldier's heart, shell shock, battle fatigue, and war neurosis, among other diagnoses.

extreme wartime conditions may be largely attributable to the neuro-chemicals you bring to the battle, and these are partly a product of your genes.

Andy Morgan, a psychiatrist at the Yale School of Medicine, has studied the Special Operations Forces trainees at Fort Bragg who undergo the famous SERE (Survival, Evasion, Resistance, and Escape) program. These aspiring Navy SEALs and Green Berets are exposed to three weeks of extreme physical and psychological hardship to deter-mine whether they could withstand the stress of being a prisoner of war. They endure pain, sleep deprivation, isolation, and interrogation—including "advanced techniques" such as waterboarding. The trainees selected for the program have already made it through a couple of years of training at places such as Fort Bragg's John F. Kennedy Special Warfare Center and School. The physically and psychologically weak get weeded out long before SERE. But even for the elite troops who make it this far, SERE can be astonishingly stressful. In a 2001 paper, Morgan and his collaborators noted that recorded changes in the stress hormone cortisol during SERE "were some of the greatest ever docu-mented in humans"—greater even than those associated with open-heart surgery.

Morgan recently discovered that the Special Forces recruits who performed most effectively during SERE had significantly higher levels—as much as one-third higher—of a brain chemical called neuro-peptide Y than the poorer-performing recruits did. Discovered in 1982, neuropeptide Y (or NPY, as the researchers call it) is the most abundant peptide in the brain, involved in regulating diet and balance—and the stress response. Some individuals with high NPY levels seem *completely immune to* developing post-traumatic stress disorder—no amount of stress can break them. The correlation between NPY and stress resis-tance is so strong that Morgan has found he can predict with remark-able accuracy who will graduate from Special Forces training and who will not simply by performing a blood test. Those with high NPY levels will graduate; those with low levels will not. Somehow, NPY confers psychological resistance and resilience.*

---

* Researchers are currently investigating whether administering NPY via a nasal spray could help block the development of post-traumatic stress disorder.

It's possible that those in the Special Forces who thrive under pressure have *learned* to be resilient—that their high NPY levels are the product of their training or their upbringing. Resilience is a trait that can be taught; the Pentagon is spending millions trying to figure out how to do that better. But studies suggest that a person's allotment of NPY is relatively fixed from birth, more a function of heredity than of learning. Researchers at the University of Michigan have found correlations not only between which variation of the NPY gene you have and how much of the neurotransmitter you produce but also between how much NPY you produce and how intensely you react to negative events. People with low levels of NPY showed more hyperreactivity in the "negative emotion circuits" of the brain (such as the right amygdala) than people with high NPY levels and were much slower to return to calm brain states after a stressful event. They were also more likely to have had episodes of major depression—and that was independent of anything having to do with their serotonin systems, which is where much of the neuroscience research over the last few decades has been concentrated. Conversely, having ample quantities of NPY seems to prepare you to thrive under stress.

Other research has found that soldiers whose bodies are more reactive to stress hormones are more likely to crack under pressure. A 2010 study published in *The American Journal of Psychiatry* concluded that soldiers with more glucocorticoid receptors in their blood cells were at greater risk for developing PTSD after combat. Studies like this tend to validate the idea that how likely you are to break down under pressure is largely determined by the relative sensitivity of your hypothalamic-pituitary-adrenal axis: if you have a hypersensitive HPA axis, you're much more likely to develop PTSD or some other anxiety disorder in the aftermath of a traumatic experience; if you have a low-reactive HPA axis, you will be much more resistant, if not largely immune, to developing PTSD. And while we know that lots of things condition the sensitivity of your HPA axis—from how much affection your parents gave you to your diet to the nature of the trauma itself—your genes are a major determinant. All of which suggests a strong correlation between your genetically conferred physiology and how likely you are to crack under stress.

But if grace under pressure is largely a matter of the quantity of a certain peptide in the brain, or of your inborn level of HPA sensitivity, what kind of grace is that?

The hero and the coward both feel the same thing, but the hero uses his fear, projects it onto his opponent, while the coward runs. It's the same thing, fear, but it's what you do with it that matters.
—CUS D'AMATO, BOXING MANAGER WHO TRAINED
FLOYD PATTERSON AND MIKE TYSON

Are those of us with hypersensitive HPA axes, our bodies set to quivering like mice in response to the mildest perturbances, doomed to falter at the moments of greatest importance? Destined, like Aristodemus the Trembler and Roberto Durán, for shame and humiliation? Fated always to be victims of our twitchy bodies and unruly emotions?

Not necessarily. Because when you begin to untangle the relationships between anxiety and performance, and between grace and courage, they turn out to be more complicated than they at first seem. Maybe it's possible to be simultaneously anxious and effective, cowardly and strong, terrified and heroic.

Bill Russell is a Hall of Fame basketball player who won eleven championships with the Boston Celtics (the most by anyone in any major American sport, ever), was selected to the NBA All-Star team twelve times, and was voted the league's most valuable player five times. He is generally acknowledged to be the greatest defender and all-around winner of his era, if not of all time. He is the only athlete in history, in any sport, to win a national college championship, an Olympic gold medal, and a professional championship. No one would question Russell's toughness or his championship qualities or his courage. And yet, to my amazement, this is a man who vomited from anxiety before the majority of the games he played in. According to one tabulation, Russell vomited before 1,128 of his games between 1956 and 1969, which would put him nearly in Charles Darwin territory. "[Russell] used to throw up all the time before a game, or at halftime," his teammate John Havlicek told the writer George Plimpton in 1968. "It's a welcome sound, too, because it means he's keyed up for the game and around the locker room we grin and say, 'Man, we're going to be all right tonight.'"

Like someone with an anxiety disorder, Russell had to contend with nerves that wreaked havoc with his stomach. But a crucial difference between Russell and the typical anxiety patient (aside, of course, from Russell's preternatural athleticism) was that there was a positive correlation between his anxiety and his performance—and therefore between his upset stomach and his performance. Once, in 1960, when the Celtics' coach noted with concern that Russell *hadn't* vomited yet, he ordered that the pregame warm-up be suspended until Russell could regurgitate. When Russell stopped throwing up for a stretch at the end of the 1963 season, he suffered through one of the worst slumps of his career. Fortunately, when the play-offs started that year and he saw the crowd gathering before the opening game, he felt his nerves jangling, and he resumed his nervous vomiting—and then went out and gave his best performance of the season. For Russell, a nervous stomach correlated with effective, even enhanced, performance.*

Nor is cowardice always necessarily an impediment to greatness. In 1956, Floyd Patterson, at the age of twenty-one, became the youngest world heavyweight boxing champion. Then, in a series of classic bouts with Ingemar Johansson between 1959 and 1961, he became the first boxer in history to regain the title after losing it. The following year he lost the title for good in a match against Sonny Liston, but he remained an intermittent contender for another decade, fighting against Liston, Jimmy Ellis, and Muhammad Ali.

Patterson was tough and fierce and strong—for several years, by

---

* Of course, when a nervous stomach impairs performance, the complexion changes dramatically. Consider the difference between Bill Russell and Donovan McNabb, the quarterback for the Philadelphia Eagles during the 2005 Super Bowl. Like Russell, McNabb was an elite athlete. A six-time Pro Bowler and the holder of almost all the Eagles' passing records, McNabb was one of the most successful college and pro quarterbacks of his generation. Yet despite many playoff victories, McNabb, unlike Russell, never won a championship—and ever since his team lost that 2005 Super Bowl game, he has been dogged by the claims of several teammates (which McNabb denies) that he was vomiting in the huddle and couldn't call plays. (The debate over whether McNabb did or did not vomit in the huddle still continues eight years after the game, and has been called "one of the great mysteries in the history of sport.") The implication is that McNabb, for all his athletic talent, was overwhelmed by the pressure of the occasion and succumbed to nerves, that he lacked the leadership qualities, the toughness—the literal intestinal fortitude—to keep his stomach in check and lead the Eagles to victory. McNabb has never been seen the same way since. (Augmenting his reputation as a choker: McNabb's stats in crucial playoff games were markedly worse than his stats in ordinary regular-season games.)

dint of being heavyweight champion, probably among the toughest and fiercest and strongest men in the world. Yet he was also, by his own account, a coward. After his first defeat by Liston, he took to bringing disguises—fake beards and mustaches, hats—to his fights, in case he lost his nerve and wanted to slip out of the dressing room before the bout or to hide afterward if he lost. In 1964, the writer Gay Talese, who was profiling Patterson for *Esquire,* asked him about his penchant for carrying disguises.

"You must wonder what makes a man do things like this," Patterson said. "Well, I wonder too. And the answer is, I don't know . . . but I think that within me, within every human being, there is a certain weakness. It is a weakness that exposes itself more when you're alone. And I have figured out that part of the reason I do the things I do, and cannot seem to conquer that one word—*myself*—is because . . . is because . . . I am a coward."

Of course, Patterson's definition of cowardice might be different from yours or mine; it's hardly conventional.* But it nevertheless suggests that inner anxiety can be coupled with the outer appearance of physical bravery, that weakness is not incompatible with strength.

In rare instances, anxiety can even be the source of heroism. During the 1940s, Giuseppe Pardo Roques was the leader of the Jewish community in Pisa, Italy. He was widely respected as a spiritual guide—but he was also impaired by crippling anxiety, in particular by an overwhelming phobia of animals. Hoping to conquer his anxiety, he tried everything: sedatives, "tonics" (neurophosphates meant to strengthen the nervous system), psychoanalysis with one of Freud's protégés, and—in an endeavor I can relate to—reading everything he could get his hands on, from Hippocrates to Freud, about the theory and science of phobias. Nothing worked; his phobia dominated his life. He was unable to travel—was barely able to leave his house—because of the irrational fear that he would be set upon by dogs. When he did muster the courage to walk the streets, he would swing a cane wildly around

---

* "When did you first think you were a coward?" Talese asked him. "It was after the first Ingemar fight," Patterson said. "It's in defeat that a man reveals himself. In defeat, I can't face people. I haven't the strength to say to people, 'I did my best, I'm sorry,' and whatnot."

himself at all times to fend off the animals he feared might attack. After neighbors acquired a pet dog, he contrived a reason to get them evicted because he couldn't bear to have an animal so close by. He spent hours every day completing elaborate rituals meant to assure him there were no animals in his house. (Today, he would be diagnosed with OCD.)

Roques recognized the irrationality of his fear but was powerless to overcome it. "Its intensity is just as great as its absurdity," he once said. "I am lost. My heart beats fast; my face no doubt changes expression. I am no longer myself. The panic increases, and the fear of the fear increases the fear. A crescendo of suffering engulfs me. I believe I will not be able to hold my own. I search for help; I don't know where to find it. I am ashamed to ask for help, and yet I am afraid the fear will make me die. I do die, like a coward, a thousand deaths."

Silvano Arieti, a young man who lived in the community, was fascinated by Roques. How was it, Arieti asked himself, that a man as brilliant and wise as Roques could allow his life to be circumscribed by so irrational a fear? Roques was afraid to travel—he had never left Pisa in all his sixty years—and there were days when his anxiety was so bad that he couldn't even leave his bedroom. But—and here's what was so fascinating to Arieti—Roques showed himself in other ways "to be an utterly fearless man, courageously prepared to defend the underprivileged, the underdog, the distressed in any way. . . . His almost constant fear was accompanied by a constantly available courage." He could handle "real" fears and, in fact, would bravely help others beset by them. But his own phobias, "in their fully tragic intensity," he was helpless to do anything about. Was there a link, Arieti wondered, between Roques's moral strength and his mental illness?

Many years later, after he had moved to America and become one of the world's foremost scholars on mental illness, Arieti would publish a book, *The Parnas: A Scene from the Holocaust* (1979), in which he recounted what happened in Pisa after the Germans occupied part of Italy. Throughout 1943 and 1944, as first the Italian Fascists and then the Nazis terrorized Pisa's Jewish community, most Jews fled. But Roques, prevented by his anxiety from traveling, stayed in Pisa. "The idea of going far away from home, to another city, or to the country, increases my anxiety to the point of panic," Roques told six friends who chose for various reasons to remain in the city with him. "I know that these fears are absurd to the point of being ridiculous, but it is useless to tell myself so. I cannot overcome them." When his followers tried to attribute his willingness to brave bombs and Nazis to courage or spiritual grace, Roques demurred. His illness, he said, "has caused such a narrowing of my life, not to mention gossip and ridicule, and has shadowed my whole existence. I live, trembling, with a totally irrational fear of animals, especially of dogs. I also have a fear of the fear itself.... Had I not felt this sick fear constantly, I would not be here; I would be far away. What you call a special gift is illness." But the fact that his fear of dogs was greater than his fear of bombs and Nazis made him appear brave.

Early on the morning of August 1, 1944, the Nazis arrived at Roques's home and demanded that he surrender the guests who were staying with him. He refused.

"Aren't you afraid of dying?" the Nazis demanded. "We will kill you, you filthy Jew."

"I am not afraid," he told them.

And according to those who survived and were later interviewed by Arieti, Roques manifestly was not afraid, even though he knew the Nazis were about to murder him. As real danger approached, he appeared to be free of fear.*

Giuseppe Pardo Roques was not the only Pisan imprisoned by his

---

* In his book, Arieti elaborates a theory about why this should have been the case. His view was that Roques's phobia of and disgust at animals was a displacement of his disgust at the evil inherent in man. As a young boy, Roques had been happy and optimistic. But during his studies as an adolescent, he discovered the facts of the Crusades, the Inquisition, and the myriad other horrors that man has visited upon man across history. He couldn't bear this. To preserve a loving view of humankind, and a view of the world as a friendly place, Arieti theorizes, Roques projected onto animals the evil that is in man, preferring to fear animals rather than give up his view of mankind as essentially good. When Roques was confronted unavoidably with evil in the form of the Nazis, his animal phobia disappeared. This, Arieti argues, gives his phobic anxiety an almost spiritual quality, since it permitted him to displace revulsion and anxiety onto insentient creatures, allowing him to retain love for humankind.

"When the sensitive youngster has made these unpleasant realizations [about the evil in man and the danger and hardship of existence]," Arieti writes, "he has difficulties in facing life. How can he trust, how can he love or retain a loving attitude towards fellow human beings? He might then become suspicious and paranoid; he might become a detached person unable to love. But this is not the case with the phobic. The phobic is a person who retains his ability to love. As a matter of fact, in my long psychiatric career I have never seen a phobic person who was not a loving person." We are born, it seems, into a Rousseauian state of innocence, but if we accurately observe life and human nature, we must adopt a Hobbesian defensive crouch against life's depredations. Phobias sublimate our Hobbesian horror into neurotic and irrational fears, Arieti argues, allowing us to preserve a more innocent and loving stance toward the world.

anxiety during the war. When the bombs started falling, reducing parts of the city to rubble, most people left. But Pietro, a young man who lived not far from Roques, could not go more than a block from his house; his agoraphobia would not permit it. So he stayed home. Pietro would sooner have had a bomb dropped on his head than endure the terror that seized him when he walked too far from his house. "The fear caused by the neurosis was stronger than the fear of the dangers of the war," Arieti observes.

Pietro survived the war—and ended up decorated as a hero for his courage. After each bombing, he would run out into the ruins (so long as they were within a block of his house) and free people trapped in them. In this way, he saved several lives. Only because he was constrained by his phobia was he available to help the bombing victims. "His illness made him become a hero," Arieti writes.

To someone who suffers from anxiety, the stories of Roques and Pietro, and of Bill Russell and Floyd Patterson, hold obvious appeal; in their anxiety lies not just redemption but a source of moral heroism and even, perhaps, a strange sort of courage.

PART III

Drugs

CHAPTER 5

"A Sack of Enzymes"

From time immemorial, [drugs] have been making possible some degree of self-transcendence and a temporary release from tension.
—ALDOUS HUXLEY, IN A MAY 9, 1957, PRESENTATION TO THE NEW YORK ACADEMY OF SCIENCE

Wine drunk with an equal quantity of water puts away anxiety and terror.

—HIPPOCRATES, *APHORISMS* (FOURTH CENTURY B.C.)

In anticipation of the release of my first book, in the spring of 2004, my publisher arranged a modest publicity tour that entailed national television and radio appearances, as well as bookstore readings and public lectures around the country. This should have been a delightful prospect—the chance to promote my book, to travel on someone else's nickel, to connect with readers, to achieve a kind of temporary, two-bit celebrity. But I can scarcely convey what powerful dread this book tour conjured in me.

In desperation, I sought help from multiple sources. I first went to a prominent Harvard psychopharmacologist who had been recommended by my principal psychiatrist a year earlier. "You have an anxiety disorder," the psychopharmacologist had told me after taking my case history at our initial consultation. "Fortunately, this is highly treatable. We just need to get you properly medicated." When I gave him my standard objections to reliance on medication (worry about side effects, concerns about drug dependency, discomfort with the idea of taking pills that might affect my mind and change who I am), he resorted to the clichéd—but nonetheless potent—diabetes argument, which goes like this: "Your anxiety has a biological, physiological, and genetic basis; it is a medical illness, just like diabetes is. If you were a diabetic, you wouldn't have such qualms about taking insulin, would you? And you wouldn't see your diabetes as a moral failing, would you?" I'd had versions of this discussion with various psychiatrists many times over the years. I would try to resist whatever the latest drug was, feeling that this resistance was somehow noble or moral, that reliance on medication evinced weakness of character, that my anxiety was an integral and worthwhile component of who I am, and that there was redemption in suffering—until, inevitably, my anxiety would become so acute that I would be willing to try anything, including the new medication. So, as usual, I capitulated, and as the book tour loomed, I resumed a course of benzodiazepines (Xanax during the day, Klonopin at night) and increased my dosage of Celexa, the SSRI antidepressant I was already taking.

But even drugged to the gills, I remained filled with dread about the impending book tour, so I went also to a young but highly regarded Stanford-trained psychologist who specialized in cognitive behavioral therapy, or CBT. "First thing we've got to do," she said in one of my early sessions with her, "is to get you off these drugs." A few sessions later, she offered to take my Xanax from me and lock it in a drawer in her desk. She opened the drawer to show me the bottles deposited there by some of her other patients, holding one up and shaking it for effect. The drugs, she said, were a crutch that prevented me from truly experiencing and thereby confronting my anxiety; if I didn't expose myself to the raw experience of anxiety, I would never learn that I could cope with it on my own.

She was right, I knew. Exposure therapy is based on fully experiencing your anxiety, which is hard to do if you're taking antianxiety medications. But with the book tour looming, my fear was that I might *not*, in fact, be able to cope with it.

I went back to the Harvard psychopharmacologist (let's call him Dr. Harvard) and described the course of action the Stanford psychologist (let's call her Dr. Stanford) had proposed. "It's your call," he said. "You could try giving up the medication. But your anxiety is clearly so deeply rooted in your biology that even mild stress provokes it. Only medication can control your biological reaction. And it may well be that your anxiety is so acute that the only way you'll be able to get to the point where any kind of behavioral therapy can begin to be effective is by taking the edge off your physical symptoms with drugs."

"What if I get addicted to Xanax and have to be on it all my life?" I asked. Benzodiazepines are notorious for inducing dependency. Withdrawing too suddenly from them can produce horrific side effects.

"So what if you do?" he said. "I have a patient coming in this afternoon who's been taking it for twenty years. She couldn't live without it."

At my next session with Dr. Stanford, I told her I was afraid to give up my Xanax and related what Dr. Harvard had said to me. She looked betrayed. I thought for a moment that she might cry. After that, I stopped telling her about my visits to Dr. Harvard. My continued consultations with him felt illicit.

Dr. Stanford was more likable, and more pleasant to talk to, than Dr. Harvard; she tried to understand what caused my anxiety and seemed to care about me as an individual personality. Dr. Harvard, on the other hand, seemed to see me as a type—an anxiety patient—to be treated with a one-size-fits-all solution: drugs. One day I read in the newspaper that he was treating a depressed gorilla at the local zoo. Dr. Harvard's treatment of choice for the gorilla in question? Celexa, the same SSRI he was prescribing for me.

I can't say for certain whether the drug worked for the gorilla. Reportedly, it did. But could there be a more potent demonstration that Dr. Harvard's approach to treatment was resolutely biological? For him, the content of any psychic distress—and certainly the meaning of it—mattered less than the fact of it: such distress, whether in a human or some other primate, was a medical-biological malfunction that could be fixed with drugs.

What to do? Dr. Harvard was telling me that I, like the gorilla, had a medical problem in need of pharmaceutical intervention. Dr. Stanford was telling me that my problem was not principally biological but rather cognitive: if I could simply correct dysfunctions in how I thought (through force of will and cognitive retraining and direct exposure to my greatest fears), then my anxiety would be reduced. But the drugs I was on, Dr. Stanford said, were impeding my ability to address those dysfunctions in an effective way.*

I kept trying to give up my Klonopin and Xanax in order to do proper cognitive retraining, and I would sometimes even succeed at this in small ways—only to be overwhelmed with anxiety again and resort to fumbling miserably through my pockets for the Xanax. As much as I would have liked to have cured myself through fixing my thinking, or achieving spiritual peace, or simply learning to cope, I seemed always to be ending up like the depressed gorilla, in need of artificial adjustments to my neurotransmitters to fix my anxious, broken brain.

> *Tranquilizers, by attenuating the disruptive influence of anxiety on the mind, open the way to a better and more coordinated use of the existing gifts. By doing this, they are adding to happiness, human achievement, and the dignity of man.*
> —FRANK BERGER, "ANXIETY AND THE DISCOVERY OF TRANQUILIZERS," IN *Discoveries in Biological Psychiatry* (1970)

> *To what extent would Western culture be altered by widespread use of tranquilizers? Would Yankee initiative disappear? Is the chemical deadening of anxiety harmful?*
> —STANLEY YOLLES, DIRECTOR OF THE NATIONAL INSTITUTE OF MENTAL HEALTH, IN TESTIMONY GIVEN TO THE U.S. SENATE SELECT COMMITTEE ON SMALL BUSINESS, MAY 1967

Sigmund Freud, the father of psychoanalysis, relied heavily on drugs in managing his anxiety. Six of his earliest scientific papers were on the benefits of cocaine, which he used regularly for at least a decade beginning in the 1880s. "In my last serious depression I took cocaine again," he wrote to his wife in 1884, "and a small dose lifted me to the heights in a wonderful fashion. I am just now collecting the literature

---

* Actually, Dr. Stanford also conceded a strong biological component to anxiety; her view was that biology can be overcome by cognitive retraining. And research does suggest that cognitive retraining, as well as other forms of talk therapy, can *change* biology in the same way that medication does, sometimes more profoundly and enduringly—a literal manifestation of mind over matter.

for a song of praise to this magical substance." He believed his research on the drug's medicinal properties would make him famous. Deeming the drug to be no more addictive than coffee, he prescribed it, to himself and to others, as a treatment for everything from nervous tension and melancholy to indigestion and morphine addiction. Freud called cocaine a "magic drug": "I take very small doses of it regularly against depression and against indigestion, and with the most brilliant success." He also took it to alleviate his social anxiety before the evening salons he attended at the Paris home of his mentor Jean-Martin Charcot.* Only after he prescribed cocaine to a close friend who went on to become fatally addicted did Freud's enthusiasm for the drug wane. But by then Freud's own experience with cocaine had solidified his conviction that some mental illnesses have a physical basis in the brain. It is an irony of medical history that even as Freud's later work would make him the progenitor of modern psychodynamic psychotherapy, which is generally premised on the idea that mental illness arises from unconscious psychological conflicts, his papers on cocaine make him one of the fathers of biological psychiatry, which is governed by the notion that mental distress is partly caused by a physical or chemical malfunction that can be treated with drugs.

Much of the history of modern psychopharmacology has the same ad hoc quality as Freud's experimentation with cocaine. Every one of the most commercially significant classes of antianxiety and antidepressant drugs of the last sixty years was discovered by accident or was originally developed for something completely unrelated to anxiety or depression: to treat tuberculosis, surgical shock, allergies; to use as an insecticide, a penicillin preservative, an industrial dye, a disinfectant, rocket fuel.

Yet despite its haphazardness, the recent history of psychopharmacology has shaped our modern understanding of mental illness. Recall that neither "anxiety" nor "depression"—two terms that today have become part of both the medical and the popular lexicon—existed as clinical categories half a century ago. Before the 1920s, no one had ever

---

* Freud was also, by his own admission, addicted to nicotine, smoking twenty or more cigars a day for most of his life, a habit that would reward him with mouth cancer in his sixties.

been diagnosed with depression; before the 1950s, hardly anyone was diagnosed with straightforward anxiety.

So what changed? One answer is that pharmaceutical companies in effect *created* these categories. What began as targets for marketing campaigns eventually became reified as diseases.

By this I do not mean to suggest that before the 1950s people were not "anxious" or "depressed" in the senses we understand those words today. Some people, some percentage of the time, have always felt pathologically unhappy and afraid. This was the case for millennia before the terms "anxiety" and "depression" were popularized to describe emotional states or clinical disorders. ("The tears of the world are a constant quantity," as Samuel Beckett put it.) But not until the middle of the last century, when new drugs geared toward mitigating these emotional states were concocted, did these states get delimited as the "diseases" we understand them to be today.

Before 1906, when the fledgling Food and Drug Administration started requiring drugmakers to list their products' ingredients, consumers didn't realize that in taking some of the most popular antianxiety remedies of the time—such as Neurosine or Dr. Miles's Nervine (advertised as "the scientific remedy for nervous disorders") or Wheller's Nerve Vitalizers or Rexall's Americanitis Elixir—they were ingesting alcohol or marijuana or opium.* In 1897, the German drug company Bayer began marketing diacetylmorphine, a compound that had been widely used on the battlefields of the American Civil War and the Franco-Prussian War, as a painkiller and cough suppressant. This new medication—under the trade name Heroin—was available in American pharmacies without a prescription until 1914.† The 1899 edition of

---

* Some doctors prescribed straight alcohol. In the 1890s, Adolphus Bridger, an influential London physician and the author of such popular medical books as *The Demon of Dyspepsia* and *Man and His Maladies*, told patients suffering from tension and melancholy to drink port and brandy. He wrote that "a suitable form of alcohol"—especially "full-bodied Burgundy, high class claret, port, the better white French, German, and Italian wines, stout or good brandy"—would "do more to restore nervous health" than any other medicine.

† Two years later, Bayer brought out another analgesic, acetylsalicylic acid, under the brand name Aspirin. In time, as Heroin and Aspirin became ubiquitous, both went from being brand names to generic terms. Turn-of-the-century physicians in America and England had a somewhat backward understanding of these medications, often giving Heroin to their patients for physical pain (which, in fairness, made a certain sense) and administering Aspirin for "nervousness" (which did not).

The Merck Manual, then as now a respected compendium of the most up-to-date medical information, recommended opium as a standard treatment for anxiety.

The serene confidence with which *The Merck Manual*—as well as the physicians and apothecaries of the time—glibly dispensed recommendations for drugs we now know to be addictive, unhealthy, or useless raises the question of whether we should place much trust in the similarly serene confidence of the physicians and drug manuals of today. Yes, today's researchers and clinicians are armed with data from controlled studies and findings from neuroimaging and blood assays, and they are buttressed—or held back, depending on your perspective—by a more cautious FDA that demands years' worth of animal testing and clinical trials before a drug can be approved for sale. But a hundred years from now, medical historians may once again be marveling at the addictive, toxic, or useless substances we consume in such great quantities today.

For the first half of the twentieth century, barbiturates were the most popular remedy for strained nerves. Originally synthesized in 1864 by a German chemist who combined condensed urea (found in animal waste) with diethyl malonate (which derives from the acid in apples), barbituric acid seemed, at first, to have no productive use. But in 1903, when researchers at Bayer gave barbituric acid to dogs, the dogs fell asleep. Within months, Bayer was marketing barbital, the first commercially available barbiturate, to consumers. (Bayer named the drug Veronal because one of its scientists believed Verona, Italy, to be the most peaceful city on earth.) In 1911, the company released a longer-acting barbiturate, phenobarbital, under the trade name Luminal, which would go on to become the most popular drug in the category. By the 1930s, barbiturates had almost completely displaced their late nineteenth-century predecessors—chloral hydrate and bromides, as well as opium—as the treatment of choice for "nerve troubles."*

---

* Potassium bromide, a compound introduced at a British medical conference in 1857, was originally used as an antiseizure medication and was, from the late nineteenth century into the early twentieth, popular as a sedative. Eventually, the toxicity and side effects of bromides, ranging from a bitter aftertaste and acne to dizziness, severe nausea, and vomiting, led to their abandonment (today they are used almost exclusively in veterinary medicine for dogs and cats with epilepsy), but their use was widespread enough for long enough that the word "bromide" also came to mean a soporific platitude. Chloral

As early as 1906, so many Americans were taking, and sometimes overdosing on, Veronal that *The New York Times* editorialized against the overprescription of such "quick-cure nostrums," but to little effect: in the 1930s, *The Merck Manual* was still recommending Veronal for the treatment of "extreme nervousness, neurasthenia, hypochondria, melancholia," and other "conditions of anxiety." Veronal and Luminal—advertised as "aspirin for the mind"—dominated what would today be called the anxiety medication market for decades. By 1947, there were thirty different barbiturates being sold under separate trade names in the United States; the three most popular were Amytal (amobarbital), Nembutal (pentobarbital), and Seconal (secobarbital). Since "anxiety" and "depression" didn't officially exist yet, the barbiturates tended to be prescribed for "nerves" (or "nerve troubles"), "tension," and insomnia.

But the barbiturates had two big drawbacks: they were highly addictive, and accidental overdoses were common and often lethal. In 1950, at least a thousand Americans fatally overdosed on barbiturates. (My great-grandmother and Marilyn Monroe, among many others, would go on to do so in the 1960s.) In 1951, *The New York Times* called barbiturates "more of a menace to society than heroin or morphine" and declared that "the matron who regards a pink pill as much of a bedtime necessity as brushing her teeth, the tense business man who gulps a white capsule to ease his nerves before an important conference, the college student who swallows a yellow 'goof ball' to breeze through an examination, and the actor who takes a 'blue angel' to bolster his self-confidence are aware that excessive use of barbiturates is 'not good for the system,' but are ignorant of the extent of the hazard."

You would think that such heavy consumption of barbiturates would have made drug companies keen to develop new and better nostrums. But when Frank Berger, a research scientist at the Wallace Laboratories subsidiary of Carter Products, tried to interest company executives in a new antianxiety medication he had synthesized in the late 1940s, they

---

hydrate, a sleep-inducing agent first synthesized in 1832, was added to doctors' psychotropic toolkit in 1869 after Otto Liebrich, a professor of pharmacology in Berlin, gave the substance to melancholic patients and observed that it alleviated their insomnia. A hundred years later, my great-grandfather would be prescribed chloral hydrate for his tension and insomnia. (Chloral hydrate was also one of the active ingredients, along with alcohol, in the Mickey Finn, a doctored drink that often featured in Depression-era potboilers.)

showed no interest. For one thing, they argued, therapy for anxiety was supposed to focus on psychological issues or unresolved personal problems, not on biology or chemistry—a distinction that from the vantage point of modern biological psychiatry seems quaint. Besides, psychoactive drugs lay outside Carter's usual commercial domain, which consisted of such things as laxatives (Carter's Little Liver Pills), deodorant (Arrid), and depilatory cream (Nair).

Berger had stumbled on the antianxiety properties of this new substance entirely by accident. Born in what is now the Czech Republic in 1913, Berger had, after earning his medical degree at the University of Prague, conducted immunology research that established him as a promising scientist. But when Hitler annexed Austria and seemed poised to claim Czechoslovakia, Berger, who was Jewish, escaped to London.

Unable to find work there, Berger and his wife became homeless, sleeping on park benches and eating at soup kitchens. Eventually, Berger got a job as a doctor in a refugee camp, where he learned English, and then moved on to a job as an antibiotics researcher at the Public Health Laboratory near Leeds.

By 1941, penicillin had been demonstrated to be an effective treatment for bacterial infections. But manufacturing and preserving penicillin in quantities large enough to be useful in fighting infections among Allied soldiers proved vexing. "The mold is as temperamental as an opera singer," lamented one pharmaceutical executive. So Berger, along with hundreds of other scientists, went to work trying to find better extraction and purification techniques for the revolutionary antibiotic. He was particularly successful in developing a method for preserving the mold long enough to distribute it more widely. After his research was published in prestigious scientific journals, a British drug company offered the once-homeless chemist a high-ranking position.

One of the penicillin preservatives Berger tested was a compound called mephenesin, which he had synthesized by modifying a commercially available disinfectant. When he injected mice with mephenesin to test its toxicity, Berger observed something he'd never seen before: "The compound had a quieting effect on the demeanor of the animals."

Berger had, quite by accident, discovered the first of a revolutionary new class of drugs. When mephenesin was found to have a similar sedating effect on humans, the Squibb Corporation, recognizing a commercial opportunity, began distributing mephenesin as a drug to induce relaxation before surgery. Sold under the trade name Tolserol, mephenesin had by 1949 become one of Squibb's most prescribed drugs.

But mephenesin wasn't very potent in pill form, and its effects were short-lived. Berger resolved to develop a more powerful version. In the summer of 1949, he took a job as the president and medical director of Carter's Wallace Labs subsidiary in New Brunswick, New Jersey. There, Berger and his team set to work synthesizing and testing compounds that might prove more potent than mephenesin. Eventually, they identified a dozen (out of the roughly five hundred they synthesized) that seemed promising; after more experiments on animals, they narrowed the list down to four and then to one, called meprobamate, which they patented in July 1950. Berger's team found that meprobamate relaxed mice. The effect on monkeys was even more vivid. "We had about twenty Rhesus and Java monkeys," Berger would later tell the medical historian Andrea Tone. "They're vicious, and you've got to wear thick gloves and a face guard when you handle them." But after they were injected with meprobamate, they became "very nice monkeys—friendly and alert." Further testing revealed meprobamate to be longer lasting than mephenesin and less toxic than barbiturates.

Meanwhile, two new papers in top medical journals were providing the first reports of the therapeutic effects of mephenesin—which, remember, was less potent than meprobamate. One of the studies, conducted by doctors at the University of Oregon, found that when mephenesin was given to 124 patients who had sought treatment from their physicians for "anxiety tension states," more than half experienced a significant reduction in anxiety—to the point where they resembled, in the words of the researchers, "individuals who are pleasantly and comfortably at ease." Other reports from mental hospitals showed similar results. Soon the first small-scale studies of meprobamate were finding the same thing: the drug significantly reduced what doctors of the time tended to call "tension."

These studies were among the first to measure in any kind of systematic way the effects of a drug on the mental states of human beings. Today, when reports on randomized controlled trials of the efficacy of various psychotropic drugs are published by the score every month in newspapers and medical journals, this kind of study seems routine. But at midcentury the notion that psychiatric drugs could be widely and safely prescribed—let alone scientifically measured—was novel.

So novel, in fact, that Carter executives didn't believe there was a market for such a drug. They retained a polling company to ask two hundred primary care physicians whether they would be willing to prescribe a pill that would help patients with the stresses of day-to-day life—and a large majority of them said they would not. Frustrated, Berger persisted on his own, sending meprobamate pills to two psychiatrists he knew, one in New Jersey and one in Florida, for testing. The New Jersey psychiatrist reported back that meprobamate had helped 78 percent of his patients suffering from what we would today call anxiety disorders—they became more sociable, slept better, and in some cases returned to work after being housebound. The psychiatrist in Florida gave the drug to 187 patients and found that 95 percent of those with "tension" improved or recovered on meprobamate.

"When I first came in here, I couldn't even listen to the radio. I thought I was going crazy," one of the Florida psychiatrist's patients reported after a few months on meprobamate. "I now go to football games, shows, and even watch TV. My husband can't get over how relaxed I am."

Berger showed these results—which *The Journal of the American Medical Association* would publish in April 1955—to Henry Hoyt, the president of Carter Products, who finally allowed meprobamate to be submitted for FDA approval. The custom at Carter had been to name compounds after local towns, and so meprobamate had been internally dubbed Milltown, after a small hamlet about three miles from Berger's lab that a guidebook called "tranquil little Milltown." Since place-names cannot be trademarked, Hoyt dropped an *l*, and when the pill came to market in May 1955, meprobamate was called Miltown.

In 1955, barbiturates were still the most popular antianxiety medication; they were marketed as sedatives and had dominated the pharmacy shelves for several decades. Because they had a proven sales record, Berger wanted to market Miltown as a sedative, too. But one night over dinner in Manhattan, his friend Nathan Kline, the research director of Rockland State Hospital, advised against that. "You are out of your mind," Kline said. "The world doesn't need new sedatives. What the world really needs is a tranquilizer. The world needs tranquility. Why don't you call this a tranquilizer? You will sell ten times more." Out of such contingencies—an unexpected side effect of a penicillin preservative, a stray remark at dinner—is the history of psychopharmacology made.

Miltown was brought quietly to market on May 9, 1955. Carter Products sold only $7,500 worth of the drug in each of the first two months it was available. But sales of the compound—which was advertised as being effective for "anxiety, tension, and mental stress"—soon accelerated. In December, Americans bought $500,000 worth of Miltown—and before long they were spending tens of millions of dollars a year on Miltown prescriptions.

In 1956, the drug became a cultural phenomenon. Movie stars and other celebrities sang the praises of the new tranquilizer. "If there's anything this movie business needs, it's a little tranquility," a Los Angeles newspaper columnist declared. "Once you're big enough to be 'somebody' in filmtown you've just got to be knee-deep in tension and mental and emotional stress. The anxiety of trying to make it to the top is replaced by the anxiety of wondering if you're going to stay there. So, big names and little alike have been loading their trusty pillboxes with this little wonder tablet." Lucille Ball's assistant kept a supply of Miltown on the set of *I Love Lucy* to help the actress calm down after spats with her husband, Desi Arnaz. Tennessee Williams told a magazine that he needed "Miltowns, liquor, [and] swimming" to get him through the stress of writing and producing *The Night of the Iguana*. The actress Tallulah Bankhead joked that she ought to have been paying taxes in New Jersey, home of Wallace Labs, because she was consuming so much Miltown. Jimmy Durante and Jerry Lewis publicly praised the drug on televised awards shows. The comedian Milton Berle took to beginning the monologues on his Tuesday night television show with "Hi, I'm Miltown Berle."

With so many prominent champions, Miltown's popularity spread nationally. Magazines wrote about "happy pills" and "peace of mind drugs" and "happiness by prescription." Gala Dalí, the wife of the surrealist painter Salvador Dalí, was such a devotee of Miltown that she convinced Carter Products to commission a $100,000 Miltown art installation from her husband.* Aldous Huxley—whom, based on the drug-addled dystopia he painted in *Brave New World*, you might have expected to be a stern Cassandra about such things—proselytized that the synthesis of meprobamate was "more important, more genuinely revolutionary, than the recent discoveries in the field of nuclear physics."

Within eighteen months of its introduction, Miltown had become the most prescribed and—with the possible exception of aspirin—the most consumed drug in the history of the world. At least 5 percent of Americans were taking it. "For the first time in history," the neurologist Richard Restak would later observe, "the mass treatment of anxiety in the general community seemed possible."

Miltown contributed to a wholesale transformation of the way we think about anxiety. Before 1955, there was no such thing as a tranquilizer—no medication that was designed to treat anxiety per se. (The first use of the word "tranquilizer" in English was by Benjamin Rush, a physician and signatory of the Declaration of Independence, who used the term to describe a chair he had invented to restrain psychotic patients.) But within a few years, American pharmacies were full of dozens of different tranquilizers, and companies were spending hundreds of millions of dollars to develop more.

The confidence of psychiatrists in the new drugs could be overweening. Testifying before Congress in 1957, Frank Berger's friend Nathan Kline enthused that the advent of psychiatric drugs may "be of markedly greater import in the history of mankind than the atom bomb since if these drugs provide the long-awaited key which will unlock the mysteries of the relationship of man's chemical constitution to his psychological behavior and provide effective means of correcting pathological needs there may no longer be any necessity for turning thermonuclear energy to destructive purposes." Kline told a journalist from *BusinessWeek* that meprobamate was good for both economic productivity (because it restored "full efficiency to business executives") and artistic creativity (because it helped writers and artists break free

---

* *Crisalida,* an undulating two-and-a-half-ton tunnel meant to symbolize the Miltown-aided passage to what the painter called "the nirvana of the human soul," stood in the exhibition hall at the annual meeting of the American Medical Association in 1958, surely one of the more avant-garde exhibits ever to grace a medical convention.

of their neuroses and overcome "mental blocks"). This utopian vision of better living through chemistry may have been overblown, but it was broadly shared. By 1960, some 75 percent of all doctors in America were prescribing Miltown. The treatment of anxiety had begun to migrate from the psychoanalyst's couch to the family doctor's office. Soon attempts to resolve conflicts between the id and the superego were being displaced by efforts to better calibrate the neurochemistry of the brain.

> *The deficiencies in our description [of the mind] would probably vanish if we were already in a position to replace the psychological terms by physiological or chemical ones.*
> —SIGMUND FREUD, *Beyond the Pleasure Principle* (1920)

> *The insulin of the nervous.*
> —FRENCH PSYCHIATRIST JEAN SIGWALD'S CHARACTERIZATION OF THE NEWLY DISCOVERED DRUG CHLORPROMAZINE (THORAZINE), 1953

Meanwhile, a series of unexpected pharmacological discoveries in France were to have medical and cultural consequences that were perhaps even further reaching than Miltown's.

In 1952, Henri Laborit, a surgeon in Paris, decided to experiment on some of his patients with a compound called chlorpromazine. Chlorpromazine, like so many drugs that would find their way into the modern psychotropic arsenal, had its origins in the rapid growth of the German textile industry in the late nineteenth century—specifically in the industrial dyes developed by chemical companies starting in the 1880s.* Chlorpromazine came into being in 1950, when French researchers synthesized the new compound from phenothiazine, intending to create a more powerful antihistamine. But chlorpromazine failed to

---

* First synthesized as a blue dye in the 1880s, phenothiazine, chlorpromazine's parent compound, was over the decades that followed discovered to have an unlikely array of medicinal properties: it worked as an antiseptic (reducing the risk of infection), an anthelmintic (expelling parasitic worms from the body), an antimalarial (combating malaria), and an antihistamine (preventing allergic reactions). Capitalizing on its bug-killing powers, DuPont started selling phenothiazine to farmers as an insecticide in 1935.

improve on existing antihistamines, so they quickly put it aside. When Laborit asked the chemical company Rhône-Poulenc for some chlorpromazine, he was hoping he would find that its purported qualities as an antihistamine would help mitigate surgical shock by reducing inflammation and suppressing the body's autoimmune response to the trauma of surgery. It did—but to Laborit's surprise, the drug also sedated his patients, relaxing some of them to the point where they were, as he put it, "indifferent" toward the major surgical procedures they were about to undergo.

"Come look at this," Laborit reportedly said to one of the army psychiatrists on the staff of the Val-de-Grâce military hospital, pointing out that the "tense, anxious, Mediterranean-type patients" had become completely calm, even in the face of major threats to their health.

Word got around the hospital, and one of Laborit's surgical colleagues would soon tell his brother-in-law, the psychiatrist Pierre Deniker, about the effects of this new compound. Intrigued, Deniker administered the drug to some of his most psychotic patients on the back wards of a Parisian mental hospital. The results were astounding: violently agitated patients calmed down; the crazy became sane. When one of Deniker's colleagues gave it to a patient who had been nonresponsive for years, the man emerged from his stupor and wanted to leave the hospital and return to his work as a barber. The doctor asked him for a shave, which the patient carefully gave him, and so the doctor discharged him. Not every case was as dramatic, but the calming effects of the drug were powerful. Neighbors reported that the noise emanating from the asylum had dropped significantly. Other small-scale experiments with the drug showed similarly potent results. In 1953, Jean Sigwald, a psychiatrist in Paris, gave chlorpromazine to eight patients suffering from "melancholia with anxiety," and five of them got better. Chlorpromazine was, Sigwald declared, "the insulin of the nervous."

Chlorpromazine came to North America when, one Sunday evening in the spring of 1953, Heinz Edgar Lehmann, a psychiatrist at McGill University in Montreal, read an article while luxuriating in his bath. The article, which had been left in his office by a drug company sales representative, reported on chlorpromazine's effect on French psychotics. ("This stuff is so good that the literature alone will convince him," the salesman had told Lehmann's secretary.) When Lehmann got out of the bath, he ordered a shipment of the compound, and he used it to launch the first North American trial of chlorpromazine, administering it to seventy mentally ill patients at nearby Verdun Protestant Hospital, where he served as clinical director. The results amazed him: within weeks, patients who had been suffering from schizophrenia, major depression, and what we would today call bipolar disorder, among other psychiatric ailments, seemed effectively cured. Many found themselves completely symptom-free; some of those who doctors had thought would be confined to asylums for life left the hospital. It was, Lehmann would later say, "the most dramatic breakthrough in pharmacology since the advent of anesthesia more than a century before."

Smith, Kline & French Laboratories, an American drug company, licensed chlorpromazine and in 1954 brought it to market with the trade name Thorazine. Its arrival transformed mental health care. In 1955, for the first time in a generation, the number of hospitalized mentally ill in the United States declined.*

Together, Thorazine and Miltown reinforced a culturally ascendant new idea—that mental illness was caused not by bad parenting or unresolved Oedipus complexes but by biological imbalances, organic disturbances in the brain that could be corrected with chemical interventions.

For me, the watches of that long night passed in ghastly wakefulness; strained by dread: such dread as children only can feel.
    —CHARLOTTE BRONTË, *Jane Eyre* (1847)

As it happens, my own decades-long experience with chemical interventions would begin, some twenty-five years later, with Thorazine.

As I approached the end of elementary school, my proliferating array of tics and phobias drove my parents to take me to the psychiatric hospital for the evaluation where it was determined I needed intensive psychotherapy. In seventh grade, I started at a new school. One Mon-

* This revolutionized psychiatry. Before 1955, both the acutely psychotic and the moderately neurotic were treated mainly by psychoanalysis or something like it; the working out of psychological issues or childhood traumas in talk therapy was the accepted route to mental health. "No one in their right mind in psychiatry was working on drugs," Heinz Lehmann would later say of the field before the 1950s. "You used shock, or various psychotherapies."

day morning in October, I refused to go. The prospect of separation from my parents, and of exposure to germs, felt too terrifying to endure. But my parents, after calling Dr. L. (the psychiatrist who had conducted the Rorschach test during my evaluation at McLean Hospital and whom I was now seeing for weekly psychotherapy sessions) and Mrs. P. (the social worker who was supposed to be counseling my mother and father about how to be less anxiety-inducing parents), refused to let me refuse. Which led to a melodramatic standoff that would replay itself most mornings for the rest of that school year.

I would wake up crying and clutching my covers, saying I was too scared to go to school. After failing to reason me out of bed, my parents would tear the covers off, and the wrestling match would begin: my father would hold me down while my mother forced me into my clothes as I struggled to escape. Then they'd frog-march me out to the car while I tried to wriggle free. During the seven-minute drive to school, I would sob and beg my parents not to make me go.

As we'd pull into the school parking lot, my moment of reckoning would arrive: Would my parents have to physically remove me from the car, humiliating me in front of merciless schoolmates? School was terrifying—but so was the threat of humiliation. Wiping my tears, I'd get out of the car and begin the gangplank walk to my homeroom. My anxiety was not rational; I had nothing, really, to fear. Yet anyone who has suffered the torments of acute pathological anxiety knows that I am not exaggerating when I say I do not think I would have felt much worse had I been walking to my own beheading.

Stunned by despair, blinking back tears, struggling to control my roiling bowels, I'd sit mutely at my desk, trying not to embarrass myself by bursting into sobs.*

By January, my phobias and separation anxieties had become so consuming that I had begun to drop my friends, and they to drop me; I scarcely socialized with my peers anymore. Engaging in the give-and-

---

* My first glimpse of clinical depression came as I was sitting in class one Friday afternoon that year. I was experiencing my characteristic relief at the prospect of being sprung for the weekend when I had the thought *But on Sunday night this starts all over again,* and I was chilled by the infiniteness of my plight, by the notion that Sunday nights—and Monday mornings—eternally return, and that only death would put a stop to them, and that therefore there was nothing, ultimately, to look forward to that might help me transcend my dread about bad things to come.

take of schoolboy banter had become too stressful, so at lunchtime I preferred to sit quietly beside a teacher. This put me in a position, on the first day back after holiday break that year, to overhear the Spanish teacher tell the French teacher a graphic tale of spending the holidays with friends in Manhattan, where she and her companions had been stricken by a stomach virus that had included prolific amounts of vomiting.*

This was more than I could bear on the first day back after vacation; I left school, went home, and pretty much lost my mind.

Here are the snapshots I can remember from that evening: me throwing things around the house, smashing everything I can get my hands on, while my father tries to grapple me into submission; me lying on the floor, pounding it with my fist, screaming so hard that drool froths from my mouth, yelling that I am so scared and can't take it anymore and want to die; my father, on the phone with Dr. L., talking about whether I should be committed (there is mention of straitjackets and ambulances); my father going to Corbett's, the local drugstore, and coming back with emergency doses of Valium (a minor tranquilizer of the benzodiazepine class, about which more shortly) and liquid Thorazine (which was then known as a major tranquilizer and is now classified as an antipsychotic).

The Thorazine tasted awful. But I was desperate for relief, so I drank it in some orange juice. For the next eighteen months, I was on Thorazine around the clock. And starting later that week, I began also taking imipramine, the tricyclic medication that was the antidepressant of choice prior to the arrival of Prozac in the late 1980s.†

Every day for the next two years, my mother would place one large orange Thorazine pill and an assortment of smaller green and blue imipramine pills on the edge of my plate at breakfast and at dinner. The medication reduced my anxiety enough to keep me out of the hospital. But at a cost: on Thorazine, I became foggy and dehydrated, shuffling along with a dry mouth and hollowed-out emotions and twitching fingers, the result of a common Thorazine side effect known as tardive

---

* Yes, it is a mark of the intensity of my phobic preoccupations that I can today, some thirty years later, still remember the conversation almost verbatim.

† Imipramine did more to determine the modern conception of panic anxiety than any other drug. (More about that in the next chapter.)

dyskinesia. A year earlier, prior to going on Thorazine and imipramine, I had been selected for an elite soccer team. When I showed up the following autumn in a Thorazine stupor, the coaches were baffled. What had happened to the short kid who had embarrassed older players by dribbling circles around them? They now had a kid, still short, who moved slowly, tired easily, and became rapidly dehydrated, a gluey white mucus encrusted around his lips.

Even after I was heavily medicated, my anxiety persisted. I'd make it to school but then get overwhelmed by fear, leave class, and end up in the infirmary with the school nurse, begging her to let me go home. When the confines of the infirmary came to feel too claustrophobic to contain my antic pacing, she would kindly walk around school with me while I tried to calm down.*

Seeing me wandering the campus with the nurse when I should have been in class, my peers naturally wondered what was wrong with me. The mother of an erstwhile friend ran into my mother and asked if I was ill. My mother, prevaricating, said I was fine.

But I was not fine; I was miserable. In photographs from that time, I look hunched and hangdog and sickly, like I am shrinking into myself. I was on antipsychotics and antidepressants and tranquilizers, and I was taking daily walks with the school nurse instead of attending class.

Without Thorazine and imipramine and Valium, I don't know that I would have survived seventh grade. But I did, and by the end of eighth grade my anxious misery had relented somewhat. Dr. L. weaned me off the Thorazine. But since that winter some thirty years ago, I have been on one psychiatric medication or another—and often two,

---

* Compounding matters, my phobia of vomiting metastasized around this time into a fear of choking; I started having trouble swallowing. (Difficulty in swallowing has been a well-recognized symptom of anxiety since at least the late nineteenth century and is known clinically as dysphagia.) I became afraid to eat. My skinny adolescent frame, worn ever thinner by nervous fidgeting, became emaciated. I stopped eating lunch at school. The more trouble I had swallowing, the more I'd obsess about my trouble swallowing, and the worse the trouble would get. Soon I was having trouble swallowing even my saliva. I'd sit there in history class, my mouth full of spit, terrified that if I were called upon to speak, I would choke on my mouthful of saliva or spew it all over my desk—or both. I took to carrying wads of Kleenex around with me everywhere I went, discreetly drooling into them so that I wouldn't have to swallow. By lunchtime each day, my pockets would be full of drenched tissues, which would leach into my pants and make them smell like saliva. Over the course of the day, the tissues would disintegrate, so by evening bits of slobbery Kleenex would be spilling out of my pockets.

Are you surprised to learn that I had but one date in all of middle school and high school?

three, or more at a time—more or less continuously, making me a living repository of the pharmacological trends in anxiety treatment of the last half century.

> *Drug discoveries were of sensational importance for understanding psychiatric illness and the basic nature of the human condition: Our personalities, our intellects, our very culture could presumably be boiled down to a sack of enzymes.*
> —EDWARD SHORTER, *Before Prozac* (2009)

For a brief period in the 1980s, I took phenelzine, a monoamine oxidase inhibitor, or MAOI, whose trade name is Nardil. My experience on MAOIs was not notably successful. I didn't feel any less anxious—but I did do a lot of worrying about whether I would die from complicating side effects of the drug. This is because MAOIs can have dangerous, even lethal, side effects, especially when combined with the wrong elements. When patients taking MAOIs ingest things—such as wine and other fermented alcohol, aged cheeses, pickled foods, some kinds of beans, and many over-the-counter medications—that contain high levels of an amino acid derivative called tyramine, the health effects can be serious: painful headaches, jaundice, a spike in blood pressure, and in some cases severe internal hemorrhaging. Which means MAOIs may not be ideal for people like me who are, even in the best of circumstances, prone to hypochondria and health anxiety.

For this reason, among others, while there are still depressed and anxious patients for whom MAOIs remain the most, or the only, effective pharmacological treatment, MAOIs have not been considered a first-line treatment for mood disorders for many years now.* Though MAOIs played only a cameo role in my own psychiatric history, they are important in the scientific and cultural history of anxiety because they were among the first drugs to be specifically tied to a just-emerging neurochemical theory of mental illness. At midcentury the advent of

---

* After trying many alternative remedies, including electroshock therapy, the novelist David Foster Wallace found Nardil to be the most effective treatment for his anxiety and depression. Going off Nardil, after experiencing what seems to have been a tyramine-induced side effect, may have precipitated Wallace's downward spiral to suicide in 2008.

MAOIs, in conjunction with the arrival of imipramine and the other tricyclics (about which more shortly), helped create the modern scientific understanding of depression and anxiety.

MAOIs have their origins in the later years of the Second World War, when the German Luftwaffe, bombarding English cities with V-2 rockets, ran low on conventional fuel and had to resort to propelling the rockets with a fuel called hydrazine. Hydrazine is poisonous and explosive, but scientists had found that they could modify it in ways that might be medically useful. When the war ended, drug companies bought the leftover hydrazine supplies at a steep discount. The investment paid off. In 1951, scientists working at Hoffmann–La Roche in Nutley, New Jersey, discovered that two modified hydrazine compounds, isoniazid and iproniazid, inhibited the growth of tuberculosis. Clinical trials ensued. By 1952, both isoniazid and iproniazid were on the market for treatment of tuberculosis.

But these antibiotics had an unexpected side effect. After being treated with them, some patients would become, as newspapers recounted, "mildly euphoric," dancing through the hallways of the tuberculosis wards. Reading these reports, psychiatrists wondered if this mood-elevating effect meant that isoniazid and iproniazid might be used as psychiatric medications. In a 1956 study at Rockland State Hospital in New York, patients with various psychiatric disorders were given iproniazid for five weeks; toward the end of that period the depressed patients had improved markedly. Nathan Kline, the hospital's research director, observed what he called a "psychic energizing" effect, and he began prescribing iproniazid to the melancholic patients in his private practice. Some of these patients, he subsequently reported, experienced "a complete remission of all symptoms." Kline would later declare that iproniazid "was the first cure in all of psychiatric history to act in such a manner." In April 1957, Hoffmann–La Roche began marketing iproniazid with the trade name Marsilid, and it was featured on the front page of *The New York Times*. Marsilid was the first of the MAOIs and one of the first drugs to become known as an antidepressant.

At midcentury the history of neuroscience, such as it was, was brief. Knowledge of how the brain worked was primitive. Debate churned between the "sparks" and the "soups"—between those scientists who believed that transmission of impulses between neurons was electrical and those who believed it was chemical. "When I was an undergraduate student at Cambridge," Leslie Iversen, a professor of pharmacology at Oxford recalled of his time there in the 1950s, "we were taught . . . there was no chemical transmission in the brain—that it was just an electrical machine."

English physiologists had done primitive research on brain chemistry in the late nineteenth century. But not until the 1920s did Otto Loewi, a professor of pharmacology at the University of Graz in Austria, isolate the first neurotransmitter, arguing in a 1926 paper that a chemical called acetylcholine was what mediated the transmission of impulses between one nerve ending and the next.*

Even as sales of Thorazine and Miltown were taking off, the concept of a neurotransmitter—of a chemical that transmitted impulses between brain cells—had not been definitively established.† (The psychiatrists who prescribed these drugs, and even the biochemists who developed them, generally had no idea why the drugs had the effects they did.) But discoveries by two researchers in Scotland swung the pendulum forcefully toward the "soups." In 1954, Marthe Vogt, a German neuroscientist at the University of Edinburgh, discovered the first convincing evidence of a neurotransmitter—norepinephrine. Later that year, John Henry Gaddum, a colleague of Vogt's, discovered through a series of unorthodox experiments that serotonin, which until that point was thought to be a gut-based compound involved in digestion, was also a neurotransmitter.‡ Gaddum took LSD—which he reported made him feel crazy for forty-eight hours and which also, according to labo-

* Loewi famously claimed he conceived the experiment, which involved artificially raising and lowering the heart rate of frogs, in a dream he had on Easter Sunday 1923. Thrilled, he scribbled the experiment on a piece of paper by his bed—only to awake the next morning to find that he could neither remember his dream nor decipher his own handwriting. Fortunately, he dreamed the same experiment the following night. This time he remembered it, performed it, and demonstrated for the first time the chemical basis of nerve transmission—work for which he would later be awarded a Nobel Prize.
† Otto Loewi and others had found suggestive evidence of neurotransmitters such as norepinephrine in the bloodstream—but no one had yet isolated any in the brain.
‡ A brief history of early serotonin research: In 1933, the Italian researcher Vittorio Erspamer isolated a chemical compound in the stomach that he named enteramine because it seemed to promote the gut contraction involved in digestion. In 1947, two American physiologists studying hypertension at the Cleveland Clinic found enteramine in the platelets of the blood. Noticing that enteramine caused blood vessels to contract, they renamed the compound serotonin (*sero* for "blood," from the Latin word *serum*, and *tonin* for muscle tone, from the Greek word *tonikos*, tonic). In 1953, when researchers for the first time found traces of serotonin in the brain, they still assumed it was merely the residue of what

ratory measurements, decreased the level of serotonin metabolites in his cerebrospinal fluid. His broad conclusion: Serotonin helps keep you mentally healthy—and therefore a deficiency of serotonin can make you mentally ill. Thus was born the neurotransmitter-based theory of mental health. This would transform the scientific and cultural view of anxiety and depression.

> *Canst thou not . . .*
> *Raze out the written troubles of the brain*
> *And with some sweet oblivious antidote*
> *Cleanse the stuff'd bosom of that perilous stuff*
> *Which weighs upon the heart?*
> —WILLIAM SHAKESPEARE, *Macbeth* (CIRCA 1606)

Bernard "Steve" Brodie had built his reputation as a biochemist making antimalarial drugs during World War II. When Thorazine and Miltown came on the market in the 1950s, he was running a lab at the National Heart Institute of the National Institutes of Health in Bethesda, Maryland. Over the next decade, that lab would revolutionize psychiatry.

The seminal experiments were on reserpine. An extract from the plant *Rauwolfia serpentina* (its root looks like a snake), reserpine had been used for more than a thousand years in India, where it was prescribed for everything from high blood pressure and insomnia to snakebite poisonings and infant colic. But it had also been used, evidently with some success, according to Hindu writings, for treating "insanity." Reserpine had never gotten much attention in the West. But when Thorazine produced such striking results, executives at Squibb wondered if reserpine could compete with it. They provided funding to Nathan Kline, who tested the compound on a group of his patients at Rockland State Hospital: several of them improved dramatically, and a few whose case reports had described them as "crippled" by anxiety became relaxed enough to leave the hospital and resume their lives.

---

had been carried through the bloodstream from the stomach. Only in the ensuing years did serotonin's role as a neurotransmitter become evident.

This led to a much larger study. In 1955, Paul Hoch, the commissioner of mental hygiene for New York, arranged with Governor W. Averell Harriman for $1.5 billion in funding to give reserpine to *every single one* of the ninety-four thousand patients in all of the state's psychiatric hospitals. (FDA regulations would never allow a study like this to be conducted today.) The results: Reserpine worked for some patients but not quite as well as Thorazine—and it had serious, sometimes lethal, side effects. Clinicians largely set it aside as a psychiatric drug.

But not before Steve Brodie and his NIH colleagues had used reserpine to establish a clear link between biochemistry and behavior. Inspired by what John Gaddum had learned about the relationship between LSD and serotonin, Brodie gave reserpine to rabbits to see what it did to their serotonin levels. Brodie found two interesting things: administering reserpine to rabbits decreased the amount of serotonin in their brains, and this decrease in serotonin seemed to produce rabbits who were "lethargic" and "apathetic," mimicking the behavior of people we would today call depressed. Moreover, Brodie and his colleagues found they could induce and diminish "depressed" behavior in the rabbits by manipulating their serotonin levels. Brodie's 1955 paper in *Science* reporting these findings was the first to tie levels of a specific neurotransmitter to behavioral changes in animals. Brodie had, as one medical historian later put it, built a bridge from neurochemistry to behavior.

Brodie's reserpine research intersected in intriguing ways with what psychiatrists were then discovering about MAOIs. To oversimplify a little, brain researchers in the 1950s were just figuring out that neurotransmitters are discharged by "upstream" neurons into the synapses—the tiny spaces between nerve cells—in order to make "downstream" neurons fire. Each neurotransmitter travels quickly from one neuron to the next, where it attaches to a receptor—its molecular mirror image—embedded in the neuron's membrane. Each time one of these neurotransmitters latches onto its receptor on the postsynaptic neuron (serotonin attaching to serotonin receptors, norepinephrine to norepinephrine receptors), the receiving neuron changes shape: its membrane becomes porous, allowing atoms from the outside of the neuron to rush toward the interior, causing a sudden change in the neuron's electric voltage. This change causes the receiving neuron to fire, releasing its own supply of neurotransmitters into the surrounding synapses. These neurotransmitters then land on receptors on still other neurons. This cascade of activity—neurons firing, releasing neurotransmitters, causing other neurons to fire—throughout the one hundred billion neurons and the trillions of synapses in our brain is what gives rise to our emotions, perceptions, and thoughts. Neurons and neurotransmitters are, in ways scientists are still struggling to understand, the physical stuff of emotion and thought.

Early research on iproniazid had revealed that the antibiotic inactivated an enzyme called monoamine oxidase (MAO), whose function is to break down and clear away the serotonin and norepinephrine that build up in the synapses. After a neurotransmitter is squirted into the synapse, it ordinarily gets quickly cleared out by MAO, allowing for the next transmission to happen. But the "inhibition" of the monoamine oxidase enzyme by iproniazid allowed the neurotransmitters to remain in the nerve terminals longer. The extra buildup of these neurotransmitters in the synapses, Brodie's researchers theorized, accounted for iproniazid's antidepressant effects. Sure enough, when rabbits were given iproniazid before reserpine was administered, these rabbits did not become lethargic the way the other reserpine rabbits did. The iproniazid, Brodie and his colleagues concluded, kept the rabbits from getting "depressed" by boosting the levels of norepinephrine and serotonin in their synapses.

This was the moment the pharmaceutical industry awoke to the idea that it could sell psychiatric drugs by marketing them as correcting "chemical imbalances," or deficiencies of certain neurotransmitters. In one of its first advertisements for iproniazid, in 1957, Hoffmann–La Roche promoted the drug as "an amine oxidase inhibitor which affects the metabolism of serotonin, epinephrine, norepinephrine and other amines."

Research on another new drug lent further support to this idea. In 1954, Geigy, a Swiss pharmaceutical company, had tweaked Thorazine's chemical structure to create the compound G22355, which it called imipramine, the first tricyclic. (Drugs in this category have a three-ring chemical structure.) Roland Kuhn, a Swiss psychiatrist who was trying to develop a better sleeping pill, had tried giving imipramine to some of his patients. Because Thorazine and imipramine were chemically similar (only two atoms were different), Kuhn assumed that imipramine, like Thorazine, would have a sedating effect. It didn't: rather than putting patients to sleep, imipramine energized them and elevated their moods. In 1957, after treating more than five hundred patients with imipramine, Kuhn delivered a paper to the International Congress of Psychiatry in Zurich, reporting that even deeply depressed patients had improved dramatically after several weeks on the drug. Their moods lifted, their energy surged, their "hypochondriacal delusions" disappeared, and their "general inhibition" dissipated. "Not infrequently the cure is complete, sufferers and their relatives confirming the fact that they had not been so well for a long time," he declared. Geigy took imipramine out of mothballs and brought it to the European market in 1958 under the trade name Tofranil.*

On the day imipramine was released in the United States, September 6, 1959, *The New York Times* published an article headlined "Drugs and Depression" about both Marsilid (iproniazid, the first MAOI) and Tofranil (imipramine, the first tricyclic). The *Times* called these drugs "anti-depressants"—seemingly the first use of the term in the press or in popular culture.

While some estimates put the number of Americans taking antidepressant medications today at over forty million, there was no such thing as an antidepressant when Roland Kuhn addressed the International Congress of Psychiatry in 1957. The concept simply didn't exist. The MAOIs and the tricyclics had created a new drug category.

---

* Imipramine might never have made it to pharmacies—and the history of biological psychiatry might have been quite different—if not for another accident of history. Kuhn's presentation to the International Congress of Psychiatry was met, as he put it, "with a great deal of skepticism" because "of the almost completely negative view of drug treatment of depression up to that time." In fact, such was the lack of psychiatric interest in drugs that only twelve people attended Kuhn's talk in Zurich. (His talk has since been referred to as the Gettysburg Address of pharmacology—little noted at the time but destined to become a classic.) Geigy, too, was unimpressed. The company shared psychiatry's skepticism about a medicine that could treat an emotional disorder. It had no plans to market imipramine. But one day Kuhn happened to run into Robert Bohringer, a powerful Geigy shareholder, at a conference in Rome. When Bohringer mentioned that he had a deeply melancholic relative in Geneva, Kuhn handed him a bottle of imipramine. Within a few days of starting on it, Bohringer's relative had recovered. "Kuhn is right," Bohringer declared to Geigy executives. "Imipramine *is* an antidepressive." Geigy executives relented and brought the drug to market.

In the early 1960s, Julius Axelrod, an NIH biochemist and a veteran of Steve Brodie's lab, began to identify the effects of imipramine on various chemicals in the brain. Axelrod discovered that imipramine blocked the reuptake of norepinephrine in the synapses. (A few years later, he would find that it also blocked the reuptake of serotonin.) Axelrod theorized that antidepressants' effect on the reuptake of norepinephrine was what accounted for the elevation of mood and the relief of depression. This was a transformative idea: if imipramine blocked the reuptake of norepinephrine, and if it made patients less anxious and depressed, that meant there must be a correlation between norepinephrine and mental health. Marsilid or Tofranil—or cocaine, for that matter, which has a similar effect—seemed to cure anxiety and depression by boosting the levels of norepinephrine in the synapses, delaying its reuptake into the neurons.

Around this time, Joseph Schildkraut was a psychiatrist at the Massachusetts Mental Health Center who believed that anxiety and psychoneurosis were caused by childhood trauma or unresolved psychic conflicts and were therefore best treated by Freudian psychotherapy. Then he gave imipramine to a few of his patients. "These drugs seemed like magic to me," he would say later. "I became aware that there was a new world out there, a world of psychiatry informed by pharmacology." In 1965, he published an article in *The American Journal of Psychiatry*, "The Catecholamine Hypothesis of Affective Disorders: A Review of the Supporting Evidence"; building on the work of Steve Brodie and Julius Axelrod, he argued that depression was caused by elevated brain levels of catecholamines, the fight-or-flight hormones (such as norepinephrine) that are released by the adrenal glands in times of stress. Schildkraut's paper became one of the most cited journal articles in the history of psychiatry, enshrining the chemical imbalance theory of anxiety and depression at the center of the field.

The first pillar of biological psychiatry had been constructed. The Freudian model of psychiatry had sought to treat anxiety and depression by resolving unconscious psychic conflicts. With the advent of the antidepressants, mental illness and emotional disorders were increasingly attributed to malfunctions of specific neurotransmitter systems: schizophrenia and drug addiction were believed to be caused by problems in the dopamine system; depression was a consequence of stress hormones released by the adrenal glands; anxiety resulted from defects in the serotonin system.

But pharmacology's most transformative effect on the history of anxiety was still to come, beginning with studies on imipramine that would reshape the psychiatric establishment's understanding of anxiety.

CHAPTER 6

A Brief History of Panic; or, How Drugs Created a New Disorder

An anxiety attack may consist of a feeling of anxiety alone, without any associated ideas, or accompanied by the interpretation that is nearest to hand, such as the ideas of the extinction of life, or a stroke, or the threat of madness, or the feeling of anxiety may have linked to it a disturbance of one or more of the bodily functions—such as respiration, heart action, vasomotor innervation or glandular activity. From this combination the patient picks out in particular now one, now another, factor. He complains of "spasms of the heart," "difficulty in breathing," "outbreaks of sweating," . . . and such like.

—SIGMUND FREUD, "ON THE GROUNDS FOR DETACHING
A PARTICULAR SYNDROME FROM NEURASTHENIA UNDER
THE DESCRIPTION OF ANXIETY NEUROSIS" (1895)

The bases of mental illness are chemical changes in the brain. . . . There's no longer any justification for the distinction . . . between mind and body or mental and physical illness. Mental illnesses are physical illnesses.

—DAVID SATCHER, U.S. SURGEON GENERAL (1999)

One day I am sitting in my office reading e-mail when vaguely, at the edges of my awareness, I notice I am feeling slightly warm.

Is it getting hot in here? Suddenly awareness of the workings of my body moves to the center of my consciousness.

Do I have a fever? Am I getting sick? Will I pass out? Will I vomit? Will I, in one way or another, be incapacitated before I can escape or get help?

I am writing a book about anxiety. I am steeped in knowledge of the phenomenon of panic. I know as much as any layperson about the neuromechanics of an attack. I have had thousands of them. You would think that this knowledge and experience would help. And, to be sure, occasionally it does. By recognizing the symptoms of a panic attack early on, I can sometimes head it off, or at least restrict it to what's known as a limited-symptom panic attack. But too often my internal dialogue goes something like this:

You're just having a panic attack. You're fine. Relax.

But what if it's not a panic attack? What if I'm really sick this time? What if I'm having a heart attack or a stroke?

It's always a panic attack. Do your breathing exercises. Stay calm. You're fine.

But what if I'm not fine?

You're fine. Every one of the last 782 times when you were having a panic attack and you thought it might not be a panic attack, it was a panic attack.

Okay. I'm relaxing. Breathing in and out. Thinking the calming thoughts the meditation tapes have taught me. But just because the last 782 instances were panic attacks, that doesn't mean the 783rd one is too, right? My stomach hurts.

You're right. Let's get outta here.

Sitting in my office while something like this sequence of thoughts flows through my head, I go from feeling moderately warm to feeling hot. I begin to perspire. The left side of my face starts to tingle, then goes numb. (*See,* I say to myself, *maybe I* am *having a stroke!*) My chest tightens. I am suddenly aware that the fluorescent lights in my office have a strobelike quality and are flickering dizzyingly. I feel a terrible vertiginous teetering, like the furniture in my office is moving around, like I am about to topple forward onto the ground. I grip the sides of my chair for stability. As my dizziness increases and my office swirls around me, my physical surroundings no longer feel quite real; it's as though a scrim has come between me and the world.

My thoughts race, but the three most prominent are: *I'm going to vomit. I'm about to die. I've got to get out of here.*

I bolt unsteadily from my chair, perspiring heavily now. All my focus is on escape: I need to get out—out of my office, out of the building, out of this situation. If I'm going to have a stroke or vomit or die, I want to be out of the building. I'm going to make a break for it.

Desperately hoping that I'm not accosted on my way to the stairs, I open the door and sprint-walk to the elevator vestibule. I push through the fire door to the stairwell and, with a small feeling of relief at having made it this far, begin to climb seven flights down. By the time I reach the third floor, my legs are quaking. If I were thinking rationally—if I could calm my amygdala and make better use of my neocortex—I would conclude, correctly, that this quaking is the natural result of an autonomic fight-or-flight response (which causes trembling in the skeletal muscles) combined with the effects of physical exertion. But too far gone into the catastrophizing logic of panic to access my rational brain, I conclude instead that my quaking legs are a symptom of complete physical breakdown and that I am indeed about to die. As I descend the final two flights, I am wondering whether I will be able to reach my wife from my cell phone to tell her I love her and to ask her to send help before I lose consciousness and possibly expire.

The door from the stairwell to the outside is kept locked. Motion detectors are supposed to sense you coming from the inside and automatically unlock it. For some reason, perhaps because I am going too fast, they fail to activate. I slam into the door at high speed and bounce off, falling backward onto my rear.

I have hit the door with sufficient force to dislodge the plastic frame around the exit sign glowing red above it. The frame falls onto my head with a thud and then clatters to the floor.

The lobby security guard, hearing the racket, pokes his head into the stairwell to find me sitting on the floor in a daze, the exit sign frame by my side. "What's going on in here?" he says.

"I'm sick," I say, and who would say that I am not?

The ancient Greeks believed that Pan, the god of nature, ruled over shepherds and their grazing flocks. Pan was not a noble god: he was short and ugly, ran on stubby goatlike legs, and liked to take naps in caves or bushes by the side of the road. When awakened by passersby, he would issue a bloodcurdling scream that made the hair of anyone who heard it stand on end. Pan's scream, it was said, caused travelers to drop dead from fright. Pan induced terror even in his fellow gods. When the Titans assaulted Mount Olympus (as myth would have it), Pan assured their defeat by sowing fear and confusion in their ranks. The Greeks also credited Pan with their victory at the Battle of Marathon in 490 B.C., where he was said to have put anxiety in the hearts of the enemy Persians. The experience of sudden terror—especially in crowded places—became known as panic (from the Greek *panikos*, literally "of Pan").

Anyone who has suffered the torments of a panic attack knows the turmoil it can unleash—physiological as well as emotional. The palpitations. The sweating. The shaking. The shortness of breath. The feeling of choking and tightness in the chest. The nausea and general gastric distress. The dizziness and blurring of vision. The tingling sensations in the extremities ("paresthesias" is the medical term). The chills and hot flashes. The feelings of doom and gaping existential awfulness.*

David Sheehan, a psychiatrist who has studied and treated anxiety for forty years, tells a story that captures how awful the experience of panic can feel. In the 1980s, a World War II veteran, one of the first infantrymen to land at Normandy on D-day, came to see Sheehan, seeking therapy for panic attacks. Wasn't the experience of storming the beach at Normandy, Sheehan asked him, bullets and blood and bodies flying and falling all around him—with the prospect of his own injury or death quite real, even likely—more frightening and miserable than enduring a panic attack at the dinner table, however ravaged he might feel by the neurotic circuitry of his own mind? Not at all, the man said. "The anxiety he felt landing on the beaches was mild compared to the sheer terror of one of his bad panic attacks," Sheehan reports. "Given the choice between the two, he would gladly again volunteer to land in Normandy."

Today, panic attacks are a fixture of psychiatric medicine and of popular culture. As many as eleven million Americans today will, like me, at

---

* I've just listed ten of the thirteen *DSM* criteria for a panic attack; the other three symptoms are feelings of depersonalization or unreality, fear of losing control or going crazy, and fear of dying. At least four of these thirteen symptoms must be present for a panic attack to have occurred, according to the *DSM*.

some point be formally diagnosed with panic disorder. Yet as recently as 1979, neither panic attacks nor panic disorder officially existed. Where did these concepts come from?

Imipramine.

In 1958, Donald Klein was a young psychiatrist at Hillside Hospital in New York. When imipramine became available, he and a colleague began administering it willy-nilly to most of the two hundred psychiatric patients in their care at Hillside. "We assumed it would be some sort of supercocaine, blasting the patients out of their rut," Klein recalled. "Remarkably, these anhedonic, anorexic, insomniac patients began to sleep better, eat better, after several weeks . . . saying 'the veil has lifted.'"

What most interested Klein was that fourteen of these patients—who had previously been suffering from intermittent acute episodes of anxiety characterized by "rapid breathing, palpitations, weakness, and a feeling of impending death" (symptoms of what was then called, in the Freudian tradition, anxiety neurosis)—experienced significant or complete remission of their anxiety. One patient in particular drew Klein's attention. He would rush in a panic to the nurses' station, saying he was afraid he was about to die. A nurse would hold his hand and talk to him soothingly, and within a few minutes the attack would pass. This recurred every few hours. Thorazine hadn't worked for him. But after the patient had been on imipramine for a few weeks, the nurses noticed that his regular panicky visits to their station stopped. He still reported a generally high level of *chronic* anxiety, but the *acute* paroxysms of it had stopped completely.

This got Klein thinking. That imipramine could block paroxysmal anxiety without stopping general anxiety or chronic worrying suggested there was something wrong with the prevailing theory of anxiety.

When Freud had hung out his shingle as a "nerve doctor" in the late 1880s, the most common diagnosis among the patients he and his peers saw was neurasthenia, a term popularized by the American physician George Miller Beard to refer to the mixture of dread, worry, and fatigue that Beard believed the stresses of the Industrial Revolution had produced. The root cause of neurasthenia was thought to be nerves that had been overstrained by the pressures of modern life; the prescribed remedies for these "tired nerves" were "nerve revitalizers"—nostrums such as mild electrical stimulators or elixirs tinged with opium, cocaine, or alcohol. But Freud became convinced that the feelings of dread and worry that he was seeing in the neurasthenic patients he consulted were based not in tired nerves but in problems of the psyche, which could be resolved through psychoanalysis.

In 1895, Freud wrote a paper about anxiety neurosis, a condition he sought to differentiate from neurasthenia and whose symptoms, as he described them, conform quite closely to the *DSM-V* checklist for panic disorder: rapid or irregular heartbeat, hyperventilation and breathing disturbances, perspiration and night sweats, tremor and shivering, vertigo, gastrointestinal disturbances, and a feeling of impending doom that he called "anxious expectations."

Nothing in all this necessarily contradicted anything that Donald Klein would later glean from his imipramine experiments. But that's because in 1895 Freud still considered anxiety neurosis to be the product not of a "repressed idea" (which is what he believed underlay most psychopathology) but of a biological force. Anxiety neurosis, Freud theorized in these early writings, was the result of either genetic predisposition (a theory that modern molecular genetics supports) or some kind of pent-up physiological pressure—most notably, in Freud's imagining, the pressure caused by thwarted sexual desire.

But in many of his subsequent writings (starting with *Studies on Hysteria* from around this same time), Freud asserted instead that attacks of anxiety—even ones that manifested themselves in acute physical symptoms—emanated from unresolved, and often unconscious, inner psychic conflicts. For nearly thirty years, Freud effectively abandoned the argument that anxiety attacks were a biological problem. He and his followers replaced anxiety neurosis with plain neurosis—a problem that had its basis in psychic discord, not in genes or biology. By the mid-twentieth century, the overwhelming psychiatric consensus was that anxiety was the result of a conflict between the desires of the id and the repressions of the superego—and that, furthermore, anxiety was the foundation of almost all mental illness, from schizophrenia to psychoneurotic depression. One of the main purposes of psychoanalysis—and of most forms of talk therapy—was to help the patient become aware of and contend with the underlying anxiety against which all of his various maladaptive "ego defenses" had been mustered. "The predominant American psychiatric theory was that all psychopathology was secondary to anxiety," Klein later recalled, "which in turn was caused by intrapsychic conflict."

But this didn't square with what Klein was finding in his imipramine studies. If anxiety was the animating force behind all psychopathology, then why didn't imipramine—which seemed to eliminate the panic suffered by patients with anxiety neurosis—help schizophrenics with their psychosis? Maybe, Klein ventured, not all mental illnesses lay on the spectrum of anxiety the way the Freudians thought they did.

The spectrum theory of anxiety held that what determined a mental illness's severity was the intensity of the underlying anxiety: mild anxiety led to psychoneurosis and various neurotic behaviors; severe anxiety led to schizophrenia or manic depression. For many traditional Freudians, the settings—like bridges or elevators or airplanes—that tended to produce acute anxiety attacks had symbolic, and often sexual, significance that accounted for the anxiety they caused.

Balderdash, Klein said. Childhood trauma or sexual repression didn't cause panic; a biological malfunction did.

Klein concluded that these attacks of paroxysmal anxiety—which he would come to call panic attacks—originated in a biological glitch that produced a suffocation alarm response, his term for the cascade of physiological activity that leads to, among other things, what feels like a spontaneous attack of overwhelming terror. Anytime someone starts to asphyxiate, internal physiological monitors detect the problem and send messages to the brain, causing intense arousal, gasping for breath, and an urge to flee—an adaptive survival mechanism. But some people, according to Klein's false suffocation alarm theory, have defective monitors that occasionally fire even when the individual is getting enough oxygen. This causes the person to experience the physical symptoms that make up an anxiety attack. The source of panic is not psychic conflict but crossed physiological wires—wires that imipramine somehow untangled. Klein's data suggested that imipramine eliminated spontaneous anxiety attacks in most patients who suffered them.

When Klein published an initial report on imipramine in *The American Journal of Psychiatry* in 1962, it was received, as he recalled, "like the proverbial lead balloon." Subsequent articles over the next several years, in which he argued that panic anxiety was an illness distinct from chronic anxiety, were received with similar *froideur*. He was attacked from all sides, accused of being an apostate. But because imipramine seemed to cure panic anxiety without affecting feelings of general apprehension and neurosis, Klein remained convinced that panic anxiety had symptoms and physiological causes that were different in kind and not just in degree from other forms of anxiety.

Though he hadn't set out to, Klein had achieved what's known as the first pharmacological dissection: working backward from the effects of drug treatment, he had defined a new illness category, carving out panic anxiety from the more general anxiety that was supposed to underlie the Freudian neuroses.

Klein's pharmacological dissection of anxiety met with enormous hostility from his colleagues. At a conference in 1980, just as the publication of the *DSM-III* was bringing panic disorder into existence, Klein's presentation on how the suffocation alarm response caused panic anxiety was followed immediately by a lecture from John Nemiah, the longtime editor of the prestigious *American Journal of Psychiatry*. Rebutting Klein, Nemiah said that panic anxiety had nothing to do with a suffocation alarm response or problems of biological hardwiring but rather was "the reaction of the individual's ego . . . to the threatened emergence into conscious awareness of unpleasant, forbidden, unwanted, frightening impulses, feelings, and thoughts."

Though Klein's theory has been to some degree officially adopted by American psychiatry since 1980, it remains controversial today. My own current therapist, Dr. W., a PhD psychologist who did his training in the 1960s, laments that Klein's work led to a fundamental shift in how we think about mental illness, moving us from the dimensional model that prevailed through the age of the *DSM-II* to the categorical model that began with the publication of the *DSM-III* in 1980. According to the dimensional model, depression, neurosis, psychoneurosis, panic anxiety, general anxiety, social anxiety, obsessive-compulsive disorder, and so forth all exist along a spectrum emanating from the same roots in what Freud called intrapsychic conflicts (or Dr. W.'s "self-wounds"). According to the categorical model, as laid out in the *DSM* since its third edition, depression, panic anxiety, general anxiety, social anxiety, obsessive-compulsive disorder, and so forth are carved up into discrete categories based on distinctive symptom clusters that are believed to have different underlying biophysiological mechanisms.

Between 1962, when Klein published his first imipramine study, and 1980, when the *DSM-III* was published, the way psychiatry (and the culture generally) thought about anxiety underwent an enormous transformation. "It is hard to recall that fifteen or twenty years ago there was no such concept [as panic anxiety]," marveled Peter Kramer, a psychiatrist at Brown University, in his 1993 book, *Listening to Prozac.* "Neither in medical school nor psychiatry residency, both in the 1970s, did I ever meet a patient with 'panic anxiety.'" Yet today panic disorder is a frequently diagnosed disease (some 18 percent of Americans are estimated to suffer from it), and "panic attack" has transcended the psychiatric clinic to become part of our lingua franca.

Panic disorder was the first psychiatric disease for which the determining factor in its creation was a drug reaction: imipramine cures panic; ipso facto panic disorder must exist. But this phenomenon—in which a drug effectively defined the syndrome for which it was prescribed—would soon recur.

DSM assigns each slice of craziness with a name and a number. Panic disorder, for example, is disease number 300.21, a diagnostic code. . . . But just because it has a name, is it actually a disease?
—DANIEL CARLAT, *Unhinged: The Trouble with Psychiatry— a Doctor's Revelations About a Profession in Crisis* (2010)

An advertisement for an October 1956 public talk by Frank Berger, the inventor of Miltown, stated that tranquilizers were effective in treating high blood pressure, worry, jitters, "executive stomach," "boss nerves," and "housewife nerves." None of these ailments were then, or are now, listed as illnesses in the American Psychiatric Association's *Diagnostic and Statistical Manual*—which raises the question of whether Miltown prescriptions were aimed less at treating actual psychiatric disorders than at treating the age itself—at mitigating the effects of what Berger in this talk called "today's pressure living."

Every time new drug therapies come along, they raise the question of where the line between anxiety as psychiatric disorder and anxiety as a normal problem of living should get drawn. We see this again and again throughout the history of pharmacology: the rise of tranquilizers is followed by an increase in anxiety disorders diagnoses; the rise of antidepressants is followed by an increase in the rate of depression.

When the APA published the first edition of the *DSM* in the aftermath of World War II, the governing infrastructure of the profession was still Freudian: the first edition placed all disorders along a spectrum of anxiety. "The chief characteristic of [neurotic] disorders is 'anxiety,'" the manual declared, "which may be directly felt and expressed or which may be unconsciously and automatically controlled by the utilization of various defense mechanisms." The second edition, published in 1968, was even more explicitly psychoanalytic. When the APA decided in the 1970s that it was time for a third edition, the Freudians (who had dominated the task forces that wrote the first two editions) and the biological psychiatrists (who had gotten a boost from the recent findings of pharmacology research) prepared for a pitched battle.

The stakes were high. Doctors and therapists of different schools would see their professional fortunes rise or fall depending on whether the definitions of the diseases they specialized in were narrowed or expanded. Drug company profits would spike or plummet depending on whether the categories that were created could be targeted by—and could help secure FDA approval for—the medications they manufactured.

The publication of the *DSM-III* in 1980 represented at least a partial repudiation of Freudian concepts and a victory for biological psychiatry. (One medical historian called the *DSM-III* a "death thrust" for psychoanalysis.) Out went the neuroses, and in their place came the anxiety disorders: social anxiety disorder, generalized anxiety disorder, post-traumatic stress disorder, obsessive-compulsive disorder, and both panic disorder with agoraphobia and panic disorder without agoraphobia. Donald Klein's pharmacological dissection of panic had prevailed.*

---

* Another way of characterizing this was as a victory of the neo-Kraepelinians over the Freudians. Many scholars consider Emil Kraepelin, not Sigmund Freud, to be the crucial figure in the history of psychiatry. Psychoanalysis, these scholars say, was just a blip; Kraepelin's system of disease classification both predated Freudianism and outlasted it.

But in moving mental illness away from Freudianism and into the realm of medical diagnosis, the new *DSM* pathologized as "disordered" or "ill" many people who once would have been considered merely "neurotic." This was a boon for the drug companies, which now had many more "sick" people for whom to develop and market medication. But did it benefit patients?

That's a complicated question. On the one hand, the medicalization of depression and anxiety helped destigmatize conditions once regarded as shameful character weaknesses, and it allowed people to find relief (often pharmacological) from their misery. The number of

---

In 1890, when Freud was setting up his practice in Vienna, Kraepelin, then a thirty-four-year-old physician, took a professorship in psychiatry at Heidelberg University. While there, Kraepelin became interested in the symptoms of various mental illnesses. He and his residents would draw up a note card for each patient who entered his clinic at Heidelberg and would record on it symptoms and a preliminary diagnosis. Each card would then be placed in the "diagnosis box." Every time a new symptom appeared, and every time a diagnosis was revised, the patient's card would be taken from the box and updated. When the patient was released from the hospital, his or her disposition and final diagnosis would be recorded. Over the years, Kraepelin accumulated many hundreds of such cards, which he would take on vacation to study. "In this manner we were able to get an overview and see which diagnoses had been incorrect and the reasons that had led us to this false conception," he wrote.

This systematic recording of patient symptoms and diagnoses may not seem novel today, but no one had attempted to apply such thorough observation and classification to mental illness before Kraepelin. (Actually, one exception here was astrologers. Through the Enlightenment, astrologers kept meticulous medical records so they could chart symptoms against astrological alignments, looking for correlations that would be useful to them in future diagnoses and treatments. This record keeping may in fact have made astrologers better able to prognosticate the course of diseases than doctors, who acted on intuition rather than systematic observation. Astrologers, in other words, may have been more likely to provide evidence-based medicine than doctors were.) Diagnoses were haphazard and random. Kraepelin's goal in gathering all this data was to try to cleave nature at the joints—to identify the cluster of symptoms that characterized each mental disease and to project their development over the life course. Unlike Freud (who was ambiguous about whether mental illness was a medical disease or a psychosocial problem of "adjustment"), Kraepelin came to believe strongly that psychiatry was a subfield of medicine. Emotional disorders were biological entities that could be identified and differentiated the way measles and tuberculosis were.

Kraepelin used the symptom data he accumulated on his cards as the basis of the psychiatry textbook he published in 1883. Revised multiple times over the years, his *Compendium der Psychiatrie* came to be the most influential psychiatric textbook ever published. By the time of the sixth edition in 1899, it had become the urtext of psychiatric classification.

Even through the middle years of the twentieth century, when psychoanalysis pushed Kraepelin's biological psychiatry to the margins, the Kraepelinian and Freudian systems of disease classification existed side by side. When the first edition of the *Diagnostic and Statistical Manual* was published in 1952, it divided diseases into different illness categories based on symptom clusters, very much the way Kraepelin's nineteenth-century textbooks had. But the terminology that described most of those illnesses was psychoanalytic, so almost everything in the first two editions of the *DSM* blended together into a soup of medical and psychoanalytic nomenclature.

people seeing depression or anxiety disorders as a health problem—as opposed to evidence of personal weakness—grew dramatically between 1980 and 2000, as Prozac and other SSRIs provided additional evidence for the idea of depression as a problem of chemical imbalance.* On the other hand, the expansion of medical categories of mental illness had the effect of drawing countless mentally healthy people into the nets of the pharmaceutical companies. Before the arrival of MAOIs and tricyclics in the late 1950s, depression (and its predecessors) was a rare diagnosis, given to only about *1* percent of the U.S. population. Today, by some official estimates, it's a diagnosis given to up to *15* percent of us. Are we truly that much more depressed in 2011 than we were in 1960? Or have we defined depression and anxiety disorders too broadly, allowing the drug companies to bamboozle us (and our insurance companies) into paying for pills that treat diseases we didn't know we had, diseases that didn't exist before 1980?

The publication of each successive edition of the *DSM* has intended to convey the impression of science advancing. And, to be sure, the *DSM-III, DSM-IV* (which came out in 1994), and *DSM-V* (which came out in 2013) were more empirically grounded than the first two editions. They placed much less influence on etiology—that is, on the presumed causes of different illnesses—and much more on simple symptom description.† But they were still political documents as much as scientific ones, representing the claims of one psychiatric school over another—and the professional interests of psychiatrists above everything else. "It is the task of the APA"—and therefore of the *DSM*—"to protect the earning power of psychiatrists," Paul Fink, the vice president of the American Psychiatric Association, declared in 1986. Stuart Kirk and Herb Kutchins, social workers who have together written two books about the history of the *DSM*, say that the APA's so-called bible is "a book of tentatively assembled agreements" that has led to the "pathologizing of everyday behaviors."

When you probe more deeply into the process that produced

---

* I will say more about this in chapter 7.

† The distinction between, say, generalized anxiety disorder and panic disorder lies not in how the disease is acquired—whether by genes or childhood trauma or unreleased libido—but on whether a person experiences a certain minimum number of symptoms from a checklist.

the *DSM-III*, its pretensions to scientific rigor begin to seem rather strained. For starters, some of its new category distinctions appear awfully arbitrary. (Why does panic disorder require the presence of four symptoms, rather than three or five, from the list of thirteen? Why do symptoms have to persist for six months, and not five or seven, for an official diagnosis of social anxiety disorder?) The head of the *DSM-III* task force, Robert Spitzer, would concede years later that many of its decisions were made haphazardly. If a constituency lobbied hard enough for a disease, it tended to get incorporated—which helps explain why between its second and third editions the *DSM* grew from 100 to 494 pages and from 182 to 265 diagnoses.

David Sheehan worked on the *DSM-III* task force. One night in the mid-1970s, Sheehan recalls, a subset of the task force got together for dinner in Manhattan. "As the wine flowed," Sheehan says, the committee members talked about how Donald Klein's research showed that imipramine blocked anxiety attacks. This did seem to be pharmacological evidence of a panic disorder that was distinct from other kinds. As Sheehan puts it:

> Panic disorder was born. And then the wine flowed some more, and the psychiatrists around the dinner table started talking about one of their colleagues who didn't suffer from panic attacks but who worried all the time. How would we classify him? He's just sort of *generally* anxious. Hey, how about 'generalized anxiety disorder'? And then they toasted the christening of the disease with the next bottle of wine. And then for the next thirty years the world collected data on it.

Sheehan, a tall Irishman who today runs a psychiatric center in Florida, is regarded as something of an apostate by the profession. He cheerfully admits he is out to "sabotage the notion" that panic disorder is truly distinct from generalized anxiety disorder. So his jaundiced version of how generalized anxiety disorder was born should perhaps be viewed with some skepticism. But Sheehan, who has been studying and treating anxiety for decades, makes an important point: Once you create a new disease, it starts to take on a life of its own. Research studies accrete around it, and patients get diagnosed with it, and the concept saturates the psychiatric and popular culture. Generalized anxiety disorder, a disease conceived over a boozy dinner and written into the *DSM* with a fairly arbitrary set of criteria, has now had thousands of studies applied to it, and the FDA has approved multiple drugs for treating it. But what if, as Sheehan contends, there is *no such thing* as generalized anxiety disorder—at least not as a disease distinct from panic disorder or major depression?* If Sheehan is right, a large edifice of diagnosis, prescription, and academic study has been built upon something—generalized anxiety disorder—that is presumed to exist in nature but that in fact does not.

> [*At current rates of Valium use*], *the arrival of the millennium would coincide with the total tranquilization of America.*
> —"BENZODIAZEPINES: USE, OVERUSE, MISUSE, ABUSE,"
> EDITORIAL IN *THE LANCET* (MAY 19, 1973)

Even as Thorazine emptied the asylums and antidepressant prescriptions grew exponentially through the late 1950s, nothing approached the runaway commercial success of Miltown. Hence the instructions given to Leo Sternbach, a chemist at Hoffmann–La Roche in New Jersey: "Invent a new tranquilizer," his bosses told him. So Sternbach thought back to research he had done on heptoxdiazine-based dyes while a postdoctoral student in Poland in the 1930s. What would happen if he chemically modified them a little? He tested more than forty different variations on animals—but none seemed to have a tranquilizing effect. Hoffmann–La Roche abandoned the project. Sternbach was reassigned to work on antibiotics.

But one day in April 1957, a research assistant who was cleaning Sternbach's lab came across a powder (official name: Ro-5-090) that had been synthesized a year earlier but was never tested. Without hope, as Sternbach said later, he sent it over to the animal testers on May 7,

---

* Recall from chapter 2 that some genetic research suggests there is in fact no meaningful difference between depression and generalized anxiety disorder.

his forty-ninth birthday. "We thought that the expected negative result would complete our work with this series of compounds and yield at least some publishable material. Little did we know that this was the start of a program which would keep us busy for many years."

Happy birthday. Sternbach had, mostly by accident and nearly without realizing it, invented the first benzodiazepine: chlordiazepoxide, which would be given the trade name Librium (derived from "equilibrium") and was the forerunner of Valium, Ativan, Klonopin, and Xanax, the dominant antianxiety medications of our age. Because of an error in his chemical process, Ro-5-090 had a molecular structure different from the other forty compounds Sternbach had synthesized. (It had a benzene ring of six carbon atoms connected to a diazepine ring of five carbon atoms and two nitrogen atoms—thus "benzodiazepine.") The director of pharmacological research at Hoffmann–La Roche tested the new substance on cats and mice and discovered, to his surprise, that although it was ten times more potent than Miltown, it did not notably impair the animals' motor function. *Time* reported that keepers at the San Diego Zoo had tamed a wild lynx with Librium. A newspaper headline blared: "The Drug That Tames Tigers—What Will It Do for Nervous Women?"

To gauge chlordiazepoxide's toxicity to humans, Sternbach performed the first test on himself. He reported feeling "slightly soft in the knees" and a little bit drowsy for a few hours, but otherwise he experienced no ill effects. By the time the FDA approved the drug, on February 24, 1960, Librium had already been administered to some twenty thousand people. The early reports in the medical journals raved about its effectiveness. Patients who had previously found that only electroshock therapy could control their anxiety declared that Librium was equally or more effective. A study published in *The Journal of the American Medical Association* in January 1960 reported that when 212 outpatients in New Jersey with a range of psychiatric ailments were given Librium, 88 percent of those with "free-floating anxiety" received some degree of relief. The researchers also found that the drug was effective in treating "phobic reactions," "compulsions" (what we would today label obsessive-compulsive disorder), and "tension." The lead researcher of a separate study proclaimed the development of Librium to be "the most significant advance to date in the psychopharmaceutical treatment of anxiety states."

The drug was shipped to American pharmacies in March 1960. The first Hoffmann–La Roche advertisement for Librium said it was for "the treatment of common anxieties and tension." Within three months, sales of Librium were outpacing sales of Miltown; by the end of the decade, more prescriptions had been written for Librium than for any other medication on earth. Physicians prescribed it for everything from hangovers, upset stomachs, and muscle spasms to all varieties of "tension," "nerves," "neurosis," and "anxiety." (One doctor noted that Librium had the same range of indications as gin.)

Librium remained the most prescribed drug in America until 1969—when it was displaced by another compound synthesized by Leo Sternbach, this one with the mellifluous chemical name 7-chloro-1, 3-dihydro-1-methyl-5-phenyl-2H-1, 4-benzodiazepin-2-one. This new drug lacked Librium's bitter aftertaste, and studies found it to be two and a half times as potent. The marketing department at Hoffman–La Roche dubbed it Valium (from the Latin *valere*, "to fare well" or "to be healthy"), and Valium, in turn, remained America's most popular drug until 1982.* In 1973, Valium became the first drug in the United States to exceed $230 million in sales (more than $1 billion in today's dollars)—even as its predecessor, Librium, continued to remain among the five most prescribed drugs in the country. In 1975, it was estimated that one in every five women and one in every thirteen men in America had taken Librium, Valium, or some other benzodiazepine. One study found that 18 percent of all American *physicians* were regularly taking tranquilizers in the 1970s. Advertisements for the drugs became ubiquitous in the medical journals. "It is ten years since Librium became available," went the text of a typical Librium advertisement from the 1970s. "Ten anxious years of aggravation and demonstration, Cuba and Vietnam, assassination and a devaluation, Biafra and Czechoslovakia. Ten turbulent years in which the world-wide climate of anxiety and aggression has given Librium—with its specific calming action and its

---

* Sternbach would also develop flurazepam (marketed as Dalmane) and clonazepam (marketed as Klonopin). Klonopin, like Valium, is still frequently prescribed today as a long-acting benzodiazepine.

remarkable safety margin—a unique and still growing role in helping mankind to meet the challenge of a changing world."

By the end of the decade, Librium and Valium had made Hoffman–La Roche—"the house that Leo built"—the biggest pharmaceutical company in the world. The benzodiazepines had become the greatest commercial success in the history of prescription drugs.

But as benzodiazepine sales grew through the 1960s and 1970s, so did the backlash against them. Some doctors warned that the drugs were being overprescribed. In 1973, Leo Hollister, a psychiatrist at Stanford, mused, "Whether the increase [in the use of antianxiety agents] is the result of the generally turbulent times which have prevailed in the past decade, or the introduction of new drugs and their widespread promotion, or of sloppy prescribing practices of physicians is uncertain." (If 18 percent of doctors were themselves taking Valium, that might account for some of the sloppiness.)

By the middle of the 1970s, the FDA had collected numerous reports of benzodiazepine dependence. Many patients who had been on high dosages of Valium or Librium for long periods of time would experience excruciating physical and psychological symptoms when they stopped taking the medication: anxiety, insomnia, headaches, tremors, blurred vision, ringing in the ears, the feeling that insects were crawling all over them, and extreme depression—and, in some cases, seizures, convulsions, hallucinations, and paranoid delusions. By the time Ted Kennedy led the 1979 Senate hearings on the hazards of benzodiazepines, critics had a rich literature of horror stories to draw on. Judy Garland's death, among others, was attributed to a toxic combination of benzodiazepines and alcohol. Fears about benzodiazepines were given a broad airing by Barbara Gordon, a star television writer at CBS who had been nearly destroyed by addiction to Valium. Gordon's experience with benzodiazepine dependence, as recounted in her memoir, *I'm Dancing as Fast as I Can,* resonated widely. The book became a *New York Times* best seller in 1979 and a feature film starring Jill Clayburgh in 1982. That was the year Public Citizen, the organization led by the consumer advocate Ralph Nader, published *Stopping Valium,* which alleged rampant benzodiazepine addiction.

Social critics worried that the rampant prescription of Valium was papering over the rough edges of society, medicating away radicalism, dissent, and creativity. "One must consider the broader implications of a culture in which tens of millions of adult citizens have come to use psychoactive drugs to alter virtually every facet of their waking (and sleeping) behavior," warned one doctor at a 1971 academic conference on drug use. "What does that say about the impact of modern technology on our style of life? What changes may be evolving in our value system?"[*] Marxist intellectuals like Herbert Marcuse attributed widespread pill popping to capitalist alienation. Conspiracy theorists invoked Aldous Huxley's dystopian *Brave New World*, alleging that the government was exerting social control by tranquilizing the masses (which was ironic because Huxley himself was an enthusiastic promoter of tranquilizers). An editorial published in the prestigious British medical journal *The Lancet* in 1973 fretted that at current rates of Valium use, which up to that point had been growing at a clip of seven million prescriptions a year, "the arrival of the millennium would coincide with the total tranquilization of America."[†]

The looming expiration of Valium's patent in 1985 helped spur the rise of a new benzodiazepine, alprazolam, which the Upjohn Company released with the trade name Xanax in 1981. Entering the market just after the *DSM-III* had introduced anxiety disorders as a clinical category, Xanax got a huge commercial boost from being the first drug specifically approved by the FDA for the treatment of the newly created panic disorder.[‡]

Many patients—and before long I was one of them—found that

---

[*] Feminists had related concerns. A series of ads run by Roche in the early 1970s presumed to offer a treatment for spinsterhood: "35, single and psychoneurotic," began a typical full-page advertisement, this one telling the sad story of Jan. "You probably see many . . . Jans in your practice," the ad went on. "The unmarrieds with low self-esteem. Jan never found a man to measure up to her father. Now she realizes she's in a losing pattern—and that she may *never* marry." The cure? Valium. ("You wake up in the morning, and you feel as if there's no point in going on another day like this," Betty Friedan had written in 1963 in *The Feminine Mystique*. "So you take a tranquilizer because it makes you not care so much that it's pointless.")

[†] As it turned out, Valium use peaked in 1973.

[‡] This approval was not without controversy. The first favorable studies of Xanax's effect on panic were published in the *Archives of General Psychiatry*, whose editor at the time, Daniel Freedman, turned out to be on Upjohn's payroll as a member of its Division of Medical Affairs. Critics said this had unduly biased him and that the studies should not have been published because they were poorly constructed and therefore did not actually demonstrate that the drug was effective.

Xanax cut down on panic attacks and reduced physical symptoms like dizziness, palpitations, and gastrointestinal distress, as well as psychological ones like excessive timidity and feelings of dread. (The poet Marie Howe once told a friend of mine who was afraid to fly after 9/11: "You know that little door in your brain marked *Fear*? Xanax closes it.") By 1986, Xanax had overtaken Miltown, Librium, and Valium to become the best-selling drug in history. It has dominated the tranquilizer market ever since.*

> *Anxiety and tension seem to abound in our modern culture and the current trend is to escape the unpleasantness of its impact. But when has life ever been exempt from stress? In the long run, is it desirable that a population be ever free from tension? Should there be a pill for every mood and occasion?*
> —FROM A DECEMBER 1956 REPORT BY THE NEW YORK ACADEMY OF MEDICINE

Benzodiazepines have been a leading pharmaceutical treatment for anxiety for more than half a century. But not until the late 1970s did the Italian neuroscientist Erminio Costa—yet another veteran of Steve Brodie's lab at the National Institutes of Health—finally home in on their salient chemical mechanism: their effect on a neurotransmitter called gamma-aminobutyric acid, or GABA, which inhibits the rate at which neurons fire.

Some brief and oversimplified neuroscience: A neurotransmitter called glutamate excites neurons, causing them to fire more rapidly; GABA, on the other hand, inhibits neurons, slowing their firing and calming brain activity. (If glutamate is the main accelerator of the brain circuitry, GABA is the main brake.) Costa discovered that benzodiazepines bind to GABA receptors found on every neuron, amplifying GABA's inhibitory effects and suppressing activity of the central nervous system. In binding to the GABA receptors, benzodiazepines

---

* In 2010, Xanax was the twelfth most commonly prescribed drug in America and the most frequently prescribed psychotropic medication—more widely prescribed than Prozac or any other single antidepressant.

change the receptors' molecular structure in a way that causes the GABA signal to last longer, which in turn causes the neuron to continue firing at a lower rate, calming brain activity.

Knowing even this superficial bit of neuroscience has given me a serviceable metaphor for understanding how my brain produces anxiety and how Xanax reduces it. When my anxiety mounts, my autonomic nervous system gets kicked into fight-or-flight mode, my thoughts start racing, and I start imagining all kinds of catastrophic things; my body feels like it's going haywire. I imagine the firing of my synapses getting faster and faster, like an overheating engine. I take a Xanax, and about thirty minutes later, if I'm lucky, I can almost feel the GABA system putting on the brakes as the benzodiazepines bind to their receptors and inhibit neuronal firing. Everything . . . slows . . . down.

Of course, this is a rather reductionist metaphor. Can my anxiety really be boiled down to how effectively gated my chloride ion channels are or to the speed of neuronal firing in my amygdala? Well, yes, at some level it can. Rates of neuronal firing in the amygdala correlate quite directly with the felt experience of anxiety. But to say that my anxiety is reducible to the ions in my amygdala is as limiting as saying that my personality or my soul is reducible to the molecules that make up my brain cells or to the genes that underwrote them.

In any case, I have a more practical concern: What is this long-term reliance on benzodiazepines doing to my brain? By this point, I have taken benzodiazepines (Valium, Klonopin, Ativan, Xanax) at varying doses and frequencies for more than thirty years. For several years during that time, I have been on tranquilizers around the clock for months at a time.

"Valium, Librium, and other drugs of that class cause damage to the brain. I have seen damage to the cerebral cortex that I believe is due to the use of these drugs, and I am beginning to wonder if the damage is permanent," David Knott, a physician at the University of Tennessee, warned back in 1976. In the three decades since then, scores of articles in scientific journals have reported on the cognitive impairment observed in long-term benzodiazepine users. A 1984 study by Malcolm Lader found that the brains of people who took tranquilizers for a long time physically shrank. (Subsequent studies have shown that different benzodiazepines seem to concentrate the shrinkage in different parts of the brain.) Does this explain why at the age of forty-four, after several decades of intermittently continuous tranquilizer consumption, I feel stupider than I used to?

CHAPTER 7

Medication and the Meaning of Anxiety

When Valium came along, both patients and their doctors were will-ing to define their problems in terms of anxiety. . . . When Prozac, a drug for depression, arrived on the scene, the accent fell on depression as the hallmark of distress.
—EDWARD SHORTER, *A History of Psychiatry* (1997)

In the spring of 1997, after a difficult year—my parents' divorce, an unhappy job situation, a bad romance—and some months off psychiat-ric medications, I began, at my therapist's urging, to take Paxil, an SSRI whose generic name is paroxetine.

After a week or so on Paxil, I experienced an infusion of energy that bordered on manic: I slept fewer and fewer hours, but without feeling tired during the day; I could, for the first time in my life, regu-larly awake in the morning feeling energetic. The mild mania passed, but what followed was a slow brightening of my mood. I ended—finally, after several unsuccessful attempts—my codependent and dys-functional relationship with my girlfriend of nearly two years. I got a promotion at the small magazine where I was working. I started dating.

At some point that fall, I realized I had not experienced a full-blown panic attack since I'd started on Paxil in April—by far my lon-gest such stretch since middle school. I was experiencing less anxiety, feeling productive and engaged in my work, and enjoying an active social life. My stomach settled. Paxil was magic.

Or was it? Because what was cause and what was effect? That pro-motion I got at work came along after someone left and I was elevated to fill the position; that would likely have happened even if I hadn't gone on Paxil. Maybe that small boost in my professional status, along with the more interesting and empowering day-to-day responsibilities of the job, bolstered my self-esteem, which in turn gave me the confidence to start sending out freelance work, which in turn made me feel professionally engaged. And while I felt like the Paxil had somehow given me the strength to finally break the stubborn cord of neurotic codependence that had tied me to my girlfriend, maybe I would have done that anyway—and there is no question that, Paxil or no Paxil, being out of that relationship was liberating. (For her, too, I'm sure; we haven't spoken since.) So maybe it was the particular constellation of events that came together that spring—the promotion, the breaking off of a dysfunctional relationship, the end of a dark Boston winter and the arrival of spring—that lifted my anxiety and depression. Maybe Paxil had nothing to do with it.

But I think it did. Beginning with that brief manic boost, my lived experience felt like it was Paxil inflected—and I now know that my clinical trajectory (mild mania, lifting of mood, effecting of positive life changes) is a fairly common one. Of course, another possibility is that what I enjoyed that spring and summer was the placebo effect— the Paxil worked because I *believed* it would work. (With the placebo effect, the power of belief itself, rather than the chemical content of any medication, is the salient mechanism.)

But the Paxil was not magic—or if it was, its magic ran out. Because after trundling merrily along in medicated contentment for ten months, my short-lived feeling of invulnerability was punctured within a period of ten minutes.

In those first months on Paxil, I had—for the first time in twenty years—been able to fly with only moderate anxiety. So one February morning, I drove heedlessly through a fierce New England rainstorm to the airport (how nice not to be in a nervous swivet for days before every plane ride!), boarded my flight, and settled in with my newspaper for the hour-long trip to Washington, D.C. I can't say that I was ever, even in those glorious early days on Paxil, free of flying anxiety. But it was a gentler experience, manifesting itself as butterflies in my stomach, sweat on my palms, and a mild feeling of apprehension—what I imagine many people feel upon takeoff. So there I sat, twenty-eight years old, feeling relatively competent and grown-up (*Here I am,* I thought, *the executive editor of a magazine, flying to Washington on business, reading my* New York Times), confidently insulated from terror by my morning dose of twenty milligrams of Paxil, that little pink pill that had kept me panic-free for a blissful few months, as we taxied and took off.

And then, passing through the dark clouds that were producing the rainstorm below, we ran into turbulence.

It lasted all of ten minutes. Fifteen at most. But the whole time I was convinced we were going to crash—or, worse, that I would get airsick and throw up. Hands shaking, I gulped two Dramamine. Beverage service had been suspended—the flight attendants had been asked to stay seated, which terrified me. But as I looked around the cabin, none of my fellow passengers seemed unduly perturbed. To my left, a man tried to read his newspaper, despite the thrashing and dipping of the plane; to my right, across the aisle, a woman appeared to doze. I, meanwhile, wanted to scream. I desperately wanted the turbulence to end (*Please, God, please make it end now and I'll believe in you and be good and pious forever*) and the Dramamine to take effect, and I craved, above all, unconsciousness, an end to the misery.

Of course, my fears of crashing must not have been completely consuming, because I had, even in that moment, an additional worry: Was my panic so obvious that the other passengers would see it? Logically, one anxiety should have canceled out the other: if we were all going to die, I shouldn't have been worried about an ephemeral moment of earthly embarrassment before plunging into eternal oblivion, right? On the other hand, if I was going to end up embarrassed after the flight, that would mean we *weren't* going to die, right? And at that moment, to be safely on the ground and to not be dead—no matter how embarrassed—was a condition greatly to be desired. But in my amygdala-controlled brain, with my sympathetic nervous system on full alert, there was no room for such clarity of logic. All I could think was, *I'm going to throw up and I'm going to be humiliated and I'm going to die and I'm terrified and all I want is to be out of this situation and never to get on a plane again.*

Then we passed above the clouds, and there was clear sky and sun outside the window, and the ride was completely smooth. The seat belt sign was turned off. Beverage service resumed. My parasympathetic nervous system kicked in, arresting the firing rate of the hyperactive neurons in my turbocharged amygdala, and I sank into a relieved, Dramamine-enhanced exhaustion. Half an hour or so later, we landed uneventfully in Washington.

But the Paxil had stopped working.

Not completely, at least not right away. But the illusion of being surrounded by an invincible anxiety-repelling Paxil force field had been dispelled. This, I now know, is not an infrequent occurrence. Certain SSRI medications can reduce anxiety and cut down on panic attacks—but according to the stress-diathesis model of panic, strong stimuli (like a turbulent flight) are potent enough to break through even medication-adjusted brain chemistry to produce intense anxiety. And this can be, because of the effect the breakthrough has on the thinking (or the "cognitions") of the individual, like a magical spell being broken. (Other times, certain drugs just stop working without such stressful provocation; this phenomenon has been called "the Prozac poop-out.")

After that day, my general anxiety level slowly rose again. My panic attacks began to recur—mild and infrequent at first, then more severe and more often. My flying phobia resurged—I needed to take a large dose of Xanax or Klonopin or Ativan before getting on any flight, and sometimes even that wasn't enough. On my first airplane trip with Susanna, who was later to become my wife, my anxiety got so bad soon after takeoff that I began shaking and gasping frantically, and then, as Susanna looked on in bewilderment, my stomach cramped and I lost control of my bowels. I had planned the trip—three days in London— as a romantic vacation, an attempt to woo and impress her. This was not a good start. Nor was the rest of the trip much better: those parts of the vacation that I did not spend sedated into near catatonia by massive quantities of Xanax I spent quaking in mortal dread of the return flight.

I kept taking Paxil for several years, even after it had lost its panic-repelling magic, out of a combination of inertia and the fear of what might happen if I stopped. But by the spring of 2003, I had been on Paxil for six years, and my anxiety was once again in full bloom. It was time to try something new.

This is what prompted me to see Dr. Harvard, the psychopharmacologist. During my first visit, he was taking my case history when, as if to demonstrate my disorder, I had a florid panic attack that rendered me breathless and tearful, unable to continue. "Take your time," Dr. Harvard said. "Continue when you're ready." Whether it was the facts of my case history or the vividness of the panic attack I unwillingly displayed for him, Dr. Harvard seemed surprised to learn that I had gone completely unmedicated for stretches of my life. He seemed amazed. To him, I was a hard case, not equipped for normal human functioning without pharmaceutical assistance.

We discussed the pharmacological options, eventually settling on Effexor, the trade name for venlaxafine, a serotonin-norepinephrine reuptake inhibitor (SNRI), which impedes the absorption—and therefore boosts the intrasynaptic levels of—both serotonin and norepinephrine in the brain. We talked about how to taper slowly off the Paxil, which I did, carefully following his instructions, decreasing the dosage bit by tiny bit over a period of several weeks.

Over the years, I had from time to time considered trying to wean myself off psychiatric medication completely. *After all,* I reasoned, *I'm pretty anxious on medication—how much worse can I be off of it?* So once I finally did manage to taper most of the way off the Paxil, I thought, *Why not, let's try flying solo for a while—no more drugs.* I stopped taking the Paxil and didn't start the Effexor.

Here is what you don't see in those TV and magazine advertisements for psychotropic drugs or even, with any real specificity or sympathetic understanding, in the clinical literature: the hell of going off them. I've never taken heroin, so I can't say whether this is true (I suspect it isn't), but many people claim that withdrawal from Paxil is as bad as withdrawal from heroin. The headaches. The exhaustion. The nausea and stomach cramps. The knee-buckling vertigo. The electric zapping sensation in your brain—a weird but common symptom. And, of course, the surge of anxiety: waking up at dawn every morning to a pounding heart and terrible dread; multiple panic attacks daily.

Despite my desire to try to "be myself" and function without pharmacological assistance for the first time in six years, I couldn't hack it, and so one morning after barely a week off the Paxil, I took my first dose of Effexor. Within minutes, literally, I felt much better: the physical symptoms receded; my state of mind improved.

This cannot actually have been due to the Effexor's therapeutic action—SSRIs and SNRIs generally need several weeks to build up in the synapses enough to start working. More likely, something in the Effexor somehow alleviated the effects of chemical withdrawal from Paxil. But what is cause and what is effect? Were the emotional anxiety and physical misery I felt after going off the Paxil really the effect of chemical withdrawal? Or was this simply what it feels like to be me undrugged? After all, I had been on psychiatric medication for long enough that maybe I had forgotten what it feels like to live in my naked brain.

Or was my misery that spring less the result of ill-fated drug-switching experiments than of the stress in my life? Two dates loomed at the end of that summer. The first was the deadline for the delivery of the manuscript of my first book, which by then had been in gestation for six years (roughly the length of time I'd been on Paxil) and had endured a harrowing journey—from editor to editor and publishing house to publishing house, through the descent into Alzheimer's of my biography's subject and the increasingly intrusive involvement of my subject's powerful family—to get to this point. The other was my wife's due date for the delivery of our first child.* Of the difficulties I endured that summer, it's hard to know exactly which were a response to external stressors and which were drug related. And of those drug-related difficulties, it's hard to know which were withdrawal effects from drugs I was weaning *off* and which were side effects from drugs I was going *on*.

The contrast between what the pharmaceutical industry's promotional materials and the clinical research papers (many of them subsidized by grants from the pharmaceutical industry) say and what the roiling online communities of actual patients say is large. I believe both sides are generally honest and accurate as far as they go (the drugs can have measurable therapeutic benefits; the side effects and withdrawal

---

* The birth of a child ranks high on the famous Holmes and Rahe Stress Scale, which attempts to quantify the effects of various kinds of life stresses on mental and physical health.

symptoms can be awful), but neither one is wholly trustworthy. The drug companies, and the doctors subsidized by them, have a profit-motivated interest in pushing pills; the drug takers are pretty much by definition an unhappy and unstable bunch prone, like me, to being easily thrown by physical symptoms. Studies have shown that people who score high on scales of anxiety sensitivity tend to suffer drug side effects more severely. (A bunch of nonanxious people who took an SSRI would likely be much less bothered by any side effects and would therefore be less likely to complain about them in online forums.) So the antidrug rants of the pill-popping community cannot be taken at face value any more than can the assessment of side effects and withdrawal symptoms in the sometimes boosterish clinical literature.

Though the Effexor eased what seemed to be the physical symptoms of my withdrawal from Paxil, my anxiety and panic persisted—and then increased. When I told Dr. Harvard about this, his response, as the response of psychiatrists and psychopharmacologists so often tends to be, was, "We need to elevate your dosage." The quantity of Effexor I was taking was not sufficient, he said, to correct the "chemical imbalance" in my serotonergic and noradrenergic systems. So I went from taking thirty-seven and a half milligrams to seventy-five milligrams of Effexor three times a day.

At which point my anxiety levels shot through the roof. At night, I would awaken in the grip of a raging panic attack. During the day, I was having multiple panic attacks—and even when I wasn't having one, I felt as though I were about to. Never had I felt such chronic, persistent agitation; I couldn't stop moving and twitching, couldn't bear the feeling of being in my own skin. (The clinical term for this is "akathisia.") Glimmerings of suicide began twinkling at the edge of my consciousness.

I called Dr. Harvard. "I can't take it," I told him. "I think maybe I need to get off the Effexor. I feel like I'm going crazy." "You need to give it more time," he said. And he gave me a prescription for Xanax, which he said would take the edge off my anxiety while giving the Effexor time to work.

Prescribing a benzodiazepine (like Xanax) to overcome the anxiety produced when a patient starts taking an antidepressant SSRI or SNRI (like Effexor) has been standard practice since the late 1990s.

And in my case this worked—a little, for a short time. My anxiety receded somewhat, and the panic subsided, but only if I faithfully took my Xanax around the clock.

To work on my book, I had rented a decrepit office on the third floor of a crummy building in Boston's North End, and to hasten my progress, I had hired a research assistant, Kathy, who shared the space with me. Kathy was an excellent researcher and, when I wasn't feeling panicky, delightful company. But I was embarrassed about my anxiety and felt I had to hide it, which meant leaving when I felt panic coming on. So I was forever contriving errands to get me out of the office.*

Yet again I called Dr. Harvard. And yet again he said, "You're not at a therapeutic level of the Effexor yet. Let's increase the dosage." So I started taking more Effexor, and a few days later my vision blurred and I couldn't urinate. I called Dr. Harvard, and for once he sounded alarmed. "Maybe we'd better get you off the Effexor," he said. But I'd been traumatized by the withdrawal symptoms I'd suffered when I'd stopped taking Paxil, and I told him so. (Discontinuation syndrome is now a clinically acknowledged Paxil phenomenon.) "I'm giving you a prescription for Celexa," he said, using the brand name for citalopram, another SSRI. "Start taking it right away, and continue taking the Xanax."

I did, and within a day my vision cleared and my urine again

---

* Often, escaping the office wasn't enough to stem the tide of panic, so I took to walking several blocks to Old North Church, where Paul Revere's famous one-if-by-land-and-two-if-by-sea lanterns had supposedly been hung in 1775. I'd sit in an austere wooden pew in the back and gaze at the oil painting of Jesus that hangs behind the altar. In that painting, Christ's face looks kindly, his eyes sympathetic. I am not a hard-core atheist, but nor am I a believer—I'm a who-knows-what-explains-all-this agnostic, a skeptic who out of my usual abundance of caution refuses to brazenly deny that God exists for fear of losing Pascal's wager and discovering too late that he does. Yet in those desperate weeks in the summer of 2003, I would sit in Old North Church and pray forthrightly to that painting of Jesus. I'd ask it to please give me peace of mind, or a sign that God existed, something I could grab hold of to steady myself against the assault of my nerves. In my quest for succor, I started reading my way through the Bible and a history of early Christianity, trying to see if I could somehow reason my way to faith and the psychic and existential serenity I thought it might provide.

I couldn't. And while I did find something about the unadorned Puritan simplicity of the church to be calming, my visits there didn't really help, either, especially during the nadir of my Effexor experience. I'd try to calm my breathing—but then I'd get overwhelmed by claustrophobia and panic and have to rush out of the church. I'd often end up shaking on a park bench, probably looking to passing tourists like a homeless person suffering delirium tremens.

flowed, which would seem to suggest those problems had been side effects of the drug. But they might not have been: the tendency of anxiety sufferers to "somaticize"—to convert their neuroses into physical symptoms—means it's possible my blurred vision and recalcitrant bladder were simply physical representations of my anxiety.

The transition from Effexor to Celexa was smoother than the transition from Paxil to Effexor had been, perhaps because I didn't wean off one before going on the other. But since then, despite chronic and intermittently severe anxiety, I've not gone a day without taking an SSRI antidepressant, and I've not adjusted my dosage much, for fear of repeating the Paxil-to-Effexor experience. At times I think wistfully about my early days on Paxil, when I found a modicum of relief, and wonder if I shouldn't switch back and try to achieve again that panic-free nirvana. But the clinical research is full of people who return to drugs they had taken earlier only to find them no longer effective.

And in any case, the experience of weaning off Paxil is not one I want to repeat.

Medication, medication, medication! What do I got to show for it?
—*THE SOPRANOS'* TONY SOPRANO TO DR. MELFI AFTER A YEAR ON
PROZAC FOR HIS PANIC ATTACKS

Exploding into the national consciousness with the March 26, 1990, edition of *Newsweek,* whose cover featured a green-and-white capsule alongside the words "A Breakthrough Drug for Depression," fluoxetine, under its trade name Prozac, would become the iconic antidepressant of the late twentieth century—a blockbuster for its manufacturer, Eli Lilly. The first selective serotonin reuptake inhibitor (SSRI) to be released in the United States, Prozac would before long surpass Xanax as the best-selling psychotropic drug in history—even as competing SSRIs (among them Zoloft, Paxil, Celexa, and Lexapro) would soon be on their way to outpacing Prozac.

With the possible exception of antibiotics, SSRIs are the most commercially successful class of prescription drugs in history. By 2002, according to one estimate, some twenty-five million Americans—more than 5 percent of all men and 11 percent of all women—were taking an SSRI antidepressant. The numbers have only grown since then—a 2007 estimate put the number of Americans on SSRIs at thirty-three million. These drugs dominate not only hospital psychiatry and our medicine cabinets but also our culture and natural environment. Books like *Prozac Nation, Prozac Diary,* and *Listening to Prozac* (and, of course, *Talking Back to Prozac*) populated the best-seller lists throughout the 1990s, and Prozac and Lexapro jokes remain a fixture of movies and *New Yorker* cartoons. Trace elements of Prozac, Paxil, Zoloft, and Celexa have been found in the ecosystems of American frogs (causing them developmental delays and anomalies), in the brains and livers of fish in North Texas, and in Lake Mead, America's largest reservoir, which supplies drinking water to Las Vegas, Los Angeles, San Diego, and Phoenix.

Given how completely SSRIs have saturated our culture and our environment, you might be surprised to learn that Eli Lilly, which held the U.S. patent for fluoxetine, killed the drug in development *seven times* because of unconvincing test results. After examining tepid fluoxetine trial outcomes, as well as complaints about the drug's side effects, German regulators in 1984 concluded, "Considering the benefit and the risk, we think this preparation totally unsuitable for the treatment of depression." Early clinical trials of another SSRI, Paxil, were also failures.*

How did SSRIs go from being considered ineffective to being one of the best-selling drug classes in history? In the answer to that question lies a story about how dramatically our understanding of anxiety and depression has changed in a short period of time.

Once again the story begins at Steve Brodie's laboratory at the National Institutes of Health. After leaving Brodie's lab for the University of Gothenburg in Sweden in 1959, Arvid Carlsson gave tricyclic antidepressants to mice with artificially depleted serotonin levels.

---

* A series of studies in the 1980s found imipramine, the tricyclic antidepressant, to be more effective than Prozac for treating patients with depression or panic disorder. Imipramine also trounced Paxil in two studies in the early 1980s of patients with depression. In 1989, Paxil failed to beat a placebo in more than half its trials. Yet four years later, Paxil was approved by the FDA—and by 2000 it was the best-selling antidepressant on the market, outselling Prozac and Zoloft.

Would the antidepressants boost serotonin levels? Yes; imipramine had serotonin-reuptake-inhibiting effects. In the 1960s, Carlsson tried similar experiments with antihistamines. Would they also inhibit the reuptake of serotonin? Again, yes. Carlsson found that an antihistamine called chlorpheniramine had a more powerful and precise effect on the brain's serotonin receptors than did either imipramine or amitriptyline, the two most commonly prescribed tricyclics. Carlsson invoked this finding as evidence to support what he called the serotonin hypothesis of depression. He then set about applying this discovery in pursuit of a more potent antidepressant. "This," the medical historian Edward Shorter has written, "was the birthing hour of the SSRIs."*

Carlsson next experimented with a different antihistamine, brompheniramine (the active ingredient in the cough medication Dimetapp). It, too, blocked the reuptake of serotonin and norepinephrine more robustly than imipramine did. He modified the antihistamine to create compound H102-09, which blocked only the reuptake of serotonin. Working with a team of researchers at Astra, a Swedish pharmaceutical company, Carlsson applied for a patent for H102-09—which had by then been renamed zimelidine—on April 28, 1971. Early clinical trials suggested zimelidine had some effectiveness in reducing depres-

---

* Carlsson wanted to pursue chlorpheniramine clinical trials for patients with anxiety and depression, but he never did. His own lab research, as well as subsequent naturalistic observations, showed that chlorpheniramine may, without any modifications, be as effective as any existing SSRI—which is intriguing because chlorpheniramine has been on the market, under the trade name Chlor-Trimeton, as an over-the-counter medicine for pollen allergies since 1950. In 2006, Einar Hellbom, a Swedish researcher, published a study suggesting that patients diagnosed with panic disorder who took chlorpheniramine for their hay fever experienced a remission of their panic symptoms while on the drug; when the patients went off Chlor-Trimeton, even if they switched to another antihistamine, many of them found their panic attacks returning. Hellbom suggested that perhaps this means an effective nonprescription SSRI antidepressant is sitting on the allergy remedy shelf of your local pharmacy today—even though scarcely any doctors, and certainly no consumers, are aware of its potential in this regard. "If chlorpheniramine had been tested on depression in the nineteen seventies," Hellbom writes, "it is probable that a safe, inexpensive SSRI drug could have been used some 15 years earlier than [Prozac]. . . . Chlorpheniramine might have been the first safe, non-cardiotoxic and well-tolerated antidepressant. Billions of dollars in the development and marketing costs would have been saved, and the suffering of millions of patients alleviated."

This is striking to me because I took Chlor-Trimeton regularly each spring throughout my childhood. I had always attributed the lifting of my depression and anxiety in April and May to the lengthening of the daylight and the approaching end of the school year. But Hellbom's paper leads me to wonder if my brightening mood and decreasing tension each spring were a result of my exposure to Chlor-Trimeton, the accidental SSRI.

sion, and in 1982 Astra started selling it in Europe as the antidepressant Zelmid. Astra licensed Zelmid's North American rights to Merck, which began preparing to release the drug in the United States. Then tragedy struck: some patients taking Zelmid became paralyzed; a few died. Zelmid was pulled from pharmacy shelves in Europe and was never distributed in America.

Executives at Eli Lilly watched these developments with interest. Some ten years earlier, biochemists at the company's labs in Indiana had fiddled with chemical derivatives of a different antihistamine, diphen-hydramine (the active ingredient in the allergy medication Benadryl), to create a compound called LY-82816, which had a potent effect on serotonin but only a weak effect on norepinephrine levels. This made LY-82816 the most "clean," or "selective," of the several compounds the researchers tested.* David Wong, an Eli Lilly biochemist, reformu-lated LY-82816 into compound LY-110140 and wrote up his findings in the journal *Life Sciences* in 1974. "At this point," Wong would later recall, "work on [LY-110140] was an academic exercise." Nobody knew whether there would be a market for even one serotonin-boosting psy-chiatric medication—and since Zelmid already had a head start of sev-eral years in getting through clinical trials and onto the market, Eli Lilly put LY-110140, now called fluoxetine, aside.

But when Zelmid started paralyzing people, Eli Lilly executives realized fluoxetine now had a chance to be the first SSRI on the mar-ket in America, so they restarted the research machinery. Though many of the early clinical trials were not notably successful, the drug was approved and released in Belgium in 1986. In January 1988, fluox-etine was released in the United States, marketed as "the first highly specific, highly potent blocker of serotonin uptake." Eli Lilly gave it the trade name Prozac, which a branding firm had thought had "zap" to it.

Two years later, the pill graced the cover of *Newsweek*. Three years after that, Peter Kramer, the Brown psychiatrist, published *Listening to Prozac*.

---

* The tricyclics and MAOIs, in contrast, were "dirty," or "nonselective," in that they affected not just serotonin but also norepinephrine, dopamine, and other neurotransmitters, a fact that was thought to account for their wide range of unpleasant side effects.

When *Listening to Prozac* came out in the summer of 1993, I was twenty-three and on my third tricyclic antidepressant—this time desipramine, whose trade name is Norpramin. I read the book with fascination, marveling at the transformative effects Prozac had had on Kramer's patients. Many of his patients became, as he put it, "better than well": "Prozac seemed to give social confidence to the habitually timid, to make the sensitive brash, to lend the introvert the social skills of a salesman." *Hmm*, I thought. *This sounds pretty good.* My longtime psychiatrist, Dr. L., had been suggesting Prozac to me for months. But reading Kramer, I worried about what Faustian exchange was being made here—what got lost, in selfhood or the more idiosyncratic parts of personality, when Prozac medicated away the nervousness or the melancholy. In his book, Kramer concluded forcefully that for most severely anxious or depressed patients, the bargain was worthwhile. But he worried, too, about what he called "cosmetic psychopharmacology"—the use of psychiatric drugs by "normal" or "healthy" people to become happier, more social, more professionally effective.

Before long, I joined the millions of other Americans taking SSRIs—and I've been on one or another pretty much continuously for going on twenty years. Nevertheless, I can't say with complete conviction that these drugs have worked—or that they've been worth the costs in terms of money, side effects, drug-switching traumas, and who knows what long-term effects on my brain.

After the initial flush of enthusiasm for SSRIs, some of the fears that had surrounded tranquilizers in the 1970s began clustering around antidepressants. "It is now clear," David Healy, the historian of psychopharmacology, has written, "that the rates at which withdrawal problems have been reported on [Paxil] exceed the rates at which withdrawal problems have been reported on any other psychotropic drug ever."*

---

* Ironically, the early commercial success of SSRIs owed a lot to the public furor over Valium addiction in the early 1970s, which had driven benzodiazepines out of favor. When the FDA approved SSRIs for the treatment of depression, that caused the number of depression diagnoses to skyrocket, even as rates of anxiety diagnosis fell. But when the FDA subsequently approved SSRIs for the treatment of anxiety, the number of anxiety diagnoses rose again.

"Paxil is truly addictive," Frank Berger, the inventor of Miltown, said not long before his death in 2008. "If you have somebody on Paxil, it's not so easy to get him off. . . . This is not the case with Librium, Valium and Miltown." A few years ago, my primary care physician told me she had stopped prescribing Paxil because so many of her patients had reported such severe withdrawal effects.

Even leaving aside withdrawal effects, there is now a large pile of evidence suggesting—in line with those early studies of the ineffectiveness of Prozac and Paxil—that SSRIs may not work terribly well. In January 2010, almost exactly twenty years after introducing Americans to SSRIs, *Newsweek* published a cover story reporting on studies that suggested these drugs are barely as effective as sugar pills for the treatment of anxiety and depression. Two massive studies from 2006 showed most patients do not get better taking antidepressants; only about a third of the patients in these studies improved dramatically after a first trial. After reviewing dozens of studies on SSRI effectiveness, the *British Medical Journal* concluded that Prozac, Zoloft, Paxil, and the other drugs in the SSRI class "do not have a clinically meaningful advantage over placebo."*

How can this be? Tens of millions of Americans—including me and many people I know—collectively consume billions of dollars' worth of SSRIs each year. Doesn't this suggest that these drugs are effective?

Not necessarily. At the very least, these massive rates of SSRI consumption have not caused rates of self-reported anxiety and depression to go down—and in fact all this pill popping seems to correlate with substantially higher rates of anxiety and depression.

"If you're born around World War I, in your lifetime the prevalence of depression is about 1 percent," says Martin Seligman, a psychologist at the University of Pennsylvania. "If you're born around World War II the lifetime prevalence of depressions seemed to be about 5 percent. If you were born starting in the 1960s, the lifetime prevalence seemed to be between 10 percent and 15 percent, and this is with lives incomplete"—meaning that in the end the actual rates will be higher.

---

* These findings are controversial and continue to be debated fiercely on psychiatry and psychology blogs.

That's at least a tenfold increase in the diagnosis of depression across just two generations.

The same trend is evident in other countries. In Iceland, the incidence of depression nearly doubled between 1976 (before the arrival of SSRIs) and 2000. In 1984, four years before the introduction of Prozac, Britain reported 38 million "days of incapacity" (sick days) resulting from depression and anxiety disorders; in 1999, after a decade of widespread SSRI use, Britain attributed 117 million days of incapacity to the same disorders—an increase of 300 percent. Health surveys in the United States show that the percentage of working-age Americans who reported being disabled by depression tripled in the 1990s. Here's the most striking statistic I've come across: Before antidepressants existed, some fifty to one hundred people per million were thought to suffer from depression; today, between *one hundred thousand and two hundred thousand* people per million are estimated to have depression. In a time when we have more biochemically sophisticated treatments than ever for combating depression, that's a *1,000 percent increase* in the incidence of depression.

In his 2010 book, *Anatomy of an Epidemic,* the journalist Robert Whitaker marshaled evidence suggesting that SSRIs actually *cause* depression and anxiety—that SSRI consumption over the last twenty years has created organic changes in the brains of tens of millions of drug takers, making them more likely to feel nervous and unhappy. (Statistics from the World Health Organization showing that the worldwide suicide rate has increased by *60 percent* over the last forty-five years would seem to give weight to the idea that the quotient of unhappiness in the world has risen in tandem with SSRI consumption.) Whitaker's argument about drugs causing mental illness is controversial—most experts would dispute it, and it's certainly not proven. What's clear, though, is that the explosion of SSRI prescriptions has caused a drastic expansion in the *definitions* of depression and anxiety disorder (as well as more widespread acceptance of using depression and anxiety as excuses for skipping work), which has in turn caused the number of people given these diagnoses to increase.

We may look back 150 years from now and see antidepressants as a dangerous and sinister experiment.
—JOSEPH GLENMULLEN, *Prozac Backlash* (2001)

In America, the question of when and whether to prescribe medications for routine neurotic suffering is bound up with two competing intellectual traditions: our historical roots in the self-denial and asceticism of our Puritan forebears versus the post-baby-boom belief that everyone is entitled to the "pursuit of happiness" enshrined in our founding document. In modern psychiatry, the tension between these two traditions plays out in the battle between Peter Kramer's cosmetic psychopharmacology and what's known as pharmacological Calvinism.

Critics of cosmetic psychopharmacology (including, to some extent, Kramer himself) worry about what happens when millions of mildly neurotic patients seek medication to make themselves "better than well" and when competition to get and stay ahead in the workplace creates a pharmaceutical arms race. The term "pharmacological Calvinism" was coined in 1971 by Gerald Klerman, a self-described "angry psychiatrist" who was out to combat the emerging consensus that if a drug makes you feel good, it must be bad. Life is hard and suffering is real, Klerman and his allies argued, so why should ill-founded Puritanism be allowed to interfere with nervous or unhappy Americans' quest for peace of mind?

The pharmacological Calvinists believe that to escape psychic pain without quest or struggle is to diminish the self or the soul; it's getting something for nothing, a Faustian bargain at odds with the Protestant work ethic. "Psychotherapeutically," Klerman wrote sardonically, "the world is divided into the first-class citizens, the saints who can achieve their cure or salvation by willpower, insight, psychoanalysis or by behavior modification, and the rest of the people, who are weak in their moral fiber and need a crutch." Klerman angrily dismissed such concerns, wondering why we would, out of some sense of misguided moral propriety, deny anxious, depressed Americans relief from their suffering and the opportunity to pursue higher, more meaningful goals.

Why remain mired in the debilitating self-absorption of your neuroses if a pill can free your mind?

Americans are ambivalent about all this. We pop tranquilizers and antidepressants by the billions—yet at the same time we have historically judged reliance on psychiatric medication to be a sign of weakness or moral failure.* A study conducted by researchers at the National Institute of Mental Health in the early 1970s concluded that "Americans believe tranquilizers are effective but have serious doubts about the morality of using them."

Which sounds like a somewhat illogical and self-contradictory position—but it happens to be the one I hold myself. I reluctantly take both tranquilizers and antidepressants, and I believe that they work—at least a little, at least some of the time. And I acknowledge that, as many psychiatrists and psychopharmacologists have told me, I may have a "medical condition" that causes my symptoms and somehow "justifies" the use of these medications. Yet at the same time, I also believe (and I believe that society believes) that my nervous problems are in some way a character issue or a moral failing. I believe my weak nerves make me a coward and a wimp, with all the negative judgment those words imply, which is why I have tried to hide evidence of them—and which is why I worry that resorting to drugs to mitigate these problems both proves and intensifies my moral weakness.

"Stop judging yourself!" Dr. W. says. "You're making your anxiety worse!"

He's right. And yet I can't help concurring with the 40 percent of respondents to that NIMH survey who agreed with the statement "Moral weakness causes mental illness and taking tranquilizers to correct or ameliorate the condition is further evidence of that weakness."

Of course, as we learn more about how genes encode certain temperamental traits and dispositions into our personalities, it becomes harder to sustain the moral weakness argument in quite the same way. If my genes have encoded in me an anxious physiology, how responsible can I be held for the way that I quiver in the face of frightening situations or tend to crumble under stress? With the evidence for a

---

* Much more so than in, say, France, where tranquilizer consumption rates are higher, but perhaps even less so than in Japan, where SSRI consumption rates are much lower.

strong genetic basis to psychiatric disorders accumulating, more recent surveys about American attitudes toward reliance on psychiatric medication reveal a dramatic shift of opinion. In 1996, only 38 percent of Americans saw depression as a health problem—versus 62 percent who saw depression as evidence of personal weakness. A decade later, those numbers had more than reversed: 72 percent saw depression as a health problem, and only 28 percent saw it as evidence of personal weakness.

The serotonin theory of depression is comparable to the masturbatory theory of insanity.
—DAVID HEALY, IN A 2002 SPEECH AT THE INSTITUTE OF PSYCHIATRY IN LONDON

The deeper one digs into the entwined histories of anxiety and psychopharmacology, the clearer it becomes that anxiety has a direct and relatively straightforward biological basis. Anxiety, like all mental states, lives in the interstices of our neurons, in the soup of neurotransmitters that bathes our synapses. Relief from anxiety comes from resetting our nervous thermostats by adjusting the composition of that soup. Perhaps, as Peter Kramer mused in *Listening to Prozac,* what ailed Camus's stranger—his anhedonia, his anomie—was merely a disorder of serotonin.

And then one digs a little deeper still and none of that is very clear at all.

Even as advances in neuroscience and molecular genetics have allowed us to get more and more precise in drawing connections between this protein and that brain receptor, or between this neurotransmitter and that emotion, some of the original underpinnings of biological psychiatry have been unraveling.

The exaltation of Prozac a quarter century ago created a cult of serotonin as the "happiness neurotransmitter." But from the start, some studies were failing to find a statistically significant difference between the serotonin levels of depressed and nondepressed people. One early study of a group of depressed patients, reported in *Science* in 1976, found that only half had atypical levels of serotonin—and only half of those had serotonin levels that were lower than average, meaning that only a quarter of the depressed patients could be considered serotonin deficient. In fact, an equally large number had serotonin levels that were *higher* than average. Many subsequent studies have produced results that complicate the notion of a consistent relationship between serotonin deficiency and mental illness.

Evidently, the correlation between serotonin and anxiety or depression is less straightforward than once thought. None other than the father of the serotonin hypothesis of depression, Arvid Carlsson, has announced that psychiatry must relinquish it. In 2002, at a conference in Montreal, he declared that we must "abandon the simplistic hypothesis" that a disordered emotion is the result of "either an abnormally high or abnormally low function of a given neurotransmitter." Not long ago, George Ashcroft, who as a research psychiatrist in Scotland in the 1960s was one of the scientists responsible for promulgating the chemical imbalance theory of mental illness, renounced the theory when further research failed to support it. In 1998, Elliot Valenstein, a neuroscientist at the University of Michigan, devoted a whole book, *Blaming the Brain,* to arguing that "the evidence does not support any of the biochemical theories of mental illness."

"We have hunted for big simple neurochemical explanations for psychological disorders," Kenneth Kendler, the editor in chief of *Psychological Medicine* and a professor of psychiatry at Virginia Commonwealth University, conceded in 2005, "and we have not found them."

What if the reason we haven't been able to pinpoint how Prozac and Celexa work is that, in fact, they don't work? "Psychiatric drugs do more harm than good," says Peter Breggin, the Harvard-trained psychiatrist who is a frequent witness in lawsuits against the drug companies. He's backed up by those studies showing that only about a third of patients get better on antidepressants.

But studies have generally not found the response rates to other forms of treatment to be all that much better. And the psychiatrists and psychopharmacologists on the front lines who consistently say that they have seen these drugs work time after time cannot all have been fatally duped by the drug industry's marketing campaigns. Sometimes the statistical reality of the randomized double-blind controlled studies says one thing while the clinical reality (what psychiatrists and primary care physicians observe in and hear from their patients) says another. What to make of all this?

I am willing to believe that, for the most part anyway, both sides in these debates are arguing in good faith. The promedication advocates—the Gerald Klermans and Frank Bergers and Peter Kramers and Dr. Harvards of the world—have a compassionate Hippocratic desire to reduce their patients' anxious suffering with drugs, and they are sincere in their desire to destigmatize anxiety disorders and clinical depression by classifying them as medical problems. The antimedication crusaders—the Peter Breggins and Dr. Stanfords of the world—are sincere in their desire to protect patients and would-be consumers against what they believe to be the profit-minded rapaciousness of the drug companies and to help patients recover from their anxiety on the strength of their own inner resources, rather than on potentially dependency-inducing medications.

I have sympathy for the more reasonable drug industry critics. I can say based not only on the thousands of studies I've pored over but on my own lived experience that in some ways the critics are clearly right—right about the debilitating side effects, right about dependency and withdrawal problems, right to express skepticism about whether these drugs work as well as they're advertised to, right to worry about what the long-term effects of such a heavily medicated society will be. But in some ways, too, I believe, they are wrong. The drugs, many other studies suggest, *can* work—yes, only some of the time, in some people, with sometimes rotten side effects and bad withdrawal symptoms and dependency problems. And, yes, we don't know what long-term damage they're wreaking on our brains. And, yes, the diagnostic categories have been artificially inflated or distorted by the drug companies and the insurance industry. But I can tell you with hard-won personal authority that there is legitimate underlying emotional distress here, which can be quite debilitating, and which these drugs can mitigate, sometimes only a little, sometimes profoundly.

When I talk to Dr. W. about this, he reports that his own clinical experience comports with what I have been finding in my research: there is enormous variability in how different patients respond to different drugs. He once treated a patient whose parents were Holocaust survivors. This woman was deeply depressed; it was clear to Dr. W. that she had internalized their survivors' guilt, a common phenomenon. He worked with her for months to get her to recognize this in an effort to dispel her unhappiness. Nothing helped; her devastating depression persisted week after week. Then she tried Prozac. After a few weeks on the drug, she came for her appointment one day and said, "I feel great." A few weeks later, she deemed herself cured and terminated treatment. Score one for the SSRIs.

But around that same time, Dr. W. had another patient, a man suffering from obsessive-compulsive disorder and low-grade depression. That patient, too, started on Prozac—and within forty-eight hours was in the hospital with acute suicidal ideation. Score one against the SSRIs.*

Dr. W. has a psychopharmacologist colleague with whom he has collaborated for years. Together they have successfully treated many patients with anxiety disorders. Whenever one of their patients gets better, Dr. W. will say to the psychopharmacologist, "It was clearly your drugs that did it." And he will respond to Dr. W., "No, it was clearly your psychotherapy that did it." And then they laugh and congratulate each other on another successful case. But the truth is, as Dr. W. acknowledges, they don't really know what made a given patient recover.

It is much cheaper to tranquilize distraught housewives living in isolation in tower-blocks with nowhere for their children to play than to demolish these blocks and to rebuild on a human scale, or even to provide play-groups. The drug industry, the government,

---

* Another colleague of Dr. W.'s—let's call him Dr. G.—was an eminent psychoanalytically trained psychiatrist who, late in his career, fell into a severe clinical depression. Dr. G. checked himself into Chestnut Lodge, a psychoanalytically oriented psychiatric hospital in Rockville, Maryland. For years, Dr. G. had been a professional opponent of biological psychiatry, arguing that Freudian talk therapy was the best way to treat anxiety and depression. But daily sessions of analytic psychotherapy provided Dr. G. no relief from his suffering. Only when he consented to go on antidepressants did his condition improve. Dr. G.'s depression lifted—but he now found himself confronted with a professional crisis: Was psychoanalytic psychotherapy, the foundation on which he'd built his career, a chimera? He died not long thereafter.

the pharmacist, the tax-payer, and the doctor all have vested interests in "medicalizing" socially determined stress responses.

—MALCOLM LADER, "BENZODIAZEPINES:
OPIUM OF THE MASSES" (1978)

Just because I can explain your depression using terms such as "serotonin reuptake inhibition" doesn't mean you don't have a problem with your mother.

—CARL ELLIOTT, *The Last Physician: Walker Percy and the Moral Life of Medicine* (1999)

Before Donald Klein's imipramine experiments, interpreting the content of one's anxiety mattered a lot: What does your phobia of heights or rats or trains *mean*? What is it trying to communicate to you? Imipramine drained anxiety of much of its philosophical meaning. Developments in pharmacology were showing anxiety to be merely a biological symptom, a physiological phenomenon, a mechanical process whose content didn't matter.

Yet for philosophers like Kierkegaard and Sartre, anxiety resolutely *does* have meaning. For them, as well as for psychotherapists who resist reducing brain states to biology, anxiety is not something to be avoided or medicated but rather the truest route to self-discovery, the road to (in the sixties-inflected version of this idea) self-actualization. Dr. W. believes this.

"Go into the heart of danger," he likes to say, quoting a Chinese proverb, "for there you will find safety."

For evolutionary biologists, anxiety is a mental and physiological state that evolved to keep us safe and alive. Anxiety enhances our vigilance, prepares us to fight or flee. Being anxious can helpfully attune us to physical threats from the world. Freud believed anxiety attunes us not just to threats from the world but to threats from within ourselves. Anxiety, in this view, is a sign that our psyche is trying to tell us something. Medicating away that anxiety instead of listening to what it's trying to tell us—listening to Prozac, as it were, instead of listening to our anxiety—might not be what's called for if we want to become our best selves. Anxiety can be a signal that something needs to change—

that we need to change our lives. Medication risks blocking that signal.*

In *Listening to Prozac,* Peter Kramer engages the work of the novelist Walker Percy, whose writing grapples with how to cope with emotional pain and spiritual longing in the age of biological psychiatry. What gets lost, Percy's stories and essays ask, when anxiety and anomie are medicated away?

Percy was well situated to tackle these issues. The "hereditary taint" (as Freud called it) of melancholy ran thick through the bloodlines of his Southern family. His grandfather, his father, and possibly his mother (who drove herself off a bridge) committed suicide; two of his uncles had nervous breakdowns. Percy's father, LeRoy, a lawyer, medicated his depression with alcohol and sought treatment from specialists, traveling to Baltimore to meet with the leading psychiatrists at Johns Hopkins in 1925. But modern psychopharmacology was not yet available, and in 1929 LeRoy succeeded in his second attempt at killing himself, shooting himself in the head with a 20-gauge shotgun.

Walker's response was to study science. Believing that science would eventually explain everything in the cosmos, including the nature of the melancholy that killed so many members of his family, he decided to become a doctor. His medical training hardened his scientific materialism. "If man can be reduced to the sum of his chemical and biological properties," as one of his biographers characterized Percy's reasoning as a young man, "why worry about ideals, or lack thereof?"

But in 1942, Percy contracted tuberculosis and had to drop out of medical school, repairing to a sanatorium in Saranac Lake, New York, to recover. Streptomycin and—note this—isoniazid and iproniazid were still a few years away from being available as tuberculosis remedies, so the prescribed treatment was rest. While at the sanatorium, he fell into a depression and read intensively—lots of Dostoyevsky and Thomas Mann, as well as Kierkegaard and Thomas Aquinas. Feeling physically and emotionally unwell, he underwent a spiritual crisis in

---

* Edward Drummond, a psychiatrist in New England, used to regularly prescribe benzodiazepine tranquilizers to his patients in order to reduce their anxiety. Today, he strongly believes tranquilizers are a significant *cause* of chronic anxiety. Taking Xanax or Ativan can temporarily alleviate acute anxiety, Drummond says, but at the cost of allowing us to avoid dealing with whatever issues are causing that anxiety.

which he determined that science could not, after all, solve the problem of human unhappiness. Eventually, influenced especially by the writings of Kierkegaard, he decided to make a leap of faith and become a Catholic.* How differently might Percy's life and philosophy have turned out if he had been treated with iproniazid instead of with a curriculum of European novels and existential philosophy? Iproniazid, we now know, would shortly become the MAOI antidepressant Marsilid—a drug that might quickly have both cured his tuberculosis and dispelled his melancholy. He might well have returned to his medical training and never become a novelist. His opinion of biological psychiatry might have become considerably warmer.†

Percy never lost his respect for the scientific method. But he came to distrust the reductionist worldview that claimed science as the philosophical basis of ethics and of all human knowledge. In fact, he came to believe that the high rates of depression and suicide in modern society were owed in part to the cultural triumph of the scientific worldview, which reduced man to a collection of cells and enzymes, without supplying an alternative repository of meaning.

In 1957, Percy wrote a two-part article for *America*, the weekly Jesuit magazine. By focusing on the biological, he said, psychiatry becomes "unable to account for the predicament of modern man." Guilt, self-consciousness, sadness, shame, anxiety—these were important signals from the world and from our souls. Medicating these signals away as symptoms of organic disease risks alienating us further from ourselves. "Anxiety is," Percy wrote, "under one frame of reference a symptom to be gotten rid of; under the other, it may be a summons to an authentic existence, to be heeded at any cost."‡

---

* Percy's conversion prompted his best friend, the novelist and Civil War historian Shelby Foote, to tell him, "Yours is a mind in full intellectual retreat."

† Peter Kramer makes observations along these lines in *Listening to Prozac*.

‡ Themes of anxiety, nervous disorders, and existential dread run through much of Percy's writing. In *The Second Coming*, Will Barrett, a retired lawyer, must cope with a strange affliction that descends on him after the death of his wife, a feeling of depression accompanied by a disturbance of his internal gyroscope, a hitch in his golf swing, and what his doctors believe may be petit mal seizures. Will suspects his neurotic ailment is caused by the world's being "farcical." But one doctor suspects "a small hemorrhage or arterial spasm near the brain's limbic system." Is Will's unhappiness a problem of meaning? Or a quirk of biology?

As the novel progresses, Will's malaise deepens; his fainting spells become more frequent, and he becomes filled with religious yearning. Eventually, his family commits him to the hospital, where

Many times in his writing, Percy alludes to Kierkegaard's idea that worse than despair is to be in despair and not realize it—to have anxiety but to have built your life around not experiencing it. "We all know perfectly well that the man who lives out his life as a consumer," he writes in "The Coming Crisis in Psychiatry," "a sexual partner, an

---

a doctor diagnoses him with Hausmann's syndrome, a disease (invented by Percy) whose symptoms include, in addition to seizures, "depression, fugues, certain delusions, sexual dysfunction alternating between impotence and satyriasis, hypertension, and what [Dr. Hausmann] called *wahnsinnige Sehnsucht*"—"inappropriate longing." The disease is caused, Will's doctors explain, by a simple pH imbalance and is treated by the simplest of drugs—a hydrogen ion, a single nucleus of one proton. Will is consigned to a nursing home, where his pH levels can be checked every few hours. "Remarkable, don't you think," says his doctor, "that a few protons, plus or minus, can cause such complicated moods? Lithium, the simplest metal, controls depression. Hydrogen, the simplest atom, controls *wahnsinnige Sehnsucht*." Will, ostensibly cured and living his circumscribed nursing-home existence, marvels: "How odd to be rescued, salvaged, converted by the hydrogen ion! A proton as simple as a billiard ball! Did it all come down to chemistry after all? Had he . . . pounded the sand with his fist in a rage of longing . . . because his pH was 7.6?"

Percy, writing here in the late 1970s, when the "catecholamine hypothesis of affective disorders" and "norepinephrine theory of depression" were taking hold, is mocking the pretensions of biological reductionism. By reducing Will's humanity—not only his depression but his ideas and his longings—to his hydrogen molecules, Percy is essaying a critique of modern psychopharmacology, which in his view pathologizes alienation.

Seven years later, on the eve of Prozac's American launch, Percy published an even blunter critique of biological materialism. *The Thanatos Syndrome* featured a character named Thomas More, a psychiatrist who had appeared in an earlier novel, *Love in the Ruins*. In *The Thanatos Syndrome*, Dr. More, who has recently been released from jail, where he had been serving time for illegally selling the benzodiazepine Dalmane at truck stops, returns to his hometown of Feliciana, Louisiana, to find everyone acting strangely. The women of his town have developed a propensity for presenting themselves rearward for sex. His own wife, in addition to exhibiting this predilection, has developed a computerlike aptitude for playing bridge that has propelled her to success in national tournaments. He notes that anxious women have suddenly lost weight and self-consciousness while gaining boldness, sexual voracity, and emotional insensitivity. They shed "old terrors, worries, rages . . . like last year's snakeskin, and in its place is a mild fond vacancy, a species of unfocused animal good spirits." It turns out that some supercilious civic leaders—including the director of the Quality of Life Division, a federal agency that oversees euthanasia programs—have taken it upon themselves to introduce a chemical called heavy sodium into the water supply, like fluoride, in an effort to "improve" the social welfare. Heavy sodium makes people more placid, less self-conscious, and more content. This is not necessarily a good thing: in losing their anxiety and self-consciousness, the citizens of Feliciana are becoming less human. Dosed with heavy sodium, Feliciana's women are no longer "hurting, they are not worrying the same old bone, but there is something missing, not merely the old terrors, but a sense in each of her—her what? her self?" Dr. More is skeptical, but the heavy sodium advocates try to argue him around to their way of thinking. "Tom, we can see it!" one zealous champion tells him. "In a PETscanner! We can see the glucose metabolism of the limbic system raising all kinds of hell and getting turned off like a switch by the cortex. We can see the locus ceruleus and the hypothalamus kicking in, libido increasing—healthy heterosexual libido—and depression decreasing—we can see it!" Mocking the arrogance of biological psychiatry, Percy means to warn that to medicate away guilt, anxiety, self-consciousness, and melancholy is to medicate away the soul.

'other-directed' executive; who avoids boredom and anxiety by consuming tons of newsprint, miles of film, years of TV time; that such a man has somehow betrayed his destiny as a human being."

If anxiolytic medication mutes our anxiety, deafens us to it—allows us to be in despair without knowing it—does that somehow deaden our souls? Percy would seem to believe that it does.

I believe all of this, as far as it goes. I endorse the philosophical stances of Walker Percy and Søren Kierkegaard. And yet how much credibility do I have? After all, here I am, in my thirtieth year of taking psychiatric medications, with citalopram and alprazolam and possibly still some of last night's clonazepam flowing through my bloodstream as I write this—my serotonergic and GABAnergic systems boosted, my glutamate inhibited—agreeing with Peter Breggin that drugs are toxic and with Walker Percy that they diminish the soul. Am I not a terribly compromised vessel for delivering this argument?

And yet so, one might say, was Percy, who took sleeping medications for his chronic insomnia. (And with good reason: his father's brutal insomnia played a large role in driving him to suicide.) Psychiatric medications—for some people, in some situations, some of the time—work. To deny the schizophrenic chemical remission from his psychotic delusions, or the bipolar patient pharmacological relief from his self-endangering manias and crushing depressions—or, yes, the panic-ravaged and housebound individual some medical defense against anxiety—would be cruel. One can be, I believe, skeptical about the claims of the pharmaceutical industry, concerned about the sociological implications of a population that is so heavily medicated, and attuned to the existential trade-offs involved in taking psychiatric medications without being ideologically in opposition to the judicious use of these drugs.

On the other hand, I know I would do well to heed Percy, as well as modern Big Pharma critics like Edward Drummond and Peter Breggin, because the irony of what I have had to ingest in order to write this section on drugs is obvious. I elevated my Celexa dosage, became dependent on Xanax and Klonopin, and consumed heroic quantities of alcohol to keep my anxiety at bay. After forty years of never smoking a single cigarette (because after getting my grandmother to quit smoking in her sixties, I'd promised to never take up the habit myself), I smoked my first one at forty-one. After having been so afraid of recreational narcotics (perhaps an instance of the evolutionary adaptiveness of my innate caution) that I'd never for forty years taken so much as a puff of marijuana nor indulged in any other nonprescribed drug, I resorted in desperation (after reading Freud's enthusiastic papers about it) to trying cocaine and also amphetamines. Many nights I would begin the evening fueled by caffeine and nicotine, which I needed to propel me out of torpor and hopelessness—only to overshoot into quaking, quivering anxiety. Thoughts racing, hands shaking, I would end the evening taking a Klonopin and then perhaps a Xanax and drinking a scotch (and then another and another) to settle down. This is not healthy.

More constructively, I have tried to draw on Kierkegaard and Percy for backbone and solace, and I have also tried yoga and acupuncture and meditation. I would very much like to unlock my "inner pharmacy"— that repository of healthy, natural hormones and neurotransmitters that can be activated, the antidrug New Age healers say, with meditation and biofeedback and better "inner balance"—but despite my best efforts, I'm fumbling with the keys.

PART IV

Nurture Versus Nature

CHAPTER 8

Separation Anxiety

The great source of terror in infancy is solitude.
—WILLIAM JAMES, *The Principles of Psychology* (1890)

When did my anxiety begin?

Was it when I, as a toddler, would throw epic tantrums, screaming relentlessly and banging my head on the floor?

The questions that confronted my parents were these: Was my behavior merely a slightly extreme but nonetheless typical manifestation of the terrible twos—or did it lie outside the band of the normal? What is the difference between childhood separation anxiety as a normal developmental stage and separation anxiety as a clinical, or preclinical, condition? Where is the line between temperamental inhibition as a normal personality trait and inhibition as a symptom of pathology—a sign of, say, incipient social anxiety disorder?

On the matter of my tantrums, my mother's Dr. Benjamin Spock manual was not dispositive, so she took me to the pediatrician and described my behavior. "Normal," was his conclusion, and his advice, in keeping with the laissez-faire approach to child rearing of the early 1970s, was to let me "cry it out." So my parents would watch in distress as I lay on the floor, screaming and writhing and smashing my head on the ground, sometimes for hours at a time.

Then what to make of my extreme shyness at age three? When my mother took me to my first day of nursery school, she couldn't (or wouldn't—separation anxiety cuts both ways with children and parents) leave because I clung to her leg and whimpered. Still, separation anxiety in a three-year-old is well within the spectrum of normal developmental behavior, and eventually I was able to stay at school for two afternoons a week by myself. And while I clearly exhibited signs of an "inhibited temperament"—shy, introverted, withdrawing from unfamiliar situations (and in a lab I probably would have displayed a hair-trigger startle reflex and high levels of cortisol in my blood)—none of this was necessarily evidence of emerging psychopathology.

Today, it's not hard to see that my early behavioral inhibition was a harbinger of my adult neurosis—but that's only in retrospect, seeing my anxiety as an unfolding narrative.

At age six, when I was in first grade, two new problems set in. The first was an intensified resurgence of my separation anxiety (about which more in a moment). The second was the onset of emetophobia, or the fear of vomiting, my original, most acute, and most persistent specific phobia.

The first presenting symptom for some 85 percent of adults with anxiety disorders, according to data collected by Harvard Medical School researchers, is a specific phobia developed as a child. The same data, based on interviews with a quarter of a million people around the world, has also revealed that early experiences with anxiety tend to compound and metastasize. A child who develops a specific phobia—say, a fear of dogs—at age six is nearly five times more likely than a child without a fear of dogs to develop social phobia in her teenage years; that same child is then 2.2 times more likely than a child without an early dog phobia to develop major depression as an adult.

"Fear disorders," says Ron Kessler, the head of the Harvard study, "have a very strong pattern of comorbidity over time, with the onset of the first disorder strongly predicting the onset of a second, which strongly predicts the onset of a third, and so on." ("Comorbidity" is the medical term for the simultaneous presence of two chronic diseases or conditions in a patient; anxiety and depression are often comorbid, with the presence of one predicting the presence of the other.) "Fear of dogs at age five or ten is important not because fear of dogs impairs the quality of your life," Kessler says. "Fear of dogs is important because it makes you *four times more likely* to end up a 25-year-old, depressed, high-school dropout single mother who is drug dependent."*

---

* The strong predictive association between a childhood fear of dogs and adult dysfunction might mean that a dog phobia somehow *causes* later social phobia, depression, or drug addiction. Or it might

While the nature of the link between childhood phobia and adult psychopathology is not clear, the fact of it is—which is why Kessler insists that early diagnosis and treatment is so important. "If it turns out that dog phobia does somehow cause adult psychopathology, then the successful early treatment of phobic children could reduce later incidence of depression by 30 to 50 percent. Even if it's only by 15 percent, that's significant."

The numbers from Kessler's study would seem to lend a statistical fatedness to the progression of my anxiety: from specific phobia at age six to social phobia starting around age eleven to panic disorder in my late teens to agoraphobia and depression in young adulthood. I have been, in my pathogenesis—the development of my pathology—a textbook case.

> *Missing someone who is loved and longed for is the key to an understanding of anxiety.*
> —SIGMUND FREUD, *Inhibitions, Symptoms, and Anxiety* (1926)

When I was six years old, my mother started attending law school at night. My father says this was at his instigation, because he'd seen how my mother's mother had become depressed and alcoholic as a stay-at-home suburban housewife without professional aspirations. My mother, for her part, says that mother was neither depressed nor an alcoholic. (My mother is presumably the better authority here, but for what it's worth, my grandmother, whom I loved dearly, often did smell appealingly of gin.)

---

mean that a childhood fear of dogs and adult depression tend to be produced by the same kinds of environmental circumstances—an impoverished inner-city childhood, say, where dangerous pit bulls are a real threat and where early trauma or deprivation can lay the neural groundwork for later depression. Or it might mean that a fear of dogs and adult depression or drug addiction are different behavioral markers of a shared genetic underpinning—the same genetic coding that predisposes you to fear dogs might also predispose you to depression. Or, finally, maybe a childhood fear of dogs is actually *the very same thing as* adult panic disorder or depression. That is, it might be that childhood phobia and adult depression are the same disease, unfolding over the life cycle through different developmental stages, each stage expressing different symptoms. As I've noted, specific phobias tend to appear early in life—half of all people who will ever have a phobia in their lives first develop it between the ages of six and sixteen—so perhaps a dog phobia is simply the first symptom of a broader disorder, the way a sore throat can augur the onset of a cold.

The powerful recrudescence of my separation anxiety coincided with the beginning of my mother's first year in law school. Each day during first grade, I would be driven home from school in a car pool to be greeted by one of a series of neighborhood babysitters. The babysitters were all very nice. Nevertheless, nearly every evening ended the same way: with me pacing around my bedroom waiting desperately for my father to come home from work. Because nearly every night for about four years—and then intermittently for about ten more years after that—I was convinced that my parents were not coming home, that they had died or abandoned me, and that I had been orphaned, a prospect that was unbearably terrifying to me.

Even though every night provided yet another piece of evidence that my parents always did come home, that never provided reassurance. *This time*, I was always convinced, *they're really not coming back*. So I would pace around my room, and sit on the radiator peering hopefully out the window, and listen desperately for the rumble of my father's Volkswagen. He was supposed to be home by no later than 6:30, so as the clock clicked past 6:10 and 6:15, I would begin suffering my nightly paroxysms of anxiety and despair.

Sitting on the radiator, nose pressed up against the window, I'd try to will him home, mentally picturing his return—the Volkswagen turning off Common Street and onto Clark Street, heading up the hill and left onto Clover, then right onto our street, Blake—and then I'd look down the street and listen for the rumble of the car. And . . . nothing. I'd stare at my bedroom clock, my agitation increasing as the seconds ticked by. Imagine you have just been told that a loved one has died in a car crash. Every night produced the same fifteen to thirty minutes of effectively believing I had been told just that—a half hour of exquisite agony during which I was absolutely, resolutely convinced that my parents had died or that they had abandoned me—even as the babysitter blandly played board games with my sister downstairs. And then finally, usually by six-thirty and almost always by seven, the Volkswagen would come motoring down the street and turn into the driveway, and a burst of relief-borne euphoria would cascade through me: *He's home, he's alive, I haven't been abandoned!*

And then the next night I would go through this all over again.

Weekends when my parents went out together were even worse.

My fears of abandonment were not rational. Most of the time I was convinced my parents had died in a car crash. Other times I was sure they had simply decided to leave—either because they didn't love me anymore or because they weren't really my parents after all. (Sometimes I thought they were aliens; sometimes I thought they were robots; at times I was convinced that my sister was an adult midget who had been trained to play the part of a five-year-old girl while her colleagues, my parents, performed whatever experiments they were carrying out before abandoning me.)

My mother, more attuned to my anxiety than my father was, clued into how I would start my worrying well in advance of when they had promised to be home. So when they were leaving and I would ask, ritually, "What's the latest you'll be back?" my mother would announce a time fifteen or twenty minutes later than when she actually estimated they would return. But I cottoned on to this gambit soon enough, so I would factor in that extra time and begin my worried pacing forty-five minutes or an hour before the stated latest time. And my mother, picking up on *this,* moved her stated return time still later, but I would pick up on *that*—and we were off and running on a kind of arms race of stated and assumed return times that eventually rendered anything she said meaningless to me, so my anxiety would rise from the moment they left.

This weekend worrying went on, I hate to say, for a long time. As a young teenager, I sometimes called (or forced my sister to call) parties my parents were at to make sure they were still alive. On several occasions I woke neighbors (and once the minister of the Episcopal church around the block) by banging on their doors late in the evening to tell them that my parents weren't home and that I thought they might be dead and to please call the police. When I was six, this was embarrassing to my parents; when I was thirteen, it was mortifying.

By the time I was twelve, even being alone in my room at night—down the hall from my parents, less than fifteen feet away—had become an ordeal. "Do you *promise* everything will be okay?" I would ask my mother when she tucked me in at night. As my emetophobia got worse, I worried I would wake up vomiting. This made me anxious and queasy at bedtime. Feeling that way one night, I told my mother, "I'm not feeling well. Can you please be especially on the alert tonight?" She said she would be. But then a few nights later, I must have been feeling even more nervous than usual, because I said, "Can you please be especially, especially, *especially* on the alert tonight?" I remember the exact wording because I began asking that question every night. Eventually, this escalated into a ritual, one with a precise and weird sequence to it, that persisted until I went to college.

"Do you *promise* everything will be okay?"

"I promise."

"And will you be especially, especially, especially, especially, *especially* three hundred fifty-seven and a quarter times on the alert?"

"Yes."

Like a psalm, with the stress always on the fifth "especially," every night for years.

My separation anxiety affected nearly every aspect of my life. I was a reasonably coordinated athlete as a preadolescent, but here's how my first baseball practice ended: with me, age six, crying in the dugout, alongside a kindly but puzzled coach. (I never went back.)

Here's how my first beginners' swimming lesson ended: with me, age seven, fearfully, tearfully refusing to get in the pool with the other children.

Here's how my first soccer practice ended: with me, age eight, crying on the sideline with the babysitter who'd brought me, resisting entreaties to join the other boys doing drills.

Here's how I spent my first morning at day camp, when I was five: sobbing by my cubby, crying that I missed my mommy and wanted to go home.

Here's how I spent the first two hours at my first (and only) overnight at camp, when I was seven: sobbing in the corner with a passel of befuddled counselors trying, serially and without success, to console me.

Here's how I spent the drive to college with my parents: sobbing in the backseat, consumed by anxiety and anticipatory homesickness, worried that my parents would not love me after I went away to college—"away," in this case, being a mere three miles from my parents' house.

Why could I never feel assured of my parents' love or protection? Why were ordinary childhood activities so difficult? What existential reassurance was I seeking in my nightly call-and-response with my mother?

The first anxiety is the loss of the object in the form of maternal care; after infancy and throughout the rest of life loss of love ... becomes a new and far more abiding danger and occasion for anxiety.
—SIGMUND FREUD, *The Problem of Anxiety* (1926)

In 1905, Sigmund Freud wrote, "Anxiety in children is nothing other than an expression of the fact that they are feeling the loss of the person they love," and so-called separation anxiety has remained a focus of researchers and clinicians ever since. Decades of studies by psychologists, primatologists, anthropologists, endocrinologists, ethologists, and others have revealed again and again, in myriad ways, the paramount significance of the early mother-child bond in determining the lifelong well-being of the child. The nature of that mother-child relationship starts getting established at the moment the infant enters the world—with "the trauma of birth," as the early Freudian psychoanalyst Otto Rank put it—if not earlier than that. Experiences in the womb and during infancy can have profound effects on a child's sense of well-being that last for decades—and that can even, according to recent research, persist into subsequent generations of offspring.

Yet for all his astuteness about the role of early childhood experiences in predicting lifelong emotional health, Freud was for most of his career strangely blind to the ways early parent-child relationships affect the human psyche. This seems to have been especially true in the case of his own psyche.

For many years, Freud endured a debilitating phobia of train travel. The train phobia first presented itself, according to Freud's own account, in 1859, when he was three years old. His father's wool business had collapsed, prompting the Freuds to relocate from Freiberg, a small Austro-Hungarian town (now Příbor, in the Czech Republic), to Vienna. When the family arrived at the train station in Freiberg, young Sigmund was filled with dread: the gas-jet lights that illuminated the station made him think of "souls burning in hell"; he was terrified that the train would depart without him, taking his parents and leaving him behind. For years thereafter, train travel caused him anxiety attacks.

His life was circumscribed by his travel phobia. For a long time, he professed a desire to visit Rome—but was deterred from going by what he came to call his "Rome neurosis." When compelled to travel anywhere by train with his family, he would book himself into a separate compartment from his wife and children because he was ashamed to have them witness his fits of anxiety. He compulsively insisted on getting to railway stations hours in advance of departure because he forever retained the intense fear of being left behind that he first experienced as a three-year-old.

A modern therapist might naturally attribute Freud's travel phobia to his childhood fears of abandonment. Freud himself did not. Rather, as he wrote to his friend Wilhelm Fliess in 1897, he believed that what prompted his anxiety was seeing his mother naked in their train compartment while en route from Freiberg to Vienna. Witnessing this at a time when his "libido toward matrem had awakened" must have aroused him sexually, Freud surmised, and even as a three-year-old he would have known the taboo nature of such incestuous desire and would therefore have repressed it. This act of repression, he theorized, generated anxiety that he neurotically transmuted into a phobia of trains. "You yourself have seen my travel anxiety at its height," he reminds Fliess.

Tellingly, Freud couldn't actually recall seeing his mother nude on the train; he just supposed that he must have and that he'd then pushed the image down into his unconscious. From this (strained) supposition he generalized that all train phobia derives from repressed sexual desire and that those who are "subject to attacks of anxiety on the journey" are actually protecting themselves "against a repetition of the painful experience by a dread of railway-travel."

On the basis of this (quite likely imagined) experience, Freud over the years elaborated his Oedipus complex and concluded that this was "a universal event in early childhood." He would eventually make the Oedipus complex the centerpiece of his psychoanalytic theory of neurosis.*

---

* According to Freud's theory of the Oedipus complex, a boy's greatest anxiety is that his father will castrate him as punishment for sexually desiring his mother, and a girl's greatest anxiety is generated by her envy of the penis she lacks. This was largely derived from Freud's own recollection of, as he wrote Fliess, "being in love with my mother and jealous of my father."

Was my own separation anxiety as a young boy—and are my abiding anxiety and dependency issues as an adult—attributable to my repressed sexual feelings for my mother? It certainly never felt that way to me. Of course, Freud would say that it *wouldn't* have felt that way: his whole point was that such feelings are repressed into the unconscious and transmuted into anxiety about other things—trains or heights or snakes or whatever. And in support of Freud, I confess there is this: The name of my first crush, in fifth grade, was Anne; the name of my first postcollege girlfriend, whom I dated for three years, was Ann; the girl I dated immediately after Ann, for nearly two years, was named Anna; the girl I left Anna for was named Anne; and my wife's name is Sus*anna*. My mother's name? Anne, of course. I used to joke that dating all those Anns, Annes, and Annas reduced the likelihood I would call any of them by the wrong name—because even the wrong name would sound like the right one. But Freud would say that what I was really in danger of calling them—that what I was seeking with all those Anns, Annes, and Annas—was Mom. Lending still further Oedipal determinism to my romantic relations is the fact that my paternal grandmother was also named Anne—meaning that my father also married a woman with the same name as his mother.

But there is, of course, a less sexual explanation for how Freud's early childhood experiences might have produced his lifelong anxiety and train phobia.

The first years of Freud's life were colored by loss, and by the wavering attention of his mother, Amalia. Shortly after he was born, in 1856, his mother got pregnant again, giving birth to another son, Julius. Less than a year later, Julius died, felled by an intestinal infection. At the time, the Freud family lived in a one-room apartment, so it's likely that Sigmund, as a toddler, witnessed at close hand his brother's death and his parents' reaction to it. Some of Freud's biographers have suggested that Julius's death sent Amalia into a depression that would have made her remote and unavailable to Sigmund. (Depression in mothers of children this age can be highly predictive of anxiety and depression in those children later in life.) With his mother emotionally unavailable, Freud naturally turned to an alternative maternal figure—the nursemaid, a Czech Catholic woman, who cared for him in the early years of his life. But while Sigmund was still a small child, the nursemaid was caught stealing and sent to jail; he never saw her again.

The logical conclusion here would seem to be that Freud's train phobia was a response to the fear of abandonment produced by this string of childhood losses—the death of his brother, the emotional unavailability of his mother, and the sudden disappearance of his primary caretaker. But Freud remained fixated on proving the rightness of his sexual explanations of anxiety and his Oedipus complex. He would exile from the fold anyone (including Alfred Adler, Carl Jung, and Otto Rank) who dared question their centrality.

> *All anxiety goes back to the anxiety at birth.*
> —OTTO RANK, *The Trauma of Birth* (1924)

Later in his career, as Freud moved from his repressed libido theory of anxiety to his intrapsychic conflict theory, he began to take more account of the way in which parent-child relations—"object relations," in the psychoanalytic argot—related to anxiety.

The final shifts in Freud's theory of anxiety were motivated by his disavowal of a book written by one of his most devoted acolytes. Otto Rank, the secretary of Freud's Vienna Psychoanalytical Society, had intended *The Trauma of Birth*, published in 1924, as a tribute to his mentor. (The book is dedicated to Freud, "the explorer of the unconscious, creator of psychoanalysis.") Rank's basic argument, elaborated at great length, was that birth—both the physical act of passing through the uterine canal and the psychological fact of separation from the mother—is so traumatic that the experience becomes the template for all future experiences of anxiety. In making this claim, Rank was building on what Freud himself had already argued. "The act of birth is the first experience of anxiety, and thus the source and prototype of the affect of anxiety," Freud had written in a footnote to the second edition of *The Interpretation of Dreams* in 1908, and he repeated this notion in a speech he gave to the Vienna Psychoanalytical Society the following year.*

---

* James Strachey, a British psychoanalyst and translator of Freud's works, speculated that Freud's linking of childbirth and anxiety dated to the early 1880s, when, while working as a physician, he heard

But *The Trauma of Birth* was a work of such extravagant interpretive brio that Freud, though no stranger to extravagant interpretive leaps himself, found it alienating and bewildering, and he devoted a full chapter of *The Problem of Anxiety* to renouncing it.* Rank's arguments forced Freud to wrestle once more with the ways in which early life experiences are relevant to anxiety. This led him to revise his own theory of it.

In the final chapter of *The Problem of Anxiety*, Freud gives brief attention to what he called the "biological factor," by which he meant "the protracted helplessness and dependence of the young of the human species."

Freud writes that "the human infant is sent into the world more unfinished than the young [of other species]"—meaning that humans emerge much more highly dependent on their mothers for their survival than do other animals.† The infant seems to be born with an instinctive sense that the mother can provide sustenance and succor, and learns very quickly that whereas the mother's presence equals safety and comfort, her absence equals danger and discomfort. Observing this, Freud concluded that the earliest human anxiety, and thus to some degree the source of all subsequent ones, is a reaction to "the loss of the object"—the "object" being the mother. "This biological factor of helplessness thus brings into being the need to be loved which the human being is destined never to renounce," Freud writes. The first anxiety is about the loss of a mother's care; throughout the balance of life, "loss of love . . . becomes a new and far more abiding danger and occasion for anxiety."

In the final pages of *The Problem of Anxiety*, Freud briefly develops the idea that phobic anxiety in adults is the residue of human evolu-

---

secondhand about a midwife who had declared that there is a lifelong connection between birth and being frightened.

* Rank believed the birth trauma explained everything—from territorial conquests like Alexander the Great's (motivated by an "attempt to gain sole possession of the mother" from the father) to revolutions like the French (an attempt to overthrow "masculine dominance" and return to the mother) to phobia of animals ("a rationalization . . . of the wish—through the desire to be eaten—to get back again into the mother's womb") to the apostles' dedication to Jesus Christ ("they could see in him one who had overcome the birth trauma"). Some of Freud's later disciples would denounce Rank, not without reason, as insane.

† Most animals emerge from the uterus or the egg dependent to some extent on parental care for their survival, but the majority of them are relatively less dependent than humans are at birth.

tionary adaptations: phobias of such things as thunderstorms, animals, strangers, being alone, and being in the dark represent "the atrophied remnants of innate preparedness" against real dangers that existed in the state of nature. For early man and woman, being alone, or in the dark, or bitten by a snake or a lion—and, of course, the separation of an infant from his mother—were legitimate mortal threats. In all of this, Freud was anticipating the work of the biologists and neuroscientists who would study phobias in the decades ahead.*

In other words, Freud was, in his seventies, in an addendum to one of his final works, finally moving closer to what would become the modern scientific understanding of anxiety. But by then it was too late. Freud's followers were off to the races with "Oedipus conflicts" and "penis envy" and "castration anxiety"—and "inferiority complexes" (Adler) and the "collective unconscious" (Jung) and "death instincts" (Melanie Klein) and "oral and anal fixations" (Karl Abraham) and so-called "phantasies" about "the good breast and the bad breast" (Klein again). For a generation, as the field grew in the years leading up to and following the Second World War, the prevailing psychoanalytic view was that anxiety was caused by dammed-up sexual drives.

While parents are held to play a major role in causing a child to develop a heightened susceptibility to fear, their behaviour is seen not in terms of moral condemnation but as having been determined by the experiences they themselves had as children.
—JOHN BOWLBY, *Separation: Anxiety and Anger* (1973)

The person most responsible for unlocking the mysteries of separation anxiety, and for installing the concept near the center of mod-

---

* Freud did retain for psychoanalysis some interpretative élan by positing that childhood phobias become overly severe or persist into adulthood only when they become the outer fears (of rats or heights or darkness or thunder or open spaces—or mayonnaise, a noted phobia in the literature) onto which inner psychic conflicts get projected. Phobias, in this view, are the outward symbolic representations of the threats that the id (with its wanton impulses that must be repressed) and the superego (with its strict demands of conscience and morality) place on the ego.

ern psychiatry, was the British psychoanalyst John Bowlby, who did as much as anyone to rescue psychoanalysis from its more torturous theoretical overreaching. Trained in the 1930s by Freud's protégé Melanie Klein, Bowlby would go on to develop what has become known as attachment theory—the idea that an individual's anxiety level derives largely from the nature of the relationship with early attachment figures, most commonly the mother.

Bowlby was born in 1907 to an aristocratic surgeon who ministered to the king of England, and he would later claim that his "was a very stable background." But it's not hard to see that Bowlby's clinical and research interests, like Freud's, were informed by his own childhood experiences. Bowlby's mother, according to the psychologist Robert Karen, was "a sharp, hard, self-centered woman who never praised the children and seemed oblivious to their emotional lives"; Bowlby's father, generally absent, was "something of an inflated bully." The Bowlby children ate completely apart from their parents until they were twelve years old—at which age they would be permitted to join their parents only for dessert. By the time Bowlby turned twelve, he'd already been away from home, at boarding school, for four years. Publicly, he would always say his parents had sent him away because they wanted to protect him from the bombs they feared German zeppelins would drop on London during the First World War; in private, however, he confessed that he'd hated boarding school and that he wouldn't send a dog away so young.*

Psychoanalysts before Bowlby were generally uninterested in the day-to-day relationship between parents and children. What interest they did have was focused on breast-feeding, toilet training, and (especially) instances in which a child witnessed his parents having sexual intercourse. Anyone who placed undue emphasis on a child's real experience—as opposed to on his internal fantasies—"was regarded as pitifully naive," Bowlby would later recall. Once, while still a medical student, he watched with dismay as a series of case studies presented at

---

* Robert Karen observes that almost everything Bowlby wrote about the needs of young children throughout his long career "could be seen as an indictment of the type of upbringing to which he'd been subjected."

the British Psychoanalytic Society traced patients' emotional disorders to childhood fantasies. Unable to bear it any longer, he blurted: "But there *is* such a thing as a *bad* mother!" This sort of thing did not endear him to the psychoanalytic establishment.

In 1938, while still in good standing with the mandarins of psychoanalysis, he was assigned as a supervisor a doyenne of the Freudian establishment, Melanie Klein.*

Bowlby would soon come to find himself at odds with many of Klein's views—such as that babies were seething miasmas of hatred, libido, envy, sadism, death instincts, and rage against the restraining superego and that neuroses arose because of conflicts between the "good breast" and the "evil breast." Klein herself was by most accounts an unpleasant person; Bowlby would later describe her as "a frightfully vain old woman who manipulated people." But what most appalled him was Klein's disregard for the actual relationship between mother and child. The first case he treated under Klein's supervision was an anxious, hyperactive young boy. Bowlby noticed right away that the boy's mother was "an extremely anxious, distressed woman, who was wringing her hands, in a very tense, unhappy state." To him it seemed obvious that the mother's emotional problems were contributing to the boy's and that a sensible course of treatment would include counseling for the mother. But Klein forbade Bowlby to talk to the woman. When the mother was eventually admitted to a mental hospital after a nervous breakdown, Klein's response was exasperation at having to find a new patient, since there was no longer anyone who could bring the boy to his appointments. "The fact that this poor woman had had a breakdown was of no clinical interest to [Klein] whatever," Bowlby would say later. "This horrified me, to be quite frank. And from that point onwards my mission in life was to

---

* Born in Vienna and trained as a nursery school teacher, Klein would go on, after the end of an unhappy marriage, to be psychoanalyzed by two of Freud's closest disciples, Sándor Ferenczi and Karl Abraham, and then herself to become one of Freud's most important followers and interpreters. In 1926, Klein, forty-four years old, moved to London, where she was exalted by Ernest Jones, the head of the British Psychoanalytic Society and the most ardent protector of Freud's legacy. Klein's arrival in London—and in particular her disagreements with Freud's daughter Anna Freud over the analysis and treatment of children—precipitated a rift in the society between the Kleinians and the (Anna) Freudians that would last through World War II.

demonstrate that real-life experiences have a very important effect on development."

In 1950, the chief of the mental health section of the World Health Organization, Ronald Hargreaves, commissioned from Bowlby a report on the psychological problems of the thousands of European children rendered homeless by the disruptions of World War II. Bowlby's report, *Maternal Care and Mental Health*, urged governments to recognize that a mother's affection was as important for mental health "as are vitamins and proteins for physical health." Strange as it may seem now, in 1950 there wasn't much recognition of the effects of parenting on psychological development—especially within psychiatry, where treatment still often focused on the processing of inner fantasies.*

Bowlby's early research focused on what happened when children, through the intrusions of war or illness, were separated from their mothers. Psychoanalytic and behaviorist theory held that separations from the mother didn't really matter as long as the child's basic needs (food, shelter) were taken care of. Bowlby found that not to be true at all: when young children were separated from their mothers for any substantial period of time, they tended to display acute distress. Bowlby wondered if the effects of prolonged separation in young childhood could lead to mental illness later on. The children who became clingy upon postseparation reunions, Bowlby suspected, were those who would grow up to be needy, neurotic adults; those who became hostile were those who would eschew intimacy and have difficulty forming deep relationships.

Throughout the 1940s and 1950s, while serving as head of the children's department at a health clinic in London, he began to explore how the early day-to-day relationship between mother and child—what he would come to call the attachment style—affected the child's psychological well-being. He found the same patterns again and again.

---

* In his initial work on hysteria, in the early 1890s, Freud had argued that adult neuroses were the product of *actual* early childhood traumas, mostly of a sexual nature—but by 1897 he had revised his view to support his emerging notion of the Oedipus complex, arguing now that adult neuroses were the result of repressed childhood *fantasies* about having sex with the opposite-sex parent and murdering the same-sex parent. Adults without neuroses were those who had successfully worked through their Oedipus complexes; adults with neuroses were those who hadn't.

When mothers had "secure attachment" relationships with their infants or toddlers—the mothers calm and available but not smothering or overprotective—the children were calmer, more adventurous, happier; they struck a healthy balance between maintaining proximity to their mothers and exploring their environment.

Securely attached children were able to create what Bowlby called "an internal working model" of their mothers' love that they could carry out into the world with them throughout their lives—an internalized feeling of psychological security, a sense of being loved and of being safe in the world. But when the mothers had "insecure" or "ambivalent" attachment relationships with their toddlers—if the mothers were anxious and overprotective or emotionally cold and withdrawn— the children were more anxious and less adventurous; they would cling to their mothers and become very agitated in response to any separation.

Over the next four decades, Bowlby and his colleagues would develop a typology of attachment styles. Secure attachment in childhood predicted low anxiety levels and a healthy degree of intimacy in adult relationships. Ambivalent attachment—which described those children who clung most anxiously, who displayed high levels of physiological arousal in novel situations, and who were much more concerned with monitoring their mothers' whereabouts than in exploring the world—predicted high levels of anxiety in adulthood.* Avoidant attachment in a child—which described those kids who tended to withdraw from their mothers after separations—predicted a dislike of intimacy in adulthood.†

The person most responsible for helping Bowlby develop this tax-

---

* Adult romantic relationships among those with ambivalent attachment styles tend to be characterized by clinginess and fear of abandonment.

† Adult avoidants tend to shun close relationships and are often workaholics; just as they preferred their toys to their mothers as children, they prefer work to family as adults. (Though those with avoidant attachment styles appear to be less anxious than those with ambivalent attachment styles, Bowlby came to believe that was not the case; a series of studies beginning in the 1970s have demonstrated that during separations the avoidant children exhibited increased levels of physiological arousal— elevated heart rates, increased excretion of stress hormones in the bloodstream, and so forth—of the sort associated with anxiety. The child seems to be feeling a physically manifested distress, but he is able—adaptively, or not—to suppress visible expression of the emotion.)

onomy of attachment styles was the psychologist Mary Ainsworth. In 1929, Ainsworth was a freshman at the University of Toronto plagued by feelings of inadequacy. That year she took a course in abnormal psychology from William Blatz, a psychologist whose security theory held that a young child's sense of well-being derives from proximity to his parents and that the child's ability to grow and develop depends on the constancy of his parents' availability. Drawn to Blatz by her own abiding sense of insecurity, Ainsworth went on to do graduate work in psychology, eventually becoming, in 1939, a lecturer in the University of Toronto's psychology department. But when her husband decided to attend graduate school in England, she had to find work in London. A friend directed her to an advertisement in *The Times*, placed by a psychoanalyst seeking research help on a project about the developmental effects of early childhood separation from the mother. Keen to understand her relationship with her own mother, who had been self-absorbed and distant, Ainsworth applied. John Bowlby hired her—and with that began the central partnership in the development of attachment theory.

Ainsworth made two signature contributions to the field. The first was in the mid-1950s, when she accompanied her husband to Kampala, Uganda. In Kampala, Ainsworth identified twenty-eight unweaned babies from local villages and began observing them in their homes, studying attachment behavior in a natural environment. She kept meticulous records, tracking breast-feeding, toilet training, bathing, thumb sucking, sleeping arrangements, expressions of anger and anxiety, and displays of happiness and sadness, and she watched how the mothers interacted with the children. It was the most extensive naturalistic observation of this sort yet conducted.

When Ainsworth first arrived in Uganda, she agreed with both the Freudians and the behaviorists that the emotional attachment babies invested in their mothers was a secondary association with feeding: mothers provided breast milk, which provided comfort, so babies came to associate that feeling of comfort with the mother; there was nothing inherent in the maternal relationship itself, distinct from the provision of food, that was psychologically significant. But as Ainsworth totted up her meticulous observations, she changed her mind. The Freudians and behaviorists were wrong, she concluded, and Bowlby was right. When the babies began to crawl on their own and to explore the world around them, they would repeatedly return to their mothers—either physically or by exchanging a reassuring glance and a smile—and appeared always to remain conscious of exactly where their mothers were. Describing what she observed when the babies first began to crawl, Ainsworth wrote that the mothers seemed to provide the "secure base" from which these excursions can be made without anxiety. The secure base would go on to become a crucial element of Bowlby's attachment theory.

Ainsworth noticed that whereas some babies clung fiercely to their mothers at almost all times and cried inconsolably when separated from them, others seemed indifferent, tolerating separations without evident distress. Did this mean that the uninterested babies loved their mothers less than the clinging babies and were somehow less attached to them? Or, as Ainsworth came to suspect, did this mean that the clinging babies were in fact the *less* securely attached ones?

Ainsworth ultimately deemed seven of the twenty-eight Ugandan babies "insecurely attached." She studied them carefully. What made them so anxious and clingy? For the most part, these insecure babies seemed to receive the same quantity of maternal care as the other ones; the insecure babies had not suffered inordinate or traumatic separations that would explain their anxiety. But as she looked more closely, Ainsworth began to notice things about the mothers of these insecure babies: some of them were "highly anxious," distracted by their own preoccupations—often they had been deserted by their husbands or had disordered family lives. Still, she wasn't able to point conclusively to specific maternal behaviors that generated separation anxiety or insecure attachment.

In 1956, Ainsworth moved to the United States and began teaching at Johns Hopkins. Determined to find out whether attachment behaviors were culturally universal, she decided to contrive an experiment that could test this.

Thus was born what Ainsworth called the strange situation experiment, which has been a staple of child development research ever since. The procedure was simple. A mother and child would be placed in an unfamiliar setting—a room with a lot of toys in it—and the baby would be free to explore. Then, with the mother still present, a stranger would enter the room. How would the baby react? Then the mother would exit the room, leaving the baby with the stranger. How would the baby react to that? Then the mother would come back. How would the baby respond to the reunion? This could be repeated without the stranger—the mother would leave the child alone in the room and then return a while later. All of this would be observed by researchers sitting behind a two-way mirror. Over the ensuing decades, thousands of repetitions of this experiment produced mountains of data.

The experiments yielded some interesting insights. In the first phase of the experiment, the babies would explore the room and look at the toys while checking in frequently with the mothers—suggesting that babies' psychological need to operate from a "secure base" is indeed universal across cultures. But babies varied a lot in how distressed they would become when separated from their mothers: about half of them cried after their mothers left the room, and some babies became severely distressed and had a hard time recovering. When their mothers returned, the distressed babies would both cling to and hit them, displaying both anger and anxiety. Ainsworth labeled these insecure babies "ambivalent" in their attachment. Even more fascinating to Ainsworth than the ambivalent babies were those she would come to label "avoidant" in their attachment style: these babies seemed completely indifferent to their mothers' departures and rarely got perturbed. Superficially, they seemed quite healthy and well adjusted. But Ainsworth would come to believe—and a lot of research would eventually be produced to support the idea—that the independence and equanimity these avoidant babies displayed were in fact the product of a defense mechanism, an emotional numbing designed to cope with maternal rejection.

As Ainsworth collected her data, the most telling fact to emerge was the powerful correlation between a mother's parenting style and her child's general level of anxiety. Mothers of the children identified by researchers as securely attached were quicker to respond to their children's signals of distress, tended to hold and caress their children for longer, and derived more apparent pleasure from doing so than did the mothers of the ambivalent and avoidant children. (The mothers of securely attached children didn't necessarily interact *more* with them, but they interacted *better*, being more affectionate and responsive.) The mothers of the avoidant children displayed the most rejecting behavior; the mothers of the ambivalent children displayed the most anxiety and also by far the most unpredictability in their responses to their children—sometimes they were loving, sometimes rejecting, sometimes distracted. Ainsworth would later write that the predictability of maternal response helped dictate a child's confidence and self-esteem later in life; those mothers who predictably responded to distress signals quickly and warmly had calmer, happier babies who became more confident, independent children.

Over the next few decades, the connection between attachment style and psychological health was repeatedly confirmed by a host of different measures.* A series of influential longitudinal studies begun by researchers at the University of Minnesota in the 1970s have found that securely attached children are happier, more enthusiastic, and more persistent and focused when working on experimental tasks than anxiously attached children are and that they have better impulse control. On almost every test the researchers devised, the securely attached children did better than the ambivalently attached ones: they had higher self-esteem, stronger "ego resiliency," and less anxiety and were more independent; they were even better liked by their teachers. They also displayed greater empathy for others—probably because the insecurely attached children were too self-preoccupied to be much attuned to anyone else. The securely attached children just seemed to enjoy life more: none of the ambivalently attached children smiled, laughed, or expressed delight at the same level as the securely attached children. Many of the ambivalently attached children tended to fall apart when subjected to even minor stress.

These effects persisted for years, even decades. Teenagers who had been securely attached as toddlers had an easy time making friends—but those who had been ambivalently attached were overwhelmed by the anxiety of navigating social groups and often ended up friendless and alienated. Studies found that adults with mothers who had ambivalent attachment styles tended to procrastinate more, to have more difficulty concentrating, to be more easily distracted by concerns about their interpersonal relations, and—perhaps as a result of all this—to have

---

* As a result of Bowlby and Ainsworth's influence, by the 1980s the psychology departments of American universities were thickly populated with attachment scholars.

lower average incomes than those with mothers who had either secure or avoidant attachment styles. Many studies from the last thirty years have suggested that insecure attachment as a baby and young child is highly predictive of emotional difficulty as an adult. A two-year-old girl with an ambivalent attachment to her mother is on average much more likely to become an adult whose romantic relations are plagued by jealousy, doubt, and anxiety; she will always be seeking—likely without success—the secure, stable relationship that she did not have with her mother. The daughter of an anxious and clingy mother will herself likely grow up to be an anxious and clingy mother.

> *A mother who, due to adverse experiences during childhood, grows up to be anxiously attached is prone to seek care from her own child and thereby lead the child to become anxious, guilty, and perhaps phobic.*

> —JOHN BOWLBY, *A Secure Base* (1988)

During the postwar decades, neurochemical research would demonstrate that when an infant or an adult is stressed, a cascading series of chemical reactions in the brain produces anxiety and emotional distress; returning to a secure base (the mother or a spouse) releases endogenous opiates that make the individual relax and feel safe. Why should this be so?

Back in the 1930s, John Bowlby, already absorbed in his studies of the mother-child bond, discovered the work of the early ethologists. Ethology, the scientific study of animal behavior, suggested that many of the attachment behaviors Bowlby had been observing in humans were universal to all mammals, and it supplied an evolutionary explanation for these behaviors.

The evolutionarily adaptive benefit of early attachment behaviors is not hard to figure: holding offspring near helps a mother to keep them safe until they are fit to fend for themselves. Thus it was possible, Bowlby realized, to explain separation anxiety almost purely in terms of natural selection: there's an adaptive value to psychological mechanisms that encourage mothers and children of whatever species to stick close to one another by producing distress when they are separated; those children most predisposed to cling to their mothers in times of distress may gain a Darwinian advantage over their peers.

In yanking the sources of anxiety out of the realm of fantasy and into the world of ethology, Bowlby alienated his psychoanalytic colleagues.* When Bowlby first presented his emerging research findings in the early 1950s, he was attacked from two sides—by the psychoanalysts and the behaviorists. For the behaviorists, the mother-child bond had no inherent importance; its relevance to separation anxiety derived from the "secondary gains"—the provision of food, the soothing presence of the breast—that the child came to associate with his mother's presence. For the behaviorists, an attachment wouldn't even exist distinct from the specific needs—mainly for food—that the mother met. Bowlby disagreed. Attachment behaviors—and separation anxiety—were biologically hardwired into animals, including humans, independent of the association between food and mothers. In defense of this argument, Bowlby cited Konrad Lorenz's influential 1935 paper "The Companion in the Bird's World," in which Lorenz had revealed that goslings could become attached to geese, and sometimes even to objects, that did *not* feed them.†

Freudians argued that Bowlby's reliance on animal models of behavior gave short shrift to the intrapsychic processes—such as the battle between the id and superego—that set the human mind apart from other animals'. Once, after Bowlby presented an early paper on separation anxiety to the British Psychoanalytic Society, the organization dedicated multiple subsequent sessions to the presentations of all the critics who wanted to "bash" him. There were calls to "excommunicate" him for his apostasy.

---

* Despite what Freud wrote late in his life about the evolutionary roots of phobic anxiety, his conversion to this line of thinking came too late to influence his followers, who were now spreading the gospel of psychoanalysis around the globe. Through at least World War II, psychoanalytic theorists still viewed castration fears, the repressive superego, and the sublimated death instincts as the "cornerstones"—in Bowlby's word—of anxiety. (Bowlby believed that if Freud had had a fuller understanding of Darwin's work, psychoanalysis would have more convincingly incorporated biological principles into its corpus.)
† When Bowlby made a series of presentations, "The Nature of the Child's Tie to His Mother," to his colleagues in the British Psychoanalytic Society in the late 1950s, he tried to place himself and his work squarely within the Freudian tradition. The reactions against him were harsh. "What's the use to psychoanalyze a goose?" the psychoanalyst Hanna Segal would later ask (channeling Ogden Nash), mocking Bowlby's resort to ethology. "An infant can't follow its mother; it isn't a duckling," another analyst said dismissively.

As psychoanalytic criticism of Bowlby swelled, he received a bracing injection of support from the world of animal research when, in 1958, Harry Harlow, the president of the American Psychological Association and a psychologist at the University of Wisconsin, published an article in the *American Psychologist* called "The Nature of Love." In it, Harlow described the series of experiments that are now a fixture of every introductory psychology course.

The experiments came about by happenstance. Many of the rhesus monkeys in Harlow's lab had been contracting fatal diseases, so he took sixty infant monkeys from their mothers a few hours after birth to be raised in a germ-free environment. It worked: the separated monkeys stayed free of disease, and their physical development seemed normal, even though they remained apart from their mothers. But Harlow observed some strange things about their behavior. For one, they clung desperately to the cloth diapers used to line the cage floors. Those monkeys who were placed in mesh cages without diapers seemed to struggle physically to survive; they did better if given a mesh cone covered in terry cloth.

This gave Harlow an idea for how he might test a hypothesis that he, like Bowlby, had always found suspect: the notion, advanced by both the psychoanalysts and the behaviorists, that a baby becomes attached to his mother only because she feeds him. Even granting that the mother's association with food may provide a "secondary-reinforcing agent" (in behaviorist terminology), Harlow didn't think that those early feedings were enough to account for the maternal bond—the love and affection—that persisted for decades afterward. Could his separated rhesus monkeys, Harlow wondered, be used to research the origins of a child's love of his mother? He decided to try.

He separated eight rhesus babies from their mothers and placed each in its own cage, along with two contraptions he called surrogate mothers. One of the two mothers in each cage was made of wire mesh; the other was made of wood but was covered with terry cloth. In four of the cages, a rubber nipple offering milk was affixed to the mesh surrogate; in the other four, the nipple was affixed to the cloth-covered one. If the behaviorist supposition was correct and attachment was merely a by-product of association with feeding, then the infants should always have been drawn to the surrogate possessing the nipple.

That's not what happened. Instead, all eight monkeys bonded with the cloth mother—and spent sixteen to eighteen hours a day clinging to it—*even when the wire mother provided the feeding nipple*. This was a devastating blow to the behaviorist theory of separation anxiety. If the monkeys were more likely to bond with a soft and cuddly object that *didn't* feed them than with a wire one that *did*, hunger relief could not be the operative association in the bonding process, as the behaviorists had assumed.*

By coincidence, Bowlby attended the American Psychological Association meeting in Monterey, California, where Harlow first presented his "Nature of Love" paper. Bowlby immediately recognized the relevance of Harlow's work to his own, and the two men made common cause. In the ensuing years, other studies would replicate Harlow's initial findings. For Bowlby, this was vindication, armor against the assaults of the Freudians and the behaviorists. "Thereafter," Bowlby would later write, "nothing more was heard of the inherent implausibility of our hypotheses; and criticism became more constructive."

The Harlow study would prove even more relevant to Bowlby's ideas about attachment relationships than either man knew at the time. In later years, the monkeys from Harlow's initial study suffered lasting effects from the separation experiment. As intensely as the babies had seemed to bond with the inanimate cloth surrogates, this was clearly no replacement for a real mother-child relationship: for the remainder of their lives, these monkeys had trouble relating to their peers and exhibited abnormal social and sexual behavior. They were abusive, even murderous, parents. When presented with novelty or stress, they became much more anxious, inhibited, and agitated—which is exactly what Bowlby had observed in his studies of humans who had endured separations or difficult relations with their mothers. All of this was haunting confirmation of the long-term effects of early experiences with separation and attachment.[†]

---

* There were other parallels between the monkeys' behavior and what Bowlby had observed in human babies. When Harlow introduced a new object into their cages, the monkeys would rush to the cloth mother in agitation and rub up against it until they felt soothed; after they calmed down, they would begin to investigate and play with the object, using the cloth mother as—to invoke the phrase that Bowlby and Ainsworth would soon be using—"a secure base."

† As so often seems to be the case across the history of psychology, Harlow was unable to apply to

In the ensuing decades, hundreds of other animal experiments have supported these findings. Robert Hinde, an ethologist at Cambridge University, showed that when infant monkeys were separated from their mothers for only a few days, they were still more timid than control monkeys when placed in a novel situation five months later. A subsequent paper by Harry Harlow observed that certain key maternal styles—such as "near total acceptance of her infant (the infant can do no wrong)" and close supervision of the infant's "beginning sallies beyond her arm's reach"—were predictive of well-adjusted adult monkeys. Recent studies of rhesus monkeys have found that the "initiation of ventral contact" (or hugging, in plain English) reduces sympathetic nervous system arousal; those monkeys that received fewer hugs from their mothers were less likely to explore the environment—and were more likely to display anxious or depressive behavior as adults. In other words, when monkey mothers coddled and protected their babies, those babies grew up healthy and happy—which is precisely what Mary Ainsworth noted in her meticulous long-term observations of mother-infant interactions among humans.

Remember when you are tempted to pet your child that mother love is a dangerous instrument.
—JOHN WATSON, *Psychological Care of Infant and Child* (1928)

The experiments of Harlow, Hinde, and their contemporaries had been fairly crude; the separations they forced were severe, and the situations they set up were not analogous to real life. But in 1984, a group of researchers at Columbia University devised a way of approximating more closely the range of separation and attachment behaviors that occur in the wild.

The idea behind the variable foraging demand (VFD) paradigm, as the researchers called it, was that changing the availability of the mother's food supply could produce changes in the way she interacted with her offspring. (Primatologists already knew this from extensive

---

his own life what he learned from his research on parent-child relationships: he died alcoholic and depressed, estranged from his children.

observations in the wild.) In what have become known as VFD experiments, researchers manipulate how easy or hard it is for monkey mothers to get food: during low-foraging-demand periods, food is left freely exposed in containers strewn around the primates' enclosure; during high-foraging-demand periods, food is more difficult to get, buried in wood chips or hidden under sawdust. In a typical VFD experiment, a two-week period during which food is easy to find is followed by a two-week period when it's hard to find.

Unsurprisingly, the mothers are more stressed, and less available to tend to their offspring, during high-foraging-demand periods than they are during low-foraging-demand periods. Bonnet macaques whose mothers are subjected to extended high-foraging-demand periods have, on average, more social and physical problems growing up. But episodes of *variable* foraging demand turn out to be even more stressful than extended high-foraging-demand periods—that is, the mothers are more stressed when food is unpredictably unavailable than when it is consistently hard to find.

Jeremy Coplan, the director of neuropsychopharmacology at State University of New York Downstate Medical Center, has been conducting VFD experiments for fifteen years. He says that these experiments appear to induce a "functional emotional separation" between mother and infant. The stressed mother becomes "psychologically unavailable" to her infant, in the way that a stressed-out human mother (like Amalia Freud) might become distracted and inattentive to her children.

The shifts in behavior might appear subtle—the stressed mothers still respond to the babies, they just tend to do so more slowly and less effectively than the unstressed mothers—but the effects can be potent. In a series of experiments, Coplan and his colleagues found that the children of the VFD mothers had higher levels of stress hormones in their blood than the children of the non-VFD mothers—an indication that the mother's anxiety was being transmitted to the child. The remarkable thing was the duration of the correlation between the mother's anxiety and the child's stress hormones: when Coplan examined those original VFD children ten years after the first experiment, their levels of stress hormones were still higher than those of a control group. When they were injected with anxiety-provoking chemicals, their responses were hyperreactive compared with other monkeys'.

Evidently, these VFD monkeys had become permanently more anxious: they were less social, more withdrawing, and more likely to display subordinate behavior; they also showed an elevated level of autonomic nervous system activity and a compromised immune response. Here was powerful physiological evidence of what Bowlby had argued half a century earlier: early child-rearing experiences—not just the obviously traumatic ones but subtle ones—have psychological and physical effects on the well-being of the child that persist even into adulthood. Coplan's team concluded that even brief disruptions in the mother-child relationship can alter the development of neural systems "central to the expression of adult anxiety disorders."*

Versions of this experiment repeated many times over the last twenty years have continually found similar results: brief periods of childhood stress, and even mild strains on the mother-child relationship, can have lasting consequences on a primate's neurochemistry.† There's even some evidence that the *grandchildren* of the VFD mothers will have elevated cortisol levels from birth, as the effects of those brief early weeks of mild stress get transmitted from generation to generation.

Researchers have found analogous evidence in the descendants of

* Related research on rodents finds the same thing: the amount of licking and grooming that a mother rat lavishes on her pups has a powerful effect on the pups' tolerance for stress throughout their lifetimes—the more licking and grooming a rat receives as a pup, the more resistant to stress it will be as an adult. The rats who receive extra maternal licking display reduced autonomic nervous system activity—a diminished level of activity in the hypothalamic-pituitary-adrenal axis—and a concomitant increased tolerance for stress. These well-licked rats have what researchers call an "augmented 'off' switch" for the stress response; after just four days of extra maternal licking, they show reduced activity in the amygdala. In contrast, those rats that receive low levels of maternal grooming exhibit an exaggerated stress response.

These effects can be adaptive even when they might seem to be negative. Rats who as pups received low levels of grooming and licking are more fearful and quicker to learn to avoid frightening environments—a useful adaptation in a harsh or dangerous environment. In fact, that dangerous environment may, in the state of nature, have been what produced the low levels of licking and grooming in the first place, as the mothers were focused on finding food or avoiding external threats rather than on lavishing affection on their children. Rats who receive high levels of maternal affection are less fearful, more adventurous, and slower to learn to avoid threats—useful adaptations in a stable environment but liabilities in a dangerous one.

† Neuroscience research has begun to find suggestive evidence for the specific mechanisms by which early life stress generates later psychopathology. In essence, elevated levels of stress hormones in childhood correlate with adverse effects on the brain's serotonin and dopamine systems, which are strongly implicated in clinical anxiety and depression. Neuroimaging studies also show that protracted childhood stress tends to have what scientists call neuropathological consequences: for instance, the hippocampus, a part of the brain crucial to creating new memories, shrinks.

trauma victims: the children and even grandchildren of Holocaust survivors exhibit greater psychophysiological evidence of stress and anxious arousal—such as elevated levels of various stress hormones—than do ethnically similar children and grandchildren of cohorts who were not exposed to the Holocaust. When these grandchildren are shown stressful images having nothing directly to do with the Holocaust—for instance, of violence in Somalia—they display more extreme responses, both in behavior and physiology, than do their peers. As John Livingstone, a psychiatrist who specializes in treating trauma victims, told me, "It's as though traumatic experiences get plastered into the tissues of the body and passed along to the next generation."

By now scores of studies support the idea that the quantity and quality of a mother's affection toward her children has a potent effect on the level of anxiety those children will experience later in life. A recent study published in the *Journal of Epidemiology and Community Health* followed 462 babies from their birth in the early 1960s in Providence, Rhode Island, through their midthirties. When the study subjects were infants, researchers observed their interactions with their mothers and rated the mothers' level of affection on a scale ranging from "negative" to "extravagant." (Most mothers—85 percent of them—were rated "warm," or normal.) When psychologists interviewed the study subjects thirty-four years later, those whose mothers had shown affection that was "extravagant" or "caressing" (the second highest level) were less likely to be anxious or to experience psychosomatic symptoms than their peers.

This would seem to suggest that John Bowlby was right—that if you want to raise a well-adjusted, nonanxious child, the best approach is *not* the one prescribed by the ur-behaviorist John Watson, who once averred, "Remember when you are tempted to pet your child that mother love is a dangerous instrument." In his famous 1928 book on child rearing, Watson warned that a mother's affection could have dangerous effects on a child's developing character. "Never hug and kiss them, never let them sit in your lap," he wrote. "If you must, kiss them once on the forehead when they say good night. Shake hands with them in the morning. Give them a pat on the head if they have made an extraordinarily good job of a difficult task." Treat children, in other words, "as though they were young adults." Bowlby, who had himself been treated that way as a boy, believed more or less the opposite: if you want to instill a secure base in the child and a resistance to anxiety and depression, be unstinting in the provision of love and affection.

By 1973, when he published his classic *Separation: Anxiety and Anger*, Bowlby was convinced that almost all forms of clinical anxiety in adults* could be traced to difficult early-childhood experiences with the primary attachment figure—almost always the mother. Recent research continues to add to the substantial pile of evidence supporting this idea. In 2006, new results from the forty-year longitudinal Minnesota Study of Risk and Adaptation from Birth to Adulthood found that infants with insecure attachments were significantly more likely than infants with secure or avoidant attachments to develop anxiety disorders as adolescents. Insecure attachment in infancy leads to fears of abandonment in later childhood and adulthood and gives rise to a coping strategy based on "chronic vigilance"—those babies who anxiously scan the environment to monitor the presence of their erratically available mothers tend to become adults who are forever anxiously scanning the environment for possible threats.

Bowlby's attachment theory has an elegant simplicity and a plausible, easily understood evolutionary basis. If your parents provided a secure base when you were an infant and you were able to internalize it, then you will be more likely to go through life with a sense of safety and psychological security. If your parents failed to provide one, or if they did provide one but it was disrupted by trauma or separation, then you are more likely to endure a life of anxiety and discontent.

> *They fuck you up, your mum and dad.*
> *They may not mean to, but they do.*
> —from PHILIP LARKIN, "THIS BE THE VERSE" (1971)

I recently came across a diary that I kept briefly in the summer of 1981, when I was eleven years old. Some months earlier I had started

---

* The exception was specific animal phobias, which Bowlby, like Freud, believed came from evolutionary adaptations gone awry.

seeing the child psychiatrist who would treat me for twenty-five years, Dr. L., who was trained as a Freudian. At his instigation, I was using the diary to free-associate in pursuit of the root cause of my emotional problems. I must say it was somewhat dispiriting for my early middle-aged self to discover my eleven-year-old self already so anxious and self-absorbed, wondering on the pages of the journal which source bore greater responsibility for my abiding anxiety and discontent: Was it the tyrannical camp counselor who had, when I was six, yelled at me and sent me—alone among the merry campers of the Sachem tribe at the Belmont Day Camp—to the baby pool because I was shaking and crying, afraid to get into the big pool on my own? Or was it the neighbor who had, when I was four, slapped me in the face in front of all my preschool peers when I broke down into hysterical sobs at the birthday party for her son Gilbert because I was scared and wanted my mommy?

Evidently, my narcissism and quest for self-knowledge are endlessly recursive: I dig back into the past at age forty-three, seeking the roots of my anxiety, and discover . . . myself, at age eleven, digging back into the past, seeking the roots of my anxiety.

We had just returned from a family vacation, and much of the diary is an enumeration of the fears and perceived injustices I had endured on the trip.

1. Afraid of motion sickness on plane.
2. 1st night homesickness, can't sleep.
3. Don't like the food.
4. Restaurant: mummy getting mad and not talking to me because I complained about wanting to go home.
5. Afraid of unsanitariness.
6. Afraid thin air in mountains will make me sick.
7. Daddy forcing me to eat. Getting mad when I eat and not letting me eat when I complain . . .
8. Dad not listening to me, and hitting me when I persisted in asking.
9. I was really scared and upset when I saw what may have been throw up on the rug downstairs. I felt awful and scared.

10. On the plane ride back, person throws up. I am terrified.
Feel sad, depressed, and scared.

The trip diary ends: "I just feel like hiding my head and being hugged and loved by my mummy and daddy but they are not sympathetic about my fear at all."

Not long ago, I e-mailed my mother a transcription of the diary and then called to ask if she thought that she had expressed more or less affection for my sister and me than her peers had for their children.

"About the same," she said. Then she thought for a moment. "Actually," she said, "I consciously withheld affection."

Stunned, I asked her why.

"I thought it was for your own good," she said, and went on to explain.

Her own mother, my grandmother Elaine Hanford, had expressed ample affection for my mother and her sister and had always been present for them, physically and otherwise. Elaine built her life around catering to her daughters' needs. Every day when my mother came home from elementary school for lunch, Elaine was there to make it for her. My mother felt loved and cared for—and coddled. And so when she started to struggle with panic attacks and emetophobia and other phobias as a young adult, she wondered if maybe her anxiety was so intense because she had felt *too* loved and safe in her mother's abundant care. So in an effort to spare my sister and me the anxiety she endured, she denied us the outward expressions of unconditional love she had received.

John Watson would have approved.

But while my mother spared us affection, she didn't spare us overprotection. Overprotection and withheld affection can be a pernicious combination. It can lead to feeling not only unloved (because you're not receiving affection) but also incompetent and helpless (because someone's doing everything for you and assuming you can't do it yourself).

My mother physically dressed me until I was nine or ten years old; after that, she picked out my clothes for me every night until I was fifteen. She ran my baths for me until I was in high school. By middle school, many of my friends were taking public transportation to downtown Boston to hang out, staying home alone during school vacations while their parents were at work, and shopping for (and buying and riding) motorbikes. Even if I had been inclined to take the subway to Boston or to ride motorbikes—and, believe me, I wasn't—I wouldn't have been allowed to. Anytime my sister and I were home while my parents were at work, we had the company of a babysitter. By the time I was in middle school, this was getting a bit weird—as I realized one day when I discovered, to our mutual discomfort, that the babysitter was only a year older than I was (twelve).

My mother did all this out of genuine anxious concern. And I welcomed the excess of solicitude: it kept me swaddled in a comforting dependency. As embarrassing as it was to be told in front of my peers that I couldn't walk downtown with them unless my mother came with us, I didn't want her to relinquish her protective embrace. The dyad between mother and child implicates the behavior of each—I craved overprotection; she offered it. But our relationship deprived me of autonomy or a sense of self-efficacy, and so I was a clingy and dependent elementary school student, and then a clingy and dependent teenager, and I then grew up to be—as my long-suffering wife will tell you—a dependent and anxious adult.

"Adults with agoraphobia are more likely to rate their parents as low on affection and high on overprotection." (That's from a 2008 paper, "Attachment and Psychopathology in Adulthood.") "Adults with agoraphobia report more childhood separation anxiety than a control group." (A 1985 study published in *The American Journal of Psychiatry*.) "[Infants with insecure] attachments [are] significantly more likely than infants with secure attachments to be diagnosed with anxiety disorders." (A 1997 study published in the *Journal of the American Academy of Child and Adolescent Psychiatry*.) "Your parents—anxious, overprotective mother and alcoholic, emotionally absent father—were a classically anxiety-producing combination." (That's from my first psychiatrist, Dr. L., whom I recently tracked down and interviewed, nearly thirty years after my first appointments with him.) And then there's the neurobiological evidence for all this: "Human adults who reported extremely low-quality relationships with their parents evidenced significantly more release of dopamine in the ventral striatum [a portion of subcortical material deep in the forebrain] and a higher increase in salivary cortisol [a stress hormone] during a stressful event than individuals who reported extremely high-quality parental relations. Such an effect suggests that early human caregiving may similarly affect the development of systems that underlie stress reactivity." (A 2006 study published in *Psychological Science.*) As I write this, I have in my office a stack of articles nearly two feet high reinforcing these and related findings. Which proves that my anxiety is largely a function of my childhood relationship with my mother.

Except, of course, that it doesn't prove anything of the sort.

CHAPTER 9

Worriers and Warriors: The Genetics of Anxiety

The manner and conditions of mind are transmitted to the children through the seed.
— HIPPOCRATES (FOURTH CENTURY B.C.)

Such as the temperature of the father is, such is the son's, and look what disease the father had when he begot him, his son will have after him. I need not therefore make any doubt of melancholy, but that it is an hereditary disease.
— ROBERT BURTON, *The Anatomy of Melancholy* (1621)

Daddy, I'm nervous.
— MY DAUGHTER, AT AGE EIGHT

I could blithely blame my anxiety on the behavior of my parents—my father's drinking, my mother's overprotectiveness and phobias, their unhappy marriage and eventual divorce—were it not for, among other reasons, this inconvenient fact: my children, now nine and six, have recently developed anxiety that, to a distressing degree, parallels my own.

My daughter, Maren, has always had, like me, an inhibited temperament—shy and withdrawing in unfamiliar situations, risk averse in her approach to the world, and highly reactive to stress or any kind of novelty. More strikingly, when she was in first grade she developed an obsessive phobia of vomiting. When a classmate of hers threw up during math, she couldn't get the image out of her head. "I can't stop thinking bad thoughts," she said, and my heart broke.

Have I—despite my decades of therapy, my hard-won personal and scholarly knowledge of anxiety, my wife's and my informed efforts at inoculating our children against it—bequeathed to Maren my disorder, as my mother bequeathed it to me?

Unlike my mother, I never revealed my emetophobia to my daughter before she developed it herself. I have tried not to betray evidence of my anxiety to Maren, knowing that to do so might be to pass it on to her through what psychologists call modeling behavior. My wife is not an anxious person; she has none of the nervously overprotective tendencies that, expressed for so many years by my mother, I had thought reduced my sister and me to such states of neurotic dependency. And we are both, my wife and I, loving and nurturing, and we strive to be emotionally present for our kids in ways that my parents sometimes were not.

Or so we like to think.

And yet here is my daughter exhibiting symptoms very similar to mine and at almost the same age I first developed them. Somehow, despite our best efforts at providing emotional prophylaxis, Maren seems to have inherited my nervous temperament—and, remarkably, *the exact same phobic preoccupation.* Which happens to be, moreover, a preoccupation I share with my mother.

Is it possible, my wife asks, that so idiosyncratic a phobia can be genetically transmitted?

One would think not. And yet we have here the evidence of three generations on my mother's side with the same phobia. And unless Maren has picked up on subtle or unconscious cues (which, I concede, is possible), she cannot have "learned" the phobia from me through some kind of behavioral conditioning, as I thought I might have learned mine from my mother.

While observers since Hippocrates have noted that temperaments are heritable, and while the modern field of behavioral genetics is revealing with increasing precision—down to the individual nucleotide—the relationship between the molecules we inherit and the emotions we're predisposed to, no one has yet identified a gene, or even a set of genes, for emetophobia. Nor, for that matter, has anyone reduced anxiety—or any behavioral trait—to pure genetics. But in recent years, thousands of studies have pointed to various genetic bases for clinical anxiety in its different forms.

Some of the earliest research on the genetics of anxiety studied twins. In the most basic studies, researchers compared rates of anxiety disorder between sets of identical and fraternal twins. If, say, panic disorder were completely genetic, that would mean in a set of identical twins—genetic copies—you would never find just one with the disease. But that's not the case. When one twin has the disorder, the other is much more likely than a randomly selected person from the population to have the disease—but not *guaranteed* to have it. This suggests that while panic disorder—like height or eye color—has a powerful genetic component, the disease is not completely genetic.

In 2001, Kenneth Kendler, a psychiatrist at Virginia Commonwealth University, compared the rates of phobic disorders among twelve hundred sets of fraternal and identical twins, determining that genes account for about 30 percent of the individual differences in vulnerability to anxiety disorders. Subsequent studies have tended to roughly support Kendler's findings. Meta-analyses of genetic studies conclude that if you don't have any close relatives with generalized anxiety disorder, your odds of having it yourself are less than one in twenty-five—but having a single close relative with the disorder boosts your odds of developing it to one in five.

Wait, you might object, this doesn't prove a genetic basis for anxiety. Couldn't the high probability of the same mental illness occurring in members of the same family be a result of their sharing what researchers call a pathogenic environment, one that is predictive of anxiety or depression? If twins share a traumatic upbringing, mightn't that engender in both of them a higher susceptibility to mental illness?

Certainly. While genes may predispose a person to schizophrenia or alcoholism or anxiety, there is almost always some environmental contribution to the disease. Still, the number of studies on the heritability of anxiety is climbing into the tens of thousands, and the overwhelming conclusion of almost all of them is that your susceptibility to anxiety—both as a temperamental tendency and as a clinical disorder—is strongly determined by your genes.

This would not have surprised Hippocrates or Robert Burton or Charles Darwin or any number of observers who long predate the era of molecular genetics. Once a family tree has one or two individuals with anxiety disorder or depression, then you will likely find the rest of the tree stippled with anxiety and depression. Researchers call this phenomenon "familial aggregation due to genetic risk."*

Does "familial aggregation" mean that my daughter, like my mother and me, is biologically predestined to be anxious, perhaps genetically fated to develop nervous illness? On my mother's side of the family alone, there is, in addition to my mother and my daughter and me, my son, Nathaniel, now six, who has separation anxiety that threatens to become as bad as mine ever was; my sister, who has struggled since age twelve with anxiety and has tried as many drug treatments as I have; another blood relative who has similarly wrestled his whole life with anxiety and depression and a nervous stomach and who has been medicated off and on for decades; that relative's older brother, who was diagnosed with clinical depression in the early 1980s, at the tender age of eight, and who vomited from anxiety before school nearly every day for a year; and my mother's father, ninety-two years old, who today takes a variety of antianxiety and antidepressant medications. Looking further back into my ancestry, I have discovered that my mother's father's grandfather was painfully reserved and hated dealing with people, dropping out of Cornell to start a "quiet life" cultivating fruit orchards ("The outdoor life saved him," his daughter-in-law would say later), and that my grandfather's aunt suffered from severe anxiety, depression, and a famously nervous stomach.

And then there is my grandfather's father Chester Hanford, whose anxiety and depression were severe enough that he had to be institutionalized multiple times, leaving him frequently incapacitated during the last thirty years of his life.

---

* In 2011, Giovanni Salum, a Brazilian psychiatrist, released the results of one of the largest-scale studies of the heritability of anxiety disorders ever conducted. Surveying data on ten thousand people, Salum found that a child who has no relatives with an anxiety disorder has only a one-in-ten chance of developing one himself. If that same child has one relative with an anxiety disorder in his family, his odds of developing an anxiety disorder rise to three in ten. And if a large majority of members have an anxiety disorder, the child's odds rise to *eight* in ten.

I suspect that most, but not all, of the large number of human temperaments are the result of genetic factors that contribute to the profiles of molecules and receptor densities that influence brain function.
—JEROME KAGAN, *What Is Emotion?* (2007)

It frequently happens that hysteria in the mother frequently begets hysteria in the son.
—JEAN-MARTIN CHARCOT, *Lectures on Diseases of the Nervous System,* VOLUME 3 (1885)

Jerome Kagan, a developmental psychologist at Harvard, has spent sixty years studying the effect of heredity on human personality. In longitudinal studies extending across decades, he has consistently found that about 10 to 20 percent of infants are, from the time they are a few weeks old, demonstrably more timid than other infants. These infants are fussier, sleep more poorly, and have faster heart rates, more muscle tension, and higher levels of cortisol in their blood and of norepinephrine in their urine. They exhibit faster startle reflexes (meaning that in response to a sudden noise they twitch nanoseconds faster and show greater increases in pupil dilation). In fMRI scans, the fear circuits of their brains—namely, the amygdala and the anterior cingulate—show higher-than-normal neuronal activity. These physiological measures remain consistently higher for these children than for other children throughout their lifetimes. Whether they are tested at six weeks, seven years, fourteen years, twenty-one years, or older, they continue to have higher heart rates, faster startle reflexes, and more stress hormones than their low-reactive peers.

Kagan has labeled as inhibited the temperament of these children with high-reactive physiology. "We believe that most of the children we refer to as 'inhibited' belong to a qualitatively distinct category of infants who were born with a lower threshold for arousal to unexpected changes in the environment or novel events," Kagan says. "For these children, the prepared reaction to novelty that is characteristic of all children is exaggerated."

A few years ago, Kagan and his colleagues took brain scans of a group of twenty-one-year-olds they had been studying for nineteen years. In 1984, when Kagan had first observed these subjects as two-year-olds, he had described thirteen of them as inhibited and the other nine as uninhibited. Two decades later, when Kagan showed pictures of unfamiliar faces to all twenty-two test subjects, now young adults, the thirteen who had been identified as inhibited displayed significantly more amygdala response than the nine who had been identified as uninhibited. Kagan believes that your genes determine the reactivity of your amygdala—and we know from other research that the reactivity of your amygdala, in turn, helps determine how you will react to stress.

Those infants or toddlers identified as inhibited are more likely to become shy, nervous adolescents—and then shy, nervous adults—than their peers. They are much more likely to develop clinical anxiety or depression as teens or adults than their less physiologically reactive peers. Even those high-reactive babies who don't grow up to get officially diagnosed with anxiety disorders tend to remain more nervous, on average, than their peers.

In believing that temperament is innate and largely fixed from birth, Kagan falls squarely in the intellectual tradition that stretches back to Hippocrates, who in the fourth century B.C. argued that personality and mental health derived from the relative balance of the four humors in the body: blood, phlegm, black bile, and yellow bile. According to Hippocrates, as noted in chapter 1, a person's relative humoral balance accounted for his temperament: whereas someone with relatively more blood might have a lively or "sanguine" temperament and be given to hot-blooded explosions of temper, someone with relatively more black bile might have a melancholic temperament. Hippocrates's theory of humoral balance directly anticipates, metaphorically anyway, the serotonin hypothesis of depression and other modern theories of the relation between chemical imbalances in the brain and mental health. For instance, Hippocrates attributed what we would by the mid-twentieth century be calling neurotic depression—and what we would today call generalized anxiety disorder (*DSM* code 300.02)—to an excess of black bile (*melain chole*). As Hippocrates described it, this condition was characterized by both physical symptoms ("pains at the abdomen, breathlessness . . . frequent burps") and emotional ones ("anxiety, restlessness, dread . . . fear, sadness, fretfulness" often accompanied and usually caused by "meditations and worries exaggerated in fancy").

Hippocrates may have had the wrong explanatory metaphor, but modern science is proving him to have been basically right about temperament's fixity and biological basis. Kagan, now in his eighties, is semiretired, but four major longitudinal studies started by him or by a former protégé, Nathan Fox at the University of Maryland, are still under way. All four are reaching conclusions that support Kagan's longheld theory that the anxious temperament is an innate, genetically determined phenomenon that characterizes a relatively fixed percentage of the population.* His studies have repeatedly found that those 15 to 20 percent of infants who react strongly to strangers or novel situations are much more likely to grow up to develop anxiety disorders than their less physiologically reactive peers. If you are born highly reactive and inhibited, you tend to stay highly reactive and inhibited. In decades of longitudinal studies, only rarely has Kagan seen anyone move from one temperamental category to another.

All of which would seem to complicate, if not undermine, what I said about attachment theory in the previous chapter. Indeed, Kagan believes John Bowlby, Mary Ainsworth, and their colleagues were largely wrong about how anxiety gets transmitted from one generation to the next. In Kagan's view, insecure attachment style per se does not produce an anxious child. Rather—and I'm oversimplifying a little—*genes* produce a mother with an anxious temperament; that temperament, in turn, leads her to demonstrate an attachment style that psychologists observe to be insecure. The mother then transmits this anxiety to her children—not primarily, as Bowlby and Ainsworth would have it, through her nervous parenting style (though, to be sure, that may intensify the transmission), but rather by the passing on of her anxious genes. Which, if true, would make it harder to break the transmission of anxiety from generation to generation through changes

---

* This squares with what studies have found about the relatively fixed percentage of soldiers who are especially prone to break down when exposed to combat stress.

in parenting behavior—and which might explain why, despite our best efforts, my wife and I have been unable to prevent our children from developing signs of incipient anxiety disorders.

John Bowlby cited animal studies to buttress his theory of attachment. But Jerome Kagan can also cite animal studies to rebut Bowlby and support his own theory of temperament. In the 1960s, researchers at the Maudsley Hospital in London bred what became known as the Maudsley strain of reactive rats, which responded to stress with pronounced anxious behavior. These breeding experiments were performed without the benefit of modern genomics. Researchers simply observed rat behavior, noted the "emotionally reactive" ones (mainly by measuring their defecation rates when placed in open spaces), and mated them with one another—and in so doing managed to produce this highly anxious strain. (By the same selective breeding technique, they also produced a strain of nonreactive rats, which responded *less* fearfully than average to open spaces and other stressors.) This seemed to be evidence of a potent hereditary component to anxiety in rat populations.

Modern experimental techniques have advanced beyond selective breeding. Scientists are now able to chemically switch different mouse genes on or off, allowing researchers to observe how the genes affect behavior. By deactivating certain genes, researchers have created mice that, for instance, no longer experience anxiety, and in fact cannot recognize real danger, because their amygdalae have stopped working. Researchers, churning out hundreds of studies of this sort a year, have so far identified at least seventeen genes that seem to affect various parts of the fear neurocircuitry in mice.

For instance, Eric Kandel, a Nobel Prize–winning neuroscientist at Columbia, has discovered one gene (known as *Grp*) that seems to encode a mouse's ability to acquire new phobias through fear conditioning and another gene (known as stathmin) that regulates innate levels of physiological anxiety. Mice whose *Grp* gene has been switched off cannot learn to associate a neutral tone with an electric shock the way normal mice do. Mice whose stathmin gene has been switched off become daredevils: instead of instinctively cowering on the edge of open spaces like normal mice, they venture boldly into exposed areas.

Evolution has conserved many genes, so humans and rodents share many of the same ones. Consider *RGS2*, a gene that in both mice and humans seems to regulate the expression of a protein that modulates serotonin and norepinephrine receptors in the brain. After it was noted that mice without the *RGS2* gene displayed markedly anxious behavior and "elevated sympathetic tone" (meaning their bodies were on constant low-grade fight-or-flight alert), a series of studies on humans by Jordan Smoller and his team at Harvard Medical School found a relation between certain variations of the *RGS2* gene and human shyness. In one study of children from 119 families, the kids who displayed characteristics of a "behaviorally inhibited" temperament tended to have the same variant of the *RGS2* gene. Another study, of 744 college students, found that students with the "shy" variant of the gene were more likely to describe themselves as introverted. A third study revealed how the gene exerts its effect on the brain: when fifty-five young adults were placed in a brain scanner and shown pictures of angry or fearful faces, those with the relevant *RGS2* variation were more likely to show increased "neuronal firing" in the amygdala and the insula, a part of the cortex associated not only with limbic system expressions of fear but also with "interoceptive awareness," that explicit consciousness of inner bodily functions that can give rise to "anxiety sensitivity." A fourth study, of 607 people who lived through the severe Florida hurricane season of 2004, found that those who had the relevant variant of the *RGS2* gene were more likely to have developed an anxiety disorder in the aftermath of the hurricanes.

None of these studies prove that simply having a certain variant of the *RGS2* gene *causes* anxiety disorder. But they do suggest that the *RGS2* gene affects the functioning of fear systems in the insula and the amygdala—and that individuals who have the "shy" variant of the gene are more likely to have hyperactive amygdalae and to experience higher levels of autonomic arousal in social situations and therefore to be shy or introverted. (Shyness and introversion are both predisposing factors in the anxiety disorders.)

Lauren McGrath, a researcher in the Psychiatric and Neurodevelopmental Genetics Unit at Massachusetts General Hospital, studied 134 babies over nearly twenty years. When the babies were four months old, McGrath's team divided them into groups of (using Kagan's terms) "high-reactives" and "low-reactives." At four months, the high-reactives cried and moved more in response to the movement of a mobile than the low-reactives did; at fourteen and twenty-one months, those same high-reactives still tended to demonstrate fearful reactions in response to novel situations. Eighteen years later, McGrath's team tracked down the original study subjects and looked at the structure and reactivity of their amygdalae. Sure enough, the babies identified as high-reactives at four months had larger, more hyperactive amygdalae at age eighteen than the low-reactives did—yet more evidence that the amygdala's response to novelty is a strong predictor of temperamental anxiety level. In a final wrinkle, McGrath's team, using new genetic coding techniques, discovered that high amygdala reactivity at age eighteen was highly correlated with a particular variation on a specific gene known as *RTN4*. McGrath and her colleagues hypothesize that the *RTN4* gene helps determine how hyperreactive your amygdala will be, which in turn helps determine whether your temperament will be high-reactive or low-reactive—which in turn helps determine your vulnerability to clinical anxiety.

This alphabet soup of genetic studies—hundreds if not thousands of which are being conducted at any given time—can seem inanely reductionist. A few years ago, I read a *New York Times* article about studies attributing a correlation between certain variants of two human genes—*AVPR1a* and *SLC6A4*—and a "talent for creative dance performance."* The good news, I suppose, is that if this changes how we think about character and fate, it might also change how we think about courage and cowardice, shame and disease, stigma and mental illness. If extreme anxiety is owed to genetic anomalies, should it be any more shameful than multiple sclerosis or cystic fibrosis or black hair, all diseases or traits encoded by the genes?

Fifty years ago, we could plausibly blame the behavior of our mothers for all manner of neuroses and unhappiness and bad behavior. Today,

---

* To be sure, genetic researchers grant that anxious emotion, or a talent for dancing, must have multiple genetic (and environmental) causes. But the trend toward reducing emotions to their underlying neurochemical correlates, and to the genes that underwrote them, can seem inexorable.

we can perhaps still blame our mothers—but it may be more plausible to blame the *genes* they conferred upon us than the *behaviors* they displayed or the emotional wounds they inflicted.

> *For that which is but a flea-biting to one, causeth insufferable torment to another.*
> —ROBERT BURTON, *The Anatomy of Melancholy* (1621)

A number of private companies will, in exchange for a drop of your saliva and a hefty fee, sequence part of your genome in order to provide information about your relative risk factor for various diseases. A few years ago, I paid a few hundred dollars to a company called 23andMe, and so I now know that my genes have left me with, all things being equal, a modestly higher than average likelihood of getting gallstones, a modestly lower than average likelihood of developing type 2 diabetes or skin cancer, and a roughly average likelihood of suffering a heart attack or developing prostate cancer. I also learned that I am, according to my genotype, a "fast caffeine metabolizer," that I am at "typical" risk for heroin addiction and alcohol abuse, and that I have fast-twitch sprinter's muscles. (I also learned that I have "wet" earwax.)

I was hoping to find out which variants I have of two particular genes, each of which has at different times been dubbed the "Woody Allen gene." The first gene, known as *COMT,* is found on chromosome 22 and encodes the production of an enzyme (catechol-O-methyltransferase) that breaks down dopamine in the prefrontal cortex of the brain. The second gene, *SLC6A4,* also known as the *SERT* gene, is found on chromosome 17 and encodes for how efficiently serotonin gets ferried across the synapses of your neurons.

The *COMT* gene has three variants.* One (known as val/val) encodes for a high level of the enzyme that breaks down dopamine very effectively; the others (val/met and met/met) encode for lower levels that break down less dopamine and leave more of it in the synapses.

---

* Let me stipulate here that I am not a genetic scientist, and that I am oversimplifying a vast and complex body of research. For an easy-to-understand book about psychiatric genetics by an expert, I recommend *The Other Side of Normal: How Biology Is Providing the Clues to Unlock the Secrets of Normal and Abnormal Behavior* by Jordan Smoller.

Recent studies have found that people with the met/met version tend to have a harder time regulating their emotional arousal. The excess levels of dopamine, researchers speculate, are linked to "negative emotionality" and to an "inflexible attentional focus" that leaves people unable to tear themselves away from obsessional preoccupation with frightening stimuli—traits that are, in turn, linked to depression, neuroticism, and, especially, anxiety. People with the met/met variant show an inability to relax after exposure to apparently threatening stimuli, even when those stimuli are revealed to be not dangerous after all. In contrast, the val/val variant was associated with *less* intense experiencing of negative emotions, a *less* reactive startle reflex, and *less* behavioral inhibition.*

David Goldman, the chief of human neurogenetics at the National Institutes of Health, has labeled *COMT* the "worrier-warrior gene." Those who possess the val/val version, according to Goldman, are "warriors": under stressful conditions, this gene variant gives them a beneficial increase in the extracellular brain level of dopamine, which presumably makes them less anxious and less susceptible to pain and allows them to focus better. The extra dopamine also gives them "better working memory" while under stress. I would imagine that, for example, the NFL quarterback Tom Brady—who is legendary for his ability to make quick, smart decisions while under tremendous pressure (throwing the ball accurately to the correct receiver even as thousands of pounds of linebacker are bearing down on him at high speed and millions of people are watching and judging him)—has the warrior variant. But there are situations in which the worrier version, which 25 percent

---

* Many studies have supported the connection between the met/met variant of the *COMT* gene and unusually high levels of anxiety—though, interestingly, mainly in women. One study, conducted by investigators at the National Institute on Alcohol Abuse and Alcoholism, looked at two disparate groups of women—Caucasians from suburban Maryland and Plains Indians from rural Oklahoma—and found that in both populations women with the met/met variant reported much higher levels of anxiety than did women with the other variants. (The met/met variant also correlated with having only a quarter to a third of the typical quantity of the catechol-O-methyltranferase enzyme in the brain.) When women with the met/met variant were placed in an EEG machine, they exhibited a "low-voltage alpha brain-wave pattern," which has been found to be associated with both anxiety disorders and alcoholism. In short, the study revealed a connection not only between the gene and enzyme levels, and between enzyme levels and brain activity, but also between brain activity and subjectively experienced levels of anxiety. Another study, conducted among both German and American populations in 2009, found that people with the met/met version of the gene exhibited higher-than-average physiological startle responses when shown a series of unpleasant pictures and were, according to standard personality tests, higher in general anxiety.

of the world population has, confers evolutionary advantages. Studies have shown that carriers of the met/met version perform better on cognitive tasks requiring memory and attention when *not* under severe stress; this suggests the worriers may be better at evaluating complex environments and therefore at avoiding danger. Each version confers a different adaptive strategy: those with the worrier variant are good at staying out of danger; those with the warrior variant act effectively once they're in danger.*

The *SERT* gene also has three variants: short/short, short/long, and long/long (these get abbreviated to s/s, s/l, and l/l). Starting in the mid-1990s, many studies have found that people with one or more short *SERT* allele (that is, those with the s/s or s/l variant of the gene) tend to process serotonin less efficiently than those with only long alleles—and that when carriers of short-allele polymorphisms are shown fear-producing images, they display more amygdala activity than carriers of the l/l pairing. This correlation between a specific gene and activity in the amygdala, researchers hypothesize, helps account for the higher rates of anxiety disorder and depression that other studies were finding in people with the s/s version.

In the absence of life stress, people with the s/s and s/l genotypes weren't any likelier to become depressed than people with the l/l genotypes. When stressful situations arose, however—whether in the form of financial, employment, health, or relationship problems—those individuals with short versions were more likely to become depressed or suicidal. Put the other way around, those people with the l/l vari-

---

* These different evolutionary strategies seem to apply even in fish. Lee Dugatkin is a professor of biology at the University of Louisville who studies guppy behavior. Some guppies are bold; some are timid. Bold male guppies, Dugatkin observes, are more likely than timid male guppies to attract females to mate with. But the bold guppies, in their brazenness, are also more likely to swim near predators and get eaten. The timid guppies thus tend to live longer—and therefore to prolong the time during which they have opportunities to mate. Both types of guppies, the bold and the timid, represent a viable evolutionary strategy: Be bold and mate more but be more likely to die young—or be timid, mate less, and be more likely to live longer. There's an adaptive value to being a bold guppy—but there's also an adaptive value to being a timid one. It's not hard to see the same evolutionary strategies at work among human populations. Some people live boldly, mate promiscuously, take risks, and tend to die young (think of the bold and tragic Kennedy clan); others live timidly, mate less, are risk averse, and tend to be less likely to die prematurely in accidents.

ant seemed partly insulated against depression and anxiety even when under stress.*

Kerry Ressler, a psychiatrist at Emory University, has produced similar findings about other genes. Ressler has discovered that whereas some genotypes seem to confer increased vulnerability to certain forms of anxiety disorder, other genotypes seem to confer *almost complete resistance to them*. For instance, a gene called *CRHR1* encodes the structure of brain receptors for corticotropin-releasing hormone (CRH), which is released during activation of the fight-or-flight response or during times of prolonged stress. To oversimplify a little, there are three variants of this gene: C/C, C/T, and T/T (the letters refer to the sequence of proteins that encode the amino acids that make up your DNA). Looking at a group of five hundred people from inner-city Atlanta who had suffered high rates of poverty, trauma, and child abuse, Ressler found that the variant of the *CRHR1* gene you inherited strongly predicted the likelihood of your developing depression as an adult if you were abused as a child. One homozygous version of the gene (C/C) was associated with child abuse victims being *very likely* to develop clinical depression in adulthood; the heterozygous version of the gene (C/T) was associated with a *moderate likelihood* of depression in adulthood; and, most fascinatingly, the other homozygous version of the gene (T/T) was *not associated at all* with depression in adulthood—the T/T version of the gene seems to confer on these child abuse victims almost complete immunity to depression. Child abuse seemed to have had *no long-term psychological effect at all* on those with this version of the gene.

Ressler has also discovered similar findings in studies on the gene responsible for coding the feedback sensitivity of glucocorticoid receptors. Variations in this gene, known as *FKBP5*, seem to have a powerful effect on the susceptibility of children to post-traumatic stress disorder.

---

* Not every study has borne out the initial hypothesis that having a short version of the *SERT* allele makes you more susceptible to anxiety or depression. For instance, while epidemiological studies consistently find that rates of clinical anxiety and depression are *lower* in Asia than in Europe and North America, genetic testing has found that the prevalence of the s/s *SERT* allele is markedly *higher* among East Asian populations than among Western ones—which raises intriguing questions about how culture and social structure interact with genetics to affect the rates and intensity of anxiety among individuals in different societies.

Whereas one variant of the *FKBP5* gene seems to be associated with high rates of PTSD, another variant seems to confer strong resistance: kids with the G/G variant developed PTSD at only around a third the rate of kids with other variants.

Research like this suggests that your susceptibility to nervous breakdown is strongly determined by your genes. Certain genotypes make you especially vulnerable to psychological breakdown when subjected to stress or trauma; other genotypes make you naturally resilient. No single gene, or even set of genes, programs you to be anxious per se. But certain gene combinations program you to have either a high or a low level of hypothalamic-pituitary-adrenal activity: if you were born with a sensitive autonomic nervous system and then get exposed to stress in early childhood, your HPA system gets sensitized even further, so it's always hyperactive later in life, producing an excessively twitchy amygdala—which in turn primes you to develop depression or anxiety disorders. If, however, you were born with genes encoding low baseline levels of HPA activity, you will tend to have a high level of immunity to the effects of even severe stress.

Here, it seems, is at least a partial explanation for what the Oxford scholar Robert Burton had observed back in 1621 in *The Anatomy of Melancholy:* "For that which is but a flea-biting to one, causeth insufferable torment to another."

Would finding out that I have the warrior version of the *COMT* gene be a relief because it would mean that I am not, after all, genetically doomed to high levels of "neuroticism" and "harm avoidance"? Or would discovering that I have, say, the long/long version of the *SERT* gene make me feel even worse than I already do: to be blessed with the genes for easygoingness and resilience and yet to feel so anxious and neurotic—how pathetic would that be? I'd be learning that I had somehow managed to squander a generous genetic inheritance.

In her 1937 book, *The Neurotic Personality of Our Time*, Karen Horney, a disciple of Freud, writes about how a standard behavioral tic of the neurotic is to reduce himself to nothing—*I am such a loser*, he says to himself, *look at all the obstacles that impede me and the handicaps that confine me; it's a wonder that I can function at all*—in order to relieve the pressure to accomplish anything. The neurotic secretly (sometimes without even knowing it) nurtures a powerful ambition to achieve as a means of compensating for a weak sense of self-worth. But the fear of failing to accomplish, or of having his poor self-worth confirmed by manifest lack of achievement despite a sincere effort to succeed, is too unbearable to abide. So as a psychological self-defense tactic, the neurotic plays up the infirmities that ostensibly make achieving success difficult. Once these handicaps and disadvantages are established, the pressure is off: anything a neurotic accomplishes merits extra credit. And if the neurotic fails? Well, that's what playing up all these deficits has aimed to prepare for: How could you expect anything but failure given the barriers stacked against him? Thus to discover that I have the neurotic version of the *COMT* gene or the anxious-depressive *SERT* gene might at some level prove to be a relief. *See,* I could say, *here's proof that my anxiety is "real." It's right there in my genes. How can anyone expect me—how can I expect myself—to do anything much more than muddle anxiously along? It's a wonder I've been able to accomplish anything given my disordered constellation of genes! Now let me huddle under the covers and watch soothing television shows.*

Late one night, the report on my *COMT* gene arrived.* I am heterozygous (val/met), which means, based on the limited data so far, I am neither warrior nor worrier but something in between. (A 2005 study at San Diego State University did find that people—mainly women— with the val/met variant tended to be more introverted and neurotic.) Some time later, I received the results from the genotyping of my *SERT* gene: I'm short/short—meaning I've got the variant that many studies have found is predictive of anxiety disorders and depression when coupled with life stress. If current genetic research is to be believed, I should—based on my genotype—be anxious and harm avoidant, inordinately susceptible to suffering and pain.

Shouldn't this be liberating? If being anxious is genetically encoded,

---

* I asked my brother-in-law, a medical student and former biochemistry major, to take the raw genomic data that 23andMe provided and plug it into open-source genome databases to figure out what variant I have of the *COMT* gene. And though 23andMe does not currently provide clients with even the raw data on *SERT* variants, I prevailed upon some neuroscientist friends of mine to test me for it, on the condition that I not reveal their names since they receive federal grant funding and are not supposed to perform the test on anyone who is not officially part of a study.

a medical disease, and not a failure of character or will, how can I be blamed or shamed or stigmatized for it?

But ceding responsibility for your temperament and personality and baseline level of anxiety to hereditary bad luck—however well based in genetic science this may be—quickly bleeds into vexing philosophical territory. The same building blocks of nucleotides, genes, neurons, and neurotransmitters that make up my anxiety also make up the rest of my personality. To the extent that genes encode my anxiety, they also encode my self. Do I really want to attribute the "me-ness" of me to genetic factors completely beyond my control?

> *The enigmatic phobias of early childhood deserve mention once again. . . . Certain of them—the fear of being alone, of the dark, of strangers—we can understand as reactions to the danger of object loss; with regard to others—fear of small animals, thunderstorms, etc.—there is the possibility that they represent the atrophied remnants of an innate preparedness against reality dangers as is so well developed in other animals.*
>
> —SIGMUND FREUD, *The Problem of Anxiety* (1926)

How could something as idiosyncratic as a specific phobia have gotten passed from my mother to me to my daughter? Can a simple phobia be genetic?

Recall that Freud, late in his career, observed that certain common phobias—fear of the dark, fear of being alone, fear of small animals, fear of thunderstorms—seem to have evolutionarily adaptive roots, representing "the atrophied remnants of an innate preparedness against reality dangers such as is so well developed in other animals." By this logic, certain phobias are so common because they arise from instinctive fears that have been evolutionarily selected for.

In the 1970s, Martin Seligman, a psychologist at the University of Pennsylvania, elaborated this notion into what he called preparedness theory: certain phobias are common because evolution has selected for brains primed to have exaggerated fear responses to dangerous things. Cro-Magnons who innately feared—and who therefore avoided—

falling off cliffs or getting bitten by poisonous snakes or bugs or being exposed to predators in open fields were more likely to survive.

If the human brain is predisposed to develop fears of certain things, that casts one of the most famous experiments in the history of psychology in a new light. What if John Watson misinterpreted the Little Albert experiment that I discussed in chapter 2? What if the real reason Albert developed such a profound phobia of rats, and so readily generalized it to other furry creatures, was not that behavioral conditioning is so powerful but that the human brain has a natural predisposition to fear small furry things? Rodents, after all, can carry lethal diseases. Early humans who acquired a prudent fear of rats would have had an evolutionary advantage that made them more likely to survive. So it may be that neither the outward projections of inner psychic conflict (as the early Freud would have it) nor the power of behavioral conditioning (as Watson had it) is the primary reason so many people today develop rodent phobias; rather, it may be the connection of such fears to an atavistic response that is readily triggered.

For a long time, primatologists believed monkeys emerged from the womb with an innate fear of snakes. When researchers would observe a monkey encounter a snake (or even a snakelike object), the monkey would react fearfully—seemingly a clear instance of purely innate preparedness, of an inborn fear somehow handed down through the genes. But Susan Mineka, a psychologist at Northwestern University, discovered that monkeys who have been separated from their mothers and raised in captivity display no fear when they first encounter a snake. Only after infant monkeys have observed their mothers reacting fearfully to a snake—or after they have watched a video of another monkey reacting fearfully to a snake—do they later exhibit fearful behavior when exposed to a snake themselves. This suggests young monkeys *learn* to be afraid of snakes from watching their mothers—which in turn would seem to be strong evidence that the phobia is acquired by environmental learning rather than through the genes. But Mineka discovered another wrinkle: she found that monkeys could *not* easily acquire fears of things that were not intrinsically dangerous. Young monkeys who were shown videos of other monkeys reacting fearfully to a snake subsequently developed the fear of snakes—but monkeys shown (artfully spliced) videos of other monkeys reacting fearfully to flowers or rabbits did *not* develop fears of flowers or rabbits. Evidently, a combination of social observation and intrinsic danger is necessary to produce phobic-like behavior in monkeys.

Arne Öhman, the Swedish psychologist whose work on social anxiety I mentioned in chapter 4, points out that while all humans are evolutionarily primed to acquire certain adaptive fears, most people do not develop phobias. This is evidence, Öhman argues, that there is genetic variation in how sensitive our brains are to even those stimuli we are evolutionarily primed to fear. Some people—like my mother, my daughter, my son, and me—have a genetically encoded propensity to acquire fears and to have them be more intense than average.*

In support of Seligman's preparedness theory, Öhman found that those phobias—including acrophobia (fear of heights), claustrophobia (enclosed spaces), arachnophobia (spiders), murophobia (rodents), and ophidiophobia (snakes)—that would have had clear adaptive relevance in our early evolutionary history were much harder to extinguish with exposure therapy than phobias of objects like horses or trains that were not historically "fear relevant." Furthermore, Öhman found that even phobias of guns and knives—which are clearly "fear relevant" today but would not have been for Neanderthals and other evolutionary forebears—were much easier to extinguish than fears of snakes and rats, suggesting that the fears we are most readily primed for, and least easily rid of, were inscribed in our genes relatively early in primate evolution.

But what, if anything, is evolutionarily useful about emetophobia? Vomiting is adaptive; it can rid us of toxins that could kill us. What would account for a genotype for such a phobia?

One speculative possibility is that emetophobia is genetically

---

* Interestingly, different phobias seem to trigger different parts of our neurocircuitry and to have different genetic roots. This is true to my own experience. As phobic as I am of flying and of heights and of vomiting and of cheese, I have no inordinate fear of snakes or rats or other animals; in fact, the animal kingdom may be one of the few areas where I'm actually less fearful than I ought to be. I have been badly bitten by a dog (which resulted in a trip to the emergency room when I was eight), by a snake (I once had a pet bull snake named Kim), and was once viciously attacked by, of all things, a kangaroo, which I'd mistakenly thought wanted a hug. (Long story.) I'd be much happier covered in a pile of (nonpoisonous) snakes and rats than flying through even the mildest turbulence.

derived from an impulse that *is* evolutionarily adaptive: avoiding *other people* who are vomiting. Instinctively running away from regurgitating peers might have saved those early hominids from being exposed to ambient toxins that could have poisoned them. Another possibility is that an array of genetically conferred temperamental traits and behavioral and cognitive predispositions, plus a high innate level of physiological reactivity, combined to enhance a vulnerability to phobic anxiety—and maybe especially, somehow, to this particular phobic anxiety. My mother, my daughter, and I all have high-reactive physiologies, with jittery amygdalae and bodies always on DEFCON 4 alert, which make us constantly hypervigilant about danger. My mother—like my daughter and like me—is a high-octane worrier; at times, she emits a nervous thrum that is practically audible. Our physiological reactivity and inhibited temperaments make all three of us more generally nervous, and more likely to experience intense negative emotion when exposed to a frightening stimulus, than someone with a low-reactive, uninhibited temperament.

Here's a conversation I had with my daughter the night before a trip to Florida not long after she turned six.

"I'm afraid of the plane ride tomorrow."

"There's nothing to be afraid of," I say, trying to project calm. "What is it about the plane that makes you scared?"

"The safety instructions."

"The *safety instructions*? What about the safety instructions?"

"The part where they talk about crashing."

"Oh, planes are very safe. The plane's not going to crash."

"Then why do they have the instructions telling you what to do if it *does* crash?"

"That's just because there's special rules that say flight attendants have to give us the instructions in order to keep us extra safe. But flying is much safer than driving in a car."

"Then how come we don't have to listen to safety instructions when we get in the car?"

"Susanna," I yell down the stairs, "can you come talk to Maren about something?"

Maren seems to have come by her fear of flying without any overt instruction from me. She was already temperamentally equipped to worry about things, to scan the environment for potential threats; the natural cast of her mind—like mine, like my mother's, like those of typical patients with generalized anxiety disorder—is such that she seeks out and worries (in the original sense of "playing with it," turning it over in her mind to consider it from every angle) every worst-case scenario. Her dawning awareness of the safety instructions, with their references to water landings and crash positions, stimulated her anxiety.

Both my children share my gift for catastrophizing—for always imagining, and worrying about, the worst-case scenario, even if that scenario is not statistically likely. If I detect a small bump on my face while shaving, I immediately worry that it is not (as is most likely) a burgeoning pimple but rather a malignant and possibly fatal tumor. If I feel a twinge in my side, I instantly worry that it is not a strained muscle or a digestive blip but rather the onset of acute appendicitis or liver cancer. If, while driving into the sunlight, I feel a bit of dizziness, I am convinced that it is not a trick of the flickering light but rather an early sign of a stroke or a brain tumor.

Some time later, we were once again preparing to fly off for a family vacation. Maren clutched the armrests on the plane before takeoff, keenly attentive to every clank and whir from the aircraft's innards, asking after each one if the noise meant that the plane was broken.

"No, it doesn't," my wife said.

"But how do you *know*?"

"Maren, would we ever put you somewhere that was dangerous?"

Another noise from the engine: *Clank!* "But what about *that* noise," Maren says, tears in her eyes. "Does *that* noise mean the plane is broken?"

Sigh. The apple has fallen all too close to the tree.*

---

* I should say here that perhaps because both my children have received early psychotherapy for their anxiety—to help them take control of what we call their "worry brains"—they both seem to be less anxious than they were a few years ago. Maren is still emetophobic, but she's developed techniques for managing her fear, and she's less anxious—and in fact quite self-confident—in most areas of her life. Nathaniel remains an imaginative catastrophizer, but his separation anxiety has become a little less severe. Temperamentally, they will probably remain prone to anxiety for their entire lives—but my hope is that they will be able to manage their fear, and even harness it in productive ways, in such a fashion that they will be able to thrive despite it.

And that which is more to be wondered at, [melancholy] skips in some families the father, and goes to the son, "or takes every other, and sometimes every third in a lineal descent, and doth not always produce the same, but some like, and a symbolizing disease."
—ROBERT BURTON, *The Anatomy of Melancholy* (1621)

The patient has been shown to be a perfectionist, ambitious to succeed though not in an egocentric way, and sensitive to small degrees of failure. Whether such psychodynamic explanations give the cause of the depression is not known. Anxiety seems the larger feature.
—FROM CHESTER HANFORD'S 1948 MCLEAN HOSPITAL REPORT

As unnerving as it has been to watch my children's anxiety develop along lines similar to mine, it's been equally so to discover the similarities between my great-grandfather's neuroses and my own. If there is such behavioral similarity between my mother and me, and between me and my kids, then mightn't the anxious genotype run all the way from my great-grandfather through my children—five generations (at least) of the hereditary taint?

Chester Hanford died the summer I turned six. I mainly recall him as a gentle, kindly presence, simultaneously distinguished and decrepit, sitting in his wheelchair in my grandparents' living room in suburban New Jersey, or in his room at the nursing home nearby, wearing a burgundy blazer, a dark tie, and gray flannel slacks. After his death in 1975, he remained a presence in our house, gazing out with wise, sad eyes from various photos and living on in a letter to him from President Kennedy that hung on the living room wall alongside a picture of the two of them campaigning together with Jacqueline Kennedy.

When I was growing up, I knew only about Chester's accomplishments: his long and successful deanship at Harvard; his respected academic publications on municipal government; his association with JFK over the course of several decades, from Kennedy's undergraduate years to his time in the White House. Only when I got older did I begin to glean the dark bits: that he had suffered from anxiety and depression; that he had undergone multiple courses of electroshock therapy; that he had been institutionalized for extended periods many times between the late 1940s and the mid-1960s and had been forced into premature semiretirement (giving up his deanship) and then full retirement (leaving Harvard) as a result; and that he had spent some portion of his final decades moaning in a fetal ball in the bedroom of his home in western Massachusetts.

What was the cause of Chester's afflictions? Was the problem primarily what we would today call an anxiety disorder or clinical depression? How closely did his anxieties resemble mine?

According to his psychiatric records from several hospitals, Chester's general existential fears and anxieties were akin to my own. Does this mean I share—whether owing to the transmission of specific genes or to a neurotic family culture established by our ancestors—a specific psychiatric disease in common with my great-grandfather? Or merely that, in an inversion of Tolstoy, all psychoneurotics are unhappy in the same way?

Reading about my great-grandfather—especially after having learned a little bit about behavioral genetics—has kindled a sense of deep uneasiness, because so much about him reminds me of myself. His nervousness. His fears of public speaking. His tendency to procrastinate.* His obsessive hand washing.† His fixation on his bowels.‡ His relentless self-criticism. His lack of self-esteem despite his respectable job. His ability to project a demeanor of seeming imperturbability and good cheer while roiling with internal torment.§ His emotional and practical dependence on his more outgoing, more together wife.¶

His first institutionalization, at age fifty-six, seems to have been

* From a 1948 "diagnostic impressions" report: "He was overconscientious and overly self-critical, a person of high energy and work output, but a procrastinator."
† From a report by his principal psychiatrist during his sojourn at McLean in May 1953: "It has been noted that he is developing an increasing hand-washing ritual. This has not been taken up in psychotherapy sessions since I feel it is important not to give him the impression that we are unduly critical of his personal activities."
‡ From a handwritten physician's note from the spring of 1948: "The patient has had an irritable large bowel . . . for years." From another note some years later: "Patient chronically worried about his bowels."
§ "Patient is very pleasant," a nurse noted, observing Chester as he ambled around the ward during his second stint at McLean. "Gives the impression that nothing could upset him."
¶ "He has also been quite a burden on his wife." That's from a psychiatrist's notes during Chester's third stay at McLean.

precipitated by the anxiety he felt about a series of lectures he was to give to graduate students. "He had read a good deal this past fall," his principal psychiatrist wrote after Chester was admitted to McLean Hospital in 1948, "but began to fear that he could not organize the material into lectures." He felt that other professors were better than he was and that he was not enough of a scholar to produce satisfactory lectures. In the late spring of 1947, Chester "became very upset over his inability to organize his work and be creative. Anxiety overwhelmed him. He became quite depressed and wept at times."

Chester's psychotherapists tried to get him to quiet his superego. "The patient's sense of self-criticism has been attacked as a factor in his depression, and shows itself to be more rigid and excessive than his talents and virtues warrant." (Over the years, my own therapists have tried to do the same thing—only they generally don't call it a superego anymore; they call it an "inner critic" or a "critical self.") In my great-grandfather's case, this didn't work. Despite abundant evidence of his effectiveness as a scholar and an administrator, he couldn't subdue his feelings of ineffectuality and inferiority. ("He is not glad to think back over his great usefulness to the college as in any way ameliorating his present plight of uselessness," his psychiatrist wrote.) The objective evidence suggests that he was a figure who commanded considerable respect among both students and academic peers. Yet by the fall of 1947, he had come to believe himself a fraud, unequal to the task of composing lectures of sufficient interest and cogency for his students.

How did this happen? This was a man who had manifestly thrived in his professional and family life. He had had tenure at Harvard for decades, had written a well-used political science textbook, and had been the academic dean of the college for many years. He had been married for thirty-two years. He enjoyed an active social life as a modest grandee of the Cambridge scene and often presided over morning chapel services for undergraduates. A father, a grandfather, a Harvard professor and dean, a member in good standing of the community—he had all the outward trappings of success, stability, and happiness. Yet inwardly he was crumbling.

Today, my grandfather says that until his father broke down completely for the first time in the late 1940s, he had never seen any evidence that his father was anxious or depressed. Yet, according to his medical records, Chester had always been "a rather nervous person," with a habit of—as his wife, Ruth, had first noticed when they were courting—constantly blinking his eyes. (Modern researchers sometimes use a measurement they call eyeblink frequency as a gauge of physiological anxiety.) Ruth also recalled the anxiety he had suffered over a series of lectures he had to give as a young assistant professor, reporting to his doctors that he had become "quite apprehensive and sleepless" for days in advance. Combing through old correspondence, I came across a letter Chester had written to Ruth while he was a junior professor at Harvard during the First World War, in which he declared that he almost hoped to be drafted for combat—because dodging bullets on the battlefield would be less nerve-racking than having to give lectures to undergraduates.

All of this suggests that Chester had a nervous disposition—what Jerome Kagan would call a behaviorally inhibited temperament—that was almost certainly, to some degree, hereditary. Both his father and a maternal aunt were prone to various forms of anxiety and depression. But this nervous disposition, this behavioral inhibition, was not, for the first fifty years of his life, unduly debilitating: as apprehensive and susceptible to worry and insomnia as he could sometimes be, he progressed steadily along a dignified professional path, gaining esteem and respect as he went.

So why, after more than five decades of managing his worry and melancholy, did he finally crack in the winter of 1947, surprising even himself?* According to the stress-diathesis model of mental illness, clinical disorders like anxiety and depression often erupt when a genetic susceptibility to psychiatric disease combines with life stressors that overwhelm the individual's ability to cope. Certain people are blessed with genotypes programmed to withstand even severe trauma; other people, like my great-grandfather (and, presumably, me), are less naturally resilient and lose the ability to cope when the stress of life becomes too heavy.

---

* "Mr. Hanford remarked that he had once visited one of his students in the [neuropsychiatric] ward at the Mass General and was quite impressed with the way the doors, etc., were kept locked," his psychiatrist noted. "He said, 'I never expected that I would find myself under the same circumstances; I always felt that I could take care of myself.'"

My great-grandfather was able to carry on his work until the Second World War. But as various colleagues were deployed to the war effort, his teaching load increased. "This put added strain on him," his principal psychiatrist later reported, "and he became quite nervous and anxious about his ability to continue." He became chronically tired. After years of hosting a salon at his home in Cambridge, he found himself too fatigued to entertain or even to socialize at all; dealing with people was too much of a strain. He suggested to James Conant, the president of Harvard, that he might resign. (For the moment, Conant requested that he stay on as dean.)

In the spring of 1945, a close friend died. Already feeling worried and on edge, he became after this (according to his wife) perpetually "jittery"—a condition that was compounded as he surveyed the casualty lists from the war and saw the names of many of his former students. After years of teaching undergraduates, Chester suddenly could no longer organize his lectures. On several occasions, his wife had to write the lectures for the freshman seminar he taught.

At the urging of his family physician, Roger Lee, he took a month off in the summer of 1946. "He felt better after this," his records report, "and was able to continue fairly well through the next school year." But the following spring, he again became upset over his inability to organize his work; he worried his lectures were inferior. He also worried obsessively about a trivial financial matter. Depression descended. He was able to carry out his teaching and administrative duties during the day, but at night he was driven to weeping by tension and sadness. Dr. Lee advised him to cut back on his workload, and so, in the fall of 1947, he retired as dean and returned to his full-time position in the government department, teaching courses in political science.

At which point he deteriorated rapidly. By mid-October, he had become "overtired, nervous, and upset about his lectures and felt that he could not carry on." He would stay up until two in the morning revising his lectures and yet still could not sleep because he was dissatisfied with his drafts, and so he would rise early the next day to begin work again. "He began to think he was not any good any more as a lecturer," his McLean Hospital records say. "He began to think that other professors were better and that he was not up to his own standard." The week before he was finally admitted to the hospital for the first time, he had become "even more apprehensive" about his lectures. At times he "wept bitterly," and he had begun talking of suicide.

In the "diagnostic impressions" section of Chester's intake file, the hospital's psychiatric director reports: "The patient gives the impression of having been an extremely valuable person in his professional life, as well as very kindly and helpful in his personal relations. He was overconscientious and overly self-critical, a person of high energy and work output, but a procrastinator. He was a worrier, and has a history of previous depression. Thus he has anxious and obsessional character traits. The change back from administrative to scholastic duties cut down the amount of satisfactory activity and of personal contacts, and increased the amount of contemplative, self-conscious and self-critical thinking. Dependent and despairing attitudes increased. He might be diagnosed as *psychoneurosis, reactive depression*. The prognosis seems fairly good for an easing of the present symptoms but the future of his adjustment is doubtful."

If Chester Hanford's psychoneurotic ailments and his genotype—and, to a lesser degree, his life circumstances—are similar to my own, does that mean a fate like his awaits me? ("The future of his adjustment is doubtful.") Does my heredity doom me to a similar downward spiral if I am subjected to too much stress? What might already have become of me if I had not had recourse to, at various times, the readily available antipsychotics, tricyclic and SSRI antidepressants, and benzodiazepines that were unavailable to my great-grandfather, who developed his affliction before the flowering of modern psychopharmacology? If my great-grandfather had had access to, say, Xanax or Celexa, would he have been spared the multiple rounds of electroshock and insulin coma therapy, not to mention the months spent moaning in his bed in a fetal ball?

Impossible to say, of course. Whatever quotient of anxious and depressive genes we may share, Chester Hanford and I are different people, living in different times under different cultural conditions, with different experiences and different stresses. Maybe Celexa wouldn't have worked on Chester Hanford. (As we have seen, the clinical evidence on SSRIs is mixed.) And, who knows? Maybe I could have muddled through without Thorazine and imipramine and Valium and desipramine and Prozac and Zoloft and Paxil and Xanax and Celexa and Inderal and Klonopin.

But somehow I don't think so. Which is what makes the similarities between us so disconcerting—and what makes me wonder if the difference between Holding It Together (as I'm doing now and as Chester Hanford anxiously did for so many years before finally breaking down) and Failing to Do So is some ingested chemical compounds that in whatever mysterious and imperfect way interact with my genotype to keep me suspended, tenuously, over the abyss.

My great-grandfather's first stay at McLean Hospital was relatively Edenic compared with his subsequent ones. Over the course of seven weeks, he had daily psychotherapy sessions, swam, played badminton and cards, read books, and listened to the radio. He also took various medications, which provide a representative snapshot of the pharmaco-therapy of the time.*

In Chester's daily psychotherapy sessions, his psychiatrist tried to boost his self-esteem and to reduce his anxiety by getting him to be less rigid in his thinking. Gradually, whether it was the talk therapy, the badminton, the drugs, the respite from work, or the passage of time, his anxiety lifted. (For what it's worth, his principal psychiatrist gave greatest credit to the testosterone injections and the regular physical exercise.) He was released from the hospital on April 12, less depressed and no longer actively suicidal. But in his discharge records, his psychiatrist stated ominously that while the symptoms of anxiety had momentarily abated, his worry-prone temperament would likely trouble him again.

A year later, he was back, readmitted on March 28, 1949, feeling, as the hospital director noted, "tense, anxious, depressed, and self-deprecatory" and suffering from "insomnia and an inability to concen-

---

* He took methyltestosterone, an anabolic steroid given to him by injection, which at midcentury was considered a standard treatment for depression in men; Oreton, a synthetic testosterone that today seems to be prescribed only to boys suffering delayed puberty; chloral hydrate, the old-fashioned nineteenth-century ethanol-chlorine derivative that remained popular as a sedative and sleep aid until the arrival of benzodiazepines; and Donatal, a potent combination of phenobarbital (the barbiturate in Luminal) and hyoscyamine and atropine (which are both plant derivatives from the deadly nightshade family), which was prescribed for his agitated bowels and nerves.

trate on his work." The day before returning to McLean, he had told Roger Lee, his family physician, that he wanted to kill himself but "did not have the guts for suicide." Dr. Lee advised that he admit himself again to the hospital.

Chester acclimated to life in a psychiatric hospital more quickly this time, and within ten days he already seemed to the staff to be more relaxed. But he was still talking about the same issues as on his previous admission—the anxiety, tension, and practical difficulties he was having in composing his lectures and the general inferiority he felt relative to his faculty peers.*

As the doctors successfully "reassured him as to his own considerable value in the college community," he became within a few weeks "a good deal more sociable and relaxed." His psychiatrists believed that the combination of "relief from the responsibilities of work" and the positive boost he got from the injections of testosterone allowed his confidence to build up fairly quickly, and he was able to leave the hospital within a month.†

My great-grandfather was at least somewhat improved for a time. He resumed his full teaching responsibilities at the college and returned to his scholarly work. For several years, it seems, he felt well and worked productively and effectively.

Then he fell to pieces.

At a faculty meeting on January 22, 1953, his colleagues noticed that he seemed "very tense," "depressed," and "disturbed." That spring, his depression became severe and his anxiety rose; he couldn't work. Most alarmingly, as his wife reported, he spent his days walking around the house "shrieking." "Oh! Lord, lift up my soul," he would moan loudly. "Today, this is the end of everything, this is the end of everything. I

---

* As his principal psychiatrist writes, "In talking with him I have laid a good deal of stress on his previous value as an individual in his work for the college. I have led him to take more satisfaction in his executive and teaching accomplishments. Thus it has been possible to somewhat relax his self-critical attitude."

† On April 29, 1949, Chester was returned to the care of his wife and his personal physician, Dr. Lee, his file noting, "There are some evidences of tension and depression still present, but it has been possible for him to be discharged home as improved."

shouldn't have let myself go." Feeling "very strongly that he was losing control of himself," he sought an emergency consultation with Dr. Lee, who recommended that he return to the hospital. On May 5, 1953, he was admitted to McLean for the third time in five years.

During his psychiatric exam upon admission, he was terribly anxious, and his sense of shame about his anxiety and depression was palpable.* By now he had developed symptoms of what would today be called obsessive-compulsive disorder: he washed his hands constantly, and he shaved and changed shirts multiple times a day.

Because testosterone injections seemed to have relieved his depression during his earlier stints at McLean, the doctors started him on a large dose. This time, however, "the sense of well-being engendered by the testosterone" could not overcome his symptoms. His psychiatrists judged that talk therapy and drugs would be insufficient to elevate his mood.

And so, on May 19, with his ready acquiescence, Chester Hanford underwent his first round of electroshock therapy with Kenneth Tillotson.† During each session, Chester would be sedated and strapped tightly to a bed. Orderlies would attach electrodes to various points on his skin and slip in a mouth guard so he wouldn't bite off his own tongue. Then a switch would be flipped, and several hundred volts of current would pass through his body, which would twitch and convulse on the bed.

After each session, he would feel a little confused and have a mild headache—both common symptoms of electroshock. But within a day of his first session, he told his doctors he was feeling considerably better. A few days later, he had his second round of treatment. After that, the nurses on his ward noticed that he seemed "more relaxed, more pleasant, and more outgoing." He stopped ruminating about his problems. He seemed markedly less anxious. A week later, after a third round of electroshock, the transformation was profound: he "looked well," was sleeping and eating, and was "laughing a great deal." The

---

* "His colleagues recently have given him support during his illness these past five years, and actually he is not carrying the workload he should, and he knows it," one psychiatrist noted. "He has also been quite a burden on his wife who has found it necessary to prepare some of his lectures for him."
† During this same period, Dr. Tillotson also administered electroshock treatment to the poet Sylvia Plath, who recorded the experience in her novel, *The Bell Jar.*

nurses reported him to be "much less fearful than when he came in," no longer "running around asking the nurses whether he can do this or that." He began spending a great deal of time in the gym with other patients, playing badminton and bowling—activities that he had earlier implied to his psychiatrist were beneath the dignity of a sixty-two-year-old Harvard professor. The electroshock therapy, it seemed, had restored (or injected) a sense of fun.

After a fourth round of treatment, on June 2, he reported himself "relaxed" and eager to return to work. His wife, who visited him frequently, was amazed: her husband was, she told his psychiatrists, "more the way he was many years ago." Chester himself told the staff that he felt "more like himself." To me this sounds uncannily like what Peter Kramer reported in *Listening to Prozac:* that the patients he put on Prozac in the 1990s had told him the medication made them feel "more like themselves."

We still have remarkably little understanding of how electroshock therapy works. Metaphorically, electroshock seems to function the way hitting Ctrl+Alt+Delete on your computer does; it reboots the system, restoring the settings on the neural operating system. The outcome statistics are compelling. Though the practice went out of vogue in the 1970s and 1980s—in part because Jack Nicholson's portrayal of an electroshock patient in the movie version of Ken Kesey's novel *One Flew over the Cuckoo's Nest* convinced people the technique was barbaric—modern studies show that the recovery rates from severe depression may be higher with electroshock than with any kind of drug or talk therapy. The experience of my great-grandfather, at least in the short term, would seem to bear that out.

Could there be any more compelling evidence that anxiety and depression are irreducibly "embodied" or "enmattered," in the fashion observed since Aristotle? By his third trip to the psychiatric hospital, Chester Hanford's psychiatrists seem largely to have given up on talking or psychoanalyzing him out of his depression and anxiety; his personality and character seemed so fixed as to resist "adjustment." But zapping his brain with a few hundred volts of electricity, on the other hand—rewiring the connections—seemed to do the trick just fine. After four electroshock treatments, the hospital director wrote that Chester "showed tremendous improvement."

On June 9, 1953, about a month after entering the hospital, a cheerful Chester was discharged into the care of his wife. They promptly left for vacation in Maine, where for the first time in years he eagerly anticipated the arrival of the fall semester and a new crop of students to teach.

I wish Chester Hanford's story ended on this hopeful note. But in time his anxiety returned, and he was compelled to retire. Throughout the 1950s and 1960s, he went regularly to McLean—and, later, to the New England Deaconess Hospital in downtown Boston—for more electroshock therapy. At one point, a too-potent drug cocktail nearly killed him. For a period in the late 1950s, his anxieties and compulsions got so bad that his doctors considered performing a prefrontal leucotomy—a partial lobotomy. (Ultimately, he was spared.)

For the balance of his lifetime, he kind of limped along. He would be okay for stretches—and then for stretches he wouldn't be. Even when he wasn't okay, he could pull himself together for appearance's sake. My grandmother recalled a summer day in the mid-1960s when a party was planned at the Hanford home in western Massachusetts. Family and friends from all over New England were to be gathering that evening. Throughout the day of the party, a haunted moaning emanated from Chester's bedroom; my grandmother cringed to think what his appearance at the party would be like—if he could manage an appearance at all. Yet as twilight fell and the party began, he emerged downstairs as a gracious, even sociable host. And then the next day he retreated again to his room, to his fetal curl and his moaning.

My parents recall Chester seeming less anxious and agitated during his years in the nursing home—a fact that my father suspects may be explained by the generous doses of Valium administered there. Benzodiazepines may, finally, have successfully tranquilized his anxiety into submission. Or perhaps being liberated from the stresses of work relaxed him.

In immersing myself so deeply in the psychopathologies of my great-grandfather, and in identifying rather strongly with them, I—as hypochondriacal and prone to worry as I am—have naturally grown concerned that the hereditary taint will soon reduce me, too, to permanent weeping and shaking in my room.

When I tell Dr. W. about this, he says, "As you know, I don't place a lot of stock in genetic determinism."

I cite some of the recent studies suggesting a powerful heritable component to anxiety disorders and depression.

"Okay, but you're three generations removed from your great-grandfather," he says. "You share only a fraction of his genes."

True enough. And in any case, genes and environment interact in complex ways. "[A genetically] inherited reaction to potential danger may be a boon or a bane," says Daniel Weinberger, the lead researcher on one of the first *SERT* gene studies. "It can place us at risk for an anxiety disorder, or in another situation it may provide an adaptive positive attribute such as increased vigilance. We have to remember that anxiety is a complicated multidimensional characteristic of human experience and cannot be predicted by any form of a single gene."

Dr. W. and I talk about the way academic conferences on anxiety have been placing increasing emphasis on how the psychological traits of resilience and acceptance can be crucial bulwarks against both anxiety and depression; much of the cutting-edge research and treatment focuses in particular on the importance of cultivating resilience.

"Yes!" Dr. W. says. "We need to work on making you more resilient."

When I tell him what I've learned about the serotonin transporter gene, and about how people with certain genotypes are far more likely to live anxious, unhappy, and unresilient lives, Dr. W. reminds me how much he dislikes the modern emphasis on the genetics and neurobiology of mental illness because it hardens the notion that the mind is a fixed and immutable structure, when in fact it can change throughout a lifetime.

"I know," I say. I've read about the recent findings on neuroplasticity—about the way the human brain can keep forming new neuronal connections into old age. I tell him that I understand the importance of resilience in combating anxiety. But how, I ask, do I gain that quality?

"You're already more resilient than you know," he said.

CHAPTER 10

Ages of Anxiety

The philosophic study of the several branches of sociology, politics, charities, history, education, shall never be even in the direction of scientific precision or completeness until it shall have absorbed some, at least, of the suggestions of this problem of American nervousness.
—GEORGE MILLER BEARD, *American Nervousness* (1881)

In April 1869, a young doctor in New York named George Miller Beard, writing in the *Boston Medical and Surgical Journal,* coined a term for what he believed to be a new and distinctively American affliction, one he had seen in thirty of his patients: "neurasthenia" (from *neuro* for "nerve" and *asthenia* for "weakness"). Referring to it sometimes as "nervous exhaustion," Beard argued that neurasthenia afflicted primarily ambitious, upwardly mobile members of the urban middle and upper classes—especially "the brain-workers in almost every household of the Northern and Eastern States"—whose nervous systems were overtaxed by a rapidly modernizing American civilization. Beard believed that he himself had suffered from neurasthenia but had overcome it in his early twenties.

Born in a small Connecticut village in 1839, Beard was the son of a Congregational minister and the grandson of a physician. After attending prep school at Phillips Academy in Andover, Massachusetts, he went on to Yale, where he began to suffer from the array of nervous symptoms that would afflict him for the next six years and that he would later observe in his patients: ringing in the ears, pains in the side, dyspepsia, nervousness, morbid fears, and "lack of vitality." By his own account, Beard's anxious suffering was prompted largely by his uncertainty about what career to pursue—though there is also evidence that he anguished over his lack of religious commitment. (Two of Beard's older brothers had followed his father into the ministry; in his diary, he chastises himself for his indifference to spiritual concerns.) Once he decided to become a physician, however, his doubts left him and his anxiety dissipated. He entered medical school at Yale in 1862, determined to help others plagued by the anxious suffering that had once afflicted him.

Influenced by Darwin's recent work on natural selection, Beard came to believe that cultural and technological evolution had outstripped biological evolution, putting enormous stress on the human animal—particularly those in the business and professional classes, who were most driven by status competition and the burgeoning pressures of capitalism. Even as technological development and economic growth were improving material well-being, the pressure of market competition—along with the uncertainty that took hold as the familiar verities fell away under the assault of modernity and industrialization—produced great emotional stress, draining American workers' stock of "nerve force" and leading to acute anxiety and nervous prostration. "In the older countries, men plod along in the footsteps of their fathers, generation after generation, with little possibility and therefore little thought of entering a higher social grade," Beard's colleague A. D. Rockwell wrote in the *New York Medical Journal* in 1893. "Here, on the contrary, no one is content to rest with the possibility ever before him of stepping higher, and the race of life is all haste and unrest. It is thus readily seen that the primary cause of neurasthenia in this country is civilization itself, with all that term implies, with its railway, telegraph, telephone, and periodical press intensifying in ten thousand ways cerebral activity and worry."*

Beard believed that constant change, combined with the relentless striving for achievement, money, and status that characterized American life, produced rampant nervous weakness.† "American nervous-

---

* Anxiety seems to be woven into the American spirit—as Alexis de Tocqueville observed as early as the 1830s. "Life would have no relish for the [people who live in democracies] if they were delivered from the anxieties which harass them, and they show more attachment to their cares than aristocratic nations to their pleasures," he wrote in *Democracy in America*.

† It also produced drug dependence. Just as the postwar affluence of the 1950s would lead to the frantic gobbling of Miltown, Librium, and Valium, the competitive pressures of the late nineteenth century

ness is the product of American civilization," he wrote. The United States had invented nervousness as a cultural condition: "The Greeks were certainly civilized, but they were not nervous, and in the Greek language there is no word for that term."* Ancient cultures could not have experienced nervousness, he argued, because they didn't have steam power, the periodical press, the telegraph, the sciences, and the mental activity of women: "When civilization, plus these five factors, invades any nation, it must carry nervousness and nervous disease along with it." Beard also argued that neurasthenia affected only the more "advanced" races—especially the Anglo-Saxon—and religious persuasions; he observed that "no Catholic country is very nervous." (On its face, this is a dubious proposition, and Beard had no real evidence to buttress it. On the other hand, rates of anxiety in modern Mexico, a primarily Catholic country, are much lower than in the United States. A 2002 World Health Organization study found that Americans are four times more likely to suffer from generalized anxiety disorder than Mexicans—and some research has found that Mexicans recover from anxiety attacks twice as quickly as Americans. Interestingly, when Mexicans immigrate to the United States, their rates of anxiety and depression soar.)

Neurasthenia was a self-flattering diagnosis, since it was thought to affect primarily the most competitive capitalists and those with the most refined sensibilities. It was a disease of the elites; in Beard's estimation, 10 percent of his own patient load was made up of other physicians, and by 1900 "nervousness" had definitively become a mark of distinction—a signifier of both high class and cultural refinement.†

---

produced an alarming rise in the number of "opiate eaters." Writing in *Confessions of an American Opium Eater: From Bondage to Freedom* in 1895, Henry G. Cole argued that "our mechanical inventions, the spread of our commerce . . . our ambition for political honors; and grasping for petty offices for gain; our mad race for speedy wealth, which entails feverish excitements . . . [and] a growth so rapid, and in some ways so abnormal, [have combined to produce] the mental strain [that] has been too much for the physical system to bear; till finally, the overworked body and the overtaxed body must . . . find rest in the repeated use of opium or morphine."

* Elsewhere, Beard wrote that anxiety was "modern, and originally American; and no age, no country, and no form of civilization, not Greece, not Rome, nor Spain, nor the Netherlands, in their days of glory, possessed such maladies."

† Some years earlier, the elites of Georgian Britain—the period extending from the early 1700s until Queen Victoria ascended to the throne in 1837—had adopted a similar "nervous culture," which claimed for itself the same kind of self-flattering class connotations that would be characteristic of

Beard's books contain case studies and elaborate symptomatologies that sound strikingly contemporary to the modern ear. In *A Practical Treatise on Nervous Exhaustion,* published in 1880, he expatiates for hundreds of pages on the symptoms of nervous exhaustion. "I begin with the head and brain," he writes, "and go downwards." The list includes tenderness of the scalp; dilated pupils; headache; "*Muscoe Volitantes,* or floating specks before the eyes"; dizziness; ringing in the ears; softness of voice (a voice "wanting in clearness and courage of tone"); irritability; numbness and pain in the back of the head; indigestion;

American neurasthenia: the idea that the nervous systems of those of better breeding and more creative sensibilities were unusually susceptible to hypochondriasis and nervous collapse. This culture, like that of the Renaissance, tended to glamorize individuals with sensitive nervous systems while providing both medical and psychological explanations for their delicate constitutions. As anatomists continued to unlock the secrets of the human nervous system, scientists of this era variously described the nerve network as a system of fibers, strings, pipes, and cords, venturing explanations that attributed the system's functioning to hydraulics, electricity, mechanics, and so forth. The crucial concept in all these explanations was the nervous breakdown—the idea being that when the nervous system was overstrained, it would break down, producing both mental and physical symptoms and often general prostration. Beginning in the 1730s, the malfunctions of the nervous system that led to breakdown were often called "nervous distempers," which encompassed everything from hysteria and hypochondria to "the vapors"—mental and physical complaints that in more recent times would be labeled psychoneurotic or psychosomatic.

In striking contrast to the stiff-upper-lip ideals of the Victorian era that would follow, the British elites of the eighteenth century wallowed in, and even cultivated, their nervous disabilities. "Nervous self-fashioning"—painting oneself as the victim of one's nerves—was common. From 1777 to 1783, James Boswell, Samuel Johnson's biographer, wrote a monthly essay for *The London Magazine* under the pen name the Hypochondriack, and in his own diary he minutely tracked every subtle shift in his endless litany of emotional and physical symptoms. Boswell was obsessed with his digestive system. "From this day follow Mr. [John] Locke's prescription of going to stool every day regularly after breakfast," he wrote in his journal early in October 1764. "It will do your health good, and it is highly necessary to take care of your health." (Yes, that John Locke—the one who wrote *Two Treatises of Government* and is the father of constitutional liberalism. Most people turn to Locke for his thoughts on political philosophy; Boswell did so for his advice on digestive hygiene. If you're curious what Locke's prescription was, well, so was I—so I tracked it down, and here's what I found in section 24 of *Some Thoughts Concerning Education:* "If a man, after his first eating in the morning, would presently solicit nature, and try whether he could strain himself so as to obtain a stool, he might in time, by constant application, bring it to be habitual.")

Nervous disorders of various kinds were believed to be so widespread during this time that, despite the various physiological explanations given for them, they were viewed as a cultural condition as much as a medical one. One prominent British physician claimed that a third of the population was "destroyed or made miserable by the Diseases." (The popularity of nervous illness during this time was not confined to England. In 1758, Joseph Raulin, the personal physician to Louis XV of France, wrote that "the vapors" had become "a veritable social plague, an endemic disease in the cities [of the Continent].")

nausea; vomiting; diarrhea; flatulence ("with annoying rumbling in the bowels these patients complain of very frequently"); frequent blushing ("I have seen very strong, vigorous men, who have large muscular power and great capacity for physical labor, who, while in a neurasthenic state, would blush like young girls"); insomnia; tenderness of the teeth and gums; alcoholism and drug addiction; abnormal dryness of the skin; sweating of the hands and feet ("A young man under my care is so distressed [by his sweating] that he threatens suicide unless he is permanently cured"); excess salivation (or, alternatively, dry mouth); back pain; "heaviness of the loins and limbs"; heart palpitations; muscle spasms; dysphagia (difficulty swallowing); cramps; tendency to get hay fever; sensitivity to changes in the weather; "profound exhaustion"; ticklishness; itching; hot flashes; cold chills; cold hands and feet; temporary paralysis; and gaping and yawning. On the one hand, this panoply of symptoms is so broad as to be meaningless; these are the symptoms, more or less, of being alive. On the other hand, this litany resonates with the twenty-first-century neurotic's—it sounds, in fact, not unlike my weekly catalog of hypochondriacal complaint.

Neurasthenia also encompassed what we would today call phobia. Beard's case studies range from the lightning phobic ("One of my patients tells me she is always watching the clouds in summer, fearing that a storm may come. She knows this is absurd and ridiculous, but she declares she cannot help it. In this case the symptom was inherited from her grandmother; and even in her cradle, as she is informed by her mother, she suffered in the same way") to the agoraphobic ("One of my cases, a gentleman of middle life, could walk up Broadway without difficulty, because shops and stores, he said, offered him an opportunity of retreat, in case of peril. He could not, however, walk up Fifth Avenue, where there are no stores, nor in side streets, unless they were very short. He could not pay a visit to the country in any direction, but was hopelessly shut up in the city during the hot weather. One time, in riding in the stage up Broadway, on turning onto Madison Square, he shrieked with terror, to the astonishment of the passengers. The man who possessed this interesting symptom was tall, vigorous, full-faced, and mentally capable of endurance"); from the claustrophobic (who fear enclosed spaces) to the monophobic (who fear being alone; "One man was so afraid to leave the house alone he paid a man $20,000 to be his constant companion"); from the mysophobic (who fears contamination and must wash her hands two hundred times a day) to the panophobic (who fears everything). One of Beard's patients had a morbid fear of drunken men.

By the turn of the century, the language and imagery of neurasthenia had permeated deep into American culture. If you yourself didn't suffer from it, you surely knew people who did. Political rhetoric and religious sermons addressed it; consumer advertisements offered remedies for it. Magazines and newspapers published articles about it. Theodore Dreiser and Henry James populated their novels with neurasthenic characters. The language of neurasthenic distress ("depression," "panic") crept into economic discourse. Nervousness, it seemed, had become the default psychological state and cultural condition of modern times. Disrupted by the transformations of the Industrial Revolution and riven by Gilded Age wealth inequality, the United States was rife with levels of anxiety unmatched in human history.

Or so Beard claimed. But was it really?

According to the latest figures from the National Institute of Mental Health, some forty million Americans, or about 18 percent of the population, currently suffer from a clinical anxiety disorder. Recent editions of *Stress in America,* a report produced each year by the American Psychological Association, have found a badly "overstressed nation" in which a majority of Americans describe themselves as "moderately" or "highly" stressed, with significant percentages of them reporting stress-related physical symptoms such as fatigue, headache, stomach troubles, muscle tension, and teeth grinding. Between 2002 and 2006, the number of Americans seeking medical treatment for anxiety increased from 13.4 million to 16.2 million. More Americans seek medical treatment for anxiety than for back pain or migraine headaches.

Surveys by the Anxiety and Depression Association of America find that nearly half of all Americans report "persistent or excessive anxiety" in their daily work lives. (Other surveys find that three out of four Americans believe there is more workplace stress today than in the past.) A study published in the *American Psychologist* found that 40 percent more people said they'd felt an impending nervous breakdown in 1996 than had said so in 1957. Twice as many people reported experiencing symptoms of panic attacks in 1995 as in 1980.* According to a national survey of incoming freshmen, the anxiety levels of college students are higher today than at any time in the twenty-five-year history of the survey. When Jean Twenge, a professor of psychology at San Diego State University, looked at survey data from fifty thousand children and college students between the 1950s and the 1990s, she found that the average college student in the 1990s was more anxious than 85 percent of students in the 1950s and that "'normal' schoolchildren in the 1980s reported higher levels of anxiety than child psychiatric patients in the 1950s." (Robert Leahy, a psychologist at Weill Cornell Medical College, characterized this finding colorfully in *Psychology Today:* "The average high school kid today has the same level of anxiety as the average psychiatric patient in the 1950s.") The baby boomers were more anxious than their parents; Generation X was more anxious than the boomers; the millennials are turning out to be more anxious than Generation X.

Rates of anxiety seem to be increasing all around the world. A World Health Organization survey of eighteen countries concluded that anxiety disorders are now the most common mental illness on earth, once again overtaking depression. Statistics from the National Health Service reveal that British hospitals treated four times as many people for anxiety disorders in 2011 as they did in 2007 while issuing record numbers of tranquilizer prescriptions. A report published by Britain's Mental Health Foundation in 2009 concluded that a "culture of fear"—marked by a shaky economy and hyperbolic threat-mongering by politicians and the media—had produced "record levels of anxiety" in Great Britain.

Given the "record levels of anxiety" we seem to be seeing around the world, surely we must today be living in the most anxious age ever—more anxious even than George Beard's era of neurasthenia.

How can this be? Economic disruption and recent global recession notwithstanding, we live in an age of unprecedented material affluence.

---

* This is not surprising, considering that panic attacks did not officially exist until the publication of the *DSM-III* in 1980.

Standards of living in the industrialized West are, on average, higher than ever; life expectancies in the developed world are, for the most part, long and growing. We are much less likely to die an early death than our ancestors were, much less likely to be subjected to the horrors of smallpox, scurvy, pellagra, polio, tuberculosis, rickets, and packs of roving wolves, not to mention the challenges of life without antibiotics, electricity, or indoor plumbing. Life is, in many ways, easier than it used to be. Therefore shouldn't we be *less* anxious than we once were?

Perhaps in some sense the price—and surely, in part, the source—of progress and improvements in material prosperity has been an increase in the average allotment of anxiety. Urbanization, industrialization, the growth of the market economy, increases in geographic and class mobility, the expansion of democratic values and freedoms—all of these trends, on their own and in concert, have contributed to vastly improved material quality of life for millions of people over the last several hundred years. But each of these may also have contributed to rising anxiety.

Until the Renaissance, there was scarcely any concept of social, political, technological, or any other kind of progress. This lent a kind of resignation to medieval emotional life that may have been adaptive: the sense that things would always be as they were was depressing but also comforting—there was no having to adapt to technological or social change; there were no hopes for a better life in danger of being dashed. While life was dominated by the fear—and expectation—of eternal damnation (one Franciscan preacher in Germany put the odds in favor of damnation for any given soul at a hundred thousand to one), medieval minds were not consumed, as ours are, with the hope of advancement and the fear of decline.

Today, especially in Western capitalist democracies, we also probably have more choice than ever in history: we are free to choose where to live, whom to court or marry, what line of work to pursue, what personal style to adapt. "The major problem for Americans is that of choice," the late sociologist Philip Slater wrote in 1970. "Americans are forced into making more choices per day, with fewer 'givens,' more ambiguous criteria, less environmental stability, and less social structural support, than any people in history." Freedom of choice generates great anxiety. Barry Schwartz, a psychologist at Swarthmore College, calls this "the paradox of choice"—the idea that as the freedom to choose increases, so does anxiety.

Maybe anxiety is, in some sense, a luxury—an emotion we can afford to indulge only when we're not preoccupied by "real" fear. (Recall that William James made a version of this argument in the 1880s.) Perhaps precisely because medieval Europeans had so many genuine threats to be *afraid* of (the Black Death, Muslim invaders, famine, dynastic turmoil, constant military conflict, and death, always death, imminently present—the average life expectancy during the Middle Ages was thirty-five years, and one out of every three babies died before reaching the age of five), they were left with little space to be *anxious,* at least in the sense that Freud, for example, meant neurotic anxiety— anxiety generated from within ourselves about things we don't really have rational cause to be afraid of. Perhaps the Middle Ages were relatively free of neurotic anxiety because such anxiety was a luxury no one could afford in their brief, difficult lives. In support of this proposition are the surveys showing that people in developing nations have lower rates of clinical anxiety than Americans despite life circumstances that are materially more difficult.

Moreover, political and cultural life in the Middle Ages was largely organized to minimize, even eliminate, the sorts of social uncertainties we contend with today. "From the moment of birth," the psychoanalyst and political philosopher Erich Fromm observed, "[the medieval person] was rooted in a structuralized whole, and thus life had a meaning which left no place, and no need, for doubt. A person was identical with his role in society; he was a peasant, an artisan, a knight, and not *an individual* who *happened* to have this or that occupation." One argument for why twenty-first-century life produces so much anxiety is that social and political roles are no longer understood to have been ordained by God or by nature—we have to *choose* our roles. Such choices, research shows, are stressful. As sodden with fear and darkness and death as the Middle Ages were, Fromm and others argue, they were likely freer of anxiety than our own time is.

The "dizziness of freedom," as Kierkegaard described it, produced by the ability to make choices, can have political implications: it can generate anxiety so intense that it creates a yearning to return to the comforting certainties of the primary ties—a yearning for what Fromm called "the escape from freedom." Fromm argued that this anxiety led many working-class Germans to willingly submit to Hitler in the 1930s. Paul Tillich, a theologian who grew up in Weimar Germany, similarly explained the rise of Nazism as a response to anxiety. "First of all a feeling of *fear* or, more exactly, of indefinite anxiety was prevailing," he writes of 1930s Germany. "Not only the economic and political, but also the cultural and religious, security seemed to be lost. There was nothing on which one could build; everything was without foundation. A catastrophic breakdown was expected every moment. Consequently, a longing for security was growing in everybody. A freedom that leads to fear and anxiety has lost its value; better authority with security than freedom with fear." Herbert L. Matthews, a *New York Times* correspondent who covered Europe between the wars, also observed that Nazism provided relief from anxiety: "Fascism was like a jail where the individual had a certain amount of security, shelter, and daily food." Arthur Schlesinger, Jr., writing a few years after the end of the Second World War, observed the same thing about Soviet Communism: "It has filled the 'vacuum of faith' caused by the waning of established religion; it provides the sense of purpose which heals internal agonies of anxiety and doubt." In periods of social disruption, when old verities no longer obtain, there's a danger that, as Rollo May put it, "people grasp at political authoritarianism in their desperate need for relief from anxiety."

One implication of the neurobiologist Robert Sapolsky's work is that human social and political systems that are highly fluid and dynamic generate more anxiety than systems that are static. Sapolsky points out that "for 99 percent of human history" society was "most probably strikingly unhierarchical" and therefore probably less psychologically stressful than in the modern era. For hundreds of thousands of years, the standard form of human social organization was the hunter-gatherer tribe—and such tribes were, judging from what we know of the bands of hunter-gatherers that still exist today, "remarkably egalitarian." Sapolsky goes so far as to say that the invention of agriculture, a relatively recent development in the scope of human history, "was one of the great stupid moves of all times" because it allowed for the stockpiling of food and, for the first time in history, "the stratification of society and the invention of classes." Stratification created relative poverty, making possible the invidious comparison and producing the occasion for status anxiety.

Jerome Kagan, among others, has argued that historical changes in the nature of human society have led to mismatches between our evolutionary hardwiring and what modern culture values. Qualities such as excessive timidity, caution, and concern with the opinions of others that would have been socially adaptive in early human communities are much "less adaptive in an increasingly competitive, mobile, industrialized, urban society than these traits had been several centuries earlier in a rural, agricultural economy of villages and towns," Kagan writes. In preliterate cultures, all members of a community generally shared the same values and sources of meaning. But starting sometime around the fifth century B.C., humans have increasingly lived in communities of strangers with diverse values—a trend that hyperaccelerated during the Renaissance and again during the Industrial Revolution. As a result, and especially since the Middle Ages, "a different kind of uncomfortable feeling was evoked by reflection on the adequacy of self's skills or status and the validity of one's moral premises," Kagan argues. "These feelings, which were labeled anxiety, ascended to the position of the alpha emotion in the hierarchy of human affects." Perhaps the human organism is not equipped to live life as society has lately designed it—a harsh zero-sum competition where the only gains to be had are at the expense of someone else, where "neurotic competition" has displaced solidarity and cooperation. "Competitive individualism militates against the experience of community, and the lack of community is a centrally important factor in contemporaneous anxiety," Rollo May argued in 1950.

By 1948, when W. H. Auden won the Pulitzer Prize for *The Age of Anxiety*, his six-part poem depicting man adrift ("as unattached as tumbleweeds") in an uncertain industrial world, anxiety seemed to have leached out of the realm of psychiatry to become a general cultural condition. During the 1950s, with America newly ascendant after the Second World War, the best-seller list was already stippled with books about how to achieve nervous relief. On the heels of Dale Carnegie's best-selling 1948 *How to Stop Worrying and Start Living* came a passel of books bearing titles like *Relax and Live* and *How to Con-*

trol Worry and Cure Your Nerves Yourself and *The Conquest of Fatigue and Fear,* suggesting that America was in the grip of what one social historian called "a national nervous breakdown." On March 31, 1961, a *Time* magazine cover story (featuring an image of Edvard Munch's *The Scream*) declared that the present era "is almost universally regarded as the Age of Anxiety." The British and American best-seller lists of the 1930s, a much more unstable time, were similarly populated with self-help books about "tension" and "nerves." *Conquest of Nerves: The Inspiring Record of a Personal Triumph over Neurasthenia* went through multiple printings in 1933 and 1934. *You Must Relax: A Practical Method of Reducing the Strains of Modern Living,* a book by an American physician named Edmund Jacobson, reached the top of the *New York Times* best-seller list in 1934.

In linking anxiety to uncertainty, Auden was both falling into a long historical tradition and anticipating modern neuroscience. One of the earliest uses of the word "anxiety" in English associated it with chronic uncertainty: the seventeenth-century British physician and poet Richard Flecknoe wrote that the anxious person "troubles herself with every thing" or is "an irresolute person" who "hovers in his every choice like an empty Ballance with no weight of Judgment to incline him to either scale. . . . When he begins to deliberate he never makes an end." (The first among the *Oxford English Dictionary*'s definitions of "anxiety" is "uneasiness about some *uncertain* event" [emphasis added].) Recent neurobiological investigations have revealed that uncertainty activates the anxiety circuits of the brain; the amygdalae of clinically anxious people are unusually sensitive to uncertainty. "Intolerance of uncertainty appears to be the central process involved in high levels of worry," Michel J. Dugas, a psychologist at Penn State, has written. Patients with generalized anxiety disorder "are highly intolerant of uncertainty," he says. "I use the metaphor of 'allergy' to uncertainty . . . to help them conceptualize their relationship with uncertainty." Between 2007 and 2010, there was a 31 percent increase in the number of news articles employing the word "uncertainty." No wonder we're so anxious.

Except maybe we're relatively less anxious than we think. Because if you read far enough back into the cultural history of nervousness and melancholy, each successive generation's claim to be the most anxious starts to sound much like the claims of the generations that preceded and followed it. When the British physician Edwin Lee, writing in *A Treatise on Some Nervous Disorders* in 1838, argued that "nervous complaints prevail at the present day to an extent unknown at any former period, or in any other nation," he sounds not only like George Miller Beard after him but also like the British naval surgeon Thomas Trotter before him. "At the beginning of the nineteenth century, we do not hesitate to affirm that nervous disorders . . . may now be justly reckoned two thirds of the whole with which civilized society is afflicted," Trotter wrote in *A View of the Nervous Temperament*, published in 1807.* Eighty years before Trotter, George Cheyne, the most prominent "nerve doctor" of his day, argued that the "atrocious and frightful symptoms" of the nervous affliction he had dubbed "the English Malady" were "scarce known to our ancestors, and never r[ose] to such fatal heights nor afflict[ed] such numbers and any other known nation."[†]

Some intellectual historians have traced the birth of modern anxiety to the work of the seventeenth-century Oxford scholar Robert Burton.[‡] Burton was not a doctor, and he scarcely left his study, so busy was he for dozens of years reading astonishingly widely and scribbling away at his mammoth tome, *The Anatomy of Melancholy*, but his influence on Western literature and psychology has been lasting. Sir William Osler, the inventor of the medical residency system and one of the most influential doctors of the late nineteenth century, called *The Anatomy of Melancholy* "the greatest medical treatise ever written by a layman." John Keats, Charles Lamb, and Samuel Taylor Coleridge all treasured it and drew on it for their own work. Samuel Johnson, for his

---

* Trotter warned that an "epidemic" of nervousness threatened not only the "national character" of Britain but also its national security, since in their weakened states, British citizens were ripe for being invaded and conquered. (Trotter's fears about the country's epidemic of nervous weakness were intensified by Napoleon, who was marauding around the Continent.)

† Cheyne claimed that a third of the British population was afflicted with the nervous condition known variously as "spleen," "the vapours," or "hypochondria"—what would today be clustered in the *DSM* under the umbrellas of the anxiety or depressive disorders. (Note that Cheyne is claiming a level of anxious affliction for the England of the 1730s that is comparable to what the National Institute of Mental Health claims for America today.)

‡ Citing the reports of other writers, Burton claimed that the frequency of melancholia—which subsumed the modern diagnoses of both anxiety and depression—was "so common in this crazed age of ours" that "scarce one in a thousand is free from it."

part, told James Boswell that it was "the only book that ever took him out of bed two hours sooner than he wished to rise." Completed in 1621, when Burton was forty-four and then revised and expanded multiple times over the following seventeen years, *The Anatomy of Melancholy* is an epic work of synthesis that ranges across all of history, literature, philosophy, science, and theology up to that time. Originally published in three volumes, the work swelled as Burton tinkered and added (and added some more) in the years before his death in 1640; my own copy, a paperback facsimile of the sixth edition, is 1,382 pages of very small type.

Much of what Burton writes is absurd, nonsensical, self-contradictory, boring, in Latin, or all of the above. But it is also full of good humor and dark pessimism and consoling wisdom about the human condition (it's easy to see why Samuel Johnson was so taken with it), and in his exuberant travels through what seems like everything ever written, he managed to gather all of the extant human knowledge about melancholy in a single work and to establish for later writers and thinkers the terrain on which they would operate. The work is also clearly informed by his own depression and, like Augustine's *Confessions* and Freud's *Interpretation of Dreams*, draws insight not only from the expert testimony of others but from his own deep introspection. "Other men get their knowledge from books," he writes. "I get mine from melancholizing." Of course, a lot of Burton's knowledge does come from books—he cites thousands of them—and part of what makes the book so interesting is Burton's ability to objectify his subjective experience.*

Though parts of Burton's book were already outdated and ridiculous when he published it, some of his insights and observations are quite modern. His clinically precise description of a panic attack would pass muster with the *DSM-V:* "Many lamentable effects this fear causeth in men, as to be red, pale, tremble, sweat; it makes sudden cold and heat to come over all the body, palpitation of the heart, syncope, etc."

---

* I feel a kinship with Burton because he freely conceded that he wrote about melancholy to combat his own: "I write of melancholy, by being busy to avoid melancholy." (I write of anxiety to avoid being anxious.)

And here's a passable description of what would today be diagnosed as generalized anxiety disorder: "Many men are so amazed and astonished with fear, they know not where they are, what they say, what they do, and that which is worst, it tortures them many days before with continual affrights and suspicion. It hinders most honourable attempts, and makes their hearts ache, sad and heavy. They that live in fear are never free, resolute, secure, never merry, but in continual pain: that, as Vives truly said, *Nulla est miseria major quam metus,* no greater misery, no rack, nor torture like unto it; ever suspicious, anxious, solicitous, they are childishly drooping without reason, without judgment, 'especially if some terrible object be offered,' as Plutarch hath it."*

Burton piles up hundreds upon hundreds of theories about anxiety and depression, many of which contradict each other, but in the end the treatments he emphasizes might be boiled down to getting regular exercise, playing chess, taking baths, reading books, listening to music, using laxatives, eating right, practicing sexual moderation, and, above all, keeping busy. "There is no greater cause of melancholy than idleness, 'no better cure than business,'" he wrote, citing the Arabian physician Rhasis. Channeling the wisdom of the Epicureans and the Stoics (and, from the East, the Buddhists), he advises modesty of ambition and an acceptance of what one has as a path to happiness: "If men would attempt no more than what they can bear, they should lead contented lives and, learning to know themselves, would limit their ambition; they would perceive then that nature hath enough without seeking such superfluities and unprofitable things, which bring nothing

---

* Plutarch, the biographer and historian, described vividly and accurately how what we would today call clinical depression can bring with it an escalation of anxiety. Anyone who has suffered the torturous insomnia of agitated depression—where anxiety begets sleeplessness and sleeplessness begets more anxiety—will recognize the clinical aptness of Plutarch's description. To the depressed person, he writes, "every little evil is magnified by the scaring spectres of his anxiety. . . . Asleep or awake he is haunted alike by the spectres of his anxiety. Awake, he makes no use of his reason; and asleep, he enjoys no respite from his alarms. His reason always slumbers; his fears are always awake. Nowhere can he find an escape from his imaginary terrors."

Plutarch was not a physician—but Galen, born not long after Plutarch died, was. Describing an epidemic of anxiety that sounds remarkably modern, Galen wrote of having seen "tremors in the hearts of healthy young people and adolescents weak and thin from anxiety and depression" and patients with "scarce, turbulent, and interrupted sleep, palpitations, vertigo" and "sadness, anxiety, diffidence, and the belief of being persecuted."

with them but grief and molestation. As a fat body is more subject to diseases, so are rich men to absurdities and fooleries, to many casualties and cross inconveniences."

Trying to directly compare levels of anxiety between eras is a fool's errand. Modern poll data and statistics about rising and falling levels of tranquilizer consumption aside, there is no magical anxiety meter that can transcend the cultural particularities of place and time to objectively measure levels of anxiety—which, like any emotion, is in some sense an inherently subjective and culturally bound thing. But if anxiety is a descendant of fear, and if fear is an evolutionary impulse designed to help prolong the survival of the species, then anxiety is surely as old as the human race. Humans have always and ever been anxious (even if that anxiety gets refracted in different ways in different cultures); some relatively fixed proportion of us have always been more anxious than others. As soon as the human brain became capable of apprehending the future, it became capable of being apprehensive about the future. The ability to plan, the ability to imagine the future—with these come the ability to worry, to dread the future. Did Cro-Magnons suffer nervous stomachs when predators lurked outside the cave? Did early hominids find their palms getting sweaty and their mouths dry when interacting with higher-status members of the tribe? Were there agoraphobic cavemen or Neanderthals who endured performance anxiety or fear of heights? I imagine there were, since these proto–*Homo sapiens* were the products of the same evolution that has generated our own capacity for anxiety, and they possessed the same, or very similar, physiological equipment for fear.

Which suggests that anxiety is an abiding part of the human condition. "In our day we still see our major threats as coming from the tooth and claw of physical enemies when they are actually largely psychological and in the broadest sense spiritual—that is they deal with meaninglessness," Rollo May wrote in 1977 in the foreword to his revised edition of *The Meaning of Anxiety*. "We are no longer prey to tigers and mastodons but to damage to our self-esteem, ostracism by our group, or the threat of losing out in the competitive struggle. The form of anxiety has changed, but the experience remains relatively the same."

PART V

Redemption and Resilience

CHAPTER 11

Redemption

The capacity to bear anxiety is important for the individual's self-realization and for his conquest of his environment. . . . Self-actualization occurs only at the price of moving ahead despite such shocks. This indicates the constructive use of anxiety.
  —KURT GOLDSTEIN, *Human Nature in the Light of Psychopathology* (1940)

Starting when I was ten years old, I saw the same psychiatrist once or twice a week for twenty-five years. Dr. L. was the psychiatrist who, when I was taken to McLean Hospital as a comprehensively phobic ten-year-old, administered my Rorschach test. When I started therapy with him in the early 1980s, he was approaching fifty, tall and lanky, balding a little, with a beard in the classic Freudian style. Over the years, the beard came and went a few times, and he lost more of his hair, which turned, over time, from brown to salt-and-pepper to white. He moved his office from one place (where he lived with his first wife) to another (where he lived with his second wife) to a third (where he leased space from an eye doctor) to a fourth (where, in keeping with his migration in a New Age direction, he shared a waiting room with a massage therapist and an electrologist) to, finally, the last time I visited him, a building by the ocean on Cape Cod (where he'd moved his practice and where his office is once again connected to his house).

Trained at Harvard in the 1950s and early 1960s, Dr. L. came of professional age in the late stages of the psychoanalytic heyday, when Freudianism still dominated. When I first encountered Dr. L., he was a believer both in medication and in such Freudian concepts as neurosis and repression, Oedipus complexes and transference. Our first sessions, in the early 1980s, were filled with Rorschach tests and free-associating and discussions of early memories from my youngest years. Our last sessions, in the mid-2000s, were focused on role-playing and "energy work"; he also spent a lot of time during those latter years trying to get me to sign up for a special kind of yoga program that is today defending itself in federal court against multiple allegations that it is a brainwashing cult.

Here's some of what we did in our sessions together over a quarter century: looked at picture books (1981); played backgammon (1982–85); played darts (1985–88); experimented sporadically with various cutting-edge psychotherapeutic methods of a progressively more New Age complexion, such as hypnotism, facilitated communication, eye movement desensitization and reprocessing, inner-child therapy, energy systems therapy, and internal family systems therapy (1988–2004). I was the beneficiary, or possibly the victim, of seemingly every passing trend in psychotherapy and psychopharmacology.

A few years ago, when embarking on the research for this book, I decided to track down Dr. L. for an interview. His inability to cure me notwithstanding, who better to help me figure out my anxiety than the man who had worked for decades to treat me? So I wrote to him to tell him what I was working on and to ask if I might interview him about my many years of therapy with him and look at any old case files of mine he still had. He said he didn't have my files anymore but that he would be happy to talk. So on a cold afternoon in late November, I drove from Boston out the length of Cape Cod to Provincetown, brisk and barren in the off-season. It had been more than five years since I'd last seen or spoken to him, and I was anxious (of course) about how the meeting would go. Wanting to maintain a journalistic composure—and to avoid falling into old dependent habits of relating to him (he'd been a father figure for twenty-five years)—I popped a Xanax beforehand and briefly considered stopping at a liquor store for a sedating nip of vodka.* I pulled into his driveway in the midafternoon.

Waiting on his back deck, he waved and gestured me up the steps and into his office, where he greeted me warmly, if a little warily, won-

---

* That I even contemplated this, of course, suggests that those decades of therapy with Dr. L. were not terribly effective; my dependencies are now chemical.

dering, I suspect, if I had come to gather evidence for a malpractice suit. (His e-mail correspondence leading up to this meeting, about my case files and so forth, had all seemed carefully worded, as though vetted by a lawyer.) By then in his late seventies, he still looked lithe and fit and appeared younger than his years. We sat down and I caught him up on what I'd been doing the past few years, and then we began talking about my anxiety.

What, I asked, did he remember about my case from when I originally showed up at the psychiatric hospital more than two decades earlier?

"I remember it pretty clearly," he said. "You were a very distressed child."

I asked him about my emetophobia, which had already presented itself forcefully by the time I was ten. "It was a dramatic fantasy that vomiting would make your body come apart," he said. "Your parents didn't help you to reality-test, and you merged with that phobia."

Did he remember how he and the team at the mental hospital interpreted my Rorschach test? I had recently approached the records department at McLean Hospital to ask whether archivists could find my original evaluation file, but it had been moved off-site some years ago, and no one had been able to track it down. The only image I could recall was one that I remembered looking like a wounded bat, its wings torn, unable to escape from its cave. "That likely had something to do with your feelings of being abandoned or being enveloped," Dr. L. said. "A sense of lack of safety and of enormous vulnerability."

I asked him what he thought had produced that vulnerability.

"There was a whole host of causal factors. We knew there were deficits in the parents."

He spoke first about my father, whom he knew very well, having counseled him when my mother left him for the managing partner of her law firm.* "When you were growing up, your father had a very

---

* This, by the way, led to a rather complex web of conflicts of interest. On the Sunday in the autumn of 1995 that my mother announced to him she might want a divorce, my father, desperate to save the marriage, stopped drinking completely for the first time in years and, in a gesture that was completely out of character, acquiesced to emergency couples' counseling. For years before that, my father, despite footing the bill for my sister's and my shrinks, disdained psychotherapy. "How was your wacko lesson?" he'd ask jeeringly after I'd had an appointment. He did this so often that the term became a part of the

strong 'knower,' which meant that parts of himself stood strongly in judgment. He didn't have a lot of tolerance for anxious behavior. Your

---

family's lingua franca, and eventually my sister and I were referring without irony to our wacko lessons. ("Mom, can you give me a ride to my wacko lesson on Wednesday?") In 1995, Dr. L. had recently hung out a shingle—with his new wife, Nurse G.—as a relationship counselor. So my parents began seeing Dr. L. and Nurse G. (who was also a licensed clinical social worker) in intensive couples' therapy. Which would have been fine except that I—by then in my midtwenties—was still seeing Dr. L. as my principal psychotherapist. So my appointments with Dr. L. started to run something like this:

> DR. L.: How are you?
>   ME: Well, I had kind of a rough week. I had a panic attack when—
> DR. L.: How are your parents doing?
>   ME: What?
> DR. L.: Have you talked to your mother or father in the last couple of days? Has your mother said anything about whether she's still seeing Michael P.?

As it happened, my mother *was* still seeing Michael P. and in fact would soon be setting up house with him.

Unmoored by my mother's departure, my father started seeing Dr. L. for psychotherapy on an individual basis. By this point, we might as well have had Dr. L. on family retainer. He had just provided six months of marriage counseling to my parents, was seeing my father at least once a week, and was still seeing me. To make this web of psychopathology even more incestuous, my mother had started seeing Nurse G. on an individual basis.

My own therapy sessions with Dr. L. came to be dominated by his questions about his new star patient, my father. I couldn't blame Dr. L. for finding my father the more interesting patient. After all, while he'd been seeing me for more than fifteen years, he'd only been seeing my dad for a few months. Being able to talk to my father about his relationship with me, and then to talk to me about my relationship with my father, surely provided an intriguing *Rashomon*-like fascination for Dr. L. He was seeing my father, his wife was seeing my mother, he and his wife were seeing my mother and father together, and he was seeing me—a kaleidoscopic game of family telephone, with Dr. L. and Nurse G. as the switchboard operators.

My dad entered therapy emotionally wrecked by his separation, profoundly shaken, and drinking heavily. He completed therapy less than two years later, happy, productive, remarried, and deemed (by himself and by Dr. L.) to be much more "self-actualized" and "authentic" than he had been. He was in and out of therapy with Dr. L. in eighteen months. Whereas I was entering my nineteenth year of therapy with Dr. L. and was still as anxious as ever.

A few years ago, my wife asked my father what had happened when he graduated from therapy with Dr. L. Had Dr. L. said anything about me when he did? He had. Dr. L., my father recalled, had told him that I wasn't anywhere near ready to graduate and that I had "serious issues" I still needed help with.

Which, I suppose, was manifestly the case. But wasn't one of those issues the fact that my own father—whose stern critical assessments of my life and work over the years had likely contributed to the leakiness of my self-esteem—had, in borrowing my therapist and advancing from temporary basket case to cured in no time at all as I languished in purgatorial neurotic stasis, confirmed yet again my general inferiority and incompetence? When my father graduated, I felt like a schoolchild whose younger sibling has just sped past him in the accelerated class: my father, starting therapy years (decades!) after me, shot through quickly to graduation with honors, while I, trapped in remedial classes, repeated third grade for the nineteenth time.

anxiety would make him blow up with anger. He had no empathy. When you got anxious, he would judge it and want to fix it. He couldn't just help you sit with it. He couldn't soothe you."

Dr. L. paused for a moment. "He couldn't soothe himself, either. He would judge his anxiety. In his mind, anxiety is weakness. It makes him angry."*

What about my mother?

"She was too anxious herself to be very effective at helping you cope with your own anxiety," Dr. L. said. "She organized her life around trying not to be anxious. So when *you* got anxious, *she* would get anxious. A parent-child unit like that, the child takes on the anxiety of the parent but doesn't know where it came from. Her anxiety became yours, and you couldn't handle it, and she couldn't help you.

"You had problems with 'object constancy,'" he continued. "You couldn't carry an internal image of your parents. Whenever you were away from them, you were in fundamental doubt about whether you were being abandoned. Your parents could never settle down enough to give you the assurance they were on the planet."†

Dr. L. said he believed this separation anxiety was compounded by my mother's overprotectiveness. "The message you got from your mother was, *You can't take it—don't take risks because the anxiety will be too overwhelming.*"

I tell him it sounds like he's mainly attributing my anxiety to psycho-

---

* *My father's anger.* Among the darker moments of my childhood was this: One night when I was fourteen, I woke up at three in the morning with one of my bouts of screaming panic. Hearing me cry, my father lost control. He stormed into my room, trailed by my mother, and started hitting me repeatedly, telling me to shut up. This made me cry harder. "You twerp, you pathetic little twerp!" he shouted as he picked me up and threw me. I hit the wall and slid to the floor. As I lay there, racked by sobbing while my father looked down at me, I could see my mother standing impassively in the doorway. I have a predisposition toward feeling lonely even when surrounded by friends and family; in that moment, I felt more lonely than ever before or since. (Here, for confirmation-of-memory purposes, is an entry from my dad's diary, which he began keeping after my mother left him and which he kindly shared with me a few years ago: "At about age 11, however, Scott began to become very anxious and was particularly phobic about vomiting. He began to manifest some behavioral oddities that Anne detected and which I denied. Anne was right, and, acerbically reviling my psychological blindness, Dr. Sherry [a pediatric psychiatrist] recommended an evaluation at McLean. This process led into Scott's now extended psychotherapy with Dr. [L.]. The initial rigmarole was terrible, however. Scott got much worse and in particular couldn't sleep at night. He had to take Thorazine and imipramine. In frustration I often got verbally and even physically abusive.")

† This comports with the Bowlby-Ainsworth attachment theory concept of the secure base.

dynamic issues—to the relationship I had with my parents. But doesn't modern research suggest that vulnerability to anxiety is largely genetic? Doesn't, for instance, Jerome Kagan's work on the links between genes and temperament, and between temperament and anxiety, suggest that anxious character is hardwired into the genome?

"Look, maybe having an 'inhibited temperament' made things worse for you," he said. "But my own view is that even if you hadn't had that kind of genetically produced temperament, your mother's personality might still have given you issues. Neither she nor your father could offer what you needed. You couldn't soothe yourself.

"Yes," he continued, "there's evidence that you've got neurochemical problems produced by your genes. And your mother's personality was a bad match for your genetic temperament. But a gene predisposing you to an illness doesn't necessarily give you that illness. Geneticists say, 'We'll map the genes and find out the trouble.' *No! Not true!* Even with breast cancer, sometimes only an environmental factor—like nutrition—will catalyze a genetic predisposition to cancer into actual cancer."

I observe that medication—Xanax, Klonopin, Celexa, alcohol—is more effective at soothing me than my parents ever were, or than Dr. L. was, or than my own self-will (whatever that may consist of) is. Doesn't that suggest that my anxiety is a medical problem more than a psychological one, regardless of what my parents' shortcomings may have been? That anxiety is a problem embedded in the body, in the physical brain rather than some disembodied mind or psyche—a problem that leaches up from body to brain to mind rather than seeping down from mind to brain to body?

"False dichotomy!" he says emphatically, standing up to pull a book off his shelf: *Descartes' Error.* In it, the neurologist Antonio Damasio explains that Descartes was wrong to argue that the mind and body are distinct. The mind-body duality is not in fact a duality, Dr. L. says, paraphrasing Damasio. The body gives rise to the mind; the mind imbues the body. The two cannot be differentiated. "Neocortical function"—that is, the mind—"makes us who we are," Dr. L. says. "But the limbic system"—which is autonomic and unconscious—"may be just as relevant, if not more, in determining who we are. The neocortex can't make a decision without the emotional system playing in."

To illustrate the inseparability of body and mind, Dr. L. talked about the effects of trauma. (He had recently been to Sri Lanka, where he coached psychotherapists on how to work with survivors of the 2004 tsunami.) The experience of trauma or abuse, he explained, gets stored in the body, "woven into the bodily tissue."

"Consider Holocaust survivors," he said. "Even grandkids of Holocaust survivors carry extra anxiety that is measurable at a physiological level. They tend to have more anxious triggers. If they see a movie with victims of violence in Somalia, they respond to it much more strongly." This is true, he said, not just of the children of Holocaust survivors but of their grandchildren and even great-grandchildren. "They've got something plastered into their bodies via the experience of their parents or grandparents. The trauma doesn't even belong to them, but it affects them." (I think here of my father's Holocaust fixation, the books about Nazis piled always on his bedside table, the World War II documentaries always running on the TV. His mother and father had escaped Germany before the Holocaust; so did much of the rest of the family, but not before his uncles and grandfather were beaten up on Kristallnacht.)

I asked Dr. L. how much he thought the psychiatric field had changed since he entered it nearly fifty years ago, especially regarding its thinking about the causes and treatment of anxiety.

"Freudians were about 'insight' über alles," he said. "If you had insight about your neurosis, the expectation was that you could control it. *Wrong!*"

Dr. L.'s treatments of choice these days are, depending on your point of view, either high-tech and cutting-edge or New Age and weird: for instance, eye movement desensitization and reprocessing, which involves moving your eyes back and forth while reliving a trauma, and internal family systems therapy, based on the work of the psychiatrist Richard Schwartz, which involves training a patient to gain control of his multiple selves through the "conducting self" and helping him to develop a better, more strengthening relationship with his vulnerable inner child. In my latter years of therapy with Dr. L., I spent a lot of time moving from chair to chair in his office, inhabiting different "selves" and "energies," and talking to my inner child.

"We used to have a monolithic view of mood and personality disorders," Dr. L. continued. "But now we realize we have little packets of personality; they have their own sets of beliefs and values." The key to treatment, he says, is to make the patient conscious of these multiple selves and to help him manage the selves that carry trauma or anxiety.

"Today," he said, "we now know much more about the neurocircuitry of anxiety. Sometimes you need to medicate. But newer, better psychiatry alters the brain chemistry—alters it in the same way drugs do."

"Am I doomed by my neurocircuitry?" I asked. "I went to therapy with you for twenty-five years, and have seen multiple other therapists, and have tried multiple methods of treatment. And yet here I am, advancing into middle age, and still suffering from chronic and often debilitating anxiety."

"No, you're not doomed," Dr. L. said. "We now know enough about neuroplasticity to understand that the circuitry is always growing. You can always modify the software."

Even if I can't fully recover from my anxiety, I've come to believe there may be some redeeming value in it.

Historical evidence suggests that anxiety can be allied to artistic and creative genius. The literary gifts of Emily Dickinson, for example, were inextricably bound up with her anxiety. (She was completely housebound, and in fact rarely left her bedroom, after age forty.) Franz Kafka yoked his neurotic sensibility to his artistic sensibility; so, of course, did Woody Allen. Jerome Kagan, the Harvard psychologist, argues that T. S. Eliot's anxiety and high-reactive physiology helped make him a great poet. Eliot was, Kagan observes, a "shy, cautious, sensitive child"—but because he also had a supportive family, good schooling, and "unusual verbal abilities," Eliot was able to "exploit his temperament" to become an outstanding poet.

Perhaps most famously, Marcel Proust transmuted his neurotic sensibility into art. Marcel's father, Adrien, was a physician specializing in nervous health and the author of an influential book called *The Hygiene of the Neurasthenic.* Marcel read his father's work, as well as books by many of the other leading nerve doctors of his day, and incorporated their work into his; his fiction and nonfiction are "saturated with the vocabulary of nervous dysfunction," as one critic has put it. At various points throughout *Remembrance of Things Past,* characters either comment on or embody the idea that, as Aristotle first observed, nervous suffering can give rise to great art. For Proust, refinement of artistic sensibility was directly tied to a nervous disposition. From the high-strung comes high art.*

From the high-strung can also come, at least some of the time, great science. Dean Simonton, a psychologist at the University of California, Davis, who has spent decades studying the psychology of genius, estimates that a third of all eminent scientists suffer from anxi-

---

* Consider also such nervous invalid intellectuals as David Hume, James Boswell, John Stuart Mill, George Miller Beard, William James, Alice James, Gustave Flaubert, John Ruskin, Herbert Spencer, Edmund Gosse, Michael Faraday, Arnold Toynbee, Charlotte Perkins Gilman, and Virginia Woolf, every single one of whom suffered debilitating nervous prostration early (and sometimes late) in their careers. During young adulthood, David Hume, who would become one of the bright stars of the Scottish Enlightenment, abandoned his studies in the law and entered upon a far more precarious career in philosophy. In the spring of 1729, following a period of intense intellectual exertion, Hume broke down. He felt, as he later wrote in a letter to a doctor documenting his ills, physically exhausted and emotionally distraught; he couldn't concentrate on the book he was trying to write (which would eventually become the famous *Treatise of Human Nature*), and he suffered terrible stomach pains, rashes, and heart palpitations that incapacitated him for the better part of five years. Much in the way Darwin later would, Hume sampled the full range of remedies on offer in the hope of finding a cure for what he called his nervous "distemper": he took water treatments at spas and went for walks and rides in the country; he took the "Course of Bitters and Anti-hysteric Pills" and "an English Pint of Claret Wine every Day" prescribed by his family's physician. Writing to another doctor in search of succor, Hume asked "whether among all those Scholars you have been acquainted with you have ever known any affected in this manner? Whether I can ever hope for a Recovery? Whether I must long wait for it? Whether my Recovery will ever be perfect, and my Spirits regain their former Spring and Vigor, so as to endure the Fatigue of deep and abstruse thinking?" In the event, Hume did recover: after he published *A Treatise of Human Nature* in 1739, he seems not to have suffered further, and he went on to become perhaps the most important philosopher ever to write in English.

The political philosopher John Stuart Mill endured a similar nervous breakdown. In the fall of 1826, when he was twenty years old, Mill experienced a complete emotional collapse, which he would years later recount in the famous fifth chapter, "A Crisis in My Mental History," of his autobiography. Through the "melancholy winter" of that year, he was, he writes, in an unrelenting state of "depression," "dejection," and "dulled nerves." He found himself so paralyzed by his "irrepressible self-consciousness" that he could scarcely function. (This puts one in mind of the novelist David Foster Wallace, another genius done in by his acute anxiety.) After eighteen months of this unremitting misery, Mill wrote, "a small ray of light broke in upon my gloom" while he was reading the memoirs of a French historian: he needed, he decided, to become less repressed and analytic and to develop his emotional and aesthetic faculties. The arduous education imposed on him by his "grim and exacting" father had, he realized, robbed him of a normal childhood and of an inner emotional life. "The cultivation of the feelings became one of the cardinal points in my ethical and philosophical creed," he wrote. By becoming more attuned to his emotions (which he cultivated by, for instance, reading the poetry of Wordsworth), he was evidently able to leave anxiety and depression behind.

ety or depression or both. He surmises that the same cognitive or neurobiological mechanisms that predispose certain people to developing anxiety disorders also enhance the sort of creative thinking that produces conceptual breakthroughs in science. When Sir Isaac Newton invented calculus, no one knew about it for ten years—because he was too anxious and depressed to tell anyone. (For several years, he was too agoraphobic to leave his house.) Perhaps if Darwin had not been forcibly housebound by his anxiety for decades on end, he would never have been able to finish his work on evolution. Sigmund Freud's career was nearly derailed early on by his terrible anxiety and self-doubt; he overcame it to become a cult figure and a major intellectual influence on generations of psychotherapists. Once his reputation as a great man of science had been established, Freud and his acolytes sought to engrave in stone the image of him as the eternally self-assured wise man. But his early letters reveal otherwise.*

---

* Ernest Jones, the original guardian of Freud's legacy, once claimed that only "uninteresting details" had been excised from the collection of Freud's letters he published. But among those strategically omitted letters were some 130 to his friend Wilhelm Fliess, many of them consisting of a litany of neurotic, hypochondriacal complaint.

"I have not been free of symptoms for as much as half a day, and my mood and ability to work are really at a low ebb," Freud wrote Fliess in early May 1894. The omitted letters are full of symptom reports, repeated over and over again. By his own account, Freud suffered migraine headaches, pains all over his body, all kinds of stomach distress, and endless heart palpitations that led him to predict in one letter that he would die in his early fifties of a "ruptured heart." His (failed) attempts to wean himself from cigar smoking would cause a resurgence of physical symptoms: "I feel aged, sluggish, not healthy." When his father died in 1896, he reported a seemingly phobic preoccupation with death, what he called his "death delirium."

This is hardly the image of the stoical, self-assured master of the mind that he sought to project. "It is too distressing for a medical man who spends every hour of the day struggling to gain an understanding of the neuroses not to know whether he is suffering from a justifiable or a hypochondriacal mild depression," Freud told Fliess. His letters are replete with melancholic, self-lacerating thoughts: he believes that he will die in obscurity, that his work is "rubbish," that all his labors will amount to nothing. At times, it seems he cannot possibly survive, let alone thrive, in the field he has chosen. "I have been through some kind of neurotic experience," he wrote on June 22, 1897, plagued by "twilight thoughts, veiled doubts, with barely a ray of light here or there."

"I still do not know what has been happening to me," he noted a couple of weeks later. "Something from the deepest depths of my own neurosis set itself against any advance in the understanding of the neuroses."

In August 1897, Freud wrote to Fliess from Bad Aussee, Austria, where he was vacationing with his family. Freud was not happy: he was "in a period of bad humor" and "tormented by grave doubts about my theory of the neuroses." His vacation was doing nothing toward "diminishing the agitation in my head and feelings." Despite his growing practice, Freud wrote, "the chief patient I am preoc-

No, anxiety is not, by itself, going to make you a Nobel Prize–winning poet or a groundbreaking scientist. But if you harness your anxious temperament correctly, it might make you a better worker. Jerome Kagan, who has spent more than sixty years studying people with anxious temperaments, believes that anxious employees are better employees. In fact, he says, he learned to hire only people with high-reactive temperaments as research assistants. "They're compulsive, they don't make errors, they're careful when they're coding data," he told *The New York Times.* They "are generally conscientious and almost obsessively well-prepared." Assuming they can avoid succumbing to full-blown anxiety disorders, "worriers are likely to be the most thorough workers and the most attentive friends," as *The Times* put it. Other research supports Kagan's observation. A 2012 study by psychiatrists at the University of Rochester Medical Center found that conscientious people who were highly neurotic tended to be more reflective, more goal oriented, more organized, and better at planning than average; they tended to be effective, "high-functioning" workers—and to be better at taking care of their physical health than other workers. ("These people are likely to weigh the consequences of their actions," Nicholas Turiano, the lead researcher, said. "Their level of neuroticism coupled with conscientiousness probably stops them from engaging in risky behaviors.") A 2013 study in the *Academy of Management Journal* found that neurotics contribute more than managers predicted to group projects, while extroverts contribute less, with the contributions of the neurotics becoming even more valuable over time. The director of the study, Corinne Bendersky, an associate professor at UCLA's Anderson School of Management, says that if she were staffing a team for a group project, "I would staff it with more neurotics and fewer extroverts than my initial instinct would lead me to do." In 2005 researchers at the University of Wales published a paper, "Can Worriers Be Winners?," reporting that financial managers high in anxiety tended to be the best, most effective money managers, as long as their worrying was accom-

---

cupied with is myself." The following summer, on another vacation, he reported unhappily that his work was progressing poorly and that he was bereft of motivation. "The secret of this restlessness is hysteria," he concluded remarkably, assigning to himself the affliction that he had staked his career on curing.

panied by high IQs. Smart people who worry a lot, the researchers concluded, tend to produce the best results.*

Unfortunately, the positive correlation between worrying and job performance disappeared when the worriers had low IQs. But some evidence suggests that excessive worrying is itself allied to high IQ. Dr. W. says that his anxious patients tend to be his smartest patients. (In his experience, anxious lawyers have tended to be particularly smart—skilled not only at foreseeing complex legal eventualities but also at imagining worst-case scenarios for themselves.) Dr. W.'s anecdotal observations are supported by recent scientific data. Some studies have found the correlation to be quite direct: the higher your IQ, the more likely you are to worry; the lower your IQ, the less likely you are to worry. A study published in 2012 in *Frontiers in Evolutionary Neuroscience* found that high IQ scores correlated with high levels of worry in people diagnosed with generalized anxiety disorder. (Anxious people are very smart at plotting out possible bad outcomes.) Jeremy Coplan, the lead author of that study, says that anxiety is evolutionarily adaptive because "every so often there's a wild-card danger." When such a danger arises, anxious people are more likely to be prepared to survive. Some people, Coplan says, are effectively stupid enough that they are "incapable of seeing any danger, even when danger is imminent"; moreover, "if these folks are in positions as leaders, they are going to indicate to the general populace that there's no need to worry." Coplan, a professor of psychiatry at the State University of New York Downstate Medical Center, says that anxiety can be a good trait in political leaders—and that lack of anxiety can be dangerous. (Some commentators have suggested, based on findings like Coplan's, that the main cause of the economic crash of 2008 was politicians and financiers who were either stupid or insufficiently anxious or both.)

The correlations aren't universal, of course: there are plenty of brilliant daredevils and stupid worriers. And, as always, this comes with the proviso that anxiety is productive mainly when it is not so excessive

---

* "Anxiety is an important component of motivated cognition, essential for efficient functioning in situations that require caution, self-discipline and the general anticipation of threat," the researchers wrote.

as to be debilitating. But if you are anxious, perhaps you can take heart from the growing collection of evidence suggesting that anxiety and intelligence are linked.

Anxiety may also be tied both to ethical behavior and to effective leadership. My wife once mused aloud about what I might lose if I were to be fully cured of my anxiety—and about what *she* might lose if I were to lose my anxious temperament.

"I hate your anxiety," she said, "and I hate that it makes you unhappy. But what if there are things that I love about you that are connected to your anxiety? What if," she asked, getting to the heart of the matter, "you're cured of your anxiety and you become a total jerk?"

I suspect I might—because it may be that my anxiety lends me an inhibition and a social sensitivity that make me more attuned to other people and a more tolerable spouse than I otherwise would be. Evidently, fighter pilots have unusually high divorce rates—a fact that may be tied to their having low levels of anxiety and a corresponding low baseline autonomic arousal, which together are tied not only to a need for adventure (indulged by flying a fighter plane or having extramarital affairs) but also to a certain interpersonal obtuseness, a lack of sensitivity to their partners' subtle social cues.* Anxious people, because they are vigilantly scanning the environment for threats, tend to be more attuned than adrenaline junkies to other people's emotions and social signals.

The notion of a connection between anxiety and morality long predates the findings of modern science or my wife's intuition. Saint Augustine believed fear was adaptive because it helps people behave morally. (That's also what both Thomas Burgess and Charles Darwin believed about anxiety and blushing: fear of misbehavior helps primates and humans behave "rightly," preserving social comity.) The pragmatist philosophers Charles Sanders Peirce and John Dewey believed that the human aversion to experiencing negative emotions like anxiety, shame, and guilt provides a kind of internal psychological incentive to behave ethically. Furthermore, psychological studies of criminals have found

---

* The Air Force reportedly has the highest divorce rate in the U.S. armed services, and nine out of ten fighter-pilot divorces are initiated by wives.

them to be low in anxiety, on average, and to have low-reactive amygdalae. (Criminals also tend to have lower-than-average IQs.)

In earlier chapters, I discussed how hundreds of studies on primates conducted over the last half century have found in various ways that the combination of certain genes and small amounts of early life stress can lead to lifelong anxious and depressive behavior in humans and other animals. But studies on rhesus monkeys by Stephen Suomi, the chief of the Laboratory of Comparative Ethology at the NIH, have found that when anxious monkeys were taken in early life from their anxious mothers and given to nonanxious mothers to be raised, a fascinating thing happened: these monkeys grew up to display *less* anxiety than their peers with the same genetic markers—and many also, intriguingly, became leaders in their troop. This suggests that some quotient of anxiety not only enhances your odds of living longer but also, under the right circumstances, can equip you to be a leader.

My anxiety can be intolerable. It often makes me miserable. But it is also, maybe, a gift—or at least the other side of a coin I ought to think twice about before trading in. Perhaps my anxiety is linked to whatever limited moral sense I can claim. What's more, the same anxious imagination that sometimes drives me mad with worry also enables me to plan effectively for unforeseen circumstances or unintended consequences that other, less vigilant temperaments might not. The quick social judging that is allied to my performance anxiety is also useful in helping me to size up situations quickly and to manage people and defuse conflict.

Finally, at some brute evolutionary level, my anxiety might actually help keep me alive. I am less likely than you bold and heedless people (you fighter pilots and con artists, with your low baseline autonomic arousal) to die in an extreme sporting accident or to provoke a fight that leads to my getting shot.*

In his 1941 essay "The Wound and the Bow," the literary critic Edmund Wilson writes of the Sophoclean hero Philoctetes, the son of a king, whose suppurating, never-healing snakebite wound on his

---

* On the other hand, I'm more likely to die prematurely from some stress-related disease.

foot is linked to a gift for unerring accuracy with his bow and arrow—his "malodorous disease" is inseparable from his "superhuman art" for marksmanship.* I have always been drawn to this parable: in it lies, as the novelist Jeanette Winterson put it, "the nearness of the wound to the gift," the insight that in weakness and shamefulness is also the potential for transcendence, heroism, or redemption. My anxiety remains an unhealed wound that, at times, holds me back and fills me with shame—but it may also be, at the same time, a source of strength and a bestower of certain blessings.

* Wilson's essay is about how art and psychological suffering are linked in writers like Sophocles, Charles Dickens, Ernest Hemingway, James Joyce, and Edith Wharton.

CHAPTER 12

Resilience

Anxiety cannot be avoided, but it can be reduced. The problem of the management of anxiety is that of reducing anxiety to normal levels, and then to use this normal anxiety as stimulation to increase one's awareness, vigilance, zest for living.
—ROLLO MAY, *The Meaning of Anxiety* (1950)

The essayist, poet, and lexicographer Samuel Johnson was, famously, a melancholic intellectual in the classic mode, suffering badly from what Robert Burton called the "Disease of the learned." In 1729, when he was twenty years old, Johnson found himself "overwhelmed with an horrible hypochondria, with perpetual irritation, fretfulness, and impatience; and with a dejection, gloom, and despair, which made existence misery," as James Boswell reported in his *Life of Samuel Johnson*. "From this dismal malady he never afterwards was perfectly relieved." ("That it was, in some degree, occasioned by a defect in his nervous system appears highly probable," Boswell surmised.) It was, as another biographer records, "an appalling state of mind, in which feelings of intense anxiety alternated with feelings of utter hopelessness." Many contemporaries noted Johnson's strange tics and twitches, which suggests he may have had OCD. He also seemed to have what would today be called agoraphobia. (He once wrote to the local magistrate asking to be excused from jury duty because "he came very near fainting . . . in all public places.") Johnson himself refers to his "morbid melancholy" and was ever worried that his dejection would tip over into full-blown madness. In addition to dipping regularly into Burton's *Anatomy of Melancholy*, Johnson read widely in both classic and contemporary medical texts.

Desperate to hold on to his sanity, Johnson—like Burton before him—seized on the idea that idleness and slothful habits were breeding grounds for anxiety and madness and that the best way to combat them was with steady occupation and regular habits, such as rising at the same time early each morning. "Imagination," he would say, "never takes such firm possession of the mind, as when it is found empty and unoccupied." So he was always at pains to occupy himself and to try to impose a regimen on his daily habits. What most endears Johnson to me is his lifelong, and plainly futile, attempts to start getting up earlier in the morning. A representative sampling from his journals:

September 7, 1738: "O Lord, enable me . . . in redeeming the time which *I have spent in Sloth.*"

January 1, 1753: "To rise early To lose no time."

July 13, 1755: "I will once more form *a scheme of life* . . . (1) to rise early."

Easter Eve 1757: "Almighty God . . . *Enable me to shake off sloth.*"

Easter Day 1759: "Give me thy Grace to break the chain of evil custom. Enable me to shake off idleness and Sloth."

September 18, 1760: "Resolved . . . To rise early . . . To oppose laziness."

April 21, 1764: "My purpose is from this time (1) To reject . . . idle thoughts. To provide some useful amusement for leisure time. (2) To avoid Idleness. To rise early."

The next day (3:00 a.m.): "Deliver me from the distresses of vain terrour . . . Against loose thoughts and idleness."

September 18, 1764: "I resolve to rise early, *Not later than six if I can.*"

Easter Sunday 1765: "I resolve *to rise at eight* . . . I purpose to rise at eight because though I shall not yet rise early it will be much earlier than I now rise, for I often lye till two."

January 1, 1769: "I am not yet in a state to form many resolutions; I purpose and hope to *rise . . . at eight, and by degrees at six.*"

January 1, 1774 (2:00 a.m.): "To rise at *eight* . . . The chief cause of my deficiency has been a life *immethodical and unset-*

tled, which breaks all purposes . . . and perhaps leaves too much leisure to imagination."

Good Friday 1775: "When I look back upon resoluti[ons] of improvement and amendments, which have year after year been broken . . . why do I yet try to resolve again? I try because Reformation is necessary and despair is criminal . . . My purpose is from Easter day to rise early, not later than eight."

January 2, 1781: "*I will not despair.* . . . My hope is (1) to rise at eight, or sooner. . . . (5) to avoid idleness."

Johnson never was able to sustain his early rising, and he spent many nights working until nearly dawn or roaming the streets of London tormented by his fears and phobias.*

Johnson's journal entries, you will have noted, span more than forty years—from his twenties until his early seventies—and it is hard to know which is more affecting: the futility of his efforts to shake off sloth and to rise early or his earnest commitment to continuing to try despite his knowledge of that futility. (As he wrote in his journal on June 1, 1770, "Every Man naturally persuades himself that he can keep his resolutions, nor is he convinced of his imbecility but by length of time and frequency of experiment.") Walter Jackson Bate, Johnson's greatest modern biographer, first compiled many of these entries in the 1970s, when psychobiography in the Freudian mode was in vogue. Bate suggested that these entries—and Johnson's continuing exhortations to improve himself generally—were evidence of a superego that was too perfectionistic in its demands, and he argued that the constant berating by Johnson's superego, along with the low self-esteem that naturally accompanied it, accounted for Johnson's "depressive anxiety" and his many psychosomatic symptoms. For Johnson, the "danger" of indolence was that, as his friend Arthur Murphy noted, "his spirits, not employed abroad, turned inward with hostility against himself. His reflections on his own life and conduct were always severe; and, wishing

---

* Recent research on sleep cycles suggests that difficulty in rising early is not (entirely) a character failing but rather a biologically hardwired trait: some people's circadian rhythms make them what researchers call "morning doves," leaping easily out of bed in the morning and fading at night, whereas other people are "night owls," productively burning the midnight oil and unable to get out of bed in the morning.

to be immaculate, he destroyed his own peace by unnecessary scruples."
When Johnson surveyed his life, Murphy wrote, "he discovered nothing but a barren waste of time, with some disorders of body, and disturbances of mind, very near to madness. His life, he says, from his earliest
youth, was wasted in a morning bed; and his reigning sin was a general
sluggishness, to which he was always inclined, and, in part of his life,
almost compelled, by morbid melancholy and weariness of mind." In
this striving for perfection in order that he might think well of himself,
Johnson exhibits the classic traits of what Karen Horney, the influential
Freudian psychoanalyst, called the neurotic personality. According to
Bate, Johnson's writing, "which often anticipates . . . modern psychiatry," was concerned with "how much of the misery of mankind comes
from the inability of individuals to think well of themselves, and how
much envy and other evils spring from this." As Johnson himself put it,
his strong interest in biography as a literary form—his work includes
The Lives of the Poets and other biographical sketches—was motivated
by an interest not so much in understanding how a man "was made
happy" or how "he lost the favour of his prince" but in understanding
"how he became discontented with himself."

But here's an instructive fact: As unhappy with himself as he was,
and as frequently as he berated himself for his lassitude and for lying
in bed until two, Johnson was enormously productive. Johnson, despite
churning out essays for money ("no man but a blockhead" would ever
do otherwise, as he famously said), was no mere hack. Some of his
writings—his protonovel *Rasselas*, his poem *The Vanity of Human
Wishes*, the best of his essays—are fixtures of the Western canon. *The
Works of Samuel Johnson* occupies sixteen thick volumes on my shelf—
and that's not even including the work for which he is most famous, the
massive dictionary he compiled. Clearly, Johnson's self-assessments of
skillfulness and accomplishment were at odds with the reality—which,
modern clinical research has shown, is often the case in people of melancholy disposition.*

In his persistent efforts toward self-improvement, and in keeping

---

* Actually, an intriguing body of research has found that clinically depressed people tend to be *more*
accurate in their self-assessments than healthy people, suggesting that an ample quotient of self-
delusion—of thinking you're better or more competent than you in fact are—is useful for good mental
health and professional success.

up his great writerly productivity in the face of emotional torment, Johnson exhibited a form of resilience—a trait that modern psychology is increasingly finding to be a powerful bulwark against anxiety and depression. Anxiety research, which has traditionally focused on what's wrong with pathologically anxious people, is focusing more and more on what makes healthy people resistant to developing anxiety disorders and other clinical conditions. Dennis Charney, a professor of psychiatry and neuroscience at the Ichan School of Medicine at Mount Sinai, has studied American prisoners of war in Vietnam who did *not*, despite the traumas they endured, become depressed or develop PTSD. A number of studies by Charney and others have found that the qualities of resilience and acceptance were what allowed these POWs to ward off the clinical anxiety and psychological breakdown that afflicted many others. The ten critical psychological elements and characteristics of resilience that Charney has identified are optimism, altruism, having a moral compass or set of beliefs that cannot be shattered, faith and spirituality, humor, having a role model, social supports, facing fear (or leaving one's comfort zone), having a mission or meaning in life, and practice in meeting and overcoming challenges. Separate research has suggested that resilience is associated with an abundance of the brain chemical neuropeptide Y—and while it's unclear which way the causation goes (does a resilient temperament produce NPY in the brain, or does NPY in the brain produce a resilient temperament, or is it, most likely, a combination of both?), some evidence suggests NPY levels have a strong genetic component.*

I lament to Dr. W. that, based on thirty years of futile effort so far, my prospects for achieving a recovery from anxiety sufficiently transcendent to provide an uplifting ending to this book seem dismal. I talk to him about the emerging research on resilience, which is fascinating and hopeful—but then I note, as I've done before, that I don't feel very resilient. In fact, I say, I've now got tangible proof that I'm genetically

---

* As we saw in chapter 9, the research of Jerome Kagan, Kerry Ressler, and others suggests that genes play a large role in determining one's innate levels of nervousness and resilience.

predisposed to be *not* resilient: I'm biologically hardwired, at a cellular level, to be anxious and pessimistic and *non*resilient.

"This is why I keep telling you I hate all the modern emphasis on the genetics and neurobiology of mental illness," he says. "It hardens the notion that the mind is a fixed and immutable structure, when in fact it can change throughout the life course."

I tell him that I know all that. And I know, furthermore, that gene expression is affected by environmental factors and that, in any event, reducing a human being to either genes or environment is absurdly reductionist.

And yet I still don't feel much capacity for resilience.

"You're more resilient than you know," he says. "You're always saying 'I can't handle this' or 'I can't handle that.' Yet you handle a lot for someone with anxiety—you handle a lot, period. Just think about what you've had to deal with while trying to complete your book."

As my deadline for delivering this book crept paralyzingly closer, I took a part-time leave from my day job as a magazine editor so I could focus on writing. This decision was not without risk: advertising my dispensability at a company that had been downsizing, in an industry (print journalism) that was radically contracting and possibly dying, and in an economy that was the worst since the Great Depression was hardly the best way to maximize my job security. But increasingly panicked that I was going to miss my deadline and have to plunge my family into bankruptcy, I calculated that the leave was a necessary gamble. My hope was that the time freed up by going on temporary leave, combined with the pressure of the looming deadline, would create the conditions necessary for a spasm of productivity.

That didn't happen. This did:

The very day that my leave was to begin, my heretofore healthy wife fell ill with a mysterious and protracted ailment that led to multiple doctor's appointments (internists, allergists, immunologists, endocrinologists) and a series of inconclusive diagnoses (lupus, rheumatoid arthritis, Hashimoto's thyroiditis, Graves' disease, and others). A few days after that, my completely law-abiding wife was charged (wrongly and absurdly; it's a long story) with a felony that required thousands of dollars in legal expenses and several trips to court to combat. Around this same time, my mother's second husband left her for another woman, and they (my mother and my soon-to-be ex-stepfather) began divorce proceedings that I feared would leave her impoverished. My father's start-up company, which I had hoped would help fund my kids' college education, lost its funding and folded. And so as I sat at my computer day after day on my ostensible book leave, I spent less time writing than I did worrying about my wife's health and compulsively checking our dwindling bank balances as money flowed out much faster than it was flowing in.

And then one early morning in August—the final month of my leave—I awoke to crashing thunder and a driving rain. Suddenly branches and stones started pummeling my bedroom window. As I leapt from bed and ran from the room, the window exploded inward. (My wife and kids were out of town.) I made for the basement, passing the kitchen just as the ceiling caved in—a tree had fallen on the roof. Cabinets were ripped from the walls and pitched to the floor. Light fixtures dropped from above and dangled in the air, suspended by sizzling wires. A swath of insulation unfurled from what remained of the ceiling, hanging there like a panting tongue. Shingles rained from above, splattering onto the linoleum. Rain poured through the gaping hole in the roof.

I ran through the living room just as another tree toppled onto the house. All four windows in the room shattered at once, glass flying everywhere. Dozens of trees were falling, some of them pulled up by their roots, others split in two about eighty feet up from the ground.

I scrambled down the stairs, intending to take refuge underground. But when I got to the basement, three inches of water already covered the ground, and the level was rising fast. I stood on the bottom step, thoughts racing, wondering what was going on (hurricane? nuclear attack? earthquake? tornado? alien invasion?)* and trying to figure out what to do.

Standing there in my boxer shorts, I became conscious of the thunderous pounding of my heart. My mouth was dry, my breathing was quick, my muscles were tense, my heart was racing, adrenaline was coursing through my bloodstream—my fight-or-flight response was

* It was, my insurance company would later conclude, "a tornadic event."

fully activated. As I felt my heart thudding, it occurred to me that my physical sensations were like those of a panic attack or an episode of phobic terror. But even though the danger now was so much more real than during a panic attack, even though I was aware that I might get hurt or even (who knows?) die as the roof caved in and giant trees tumbled, I was less unhappy than I would be during a panic attack. I was scared, yes, but I was marveling at Nature's force, her ability to tear down my seemingly solid house around me and to knock down scores of big trees. It was actually sort of . . . exciting. A panic attack is worse.*

The next several weeks were spent dealing with insurance claims and disaster recovery technicians and real estate agents and movers—and not at all working on my book. As the precious days of my dwindling leave ticked away, I again found myself in an excruciating bind. If I didn't go back to work, I feared, I would lose my job; if I did go back to work, I'd probably miss my book deadline (and maybe lose my job anyway). Worse still would be to finally receive the external confirmation of my inner conviction all these years: that I am a failure—weak, dependent, anxious, shameful.

"Scott!" Dr. W. said when I was going on in this fashion. "Are you listening to yourself? You've already written one book. You're supporting a family. You *have* a job."

Later that day he e-mailed me:

> *As I was writing my notes today after we met, it occurred to me that you need to better internalize positive feedback. . . . Your capabilities are far from the picture of inadequacy that you carry around in your head. Please try and absorb.*

I wrote back:

> *I'll try to absorb these comments—but I immediately discount or back away or rationalize them.*

---

* As if to confirm that, two nights later I woke up with a stomachache, which instantly triggered miserable body-quaking panic that had me desperately gulping vodka and Xanax and Dramamine in headlong pursuit of unconsciousness—probably putting myself at more risk of death than the house-destroying storm did.

He responded:

Scott, the automatic response is to discount positive feedback. That is why it is so difficult to change. But the beginning of that process is a pushback against the negative juggernaut.

Trying is all anyone can ask.

The irony, of course, is that, as Dr. W. keeps telling me, the route to mental health and freedom from anxiety is to deepen my sense of what he calls, drawing on the work of the cognitive psychologist Albert Bandura, self-efficacy. (Bandura believed that repeatedly proving to oneself one's competence and ability to master situations, and doing so in spite of feelings of anxiety, depression, or vulnerability, builds up self-confidence and psychological strength that can provide a bulwark against anxiety and depression.) Yet writing this book has required me to wallow in my shame, anxiety, and weakness so that I can properly capture and convey them—an experience that has only reinforced how deep and long-standing my anxiety and vulnerability are. Of course, I suppose that even as writing this book has intensified my sense of shame, anxiety, and weakness and has accentuated those feelings of "helpless dependency" that, according to the psychiatrists at McLean Hospital, did in my great-grandfather, it has also helped me appreciate that my efforts to withstand their corrosive effect provide some evidence that I have the resources to overcome them. Maybe by tunneling into my anxiety for this book I can also tunnel out the other side. Not that I can escape my anxiety or be cured of it. But in finishing this book, albeit a book that dwells at great length on my helplessness and inefficacy, maybe I am demonstrating a form of efficacy, perseverance, productivity—and, yes, resilience.

Maybe I am not, for that matter—despite my dependency on medication, despite my flirtations with institutionalization, despite the genotype of pathology handed down to me by my ancestors, despite the vulnerability and what sometimes feels like the unbearable physical and emotional agony of my anxiety—as weak as I think I am. Consider the opening sentence of this book: "I have an unfortunate tendency to falter at crucial moments." That statement feels true to me. ("The neurotic,"

Karen Horney writes in *The Neurotic Personality of Our Time,* "tenaciously insists on being weak.") And yet, as Dr. W. is always pointing out, I *did* survive my wedding and have managed (so far) to remain productive and gainfully employed for more than twenty years despite often debilitating anxiety.

"Scott," he says. "Over the last few years, you've run a magazine and edited many of its cover stories, worked on your book, taken care of your family, and coped with the destruction of your house and with the normal vicissitudes and challenges of life." I point out that I've managed all this only with the help of (sometimes heavy) medication—and that anything I've accomplished has been accompanied by constant worry and frequent panic and has been punctuated by moments of near-complete breakdown that leave me always at risk of being exposed for the anxious weakling that I am.

"You have a handicap—anxiety disorder," he says. "Yet you manage it and, I would say, even thrive despite it. I still think we can cure you of it. But in the meantime, you need to recognize that, given what you're up against, you've accomplished a lot. You need to give yourself more credit."

Maybe finishing this book and publishing it—and, yes, admitting my shame and fear to the world—will be empowering and anxiety reducing.

I suppose I'll find out soon enough.

Acknowledgments

This book might not exist if Kathryn Lewis had not, unbeknownst to me, shown an e-mail with my inchoate thoughts to Sarah Chalfant of the Wylie Agency—and it would almost certainly not exist if Sarah had not then tracked me down and spurred me, patiently but relentlessly, to produce an actual proposal. Scott Moyers, during his stint at the Wylie Agency, held my hand through some dark times, providing both wisdom and invaluable practical advice. Andrew Wylie is as legend has him: a great and fearsome agent—you want him on your side. No one is a greater champion of writers than Andrew.

Marty Asher, a sympathetic editor, immediately grasped what I was trying to do, and his enthusiasm for the book brought it to Knopf. Marty's warmth and his many kindnesses sustained the book (and me) through some difficult stretches.

I owe Sonny Mehta triply: first for signing off on Marty's original acquisition of the book; second for his patience as the writing dragged on; and third for assigning the manuscript to Dan Frank for editing. Dan's ministrations made this book so much better. I have worked as an editor for twenty years, so I like to think I know good editing when I encounter it: Dan is a brilliant editor and a kind man. Amy Schroeder helped untangle my prose. Jill Verrillo, Gabrielle Brooks, Jonathan Lazzara, and Betsy Sallee, among others, make it a pleasure to be a Knopf author.

I am grateful for fellowships at the Yaddo and MacDowell colonies, which gave me time and space to work.

Lots of people contributed ideas, steered me to useful sources, or provided support in other ways: Anne Connell, Meehan Crist, Kathy Crutcher, Toby Lester, Joy de Menil, Nancy Milford, Cullen Murphy, Justine Rosenthal, Alex Starr, and Graeme Wood. Alane Mason, Jill Kneerim, and Paul Elie all provided helpful early feedback on the book proposal before it was fully formed. Alies Muskin, executive director at the Anxiety and Depression Association of America, was generous with her time and her Rolodex.

My brother-in-law, Jake Pueschel, provided valuable research assistance, tracking down hundreds of scholarly articles for me and, more essentially, helped me to process and interpret my genetic data. Jake's parents, my mother- and father-in-law Barbara and Kris Pueschel, provided both child care and moral support—and tolerated my too-frequent absences from family events while I raced to meet deadlines.

At *The Atlantic*, I am grateful to colleagues (and former colleagues) who endured my periodic absences and filled in for me while I worked on the book, among them Bob Cohn, James Fallows, Geoff Gagnon, James Gibney, Jeffrey Goldberg, Corby Kummer, Chris Orr, Don Peck, Ben Schwarz, Ellie Smith, and Yvonne Rolzhausen. (On the business side, *Atlantic* president Scott Havens, Atlantic Media president Justin Smith, and Atlantic Media chairman and owner David Bradley showed blessed forbearance in allowing me time to work on this book.) More than any other *Atlantic* colleagues, though, I owe Jennifer Barnett, Maria Streshinsky, and James Bennet, who were exceedingly generous in working around the problems my absences caused. I worry I've taken years off James's life.

Despite everything, I am grateful to Dr. L., Dr. M., Dr. Harvard, Dr. Stanford, and various other therapists and social workers and hypnotists and pharmacologists who are not named or got left on the cutting room floor. I am unreservedly and ongoingly grateful to Dr. W.: thank you for helping keep me afloat.

I want to thank my family—especially my dad, my mom, my sister, and my grandfather. I love them all. None of them (with the qualified exception of my father) were happy I was writing this book—and they were all even unhappier to be included in it themselves. (I am especially grateful to my father for sharing his diary with me.) I have tried to be as accurate and objective as my memory and the limited documentary record permit. Some family members would dispute aspects of what I have written here. I worry that some in my family view my revelations about Chester Hanford as a desecration of his memory and a posthumous despoiling of his dignity. For what it's worth, I respect him tremendously, and I hope that in my own anxious struggle I can live up to the standards of grace, decency, kindness, and perseverance he embodied. (I owe special thanks to my grandfather, who—though he made clear he didn't want to know what was in his father's psychiatric records—was willing to let me find out and helped me navigate probate court to secure them.)

As ever, my deepest thanks go to my wife, Susanna. Early on, she logged many hours at the National Institutes of Health Library, tracking down scientific articles and books. She also went far beyond any reasonable expectation of spousal support in helping me fight through legal thickets and bureaucratic impediments to gain access to the mental health records of my great-grandfather. Most important, if you've read this book, you know that holding me together can sometimes be challenging, unrewarding work. That work falls most heavily on Susanna—and for that I owe her more than I can ever repay.

Notes

CHAPTER I: THE NATURE OF ANXIETY

8 accounting for 31 percent of the expenditures: Figure on anxiety and mental health care expenditures comes from "The Economic Burdens of Anxiety Disorders in the 1990s," a comprehensive report published in *The Journal of Clinical Psychiatry* 60, no. 7 (July 1999).

8 "lifetime incidence" of anxiety disorder: Ronald Kessler, an epidemiologist at Harvard, has spent decades studying this. See, for instance, his paper "Lifetime Prevalence and Age-of-Onset Distributions of DSM-IV Disorders in the National Comorbidity Survey Replication," *Archives of General Psychiatry* 62, no. 6 (June 2005): 593–602.

8 A study published: R. C. Kessler et al., "Prevalence and Effects of Mood Disorders on Work Performance in a Nationally Representative Sample of U.S. Workers," *The American Journal of Psychiatry* 163 (2006): 1561–68. See also "Economic Burdens."

8 the median number of days: U.S. Bureau of Labor Statistics, "Table R67: Number and Percent Distribution of Nonfatal Occupational Injuries and Illnesses Involving Days Away from Work by Nature of Injury or Illness and Number of Days Away from Work, 2001."

8 Americans filled fifty-three million prescriptions: *Drug Topics,* March 2006.

8 Xanax prescriptions jumped 9 percent nationally: "Taking the Worry Cure," *Newsweek,* February 24, 2003. See also Restak, *Poe's Heart,* 185.

8 the economic crash caused prescriptions: Report from Wolters Kluwer Health, a medical information company, cited in Restak, *Poe's Heart,* 185.

9 A report published in 2009: Mental Health Foundation, *In the Face of Fear,* April 2009, 3–5.

9 A recent paper: "Prevalence, Severity, and Unmet Need for Treatment of Mental Disorders in the World Health Organization World Mental Health Surveys," *The Journal of the American Medical Association* 291 (June 2004): 2581–90.

9 A comprehensive global review: "Prevalence and Incidence Studies of Anxiety Disorders: A Systematic Review of the Literature," *The Canadian Journal of Psychiatry* 51 (2006): 100–13.

9 other studies have reported similar findings: For instance, "Global Prevalence

of Anxiety Disorders: A Systematic Review and Meta-regression," *Psychological Medicine* 10 (July 2012): 1–14.

9   Primary care physicians report: See, for instance, "Content of Family Practice: A Data Bank for Patient Care, Curriculum, and Research in Family Practice—526,196 Patient Problems," *The Journal of Family Practice* 3 (1976): 25–68.

9   One large-scale study from 1985: "The Hidden Mental Health Network: Treatment of Mental Illness by Non-psychiatric Physicians," *Archives of General Psychiatry* 42 (1985): 89–94.

9   one in three patients complained: "Panic Disorder: Epidemiology and Primary Care," *The Journal of Family Practice* 23 (1986): 233–39.

9   20 percent of primary care patients: "Quality of Care of Psychotropic Drug Use in Internal Medicine Group Practices," *Western Journal of Medicine* 14 (1986): 710–14.

11 "Woody Allen gene": See, for instance, Peter D. Kramer, "Tapping the Mood Gene," *The New York Times,* July 26, 2003. See also Restak, *Poe's Heart,* 204–12.

11 "The real excitement here": Thomas Insel, "Heeding Anxiety's Call" (lecture, May 19, 2005).

13 "as vain as a child's story": Roccatagliata, *History of Ancient Psychiatry,* 38.

14 "if one's body and mind": Maurice Charlton, "Psychiatry and Ancient Medicine," in *Historical Derivations of Modern Psychiatry,* 16.

14 "All that philosophers have written": Charlton, "Psychiatry and Ancient Medicine," 12.

17 One study found that children: See, for instance, Rachel Yehuda et al., "Transgenerational Effects of Posttraumatic Stress Disorder in Babies of Mothers Exposed to the World Trade Center Attacks During Pregnancy," *The Journal of Clinical Endocrinology and Metabolism* 90, no. 7 (July 2005): 4115 Rachel Yehuda et al., "Gene Expression Patterns Associated with Posttraumatic Stress Disorder Following Exposure to the World Trade Center Attacks," *Biological Psychiatry* 66(7)(2009): 708–11.

17 "Myself and fear were born twins": Quoted in Hunt, *Story of Psychology,* 72.

18 There's also evidence that: See, for instance, "The Relationship Between Intelligence and Anxiety: An Association with Subcortical White Matter Metabolism," *Frontiers in Evolutionary Neuroscience* 3, no. 8 (February 2012). (Also on high Jewish IQ: Steven Pinker, who in 2007 gave a lecture called "Jews, Genes, and Intelligence," says "their average IQ has been measured at 108 to 115." Richard Lynn, author of the 2004 article "The Intelligence of American Jews," says Jewish intelligence is half a standard deviation higher than the European average. Henry Harpending, Jason Hardy, and Gregory Cochran, University of Utah authors of the 2005 research report "Natural History of Ashkenazi Intelligence," state that their subjects "score .75 to 1.0 standard deviations above the general European average, corresponding to an IQ of 112–115.")

19 An influential study: "The Relation of Strength of Stimulus to Rapidity of Habit-Formation," *The Journal of Comparative Neurology and Psychology* 18 (1908): 459–82.

19 "We then face the prospect": *Los Angeles Examiner,* November 4, 1957, quoted in Tone, *Age of Anxiety,* 87.

19 "Van Gogh, Isaac Newton": *Los Angeles Examiner,* March 23, 1958, quoted in Tone, *Age of Anxiety,* 87.

19 "Without anxiety, little would be accomplished": Barlow, *Anxiety and Its Disorders,* 9.

22 "I awoke morning after morning": James, *Varieties of Religious Experience,* 134.

28 Petraeus . . . "rarely feels stress at all": Steve Coll, "The General's Dilemma," *The New Yorker,* September 8, 2008.

CHAPTER 2: WHAT DO WE TALK ABOUT WHEN WE TALK ABOUT ANXIETY?

35 "usually linked with a strong": Jaspers, *General Psychopathology,* 113–14.

36 "a sense of foreboding": Lifton, *Protean Self,* 101.

36 "the internal precondition of sin": Niebuhr, *Nature and Destiny,* vol. 1, 182.

36 "the most pervasive psychological phenomenon": Hoch and Zubin, *Anxiety,* v.

36 "The mentalistic and multi-referenced term": Theodore R. Sarbin, "Anxiety: Reification of a Metaphor," *Archives of General Psychiatry* 10 (1964): 630–38.

36 "to feelings": Kagan, *What Is Emotion?,* 41.

37 "as wine to vinegar": See, for instance, "Three Essays on the Theory of Sexuality," in Freud, *Basic Writings.*

37 "with a manual stimulation": Quoted in Roccatagliatia, *History of Ancient Psychiatry,* 204.

37 "It is almost disgraceful": Freud, *Problem of Anxiety,* 60.

38 "When a mother is afraid": Horney, *Neurotic Personality,* 41.

39 Studies of the: *DSM-II:* See, for instance, R. Spitzer and J. Fleiss, "A Re-analysis of the Reliability of Psychiatric Diagnosis," *The British Journal of Psychiatry* 125 (1974): 341–47; Stuart A. Kirk and Herb Kutchins, "The Myth of the Reliability of *DSM,*" *Journal of Mind and Behavior* 15, nos. 1–2 (1994): 71–86.

40 "stress tradition": For more on the stress tradition, see the section "Anxiety and the Stress Tradition" in Horwitz and Wakefield, *All We Have to Fear,* 200–4.

40 "a sister, *fidus Achates*": Burton, *Anatomy,* 261.

40 "are affrighted still": Ibid., 431.

40 "Don't allow the sum total": Breggin, *Medication Madness,* 331.

42 Moreover, the brain of a research subject: Kagan, *What Is Emotion?,* 83.

43 humans whose amygdalae get damaged: See, for instance, "Fear and the Amygdala," *The Journal of Neuroscience* 15, no. 9 (September 1995): 5879–91.

44 "the final and most exciting contest": Cannon, *Bodily Changes,* 74.

45 "The progress from brute to man": James, *Principles of Psychology,* 415.

45 "One day": Quoted in Fisher, *House of Wits,* 81.

47 "Contrary to the view of some humanists": LeDoux, *Emotional Brain,* 107.

47 Even *Aplysia californica:* This comes from the research of Eric Kandel, which is described in Barber, *Comfortably Numb,* 191–96.

47 "It is not obvious": Kagan, *What Is Emotion?,* 17.

47 "entering a seemingly involuntary state": Barlow, *Anxiety and Its Disorders,* 35.

48 "How many hippos worry": Sapolsky, *Zebras,* 182.

48 "A rat can't worry": Quoted in Stephen Hall, "Fear Itself," *The New York Times Magazine,* February 28, 1999.

51 "Theta activity is a rhythmic burst": Gray and McNaughton, *Neuropsychology of Anxiety*, 12.

53 "This remark of Plato": Maurice Charlton, "Psychiatry and Ancient Medicine," in Galdston, *Historic Derivations*, 15.

54 Meditation led to decreased density: G. Desbordes et al., "Effects of Mindful-Attention and Compassion Meditation Training on Amygdala Response to Emotional Stimuli in an Ordinary, Non-meditative State," *Frontiers of Human Neuroscience* 6 (2012): 292.

54 Other studies have found that Buddhist monks: See, for instance, Richard J. Davidson and Antoine Lutz, "Buddha's Brain: Neuroplasticity and Meditation," *IEEE Signal Processing Magazine* 25, no. 1 (January 2008): 174–76.

54 suppress their startle response: See, for instance, R. W. Levenson, P. Ekman, and M. Ricard, "Meditation and the Startle Response: A Case Study," *Emotion* 12, no. 3 (June 2012): 650–58; for additional context, see Tom Bartlett, "The Monk and the Gunshot," *The Chronicle of Higher Education*, August 21, 2012.

54 even old-fashioned talk therapy: Richard A. Friedman, "Like Drugs, Talk Therapy Can Change Brain Chemistry," *The New York Times*, August 27, 2002.

54 "My theory": William James first articulated this in "What Is an Emotion?," an article he published in *Mind*, a philosophy journal, in 1884.

55 When researchers at Columbia: S. Schachter and J. E. Singer, "Cognitive, Social, and Physiological Determinants of Emotional State," *Psychological Review* 69, no. 5 (1962): 379–99. Joseph LeDoux has a good description of this experi-ment, and of the history of the James-Lange theory, in *Emotional Brain*, 46–49.

55 "fear of death, conscience, guilt": Tillich, "Existential Philosophy," *Journal of the History of Ideas* 5, no. 1 (1944): 44–70. (This later appeared in Tillich's 1959 book *Theology of Culture*.)

57 the moment an anxious patient: See, for instance, Gabbard, "A Neurobiologi-cally Informed Perspective on Psychotherapy," *The British Journal of Psychiatry* 177 (2000): 11; A. Öhman and J. J. F. Soares, "Unconscious Anxiety: Phobic Responses to Masked Stimuli," *Journal of Abnormal Psychology* (1994); John T. Cacioppo et al., "The Psychophysiology of Emotion," *Handbook of Emotions* 2 (2000): 173–91.

58 Richard Burton could not bear: Shawn, *Wish*, 10.

59 how to eliminate fear responses in cats: Joseph Wolpe, *Psychotherapy by Reciprocal Inhibition* (Stanford, Calif.: Stanford University Press, 1958), 53–62.

61 "chimney sweeping": Breger, *Dream*, 29.

CHAPTER 3: A RUMBLING IN THE BELLY

69 "scare the hell out of the patient": David Barlow "Providing Best Treatments for Patients with Panic Disorder," Anxiety and Depression Association of American Annual Conference, Miami, March 24, 2006.

69 phobia cure rate of up to 85 percent: Lauren Slater, "The Cruelest Cure," *The New York Times*, November 2, 2003.

69 Barlow himself has a phobia: "A Phobia Fix," *The Boston Globe*, November 26, 2006.

70 "It's from 1979": J. K. Ritow, "Brief Treatment of a Vomiting Phobia," *American Journal of Clinical Hypnosis* 21, no. 4 (1979): 293–96.

75 "a phobia and a beef-steak": Northfield, *Conquest of Nerves*, 37.

75 as many as 12 percent: Harvard Medical School, *Sensitive Gut*, 71.

75 First identified in 1830: Ibid., 72.

75 In one well-known set of experiments: William E. Whitehead et al., "Tolerance for Rectosigmoid Distention in Irritable Bowel Syndrome," *Gastroenterology* 98, no. 5 (1990): 1187; William E. Whitehead, Bernard T. Engel, and Marvin M. Schuster, "Irritable Bowel Syndrome," *Digestive Diseases and Sciences* 25, no. 6 (1980): 404–13.

76 an article in the medical journal *Gut:* Ingvard Wilhelmsen. "Brain-Gut Axis as an Example of the Bio-psycho-social Model," *Gut* 47, supp. 4 (2000): 5–7.

77 "nervous in origin": Walter Cannon, "The Influence of Emotional States on the Functions of the Alimentary Canal," *The American Journal of the Medical Sciences* 137, no. 4 (April 1909): 480–86.

77 between 42 and 61 percent: Andrew Fullwood and Douglas A. Drossman, "The Relationship of Psychiatric Illness with Gastrointestinal Disease," *Annual Review of Medicine* 46, no. 1 (1995): 483–96.

77 40 percent overlap between patients: Robert G. Maunder, "Panic Disorder Associated with Gastrointestinal Disease: Review and Hypotheses," *Journal of Psychosomatic Research* 44, no. 1 (1998): 91.

78 "Fear brings about diarrhea": Quoted in Roccatagliata, *History of Ancient Psychiatry*, 106.

78 "People attacked by fear": Quoted in Sarason and Spielberger, *Stress and Anxiety*, vol. 2, 12.

79 "90 percent redness": Wolf and Wolff, *Human Gastric Function*, 112.

85 One of the more alarming: Richard W. Seim, C. Richard Spates, and Amy E. Naugle, "Treatment of Spasmodic Vomiting and Lower Gastrointestinal Distress Related to Travel Anxiety," *The Cognitive Behaviour Therapist* 4, no. 1 (2011): 30–37.

85 weeping at a sad play: Alvarez, *Nervousness*, 123.

85 The nervousness and hypersensitivity: Ibid., 266.

85 "The stomach specialist has to be": Ibid., 11.

85 "day and night for a week": Ibid., 22.

86 "a tense, high-pressure type of sales manager": Ibid., 17.

86 "the cruelest prank of nature": Ibid.

87 A study published in: Angela L. Davidson, Christopher Boyle, and Fraser Lauchlan, "Scared to Lose Control? General and Health Locus of Control in Females with a Phobia of Vomiting," *Journal of Clinical Psychology* 64, no. 1 (2008): 30–39.

88 As the British physician and philosopher: Tallis, *Kingdom of Infinite Space*, 193.

89 "Age 56–57": Quoted in Desmond and Moore, *Darwin*, 531.

89 "Diary of Health": Cited at length in Colp, *To Be an Invalid*, 43–53.

90 "knocked up": Desmond and Moore, *Darwin*, 530.

90 "We liked Dr. Chapman": Quoted in Colp, *To Be an Invalid*, 84.

91 "What the devil is this": Hooker, *Life and Letters of Joseph Dalton Hooker*, vol. 2, 72.

91 "Darwin's Illness Revealed": Anthony K. Campbell and Stephanie B. Matthews, "Darwin's Illness Revealed," *Postgraduate Medical Journal* 81, no. 954 (2005): 248–51.

91 "bad headache": Bowlby, *Charles Darwin*, 229.

91 "Charles Darwin and Panic Disorder": Thomas J. Barloon and Russell Noyes Jr., "Charles Darwin and Panic Disorder," *The Journal of the American Medical Association* 277, no. 2 (1997): 138–41.

91 "neurotic hands": Edward J. Kempf, "Charles Darwin—the Affective Sources of His Inspiration and Anxiety Neurosis," *The Psychoanalytic Review* 5 (1918): 151–92.

91 one pseudoscholarly paper: Jerry Bergman, "Was Charles Darwin Psychotic? A Study of His Mental Health" (Institute of Creation Research, 2010).

92 "the most miserable which I ever spent": Darwin, *Autobiography*, 28.

92 "I was out of spirits": Ibid., 28.

92 "I dread going anywhere": *Life and Letters of Charles Darwin*, vol. 1, 349.

92 "I have therefore been compelled": Darwin, *Autobiography*, 39.

92 He installed a mirror: Quammen, *Reluctant Mr. Darwin*, 62.

93 In addition to Dr. Chapman's ice treatment: Sources include Bowlby, *Charles Darwin*; Colp, *To Be an Invalid*; Desmond and Moore, *Darwin*; Browne, *The Power of Place*; and Quammen, *The Reluctant Mr. Darwin*; among others.

93 "a very bad form of vomiting": Bowlby, *Charles Darwin*, 300.

93 "I have been bad": Ibid., 335.

93 "I have been very bad": Ibid., 343.

93 "strive to suppress their feelings": Ibid., 11.

94 "I must tell you": Ibid., 375.

94 "Without you, when I feel sick": Desmond and Moore, *Darwin*, 358.

94 "O Mammy I do long": Bowlby, *Charles Darwin*, 282.

CHAPTER 4: PERFORMANCE ANXIETY

98 Starting when he was thirty: Oppenheim, *"Shattered Nerves,"* 114.

98 "To that": Davenport-Hines, *Pursuit of Oblivion*, 56.

98 "mystifying and scandalously sudden retirement": Quoted in Marshall, *Social Phobia*, 140.

99 "They . . . to whom a public examination": "Memoir of William Cowper," *Proceedings of the American Philosophical Society* 97, no. 4 (1953): 359–82.

99 "My head was reeling": Gandhi, *Autobiography*. (I was pointed to this source by chapter 5 of Taylor Clark's *Nerve*.)

99 "Thomas Jefferson, too, had his law career disrupted": All Jefferson material here is drawn from Joshua Kendall's *American Obsessives*, 21.

100 a career-ending panic attack: Mohr, *Gasping for Airtime*, 134.

100 "I had all these panic attacks": "Hugh Grant: Behind That Smile Lurks a Deadly Serious Film Star," *USA Today*, December 17, 2009.

100 Elfriede Jelinek, the Austrian novelist: "A Gloom of Her Own," *The New York Times Magazine*, November 21, 2004.

102 Sigmund Freud took cocaine to medicate: See, for instance, Kramer, *Freud,* 42.

102 The first case study of erythrophobia: Casper, Johann Ludwig, "Biographie d'une idée fixe" (translated into French, 1902), *Archives de Neurologie,* 13, 270-287.

102 "It is not a simple act": Darwin, *Expression,* 284.

103 "the soul might have sovereign power": Burgess, *Physiology or Mechanism of Blushing,* 49.

103 Writing in 1901, Paul Hartenberg: Hartenberg, *Les timides et la timidité* (Félix Alcon, 1901).

103 The term "social phobia" first appeared: Pierre Janet, *Les obsessions et la psychiatrie* (Alcan, 1903).

104 "the socially promoted show of shame": Ken-Ichiro Okano, "Shame and Social Phobia: A Transcultural Viewpoint," *Bulletin of the Menninger Clinic* 58, no. 3 (1994): 323-38.

105 In 1985, Liebowitz published an article: Michael Liebowitz et al., "Social Phobia," *Archives of General Psychiatry* 42, no. 7 (1985): 729-36.

105 As recently as 1994: "Disorders Made to Order," *Mother Jones,* July/August 2002.

107 One study has found: See Manjula et al., "Social Anxiety Disorder (Social Phobia)—a Review," *International Journal of Pharmacology and Toxicology* 2, no. 2 (2012): 55-59.

110 Studies at the University of Wisconsin: See Davidson et al., "While a Phobic Waits: Regional Brain Electrical and Autonomic Activity in Social Phobias During Anticipation of Public Speaking," *Biological Psychiatry* 47 (2000): 85-95.

111 "When I see anyone anxious": "On Anxiety," in Epictetus, *Discourses,* ch. 13.

112 Kathryn Zerbe, a psychiatrist: See, for instance, Kathryn J. Zerbe, "Uncharted Waters: Psychodynamic Considerations in the Diagnosis and Treatment of Social Phobia," *Bulletin of the Menninger Clinic* 58, no. 2 (1994): A3. See also Capps, *Social Phobia,* 120-25.

113 "Highly anxious people read facial expressions": "Anxious Adults Judge Facial Cues Faster, but Less Accurately," *Science News,* July 19, 2006.

113 "this barometer can cause them": "Whaddya Mean by That Look?," *Los Angeles Times,* July 24, 2006.

114 Arne Öhman, a Swedish neuroscientist: See, for instance, Arne Öhman, "Face the Beast and Fear the Face: Animal and Social Fears as Prototypes for Evolutionary Analyses of Emotion," *Psychophysiology* 23, no. 2 (March 1986): 123-45.

114 "doing something foolish": Marshall, *Social Phobia,* 50.

114 A National Institute of Mental Health study: K. Blair et al., *The American Journal of Psychiatry* 165, no. 9 (September 2008): 193-202; K. Blair et al., *Archives of General Psychiatry* 65, no. 10 (October 2008): 1176-84.

115 "Generalized-social-phobia-related dysfunction": K. Blair et al., "Neural Response to Self- and Other Referential Praise and Criticism in Generalized Social Phobia," *Archives of General Psychiatry* 65, no. 10 (October 2008): 1176-84.

115 they are not consciously aware of seeing: For instance, Murray B. Stein et al., "Increased Amygdala Activation to Angry and Contemptuous Faces in Generalized Social Phobia," *Archives of General Psychiatry* 59, no. 11 (2002): 1027.

116 "Unconsciously perceived signals of threat": Zinbarg et al., "Neural and Behavioral Evidence for Affective Priming from Unconsciously Perceived Emotional

Facial Expressions and the Influence of Trait Anxiety," *Journal of Cognitive Neuroscience* 20, no. 1 (January 2008): 95–107.

117   Murray Stein, a psychiatrist: Murray B. Stein, "Neurobiological Perspectives on Social Phobia: From Affiliation to Zoology," *Biological Psychiatry* 44, no. 12 (1998): 1277.

118   the social hierarchies of particular baboon populations: See, for instance, Robert Sapolsky, "Testicular Function, Social Rank and Personality Among Wild Baboons," *Psychoneuroendocrinology* 16, no. 4 (1991): 281–93; Robert Sapolsky, "The Endocrine Stress-Response and Social Status in the Wild Baboon," *Hormones and Behavior* 16, no. 3 (September 1982): 279–92; Robert Sapolsky, "Stress-Induced Elevation of Testosterone Concentrations in High Ranking Baboons: Role of Catecholamines," *Endocrinology* 118 no. 4 (April 1986): 1630.

118   the happiest-seeming and least stressed monkeys: Gesquiere et al., "Life at the Top: Rank and Stress in Wild Male Baboons," *Science* 333, no. 6040 (July 2011): 357–60.

119   monkeys with enhanced serotonergic function: See, for instance, Raleigh et al., "Serotonergic Mechanisms Promote Dominance Acquisition in Adult Male Vervet Monkeys," *Brain Research* 559, no. 2 (1991): 181–90.

119   altered serotonin function in certain brain regions: For instance, Lanzenberger et al., "Reduced Serotonin-1A Receptor Binding in Social Anxiety Disorder," *Biological Psychiatry* 61, no. 9 (May 2007): 1081–89.

119   Prozac and Paxil can be: See, for instance, van der Linden et al., "The Efficacy of the Selective Serotonin Reuptake Inhibitors for Social Anxiety Disorder (Social Phobia): A Meta-analysis of Randomized Controlled Trials," *International Clinical Psychopharmacology* 15, supp. 2 (2000): S15–23; Stein et al., "Serotonin Transporter Gene Promoter Polymorphism Predicts SSRI Response in Generalized Social Anxiety Disorder," *Psychopharmacology* 187, no. 1 (July 2006): 68–72.

119   when nonanxious, nondepressed people take SSRIs: See, for instance, Wai S. Tse and Alyson J. Bond, "Serotonergic Intervention Affects Both Social Dominance and Affiliative Behaviour," *Psychopharmacology,* 161 (2002): 324-330

119   the monkeys that rise the highest: See, for instance, Morgan et al., "Social Dominance in Monkeys: Dopamine D2 Receptors and Cocaine Self-Administration," *Nature Neuroscience* 5 (2002): 169–74; Morgan et al., "Predictors of Social Status in Cynomolgus Monkeys (*Macaca fascicularis*) After Group Formation," *American Journal of Primatology* 52, no. 3 (November 2118): 115–31.

119   people diagnosed with social anxiety disorder: See, for instance, Stein and Stein, "Social Anxiety Disorder," *Lancet* 371 (2008): 1115–25.

119   One 2008 study found that half: Arthur Kummer, Francisco Cardoso, and Antonio L. Teixeira, "Frequency of Social Phobia and Psychometric Properties of the Liebowitz Social Anxiety Scale in Parkinson's Disease," *Movement Disorders* 23, no. 12 (2008): 1739–43.

119   Multiple recent studies have found: See, for instance, Schneier et al., "Low Dopamine D2 Reception Binding Potential in Social Phobia," *The American Journal of Psychiatry* 157 (2000): 457–59.

120   Murray Stein, among others: Stein, Murray B., "Neurobiological Perspectives on Social Phobia: from Affiliation to Zoology," *Biological Psychiatry* 44, no. 12

(1998): 1277–85. See also David H. Skuse and Louise Gallagher, "Dopaminergic-Neuropeptide Interactions in the Social Brain," *Trends in Cognitive Sciences* 13, no. 1 (2009): 27–35.

121 where you fall on the spectrum: See, for instance, Seth J. Gillihan et al., "Association Between Serotonin Transporter Genotype and Extraversion," *Psychiatric Genetics* 17, no. 6 (2007): 351–54.

121 But Robert Sapolsky has found: Sapolsky, "Social Status and Health in Humans and Other Animals," *Annual Review of Anthropology* 33 (2004): 393–418.

121 In the late 1990s, Dirk Hellhammer: Dirk Helmut Hellhammer et al., "Social Hierarchy and Adrenocortical Stress Reactivity in Men," *Psychoneuroendocrinology* 22, no. 8 (1997): 643–50.

125 In 1908, two psychologists: Robert M. Yerkes and John D. Dodson, "The Relation of Strength of Stimulus to Rapidity of Habit-Formation," *The Journal of Comparative Neurology and Psychology* 18, no. 5 (1908): 459–82.

125 Bertoia . . . "couldn't hit and sometimes bobbled fielding plays": Tone, *The Age of Anxiety*, 113–14.

130 "like a song that got in my head": Quoted in Ballard, *Beautiful Game*, 76.

131 "disreturnophobia": "Strikeouts and Psych-Outs," *The New York Times Magazine*, July 7, 1991.

131 The explicit monitoring theory of choking: Sian L. Beilock and Thomas H. Carr, "On the Fragility of Skilled Performance: What Governs Choking Under Pressure?," *Journal of Experimental Psychology: General* 130, no. 4 (2001): 701.

131 Beilock has found that she can: For more on this, see Beilock, *Choke*.

132 a neural "traffic jam" of worry: Quoted in Clark, *Nerve*, 208.

133 "found himself in such disgrace": Herodotus, *Histories*, vol. 4, bk. 7.

133 inure their soldiers to anxiety: Gabriel, *No More Heroes*, 104.

133 and also valerian, a mild tranquilizer: Ibid., 139.

133 Researchers at Johns Hopkins University: "Stress Detector for Soldiers," *BBC World News*, May 29, 2002.

134 The *Anglo-Saxon Chronicle* recounts: Cited in Gabriel, *No More Heroes*, 51.

134 "at best a constitutionally inferior human being": Herman, *Trauma and Recovery*, 21.

134 A 1914 article: "The Psychology of Panic in War," *American Review of Reviews* 50 (October 1914): 629.

134 "hyperconsiderate professional attitude": Quoted in Barber, *Comfortably Numb*, 73.

134 "because only such a measure would prevent": Quoted in Bourke, *Fear*, 219.

134 "It is now time that our country": Ibid.

135 General George Patton of the U.S. Army denied: Shephard, *War of Nerves*, 219.

135 dishonorably discharged for cowardice: Jeffrey Gettleman, "Reduced Charges for Soldier Accused of Cowardice in Iraq," *The New York Times*, November 7, 2003.

135 the first person to be formally diagnosed: Jacob Mendes Da Costa, "On Irritable Heart: A Clinical Study of a Form of Functional Cardiac Disorder and Its Consequences," *The American Journal of the Medical Sciences* 121, no. 1 (1871): 2–52.

135 Studies of "self-soiling rates": Collins, *Violence*, 46.

135 A survey of one U.S. combat division: Paul Fussell, "The Real War, 1939–45," *The Atlantic,* August 1989.

136 Another survey of World War II infantrymen: Kaufman, "'Ill Health' as an Expression of Anxiety in a Combat Unit," *Psychosomatic Medicine* 9 (March 1947): 108.

136 "Hell . . . all that proves": Quoted in Clark, *Nerve,* 234.

136 "I could feel a twitching": Manchester, *Goodbye, Darkness,* 5.

136 "Now, those who fail to register": Christopher Hitchens, "The Blair Hitch Project," *Vanity Fair,* February 2011.

136 needed a man "with iron nerve": Alvarez, *Nervousness,* 18.

137 Comprehensive studies conducted during World War II: See, for instance, Grinker and Spiegel, *Men Under Stress.*

138 "These people will be able to collect": Leach, *Survival Psychology,* 24.

138 "uncontrolled weeping": Ibid., 25.

138 civilians with preexisting neurotic disorders: Janis, *Air War,* 80.

138 "Neurotics turned out to be": Bourke, *Fear,* 231.

138 "looking as worried as they have felt": Felix Brown, "Civilian Psychiatric Air-Raid Casualties," *The Lancet* 237, no. 6144 (May 1941): 689.

138 One fascinating study of stress: V. A. Kral, "Psychiatric Observations Under Severe Chronic Stress," *The American Journal of Psychiatry* 108 (1951): 185–92.

139 "unprecedented in over 30 years": Kathleen E. Bachynski et al., "Mental Health Risk Factors for Suicides in the US Army, 2007–8," *Injury Prevention* 18, no. 6 (2012): 405–12.

139 more than 10 percent of Afghanistan veterans: Hoge et al., "Mental Health Problems, Use of Mental Health Services, and Attrition from Military Service After Returning from Deployment to Iraq or Afghanistan," *JAMA* 259, no. 9 (2006): 1023–32.

140 army veterans diagnosed with post-traumatic stress disorder: Boscarino, Joseph, "Post-traumatic Stress Disorder and Mortality Among U.S. Army Veterans 30 Years After Military Service," *Annals of Epidemiology* 16, no. 4 (2006): 248–56.

140 the suicide rate reached a ten-year high: "Mike Mullen on Military Veteran Suicide," Huffington Post, July 2, 2012.

141 "were some of the greatest": Charles A. Morgan et al., "Relationship Among Plasma Cortisol, Catecholamines, Neuropeptide Y, and Human Performance During Exposure to Uncontrollable Stress," *Psychosomatic Medicine* 63, no. 3 (2001): 412–22.

141 Some individuals with high NPY: "Intranasal Neuropeptide Y May Offer Therapeutic Potential for Post-traumatic Stress Disorder," *Medical Press,* April 23, 2013.

141 Administering NPY via a nasal spray: Charles A. Morgan III et al., "Trauma Exposure Rather Than Posttraumatic Stress Disorder Is Associated with Reduced Baseline Plasma Neuropeptide-Y Levels," *Biological Psychiatry* 54, no. 10 (2003): 1087–91.

142 Researchers at the University of Michigan: Brian J. Mickey et al., "Emotion Processing, Major Depression, and Functional Genetic Variation of Neuropeptide Y," *Archives of General Psychiatry* 68, no. 2 (2011): 158.

142 with more glucocorticoid receptors: Mirjam van Zuiden et al., "Pre-existing High Glucocorticoid Receptor Number Predicting Development of Posttraumatic Stress Symptoms After Military Deployment," *The American Journal of Psychiatry* 168, no. 1 (2011): 89–96.

143 "[Russell] used to throw up all the time": George Plimpton, "Sportsman of the Year Bill Russell," *Sports Illustrated*, December 23, 1968.

144 he ordered that the pregame warm-up: See, for instance, John Taylor, *The Rivalry: Bill Russell, Wilt Chamberlain, and the Golden Age of Basketball* (New York: Random House, 2005).

144 "one of the great mysteries in the history of sport": "Lito Sheppard Says Donovan McNabb Threw Up in the Super Bowl," *CBSPhilly*, July 8, 2013.

145 "You must wonder what makes a man": Gay Talese, "The Loser," *Esquire*, March 1964.

145 Hoping to conquer his anxiety: This section on Pisa in wartime is drawn from Arieti, *Parnas*.

CHAPTER 5: "A SACK OF ENZYMES"

153 Reportedly, it did: "Restless Gorillas," *Boston Globe*, September 28, 2003; "Restless and Caged, Gorillas Seek Freedom," *Boston Globe*, September 29, 2003.

154 "In my last serious depression": Quoted in, among many other places, Kramer, *Freud*, 33. For more on Freud's use of cocaine, see Markel, *An Anatomy of Addiction*.

155 "I take very small doses": Davenport-Hines, *Pursuit of Oblivion*, 154.

155 It is an irony of medical history: This irony has been noted by Peter Kramer, among others.

156 they were ingesting alcohol: Tone, *Age of Anxiety*, 10.

156 "a suitable form of alcohol": Quoted in Shorter, *Before Prozac*, 15.

156 The 1899 edition of *The Merck Manual:* Tone, *Age of Anxiety*, 10.

158 "quick-cure nostrums": Topics of the Times, *The New York Times*, January 23, 1906.

158 *The Merck Manual* was still recommending: Tone, *Age of Anxiety*, 22.

158 "more of a menace to society": Quoted in Tone, *Age of Anxiety*, 25.

158 But when Frank Berger: Much of the history of Frank Berger and Miltown in these pages draws heavily from Andrea Tone's *Age of Anxiety*, Edward Shorter's *Before Prozac*, and Mickey Smith's *Small Comfort*.

159 "The mold is as temperamental": Quoted in Tone, *Age of Anxiety*, 34.

159 "The compound had a quieting effect": Taylor Manor Hospital, *Discoveries in Biological Psychiatry*, 122.

160 "We had about twenty Rhesus": Quoted in Tone, *Age of Anxiety*, 43.

160 "individuals who are pleasantly": Henry H. Dixon et al., "Clinical Observations on Tolserol in Handling Anxiety Tension States," *The American Journal of the Medical Sciences* 220, no. 1 (1950): 23–29.

161 The New Jersey psychiatrist reported back: Borrus, "Study of Effect of Miltown (2-Methyl-2-n-Propyl-1,3-Propoanediol Dicarbamate) on Psychiatric States," *The Journal of the American Medical Association*, April 30, 1955, 1596–98.

161 The psychiatrist in Florida: Lowell Selling, "Clinical Use of a New Tranquilizing Drug," *The Journal of the American Medical Association,* April 30, 1955, 1594–96.

161 "You are out of your mind": Quoted in Tone, *Age of Anxiety,* 52.

162 Carter Products sold only $7,500: "Onward and Upward with the Arts: Getting There First with Tranquility," *The New Yorker,* May 3, 1958.

162 In December, Americans bought $500,000: Restak, *Poe's Heart,* 187.

162 "If there's anything this movie business needs": Quoted in Tone, *Age of Anxiety,* 57.

162 Lucille Ball's assistant kept a supply: Tone, *Age of Anxiety,* 57.

162 "Miltowns, liquor, [and] swimming": Ibid.

162 The actress Tallulah Bankhead: Ibid., 58.

162 "Hi, I'm Miltown Berle": Restak, *Poe's Heart,* 187.

162 a $100,000 Miltown art installation: Tone, *Age of Anxiety,* 76.

163 "For the first time in history": Restak, *Poe's Heart,* 187.

163 "be of markedly greater import": Testimony of Nathan S. Kline, *False and Misleading Advertisements (Prescription Tranquilizing Drugs): Hearings Before a Subcommittee of the Committee on Government Operations,* 4.

163 Kline told a journalist: "Soothing, but Not for Businessmen," *BusinessWeek,* March 10, 1956.

164 By 1960, some 75 percent: Tone, *Age of Anxiety,* 90.

165 "tense, anxious, Mediterranean-type patients": Shorter, *History of Psychiatry,* 248.

165 "the insulin of the nervous": Shorter, *Before Prozac,* 49.

165 "This stuff is so good": Valenstein, *Blaming the Brain,* 27.

166 "the most dramatic breakthrough": Tone, *Age of Anxiety,* 80.

166 "No one in their right mind": Valenstein, *Blaming the Brain,* 27.

170 may have precipitated Wallace's downward spiral: See, for instance, D. T. Max, "The Unfinished," *The New Yorker,* March 9, 2009.

171 "was the first cure": Kline, *From Sad to Glad,* 122.

171 the "sparks" and the "soups": Valenstein, *Blaming the Brain,* 60–62.

172 "When I was an undergraduate student": Quoted in Abbott, Alison, "Neuroscience: The Molecular Wake-up Call," *Nature* 447, no. 7143 (2007): 368–70.

172 Gaddum took LSD: Shorter, *Before Prozac,* 69.

174 to give reserpine to *every single one:* Valenstein, *Blaming the Brain,* 69–70.

174 administering reserpine to rabbits: Healy, *Creation of Psychopharmacology,* 106, 205–6.

174 Brodie's 1955 paper: Alfred Pletscher, Parkhurst A. Shore, and Bernard B. Brodie, "Serotonin Release as a Possible Mechanism of Reserpine Action," *Science* 122, no. 3165 (1955): 374–75.

174 built a bridge from neurochemistry to behavior: Healy, *Antidepressant Era,* 148.

175 In one of its first advertisements: Shorter, *Before Prozac,* 52.

176 "Not infrequently the cure is complete": Roland Kuhn, "The Treatment of Depressive States with G 22355 (Imipramine Hydrochloride)," *The American Journal of Psychiatry* 115, no. 5 (1958): 459–64.

176 another accident of history: Healy, *Antidepressant Era,* 52, 58; Barondes, *Better Than Prozac,* 31–32; Shorter, *Before Prozac,* 61.

177 "These drugs seemed like magic to me": Shorter, *Before Prozac,* 62.

177 In 1965, he published an article: Joseph J. Schildkraut, "The Catecholamine

Hypothesis of Affective Disorders: A Review of Supporting Evidence," *The American Journal of Psychiatry* 122, no. 5 (1965): 509–22.

CHAPTER 6: A BRIEF HISTORY OF PANIC

182 "The anxiety he felt landing": Sheehan, *Anxiety Disease,* 37.

183 "We assumed it would be": Donald F. Klein, "Commentary by a Clinical Scientist in Psychopharmacological Research," *Journal of Child and Adolescent Psychopharmacology* 17, no. 3 (2007): 284–87.

183 significant or complete remission of their anxiety: Donald F. Klein, "Anxiety Reconceptualized," *Comprehensive Psychiatry* 21, no. 6 (1980): 411.

184 "The predominant American psychiatric theory": Quoted in Kramer, *Listening to Prozac,* 80.

185 an initial report on imipramine: Donald F. Klein and Max Fink, "Psychiatric Reaction Patterns to Imipramine," *The American Journal of Psychiatry* 119, no. 5 (1962): 432–38.

185 "like the proverbial lead balloon": Quoted in Kramer, *Listening to Prozac,* 84.

185 Subsequent articles over the next several years: Donald F. Klein, "Delineation of Two Drug-Responsive Anxiety Syndromes," *Psychopharmacology* 5, no. 6 (1964): 397–408; Klein and Oaks, "Importance of Psychiatric Diagnosis in Prediction of Clinical Drug Effects," *Archives of General Psychiatry* 16, no. 1 (1967): 118.

186 "the reaction of the individual's ego": Quoted in Kramer, *Listening to Prozac,* 84.

187 "It is hard to recall": Kramer, *Listening to Prozac,* 77.

187 An advertisement for an October 1956 public talk: Tone, *The Age of Anxiety,* 111.

189 "In this manner we were able": Shorter, *History of Psychiatry,* 105.

189 Actually, one exception here was astrologers: MacDonald, *Mystical Bedlam,* 13–35.

190 "It is the task of the APA": Caplan, *They Say You're Crazy,* 234.

190 "a book of tentatively assembled agreements": Kutchins and Kirk, *Making Us Crazy,* 28.

191 "As the wine flowed": David Sheehan, "Rethinking Generalized Anxiety Disorder and Depression" (remarks at a meeting of the Anxiety Disorders of America Association, Savannah, Ga., March 7, 2008).

192 "Invent a new tranquilizer": The account of Sternbach's discoveries is drawn from, among other sources, Baenninger et al., *Good Chemistry,* 65–78; Tone, *Age of Anxiety,* 120–40.

193 "We thought that the expected negative result": Leo Sternbach, "The Discovery of Librium," *Agents and Actions* 2 (1972): 193–96.

193 tamed a wild lynx with Librium: Smith, *Small Comfort,* 74.

193 "The Drug That Tames Tigers": Quoted in Davenport-Hines, *Pursuit of Oblivion,* 327.

193 "slightly soft in the knees": Tone, *Age of Anxiety,* 130.

193 88 percent of those with "free-floating anxiety": Joseph M. Tobin and Nolan D. C. Lewis, "New Psychotherapeutic Agent, Chlordiazepoxide Use in Treatment of Anxiety States and Related Symptoms," *The Journal of the American Medical Association* 174, no. 10 (1960): 1242–49.

194 "the most significant advance to date": Harry H. Farb, "Experience with Librium in Clinical Psychiatry," *Diseases of the Nervous System* 21 (1960): 27.

194 "the treatment of common anxieties": Shorter, *Before Prozac*, 100.

194 Librium had the same range: M. Marinker, "The Doctor's Role in Prescribing," *The Journal of the Royal College of General Practitioners* 23, supp. 2 (1973): 26.

194 Valium became the first drug: Restak, *Poe's Heart*, 191.

194 one in every five women: Valenstein, *Blaming the Brain*, 56.

194 18 percent of all American *physicians*: George E. Vaillant, Jane R. Brighton, and Charles McArthur, "Physicians' Use of Mood-Altering Drugs: A 20-Year Follow-up Report." *The New England Journal of Medicine* (1970).

194 "It is ten years since Librium": Quoted in Smith, *Small Comfort*, 113.

195 "Whether the increase": Hollister, *Clinical Use of Psychotherapeutic Drugs*, 111.

196 "One must consider the broader implications": D. Jacobs, "The Psychoactive Drug Thing: Coping or Cop Out?," *Journal of Drug Issues* 1 (1971): 264–68.

196 "35, single and psychoneurotic": See, for instance, *The American Journal of Psychiatry* 126 (1970): 1696. The advertisement also ran in the *Archives of General Psychiatry*.

196 "the arrival of the millennium": Quoted in Smith, *Small Comfort*, 91.

198 "Valium, Librium, and other drugs": Quoted in Whitaker, *Anatomy of an Epidemic*, 137.

198 the brains of people who took tranquilizers: M. H. Lader, M. Ron, and H. Petursson, "Computed Axial Brain Tomography in Long-Term Benzodiazepine Users," *Psychological Medicine* 14, no. 1 (1984): 203–6. For additional overview, see "Brain Damage from Benzodiazepines," *Psychology Today*, November 18, 2010.

CHAPTER 7: MEDICATION AND THE MEANING OF ANXIETY

208 By 2002, according to one estimate: M. N. Stagnitti, *Trends in Antidepressant Use by the U.S. Civilian Non-institutionalized Population, 1997 and 2002*, Statistical Brief 76 (Rockville, Md.: Agency for Healthcare Research and Quality, May 2005).

209 a 2007 estimate put the number: United Press International, "Study: Psych Drugs Sales Up," March 28, 2007.

209 Trace elements of Prozac: See, for instance, "In Our Streams: Prozac and Pesticides," *Time*, August 25, 2003; "River Fish Accumulate Human Drugs," *Nature News Service*, September 5, 2003; "Frogs, Fish, and Pharmaceuticals: A Troubling Brew," CNN.com, November 14, 2003; "Prozac in the Water," *Governing* 19, no. 12 (September 2006); "Fish on Prozac Are Violent and Obsessive," Smithsonian.com, November 12, 2012.

209 "Considering the benefit and the risk": Healy, *Let Them Eat Prozac*, 39.

209 A series of studies in the 1980s: Breggin, *Talking Back to Prozac,* 49. See also Healy, *Let Them Eat Prozac*, 37.

210 "This": Shorter, *Before Prozac*, 172.

210 In 2006, Einar Hellbom: Einar Hellbom, "Chlorpheniramine, Selective Serotonin-Reuptake Inhibitors (SSRIs) and Over-the-Counter (OTC) Treatment," *Medical Hypotheses* 66, no. 4 (2006): 689–90. See also Einar Hellbom and

Mats Humble, "Panic Disorder Treated with the Antihistamine Chlorphenira-mine," *Annals of Allergy, Asthma, and Immunology* 90 (2003): 361.

211 David Wong, an Eli Lilly biochemist: Healy, *Let Them Eat Prozac,* 39.

211 a branding firm had thought: "Eternal Sunshine," *The Observer,* May 12, 2007.

212 "It is now clear": Quoted in Barber, *Comfortably Numb,* 55.

213 "Paxil is truly addictive": Quoted in Shorter, *Before Prozac,* 44.

213 "do not have a clinically meaningful": Joanna Moncrieff and Irving Kirsch, "Efficacy of Antidepressants in Adults," *British Medical Journal* 331, no. 7509 (2005): 155.

213 "If you're born around World War I": Quoted in Barber, *Comfortably Numb,* 106.

214 In Iceland, the incidence of depression: Tómas Helgason, Helgi Tómasson, and Tómas Zoega, "Antidepressants and Public Health in Iceland: Time Series Analysis of National Data," *The British Journal of Psychiatry* 184, no. 2 (2004): 157–62.

214 Britain reported 38 million: Joanna Moncrieff and Joceline Pomerleau, "Trends in Sickness Benefits in Great Britain and the Contribution of Mental Disorders," *Journal of Public Health* 22, no. 1 (2000): 59–67.

214 depression tripled in the 1990s: Robert Rosenheck, "The Growth of Psycho-pharmacology in the 1990s: Evidence-Based Practice or Irrational Exuberance," *International Journal of Law and Psychiatry* 28, no. 5 (2005): 467–83.

214 *1,000 percent increase:* See, for instance, Healy, *Let Them Eat Prozac,* 20. See also McHenry, "Ethical Issues in Psychopharmacology," *Journal of Medical Ethics* 32 (2006): 405–10.

214 the worldwide suicide rate has increased: www.who.int.

215 if a drug makes you feel good: Greenberg, *Manufacturing Depression,* 193.

215 "Psychotherapeutically": Gerald L. Klerman, "A Reaffirmation of the Efficacy of Psychoactive Drugs," *Journal of Drug Issues* 1 (1971): 312–19.

216 "Americans believe tranquilizers are effective": Dean I. Manheimer et al., "Popular Attitudes and Beliefs About Tranquilizers," *The American Journal of Psychiatry* 130, no. 11 (1973): 1246–53.

217 only 38 percent of Americans: Mental Health America, Attitudinal Survey 2007.

217 only half had atypical levels of serotonin: Marie Asberg et al., "'Serotonin Depression'—a Biochemical Subgroup Within the Affective Disorders?," *Science* 191, no. 4226 (1976): 478–80.

218 "abandon the simplistic hypothesis": "CINP Meeting with the Nobels, Montreal, Canada, June 25, 2002: Speaker's Notes—Dr. Arvid Carlsson," *Collegium Internationale Neuro-Psychopharmacologicum Newsletter* (March 2003).

218 Not long ago, George Ashcroft: L. McHenry, "Ethical Issues in Psychopharmacology," *Journal of Medical Ethics* 32, no. 7 (2006): 405–10.

218 "the evidence does not support": Valenstein, *Blaming the Brain,* 96.

218 "We have hunted for big simple": Kenneth S. Kendler, "Toward a Philosophical Structure for Psychiatry," *The American Journal of Psychiatry* 162, no. 3 (2005): 433–40. For more on the decaying of the serotonin hypothesis, see Jeffrey R. Lacasse and Jonathan Leo, "Serotonin and Depression: A Disconnect Between the Advertisements and the Scientific Literature," *PLoS Medicine* 2, no. 12 (2005): e392.

222 "If man can be reduced": Tolson, *Pilgrim,* 129.

223 "Yours is a mind": Quoted in Ibid., 191.

223 His opinion of biological psychiatry: Peter Kramer makes observations along these lines in *Listening to Prozac.*

223 "unable to account for the predicament": This essay is reprinted in Percy's collection *Signposts in a Strange Land.*

224 "We all know perfectly well": Quoted and discussed in, among other sources, Elie, *The Life You Save,* 276; Elliott and Chambers, *Prozac as a Way of Life,* 135.

CHAPTER 8: SEPARATION ANXIETY

230 "Fear disorders": Ron Kessler, "Comorbidity of Anxiety Disorders with Other Physical and Mental Disorders in the National Comorbidity Survey Replication" (presentation at ADAA conference, Savannah, Ga., March 7, 2008).

235 "Anxiety in children": Freud, *Three Essays.*

235 "souls burning in hell": Breger, *Dream of Undying Fame,* 9.

236 "libido toward matrem had awakened": Gay, *Freud,* 11.

236 "You yourself have seen": Breger, *Freud,* 18.

236 "subject to attacks of anxiety": Kramer, *Freud,* 20.

236 "a universal event in early childhood": *Complete Letters of Freud to Fliess,* 272.

239 "biological factor": Freud, *Problem of Anxiety,* 99.

239 "the human infant is sent": Ibid.

239 "loss of love": Ibid., 119.

240 "the atrophied remnants of innate preparedness": Ibid., 117.

241 "was a very stable background": Karen, *Becoming Attached,* 30.

241 "a sharp, hard, self-centered woman": Ibid., 31.

241 "could be seen as an indictment": Ibid.

242 "But there *is* such a thing": Bowlby, *Separation,* viii.

242 "a frightfully vain old woman": Karen, *Becoming Attached,* 44.

242 "an extremely anxious, distressed woman": Ibid., 45.

242 "The fact that this poor woman": Ibid.

245 When Ainsworth first arrived in Uganda: This account of Ainsworth's time in Uganda draws heavily on her book *Infancy in Uganda* and on chapter 11 of Robert Karen's *Becoming Attached.*

248 none of the ambivalently attached children: Karen, *Becoming Attached,* 180.

250 Konrad Lorenz's influential 1935 paper: Konrad Z. Lorenz, "The Companion in the Bird's World," *The Auk* 54, no. 3 (1937): 245–73.

250 "What's the use to psychoanalyze a goose?": Quoted in Karen, *Becoming Attached,* 107.

250 calls to "excommunicate" him: Issroff, *Winnicott and Bowlby,* 121.

251 published an article in: Harry Frederick Harlow, "The Nature of Love," *American Psychologist* (1958): 673–85.

252 "Thereafter": Bowlby, *Secure Base,* 26.

253 when infant monkeys were separated: See, for instance, Yvette Spencer-Booth and Robert A. Hinde, "Effects of 6 Days Separation from Mother on 18- to 32-Week-Old Rhesus Monkeys," *Animal Behaviour* 19, no. 1 (1971): 174–91.

253 A subsequent paper by Harry Harlow: Harry F. Harlow and Margaret Harlow, "Learning to Love," *American Scientist* 54, no. 3 (1966): 244–72.

253   "initiation of ventral contact": See, for instance, Stephen J. Suomi, "How Gene-Environment Interactions Can Shape the Development of Socioemotional Regulation in Rhesus Monkeys," *Emotional Regulation and Developmental Health: Infancy and Early Childhood* (2002): 5–26.

253   The idea behind the variable foraging demand: See, for instance, Mathew et al., "Neuroimaging Studies in Nonhuman Primates Reared Under Early Stressful Conditions," *Fear and Anxiety* (2004).

253   he died alcoholic and depressed: See, for instance, Blum, *Love at Goon Park.*

255   the amount of licking and grooming: See, for instance, Christian Caldji et al., "Maternal Care During Infancy Regulates the Development of Neural Systems Mediating the Expression of Fearfulness in the Rat," *Proceedings of the National Academy of Sciences* 95, no. 9 (1998): 5335–40.

255   lasting consequences on a primate's neurochemistry: See, for instance, Jeremy D. Coplan et al., "Variable Foraging Demand Rearing: Sustained Elevations in Cisternal Cerebrospinal Fluid Corticotropin-Releasing Factor Concentrations in Adult Primates," *Biological Psychiatry* 50, no. 3 (2001): 200–4.

255   There's even some evidence: See, for instance, Tamashiro, Kellie L. K., "Metabolic Syndrome: Links to Social Stress and Socioeconomic Status," *Annals of the New York Academy of Science* 1231, no. 1 (2011): 46–55.

256   the children and even grandchildren: See, for instance, Joel J. Silverman et al., "Psychological Distress and Symptoms of Posttraumatic Stress Disorder in Jewish Adolescents Following a Brief Exposure to Concentration Camps," *Journal of Child and Family Studies* 8, no. 1 (1999): 71–89.

256   A recent study published: Maselko et al., "Mother's Affection at 8 Months Predicts Emotional Distress in Adulthood," *Journal of Epidemiology & Community Health* 65, no. 7 (2011): 621–25.

257   a coping strategy based on "chronic vigilance": See, for instance, L. Alan Sroufe, "Attachment and Development: A Prospective, Longitudinal Study from Birth to Adulthood," *Attachment and Human Development* 7, no. 4 (2005): 349–67.

260   "Adults with agoraphobia are more likely": Corine de Ruiter and Marinus H. Van Ijzendoorn, "Agoraphobia and Anxious-Ambivalent Attachment: An Integrative Review," *Journal of Anxiety Disorders* 6, no. 4 (1992): 365–81.

260   "Adults with agoraphobia report": Dozier et al., "Attachment and Psychopathology in Adulthood," in *Handbook of Attachment,* 718–44.

260   "[Infants with insecure] attachments": Warren, et al., "Child and Adolescent Anxiety Disorders and Early Attachment," *Journal of the American Academy of Child & Adolescent Psychiatry* 36, no. 5 (1997): 637–44.

260   "Human adults who reported": Hane, Amie Ashley, and Nathan A. Fox, "Ordinary variations in maternal caregiving influence human infants' stress reactivity," *Psychological Science* 17.6 (2006): 550–556.

CHAPTER 9: WORRIERS AND WARRIORS

264   In 2001, Kenneth Kendler: Kenneth S. Kendler et al., "The Genetic Epidemiology of Irrational Fears and Phobias in Men," *Archives of General Psychiatry* 58, no. 3 (2001): 257. See also Kenneth S. Kendler, John Myers, and Carol A. Prescott,

"The Etiology of Phobias: An Evaluation of the Stress-Diathesis Model," *Archives of General Psychiatry* 59, no. 3 (2002): 242.

264 Meta-analyses of genetic studies: See, for instance, Hettema et al., "A Review and Meta-Analysis of the Genetic Epidemiology of Anxiety Disorders," *The American Journal of Psychiatry* 158, no. 10 (2001) 1568–78.

265 one of the largest-scale studies: Giovanni Salum, "Anxiety 'Density' in Families Predicts Disorders in Children" (presentation at ADAA conference, March 28, 2011).

266 "We believe that most of the children": quoted in Restak, *Poe's Heart,* 64; see also Kagan, *Unstable Ideas,* 161-163.

267 Kagan and his colleagues took brain scans: These studies are described in Robin Marantz Henig, "Understanding the Anxious Mind," *The New York Times Magazine,* September 29, 2009.

269 Mice whose *Grp* gene: See, for instance, Gleb P. Shumyatsky et al., "Identification of a Signaling Network in Lateral Nucleus of Amygdala Important for Inhibiting Memory Specifically Related to Learned Fear," *Cell* 111, no. 6 (2002): 905–18.

269 Mice whose stathmin gene: See, for instance, Gleb P. Shumyatsky et al., "Stathmin, a Gene Enriched in the Amygdala, Controls Both Learned and Innate Fear," *Cell* 123, no. 4 (2005): 697–709.

270 In one study of children: Smoller et al., "Influence of *RGS2* on Anxiety-Related Temperament, Personality, and Brain Function," *Archives of General Psychiatry* 65, no. 3 (2008): 298–308.

270 Another study, of 744 college students: Cited in Smoller et al., "Genetics of Anxiety Disorders: The Complex Road from DSM to DNA," *Depression and Anxiety* 26, no. 11 (2009): 965–75.

270 A third study revealed: Leygraf et al., "*RGS2* Gene Polymorphisms as Modulators of Anxiety in Humans," *Journal of Neural Transmission* 113, no. 12 (2006): 1921–25.

270 A fourth study, of 607 people: Koenen et al., "*RGS2* and Generalized Anxiety Disorder in an Epidemiologic Sample of Hurrican-Exposed Adults," *Depression and Anxiety* 26, no. 4 (2009): 309–15.

270 Lauren McGrath, a researcher: "Unique Study Identifies Gene Associated with Anxious Phenotypes," *Medscape News,* March 29, 2011.

271 "talent for creative dance performance": R. Bachner-Melman et al., "*AVPR1a* and *SLC6A4* Gene Polymorphisms Are Associated with Creative Dance Performance," *PLoS Genetics* 1, no. 3 (2005): e42.

273 tend to have a harder time: See, for instance, "Catechol O-methyltransferase Val158met Genotype and Neural Mechanisms Related to Affective Arousal and Regulation," *Archives of General Psychiatry* 63, no. 12 (2006): 1,396. Also, Montag et al., "COMT Genetic Variation Affects Fear Processing: Psychophysiological Evidence," *Behavioral Neuroscience* 122, no. 4 (1008): 901.

273 One study, conducted by investigators: Enoch et al., "Genetic Origins of Anxiety in Women: A Role for a Functional Catechol-o-methyltransferase Polymorphism," *Psychiatric Genetics* 13, no. 1 (2003): 33–41.

273 Another study, conducted among both: Armbruster et al., "Variation in Genes

Involved in Dopamine Clearance Influence the Startle Response in Older Adults," *Journal of Neural Transmission* 118, no. 9 (2011): 1281–92.

273 David Goldman, the chief of human neurogenetics: See, for instance, Stein et al., "Warriors versus Worriers: The Role of COMT Gene Variants," *CNS Spectrums* 11, no. 10 (2006): 745–48. Also, "Finding the 'Worrier-Warrior' Gene," *Philadelphia Inquirer,* June 2, 2003.

274 These different evolutionary strategies: Cited in Stein and Walker, *Triumph over Shyness,* 21.

274 Starting in the mid-1990s: For instance, Lesch, et al., "Association of Anxiety-Related Traits with a Polymorphism in the Serotonin Transporter Gene Regulatory Region," *Science* 274, no. 5292 (1996): 1527–31. Also, Hariri, Ahmad R., et al., "Serotonin Transporter Genetic Variation and the Response of the Human Amygdala." *Science* 297, no. 5580 (2002): 400–403. (For a good, non-technical overview of this research, see Dobbs, "The Science of Success," *The Atlantic,* December 2009.)

275 Ressler found that the variant: Charles F. Gillespie et al., "Risk and Resilience: Genetic and Environmental Influences on Development of the Stress Response," *Depression and Anxiety* 26, no. 11 (2009): 984–92. See also Rebekah G. Bradley et al., "Influence of Child Abuse on Adult Depression: Moderation by the Corticotropin-Releasing Hormone Receptor Gene," *Archives of General Psychiatry* 65, no. 2 (2008): 190; Kerry J. Ressler et al., "Polymorphisms in CRHR1 and the Serotonin Transporter Loci: Gene× Gene× Environment Interactions on Depressive Symptoms," *American Journal of Medical Genetics, Part B: Neuropsychiatric Genetics* 153, no. 3 (2010): 812–24.

275 Variations in this gene: Ibid. See also Elisabeth B. Binder et al., "Association of FKBP5 Polymorphisms and Childhood Abuse with Risk of Posttraumatic Stress Disorder Symptoms in Adults," *The Journal of the American Medical Association* 299, no. 11 (2008): 1291–305; Divya Mehta et al., "Using Polymorphisms in FKBP5 to Define Biologically Distinct Subtypes of Posttraumatic Stress Disorder: Evidence from Endocrine and Gene Expression Studies," *Archives of General Psychiatry* (2011): archgenpsychiatry-2011.

277 A 2005 study at San Diego State University: Stein, Murray B., Margaret Daniele Fallin, Nicholas J. Schork, and Joel Gelernter. "COMT Polymorphisms and Anxiety-related Personality Traits." *Neuropsychopharmacology* 30, no. 11 (2005): 2092–2102.

278 In the 1970s, Martin Seligman: Martin E. P. Seligman, "Phobias and Preparedness," *Behavior Therapy* 2, no. 3 (1971): 307–20.

279 monkeys could *not* easily acquire fears: Susan Mineka and Arne Öhman, "Born to Fear: Non-associative Vs. Associative Factors in the Etiology of Phobias," *Behaviour Research and Therapy* 40, no. 2 (2002): 173–84.

280 This is evidence, Öhman argues: Öhman and Mineka, "Fears, Phobias, and Preparedness: Toward an Evolved Module of Fear and Fear Learning," *Psychological Review* 108, no. 3 (2001): 483.

CHAPTER 10: AGES OF ANXIETY

295 "the brain-workers in almost every household": Beard, *A Practical Treatise,* 1.

296 "In the older countries": A. D. Rockwell, "Some Causes and Characteristics of Neurasthenia," *New York Medical Journal* 58 (1893): 590.

296 "American nervousness is the product": Beard, *American Nervousness,* 176.

297 "The Greeks were certainly civilized": Ibid., 96.

297 "modern, and originally American": Ibid., vii–viii.

297 "When civilization, plus these five factors": Ibid., 96.

298 The crucial concept in all these explanations: See, for instance, Micale, *Hysterical Men,* 23.

298 "I begin with the head and brain": Beard, *Practical Treatise,* 15.

298 "destroyed or made miserable": Quoted in Micale, *Hysterical Men,* 35.

298 "a veritable social plague": Quoted in Micale, *Hysterical Men,* 35.

299 "One of my patients tells me": Ibid., 53.

299 "One of my cases": Ibid., 54.

299 "One man was so afraid": Ibid., 60.

300 neurasthenia had permeated deep: For a detailed exploration of this, see Lutz, *American Nervousness;* Schuster, *Neurasthenic Nation.*

300 "overstressed nation": American Psychological Association, *Stress in America,* 2010.

300 increased from 13.4 million to 16.2 million: IMS Health Data, National Disease & Therapeutic Index, Diagnosis Visits, 2002–2006.

300 More Americans seek medical treatment: Ibid.

300 A study published in the *American Psychologist:* Swindle et al., "Responses to Nervous Breakdowns in America over a 40-year period," *American Psychologist* 55, no. 7 (2000): 740.

301 Twice as many people reported: Goodwin, Renee D., "The Prevalence of Panic Attacks in the United States: 1980 to 1995," *Journal of Clinical Epidemiology* 55, no. 9 (2003): 914–16.

301 the average college student in the 1990s: Twenge, *Generation Me,* 107.

301 "The average high school kid today": "How Big a Problem is Anxiety?" *Psychology Today,* April 30, 2008.

301 A World Health Organization survey: Kessler et al., "Lifetime Prevalence and Age-of-Onset Distributions of Mental Disorders in the World Health Organization's World Mental Health Survey Initiative," *World Psychiatry* 6, no. 3 (207): 168.

301 Statistics from the National Health Service: "Anxiety Disorders Have Soared Since Credit Crunch," *The Telegraph,* January 1, 2012.

301 "culture of fear": Mental Health Foundation, *Facing the Fear,* April 2009.

302 the odds in favor of damnation: LeGoff, *Medieval Civilization,* 325.

302 "The major problem for Americans": Slater, *Pursuit of Loneliness,* 24.

303 "the paradox of choice": Schwartz, *Paradox of Choice,* 2, 43.

303 "From the moment of birth": Fromm, *Escape from Freedom,* 41.

304 "First of all a feeling": Tillich, *Protestant Era,* 245.

304 "Fascism was like a jail": Quoted in May, *Meaning of Anxiety,* 12.

304 "It has filled the": *The New York Times,* February 1, 1948.

304 "people grasp at political authoritarianism": May, *Meaning of Anxiety,* 12.

304 "for 99 percent of human history": Sapolsky's discussion of this appears in *Zebras,* 378–83.

305 excessive timidity, caution, and concern: Kagan, *What Is Emotion?,* 14.

305 "Competitive individualism militates against": May, *Meaning of Anxiety*, 191.

306 "troubles herself with every thing": Hunter and Macalpine, *Three Hundred Years of Psychiatry*, 116.

306 "Intolerance of uncertainty appears to be": Michel J. Dugas, Mark H. Freeston, and Robert Ladouceur, "Intolerance of Uncertainty and Problem Orientation in Worry," *Cognitive Therapy and Research* 21, no. 6 (1997): 593–606.

306 a 31 percent increase: Scott Baker, Nicholas Bloom, and Steven Davis, "Measuring Economic Policy Uncertainty" (Chicago Booth Research Paper 13-02, 2013).

307 "nervous complaints prevail at the present day": Quoted in Oppenheim, *"Shattered Nerves,"* 14.

307 "At the beginning of the nineteenth century": Quoted in Micale, *Hysterical Men*, 81.

307 "atrocious and frightful symptoms": Cheyne, *The English Malady*, xxx.

308 "Other men get their knowledge": Burton, *Anatomy*, Book I, 34.

308 "I write of melancholy": Ibid., 21.

308 "Many lamentable effects this fear causeth": Ibid., 261.

309 "Many men are so amazed": Ibid.

309 "There is no greater cause": Ibid., 21.

309 "If men would attempt no more": Ibid., 50.

310 "In our day we still see": May, *Meaning of Anxiety*, xiv.

CHAPTER 11: REDEMPTION

320 Eliot was, Kagan observes: Kagan has made this observation in numerous places.

320 "saturated with the vocabulary": Micale, *Hysterical Men*, 214.

321 "whether among all those Scholars": Quoted in Ibid.

321 Dean Simonton, a psychologist: Simonton, "Are Genius and Madness Related? Comtemporary Answers to an Ancient Question," *Psychiatric Times* 22, no. 7 (2005): 21–23. See also "The Case for Pessimism," *Businessweek*, August 13, 2004.

322 But his early letters reveal otherwise: Letters quoted here are from Masson, *Complete Letters*.

323 "They're compulsive, they don't make errors": Quoted in Robin Marantz Henig, "Understanding the Anxious Mind," *The New York Times Magazine*, September 29, 2009.

323 A 2012 study by psychiatrists: Nicholas A. Turiano et al., "Big 5 Personality Traits and Interleukin-6: Evidence for 'Healthy Neuroticism' in a US Population Sample," *Brain, Behavior, and Immunity* (2012).

323 A 2013 study in the *Academy of Management Journal:* Corrine Bendersky and Neha Parikh Shah, "The Downfall of Extroverts and the Rise of Neurotics: The Dynamic Process of Status Allocation in Task Groups, Academy of Management Journal," AMJ-2011-0316.R3.

323 "I would staff it with more neurotics and fewer extroverts": "Leadership Tip: Hire the Quiet Neurotic, Not the Impressive Extrovert," *Forbes*, April 11, 2013.

323 In 2005, researchers at the University of Wales: Adam M. Perkins and Philip J. Corr, "Can Worriers Be Winners? The Association Between Worrying and Job Performance," *Personality and Individual Differences* 38, no. 1 (2005): 25–31.

324 high IQ scores correlated with high levels: Jeremy D. Coplan et al., "The Relationship Between Intelligence and Anxiety: An Association with Subcortical White Matter Metabolism," *Frontiers in Evolutionary Neuroscience* 3 (2012).

325 a certain interpersonal obtuseness: See Winifred Gallagher, "How We Become What We Are," *The Atlantic,* September 1994.

326 But recent studies on rhesus monkeys: Stephen J. Suomi, "Risk, Resilience, and Gene-Environment Interplay in Primates," *Journal of the Canadian Academy of Child and Adolescent Psychiatry* 20, no. 4 (November 2011): 289–97.

CHAPTER 12: RESILIENCE

330 the constant berating by Johnson's superego: Bate, *Samuel Johnson,* 117–27.

332 The ten critical psychological elements: Charney, "The Psychobiology of Resilience to Extreme Stress: Implications for the Treatment and Prevention of Anxiety Disorders," keynote address at ADAA conference, March 23, 2006.

336 the work of the cognitive psychologist: See, for instance, Albert Bandura, "Self-Efficacy: Toward a Unifying Theory of Behavioral Change," *Psychological Review* 84, 191–215; Albert Bandura, "The Assessment and Predictive Generality of Self-Percepts of Efficacy," *Journal of Behavior Therapy and Experimental Psychiatry* 13, 195–99.

Bibliography

Aboujaoude, Elias. *Compulsive Acts: A Psychiatrist's Tales of Ritual and Obsession.* Berkley: University of California Press, 2008.

Ackerman, Diane. *An Alchemy of Mind: The Marvel and Mystery of the Brain.* New York: Scribner, 2004.

Adler, Alfred. *The Neurotic Constitution: Outlines of a Comparative Individualistic Psychology and Psychotherapy.* Translated by Bernard Glueck. New York: Moffat, Yard, 1917.

———. *Problems of Neurosis.* New York: Cosmopolitan Book Corporation, 1930.

———. *Understanding Human Nature.* Greenberg Publishers, 1927.

Aggleton, John, ed. *The Amygdala: A Functional Analysis.* 2nd ed. New York: Oxford University Press, 2000.

Ainsworth, Mary D. Salter. *Infancy in Uganda: Infant Care and the Growth of Love.* Baltimore: Johns Hopkins University Press, 1967.

Alexander, Franz G., and Sheldon T. Selesnick. *The History of Psychiatry: An Evaluation of Psychiatric Thought and Practice from Prehistoric Times to the Present.* Northvale, N.J.: James Aronson, 1995 (original 1966).

Alvarez, Walter C. *Nervousness, Indigestion, and Pain.* New York: Collier Books, 1962.

Ameisen, Olivier. *The End of My Addiction.* New York: Farrar, Straus and Giroux, 2009.

Andreasen, Nancy C. *The Broken Brain: The Biological Revolution in Psychiatry.* New York: Harper and Row, 1984.

Arieti, Silvano. *The Parnas: A Scene from the Holocaust.* Philadelphia: Paul Dry Books, 2000.

Arikha, Noga. *Passions and Tempers: A History of the Humours.* New York: Ecco, 2007.

Attwell, Khleber Chapman. *100 Questions and Answers About Anxiety.* Jones and Bartlett, 2006.

Auden, W. H. *The Age of Anxiety.* New York: Random House, 1946.

Augustine, *Confessions.* New York: Dover Editions, 2002.

Backus, William. *The Good News About Worry: Applying Biblical Truth to Problems of Anxiety and Fear.* Minneapolis: Bethany House, 1991.

Baenninger, Alex, Joseph Alberto Costa e Silva, Ian Hindmarch, Hans-Juergen Moeller, and Karl Rickels. *Good Chemistry: The Life and Legacy of Valium Inventor Leo Sternbach.* New York: McGraw-Hill, 2004.

Ballard, Chris. *The Art of a Beautiful Game: The Thinking Fan's Tour of the NBA.* New York: Simon and Schuster, 2009.

Balthasar, Hans Urs von. *The Christian and Anxiety*. San Francisco: Ignatius Press, 2000.

Barber, Charles. *Comfortably Numb: How Psychiatry Is Medicating a Nation*. New York: Pantheon, 2008.

Barbu, Zevedei. *Problems of Historical Psychology*. New York: Grove Press, 1960.

Barlow, David. *Anxiety and Its Disorders*. 2nd ed. Guilford Press, 2002.

Barlow, David, and Michelle G. Craske. *Mastery of Your Anxiety and Panic*. 3rd ed. Graywind Publications, 2000.

Barnes, Julian. *Nothing to Be Frightened Of*. New York: Alfred A. Knopf, 2008.

Barondes, Samuel H. *Better Than Prozac: Creating the Next Generation of Psychiatric Drugs*. Oxford University Press, 2003.

———. *Molecules and Mental Illness*. Delhi, India: Indo American Books, 2007.

Bassett, Lucinda. *From Panic to Power: Proven Techniques to Calm Your Anxieties, Conquer Your Fears, and Put You in Control of Your Life*. Quill, 1995.

Bate, Walter Jackson. *Samuel Johnson*. Harcourt, Brace, 1977.

Battie, William. *A Treatise on Madness*. Brunner/Mazel, 1969.

Baumer, Franklin L. *Religion and the Rise of Skepticism*. Harcourt, Brace, 1960.

Beard, George Miller. *American Nervousness, Its Causes and Consequences*. New York: G. P. Putnam's Sons, 1881.

———. *A Practical Treatise on Nervous Exhaustion (Neurasthenia), Its Symptoms, Nature, Sequences, and Treatment*. New York: William Wood, 1880.

Beatty, Jack. *Age of Betrayal: The Triumph of Money in America, 1865–1990*. New York: Alfred A. Knopf, 2007.

Beck, Aaron T. *Depression: Causes and Treatment*. Philadelphia: University of Pennsylvania Press, 1967.

Beck, Aaron T., and Gary Emery. *Anxiety Disorders and Phobias: A Cognitive Perspective*. New York: Basic Books, 1985.

Beck, Aaron T., and Arthur Freeman. *Cognitive Therapy of Personality Disorders*. New York: Guilford Press, 1990.

Becker, Dana. *One Nation Under Stress: The Trouble with Stress as an Idea*. Oxford University Press, 2013.

Becker, Ernest. *The Denial of Death*. Free Press, 1973.

Beilock, Sian. *Choke: What the Secrets of the Brain Reveal About Success and Failure at Work and at Play*. Free Press, 2010.

Berger, Peter L., Brigitte Berger, and Hansfried Kellner. *The Homeless Mind: Modernization and Consciousness*. New York: Random House, 1973.

Berrios, German E. *The History of Mental Symptoms: Descriptive Psychopathology Since the Nineteenth Century*. Cambridge University Press, 1996.

Bertin, Celia. *Marie Bonaparte: A Life*. New Haven, Conn.: Yale University Press, 1982.

Bettelheim, Bruno. *Freud and Man's Soul*. New York: Vintage Books, 1982.

Blanchard, Robert J., Caroline Blanchard, Guy Griebel, and David Nutt. *Handbook of Anxiety and Fear*. Academic Press/Elsevier, 2008.

Blum, Deborah. *Love at Goon Park: Harry Harlow and the Science of Affection*. New York: Basic Books, 2002.

Blythe, Jamie. *Fear Is No Longer My Reality: How I Overcame Panic and Social Anxiety Disorder—and You Can Too*. With Jenna Glatzer. McGraw-Hill, 2005.

Borch-Jacobsen, Mikkel. *Making Minds and Madness: From Hysteria to Depression.* Cambridge University Press, 2009.

Bourke, Joanna. *Fear: A Cultural History.* Virago, 2005.

Bourne, Edmund, and Lorna Garano. *Coping with Anxiety: 10 Simple Ways to Relieve Fear, Anxiety, and Worry.* New Harbinger, 2003.

Bowlby, John. *Charles Darwin: A New Life.* New York: W. W. Norton, 1990.

———. *A Secure Base.* London: Routledge, 1988.

———. *Separation: Anxiety and Anger.* New York: Basic Books, 1973.

Braund, Susanna, and Glenn W. Most, eds. *Ancient Anger: Perspectives from Homer to Galen.* Cambridge University Press, 2003.

Breger, Louis. *A Dream of Undying Fame: How Freud Betrayed His Mentor and Invented Psychoanalysis.* New York: Basic Books, 2009.

———. *Freud: Darkness in the Midst of Vision.* New York: John Wiley and Sons, 2000.

Breggin, Peter R. *Medication Madness: A Psychiatrist Exposes the Dangers of Mood-Altering Medications.* New York: St. Martin's Press, 2008.

———. *Talking Back to Prozac: What Doctors Aren't Telling You About Today's Most Controversial Drug.* New York: St. Martin's Press, 1994.

Bremner, J. Douglas. *Does Stress Damage the Brain? Understanding Trauma-Related Disorders from a Mind-Body Perspective.* New York: W. W. Norton, 2002.

Bretall, Robert. *A Kierkegaard Anthology.* Princeton, N.J.: Princeton University Press, 1936.

Briggs, Rex. *Transforming Anxiety, Transcending Shame.* Health Communications, 1999.

Browne, Janet. *Charles Darwin: The Power of Place.* Princeton, N.J.: Princeton University Press, 2002.

———. *Charles Darwin: Voyaging.* Princeton, N.J.: Princeton University Press, 1995.

Bruner, Jerome. *Acts of Meaning.* Cambridge, Mass.: Harvard University Press, 1990.

Burgess, Thomas H. *The Physiology or Mechanism of Blushing, Illustrative of the Influence of Mental Emotion on the Capillary Circulation, with a General View of the Sympathies.* John Churchill, 1839.

Burijon, Barry N. *Biological Bases of Clinical Anxiety.* New York: W. W. Norton, 2007.

Burns, David D. *When Panic Attacks: The New, Drug-Free Anxiety Therapy That Can Change Your Life.* Morgan Road Books, 2006.

Burton, Robert. *The Anatomy of Melancholy.* New York Review of Books, 2001.

Cannon, Walter B. *Bodily Changes in Pain, Hunger, Fear and Rage.* New York: Harper Torchbooks, 1963 (original edition 1915).

Cantor, Norman F. *The Civilization of the Middle Ages.* New York: HarperCollins, 1993.

Caplan, Paula J. *They Say You're Crazy: How the World's Most Powerful Psychiatrists Decide Who's Normal.* Da Capo Press, 1995.

Capps, Donald. *Social Phobia: Alleviating Anxiety in an Age of Self-Promotion.* St. Louis: Chalice Press, 1999.

Carlat, Daniel. *Unhinged: The Trouble with Psychiatry—a Doctor's Revelations About a Profession in Crisis.* Free Press, 2010.

Carlstedt, Roland A. *Critical Moments During Competition: A Mind-Body Model of Sports Performance When It Counts the Most.* Psychology Press, 2004.

Carter, Rita. *Mapping the Mind.* University of California Press, 1998.

Cassidy, Jude, and Phillip R. Shaver. *Handbook of Attachment: Theory, Research, and Clinical Applications.* 2nd ed. Guilford Press, 2008.

Cassirer, Ernst. *An Essay on Man.* New Haven, Conn.: Yale University Press, 1944.

Chansky, Tamar E. *Freeing Yourself from Anxiety.* Da Capo, 2012.

Charney, Dennis S., and Eric J. Nestler. *Neurobiology of Mental Illness.* 3rd ed. Oxford University Press, 2009.

Cheyne, George. *The English Malady (1733).* Tavistock/Routledge, 1991.

Clark, Taylor. *Nerve: Poise Under Pressure, Serenity Under Stress, and the Brave New Science of Fear and Cool.* Boston: Little, Brown, 2011.

Coleman, Penny. *Flashback: Posttraumatic Stress Disorder, Suicide, and the Lessons of War.* Beacon Press, 2006.

Coles, Robert. *The Mind's Fate: A Psychiatrist Looks at His Profession.* Back Bay Books, 1975.

————. *Walker Percy: An American Searcher.* Boston: Little, Brown, 1978.

Collins, Randall. *Violence: A Micro-sociological Theory.* Princeton, N.J.: Princeton University Press, 2008.

Colp, Ralph, Jr. *To Be an Invalid: The Illness of Charles Darwin.* Chicago: University of Chicago Press, 1977.

Conley, Dalton. *Elsewhere, U.S.A: How We Got from the Company Man, Family Dinners, and the Affluent Society to the Home Office, BlackBerry Moms, and Economic Anxiety.* New York: Pantheon, 2009.

Contosta, David R. *Rebel Giants: The Revolutionary Lives of Abraham Lincoln and Charles Darwin.* Amherst, N.Y.: Prometheus Books, 2008.

Coolidge, Frederick L., and Thomas Wynn. *The Rise of Homo Sapiens: The Evolution of Modern Thinking.* Chichester, U.K.: Wiley-Blackwell, 2009.

Cozolino, Louis. *The Neuroscience of Psychotherapy: Building and Rebuilding the Human Brain.* New York: W. W. Norton, 2002.

Crick, Francis. *The Astonishing Hypothesis: The Scientific Search for the Soul.* New York: Touchstone, 1994.

Cuordileone, Kyle A. *Manhood and American Political Culture in the Cold War.* New York: Routledge, 2005.

Cushman, Philip. *Constructing the Self, Constructing America: A Cultural History of Psychotherapy.* Addison-Wesley, 1995.

Damasio, Antonio. *Descartes' Error: Emotion, Reason, and the Human Brain.* Grosset/Putnam, 1994.

————. *The Feeling of What Happens: Body and Emotion in the Making of Consciousness.* Harcourt, 1999.

————. *Looking for Spinoza: Joy, Sorrow, and the Feeling Brain.* New York: Harcourt, 2003.

Darwin, Charles. *The Autobiography of Charles Darwin, 1809–1882.* New York: Classic Books International, 2009.

————. *The Expression of the Emotions in Man and Animals.* BiblioBazaar (originally published 1872), 2007.

Davenport-Hines, Richard. *The Pursuit of Oblivion: A Global History of Narcotics.* New York: W. W. Norton, 2001.

Davey, Graham C. L., ed. *Phobias: A Handbook of Theory, Research and Treatment.* Chichester, U.K.: Wiley, 1997.

Davey, Graham C. L., and Adrian Wells, eds. *Worry and Its Psychological Disorders.* Wiley, 2006.

Davidson, Jonathan, and Henry Dreher. *The Anxiety Book: Developing Strength in the Face of Fear.* Riverhead Books, 2003.

Davidson, Richard J., and Sharon Begley. *The Emotional Life of Your Brain.* Hudson Street Press, 2012.

Davis, Lennard J. *Obsession: A History.* Chicago: University of Chicago Press, 2008.

Davison, Gerald D., and John M. Neale. *Abnormal Psychology.* 5th ed. John Wiley and Sons, 1990.

Dayhoff, Signe A. *Diagonally-Parked in a Parallel Universe: Working Through Social Anxiety.* Effectiveness-Plus Publications, 2000.

de Botton, Alain. *Status Anxiety.* New York: Pantheon Books, 2004.

DeGrandpre, Richard. *The Cult of Pharmacology: How America Became the World's Most Troubled Drug Culture.* Durham, N.C.: Duke University Press, 2006.

Descartes, René. *Discourse on Method and Meditations.* Library of Liberal Arts, 1960.

Desmond, Adrian, and James Moore. *Darwin: The Life of a Tormented Evolutionist.* New York: W. W. Norton, 1991.

Dessoir, Max, and Donald Fisher. *Outlines of the History of Psychology.* New York: Macmillan, 1912.

Dillon, Brian. *The Hypochondriacs: Nine Tormented Lives.* New York: Faber and Faber, 2010.

Doctor, Ronald M., and Ada P. Kahn. *The Encyclopedia of Phobias, Fears, and Anxieties.* Facts on File, 1989.

Dodds, E. R. *The Greeks and the Irrational.* Berkeley: University of California Press, 1951.

Doi, Takeo. *The Anatomy of Dependence.* Kodansha, 1971.

Dollard, John. *Victory over Fear.* Reynal and Hitchcock, 1942.

Dollard, John, and Neal A. Miller. *Personality and Psychotherapy: An Analysis in Terms of Learning, Thinking, and Culture.* McGraw-Hill, 1950.

Dozois, David J. A., and Keith S. Dobson. *The Prevention of Anxiety and Depression: Theory, Research, and Practice.* American Psychological Association, 2004.

Drinka, George Frederick. *The Birth of Neurosis: Myth, Malady, and the Victorians.* New York: Simon & Schuster, 1984.

Drummond, Edward H. *Overcoming Anxiety Without Tranquilizers.* Dutton, 1997.

Dukakis, Kitty, and Larry Tye. *Shock: The Healing Power of Electroconvulsive Therapy.* Avery, 2006.

Dumont, Raeann. *The Sky Is Falling: Understanding and Coping with Phobias, Panic, and Obsessive-Compulsive Disorders.* New York: W. W. Norton, 1996.

Eghigian, Greg. *From Madness to Mental Health: Psychiatric Disorder and Its Treatment in Western Civilization.* New Brunswick, N.J.: Rutgers University Press, 2010.

Elie, Paul. *The Life You Save May Be Your Own: An American Pilgrimage.* New York: Farrar, Straus and Giroux, 2003.

Ellenberger, Henri F. *The Discovery of the Unconscious: The History and Evolution of Dynamic Psychiatry.* New York: Basic Books, 1970.

Elliott, Carl, and Tod Chambers. *Prozac as a Way of Life.* Chapel Hill: University of North Carolina Press, 2004.

Ellman, Richard. *Yeats: The Man and the Masks.* New York: Macmillan, 1948.

Engel, Jonathan. *American Therapy: The Rise of Psychotherapy in the United States.* Gotham Books, 2008.

Epictetus. *Discourses and Enchiridion.* New York: Walter J. Black, 1944.

Erikson, Erik H. *Childhood and Society.* New York: W. W. Norton, 1950.

Esposito, Janet. *In the Spotlight: Overcome Your Fear of Public Speaking and Performance.* Strong Books, 2000.

Eysenck, H. J., and S. Rachman. *The Causes and Cures of Neurosis.* San Diego: Robert R. Knapp, 1965.

Fann, William E., Ismet Karacan, Alex D. Pokorny, and Robert L. Williams, eds. *Phenomenology and Treatment of Anxiety.* Spectrum Publications, 1979.

Farnbach, Rod, and Eversley Farnbach. *Overcoming Performance Anxiety.* Simon and Schuster Australia, 2001.

Fisher, Paul. *House of Wits: An Intimate Portrait of the James Family.* New York: Henry Holt, 2008.

Ford, Emily. *What You Must Think of Me: A Firsthand Account of One Teenager's Experience with Social Anxiety Disorder.* With Michael R. Liebowitz and Linda Wasmer Andrews. Oxford University Press, 2007.

Forrester, John. *Dispatches from the Freud Wars: Psychoanalysis and Its Passions.* Cambridge, Mass.: Harvard University Press, 1997.

———. *Truth Games: Lies, Money, and Psychoanalysis.* Cambridge, Mass.: Harvard University Press, 1997.

Foxman, Paul. *Dancing with Fear: Overcoming Anxiety in a World of Stress and Uncertainty.* Jason Aronson, 1997.

———. *The Worried Child: Recognizing Anxiety in Children and Helping Them Heal.* Hunter House, 2004.

Frankl, Viktor E. *The Doctor and the Soul: From Psychotherapy to Logotherapy.* New York: Vintage Books, 1986.

———. *Man's Search for Meaning.* New York: Washington Square Press, 1985 (copyright 1959).

Frattaroli, Elio. *Healing the Soul in the Age of the Brain: Why Medication Isn't Enough.* Penguin, 2001.

Freeman, Daniel, and Jason Freeman. *Anxiety: A Very Short Introduction.* Oxford University Press, 2012.

Freud, Sigmund. *The Basic Writings of Sigmund Freud.* Modern Library, 1995.

———. *Beyond the Pleasure Principle.* New York: W. W. Norton, 1961.

———. *Character and Culture.* Collier Books, 1963.

———. *Civilization and Its Discontents.* New York: W. W. Norton, 1961.

———. *The Complete Letters of Sigmund Freud to Wilhelm Fliess, 1887–1904.* Translated and edited by Jeffrey Moussaieff Masson. Cambridge, Mass.: Harvard University Press, 1985.

————. *Five Lectures on Psycho-Analysis.* New York: W. W. Norton, 1989.

————. *The History of the Psycho-Analytic Movement and the Origin and Development of Psychoanalysis.* New York: W. W. Norton, 1990.

————. *The Interpretation of Dreams.* London: Hogarth Press, 1953.

————. *The Problem of Anxiety.* Psychoanalytic Quarterly Press, 1936.

————. *Three Essays on the Theory of Sexuality.* New York: Basic Books, 2000.

————. *Totem and Taboo: Some Points of Agreement Between the Mental Lives of Savages and Neurotics.* Routledge and Kegan Paul, 1950.

Friedman, Steven, ed. *Cultural Issues in the Treatment of Anxiety.* Guilford Press, 1997.

Frink, H. W., and James J. Putnam. *Morbid Fears and Compulsions: Their Psychology and Psychoanalytic Treatment.* Moffat, Yard, 1918.

Fromm, Erich. *Escape from Freedom.* New York: Owl Books, 1969.

————. *Man for Himself: An Inquiry into the Psychology of Ethics.* New York: Henry Holt, 1947.

Furedi, Frank. *Therapy Culture: Cultivating Vulnerability in an Uncertain Age.* London: Routledge, 2004.

Furer, Patricia, John R. Walker, and Murray B. Stein. *Treating Health Anxiety and Fear of Death: A Practitioner's Guide.* New York: Springer, 2007.

Gabriel, Richard A. *No More Heroes: Madness and Psychiatry in War.* Hill and Wang, 1987.

Galdston, Iago, ed. *Historic Derivations of Modern Psychiatry.* New York: McGraw-Hill, 1967.

Gamwell, Lynn, and Nancy Tomes. *Madness in America: Cultural and Medical Perceptions of Mental Illness Before 1914.* Ithaca, N.Y.: Cornell University Press, 1995.

Gandhi, Mohandas K. *An Autobiography: The Story of My Experiments with Truth.* Beacon Press, 1993.

Gardner, Daniel. *The Science of Fear.* Dutton, 2008.

Garff, Joakim. *Søren Kierkegaard: A Biography.* Princeton, N.J.: Princeton University Press, 2005.

Gay, Peter. *Freud: A Life for Our Time.* New York: W. W. Norton, 1988.

Gazzaniga, Michael S. *Nature's Mind: The Biological Roots of Thinking, Emotions, Sexuality, Language, and Intelligence.* New York: Basic Books, 1992.

Gershon, Michael D. *The Second Brain: The Scientific Basis of Gut Instinct and a Groundbreaking New Understanding of Nervous Disorders of the Stomach and Intestine.* New York: HarperCollins, 1998.

Gerzon, Robert. *Finding Serenity in the Age of Anxiety.* New York: Macmillan, 1997.

Gewirtz, Jacob, ed. *Attachment and Dependency.* V. H. Winston and Sons, 1972.

Ghinassi, Cheryl Winning. *Anxiety.* Greenwood, 2010.

Gifford, Frank. *Gifford on Courage.* With Charles Mangel. M. Evans, 1976.

Gijswijt-Hofstra, Marijke, and Roy Porter. *Cultures of Neurasthenia: From Beard to the First World War.* Rodopi, 2001.

Glantz, Kalman, and John K. Pearce. *Exiles from Eden: Psychotherapy from an Evolutionary Perspective.* New York: W. W. Norton, 1989.

Glatzer, Jenna, ed. *Conquering Panic and Anxiety Disorders: Success Stories, Strategies, and Other Good News.* Hunter House, 2002.

Gleick, James. *Faster: The Acceleration of Just About Everything.* New York: Vintage Books, 1999.

Glenmullen, Joseph. *The Antidepressant Solution: The Only Step-by-Step Guide to Safely Overcoming Antidepressant Withdrawal, Dependence, and "Addiction."* New York: Free Press, 2005.

Goldstein, Kurt. *Human Nature in the Light of Psychopathology.* 1940. New York: Schocken Books, 1963.

Goldstein, Michael J., and James O. Palmer. *The Experience of Anxiety: A Casebook.* New York: Oxford University Press, 1963.

Goodwin, Donald W. *Anxiety.* Oxford University Press, 1986.

———. *Phobia: The Facts.* Oxford University Press, 1983.

Gordon, James S. *Unstuck: Your Guide to the Seven-Stage Journey Out of Depression.* New York: Penguin, 2008.

Gorman, Jack, ed. *Fear and Anxiety: The Benefits of Translational Research.* Washington, D.C.: American Psychiatric Publishing, 2004.

Gosling, F. G. *Before Freud: Neurasthenia and the American Medical Community, 1870–1910.* University of Illinois Press, 1987.

Gould, James L. *Ethology: The Mechanisms and Evolution of Behavior.* New York: W. W. Norton, 1982.

Goulding, Regina A., and Richard C. Schwarz. *The Mosaic Mind: Empowering the Tormented Selves of Child Abuse Survivors.* New York: W. W. Norton, 1995.

Gray, Jeffrey A., and Neil McNaughton. *The Neuropsychology of Anxiety.* 2nd ed. Oxford: Oxford University Press, 2000.

Greenberg, Gary. *The Book of Woe: The "DSM" and the Unmaking of Psychiatry.* Blue Rider Press, 2012.

———. *Manufacturing Depression: The Secret History of a Modern Disease.* New York: Simon and Schuster, 2010.

Greist, John H., James W. Jefferson, and Isaac M. Marks. *Anxiety and Its Treatment.* New York: Warner Books, 1986.

Grinker, Roy R., and John P. Spiegel. *Men Under Stress.* Philadelphia: Blakiston, 1945.

Grob, Gerald N. *Mental Illness and American Society, 1875–1940.* Princeton, N.J.: Princeton University Press, 1983.

Grosskurth, Phyllis. *Melanie Klein: Her World and Her Work.* New York: Alfred A. Knopf, 1986.

Hallowell, Edward M. *Worry: Hope and Help for a Common Condition.* New York: Random House, 1997.

Handly, Robert. *Anxiety and Panic Attacks: Their Cause and Cure.* With Pauline Neff. Fawcett Crest, 1985.

Hanford, A. Chester. *Problems in Municipal Government.* A. W. Shaw, 1926.

Harrington, Anne. *The Cure Within: A History of Mind-Body Medicine.* New York: W. W. Norton, 2008.

Hart, Archibald D. *The Anxiety Cure.* New York: Thomas Nelson, 2001.

Harvard Medical School. *The Sensitive Gut.* New York: Fireside Books, 2000.

Hayes, Steven C. *Get Out of Your Mind and into Your Life: The New Acceptance and Commitment Therapy.* New Harbinger, 2005.

Hayes, Steven C., Kirk D. Strosahl, and Kelly G. Wilson. *Acceptance and Commitment Therapy: An Experiential Approach to Behavior Change.* Guilford Press, 1999.

Healy, David. *The Antidepressant Era.* Cambridge, Mass.: Harvard University Press, 1997.

———. *The Creation of Psychopharmacology.* Cambridge, Mass.: Harvard University Press, 2002.

———. *Let Them Eat Prozac.* James Lorimer, 2003.

Heimberg, Richard G., Cynthia L. Turk, and Douglas S. Mennin, eds. *Generalized Anxiety Disorder: Advances in Research and Practice.* Guilford Press, 2004.

Herman, Judith Lewis. *Trauma and Recovery.* New York: Basic Books, 1992.

Heston, Leonard L. *Mending Minds: A Guide to the New Psychiatry of Depression, Anxiety, and Other Serious Mental Disorders.* W. H. Freeman, 1992.

Hobson, J. Allan, and Jonathan A. Leonard. *Out of Its Mind: Psychiatry in Crisis.* Cambridge, Mass.: Perseus Books, 2002.

Hoch, Paul, and Joseph Zubin, eds. *Anxiety.* New York: Grune and Stratton, 1950.

Hofstadter, Richard. *The Age of Reform.* New York: Vintage, 1955.

———. *The American Political Tradition.* New York: Alfred A. Knopf, 1948.

Hollander, Eric, and Daphne Simeon. *Concise Guide to Anxiety Disorders.* American Psychiatric Publishing, 2003.

Hollister, Leo. *Clinical Use of Psychotherapeutic Drugs.* Charles C. Thomas, 1973.

Holmes, Jeremy. *The Search for the Secure Base: Attachment Theory and Psychotherapy.* Routledge, 2001.

Horney, Karen. *Neurosis and Human Growth: The Struggle Toward Self-Realization.* New York: W. W. Norton, 1950.

———. *The Neurotic Personality of Our Time.* New York: W. W. Norton, 1937.

———. *New Ways in Psychoanalysis.* New York: W. W. Norton, 1939.

———. *Our Inner Conflicts.* New York: W. W. Norton, 1945.

———. *Self-Analysis.* New York: W. W. Norton, 1942.

Horstmann, Judith. *Brave New Brain: How Neuroscience, Brain-Machine Interfaces, Psychopharmacology, Epigenetics, the Internet, and Our Own Minds Are Stimulating and Enhancing the Future of Mental Power.* John Wiley and Sons, 2010.

Horwitz, Allan V., and Jerome C. Wakefield. *All We Have to Fear: Psychiatry's Transformation of Natural Anxieties into Mental Disorders.* New York: Oxford University Press, 2012.

———. *The Loss of Sadness: How Psychiatry Transformed Normal Sorrow into Depressive Disorder.* New York: Oxford University Press, 2007.

Huizinga, Johann. *The Waning of the Middle Ages.* 1924. Mineola, N.Y.: Dover Books, 1999.

Hunt, Joseph McVicker, ed. *Personality and the Behavior Disorders: A Handbook Based on Experimental and Clinical Research.* Ronald Press, 1944.

Hunt, Morton. *The Story of Psychology.* New York: Doubleday, 1993.

Hunter, Richard, and Ida Macalpine. *Three Hundred Years of Psychiatry, 1535–1860.* Carlisle Publishing, 1982.

Hustvedt, Siri. *The Shaking Woman; or, A History of My Nerves.* New York: Henry Holt, 2010.

Issroff, Judith, ed. *Donald Winnicott and John Bowlby: Personal and Professional Perspectives.* H. Karnac, 2005.

Izard, Carroll E. *Human Emotions.* Plenum, 1977.

Jackson, Stanley W. *Melancholia and Depression: From Hippocratic Times to Modern Times.* New Haven, Conn.: Yale University Press, 1986.

Jacobson, Edmund. *You Must Relax: A Practical Method for Reducing the Strain of Living.* 1934. Whittsley House, 1942.

James, Oliver. *The Selfish Capitalist.* Vermillion, 2008.

James, William. *Principles of Psychology.* New York: Henry Holt, 1890.

———. *The Varieties of Religious Experience.* Longmans, Green, 1902.

Jamison, Kay Redfield. *An Unquiet Mind: A Memoir of Moods and Madness.* New York: Vintage, 1995.

Janis, Irving L. *Air War and Emotional Stress: Psychological Studies of Bombing and Civilian Defense.* New York: McGraw-Hill, 1951.

Jaspers, Karl. *General Psychopathology.* Vol. 1. Baltimore: Johns Hopkins University Press, 1997.

Jaynes, Julian. *The Origins of Consciousness in the Breakdown of the Bicameral Mind.* New York: Mariner Books, 1990 (original copyright 1976).

Johnson, Haynes. *The Age of Anxiety: From McCarthyism to Terrorism.* Harcourt, 2005.

Jones, Edgar, and Simon Wessely. *Shell Shock to PTSD: Military Psychiatry from 1900 to the Gulf War.* Psychology Press, 2005.

Jordan, Jeanne, and Julie Pederson. *The Panic Diaries: The Frightful, Sometimes Hilarious Truth About Panic Attacks.* Octopus Publishing Group, 2004.

Kagan, Jerome. *An Argument for Mind.* New Haven, Conn.: Yale University Press, 2006.

———. *Galen's Prophecy: Temperament in Human Nature.* New York: Basic Books, 1994.

———. *Psychology's Ghosts: The Crisis in the Profession and the Way Back.* New Haven, Conn.: Yale University Press, 2012.

———. *Unstable Ideas: Temperament, Cognition, and Self.* Cambridge, Mass.: Harvard University Press, 1989.

———. *What Is Emotion?* New Haven, Conn.: Yale University Press, 2007.

Kagan, Jerome, and Nancy Snidman. *The Long Shadow of Temperament.* Cambridge, Mass.: Harvard University Press, 2004.

Kahn, Jeffrey P. *Angst: The Origins of Anxiety and Depression.* Oxford University Press, 2012.

Kardiner, Abram. *The Individual and His Society: The Psychodynamics of Primitive Social Organization.* New York: Columbia University Press, 1939.

Karen, Robert. *Becoming Attached: First Relationships and How They Shape Our Capacity to Love.* Oxford University Press, 1994.

Karp, David A. *Is It Me or My Meds? Living with Antidepressants.* Cambridge, Mass.: Harvard University Press, 2006.

Kasper, Siegfried, Johan A. den Boer, and J. M. Ad Sitsen, eds. *Handbook of Depression and Anxiety.* 2nd ed. Marcel Dekker, 2003.

Kassirer, Jerome P. *On the Take: How Medicine's Complicity with Big Business Can Endanger Your Health.* Oxford University Press, 2005.

Kaster, Robert A. *Emotion, Restraint, and Community in Ancient Rome.* Oxford University Press, 2005.

Kendall, Joshua. *American Obsessives: The Compulsive Energy That Built a Nation.* New York: Grand Central Publishing, 2013.

Kierkegaard, Søren. *The Concept of Anxiety: A Simple Psychologically Orienting Deliberation on the Dogmatic Issue of Hereditary Sin.* Princeton, N.J.: Princeton University Press, 1980.

———. *Fear and Trembling.* New York: Penguin Books, 1985.

Kirk, Stuart A., and Herb Kutchins. *The Selling of "DSM": The Rhetoric of Science in Psychiatry.* Transaction Publishers, 1992.

Kirsch, Irving. *The Emperor's New Drugs: Exploding the Antidepressant Myth.* New York: Basic Books, 2010.

Klausner, Samuel Z., ed. *Why Man Takes Chances: Studies in Stress-Seeking.* New York: Doubleday Anchor, 1968.

Kleinman, Arthur. *Rethinking Psychiatry: From Cultural Category to Personal Experience.* New York: Free Press, 1988.

Kleinman, Arthur, and Byron Good, eds. *Culture and Depression: Studies in the Anthropology and Cross-Cultural Psychiatry of Affect and Disorder.* Berkeley: University of California Press, 1985.

Kline, Nathan S. *From Sad to Glad: Kline on Depression.* New York: Putnam, 1974.

Kramer, Peter. *Freud: Inventor of the Modern Mind.* Atlas Books/HarperCollins, 2006.

———. *Listening to Prozac.* Viking, 1993.

Kuijsten, Marcel, ed. *Reflections on the Dawn of Consciousness: Julian Jaynes's Bicameral Mind Theory Revisited.* Julian Jaynes Society, 2006.

Kurzweil, Edith. *The Freudians: A Comparative Perspective.* New Haven, Conn.: Yale University Press, 1989.

Kutchins, Herb, and Stuart A. Kirk. *Making Us Crazy: "DSM"; The Psychiatric Bible and the Creation of Mental Disorders.* New York: Free Press, 1997.

Lane, Christopher. *Shyness: How Normal Behavior Became a Sickness.* New Haven, Conn.: Yale University Press, 2007.

Lasch, Christopher. *The Culture of Narcissism: American Life in an Age of Diminishing Expectations.* New York: Warner Books, 1979.

Last, Cynthia, ed. *Anxiety Across the Lifespan: A Developmental Perspective.* New York: Springer, 1993.

Lazarus, Richard S. *Stress and Emotion: A New Synthesis.* Springer, 1999.

Lazarus, Richard S., and Bernice Lazarus. *Passion and Reason: Making Sense of Our Emotions.* Oxford University Press, 1994.

Leach, John. *Survival Psychology.* Palgrave Macmillan, 1994.

LeDoux, Joseph. *The Emotional Brain: The Mysterious Underpinnings of Emotional Life.* New York: Simon and Schuster, 1996.

LeGoff, Jacques. *Medieval Civilization.* Cambridge, Mass.: Basil Blackwell, 1988 (translated from French edition of 1964).

Levy, David. *Maternal Overprotection.* New York: Columbia University Press, 1943.

Lewis, Marc. *Memoirs of an Addicted Brain: A Neuroscientist Examines His Former Life on Drugs.* Public Affairs, 2012.

Lewis, Nolan. *A Short History of Psychiatric Achievement.* New York: W. W. Norton, 1941.

Lifton, Robert Jay. *The Protean Self: Human Resilience in an Age of Fragmentation.* New York: Basic Books, 1993.

Linton, Ralph, ed. *The Science of Man in the World Crisis.* New York: Oxford University Press, 1945.

Lloyd, G. E. R., ed. *Hippocratic Writings.* London: Penguin Books, 1983.

Lowrie, Walter. *A Short Life of Kierkegaard.* Princeton, N.J.: Princeton University Press, 1942.

Luhrmann, T. M. *Of Two Minds: An Anthropologist Looks at American Psychiatry.* New York: Vintage Books, 2000.

Lutz, Tom. *American Nervousness, 1903: An Anecdotal History.* Ithaca, N.Y.: Cornell University Press, 1991.

MacArthur, John. *Anxiety Attacked: Applying Scripture to the Cares of the Soul.* Victor Books, 1993.

———. *Anxious for Nothing: God's Cure for the Cares of Your Soul.* Colorado Springs, Colo.: Cook Communications Ministries, 2006.

MacDonald, Michael. *Mystical Bedlam: Madness, Anxiety, and Healing in Seventeenth-Century England.* Cambridge University Press, 1981.

Makari, George. *Revolution in Mind: The Creation of Psychoanalysis.* New York: Harper-Collins, 2008.

Malone, John C. *Psychology: Pythagoras to Present.* MIT Press, 2009.

Manchester, William. *Goodbye, Darkness: A Memoir of the Pacific War.* Back Bay Books, 2002.

Mannheim, Karl. *Man and Society in an Age of Reconstruction.* Harcourt, Brace, 1940.

Manning, Martha. *Undercurrents: A Life Beneath the Surface.* New York: Harper-Collins, 1994.

Markel, Howard. *An Anatomy of Addiction: Sigmund Freud, William Halsted, and the Miracle Drug Cocaine.* New York: Pantheon, 2011.

Marks, Isaac M. *Fears, Phobias, and Rituals: Panic, Anxiety, and Their Disorders.* Oxford University Press, 1987.

Markway, Barbara G., Cheryl N. Carmin, C. Alec Pollard, and Teresa Flynn. *Dying of Embarrassment: Help for Social Anxiety and Phobia.* Oakland, Calif.: New Harbinger Publications, 1992.

Markway, Barbara G., and Gregory P. Markway. *Painfully Shy: How to Overcome Social Anxiety and Reclaim Your Life.* New York: St. Martin's Press, 2001.

Marmor, Judd, and Sherwyn M. Woods, eds. *The Interface Between the Psychodynamic and Behavioral Therapies.* New York: Plenum Medical, 1980.

Marshall, John R. *Social Phobia.* New York: Basic Books, 1994.

Maudsley, Henry. *The Pathology of Mind.* D. Appleton, 1860.

Mavissakalian, Matig, and David H. Barlow, eds. *Phobia: Psychological and Pharmacological Treatment.* New York: New York University Press, 1981.

May, Rollo. *The Discovery of Being.* New York: W. W. Norton, 1983.

———. *Love and Will.* New York: W. W. Norton, 1969.

———. *Man's Search for Himself.* New York: W. W. Norton, 1953.

———. *The Meaning of Anxiety.* Rev. ed. New York: W. W. Norton, 1977.

———. *Psychology and the Human Dilemma.* New York: W. W. Norton, 1979.

McEwen, Bruce. *The End of Stress as We Know It.* Washington, D.C.: Joseph Henry Press, 2002.

McGlynn, Thomas J., and Harry L. Metcalf, eds. *Diagnosis and Treatment of Anxiety Disorders: A Physician's Handbook.* American Psychiatric Publishing, 1992.

McKay, Dean, Jonathan S. Abramowitz, Steven Taylor, and Gordon J. G. Asmundson. *Current Perspectives on the Anxiety Disorders: Implications for "DSM-V" and Beyond.* New York: Springer, 2009.

McLean, Peter D., and Sheila R. Woody. *Anxiety Disorder in Adults: An Evidence-Based Approach to Psychological Treatment.* Oxford University Press, 2001.

Menninger, Karl. *The Human Mind.* 3rd ed. New York: Alfred A. Knopf, 1946.

———. *Man Against Himself.* Harcourt, Brace, 1938.

———. *Whatever Became of Sin?* Hawthorn Books, 1973.

Messer, Stanley B., Louis Sass, and Robert Woolfolk. *Hermeneutics and Psychological Theory: Interpretive Perspectives on Personality, Psychotherapy, and Psychopathology.* New Brunswick, N.J.: Rutgers University Press, 1988.

Micale, Mark S. *Hysterical Men: The Hidden History of Male Nervous Illness.* Cambridge, Mass.: Harvard University Press, 2008.

Millon, Theodore. *Masters of the Mind: Exploring the Story of Mental Illness from Ancient Times to the New Millennium.* Hoboken, N.J.: Wiley, 2004.

Mohr, Jay. *Gasping for Airtime: Two Years in the Trenches of "Saturday Night Live."* New York: Hyperion, 2005.

Morita, Shoma. *Morita Therapy and the True Nature of Anxiety-Based Disorders.* Albany: State University of New York Press, 1998.

Morris, Colin. *The Discovery of the Individual, 1050–1200.* Toronto: University of Toronto Press, 1972.

Mumford, Lewis. *The Condition of Man.* Harcourt, Brace, 1944.

Murphy, Gardner. *Historical Introduction to Modern Psychology.* Harcourt, Brace, 1949.

Newman, Paul. *A History of Terror: Fear and Dread Through the Ages.* Sutton Publishing, 2000.

Niebuhr, Reinhold. *The Nature and Destiny of Man.* 2 vols. New York: Scribner, 1941–43.

Northfield, Wilfrid. *Conquest of Nerves: The Inspiring Record of a Personal Triumph over Neurasthenia.* London: Fenland Press, 1933.

Opler, Marvin K. *Culture, Psychiatry, and Human Values: The Methods and Values of a Social Psychiatry.* Charles C. Thomas Publisher, 1956.

Oppenheim, Janet. *"Shattered Nerves": Doctors, Patients, and Depression in Victorian England.* Oxford University Press, 1991.

Parkes, Henry Bamford. *Gods and Men: The Origins of Western Culture.* New York: Alfred A. Knopf, 1959.

Pearson, Patricia. *A Brief History of Anxiety.* Bloomsbury, 2008.

Percy, Walker. *Lancelot.* New York: Farrar, Straus and Giroux, 1977.

———. *The Last Gentleman.* New York: Farrar, Straus and Giroux, 1966.

———. *Lost in the Cosmos: The Last Self-Help Book.* New York: Farrar, Straus and Giroux, 1983.

———. *The Message in the Bottle: How Queer Man Is, How Queer Language Is, and What One Has to Do with the Other.* New York: Farrar, Straus and Giroux, 1975.

———. *The Moviegoer.* New York: Alfred A. Knopf, 1961.

———. *The Second Coming.* New York: Farrar, Straus and Giroux, 1980.

———. *Signposts in a Strange Land.* Picador, 1991.

———. *The Thanatos Syndrome.* New York: Farrar, Straus and Giroux, 1987.

Peurifoy, Reneau. *Anxiety, Phobias, and Panic: A Step-by-Step Program for Regaining Control of Your Life.* New York: Warner Books, 1988.

Pfister, Oscar. *Christianity and Fear: A Study in the History and in the Psychology and Hygiene of Religion.* Unwin Brothers, 1948.

Phillips, Bob. *Overcoming Anxiety and Depression: Practical Tools to Help You Deal with Negative Emotions.* Harvest House, 2007.

Pinero, Jose M. Lopez. *Historical Origins of the Concept of Neurosis.* Cambridge University Press, 1983.

Pinker, Steven. *How the Mind Works.* New York: W. W. Norton, 1997.

Pirenne, Henri. *Medieval Cities.* Princeton, N.J.: Princeton University Press, 1925.

Pollino, Sandra M. *Flying Fear Free: 7 Steps to Relieving Air Travel Anxiety.* New Horizon Press, 2012.

Porter, Roy. *Madness: A Brief History.* New York: Oxford University Press, 2002.

Pressman, Jack D. *Last Resort: Psychosurgery and the Limits of Medicine.* Cambridge University Press, 1998.

Prinz, Jesse J. *Gut Reactions: A Perceptual Theory of Emotion.* Oxford University Press, 2004.

Prochnik, George. *Putnam Camp: Sigmund Freud, James Jackson Putnam, and the Purpose of American Psychology.* Other Press, 2006.

Quammen, David. *The Reluctant Mr. Darwin.* New York: W. W. Norton Books, 2006.

Quinlan, Kieran. *Walker Percy: The Last Catholic Novelist.* Baton Rouge: Louisiana State University Press, 1996.

Quinodoz, Jean-Michel. *The Taming of Solitude: Separation Anxiety in Psychoanalysis.* London: Routledge, 1993.

Rachman, Stanley. *Anxiety.* East Sussex, U.K.: Psychology Press, 1998.

———. *Phobias: Their Nature and Control.* Springfield, Ill.: Charles C. Thomas Publisher, 1968.

Rachman, Stanley, and Padmal de Silva. *Panic Disorder: The Facts.* 2nd ed. New York: Oxford University Press, 2004.

Radden, Jennifer, ed. *The Nature of Melancholy: From Aristotle to Kristeva.* New York: Oxford University Press, 2000.

Radin, Paul. *Primitive Man as Philosopher.* New York: Dover Publications, 1957.

Rank, Otto. *The Trauma of Birth.* New York: Dover Editions, 1993 (original edition 1929).

Rapee, Ronald M. *Overcoming Shyness and Social Phobia.* Rowman and Littlefield, 1998.

Raskin, Marjorie. *The Anxiety Expert: A Psychiatrist's Story of Panic.* AuthorHouse, 2004.

Reich, Wilhelm. *The Mass Psychology of Fascism.* New York: Farrar, Straus and Giroux, 1970.

Reiser, Morton F. *Mind, Brain, Body: Toward a Convergence of Psychoanalysis and Neurobiology.* New York: Basic Books, 1984.

Restak, Richard. *Poe's Heart and the Mountain Climber: Exploring the Effects of Anxiety on Our Brains and Our Culture.* Harmony Books, 2004.

Richardson, Robert D. *William James: In the Maelstrom of American Modernism.* Boston: Houghton Mifflin, 2006.

Riesman, David. *Abundance for What?* Garden City, N.Y.: Doubleday, 1964.

———. *Individualism Reconsidered.* New York: Free Press, 1954.

———. *The Lonely Crowd.* New Haven, Conn.: Yale University Press, 1961.

Roazen, Paul. *Freud and His Followers.* New York: Da Capo Press, 1992.

Robin, Corey. *Fear: The History of a Political Idea.* Oxford: Oxford University Press, 2004.

Roccatagliata, Giuseppe. *A History of Ancient Psychiatry.* New York: Greenwood Press, 1986.

Roche Laboratories. *Aspects of Anxiety.* J. B. Lippincott, 1965.

Rorty, Amelie Oskenberg, ed. *Explaining Emotions.* Berkeley: University of California Press, 1980.

Rosenberg, Charles E., and Janet Golden, eds. *Framing Disease: Studies in Cultural History.* New Brunswick, N.J.: Rutgers University Press, 1997.

Rousseau, G. S., and Roy Porter, eds. *The Ferment of Knowledge: Studies in the Historiography of Eighteenth-Century Science.* Cambridge University Press, 1980.

Rycroft, Charles. *Anxiety and Neurosis.* Middlesex, U.K.: Penguin Books, 1968.

Rygh, Jayne L., and William G. Sanderson. *Treating Generalized Anxiety Disorder: Evidence-Based Strategies, Tools, and Techniques.* Guilford Press, 2004.

Salecl, Renata. *On Anxiety.* London: Routledge, 2004.

Samway, Patrick. *Walker Percy: A Life.* Loyola Press, 1999.

Sapolsky, Robert M. *Monkeyluv and Other Essays on Our Lives as Animals.* New York: Scribner, 2005.

———. *Why Zebras Don't Get Ulcers.* New York: Henry Holt, 2004.

Sarason, Irwin, and Charles Spielberger, eds. *Stress and Anxiety.* Vols. 2, 4, and 5. Washington, D.C.: Hemisphere Publishing, 1975–78.

Satel, Sally, and Scott O. Lilienfeld. *Brainwashed: How We Are Seduced by Mindless Neuroscience.* New York: Basic Books, 2013.

Saul, Helen. *Phobias: Fighting the Fear.* New York: Arcade, 2002.

Schlesinger, Arthur M., Jr. *The Cycles of American History.* Boston: Houghton Mifflin, 1986.

———. *The Vital Center: The Politics of Freedom.* Riverhead Press, 1949.

Schneier, Franklin, and Lawrence Welkowitz. *The Hidden Face of Shyness: Understanding and Overcoming Social Anxiety.* New York: Avon Books, 1996.

Schreber, Daniel Paul. *Memoirs of My Nervous Illness.* New York Review of Books, 2000.

Schuster, David G. *Neurasthenic Nation: America's Search for Health, Happiness, and Comfort, 1869–1920.* New Brunswick, N.J.: Rutgers University Press, 2011.

Schwartz, Barry. *The Paradox of Choice: Why More Is Less.* HarperPerennial, 2004.

Seeley, Karen M. *Therapy After Terror: 9/11, Psychotherapy, and Mental Health.* Cambridge University Press, 2008.

Selye, Hans. *The Physiology and Pathology of Exposure to Stress: A Treatise Based on the Concepts of the General Adaptation Syndrome and the Diseases of Adaptation.* Acta, 1950.

———. *The Stress of Life.* New York: McGraw-Hill, 1956.

———. *Stress Without Distress.* Signet, 1974.

Shapiro, David. *Neurotic Styles.* New York: Basic Books, 1965.

Sharpe, Katherine. *Coming of Age on Zoloft: How Antidepressants Cheered Us Up, Let Us Down, and Changed Who We Are.* HarperPerennial, 2012.

Shawn, Allan. *Wish I Could Be There: Notes from a Phobic Life.* Viking, 2007.

Shay, Jonathan. *Achilles in Vietnam: Combat Trauma and the Undoing of Character.* New York: Scribner, 1994.

Sheehan, David V, *The Anxiety Disease.* New York: Bantam Books, 1983.

Shephard, Ben. *War of Nerves: Soldiers and Psychiatrists in the Twentieth Century.* Cambridge, Mass.: Harvard University Press, 2001.

Shinder, Jason, ed. *Tales from the Couch: Writers on Therapy.* New York: William Morrow, 2000.

Shorter, Edward. *Before Prozac: The Troubled History of Mood Disorders in Psychiatry.* New York: Oxford University Press, 2009.

———. *A History of Psychiatry: From the Age of the Asylum to the Age of Prozac.* New York: Wiley, 1997.

———. *How Everyone Became Depressed: The Rise and Fall of the Nervous Breakdown.* Oxford University Press, 2013.

Shute, Clarence. *The Psychology of Aristotle: An Analysis of the Living Being.* New York: Russell and Russell, 1964.

Simon, Bennett. *Mind and Madness in Ancient Greece: The Classical Roots of Modern Psychiatry.* Ithaca, N.Y.: Cornell University Press, 1978.

Simon, Linda. *Genuine Reality: A Life of William James.* Harcourt, Brace, 1997.

Slater, Lauren. *Prozac Diary.* New York: Random House, 1998.

Smail, Daniel Lord. *On Deep History and the Brain.* Berkeley: University of California Press, 2008.

Smith, Daniel. *Monkey Mind: A Memoir of Anxiety.* New York: Simon & Schuster, 2012.

Smith, Mickey C. *Small Comfort: A History of the Minor Tranquilizers.* Praeger, 1985.

Smoller, Jordan, *The Other Side of Normal: How Biology Is Providing the Clues to Unlock the Secrets of Normal and Abnormal Behavior.* New York: William Morrow, 2012.

Snell, Bruno. *The Discovery of Mind in Greek Philosophy and Literature.* New York: Dover Publications, 1982 (first published 1953).

Solomon, Andrew. *The Noonday Demon: An Atlas of Depression.* New York: Scribner, 2001.

Solomon, Robert. *What Is an Emotion? Classic and Contemporary Readings.* New York: Oxford University Press, 1984.

Spielberger, Charles D., ed. *Anxiety: Current Trends in Theory and Research.* Vol. 1. Academic Press, 1972.

————, ed. *Anxiety and Behavior.* Academic Press, 1966.

————. *Understanding Stress and Anxiety.* New York: Harper and Row, 1979.

Spielberger, Charles D., and Rogelio Diaz-Guerrero, eds. *Cross-Cultural Anxiety.* Vol. 3. Hemisphere Publishing, 1986.

Spinoza, Baruch. *Ethics: Treatise on the Emendation of the Intellect.* Hackett Publishing, 1992.

Stein, Dan J. *Clinical Manual of Anxiety Disorders.* Washington, D.C.: American Psychiatric Publishing, 2004.

Stein, Dan J., and Eric Hollander. *Anxiety Disorders Comorbid with Depression: Social Anxiety Disorder, Post-traumatic Stress Disorder, Generalized Anxiety Disorder and Obsessive Compulsive Disorder.* Martin Dunitz, 2002.

————. *Textbook of Anxiety Disorders.* Washington, D.C.: American Psychiatric Publishing, 2002.

Stein, Murray B., and John R. Walker. *Triumph over Shyness: Conquering Shyness and Social Anxiety.* McGraw-Hill, 2002.

Stekel, W. *Conditions of Nervous Anxiety and Their Treatment.* New York: Dodd, Mead, 1923.

Stepansky, Paul E. *Psychoanalysis at the Margins.* New York: Other Press, 2009.

Stone, Michael. *Healing the Mind: A History of Psychiatry from Antiquity to the Present.* New York: W. W. Norton, 1997.

Stoodley, Bartlett H. *The Concepts of Sigmund Freud.* Glencoe, Ill.: Free Press, 1959.

Strupp, Hans H., Leonard M. Horowitz, and Michael J. Lambert, eds. *Measuring Patient Changes in Mood, Anxiety, and Personality Disorders.* American Psychological Association, 1997.

Sullivan, Paul. *Clutch: Why Some People Excel Under Pressure and Others Don't.* New York: Penguin Books, 2010.

Sulloway, Frank. *Freud, Biologist of the Mind.* Cambridge, Mass.: Harvard University Press, 1979.

Summers, Christina Hoff, and Sally Satel. *One Nation Under Therapy: How the Helping Culture Is Eroding Self-Reliance.* New York: St. Martin's Press, 2005.

Symonds, Percival M. *The Dynamics of Human Adjustment.* New York: Apple-Century-Crofts, 1946.

Szasz, Thomas S. *The Myth of Mental Illness.* New York: HarperPerennial, 1974.

Tallis, Raymond. *The Kingdom of Infinite Space: A Portrait of Your Head.* New Haven, Conn.: Yale University Press, 2008.

Tanielian, Terri, and Lisa H. Jaycox, eds. *Invisible Wounds of War: Psychological and Cognitive Injuries, Their Consequences, and Services to Assist Recovery.* RAND, 2008.

Taylor Manor Hospital, *Discoveries in Biological Psychiatry.* Lippincott, 1970.

Taylor, Steven, ed. *Anxiety Sensitivity: Theory, Research, and Treatment of the Fear of Anxiety.* Mahwah, New Jersey: Lawrence Erlbaum Associates, 1999.

Thomson, Keith. *The Young Charles Darwin.* New Haven, Conn: Yale University Press, 2009.

Tillich, Paul. *The Courage to Be.* New Haven, Conn.: Yale University Press, 1952.

————. *A Theology of Culture.* Oxford University Press, 1959.

Tolson, Jay, ed. *The Correspondence of Shelby Foote and Walker Percy.* New York: W. W. Norton, 1997.

———. *Pilgrim in the Ruins: A Life of Walker Percy*. New York: Simon & Schuster, 1992.

Tone, Andrea. *The Age of Anxiety: A History of America's Turbulent Affair with Tranquilizers*. New York: Basic Books, 2009.

Torrey, E. Fuller, and Judy Miller. *The Invisible Plague: The Rise of Mental Illness from 1750 to the Present*. New Brunswick, N.J.: Rutgers University Press, 2001.

Tseng, Wen-Shing. *Clinician's Guide to Cultural Psychiatry*. Academic Press, 2003.

Tuan, Yi-Fu. *Landscapes of Fear*. New York: Pantheon Books, 1979.

Twenge, Jean M. *Generation Me: Why Today's Young Americans Are More Confident, Assertive, Entitled—and More Miserable Than Ever Before*. New York: Free Press, 2006.

Valenstein, Elliot S. *Blaming the Brain: The Truth About Drugs and Mental Health*. New York: Free Press, 1998.

van den Berg, J. H. *The Changing Nature of Man: Introduction to Historical Psychology*. New York: W. W. Norton, 1961.

Vasey, Michael M., and Mark R. Dadds, eds. *The Developmental Psychopathology of Anxiety*. Oxford University Press, 2001.

Wain, Martin. *Freud's Answer: The Social Origins of Our Psychoanalytic Century*. Ivan R. Dee, 1998.

Wallin, David. *Attachment in Psychotherapy*. New York: Guilford Press, 2007.

Watt, Margo, and Sherry Stewart. *Overcoming the Fear of Fear: How to Reduce Anxiety Sensitivity*. Oakland, Calif.: New Harbinger, 2008.

Watters, Ethan. *Crazy Like Us: The Globalization of the American Psyche*. New York: Free Press, 2010.

Weatherhead, Leslie D. *Prescription for Anxiety: How You Can Overcome Fear and Despair*. Pierce and Washabaugh, 1956.

Weekes, Claire. *Hope and Help for Your Nerves*. Signet, 1969.

Wehrenberg, Margaret, and Steven Prinz. *The Anxious Brain: The Neurological Basis of Anxiety Disorders and How to Effectively Treat Them*. New York: W. W. Norton, 2007.

Wellman, Lee. *My Quarter-Life Crisis: How an Anxiety Disorder Knocked Me Down, and How I Got Back Up*. Tuckett Publishing, 2006.

Wender, Paul H., and Donald F. Klein. *Mind, Mood, and Medicine: A Guide to the New Biopsychiatry*. New York: Farrar, Straus and Giroux, 1981.

Wexler, Bruce E. *Brain and Culture: Neurobiology, Ideology, and Social Change*. Cambridge, Mass.: MIT Press, 2006.

Whitaker, Robert. *Anatomy of an Epidemic: Magic Bullets, Psychiatric Drugs, and the Astonishing Rise of Mental Illness in America*. New York: Crown, 2010.

Wilkinson, Richard, and Kate Pickett. *The Spirit Level: Why Greater Equality Makes Societies Stronger*. London: Bloomsbury, 2010.

Winik, Jay. *The Great Upheaval: America and the Birth of the Modern World, 1788–1800*. New York: HarperCollins, 2007.

Wolf, Stewart, and Harold Wolff. *Human Gastric Function: An Experimental Study of Man and His Stomach*. New York: Oxford University Press, 1943.

Wolfe, Barry E. *Understanding and Treating Anxiety Disorders*. American Psychological Association, 2005.

Wood, Gordon. *The Radicalism of the American Revolution*. New York: Random House, 1991.

Wullschlager, Jackie. *Hans Christian Andersen: The Life of a Storyteller*. New York: Penguin Books, 2000.

Wurtzel, Elizabeth. *Prozac Nation*. Houghton Mifflin, 1994.

Yapko, Michael D. *Depression Is Contagious: How the Most Common Mood Disorder Is Spreading Around the World and How to Stop It*. New York: Free Press, 2009.

Young, Allan. *The Harmony of Illusions: Inventing Post-traumatic Stress Disorder*. Princeton, N.J.: Princeton University Press, 1995.

Young-Bruehl, Elisabeth. *Anna Freud*. 2nd ed. New Haven, Conn.: Yale University Press, 2008.

Zane, Manuel D., and Harry Milt. *Your Phobia: Understanding Your Fears Through Contextual Therapy*. American Psychiatric Press, 1984.

Zeman, Adam. *A Portrait of the Brain*. New Haven, Conn.: Yale University Press, 2008.

Zilboorg, Gregory. *A History of Medical Psychology*. New York: W. W. Norton, 1941.

Zolli, Andrew, and Ann Marie Healy. *Resilience: Why Things Bounce Back*. New York: Free Press, 2012.

Index

A NOTE ON THE TYPE

This book was set in a modern adaptation of a type designed by the first William Caslon (1692–1766). The Caslon face, an artistic, easily read type, has enjoyed more than two centuries of popularity in the United States. It is of interest to note that the first copies of the Declaration of Independence and the first paper currency distributed to the citizens of the newborn nation were printed in this typeface.

Typeset by Scribe,
Philadelphia, Pennsylvania